I0788596

CRAIG HALLORAN

THE SUPERNATURAL BOUNTY HUNTER FILES

BOXED SET
BOOKS 1-10

The Supernatural Bounty Hunter Files Boxed Set
Books 1-10
By Craig Halloran

Copyright © 2017 by Craig Halloran
Print Edition

TWO-TEN BOOK PRESS
P.O. Box 4215, Charleston, WV 25364

ISBN eBook: 978-1-946218-18-6
ISBN Paperback: 978-1-946218-19-3
ISBN Hardback: 978-1-946218-20-9

www.craighalloran.com

Publisher's Note

This book is a work of fiction. Names, characters, places, and incidents either are the product of the author's imagination or are used fictitiously, and any resemblance to actual persons, living or dead, events, or locales is entirely coincidental.

TABLE OF CONTENTS

CRAIG HALLORAN

THE SUPERNATURAL BOUNTY HUNTER FILES

SMOKE RISING

BOOK 1

PROLOGUE

THE MAN-LIKE THING LURCHED UP and smacked Smoke in the chin.

He staggered back.

It started walking down the hall, arms dangling at its sides and a hole clean through its back and chest.

Sidney took aim.

Blam! Blam! Blam!

It tumbled over with its kneecap blasted apart.

"Good shot." Smoke wiped his brow and headed after their fallen attacker where it writhed on the floor. "I think it's a zombie." He pointed his weapon at its head.

Blam!

"Zombies aren't real," she said, catching her breath and holstering her gun.

CHAPTER 1

HUNTSVILLE DETENTION FACILITY, ALABAMA

"ARE YOU NERVOUS?" THE WARDEN asked.

"No," Sidney said. "Why would I be?"

Warden Decker shrugged. Dabbing the sweat on his brow with his handkerchief and tucking it back in his pocket, he hustled forward and swiped his card. Nothing happened. He swiped it again and again. An unseen latch popped.

"Ah, there we go." He opened one of two heavy metal doors and stepped aside. "It's an old place. Not made for all this technology. I miss the sound of those keys jangling on my hip some days."

"Thank you," she said, crossing into the next room.

"You're welcome, Agent Shaw."

The pair entered a long hall made of cinderblock wall, lined with barred windows. Agent Shaw's short heels echoed on the marble floor. The prison was old, but it had the smell of fresh paint that still lingered on the pale grey walls.

The thickset black man cleared his throat. "I've been the warden these ten years, and I have to admit, I've never had a situation like this."

"Like what?" She adjusted the strap of her black leather satchel on her shoulder.

"We just don't get a lot of visitors from the FBI, that's all. And you have to admit, the situation is very unique." He was smiling as he glanced over at her. "Isn't it?"

"For you, I suppose, but I've been doing this for quite some time."

"Visiting prisoners in sweat-rank prisons?" He huffed. "You didn't sign up for that, did you?" He let out a little laugh. "Sounds more like something a foolish young man would do, like me."

She showed the slightest smile on her face. Dark hair was pinned up behind her head. She wore a dark-blue pants suit with a white shirt. She reminded him of his daughter, in a white sort of way. Too confident for her own good.

"My job requires me to go to a lot of unique places, but I'll admit, Warden Decker, I don't think I've been to a place as humid as this."

"They've been working on the A/C for twenty years, and it still never works right. I'm from the South, and I still never get used to it." He dashed the sweat from his eyes. "Sorry. But this hallway has no ventilation at all."

"It's all right. The academy's prepared me for worse."

He stopped at the next set of doors, readied his swipe key, and paused.

She dipped her chin and eyed him. "Something on your mind, Warden?"

He leaned on the door, took out his blue handkerchief, and wiped his neck. "I just got to know. Why do you need to see him?"

"That's confidential."

"I know that, but … it's so strange. Listen, Agent Shaw. I'm the warden. Certainly you can give me some nugget of information. After all, he's my prisoner. I'm pretty familiar with him. I'm pretty familiar with all of them. We have the worst of all sorts here: dangerous maniacal bloodthirsty killers. Of course, I've seen some of them cry like babies before." He gave her a quick finger shake. "But we don't have—and never have had—anyone like him."

"Sorry," she said, looking at the next set of doors.

They were painted white, with the word "LIBRARY" stenciled in black where the window glass had been replaced with steel.

"Is this really a library?"

"It is." He tapped on the metal. "This is how we make do. I don't think we get the same level of funding as the G-Men"—he looked her up and down—"or G-Women do. Are you sure I can't stay inside with you?"

"I'll be fine." She shifted her satchel from one side to the other.

He took a breath and swiped his card. "All right then."

CHAPTER 2

THE LATCH POPPED, AND THE warden pushed the door open. It was a library as expected, with stacks and rows of books. The musty smell reminded Sidney of her days in high school. She'd done a lot of reading back then. Large wooden tables were lined up neatly, resting on old hardwood floors.

Two correction officers in grey shirts and black pants held synthetic stocked shotguns on either side of a table. A man in an orange jumper sat there between them. His head was down over a newspaper and his dark straight hair dangled over his face.

Her heart thumped behind her temples.

"I can stay inside, just out of earshot," the warden said, patting the semiautomatic pistol on his hip.

She lifted a brow. "I don't think he'll try to escape, or even to hurt me, for that matter. It's not in his profile."

The warden blocked her view of the prisoner and whispered, "I've read his profile too. Several times. He has a dark side to him."

"I know, but don't all men?"

Warden Decker nodded and stepped aside. "Come on, men." But at the last second, he turned to her and said, gradually getting loud enough for the prisoner to hear, "As long as you stay out of the stacks, I've got eyes on everything. Just signal when you're finished."

The guards came forward, eyeing her as they passed the threshold.

"Uh, Warden—"

Warden Decker held his hand up and led them out.

Sidney glanced over her shoulder as the doors began to close, just in time to see Warden Decker swallow. Her heart skipped a beat as the door sealed shut. She turned and faced the prisoner.

Pull it together. He's just another creep, Sidney.

She approached him, heart thumping. It was even hotter in the library, and she could feel the sweat beading above her lip. Her eyes slid toward the camera globes above. *Those things better be on.* She dropped her file on the table, dragged a chair back, and sat down. The man across from her, eyes still down, turned a page of the newspaper.

"John Smoke," she said, scooting her file in front of her and opening it. "I'm Agent Shaw with the FBI. How are you doing today?"

Without glancing up, he said, "You're different than what I expected. What are you, about five foot eleven? That's tall for a gal. And you're even wearing flat shoes. The last one I met was a sawed-off dumpling with Coke-bottle glasses. I didn't like her so well." He scanned the paper, turned the last page, folded it up, and pushed it aside. He clasped his fingers together and looked down into her eyes. "Volleyball. I bet you played collegiate volleyball."

Smoke was hawkish, but handsome. His chestnut hair was thick and cut just above the neck. His eyes were dark with a burning fire behind them. He was a strong-chinned, lean, well-knit man with hands the size of mitts.

"This is business, Mister Smoke, not a social call."

"You know"—he eased back in his chair—"you aren't exactly what I figured for an FBI woman. I was expecting someone a little less, well, a lot less—to keep it professional— appealing. I have to say, it's a nice surprise." He scratched the scruff on his cheeks. "Shaw. Is that your maiden name?"

Sidney didn't have a ring on. "I'll ask the questions. You just answer them."

"Well, you haven't asked anything yet." His voice was a little rough, with a hair of charm behind it. He clasped his fingers together and rested them on his head. "I'm all yours."

"All right, Mister Smoke—"

"Smoke," he interrupted.

"Excuse me?"

"Just call me Smoke." He winked. "That's what everyone calls me."

"Sure," she said. "First question then. Are you interested in getting your sentence commuted?"

He shrugged.

I'm starting to hate this guy. Sidney had interviewed dozens of prisoners over her career. She'd negotiated deals with many. Every time she mentioned someone getting their sentence commuted, their eyes lit up. Smoke's hadn't.

"You're less than a year into a three-year sentence," she continued. "And when I say commute, I'm not talking about months off. I'm talking about years."

Rubbing a bruise on his cheek just below the ear, he said, "I've become pretty fond of the old place." He glanced around. "It speaks to me."

"Warden Decker says you and the other prisoners don't get along so well."

"He's such a worrywart. Nice guy, though."

"I've been informed that there's a bounty on your head." She leaned forward. "In most cases, the superior numbers get you. One slip-up or payoff of the guards will get you killed in here."

"It keeps me sharp," he said.

"Getting killed?"

"People trying to kill you is always the best training."

"I see," she said. "And I guess I shouldn't be surprised after reading your file." She leafed through some pages. "You've had quite a career for a man under thirty. Navy SEAL. Ex-Washington PD. Bounty Hunter. Prisoner. Now that's a resume."

"Chicks dig it."

"There aren't any *chicks* around here, and there won't be for the next two years. The funny thing I came across is how you wound up here in the first place. You are a decorated veteran, though not without some marks. Tell me, why'd you leave the SEALs?"

"I didn't like the pay."

"Oh, the pay," she said, eyeing the file and nodding, "but that's not what it says here. The gist I got was that you are difficult to control. Insubordinate. You struck an officer."

"He had a big mouth."

"He was a general."

"He had a really big mouth." He shrugged. "And I got an honorable discharge. I hope you read that far."

"I see," she said. "So you didn't like the military?"

"Listen, Agent Shaw. I loved the military. But there is a lot of standing around, training, and waiting. I got bored."

"It doesn't say that here."

"Do you believe everything you read?"

Interesting. But at least he's talking. "Let's skip over the Washington PD and talk about why you became a bounty hunter."

"Better money."

"Really? So you're all about the money?"

"Yes."

"I don't believe you."

"I don't care."

Typical stubborn man.

"Fine. Let's talk money then. The last goon you brought in was worth ten thousand."

"It should have been fifty, and I still haven't received payment for that."

"No?" Sidney said, cocking her head. "Well, I wonder why *that* is?"

Smoke looked away and growled in his throat a little. He mumbled something.

Sidney leaned forward and turned her ear toward him. "What was that?"

The room seemed to darken when Smoke's eyes narrowed. He slammed his fist on the table. *Wham!* "He had it coming!"

CHAPTER 3

H EART RACING, SIDNEY FLINCHED BACK. Smoke's eyes were smoldering fires. Behind her, the doors burst open, and two guards dashed in. The first one drove the butt of his shotgun into Smoke's chest, toppling him over. In a second, both barrels were lowered toward his chest.

"Don't you move, Smoke," the first guard said. "Not an inch."

"Are you all right, Miss?"

Face flushed red, Sidney jumped from her chair. "Get your sorry asses out of here!"

"What?"

"Did I signal for the cavalry?"

"Well…"

"Did I?" She pointed at the cameras.

"But—" the first guard started.

"Jeff," a voice shouted from just outside the library doors. "Moe! Let's go!" It was Warden Decker. His chest was heaving and his face beaded in sweat. He loosened his tie. "Now!"

With hesitation, the guards lifted their barrels and backed off, eyes never leaving Smoke.

"Sorry, Miss."

Sidney glared at him.

"Er … Sorry, Agent Shaw."

Sidney waved the warden off, and he showed her a squeamish grin. Seconds later, the doors closed again, leaving her all alone with Smoke. She turned and found him in the chair, with a slight smile on his face. She hid a gasp. She hadn't even heard him move. No rattle of metal nor scuff of chair. Nothing. She resumed her seat.

"How's your chest? I bet that hurt."

"I've been hurt worse." His eyes were dancing. "You're prior military too, aren't you?"

"Let's pick up where we left off before you had your little tantrum, shall we? I believe you were saying you're upset that you haven't been paid."

"I took a major thug off the streets. A top dealer." He rolled his shoulders and grimaced a little. "I should have been paid. I was tossed in here instead."

"The judge didn't see it that way." She glanced through the file. "It says you acted with extreme prejudice."

"The man's a killer. A murderer."

"That's for the courts to decide. And we can't just go around maiming people."

Smoke lifted his brows. "Even if it saves a life?"

"You cut off his index finger."

"No, I cut off his trigger finger."

She wanted to laugh but held it back. "Most people only have one trigger finger. You cut off two."

"I can shoot right- or left-handed. Can't you?"

"I've never had the need. As for you, well, I'd venture to guess your little act of mutilation didn't sit well with Mister Durn. That's probably why he put the prison hit on you."

"Huh, well, I've been a bounty hunter a long time."

"You've been one four years."

"That's a long time." He crinkled his brow. "Anyway, I've achieved a lot in that time. Helped a lot of people. But some of those judges aren't so helpful. Durn has deep pockets. It's no surprise he paid the judge off and got me sent inside here."

"Maybe the judge was coerced."

"He should be willing to die first."

Sidney nodded. Smoke had a point, but it was all speculation. She picked up the file and fanned herself with it.

"It's in the past now. Let's talk about the future. Are you interested in hearing what I have to offer or not?"

He shrugged.

"Yes or no, if you please."

"Does it involve working with the FBI or any other law enforcement agency?"

"Absolutely."

"Then no."

"Why?"

"You've read my file. I don't play well with others. Too many rules. Not enough action. That's why the bad guys get away. Besides, I don't trust them. If I did, I'd probably be doing what you're doing."

"Come on." She leaned back. "We aren't all bad."

"See, you just admitted it."

"Admitted what?"

"That most of you are bad." He tilted his head back and let out a laugh. "Hah."

"That's a common expression."

"Says the girl scout. And I bet you think those cookies you're selling are good for me, too." He shook his head. "No one is as blind as he who will not see."

"My eyes are wide open."

"I'm sure they are, but my answer is still no."

"So, you'd rather sit in here for two more years plus and let more criminals get away?"

"There are plenty of criminals inside here that are in need of my correction."

Difficult. Difficult. Difficult. The man across from her seemed content, however. It was weird.

"So long as I'm here, will you just listen to my offer?"

He shrugged. "Sure."

"The FBI has a list." She clasped her hands together and rested them on the table. "The typical America's Most Wanted. You're familiar with it, I'm sure."

"Uh-huh. Say, what kind of perfume are you wearing?" He sniffed the air. "It's different. Good, but different."

"The Marshalls have their lists. The Washington PD has their lists too," she continued, "more on the local level. You've dealt with them all, and disregarding the last case, you've done an exemplary job."

"Yeah." He yawned and eased back until he lifted the front legs of his chair from the floor, then started gazing around. "I know all of the lists. It's what I do."

"But there's another list, one that isn't on the public record. It's called—"

Smoke's brows lifted, and his chair legs hit the floor. He leaned over the table and spoke.

"The Black Slate."

CHAPTER 4

I'VE GOT HIM.

"Let me see the list," Smoke said, unable to hide the excitement in his voice. "I knew it existed."

"Oh, did you now? You don't sound so sure."

"It was a theory."

"Based off what? The Black Slate has very little activity. It's very low profile."

"True, but I know all the lists pretty well. I've studied the cases, the files, at least whatever I could get ahold of. But there was always something missing. I don't look for what they show or say, I look for what they don't show or say." He drummed his fingers on the table and stared at the file. "All of those lists I figured were nothing but busywork that hid the real people. Good for the papers. Good for accolades and medals. But they never bring in the top-dog criminals." He stretched his fingers toward the file. "May I?"

Sidney slid the file away. She wanted to give it to him, he seemed so eager, child-like even.

"Not without clearance, and I don't see that happening if you aren't on board with this. Don't fret it. The list isn't in here, just the first assignment. Are you interested or not?"

Smoke pulled his fingers back. "Tell me more. I'm curious. Why does the FBI want to use me as a resource?"

"All right, I can answer that. Let's just say that our resources are stretched thin. Even though the Black Slate, as you call it, is important, other matters have higher priority: border security, domestic terrorism, cyber-attacks, white collar crime. There are only so many agents, and they can only keep tabs on so many things."

"Sure, sure, and I'm supposed to believe the NSA doesn't keep tabs on any of these things? Don't you share information with each other?"

"Like I said, the FBI has priorities, but the Black Slate is still a threat, it just isn't as high up on DC's agenda."

"Ah," Smoke said, "Washington DC, home of the greatest truths and the greatest lies."

"You have a skewed outlook on things," she said. "Where does all this come from?"

"I read a lot of books."

"What kind of books?"

"The kind that aren't on the bestseller lists."

"I see." She nodded. "Is there anything you care to recommend?"

"Nope." Smoke's chair groaned as he shifted. "So this character on the wanted list, tell me about him. Has the FBI tried to catch him?"

"Yes, for years and without success. I've studied the file. We've gotten close, only to see him slip from our grasp time and time again. And these are veteran agents. They speak as if he's a ghost or something."

Smoke tilted his head. "Maybe he is?"

"I don't think so."

"Maybe he's like Bruce Lee and they just can't handle him?" He made some quick chops with his hands. "Wah-tah!"

"I'm certain that's not the case, but several agents were wounded in hand-to-hand combat."

Smoke's eyes widened. "Maybe it's the ghost of Bruce Lee?"

"You are a strange man."

"So, do you have a picture? A name?"

"Are you in?"

Smoke beckoned with his fingers.

Sidney pulled a picture from the file and shoved it over. It was a surveillance shot of a small dark-haired man in a blue suit, stepping out of an SUV. "His name is Vaughn, Adam Vaughn. They call him AV."

Smoke's brows buckled as he studied the picture.

"Is this the only picture you have?"

"The only one on me, and it's the best one we have."

"This guy's about five foot five. Hmmm, and he almost has the unibrow thing going. Spanish descent. Sharp features. Hard-eyed." He rubbed his chin. "Where's the last place they cornered him?"

"DC."

"And what is he suspected of?"

"Trafficking."

"Trafficking what?"

"Everything."

"So you have testimonials?"

"Some living and some dead."

Smoke shoved the picture back across the table.

"All right."

"All right. Does that mean you're in?"

"No, all right as in I'm thinking about it."

CHAPTER 5

SIDNEY JOGGED THE MONUMENTS ROUTE in DC. She checked her watch and heart rate. She was thirty minutes into the run, and her thighs and legs were starting to burn.

Thirty more to go.

It was Saturday, mid-morning, and the sun almost warmed the fall air. She hated running when it was too cold. She didn't like getting up early either, not on Saturday. There were other tasks at home she liked to do. But today was different. This wasn't her usual route or scene. She had another meeting. Her former boss wanted to meet. Outside the office. Privately. First time for everything.

Wiping the sleeve of her grey hoodie across her brow and picking up the pace, she passed two joggers, older, wearing 80s Adidas leisure. She smiled as she ran by. They probably moved much faster thirty years ago. She jogged by several people, strollers, tourists. It wasn't the best time to run, but she liked the extra work that came with running through the slow masses. She picked up on things.

A man sitting on a bench wearing a leisure suit and winding his watch. A group of older women walking at a brisk pace and laughing. One had purple leggings on. Another straightened her red wig from time to time.

She weaved her way around the reflecting pool three more times. Her lungs labored, and her feet burned. She checked her time, pushed on, passed the World War II Memorial and sprinted across the street toward the Washington monument, where she slowed to a walk. Hands on her hips, she strolled toward the monument until she saw a man sitting on a bench, waving.

"Sid! Sid!"

Soaked in sweat, she trotted over. He stood up and opened his arms wide. He was as tall as her, broad and heavy, balding with a handsome smile on his face. She stopped short of him.

"I'm soaked in sweat."

"It's all right," he said in a comforting voice, "I have my raincoat on. Come here."

She sighed and made her way into his arms, which braced her in a bear hug, taking more wind from her. "Easy now, Ted." She patted his back.

"Sorry." He released her. He was still smiling. "I've missed my favorite trooper. It's been awhile." He clasped her hands and held them tight. "You look great."

"Sure I do," she said, brushing the damp hair from her eyes. "You look great yourself."

He patted his stomach. "Maybe twenty, thirty, forty pounds ago." He lumbered back to his seat and sat down with a groan. He patted the bench. "The desk and meetings are killing me."

"Are you sure it isn't the burgers and French fries?" She took a seat.

"It's those buffets at the lunch meetings, I swear it. Marge keeps me on a strict diet." He scratched the top of his head and squinted one eye. "But that diet's not very tasty. Salad, salad and more salad. I try, but I can't figure it out."

"Maybe you should start running again, like we used to."

"Ah," he nodded, "I miss that. Well, your company, not so much the running."

His full name was Ted C. Howard, and Sidney still didn't know what the C stood for. He was the first assistant director she'd worked for. Over fifty years old now, Ted still had the thick-set frame of his football days that he always loved to talk about. He was a good man. Energetic. A good mentor. He'd taught her a little about everything—and a lot about little, when he started to ramble. He was like family. An uncle of sorts.

"So, how was Alabama?" he asked.

"Hot."

"Good country down there," he said. "Nice fishing. Nice people."

"Not where I was," she said, smiling. She bent over and redid the laces on her shoes. "But I'm sure you'd find good company."

"True," he said. "Did I ever tell you about the last time I was down there? I was thirty-nine and …"

Aw crap. Here we go. Cut him off before you end up in tomorrow.

"Yes, you told me," she interrupted. Maybe Ted had told the story, and maybe he hadn't, but she was pretty sure she'd heard them all. Some of them two or three times, as he'd told them to other people when she was around. "What's this about, Ted?"

"Oh." He seemed disappointed. "How'd your interview with Mister Smoke go?"

Cocking her head, she looked him in the eye. "You know about that?" All she had told him was that she'd come back from Alabama. She hadn't mentioned anything about anyone she'd met.

"I spoke with Warden Decker. We go way back."

"Of course you do." Ted had a catalog of contacts. He had access. If he wanted to know something, he'd find it. "And does your office have an interest in my case? I thought you were handling more of the border cases."

Ted reached into the pocket of his navy trench coat and pulled out a paper bag. It was full of nuts. He tossed one toward the nearest squirrel that was skirting by.

"I'm not keeping tabs on you, Sid, but I have checked up on you from time to time." He flicked another nut out. "But this was different. A little bird dropped me a wire of peculiar interest. I felt compelled to look into it."

"And?"

"The Black Slate. I know a little something about that." The creases deepened over his eyes. "I don't like the idea of you working on this. The way they're going about it is peculiar. It seems … dangerous."

Ted had never been like this before, and they'd navigated some dangerous waters. Why the concern now?

"Danger's part of the job. You told me that."

He laughed. "I think that's a quote from a movie. It's true, but probably much shorter and more eloquent than I would have put it." He flung out a few more nuts where many squirrels had now gathered. "Don't take me wrong. You're as fit to do this as any. If I was in the field, I'd want a piece of the action too." He groaned. "Don't ever get promoted, Sid. They anchor you with cinderblocks to that desk. I should have been a cop. Did I ever tell you—"

She grabbed his shoulder. "Back to the Black Slate, please. John Smoke? You wanted to talk about him."

"Yes, John Smoke. Now that's an odd one. A good candidate on the surface, but all the paperwork below the surface is blacked out or missing."

"You mean I didn't get the entire file?"

"You got enough. I got a little more. That's why I talked to Warden Decker." He pointed at the squirrels. "Look at them. I haven't done this in years. Crazy little rodents. I met a man once who had a squirrel living in the hood of his hoodie. It was after Hurricane Hugo hit Charleston. Construction guy. One of the strangest things I ever saw." He turned and smiled at her. "In a good way."

She glared at him.

"Sorry." He flung the rest of the nuts aside and dusted his hands off. "Truth. Warden Decker likes the guy. But, we aren't the only people taking an interest in him. Decker clammed up when I prodded him. Leaves me uneasy."

"Well, Smoke has neither accepted nor declined my offer, so maybe there's nothing to worry about."

"Interesting, but I assume he'll take it."

"Why's that?"

"I just have a feeling. That said, be careful. I did some deeper research on similar projects like this that failed. The Black Slate is marred with a dark history. They've tried mercs, bounty hunters, and others of their ilk before."

"And what happened? It didn't work out?"

"They're dead. Some, not to mention many of our agents—who aren't even in that file you were toting—are gone without a trace." He peered up at the Washington Monument. "I don't like this, Sid. Just use extraordinary caution." He got up and extended his hand. She took it, and he pulled her up with ease. "I'm serious." He patted her shoulder and started to walk away. He stopped and turned. "Say, how's the Hellcat doing?"

Unable to contain her smile, she said, "Doing great."

"Hah. You stole her from me. I'll never forget that." Moving on, he waved. "Call me if you need anything."

"Good seeing you, Ted. And thanks."

I think.

CHAPTER 6

S IDNEY'S EYES POPPED OPEN. SHE rolled over and grabbed her buzzing phone. Sitting up in bed, blinking, she read the screen. There was an address. A time. And the text came from her supervisor, Dydeck.

"Are you shitting me?" She checked the time. 4:30 a.m. She groaned and fell back into her goose-down pillows. "What does he want now?" she mumbled. "Ugh. Why does he get up so early? Why does he feel compelled to bother me? So early!"

Her toes touched the cold hardwood floor, and she crept into the bathroom and started the shower. The small bath steamed up quick, and into the hot water she went and soaked it up. Five minutes later she was out, drying off, and on the go. She tore the plastic off her dry-cleaned clothes. Seconds later, she had everything on but her shoes and headed for the kitchen.

The studio apartment west of Reston, Virginia didn't offer much. Its eight hundred square feet was furnished from secondhand shops and goodwill stores. A mid-size bed, a small sofa, recliner and a kitchenette with two stools under the bar.

She turned on the television and followed the blurbs on the news. It was Monday. Forty-five degrees and a rainstorm was coming.

"Great."

She grabbed the blender out of the sink and loaded it with ice, protein mix, two eggs, fresh veggies and ice and blended it all up. Eyes intent on the news, she poured the mixture into a travel mug and rinsed the blender out before abandoning it in the sink. She snatched her bag from the kitchen bar, clicked the television off, and headed for the front door. She opened it and stopped. Something didn't feel right. He fingers fell to her waist.

"Ah!"

She shuffled back to the bed and grabbed her weapon from under the pillow. A Glock 22. .40 S&W. Inside her closet, she took her shoulder holster and strapped it on. She paused, staring into the small closet. Another pistol and shoulder holster hung ready. What Ted had said hung in her thoughts. *Use extraordinary caution.* It was a strange phrase. The way he'd said it even more so. At 4:42 am, she was inside an FBI-issued Crown Victoria and rolling down the road. Fifteen minutes into the ride, the rain started in heavy splatters on the windshield. She turned on the wipers, which left streaks of rain, and the defroster wasn't working well either. She wiped the condensation with her hand and sighed. The rising sun was a blur in her eyes. She slipped on her sunglasses.

It's going to be a long week.

While she drove down the road, Sidney's thoughts were heavy. Typically, she headed into the office at 8 a.m. She'd push paperwork for a few hours then go to meetings and briefings. That was seventy percent of the job, maybe eighty. The rest of the time she was in the field. When Dydeck called her out in the field, it could mean anything. Homicide. Drug busts. Stake outs. Talking to clients and informants. Anything dealing with problems or potential problems at the federal level. From time to time they were a cleanup crew of sorts, when the local brass of Washington got their hands too dirty. It was a part of the job she didn't care for.

Two hours later and south of DC, she exited the highway and entered a residential neighborhood along the Potomac.

Homicide?

Dydeck liked to surprise her. He was good about that. He had a way of working them into a little bit of everything, which she liked. Most of the agents were assigned to a particular unit, but Sidney floated along the rim, where the full range of her talents could be put to use. She was classified as special field ops. Not to mention her paperwork. She was thorough, her wording in sync just the way the top brass liked it. The Bureau loved paperwork. Without it, they'd eliminate most of what they did. She hated it.

Her brakes squeaked to a halt as she parked in the driveway of a contemporary one-level home in a lower-middle-class neighborhood. A For Sale sign was in the yard, and there were also signs in the other two yards at the end of the cul-de-sac. Two other cars were there, black SUVs.

Why don't I have one of those?

Through the rain, she could make out one man on the porch in a dark trench coat, standing by the door. She didn't know him.

Aw, great.

No uniformed local law enforcement. That ruled out homicide, but she'd been to plenty of these scenes before. The estranged family members or children of Washington's finest often wound up in dark places: overdoses, suicide, domestic squabbles. The FBI often covered it up before the news outlets caught wind of it.

She grabbed her gear, popped open the door, and dashed through the sloppy wet grass and onto the covered porch.

"Agent Shaw?" the stocky man said, smiling. He had a warmth about him.

She showed her ID.

He glanced at it. "Lousy morning, isn't it."

"You bet."

"I'm Tommy," he said, extending his hand. "Nice to meet you."

She shook it.

"You too."

He opened the door. "They're all waiting for you."

Inside, the house was dimly lit by a lone floor lamp in the living room. There, three men in dark suits waited. Sitting on the large raised hearth was a fourth man in an orange jumpsuit, shackled with his head down.

"Welcome, Sidney," said a man standing off in the corner and putting away his phone. He was in his forties, well-knit, with his head shaven. His eyes slid over to Smoke and back to her. "Well, what do you think?"

"I have to admit, I'm surprised, Jack. And I'm not even including the location. I was under the impression this would be handled downtown. Aren't we outside of protocol?"

"Yes and no. All the paperwork is covered on my end. On the prison end. At the assistant director's end. But hey, it's the list. We have to keep it low." He scratched his head. "And I have to admit, I didn't even know there was a list until a month ago. Huh. Gum?"

"No thanks." She folded her arms over her chest. "So, where do we stand? I'm not really familiar with running things without explicit directives."

"I know that." He nodded to one of the other agents. The man handed another file over. "The directives are in here. Everything we have on the mark as well, including his last known location." He approached and brushed his shoulder against hers. Tapped the file. "Never seen anything like this in twenty years, plucking a low-life out of the prisons to do our job." He sneered at Smoke. "You have two weeks, pal, and then it's back in the hole." He winked at Sidney. "If he gives you any crap, just call and we'll cut this silly mission short." He walked over to Smoke and kicked the man's foot with his boot. "Mind yourself."

The door opened, and another man in a trench coat entered, holding a newspaper over his head with one hand and a briefcase in the other. The man was slender and stoop shouldered, and he wore glasses that looked too heavy for his nose. His frosty eyes met hers.

"Agent Shaw, what a displeasure."

"Agree, Agent Tweel. I couldn't be less happy to see you."

Agent Cyrus Tweel didn't look like much, but he was proven. Sidney had graduated from the academy with him.

Agent Tweel dropped to a knee and popped his briefcase open. "Let's get on with this, shall we? I have more important things to do than waste time on experiments."

Smoke's head tilted up. His gaze fell on Cyrus.

"Jack," Sidney said, "What's going on here?"

"Tracking," Jack said. "We can't lose sight of him. Not for a second. Surely you know that."

Cyrus held up a two-inch needled syringe filled with clear liquid. He flicked it with his fingers.

Smoke rose to his feet. "No one is going to Snake Plissken me!"

"You'll do what you agreed to," Jack said. He nodded to the other agents, who seized Smoke by the arms. "Now be still." Jack pulled out a stun gun. "Or it'll be my pleasure to use this on you."

"No!" Smoke said, struggling against the agents. "No!"

CHAPTER 7

"T HAT NEEDLE BETTER NOT GET within a foot of me!" Smoke said.

"What's going on here, Jack?" Sidney said. "What the hell is in there?"

"Something new," Jack said. He pointed to Smoke. "You agreed to this. You better settle yourself."

"I didn't agree to any injections! Screw this! Put me back in prison."

"Jack!" Sidney said, stepping in front of him. "What is it?"

"A vaccination."

"No one is giving me any shots!" Standing taller than the rest, hands cuffed behind his back, Smoke squatted down and drove his shoulder into the agent on his left. The man teetered over but held on, dragging the three of them down in a heap.

"You're going to regret that," Jack said. He stepped around Sidney and pointed the stun gun at Smoke. "I don't have time for this."

Sidney shoved his hand aside.

Jack misfired. The taser prods buried themselves in one of the agents. He jerked, spasmed, and writhed on the floor.

"Dammit, Sid! What did you do that for?"

"This isn't protocol!"

"It is. Read the file. I tell you it is." He shoved by Sidney and drove his toe into Smoke's gut.

"Oof!"

"Settle down, hot dog! Take your medicine!" Jack said. He put his knee on Smoke's neck. "Cyrus!"

Smoke bucked and squirmed.

Zap!

Smoke jerked and writhed.

Behind Sidney, Cyrus had tased him.

"Give him more juice," Jack said. "He's still squirming."

"Gladly," Cyrus said, squeezing the trigger.

Pop. Pop. Pop.

Smoke screamed out, "Aaargh!" A second later he collapsed on the floor, disheveled and coated in sweat.

"Whew!" Jack said, getting up. He ran his forearm across his brow. "What is that man made of?" He helped up the agent who'd caught some juice from his taser. "Sorry about that." He let out a heavy sigh. "Agent Shaw, I'm letting this incident go. But if you ever act insubordinate again, I'll black mark your file."

"But Jack—"

He stepped up to her.

"But Sir!"

He reached into his pocket and grabbed a handkerchief. "Get in line, or I'll withdraw my consideration."

Sidney started to say, *Yes, Sir*, but held her tongue.

"You go right ahead, *Sir*. This entire incident is way out of bounds."

"No, you're out of bounds, Sid."

"I'm not the one who lost control of this situation. That's on you, not me. That's no way to treat a person. He's a decorated veteran."

"He *was* a decorated veteran. Now he is some ex-con vigilante hot dog idiot."

She glanced at Smoke. Cyrus was driving the needle into him. "Hey!"

"Back off, Sid," Jack said. "Tohms! Yo, Tommy!"

The man she'd met outside came in.

"What the hell are you doing out there? Didn't you hear the racket?"

"Er …"

"Never mind," Jack said. "Just help Muldoon to the car. He's shaken up."

"Right," Tommie said. He glanced at Sid. There was a bit of sympathy in his eyes. He mumbled as he passed. "Cyrus is an a-hole."

"I heard that," Cyrus said.

"Good," Tommy replied. He helped Muldoon back outside, closing the door behind him.

Jack raised his palms up. "Let's start over. The vaccination. I had to do it. Orders. And that's all I know. It's a vaccination."

"Is there something wrong with him?" Sid said.

"Well, I'm just assuming it's for your protection … and his."

Smoke groaned on the floor.

Cyrus locked an ankle tracker on him.

"Who's keeping tabs on him," Sid said, "me or you?"

"Check your phone?" Cyrus said. "There's an app you need to download. Twenty four seven location. Just don't let your phone go dead. Don't lose it like the last time, either."

"Shut up, Cyrus."

"Listen, Sid," Jack intervened. "This is a strange case. I have my orders. You have yours. Execute them, and I'm sure it will all make sense after everything hashes out. Got it?"

"Sure, I got it."

"Good."

"So," Sid said, "is this headquarters?"

He pointed to a peg on the wall.

"Those are the keys. You can work out of here, or you can work out of his place."

"I'm sure she'd like to take him back to her place." Cyrus snapped his briefcase shut. "Probably why she took the assignment. She always had a thing for damaged guys."

"Cyrus, get going," Jack said.

Agent Tweel departed with a frown, slamming the door behind him. That left only Jack, Smoke, the other agent, and herself in the room.

"Get the car warmed up, Danny," Jack said.

That left only three.

"Sid, I'm sorry for how this went down. You're my best. You know that. But I can't have you questioning me in front of others. Not like that. Respect the chain."

"I know, but—"

"No, the only butt I'm going to have is yours if you cross that line again. Capisce?"

She nodded.

"Good." His eyes slid over to Smoke and back. "I don't know what to make of this. He's all yours though. Read the file. Stay away from the office. Don't hesitate to call. In two weeks this will all be over. Things will be back to normal."

"You say that as if you don't think we can bring this guy in."

"Well, the odds are against you. I'm told no one has ever brought one in. And by the look of things, I don't see that changing." He squeezed her shoulder. "Good luck, Sid."

She could feel his heavy gaze on her back as he headed for the door. It sent a chill through her. She didn't turn.

"Goodbye, Sir."

CHAPTER 8

SID PEEKED OUT THE CURTAIN in the bay window and watched the black SUV back out of the driveway and roll out. The chill between her shoulders didn't ease. It seemed everyone knew something they weren't telling. First her old boss, Ted, and now her current boss, Jack.

Behind her, metal clanked on the floor.

In a single motion, she spun around and ripped her pistol out. Smoke sat on the hearth, undoing the cuffs on his ankles.

"Freeze!"

He didn't move a muscle.

"Key. Toss it over to me."

He flicked it at her feet. "You don't think I can work shackled and with this prison garb on, do you?"

"No." She holstered her weapon. "But I won't have you playing pickpocket either. Just be still." She gave him a once-over. A moment ago, he'd been completely disheveled, and now he seemed perfectly fine. He should have been laid out still. "Are you all right?"

Smoke nodded. "Maybe a little achy, but that's more from the vaccination than the taser."

"I don't know what that's about."

"Don't worry about it."

She cocked her head. "You seemed pretty upset about it, and now you're not worried."

"Nope."

"So that was a show?"

"Yep." He held his arms out. "Can you please unlock these?"

"So, you know what the shot was?"

"Yep."

"And they don't?"

"That's right."

"Are you going to tell me?"

"Are you going to take these cuffs off?"

"Answer my question first."

"No, I'm not going to tell you what the shot was for. But I will tell you I have a condition. Nothing contagious, but I've had that shot before."

"Who makes those shots?"

"Don't worry about it." He extended his wrists. "It's just a thing. A private thing. I have my right to privacy, you know."

She tossed him the key.

What in the world is going on?

Smoke had been injected with something, and he was the only one who knew what. He had a fit and had taken a walloping for it. Someone beyond pay grades was overseeing this. Watching Smoke. And so far, everything that was going on made absolutely no sense to her.

Smoked unlocked the last set of cuffs and tossed them on the floor. He unzipped his jumpsuit and slipped out of it.

"What are you doing?" she said, averting her eyes. Her glance revealed his lean body was packed with hard muscle.

"Changing," he said, walking over and grabbing a duffle bag in the corner. He emptied the contents of his bag and slipped on a pair of jeans, a black t-shirt, and work boots. "So, you and Cyrus have a past." He repacked the bag and threw in the jumpsuit. "He doesn't seem like your type."

"I beg your pardon?"

Smoke tossed his duffle bag on the counter. "Aw, come on. It's obvious you two dated. But I can't imagine why you broke it off. He seemed so … charming. Beady eyes and all."

"You have wonderful powers of perception." She opened the file and set it on the kitchen table. "But if it's not related to this case, keep it to yourself."

"Sure." He walked over and stood by her side. "But tell me, why did you go out with him? Let me guess: you thought his drive and intelligence outweighed his meager frame and uber-bland personality."

"No." She kept her eyes on the papers in the file.

"You have a thing for short guys?"

"Mister Smoke—"

"Smoke." He smiled. "Just call me Smoke."

"Grab a chair."

Smoke took a seat and hitched one booted foot on the table. It had the ankle tracker on it. "They might as well have left the handcuffs on. Ridiculous."

Sid downloaded the application Cyrus had sent her. A minute later, Smoke's location was on the screen. She showed it to him. "Works great. Things are looking up. Now, let's discuss our current situation… First, whatever you have in mind, you run by me first. Second, you don't go anywhere without me."

"I need to hit the head."

"Third." She looked at his boot on the table. "Keep it professional."

He dropped his foot on the floor.

"All right, but I really do."

"Make it quick."

He got up. "I missed prison chow this morning too." He patted his stomach. "I'd really like to have some pancakes."

She looked at him. "I don't care."

He picked up his duffle bag.

"Where are you going with that?"

"If you don't mind, I'm going to shave." He rubbed his chin. "This scruff makes me feel dirty. Now that I'm out of prison, I want to feel clean again."

"That really doesn't matter to me."

Smoke walked away and flipped a hallway switch.

"No bulbs."

Sid heard him checking switches until he finally stopped and a door near the back of the house closed. She checked the monitor on her phone. *Good.* Inside the file were more pictures of Adam Vaughn. He wore plain clothes and kept a personal network of goons close by. Most of the footage wasn't the best, as it came from security cameras and the locations were erratic. Different banks. Restaurants—some expensive, others dives. AV seemed to have friends in high and low places. She became engrossed. There were pictures of weapons caches. Unidentified men slaughtered. There were pages of documentation with the letters blacked out.

What good is this?

There was an envelope inside she'd overlooked. She opened it. A brief letter was typed out on bureau letterhead.

Agent Shaw,

Due to the unorthodox arrangement of this assignment, you will need to keep the following items under consideration.

John Smoke is a convicted criminal with special skills. Don't underestimate him.

You have eyes on him and we have eyes on him. Allow him free range. We'll let you know if he needs to be reeled in.

If any alien objects or circumstances or individuals are encountered, notify your superiors immediately.

Trust your instincts and good hunting,

The Bureau

"Who on earth wrote this?" She glanced at her phone. Smoke's beacon hadn't moved. "It can't be from the bureau."

It was a first: a cryptic, unprofessional, unsigned letter. It made her wonder if Cyrus or Jack were playing a joke on her. But the bureau stamp. The make of the paper. She'd seen it before. It was nothing short of top brass bonding. She shook her head.

I guess there's a first time for everything.

She put the letter back inside the envelope and slipped it into her bag. *'Allow him free range', it says.* She smirked. *He doesn't need to know that.*

There was a squeak from down the hall. The turn of a faucet. The faint sound of water echoing.

Are you kidding me? A shower? Really? I thought he was hungry.

She glanced at the tracker on her phone. Nothing had changed.

One by one, she entered the location coordinates into her phone. Ten minutes later she was done.

Sidney brushed her hair aside. "I need a map." Her belly groaned. "Someone needs another shake." She gathered all the items up and stuck them back in the file folder. Calling out, "Let's get this show on the road," she made her way down the hall and listened at the door. The shower was still running. She rapped her knuckles on it. "Hey."

No reply.

She checked her tracker, and it showed no changes. She knocked again.

Her fingertips started to tingle. She drew her gun and tested the door handle. Locked.

"John? John Smoke?"

No reply.

She stepped back and delivered a heavy kick. The hollow door burst open. The mirror was steamed up, and the ankle tracker lay resting on the back of the toilet. She picked it up.

Damn. How'd he do that?

CHAPTER 9

A NGRY, SIDNEY RIPPED THE SHOWER curtain back.

Smoke was in there.

"Hey! Do you mind?"

"What! Do I mind?" She looked away and slung the ankle tracker at him. "Put that back on!"

"I didn't want to get it wet," he said, chuckling.

"It's waterproof, imbecile!" Sidney left the room. Her face was flushed red. *How in the world did he do that?* "Get dressed and get out here!"

"I'm coming," he said from inside the bathroom. "What's the matter, Agent Shaw? Did you think all of your plans had gone up in Smoke?"

How did he do that? She stormed down the hall. Paced back and forth. Smoke rattled her. Nothing ever rattled her—until this assignment. *Get it together, Sid. Get it together.*

A few minutes later, Smoke came out. He was drying his dark hair off with his towel.

"Sorry about that," he said. "I didn't mean to startle you."

"I kicked the door in. You didn't hear that?"

"I was singing," he said, screwing up his face, "I think. Sometimes I get really into it."

"I didn't hear any singing." She glanced down at his ankle. The ankle tracker was back. "Care to explain?"

"I have my secrets."

"Do you want pancakes, little boy?"

"Okay, I made some calls."

Her head tilted over. "How did you do that?"

"I borrowed one of those agents' phones. The one who got a piece of taser." He held it out. "He can have it back now."

She snatched it from his hand and slipped it in her bag. "Who did you call?"

"My crew."

"And they remotely disarmed the ankle tracker?"

"Sure. Not a problem. And this model isn't one of the best ones. As soon as I gave them a model number, they laughed. So, they looped the signal and I unsnapped it. Easy peasy."

"Are you testing me, Mister Smoke?"

"I'm just knocking some dust off, Agent Shaw. We're going up against something big, and I need to be sharp." He tossed the towel aside and came closer. "I could have just vanished, you know."

"True, but then I wouldn't buy you any pancakes."

"Mmm," Smoke said. "That's good." He stuffed in another forkful of buttermilk pancakes slathered in syrup. He was half through his second stack. "You really should try some."

"No thanks," Sidney said again. She took a sip of coffee. She hadn't been inside an IHOP since she was a teenager. "I'm fine."

Smoke shrugged and stuffed in another mouthful. Over the past hour he'd proven himself to be the most elusive garbage disposal she'd ever known. He was a bit of a chatterbox too, asking her bizarre question after question that she ignored and dodged until they arrived at their high-carb destination.

She checked messages on her phone. Text. Email. Her niece, Megan, had dropped her a quick text that said 'Hi' with a smile and a unicorn. It had been a while since she heard from her. Her sister, Allison, had issues.

"What's the matter?" Smoke said, gulping down his second Coke and motioning for the waitress.

"Nothing." She set down her phone. "Tell me about this crew of yours."

A waitress took away his glass. "I'll be right back, Hun."

"Thanks," he said. "Sure, my crew. Right. Well, not much to tell. Just two friends that help me track things down. They work the inside, and I work the outside."

"Do they have names?"

"Fat Sam and Guppy."

"And this Fat Sam and Guppy are the ones that helped you hack into FBI property."

He nodded and shoved more pancake in his mouth. "Mmm! I swear, this makes me feel like I haven't eaten in months. Prison food has no flavor to it. And we never get pancakes or waffles, either. Which do you prefer?"

"Neither." She straightened herself in her seat. "Are you about finished?"

"Huh? Well, no. This is a carb load. The protein load comes next." He eyed her and her plate of half-eaten bacon. "You look like someone who knows something about that."

"Are your friends criminals?"

Smoke sat up and leered down. "No. Why would you say that?"

"I need to know what I'm dealing with. 'Fat Sam and Guppy' doesn't tell me much of anything." She took another sip of coffee. "You have to admit, it sounds shady."

"'Fat Sam and Guppy' sounds shady to you?"

"Yeah."

He shook his head. "Well, they say perception is everything."

The waitress returned with his third Coke. "Anything else, hun?"

Smoke looked at Sidney.

She glanced at the windows. The rain was pouring down, and the chill in her bones had finally faded. She gave him a nod.

Smoke held up the menu and pointed.

"I want this and this."

"Anything else?"

"I'll let you know when I'm through."

The waitress brushed by him. "You do that."

"Sure," Sidney said. "You do that. So, you were talking about Sam and Guppy?"

"No, you were talking about them." He took a drink. "Listen, they are legit. No record."

"Which implies they haven't been caught."

"Sort of, Agent Shaw … or Sidney … or Sid—can I call you that?"

"Let's keep it professional."

"Ugh … Agent Shaw, how suspicious are you of this hunt? I mean, think about it. They don't want you in the office. That limits resources. Instead, they want you to tail me as I go on a hunt. And you said yourself they weren't following protocol. Doesn't that worry you?"

"A little, maybe."

"Good. You're honest. Frankly I'm a bit worried too. Not in a scared way, but in a 'I'm pretty sure I'm being manipulated' kind of way."

"Then why do it?"

"It's the Black Slate. Bad people are on that list, and I like the idea of putting them away. Say, mind if I take a look at that file now?"

"Can you handle it while you're eating?"

"I'm a multitasker," he said, taking another big bite of pancakes.

She opened her bag and handed over the file. Smoke rummaged through it, his dark eyes scanning the contents. He was an attractive man. Boyish, yet dark. She noted white scar lines on his hands. A broken finger that hadn't healed well.

"He's a swarthy-looking Spaniard."

"Why do you say he's a Spaniard?"

Smoke shrugged. "He has some interesting haunts, too. Ew, look at all these dead guys. That's not good. Why did you show me this while I was eating?" He stuffed the papers inside the envelope. "I'm going to need a copy of this."

"It's confidential."

"Really?" He laughed. "I don't think there *is* such a thing these days."

The waitress returned and set down two steaming omelets surrounded by hash browns, all on one plate.

"Aw, you put them on one plate. That was really sweet of you. Thanks, sugar."

The waitress pinched his cheek. "If you weren't my son's age, I'd take you home with me." She looked at Sidney. "You found yourself a good one here. Big eater. I like a man that lets you feed him."

"Uh, we're not …" Sidney started, but the waitress moved on.

"Are you a good cook?" Smoke said, sharpening his knife with his fork.

"I can make an omelet."

"Well that's better than the last girl I dated."

"This isn't a date."

"Easy, I'm just making conversation."

"Let's stay on point, Mister Smoke."

"You see, there you go again. Just call me Smoke."

She held her tongue. She wanted to call him something else, but didn't.

"Agent Shaw, let me tell you how I expect things to go. I need information and a couple of days. I want to go to my place. Sort through some things. When I'm ready to move, I'll let you know and … we go."

"That's not going to happen. We're going to go back to the house and plan things out. We only have two weeks to resolve this."

He tilted his head back and closed his eyes. "Ugh. This is why I work alone."

"And you'd still be working alone if you hadn't gotten carried away with your last job."

"Just two days, that's all I ask. You take some time and I take some time. After that, I'll fill you in and be more willing to cooperate. Please."

The letter did say to turn him loose, but she wanted to hang on. That was her nature. Her training. This scenario was the complete opposite of everything she'd been taught. It irked her.

"You can take the ankle tracker off. That's the biggest problem. Why did you show your cards on that one?"

"Perhaps I was showing off a little."

"Here's the deal. You stay in the house. I drop you off. I pick you up. If I show up and the ankle tracker is there but you aren't, it's over."

"I'll keep it on if you insist, but take a moment. Don't you see the problem this ankle tracker presents? It's a distraction for us, nothing more. It doesn't benefit either of us. It only benefits *them*."

"Them?"

"You know," he said, eyeballing around. "Them."

I actually understand his point. "I tell you what, Mister Smoke. You finish your meal, we go back to the house, lay out a plan, and we'll see how it goes. Easy peasy?"

He dug into his omelet. "Good enough for me."

Her phone buzzed. It was another text from her niece, Megan. Her heart stopped. The text read:

Sorry to bother you, but I haven't seen Mommy in three days. I'm scared. A frowning icon followed.

CHAPTER 10

"**W**HAT'S GOING ON?" SMOKE SAID.

Sidney pulled the sedan into the driveway of the house, put it in park, and looked at him.

"Here's the deal. You go inside. You don't leave."

"Come on," he said. "You've been frosty the entire ride. What's going on? I can help."

"Get your bag. Get out of the car. Get inside the house."

Nodding and raising his hands in surrender, Smoke reached into the back seat and grabbed his duffle bag. He popped the door open to the sound of pouring rain outside. "Let me come."

"I'll be back tonight. Just go."

Smoke stepped into the rain, shut the door, and dashed onto the covered porch.

Sidney didn't wait to see if he went inside. She hit the gas, squealed out of the driveway, and blasted the car through the rain.

"Dammit!"

She was torn. On the one hand, she hated to let Smoke out of her sight. On the other, she didn't want him in her personal business.

It took her an hour and a half to get to her sister's apartment, talking to Megan the entire ride. The nine-year-old was tough, but scared. Sidney wheeled into the apartment complex, which consisted of twenty three-story brick buildings, a pool, tennis courts, and a gym—all of which were long past their glory days.

She parked, headed up the grass to the screened patio of her sister's porch, and knocked on the metal frame of the screen door.

"Megan? It's me, Aunt Sid."

A cute little face peeked through the blinds, and its watery eyes brightened. Megan unlocked the door, flung it open, ran outside, and hugged Sidney.

Sidney picked her up and carried her inside.

"It's all right. It's going to be all right."

Using her foot, she closed the door behind her and sat down on the couch with Megan latched onto her. Sidney's heart burst in her chest.

Allison had better not be using again.

"All right, Megan, all right. You're safe. I'm here." She pushed Megan back and wiped the tears from her eyes. The little girl's long brown hair was braided back in a ponytail. Her face was sweet and innocent with freckles on her nose. "I'm going to take care of you."

"I-I was doing fine. I even made it to school the last two days, but the storm scared me. I thought Mommy would be home by now, but she isn't. Do you think she's mad at me?"

"No, no, no, of course not." Sidney took a breath. Megan was a capable little girl. She'd learned how to take care of herself when she was little. An independent little thing. "She probably got lost again."

"Will you find her, Aunt Sid?"

"I will." She hugged her niece again. "I will."

Her sister, Allison, was younger. She was a runaway. An addict. A mess. Sidney could never make heads or tails of her problems, but she always tried to protect her. No matter what, Allison stayed in trouble. It was heartbreaking and infuriating.

"Are you hungry?"

"No," Megan said, "I had some cereal."

"Do you want to go stay with Nanny and Grandpa?"

"Can't you just stay here with me?" Megan looked at her with sad eyes. "Until Mommy comes back?"

"I'll see what I can do, but I have to call Nanny and Grandpa first."

Megan shrugged. She looked adorable. Little blue jeans. A flowery pink-and-purple shirt. "They'll do."

Sidney didn't stick around after her mother arrived. Keeping the reunion short, she hit the road and headed to Allison's ex-boyfriend's … Dave was his name. According to Megan, he'd been coming around and staying over from time to time. The last time she'd seen Dave and Megan together, it hadn't ended well.

If she's with him, I might kill both of them.

She drove the car into another neighborhood a little better than the one where she'd left Smoke. The sidewalks and driveways made up the edges of well-kept lawns. Leaves were in piles and bagged at the end of the drives. She pulled along the sidewalk across the street from Dave's house, 104 Dickers Street. The windows were barred. The screen door was a wrought-iron security door. The garage door was closed.

Somebody's made some changes since the last time I was here.

She checked her phone. Smoke's beacon remained in place.

He'd better be there.

The blinds were shut, but light peeked out at the corners. She waited. Dave was a dealer. A clever one. He moved small quantities to subsidize his government assistance. He hadn't worked in years—or ever, for all she knew. She waited another hour. Cars splashed by. Water poured into the grates. It was 2:15 p.m. when she looked again. She needed to get back to Smoke. She needed to find her sister.

I need to put an ankle tracker on her!

She drummed her fingernails on the steering wheel. Chewed on her lip.

Aw, screw it.

She popped the trunk, opened her door, and stepped out into the rain. From the trunk she grabbed an umbrella and opened it up. A car rolled by, splashed her legs, and pulled into Dave's driveway. She noted the plate.

A couple of young men in hoodies jumped out of the car and rushed onto the stoop. One started pounding on the door. The other was yelling.

"Hurry up! It's cold as hell out here!"

The door opened. Sidney hid behind the umbrella until she heard the door close, then made her way across the street and waited beside the front door on the stoop, craning her neck toward the window. The voices were muffled, and the driving rain splattering all around drowned out the details. She closed the umbrella, shook it off, and waited. Ten minutes later, the door opened. She stepped back and whipped out her badge.

The dilated eyes of the young men lifted toward her.

Sidney held her badge up and said quietly, "Disappear."

The two scurried through the rain without a glance backward.

Sidney caught the door with her umbrella and slipped inside.

"Shut the door, you idiots!" a voice said. Dave appeared in the foyer. His eyes widened. He dropped his can of beer. "Aw shit! How'd you get in here?"

Sidney closed the door behind her and locked it.

"Hey, hey," Dave said, holding his hands up and backing away into the living room. "I didn't do anything."

"Sure you didn't, Dave. Sure."

Dave wasn't a bad-looking guy. He had a mop of brown hair and strong features. A scruffy beard. The plaid pajama pants and Bob Marley T-shirt did little to enhance his demeanor. His eyes were weak and yellow, and he smelled like reefer.

"You can't be in here," he said. "It's illegal."

"Where is Allison, Dave?"

His eyes flitted around the room. A bong sat on the coffee table in front of a new plush sectional sofa. A video game was playing on a seventy-inch flat-screen TV.

"I haven't seen her."

"Do you remember what happened the last time you lied to me about her?"

Grimacing, he rubbed the white scar on his forehead.

"Yes."

Sidney got closer and bounced the handle of the umbrella on his shoulder.

"Don't make me use this."

"What are you going to do with an umbrella?" He laughed. "Let me guess. Stick it where the sun don't shine and open it?"

"Aw, that's my darling Dave. Smart-ass dope head and everything." She stepped on his toe. "You know what, Dave? I really like your idea."

"You would, seeing how you don't have any of your own." He tugged his foot out. "And as I recall, you got into quite a bit of trouble the last time you barged in here, didn't you?"

"Oh, you gonna call your uncle again, the congressman?"

"Yep."

"Hmmm," she said, tapping the umbrella on his shoulder. "I think he's in danger of losing this next election. Yes, I'm pretty sure he's done for."

"No he isn't. He's up in the polls."

She smiled.

"I'll take my chances."

She brought the umbrella handle down between his eyes.

Crack!

"Ow! You bitch!"

Crack!

"Ugh! Stop it!"

"Stop it what?"

"Sid!"

Crack!

"Agent Shaw! Okay? Agent Shaw!"

"Dave, this is the last time that I ask. Where is she?"

He swallowed hard and looked away.

Sidney made it over to the coffee table, picked up the bong, and started to pour the water out on his new couch.

"Be nice, now. I didn't do this. I swear it's not my fault."

"Where IS she?"

"I-I..."

Sidney dropped some more water on the sofa.

"Aw ..." Dave moaned.

"If you like, Dave, I'll be more than happy to confiscate your inventory."

"Not without a warrant."

She poured out the bong and dropped it on the couch.

"Dammit, that's new!"

She took out her phone.

"I'm out of patience. One call, and a swarm of local law enforcement will be here."

"You wouldn't dare. Not after the last time."

She started to dial.

Dave turned tail and ran up the steps.

"Allison! Allison! Run!"

Sidney surged up the stairs and stormed down the hallway just as Dave jetted into a bedroom and slammed the door behind him.

Sidney pounded on the door.

"Open up! I'm not playing any games! Get out of there, Allison!"

"Screw you, *Agent* Shaw!" Dave yelled.

She kicked the door in.

Dave stood inside an unkempt bedroom with the window wide open. One leg hung outside the sill.

She grabbed him by the arm, jerked him inside, and wrestled him to the floor.

"No more games, Dave."

"You're too late," he said, laughing. "She's already gone."

She checked outside the window. There was a deck and stairs that led down into the backyard. There was no sign of Allison.

"She left you a message, Sid," Dave said, sitting up and rubbing his head.

"Really, what was that?"

He giggled. "You are so stupid."

"Am I? Why is that?"

She heard the rumble of a garage door opening.

"Because," Dave said, "she was never up here to begin with. It was all a distraction, you stupid b—"

She socked him in the jaw, rocking his head back to the carpet. *Whap!* She dashed downstairs and opened the front door. A jungle-green Jeep Wrangler sped out of the garage down the street and disappeared around the corner.

"Damn!"

CHAPTER 11

Sidney rushed to her car and slung open the door. Taking a seat, she glanced back at Dave's house. A blind in one of the top bedrooms peeked open. She saw the faint outline of two fingers.

Wait a minute.

She took a second and closed her eyes, envisioned the Jeep Wrangler speeding away. There was a lone driver hunched over the wheel. Big. Husky. Allison could have been hidden in the back seat. Or maybe not. She had a feeling. An instinct.

That little dope-headed witch is still in there.

The garage door started to close.

Crap! Move it, Sid!

She couldn't let Dave lock her out again. And she dared not force herself in, not after the last time. She was probably in enough trouble already. She sprinted across the street, right in front of an oncoming car. It squealed to a stop, and the driver laid on the horn. She kept moving, eyes intent on the lowering garage door. She wasn't going to make it. She made a decision and did a stupid thing.

Sidney drew her gun and slung it under the garage door. It skidded over the driveway, clearing the opening by inches and disappearing inside. The door stopped, rattled … and began to lift. She heard a voice inside scream. Up the door went. One foot. Two feet. It stopped and renewed its descent. Sidney rolled underneath it and inside. She spied her gun, scrambled to it, and found Dave's wide eyes.

"No!" he said, making his way back inside through the door. "No! Get out of here!"

Sidney snatched up her weapon and charged the closing door that was slamming shut. She lowered her shoulder and plowed into it. The impact jarred the door open. It jarred Dave.

"You get out of here! This is illegal!"

She drove her knee into his crotch. She shoved him inside the garage and watched him spill onto the floor, cry out, and writhe. She slammed the door shut and locked it.

Upstairs, she heard footfalls scampering over the floor. There was something about them—lithe, child-like, familiar. She made it upstairs in seconds. A woman with long dark hair, blue jeans, and a black T-shirt ambled across the hall into another room and stumbled inside the door.

"Allison!"

Two bare feet slipped into the frame, and the bedroom door started to close. Sidney stopped it with her foot and shoved it open. She looked down at her sister. Allison was a smaller version of herself, but soft and supple. She was shaking. Her face was sad. Tears streamed out of her eyes. There were needle tracks on one arm.

"I'm sorry, Sid. I'm sorry."

"Shut up," Sidney said. "Do you know how long it's been since you left Megan?"

"A day?" Allison sniffed.

"Three days!"

"No," Allison said, shaking her head. "It, it can't have been."

"Well, it has."

Allison started to bawl. Tears streamed out of her sunken eyes and over her pouting lips. "I'm a lousy mother."

"You're a lousy sister too. Get up!"

"What? Why? I'm not leaving. I don't deserve to go back."

Sidney reached down and grabbed her arm.

"Get up!"

Allison jerked away. "No!"

Here we go. Her little claws are coming out.

"I'll take you out of here in handcuffs."

Allison pounced on her legs and drove her to the floor. Sidney cracked her head on the door frame, drawing spots in her eyes.

"No you won't!" Allison screamed. She sprang out of the door.

Angry, Sidney snatched her sister's ankle and climbed onto her back.

"Get off me! Get off me! Dave!"

Sidney wrenched Allison's arms behind her back. Her sister squealed. She bound up her wrists and slipped the flexi-cuffs on her. Allison resumed her bawling.

"Get up. I'm not carrying you."

"No," Allison said with a defiant sob. "No."

She grabbed Allison by the ankles and started dragging her toward the stairs. Her sister kicked at her and yelled.

"I hate you! I hate you, Sid! I hate you! Why can't you mind your own business? Why can't you leave me alone!"

This wasn't the first time the sisters had gone round and round. It all started in their teens. Allison liked to party. She liked the attention. She liked boys. Drugs. Excitement. Sidney bailed her little sister out time and again. It got old. It had made her mom and dad old.

"Why don't you grow up, you little brat! You have a daughter. Go to church and find Jesus or something." She hauled Allison down the carpeted stairs.

"Hey!"

"Get up, then!"

At the landing, Allison started to rise. She eyeballed Sidney. She spat in her face.

Sidney slapped her across the jaw, and Allison stumbled back to the floor. Her little sister wailed. "I hate you, Sid. I hate you."

Sidney dragged her to her feet and said, "You don't hate me. You hate yourself."

Family. It mattered, even though her sister was a wild one who often ruined the best-planned Thanksgiving. Sidney loved her sister, even though for the last decade she'd wanted to choke her. And there was Megan. How could Allison neglect Megan? The little beauty was about one step from a foster home if she and their parents didn't intervene.

Please God. Please don't let that happen.

Sidney pulled into a gas station alongside the pumps. It was evening now, and she'd just spent the last three hours helping her parents get Allison settled down. They were all distraught, and none more so than Allison had been when she was finally reunited with Megan. She had shaken all over and sobbed, begging forgiveness. All Megan had said was, "It's going to be okay, Mommy."

Megan was a strong little lady.

Sidney whipped out her credit card, pumped gas, ran inside the station, and grabbed some coffee. Black. No cream. No sugar. No straws. She dropped two bucks on the counter and left, ignoring the greasy-haired clerk's toothy smile at her.

Creep.

She racked the nozzle, grabbed her receipt, and hopped back inside the car to lean back against the headrest and take a long sigh.

Lousy weather. Lousy day. I should have transferred south when I had the chance. What was I thinking?

Family. She rubbed the knot on the side of her head.

Love hurts.

She took a sip of coffee and checked her phone. Smoke's location hadn't changed.

He'd better be there—probably wants more pancakes.

She put the car in drive, sped out onto the main drag, and gunned it onto the highway. Her thoughts were riddled with her family. The burden on Mom and Dad. Dealing with Allison's problems. And Megan. This was one of the things she hated about her job. She loved her duty. She loved her family. But duty presided over family, and it hurt in times like this when they needed her.

"It's all right," her mother, Sally, had assured her. "We understand. It's our job to handle this. We'll get her on the mend."

Her father, Keith, had agreed and nodded his head. Both of her parents were strong, but they were heartbroken, and they weren't getting any younger. She could see it in their eyes. She heard the worry in their voices, not just for Allison, but for her. They didn't like the job she did. It was dangerous. And oftentimes Sidney felt selfish. It tore at her.

Block it out. Block it out, Sid. You can't take care of everybody.

Sidney had to live her life and be available when she could.

"Just do the best you can, Sid," her father had said, giving her one last hug. His hugs were always warm and comforting. "Do the best you can."

I try, but it never feels like enough.

CHAPTER 12

I T WAS 8:14 P.M. WHEN she pulled into the driveway of the FBI house. Smoke's beacon was still strong, but the porch lights were out, and so was the lamppost at the end of the drive.

He's not here. I know it.

The front door was locked, and none of the inside lights shone. She took out the house key that Jack had given her and fumbled around with the lock until she got it. Inside she went, testing the switches until she made it to the lamp between the living room and kitchen and switched it on.

With caution she made her way down the hallway. A dim light showed beneath one of the doors. She put her ear to it and heard voices on the other side. She drew her weapon, turned the knob, and opened the door. A set of wooden stairs led into a basement she hadn't accounted for. Weapon first, she crept down them.

The basement was partially finished. There were hook-ups for laundry and an unfinished shower. The framework of two-by-four walls was laid out. There was an empty fireplace and a rec room or den of some sort. A flat-screen TV was on. In front of it was a plaid sofa, and there was an old recliner that didn't match beside it. A news show was on the screen. A lady doing the weather.

What is going on here?

She noticed a wooden kitchen table with some papers fanned out on it. A pizza box and a two-liter of soda. Some power tools and drywall were lying nearby on the floor. There was a map hanging on a plywood wall.

A commode flushed.

Sidney whirled around.

Smoke stepped out from behind a narrow bathroom door. He lifted his hands up.

"Easy, Shooter. I'm just taking a ten-fourteen, is all." He eyed the gun and cocked a feeble smile. "Glad you're back. Is everything okay? You look like you've had a long day."

She holstered her weapon.

"What is going on here?" She glided back to the table and took a closer look at the contents. The file folder was on the table. Her blood pressure spiked. "You stole my file."

Hands still up, Smoke said, "I can explain."

"Can you now?"

"Sure, I, er ... okay, I stole it, but only so that I could work on things while you were gone." He walked over to his map and pointed at the red circles. "See, now we can take another angle on things."

"You made a mistake."

"I'm sorry," he said, "but I stayed put. I bet you thought I wouldn't, didn't you?"

Her stomach gurgled.

Smoke opened the pizza box. "Half ham and onions and half Hawaiian. Please, have some."

"How did you get this?"

"Uh ... Delivery."

"And how did you pay for it? Did you spend my money too?"

"No," he said, "I'd never do that." He tapped his head. "I have many numbers in my head. Hey, my accounts are still good."

"Well, you did one thing right today."

"I did? What's that?"

Sidney picked up a slice of pizza and took a seat on the sofa.

"I like Hawaiian."

The old sofa was comfortable. It reminded her of the times she and Allison would stay in their grandparents' basement for long weekends. She bit into the pizza.

"I could warm it up," Smoke said. "I came down here and saw that some of the breakers were off, but I let them be. I didn't want any nosy neighbors dropping by for a greeting. I like my privacy."

Sidney yawned. An image of Megan came to mind, and she forced it out again. She studied the television. "So, you're getting reception down here."

"I spliced into the box."

"Cable theft is a crime," she said with a laugh.

Smoke eased into the recliner.

"So, I'm here. You're here. What's the next move?"

I have no idea.

"You look beat," he continued.

"I look beat? Really?"

"Sorry, I guess *tired* is a better word."

She finished off the pizza and dusted off her hands. She wanted to lie down, but she forced herself off the sofa instead and headed toward the map.

"Where did you get the map? Did the pizza guy deliver that too?"

"Er … well, you shouldn't be surprised at what you can get delivered these days. As a matter of fact, Amazon—"

"Save it. I don't care to know." She eyed the map that was tacked to the wall. Smoke had seven locations circled and named in colored Sharpie. "I guess they delivered the thumb tacks and pens, too." She faced him. He sat with an innocent look on his face. "Is there anything else you care to share that you *ordered*? Should I expect a delivery from QVC?"

"No."

Her thoughts raced.

He could have had a gun delivered. Anything! "Get up!"

"What?"

"I said, 'get up'!"

"But—"

She drew her gun. "Now!"

Slowly he came out of the chair.

"Put your hands on your head."

"Okay."

She held her weapon barrel up under his neck, kept her eyes on him, and patted him down. Her fingers found a gun tucked in the back of his pants.

"Sit."

Smoke obeyed.

"Where did you get this?"

"From the same agent that I got the handcuff keys from. Smith & Wesson .45 ACP." He smiled. "A fine weapon. But he doesn't deserve it if he can't secure it."

"And you don't deserve it either."

"You can't expect me to traverse troubled waters without a weapon in hand."

"No one said anything about you getting a weapon. It's illegal for a convict to possess one."

"I'm not a—oh, never mind." He flopped back into his seat. "Fine. Keep it."

She stuffed it in the back of her pants.

"Thank you."

How did he steal a weapon from an agent? She turned and faced the map again, hiding the grin on her face. *Impressive. I wish I could see Jack's face when he finds out.*

"So tell me, Mister Smoke, what have you learned from all of these locations?"

"Smoke, and they have nothing of use whatsoever."

"What do you mean? There has to be something here."

He got up and picked up the pictures from the table. "All of these pictures of Adam Vaughn at all of these locations. Well, guess what."

"Humor me?"

"These photos are doctored."

CHAPTER 13

SIDNEY STUDIED THE PHOTOS.

"You have to be kidding me."

"I wish I was," Smoke said.

She took a seat at the kitchen table and eyed each photo one by one. Smoke was right. The shadows were bad. The angles off. Faint white lines showed where images had been trimmed and cropped. Repetition of pixels. A lack of reflections. They were good fakes, really good. She'd spent months working with the FBI's digital forensics labs. She should have caught this right off the bat. She pushed her hair back from her eyes.

I'm an idiot.

Ever since Jack woke her up, her entire day had been rush, rush, rush. Everything was off beat. Unorthodox. She liked order. She liked a plan. She liked to be in charge.

Today is not my day.

"You have a good eye," she said. "I have to admit I'm surprised. And I hate to admit that I missed it."

"You hardly looked at them." He cleared his throat. "Given the evidence, I have a suggestion."

Sidney sifted through the file. There were rap sheets on some of the faces that accompanied Adam Vaughn.

"We'll go after them," she said.

"We?"

"Sure. You're used to stakeouts, aren't you?"

"Not with a partner. And I thought I was going this alone and reporting back to you."

"Given the circumstances, I think it's best that we stay together. I feel more comfortable keeping an eye on things."

Smoke scratched his forehead. "So, when do we start this stakeout?"

"When I say so."

The couch groaned when Smoke lay down. "Great, wake me up when you're ready to go."

Sidney continued her closer inspection of the papers in the file. Pictures. Names. Places. Drug labs. Murder scenes. Illegal arms. Adam Vaughn was in a mish-mash of illegal behavior.

"You know," Smoke said, "I'm sure you know we're being set up to fail. Or at least I am."

"I thought you were taking a nap."

"No, I was just thinking. Honestly, Agent Shaw, just let me go at this alone. There's no reason you need to get hurt."

She began organizing the papers and pictures in neat little piles.

"I beg your pardon?"

"Think about it, The Black Slate, it's just a ruse. They don't really want us to find those criminals. Or at least not AV. They just want paperwork for the files so that it looks like they're trying to put them down. It's all baloney."

Oh Lord, that's exactly what I was thinking ... Quick, find a reason to not like this guy.

"Sounds like you read a lot of conspiracy books in prison." She plucked out the picture of a beefy dog-faced man named Rod Brown. "Do you lose a lot of sleep over it?"

"I always sleep like a baby."

"Except now, unfortunately."

"You really don't have to be so defensive," he said. We're on the same team, remember?"

"We aren't a team."

"Then what are we?"

She found his eyes. "Screwed." She held up the picture of Rod Brown. "But not as bad as this guy when we find him."

"So this is your plan, stake out this Rod Brown fella?" Smoke sat in the passenger seat with a frown on his face. "With a face like that, he must have had a hard life. He looks like a bulldog. Maybe a Rottweiler. Why'd you pick him?"

"He looks stupid."

"Man, why didn't I think of that? Wow, you really learn great things at the academy." He fanned the photo. "Just shake down the stupid-looking people."

Sidney wanted to laugh, but she didn't. It was difficult because she liked joking around. She often did with the people she worked with once she got to know them. Yawning, she focused on the road.

"You'll be sharper if you get some rest," Smoke suggested. "Tell you what. How about you let me drive this racing machine. Crown Vic. Rear wheel drive. Small block V-8. Pretty slow muscle if you ask me, but I can make it fun." He toyed with the dash. "What year is this thing? Two thousand eight?"

"Nine."

"Oh. Seems older. How about I put some music on. What kind do you like?"

She could feel his eyes on her. "How about you leave it alone."

"I bet you like talk radio."

"No, what I like is *no talking about the radio*."

Smoke blanched. "Wow. That was almost funny." Smoke leaned back in his seat and perused the file. "So are we going to Mister Brown's apartment or hangout? I'd try the apartment first. It's too early for the hangout. What do you think?"

"I think you'll know when we get there."

"That isn't exactly fair," he said. "I need a little time to visualize and prepare. You know, a heads up."

Sidney laid down the accelerator and zoomed up the interstate's passing lane. She loved the feeling of the car pushing forward.

"You're breaking the speed limit," Smoke said. "Huh, I bet you're one of those speed demons. Where did you say you were from? Bristol?"

He's annoying. Perhaps I should let him work alone.

Smoke kept talking and she continued her silence. Too many things were running through her mind. The doctored pictures were a problem. Surely someone else had studied them, Jack perhaps. The digital forensics lab. Who had made them? Why the deception? She had been with the FBI five years, and until today, the job had been cut and dried. And that begged another question. Why her? And why had her old boss, Ted, recommended extraordinary caution?

"So, how's your family?" Smoke said.

"Great."

He bobbed his head. "That's good to hear. Do they live in the area?"

"No."

"Well, not the immediate area, but maybe within a few counties or so? You sound local. Very, very local."

"A lot of people say that about me."

"A lot of people such as ... friends?"

I'm going to shoot him.

"I noticed a little indentation on your ring finger," Smoke continued. "Are you divorced? It's funny how that ring seems permanent. It wasn't Cyrus, was it?" Smoke pulled down his visor and checked his hair in the mirror. "No, it's been a while since you two had your thing. But I have to say, you and Cyrus ... you have to admit that was a huge mismatch."

"Shut up."

"Fine." Smoke zipped his mouth shut, locked it, powered down the window, and tossed out the imaginary key. He closed the window and held out his hands.

And this guy used to be a Navy SEAL? Geez.

She blocked Smoke's humming out until they arrived at Rod Brown's condominium and parked on the street just outside the parking lot. The record didn't state whether he drove a car or not. She checked the address in the file. Unit 12, room 11. She checked her watch. 10:35 p.m.

"If you stop humming, I'll let you listen to the radio while we wait."

Smoke mumbled from behind his sealed lips.

"Enough, please," she said.

"So, now what? We're just going to sit here?"

"Yep."

"Uh ... and what if he's on vacation or out on the job?"

She shrugged. "We'll see."

Smoked stared out his window. "Why don't you let me go and see if he's in his condo?"

"No."

"Come on. Just give me a little bit of leash. It's not like I haven't ever performed recon before. Please."

His words softened her. She didn't like it. "Ten minutes—"

Smoke popped open the door.

"Stop right there!"

He shut the door in her face and disappeared between the buildings.

Sidney closed her hanging jaw.

I'll give him ten minutes. If he's not back by then, I'm going to catch him and kill him. She pounded her fist on the dash. *Men!*

She took out her phone. Smoke's beacon remained in the area. A text message popped up from her mother.

"It's going to be a long few nights, but we'll be fine. Jeff is here. Don't worry."

Jeff was a lifelong friend who had handled Allison before. A good guy. Calm under pressure.

Sidney didn't respond. If she did, her mother would keep texting all night.

I'll check tomorrow.

She checked the time. 10:41 p.m. Smoke's beacon was unmoving.

Maybe this is a good thing. Let go, Sid. Let go. You can't control everybody. Just like you can't control Allison.

She drummed her fingers on the steering wheel. The car was fogging up, so she rolled down the window. There were more than a dozen buildings in the complex. Rod's was one away from the highway. His place was on the first floor. The file said he was a very husky guy, three hundred pounds or so.

Sidney reached into the back seat and dug a pair of binoculars out of a gym bag. She spied on the sidewalk that led in front of the condo. It was dark, but the lamp posts gave off a dim light in the steady rain.

10:44.

One more minute and it's go time.

She kept the binoculars up. A hulking figure stepped into view.

What in the...

Smoke was running straight for her with a large man hefted over his shoulder.

He's insane!

CHAPTER 14

"**O**PEN THE DOOR! OPEN THE door!" Smoke yelled.

Sidney popped the locks.

Smoke swung open the back door and stuffed the hefty body inside. The back sagged and bounced with the impact. Smoke shoved the man over, hopped in the back seat with him, and shut the door.

"What are you doing? Have you gone mad?"

"Did I make it?" Smoke asked, scanning the dash.

"Make what?"

"Make it back in ten minutes?"

"Are you kidding me?"

"No, you said ten minutes. I made it, didn't I?" He pumped his fist. "Yes, one of my best extractions ever!"

Sidney stared at the man in the back seat. It was Rod Brown. A white cotton tank-top barely contained his belly. His plaid boxer shorts were half turned around. He was out. Out cold.

"Go," Smoke said. "Go! I think someone might have seen me."

"No."

"Yes!" Smoke said. "I see someone coming."

A flashlight coming from the condos cut through the dank night.

Sidney dropped the transmission into drive and sped away. "Do you know how many laws you've broken?"

"Let's see ..." He counted on his fingers. "Breaking and entering, and kidnapping. Two."

"Two to start with."

Rod Brown groaned.

Smoke socked him in the jaw. *Whap!* "And battery."

"You're an idiot!"

"Look," Smoke said, "the way I see it, he's a criminal."

"So are you."

"No—aw, let's not get into that. That said, guys like him don't operate within the rules you hold so dear. They break them. And we aren't going to get anywhere following the FBI playbook." Smoke huffed. "Guys like this laugh at those tactics. If you want to get this done, then we need to fight fire with fire."

"We need to not break the law."

"Then you shouldn't have come along, Agent Shaw. I'm pretty sure that's the reason they hired me to do this: I can get my hands dirty. You can't." He shoved Rod's sagging body over toward the window. "Let me out, and you walk away from this."

"No." In the rearview mirror, she saw Smoke banging his head against his headrest.

I'm in charge, not you.

"So what's the next step in your brilliant plan? Are we going to beat the whereabouts of AV out of him?" she asked.

"Something like that, but my methods of intimidation are a bit more subtle."

"Waterboarding?"

Smoke laughed. "Sure. Why not? Let's swing by Walmart and pick up some bottled water and towels."

Sidney drove the car down into a marina along the Potomac and parked in the shadows where a stretch of highway passed over. She turned and faced Smoke. "Next time, let's put him in the trunk."

"Next time, huh?"

"You know what I mean."

"Sure. Say, where are your flex cuffs?"

She popped open the glove box and handed him two pairs.

Smoke fastened Rod's arms behind his back and bound his ankles. He rummaged through Sidney's gym bag.

"Hey!" She snatched a pair of her panties from his hand. "Do you mind?"

"No," Smoke said. He found a sweatshirt and covered Rod's head. "There. I think we're ready to go now." He handed over her gym bag. "All set. Time to wake him up." He put his finger to his lips. "Let me do the talking."

"Fine. Just don't get carried away." Interrogations. She'd conducted plenty. *Let's see how you handle this.*

"Great, now turn the heater up."

She did.

Smoke nodded. "And cover your ears."

"Why?"

Smoke pinched Rod's inner thigh.

The big man bucked in his seat and let out an ear-splitting howl.

Sidney covered her ears.

Smoke grabbed Rod by his neck and squeezed. "Quiet, Rod, and we'll make this quick."

"Who-who are you?" Rod stammered. "What's going on?"

"I just have a few questions." Smoke changed his voice to something, rougher, darker. "Tell me what I need to know, and I'll let you go."

"Screw you! Do you know who I am?"

"You're Rod Brown. Another one of AV's disposable buttholes."

"Huh? What did you call me? A disposable—"

Smoke punched his face through the sweatshirt. "Shut up!"

"But—"

Punch!

"I don't like your accent. Where are you from, Rod? Pennsylvania? Jersey?"

"Baltimore."

Punch!

"I thought I told you to keep quiet. And I hate Baltimore." Smoke winked at Sidney. "Now, simple question. Where can I find AV?"

Rod remained still and silent. The rising heat was fogging up the windows. Sidney fanned her neck.

"I asked you a question, Rod."

Rod said nothing.

"Oh, I see. Now you're going to be quiet."

Punch.

"Listen, moron," Rod said. "You can punch me all you want, but I don't know any AV."

"Sure, sure you don't. And I'm Mary Poppins."

"You sound like her to me, you frigging putz!" Rod thrashed at his bonds. "Now let me out of these things, you idiot, and I won't have to frigging kill you!"

Smoke reached under the sweatshirt, hooked his fingers into Rod's nose, and lifted him up out of his seat. It was one of Sidney's favorite pressure points. A simple restraining technique. *Impressive.*

"Ow! Ow! Ow!"

"Do you know who AV is, or don't you?"

"Yes! Yes!"

"Are you going to sit still?"

"Yes! Ow! Yes!"

Smoke released him.

"Good, Baltimore Rod. Now we're getting somewhere. So tell me—you're one of his crew—where is he?"

"Look," Rod said, huffing for breath, "Let me do both of us a favor. Whatever you have with AV, drop it. If you pursue it, then you're dead already."

"So you know where he is?"

"All I know is when and where I'm supposed to be. He may or may not be there. Listen, whoever you are, I don't care." Rod's voice started to break. He balled up a little. "Don't cross AV. Don't make me cross AV. It's worse than death, what he does to people who cross him. Worse than death."

An uncanny chill raced down Sidney's spine. She glanced at Smoke. One of his brows was cocked over his eye. He mouthed some words to her. "What do you make of that?"

She shrugged.

He held a finger up, reached into his pocket and handed her a smartphone. He nodded to Rod.

Sidney turned it on. It needed a passcode. *Great.* She thought about it as Smoke went back to work.

"When's your next meeting with AV?"

"Two days."

"Oh, that was pretty quick. I think you're lying, Baltimore Rod." Smoke lightly touched his fingers on Rod's leg.

"Eek! What was that?"

"A spider. Well, a tarantula to be exact." He tickled Rod's leg again.

Rod screamed. "Get it off me! Please! Get it off me!"

"What's the matter, Rod? Are you scared of a little, er, well, a big bug with eight hairy legs?" He barely touched the hair on Rod's leg again.

"Ah!" The big man bucked and twitched. "Stop it! I meet him tomorrow. Late afternoon! Stop it!"

"Where?"

Rod fell silent.

"My spider is a biter, Rod."

"Please, man, please. You don't want to do this. If I tell you, AV will figure it out. AV knows everything. No one can get close to him, no matter how hard they try. Trust me, man. Trust me!" He sobbed. "It's a death wish."

Sidney had seen plenty of men under duress before, but she hadn't expected this. Given enough pressure, loyal foot soldiers rolled on their bosses all the time. This was different. Rod had fear. Real, earnest fear.

*Hmmm…*She decided to try a passcode on Rod's phone. *Let's see how dumb you are.* She typed in his building and room number. 1211. She got access. *Yes!* She showed Smoke. His brows lifted. She began sifting through Rod's emails, contacts, texts, and interesting applications. It was sparse. *Great. A burner.*

"Where are you meeting tomorrow?" Smoke said.

"Aw geez, don't make me, please."

"I'm going to leave you in here with Mister Tarantula. Leave him on your face. How does that sound, Rod?" Smoke tickled his leg.

"Ah! No! No!"

"Ah, yes, yes," Smoke said.

"It's Drake. A club called Drake. He meets us there. Oh man. Oh man, I can't believe I told you." He balled up and started to rock. "I'm a dead man. You're a dead man. All loose ends must go."

CHAPTER 15

S MOKE PUT ROD IN A sleeper hold and silenced the man's hysteria. "Sorry," he said, "that was getting old."

"Agreed." Sidney tossed the phone back to Smoke. "So what's the plan now? Are you going to tuck him back in bed?"

"We could drug him."

"I don't have any drugs. Do you?"

"I was thinking we could buy some."

"Dumb idea. I guess you didn't think things through." Sidney fastened her belt and put the car in drive. In two minutes they were back on the highway.

This is a mess. A total mess.

"You did good," Smoke said.

"I beg your pardon?"

"You did good. You have good instincts. Going after Baltimore Rod was a good call. He *is* stupid, and he was easy to break."

"I think some luck should be factored in there, seeing as he was home. What if he hadn't been?"

"Well, he was though, wasn't he?"

Sidney fought off a yawn.

"Tired?"

She ignored him. Exhausted was more like it. It had been an unexpectedly emotional day, and she hadn't handled it well. *I need to get better at this.*

"I think we should follow your suggestion and tuck Baltimore Rod back in bed."

Sidney caught Smoke's eyes in the rearview mirror. "Why is that?"

"Why do you think? You suggested it."

"You first."

"Aw, can you just be forthcoming for once and let me be the devil's advocate for a change?"

"All right, Mister Smoke, let me share my thoughts. You're an idiot! All you had to do was verify that Rod was in there. We could have tailed him. Bugged him. Done something vastly more subtle."

"That might have taken days. Maybe weeks."

"And after a few days we could have improvised," she said.

"I improvised early. Now we know where AV will be."

"Might be. And that's assuming Rod isn't lying."

"He's not."

"Why, because you pretended to put a spider on his leg?"

"You have to admit, it was pretty effective, one of my better ones." He leaned forward. "It's called entomophobia. People that are raised in the city are twice as likely to get big heebie-jeebies as folks in the country. It pays off for me most times."

"Luck."

"Fate," he said.

"Well, I think the mentioning of AV shook him," she said, hitting the car's blinker and switching lanes. "And to your point, I think that gives us an advantage. He won't tell AV. That would be bad for him too. You can just put him back in his apartment. He's so scared of AV that I'm betting he'd rather hide his secret than go on the run. It at least gives him a pleading chance."

Smoke eased into his seat. "My thoughts exactly, Agent Shaw. Well done."

"Shut up."

It was 12:42 am when they got back to the FBI house. Baltimore Rod was back in his condo asleep—with the help of some Sominex Smoke had forced down his throat.

"He'll sleep like a baby," Smoke said. "He might even forget the whole thing."

I'd like to forget this whole thing.

Sidney sat on the basement couch while Smoke started up the gas fireplace in the corner. The warm light was soothing. Too soothing. She yawned again.

"If you're going to stay over," Smoke said, taking a place on the recliner, "you might as well catch some *z's.*"

Sidney sat up and toggled through her phone. She'd downloaded all of Baltimore Rod's information from his burner before she returned it. There were a few nuggets that were useful. Times. Locations. A month's worth of data. It was a stroke of luck that he hadn't pitched it by now. She covered her mouth and yawned.

I need sleep. I need to be sharp tomorrow.

She was heading into a twenty-four-hour day, and it had been a while. At least a year. She'd gotten used to six hours of sleep during the week—eight on the weekends. In the Air Force, when she was law enforcement, there had been days that lasted forty-eight to seventy-two hours. There were long stake-outs with the FBI, but they weren't so bad.

I've gotten soft.

She rubbed her blurry eyes and took a glance at Smoke. He sat rubbing the grizzle on his chin, with the fire's flame reflecting in his dark eyes.

Well, look at Mister Bright-eyed and Bushy-tailed.

"This reminds me of my grandmother's place," he said. "She had a basement I'd stay in whenever Mom and Dad took trips out of town." He started to rock a little in the recliner. "It was so easy to start a fire with a gas line built in. I'd play with the flames all night. Huddle in front of the TV and play Nintendo. And Nanny, she fed us hot chocolate with ice cream."

Sidney rose up off the sofa. "I'll see you in the morning."

"You're leaving? Why?"

"Because you're ruining my image of the Navy SEALs."

"Because I like Nintendo?"

"No, because I don't want to know what your favorite ice cream is."

"It's—"

"See you tomorrow," she said, heading up the steps.

"What time?"

"Morning time." She stopped at the upper stoop. "And don't you go anywhere until I return."

She made it outside through the rain and into her car, thinking about the long drive home. If the house had a few beds, she probably would have stayed. *FBI idiots. They could have rented a furnished house at least.* She backed out of the drive and roared down the street. The good-looking image of Smoke sitting in the recliner was branded in her mind. *Hot chocolate and ice cream.* She shook her head in self-defense. *Don't warm up to him.*

CHAPTER 16

Buzz. *Buzz. Buzz.*
Sidney pushed her face out of her pillow and checked the clock on the nightstand. 5:34 a.m. Not even four hours' sleep. With a groan, she sat up. Her eyelids were heavy. She rubbed her neck, stretched out her arms, and yawned.

If that's you, Jack, I'm going to kill you.

Rubbing her eyes, she checked her text messages. There weren't any.

"Great. Phantom buzzing in my sleep now."

She toggled through her features. There was a red update on the tracking app. "What's this?"

She opened it up. Smoke's beacon had moved. It was no longer sitting safely at Benson Park Estates. It was on the move. Miles away. Sidney jumped to her feet.

"Sonuvabitch!"

She stubbed her toe on her bed post.

"Dammit!"

She limped to her closet, grabbed a pair of jeans and a pullover shirt, and slipped them on. She holstered up and tied on her shoes. Inside of two minutes she was squealing out of her parking spot and then back on the road.

She tied her hair back in a ponytail, then rubbed her puffy eyes. It wasn't raining, but the window was frosted up. She rubbed it with her hand and turned up the heater.

"Piece of crap car."

She shivered and checked the beacon. Smoke was moving. West. Toward Annapolis. She laid on the gas.

I'll intercept him in the Interceptor. She laughed. It was a long-standing joke that cops and agents made about the old cars. *Then I'll kill him.*

Hankering for coffee and listening to the moan in her stomach, she plowed down the road. She was angry. Jack. Cyrus. Smoke. They all made her mad. Each was unreliable. Unpredictable. She didn't like it. But she didn't mind the excitement that came with it.

I'll show 'em.

She eased back in her seat and turned on some talk radio. The aggravating conversations were certain to keep her alert. Awake. Promises and failures. A chronic rinse-and-repeat cycle of wasted taxpayer dollars.

Clear your mind, Sid. Focus.

There were a lot of things to take in. Change was one of them. She didn't like change. She liked routine. She liked a plan.

"Some things you just can't plan for," her father often said. "Always assume everything is out of your control, aside from yourself."

She hated it when he said that, right along with the smile that came with it. It made her feel like she was doing something wrong. She did things right. She saw to it others did things right as well.

Cruising down the road, she regained her focus. She'd been off her game.

Too much time behind the desk.

She had yelled and cussed. It showed a lack of self-control.

No more of that. You're a pro, Sid. Be a pro. No surprises. No letdowns.

She unholstered her Glock, ran her fingers over the barrel, and stuffed it back in the holster.

I need to get to the range.

She felt jumpy. Edgy.

I don't like feeling this way.

The frost on the windows cleared, revealing the moon's bright glow. An eerie haze hung in the sky, concealing parts of it. Up ahead, a pack of animals darted across the highway. She squinted.

"What the heck?"

The dogs were big dark silhouettes padding across the concrete and vanishing over the guard rail and into the woods. A chill went through her.

Those were wolves.

She shook her head. *Maybe coyotes. No, coyotes aren't that big.* She slowed the car down and eased onto the berm. *No. Get after Smoke, Sid. No time to fool around.* She laid the gas back on and zoomed up the road. *Those were wolves, though. I know it.* Ted's words came to mind. *Extraordinary caution.*

Cruising at ninety, she closed in on Smoke's beacon, which had come to a stop off somewhere south of the John Hanson Highway. She took the machine up to ninety-five before slowing for the next exit, then followed the beacon down the greenway beyond the condos and plaza to a lonely stretch of road miles from the nearest highway.

What on earth is he doing out here?

That's when another thought crossed her mind. What if it wasn't him at all? What if one of his crew was leading her on a wild goose chase? It had been at least twenty minutes since his beacon stopped moving.

Erase your doubt. Follow your leads.

The beacon led her down a grave stretch of road that ended in a grove of tall trees. A gravel parking lot greeted her, accompanied by a lone warehouse lit up with neon signs. One sign read Chester's in bright orange and green flames. There were a few motorcycles and muscle cars on the scene. Beer cans and broken glass littered the parking lot.

What is he doing here?

Sidney checked the beacon. She was on target. She brought the Interceptor to a halt a hundred feet from the front doors. Fog was lifting into the early sunrise. A man in jeans and a leather vest lay face down in the parking lot. Fresh blood from a broken nose dripped on the ground. There was a gentle rise in his chest. She took out her weapon and crept to the doorway.

What have you gotten into, Smoke?

Inside the bar she could hear loud hillbilly rock playing.

Just when I thought it couldn't get any worse.

She pushed the door open and peeked inside. A gunshot cracked out.

Blam!

CHAPTER 17

S IDNEY CROUCHED DOWN OUTSIDE THE door.

Blam! Blam!

The shots were coming from inside the warehouse, somewhere above her head. Adrenaline pumped through her veins.

Crash!

Glass rained down into the parking lot from above her head. A man fell onto the hood of an old white Camaro. Groaning, he rolled off the hood and onto the ground.

Sidney peeked up and around the corner. A figure stood looking out of the oversized window pane. It was Smoke.

"Freeze!" she said. He vanished. She turned her attention to the other man, who was stumbling away. He hopped onto a motorcycle and started it up. "FBI! Freeze!"

He revved the engine.

"Don't make my day," she said, pointing her weapon at him. "The first hole goes in your gas tank. The next hole goes in your head."

He raised his hands over his head. His sagging face was skinned up, and his chin was bleeding.

"Sure thing, lady. Sure thing."

"Aiiyee!" a man screamed.

Sidney turned just in time to see another man flying through the window. He crushed the roof of the Camaro.

Vrooom!

The biker revved up his engine and started to speed out of the parking lot.

Blam! Blam!

Sidney put a bullet in his tank and another in his back tire.

"Get on the ground now!" she said.

The man obeyed.

She bound his legs and wrists with flex-cuffs.

"You didn't have to shoot my bike," he said. "Stupid bi—"

She shoved his face in the ground and rubbed it in the gravel.

"What was that?"

"Nothin'."

Smoke landed on the Camaro's hood, a tall figure in a dark shirt and jeans. He dragged the man who had crunched in the roof to the ground.

Sidney trotted over. "What are you doing?"

Smoke had a dangerous look his eye. He punched the man in the face. *Whap!*

"Taking care of unfinished business."

"Stop!" Sidney said, holding her weapon on him. "Stop now!"

Smoke let go, and the man sagged to the ground.

"Who is he?" Sidney watched the man gather himself into a sitting position.

The man was in his forties, shaven head and black bearded. Dusky skinned. Tattoos covered his naked arms. He was thickset. Formidable. Valuable rings dressed his fingers below all of the knuckles except for two of them. His trigger fingers were missing.

"Ray Cline?"

"Sting Ray," Ray interrupted, spitting blood. "You're going to die, Smoke. Die in a horrible way! Oof!"

Smoke kicked him in the gut.

"What was that, Ray? Say, how did that hit that you put on me go down, in prison? Not so well, did it?"

"Back off," Sidney stepped between them, keeping her eyes on Ray. She had become familiar with his file when she studied up on Smoke. He was a killer. A drug lord. A career criminal. For some insane reason, the system had let him out. "I'll handle this."

Ray started laughing.

"You want to handle me, Pretty?" He winked at her. Blood dripped off his chin. "Help yourself then."

She handed Smoke another pair of flex cuffs and covered Ray with her weapon.

"Secure him."

Smoke slipped the flex cuffs around Ray's neck.

"No, no, no!" Ray said.

"Yes, yes, yes," Smoke replied.

"No," Sidney said. "Just the wrists."

"I can make it look like an accident," Smoke said.

"The wrists," Sidney said. "Take care of it while I call this in."

"Wait," Smoke said, cuffing Ray's wrists behind his back. "Before you do that, let me show you something."

"Yeah," Ray said, "let me show you something too, Pretty."

Smoke rabbit-punched Ray's ribs and hauled him up to his feet.

"Not another word, fiend," he said in his ear. "Not another syllable." He shoved Ray back toward the warehouse bar.

"Are you coming or not? You need to see this."

Sidney followed. The intensity in Smoke's voice compelled her. He was angry. It stirred her.

Inside, there was a long bar, a band stage with instruments, high tables scattered about, and a checkered dance floor. Smoke pushed Ray toward a metal stairwell that led up. Two goons were knocked out cold by the threshold.

"Watch your step." Smoke banged Ray's head into the doorframe. "I'd hate to see you get hurt more than you already are." He banged his head into the door frame again. "No, I wouldn't."

At the top of the stairs they entered an office with a large one-way mirror overlooking the dance floor. The furnishings were fine leather and well-crafted oak. A kitchenette. A bar. An apartment of sorts. Bags of cocaine and cash were on a black velvet pool table, along with dozens of small bottles full of pills.

At least a million worth of dope and cash.

Sidney stepped over another prone body, one of three more men whose blood had been spilt on the floor.

"He has a nice little empire here, doesn't he?" Smoke said to her.

"I've seen bigger," she said, "But without probable cause there isn't a case here."

"That's right, Smoke," Ray said with a sneer. "You don't have a case with me, you frigging renegade. You're toast, Smoke."

Smoke shoved Ray onto the sofa and tied his legs to the sofa's foot with the man's belt. One by one, he tore open the cocaine bags and slung them out the window.

"I'm going to kill you, Smoke! Stop doing that!"

"That's evidence," Sidney added.

"Whose side are you on?"

"The law's."

"Yeah, the law's, you stupid bastard," Ray added.

Smoke chucked bundles of cash out the window.

"That's enough," Sidney said, "I'm calling this in."

"Just one more minute," Smoke said, "You haven't seen anything yet." He tilted his head toward another door. "Check there."

She eyed him.

"It's clear. Go ahead."

"Something you want to tell me, Ray?"

The drug lord looked away.

Butterflies started inside her stomach. Smoke's tone. Ray's feverish look. What was on the other side of that office door? She grabbed the brass door knob and shoved it open. A short hallway, maybe twenty feet long, greeted her. A heavy door stood at the end. On the left, or the front side of the warehouse, was an open office with computers. A black man in a biker vest was laid out on the floor. She walked up to the door and glanced back. Smoke stood just outside the doorway.

And behind door number 1 we have ...

She pulled open the door and gasped.

CHAPTER 18

CHILDREN WERE INSIDE. SIX IN all. They wore aprons and masks. Wide-eyed, frail and skinny, their hollowed eyes froze on her.

Sidney's heart sank. Blood drained from her face.

The children kept working. Scales. Baggies. Small piles of pills and cocaine. Latex gloves stretched over their little hands. Not a one of them could have been more than ten. Girls and boys. Eyes weak and glassy.

Her knees gave a little. She swallowed. "It's okay. I'm here to help. I'm the police."

A little Latino boy dropped his utensils, ran over, and hugged her. Within seconds, they had all closed in and embraced her. Tears streamed down their faces. Her own eyes watered. Her heart ached. Their lithe bony bodies pressed against hers.

"It's okay. It's okay. Let's find you something to eat." She picked two of them up in her arms. The others hung on her legs and waist. She gently yelled down the hallway, "A little help please."

Smoke picked up a few of the children and took them into the office. He peeled their tiny fingers off Sidney and set the children down at a table. There was a refrigerator that had some sodas inside. Some Doritos were in the cabinet over the bar. He filled their hands and said, "Eat."

Their fear-filled glances fell on Ray's hard eyes.

Sidney's temperature rose. Her cheeks turned red.

"You're going away for a long, long time, Ray."

"Am I, Pretty? I don't think so. You see, those kids ... heh, heh, well, they're all *my* kids."

"I'm sure that isn't so," she said, stepping between Ray and the kids. "I'll see to it this all sticks."

"Good luck with that, Pretty. The only thing that's going to get stuck, though, is you."

Her fingers danced on her gun. She wanted to wound him. Shoot him. Make him pay for all that he'd done.

"You won't shoot me." Ray chuckled. "You have a career. A pension. Hah. You wouldn't want to lose all that, would you."

"True," she said. "But that's not why."

"Really, why is it then?"

"It's because I don't want to set a bad example for the children." She looked at Smoke. "Do you mind removing him from our sight so they can eat in peace?"

"As you wish." Smoke undid the belt, picked Ray up by the scruff of the neck, shoved him toward the outside window, and leaned him over the edge. "Time to fly Smoke Airlines again."

"No! Wait! What are you doing?"

Smoke, much bigger than Ray, hoisted him up over his shoulders.

The whine of police sirens cut through the air.

Sidney rushed to the window.

Three police cruisers pulled into the parking lot. It was the county sheriff.

"Ah ha ha!" Ray laughed. "My cavalry has arrived."

A nagging feeling crept between Sidney's shoulders.

Smoke started to heave Ray out anyway.

Sidney grabbed his shoulder. "No, don't. Put him down." She messed with her phone. "We have to let the law sort this out."

"Amen to that," Ray said. "Amen to—ow!"

Sidney elbowed him in the nose.

❋ ❋ ❋

The scene was ugly. Sidney had called in her colleagues at the bureau. Ray had called in his the moment Smoke arrived. The two parties fought over jurisdiction. Possession. The children. Smoke was handcuffed in the back of a bureau SUV. The only thing going for them was that nobody had died.

"Stupid, Sid. Really stupid." That was all Jack said when he showed up an hour later. "He needs to go back in the hole."

"I'll handle the paperwork," she said. "It's not that bad. Nobody died. The media hasn't arrived."

"Oh, really. It's not that bad? You have an ex-con going vigilante. You've pissed off the county sheriff's department. I can imagine a dozen lawsuits being filed from all this." He rubbed his forehead. "None of the charges will stick!"

"I can handle it."

"You're what, going to make something up? Lie?"

"No," she sighed, "embellish."

Jack's face turned red. "Embellish!"

"Don't you raise your voice to me, Jack. You saw the drugs. The lab. The children. Don't you act like this can't stick." She poked him in the chest. "We've handled worse. I seem to remember doing a few favors for you."

"Get … get over here." He pulled her away from prying eyes and ears. "Listen to me. You are out of your lane. This is not part of the Black Slate. No, you blew it. Your little soldier over there is going back to the jail cell where he belongs. Experiment over. And you will be spending a lot more time behind the desk."

"Wait a minute. It's only been one day. I'm supposed to have two weeks."

"Tough. Now get in your car, go home, and report back to me in the office tomorrow so you can get started on all the paperwork you wanted."

"No," she argued. "We have a lead on AV."

Jack looked up into the sky and shook his head. "I could almost let this slide." He locked eyes with her. "Except there's another detail you missed. Congressman Wilhelm gave me a call late yesterday, and let's just say it wasn't so pleasant."

Crap!

Congressman Wilhelm was her brain-dead sister's boyfriend Dave's uncle.

"I gave you the benefit of the doubt, Sid. I sympathize with you regarding your sister. But now this?"

"Sir—"

"No sirs, Sid! Go home. It's over." His phone buzzed inside his suit pocket. "Excuse me." Jack walked away.

Sid headed for her car.

I can't believe this!

Smoke sat in the back of a black FBI SUV. She shot eye daggers at him through the tinted windows. She could have sworn he waved.

Good riddance.

Things were beginning to clear up. Ray and his men were gone. The children had been taken by protective services, leaving only a few men from the sheriff's department. One of them passed her by and in a low voice said, "Now you're in the crosshairs. Beware, Agent. Beware."

"What?"

He tipped his cap and kept on moving. Seconds later, the deputy sheriffs and their cruisers were gone, leaving only her, Jack, and Agent Tommy Tohms—and Smoke, but he was locked up. She popped open her car door and started inside.

Well, at least the kids are safe.

"But sir?" she heard Jack exclaim. His face reddened. "But—" He looked at his phone. "Dammit!" He started to throw it on the ground, but stopped short. He marched over to his SUV and opened Smoke's door.

"Get out!"

Smoke eased his big frame out of the car.

"Uncuff him, Tommy."

Smoke handed Tommy the cuffs.

Jack snatched them out of Tommy's hands and slung them away. He pointed his finger in Smoke's face. "Don't get my agent killed, you stupid sonuvabitch. Let's go, Tommy."

"But my cuffs!"

"Let's go!" Jack glared at Sid. "You got your wish, Sid. He's all yours."

Ten seconds later, Smoke and Sidney stood in the parking lot all alone.

She got into her car, feeling a little bit elated.

Smoke joined her.

"I have one question," she said.

"Shoot."

"How in the hell did you get here?"

CHAPTER 19

"**H**UNGRY?" SMOKE ASKED.

Sidney rolled her eyes. She was torn between mad and happy.

Smoke patted his belly. "I always get hungry after an adventure like that."

"I don't care." She accelerated up the highway.

"It's early. I know a diner around here that makes great pancakes."

"No."

"Excellent coffee too."

Yes.

"No."

"Come on, Agent Shaw. You can't be that sore at me. We did a good thing back there."

"'Sore at you?' Really? Is this the nineteen fifties? Who says that anymore?"

"I picked it up from some old timer in prison. He said that a lot. 'Don't be sore at me, boss.' It kind of stuck." He popped open the glove box. "Got any snacks in here?"

She leaned over and slammed the glove box shut.

"No."

Smoke shrugged. He adjusted his seat backward, locked his fingers behind his head, and closed his eyes. Seconds later he was snoring.

You have got to be kidding me!

She glanced over at him. His athletic frame filled out his black T-shirt and jeans. His knuckles were scuffed and swollen, and there were white scars on his bare arms.

He wouldn't be so bad if I didn't hate him.

She backhanded him in the chest.

He lurched up. "What—what?"

"You're on duty. No sleeping."

"So now we're a team, are we?"

"Where's the diner you were talking about?"

Smoke's dark eyes scanned the signs on the highway. He rubbed his jaw. "Two more exits. You'll love it."

"We'll see."

The diner wasn't much, but the silverware was clean. It was an old dining car in the front with much more built on in the back. Blue stools hugged the chrome-trimmed counter. The floor was hardwood, and the booth they sat in was a soft blue vinyl. A gas fireplace burned at one end. It was warm. Cozy.

"Nice, isn't it?" Smoke stuffed in a mouthful of pancakes that looked like they were stacked to his chin. "Ever seen a fireplace in a dining car?"

Sidney picked through her eggs and bacon. "No." She took a sip of coffee. *Mmmm ... good coffee.*

"How's the coffee?"

"It's all right."

"Would you like to try my pancakes?"

Yes.

"No." She scraped up the rest of her eggs and washed them down. "Are you about finished?"

Smoke looked at his stack. "No. Are we in a hurry?"

"Yes."

"For what? AV isn't supposed to show until five. We have plenty of time." He flagged down the waitress. "Could I get another Coke, please?"

"Sure thing."

"I'm still catching up from prison time," Smoke said to her. "I hope you don't mind, but I'm hungry."

"Fine, take your time." She checked the messages on her phone. "You clearly know what you're doing. And your friend, Ray, when he's released—say, tomorrow—will be thankful for your intervention."

"It wasn't supposed to go down that way."

"Really?" She leaned forward and looked him in the eye. "And how was it supposed to go down?"

"You weren't supposed to show up." He cut up his sausage and pointed at her with it on his fork. "I had it all under control. I told you, just leave me be."

No.

"All right, so I don't show up, what happens?"

"I have my ways. I nullify Ray and his gang and secure the kids." The waitress returned and put his Coke on the table. "Thanks. The kids are the main thing. Once they're safe, I burn the place down."

"Arson? That was your brilliant plan. Committing a felony."

"I'm just kidding."

She shook her head. "No, no you aren't."

"Come on." He tried to catch her eye. "You know you feel good that we put some bad guys down and saved some kids. Everyone is better off now."

She balled up her fist and said through her teeth, "That wasn't our mission."

"He put a hit out on me. He's slime. Do you have any idea how many people have disappeared under his watch?"

"That's not the point."

"How many women and children?"

"You don't know that."

"Yes, yes I do. I studied him for months. I have files inches thick I can show you." He reached over and grabbed her arm. "Justice was served today, and it didn't take a pile of paperwork to dispense it."

His grip was warm and strong. She pulled away.

"Let's go."

"But I'm not finished."

She tossed two twenties on the table. "You are now."

CHAPTER 20

T HE DRAKE. THAT WAS WHERE Rod had said AV would be. It wasn't at all what Sidney expected.

"That's different," Smoke said.

A series of barges formed a small city along the Potomac on the Virginia side of the river, south of the Torpedo Art Museum. A lighthouse could be seen in the distance. Standing on the wharf that jutted over the river and led to the barrages was a lone sign that pointed to the Drake.

"Let's go," Sidney said.

The Drake was a hotel-like building that sat on top of the backs of four barges. Pleasant music drifted down the pier that ran alongside it. The salivating scent of food drifted into her nostrils. She led with Smoke in tow, drifting in with the crowd that traversed the docks. Along with the hotel/restaurant getaway there were small stores and local artists. Beatniks, preppies, hippies, all sorts walked, talked and made polite conversation.

"Great," she said. A long line of people had formed outside the restaurant at the Drake.

"Shall I put our name on the list?" Smoke said.

"No, let's go around. Come on."

The Drake plaza sat on a huge boardwalk and deck. People gathered around the railing watching the boats and ferries. A few hard faces fished. A staircase led down to a boat dock and slips on the back of the floating city. Men in dark suits stood on the docks, helping men and women from their boats. Sidney could see the bulges of body holsters concealed under their jackets.

"Pretty seedy," Smoke said.

Sidney took a closer look at the men fishing. They were holstered up too. And so were some of the common folk milling about. She counted at least ten well-armed men and women. Guns for hire. Bodyguards. Goons.

"I'll be. We're on private property," she said under her breath.

"Yep," Smoke said. "It seems like AV has thought of everything. A criminal's safe house. An excellent escape route with immediate access to three states. I like it."

"It seems you convicts all think alike." She smiled up at him and hooked her arm in his. "Oh, don't frown. Buy a girl a drink, why don't you." She tugged him along. "Come on. We can't make our intentions obvious."

"I don't have any cash."

"And that's why there won't be a second date." They made their way up to the hostess stand.

"Name and how many?" the hostess said.

Sidney looked up at Smoke.

"Er, two, and the last name is Ferrigno."

The young waitress wrote it down and handed him a pager. "Okay, it will be at least an hour, Mister Ferrigno. You can get some drinks on the plaza while you wait." She smiled. "Next."

They grabbed two long-necks from a beer stand and took a seat on a bench overlooking the river.

"A toast," Smoke said.

"No."

"I'm just trying to act natural," he said. "Forgive me; I haven't been on a date in a while."

"This isn't a date." She took a sip of beer. "And don't get wasted on that beer. I might need you."

"Really?"

"It's a figure of speech."

"If you say so." He tilted the bottle to his lips and guzzled it down. "Ah!"

"What did I just say?"

"What? I've been in prison. Can you blame me?"

"No more." She eased back on the bench and crossed her legs. The chill from the river was worse than she expected. It was a starry night. "This place is full of all kinds of everything."

"It sure is." Smoke cleared his throat. "I wonder who Drake is?"

"I only care who AV is. You should too."

A group of men in tuxedos with women in fine jewels crested the steps that led down to the dock. Eyes forward and faces drawn tight, they marched straight for the restaurant.

"I'll be."

"What?"

One of the men was Congressman Wilhelm, with his troupe of lackeys. His beady eyes turned her way. There was no avoiding his gaze.

She nudged Smoke.

"Kiss me."

"Wh—"

She pulled his face down to hers and locked her lips with his. He pulled her body into his. A charge went through her. *Good kisser. Three. Two. One.* Through the corner of her eye, she saw Congressman Wilhelm move on. She held the kiss a moment longer and broke it off. "That'll do."

"Do you mind telling what that was all about?"

"Yes, I do mind." *What is Wilhelm doing here?*

"Ex-boyfriend?"

"No."

"Animal attraction?"

"Don't get any ideas. I might explain later."

Locking his fingers behind his head, he gazed upward into the stars. "Oh, at least you've given me plenty to think about."

Me too.

Smoke pulled the flashing pager out of his pocket. "That was quick."

"Sure was." Sidney felt eyes on her and noticed a few cameras on the lamp posts. A pair of eyes along the railing drifted away from her. A woman at the beer stand spoke into her wrist and looked away. "I have a feeling Rod Brown gave us up."

"Maybe." Smoke cracked his knuckles. "Say, are you going to finish that beer?"

She took a long drink and handed it over. "Knock yourself out."

Smoke chugged it down. "Ah!"

Please don't burp.

"Buuuurp! Whoa!" Smoke tapped his chest. "Sorry."

Sidney got up and started toward the restaurant. A mix of six men and women wearing dark pea coats hemmed them in with hands on their holsters.

CHAPTER 21

A DUSKY-SKINNED WOMAN WITH DARK CORNROWS stepped forward, rolling a toothpick from one side of her mouth to the other. She had a hard edge in her voice.

"My name is Gina. I speak on behalf of the Drake. You need to leave."

"I beg your pardon, Gina?"

"Listen, Miss." The woman rolled the toothpick to the other side of her mouth. "This is private property. The Drake Management doesn't want you here."

"I don't follow." Sidney glanced at the tattoos crawling up the rough-cut woman's neck.

"I don't need to explain myself. I know you saw the private property lines. You're trespassing."

No, I'm getting close to something. AV must be here.

The woman stuck her fist inside her palm and cracked her knuckles. "Now, I'm asking nicely. Don't make me mess up that pretty little face of yours." She cracked her neck from side to side. "I'd love to do it."

"I'm certain that's not going to happen."

Gina took a step closer and leaned forward. "Listen, tramp, I've busted up men and women in the octagon. These hands are lethal weapons. And here, heh, well, I'm free to use them. I've left the bloodstains of my victims on the deck before. Just ask them." She tipped her chin. "What do you think about that, Pretty?"

"I don't think a woman acting like a man makes for much of a woman."

Gina's eyes enlarged. "What!" She shoved Sidney in the chest.

Sidney absorbed the push, lowered her hip, and launched a roundhouse kick. She caught Gina flush on the chin. Gina smacked the deck face first, spilling her blood.

The men closed in with fingers itching on their weapons.

Sidney whipped out her badge. "FBI, back off!"

The wary-eyed men eased back.

"Her assault on a federal officer just gave me probable cause to search this place. Come on." She led Smoke through the gathering crowd. "He's in there. I can feel it." She rushed past the hostess stand.

Smoke tossed the hostess the pager. "The Ferrignos will be seating themselves tonight."

Sidney carefully picked her way through the tables while scanning the crowd. The Drake had two levels: the main floor of booths and tables decorated in a high-décor riverboat look, and the upstairs level, which was roped off for private parties.

"Up there." Sidney eyed a man who was quickly moving along the balcony. He spoke to another group of men who were seated. It was Congressman Wilhelm and his party. Sidney stepped under the balcony, evading their concerned glances.

"The only way out of here is back the way we came. I didn't notice a fire escape. Did you?"

Smoke was at her side. He peeked up at the next level. "Apparently the Drake doesn't like OSHA, either. I saw him."

Sidney pulled him back. "Saw who?"

"AV. He's up there at your ex-boyfriend's table."

Some of the goons in pea coats eased their way into the restaurant without creating a commotion.

"Are you sure you saw him?"

"Yep."

"Let's go up then." Heading for the stairs, she was cut off by a bald thickset bodyguard in a dark grey suit. She flashed her badge. "I need to get a message to Congressman Wilhelm. It's urgent federal business."

He took a hard look and glanced up at the balcony. Someone gave him a nod. He removed the velvet rope and stepped aside. "Go on up. But just you, lady."

Smoke's fist crashed into the man's rugged jaw.

Whop!

The henchman sagged onto the stairs.

Up they went, side by side. At the top, two other henchmen awaited them. Sidney's fingertips danced on her weapon. "Move."

The pair of men parted, and at the top a table awaited with eight guests. One of them was Congressman Wilhelm. The other face she recognized was Adam Vaughn's.

"Agent Shaw," Congressman Wilhelm said, lighting up a cigar, "may I ask what you are doing here?"

"I could ask you the same," she said.

"I don't answer to anyone less than a senator."

"I'm sure your voters would love to hear that."

The congressman chuckled. "They only hear what I want them to hear." He squeezed his date's knee with the hand bearing his wedding ring. "And they only believe what I want them to believe."

A few more henchmen crowded near the table. Congressman Wilhelm had a secret service agent on one side and his baby-doll date on the other. One seat over from AV, Rod Brown sat in a blue suit, eyeing a spot on the table.

"As always," Sidney said, "you seem to be on top of things, so I assume you know you're dining with a wanted man?"

"Beg pardon?" Wilhelm's eyes slid toward AV, but shifted back to her. "What are you talking about? You're not here to pester me?"

"No," she said, taking out her flex cuffs, "I'm here for Adam Vaughn."

"Adam? What on earth would you want with Adam?"

Adam Vaughn's fine features darkened. His eyes scoured his men.

"That isn't any of your business, Congressman. But I'm sure your spineless sources will fill you in soon enough. Mister Vaughn, I need you to come with me."

"Stay put, Adam," Wilhelm said, tossing his napkin on the table and getting up from his seat. "You listen to me, Shaw. You need to get out of here. Get out of here now. You're in deeper than you know." He plucked out his phone and started to dial. "Relax, Adam. I'll handle this."

Adam Vaughn was an attractive man, small in stature, with a head of coarse black hair and heavy eyebrows. He wore a white shirt with an open collar underneath a blue pin-striped suit. His eyes narrowed and his jaws were clenching. The atmosphere was ripe with tension. Sidney felt Smoke slide in behind her. She glanced back. His eyes were laser locked on AV.

"Let's go, Mister Vaughn," she said, using more authority this time.

AV had turned his attention to Rod. The big man's head was beaded with sweat.

"Rod," AV said in a European accent that was more deadly than charming, "look at me."

Rod lifted his chin, started to turn, and began shaking uncontrollably.

"I'm sorry, AV. I'm sorry!"

"Nobody's sorry, Adam," Wilhelm said, covering his phone. "I'll take care of this in a moment." He rolled his eyes at Sidney. "You really don't know what's good for you."

"Betrayer!" Adam jumped up from his seat and lunged at Rod.

Sidney drew her weapon. "Back off, Mister Vaughn!"

AV lifted his palms and backed off. "You're dead to me, Rod." He spat on the table. "Dead!" He came out from behind the table and faced Sidney. "You'll soon be dead to me too."

"Turn around — *oof!*"

AV kicked her in the gut, dropping her to her knees. He ducked under Smoke's lunging arms and leaped over the rail and crashed onto a table below. A cry of alarm went up all over the restaurant.

Smoke catapulted off the rail and charged after AV, who was dashing toward the exit.

Sidney scrambled to her feet and headed for the stairs, tripping over Wilhelm's feet.

"Watch your step, Agent Shaw," he said with a sinister grin. "Watch your step."

CHAPTER 22

S IDNEY HIT THE LANDING AT the bottom of the steps just as Smoke vanished through the front doors. Panicked people spilled into her way.

"Move it!"

A path slowly parted between feeble bodies and bewildered faces. She powered through them, shoving a man and two women down. "Does anyone know what move means?"

While she was rushing by the hostess stand, two peacock goons blocked her path. She blasted two warning shots into the floor.

Blam! Blam!

One goon dove left and the other dove right. Everybody screamed. Through the door Sidney went. Sprinting on long, fast legs, she surged out onto the deck and saw Smoke racing through the crowd thirty yards away. AV vanished down the steps leading to the docks. Smoke disappeared right after him.

Get down there, Sid!

At the top of the stairs, two more gunshots cracked off. The bodyguard on the dock was blasting away at the slithery Smoke.

Sidney took aim.

Blam!

Her bullet ripped through the back of the man's shoulder, spinning him to the ground. Down the stairs she went, sidestepping the big man and kicking his pistol into the water. After Smoke and AV she went, weapon ready. A pitch-black 30-foot cabin cruiser at the end of the dock started pulling out of its slip.

No you don't! She sprinted toward the end of the dock. *Faster, Sid! Faster!* Adrenaline surging through her limbs, she put everything into her jump. She sailed through the air. *I'm going to make it!*

Her foot clipped the edge of the boat, making for an ugly landing. She tumbled and bumped her head on the table. Bright starry spots drew in her eyes. She rubbed her head and forced herself up to her feet. A man in a captain's hat was up the stairs behind the wheel. She took aim and said, "FBI! Shut it down!"

The man remained unmoving. Sidney went up the steps and put the gun to his neck.

"I said, shut it down."

The man turned to face her. His face was pasty, hair ratty and stringy, eyes hollow and lifeless.

She gasped. Something evil, unnatural lurked behind his sunken eyes.

In a burst, the creepy man shoved her aside and lumbered stiffly down the stairs.

"Freeze!"

He kept going.

She fired a round at his leg.

Blam!

Unfazed, he stepped up on the edge of the boat and fell into the black water.

Sidney rushed down the steps and looked over the rail. The man was gone. Only the captain's hat remained afloat.

I know I hit him ... it.

"Sid!" a voice cried out. "Sid!"

She twisted around. Smoke's voice was coming from inside the lower cabin. She burst through the doors. Smoke's big frame had AV pinned down on the floor. The smaller man twisted away and sprinted toward Sidney. Smoke tackled his legs and launched a quick punch in AV's ribs. The man sagged.

"Cuffs!" Smoke said, chest heaving.

"What?"

"Flex cuffs!" he added, sucking for air. He wrenched AV's arms behind his back.

AV jerked them away.

"You are one strong little man!" Smoke punched both sides of his ribs again. *Whap! Whap!* "I'll have no more of that, you swarthy Spaniard."

"I'm not Spanish, you fool!" AV spat on the floor. "I'm something else."

You're something else, all right.

Sidney kneeled down and put her gun barrel to AV's temple. "If you don't remain still, something else of yours is going to be splattered all over the floor."

AV's struggles eased. He gazed up at her. His eyes were black pools. Insidious. Primal. Evil. Hair rose on her neck. Without averting her eyes, she handed Smoke the cuffs. He crisscrossed AV's wrists and bound them.

"Do you have another pair?"

"I always have another pair," she said, handing them over.

Smoke tied down AV's legs, leaned back against the bed, and caught his breath.

Winded herself, Sidney sat back on the steps and wiped her sleeve across her forehead. She then asked AV, "Is there anyone else on this boat we should know about?"

"Do you see anyone else?" he said with a sneer. "It's just me and a couple of soon-to-be dead people."

Smoke kicked him. "Where's the captain?"

"He jumped overboard."

"Really?" Smoke said, cocking his ear, "then who's driving the boat?"

The blaring sound of a boat horn ripped through the chill night air.

Sidney's eyes widened. She jumped to her feet, darted up the stairs, and raced up to the captain's chair. A river barge was almost on top of them. She spun the wheel right and pumped down the throttle. The fore of the boat rose high, and the propellers sank the aft of the boat into the water. Sidney hung onto the wheel. The massive bulk of the barge cruised by with little more than a foot to spare.

That was close.

She throttled down the cruiser and watched the barge pass by.

Too close.

She scanned the black water. The barge's wake beat against the hull. There was no sign of the captain—and she was certain the captain wasn't any man at all. Cruising down the shoreline, she caught movement along the bank. A drenched figure lumbered out of the water, up the shore, and disappeared into the woods. A chill went through her.

That's wasn't a man. I swear it!

CHAPTER 23

"**E**XCELLENT JOB, SID," SAID JACK Dydeck. "Just excellent." He paced the floor with his fingers locked behind his back. They were back at the house: Jack, Tommy Tohms, Sidney, Smoke, and a couple of other agents. AV sat cross-legged, head down, by the fireplace. "You erased a name on the Black Slate in one day?" He put his hand on her shoulder and squeezed it. "I'm proud of you, Sid."

"There's really no need. It's my job, and I can't take all the credit." She nodded at Smoke. "He helped."

Smoke sat quietly on the sofa, eyes intent on AV. He hadn't said much of anything since they journeyed back from the Potomac and Jack and his men picked them up.

"I'm sure he did," Jack said. "We'll be sure to send him some new books to read back in prison."

"Wait," Sidney said, "I thought we had two weeks?"

"Sure, to get Mister Vaughn here. That's all over now."

"Hold on." Sidney was not hiding the irritation in her voice. "There are reports. Interrogations. Investigations of his operations. The list goes on. I want to be thorough."

"We'll handle that, Sid. You go get some rest and we'll talk tomorrow."

"No, I'll handle it."

Jack offered a smile. "Tomorrow. Back in the office. Around noon. We'll await Mister Vaughn's caretakers." His tone became stern. "You look exhausted, Sid. We can stitch up this mess tomorrow. Go."

"What about him?" She looked at Smoke.

Jack sighed.

"Tell you what: seeing how the two of you caught headquarters with their pants down, well," he scratched his head, "they aren't sure what the next step is. I'm waiting on their call to advise me on what to do with Mister Smoke, so the two of you head up the road and grab a bite to eat. I'll call you back after Mister Vaughn is picked up. We'll take it from there. Fair enough?"

"I'd rather stay," Smoke said. His eyes were still glued on AV.

"I don't care." Jack glowered at him. "You can go eat or sit here handcuffed."

"Come on," Sidney said to Smoke. "Let's go."

Slowly, Smoke rose from the sofa and headed out the door. Sidney was one half-step behind.

"Give us a couple of hours, Sid," Jack said. "I should have it all wrapped up by then."

"All right," she said, glancing down at AV.

His eyes fastened on hers. "Soon, Pretty. Soon."

Goosebumps rose on her arms. She tore her gaze away and went back outside. She was short of breath.

"You okay?" Smoke said.

She swallowed and took a breath. "Yeah. Let's go."

"You've been awfully quiet," Sidney said to Smoke. They were sitting in a truck stop restaurant almost ten miles up the road from the house. Smoke's burger and fries were getting cold. "Did you lose your appetite?"

"Tell me about that captain again."

"I don't know." She covered her yawn. "It was dark. I've been tired." She took a sip of coffee. "His face was clammy. Veiny. Like a, well, I don't know."

"Like a zombie?"

"I wouldn't take it that far." She wrinkled her forehead. "Zombies don't drive boats. It might have been sick from something."

"You said *it* again."

"Him. It. It was ugly. Ugh. He was ugly. Just let it go."

"But you said you shot him. Hit his leg. But didn't slow him."

"Adrenaline."

"You said he walked up the shore and disappeared."

"It might have been someone else. It was too far to see."

"I don't think anyone else would have been swimming in the Potomac." Smoke pushed his plate aside, scooted back into the booth, and stretched his legs out.

"Make yourself comfortable, why don't you."

Smoke closed his eyes and rubbed his temples.

He's getting weird on me.

"Are you all right?"

"I have a confession." His eyes were still closed.

Oh great. Please don't give me some sappy story about the last time you ate Pop-tarts with your sister.

"Great. There's a Catholic steeple down the street."

"I'm worried." He opened his eyes and looked worried.

"So?"

"I don't get worried."

"Well, I guess you're just one of us now."

"AV. He's not normal."

"No, most criminals aren't. What's the matter? Are you afraid he won't be a good cell mate?"

Smoke raised his eyebrows at her.

"Sorry. That was uncalled for." She leaned forward. "It's been a really long day."

"Agent Shaw, did you get a good look when AV jumped off the balcony?"

"I was there."

"Well, so was I. There aren't many people aside from Olympic athletes who can jump that far in a single bound." He sat up. "He made a mistake and ran for the boat, thinking the bodyguards would stop us. If he had run into the city, we never would have caught him."

"So he's fast."

"And strong." Smoke narrowed his eyes at her. "I have a hundred pounds on him. It took all I had to wrestle him down."

"He's in shape. Adrenaline. Maybe he's on something. That wouldn't be a first. My father told me he saw a man on PCP burst out of his handcuffs once."

"No," Smoke said in a hushed voice, "I'm telling you, he's not normal. Just like that captain isn't normal."

"Don't overthink it." She finished off her coffee and checked her phone. No messages from Jack yet, and it had been two hours. She yawned. "I wonder why this is taking so long."

Smoke started to ease himself out of the booth. "I say we head back." His eyes were restless. "I have a bad feeling."

Can't disagree there. But I'm not going to let him spook me either.

"Sure, why not." Sid fetched some bills out of her bag. "Do you want a doggie bag?"

"What?"

She dropped the money on the table. "Lighten up a little, will you?"

Driving down the road, Sid couldn't shake the butterflies from her stomach. Smoke was uncomfortable. It made her uncomfortable.

What is his deal?

She'd texted Dydeck before they left and hadn't heard back. Jack was always quick to reply. Ahead, the half-moon shone brightly behind the rising mist of the late evening. She barreled down the exit ramp, merged onto the highway, cruised a few more miles down the road, and turned into Benson Estates.

A pack of dogs darted across the road. Sidney slammed on the brakes. Her heart was jumping.

"Whoa." Smoke leaned forward in his seat. "Were those coyotes?"

"Coyotes aren't that big," Sidney said, peering into the night. The pack had vanished behind the houses. "Those were wolves."

"Like timber wolves? I don't know about that. But they were big. Shepherds, maybe."

"Wolves, trust me. I'm pretty familiar with the breeds of dogs." She let off the brake pedal and eased on up the road. It was the second time she'd seen them in a day.

"Care to fill me in?"

"No."

"So, you used to be a veterinarian?"

She didn't reply.

"Really? Is it that hard to share the smallest detail of any of your history?"

"No. I'm just staying focused right now." Driving slowly, she surveyed between the houses they passed. "Just keeping it professional."

"I agree, but I think you should work on tuning up your social skills."

After a long pause, Sidney said, "I was a K-9 cop in the Air Force."

"Oh." Smoke nodded. He sniffed the air. "Funny, you don't smell like a canine cop. They usually have a scent about them."

"I'm not one now, obviously."

"Just a little humor, Agent Shaw. Take it easy."

She almost cracked a smile as she pulled the car alongside the curb of the house. The two black SUVs were still in the driveway.

Unbuckling his belt and getting out of the car, Smoke said, "It doesn't look like anyone else has shown up." He headed for the front door. Sidney followed in step behind him. The lights were on inside. The front door was wide open. No sounds came from within. "That's weird."

"Sure is," she said, drawing her weapon.

Smoke stopped at the threshold. His arms fanned out, shielding her.

"Wait."

Sidney's body tingled with tiny fires. She slipped underneath Smoke's arm and stepped inside. Blood dripped from the fireplace mantle. The stench of death was thick. She gasped.

CHAPTER 24

S IDNEY STUMBLED BACK INTO SMOKE, mumbling, "No ... no."

Blood pooled on the floor. Splattered on the walls. Two agents lay in mangled heaps of flesh. A man was disemboweled, his frozen gaze fixed on the hearth. It was Tommy Tohms. A woman lay with her elbow and neck snapped. The third agent sat on the sofa, coated in blood. His head was missing. Twisted clean off.

Sidney swallowed hard and choked out a cry when she saw the head lying on the fireplace grate. It was Dydeck.

She started shaking. This was inhuman. Uncanny. She dropped her weapon. Her knees sagged.

Smoke caught her. "Let's get you to the car."

"No." She gasped, wiped the tears from her eyes, reached down to pick up her weapon, and took a deep breath. "I can handle this."

"This is madness. Not a lot of people can handle madness."

Sidney took another deep breath and straightened herself. "Not a lot of people can handle me mad either. Let's get to the bottom of this."

AV was gone. Sidney noticed the busted flex cuffs on the floor.

Smoke was squatted down, eyeballing them. "These weren't cut, they were torn," he said, covering his nose. "Whew … Death stinks."

Sidney held her stomach.

Don't puke. Don't puke.

Blood coated the walls in the living room. It dripped from the ceiling. It looked like a Cuisinart had ripped through the agents in the room.

"What could have done this?" she asked herself.

"These are claw marks. A wild pack of canines perhaps."

"Dogs wouldn't do this."

She studied Dydeck's headless corpse. She'd lost a few friends in the field, but none that she knew well. Her heart ached. Dydeck had a wife and three children.

Lord, no. Lord, no. This can't happen. Not like this. Not to Dydeck.

He was hard-nosed. Not always right. But she liked him. She liked him a lot.

Dydeck still had his weapon in hand. It had been discharged. She turned. The same with Tommy Tohms.

"Do you see any bullet holes?" She pulled some latex gloves from her inside pocket and checked the cartridge on Dydeck's weapon. It was empty.

He couldn't have missed. Not at this close a range.

"Two in the wall over here," Smoke said, fingering the holes, "and one nick in the mantle."

"There should be more," Sidney said, brushing the hair from her eyes. "This magazine is empty."

"I don't see anything else," Smoke said. "They must have filled something with lead."

Sidney noticed a pair of holes on the blood-stained floor.

"Here's another. Geez." She took out her phone and dialed headquarters. It wasn't her first instinct, but it was protocol. She wanted to call Ted, her old boss. A woman's voice answered.

"This is Agent Sidney Shaw—"

She heard the squeal of brakes and pushed the blinds up.

"Hold on."

An unmarked black van had pulled into the driveway. Four men in FBI jackets came out and slammed the doors shut.

One of them was Cyrus. "Agents down. More agents arriving on scene at 241 Benson Estates. Send forensic team and homicide." Cyrus spilled in the doorway and stopped in his tracks. His eyes widened and his face turned ashen. "What the hell?" He jerked out his weapon and pointed it at Smoke. "Freeze!"

Smoke raised his arms over his head.

"Cyrus." Sidney cut in between the two men. "They were dead when we got here. Lower your weapon."

Three other agents poured into the room with their weapons drawn.

"Did you clear the house?" Cyrus said.

"Not yet, I just got—"

"Secure the house," Cyrus ordered his men. "Now! You," he said to Smoke. "Don't move." He grabbed one of the agents by the sleeve and said, "Cuff him."

"That's not necessary," Sidney objected. "He's done nothing wrong."

Smoke's arms were jerked behind his back and he was shackled. "Don't forget to double-lock them," he said.

"Stay with him," Cyrus said to the other agents. He looked at Sidney. "You, come with me." His eyes drifted toward the fireplace. He blinked and leaned in. "Is that … Dydeck?"

"Yes," she said. "Cyrus, I just arrived a few minutes before you. How come the transport was late? It should have been here over an hour ago to take Adam Vaughn away."

"Sir," one of the agents said, coming from downstairs. "We have another agent down, but she's breathing. The rest of the home is secure."

"Call an ambulance," Cyrus said, rushing down the hall and down the steps.

Sidney was right on his heels. At the bottom of the stairs a woman in an FBI vest lay still. Sidney swallowed. The agent—a short-haired black lady—was crumpled up in a heap.

"Back broken," said one of the agents, a short wiry man with a mustache. He shook his head. "Probably from the fall. A bad spill." He patted her leg. "Hang on, honey. Hang on."

"Don't touch her," Cyrus said, kneeling by the woman's side. "Wait for the ambulance to arrive."

"She didn't fall," Sidney said, gazing at the stairwell. There was a large indentation in the drywall. "She was thrown."

Cyrus stood up, glanced up the stairwell, and said, "That's not possible." He eyed the spot. "Maybe it was already there."

"I don't think so," Sidney said.

"Well, I don't care what you think, Agent Shaw." Cyrus's forehead started to bead with sweat. "Forensics will decide that. You need to decide how to explain all this."

"Me?"

He got in her face. "Yes, you!"

"Hey, Cyrus," the short agent said, "look at this."

Cyrus took out a pair of glasses and put them on. "What is it?"

"She has something in her hand," the agent said. "It looks like hair."

Sidney leaned in. The hair was long, dark brown, and very coarse. Cyrus scooted over and blocked her view. She said, "Do you mind?"

"As a matter of fact, I do." He rose up, stood in front of her, and pointed up the stairs. "Go."

"I beg your pardon?"

"I'm the senior agent on the scene," he said. "And you are going."

"Going where?"

"Going home."

CHAPTER 25

*W*HAP! *WHAP! WHAP!* Sidney laid into the heavy bag that hung in the gym.
Whap! Whap!

Sweat dripped from her brow.

Whap!

Chest heaving inside her Under-Armor hoodie, she walked over to a nearby bench and twisted the cap off her bottled water. It was Saturday, two days after the massacre at Benson Estates. She'd spent all day Friday doing paperwork, and she hadn't heard a word about the case since. Cyrus didn't return her texts. He'd iced her. She finished off her water, crushed the bottle, and tossed it in a can. *Damn him.*

The gym had a little bit of everything going on and was fairly busy for a Saturday. Men and women pushed weighted sleds. Cross trainers pushed their clients to the limits. Sweating bodies churned on treadmills and elliptical machines lined up row-by-row in front of the wall-mounted television. The entire gym smelled like sweat, and the music playing gave it energy.

She ripped a sidekick into the bag. Launched another and another.

A man walking by stopped and watched. He was a little shorter than her, red-faced, and all muscle in a little T-shirt. Tattoos of daggers and snakes decorated his shoulders. He nodded and smiled. "You really know how to work that bag. Impressive."

Great. "Thanks." She paused. "Are you waiting?"

"No," he said, shaking his chin. "I'm enjoying watching." He looked her up and down. "You really are something. How long have you been working out?"

"Listen—"

"Tommy. Tommy's my name." He extended his hand. "Weightlifting is my game."

She laughed. "Tommy, you really need to go."

"I can't leave without your name."

She walked over the padded floor to her gym bag, grabbed her badge, and held it in front of Tommy's widened eyes. "Here are my initials. Now beat it."

He eased back but kept smiling. "Well, FBI, you are one fine agent. You can cuff me any time."

"Can I shoot you too?"

He swallowed. "Er ... No." He blinked a couple of times, turned, and walked away.

Loser.

Sidney worked the bag again. Combos of kicks and punches. She loved kick boxing. It had been a passion of hers since she was nine. Her arms became heavy. Her black stretch pants were soaked in sweat. She unleashed some more roundhouse kicks.

Whap! Whap! WHAP!

She took the sparring gloves off, tossed them into her gym bag, and headed toward the treadmills. The ghastly images from the crime scene still burned in her mind. Dydeck was dead. Good agents were dead. One paralyzed. And somewhere, a killer was out there running free. Could it have been Adam Vaughn? It wasn't possible. But that wasn't what bothered her most.

Smoke was gone.

She climbed up on a step mill, punched in the time and intensity, and started walking.

Things had gotten ugly between her and Cyrus when he'd told her to leave. She had objected. The mousy man with frosty eyes had responded by having Smoke carted off behind her back, with no goodbyes between them.

"Your boyfriend is headed back to prison. You'll have to get your kiss goodbye some other place, some other time."

It gnawed at her gut. After a forty-five-minute workout, it still stuck in her craw.

Maybe I should go for a run. Or go shooting.

She gathered her things and exited the gym into the biting wind, headed for her car. The Interceptor wasn't alone. A man wearing a brown leather Donegal and a tweed trench stood there.

"Ted?" She looked around the parking lot. "What are you doing here?"

"I just came to see how you were doing."

"Really." She unlocked the car and tossed her gym bag inside. "Why?"

"Come on, Sid. Agents died. You were there. I saw the pictures." He grimaced. "In all my years, I've never seen ... well, never. Let's just leave it at that. How about we go and get something to eat?"

She crossed her arms. "How about you tell me what's going on? I should be in on this, you know."

"Headquarters is in turmoil at the moment. It almost takes an act of God to keep these incidents out of the papers." Hands stuffed in his pockets, he leaned his shoulder on the car. "When I heard the news, I thought it was you in that bloodbath. I'm glad you're still alive."

"Still?"

"Ah, don't start that." He rolled his eyes. "Quit picking sentences and expressions apart."

"Didn't you teach me that?"

"I don't know." Looking at her with his soft eyes, Ted reminded her of the old actor named Brian Keith from movies she watched with her father. Tough, yet soft in a very manly way. "Probably. Let's get out of this cold and go eat. There's a nice little greasy spoon around the corner."

She pushed her back off the car. "Nice little greasy spoon? I don't think so."

He chuckled and offered his elbow. "Aw, come on. I've never seen anything in there that could bite you."

They made their way out of the parking lot and down the sidewalk, brushing by many passersby.

"Sir, I have to have a part in this. I was there, I brought in AV, and now I'm cut out? It doesn't make any sense."

"The Black Slate doesn't make any sense either. Those files are off the books. I'm trying to make sense of it myself."

"And what have you learned?"

"Huh, well, from what I've gathered, the Slate precedes the FBI." He cleared his throat. "It's a mystery where it came from."

"Wouldn't that make the people on the list really old ... like you?"

He laughed.

"And," she continued, "Adam Vaughn didn't seem very old. He seemed little older than me."

"Over time, the list ... it changes, I guess. I don't know."

"Well, who keeps the list updated?"

"I don't know that either."

"What do you know?"

He pointed at the sign on the door of a restaurant. The stenciled lettering on the glass door read: The Wayfarer. He opened the door and nodded. "We're here."

The smell of fried food and cooking oil wafted into her nostrils. Soft rock music and the clinking of dishes caught her ear. She stepped inside. "Great." She shivered. "At least it's warm."

"Come on." Ted led her toward the back of the quaint but deteriorating establishment that hadn't changed since the fifties. He stopped at a booth and began speaking to someone.

She couldn't see the person until Ted stepped aside. Her eyes grew. Her heart skipped. It was Smoke.

CHAPTER 26

"HELLO, AGENT SHAW." SMOKE HOISTED a Coke. He wore jeans and a dark sweater under a black leather jacket. His face was clean shaven. "Did you miss me?"

Yes.

"No."

Ted removed his coat, hung it on a hook on the booth, and took a seat opposite Smoke. Just he and Smoke practically filled the booth. "Uh … let me scooch over."

"That's all right." Sid grabbed a chair and dragged it over to the table, closer to Ted's side. She sat down, rested her clasped fingers on the table, and looked at Ted.

"Er, well, I guess we don't need any introductions." Ted took off his cap and placed it on the table. Scratched his head. "A little stuffy in here. Waitress!"

A young man came over in a dirty apron with quaffed brown hair dominating one side of his head. The pen in his hand looked heavy. "Yeah, man."

"Er, double cheeseburger with everything, fries—no, onion rings, and a sweet tea." He eyed Sidney. "And you'll be having?"

"Nothing."

"Mister Smoke?"

"I already ordered."

It better not be pancakes.

The waiter nodded. "Coming up, man."

"All right, man." Ted glared at the waiter's back. "Man. Man. Man. Man. Doesn't anyone say sir anymore?" He looked at Sid. "All right, I'll quit. But if he screws my order up, no tip."

"Sir, can we get down to business?"

"That's my girl. Okay, they still want you on this case. You got AV before, they think you can get him again."

"*It* again," Smoke said.

"Wait a second," Sidney interrupted. "Who wants us on this?"

"One at a time." Ted held up his palm. "First, Sid, I can't tell you that. I'm not really sure myself, but for the interim, I'm your new supervisor."

Unusual, but good.

"Second," Ted said to Smoke, "Adam Vaughn is not an *it*. Some person or persons took him out of there. The evidence confirmed that."

I don't think so.

Smoke sat up. "Did the evidence lead to the discovery of Bigfoot, too? An animal or something like an animal tore through those people like the Tasmanian devil. It wasn't a person."

"Just settle down a moment. Your mission"—he pointed at Sidney and Smoke—"is to find Adam Vaughn. Bring him in. Alive. Find him, and we'll find the fiend that did this to our agents."

"Just us?" she said.

"Yes."

"What about resources? Cars? Weapons? Tactical support? Is Mister Smoke going to be armed or not? And what about his ankle tracker?"

Smoke stuck out his boot. No tracker. With a smile, he said, "All gone."

"Ted, how am I supposed to keep track of him then?"

"You'll just have to work together." He leaned forward. "Ah, food is coming."

The waiter had a tray full of food. Three hamburgers and two chili dogs and plenty of fries. He set a burger and fries down in front of Ted.

Ted's face reddened. His voice darkened as he said, "I said onion rings."

"No man, no, you didn't," the waiter said, setting the other baskets in front of Smoke. "I can get some, man, but it will be extra."

The veins in Ted's neck started to bulge. He glared at the young man.

"No, it won't."

"Take it easy, man. I'll get your rings. Stat." He sauntered off.

Smoke squirted ketchup on his fries and Sidney fought against her giggles.

"What?" Ted said, checking the contents of his burger.

"Nothing," she replied. A giggle erupted.

"All right, now what's so funny?"

"You sounded like Batman," Smoke interjected. Then he imitated. "*I said onion rings.*"

Sidney's face flushed and her giggles continued. She stopped herself. "But it was way better than 'Do you feel lucky, punk?' I thought that was coming."

Ted snatched up his burger and stuffed it into his mouth. "Screw both of you." Ketchup dripped onto his shirt. "Aw, dammit."

Sidney caught a playful look in Smoke's eyes. She felt a spark inside.

Sense of humor a plus. Stuff your face with unknown parts of a swine, minus.

"So, Ted, it's just us then? Again, who is my backup?"

"It's you and him." He swallowed his food. "And me. He reports to you. You report to me. The clock is still ticking on your two weeks. Remember, this is off the books. The less everyone else knows, the better."

Smoke dipped one of his fries in the ketchup. "So there's a mole in the FBI then?"

That's what I was thinking.

"No, there isn't any mole. Just loose lips and big-eared busybodies." Ted tucked a napkin under his chin. "I have enough on my plate without any more probing questions. And so far as I'm concerned, until it's over, the less I know, the better." He bit into his burger.

"Wherever you go, we're going together," she said to Smoke.

"Fine, but that might be a bit awkward when we're sleeping." He leaned closer. "Does that mean I'm staying at your place?"

Sidney's eyes got big. "No, you know what I meant!"

"Ha," Ted laughed. "He turned the tables on you, Sid. I like that."

"I've got everything I need: my own ways," Smoke said, tapping his head, "and my own gear. Just step aside and let me make this happen." He looked straight into her eyes. "I want this murderer as much as you do, and at some point you're going to have to put some trust in me."

Sidney shook her head. "We'll see."

Ted grumbled at the fries in his basket. "Where the heck are my onion rings?"

She glanced back at Smoke. "So, do you have any leads?"

He drained his Coke and clopped the plastic tumbler on the table. "Nope."

CHAPTER 27

"Y OU KNOW," SMOKE SAID, RIDING shotgun in the Interceptor, "there's one thing I can't figure."

"About what?" Sidney said.

"AV. If he turned into a werewolf—"

"A werewolf?" *Oh lord, please don't be some Twilight geek.*

"In theory."

"Uh, stupid theory." She pulled the car to a stop at the light. "I think I like the Bigfoot idea better."

"Well, you saw a pack of wolves for yourself. So did I."

"And you thought they were coyotes. Perhaps they were were-coyotes?" The light changed, and she eased on the gas. "That said, I'm not liking your theory. It's ludicrous."

"My point is, AV's clothes were gone. Not a stitch. If he turned into a werewolf or something else, there would have been evidence of something." He pointed up the highway. "Take the next exit."

"So, you're ruling out the supernatural then?" She nodded her head. "Good for you."

"Well—"

"Well, I won't have any of it." She accelerated. "Monsters don't roam Washington."

"Hah, Washington's full of them. They just prefer human form." His head turned right. "Uh, you missed my exit."

Sidney jammed on the brakes and shifted into reverse. She eyed the rearview mirror and gunned the gas.

"Hey," Smoke said, "there's a lot of traffic coming our way. Not a good decision."

"What's the matter, are you afraid I might run over a groovy ghoulie?"

"A what?"

"Nothing." A few car horns blared as they whizzed by. Sidney gunned the Interceptor down the exit ramp. "How much farther?"

"About three miles." He shifted in his seat. "Are you telling me your skin didn't crawl when you stood in the middle of that bloodbath?"

"No, my skin didn't crawl."

"Your friend's head was twisted clean off."

Her throat tightened a little. She thought about Dydeck's family. The funeral. A closed coffin was never a good thing. "I'll let forensics figure that out."

"And I guess you'll read it in the reports you'll never see. Ha." He pointed right. "Turn there."

She hit the blinker and turned right down a blacktopped road marred with low spots and potholes. The car plunged into a pothole and lurched upward.

Smoke stared out the window. "You just lost a cap."

She kept driving.

"Aren't you going back for it?"

"No."

"But that's littering."

"No it isn't."

"Yes—"

She hit the brakes, lunging Smoke forward. Putting the car in reverse, she hit pothole after pothole. Coming to a stop, Sidney put the car in park and got out. Outside, she located the hubcap, picked it up, walked over to Smoke's door, opened it, and dropped it in his lap. She got back in the car again.

"What do you want me to do with this?"

"Shove it."

Smoke flipped it around between his hands. "Usually these old cars are nothing but black rims. It'll probably look better without it anyway." He tossed the cap in the back seat. "Take the next left. Another mile up or so."

Sidney's knuckles were white on the steering wheel. She couldn't shake the image of Dydeck's headless body from her mind. She knew his wife, Jean, and his children, Larry and Zoey. Her heart ached for them.

"Are you all right?" Smoke said.

"Fine."

"This is strange." He cleared his throat. "And I know plenty about strange. I've seen bodies after fifty-caliber bullets ripped through them. At least, I've seen what was left of them. I saw plenty of people decapitated in the desert. It's gruesomely horrible. That said, I've never sensed anything like this before. Eerie."

Goosebumps rose on her arms as she wound the wheel to the left. Sidney couldn't deny the eeriness she felt either, or the sickness the scene stirred inside her.

They passed by some small homes and trailers.

"Next right," Smoke said.

Ahead, an old gas station sign was mounted on a light pole twenty feet in the air. Below it was an old service station, neatly kept. It had two closed garage bays on the left and the store front on the right. The gas pumps were gone, but the overhead canopy remained. It all had been converted into an apartment or house of some sort.

"This is where you live?" she said. The place was almost forty minutes from D.C., east of the Potomac. "Strange place for a gas station."

Smoke popped open his door, but before he got out he said, "It's an old place. Mostly for the locals and family. I picked it up at an estate auction several years ago." He closed the door and headed toward the apartment. "Are you coming?"

Her palms started sweating.

Strange place to be with a strange man.

CHAPTER 28

S HE PICKED UP THE FILE on AV and made her way after him, eyeing the garage bays.

"What's in there?"

"That's where I keep my friends," he said, reaching inside his pocket and producing a set of keys.

"Ah, Fat Sam and Guppy then?"

He tilted his head back and laughed. "You remember! No, but I can't wait to tell them you said that." He stood at the door beside the large block glass window. The heavy grey steel door had both a keypad and a key hole. He stepped in front of her and punched in the code. "I hate carrying keys."

Me too.

Smoke shoved the door open and stepped aside, gesturing. "After you."

Sidney crossed over the threshold. Her heart raced a little.

What is wrong with me?

She took a long draw through her nose. The glass wall offered little light to an otherwise dim room. It was quiet.

"Hold on." Smoke brushed by her. He stopped at a circuit box and pushed up the black handle. The overhead incandescent lights came on, and the room hummed with life. "That should be better."

A sofa, kitchenette, refrigerator, cupboards, and an island with two stools made for a quaint apartment remarkably similar to her own. An office desk and computer monitors filled one back corner. Two tall dark-green gun safes filled another. It was a lot more modern and cozy than she expected from seeing the outside.

No back door.

"Make yourself comfortable." He sat down and turned on the computer. "As best you can, anyway. It's not much for entertaining. And ignore the cobwebs; I haven't dusted in over a year."

"Ha ha." She took a seat on the sofa, tossed the folder on the coffee table, and opened it up. "So, bounty hunter, you don't have any leads?"

"Nuh-uh." He pecked the keyboard of his computer. "But give it some time and I'll have something."

Adjacent to him, she squinted her eyes toward the monitors. There were four in all. The biggest displayed security camera feeds from outside. Smoke's broad back blocked the front screen from her view. *This is awkward.* She pulled out a picture of Rod Brown, AV's goon.

"Maybe we should check up on Rod Brown."

Smoke stopped typing and swiveled around in his chair to face her.

"I already did."

"What? When?"

"Yesterday, right after they took the leash off." He cocked his head. "You look angry. Are you angry?"

Sidney's nails dug into her palms. She'd been put on ice, but Smoke had been given free range? *Ted's going to get it.* "What did you find?"

"Rod's dead."

She leaned forward. "Dead how? I didn't see anything in the news about it."

"FBI covered it up after I called them. Just like the other one."

Sidney's pulse quickened. Her jaw muscles clenched.

Smoke rose out of his chair and gestured at it. "Have a seat. I'll show you what I discovered."

"Oh, I can't wait to see your big discovery, but I'm fine where I am. Just tell me what you did."

"I went to Rod's apartment, picked the lock, and went inside. His blood was everywhere, just like we saw at Benson. The only difference was Rod's head was … missing." He turned and plucked away at the keyboard. "I took a few pictures of the scene before I called. Can you stomach it?"

She eased her way over and gazed at the monitor. Blood soaked the carpet and was splattered on the walls. Rod's corpse lay headless on the floor. A queasy feeling sank into her stomach and weakened her knees.

"It takes time to get used to it," Smoke said, easing back. "But it's best you don't."

"Did anyone report a disturbance? Screams? Someone must have heard something."

"Growls," he said, taking hold of the mouse.

"I don't think werewolves lock doors."

"Maybe someone else did. Besides"—he clicked on another file—"the residents did report seeing something tall and hairy sprinting through the streets."

"There are such things as bearded runners, you know."

He opened up a video file. "True. But here's a little local footage I hacked into, from the condos."

"You hacked into?"

"Sort of." He pointed at the screen. "Just watch."

The video clip showed a view of the condominium complex's parking lot. It was nighttime, and most of the spaces were filled. The lamp posts illuminated much but not all. A tall figure— distant from the camera angle—glided along the perimeter wall.

Sidney's spine tingled.

The image was unclear, but its shoulders were hulking, and a snout looked to be protruding from its face. It jumped, grasping the high wall's ledge and pulling itself over with ease. Then it vanished. It all happened in a few seconds.

"Go back," she said, "frame by frame."

Smoke toggled the keyboard. The video wound back frame by frame.

"There's something in its hand."

"Yeah, I know," Smoke said, zooming in. It looked like a dripping skull was clutched in a big paw. "I'm pretty sure that's Rod's head."

CHAPTER 29

THE HUMAN BRAIN IS A powerful organ. It can detect the difference between reality and the finest computer-generated images. What Sidney saw wasn't a hoax, but that wasn't the problem. What she saw wasn't human. The limbs were too long. The movements impossibly fluid.

"Maybe a seven-foot-tall ape escaped from the zoo," Smoke said, powering down the monitors. "Or maybe there is a Sasquatch, even though I always figured him to be bigger."

Sidney rubbed her head.

"It's a lot to take in," Smoke said. "I have some aspirin."

"No." She made her way back over to the sofa. "Just give me a moment."

Smoke turned on a TV that hung on the wall. The local news was on.

"You know, it always amazes me how deft the FBI are at covering things up. The sad thing is, I don't think there's enough news time to air all the stories they cover up. And if there were, people would be overwhelmed by the reality of the horrible world we really live in." He sat down on the other end of the sofa and kicked his boots off onto the table. "And in the last few days, I've learned the world is even worse than I thought it was."

"We need to learn what we can about the Drake." She stared at the big screen. "I spent my time poking around the last two days, and I picked up a few things. It's owned by a real estate investor. Aside from the hotel and restaurants, I found almost nothing. There isn't even a website about the barge island on the river."

"Sure, follow the money. I'm sure the IRS has something."

"I made some calls to some friends, and they're pretty tight-lipped right now." She spread some of the file pictures out on the table. "But I did learn the Drake Corporation operates a lot of subsidiary companies. They own most of these locations that Adam Vaughn frequents."

"I think he'll show up."

"Where? Here?" She shook her head. "He's hiding somewhere."

"He's cocky. He'll be out and about."

"We can't stake all of those places out, and they'll be looking for us."

"True, but that's why I have Fat Sam and Guppy on it."

She rolled her eyes and got up. *Damn, I'm still in my gym clothes.* "I'm going. If you can control yourself, stay put and I'll swing by and get you tomorrow." She looked around. "Say, do you have a phone?"

"I have a burner."

"Let me have it." She pulled her phone from her bag. "Here's mine."

They each put themselves in the other's phone as a contact.

"Wow, you just gave me your number and I didn't even ask for it. I'm flattered."

"I'm not."

Her phone buzzed. She grabbed it from him. There was a text from her mother.

It read: Allison's gone.

Racing down the road, Sidney pounded on the steering wheel. "I don't need this right now." Her phone rang. "What's going on, Mom?"

"It's been seven hours, Sidney, and we can't find her anywhere." Her mother sobbed. "I'm worried."

"This isn't the first time it's happened," Sid said, accelerating up the highway ramp. "Aren't you used to it?"

"Never, but Megan," Sally's voiced cracked, "it's not fair to Megan. It breaks my heart and makes me so angry. And sad!"

"Did she steal a car? How did she get out of there? You're five miles from anywhere."

There was a silence.

"Mom, you *are* five miles from anywhere, aren't you? The camp, not the house?"

"We thought the house would be a nice change."

Sidney squeezed her phone. Her parents used to be tough as nails, but over the past few years they'd gotten softer. Almost feeble in many ways.

God, don't let that happen to me.

"Your father and Joe are out looking for her now. I'm sure they'll find her."

No, they won't.

"Mom," Sidney softened her voice, "Allison's going to have to figure this out on her own. You've given her all the love you can. There's nothing more you can do."

Sobbing, her mother said, "You're a good girl, Sid. You know how to say the right things."

"I'm just repeating what you told me."

"Oh!" her mother said, perking up. "I hear the garage door opening." There was a pause. Suddenly, she screamed in the phone. "It's Allison! He's got Allison! She looks okay!" *Click!*

Sidney looked at her phone and said to it, "Are you frickin' kidding me?"

Buzz … Buzz … Buzz …

Sidney stretched her arms through her bedsheets, fingers searching for her phone. Bright morning light peeked in through the apartment's blinds. She found her phone. 8:00 a.m. "Ugh. Already." She'd been in bed by 2:00 am, but it felt like five minutes ago. *Screw it.* She set the snooze and sank back into her bed.

Buzz … Buzz … Buzz …

She forced her heavy eyelids open. Her phone was still clutched in her hand. 8:08 a.m. A crack of sunlight gleamed in her eye. Sidney's bare feet crossed the cold floor to the window, where she pulled the curtains closed. *That's better.* She set the snooze again and crawled back under the sheets. A few things raced through her mind. Smoke. Allison. Megan. Smoke. She drifted off to sleep. She dreamed. Smoke. Fire. Satin sheets.

Knock. Knock. Knock.

She lurched up in bed. A thin film of sweat coated her body. Her phone read 8:13 a.m. *That's odd*, she thought, panting a little. *It shouldn't have gone off yet. Sounded like a knock.* Yawning, she stretched her arms out wide. Normally she was on the move by six, except on the weekends. *I'm not even sure what day it is.*

Knock. Knock. Knock.

Her eyes widened. She grabbed her Glock and headed toward the front door in nothing but a black T-shirt and panties.

She'd been in this apartment a year, but only one time had this door been knocked on—by a couple of college guys who lived a few doors over. It had been an invitation to one of their parties. They never looked her way again after she shoved her badge and an earful of her legal authority in their faces.

Sidney checked the peephole. Smoke stood on the other side, holding a tray of coffee and wearing a pair of sunglasses. *How does he know where I live!*

CHAPTER 30

"**W**HAT ARE YOU DOING HERE?" she said through the door.

"I was in the neighborhood and thought I'd bring some coffee over."

A playful thought entered Sidney's mind. She swung the door open.

Smoke's jaw hung in the air.

She plucked a cup of coffee out of the carrier, said "Thank you," and shut the door in his face. From the other side of the door she heard him say, "I thought I'd come over and we could get a jump on things."

"Really, and what kind of things did you want to jump on?" She set down the coffee, headed to her room, grabbed a pair of jeans and a maroon sweater, and slipped them on. She could hear his reply through the door.

"It's not like that."

"You're a man, aren't you?"

There was a pause. "Well, it's kinda like that, but not the way you think. I have a lead."

She buttoned her jeans. "Hold on." Inside the bathroom she brushed her teeth and clipped her hair up. *No.* Back in the bedroom, she found an FBI-issued ball cap, put it on, and laced up some rubber-soled boots.

"Aren't you going to invite me in?" Smoke said.

And break my last seven months of chastity?

She checked herself in the mirror again and strapped her weapon on. She saw her bed reflecting in the mirror.

Just let him in. Long enough is long enough.

"Hello?" she heard him say. "The biscuits are getting cold."

The biscuits are getting cold? The fires inside her dimmed. *Cheap thrill killed.* She pulled her hat down, grabbed her coffee and bag, and opened the door.

"Don't ever do this again," she said, locking the door behind her, "and you can explain how you found me later." Her stomach growled. "Where's my biscuit?"

"Oh," he said, rubbing his neck. "I was joking about that. I ate on the way over."

She glared at him.

"Nice hat," he said, eyeing the three big letters. "Not exactly discreet considering where we're headed."

"And where might that be?" She scanned the parking lot. "And how did you get here?"

"Automobile." He pointed at the parking lot as they made their way down the stairs. "I can drive too, you know."

"Well, we won't be finding out about that anytime soon." There was an old VW bus, red with a white top, she hadn't seen before. "Please tell me you aren't driving that."

He looked at the bus. "That? No." He pointed to the space on the other side, where there was a primer-gray Camaro. A mid-eighties IROC version. "Those are my wheels."

"We'll take the Interceptor."

"It's too slow."

"I didn't think we were in a hurry." She headed for her car. The windows were frosted over. The trunk groaned when she opened it up and grabbed the ice scraper. She handed it to Smoke. "Get to work."

"My car's warm and ready. The bucket seats are cozy."

"Please stop." She grabbed her jacket from the back seat and then started up her car. "Hurry up, and then get in."

Scraping, Smoke said, "I have all my gear in my car."

"And I have all my gear in mine." She closed the door and took a sip of coffee. Flipped on the defroster. The fan rattled. Her neck tightened. Smoke's suggestion seemed more promising.

Nah, let him scrape.

Finishing up, Smoke rapped on the window with his knuckle and said with icy breath, "Why don't we take both cars?"

Her nostrils flared. *Screw it.* She shut off the engine, got out of the car, and locked it.

Smoke tossed the scraper in the trunk and started to close it.

"Hold on." She took out a black duffle bag that clattered with metal and swung it over her shoulder. "All right."

Smoke clamped the lid down, headed for his car, and opened up the passenger side door.

"This isn't a date." She placed her bag in the back seat.

"No, it's common courtesy."

Sidney took her seat and Smoke closed the door. Seconds later, they were roaring down the road. The Camaro's acceleration pinned her to her seat. It had a roll cage inside, and the dash rattled and squeaked. Smoke filled up his racing seat. His head almost touched the ceiling.

"I appreciate you letting me drive," Smoke said over the hum of the engine. "That's one thing I hate about prison. I don't get to drive anywhere."

"Don't get used to it. We have a stop to make."

"Stop, why?"

"Take the next left, a right and then another left."

"Sure, where are we going?"

"Just do it." *Turn about is fair play.*

She took the lid off her coffee and took another drink. Smoke was being extremely cooperative for a man who had problems with authority. He was up to something. His behavior was way outside of his profile. Smoke made the second left.

"Turn here."

They entered a facility full of orange-doored storage garages. He pulled his car to a stop at the key pad. "Uh …"

"Seven six seven five."

He punched it in, and the gate glided open.

"Straight back and to the right."

Smoke cruised toward the back, where cars, boats, and RVs were parked in rows. He pulled into an open slot.

She picked up her belongings, got out, and said, "Wait here."

"Can I at least get out?"

"Sure."

A few minutes later she pulled out in a Dodge Challenger Hellcat: phantom black, with flame-orange stripes on the hood and pinstripes on the side. She pushed on the gas, unleashing a throaty exhaust note.

Smoke took off his glasses. Brows up and eyes wide, he strolled over.

"I think I'm in love."

"With me, or the car?"

"Heh … I'll get my stuff."

CHAPTER 31

CRUISING DOWN THE HIGHWAY, SMOKE ran his fingers over the dash. "Seven hundred and seven horsepower, the most powerful production engine." He bobbed his chin. "Now that's something. I read about these in prison. Pretty new. How'd you come by it?"

"Police auction," she said, fingers hugging the heated steering wheel. *I've missed my baby.* "I outbid a lot of interested people. Pissed off many men."

"I bet."

"It came down to me and Ted." She plucked her shades from the console and put them on. "At the end of the day it was my Hellcat, not his."

Glasses off, Smoke inspected everything. "He missed out. So why the attraction?"

"Love cars. Love the name. My dad actually had some comics with a superhero named Hellcat I kind of liked." *Too much information, Sid.*

Smoke smiled. "Ah, very interesting."

"Not to mention the rear-wheel drive and all the awesome power. It's sort of a given."

"So, was this a drug runner's car?"

"Snagged north of the Arizona border. The auction was in Texas. I drove him all the way home."

"I thought cars were *hers?*"

"Does he look like a *her?*"

He shook his head no.

"I'm heading south, you know," she said. "Unless there's another direction I should be going."

"Right, right. No, south is good." He poked at the GPS. "Do you mind?"

"It would help to know where I'm going." She checked the speedometer. It read ninety. The feel of the road, the sound of the engine, she lost herself in it. She eased off the gas and set the cruise control at seventy. "So tell me about this lead. How did you get it?"

"Fat Sam—"

"And Guppy. Sheesh, I should have known." She switched lanes. "I'm wondering if they're even real."

"Oh, they're real, but it's important that I keep my resources secret." He finished tapping on the GPS. "There we go."

"What is that?"

"Mitchell-Bates Hospital. Closed as of 2004. One hundred and seventy-five beds. Three floors and a basement." He took a drink of coffee. "Two miles from the highway. Once public and now private property."

"And who owns it now?"

"A real estate developer, which is a subsidiary of …"

"The Drake Corporation."

"Actually, Drake Incorporated. We checked at the Secretary of State's office, which wasn't easy seeing how three states are in the immediate area."

"So there are lots of companies, different names and doing business as?"

"Yep." He nodded. "And no real names."

"And I guess they all pay their taxes."

"Do you want me to find out?"

"No." Sidney had done her share of white-collar investigations. Digging through layer after layer of false names and companies was interesting. The top lawyers and accountants dotted every 'i' and crossed every 't' on the good ones. In the most thorough cases it took an act of God to bring them down, and that was only after years were exhausted in the court systems that the enemy knew too well. *This is a lot deeper than just one man.*

"Shadow companies like the Drake probably benefit from a few congressmen and senators in their pockets."

She thought of Congressman Wilhelm and the last words he had said: "Watch your step."

Things were quiet the next ninety minutes of driving, and then she took the Grandview Road exit. A pair of steel-crafted yellow swing gates barred the road that led into the parking lot.

"Looks like we walk from here."

"I'm not leaving my car out here," Sidney said. She got out and made her way to the gates. A heavy padlock down inside a steel mesh cage held the gates together. She scanned the area. The Mitchell-Bates Hospital sign was in disrepair. No cameras were mounted on the light poles leading to the entrance. Only the sound of highway traffic caught her ears. She drew her weapon, shot the lock off, swung the gate open, and got back in the car.

"Subtle," Smoke said.

She put the car in drive. "Let's get this over with."

CHAPTER 32

"**M**AYBE HE IS, MAYBE HE isn't in here," she said, driving forward. "Perhaps Fat Sam and Guppy are wrong."

"They aren't wrong."

"Maybe there's another way out."

Smoke shrugged.

As they rolled up the road between the tall trees, the rising sun dimmed behind misty clouds. The brisk wind stirred the leaves on the parking lot as they approached. The small brick hospital stood in a woodland of falling leaves and pines. Not a car was in the lot. Patches of tall grass popped up through the blacktop.

"He's in here, huh?" she said to Smoke. "It looks pretty abandoned to me."

"It's a lead," he said. "Besides, looks can be deceiving. There's another side to the building, you know." He shook his head. "Man, this is the worst recon ever."

"What's that supposed to mean?" she said, reaching into the back seat for her gym bag. She took out another shoulder holster. A Kevlar vest. Another Glock was ready, along with two fifteen-round magazines. She slipped off her jacket, put on the Kevlar vest, and put the jacket over it. "I don't think there's that much to recon."

"Then why are you gearing up like that?"

"Because I don't normally get to." She pulled the car under the canopy that led to the emergency room entrance, opened her door, and dropped a foot outside. "Are you coming or not?"

"Pop the trunk."

She followed him to the back of the car, where he opened his oversized gym bag. He put on his own Kevlar vest and strapped a pair of 9mm Beretta pistols to his hips. He finished by stuffing a single-action army sheriff's pistol in the back of his pants.

"A revolver?" she said.

"It's sentimental."

"All right, cowboy." As she turned toward the hospital entrance, something caught her eyes. She froze.

A white-grey wolf stood twenty feet away, teeth bared. Its muscular back was more than waist tall. It was one of the biggest canines she'd ever seen.

"Uh, Smoke?"

"Yeah?" he said, turning. "Oh … that's one big dog."

Sidney's back tightened. Her fingertips tingled. She knew dogs but not wolves. They were wild. Ferocious. She reached for her weapon.

Before she could even touch it, the wolf had snarled and sprinted away.

Sidney jumped when Smoke closed the trunk.

He had a tire iron in his hand. "Let's go catch that werewolf."

"I think it will be a few more hours before any of them come out." She took the tire iron from his hand and made her way onto the landing. A set of sliding glass doors were closed, and the side entrance steel door was locked. She wedged the tire iron in between the doors and started to pry. The doors cracked open an inch. "A little help," she grunted.

Smoke gripped the door's edge and gave a powerful tug. The doors split apart another foot. Straining, he said, "Think you can fit?"

"Ha," she said, squeezing through. Smoke forced himself inside, and the doors sealed shut with the tire iron outside. "Ew," she said, covering her nose. "It smells like the dead in here."

Inside, the lighting was dim other than the natural light from the windows.

"Do you hear that?" Smoke said, tilting his head. The sound of electricity hummed inside the walls. "Something is going on in here." He started forward, shuffling by the old waiting room chairs and into the ER. There were several gurneys with rotting curtains hanging around them. "What do you think? Follow the smell?"

Sidney remained behind Smoke's shoulder and followed him into the central hall, plugging her nose. *This is disgusting.* The long hallway was darker because the patient room doors were closed, blocking the sunlight. Smoke stopped at one of them and pushed it open. It groaned on the hinges and swung inward. *Is he visiting somebody?*

It was a two-patient room with soiled linens rotting on the beds. The air was musty, rotten, and stale.

Sidney coughed. "Do you have a thing for bad smells?"

Smoke glided to the window and stood where the daylight crept in through the blinds. He pulled them aside with two fingers. "We aren't alone."

Sidney took a look. Smoke was right. More cars were parked behind the building: two navy-blue cargo vans and several dark sedans. A box truck was backed into the service drive. All of it was shadowed by the tall trees that snuffed out the bright rising light.

She glanced up at Smoke. "I can't say I'm glad that you're right. Come on."

"I'd be disappointed if I was wrong."

Heading out of the room, she came to a stop. Footsteps and the shuffle of feet came from the room above. The steps creaked and were moving down the hall. Sidney followed the sound down toward the emergency exits. Smoke was a large shadow behind her. The doors were closed at the stairwell, but she heard the latch of the doors above pop open. She slid to one side of the doors, and Smoke took the other. Her heart thumped in her chest.

After about thirty seconds, Smoke shrugged. "They either went up or went back." He popped the door open and peered inside the dark stairwell. "Huh, there's a basement too. I have a coin. Heads we go up, tails we go—*ulp*!"

A hand shot out and pulled Smoke into the stairwell. The door slammed shut behind him.

CHAPTER 33

"**S**MOKE!"

Sidney shoved on the door, but there was no give. Something blocked the other side. She thrust her shoulder into it. It cracked open and slammed shut. She could hear the scuffle of a fight on the other side. A man screamed. "Smoke!"

Wham!

A heavy body rocked the door. She heard the heavy blows of bone on bone and flesh on flesh. Hard smacks. Kicking. Punching. Wrestling. She found her flashlight and shone it through the rectangular portal. A bloodshot eye blinked in the light. The face was scarred. Subhuman. She tapped the nose of her gun on the glass.

"Back off!"

The face ducked away.

She lowered her shoulder, rammed into the door, and winced. No give. She wanted to shoot. Blast away, but Smoke was over there, fighting for his life.

Come on! Come on! Think, Sid! Think!

"Back away, Sid," Smoke roared from the other side. "Back away!"

Sidney stepped aside. The door flung inward. Smoke appeared, dragging another man in a headlock.

"Stay away from the door," Smoke warned. The door clasped shut. Footsteps scurried up the stairwell. "Stay here." Smoke wrestled the struggling man to the floor and wrenched the man's arm behind his back. *Pop!* The shoulder was dislocated, but the man didn't cry out.

"What are you doing?" Sidney said.

Chest heaving, Smoke replied, "I'm immobilizing him." He wrenched the man's other arm. *Pop.* The other shoulder gave.

Sidney's stomach turned.

The man-like thing thrashed with purpose, arms hanging limp as noodles from the sockets. Its face was ghoulish and veiny. It gathered itself on its feet.

Smoke swept the legs out from under it.

It crashed back-first to the floor.

Smoke pinned it and jammed his gun barrel in its chest.

"Don't kill him," Sidney ordered.

"I hit him with everything I had. He didn't even grunt."

"That's not a license to kill."

"You're just going to have to trust me on this, Agent Shaw." He squeezed the trigger.

Ka-blam!

The man-like thing lurched up and smacked Smoke in the chin.

He staggered back.

It started walking down the hall, arms dangling at its sides with a hole clean through its back and chest.

Sidney took aim.

Blam! Blam! Blam!

It tumbled over with its kneecap blasted apart.

"Good shot." Smoke wiped his brow and headed after their fallen attacker where it writhed on the floor. "I think it's a zombie." He pointed his weapon at its head.

Blam!

"Zombies aren't real," she said, catching her breath and holstering her gun.

"I don't know," Smoke replied.

She kneeled down. Whoever or whatever the man was, it didn't bleed: it oozed. It still moved. Her skin turned clammy. "This is sick."

"Good thing we're in a hospital."

Sidney eyed him. "How many were in there?"

"Just two. One I think was a man. I kicked him solid in the balls." He cracked his neck. "That's when I dragged this fiend out of there. Do you think it's that captain?" he said, referring to the man driving AV's boat she'd mentioned earlier.

"No, but his skin is just like what I saw." She took out her phone. "No signal."

"No surprise." He tipped his head toward the stairwell. "How about I scout it out?"

"How about we scout it out? But another approach would be better, seeing how they know we're here." She made her way into another patient room and peered out through the window. None of the cars had moved. "Doesn't look like we scared anyone off, either."

"Not yet," Smoke said, leaning on the door frame. "But I say we take it to them."

If AV was here, then he certainly knew they were here. It might take hours to clear the building, not to mention the unnatural elements that surrounded them. What kind of man had they just taken down? It had attacked, but it hadn't tried to eat them.

It's not a zombie. There's no such thing as zombies. She headed back into the hall. The man-like thing on the floor was still moving.

"Strange," Smoke said, looking down at it. "I thought the head wound would kill it."

"This isn't a movie. This is reality."

Smoke switched weapons. "And this is a forty-five automatic loaded with hollow points." He pointed at the writhing thing's heart.

Blam.

It stopped moving.

He blew the smoke rolling from the barrel. "Critical hit."

Irritated, she said, "Will you stop shooting?"

"We needed to know how to take these things out, and now we do."

"A bullet in the heart does that to anything." She made her way back down the hallway, stopping and listening at patient doors from time to time. On the other side of the hall, Smoke did the same. She traversed the hall, passing the elevators. She heard a ding and turned back.

Smoke stood in front of the elevators. The up button glowed with light. The doors split open and he half-stepped inside. He looked at her and said, "Going up?"

"I'm not taking the elevator." She crept in halfway and pressed buttons two and three, grabbed Smoke's arm, and pushed him out. She ran down the hall with Smoke on her heels. Flashlight ready, she entered the stairwell, jogged up the steps, and stopped on the second floor landing. She peered through the door's portal. Figures crowded in front of the elevator down the hall. One of them was limping.

"That's the guy," Smoke said, cocking his pistol. "It has to be."

Sidney counted four men, but she didn't see any weapons. It was odd. One of them disappeared into the elevator. Necks craned forward until the man stepped out into view again. Voices mumbled among themselves, and the group spread out, vanishing into patient rooms and behind the nurse's station.

"Ambush," she whispered to Smoke.

"I say we start at the top and work our way down. Give them something to think about."

"Agreed." She turned her flashlight up the stairwell and took it two steps at a time. She stopped halfway to the first landing. A man stood there in ragged clothes, hollow-eyed and ugly. He held a grenade-sized object in his hands.

"FBI! Hands up!"

The man's thoughtless expression didn't change as he dropped the grenade down the stairwell. It bounced off the first step.

Smoke scooped it up. "Stun grenade." He flung it back at the man.

Sidney squeezed her eyes shut and covered her ears.

Flash! Boom!

The sound inside the stairwell rocked her senses. She saw dizzying spots and sagged down the steps. There was ringing, ringing and ringing, and everything faded to black.

CHAPTER 34

A SPLASH OF COLD WATER SNAPPED Sidney out of her sleep. Wide-eyed and head aching, she tried to spit the gag from her mouth. Something bit into her wrists, which were tied behind her back. Her feet were bound as well.

"Huh, huh," a man said, lumbering by with a plastic bucket in his hands. He was thickset and bald. He wore a heavy blue sweater, grey sweatpants, and white tennis shoes. He poured the bucket of water on Smoke, who sat on the floor by her side, bound the same way.

Smoke coughed and sputtered.

The man walked away and disappeared through a double doorway.

Spitting the gag from his mouth, Smoke said, "You all right?"

Sidney nodded. Other than a piercing headache and stiff limbs, she was fine. They looked to be in the basement cafeteria, judging by the checkered tiles on the floor. They weren't alone, either. Below the incandescent lights were more people, working at tables. They wore masks, gloves, and dark-grey scrubs. Some sat at the tables and others stood. She didn't have a clear view of what they were doing. Not a one glanced their way.

"See that?" Smoke said in a low tone. Two goons in pea coats lorded over a lone table. It had their guns and gear on it. "Be patient."

It was easier said than done. Sidney had never been captured before. Never been a captive of any sort. The revolting smells didn't help, either. She strained against her bonds. Her eyes watered.

"Save your energy," Smoke advised.

Balled up, she let her body go slack. Smoke was right. She focused on what the others were doing. A small figure that looked to be a boy taped up a box the others had loaded and moved it to a stack in the corner. *Hmmm.* Five people in all were making packages of some sort. It reminded her of the scene at Sting Ray's bar. Children being exploited. She clenched her teeth.

A small bell rang. The workers stopped what they were doing, and without a glance among them they departed from the room.

With great effort, she spat the gag from her mouth and gasped.

"Feel better?" Smoke said.

"No. Hey!" she yelled over at the guards. "I'm a federal agent. I demand to know who is in charge."

The men remained frozen in place without a glance her way. Each one had a shotgun strapped over his shoulder.

She heard Smoke's belly grumble. "I don't think they're serving pancakes."

"No," Smoke said just as the set of doors that led into the hallway opened. Two ghoulish men with clammy skin, wearing denim overalls, walked in. "And I don't think they're here to take our order."

The men came toward them with strong stiff movements. The first one grabbed Smoke by the collar and heaved him up on his shoulder. The second one did the same to Sidney. Draped over the ghastly men's shoulders, they exited the room into a dark hallway and entered another. Sidney's goon set her down in a padded office chair. An antique walnut desk in a well-furnished office was in front of her.

Behind it sat AV in a high-backed leather chair.

His eerie henchmen moved to either side of him.

"I have to admit," AV said, filing his nails, "This is a surprise. I normally fetch my enemies myself. But in this case, you came straight to me." He wore a dark-purple dress shirt with rolled up sleeves, revealing his hairy arms. The glow of two floor lamps against the back wall brought out the sheen in his waves of jet-black hair. He seemed small between his goons. "Agent Shaw, didn't I mention that I would kill you?"

"Yes, I recall you threatening a federal agent."

AV laughed. "And yet, here you are." He waggled his finger at her. "Did you not see the bodies of your friends? Were they not torn to shreds?"

A coldness overcame her.

"Ah," He continued, "you look confused. He eased back in the chair and rocked a little. "Let me fill you in." He licked his teeth. "I'm a werewolf."

Sidney laughed despite the truth behind his words and the tingling that shot up her limbs. "Congratulations," she said. "That must explain the fleas."

"Good one," Smoke said with a nod. "And I told you so."

AV picked up a pistol that lay on the desk. It was Smoke's Colt .45, black matte and pearl-handled, sheriff's model. He popped open the chamber and emptied the bullets out of the cylinder. They were silver. "Either you're a fan of the Lone Ranger, or you are as stupid as most men are."

"Really?" Sidney said, looking over at Smoke. "He's not a werewolf."

"Ah, a skeptic. I love a skeptic." AV opened a drawer and pulled a knife out. The wavy blade looked ancient. He turned in his chair and grabbed the hand of one of his goons and placed it on the desk. He skinned the hair off its arm. "Sharp, isn't it?" The knife bit deeper, and he peeled off the skin, exposing the muscle beneath it.

Sidney's skin crawled.

"See, he doesn't even scream." The listless goon leaned back into attention. AV stuck the knife in its thigh. "And he makes for an excellent knife holder." His dangerous eyes narrowed on Sidney. "Can you explain that, Agent Shaw?"

No.

"We call them deaders."

We?

"Cursed flesh brought to life. Flesh automatons made for our bidding. Capable of executing simple commands. Fetch. Fight. Kill."

"That's quite an accomplishment," she said, twisting her wrists behind her. *I need to get out of here.* "Do you have a patent on it?"

"Humph," he said, plucking a pen from its holder and writing on something. "How did you find me? I need to tie up that loose end."

"It wasn't that hard," Smoke said. "Those wild wolf dogs led us here."

"I don't think so," AV said. "But no matter. I'll figure it out soon enough."

"So, who is 'we'?" she said, turning her ear to him. *Keep him talking.* "I can use all the leads I can get, because you're only the first guy, I mean werewolf, on my list."

"Your tongue is sharp, Agent." He leered at her. "I'm reconsidering."

"Reconsidering what?"

"Twisting your head off first." He picked up a phone that looked to be hers. "You have family, don't you?" He turned her phone toward her. A picture of Megan, her niece, appeared.

How'd he get in there?

"You've seen what I can do," he continued. "Imagine what I could do to her."

The blood rushed through her temples. Her heart sank. *No!*

"Of course, that would be merciful," AV said, flipping through the pictures. "Maybe I'll have her turned into a deader."

"I'm going to kill you," Sidney replied.

"No, Agent Shaw, I am going to kill you." He rose from his chair, pushing it back, and stretched out his arms. "Both of you. I've been waiting to wake you for hours." He cracked his neck from side to side. "Nighttime is my time." He crushed her phone in his fist and dropped the remains on the desk.

"Told you he was strong," Smoke said, straining at his bonds.

Sidney's heart quickened. *What is happening?!*

AV started to change. His body stretched and convulsed. Coarse hairs sprouted from his face and arms. Muscle bulged and bone groaned. His purple shirt split at the seams. A short snout protruded from his jaws, and his head stretched toward the ceiling. In seconds, AV went from a man to a full-blown werewolf. Evil and lust lurked behind the yellow eyes that rested on Sidney.

Horrified, she sagged in her seat and turned her head away.

This isn't real! This isn't real! This isn't real!

CHAPTER 35

"**W**HAT'S THE MATTER?" AV SAID, his voice now something monstrous—throaty and raw. "Has your sharp tongue dulled?"

Sidney had seen horrible things, both in real life and in the movies, but nothing compared to the supernatural transformation she'd just witnessed. It was unnatural. Evil. Yet somehow … alluring? Utterly afraid, she pulled her knees up into her chest.

"That's what I like to see," AV said, coming from around the desk. "The brave woman turned into a little girl again." He leaned over her. "Your fear feeds my craving."

She felt his hot breath on her neck. Now she couldn't deny there was something seductive and powerful about it. Her iron will started to cave.

"Yes, yes, Agent Shaw. Give yourself away." He brushed her hair aside with his clawed finger and turned her chin toward him. "Experience every pleasure I can offer that needs awakening in the dark corners of your soul."

He ran his claw down her face, over her chest, and rested his powerful hand on her thigh and squeezed.

She moaned. Dark fires ignited within. She was powerless in the clutch of the uber-man before her.

"Maybe I'll keep you around after all." He ran his finger down her thigh. With his claw, he sliced the cord that bound her ankles. He twisted her around and cut the bonds from her wrists.

Her shoulders sagged. Her body was loose. Languid.

He eased her legs apart. "It's been quite some time, hasn't it, woman?"

Lost in his power, her head fell over on her shoulder. She wanted him. She loathed him. Her eyes found Smoke's. He had a fierce look about him. Seeing the sweat bead on his forehead, a glimmer of her senses returned. AV took her chin and turned it away.

"Don't worry about him—he's a dead man, but you might have a promising future ahead."

"Sidney! Close your eyes! Think of pancakes and butterflies."

What kind of man says that?

"Deaders, kill that fool!" AV ordered. "Feed his corpse to the wolves. I'll be needing Agent Shaw all to myself."

Pancakes and butterflies? The flames of passion turned to angry fires. *Pancakes and butterflies!* She kicked AV's groin with all her force.

He slammed back into the desk.

"Fool woman!" He lurched forward and backhanded her in the face, spinning her like a top from the chair so that she tumbled over.

Her head rang, and all she saw was bright spots and stars.

AV put his big paw on her head and tugged her up to her toes by the hair. "I'm not big on second chances, Pretty."

A clamor rose. Smoke, somehow free of his bonds, wrestled against the clutches of the deaders.

"Excuse me," AV said a moment before he slung Sidney into the wall.

She smacked into it hard and sagged to the floor. Groaning, she forced herself up to her knees and spat blood.

"Run, Sidney!" Smoke urged. "Run!" He slipped away from the deaders only to find himself cornered by AV. The werewolf sneered down on him. Smoke punched him in the throat and poked him in the eye.

AV roared. His claws slashed out.

Smoke twisted away, ducked, and popped up with a knife in his hand. It was the ancient blade that AV had planted in the deader. He cut into the monster's slashing arms, spun under a powerful blow, and drove the blade home into AV's abdomen.

The werewolf staggered back against the wall.

"No! No!" AV cried. "You stabbed me with the Blade of Hoknar. Darkness falls. Darkness falls." He slumped back against the wall, and his eyes began to close.

Sidney got up and wiped the blood from her mouth.

"That was close."

Smoke skipped away from the deaders, who wandered the room but didn't attack.

Laughter rumbled in AV's throat, and his mighty form rose again. He plucked the blade from his stomach and showed a mouthful of sharp teeth.

"Fools." He hurled the blade at Smoke.

The big man plucked it out of the air, spun, and buried it hilt-deep in the heart of a deader. He ripped it out and said, "Sid, get out of here!"

"Oh please," AV said, "no one has ever escaped alive." He wiped the saliva dripping from his fangs off of his chin. "I just need to decide which one of you to kill first." He chomped his teeth. "Deader, kill her. I shall kill him." AV sprang from one side of the room to the other. His heavy frame drove the evading Smoke to the ground. His fists came down with speed and power.

Sidney ran for the door.

The dead man cut into her path. Fingers clutched at her waist and tore a belt loop off her pants.

She slugged it in the face.

It leered back into her eyes. Soulless. Empty. Its grabby hand locked around her wrist and slung her to the floor.

She hit hard. "Ugh!"

The deader held her in a fierce grip and pummeled her with its free fist. The hammering blows rocked her body.

She kept her shoulder up to absorb what she could and kicked her hardest with her legs. Her heel connected with its jaw.

"Nuh!" it said, sounding almost human.

With an angry shout, Sidney twisted her wrist free and was on her feet again.

The werewolf had Smoke pinned to the wall by the neck. Smoke's shaky hand was pointing at the desk. The gun. The bullets. Silver nodules caught her eye. She snatched the old wheel gun up. Strong hands grabbed her feet and jerked her to the floor.

"Ulp!"

Crack!

Her head bounced off the edge of the hardwood desk. She saw red.

"No!"

She kicked it in the face.

"No!"

Her heel crushed its nose in.

"NO!"

She ripped her foot out of its grip and scrambled away on all fours. The other deader lay still, with a knife stuck in its chest. She ripped it out and turned just as the deader dove on top of her. She drove the blade into its chest and pushed it off her.

Smoke!

She pushed off the floor. Smoke held on for his life against the werewolf. Sidney plucked a bullet from the desk and loaded it into the chamber. She cocked back the hammer. "Let him go, AV!"

The wolfman froze with the battered Smoke held tightly in his grip and said, "You don't really think that will work, do you?"

"Only one way to find out."

"Aren't you here to arrest me? After all, I'm no good to your handlers if I'm dead. They need the knowledge within this body."

"Shoot him," Smoke spat out from busted lips. "Shoot him now."

"Let him down," she warned. The adrenaline cleared her mind. She felt in control again.

"Certainly," AV replied, lowering Smoke's busted frame to the ground. "But I don't think you have strong enough cuffs to hold me. Remember what happened the last time. And another thing, silver bullets don't really kill werewolves."

"Then why are you doing what I say?"

"Because I enjoy the game." In a flash, he rocketed by the desk toward the office door.

Sidney fired. *Blam!*

The wolfman burst through the door with a wounded howl and vanished into the hall.

Sidney peeked down both ways. AV the werewolf was gone.

CHAPTER 36

"**T**HAT WAS FAST," SIDNEY SAID, rushing over to Smoke. She helped him to his feet. His hair was matted in blood, and his face was swelling. His Kevlar vest was all torn up. "Are you going to make it?"

He straightened up. "I had my doubts." With a bloody hand, he picked up the other bullets from the table. "Why didn't you shoot him?"

"They want him alive."

"They? Don't let your overzealous sense of duty get me or you killed, Agent Shaw. " He stepped past her and plucked the knife out of the deader's chest. He flipped it around and faced her. "He's a murderer. And murderers must die." He pointed his finger in her face. "I told you he was a werewolf. Now hand over the gun."

"No." She held out her hand. "Hand over the bullets."

"It's my gun."

"I'm not arguing with a twelve-year-old."

Smoke's face drew tight as he handed over the bullets. "Fine. Just, the next time you hesitate, remember—he twists people's heads off!" He made his way into the hall and knelt down by some blood drops on the floor. "Seems you clipped him, and my guess is he didn't like it."

"Follow the blood," she said, loading the bullets into their cylinders. As she made her way down the hall toward the cafeteria, one of the double doors squeaked open. Smoke darted in front of her. A shotgun blast rang out. She flattened on the floor. Aimed her weapon.

In a burst of motion, Smoke jerked one of the pea-coat men through the door and ripped the shotgun from his grasp. He lowered the barrel to between the man's eyes.

"No, no man! Please, don't shoot me."

Smoke kneeled down, pressing the barrel deeper into the man's face. "Where's Mister Vaughn?"

"Who?"

Smoke punched him in the gut. "The werewolf."

"Aw man, aw man, I don't know!"

"How many others?" Sidney piped in.

"Just me. Just me."

"Liar," Sidney said, backing into the cafeteria. There were no signs of anybody anywhere.

Pop! Pop! Pop! Pop! Pop!

Bullets ripped through the air from the other end of the hall.

Smoke dragged the man into the cafeteria.

"Who was that?"

"The other man, Allen. Like me, he stayed to finish you off." He chuckled. "And if he doesn't, the others will."

Smoke looked up at Sid. "We've got to go. Time's wasting."

Pop! Pop! Pop! Pop! Pop!

"Yer gonna get wasted, all right," the goon said.

Smoke took the shotgun stock and clocked the goon in the jaw. "I hate big talkers." He nodded at the table. "Get the gear. I'll cover the hall."

Sidney moved, picking up pistols and holsters.

Ka-Blam! Ka-Blam!

She whipped around. Smoke was gone. "Dammit."

He reappeared back inside the door with another shotgun strapped on his shoulder. "Got him."

She took a moment and caught her breath. *Is this really going on? Werewolves and zombie-like men called deaders?* She swooned a little.

Smoke wrapped his arms around her waist and steadied her. "We aren't finished yet. And I think you're going to have quite a shiner, but I can live with it."

"Look who's talking," she said.

Smoke's clothes were blood-soaked in some parts.

The cafeteria suddenly became quiet. She remembered what AV had said: no one ever left alive. She took a shotgun from Smoke's shoulder and pumped the handle.

"Until today."

"Until what today?"

"Nothing," she said, looking at the floor. She found AV's blood. "Let's go."

The blood trail led into the darkness of the stairwell. She turned on her flashlight.

Smoke cut in front of her. "You shine. I'll lead." He took off up the steps, clearing the first floor and heading up the second flight. He cracked the door open.

Pop! Pop! Pop! Pop!

Bullets blasted into the stairwell doors.

"Turn off the light and cover me," Smoke said.

"Wait."

He surged through the door.

Sidney laid down shotgun cover fire into the middle of the hall. Shots cracked out from everywhere. Muzzle flashes flared. Shielded behind the door, she cracked off a few more rounds and everything fell silent. Now that it was night, the hallway was almost pitch black. The seconds seemed like minutes as she peered into the shadows.

Pop!

A man cried out. A group of shadows tussled in the hall. Something cracked. Another man screamed.

Blam! Blam!

"It's clear," Smoke said, his voice hollow in the blackness of the hall. "Come on. There's still a trail of blood."

Just as Sidney eased into the hallway, the fine hairs on her neck rose. She started to turn. A hairy paw clamped down on her shoulder and dug its sharp nails into her skin.

"I'll take this," the soft savage voice of the wolfman said, sliding Smoke's pistol with the silver bullets out of the back of her pants. "Set down your weapons and stop resisting. You don't know what you're missing."

Hot saliva dripped onto her neck, arousing her carnal senses. Compelled to obey, she set the shotgun and pistol down.

"I'm not so bad, Pretty," AV said, wrapping his powerful arm around her waist. He picked her up off her feet like a child. "Come quietly now and everything will be fine."

She wanted to believe him. Her rigid body slackened. "No," she managed to say.

"Yes," he replied, moving down into the stairwell's blackness.

In a twisted moment of fate, her terror turned to attraction as she felt herself being carried over the threshold of wickedness. Everything she knew to be right suddenly turned wrong. Reaching deep inside, she found a spark and tried to cry out against her captivating bonds.

AV clamped his hand over her mouth. "Sssh…"

CHAPTER 37

THE SECOND-FLOOR DOORS TO THE stairwell flung open, and Smoke emerged. He hurled himself down the stairwell, crashing into Sidney and AV. The jolt knocked her loose from the werewolf's clutches.

"Fool!" AV roared, lashing out and striking Smoke in the chest.

The hardened soldier crashed into the wall. The stairwell lit up with bright barrel flashes.

Ka-Blam! Ka-Blam! Ka-Blam!

Smoke unloaded his shotgun into AV's chest, rocking the werewolf backward.

Click.

"You're a dead man!" AV roared.

Sidney crawled through the darkness as she heard heavy blows smacking into flesh. Man and monster cursed and snarled. *I have to help!* A clatter of metal skidded over the landing. She dove toward it and felt the cool pistol clutched in her fingers.

Whap! Whap! Whap!

Punches and angry howls filled the stairwell. The heavy scuffles and grunts were inseparable. Weapon ready, she rushed into the fray, grabbed a handful of coarse hair, and fired.

Blam!

A shrieking howl split her ears, and a swipe of claws knocked her from her feet. She fired again at the sound of feet fleeing up the stairs.

Blam!

Smoke grabbed her hand and moaned, "Stop! Only three more bullets left."

They helped each other to their feet. Smoke leaned on her, limping down the stairwell. He looked like he had crawled out of a mine field.

"We need to get you help."

He spat blood. "I'm fine."

"You don't look fine."

"Well, I look better than most guys who've slugged it out with a werewolf." He groaned. "We need to kill this guy."

"We need more help."

"Follow the blood. I think we've almost got him." He pointed at bloody footprints on the floor. "Staggered. You got him good."

The blood trail led to the emergency room and then to the door of a locked office. She peered through the portal. AV sat in a chair, digging medical pliers into an abdominal wound. He plucked out a bloody silver bullet and tossed it to the floor.

Sidney tapped on the glass and pointed the barrel at him.

The werewolf's eyes widened.

She fired.

Blam!

Cat-quick, he sprang away, crashing through the window and into the parking lot.

"Missed. Dammit!"

Smoke busted the door handle off with a fire extinguisher and kicked it open.

"True, but I think you scared him off," Smoke said, stepping inside and looking out the broken window. "And the hunt starts all over."

"Did you hear that?" she said.

An engine flared up with a gentle roar. A second later, a maroon Cadillac Escalade sped through the parking lot. AV the werewolf filled the seat.

"You've got to be kidding me." She took aim. Smoke pushed the barrel down.

"I think the Hellcat has a better chance of not missing."

She took off, racing into the ER waiting room. The sliding glass doors were sealed and the main entrance door wouldn't open.

Smoke picked up a row of seats and hurled them through the glass. "After you," he said.

Sidney jumped down the steps and flung open the car door.

Smoke slid over the hood.

"Don't you ever do that again!" she said, firing up the engine. She shifted into reverse, hit the gas, and swung the car around. Dropping the car into drive, she stomped on the gas, smoking the wheels.

"Nothing like the smell of burning rubber in the evening," Smoke said, crawling into the back seat. "Sorry about the upholstery."

"What are you doing?" she yelled at the rearview mirror.

Smoke popped down the rear seat, pulled his duffle bag from the trunk, and crawled back into the front seat. "Getting this," he said, holding an M-16 assault rifle with an M203 grenade launcher mounted under the barrel. "A real beauty, isn't it?"

"Illegal as hell!"

"I won't tell if you won't. Jealous?"

Yes. "No."

"Well, get after him. It's time to blow Fang Face away."

The engine roared as they raced up onto the highway. AV's bright red taillights weaved in and out of traffic about ten car lengths ahead.

"Looks like he knows we're coming." She changed lanes, pushing on the gas. "And don't you dare discharge your weapon. There are civilians everywhere."

Smoke rolled down the window. "Don't you have a siren or something?"

"No, Starsky, I don't."

A grin crept onto Smoke's busted lips. "Just pull alongside."

"What are you going to do?"

"Blow his doors off."

Barreling down the highway one lane over, Sidney caught up with AV.

"Perfect!" Smoke yelled.

AV slammed on his brakes.

The grenade blasted out of the barrel and tore out a section of the guard rail.

"You missed?" Sidney said.

"It happens." Smoke started firing short bursts of bullets. *Takka takka … takka takka …*

AV turned the Escalade off at the next exit.

"Great, he figured that plan out," she said, cruising after the SUV. She was three car lengths from the bumper.

"Get closer," Smoke said, shooting out the back windows. "I need to get the wheels."

"No," she said, "he might slam on the brakes."

"You're joking."

"No, wouldn't you do th—"

The SUV's brake lights blared. The huge car started to screech.

Sidney hit the brakes and slung the wheel over to the right. She hit the berm and skidded by until they came to a stop.

"Perfect," Smoke said, crawling out the window. He fired the launcher over the hood.

Toomph!

Inside the cab of the Cadillac, AV's fierce yellow eyes shone like moons. The entire front end of the SUV exploded.

Ka-Boom!

The front of the car was engulfed in flames.

"That ought to do it." She got out of her car.

Smoke approached the burning car and unloaded a few more rounds into it.

Takka takka … takka takka ….

There was nothing left but a ball of flame and black smoke. Smoke circled with wary eyes, barrel lowered toward the flames. The driver's side door opened with an eerie groan and fell onto the pavement.

AV the werewolf stepped out. All of his fur was smoking.

Smoke let him have it.

Takka takka … takka takka …

AV barked a wolfish laugh. "Fools, you can't kill me!" The werewolf's eyes narrowed on Sidney.

She went for the pistol as the monster closed in. She brought the weapon up and fired a blast into the ground where AV once stood.

Hurtling through the air, he landed on top of her. The breath was knocked out of her, and the pistol clattered over the road. AV wrapped his claws around her neck and squeezed. "Goodbye, Pretty!"

Crack!

AV's wolfish head jerked forward.

Smoke locked his rifle under AV's neck and pulled back with both arms. AV released his grip on Sidney.

Gasping for breath, she crawled away.

"Get the gun!" Smoke yelled.

The werewolf bucked and slung like a bull.

Smoke held on to the rifle and rode the werewolf like a cowboy.

Sidney searched for the pistol. A glimmer of metal rested underneath her tire. Snatching it up, she rolled to a knee and took aim. AV now had Smoke in a headlock.

"One shove," AV said, concealed behind Smoke's body, "and I break him. Walk away, and I'll let him live. I'll let both of you live."

She didn't have a clear shot. Little more than half of his head was exposed.

"Take the shot," Smoke sputtered. "You've got to take the shot and forget about me."

"Touching," AV said, applying more pressure to Smoke's head.

The large man's face turned purple. She heard bones popping and cracking.

Her eyes found Smoke's.

His lips spit out two words. "Center mass."

"Time's up, Pretty," AV said. He howled at the moon. "And I don't think you can hit me anyway."

In a burst of motion, Smoke shifted his leg behind the werewolf and flipped him over.

Sidney fired.

Blam!

Both men lay on the road, and only one of them started moving.

Smoke peeled the werewolf's arms off him. Hair, claws, and wolf face retracted. In seconds, Adam Vaughn was back, wearing only shorts made from spandex. He had a bullet hole in his heart. While examining the body, Sidney noted a strange brand on his back shoulder: a rising black sun that seemed to be bleeding.

"Good shot," Smoke said, groaning. "Can I have my gun back now?"

She started to hand it to him and stopped. "I have a question first."

"All right."

"How did you get your hands free, inside AV's office?"

"Diamond dust on my fingernails." He flashed his hands. Where there wasn't blood, they twinkled a little.

"Did you learn that in the SEALs?"

"No, it's from a Punisher comic book."

"Is that from the prison archives, Smoke?"

He smiled. "Finally."

EPILOGUE

THE NIGHT BECAME EVEN LONGER. Fire trucks arrived. Local law enforcement and the FBI followed. No one listened, and Smoke was back in handcuffs. Sidney spent an hour arguing her case, only to have Ted arrive in his brown trench coat and clear things up in five minutes.

"A werewolf?"

"Don't judge me, Ted." She yawned. She didn't really care if he believed it or not. At the moment she was happy to be alive.

"I know, but that corpse looks like a man." He watched the emergency crew bag AV up. "Next time take a picture. Maybe a video. And we wanted him alive."

"I tried. We both tried, sort of." She touched her lip and winced. "At least I don't have prom tomorrow."

"What?" Ted shook his head.

"Nothing. So what happens to him?" she said, looking at Smoke. He was sitting in the back of a police cruiser, all stitched up.

"Back to prison, I guess." Ted patted the hood of her car. "Man, I can't believe you outbid me by a dollar. A dollar! The Hellcat sure is pretty."

Sidney wasn't paying much attention. Her thoughts were on Smoke, AV, deaders, the Black Slate... Many things. But mostly Smoke.

"Go home," Ted said, rubbing her shoulder. "Come in when you feel like it tomorrow."

A wrecker hauled the SUV off and the ambulance pulled out with AV's body.

"I'd rather head back to that hospital."

"Sid, there's a dozen agents over there already. Damned if we didn't find more missing children." He scratched his head. "What you did was a good thing. Another good thing. Take comfort in that. As for your friend, I'll do what I can."

An FBI agent shut the cruiser door on Smoke, got inside the car, and sped away. Her friend had vanished. Her chin dipped and she sighed. Then the rain came down.

The next day, stiff as a board, Sidney headed into the office. Five hours later, she turned in her statement of events to Ted. It was fifteen pages long.

"Geez, Sid." He put on his glasses. "It's just a report, not a bestseller."

She scanned the trophies, pictures, and colorful memorabilia on his wall. "What's the matter? Are you worried it might cut into football?"

"No. Well, yes." He huffed a breath and looked up at her. "Sid, I'm sorry, and I want you to know that I'm glad you're all right. But deaders? What is a deader?” His desk phone rang. He picked it up. “Ted.” His face darkened and he hung up. “Dammit.” He picked up her report and grabbed his dress coat. “Got to go.”

He was gone, leaving her all alone. She slipped out of his office, grabbed her bag, took the elevator, and went to her car. The old Interceptor. *At least it's not raining.* The rattle in the dash was even worse than before. She turned up the radio and headed for Mildred Bates hospital. Driving up the entrance, the first thing she saw was a great yellow crane with a wrecking ball. She pulled into the parking lot, parked, and got out, gaping.

The entire hospital was rubble. A dump truck loaded with debris rode by. The company name and logo, she instantly recognized.

Drake.

Her phone buzzed. A picture of her sister, Allison, and niece, Megan, popped up. The text below it read: Watch your step.

CRAIG HALLORAN

THE SUPERNATURAL BOUNTY HUNTER FILES

I SMELL SMOKE

BOOK 2

CHAPTER 1

*B*uzz. *Buzz. Buzz.*

Sidney rolled over in her bed and grabbed her phone. The clock read 4:32 am, Tuesday morning. She sat up, rubbed her eyes, punched in her security code, and read the text.

It was from Cyrus Tweel, her new supervisor.

The text read:

Come immediately.

"Aw, crap."

She shuffled toward the bathroom. Inside, she turned on the shower then brushed her teeth until the mirror steamed up. She flung her garments into a hamper, and then, stooped under the showerhead, she let the hot water run down her neck.

Enjoy the little things in life.

The last two months had been lousy. Cyrus Tweel, her ex-boyfriend, had replaced Jack Dydeck as her supervisor. Every time she thought about Jack, she envisioned him sitting there with his head torn off. The funeral for him had been horrible. His wife, Jean, was a waterfall of tears. She could still see one of Jack's boys pounding on the closed coffin saying, "I want to see my daddy. I want to see my daddy." The moment shook her. It shook everybody, it seemed, but no one talked about it.

She lathered up her hair with shampoo and groaned. "Ugh." She rinsed the soap from her eyes. "Great job."

Her old supervisor, Ted Howard, had been elusive since their clash with Adam Vaughn. It was shortly thereafter that Cyrus was named as Jack's replacement, which infuriated her. Cyrus was a solid agent, but he was a suck-up. That was one of the many reasons she had stopped dating him.

She stepped out and began drying off, her thoughts still on the Black Slate. No one spoke about it. She tried to pry at Ted for information, but he gave nothing away. She worked out her frustrations at the gym, hammering away at heavy bags late in the evening. When that didn't work, she always ended up doing midnight searches about the Drake, werewolves, and deaders, trying to fit these things together. Ted had called her out for using FBI resources and tried to put an end to the searches. The trail had gone cold, but she had to keep digging.

She blow-dried her hair, which she'd had cut to a shorter length. She could still feel one of the deader's clammy hands pulling at her locks. It was a nightmare that had awoken her more than once, coated in sweat. Toweling dry, she headed into the cold air of the bedroom that rose goosebumps on her arms, grabbed some clothes, and put them on. Seconds later, she was geared up and inside the kitchen. She flipped on the switch to her coffee brewer and got a warning light.

"Great."

Sidney routinely loaded up the pot the night before and had it set on a timer. Last night wasn't her night however. She'd slogged in the door extra late before pecking at the computer a few hours and crashing on the bed. She refilled the coffee pot, loaded the grounds, and set it to brew. The aroma brought a thin smile to her lips.

Cyrus can wait.

Normally, she'd get a move on, but Cyrus was never satisfied, late or on time. He was much worse than Dydeck: emails, texts—his micro-management methods were overkill.

Maybe I should try another agency.

Five minutes later, she had the coffee in her travel cup and was headed out the door. Nearby, the Interceptor sat covered in a thin layer of frost. She shivered inside the cab, grinding the ignition until the engine fired up. Waiting for it to defrost, she sipped on her coffee. *Waiting's good.*

She texted Cyrus back.

On my way.

He replied:

You should have been here 10 minutes ago!

I can't believe I dated that guy! She put the car in reverse, backed up, slammed it into drive, and sped out of the quiet parking lot onto the highway. She turned on the radio and started singing along with a corny tune. *"I think it's gonna be a great day."*

CHAPTER 2

"**I**T'S ABOUT TIME, AGENT SHAW," Cyrus said with a sneer as he checked his watch. The sly man in round spectacles wore a dark blue suit and FBI logo'd tie. His beady eyes were calculating and penetrating. "What did you do, take the bus?"

"Traffic was really bad," she said. They were inside an apartment building that the FBI had been conducting surveillance from, overlooking a small abandoned strip mall. A chain link fence surrounded the facility, including the parking lot. Cameras and other equipment were set up in front of the window. The computers monitored the activities on the streets.

"At five in the morning? Don't feed me that load of crap."

"Just tell me why I'm here," Sidney said, rolling her eyes, "and try to tone down being such a dick."

An agent sitting at a desk snickered.

Cyrus glowered at him, and the guy's neck reddened. Then he turned back to Sidney. "Watch yourself, troop."

"Don't call me that," she said, walking away. "Ever again." She thought about Dydeck. He was a good man, and even though they had avenged him, everything still felt unfinished. "So, a move is about to be made."

"We got a transaction alert from our insider," an agent said. He was a well-knit black man in a blue FBI jacket. His name was Harvey. "The deal should go down this morning." He pointed toward the kitchenette. "Coffee?"

"Sure," she said, taking a Styrofoam cup from the stack.

The case they were on had been going for months, but she'd only been assigned to it a few weeks ago. More drugs. More problems. The cartel's smuggling operations became more sophisticated and refined with each passing day. They were impossible to keep up with. For every player the FBI took down, three more stepped up in his place. No guilt. No shame.

"So," Cyrus said, keeping his voice low and cornering her near the coffee, "you look kind of tired. Were you up all night chasing zombies? Or were they chasing you?"

"Back off, Cyrus."

"I need to make sure you aren't distracted from the mission. Are you?"

She glowered down at him. "The only thing distracting me is you."

He touched her arm, leering at her. "That's my job, Sid."

She pushed past him and stood in front of the monitors, clenching her jaw.

Harv glanced up at her and shrugged. There had been some leaks about what happened with the Adam Vaughn case, and word had spread that Sidney had reported an encounter with a zombie. She had no doubt that Cyrus has seen her report and had something to do with that. He'd been hounding her ever since. She'd hounded Ted about the leak, but he said he had nothing to do with it, so she did her best to ignore it.

"We have some movement," Harv said, adjusting his headset. "White box truck. Two in the cab."

Sidney watched the monitors. The driver hopped out of the truck and unlocked the gate. Back into the truck he went. The truck wheeled around the building and backed into the loading dock of a small abandoned department store. Cameras had been set up at adjacent buildings overlooking a long-gone strip mall.

"I don't want to miss anything," Cyrus said. "Call in a drone."

"Yes, sir," Harv said, typing into his computer. "I'm on it."

Cyrus put a headset on and tossed another set to Sidney. "Gear up," he said.

While she slipped the device on her head, another vehicle pulled inside the fence, a black Corvette.

"That's our man, McCall," Cyrus said. "Must be nice going undercover and flashing all that money. Poor bastard."

"I told you I'd do it," Harv said.

"Maybe next time."

"Count me in too," said another voice in the headset.

"And me," said another. It was a woman. They were all part of the team on the streets.

"All right, let's maintain radio discipline," Cyrus added, crossing his arms over his chest and looming over Harv's shoulder. "This is McCall's third time inside. Something has to go down at some point."

Agent McCall pulled the Corvette around back and alongside the truck. He stepped out with his briefcase in hand and gave a quick nod.

Cyrus clapped his hands. "This is it!"

Sidney's spine tingled. They'd been waiting for the signal for over a month and now it came. *I wish I was down there.* Agent McCall was good, but everyone needed back-up. High caliber traffickers were trigger happy. Agent McCall slipped out of sight, either into the building or into the truck.

The room fell quiet for a moment, then Cyrus broke the silence.

"Everyone breathe easy. This might take a while. Lacy and Carl, do either of you have an angle on McCall?"

"No."

"Ditto."

"Just remember," Cyrus continued, "once they start rolling out, McCall will send another signal, so no one get jumpy until I say go. They're probably checking for a wire now."

The operation wasn't the biggest, but it was important. The traffickers dealt in arms, munitions, and drugs. The men McCall dealt with weren't high up the chain either, but their bosses were, and that was who the FBI wanted. Get names. Get voices, and have it all recorded by a small device built into the handle of a briefcase.

"How's our signal?"

"Solid," Harv said, leaning forward, "let's hope it's recording."

"Hope's for sissies," Cyrus said, smiling over at Sidney.

Such a tool.

Five minutes turned into ten and then fifteen. Cyrus started to pace, saying from time to time, "Be patient everybody. The last few months are down to the final minutes."

Sidney's palms were sweating. *This is taking too long.* She checked her watch. 5:38 am.

"We've got movement," said one of the outside agents.

The box truck was pulling out of the dock.

"Any eyes on McCall?"

"Negative."

The box truck sped up the ramp. A spark of light on the monitors was mirrored by sharp pops of gunfire. McCall was holding his side, staggering up the ramp and blasting away in the dark.

Cyrus cried out, "Stop that truck! Execute!"

CHAPTER 3

SIDNEY BOLTED FOR THE DOOR.

"Hold it, Agent Shaw," Cyrus said, grabbing her by the arm.

She twisted out of his grasp. "Are you insane?"

"No, I'm in charge. Now stay in here!"

With an inner growl, Sidney returned to her spot behind the monitors.

Three FBI SUVs sped through the gates, and two more blocked the entrance. The box truck weaved through the parking lot in chase until one of the SUVs slammed into the driver's side. In seconds, agents in body armor and holding M-16 rifles had the truck surrounded. The drivers exited the box truck with their hands up. Instantly, the agents took them to the ground.

"Now that's a clean takedown," Cyrus said with a nod. "And I'm not even breathing heavy. Well done everyone. Someone get to McCall, pronto."

Sidney's nails dug into her palms. It was hard to watch something like this from afar and not get involved. On the screen, she watched FBI agents rushing to McCall's side. Inside her headset she heard one say, "It's bad, but he's breathing."

"All right, get him stabilized. An ambulance is on its way." Cyrus slapped Harv on the shoulder. He had a worried look in his eye. "Good work. We'll go check it out. Come on, Agent Shaw."

Finally. She followed him out the door and down the stairs. By the look of things, Cyrus had taken control and bottled up what could have otherwise been a very ugly situation. Of course, that all depended on whether McCall survived or not. Clearly something had gone wrong. *Let's see how he handles it.*

Rushing out of the stairwell and across the street, they cut between the cars blocking the gate.

"Ambulance coming," Cyrus said, slapping one of the hoods. "Move these things!"

Jogging across the parking lot, they came on the scene. Two men lay on the ground, hands cuffed behind their backs. Each wore nice street clothes. One was tattooed and bald. The other was taller, long-haired, and lanky. Each had an edge about him.

Cyrus kneeled down, grabbed the taller one by his locks, and said, "My agent better not die."

Somehow, the man shrugged. "The only good agent is a dead agent."

Cyrus stuffed the man's face in the cement and ground it in a little.

"Sir," one of the other agents said, "Come take a look at this?"

The thugs stirred on the ground, watching Cyrus walk over. Sidney made her way behind him, stopping at the back of the box truck that was wide open. Inside were munition crates and round blue barrels. Seated along the wall and wide-eyed were children.

"Aw," Cyrus said, rubbing the back of his head, "are you shitting me?" He shook his head and activated his Blue-tooth. "Call Child Services too." An ambulance with flashing lights roared into the parking lot and sped by, stirring the wind. "How's McCall?" No reply. "Carl. Lacy. What is the status on McCall?"

Carl's voice was flat. "He didn't make it, sir."

"Dammit," Cyrus whispered. Everyone's chin dipped a little.

Sidney felt her heart sink. McCall was one of their best agents. Flashy. Confident. Well-liked. His loss was a wound. Like Dydeck's.

"Heh heh heh," said the bald thug lying in the parking lot. "What's the matter, agent? Pretty Boy didn't make it? Heh heh heh … that's what you get for trying to fool us. But it looks like we fooled you."

"Somebody shut him up," Cyrus said, turning his back and rubbing his temples.

"I hear you agents have been dying like flies around here lately," said the other dealer.

Sidney's heart skipped. Something about the way the man said it jolted her. She fastened her eyes on the men and said to one of the agents, "Did you get them patted down?"

"Yes, ma'am."

"I don't think they did a very thorough job," the bald one said. He winked. "How about you come on over and pat me down, sugar. I'm pretty sure they missed my crotch, and besides, my balls are itching. Heh heh."

Sidney walked over, squatted down, and put her knee in his back. She grabbed his thumb and twisted it.

"Yeow!" the dealer cried out.

"Are they still itching?"

"Yes!" he spit out.

She cranked up the pressure.

"Argh!"

"How about now?"

"No," he puffed. "No, dammit!"

Just as she released him, she noticed a mark inside the palm of his hand, a black sun dripping blood. A sliver of ice raced down her spine, making her toes tingle. It was the same mark she had seen at the hospital where she encountered the deaders and Adam Vaughn. *This can't be a coincidence.*

"Sid," Cyrus barked at her. "Get over here."

She hated the sneering tone Cyrus used on her. It riled her up. She walked up to him and said, "Don't 'get' me again."

"Fine. Will you just take custody of the children and sort them out before Child Services arrives?"

"Sure, you're the boss."

Inside the box truck, some of the agents had cracked open the crates: assault rifles, ammo, grenades, and bags of pills and powders. It was enough to start or incapacitate a small army. Sidney climbed into the truck and crawled among the children. Each was ragged, dirty—and hungry, by the looks of them. "I'm Agent Shaw, and I'm here to help you. Can you tell me your names?"

A small black boy with lighter skin, maybe eight years old, spoke up first. "My name is James." He cocked his head and touched her cheek with a gentle hand. "Your hair is different."

She pulled back and put her hand inside his. It was fragile and cold. "I'm not sure that I follow, James. What do you mean, different?"

"I think it was longer last time."

Sidney's memory flashed. James's face was suddenly familiar. He was one of the children she and Smoke had rescued from Ray Cline's joint back in October. *Sonuvabitch, this can't be happening!* She scooped the boy up in her arms. "Cyrus, we have another problem."

CHAPTER 4

I NSIDE HER CUBICLE, SIDNEY HAMMERED at the keyboard. *This doesn't make any sense.* She'd sent emails. Made inquiries. But the children she'd rescued months earlier had disappeared into the system. She snapped the pencil in her hand and tossed it in the trash. "Dammit."

"You okay?" a woman said, walking up behind her. It was Sadie, a black co-worker, a little heavy, in a plum pantsuit. She had a warmth about her. "Because I don't think your keyboard can take much more."

Sidney spun around in her chair. "It's that noticeable?"

Sadie set down her coffee mug that had a picture of two children on it. She rested her rear end on Sidney's desk. "So what's going on? It's Cyrus, isn't it? You and him are a thing again, aren't you?"

"No," Sidney said shaking her head. "Lord no."

"Good. Because I don't like him."

"Does anybody?"

"True," Sadie said, hoisting up her coffee cup. "So, fill me in."

"Aw, just a dead end on those kids is all. Makes me wonder who's protecting the children from Protective Services."

"You don't actually think they're going to be very forthcoming about losing children, do you? After all, it is just another government agency."

"One that loses children?"

"Well, maybe they didn't. Maybe it was the foster home."

"They can't ever tell me anything about that." Sidney shook her head and clenched her fists. "I could just punch somebody."

"You know, Sid, you've been pretty frustrated lately. Are you seeing anybody?"

"What do you mean?"

"What do you mean, what do I mean? Are you getting any?"

No!

"Come on," Sadie continued with a smile. "It's just us girls talking."

"I don't have the time."

"Hah, you're single. You've got the time. Me and Reggie have two children: baseball, football, soccer, basketball," Sadie huffed, "not to mention coaching, shopping, cleaning, and cooking. And we find the time. Heck, we make the time, else we'd kill each other."

"That's different. You're married."

"And you're single." Sadie leaned closer. "A long time single, and the longer you stay single, the longer you're going to be single. Don't get set in those ways, else you're going to be an old maid forever."

"No, I won't."

"That's what my sister says, and guess what—still single. And every time she finds a good man, she picks him apart. She's set in her ways."

Great warm-up. I'm going to have to listen to this same crap from Mom over Christmas.

"You know," Sadie said, peeking around, "there's some new faces around here that I'd love to introduce you to."

"I'll never date another agent."

"They aren't *all* agents. Most of them are just nerds, college boys wanting to change the world. Look down this way." Sadie motioned her over, peering around the cubicle. "That's Greg. Blond hair. Blue eyes. Nice butt in those trousers."

Sidney wheeled her chair and looked down the aisle. "I don't see anybody."

Sadie started laughing. "You looked. Ha ha. Sid, you need a man even worse than I thought you did."

Sidney slapped Sadie's leg. "You witch!"

"Don't be disappointed. There is a Greg, as described. I'll introduce you to him."

Sid pushed back toward her desk. "No thanks. I need a matchmaker I can trust."

"Aw, that's cold. You know you can trust me."

"And why's that?"

"Cause I ain't a man."

"No, but you're just as ornery. See you around, Sadie," she said, turning around.

"Say, I didn't come over here to rile you. I want to help." Sadie looked over her shoulder. "I have a close cousin in Child Protective Services. Why don't you give me something so I can snoop around?"

Sadie was an executive secretary who had as much authorization and access as most field agents. She'd proven to be very helpful on more than one occasion, not to mention that she did most of the supervisors' and assistant directors' work for them.

Sidney jotted down some names and contacts on a legal pad, tore it off, and handed it to her. "Thanks."

Sadie snatched it out of her grip and said, "You're welcome."

Glad that's out of my hair. The last thing I need is to be reminded that I don't have a boyfriend or husband. There'll be plenty of that talk tomorrow. Ugh. She enjoyed the holidays, but things would be a little tense dealing with her sister, Allison, who was still holed up at her parents', along with Sidney's niece, Megan. Sid had made one visit for Thanksgiving, and it had turned ugly. Allison didn't hide her resentment of Sid.

Her desk phone rang. Ted Howard's name popped up. She hadn't met with him in weeks. She picked up the receiver. "Agent Shaw."

"Sid, can you swing by?" Ted sounded a little tense.

"Sure, when?"

"Now would be ideal."

"Okay, I'll be right—" The line went dead, "There? Great." Normally, Ted gave her a heads up on what he wanted to talk about. But not today. The tension in his voice left her uneasy. She picked up her bag and got up out of her seat. A nice-looking younger man was standing behind her in a white oxford shirt, burgundy checked tie, and khaki pants.

Morning glory. He's fresh out of the frat house.

"Hi," he said, rubbing the back of his blond head. "I'm Greg. Uh, Sadie says you need to see me. She says your computer needs a tune-up."

Sidney laughed out loud.

"I'm missing something," he said, swallowing. His eyes glanced down at her chest.

"Apparently not," she said, disappointed. "And my computer's just fine. Nice meeting you, Greg." She walked by Sadie's desk on the way to Ted's office, one floor up from hers. "Nice try, Sadie. It only took him five seconds to glue his eyes on my boobs." She kept going.

Sadie hollered after her, "You can't fault a young man for looking when you have a body like that, you prude."

Sid made her way to the elevator, laughing inside. Normally, her suit jacket concealed her ample curves. And it was a rare day when she wore a skirt. Waiting at the elevator, she noticed a few agents approaching. *No time for chit chat.* She took the steps and made her way to Ted's floor, stopping at his secretary's desk.

"Go on in, Sidney. He told me he was expecting you."

"Should I knock?"

"No, go on in," the secretary said, eyeing her up and down. "I like that outfit. Why don't you dress like that more often?"

Sidney grabbed the door handle and started her way inside. "Because I work here."

Inside, Ted was sitting at his desk with a stern expression on his face. Filling one of the two chairs in front of him was a man with short dark hair in a grey suit. Both men stood up as she entered and closed the door behind her. The man in the grey suit turned and fastened his engaging eyes on hers. Her heart skipped under his heavy gaze.

Glorious morning!

CHAPTER 5

"**H**ELLO, AGENT SHAW," SAID SMOKE. His presence seemed to fill up the office. "How have you been?" The tall man's suit coat bulged in the arms.

"Never better," Sidney said, taking the open seat in front of Ted's desk. "Looks like prison life has been treating you well. Did you make that suit in there yourself?"

"It was either this or vanity license plates."

"I see," she said, turning her focus to Ted. "So you surprised me. Care to fill me in?"

"The Black Slate is back on the table," Ted said, taking a black file folder from his drawer. "They appreciated the thoroughness of your report."

Sidney reached for the folder, but Ted pulled it back. She said, "Who appreciated the thoroughness of my report?"

"You'll know when they want you to know."

"Come on, Ted. It's been two months already, and now it's suddenly back on the table."

"Things take time. It could have been longer. But you two are back on it. At least, Mister Smoke has agreed to it."

"So you two have visited?" She narrowed her eyes on Ted. She'd been left in the dark again.

"We talked," Ted said, loosening his tie.

"In person or over the phone?"

"Sid, don't start this."

"First," she said, poking her finger into his desk, "you send me in to recruit him. Then, I'm sent out to hunt werewolves with him only to have him slammed back in prison again, and not a single word about it until now. I don't work like this, not with you. Not with anyone."

Ted leaned forward, resting his big elbows on the table. "Don't think you are the only one being put in an unusual predicament, Sid. You get your orders. You follow them. Or did you forget that?"

"This is why I'm a civilian," Smoke interjected.

Sidney shook her head. She hated being left in the dark about anything. Even worse, just when she'd managed to bury her memories of Smoke and everything that happened at Mildred Bateman hospital, it all cropped up again, like a volcano blasting out memories and emotion. "I'm sorry," she said to Smoke, "but didn't you volunteer for this?"

"The food's still better outside of prison."

"You don't look like you've missed any meals."

"Thanks for noticing."

She turned back to Ted. "Why the secrecy, Ted? Why?"

"They," Ted said, "who it seems I can't not mention, wanted to wait until the end of this last assignment of yours was resolved."

"And this revolves around me how?"

"As I am told, you and Mister Smoke are the first to bring in a member of the Black Slate in ten years."

"So there are other werewolves."

Ted rolled his eyes. "Man, I really hate that word. But, no, not a werewolf, just another wanted criminal. I don't know much more than you do, but I do know that."

"So I guess we aren't getting any government-issued silver bullets?" she asked.

"Aw," Ted grunted, "let's forget that last bounty and talk about the new one." He pushed the file over. "Shall we?"

Sidney snatched it up. "Hold on a second, Ted. What about the case I'm on? I can't just walk away from it. We found one of the same kids that we picked up from Ray Cline."

"We did?" Smoke said, sitting up.

"I did," Sidney added.

"Cyrus will handle that, Sid," Ted warned. "Drop it."

"I'm not going to drop it. Children are in danger. Something is wrong with the system."

"It's being taken care of."

"No it isn't."

"Sid, you have to have faith in the system."

She sat back and groaned. She'd heard that plenty of times. For the most part, the system did hold together, but in this case something was wrong. Really wrong. "I'd rather stick to the case I'm on." She looked at Smoke. "No offense."

"She doesn't play, then I don't play," Smoke said.

Ted rose out of his chair, and with a raised voice, he said, "Let me remind you that neither one of you have a choice in the matter. Mister Smoke—"

"Call me Smoke."

"*Mister* Smoke, it's the Black Slate or you go back to staring at the grey slate, not to forget the time in solitary you have coming… "

Solitary? Why would he have solitary? Sidney noticed a nasty scrape on the right side of his face that was a little swollen.

"… and you, Agent Shaw, will follow orders or be faced with insubordination. Now don't buck me on this. If I could give you another assignment, I would, but I can't. It's this or nothing. Nothing being, you might be out of a job," he said to her, "and you might go back to prison even longer," he said to Smoke. "Do I have your cooperation or not?"

Smoke shrugged.

"Sir, yes, Sir!" Sidney mocked.

"Don't push me, Sid. Don't push me."

She could see Ted's harsh expression drain a little. He didn't like this any more than she did. He had orders, and he'd follow them. It was just the way the chain of command worked, and in the grand scheme of things they were all way down on the pecking order. She opened the black file folder. Inside was the portrait of a beautiful lustrous-haired woman with a wicked look. "Interesting."

"Her name is Angi Harlow," Ted said with a sigh, "also known as Night Bird."

Smoke leaned over and glanced at the picture. "Why do they call her Night Bird?"

"I don't know," Ted mumbled, uneasy. "Maybe she can fly or something."

Sidney shuffled through the pictures. There were more crime scenes. Drug labs. Munitions. Blood. She swallowed hard. There were dead bodies too. Some disemboweled. Others in bits and pieces. The last photo was of a man, dead in a cemetery. His eyes were missing from a body half covered in ravens. Sidney's chest tightened. *This is not normal.* She glanced up at Smoke.

"Let's go find her nest," he said, "and burn it."

CHAPTER 6

"**Y**OU AREN'T BURNING ANYTHING," TED said. "Bring her in alive."

"And we have how much time to do this?" Sidney asked.

"Mister Smoke's out for two more weeks, and the clock has already started."

"Now?" Sid said. "My leave starts at the end of the day, and it's Christmas Eve tomorrow."

"Figure it out," Ted said, taking his seat and fumbling through his desk. "And thanks for reminding me." He punched keys on his desk phone. "Jane, where's my gift?"

"Bottom drawer on the left," said his secretary.

Ted reached down and produced a small flat box wrapped in bright colors. "Ah, very nice." He got up, walked across the office, and put on his coat and hat. He opened the door, turned to Sid, and said, "Everything you need to know is in the file."

"Sir, what am I supposed to do with him?" she said, throwing her thumb back at Smoke.

"You'll figure it out." Ted gestured for them to leave. "Let's go. The bad guys don't stop just because it's the holidays."

Sidney headed out of the office with Smoke right behind. *Man, this is so weird.*

"Jane," Ted said, "I'll be back in Monday. Merry Christmas everybody."

Sid saw Jane watching Ted's lumbering form dash for the steps and disappear through the doorway. Jane sighed and shook her head then glanced over at Smoke. Her smiling eyes were filled with him. Sidney tapped his arm. "We have to go."

"Sure," he said. "Nice meeting you, Jane."

"You too, Mister Smoke." She batted her eyelashes. "I hope I see you again soon."

"Come on," Sidney said, taking him by the elbow and steering him down the hall. She began nosing through the file as they headed down the stairs. The black file folder was almost a half inch thick. It had a white tab on it marked Harlow. There were names, dates, pictures, and locations. The main thing that caught her eye was the Drake logo. That and another. A black sun.

"Can I see that?"

"No," she said, pushing her way through the elevator door and heading for her desk. As soon as she got there, she put on her jacket. Smoke was watching her. His handsome face stared right into her eyes. "What?"

"You seem rattled."

Pull it together, Sid. Man, he looks nice in a suit.

She plopped down in her chair. "I'm not really big on one-eighties. Pull over a seat, why don't you."

Smoke reached across the aisle and dragged a four-legged chair into her cubicle and sat down.

"Okay," she said, scooting away, "not exactly built for two." She took half the papers out of the file and handed them over to Smoke. A sealed envelope fell out, marked Shaw. Smoke beat her to it. She snagged it away. "For my eyes only."

Inside, she found another letter like the last one, on old Bureau letterhead. It said almost the exact same thing.

Agent Shaw,

Due to the unorthodox arrangement of this assignment, you will need to keep the following items under consideration.

John Smoke is a convicted criminal with special skills. Don't underestimate him. He's dangerous. Unpredictable. Possible escape risk.

You have eyes on him and we have eyes on him. Allow him free range. We'll let you know if he needs reeling in.

If any alien objects or circumstances or individuals are encountered, you should notify your superiors immediately.

Seek Mal Carlson for assistance when needed.

Shadow cover authorized.

Trust your instincts and good hunting,

The Bureau

Whoa! Shadow cover? Who is Mal Carlson?

"What does it say?" Smoke said without glancing up from his papers. "Let me guess. I'm a dangerous criminal who can't be trusted, and if any strange circumstances arise, then notify your superiors immediately."

Sidney stuffed it back in the envelope. "It says if you don't do whatever I say, I get to shoot you."

"I like the sound of that."

"What, me shooting you?"

"No, me doing whatever you say."

Sidney flushed around the collar. "Let's get something to eat." She took his papers and put them in the folder and stuck it inside her satchel. "I imagine you're up for some pancakes."

"I was thinking milkshakes."

"Come on." As soon as she started up, a voice interrupted.

"Who do we have here?" Sadie said, warming up to Smoke with her hand extended.

He rose from his chair, took her hand, and said, "I'm Smoke."

"No, you're smoking."

"Sadie!"

"What? He is."

Sidney pushed Smoke toward the elevator. "We're going."

"Where you going? I want to come too," Sadie said, "My lunchtime just started."

"We aren't coming back."

"Now that's my girl," Sadie said with a smile. "Glad to know you're listening to your sister Sadie."

Leading Smoke away, Sidney whirled back and whispered harshly at her friend, "You're filthy."

Sadie walked away laughing.

It left Sidney smiling, but she caught herself as she turned around and entered the elevator with Smoke. They had made it down one floor when the door opened. A man with frosty eyes entered. *Morning glory!* It was her supervisor, Cyrus Tweel.

CHAPTER 7

"**W**HAT DO WE HAVE HERE?" Cyrus sneered as the elevator doors closed. "And what's the convict doing here?"

Smoke wedged himself between Sidney and Cyrus.

Cyrus leaned right; Smoke leaned right. He went left; Smoke went left. It almost made Sidney giggle. "I have new orders," she said, fanning the file out in front of Cyrus's face.

"My ass you do. You're still on a case."

I love pissing him off. "Take it up with Ted."

"Black Slate file, huh. Will you get out of my way, you goon!"

Smoke poked him in the chest, knocking Cyrus back a little. "I haven't forgotten about that injection you gave me."

"You lay another finger on me—"

Smoke crowded him against the buttons. "I'll break you."

Cyrus pushed back. "Back off, troglodyte."

"That's enough, Smoke," Sidney said. "Cyrus!"

"I'm guessing you two are going on another zombie hunt. Hah." Cyrus tightened his tie. "What a joke."

"What's the matter, Cyrus? You can't handle being in the dark on this one?"

"I know more than you know about, Sid." The elevator opened, and he stepped out. "And just so you know, I took a pass on it. It's a joke, and so are you and your ex-con—" The doors closed.

Smoke was shaking his head.

"What?" she said.

"I can't believe you dated that guy."

"Why do you care?" she said, grinding her teeth.

"It's such a mismatch, is all."

"I'd think you'd have figured out by now that it didn't work out."

"I've figured it out, but I'm pretty sure he hasn't. He eyes you like chattel."

"Chattel?"

"You know—"

"I know what chattel is." The elevator doors split apart, and out she went, with Smoke close on her heels. "A little space, if you don't mind."

"Sure," he said, eyeing the lobby of the FBI building. It wasn't the J. Edgar but one of the larger post-modern satellite offices a few miles outside DC.

"Just to be sure," she said, "you didn't drive, did you?"

"No. Are you still in the Interceptor?" He scooted ahead and opened the exit door for her.

That was nice. "Yep," she said, stepping outside into the biting cold. "Tell you what, I'll let you scrape the frost off the windows."

"It would be my pleasure."

I do not understand this man. Smoke's actions had been very contrary to everything she'd read about him in his file—and in those strange letters, too. His military record made him out to be an insubordinate hot head. A loose cannon. For the most part, he'd been nothing but amiable and reliable. To her at least. *He's playing me. He must be.* "It's pretty cold," she said, "you still in the mood for a milkshake?"

"I thought I said *milkshakes*?"

Geez, he's corny. She popped the trunk open and tossed him a scraper. "Work up that appetite, big boy." *Did I just call him big boy? Why did I say that?* Inside the car, she fired up the engine and turned on the heat. Her phone buzzed. It was her mom, Sally. *To answer, or not to answer.* With a sigh she picked up. "Hi, Mom."

"We're eating at four tomorrow." Her mother's voice was as sweet as it was lovely, but it had a pressing tone about it.

"I know, you told me."

"What's the matter, Sidney? You don't sound so well. You're still coming."

"I just got a new assignment, and I have to tidy things up."

"Don't you dare show up late, Sidney. I need you here." Sally started to whisper. "Allison is such lousy help, but Megan shows promise."

"I'll get there as soon as I can."

"You have to be here to help me cook. It's tradition."

In truth, Sally did all of the cooking while Sidney stood around listening to her talking. She was pretty sure most everything was ready already.

"I'll do my best." She covered the phone and moaned. It wasn't that she didn't want to be home with her family. She did, but Allison made for such a distraction. *I've got to be there for Mom and Dad. They'd be there for me.*

"We had some excitement around here the other day," Sally said. "A very nice man stopped by and said he was in the area looking at properties."

"Uh-huh."

"Of course we told him that we weren't interested in selling, but he was very, oh, how would you call it—suave. He seemed European. Very persistent."

"Mom, I've told you about people that run these scams. Business people like that don't just show up at your front door." *Sheesh.* "Did he try to sell you a security system too?"

"Why no, but he said his company would pay good money, and you know how much your father talks about moving to Florida this time of year."

"I wish I was in Florida this time of year," she mumbled.

"What was that?"

"Nothing. You didn't invite him in, did you?"

"It would have been rude not to, and besides your father was here." Sally sighed. "They spent an hour talking about the Redskins. The only Redskins I like are the kind that have potatoes in them. That's what I told him. The man almost spit up his tea from laughing so hard."

"Listen, Mom, quit letting strangers in. These are dangerous times we live in." Her palms became clammy as she thought about the text she had received with a picture of Megan that read

Watch your step.

Smoke opened the car door and slumped into the passenger's seat, jostling the car. He started blowing into his icy red hands.

Sidney clicked the heater up a notch.

"All right, I'll see you tomorrow, Mom."

"Wait, wait a second," Sallie said, still hanging on the line. "This man is legit. He even left a business card."

"Those aren't exactly hard to come by, Mom."

"It says Edwin Lee. And the nice logo reads ..."

Sidney lurched up in her seat as soon as her mom finished the sentence.

"... Drake Properties."

CHAPTER 8

"**I** HEARD THAT," SMOKE SAID WITH a concerned tone.

"Heard what?"

"Your Mom talks pretty loud. So, let's get up there and find out what's going on."

"Excuse me, but I'll be dropping you off, or you can get out of the car now."

"Sidney, who are you talking to?" Sally said on the other end of the line.

"Nothing, Mother. I'll see you soon." She hung up her phone, backed the car out of her spot, and sped away.

"I think I should come with you," Smoke insisted. "Anything that involves Drake is tied to our cases."

Sidney wasn't going to admit it, but she didn't really hate the idea.

"I'm dropping you off."

Smoke tossed his duffle bag into the back seat. "I'd rather you didn't. I can help."

"Maybe you should take some time to visit with family."

"I can't. Just like you, I have my orders." He buckled his seatbelt. "Just tell me what Sally said."

Sidney scowled at him. "How'd you know my mother's name?"

"You know I have my ways."

"It's kind of rude, don't you think?"

"You know everything about me, don't you? My parents. Place of birth. Every military mission?"

"I'm authorized to know that."

"That doesn't exactly seem fair now, does it?"

Sort of yes. Sort of no. "You'll get over it." She switched lanes and merged onto the interstate, then glanced over at him. "What happened to your face?"

"Oh, this." He brushed his fingers over the ragged scar. "It seems Drake has many accomplices in prison. They came after me when I asked too many questions."

Sidney's chest tightened. "What kind of questions?"

"There were a few dudes with those black-sun tattoos." He shrugged. "They weren't very forthcoming. It's okay now."

"What did Ted mean about you going into solitary confinement?"

"Well, after the fight—"

"Fight? What fight?"

"You know, the four of them cornering the one of me fight." He rubbed his scabbed knuckles. "It landed me two weeks in solitary and four of them in the hospital, but"—he smiled—"they still have solidary coming."

It made her uneasy. Were they coming after her, too? Why?

"I'm sorry to hear that."

"I'm fine. It wasn't anything I couldn't handle, considering the last scrap I was in."

"You're talking about AV."

"Yep."

Damn. I hate being reminded of him. She squeezed the wheel until her knuckles turned white. *Damn evil people. Don't swear about it. They aren't worth it. Morning Glory! I hate evil people! That doesn't exactly work, either.* "You'll be fine on your own, I assume?"

He shrugged. "I think Fat Sam and Guppy have a Christmas tree."

"What does that have to do with anything?"

"I just haven't been out for Christmas in a while. And I know a few places that make a decent home-cooked-like meal. There's this one place called Humphreys. It's all pine walls, stone fireplaces, and baskets of buttered hot rolls."

"It sounds wonderful."

"It would be if I was with my family." He tapped on the dash. "But it's better alone there than in the hole in prison.

You know, I never thought about it, but it's always possible this could be my last Christmas. After all, you never know what this new mark, uh, what's her name, Black Bird? No telling what might be in store for us, considering what we ran into the last time."

What he said made her mad. Not because of him but because her heart ached a little. It made her think of the first time she had missed Christmas with her family. It had been her first military mission, and she had thought she would never make it home ever again. "Fine," Sidney said in almost a growl, "you can come with me."

"I appreciate it," he said, nodding. "So, I take it Sally's a good cook?"

"Yes, very good." Sidney floated the car down the next exit and re-entered the interstate, heading north. Her mom would have a hundred questions for Smoke. And even more for her. "My mom's pretty nosy, so keep it professional."

"I will," he said. "So, can you tell me a little more about what she said on the phone about Drake?"

"Edwin Lee. That was the man's name."

Smoke produced a phone from his pocket and started to text.

"What are you doing?" Sidney said.

"Checking in with Fat Sam and Guppy. They worry about me."

"That's a load of crap," she said. "You don't share confidential information."

"That's not confidential. It wasn't in the file, was it?"

"No, but I have another file, my trust file, and you just broke it. I'll check into this with my own sources. "

"Aw … I'm sorry. But you can't trust your sources. That's how they track what we do."

"Tough. No more sharing our information." She held her hand out. "Now give me the phone."

"What?" he pulled it away. "No, it was hard to get this burned."

"Hand it over."

"No."

"You just lost my trust," she said. "Do you want to earn it back?"

"Maybe."

She made his window go down. The icy air battered the cabin.

"What are you doing?" Smoke said. He tried to roll up the window, but she had it locked.

"Chuck it."

"Why?"

"I told you why. Now chuck it."

"You're being a bit extreme, aren't you?"

"I have trust issues." She glowered at him.

Smoke sighed and tossed it out the window.

Good boy! "Excellent," she said, rolling up his window. "If I want you to have a phone, I'll get you one. Do you understand?"

"No, no I don't understand, but I'll live with it, your worshipfulness." He glanced at the semi-truck passing by. Its wheels were kicking up slush and salt from the road, coating the windshield. "Say, that truck … can you see the logo on it?"

Sidney turned up the wipers. "No. Why?" The semi-truck, passing on the left, swerved into her lane. She pumped the brakes and rode onto the berm.

The truck kept coming, sideswiping the Interceptor. *Wham!* Metal groaned and popped.

Sidney slammed on the brakes. The car's front end caught up underneath the trailer, and the semi-truck wheels ran over the hood, crushing it. The car did a three-sixty, spun across the road, and careened into a ditch. The air bags deployed with loud pops, busting her in the nose. Stunned and bleeding, she heard Smoke saying, "Are you okay? Are you okay?"

CHAPTER 9

T HE ENGINE CAUGHT FIRE, AND the interior started to fill with grey smoke. Sidney's fingers fumbled over her seatbelt as the heat rose. It wouldn't unbuckle.

"Hang on," Smoke said.

She started coughing. Smoke sawed at her belt with a knife. "Get the folder. The folder's in my bag!" she said. The belt came loose, and Smoke dragged her out through the passenger door.

Whoosh!

The entire car went up in flames.

"The folder," she said, coughing. "Put me down. We need that file folder. It's in my bag." She rushed back toward the car.

Smoke caught her by the arm. "Let it go," he said. "It's over. We're lucky to be alive after that hit."

Sidney watched the Interceptor go up in flames. Bright orange flames and black smoke rolled out from under the hood and through the windows. She had thought about torching it herself on more than one occasion. It was a good way for a bad car to go. Still, it shouldn't have caught fire and burned like that.

"Here," Smoke said, handing her cell phone to her. "I saved this."

"Thanks," she said, taking it and sliding it into her pocket. "Say, what were you saying before that truck ran into us?"

"I was saying that the truck, the black semi, was marked Drake Transportation Industries."

After the first fire engine arrived, it took four more hours to clear the scene. Covered in a blanket, Sidney was cold, stiff, and sore. She rubbed her head. Speaking to the officer on scene, she finished off the last of her statement. "Mind if I take a look at what's left of my car?" The tow driver was loading it up on the trailer. "Sentimental, you know."

"I don't think there's much left to see," he said, taking the report. "And you probably should go to a hospital."

"I'm okay." She limped toward the tow truck, grimacing. A fireman in a yellow coat and hard hat was standing there. "You see many cars after a wreck go up in flames like that?"

"It happens all the time in the movies but not so much in DC—or on a Crown Vic. Those are pretty safe cars. That's why cops used them. A decade ago." He tipped his hat at her. "But I've seen stranger things happen."

"Thanks," she said. She turned to the tow truck driver. He was a burly roughneck in dirty overalls. "What about you? Have you seen many cars go up in flames?"

He spat juice on the sludgy ground. "It happens. But it's odd how some of the metal just melted. Like there was an accelerant or something. I've seen paints and coating that burn like hot welds." He spat again. "That was back in my military days." He winked at her. "Hush hush. You didn't hear it from me." He hopped into his cab, hung his waving arm out the window, and said, "So long."

The tow truck pulled away, revealing Smoke standing on the other side. He had his duffle bag strapped over his shoulder. Patting it and saying, "Fireproof," he walked up and handed her what was left of her satchel. "Not fireproof. I peeled what I could off the carpet."

The satchel was charred leather, but a few pages from the file folder remained intact. She rubbed her head. "Are they trying to kill us or scare us?"

"I don't think it makes much of a difference to them."

Angry, she set her jaw. "Well, it makes a difference to me."

The police officer from a moment earlier was waving them over to his sedan. He said, "Do you two want a lift or not? I've got things to do."

Sidney sulked in the back seat. At her side, Smoke was oddly quiet and staring out the window. She'd given the policeman directions to the storage yard that housed her Dodge Hellcat. On Smoke's advice, she'd sent a text to Ted stating that the accident was only a fender bender and she had other means of transportation. *Screw 'em,* she thought. *They aren't completely honest with me, so I won't be completely honest with them.*

It was 7:32 pm when the officer dropped them off. "Are you sure you don't need anything else?"

"We're fine," she said. "Thanks, Officer Parrish."

"No problem, ma'am."

Within the next five minutes she had the Hellcat pulled out and was speeding down the highway. She passed the spot where they crashed. *Better their car than mine. RIP Interceptor.*

Sidney fumed inwardly in silence the entire ride home. Someone was coming after her, her family, and her friends. It was personal now, and all she could think of was Congressman Wilhelm's last words. "Watch your step." *Perhaps I need to pay him a visit.*

"We'll take it to them, Agent Shaw," Smoke said, resting his head against the glass and closing his eyes. "You can count on it."

She eased the car off the highway and onto a gravel road dusted in snow. It winded two miles deep through the woods until they passed by two stone pylons. The gravel road jostled Smoke from his snoring.

He sat up. "Are you a farm girl or something?"

"I think you probably already know the answer to that is no."

Ahead, some red and white lights were flashing. She wheeled around the curve and came to a stop on the edge of the gravel driveway to her parents' home. An ambulance was parked in front of the garage.

"Good Lord," Sidney said, rushing out of the car. "What now?"

CHAPTER 10

SIDNEY RUSHED INTO THE HOUSE. Her first fear was that her sister had overdosed. Instead, she found her father sprawled out on his recliner, surrounded by two paramedics.

"Will you get away from me!" Keith wore a brick-colored flannel shirt under a pair of jean overalls. The sleeves were rolled up. His grey hair was a frizzled mess. "Sally, why did you do this? I'm fine, I tell you. I'm fine."

Sally stood nearby wringing her hands. Her frosty blonde hair was up in a bun, and she wore a plum-colored apron. "You hush, Keith. I'm not having you die on me."

"I'm not dying," he growled back, rolling his eyes. "It's heartburn, I tell you."

"You're all clammy," Sally argued.

"You need to clam up. I told you I was fine." Keith rolled his thick neck around and saw Sidney. "Sid!" His face brightened. "Will you arrest these men?"

"Sidney!" Sally exclaimed, rushing over and grasping her arm. "Talk some sense into him."

"What happened?" she asked.

"He collapsed on the sofa."

"I did not," Keith said. "I just tripped because I felt a little dizzy, and your mother went into a panic." He glared at one of the blue-clad paramedics. "Let me go."

"His blood pressure is high," one of the paramedics said. She was a no nonsense burly woman. "But the heartbeat is strong. We need to take him in and run some tests on him. Be on the safe side."

"Of course my blood pressure is high. It's the holidays, isn't it. And you, ball breaker, aren't making life any easier. Now get in your death wagon and get out of here."

"Keith!" Sally said. "You settle down right now! And apologize to that young lady. They're trying to help you."

"No, they're trying to take my money." He pulled his arm away from the man who was taking his pulse. "Well, guess what? I don't have any money. No insurance, either."

Sidney walked over to the paramedics. "Give me a minute."

"And you are?" the woman paramedic said, eyeing her.

"A lot more difficult than him if you care to find out."

"We're just doing our job," the woman said, stepping aside.

Sidney kneeled alongside her father and clasped his calloused hand. It was warm but not clammy. "What's going on, Dad?"

"Nothing," he said.

Keith was a retired deputy sheriff with over thirty years on the force. Hard as nails. He once cut the tip of his finger off and tried to stitch it back on himself. Now he had a missing finger to show for it, down to the second knuckle.

"How do you feel?" she said, rubbing his palm. "Really?"

Keith looked away. "Crowded."

He looked tired, too. His grey eyes sagged a little, and deeper creases were in his face. Decades on the force had caught up with him and perhaps something else too. Allison. Sidney's stomach sank. Allison was wearing them down.

"Dad, do you really think you're all right?"

He nodded her over and whispered in her ear. "Don't tell your mother, but I think I forgot my medicine." He choked. "Don't let them take me to that hospital, Sid. I won't go. Mortimer died the last time he went. I won't go, I tell ya. I won't."

Mortimer was his younger brother, her uncle, who had died the year before from the flu. They'd taken him in for fluids, and he'd never come back out again. It had sapped a good bit of her father's hardened resolve. Her iron-clad father had become mortal.

"All right. Just sit tight."

She led the paramedics outside. "Did you pick up anything serious?"

"No," the woman said, "but you never know."

"He says he didn't take his medicine."

"That'll do, but I still advise caution," the lady said. "But I see your mind's made up, and I'm pretty sure his is too. We'll get on out of here."

Sidney handed her a business card. "Thanks. And if you can, send this bill to me."

"Sure, no problem."

Back inside, Sidney's mother was sitting on the couch talking with Smoke.

So much for introductions.

"Sidney, you didn't tell me you had a handsome new partner?" She patted Smoke's leg. "And he's a nice one. Tall, dark—"

"Mom, I think I smell something burning in the kitchen."

Sally jumped up. "What?" Her bright eyes widened. "My pies!" She shot a look at her husband and rushed into the kitchen. "You burned my pies."

"I didn't burn them." Keith let out a breath and watched the ambulance back out of the driveway. "Ah, I feel better already. Say chief," he said to Smoke, "toss me that remote. And Sid, think you can grab my pill case from the medicine cabinet?"

She started down the hall. Megan, dressed in pink and purple pajamas, wrapped her arms around Sid's legs.

"Aunt Sidney! I didn't think you were coming until tomorrow." She sniffed and looked up at her. "Why do you smell smoky? Is that blood on your nose?"

Sidney hoisted the little girl up on her hip. "You know, you're going to make a great detective some day."

"I want to be an FBI agent like you so I can waste the bad guys."

"Oh, and where did you hear I did that?"

"Grandpa," she said cheerfully.

"Well," said Sid, carrying Megan into her parents' bathroom with her. "I'm certain that you're going to grow up to be whatever you want to be." Inside the medicine cabinet she found a plastic pillbox with each day of the week. Half of the cabinet was filled with prescriptions. *Do I have this to look forward to? Insane.* She handed the pill case to Megan. "Take this to Grandpa, and don't let Grandma see. Okay?"

Megan nodded yes. "You can count on me." She saluted and disappeared into the bedroom.

Wish I could say the same about your mother. She rummaged through the cabinet. There were pain pills, muscle relaxers, high blood pressure pills, cholesterol regulators, and anti-depressants. *Geez!* She checked some of the dates. They were recent. *Allison!* She snapped the mirrored cabinet shut and began washing her face off. She scrubbed her hands with vigor.

Allison! Allison! Allison!

Her younger sister had begun the art of parental manipulation at an early age. Her being the youngest, her parents let her get away with it. Allison was every bit as charming as she was conniving. She used her beauty shamelessly to get whatever she wanted. Most mortal men found it impossible to tell her no. *Hussy. Where is she anyway?* Sid had just finished drying her face off when she heard her sister's concocted laughter coming from the living room. Sidney threw the hand towel down on the sink and headed out there.

Smoke sat in the middle of the couch smiling. Megan was on one side. Allison was on the other. Long legs crossed and brushing against his, wearing only a flimsy pink top and white cotton yoga pants, she left little to the imagination. She tossed her hair and laughed some more. "You are so funny," she said, twirling her finger in her hair. "Much more than the last one. What was his name?"

Shut up, you hussy!

CHAPTER 11

"**C**YRUS," SIDNEY'S FATHER ANSWERED.

"Frosty," Smoke said, perking up.

Sidney cut between them. "Time to change the subject."

"Cyrus Tweel?" Smoke said to Sidney.

"So you've met him," Allison said. "Too bad for you, I'd say." She checked her nails. "But he was a good match for my sister."

"Drop it, Allison," Sidney warned through her teeth.

"Oh, get over it. That was years ago, but it seems like it was yesterday." Allison giggled as she eyed Smoke. She leaned forward, offering a generous view of her ample boobs. "I was sitting right here, nursing Megan—"

Sidney closed in on her sister. "Stop it, Allison."

Allison put her hand on Smoke's thigh and let out a haughty little laugh. "You know what he looks like, right?"

Smoke nodded.

"Well, the little worm got down on one knee and proposed to my sister in front of everybody. Ha. You should have seen the look on Sidney's little face. She looked like she swallowed a rodent."

"It made for a frosty summer day," Keith said, shaking his head. "I'll never forget it."

It took all of Sidney's willpower to keep from strangling Allison. Her eyes were daggers. *I hate you.*

"So—" Smoke started.

"I said no." Sidney slunk over to the love seat adjacent to the fireplace and took a seat. It was a day she'd do anything to forget. She liked Cyrus, but the relationship had topped off after several months of dating. She'd been ready to move on but had dragged it on too long, and he had made his move.

"She really did say no," Allison said, pressing into Smoke's shoulder and eyeing her sister. "Right then and right in front of everybody. You should have seen his face: like a wounded dog that quickly became dark and angry. And my sister says I'm a tease."

"No," Sidney interjected. "I say you're a hussy."

"Sidney!" Sally exclaimed, re-entering the room with a tray of cookies. "We will not have that kind of talk in this house, especially over the holidays. Now leave your little sister alone." She set the tray down on the coffee table and faced Smoke. "What would you like to drink?"

"Milk is always best with cookies, if it's not a problem."

"Milk goes great with a lot of things," Allison said.

"Allison," Sally said, "go and put something decent on."

"This is decent, don't you think—John, is it?"

Smoke turned his head toward Sally. "I always respected my mother's wisdom, and I think your mother's is very much the same."

Sally's face lit up like a Christmas tree, and with an approving nod, she shuffled back to the kitchen.

Allison stood up with a huff, ran her fingers along the waistband of her yoga pants, and slunk out of the room, saying, "I'm sure I can find something much more traditional and boring in Sidney's room."

The tightness in Sidney's chest started to ease, and the room's atmosphere lightened. She found Smoke's eyes searching hers with a curious look in them. *What must he think of me? And Cyrus? Damn!*

"Aunt Sidney," Megan said, crawling up on the love seat and laying her head on Sid's shoulder. "What's a hussy?"

Damn.

About an hour later, Sidney sat on the hearth with Megan sleeping on a pillow in her lap. She flipped the business card her mother had let her see through her fingers. Edwin Lee with Drake Real Estate Appraisers. A voicemail picked up when she called the number.

"I can't say, Sid," Keith said, yawning. "He seemed all right. Not a twitch about him."

"So a man shows up out of the blue and you just let him inside?"

"Your mother did that."

"He was nice, and he looked cold," Sally said, knitting a bundle of bright green yarn. She glanced at Smoke. "Would you like some more cookies, John?"

"No thank you." He patted his belly. "Those were fine though. I love chocolate chips and pecans. And what were those white chocolate things with the peanut butter in them?"

"Oh, those are Ritz crackers, Jiffy dipped in melted chocolate …."

Sidney let her mom ramble on. Holidays were her thing: cooking, talking, and making merry. She hadn't always been so jovial. Her parents had been stalwart, once upon a time. They had two girls and two older boys, and her mother had taken a switch to every one of them on more than one occasion. But now her mother wouldn't swat a fly.

"Sid, I'm sorry. I don't hear so well. I can't see, either," Keith started, clearing his throat. He picked something up off of his end table by the recliner. "And I have to use this magnifying glass to read my comic books. I never believed my father when he told me, 'Getting old's not for sissies.' Well hell, he was right."

She brushed Megan's hair aside. Megan was sweet, smart, and adorable. Sid wished she had more time with her. The little girl didn't deserve the hard life Allison put her through. No one did. She sighed. "Dad, where did he sit?"

"Right there, where John is. Why?"

"Did he go anywhere else?" she asked. "Use the phone or anything?"

"No. Sally," he said, interrupting her mother's story. "Sally!"

Her mother jerked up. "What did I tell you about using that tone with me?"

"If you'd answer me the first time I wouldn't have to."

"What do you want? I'm talking."

"I know that. Everybody knows that. You're always talking." He rolled his eyes at Sidney. "Always. And it ain't to me. It's to the wall, the cat, the dog, the plants."

"What is your question?" Sally demanded.

"Did that man go anywhere else in the house besides the couch?"

"No," she said, looking up and tilting her head. "Um… Oh, yes, he asked to go to the bathroom."

"Speaking of which," Smoke said, "may I make use of your facility?"

"Certainly, John, second door on the right down the hall."

As soon as Smoke got up, the house phone started ringing. It was an olive green handset from the eighties. No caller ID to be found. Sally picked it up and in a welcoming voice said, "Hello, Shaw residence." She made a sour face. "Smoke?" Her brows buckled in concentration. "Oh, John Smoke. Yes, he's here." She made an excited face at Smoke, who'd stopped in the hall. "And may I ask who's calling?"

Sidney's eyes fastened on Smoke. He shrugged.

"Okay," Sally said. She covered the phone receiver with her hand. "Uh, John, it's a Mister Guppy for you. That's a funny name, but he sounds friendly."

Smoke walked over and took the receiver from Sally. "Thank you." He held the phone to his head. "Smoke." His eyes scanned the room. "Uh-huh … uh-huh … thanks." He hung the phone up and said to Sally. "Thank you."

"Is everything all right?" she asked.

"Just fine," he said, "but I don't think my bladder will hold out much longer." He headed for the bathroom.

"I have the same problem," Keith said.

"I really like him," Sally said to Sidney. "I hope he's your partner for a long, long time."

Sidney shook her head, gaping. *What was that all about?*

CHAPTER 12

A T 10:42 PM, EVERYONE WAS in bed asleep except Sidney and Smoke. The coals in the fireplace had gone dim. Her eyes were heavy, but inside some fires still burned. Smoke sat on the couch, still in the grey suit, but the jacket and tie were undone. He looked relaxed. Casual.

"So you grew up here," he said, glancing over at her. "It's a nice place. I like the knotty pine on the walls."

"My grandparents built it and left it to my mom. They died kinda young."

Smoke stretched back his elbows over the back of the couch. "Well, I guess I should catch some sleep. I guess the loft over the garage is that direction?" He pointed toward the kitchen.

"Just a second," she said, getting up from the hearth and taking a seat in her father's chair across from him. "Care to share what your friend Mister Guppy had to say? That was a nice trick, by the way."

"Oh, that. Sure, I thought you'd never ask."

"Sure you did." She crossed her arms over her chest. "Now out with it."

Smoke pulled a small device out from under the coffee table to show her. It was digital wire. A bug. "I'm pretty sleepy. Some fresh air would be nice."

Sidney headed for the sliding glass door and pulled it open. She shut it just as Smoke stepped outside. The frigid air felt as if it had teeth on it.

"Think there are any others?"

"No," he said, following the steps off the front porch and walking toward the triple-bay garage. "I looked, but I'd say that was it."

"Well, let's destroy it."

"Nah. Just leave it be. There's nothing for them to hear once we leave, and I doubt they'll be monitoring once we're gone. This kind only works a few weeks anyway. They're messing with you. They're messing with us."

"Who is?"

"Whoever doesn't want us to pursue the Black Slate."

Her boots crunched over the gravel path that led around the house. It was a nice moonlit evening, just freezing cold. She remembered running around this house with her brothers and sister and cousins, all playing spotlight late into the night. She accidentally brushed her hand against his as they rounded the corner. He held hers gently for a moment and let it go. *He's still warm.*

She blew her icy breath into her hands and rubbed them together. "I'm guessing someone on the Black Slate doesn't want us pursuing the Black Slate."

"The best criminals own a piece of everybody. Just look at your buddy Congressman Wilhelm. He may be the one behind it all. I can only imagine there's a bundle of money on the table. And money and blackmail win elections."

"I'd hate to think this is all about politics."

"It's always about politics. That's all DC cares about. People around here lose their minds during an election cycle."

"And their jobs." She plucked a rock off the ground and dropped it back onto the gravel pathway. "So, what did Mister Guppy say about Edwin Lee?"

Smoke made his way into the yard and leaned back on the split-rail fence. "What makes you think it was about Mister Lee?"

"Come on, I don't have time for games, Mister Smoke."

"Are we back to that again?"

"Back to what?"

"Mister Smoke? After all we've been through? At least your parents call me John."

"So I should call you John?"

"No, I like Smoke, but your parents can call me John because I'm a guest in their home."

She shivered. "What did Guppy say?"

"He wanted to wish me a Merry Christ—"

She punched him in the shoulder. "Out with it, please."

"All right, I'm just teasing. You really should loosen up over the holidays some." He cocked an eyebrow at her.

She glowered back.

"So, Guppy found Edwin Lee."

"And?" she said, shivering.

"There's several hundred in the United States, and fifteen in DC. Fourteen don't match the description." He cracked his thumbs. "The fifteenth did." He looked up at the distant tree line. "I bet you have a bundle of deer out there."

"And?" she said again, not hiding her agitation.

"And he died in 1943. Buried in a place called Red Vine Cemetery, southwest of DC."

Sidney stretched her visit as long as she could stand it and departed her parents' home late Christmas afternoon. Smoke, to her surprise, blended in quite well and was very smooth, brushing off all of Allison's advances. It pleased her, watching him handle himself so well where most men tended to stumble. Rolling onto the highway headed south, she set the Hellcat on cruise control.

"Where are we headed, Agent Shaw?" Smoke said, staring out the window.

He sat dressed in blue jeans and a black shirt under a dark leather jacket. A holster holding a gun was strapped to his side.

"Red Vine Cemetery. I want to see that grave."

"Not a bad call."

"Did you have something else in mind?"

"We have to start somewhere, but I might have picked a place out of the file folder. Out of what's left of it, anyway."

They'd gone through the remains of the file back at her parents'. There was little left to start on, but Sidney remembered plenty of what she'd seen and jotted down her notes. It was one of her things: studying something once and not forgetting. Names, places, and events easily stuck in her mind. "I'm sure there's another file."

"Well, I have a feeling those files aren't digital. Looks like it was dug out of a metal file cabinet from the old days."

"Perhaps."

Smoke patted his stomach. "I appreciate the hospitality. I haven't been a part of something like that in a long time. I like your family."

"I bet you liked Allison."

"She's something, all right. But your Mom was the one who kind of got me."

"What do you mean? What did she say?"

"She said she thought I was a *goodly* child and asked me if I had any baby pictures."

Sidney laughed. "Yes, that was strange. Try not to take it the wrong way. She's pretty old-fashioned with her words. She always says something odd about everyone. It used to be pretty embarrassing growing up."

"What did she say about Cyrus?" he said without looking at her. "Did he come over much?"

Ugh! Why did you have to ruin a perfectly normal conversation? She didn't reply.

"Did you ever envision yourself married to him?" he pressed.

"I don't want to talk about it. And why do you have such an interest in it?"

"He's a jerk. I've never understood why so many women go for such big jerks. That's all."

"There's more to him than meets the eye."

He turned his head. "Is there now?"

"Not like that."

"What do you mean, not like that? What were you talking about?"

"I thought you were—ugh, never mind. Drop it."

The next few hours were driven in silence. No radio. No chatter. Just her driving and Smoke, eyes closed and maybe sleeping. She liked him. Every time Allison neared him, a fire had lit inside her. But she couldn't blame her sister for trying, and he wasn't the first man they'd fought over. Allison hadn't flirted with Cyrus, though, and that had ended up being a confirming sign. *Quit thinking about it and get back to the business at hand.* But she didn't stop thinking about it. She couldn't. The way he'd handled himself with her parents was genuine and impressive. *And they like him.* But it was ludicrous for her to fall for a man whose home was in prison. She pulled off the highway, entered the nearest gas station, and pulled alongside the pumps.

"Why are we stopping?" Smoke asked, rubbing his eyes.

"Getting a little gas and coffee." She popped open the door. "Want some?"

"Gas, or coffee?" he said with a smile.

"Or neither."

"Large black coffee, and if you don't mind, some nacho Doritos would be nice."

At least they don't serve milkshakes.

"Just pump the gas," she said, scanning the card on the pump and walking away.

Inside the store, Sidney prepared two large coffees and paid the clerk.

He was an older black man with a lazy eye, wearing a Santa cap on his head. "I hope you've had an extraordinary day," he said with a smile. "Now you be careful out there, or the holiday spooks will get you."

That's an odd thing to say.

Back inside the car, she waited for Smoke to stop pumping and get inside. Finally he hopped in. She handed him his coffee, saying, "You used high octane, didn't you?"

"Of course," he said, taking the cup. "Hey, no Doritos."

"No," she said, putting the car in drive and motoring out of the lot. "No Doritos." *What am I, your mom? Geez, I don't get this guy.*

Another twenty minutes of driving and things remained quiet. Smoke sat huddled over his coffee, sipping and looking away.

Is he pouting?

She checked the GPS on her phone. Red Vine Cemetery was ten miles from the nearest highway in Springfield. The road leading up to it was dirt and gravel with a heavy night fog rolling over it. She pulled off to the side in the tall grasses beside a tall iron gate that was chained shut. Black gargoyles loomed on the top posts with wings spread and screeching faces. There was something alive about them. She popped the trunk and got out.

Smoke slid out of the car, eying the metal fence. "This looks like the ancient ones in Savanna."

She picked up a flashlight and checked her weapon, eyeing the moon in the sky. She grabbed another gun, a Glock 22, and clipped it on. She kept the .40 caliber ready in her free hand. She closed the trunk and Smoke was nowhere to be found.

No he didn't.

CHAPTER 13

THE FENCE AND GATE WERE eight feet high, and the top rails were spiked. It was odd. Most cemeteries didn't have fences around them. And there was something else peculiar, too. She ran her fingers over the wrought iron. The metal was in excellent condition, almost new. After pushing her gun and flashlight between the rails and setting them down on the other side, she grabbed the ice-cold rails and squeezed them. *Here we go.* She shimmied up the rails, got her boot on the topside, and swung herself over.

Rip!

One of the barbs at the top ripped through her coat and into her shoulder. Grimacing, she hopped down to the ground and grabbed the gun and flashlight. She touched the throbbing wound. Warm blood wet her fingers.

Not good. She peered through the murk. *Dammit, Smoke, where are you?* Treading through the tall lawn, she took note of the graves and markers. Many were tall limestone works with crosses and other ornate types of pylons and pillars. There were stone sarcophaguses too, with a few cracked and damaged. There were hundreds of marble headstones as far as her eyes could see, glinting faintly in the moonlight. Sidney waded through the mist that hung just above her ankles. A sound caught her ear. She stopped.

Shnnnk … Ffffp … Shnnnk … Ffffp … Shnnnk … Ffffp …

It was the steady rhythmic sound of a shovel digging into the earth. Sidney crept toward the sound.

Shnnnk … Ffffp … Shnnnk … Ffffp … Shnnnk … Ffffp …

A figure in shabby clothes stood waist-deep in a grave. A man with a broad back and hunched shoulders scooped out large shovelfuls of dirt and tossed them aside. There was something extraordinary about the man as he slung the dirt aside. The shovel was huge, almost the size of a snow shovel. The ominous silhouette kept shoveling without any source of light. Spidery legs of warning crawled up her arms.

Shnnnk … Ffffp … Shnnnk … Ffffp … Shnnnk … Ffffp …

She turned on the flashlight and readied her Glock and slid in behind him. There was a body in a burlap sack, bound up in thick cords of twine beside the grave.

"FBI," Sidney said, shining the light on the man's back. He was big-framed. Arms bulged. A nasty scar was carved deep in his bare skull. *He should be freezing.* "Drop the shovel and let me see your hands."

Shnnnk … Ffffp … Shnnnk … Ffffp … Shnnnk … Ffffp …

Dirt landed on Sidney's boots. "Drop the shovel and get out of the grave, sir."

Shnnnk … Ffffp … Shnnnk … Ffffp … Shnnnk … Ffffp …

Sidney growled in her throat. *Men never listen.* She stepped around the side of the grave to get a better look at him. He kept his head down. *He might be deaf, but he can certainly see the light.* She shined the light in his face.

The foreboding man stopped and looked up. His marred face had dead eyes. He snarled. The shovel swung.

Shit! A deader!

Sidney jumped. The shovel clipped her heel, and she pitched backward hard onto the ground. Her gun fell from her grasp. The man grabbed the hem of her pants and hauled her into the grave. She drove her heel into his mouth. Clocked him in the head with the flashlight. The deader's grip was iron, his power unnatural.

"Screw you, Frankenstein!"

She let loose a flurry of kicks in his face, rocking his thick neck back. Using a jujitsu move, she twisted her leg free of his grasp and scrambled out of the hole. In the darkness, she clutched through the tall grasses for her gun.

"Murrr!" the deader moaned, climbing out of the hole wielding the shovel. He raised it over his head and brought it down hard.

Sidney rolled left.

The shovel bit into the ground beside her head. The deader ripped it from the ground and swung another decimating blow.

She ducked under the swipe. Spying her gun, she snatched it up and blasted away.

"Eat Glock, you ugly undead sonofabitch!"

Blam! Blam! Blam! Blam! Blam! Blam!

The deader staggered backward, shovel slipping through its grasp, teetering on the lip of the grave.

Blam! Blam! Blam! Blam! Blam! Blam!

Goo oozed from the hole in its chest as it toppled into the grave.

Thud!

Chest heaving, Sidney leaned over the grave.

The deader's arms shot up.

Blam! Blam! Blam!

The deader's arms fell down.

Morning Glory. She took out another fifteen-round magazine and reloaded. *What was that goon made of?*

A man rushed toward her. She aimed for his head. He raised his arms. It was Smoke. "Where in the hell have you been?"

"Sorry," he said, peering into the grave. "Another deader?"

"I guess," she said, glaring at him. "Now, if you don't mind, where were you?"

"While you were fumbling through the trunk, I saw somebody running and went after them."

"And you didn't think to tell me."

"When a wolf chases a rabbit, he doesn't think about it."

"So you think like a dog?"

"I said I was sorry. You're a big girl, Agent Shaw. Get over it." Then he said with a little guilt in his voice. "I really didn't anticipate any danger. I should have known better. Sorry."

She could see the heavy look in his eye. He meant it. And he was right. She didn't need to get into the habit of relying on someone else. "Just give me a heads-up next time."

Smoke sauntered over to the grave marker and ran his fingers over the engraving. "You need to see this," he said.

She took out her phone, turned its light on, and shined in on the marker. Sidney read it out loud: "Edwin Lee. 1865-1945. A humble servant of the Drake Foundation." There was a black sun rising at the top. She looked at the body on the ground, covered only with the burlap sack. "You thinking what I'm thinking?"

Smoke cut away at the cords with a knife and peeled the burlap away from the face.

Just as her mother had described lay the cold dead face of Edwin Lee.

CHAPTER 14

"**W**EIRD," SMOKE SAID, LOOKING AT the dead body. "Really weird. He doesn't look like a deader. Practically a fresh corpse." He glanced at Sidney. "You're bleeding."

"I don't have time to bleed," she said.

Smoke started laughing. "I can't believe you just said that. Is there something you're not telling me? Did you used to be part of the secret SEALS or something?"

The willies that had been creeping through her bones started to subside. She needed some humor, something real and tangible in what was become a bizarre world. "My father and brothers were big fans of the movie."

"And you weren't?"

"Well, I liked it too—the first twenty times."

"It was a pretty popular phrase among the seals," he said, "I've just never heard a woman use it. I like it."

"So, assuming we haven't woken the dead, did you find what you were chasing?"

"Disappeared into a mausoleum." He pointed over a ridge of tombstones. "That's when I heard your shots." He nudged the body of Edwin Lee with his boot. "What do you want to do with him?"

Good question. According to her letter from the Bureau, she needed to call it in. Then again, this was a shadow operation, which gave her liberties with her decisions. She took some pictures of Edwin Lee, the tombstone, and the deader. "Let's go check out this mausoleum."

After traversing through fifty yards of grave markers and willow trees, she came to a stop in front of an ancient rectangular structure. Standing almost twenty feet tall and just as wide, it towered over the other structures. Gargoyles adorned the corners. Vines crept over the stained glass windows and twisted along the columns to the entrance. A pair of brass doors at the top of the steps were split open.

"In there?" she said.

Smoke nodded.

"Maybe he or she slipped back out."

"Only one way to find out," Smoke said, starting up the steps and pulling open the door. The hinges creaked from the effort. "I'll go first."

"But you don't have a light."

Smoke disappeared inside. Sidney ran up the steps after him and shined her phone light inside. It was wholly inadequate, and she regretted busting her Maglite on the deader's head. She could see Smoke well enough, however, and rows of marble burial markers. There were dates carved in them and initials but not full names. She snapped a few pictures.

"Do you mind?" Smoke said, running his fingers over the burial vaults. "You're screwing up my night vision."

"Do you have super powers I should know about?"

"Maybe," he said, tapping his knuckles on the stones. "Huh. Doesn't make sense someone would run in here without anywhere to go."

"Only those windows." She shined the light toward the top. The stained glass windows at the top were all intact. "Or down through the ground."

Smoke pressed his ear to one of the burial chambers.

"Listening for a ghoul's heartbeat?" she said, eyeing the floor and walls. There wasn't anything out of the ordinary. "I think whoever it was already left."

"I don't," Smoke said. "I can smell them."

Oh boy. Sidney sniffed the air. There was nothing extraordinary. "Really, and what do they smell like?"

"Fear." He ran his hands over the markers and started pushing. "Help me out. There has to be a catch or something."

Sidney gave it a half-hearted effort, running her fingers over cold stone after cold stone. She pushed in a little here and there. "It's just a mausoleum, not the Temple of Doom, Indiana."

"I take it you don't like my plan."

"I think we stumbled on plenty to start with already." Her shoulder throbbed, and she was getting colder. "I think it's time to go."

"You aren't all right, are you?"

"This isn't how I normally spend the holidays."

Wuppa—Wuppa—Wuppa—Wuppa—Wuppa …

"That's a chopper landing," he said, heading for the door.

Sidney followed him outside. Sure enough, a large helicopter landed in a nearby clearing. Its whirling blades pressed down the tall grass and stirred the leaves on the willow trees. Men in dark garb spilled out the chopper's doors and rushed at them with bright lights and assault rifles.

"This is bad," Smoke said as the men surrounded them from all angles. "Really bad."

Shielding her eyes, Sidney took out her badge and held it up over her head.

"Don't move another inch, lady," said a voice filled with authority.

"I'm Agent Shaw with—"

Budda-budda! Budda-budda!

One of the armed men squeezed off a few rounds at her feet.

"When I say don't move, that means not anything!" His voice was muffled by a mask of some sort. "Especially your mouth. Try me again, and I'll saw your legs off."

CHAPTER 15

"Lock your hands onto your head," the soldier demanded. "Now!"

Slowly, Sidney put her arms over her head. Smoke's hung ready at his sides. *Just do it!* she wanted to say but didn't. She had no doubt the half dozen men she could make out meant business.

"Looks like we have a wise guy on our hands," the soldier said. "Teach the trespassers a lesson."

"No!" Sidney cried out.

The muzzle flashed.

Budda-budda! Budda-budda!

Bullets tore up the landscape in front of Smoke's toes. He didn't flinch.

"I'll be," the leader said. "Plenty of guts to splatter in this one. Take him down."

Two figures darted from behind the lights. One of them launched the butt of his weapon into Smoke's belly. He doubled over.

Zap!

The second soldier prodded Smoke in the back with a stick that was some sort of taser. Smoke twitched, growled, and started to rise.

The soldiers laid into him.

Zap! Zap! Zap!

Smoke sagged to the ground, clutching at the air.

"That'll take the starch out of him," one said, twirling his stick in the air. He slapped it in his hand. "How about we take a little starch out of her, Boss? I bet Barbie pees herself."

"Just fetch me her ID," the leader said.

"Aw," the man said, strutting over. He snatched Sidney's badge. The men were soldiers of a sort, clad in dark body suits padded in body armor and wearing rectangular goggles and some sort of masks over their mouths. "Sidney Shaw, FBI agent." He glanced down her backside. "Not bad. Boss, can I keep this one? She's got a nice — *oof!*"

Sidney slammed her knee into his nuts. The other forces closed in with stun sticks ready.

Zap!

She twitched from head to toe and toppled to the ground. Everything tingled. Her bones hurt. She watched the sky above blinking as more men in strange masks crowded around her. One of them called her a bitch. She was pretty sure she knew who it was.

Just doing my job, she thought.

"What's the plan, Boss?" said one of the mercenaries. "This is a great place to bury them. Alive would be nice."

"I'm not very fond of suggestions. Perhaps I should bury you. Nothing like a shovelful of dirt to silence you," said the leader, kneeling down alongside Sid.

"Sorry, Boss."

The leader brushed Sidney's hair from her eyes. "It's so hard to find good help these days, Agent Shaw. The younger ones are so, eh, exuberant. And stupid, for that matter." There was some polish in his voice behind the mask. "I hate stupid people." He pulled out a stainless steel pistol. The muzzle flashed.

Blam!

Sidney saw the body fall.

"Leave him," the leader ordered. "The servants shall dispose of him." He ran the muzzle of the gun along Sidney's chin. The hot barrel seared her flesh.

"Uh…" The man's tone and demeanor were those of many cold-blooded killers she'd studied. Nerveless men who didn't flinch executing torture. Mutilation.

"Agent Shaw, I assume you don't have a warrant. Blink once for yes."

She did.

"Good," he said. "But I find it very strange that you are here. Why would that be?"

Can't exactly help with that right now.

"I see, you still can't speak. How rude of me. What's this?" He took off his goggles. He was fair-haired and pale, with pitch-black eyes. He fingered the wound in her shoulder. Blood was on his finger. A hunger filled his eyes. "Mmmm … delicious, I bet." He removed the mask over his mouth. His face was long and slender with a strong dimpled chin. He licked the blood and closed his eyes. "Delicious indeed."

You better not be a vampire. You can't be a vampire.

The leader gazed into her eyes, lending her a full view of his becoming face. He cradled her in his arms. Her head flopped back, exposing her neck to him. The leader bent down and brought his lips to her neck.

This can't be happening! No! She moaned. *No!*

His teeth sunk into her skin. She squirmed. "No."

"Ah-hahaha!" the leader laughed. "I'm screwing with you, Agent Shaw. I'm not a vampire, but I always wanted to be one." He cocked his head and stared hard into her eyes. "But there are worse things out there than vampires, love. Take my word for it."

I know. They're called lawyers, jerk. The numbness and pain started to wear off. *Save your energy, Sid. Save it.*

"But I do have a bit of a dilemma here. Normally, I just kill people that trespass and have them buried. You however, are a Fed." He scratched his neck. His nails were unusually long. "And the Feds cause problems. Questions. Investigations. Hmmm. My boss likes to keep things quiet. And I don't like my boss showing up, so I like to keep things quiet too." He gazed into the sky. "Damn. I really hate loose ends."

Sidney watched him stand up and hang the barrel of the gun over her face. *He's going to shoot me. God, please don't let him shoot me!*

CHAPTER 16

"H MMM …" THE BOSS SAID, tilting his head with the moon hanging over his shoulder. "I like you, Agent Shaw. You and your friend can live, for now. But I suggest you stop your snooping around. The game you're playing is far too dangerous for the common man—or woman." He motioned to his men. "Drag them outside of the gate and leave them. Maybe the cold will take them." He walked off, heading toward the chopper.

A hand clutched Sidney by the hair and dragged her limp body over the grass. Smoke was being dragged by two men behind her. His head was slumped downward. Her teeth started to chatter. It was a miserable existence, being dragged.

"Hurry up," one of them said. "The boss might leave us." The soldiers picked up the pace. "It'd go quicker if this big bastard wasn't so damn heavy. I say we kill 'em both. He'll never know."

"You saw what happened to dumbass Franklin back there, didn't you? You want a hole in your head too?"

"Good point," said the man dragging her. "But a bullet in the head's an act of mercy compared to what I've seen other upstarts get. The Cage. Ew. That's nasty."

"Clam up, will you. I don't need reminded."

They came to a stop just outside of the gate. Sidney could see the Hellcat's taillights and mufflers. The soldiers dragged Smoke by her side and kicked him in the ribs a few times.

"All right, that's enough," one said. He started closing the gate. "Let's go. I'm pretty sure they'll be dead soon enough anyway. He'll make it look like an accident is all. Enjoy the cold, agents."

They all piled in the chopper, and it took off.

Wuppa—Wuppa—Wuppa—Wuppa—Wuppa …

It was below twenty outside, and if she didn't get moving she'd be a Popsicle in an hour. *Come on, Sid. Move.* Her fingertips scraped at the dirt. Her teeth still chattered. *This sucks!*

Smoke rolled over with a heavy groan and crawled toward her.

Thank God!

"Hang in there," he said, rummaging through her pockets.

What! What in the hell are you doing?

He produced her key fob and pressed the button. The taillights flicked on.

You'd better be starting the engine.

Smoke rose to his feet, staggered toward the car, and pulled the door open. He pulled out his duffle bag and unzipped it.

Now you're pissing me off.

He produced an army green tube and stretched it out to full length.

That's a LAW rocket! He's insane! She had fired the light anti-tank weapons before during Air Base Ground Defense training in the Air Force. But those had been blasting caps. This was the real thing.

Smoke hefted it onto his shoulder and took aim at the rising helicopter.

"No," she managed to croak out. "No."

Watching the chopper rise, Smoke took his hand off the trigger and collapsed the weapon back into its compact size. Jaw jutted against the moonlit sky, he shook his head as the chopper flew out of sight.

Thank God. The men deserved it, but she didn't want their blood on her hands. She didn't want it on Smoke's either.

He walked over, picked her up, and cradled her in his arms. "I hate loose ends. It'll come back to bite us." Smoke set her down in the passenger seat and buckled her inside. "Looks like I finally get to drive."

"Don't you dare," she mumbled.

Smoke fired up the engine and pressed on the accelerator, which let out a vicious exhaust note. "What? Did you say something?"

Pinning her to her seat, the Dodge Hellcat's back wheels tore the gravel off the road. After a couple of minutes, the seat began warming her rear, and the heater thawed her icy cheeks. She glanced over at Smoke. In the dim light he reminded her of a modern-day road warrior. She kinda liked that about him. "Don't get too comfortable, Mad Max."

"Hah. Now he was an interceptor. But that wasn't a Hellcat."

She shifted in her seat and made herself a little more comfortable. Held her hands in front of the heater. The nerve-jangling effects were beginning to wear off. But Smoke had been tasered at least three times. *He shouldn't be moving.* "So, was that LAW rocket a parting gift from the SEALS?"

"Nope."

"You were about to kill all of those guys, weren't you?"

"Maybe. Don't you think they had it coming?"

"I'm not a judge. I'm an agent." She rubbed her temples. "Man, this is one rotten Christmas."

"I've had worse," Smoke said, adjusting the rearview mirror. He glanced at her shoulder. "That might need stitches. I can handle it, if you like. But you need to put some pressure on it."

Sidney had a few things to consider. A trip to the hospital would generate paperwork. She was a shadow agent now, and maintaining a low profile would take some getting used to. There were other bizarre matters too. The deader and the body of Edwin Lee. She still needed to confirm that. Grimacing, she searched her pockets. Panic seized her.

"What's wrong?" Smoke said.

"That man, the Boss, he must have taken my phone!"

On Smoke's insistence, she let him take her back to his place. It wasn't like her to not put up a fight, but his words persuaded her. Now, she sat on his kitchen counter inside his service garage apartment. The gas heater made a soft roar overhead, which gave the place a cozy feeling. Her shoulder throbbed, however. Sitting too long and staying awake on depleted adrenaline had stiffened her body.

"I'll be back," Smoke said, heading for his bathroom. "You might want to remove your jacket, and you'll probably need a clean shirt. I can help out with that one."

With a few grunts, she slid her jacket off and dropped it to the floor. The shoulder of this shirt was ripped and soaked in blood. She debated taking it off or not. *Screw it. Life's too short to be modest.* Off the shirt went, leaving her in only her bra and slacks.

Smoke returned with a towel, a damp washcloth, and a medic kit. "Did you learn that move from your sister?" he said, eyes fixed on hers.

"Ha ha. If it were my sister, there'd be no top at all and your sofa-bed would be unfolded."

"Ouch," Smoke said, inspecting the wound. "Sounds like you're feeling better, but it's pretty nasty."

"Just get on with it."

He went to work. Wiping off the blood. Cleaning the wound. Threading the needle. "Four or five should do it. It might sting a little."

She didn't look away. She looked right at him. His warm presence and rock-steady hands drew her in. Her blood began to sizzle. They'd only spent a few days together, but it felt like a lifetime. The needle dug into her arm. Her eyes watered.

"You okay?" he said, fixated like a surgeon on the wound.

"Never better," she said in his ear, eyeing the wound.

He ran another stitch through. "Good. That's two ... that's three ... and four." He knotted it off and clipped it with scissors. "All done."

"That was fast," she said with bated breath, looking into his eyes and resting her good hand on his neck. She rubbed his cheek and earlobe with her thumb. Her body was throbbing. "Good job."

"You're a wonderful patient," he said.

Her lips drew closer to his. "And you're a wonderful—"

Smoke withdrew just as the sound of an approaching car caught her ear. *Morning glory!*

CHAPTER 17

HEADLIGHTS ILLUMINATED THE WINDOW BLINDS. Smoke went for his gun. She went for hers. The sound of tires crunched over the driveway. He peeked through the blinds, pulled back, and headed to the other side of the room.

"Who is it?" she said, standing in her bra and slacks, holding her gun.

Smoke opened up a dresser drawer and withdrew a T-shirt. He tossed it to her. "Put this on. We have company."

"Good company or bad company?" she said, slipping the shirt on. It was a little tight and had a battle helmet and axe logo on it. "Whose was this, your girlfriend's?"

"I used to be smaller." He put away his weapon. "It's a sentimental treasure."

Knock! Knock! Knock!

Smoke made his way over to the door and swung it open. A short stocky man, bald-headed and bearded, bustled inside. A woman, taller, followed in behind him. Her honey blonde hair was pulled back in a long silky pony tail. Her winter jacket did little to hide her generous curves. Smoke closed the door behind them. She was older than Sid, over forty, but without a wrinkle and nary an eyelash out of place. *I hope I age that well.*

"Nice shirt," the woman said with a voice that was a little Lauren Bacall-like. She looked Sid up and down with very pretty eyes then took off her coat and handed it to the other man. She wore a sleeveless black top adorned in silver sequins and a pair of Buckle jeans. "I used to have one just like it."

"Hey," the man said to Sid, "The Darkslayer. I like that." He hung the woman's coat on the wall and did the same with his. He wasn't tall for a man but stocky as a bull, with thick forearms bulging beneath his flannel sleeves. His voice was warm and friendly. He had a rugged charm about him. He walked over and extended his hand. "They call me—"

"Guppy," Sidney said, taking his hand in hers.

Guppy's eyes lit up. "You can call me Gil if you don't like Guppy. I don't mind."

"Well, you don't look like a Guppy."

"I'd say not. I've been telling everyone that for years." He scratched his brown-red beard and glowered back at Smoke.

"So why the name then?"

"Well, it is my last name, after all."

"Ah," she said. "So it's Gilmore Guppy."

"Er, no," Guppy said, scratching the back of his bald head. He mumbled. "It's Gilligan actually. Gilligan Guppy."

"We tried Double G, but it didn't stick," Smoke said. He slapped his hand down on Guppy's brawny shoulder. "So, Guppy it is. And over there is Fat Sam."

Fat Sam had moved away and taken a seat behind the computer.

"It'll take some time, but she'll warm up to you," Guppy said with a wink.

"I have to admit," Sid said, "neither of you are what I expected, especially in her case. She's so—"

"Stacked," Smoke interjected.

Sid narrowed her eyes on him. "I was going to say gorgeous and female."

"Thank you," Fat Sam boomed, pecking away on Smoke's computer.

"Yes, she's the fat with a PH kind. Pretty hot and tempting, wouldn't you say?" Guppy said, raising his brows.

"I get it," Sidney said, glancing at the woman.

"And Sam's short for Samantha," Guppy added.

"I think she figured that out already," Sam said.

"And she's grumpy," Guppy whispered.

"I heard that."

"Well, I have to admit, your arrival is a bit peculiar." Sid made her way over to the computer desk and looked over Fat Sam's shoulder. The monitor had pictures from the Drake graveyard on it. The ones she had taken. *How in the world did she get those?* On the desk, she noticed a phone similar to the one she thought she lost. A jolt of fury went right through her. "Smoke!"

"Oh, I meant to tell you, I found your phone," he said.

She jerked her phone off the cable. "Garage! Now!" *Jerk!* Smoke made his way into the garage, and she shut the door behind them. She wanted to hit him. She poked him in the chest. "Why didn't you tell me that?"

"Easy," he said, putting his hands up, "you don't want to tear those stitches."

"I'm going to tear your tongue out if you don't give me some straight answers!"

"Is this an interrogation?"

"It's betrayal," she said, walking away. In one of the garage's double bays, his IROC Camaro was on a lift with a new fiery red paint job on it. *When did he do that?* On the other side, two motorcycles were covered in tarps. Last time there had only been one. Boxes of Snap-On Tools hugged the block walls, and long shelves were filled with neatly organized parts.

"I shouldn't have taken it," he said, "or at least I should have given it back. But I wasn't sure how forthcoming you'd be with the information. We need it."

"I'm here. We're well past that point."

Dejected, he said, "I'm sorry."

Her fires simmered down, but it still hurt a little. She wanted to trust him. Even worse, she had trusted him, letting things hang out with only a bra on. She wanted to take the T-shirt off and throw it at him. She wanted him to take her in his arms and kiss her. *Damn men!* "So, this shirt, was it Sam's?"

"Still is, I think." He stretched his arms up on the bottom of his car that hung on the lift. "We aren't a thing. Her and Guppy stay over sometimes."

"I don't want to know anything else." *Keep it professional.* She headed for the door. "But it's nice knowing you kids have sleepovers." She opened the door and stepped inside, then shut it behind her. Guppy and Fat Sam were seated at the desk, staring at her.

"Is the squabble over?" Sam said.

No! "Yes." She made her way over to them. "Care to fill me in on what you're doing?"

"Trying not to freak out," Guppy said, staring at one of the four monitors. He got up from his chair. "Please, Agent Shaw, have a seat."

"I'm all right."

"I insist."

Sidney obliged. *Nice guy but probably lying to someone.* "What are you freaking out about?"

Sam twisted her head around. "Are you shitting me?"

"Language," Guppy warned.

"Oh, I'm sorry for my French. I meant to say, are you joking?" Sam clicked on the mouse and pulled up four images, one on each monitor. The tombstone marker of Edwin Lee. Edwin Lee's corpse. The 1943 obituary and photo of Edwin Lee, and finally the deader. "That's what we're talking about. Craziest shit I ever saw."

"Ahem."

"Sorry again. Craziest slat … oh never mind. This is Nucking Futz! Yet at the same time, it's awesome."

"Sorry about her," Guppy said, shaking his head. "She's still got a lot of alley cat in her."

Sam spun around her in her seat to face Sid. "Tell me more about the werewolf." Her green eyes gleamed. "Smoke wouldn't talk about it, but you'll tell me. Tell me everything."

"I'll think about it," Sidney said, leaning toward the screen with the deader on it. "I'm curious. Do you think you can identify that guy?"

"Maybe, why?" Sam said, zooming in on the image.

"It might give us some more insight. Man, he's huge. You don't notice so much when they're trying to kill you."

Sam and Guppy gave each other odd looks. "Boy, Smoke is right," Guppy said, "you really are a Hellcat."

Sidney showed a wry smile. She squinted her eyes at another image on the screen with the tombstone. She pointed at it. "Zoom in on that."

"Okay." Sam zoomed in.

There was a figure with gleaming eyes peering at them from up in the tree. Its shape was fuzzy.

"Cat maybe," Guppy said.

The shape was odd but familiar. "Pretty big cat. Are those wings on its back?"

"Probably an owl," Sam offered.

Smoke crept back in the room and offered his insight. "Not a cat. Not an owl. It's a gargoyle."

CHAPTER 18

"**O**H, PLEASE," SIDNEY SAID. "It's not a gargoyle."

"Oh, please be a gargoyle," Sam said, toying with her onyx and diamond necklace with her eyes glued to the screen. "Smoke, this is so much more exciting than the wife-beating drug dealers we're used to."

"And stopping those people isn't a good thing?" Smoke said.

"Sure, but taking down wife-beating werewolves is so much cooler."

"Am I missing something?" Sidney asked, staring at Smoke.

"She prattles. Don't worry about it."

"Hmmm, I think it is a gargoyle," Guppy said. "Yep, I'm with Smoke. Gargoyle."

Sidney recalled a bad movie she'd seen years ago with friends, called *Gargoyles*. It had really creeped her out then, and the talk of them creeped her out now. *Strange bunch. Just a little too into this.* "I think we need a little more proof. I'm sure forensics can find a scientific explanation for what that is."

"Don't be such a Scully," Sam said, tilting back in her chair. "You've seen deaders and a werewolf. I don't see any reason you can't add a gargoyle to the supernatural kingdom."

"I know what I saw, but we don't really have proof of any of that, so don't go calling the papers."

"Not even the *Enquirer*?" Sam said with a huff.

"Or the *Sun*?" Smoke said with a laugh.

"Don't forget the *Weekly World News*," Guppy added.

"Sure, call the *Lone Gunman*, why don't you?" Sidney said, laughing at herself. They all fell silent and stared at her. "Oh, it's funny when you say stupid things, but not when I do, is it?"

Guppy shrugged his heavy shoulders. "We just weren't of the impression that you were funny is all."

Smoke nudged him.

Sidney folded her arms over her chest and cocked her head. "And why would you be under that impression?"

"Er, well …" Guppy scratched his head. "I think I hear something in the garage. I better go check it out. Probably them raccoons again."

Smoke put his finger up. "I'm going to get a shower." He tugged at the neck of his shirt. "Phew, I can almost feel what I'm smelling."

Almost instantly, Sidney found herself all alone in the studio with Sam, whose decorated fingernails were a blur on the keyboard. Sid resumed her seat beside her. Everything about Sam was impeccable, from the type of shoe she wore to the onyx wrap that held her blonde ponytail in place.

"What?" Sam said, keeping her eyes on the monitor.

"Nothing," Sidney said. "Well, not exactly nothing. I really like your fingernails."

"Thanks. Too bad I can't say the same about yours."

"Excuse —" Sidney fanned out her hands. The maroon polish was dull and chipped off. Polishing her nails wasn't one of her better habits. She was a little more practical about such things. "They do look pretty crappy, don't they?"

"Yep," Sam said, smiling out of the corner of her mouth. "But I imagine FBI girls need to be a little more practical, especially when you're fighting deaders and such. You might want to sprinkle a little diamond dust on them though."

"I suppose." She nodded. "I have a question."

"About me and Smoke I bet."

"Yes."

Sam turned in her chair and looked into Sid's eyes. "We don't have the right chemistry."

Sidney locked her fingers in her lap and leaned back with an inner sigh. But another question pecked in her mind. She opened her mouth to speak.

"No, we haven't done it," Sam said, "and let's just leave it at that. Smoke's a special guy, but even he gets a little misaligned sometimes." She resumed her pecking on the keyboard. "That's all I can say, because it's starting to get a little weird."

"Fair enough," Sidney said. "So, Sam's short for Samantha?"

"My mom was a fan of the *Bewitched* show. Well, I was too, a decade later. Huh. There I go, dating myself."

"I used to watch that with my mom and *I Dream of Jeannie* too."

"Well, at least your mom had sense enough not to name you Samantha Jean."

Sidney burst out in laughter.

"Yeah, laugh it up. Everyone else does." She started to laugh herself. "I hated it growing up, but it's kinda cool now. Goes well together. Don't you think?"

"Sure, if you live in Alabama."

"Ha ha." Sam shook her head. "I went to one of those snobby private schools. I was a little heavy, really had a thing for Little Debbies and hot donuts as a kid. My parents never told me no to anything until after they were dead."

"Oh." Sidney stopped laughing. "Sorry."

"I'm just screwing with you. Made you stop laughing, though."

"That's messed up."

"But it's effective."

It wasn't half bad having a friend to warm up with for a change. For the most part, all she had was Sadie. *Sam and Sadie. Now that would make one heckuva girls' night out together.*

"So, as I understand it, you have a file on this weird shit—I mean slat?" Sam asked.

"Yea, how'd you already know about that?"

Sam just looked at her.

"He's really sneaky, isn't he?" Sidney said.

"An oversized fox. Don't underestimate him."

Sidney made her way over to the kitchen table to pick up the charred remains of their case file. She noticed a coffee pot in the corner.

"I like the way you're thinking," she heard Sam say.

Does everyone have ESP around here? She found a pack of grounds, readied the pot, and returned to the computer station. She dumped the file on the desk. The envelope from the Bureau slipped out on the floor.

Sam snatched it up. "What's this?"

CHAPTER 19

S IDNEY SNATCHED THE CHARRED LETTER from Sam's dazzling fingertips.

"It's mine."

"Secret orders, huh?" Sam's eyes narrowed on her. "Now's not the best time to keep secrets. You need to trust someone."

The door to the garage opened, and Guppy bustled in, sniffing the air. "Is that coffee brewing?"

"Hey, Guppy," Sam said. "You'll never believe this."

"Believe what?"

"Sid has secret orders."

Smoke appeared out of the bathroom, drying his hair and wearing only a beige terrycloth towel. The strapping man's muscles flexed as he breathed in the aroma. "Ah, coffee."

Sidney unglued her eyes from his hard belly and turned back to the file on the desk. "We need to get going on this Night Bird case, before the jailbird back there has to go back to his nest." She plucked out a picture of Angi Harlow and set it on the table. The edges were crisp. "I recall seeing some notes about her being a philanthropist of sorts. There were several similar locations that she had in common with Adam Vaughn too. That might be a starting point."

Sam slid the picture over and stared at it. "She's a true beauty. Look at those cheekbones. I'll do a search and see if I can find anything on her. But I'm sure there's a thousand Angi Harlows in the system."

"Think it will get flagged?" Sid said, fanning herself with the Bureau letter. "We need to be careful."

"I'm careful," Sam said, typing.

"What's this?" Smoke said, snatching the letter from Sidney's hand.

"Hey!"

He took the letter out, held it high over his head, and started reading it out loud. "'Agent Shaw, due to the unorthodox arrangement of this assignment, you will need to keep the following items under consideration.' Interesting. 'John Smoke,' that's me, 'is a convicted criminal with special skills.'" He made a quirky face. "'Don't underestimate him.' Which you already have. Several times." He changed his voice to something dark and hoarse. "'He's dangerous,' like Batman. 'Unpredictable,' like Miley Cyrus. 'Possible flight risk,' like DB Cooper." His voice changed back. "'You have eyes on him and we have eyes on him.'" He glanced around with widened eyes and shrugged. "'Allow him free range.'" He stopped and looked at Sid. "*Allow him free range.*" He wagged his finger at her. "It seems you're not being completely honest about things either. Shame. Shame." He continued. "'We'll let you know if he needs reeling in.' Blah, blah, 'alien objects,' blah blah, 'notify your superiors. Seek Mal Carlson … for assistance when needed.' That's new. 'Shadow cover authorized.' That's cool." He switched back to his Dark Knight voice. "Trust your instincts and good hunting. The Bureau." He handed her back the letter. "Sooner or later, you're going to have to figure out who you're going to trust: us or the Bureau. I'll be back. I have to brush my teeth. I have a foul taste in my mouth for some reason."

Sidney shrank in her chair as he walked away. She swore his cheeks had reddened. "I bet I seem like a real ass, don't I?"

Sam kept up at the keyboard while Guppy poured a mug of coffee. He walked it over to her. It was a white mug with a dragon and sword logo on it.

"Thanks," she said.

"Don't mention it," he said. "And don't worry. He's only a little mad. He'll get over it."

"I've got nothing on Mal Carlson, but I've found a few good Angi's," Sam said. "I'll see if I can tie any of it in to Drake." She shook her head as she talked. "Drake has a plethora of subsidiaries. They're as bad as government pork barrel companies."

Glimpsing through the remains of the file, Sidney noticed a tattoo on a dead man's arm. "Look for anything with a black sun incorporated into it. That might help."

"Sure," Sam replied.

The bathroom door popped open. Smoke appeared in a black T-shirt and jeans. His dark brown hair was still damp but combed back. He made his way over to the kitchen counter, where Guppy had him a mug of coffee ready. "Did you bring the kit?"

"It's in the car," said Guppy. "I'll fetch it." He headed outside and returned shortly with a red medical kit in his hands. He opened it up and took out a packet with a syringe. Then he cleaned off the inside of Smoke's elbow with alcohol and a cotton swab.

"What's going on here?" Sidney said, getting up out of her chair.

"We're checking to make sure that I'm not a werewolf," Smoke said. "We have to send the bloodwork to Transylvania Labcorp."

"Ha ha," she laughed. "No really, what's going on?"

"Okay, since you seem genuinely concerned, we're testing my blood to see what your boyfriend Cyrus injected into me months ago."

Sidney had forgotten about that until Smoke brought it up again in the elevator. It was pretty clear that it agitated him. "He's not my boyfriend."

"Sorry, I meant ex-fiancé."

Sam wheeled around in her chair. "You were engaged? When did this happen?"

She shot a look at Smoke. His playful smile was showing. "I wasn't engaged." She shook her chin at him. "I said no."

"Oh," Sam said, turning back around. Her fingers became a blur on the keyboard, "Cyrus Tweel. Let's get a better look at you."

"What? Wait, what are you doing?" Sidney said. Pictures of Cyrus suddenly picked up on the monitors. *Morning glory!*

"Ew, you were engaged to this creepy little guy?" Sam said with her head cocked.

Guppy walked over for a closer look. "Him? You and him?" He pointed at the screen. "Look at those cold beady eyes. I bet his great granddaddy was a horse thief."

"Again," Sidney interjected, "we didn't get engaged. I said no."

"But you slept with him, right?"

Sidney pushed her hair back over her head. *She's worse than Sadie!* "Let's get back on the track that doesn't have anything to do with my sex life, okay?"

Sam spun back around in her chair, facing Sid. "My door's always open when you want to talk about it." She turned back around.

Behind her, Smoke was chuckling. Sidney turned and punched him in the shoulder.

"Ow," he said, flatly.

"Now what's this bloodwork all about?" she asked.

"Just a second and I'll tell you," he said.

Guppy drew blood from Smoke's arm then proceeded to inject the blood into a large glass vial of solution. He was stirring the blood in with a clear liquid when the most bizarre thing happened. It started to shine in the light.

Smoke's face turned grim.

"Yep, you were right," Guppy said to him with a frown. "They've got the Glow in you."

Smoke smacked his fist on the kitchen counter.

Wham!

CHAPTER 20

"T HE GLOW?" SID ASKED. "WHAT is that?"

"It's a tracking serum," Guppy said, disposing of the syringe in a biohazard bag. "Experimental stuff."

"I've never heard of it."

"Well, don't be surprised. It's relatively new and not used very much. Mostly tested by the Department of Agriculture on animals."

Sidney thought about the letter from the Bureau. *We've got eyes on him.* She had wondered how that could be, and now it made perfect sense.

"It'll wear off, Smoke," Guppy said, trying to sound reassuring. "And it's never been proven effective."

"Are there any side effects?" she asked.

"Don't know." Guppy rubbed his chin. "Are there, Smoke?"

"Aside from headaches, blurred vision, and nosebleeds, I'm perfectly fine." He shrugged. "Of course, fighting for your life causes some of that."

Sid wanted to reach out and touch him. She couldn't imagine how hard it would be to be used as someone's lab experiment. She noticed a sad look in Sam's eyes. Behind her was a clip of Cyrus's face. *Has he known all along where Smoke was? Where I was? The bastard!*

"I'll get more tests done and see how diluted it is. Maybe it's down to the final days."

"Apparently, it's lasted for months. I feel like a collared dog."

"How does this *Glow* work?"

"It's a bit like the dye they put in you for bloodwork. It spreads through the body and can be picked up like a radio signal. It has a frequency. *They* tune into it." He snapped up the lab kit. "But, just because it's in you doesn't mean that it works. Remember that, Smoke."

He nodded. "I've made it this far. I'll be fine."

Sidney yawned. She had another dozen questions that she'd like to ask, but she'd had enough. Their knowledge of the Glow impressed her. How did they know about it? What kind of access did they have? She had a last name now, and it was time she learned a little bit about them. "It's been a pleasure," she said, picking up her things. "But I'm going home to get some shut eye." She opened up the door. "I'll swing by tomorrow, assuming you'll still be here."

"Uh, bye," Sam said, waving her fingers with a funny look on her face.

Smoke and Guppy weren't even looking as Sid closed the door behind her. She felt a load fall from her shoulders when she fired up the Hellcat's engine. She needed space. Time to settle herself. She wanted to look into a few things on her own. Who they were and what the Glow was. She dropped the car into gear and sped off down the road. *Need to make sure they aren't all full of bullshit.*

❀ ❀ ❀

Sidney tossed all night in her sleep and woke up with a slight headache. Fully dressed, she sat on the sofa watching the TV and sipping coffee. The local news was on. She laughed a little. The lead anchor wore a burgundy tie and had a caterpillar moustache. *What a clown. I bet everyone's seen the movie but him.*

She soaked it in for almost thirty minutes, getting updates on traffic and weather before she turned the TV off. It was a habit, watching the news, but Guppy's words gave her another perspective that she hadn't given much thought to before. *Plenty of conspiracies, so little proof. Or is there?* She took a seat behind her laptop at the counter and punched in her password. Her FBI mailbox had a few canned messages and something else.

Yes!

Her shadow authorization access had come through. She began clicking through various websites, setting up passwords and entering authorization codes. After about thirty minutes of answering security questions to various sites, she sat back in her seat.

Who shall I look up first?

Being an agent of the FBI, there wasn't much you couldn't look up about an ordinary citizen. It came with the job. But any inquiries fed into the system, and those checks were reviewed by someone else in the agency. She didn't want anyone else knowing what they were doing. *I wonder what database Sam is hacking? Crap, I didn't get her last name. Way to go, Agent Shaw.* She typed Gilligan Guppy into the database.

Guppy's face, social security number, and birthday popped up. His work history was nothing out of the ordinary. If anything, it was too ordinary.

"Service Manager at Walmart?" She shook her head. "He's not working at Walmart. Auto Zone maybe." She felt a little guilty doing research on him. Clicking from link to link and place to place, she found everything she could. It was clean, all the way down to the bank records and credit cards. Guppy was just an ordinary citizen living his life day by day. Not married. Next of kin all deceased. "That's odd."

She gently rubbed her aching shoulder that itched a little and took a sip of coffee. She thought about some of the things that Guppy had said. "They only show you what they want to show you." *Huh, they could be FBI for all I know. Great.* She plugged in Angi Harlow. Nothing popped up remotely close to the pictures she'd seen.

Knock. Knock. Knock.

The knocking sounded familiar. *Smoke?* She made her way over and looked through the key hole. A courier in a blue uniform stood on the other side, holding a package. She opened the door.

"Are you Sidney Shaw?" he said with frosty breath. He had freckles, and dark red hair spilled out from underneath his cap that was almost pulled over his eyes.

"Yes."

"Special delivery. Sign here, please."

She eyed the box. The cardboard was solid black. "Does it say who it's from?"

He looked at his digital pad. "Mmmmm, an M. Carlson." He shrugged. "I guess you weren't expecting it. Do you want me to return it?"

"No." She signed the pad and took the package. "I know him. Thanks."

"Have a nice day."

She closed the door in his face, staring at the package. There weren't any postage markings on it at all, but a letter was slipped inside a sealed plastic bag stuck to the box. She shook the box. It had some heft to it. She put her ear to it. *Is that ticking?* Her fingers went numb. She closed her eyes and put her ear to it again. *Phew, nothing.* She peeked back through the keyhole. The courier's van motored out of the parking lot. It was black with white stripes along the side. The lettering on the van read Jebco Deliveries, in red.

She set the box down on the coffee table and took a seat on her couch. She tore the letter off and opened it up. The typed letter read.

Agent Shaw:

Looking forward to meeting you soon. I'll let you know when I'm available. In the meantime, take advantage of the contents of this package. You'll need it ... soon.

Regards,

Mal Carlson

CHAPTER 21

"**W**HAT COULD THIS BE? AND who is Mal Carlson?" she said, opening the briefcase-sized package. Inside was a black case with a latch on it. There was a note attached. It read:

Hold onto this case. I'll need it back.

"Sure thing, buddy."

She clicked open the clasp and lifted the lid. The inside was filled with black foam, like many gun cases she had seen. There was a knife in a case about eight inches long. The grooves in the hilt perfectly fit her hand. The curved edge was as keen as anything she'd seen. In another slot were two loaded fifteen-round magazines, fit for her FBI-issued weapon.

"Interesting."

She pushed out a bullet. It had a unique full-metal casing that had a blue sheen to it. The tip was pointed and tipped with a tiny red dot. Sidney had seen plenty of ammo in her days. It reminded her of a tracer round, but it was still unlike any ballistic she'd ever seen.

"Guess I won't know until I shoot it."

In the middle of the case was a folded shirt that felt like a thin sweater of some kind. It was dark gray, tightly woven, and flexible, if a little heavy. Its waffle texture reminded her of long underwear. Dark copper stripes ran up and down the middle and around the arms.

"What the heck is this for?"

The longer she stared at the shirt, the more compelled she felt to put it on. *Why not?* She took off Smoke's T-shirt and slipped this on like a second skin. The flexible top hugged the curves of her body. It felt warm, almost like a part of her. It breathed well too. *I like it.* Her body became more alive. The throbbing inside her stitched shoulder eased. She felt energized. There was something inside the fabric. *Copper or magnets maybe.* She picked the knife up. *Hmmm?* She ran it across the sleeve of her arm. It didn't cut the odd fabric.

"Wow."

Inside the box she noticed a pair of pants, the same make-up as the shirt. She shrugged, switched out of her jeans, and slipped them on. Her blood tingled. She wanted to run a hundred miles.

What is this stuff made of?

The heightened sense of her body was exhilarating but natural. She slipped her clothes on over the outfit and laced on her boots.

Time to go ... somewhere.

She snapped up the briefcase, grabbed a new bag out of the closet and transferred her gear, got her travel mug, and headed out the door. The bite of the icy air was muted by the suit, nipping at only her fingers and nose. She was firing up the engine of her car from the outside when she noticed a man walking down the sidewalk with his hands inside his jacket pockets. Her eyes met his. It was Smoke.

"Ah, I see you got one too," he said, looking at the briefcase. He jogged in place with high knees. "Tell me you got a suit too. It's amazing. I've heard about them but never believed they existed." He stretched his arms. "Man, I feel great in this."

An image of Smoke in only the suit flashed through her mind. *I bet you look great too.* "Did you drive?" she said, opening her door.

"No."

"And Sam and Guppy are?"

"Doing their thing." He rubbed his hands together. "Do you have any more coffee inside?"

Don't tempt me in close quarters. "No. Get in, let's go." She got in.

Smoke eased in beside her. He had a piece of paper in his hand. "Some places we might want to check out first. Philanthropies tied into Drake." He set it on the dash. "Fat Sam and Guppy are on it too."

She put the car in reverse, started to ease out, stopped, and shoved the car back into park. She turned and looked at him. "What are you doing here?"

"What do you mean?"

"You? Here? Now? Tell me why."

"I just happened to be in the —"

"Don't bullshit me!" She wasn't sure why she let it out, but it felt good. "The man I read about in your file is a lone wolf. Independent. Bucks authority. But here you are, completely out of the ordinary. What are you up to?"

"I'm changing my ways."

"I don't buy that."

"Why does it matter?" He slid a knife out of his jacket. It was like the one she'd received. "Did you get one of these, too? It's made of a unique steel alloy I haven't figured out yet."

"Listen, dude. I can't count on you one minute and not the next. I need you to be accountable."

"Well, I'm here," he put the knife away, "so I'm accountable. And being unpredictable is kind of my thing."

The muscles in her jaw tightened. The military and the Bureau were all about teamwork and reliability.

"I know what you're thinking, Agent Shaw. 'The machine breaks down, we break down.' Man, we used to love to watch that movie. Good stuff." He cleared his throat. "But too much blind loyalty also creates vulnerabilities. The element of surprise can escape us, and sometimes that's the edge you need when taking on an unknown enemy."

It made sense, but it wasn't satisfying. "Fair enough." She put the car back into reverse.

Smoke put his hand on top of hers and looked her in the eye. "You can count on me."

His words seemed to have a deeper meaning to them that penetrated her to the heart. She swallowed. "We'll see."

CHAPTER 22

THEY SPENT THE BETTER PART of the morning and afternoon chasing down dead ends. Restaurants. Hotels. A couple of local stores. Angi Harlow was a gorgeous woman. Her stunning looks would make an impression on anyone. Not one person was forthcoming with anything. No surprise. Not a flinch.

Sitting in traffic waiting on a stoplight, Sidney sighed.

"It's only the first day," Smoke said. He drummed on his knees. "In time something will reveal itself."

"What leads did Sam and Guppy take?"

"Probably the good ones."

"Great."

"I'm joking."

"No," she said, "you're probably right. I'd do the same thing." Her stomach groaned.

"I know a great place nearby called Pancakes and Butterflies."

"What?" She looked at him. "Really?"

"Yes." He shook his head. "No."

"Why'd you say that anyway?" The moment in the clutches of AV the werewolf popped in her mind.

"It was a joke. Sorry. I shouldn't have brought it up."

She could still feel the wolfman's hot breath on her neck, her will caving in. "No, it's fine. Your annoying words saved that day. It wouldn't be so bad to talk about it, maybe."

Smoke straightened up in his chair. "Really?"

Why not. After all, I don't know a lot of other people who have met a werewolf. "Let's check off the last place on the list, and then we'll go grab some chow."

"Sounds good to me. Chowabunga."

Sidney shook her head. *Please stop saying things like that.*

The last stop was the Hilton Renaissance Hotel. She pulled the car into the front. Smoke rolled down his window and flagged the valet. "I'll handle this."

"Sweet ride." The valet was Indian, pleasant faced with a broad smile. "Lots of horsepower. It would be my pleasure to park it."

"We aren't checking in." Smoke held up a picture. "Have you seen this woman?"

The valet's eyes lit up. He said, "Have I seen her. I'm pretty sure I have. You can't forget a face like that. Wowza!"

Sidney looked at Smoke, shaking her head. *I can't believe it. I've been asking questions all day to nothing, and he only asked one.*

Smoke shrugged.

"This is serious," Sidney said.

"I'm being serious," said the valet.

"When's the last time you saw her?" Smoke said.

"Can't say for sure," the valet replied, rubbing his white-gloved thumb and fingers together.

"Do you mind?" Smoke said to Sidney, "I left all my cash back at home."

"I don't have any cash either. It's the digital age, you know."

"Aw, that's too bad," the valet said. He tipped his cap. "See you later."

Smoke's hand shot out of the window, grabbed the man by his coat collar, and jerked his head inside the car window.

"Hey, man! Hey, Man! Hey!" the guy squirmed. "We can Square up on my phone?"

"Shut it," Smoke growled in his ear. "Now tell me what I want to know, unless you want me to bite your ear off."

Smoke's dark tone put a shiver through Sid. *Morning glory.*

The man went stiff, his eyes boggled in his head. He said, "Like Mike Tyson?"

"Exactly."

Sidney stuck the picture in his face.

"Yes. Yes! That's the bird lady. Very hot. Very hot. Good tipper."

"How long since you last saw her?" Smoke said.

"She like to party. She like to party," the valet sang in a jingle. "And wiggle that thang." He bobbed his head. "Can you let go of me please?"

"No."

The man made a pleading look at Sidney.

"When?" she said.

"Aw, these people are heavy hitters. She's got a serious crew. I'm talking spooky."

Smoke shook him.

"All right. They checked in last night. Went out a couple of hours ago and haven't been back since." He grimaced. "Please don't screw up my uniform. It's all I got, mean guy."

"Where'd they go?" Smoke said.

"Clubbing down the road. Took a black Jaguar. Black wheels rolling behind her. Park City Nights. You know, right? Park City. Park City."

"Never heard of it. Why don't you fill us in?"

"The underground. You know, the old place. I've been there once. They go there. Bad crews. Bad crews."

Smoke glanced at Sidney then said to the valet, "There better be a place, or I'm coming back for your ear."

"You'd really bite it off?"

Smoke held his knife up to the man's eye. "Nope." He pushed the man away.

Sidney accelerated back into the street. "A little dark, don't you think?"

"Didn't have much of a choice without any cash." He eyed his knife. "Besides, a little fear in the belly never hurt anyone. It's better than a knife anyway."

"I just never figured you for the tormenting type."

"Good. Let's keep it that way." He tucked the knife away and pulled something else out. A smart phone. He started texting. "Let's get something to eat."

"Now? We just got a lead."

"I've passed it on," he said, putting the phone away. He patted his belly. "Let's eat."

"No, we're going to pursue this lead first."

"Come on, I don't do so well on an empty stomach. I'm starving. I almost chewed that guy's ear off." He made a sour face. "And that just ain't right."

"No."

"Let Sam and Guppy do their thing. The Drake and their people know we're out here looking for someone. They might know the entire thing. Besides, I have the Glow in me. Let's lay low. When the time is right, we'll do the right thing." He pointed. "Take the next left at the light and head three miles downward. Great steaks and pancakes."

Sidney pushed her blinker down. *Fine.* "I'm only doing this because I was about ready to eat that man's ear too."

Smoke laughed. "You get cranky when you're really hungry, don't you."

"No." *Yes. Mother always said that. Allison too.* "I think it's the suit. It's like I'm burning more energy."

"If you say so. How's the shoulder?"

"Good."

Not much was said after that until they parked and went inside the restaurant. It was located beneath an apartment complex and displayed the modern décor of a restaurant chain. The food smelled good, and being just past dinner time, it was busy. The hostess sat them down in a booth in the corner.

Sidney studied the menu. "I don't see any pancakes."

"That's the dinner menu. They'll have them."

The waiter came over. "Drinks?"

"Water," Sidney said.

"Coke and two orders of pancakes." He glanced at Sidney.

"Uh … just bring me the grilled chicken salad and a cup of tomato Florentine soup."

"Certainly," the waiter said, dropping his pad back in his apron. "I'll be back with your drinks."

Sidney checked her phone. 6:33 pm. *Where does the time go?*

"So," Smoke said, easing back in his chair. "Are you ready to talk about werewolves?"

CHAPTER 23

"**I** HAVEN'T SLEPT THE SAME SINCE," Sidney said, finishing off her salad. "Not bad but not my best. It was getting better, but now after this last incident, I'm not so certain."

"I've never been much of a sleeper," Smoke said. He'd almost finished off his second stack of pancakes and downed his third Coke. "I think you're right."

"About what?"

"These suits. They burn more calories or something. I'm still hungry." He jabbed his fork into the flapjacks and stuffed them in his mouth. "Not that I mind eating."

He had a drop of syrup on his grizzled chin. It didn't bother her. Nothing about the way he ate or drank bothered her at all. It was odd. There were plenty of things she'd find to pick a person apart. But not Smoke. Not yet. Something about his raw nature was enjoyable to watch. "Maybe you aren't getting it all in your mouth." She pointed at his chin.

"Oh." He wiped off his chin with the cloth napkin. "Sorry. How barbaric of me."

"Barbarians don't use utensils."

"You're right." Smoke dropped his fork, picked up the rest of the pancakes with his hand, and stuffed them in his mouth, grunting. "Mmmm."

Why did you have to do that? Everything had gone pretty well up to that point. They'd discussed the werewolf, the deaders, and the Drake. It was all a common bond only the two of them shared, and it was comforting. Almost like a good date, and she hadn't been on one in a long time. *And now this?* Her expression didn't hide her disappointment.

"What?" Smoke said, trying to clean off his sticky hands. "It's a joke. Just lightening up the mood a little. You're looking at me like this is a bad date or something." He set down the napkin. "I don't think this is going to do it. I'll be back."

She watched him go, gently shaking her head. *Lighten up, Sid.* She'd been around plenty of frivolous men in the past. Silly gestures hadn't bothered her before, at least not during her time in the military. But in the Bureau, things were always serious. *Screw it. I'm under shadow cover now. No one else is around.* She took her fork and stabbed his last bit of pancake and stuffed it in her mouth. *Oh, that's good.* She swallowed down part of his Coke. *And that's good too. Man I wish I could put it down like he does.*

The waiter showed and said, "Can I take this out of your way?"

"Yes. Take all of it, and I'm ready for the check."

Smoke returned just as the waiter was taking everything away. "I wasn't finished," he said, taking a seat. "Or was I?"

"You were," she said.

"Fine. Well, I return bearing good news."

"Really, from a trip to the restroom?"

"It's a text from Sam." He held up his phone.

It read:

She's here and this is freaky. Laterz.

"There's a picture." He pulled it up. The image was dark, but the distinct features of Night Bird's face were defined well enough. She was dancing in a mish mash of people.

"Who parties like that at this time of day?" Sidney said.

"Freaky people."

The waiter came back and set down the check. "I'll pick it up when you're ready."

"I got it," Smoke said, reaching into his back pocket and producing a thin wallet. He removed some bills and handed them to the man. "Keep the change."

You butthole! "I thought you said you didn't have any cash."

"It slipped my mind."

"Right."

"Besides, I was saving it for our dinner."

"You tormented that poor guy."

"I gave the otherwise boring man something to talk about." He put his wallet away and got up. "We can go back and tip him if you feel so bad about it. You're driving."

She narrowed her eyes on him and sighed through her nostrils. "Let's just go."

That sat in their car across the street, eyeing the entrance to the club. Every five to ten minutes or so, an expensive car or limo would pull in front of an older office building. They'd been staking it out for over an hour.

"Here comes another one," Smoke said, using a small pair of binoculars. A dark green limousine pulled alongside the curb across the busy street.

A burly bouncer with almost as much neck as head opened the limo door and escorted three well-dressed people, a short man and two women in furs, into the alleyway that was shared with the next-door building.

"Is that all rich people do, party day and night?"

"I wouldn't know," Smoke said.

"Me neither. Though I have been at a few federally funded banquets, helping out the Secret Service."

"Ah, the Secret Servants," Smoke said with a nod.

"No, Secret Service."

"That's what I said, Secret Servants."

Here we go. Conspiracy time. "I have plenty of good friends in the service."

"Hah, that's a lie."

"No it isn't."

"It is, because I don't think you have *plenty* of friends of any kind."

True. "Fine. Acquaintances."

Smoke continued. "Unless you've spent time at home with them, you don't really know them."

"All right, all right. I don't want to get into this right now. But those guys and gals are willing to take a bullet for someone, so I'm willing to give them the benefit of the doubt."

"Touché."

Thank you, Lord. "So, mister bounty hunter, what's your next move: wait for them to leave, or go in there?"

"What do you think?"

"I'm giving you *free range* on this one, but if you'd rather I didn't—"

"Sam sent me the password," he said.

"We've been sitting here an hour when all along you had the password." *And why do you text with Sam all the time and not Guppy?*

"I didn't figure you'd let the valet park your car."

True. "Or you could give me the password and I'll go inside alone," she said.

"I was thinking it should be the other way around."

"No. I trust the valet more at this point."

Smoke gave her a look.

She gave him one back. "So what's the plan to bring her in once we're inside, bounty hunter?"

"We isolate her from the pack."

"Pack? I don't like the sound of that."

"I'm not worried." Smoke lowered his binoculars from his eyes. "Somehow I don't think someone that calls themselves Night Bird is a werewolf."

"She's on the Black Slate. I have a feeling she must be something. I'm not exactly eager to find out what that is."

"Don't worry. You can count on me. We'll take her the other way out. Easy peasy."

"Why don't we take this other way in?" she said. "I'm assuming Sam and Guppy told you where it is?"

"Now you're catching on." He showed a little teeth. "But there's a catch."

"I'm listening."

"We can't go in with any weapons."

CHAPTER 24

P ARK CITY NIGHTS. THE CLUB was expensive, yet seedy all the same. Sidney and Smoke hung back at the bar. The mirrored cabinet stocked with top shelf liquors gleamed. The wine glasses and goblets were fine crystal. The music that thumped in the room was loud but manageable for conversation.

"Would you like something to drink?" said the bartender. He was a lean black man, white shirt and black bowtie. A very clean look about him.

"Edmund Fitzgerald," Sidney said to him.

"Make it two," Smoke added.

The bartender gave them a funny look. "Coming right up." He made his way down to the end of the bar, opened up the cooler, and returned with two beer bottles with sinking ships on them. He removed the caps. "Enjoy."

Sidney took a taste.

"Interesting choice," Smoke said. His Adam's apple rolled as he gulped. "Ah. Much better than the beer they make in prison."

"Don't get carried away."

"Who, me?"

She eased up onto the stool, eyeing the dance floor. Lithe hard-bodied women danced in gleaming jewels and fine linens, their movements seductive and erotic. Sidney's throat tightened. There was something ancient and fascinating in how they moved. Almost like a ritual. *Geez.*

"I don't see her yet," Smoke said in her ear.

It brought her back to reality. She scanned the rest of the room. Half-naked women in bronze bird cages cavorted and grinded amid men huddled in conversation. The sinister atmosphere crept into Sid's bones. Stirred her soul. These were not the people of the streets she'd sworn her protection to. They were something else.

Smoke bobbed his chin to the beat. "Man, this place is filled with evil boogers. It's like I can smell it. Want to dance?"

"No," she said, taking a sip. *I want to drink.*

"I think it would be better than sitting here like a couple of toads. Come on. Show me your moves. I'm sure you have at least one."

"Oh, I've got more than one. You'll just have to take my word on that." She spied the dance floor. The women frolicked and shimmied all over the men and one another. Shameless. Inviting. "I've never seen people dance like that so early in the day before."

"It's after midnight somewhere, so I guess that's why they're letting it all hang out. Before long I bet they scream and shout."

"I bet you'd like that."

Smoke shrugged his brows and finished his beer.

A deeply tanned muscle man in a sliver of a gothic T-shirt walked by. There was a tattoo on his neck with a rising black sun on it.

"We've definitely got the right place," Smoke said, watching the man walk away. "The stink of Drake is all over it."

On the dance floor, the sultry dark and dusky women and their partners parted on the floor. A magnificent woman walked into the center. *Angi Harlow.* She wore a long silver dress trimmed in feathers and sequins with a plunging neck line. The curves of her body were without flaw. Her eyebrows sparkled with glitter. The music changed into something dark, passionate, and ceremonial. *What is going on here?*

"Night Bird is one fine lady. It's a shame she's a soul-sucking criminal," Smoke said, taking his last sip of beer. "Makes me thirsty."

Sidney had been to a Persian wedding years back and enjoyed the incredible dances. This was like that but with ten times the passion and filled with erotic steam. *Morning Glory. They're gonna rip their clothes off at any moment.* She took a long drink. Smoke nudged her out of her trance.

"Four o'clock," he said, eyeing the edges of the dance floor. "And eight o'clock. Huh, rock around the clock it seems."

Goons. Bullish men in dark suits and glasses stood around the edge of the dance floor with their arms crossed over their chests. *She really does have a lot of henchmen.* There was the bulge of a concealed gun underneath each man's jacket. Sidney knew the type. A lot of former athletes and vets who liked the spicy benefits of the macho life turned mercenary. It reminded her of a movie scene with Columbia drug lords. *The Night Bird Cartel. How nice.*

"Hey," said the man sitting beside her. "Hey, gorgeous. You want some?"

He's wasn't handsome, but his clothing and watch were exquisite. He had five lines of cocaine lined up on the bar. He seemed familiar.

"No, thanks."

He grabbed her arm. "Come on. I insist."

"No, thanks," she said, plucking his fingers away.

"Nobody tells me no, lady." He grabbed at her. She backed into Smoke. Two large bouncers appeared and locked their arms around her accoster. They picked him up off the floor. "No, no, I'm sorry guys," the man pleaded. "I was just flirting with the lady!" They escorted him out of sight.

"Interesting," Sid said, watching the bartender wipe the cocaine off the counter. She turned her attention back to the dance floor. Hips and shoulders swaying, Night Bird had her hungry eyes fastened on Smoke. One of her goons on the edge of the dance floor approached.

The bulldog of a man was bald and wore heavy rings on his fingers. "Night Bird wants to dance with you, fella," he said in a thick accent.

"I'm with someone," Smoke said, "and I'm not the best dancer."

The man, broader than Smoke but not quite as tall, cracked his neck from side to side and said, "Get out there now, before I put all those pretty teeth out."

"I—"

"Bub," the goon said, "she ain't a patient lady, and I'm not a patient man."

"Sure," Smoke said, setting his bottle on the bar. "I'm going." He eased his way around the thug, headed to the dance floor, and took Night Bird's extended hand in his.

Sidney felt flames shoot through her as the woman's hand caressed his back and went over his butt and down the backs of his legs. *Damn Dirty Bird!*

CHAPTER 25

AFTER ABOUT TWO MINUTES OF bumping and grinding, the music changed to something slower and more seductive. Ears red underneath her dark locks, Sidney was impressed with how Smoke handled himself. *He's a decent dancer. I'll give him that.* The strapping man towered over the men and women on the starlit dancefloor, except for Night Bird. In her heels, she was almost as tall as he. As the music slowed, the exotic woman wrapped her arms around his waist and drew him in close.

Can't wait to see you in your bird cage, whore.

As Sid finished her thoughts, she found Night Bird's eyes on hers. The woman's mysterious gaze was inviting as she nestled her head against Smoke's muscular chest. Like a flash of the camera, she winked. Sidney's head spun a little, and she bumped back into the bar. She felt those icy spiders crawling over the goosebumps on her arms.

What was that?

It was that same seductive power that AV had over her, paralyzing her reason and opening the gates to her lusts. She took a long draw from her beer and looked away.

Get it together, Sid. Butterflies and Pancakes!

It didn't help that Smoke seemed to be enjoying himself. He smiled as his lips moved in conversation. Sidney wanted to know what he was saying to her and what she was saying to him. She realized she needed to distract herself. She started counting. The guests. The entertainers. The staff, bouncers, and most importantly, Night Bird's bodyguards.

Eight thugs. Great.

Extracting their mark wouldn't be easy. All of the men were armed with pistols or possibly small Uzis. A single elevator, the one they had taken, led up and out. By it was posted a guard who was almost as wide as the elevator itself. She turned and motioned to the bartender.

"Another beer from the lakes, my lady friend?"

"No thanks. Um," she smiled and wiggled up to him. "I was kinda curious. What happened to that guy snorting all of those lines? I feel bad for him."

"Don't feel bad for that guy. He's a real jerk, a good tipper, but a jerk. He should have known better."

"I just don't want to see anyone get hurt. I'm a peacemaker. He'll be all right, won't he?"

The bartender's eyes drifted toward the kitchen doors. "Lady, don't ask questions that you don't want the answers to, especially in a place like this." He leaned closer. His tone became grim. "You're new, so I'm going to cut you a break and pretend you didn't ask me anything. Do you understand?'

Sidney swallowed and widened her eyes. "Sure." *You've given me all I need.* "Uh, where's the powder room?"

He pointed. "That way."

"Thanks."

Passing the kitchen on her way to the bathroom, she slowed and cracked open the windowless door. About ten people were busy at work in white outfits and red aprons. A waitress in a feathered cocktail dress bustled by. Making a quick scan of the area, Sidney noticed a service elevator in the rear. Perfect. A man was seated by it in a metal folding chair. His suit jacket was draped over the back, and he had two pistols strapped under his heavy shoulders. A shotgun rested in his lap. *Not perfect.*

She headed for the restroom and glanced at Smoke, who still danced comfortably in Angi's clutches. *Horndog.* The restroom was long, with many stalls crafted in white marble stone that rose from the floor to the ceiling. Sidney walked by a half dozen sinks in front of a huge vanity mirror trimmed in cherry wood. Beside them sat a small lithely built woman in a feathered mask. A basket of toiletries, same as those on the sinks, sat on her lap.

Weird. Too weird.

Sidney took the faucet farthest from the woman in the bird mask and turned the water on.

"Ow!"

The water was steaming hot. She glanced at the woman, who had her head cocked to the side. The black bird eyes faced her.

Get used to it. Ignore it.

She checked her face. Her make-up was a far cry from what she'd observed on the other women. Her clothes were far from up to snuff either.

How out of place must we be?

She washed her hands and had begun to rinse them off when the moaning started.

"Uh, uh, uh …"

A man and woman were cavorting in one of the stalls. Their moans got louder, the rollicking more pronounced. Sidney took a deep breath and adjusted her hair. The little attendant appeared with a steaming cloth on a plate. Sidney plucked it up with her fingers.

"Thanks."

She wiped her neck down. *I think it's going to take more than this to get the filth off of me.* She dropped it on the plate, and the little attendant walked away and put the washcloth in a bin then returned with a basket of toiletries. Sidney took a closer look at them. *Geez! Some of this stuff is a hundred dollars an ounce.* She picked out two tiny perfumes and a small shampoo bottle and crammed them in her pocket. The attendant's bird eyes were glued on her.

"Aw, you won't tell."

Sidney felt a strange compulsion overcome her, staring at the tiny woman in the mask. Something was not right. It creeped down her spine. Looking deep into the eyes, she stretched out her fingers toward the mask. The figure didn't move away. She glanced at the tiny fingers holding the basket. They reminded her of her niece, Megan. *No. Not another child.* She started to pull the mask up.

Wham!

The attendant jerked away at the sound of a stall door banging open. A giggling woman and a man with devilish good looks staggered by. Tucking his shirt in and buckling his belt, he winked at Sid and said, "Good evening."

The stall woman adjusted her skintight dress, slung her bra over her shoulder, and added as they strutted out, "Maybe next time you can join us?"

Sidney stood alongside the sinks shaking her head, thinking, *Ew, they didn't even wash up after that. Now I know why they're called the filthy rich.* Giving the little attendant no more thought, she headed back out into the club. Making her way back to the bar and spying the dance floor, she noticed something out of place. Smoke and Night Bird were gone.

CHAPTER 26

S MOKE AND NIGHT BIRD WEREN'T the only ones gone from the dance floor. The bodyguards had vanished too. *Those oxen shouldn't be too easy to hide.* She cut through the tables and patrons until she found herself on the other side of the room. Several well-concealed alcoves dotted the back. The heavy curtains were drawn on most of them. Sidney got a peek inside the closest one. Girls. Men. Sex. Drugs. She moved down the row.

Ah, follow the goons.

A pair of body guards stood on either side of the alcove at the end. The other guards were spread out nearby.

Play along, Sid. Play along.

She weaved her way toward them showing a dreamy look in her eye. She said to the nearest bodyguard, "Have you seen my friend? Tall guy. Kind of handsome?" She added a hiccup. "He was just dancing with that gorgeous lady. I want to party with them."

"Just move along," the man said. "If Night Bird wants you, she'll let you know, and I ain't heard nothing about her wanting you. Consider it a good thing. So move along now, prissy."

I am so gonna take you out first, you nose-pierced jerk.

"But," she said, batting her eyelashes, "can I at least go in and say hi?"

"No." he looked her up and down. "But, maybe on my break, if you do me a favor, I can work something out." He patted her ass.

I hate this guy. I hate this place.

"What did you have in mind?" she said.

"Well," his eyes widened. He touched his finger to his ear and cocked his head. He looked back at Sidney. "Huh, seems you have the okay to go in." He leaned in closer and whispered in her ear. His breath was heavy with cigarettes, but his soft words were perfectly clear. "That's too bad. I was doing you a favor." He pulled the heavy maroon curtain back and stepped aside. "Nice meeting you, lady."

Doing me a favor? I don't see how.

Sidney gave the man a funny look and drifted inside. Smoke sat back in a comfortable booth looking as innocent as a Boy Scout. A small round table offered drugs and drinks. Night Bird was beside him, glued to his hip. One long leg was draped over his, while her free hand toyed with the hair around his ears.

"Is this your little friend, John?" Angi said, offering a playful smile. "She's tall for a woman. Finely crafted. I like that. What is your name, dearie?"

"Sidney."

"Hmph," Night Bird said, "fitting. So, why don't you come and join us." She fanned her free arm out toward the other three people in the room. Two women's hard bodies were only clad in feathery lingerie. A chiseled man with long brown locks and the looks of a Chippendale dancer sat drinking a bottled beer in only cutoff sequined trousers.

I think I've seen enough.

"I think it's time to go, *John*," Sidney said, lifting her brows.

"Oh, dearie," Night Bird said, squeezing Smoke's thigh, "he's not going anywhere. But maybe you can have him back tomorrow. He's such a fine drink of water. I can't wait to bathe with him."

Sidney's chest tightened. "John, it's time to go."

Smoke didn't reply. Instead, he sat in a daze.

Aw, crap! She's done something to him.

"You're starting to bother me, dearie," Night Bird said. "I think it's time you moved along." She glanced at the scantily clad man. "Be a dear, Bulldog, and escort our lady friend out."

The well-defined man's bulging muscles flexed as he stood up.

Sidney laughed. He was maybe five and a half feet tall, and she towered over him. "He's cute, but really," she said, staying him with her hand. "Please, I'll show myself out. I don't want you to hurt yourself"—she glanced at his pants—"Bulldog." She backed up toward the door. "John, it's time to go. Pancakes and Butterflies."

"Pancakes and Butterflies?" the woman said. "My dear, what on earth are you talking abou—"

Night Bird slumped forward and crashed through the table.

Bulldog growled at Sidney and closed in with clutching fingers.

In a flash, Sidney put everything she had into a roundhouse kick that broke Bulldog's jaw. He collapsed on the floor and didn't move. The two women in the room started giggling, and one lit up a joint for the other.

"I take it you have a plan to get out of here," Smoke said. He had Night Bird draped over his shoulder.

"You drugged her?"

"It's an unethical method, but effective," Smoke said, staring at the curtains. "Every situation is different. So, did you disable all the bodyguards?"

"What? Disable them? Exactly how would I do that? I don't even have a gun."

"You take one of theirs."

Sidney stood by the curtain, felt the material, and listened. It was amazing how quiet the room was on account of the heavy fabric. She could barely make out the music. "I have an exit plan at least. That's more than you have, *John*."

One of the girls started clapping. She said, "I like this game. What is it?"

"Hey," the other girl said, taking a toke. "What happened to Bulldog? And why do you have Night Bird over your shoulder, new guy?"

"Where's the other exit?" Smoke said. His eyes flashed, and his tone was urgent.

"Why? What are you going to do?"

Suddenly, one of the girls let out an ear-splitting shriek.

Smoke shrugged his shoulders at Sid. "Run for it!"

CHAPTER 27

Oneof the bodyguards stepped inside the curtains. Smoke plowed over the man and kept going. Sidney didn't stick around. She burst through the curtains just as the second bodyguard lowered his gun on Smoke's back. She chopped him in the neck and twisted the weapon free of his grip. She turned.

Aw, crap!

The other four bodyguards were up, weapons drawn and moving. Alert men. Formidable. They didn't see her coming. She squeezed the trigger.

Pop! Pop! Pop! Pop!

Two men collapsed, clutching at their legs and crying out in pain. Sidney jumped over them and sprinted after Smoke and his assailants, out into the larger room of the club. That was when the music stopped and the screaming started. A sea of bodies came to life and moved in a wave of panic. A heavyset woman in a sparkly tube top crashed into Sidney, knocking her to the floor.

Hell's bells!

She scrambled to her feet and shoved her way through the throng of sweaty bodies toward the kitchen door. Two bodyguards disappeared inside. She was almost there when another woman grabbed her, yelling, "Help me! Help me!"

Sidney slapped her in the face, widening the woman's eyes. "Help yourself, halfwit!" She stormed toward the kitchen door and heard gunshots crack out on the other side.

Blaat-at-at! Blaat-at-at! Blaat-at-at!

The kitchen help dashed out as machine-gun fire ripped through the metal pots and stainless cabinets. Sid went in low, spied a man blasting away with his back to her, and fired.

Pop! Pop!

He collapsed bleeding on the floor.

Blaat-at-at! Blaat-at-at! Blaat-at-at!

She dove behind a rolling counter and peeked underneath. *Feet, feet, where are you?* She saw a pair of filthy sneakered feet shuffling over the floor tiles and took aim.

Pop!

"Ow! Sonuvabitch! My foot!" His shooting became wild.

Blaat-at-at! Blaat-at-at! Blaat-at-at! Blaat-at-at! Blaat-at-at! Blaat-at-at! Blaat-at-at! Blaat-at-at! Blaat-at-at!

"I'm gonna kill you! I'm gonna kill you good!" said the bodyguard, spraying the room with bullets. "Where are you! Where the hell are you!"

Blaat-at-at! Blaat-at-at! Blaat-at-at! Blaat-at-at! Blaat-at-at! Blaat-at-at! Blaat-at-at! Click. "Aw, hell."

Whop! Thud!

From under the counter, Sidney saw the man fall flat on the floor. *Whew!*

"Sid? Come on!" Smoke yelled out.

She popped up and saw him. "What about the guy at the elevator?"

Ka-Blam! Ka-Blam!

"You talking about me?" said a hard voice. "Come on. Take my elevator."

Ka-Blam! Ka-Blam!

"Shoot him, Sid!"

"Yeah! Go ahead! Try and shoot me!" The man started clearing the kitchen aisles, one shotgun blast at a time.

Ka-Blam! Ka-Blam! Ka-Blam!

Sidney scurried from one side of the aisle to the other and got a bead on the man. She took a knee and fired center mass.

Pop! Pop! Pop! Pop! Click.

The big fella teetered backward into the counter, jostling the shot-up pots and pans. "Oof," he said. "That stung. Good thing I'm best friends with Kevlar." He snarled and pulled his two pistols out. Lowered the barrels on her. "Your elevator's going down, lady!"

Sidney dove down the aisle.

Blam! Blam! Blam! Blam!

"Where'd you go, little rabbit?"

BLam! Blam! Blam!

Pinned down with nowhere to go, she crouched behind the counter. *Think of something, Sid. Think!*

"Last call, you squirrely little bitch!" A hail of bullets ripped through the counter.

Blam! Blam! Blam! Blam! Blam!

Bong!

The gunshots stopped.

Bong?

"Sid, are you coming?"

She glanced over the counter. Smoke was standing in the elevator, Night Bird still in tow. A huge frying pan was in his hand. He tossed it out on the floor with a clatter. She got up and ambled over. A bullet grazed her ankle.

Inside the elevator, Smoke said, "You all right?"

She pressed the button going up and glared at him.

More bodyguards spilled into the room and rushed the door, which hadn't yet started to close. Smoke filled the doorway, cradling Night Bird in his arms. "I wouldn't shoot if I were you."

The men's itchy trigger fingers froze. A few eternal seconds went by, and finally the doors closed.

"You're an idiot," Sidney said.

"Me, what did I do?"

"You started a date in the middle of a mission."

"I just went with the flow. Sometimes the best plan is to let things happen and strike when there's an opening."

"Oh, you had an opening all right," she said, looking at the woman in his arms. "A pretty big one."

"Hey, I'm dedicated to the mission, whatever it takes," he finished with a wry smile.

"This isn't On Her Majesty's Secret Service, and you aren't James Bond."

"Don't be a Moneypenny." He glanced at her ankle. "Looks like you're going to need some of my services again."

"It's barely a flesh wound."

The elevator came to a stop.

"Here," Smoke said, handing Night Bird over to Sid, "hold her."

As soon as the elevator doors parted, his hands snaked out and jerked in a man carrying a pistol. He slammed the man into the back wall and snatched up his gun. "Switch me." He hefted Night Bird over his shoulder and gave Sid the gun.

Outside the elevator, they went down the service ramp that led outside. A cold rain was pouring down. After splashing down the street, they raced up the sidewalk, crossed over the intersection, and ran to the parking spot where the Hellcat waited.

"Hurry," Sid said, opening up the door, eyeing the valet station to the club across the street. The husky bodyguard was talking into his wrist as he scanned the streets.

Smoke stuffed Night Bird in the back seat. "Let's go," he said, hopping into the passenger seat.

"Stop! Stop!" The bodyguard had spotted them. He pulled out his gun. Others came to his aid. "Stop!" *Pop! Pop! Pop!*

Sidney stomped on the gas, and the car sped away. She watched a swarm of angry figures diminish in the rearview mirror and took the next turn down the street. "I better not have any bullet holes in my car!"

"Are you blaming me?" Smoke said.

"You're the one who said to park in the street."

"It was just a suggestion—and a good one, seeing how we're making a clean getaway. You should thank me."

"We'll see after I inspect the Hellcat later." She took out her phone and said, "Call Howard mobile."

A voice grumbled on the other line, "Yeah, Sid?"

"Ted, Night Bird's in custody. Where's the safe spot?"

"Already?" he said.

"Safe spot, Ted. Safe spot."

"Oh, oh, all right. Let me see. Are you on the road?"

"Yes," she said, irritated.

"Okay, keep moving and I'll text you directions. Give me a minute. Bye." He disconnected.

Sid looked over at Smoke, who asked, "What did he say?"

"He's texting directions. It'll be a minute."

A coldness slipped into her body. In the rearview mirror, an image appeared. It was Night Bird leaning over her seat. A strange, somewhat demonic expression was creased in her face. Her lacquered lips parted, and she said in a bewitching voice, "Pardon me, but where are we going?"

CHAPTER 28

TRYING HER BEST TO KEEP her eyes on the road, Sidney said to Smoke, "I thought you sedated her."

"I did," Smoke said, looking back at Night Bird.

The woman leaned forward from the back seat and placed her hands on either side of both headrests. "Sedate me? Ha. I'm immune to your toxins and poisons."

Sid noticed the long fingernails on the woman's hands. There was something unnatural about them. "I see you didn't restrain her either?"

"I didn't feel there was a need," Smoke said. Night Bird was toying with his hair. "She shouldn't have woken up until tomorrow."

"Don't worry," Angi said to both of them, "I won't run. I never run." She eased back into the back seat. "Interesting, a little tight, but cozy." The exotic woman cocked her head in quick shifts and whistled a bird song. Her dark spacey eyes were in another world.

"I think you better restrain her," Sidney said from the corner of her mouth.

Smoke opened the glove box and took out a set of flex cuffs. He twisted his shoulders around toward the back and said, "Do you mind?"

"Oh," Angi said, offering her wrists. "I don't mind at all. I enjoy being tied up. How about you?"

He secured her. "Not so much."

"And what about your uptight friend?" Angi touched Sidney's ear.

Sid jerked away. "Sit back, bird lady."

"Humph." Night Bird eased back and resumed her bird song.

For someone who'd been apprehended, the woman was very much at ease. Not the slightest worry creased her face. *This really isn't right.* Sid's phone buzzed. Directions from Ted appeared, to the safe location. It was twelve miles away. She glanced back at Night Bird. *I can't handle her tweeting another minute longer.* "Hey! Night Bird. Shut your beak."

Night Bird quieted. "No need to be rude. I am capable of mercy, you know."

"What is that supposed to mean?"

Angi let out a frivolous laugh. "You two don't know anything about me, do you?"

"Such as?" Smoke said.

"Blind mice," the woman said. "The innocent can be so delicious." She chirped out a flittering sound. "The Black Slate. I know I'm on that dubious list. You aren't the first to find me, and you won't be the last either." She checked her nails. "I'm not one for hiding."

She's way too confident. I should probably shoot her now.

"So," Night Bird continued, "are you the pair that took down the wolf man? He was such a cock. But I admit, we were impressed. Two mortals taking down the wolf. I would have lost a bundle on that bet, not that money matters." She clapped her hands together. "Good for you."

Not good. Again, someone knew more about what was going on than Sid did. But didn't most criminals? *Keep her talking.*

Smoke beat her to it. "He wasn't so tough. Just bad dog breath walking on hind legs. I look forward to taking out more of them."

"Oh ho!" Angi leaned forward. "I like a man who is cocky. Even a mortal one."

"Everyone is mortal," Sidney chimed in.

"Really?" the woman said. "I know a lot of dead people who are still living, including me. Don't be so sure of yourself … Agent Shaw."

What is she talking about? Sid's fingernails drummed on the wheel. Night Bird had said too many odd things. *Mortals.* She talked as though she was a demi-god or something. But she was so confident when she spoke. Everything she said had the stamp of truth behind it.

And Night Bird, she sat back in her seat with a confident smile, staring out the window. The voluptuous debutante seemed invincible.

Sid stopped at a light and turned the wipers off.

"Huh," Smoke said, looking out the windshield. Large black birds flew across the night sky and landed on the nearby power lines. They squawked at the car. "Are those crows or ravens? I've never seen birds like that fly at night before."

"They do what they're told," Night Bird said. "And they are ravens."

"Aren't they the same?" Sid asked. "Black. Annoying. Ugly."

Angi sneered. Her voice became a hiss. "You had best watch your tongue, little woman. You know not of what you speak."

"No surprise that you know a lot about them," Sidney said, watching Angi in the mirror. "I've heard a lot of people call them rat birds." The light turned green, and they accelerated forward.

Smoke stared out of his window.

This is getting creepy. The birds were following them. Sidney gunned the gas a little more. "Do they like cheese?"

"I can tell you what they don't like," Night Bird said in a very dark tone. "They don't like people."

"Ah," Smoke said, looking inquisitive, "so that's why they crap on my car?"

"Oh, John, please don't you start," Night Bird said. "I've grown fond of you. Of course, I'm always fond of my pets, especially the lab rats. They're so entertaining."

"Lab rats?" Sidney said. They were approaching the safe zone drop.

"Well, it's a bit more of a modern terminology, but every decade or so, a group of fools such as yourselves shows up to take the likes of us down." Night Bird sighed then whistled a dreary tune that was impossible for a human. "We toy with them until we bore of their games. And then we wipe them out."

Sidney's hand slipped to her Glock, inside the door pocket. "So, care to fill us in a little more on who *we* is?" She glanced at the sky. It was cloudy, but no moon was out. "Would that *we* be the Drake criminal network?"

"Such children," Angi said, shaking her head. "I think it's too late for your education. Besides, some things, you are better off not knowing. Your minds aren't ready to comprehend them. But soon enough, the world will be ready. This is just the beginning."

This needs to be the end. As harmless as she seemed, Night Bird's calm cool collectedness was a tad on the frightening side. Sid looked up from the highway and noticed a black helicopter landing in the distance. It was FBI. They landed about a mile off the road at an abandoned truck stop. The tightness in her neck eased. *Good! They can have the bird-loving loon.*

"It seems my escort has arrived. I so hate those flying metal machines," Night Bird said. "So loud, and they smell nasty."

As soon as they pulled into the lot, they were surrounded by agents clad in body armor and armed with M-16 assault rifles.

What is up with all the hardware? Badge out and up, Sidney exited the car. Smoke helped Night Bird out of the back seat.

"This was fun. Too bad we'll never do it again," Night Bird said, leaning on his chest. She sucked her teeth. "I just love the dark and charming kind." Two agents pulled her away and marched her toward the chopper. "Ta ta!"

A sea of ravens landed on the truck stop's roof, on all the cars and trucks, and all over the pavement, pecking and squawking.

Sidney shooed them away from her car. "Get!" She looked around. "Who's the agent in charge?"

A Chinese man in full gear walked up with his rifle slung over his shoulder. He stood eye to eye with her and had a small mole under his left eye. He extended his hand. "Agent Ramsey."

"Do you have any paperwork or anything that needs to be signed off?"

"No. I was just told to get my ass down here ten minutes ago. We rolled off another job to come to this one." Agent Ramsey looked at the chopper. "I was expecting something a lot less fine and a lot more dangerous. Who is she?"

"Huh, well, I guess I can't really tell you that. But thanks for the back-up."

Agent Ramsey touched the microphone in his ear. "Once the bird's out of site, we're all clear." Watching the chopper lift off, he shrugged. "Nice meeting you, Agent Shaw. Nice car too. Be careful you don't get any bird poop on it." He kicked at a raven and walked off.

Sidney eased up alongside Smoke. His gaze hadn't left the chopper. "What do you think, easy peasy?"

He slowly shook his head. "Maybe too easy peasy."

Watching the helicopter drift up and away, Sid's eyes widened. An agent from inside the chopper was plummeting toward the ground. Her heart jumped. "Oh no!"

CHAPTER 29

AGENTS SPRINTED TOWARD THE BODY that had crashed to the ground, but Sidney's eyes remained transfixed on the scene above. The chopper wavered in the air, hung in place for a moment, then spun in a three sixty. Her keen eyes picked up a struggle in the cockpit. A wrestling of bodies.

What on earth is going on?

Another man was hurled out of the chopper doors. "Aaaiiyyeee!"

More agents scrambled in aid then slowed as they gazed up. Something alive emerged from the reeling chopper. A giant bird of some sort.

"My Lord," one agent said, gawping. "Are those wings?"

Among the distant commotion, a bird with the head of a woman dropped from the chopper and into the sky. Like an eagle, the bird-woman clutched a screaming agent in her talons. She soared overhead, making a cackling shriek just one hundred feet above.

"Night Bird's a harpy?" Smoke said, drawing out his pistol.

"A what?" Sid said, taking aim.

Night Bird circled above. Her great wings of black and grey feathers spanned fifteen feet. Everything from her chest down was covered in feathers, and her face was still human. It was radiant but in a dark and supernatural state. Suddenly, she dove and flung the agent from her talons. The screaming man soared head over heels and smashed into the FBI van.

"Run!" Agent Ramsey said, pointing toward the sky. "Take cover! Now!"

The helicopter descended in their direction. Legs churning, Sid sprinted away and took cover behind a parked bus. The chopper plunged into the blacktop.

Boom!

A fiery explosion erupted, spraying the parking lot with bits and pieces of metal. Black birds scattered everywhere, taking to the air in droves and diving down in a black swirl of terror on the other agents. Men and women were flayed, and they screamed.

"Come on," Smoke said, scraping Sidney off the ground and onto her feet. "Let's move!"

Wading through the sea of birds, they headed for the car. A shadow glided over them, cackling. It was Night Bird. She snatched another agent off the ground and pumped her wings, racing into the sky, up, up, up, a speck in the dim light. Suddenly, the woman dropped from high above and smashed through the truck-stop roof.

Sidney's stomach turned in the chaos. *This is mad! Hitchcock madness!*

FBI agents fired bullets into the sky. Night Bird weaved and darted with grace and speed, cackling the entire time. In a streak of feathers, she closed in on one man and sliced his throat open. Blood spilled from the gaping wound.

Sidney blasted away at the evil creature as it did aerial somersaults in the sky. Her bullets clipped off some feathers that sprinkled the air. Night Bird and her ravens continued their assault on the other agents, who scrambled for the cover of their cars, plucking the birds from their ankles and faces.

"Strange that they aren't after us," Smoke said, taking cover behind the fuel pumps beneath the canopy. "Keep an eye out for her."

Sidney dashed the sweat from her eyes. Underneath the truck depot's cover, the ravens darted in and out, squawking. She fired at three of them. *Pop! Pop! Pop!* They dropped from the sky.

"Good shooting," Smoke said, "but you might want to save your bullets. There's at least a thousand more to go."

Sidney's mind raced. Her heart pumped from terror. Nature had run wild, and she'd seen at least five agents fall in the chaos. "We have to end this!" She marched out from underneath the oversized canopy and eyed the sky. There was no sign of Night Bird. "Where are you?"

"Looking for me?" said a voice from above. It was Night Bird, standing on top of the roof in her full glory. Her feather-coated body still maintained her voluptuous figure, but her arms were turned into wings with hands, and razor-sharp talons had become her feet. The bird-woman's face was dark and twisted, yet beautiful. "Here I am!"

Sidney fired.

Pop. Pop. Pop.

The spray of bullets hit center mass, drawing a gusty laugh from Night Bird. "Your mortal weapons cannot hurt me." She took flight and disappeared into the sky.

Smoke eased along to her side and said, "Which bullets are you using?"

"Government-issued loads, why?"

Smoke popped the magazine of his weapon and showed her the blue-tipped bullets within. "I think I have a pretty good idea what these are for." He slapped the magazine back in. "If she comes back, let me take the next shot." He scanned the sky.

"Why don't you let me handle that? I think I'm a better shot."

"No," Smoke said, shaking his head, "I don't think so."

"Even if those pretty bullets work," she said, "we're supposed to take her in alive, you know."

"After she killed all those people?" Smoke set his jaw. "I don't think so."

Good point. Good men and women were down. Many dead. Ravens pecked and clawed at their flesh. Capture would be mercy to the murderous fiend.

"And to think I kinda liked birds up until now," he said. "But Night Bird is going down."

"I'm sure they aren't all bad. But I think we need to take her alive. Those are my orders."

In an instant, the ravens stopped squawking and took off in flight, disappearing into the night sky.

"That was weird," Smoke said, surveying the lot.

The surviving agents stumbled around assisting one another. In the distance, Sidney recognized the silhouette of Agent Ramsey. *Good.*

"Oh, I beg your pardon," a familiar sultry voice said. "Are you searching for me?" Night Bird stood near the pumps behind them, back in human form and completely naked. She held out her blood-caked hands and wrists. "I surrender."

Smoke aimed his gun at her chest.

"Please don't," Night Bird said, eyeing his gun. "I don't want any part of your little blue bullets." She touched her ear. "We birds have very keen hearing, you know. I'm glad I was paying attention."

"She's unarmed," Sid said, readying her own weapon.

"She only looks unarmed."

"What's the matter?" Night Bird said, approaching them, "Are my perfect breasts a threat to you?"

"Sorry, Agent Shaw," Smoke said, "but I don't play by your rules." His finger tensed over the trigger.

"Stay where you are, Night Bird," Sid said, stepping between the bounty hunter and the woman. "Smoke, ease up."

Night Bird stopped, lifted her hands above her head, and dropped to her knees. "I'm really sorry about your comrades, but my temper got the best of me when one of them groped me." She offered a coy smile. "I'm over it. I'll play nice from now on."

"Don't trust her, Sid," Smoke said in a growl.

Duty. Despite the carnage, Night Bird had to be taken in alive. Those were the orders. Sid was a good soldier, and she'd follow them as long as she could. She pulled out her flex cuffs and said, "Hands behind your back."

"You are a faithful soldier, Agent Shaw," Night Bird said, placing her hands behind her back, "but you should have listened to your friend." She opened her mouth wide, and an ear-splitting shriek came out.

Sidney's stomach turned and her knees buckled. She hit the pavement and the world started spinning. In front of her, Night Bird rose up, still unleashing the hellish sound. Sid felt bile rise up in her mouth when the horrendous sound stopped. She spat it out.

Ahead, Night Bird's body convulsed and transformed. Muscle, sinew, and bone popped and crackled. Feathers sprouted out. The bird woman shuffled over and grabbed ahold of Smoke. The big man's long limbs trembled. His gun lay inches from his fingers. Sid's ears were ringing. She tried to find her own gun but couldn't move. She couldn't feel her fingers. *Ugh!*

Night Bird was a much bigger bird than she was a woman. She scooped Smoke up in her talons, spread her great wings, took flight, and disappeared into the night sky.

Sidney's mind cried out, "Nooooooooooooooooo!"

CHAPTER 30

HEAD DOWN, SIDNEY SAT INSIDE the Wayfarer's Way restaurant, stirring her spoon in her chicken tortellini soup. It was midday, two days after Night Bird flew off with Smoke. Since the chopper crashed. Since good FBI agents died. *I can't believe he's gone. I can't believe they're all gone.*

She glanced at the front page of the Washington Post on the table. The headline read:

FBI AGENTS PERISH IN TRAGIC TRAINING INCIDENT.

Conspiracies and accusations followed. The community was shocked. Television, Internet, and radio buzzed with theories about terrorist activities. Everyone had a theory. Everyone was wrong.

How many other fabricated stories have I believed before?

There had been plenty of incidents with loose ends she had previously taken at face value but had begun to reconsider. Pan Am's Malaysia Flights. Seal Team Six. Was any of it true? Everything she read in the paper was a lie. What else was?

She rubbed her temple with one hand and took a sip of soup with the other. It tasted funny. Not that she'd eaten much. Everything tasted funny since Night Bird's screech. The jarring sound still echoed in her ears. She could still see Smoke's body being hauled through the air like a carcass. It left her cold inside. She should have trusted him. She should have let him take Night Bird down. Now, he might be gone forever. *I failed him.*

She closed her eyes and sighed. She felt as if something was eating her from the inside out. After the incident, it had taken her thirty minutes to get back on her feet. By the time that happened, help had come, sort of. Men and women covered from head to toe in hazmat-type attire administered aid and whisked the dead away in minutes. It was bizarre. Not of one of them spoke or identified themselves. Agent Ramsey did all of the talking while they patched up his bleeding arm. Sid was in a haze eyeing the sky. By the time they shook her out of it, everyone was gone. She was taken to a small hospital and released the day before with orders to stay away from headquarters and meet her boss at the Wayfarer. Finally he came.

Ted Howard entered the restaurant, hung up his coat and hat, and took a seat across from her.

"How are you doing, Sid?"

She held up the paper. "It's all a lie."

"Aw, come on. You know we can't print what you and the other agents saw, especially when none of it can be verified." A waitress approached with her honey brown hair up in a bun. "Coffee and the special," Ted said.

"Coming right up."

"I'm surprised you can eat," Sidney added, pushing her soup away.

"I'm not hungry, but I am a creature of habit. You know that." He leaned forward with an uneasy look on his face. "Sid, you're going to have to let this one go."

"What do you mean, *let it go?*"

He swallowed, and his eyes drifted before they found hers again. "The Black Slate is shut down for now. At least until the smoke clears. Ah!" He shook his head. "Sorry, bad choice of words. Let me rephrase. Until the dust settles."

"What do you mean, Ted? I have to go after him. We have to go after him."

"You know bloody well that the Pentagon is all over this one. At least until the media moves on to something else." He rolled his sleeves up, revealing his meaty forearms. "But there will be an investigation, and that will take weeks. Heck, months. This won't go away for a long time."

"I have to find him, Ted. You know that. We can't just forget about him."

"If he was an agent, sure, but he's not." He lifted his finger up. "And before you get mad at me, you know that my hands are tied on this one."

"Just because he isn't an agent doesn't mean he's worth any less."

"Yeah, well they don't see it that way. He's a convict. Expendable." He frowned. "That's probably why they signed him up for this gig."

"And what about me? Am I expendable?"

"You were his Bureau liaison, Sid. His handler, not his partner." He nodded at the waitress, who dropped off a steaming cup of coffee. "I told you to use extraordinary caution, didn't I? You jumped into the shark tank feet first. You have to back off of this."

"You know I can't do that. I'm a vet. He's a vet. You're a vet. We don't abandon one another, come hell or high water. He wouldn't do that to me."

"Sid, your report says that a giant bird flew away with him." He clenched his jaws. "I can't believe you wrote that."

"That's what happened, Ted!" She clenched her fists. She wanted to hit the table but restrained herself. "What if we can find him? When Dydeck was alive, he and Cyrus injected Smoke with a serum called the Glow."

"The Glow? I've never heard of it."

She wanted to reach across the table and slap him. All of his answers were too convenient. He had to know something. "Can you look into it?"

"Sure. All right. Fine."

"I'm being serious, Ted."

"So am I. I promise."

She picked at her lip. That might take forever, and Smoke would be long gone or dead by then. She needed something now, but she had nothing. She didn't even have a number for Fat Sam or Guppy. "What about Agent Ramsey? Why don't you talk to him? Plenty of agents saw what happened."

"And plenty of agents want to keep their jobs," he said matter-of-factly.

"Are you kidding me?"

He shook his head. "Sorry." His food arrived, a loaded cheeseburger and fries.

"So what am I supposed to do then, bury my head in the sand?"

He squirted ketchup on his plate. "Be patient and see how things turn out."

"And what about John Smoke?"

"I know you liked the guy. I liked him too. But given his background, you're just going to have to pray his own survival skills get him out okay." He took a bite of his burger. "Sometimes that's all you can do."

"Pray?"

He shrugged. "It works sometimes. I once had a friend—"

"Ted," she said, getting up from the booth. "Just check into the Glow. I'm going home ... for now."

"Aw Sid, don't go like this—"

She made it out of the restaurant before he finished and headed for her car. *I'm such a fool!* She opened the Hellcat's door, got behind the wheel, and fired the engine up. *Perhaps a long drive through pigeons will help.* Her phone buzzed. It read Unknown Caller on the screen. *Fat Sam and Guppy?*

"Hello?"

"Agent Shaw," an unfamiliar voice said. "It's time to go after Smoke."

CHAPTER 31

"**W**HO IS THIS?" SIDNEY ASKED.

"Mal. Mal Carlson," the man replied. His voice was cool but serious. "And your first question should probably be, 'Where is he?'"

"Or, maybe it should be, 'Where are you?' assuming you are Mal Carlson." She turned left on the next street. "Mister, I have no idea if you are who you say you are."

"Well, you got the case with the bullets I assume?"

True. He wouldn't know that otherwise. "Yes."

"Do you have on the *Zweite Haut* suit I made you?"

"Sweet heart?"

"*Zweite Haut* is German for second skin," he said with a testy tone. "I haven't thought up a good name for it. It's a trivial thing. Do you have it on?"

"No."

The man sighed. "Oy. Well, tell me you do have it with you."

"Why, don't you have another one?" Sid was a little irritated with all men right then.

"As a matter of fact I do, Agent Shaw, but your comrade, Mister Smoke, is wearing it, and I'd like to have them both returned intact, but I need your help."

Well, at least I'm not the only one who gives a damn. "Let's meet."

"There is no time for that, Agent Shaw. Within a day I'm certain they'll... well, we'll never see him again."

Half a dozen questions raced through her mind. How did he know where Smoke was? Why should she trust him? And who in the world *was* Mal Carlson? She pulled off to the side of the road. "I have the suit."

"And it's in the case, I assume."

"No. It's in the back seat of my car."

"You need to put it back on."

"I'm not putting it back on. It needs a wash," she said, reaching into the back and sniffing it. There was a pause on the other side of the line, followed by a groan. "Are you still there, Mister Carlson?"

"I'm here, but please don't stop by the cleaners. That's a quarter million dollar suit you've been wearing. And those bullets, a thousand dollars each. You still have those, don't you? And the case?"

"Let me guess, it's worth a million?"

"With the contents, yes, without them, well, look, it's sentimental. Don't lose it. Now, get dressed and ready to go."

"Go where? How do you even know where Smoke is? Nobody else does."

"The Glow," he replied.

She thought about Ted. Maybe he was moving faster than she thought. "How did you know about that?"

"Because I'm the one who had it put in him—and we need to get moving before the signal is lost." There was pecking on a keyboard. "I'm sending you directions."

Sid's phone buzzed inside her palm. She checked the screen. "Got them. What is this place?"

"A nineteenth-century bird sanctuary. It was an estate of an old English lord from the seventeen hundreds." He coughed. "But I don't have much history on it, just what was in the local papers that have been transferred to microfiche. It's now owned by an eccentric group of philanthropists."

"Anything tying the property to Drake?"

"Oh yes. The land is under a trust managed by Drake Property Enterprises."

Sidney pulled off the shoulder and headed down the road. The location was about 45 miles away, northwest of DC. "So Mal, now that I've seen deaders, werewolves, and now a harpy, do you care to fill me in on what is going on?"

"All in due time."

"Now is the time!" She squeezed the wheel. "Come on, Mal—Mister Carlson, you need to give me a heads-up on what's going on. I need something of substance. If I'm going to risk my neck, I'd like to know what in the heck for."

"In this case, you're doing it for your friend," he said matter-of-factly.

Sid could hear his rustlings and peckings on a computer in the background. *Morning glory! I don't need this crap!* "Just tell me more about the Black Slate and what I'm up against."

"I'd rather have you focus on the task at hand."

"Well, it's a bit of a drive, and I think I'm just as ready as I was the last time." Her car roared up the highway ramp and merged with traffic. "Just a nugget. Something meaningful."

"This enemy, the Drake—which is just a name—has been around a long, long time."

"Humor me. How long?"

"We're talking ancient times."

"Like, BC?" she said.

"I can't confirm it, but yes. There's evidence of it all over the globe, but it's never viewed in the proper light."

"Why don't you just shed some illumination on it then?"

He sighed. "All right. Just suppose that myths and legends aren't a shadow of the truth but real. At least some of them. There's a lot of silly stuff out there too, and you have to learn how to discern what should be ignored. Ahem. That said, these people, be it from fallen angels or demons, have always been among us, in one form or another, lending others their power. That's what you're dealing with here."

"Demons?"

"More like the spawn of demons. I like to think of it as manifestations of evil. It takes all sorts of forms and develops all sorts of powers. The evil seed planted in the body makes for supernatural mutations of sorts."

It was hard to hear and believe, even though she had seen it for herself. *This is too big a pill to swallow. I'd be choking on it if I hadn't seen it for myself.*

"I know what you're thinking, Agent Shaw. Even seeing is not believing. People see only what they want to see, and this enemy of which we speak, they thrive on our ignorance. Hence the world that crumbles all around you."

His words crept into her soul. "Can you tell me … why me, and why now, if this has been going on so long?"

"For the most part, men and women have fought the good fight and kept it under control. But you don't hear about these heroes in the history books. Very little is known about them at all. They've battled and driven the fiends into their dark holes, but there's always meddling underneath the surface. Like snakes, they slither out and suck good people down."

Sounds like a bad fantasy series. "And what is your part in all of this?"

"Oh, I guess it's just my predestination to find these evil toads. Keep your phone handy, Agent Shaw. I'll call you back in a few minutes. Remember, fight the good fight."

The line went dead.

"Wait!"

CHAPTER 32

THIRTY MINUTES LATER THERE WAS still no word from Mal Carlson.

Great, great, great, great, great!

Sidney followed the GPS directions and found herself traveling down a lonely stretch of roadway accompanied only by tall pines. She took the left split at the fork in the road. Dusk was settling, and the landscape was changing, revealing an assortment of trees of all shapes and sizes. There were stone markers along the road too, some bigger than cars and others the size of tires. An old split-rail fence linked them.

Things became odd as the road winded. The trees changed. Thick roots seemed to burst through the ground like animated things. The heavy brush looked ominous and impenetrable. What had been a colorful forest by day was fast becoming a deadly and dreary one by night. The kind that campers disappear in. Colorful birds darted over the road from tree top to tree top. Some seemed unusually big. Their chirping was shrill and creepy.

Bird sanctuary my butt.

As she pulled on ahead, a pair of bright yellow eyes reflected her headlights. The four-legged creature bounded away along with the rest of the pack. Wolves. Big furry bodies disappeared like shades in the forest.

Not again.

She wanted to turn around. She didn't belong here, but Smoke didn't either. Finally she found herself passing underneath an old iron archway covered in vines and ivy. The lettering read Dummerville Bird Sanctuary. Half a mile ahead a lone manor stood against a backdrop of tall creepy oaks. Made from rough-hewn stone, the estate house, the size of a small resort, became bigger as she approached. Exotic cars and limos were parked all over the huge lawn, and a few people milled about at the front entrance. One man in a tuxedo was smoking with a woman in a fur coat. Each of them wore a bird mask that covered the eyes and nose.

This must be the place.

She parked the Hellcat on the lawn, leaving some room away from the rest, and waited. Another car pulled up to where a valet waited. He took the couple's keys, took the car, and parked beside her. The man lumbered out of the car in an old doorman's uniform. His skin was clammy and pale. He glanced over at Sidney's car. She let out a soft gasp and pressed against the seat.

Deader! She closed her eyes, clutching her gun to her chest. *Look away! Look away!*

The deader's heavy footsteps crunched over the grass and back toward the estate.

Sidney let out a soft sigh and grabbed the sweetheart suit. *No back-up, Sid. No problem.* Cramped inside her car, she slipped out of her clothes, slid the suit on, and redressed. Her body began to warm and energize. She picked up her gun and readied a second magazine. *Glock is my back-up.* She slid the knives Mal had sent to her and Smoke into her boots.

Just as she started to exit her car, another one wheeled in beside her—a razor-blue Jaguar XE. Two men exited from the front, and two giggling ladies exited from the rear. All of them swayed a little. One of the men handed each of them a mask and said, "We can't forget these ladies."

Sidney got out of her car and turned on the charm. She sauntered up to the man who had handed out the masks. She fingered his chest. "You wouldn't have another one of those would you? I forgot mine, and my boyfriend, well, ex-boyfriend maybe, got mad and went inside without me."

"He left a pretty thing like you out here all by yourself?" He hiccupped. "What a dick. Sure, I have another." He popped open his trunk and gave her one that was black with feathers and silver sequins. He pointed to his face. "Find me later though. You owe me a favor."

One of the girls hooked her arm in his and said, "Come on Reggie. The only one owing you any favors is me."

"Sure sure, babe. Whatever you say," he said, winking at Sidney from behind his mask. "Come on lady. Head on inside with us. It's as cold as a snowman's ass out here."

Feeling underdressed, Sid opened up her trunk and grabbed a coat her mother had gotten her for Christmas. Still in the box, the long winter coat was deep brown with fur trim around the neck. She put it on and said to the group, "Let's go party."

Approaching the manor, Sidney stayed close to the others. An imposing man in a hawk mask gave everyone a once over. Reggie held up his ring, and the man in the mask nodded. Behind the guard, on either side of the door, were deaders in doorman uniforms that looked to be a hundred years old.

"I love the looks of these men," one girl with a squeaky voice marveled. "So undead."

"They're undead all right," Reggie said, stuffing a fifty in the hawk-masked man's breast pocket. "Just don't get too close."

"Why?" the girl said, stepping closer and cocking her head.

The young man goosed her. "Boo!"

She squealed. "Stop that Reggie! You almost made me pee myself!"

"Sorry, babe." He slung his arm over her shoulder. "But you haven't seen anything yet."

Sidney caught a glimpse of a signet ring on his finger. It was a golden head with a rising black sun stamped in the middle of it. A dreadful feeling overcame her. Not for the men so much as the girls. They had no idea what they were in for. Sheep being led by wolves to the slaughter.

Inside, the atmosphere was heavy. Dreary music filled the massive foyer made from cut stone and marble. A banquet room with buffet tables and a bar was on the right, and a huge ballroom was on the left. People didn't dance. Instead, dressed in evening attire, they talked and touched, and some kissed. Every one of them had on a bird mask. There were eagles, hawks, pigeons, ravens, cardinals, robins and even parakeets and canaries.

I bet there's a pecking order to all of this.

There seemed to be. Men in dark suits wearing hawk masks were spread out along the walls. Their builds were similar to the men from the club. Women in scanty outfits of revealing silk wore bright pink and yellow canary masks. A few muscular bruisers in blue jay masks sauntered around carrying trays with drinks and small packages of pills.

I bet Allison would love this place.

Sidney broke off from the others and began milling about, careful not to jostle anyone. She picked up on a few conversations but nothing of note. Money. Politics. Sex. That was the gist of it. She grabbed a drink from one of the trays and leaned against a post. She noticed more oversized bird cages. Inside them were bird-masked shirtless men, covered in neon colors with war paint and wearing only buckskin pants. Some danced. Others stood with their arms crossed over their bare chests.

Allison would definitely love this depraved place. Her phone buzzed.

Unknown Caller

The message read:

Are you in?

Sidney responded with a *yes.*

Describe*?*

She texted back: *The filthy rich in bird masks. Men in loincloth and cages. Want a picture?*

How many*?*

Two-hundred +.

Odd for this time of day. Something must be going on. Much artillery?

Yes.

Find Smoke and leave. Make sure you have the suit.

I didn't come to make new friends—and screw your suit. What about Night Bird?

She'll have to wait.

Sid put her phone away. These cryptic messages from Mal Carlson were of little benefit at all. Not to her anyway. But he did point out one odd thing: the unique time of day for the gathering. Unlike the late-night hours mingling at the club, this had more of the feeling of a buildup for an event. She headed for the buffet and decorated her crystal plate with extraordinary cuisine. The aroma of fine spices was arousing. She took a few bites. *This is wonderful.*

"Are you enjoying yourself?" said a man in a robin mask and a tuxedo. He sounded young and was well built. His cologne was enticing.

Sidney nodded. "Yes. You?"

He rubbed his hand up and down her arm. "Not yet. Say, aren't you hot? I bet you are." His voice was smooth and persuasive. "Why don't you let me help you take that coat off?"

"I just got here." She eased away. "Maybe later." *Never!*

"I'll be close," he said, walking away.

Find Smoke! Get out of here!

The music stopped and the chatter quickly subsided. Everyone gazed up at the balcony at the top of the stairs. There was Night Bird.

CHAPTER 33

NIGHT BIRD STOOD PROUDLY AT the top, hands on the rail, in a glorious white feathered gown. Her outstanding features almost made Sidney forget about the monster that lurked behind them. She spoke. "Guests, one and all, welcome to my abode. I'm sure you're enjoying yourselves."

Some laughter broke out, and a few cheers echoed and died.

Night Bird clapped her hands. "Are you ready for the main event?"

The crowd shouted back. "Yes!"

"Are you sure?" she said, playfully.

"Yes!"

"Then step aside, children, and let the Battle of the Bird Cages begin!"

Sid moved out of the banquet room and over to the ballroom, where the people gathered in a big circle eyeing the floor. The center of the floor slid back like a great eye, making a gaping hole in the middle.

Morning Glory!

The men and women started chanting and pumping their fists. "Bird Cage! Bird Cage! Bird Cage!"

A great raven made from blackened iron rose from the gaping floor, rising higher and higher. It was perched on a round metal bird cage maybe twenty feet wide and over ten feet tall. It filled almost a third of the room.

You have got to be kidding me.

She glanced up at the balcony. Night Bird stood looking downward with two deaders in pea coats on either side of her.

On the main floor, the serving men in hawk-masks opened up the door to the big cage. Other servants pushed the smaller bird cages with men inside over and let them out. Inside the cage they went, and the door was latched shut. The men inside—each coated in bright colorful war paint—were well built: stout and hard muscled. One shadow boxed, stretched and warmed up. The other stroked his wild beard. Somewhere a gong sounded, and the room fell silent.

Sidney controlled her gaping. *Really, they couldn't go see this anywhere else? Couldn't they just stay home and watch* Fight Club?

Night Bird spoke up. "No mercy. Winner take all!"

The crowd let out a cheer.

Sidney pushed her way through the throng. Now was the best time to find Smoke. Someone had to be holding him somewhere. *Wouldn't surprise me if there was a dungeon in here.*

Night Bird raised her arms and lowered them.

Bong!

Sid glanced back over her shoulder. Up inside the cage, the men circled. One, sleek and bald, jabbed at the brawny bearded one. His blows smacked into flesh. The bearded man snatched the man by the arms and drove his knees into his chest. In a blink, the bald man was hoisted over the bearded man's head.

The people roared.

A second later, the bearded man slammed the struggling man head first into the floor. *Crack!* The witnesses gasped, and the ballroom fell silent. The bald man moved no more.

The bearded fighter beat his chest and let out a triumphant howl. He flexed his muscles and yelled up at the balcony, "Who's next? Who's next?"

The crowd started chanting. "Wild Jack! Wild Jack! Wild Jack!"

Wild Jack? It was the name of a legendary MMA fighter. Sidney hadn't recognized him with the beard. He had been clean-shaven and worn a Mohawk, if she remembered it right. *This is insane, not to mention highly illegal.* She took out her phone and sent a text to Ted Howard. *Night Bird or no Night Bird, I'm breaking this party up. I'm a witness to a murder.* She pressed send, but the signal bar was dead. *No!*

Bong!

"Well done, Wild Jack," Night Bird said. "Are you ready for another?"

"I'm not even warmed up yet," he shouted up to her, "But yes, milady, I'm ready."

"Excellent, because we have a newcomer that I think you just might find worthy." She clapped her hands. "Bring him in!"

A pair of grand double doors opened underneath the balcony. Another bird cage was pulled in, containing a man with his back turned to them with his head down. The people murmured and pressed toward the cage.

"Make a hole! Out of the way!" said one of the hawk-masked men.

Oh no! Sidney's gut churned. She squeezed through the crowd and crept up on the cage. She got a good look at the face. It was Smoke. His shoulders were bruised, his complexion pale, and he had a sick and haggard look about him. His weak eyes met hers. "Smoke?"

His head lifted, and he coughed. "You need to go," he said in a raspy voice. "Just go."

Keeping up with the cage, she said, "What happened?"

"What didn't happen?" He winced. "Just go. They'll see you. Forget about the Slate." His eyes hardened. "Forget about all of this and go."

"But—" she stammered.

"Move it, woman," said one of the servants, shoving her aside. They started pushing the crowd back from the cage. "Clear out! All of ya!"

The throng eased back and Sidney drifted in with the masses. A hollowness filled her. Smoke's rock-solid demeanor was gone. A world champion MMA fighter waited inside the cage, grinding his fist into his paw. *I have to stop this. He'll die.*

The crowd hummed with new energy.

Smoke's disheveled form lumbered out of his cage and stepped over the bald man's dead body. Stooped over, his battered muscular body was riddled with cuts, scrapes, and bruises. He shuffled toward the center of the cage, facing his aggressor. The cage door closed with a clank.

"This is going to be a massacre," one man said.

"I hope there's blood this time," added a woman.

"There's blood. There's always blood," the man in the eagle mask replied. "Wild Jack will bring it all night long. He's never been defeated."

Sidney's chest tightened. Her fingers went to her gun. *What am I going to do? I can't watch him die.*

"Kill him, Wild Jack!" a strong voice cried out. "No mercy on that man! I want to see blood on those hands."

Sidney cocked her head and looked at the man. He had a husky bowling-pin build and meaty hands. He squeezed the hips of the women on either side of him.

"Wait till you see this, girls. Wait and see. That bastard in the cage has it coming."

Congressman Wilhelm!

CHAPTER 34

S IDNEY'S JAW MUSCLES TIGHTENED. IF Congressman Wilhelm was there, who else was? All around her, people in bird masks talked, some in different languages and others with bad American accents. They all wanted blood. Mayhem. Death.

Who are these people? Why don't they get in the cage!

She shuffled through the crowd toward the cage, bumping Congressman Wilhelm, jostling his drink.

"Idiot! Watch where you're going!"

She didn't turn.

Night Bird clapped her hands, and the crowd fell silent. "Life to the victor! Death to the fallen! Agreed?"

The people shouted back in agreement. Inside the cage, Smoke stood a few paces away from Wild Jack with his shoulder dropped. The bearded warrior, all lathered up, mopped the sweat from his brow. He spat. "This man doesn't seem fit for fighting!"

"I don't expect him to put up much of a fight," Night Bird replied. "He crossed me. That's how I want it."

"I see," Wild Jack said, stroking his beard. He pumped his fists in the air. "I'll make it a prolonged and painful death then!"

Smoke burst into motion, striking Wild Jack in the throat. The burly man's eyes popped wide. The seasoned fighter brought his fists down. Smoke slipped behind the man and locked Wild Jack's arms and neck up. The bearded warrior gagged, and his face quickly went from beet red to purple.

Get him, Smoke!

Wild Jack slapped at Smoke's arms, spat and struggled. The muscles in Smoke's corded arms bulged. His face filled with strain. Wild Jack's eyes rolled up inside his head, and Smoke took him to the floor.

The crowd unleashed a fury of angry boos and profanities. It didn't matter. It was over.

Smoke released Wild Jack, rose back to his feet wincing, looked up at Night Bird, and shrugged.

The gong sounded, and the crowd quieted.

"I didn't even give the signal to start the match, and that's cheating," Night Bird said. "Not to mention that I said it was to the death. I see Wild Jack is still breathing. Or should I say, sleeping?"

The attendees craned their necks toward the cage and murmured.

"Kill him yourself," Smoke said back to Night Bird.

Night Bird laughed. "Oh, that's noble. How quaint. But either you can kill him or I'll have to kill her." She pointed straight down at Sidney. "Take her!"

How did she know?

The array of guests turned on her. The brutes in the hawk masks shoved the masses aside and came straight for her. Sidney pulled out her gun and fired three shots into the ceiling.

Blam! Blam! Blam!

Screams and frightened cries were followed by dozens of people scrambling for the doors. Sidney lowered her head and melded in with the rampaging throng.

Try to find me now, you idiots!

As the crowd pushed toward the main entrance, she noticed two men in suits pushing Congressman Wilhelm out the door. The bodyguards in bird masks formed a blockade at the main entrance, patting everyone down with force. Above, on the balcony, Night Bird was screaming, but Sidney didn't look back. Instead, she snatched a parakeet mask from one woman's face and disappeared underneath the stairs that led up to the balcony. Gathering her thoughts and catching her breath, she waited.

I've got to get Smoke out of here.

Five minutes into the wait, she switched masks, slipped off her coat, and reentered the scene. The manor was half empty. The excitement from the gunfire had dulled. The servants were picking up the mess. Others searched. The remaining party guests had resumed their talks, making up half-baked stories. Eyeing the balcony, Sidney noticed Night Bird was gone.

Where could that bird brain be?

She huddled with a crowd of talking guests that had gathered near the cage. Smoke was still inside, sitting on the floor, head down and shivering.

What is wrong with him?

Checking her surroundings, she eased closer to the cage and cleared her throat.

Smoke didn't move.

Putting a stagger in her step, she teetered around the rim and hiccupped from time to time.

Smoke crawled over on his hands and knees, saying, "Water. I need water."

She whispered. "It's me, Sid."

"Water," he replied, then under his breath he said, "I know. I can handle this. Just go." He coughed.

"Are you all right or not?" she said, still whispering.

He cocked his head back toward Wild Jack and said, "Better than him." He coughed again. "What a tool. If you're going to stick around, get the keys. But I suggest you go. Night Bird has keen instincts."

"I'm not leaving without you."

"Then we might not be leaving at all." He looked deep into her eyes. "Are you sure you're all right with that?"

"I'm good. Let me go find you some water."

"A milkshake would be better."

Now that the crowd had settled down, the hawk-masked guards began making rounds and patting everyone down. Sidney still had her gun tucked down in her pants. *Great.* She made her way over to one of the banquet tables, kneeled down, and put her gun beneath the curtains. She then sauntered over toward one of the guards with her hands raised over her head.

"Yoo hoo, you haven't searched me yet," she said to the nearest one. She nuzzled up to him. "Pat me down, and be sure to be thorough. And if you do a good job I'll pat you down too!"

The guard grunted. "Be still."

She draped her arms over him and pulled him close. "How can I be still with a brute like you around? Hmmm?" *Lord, he smells like English Leather.*

He ran his hands over her chest and waist, taking full advantage of the moment.

"You have great hands."

"I'm a student at a massage therapy school." He patted her rear. "You're clear."

"No doubt you'll be a good one," she said, tickling his chin. "Anything else?"

"No," he said, starting to walk away.

"Oh, well, can I get that man in the cage some water? I feel sorry for the dear."

There was a grinding of gears and a clank of metal. The giant bird cage started to lower back into the floor.

"I think it's a little late for that now, but don't worry, he won't be thirsty much longer."

"Why do you say that?"

"Because dead men don't thirst."

CHAPTER 35

SIDNEY RETRIEVED HER GUN AND made her way up to a gathering crowd that stood watching the cage go down into the floor. Smoke sat inside the cage, head down.

"Bummer," someone said, "no more violence. Let's go."

The cage sunk into the darkness and rattled when it hit bottom. Gears grinded and the floor began to close.

"Wow, it looks like he's being swallowed whole. Too bad for that loser," a man said, guzzling a bottled beer. "Better him than me. I wonder where they find these goons anyway."

Sidney crept toward the rim. The hole was seconds from closing.

"Hey, lady, you better back off. That floor will cut your leg off." The man laughed. "It wouldn't be the first time that happened, either."

The light over the grand birdcage faded.

Sidney swallowed. *I'm not losing you again.* She jumped on the sliding door of the closing circle.

"Are you crazy?" the man said. "Get off of there!"

Crazy enough! She jumped through the narrowing doorway into the darkness. She hit the top of the cage with a bang and rolled down the side, hitting the floor hard. "Oof!" Slowly, she sat up, rubbing her hip and shaking her head.

"What have we here?" The man's voice was gruff. He approached, tall and lanky and wearing a pea coat. "Looks like a little bird fell out of her nest." He extended his hand. "Let me help you up, my dear."

She reached for his hand.

He took it, started to pull her up, and drove his booted toe into her gut.

She doubled over with a groan.

"Men, I got her! I got—*ulp!*"

Smoke stretched his arms through the bars and grabbed the man's neck and collar. He jerked the man's face into the metal. *Bang! Bang! Bang!*

The man sagged to the floor with his face bleeding.

"Find the key," Smoke urged. "Hurry!"

Sidney fumbled through the man's pockets and belt and found nothing. A scuffle of feet and agitated voices echoed down the corridor. "He doesn't have it."

Smoke reached into the front of her jeans and pulled her gun out.

"Hey!" she said.

He marched over to the cage door and shot the lock off. It sounded different underground.

Pop!

And then he stepped outside and tossed her back the gun. "Thanks," he said, coughing.

They stood in a cavernous room, almost the size of the ballroom above. Oaken barrels lined the walls. Shelves were stacked up to the ceiling, loaded with unknown materials. The walls were cut rock, and three stone corridors led out. Smoke took her by the wrist and pulled her toward the one farthest from the onrush of guards.

Blat—at! Blat—at! Blat—at!

Sidney's legs churned. Bullets whizzed by her head. Rock chips scattered from the wall. She returned fire.

Pop! Pop! Pop! Pop!

Smoke pushed through the exit door and bounded up the stairs. She kept pace, stumbled, bashed her knee on the metal step, and carried on, grimacing. They rushed through the door at the top and found themselves in a grand kitchen. They dashed to the other side of the room and found themselves inside one of the main halls.

Voices cried out from all over. Footsteps echoed off the hardwood floors.

"Stay close," Smoke said.

"No, you stay close," she replied. "I'm rescuing you. It's not the other way around."

Smoke coughed. "If you say so."

They took a curved stairway going up, away from the sound of voices. At the top was a long hallway with many bedroom doors. She jiggled the handles on one side. Smoke tried the other. The opposite end of the hall was a dead end.

"Any luck?" she said, glancing back over her shoulder. Smoke was gone. A door gaped open on the other side. "Smoke?" A heavy scuffle caught her ear. Inside, a deader had Smoke by the waist and picked up off the floor.

"Close the door," Smoke spit out. He drove an elbow into the deader's eye socket. The lifeless creature shrugged it off and slammed him to the floor.

Sidney closed the door and locked it, closed in, and took aim.

Smoke shook his head. "Don't shoot it!"

"Why?"

"Too loud." The deader got his tireless arms around Smoke's neck. "Knife," Smoke choked out, stretching his clutching hand and eyeing her ankle. His face reddened. "Knife, now."

She slid the blade from her boot.

"Don't just stand there, stab it!"

"Stabbing's not really my thing."

"Give it!" Smoke snatched the blade from her hand and drove it backward into the deader's eye. The creature's body stiffened, but it held on. Smoke twisted inside its grip, ripped himself free, plunged the blade into its heart, and gave it a twist.

Churk!

The deader went limp.

Gasping, Smoke wiped the blade on the bedspread. "Stabbing isn't really your thing?"

She shrugged. "It seemed weird."

He staggered toward the window. "Some rescue." Peering outside, he said, "I think you can make a break for it from here." He opened the window. "The ivy's pretty heavy on these walls."

"And just what do you think you'll be doing?"

"Bringing in Night Bird."

"You need to forget about her."

"Nah," he said, shaking his head. "Not after what she did to me. Did to those others. She's going down."

She grabbed his chin, looked straight into his eyes, and said, "There's too many, Smoke. Let's cut our losses and go. You're sick."

"I'll be fine." He tried to nudge her toward the window.

"You weren't fine five minutes ago."

"Of course I was," he said, coughing. "It was all going according to my plan until you showed up."

"Me?" She backed up into the room. "You'd be dead if not for me."

He shook his head. "No I wouldn't."

The closet door popped, and with a creak it slowly opened. It was dim inside. *Probably some partygoers.* Sidney peered inside, weapon ready. "Come out with your hands up."

A pale and ghastly figure rushed out of the closet.

Sidney's finger froze on the trigger.

A knife flashed and stabbed her in the gut.

CHAPTER 36

T HE GUT-BUSTING BLOW PICKED SIDNEY up off her feet. Agony raced through her body. Instinct took over. She fired the Glock.

Blam! Blam! Blam! Blam! Blam!

The spray of bullets blasted the deader back into the closet.

Smoke rushed over. "Sid! Sid! Are you all right?"

Clutching her stomach, she shook her head quickly, saying, "I don't know." It felt as if the monster had punched a hole through her. All of her innards ached.

Smoke pulled the belly of her sweater up. "Whoa."

"Is it that bad?"

"No. Your second skin held."

"It's called a *Zweite Haut* suit."

"Sweet heart?"

"Something like that. It's German. Where's yours?" She groaned as Smoke helped her to her feet. Her knees buckled, but Smoke caught her. *Man, it hurts.*

"Not sure. Why, am I in trouble?"

"Probably. It's worth more than the both of us put together."

"Well, at least it kept you together."

A heavy pounding came at the door.

Wham! Wham! Wham!

"Open up! Open up!"

"Just a minute," Smoke said in a feminine voice. "I'm not decent." He dragged Sidney to the window.

Gunshots cracked out from the other side of the door. Wood chips blasted through the holes.

"Hang on," Smoke said, hefting her onto his shoulder.

"Let me down, I can climb."

"You can barely move."

He eased out of the window, gripped the vines, and scaled the wall to the ground like an ape. He sprinted out into the back courtyard. Angry voices called out after them. Gunfire followed.

Feeling as if her guts were falling out, Sidney aimed her weapon and cracked off some cover fire.

Blam! Blam!

One man fell out of the window. "Ahhh!"

Nice shot, Sid! Wish my combat arms instructors could have seen that. They'd never believe it.

"Hang on!" Smoke said, running at full speed. "I'll get you to safety."

Whoooosh!

A great shadow dropped from the sky and knocked them sprawling to the ground. Sidney fought her way up to her hands and knees.

"You ruined my party!" Night Bird squawked. The bird woman's face was contorted with demonic fury. Her wings were spread, and her razor-sharp talons clawed up the dirt as she bird-walked forward. "I will make you pay!"

Sidney raised the barrel of her gun, aimed center mass, and said, "Glock you." She squeezed the trigger.

Click.

Night Bird snarled. "I'm going to rip you lab rats apart!" She lowered her head, pinned back her wings, let out a shriek, and charged with unnatural speed.

The shriek paralyzed Sidney. She hunkered down, fighting to regain her faculties.

Night Bird landed on top of her. The talons dug into her body, and Sidney cried out. She felt her body lift from the ground and rise toward the sky. Something slammed into Night Bird and dragged the monster to the grass by the neck. The talons released her.

"You dare!" Night Bird shrieked at Smoke. "I've had enough of you, mortal!" Her wings lashed out, cutting Smoke along the eyes. Bigger and stronger than the man, she pinned his legs down with her talons. Her talon-like fingernails tore into his skin. With superior strength and speed, she pummeled him.

Smoke struck back, stabbing with the knife.

Night Bird bit his wrist and wrenched it free. "Fool! For hundreds of years none of your kind have ever stopped me." She shrieked in his face.

Smoke covered his ears. He sagged to the ground, nose bleeding. His body was cut to ribbons, and he slumped over on the blood-slicked grass.

Night Bird spread her wings in triumph and squalled.

A fire lit inside Sidney. She snaked the other knife out of her boot and charged the harpy.

"Eh?" Night Bird turned her head a split second too late.

Sidney jumped and jabbed the knife deep between Night Bird's wings.

The monster let out a squawk so loud it bent the leaves on the trees. Somewhere, glass shattered. "Noooooooooooo!" Night Bird slung Sid from her back, spread her great wings, and took to the air, under the moonlight. The higher she went, the more she wavered. Finally, she spiraled in a downward cone and crashed into a storehouse nearby.

Oh, please be dead!

Sid crawled over to Smoke.

He lay prone on the ground, struggling to rise and wiggling his fingers in his ears. "Did you stab her?"

"Yes," she said, holding up the knife.

He poked the other magazine in her pocket. "Why didn't you just reload and shoot her?"

I forgot. She didn't see her gun anywhere on the ground either. "I just wanted to stab her, I guess." She shivered. "I think I've had enough of this cold. Let's make sure she's dead and get inside."

"I don't think that's our call," Smoke said. Looking over her shoulder, he raised his hands.

They were surrounded by at least a dozen gun-toting goons.

Sid's teeth chattered, and she thought, *Don't say it.*

But they did.

"Freeze!"

CHAPTER 37

"**D**ROP THE KNIFE, LADY!" ONE of the guards said.

Sidney let it slide from her fingers. "I think you can take the masks off now, bird boys. I think your boss is dead."

"She's not our boss," one man said, hauling Sidney up to her feet.

"Is that so? Then who is?"

"Button your lip," the man said, picking up her knife, "or it might get cut off." Behind her a man stuck a rifle muzzle in her back, shuffling her forward. "Let's go."

She glanced at Smoke. Blood was caked all over him. He tried to fight off the cough in his chest.

"This is a horrible rescue," he said to her. "You know that, don't you?"

"If you'd cooperate, it'd be just fine."

A rifle butt gently clocked both of them in the back of the head. "Shut it," a man said.

Whumpa! Whumpa! Whumpa! Whumpa! Whumpa! Whumpa! Whumpa!

A helicopter soared in overhead, shining its floodlight on them like a small moon in the sky.

"This is the FBI! Drop your weapons and surrender!" an amplified voice called out from it.

The guards, some in bird masks and others in pea coats, fled toward the house.

"FBI! Last warning!"

A second chopper soared over and landed closer to the house. A tactical team in gas masks spilled out of the helicopter's bay, cracked off some blasts of gunfire, and unleashed smoke grenades. Within minutes, the FBI took control of the situation. Night Bird's bodyguards were face down in the grass. FBI agents in vans and SUVs spilled into the driveway a few minutes later.

Sidney grabbed her phone. "I'll be." Her text had gone through.

"What?" Smoke said.

She showed him the phone with a reply from Section Chief Howard.

Almost there. Hang tight.

She shifted around and said to Smoke, "I told you I was rescuing you."

"No, I'm pretty sure they're rescuing you."

"So that's her, huh?" Ted said, watching Night Bird being loaded into an ambulance on a gurney. She was in human form and had an oxygen mask strapped to her nose.

"No, that's an *it*," Sidney said, pulling the blanket tighter over her shoulders. "And you better hope *it* doesn't survive."

"I look forward to you telling me all about … it," he said, patting her shoulder. "But most of all, I'm glad you're all right."

"Well, I have plenty to tell you, but I'm positive you're going to hate my report."

"At least it'll be entertaining."

The wind stirred the ground, and a bird mask made of raven feathers rolled up on Ted's shoe. He picked it up. "Strange masquerade party."

"They're strange people." Sidney looked over at the back of the other ambulance, where Smoke sat on a gurney. A paramedic was stitching him up. "Does he really have to go back … tonight? He's sick, you know."

"Afraid so. By the looks of things, he's lucky to be alive, like you." He eyed Smoke and then looked at her. "You like that guy, don't you?"

"He's a good soldier. I don't think he deserves what's being done to him."

"Probably not. I'll see what I can do about his living conditions. I figure he deserves that much." Ted surveyed the scene. "Sheesh, this is a mess. Half of these people aren't even citizens. We can't figure out where some of them are from. Some days I just don't recognize my country anymore. I swear I'm going to wake up one day and everything I knew will be gone."

"You could be right," she said.

"Ted! Ted!" Waving his hand over his head, Cyrus ran toward them. "You need to get inside and look at this place." He glanced at Sid. "Hey." Then he was back to eagerly addressing Ted. "Anyway—weapons, drugs, you-name-it's in there. All of these agents are going to be up for accomplishments after this bust!"

Just after he said it, agents came rushing out of the manor. Flames roared with fiery life in the windows. In moments, the entire manor was ablaze.

Cyrus gawped. "Oh no, oh no, oh no! Somebody call in the fire trucks!"

Boom! Boom! Boom!

The ground shook, and the manor collapsed into a pile of rubble.

"I can't believe it," Cyrus said, squeezing his head. "All of the evidence. It's gone."

Sidney walked away shaking her head and headed toward where Smoke now stood. "Are you going to make it?"

"Yea. You?"

"I think so." She extended her hand. "I guess you have to go back now."

He grabbed her hand and squeezed it in his. "Seems so."

Two agents put a coat over his shoulders and led him toward a Bureau car.

Her heart sank. She said over to him, "Until next time then?"

"You can count on me."

CRAIG HALLORAN

THE SUPERNATURAL BOUNTY HUNTER FILES

WHERE THERE'S SMOKE

BOOK 3

CHAPTER 1

A LONE INSIDE Section Chief Howard's office, Sidney sat chewing on a pen cap. She stopped and scribbled a name on her notepad.

Mal Carlson.

He had sent her several texts over the past few weeks. They didn't say much. Greetings. Almost gibberish.

How are you?

Checking in.

Anything strange?

Be alert.

Sometimes she replied, sometimes she didn't.

The office door popped open, and Ted's secretary, Jane, stepped inside. Refined in her appealing and professional dress, she said, "He just pulled in. Can I get you anything, Agent Shaw?"

"You could tell me where John Smoke is."

Jane offered a smile. "I wouldn't mind knowing where he is myself. Are you sure I can't get you anything?"

"No, thank you," she said, turning away. She heard the door close behind her. A whiff of Jane's perfume lingered in the air. *I wish I felt as together as she looks.* She sketched an hourglass on her notepad. And waited. Jane knew plenty more than she'd ever let on. That's what good secretaries do, and they are often privy to what is said and never documented. Jane always eased out of Sid's inquiries. *I hate that about her.* But she respected it too.

Buzz. A new message appeared on her phone from her mother. It read:

Don't forget to check on her.

Allison and Megan had headed back to DC. Her sister had convinced their parents that her head was better and she was ready to go back home. Supposedly she had a job lined up. Allison was well educated and capable. She had a degree in nursing, but she never really applied herself to it. Instead, she enjoyed working in campaign offices with high-profile people, and it was election season.

Sidney texted back:

I will. Love U.

She turned the phone off and tucked it away. *As if I don't have enough on my plate already. Hah!*

Life had changed, but it hadn't. She went through the routine. Eat. Work. Sleep. Good sleep was hard to come by. Now she slept with restlessness, knowing that the monsters under her bed or in her closet were real. But no one wanted to talk about them. There wasn't anyone she could confide in. Instead, she came in once a month to meet with Ted. Otherwise, she was a shadow. Sometimes as she lay in bed she wondered if any of what happened had been real.

Werewolves. Deaders. Harpies. Gargoyles. Cage fights. Plenty of other agents had also witnessed what she had seen, but no one talked about it. In today's world of mass communication, that didn't seem possible. She'd been completely cut off from the investigations and interrogations at the Drummerville Bird Sanctuary. She scratched on her pad. *Maybe they want me to think I'm crazy.*

The door opened, and Ted entered. "Sorry, Sid." He hung his coat and cap on the rack. "Got a late start with the grandkids in. Honestly, I'd forgotten about this meeting until Jane reminded me. I must be slipping." He walked over and patted her on the shoulder. "I hope you'll forgive me." He glanced at her pad. "Is that a portrait of Mr. Smoke?"

She glanced down at the paper. *Lord, it is!* "No, just another person of interest." She watched Ted take a seat behind his desk. "Nice to know you've forgotten about me. I'd like to think the Black Slate carries more interest."

He held his hands up and waved them from side to side. "It does, it does. Please don't go on the attack again. I just got here."

She leaned toward his desk. "No, it doesn't. You don't even want to think about it, and you know it. I bet we wouldn't even be meeting if you didn't have an obligation to."

His eyes drifted a moment before they found her again. "That's not true. You know how fond I am of you, Sid." He unbuttoned his sleeves and rolled them up. "But I am not now, nor have I ever been comfortable with this Black Slate stuff, not since day one. The fact that you are on it is the worst part."

"You don't think I can handle it."

"No. Well that's not entirely true. Five agents died last time, right? You were there. Not that I don't feel for those agents. I do, but you're just different." He locked his eyes on hers. "I don't ever want to go to your funeral."

"I'm touched, but it comes with the job, you know."

"Sure, all agents are at risk. We all know that. But a greater rate of mortality comes to those who deal with this Black Slate." He wiggled his mouse while he put on a pair of rectangular glasses. His monitor came to life. He logged in. "And well," he sighed, "I've lost a friend before to the peculiar circumstances that come with it."

Interesting. Sidney settled back in her chair. Ted might be a little grizzly on the outside, but he was all heart on the inside. When agents died, he felt it. "So you were close to this person? How did they die?"

"Disappeared is more like it." He rubbed his neck. "I was two years out of the academy. She was my supervisor. Deanne, one of the few people in this world who ever intimidated me." He smiled and locked his fingers behind his neck. "She was magnificent. Merciless in interrogation. The tougher they were, the harder they fell. She'd have them crying for their mommies. Confessing everything. You'd watch through the one-way glass, hear that penetrating squall that turned your guts out, and watch a man's entirety collapse."

"Wow, she really made an impact on you."

"She made an impact on everybody. One time, we were on a presidential detail, and I swear he saluted her. Ha. She was the Rambo of the interrogations unit." He got up and opened the small fridge and grabbed a water. "Want one?"

"No, thanks. So, she really got you worked up, huh Chief."

"Aw," he shooed her with his hand. "Not like that. Well, maybe. I'd be lying if I said I hadn't thought about it, but hell Sid, she scared me."

"Do I scare you?"

"No no no, that's not what I'm getting at. But your toughness makes me think about her sometimes. Not many have that edge like you have. It's a gift in this profession."

"Thanks. What did happen?"

Ted leaned his head back like he was looking for the answer on the ceiling. "Huh, good question. She called me into her office one day, sat me down, and told me she was leaving and that I would be her replacement." He rubbed his chin. "All she had was a cardboard box. You know, the kind that hold reams of paper. Her possessions didn't fill half of it. Of course, back then you were lucky to have an office with a window air conditioner in it." He glanced around his office. "Look at all the shit I have. If she came back, well, I'd be embarrassed." His eyes grew sad. "We're just so damn soft nowadays."

Sidney chuckled.

"What?"

"Nothing." She shrugged. "Just funny to hear my hard-nosed boss say that. I don't think your baubles are too much to be ashamed about."

He stuck out his chest. "No, I guess not. Besides, Margie won't let me put them up at home, so it might as well be here." He eyed a fish on the wall. A bass every bit of two feet long. "Did I ever tell you—"

"Yes!" Sid widened her eyes. "So that's it. She left, and you never heard from her again. How did you know it was the Black Slate she was involved with?"

"She left with few words, but she said, 'You'll do well.' I asked about her assignment, and all she said was 'If they wanted you to know, they'd tell you.' And out the door she went. I never saw her again. She became a ghost."

"So how do you know she was on the Black Slate?"

"I got a postcard in my mailbox at home years later." His voice became low and quiet. "It was a picture of an eerie castle somewhere in Europe I guess. Like something one would see or imagine from a scene in Transylvania. It said, 'Ted, monsters are real. Avoid the Slate.' She didn't sign it, but I knew it was her writing. I always thought it was a joke. A gag. It was almost two decades later that I learned it wasn't."

"Do you still have the postcard?"

"Yeah." He opened up his drawer, reached down, and withdrew a small yellow envelope. He tossed it to the edge of the desk. "I've never shown it to anyone, aside from Margie."

Sidney bent back the clasp and took out the postcard. The edges were still clean and crisp. The picture of the castle nestled in the hills above the fog seemed almost as real as a view from a window. She read the message. All seven words. *Seven. Interesting choice.* A small sketch in the bottom left corner shot a chill through her bones. It was a black sunrise.

CHAPTER 2

"**S**o," Sid stared at the card, "can I borrow this?"

"Uh, no." Ted said, rubbing his lip with his finger. "Why would you want to?"

"What if there's more to it than meets the eye, and you missed it?"

He reached across the desk with his hand out. "I don't think so."

"You're pretty attached to it, aren't you? I wonder what Deanne would think about that." She fanned herself with the card. "I bet she'd be touched."

Ted's forehead crinkled. "Give it back."

Boy, he really is attached to it. "Do you have a picture of her?"

"No."

"What was her last name?"

"Just forget about it, Sid." He patted his desk with his meaty fingers. "The card, please."

She took her phone out and brought up the camera.

"Don't you dare," he said. "I don't want every detail of my life to be a digital record. They have a file on me in the computers already."

She gave it one last look, dropped it back in the envelope, and handed it over. *I've seen all I need to see anyway.* "Thanks for sharing."

He stared at the envelope with a pained expression on his face. He sighed and handed it back to Sid. "Here. Just try not to lose it. So, how has the last month been?"

She tucked the postcard away. "Oh, let's see. I've been inside archives doing research as ordered. Pretty boring. Sorting. Filing."

"I thought you liked that kind of stuff."

"No, I'm just better at it than anybody else. What I like is being in the field and not shackled inside a library basement that everyone but the janitor has forgotten about. Do you have another name on the Black Slate for me or not?"

Ted looked away and wrote a note on a piece of paper. "No."

He's not telling me something. "So then I can assume that everything is suddenly right in the nefarious underworld I've discovered, the one no one else wants to talk about." She folded her arms over her chest. "I guess if no one talks about it, it's not real. Huh, Ted? Is that why I'm not in the office? Why I'm isolated? Because I might disrupt the status quo?"

"Don't get so heated. No one has forgotten about you. You just aren't a priority right now. We have borders, elections, terrorist threats, endless investigations, and budget cuts, not to mention an unruly media." He took a drink of water. "The Slate is low on the pecking order, and they haven't so much as sent me a peep about any of it. No files. No nothing."

"Do I just wait?"

"You're still under shadow cover. Why not enjoy it? And don't make it sound as if you aren't doing anything. I know you're snooping around over something."

True. She'd still been digging up all the dirt should could on Drake and its conglomerates. Black suns. They kept popping up in the shadows. "I've been practicing *extraordinary caution.*"

"And I couldn't be happier," he said, clicking through his emails. "Man, it's going to be another long day." Without taking his eyes off the screen, he said, "What you're doing is better than sitting in meetings all day. It's a wonder we get anything done around here." He clicked through a few more emails, shaking his head and muttering to himself.

Sidney sat back in her chair and watched his eyes toggle up and down the screen. A couple of minutes had gone by when she spoke up. "Excuse me, Chief? Are we finished here?"

"Oh, sorry Sid." He swung his shoulders around. "I believe we are."

"You're joking."

"I don't have anything else. I really don't."

"So you invited me to a meeting about nothing?"

"It's routine, you know that. Most meetings are about nothing. They're just a nugget on the schedule."

She got up quickly and glared at him. "Well I hope you get a medal for it." She headed for the door. "This is ridiculous!"

"You haven't been dismissed, Agent Shaw." He got up, crossed the room, and met her at the door. He put one hand on her shoulder and took her hand in the other.

She felt a piece of paper in it.

"Same time next month, Agent Shaw. Now, let me get that door for you."

"See you around next month, maybe." She nodded at Jane and made a bead straight for the elevators. Passing cubicle after cubicle, she felt eyes slide over her body and drift away when she faced them. A young woman with her head down rounded the corner and bumped into her, dropping her phone on the floor.

"Excuse me," the woman said. She was a blonde in her late twenties, dressed in an FBI polo and slacks.

"No problem," Sid said, picking up her phone and handing it to her. "Have a good day."

"Say," the woman said, "you wouldn't be Agent Shaw by any chance?"

"Yes, why?"

"Nothing. I just heard Sadie talking about you one day to some of the newer agents. And older agents. Pretty much everybody." The woman offered her hand. "I'm Rebecca Lang, data analyst." She rolled her eyes. "Pretty boring job, but I'm going to be a field agent, eventually." She pushed her glasses up. "I'm just not a very good shot, but I've also heard you're one of the best. Any chance you can teach me sometime?"

Sidney looked down at her. "There's nothing I can teach you that you haven't already been taught. Practice more, Agent Lang." *I'm going to kill Sadie.* Without another word or glance, she headed for the elevator but turned left and pushed through the fire door into the stairwell. *I suppose some time at the range wouldn't hurt me either.*

Heading down the stairs, she'd almost forgotten about the note. Given the peculiar nature of the delivery, she'd kept it tucked inside her palm. Head down, she averted her eyes from the cameras in the stairwell. That was one thing that didn't bother her about being in the remotely located archives. She didn't feel as if she was being watched all the time. But headquarters was different. Too different. If someone's eyes weren't on her, someone else's were. *They.* Ted always mentioned *them* but gave her no idea who *they* were. She wasn't even certain that *they* were agents. She still wasn't certain about a lot of things. Too many things.

She popped the fire door, crossed through the lobby, and exited through the front doors. Her breathing eased. Keeping pace with the crowd, she made her way to her car a few blocks down. That was one thing she didn't mind so much about shadow cover: blending in. Jeans. Sweater. She wasn't any different than anyone else on the street. *There's something to be said for anonymity.*

Checking traffic, she crossed the street and headed for her phantom-black Hellcat. The twenty-inch wheels on the boss machine made her smile. She unlocked the door, took her seat, and closed herself inside. With a push of a button the engine purred to life. She sank into the leather and closed her eyes. *Ah, that's better.* She rubbed the note inside her hand and tried to guess what it said. *Probably the name of a new pizza place or a microbrewery that's just opened.* Opening her eyes, she unfolded the paper and read a short list.

Alexandria Detention Center
Deanne Drukker
Extraordinary Caution

CHAPTER 3

S IDNEY DIALED UP THE ALEXANDRIA Detention Center. A man picked up. She asked, "Do you have a Deanne Drukker incarcerated?"

The man replied, coughing. "Sorry. Fighting a cold. Are you wanting to schedule a visit?"

"Maybe. Right now I'm just looking for her, actually."

"Well, the name doesn't sound familiar. Let me check." He started to hum an eighties rock melody that was broken up with coughing. "Nope. No Deanne or Drukker. Are you sure that's the right name?"

"I'm sure," she said, pulling out of her parking spot.

"You might want to call around some other places, Miss. Did you call the local police on this?"

"Not yet." She stopped the car at the red light. *Why would Ted give me her full name? Why the detention center?*

"Miss, are you there? I've got another call if we're finished here."

"Smoke," she said. "Is John Smoke housed there?"

"Oh yeah, Smoke's here. Are you family?"

Her blood pulsed through her chest. "Really. Uh, No."

"Ah, girlfriend. What's your name? I'll see if he has you scheduled."

"Does he get many visitors?"

"Not many people do, but he does better than most. I see he's expecting someone. What is your name?"

It better be Fat Sam or Guppy. "It's Sidney. I'm probably not on the list, but I'd like to see him."

"Well, Sidney, are you finally going to show up this time?"

"What do you mean?"

"Well, protocol calls for him to schedule someone before they come. He's had your name on here every Thursday for the last several weeks. Pfft. If you're coming, show up sometime between now and noon. Time's up after that. We can't wait to see you." The line went dead.

What game is he playing?

A correction officer escorted Sidney through the halls of the detention center. Their footsteps echoed off the hard white walls. He opened the door to the visitation room and stepped aside.

"He'll be with you soon, Miss."

Inside, there was a sofa, a small round table, and four chairs. The walls were painted a pale yellow, and a painting of an old man fishing in the sea hung on the wall. The checkered tile floors were scrubbed clean, and the smell of Clorox lingered in the air. It was one of the better detention centers she'd been inside. The chair scraped across the floor as she took a seat. She took off the jacket they'd given her to wear. The watch commander had said her sweater left little to the imagination. She'd told him she was FBI acting in official capacity. And he'd said he didn't care. She checked the time. 11:15 am.

Two minutes later, Smoke came through the door. He wore a beige jumpsuit, and his hair was shaved down to about a quarter inch. The imposing man took a seat across from her and looked deep into her eyes.

"So, you've been expecting me?" she said, pushing her sleeves up on her sweater.

"For about seven weeks," he said. "How have you been?"

"Bored."

"Huh-huh," Smoke laughed, tipping his head back a little. "You think you're bored. I think you miss me."

"You're the one writing me in for visitations," she said, remaining poised. "You've been here the entire time?"

"I have, and that's why I thought you'd have been here sooner." He eyed her. "You really didn't know I was here, did you."

"Not until today. A little bird told me."

"A bird, huh?"

"Not that kind of bird." She glanced at his hair. "So, are you going back in the military? You look like you're fresh off the bus and just left the base barber."

"We had a lice outbreak."

As if being almost obscene wasn't bad enough, you have to follow up with that.

He rubbed his hand over his head. "It takes some getting used to, but it will grow back."

Let's hope. "It doesn't really matter." She brushed her own hair aside. "Are you going to stay here for the duration?"

"Seventeen months to go, maybe six with good behavior, but I'm not for sure. I'm just marking the days until time is served."

Clearly Smoke didn't need to be imprisoned, and seeing him there hurt. She wanted him out. *At least I know where he is now.* "Any other visitors, Sam or Guppy?"

He shook his head. "No, they don't swing by. It's better that way." He patted the table with his fingers. "So, do you have your sweet heart suit on?"

"No, just my own skin."

He leaned forward. "Did you return it to Mal Carlson then?"

"I still don't have any idea who he is, but he sends me texts from time to time. They don't make a lot of sense."

"Can I see them?"

"No."

"Can you tell me what they say?"

"Not much of a point in it. Just weird stuff. Common courtesy and such." She crinkled her nose. "Kinda juvenile actually."

The chair groaned as Smoke eased back into his seat. "I see. So you don't have anything interesting to tell me? Black suns? Odd investigations? Semi-truck trailers running you off the road?"

"Nothing worth mentioning." An odd silence followed and the distance between them seemed to grow. On the one hand she wanted to talk to him about everything. Her family. Her work. Drake. Section Chief Howard and Deanne Drukker. But she held her tongue. "And you? I see you aren't battered up like the last time. I take it there's been no more attempts on your life?"

"Not as much hostility here." He leaned onto the back legs of his chair, stretched his long arm out, and pounded on the door. "Guard!"

"What are you doing?" Sidney said in alarm.

"Well, if you don't have anything else to say, then I guess this meeting's over."

CHAPTER 4

L ATER THAT DAY AT THE FBI's indoor shooting range, Sidney blasted away at a silhouette. She emptied her magazine on the target and snapped in another, took aim, and squeezed the trigger.

Blam! Blam! Blam! Blam! Blam... click.

She popped out the magazine and set her weapon aside on the counter. When she hit the switch, the target floated to her. Her bullet groupings were tight. Quarter-sized holes appeared inside the head, the heart, and two inches below the target's lower abdomen. She plucked the chart off the clip and replaced it with another.

"Nice grouping," said a feminine voice behind her back.

Sidney turned and found herself facing Agent Rebecca Lang. The young woman wore yellow shooting goggles and hearing protection, standard issue, like Sid's. Slight of build and wearing loose-fitting clothes, she seemed undersized for all of her gear.

"So, what's his name? Or is it a her?" Rebecca continued, gazing at Sid's target.

"Its name," Sidney said, opening up another box of bullets, "is none of your business."

"All right," Rebecca said, making a slight wave. "I'll carry on then. I just thought since I happened to be taking your advice and just happened to be down here at the same time, I'd say hi. And now that is said, I'll say goodbye." She turned her back and began to step away.

Aw, geez. "Hold on a second, Agent Lang."

The younger woman turned and faced her.

"Sorry, but it's been one of those days. I apologize." She looked at her target with the holes in it and let loose a small laugh. "Pretty obvious, isn't it?"

Rachel nodded and smiled. She was nice looking, professional, and carried a determined look about her. "I think it would make for a pretty cool poster. Maybe keep it on your wall in your cubicle. Put a note on it saying, 'Ask me what happened to the last guy I dated.'"

"Kinda dark, don't you think?"

"I'm a data analyst, not a comedian. Just trying to make some honest conversation."

"I'm not in much of a talking mood right now." She fed bullets into her magazine.

"You've got some pretty fast fingers," Rachel said. "Is there a trick to that?"

Sidney loaded one bullet in after the other, saying, "Press and slide. Press and slide. I used to fill magazines for my father when I was a kid. He was a sheriff. I'd go to the range and help him and his deputies all the time. By the time I was sixteen, I could outshoot all of them." She slapped in the magazine, twirled the gun on her finger, and stuffed it in her holster. "We watched a lot of westerns, too."

"They don't teach that at the academy. Any chance you could show me that roll?"

"Show you that roll?" Sidney shook her head and flipped the switch. The target glided out toward the back wall. She flipped the switch off. The paper silhouette lingered about twenty-five feet away. "This is how I roll." Cat quick, she slid her Glock out of the holster, took aim, and blasted away. In seconds, the magazine was empty. Empty bullet casings rattled off the floor. She holstered her gun and flipped the switch.

Rachel stepped closer, eyeballing the target.

The target had holes that formed two eyes, a nose, and a mouth.

"Is that a belly button or a bad shot?"

"It's a belly button," Sid said, taking down the target. She had a wry smile. "A little something I learned watching *Lethal Weapon*. Ever see it?"

Rachel shook her head. "No."

Sidney reloaded, twirled the gun on her finger, and holstered it. She said to the woman, "I love shooting. That's why I'm good at it. And if you don't love it, chances are you won't ever be any good at it. We're best at the things that we love most. That's not always good in some cases, but it's often true." She patted Rachel's sidearm. "Do you love that weapon?"

Rachel shrugged her brows and shoulders.

"Well, I love mine. That's the difference. Find out what you love, and do it." She gave her the ole Ted Howard squeeze on the shoulder. "Good luck with that. I've got to go."

"Is there anything you love more than shooting?" Rachel asked.

Without turning back or slowing, Sidney said, "Of course, but loving your weapon is so much easier."

"I'm an attorney."

"Oh really," Sid said, rolling her eyes. She'd stopped at a restaurant to grab a bite to eat on her way home. The place was busy. Lots of suits and ties. A working crowd. Not wanting to wait for a table, she'd settled in at the bar. "Well, let me take my panties off and give them to you right now. So impressive. Please. Your place or mine?"

"Look, I was just making conversation," he said, pushing back his hair. "I wasn't trying to brag or anything."

"Of course you were." She fixed her eyes on his and took a swig of beer. "And you said 'I'm an attorney' as if that were something rare. Have you ever picked up a phone book? Have you?"

He eased back and said, "Yes."

"There are more attorneys in there than anyone else. Almost double. So pray tell, what makes attorneys so special?"

"I-I…" he loosened his tie and took a half-step back. "I swear I didn't mean it that way."

"Yes, you did. But let me tell you what is special: plumbers. You see, plumbers are useful. They fix things. Your kind, they just make a mess of things."

"I'm not a divorce attorney. I'm not even a trial lawyer. I'm a title attorney. That's all."

She narrowed her eyes on him. "Did I say anything about divorce lawyers or trial attorneys? Are they bad or something?"

"Look, I just think there are stereotypes, and plenty of them are accurate, but that doesn't mean we're all bad. We've done plenty of good things."

"Really? Well, please tell me one good thing your profession has done."

He rubbed the back of his neck. He had a little curl in his tawny hair, soft eyes, and a gentle smile. Lean but well built. "Look. I'm sorry. I don't have very much experience in the bar scene. I just thought you were pretty and maybe I could buy you a drink." He turned away and waved. "See ya."

Sidney shrank back on the bar stool. The man, right around her age, settled back down at his table, alone. *A title attorney. Probably lying.* She drained her beer and set it back on the bar.

"Another, Miss?" the bartender said, wiping down the bar.

"Uh, sure." She didn't drink much, and when she did, usually one was her limit, but tonight was different. Smoke had given her the cold shoulder, and she suddenly felt more alone now than ever. Something needed to fill her. *Cold beer. Why not?*

Sidney stirred in her bed. There was a rattle in her bedroom. She eased her gun out from underneath her pillow, heard a soft scuffle of shoes, turned, and pointed.

"Easy! Easy!" said a man, dropping his pants to the floor and raising his hands.

She lowered her weapon and rubbed her aching eyes. "Damn." The clock on the wall read 2:10 in the morning.

"Sorry," the man said. His name was Roy, the title lawyer she'd met earlier. After another beer, she'd cozied up to him at the restaurant, and things had steamrolled from there. "I didn't want to wake you." He glanced down at his trousers. "May I?"

"Go ahead."

He slid his pants up and tucked in his shirt. "Is this a one-night thing, or can I call you again?"

"It's a moment of weakness on my part."

"You don't have to be so glum about it. I'm pretty sure we both had an excellent time."

Not going to argue there. "Just consider it your lucky night."

He tightened his belt. "Maybe you should consider it your lucky night." He flashed a nice row of teeth. "You yelled out my name a few times, as I remember."

"I don't think so."

"Hmmm." He snapped on his watch. "Maybe that was me yelling out your name. Hope I didn't disturb your neighbors. It's a nice area you live in here." He sat down on the bed and put his shoes on. "Are you sure I can't call you sometime?"

"Look, you're a nice guy, but no thanks."

"Yeah, I know. The nice guy never gets the girl. I've heard it before. Bad girls don't like nice guys."

"I'm not a bad girl."

"Uh, I just finished sleeping with you, and well, by my standards—which are well coordinated with the likes of Maxim magazine and such—you're a bad girl." He got up, slipped on his suit jacket, and said, "Are you sure you won't reconsider?"

Maybe. "I'm sure."

"Sidney, you're a magnificent woman." He started across the bed and tried to kiss her.

She placed her hand on his face and pushed him back. He mumbled a word, awkward in her hand. "Just get going, Roy. And don't swing by or look me up." She patted her gun on the pillow. *He's not a bad guy. Fit. Effective. A second time is considerable.* "I mean it."

"Loud and clear," he said, saluting. A buzz erupted inside his pocket. He fished the phone out and answered. "Yeah. Yeah."

Sidney cocked her head. There was an irritated woman's voice on the line.

"I'm on my way. Long night, it'll be fifteen minutes. Thirty tops. I love you too. Kiss. Kiss."

Sidney's eyes widened. "You're married!"

Roy started backing toward the door. "Hey, you didn't ask. I thought it was cool."

"I didn't ask because I didn't see a ring on your finger!"

"Pfft! How dated is that? Sorry, but you should have asked." He turned the doorknob and began his exit. He eyed her up and down. "Besides, bad lawyers don't wear wedding rings. Especially ones that are actually divorce attorneys." He flashed his teeth. "Thanks, you hellcat, you."

As Roy closed the door, she just shook her head.

CHAPTER 5

SIDNEY SCRUBBED A RUSTY SPOT around the drain of her bathroom sink with a Brillo pad until her elbow ached.

"Why won't you go?" she said through clenched teeth. She rinsed the spot and the rust was still there. "So be it." She removed the rubber gloves, tossed them in a plastic pail, and headed to the kitchen. There she placed another coffee pod into the machine. The coffee maker vibrated on the counter a little, and thirty seconds later she had another fresh cup of brew in her hand. She looked at the five empty pods on the counter and swept them into the trash bin. *Get it together, Sid.*

It was 6:37 in the morning, and she hadn't been back to sleep since Roy left. She'd showered. Cleaned. Washed and dried. Her apartment, normally well kept, was now spotless. Counters were wiped clean. Not a dirty dish in the washer, the sink, or on the counters. All of her clothes were folded or ironed and hung. No dust bunnies lurked under the bed. She took a drink out of her coffee mug. It was a keepsake from her Air Force days, with a logo of a skull wearing a beret and the letters ABGD. *Air Base Ground Defense. Those were the days.*

She mopped a thin film of sweat from her brow with a dishrag. *I think I may need to shower again.* Meandering into the bathroom, she thought of Smoke. She couldn't get his brush-off out of her mind. She couldn't think of anything she'd done wrong, either. *I didn't do anything wrong.* Deep inside, her feelings stirred. She'd done something. Inside the tub and shower, all of the porcelain had a nice sheen. No soap buildup surrounded the drain nor watermarks the basin. Everything smelled clean. *Not gonna be enough.*

She put on a set of gym clothes, packed a duffel bag, got in her car, and drove to the gym. The showers there were plenty hot after a good workout, and the sauna would do her good. Still, the more she tried not to think about Smoke, the more he cropped up, a stealthy intruder invading the privacy of her mind. *Why the sudden rejection? Was there a message in it? What was his reason?* They hadn't even talked about the Black Slate, AV, or Night Bird. She didn't have anyone to talk with about those things.

Inside the gym, she had a purpose-filled workout, hammering at the heavy bag. Large drops of sweat splatted on the rubber-coated floor, forming tiny puddles. She wiped it up with her towel and headed for the sauna. There, she spent twenty minutes listening to a pair of older women discussing the sexual inefficiency of their husbands and planning a girls' trip to Vegas. The shower she took was hot, pleasant, and without any busybody neighbors. Refreshed and dressed for work, she left the gym and headed for her car.

"Excuse me, Agent Shaw?"

She turned. There stood a husky man in a weather-beaten trench coat and a Redskins ski cap that hung over his ears. He had s shifty gait as he approached.

"That's close enough, Mr…"

"Davenport. Russ Davenport." He tipped his scruffy chin that went well with his scratchy voice. "I'm a reporter for *Nightfall DC.*"

"Never heard of it," she said, easing back toward her car. "Care to explain how you know who I am?"

"Well, I'm an investigative reporter in the middle of an investigation. Surely you understand, being an investigator yourself."

"Oh, I understand. You're stalking a federal officer."

"It's still a free country. I'm just making conversation with a fellow citizen with whom I might have something in common. That's all."

"So, you've been waiting for me in a parking lot?"

He glanced back at the gym and patted his tummy. "I'm not one for working out much. It interferes with my fully processed diet." His eyes darted around before they fixed back on her. "Look, I'm not a troublemaker. I just have a question."

She popped open her car door. "Then you'll have to contact the FBI and go through the proper channels. They have a media center. I'm sure you're well acquainted with the Freedom of Information Act. Go there, or else you might find yourself in prison."

"You're working on the Black Slate," he interjected. "Have you seen any werewolves lately? Giant birds, maybe?"

She froze. *No way!* She held his gaze and shook her head. "DC is full of a lot of crazy things. A lot of people see one thing, and someone else sees another."

"I got proof," he said, raising his double chin. There was a satisfied look on his chubby face. He withdrew a plastic bag from his pocket. There was a large feather in it. "Look familiar?"

"No."

"I found this at the truck stop where that FBI chopper crashed. Normally I don't report on those bigger stories, but on social media there were some tall tales—of a giant bird, for instance." He coughed into his fist. "Well, how did I come across this?"

"DC is notorious for its really big pigeons."

"True, Agent Shaw, but this isn't that kind of feather. You see, I've got a friend who works in the Smithsonian. He's in the ornithology department—that means birds. He freaked out when he saw this. He said, 'I've never seen anything on this planet like it.' I almost didn't make it back out of there. Really creepy."

"Maybe you should have just left it with them. I'm sure they would have paid good money."

"As you can see," he opened his jacket, revealing a cheap shirt and cheaper blue trousers underneath, "I'm not into money. I'm into the truth. I know there are monsters out there, and I know that you have seen them. Just tell me more about what you saw."

"Oh, there are monsters all right, Mr. Davenport. You know as well as I do that this town is full of them. But the kind you're talking about, well, I don't have any proof on anything." She got inside her car and started to close her door. Russ grabbed the door. She tried to pull it shut, but his strength was firm. "You need to let go."

"You might not have any proof, but you have your word. Eyewitness testimony is the most convicting."

"And many eyewitnesses are also known to be convicts."

"You aren't a convict."

"How do you know for sure? How do you know anything for sure?" She closed the door, started the engine, and pulled out of her spot. She heard him yell out and say, "Nice car!"

Gunfire cracked out of nowhere. *Pop! Pop! Pop!* She flinched and checked her mirror. Russ was on the ground, clutching his chest and bleeding on the pavement.

CHAPTER 6

G LOCK READY, SIDNEY RUSHED OUT of her car toward Russ. He lay on the ground, moaning. Scanning the parking lot, she didn't notice any threat, just some gaping onlookers.

She pointed at one and said, "Call 9-1-1!" She kneeled at the man's side. He had two bullet holes in his side. Placing her hands on it, she applied pressure.

"Oh!" he said in alarm. His face was ashen. Eyes wide open.

"Easy, Russ. Easy. Help's coming."

His jittery gaze held her eyes, and he said, "Why would anyone shoot me?"

Because you know something you shouldn't know. She shushed him. "Save your strength, okay? Help is on the way." A small crowd gathered. "If you can't help, step away!" Most gawked, and a couple of others pulled out their phones. *Indecent idiots!*

"Dude, I might catch a shot of him dying," said a young man in a ski cap, tank top, and baggy sweatpants. He had more tattoos than teeth. "Wouldn't that be cool?"

"Yeah, man," said another one. "Pretty sick. Get closer. I want to show my girlfriend. She loves this stuff."

Someone get here now, please! "Has anyone called 9-1-1 yet?"

"I did."

"Me too."

"Agent Shaw," Russ said in a raspy voice. Blood bubbled from his mouth. "Getting shot hurts like hell."

"Don't talk. Try not to talk. Save your energy."

"I need to tell you something, in case I don't make it." He convulsed and twitched. "Aw geez, it hurts."

"Don't say anything," she said, cocking her head. Sirens. Loud and clear. *Hurry!* She bent closer. "Just hang on Russ. Can you do that for me? Hang on."

"I'm trying." He coughed blood.

"Dude, that's sick!" the young man said. "Get closer on that. It's awesome."

Sidney clenched her jaws and checked Russ's pulse. It slowed. He was losing lots of blood. *Please don't die.*

"Agent Shaw, you must listen," Russ croaked out. "They're watching. They're always watching."

Who's watching? She wanted to ask, but she couldn't. Not when his last moments were upon him. She needed to save him. *Why shoot him and not me?* "Save your strength. Help's here. They're going to take you to the hospital and save you."

"I'm already saved," he said. His eyes fluttered. "And I hate hospitals. Fight the good fight, Agent Shaw." He reached up and touched her cheek. His eyes were glassy. "I just wanted to help." His bloodstained fingers slipped down her cheek.

"Dude, did he die? Did he die?" one punk said. "Did you get it?"

The ambulance pulled in, and the paramedics pulled out. Police officers took control of the scene.

"Miss," said a paramedic in a blue EMS uniform. "You've done all you can. We got this."

She backed off as they loaded Russ onto the gurney. He wasn't moving. Into the ambulance he went. They shut the doors, and the vehicle sped away. *What just happened?*

"I got it all, dude. I got it all."

She whirled around and faced the pair of young men. "Excuse me." *Try reason, Sid.* "That man's a friend of mine who may or may not have just died. I'd appreciate it if you'd delete that video."

"Sorry, lady, but stuff like this is too hot." He eyed her up and down, nudged his friend, and thumped his nose. "But maybe we can work something out."

She closed in, looked him in the eye, and said, "Oh yeah? What did you have in mind?"

He rubbed his lower lip with his index finger, licked his teeth, and said, "I was thinking…" He grabbed her arm.

Perfect. She grabbed him by the wrist, twisted it behind his back, and slammed him into the pavement.

"Ow! What's the deal? Get off me!"

She took out her badge and stuck it in his face. "You just assaulted a federal officer. That's the deal, worm!"

The other young man took off running. She held her badge up and said, "Officers! That man's a suspect in the shooting." She drove her knee into the punk's back and said, "So are you, maggot."

"Hey, I didn't shoot anybody!"

"That's not for me to determine. That's up to the courts. You don't have any priors, do you?"

"A couple." He struggled. "Look, I'll delete it. Just let me go. I don't want any trouble. I'm sorry. Really, I'm sorry."

"Do it," she said, lifting her knee off his back.

Chin on the ground, hands holding the phone in front of his face, he pulled up the video. He hit the trash bin icon. "There, it's gone."

"Let's hope, but this isn't the end of the investigation, just the beginning. It's gonna be a long day, bub."

"But I have class."

"No, you don't. And that's not my problem." She pulled him up to his feet. "Did it even enter your mind to do something to help the man?"

"Why? He probably wouldn't do that for me." His eyes grazed over her body. "I'd help you out though."

Loser! "Officer!" She flagged a cop over. "This one's ready to make a statement, and so am I when you're ready."

It was late Friday morning, a day after the shooting at the gym. Sidney sat inside the Wayfarer's Way, sipping coffee and picking at her plateful of eggs and bacon that was pushed off to the side. She had a newspaper under her nose. There was a little blurb about the shooting. It said Russ Davenport was in critical condition. The police blotters had it down as an accidental shooting.

This is crazy.

Two bullets in the lungs in a full parking lot wasn't an accident. Witnesses said they'd seen a car drive by, chasing after another. Both of the vehicles were SUVs, dark paint, big rims. She hadn't noticed the vehicles at all. Everyone figured it was a gang, but she knew better.

She folded up her paper and pulled her plate of food over. The portions were huge. *No wonder Ted likes to meet here so much.* She figured he dreaded meeting her anyway, but he had to, given the nature of yesterday's incident. Her name, tied with the agency, was all over the blotters. But her name wasn't in the paper. Not that it should be, but it very easily could have been. The FBI didn't want that kind of local attention.

"Can I freshen you up, honey?" asked an older woman holding a steaming pot of coffee over the table.

"That would be great, thanks." Sid shoved her mug over and watched the woman fill it to the brim.

"No cream or sugar?"

"No."

"There you go. Anything else?"

"No, thank you."

She checked the clock on the wall. 10:32 am. Ted was late, and he wasn't normally late. She shifted in the booth and pulled up a website on her iPad. www.nightfalldc.com. It was more of a tabloid than anything else, but it had a strong following. There were stories about crimes that never got reported. Strange happenings at the nightclub scene. Sidney had spent a couple of hours scanning the past year's worth of articles and stories. Russ Davenport's name was on most of them, but that wasn't all she learned. Russ Davenport wasn't his real name, rather a pseudonym. And to make things more interesting, she still didn't know what his real name was.

A text popped up on her iPad from her sister, Allison. It read:

Can you watch Megan this weekend? Need serious help. Mom and Dad in Florida.

"She must be joking." Sid started to reply no but pulled back. A weekend with Megan might be just what she needed. She didn't want Allison to know that, but why punish the kid? Megan probably needed a break too. She texted back.

I'll think about it.

Great. It could be a career-defining moment. Thanks, Sis.

That's odd. The nature of the text almost seemed cheerful. Positive. *She's probably high.* Sidney sighed. *I guess I'll find out soon enough.* She checked the time. 10:36. *Where is he? He could at least text or something.* She took out her phone and pulled up Ted's number. *Screw this. I've got things to do.* A bell rang on the old restaurant's front door, and a man in an overcoat, suit, and tie entered. Sidney frowned. It wasn't Ted, it was Cyrus Tweel.

CHAPTER 7

CYRUS SAT DOWN IN THE booth and dropped a paper satchel on the table. "Hey, Sid." He raised his finger up and half-shouted at the waitress. "Coffee. Two creams. One sugar." He drummed the table and settled himself into the booth. "I hate this place. Smells old. Feels old. Never understood why Ted's so fond of it."

"Probably because people like you don't come here."

"Oh-oh," he said, drumming the table. He pushed back his round wire-rimmed glasses. "Why the frosty reception?"

"I was expecting Ted."

"Ted was called into something bigger—we can only assume—and hence, he dispatched me, your supervisor, to have this little meeting with you." He plucked a piece of bacon off of her plate and bit into it. "Man that's greasy." He dropped it back on her plate and wiped his hands off. "You should switch to turkey bacon or no bacon at all. That would be wise."

"And you should keep your hands to yourself." She straightened up in her chair and locked her fingers together and rested her hands on the table. "What's the meeting about? I assume it involves the incident from yesterday?"

"Never assume anything," he said, smiling. "No, I've been briefed on the incident and so has Ted, but this is entirely different." He shoved the paper satchel her way. "It's the next Black Slate assignment."

"Really?" she said, staring at the file. She fixed her gaze back on him. "You seem almost chipper about it."

"Oh, not really. Look Sid, I've gotten wind of some of the reports, and maybe I haven't been very clear about what I think, but I will be now." He pecked his index finger on the file. "This is a career killer. Get away from it."

"It's my assignment. I've been picked for some reason, and truth be told"—she pulled the file toward her—"I like it."

His face deflated a little and he said with a shrug, "It's your career." The waitress delivered his coffee and set it on the table. He took a long sip and made a sour face. "Good lord, this coffee tastes as old as the building."

Sidney stared at the file. It was sealed shut. She began tearing it open.

"Ah ah ah," Cyrus said, pinning the folder down with his hand. "You can look at this bullshit after I'm gone. I don't want any of this supernatural crap rubbing off on me. I've got big plans for tonight."

"Oh I see. You have a date then?"

He lifted his chin and said with a smirk, "As a matter of fact I do, and I'm pretty excited about it. She's so interesting." His eyes were fixed on hers. "Really interesting."

Fine, I'll entertain him. "And where did you meet her?"

"Work."

"Oh, well, I think that's a bad idea." *Not that I care.* "So, what's her name?"

"Rebecca Lang, and I believe you've met her."

"Yes," she nodded. "She seems nice. Good for you, Cyrus."

He reached into his pocket and grabbed his ringing phone. "Oh, that's her." He answered. "Hey Rebecca. Uh-huh. Uh-huh. Great. Eight it is." He disconnected and got out of his seat. "Sorry, but I've got to get back out on the street. I'm knocking off a little early today."

"Wait a minute," she said to him. "What about John Smoke? Isn't he going to be a part of this?"

"Don't know, don't care." He threw a buck on the table. "Read the file."

Back home inside her apartment early that evening, Sidney sat on her sofa staring at the unopened Black Slate file. Something was different. The hand-off from Cyrus for one thing. The lack of discussion about Smoke for another. She picked at the clasp that held the paperwork inside.

What are you waiting for, Sid?

Her phone buzzed. It was another text message from her sister. It read:

I'm waiting.

Sidney texted her back:

90 min.

She'd agreed to watch Megan over the weekend, and that was part of her hesitation with the file. Once she opened it, she'd dive into it, and she just didn't want to do that right now. But what if the contents inside required immediate action? And wasn't Smoke supposed to be the bounty hunter, not her? She was just supposed to watch him. The phone buzzed again. It read: Pick up some dinner.

Sidney squeezed her phone. *That's just like her, not feeding Megan any dinner. It's 7:10 already. Geez! I suppose I might as well stock up on some groceries. Deadbeat!* She tapped the phone against her chin and stared at the file. The last two files had almost gotten her killed, not to mention all the mystery they had unfolded. What would the next file have in store for her? *A vampire? The New Jersey Devil or a Mothman?* The man from the cemetery who they called Boss had made light about one.

It's not like you to be a chicken, Sid. Go ahead. Tear Pandora's box wide open.

She ripped off the tape, peeled back the metal clasp, and dumped the contents on the table. The tab on the black folder read Mason Crow. After folding it open, she studied the portrait of a black man in sunglasses and mutton chops. "Oh Lord," she chuckled, "it's the Duke of New York." She pushed the picture aside and glanced at the next one and blanched. "On steroids."

The pictures were all labeled Mason Crow. The man was huge. Maybe seven feet tall and solid muscle. One picture was of him towering in the center of a group of men of several nationalities. They were in the bush and geared up like mercenaries. Mason Crow had an M-60 machine gun that looked like a toy resting on his brawny shoulder.

"I don't even want to know what kind of monster this guy turns into." She flipped through a few more pictures, and her stomach turned queasy. Mason Crow stood over a pile of butchered bodies with a blood-soaked machete in his hand. "He's a monster already."

CHAPTER 8

"**C**ONGRESSMAN WILHELM? YOU'RE KIDDING, ALLISON. Tell me you're kidding?"

"No," Allison said, picking up her luggage and heading for the door. "This job's paying me seven thousand a month. I can't pass that up. I can't afford to pass up anything right now."

Sidney tossed her duffel bag onto the couch and glared at her sister. Allison wore a business pantsuit and she still looked sexy in it, like an airline attendant you'd see on some billionaire's private jet. "And David? Is he going to be there?"

"Nope," Allison said, checking her hair in her mirror. "I'm done with him." She smiled at herself in the mirror. "Wow, what a great view!"

"Seven-K a month seems a bit pricey for an internship," Sidney said, rubbing Megan's head. The little eyes were glued to the TV, watching cartoons. *I might need to look into her pay stub.* "And where are you going, exactly?"

"Oh, some sort of conference in Houston, Texas. I've never been there, but I hear it's pretty exciting. Do you think they still wear cowboy hats?"

"Sure, and the governor stables his horse at the capitol."

"Really?" Allison checked her make-up. "I bet that's fascinating." She loaded her luggage onto her shoulder. "Cab's waiting. Got to go. Kiss kiss, Megan."

Megan waved her pink-sleeved arm up in the air. "Bye, Mommy."

"Allison," Sidney started to say. Her sister disappeared into the hallway, and the door closed behind her. "Be careful."

"Are you worried about Mommy?" Megan said. She was leaning over the back of the sofa and looking up at Sid with her hands cupped under her chin. "Because you look worried."

Sidney took a seat on the couch and Megan curled up into her side. "Your mommy is my little sister, so I'll always worry some. Besides, that's what women do, too much and too often."

"Well, I'm not worried." Megan turned the TV off. "Can we play dress-up now?"

"How about we eat first? I brought your favorite takeout."

Megan clapped her hands. "Chinese?"

"Uh, no, I thought you liked Mexican."

"That was last year. I'm ten now, and I'm all about some Moo Goo Gai Pan."

"But you'll still eat Mexican, won't you?"

Megan shrugged her little shoulders and said, "I guess so."

"Good." Sidney got up from the couch and made her way into the apartment's kitchen. Grimy dishes were piled high in the sink. She stuck them in the dishwasher.

"That doesn't work anymore," said Megan, taking a seat on the kitchen barstool. She held a white teddy bear in her arms. "The landlord won't fix it because Mom's behind on her rent. You won't let them kick us out, will you Aunt Sid?"

"No, of course not." *Oh, great! Seven grand a month she says, and she can't pay rent.* "Well, you can still clean dishes with soap and water."

"I know. But I've been feeling kinda lazy lately." Megan stretched her arms out and yawned. "Plus, we're out of dish soap."

"I wasn't talking about you." Sid found a stack of paper plates in the cupboard, but there were water stains on them. "I was talking about your mother." She took the stryofoam containers of Mexican food out of the plastic bag and set them on the counter. "Looks like we're going to eat in a less formal setting." She fished some plastic utensils and napkins out of the bag. "Is that all right with you?"

Megan glanced at the trash can in the kitchen corner. It was stuffed with take-out containers. "What do you think?" she said.

The lukewarm food was good and the conversation light. Megan told her about school and her upcoming science project that she needed some help on. Sid noticed that Megan yawned a lot. She'd been with her niece plenty over the years, and usually, even later in the evening, she was bright eyed and bushy tailed. Normally, she'd be alert until she zonked out.

After they finished eating, Megan asked again if they could play dress-up, and they'd spent the last thirty minutes applying makeup.

Staring into the mirror, Megan said, "I look like a hooker."

"What?" Sidney gasped. "No, no, you don't." She started rubbing off some of the blush on her cheeks. *Morning Glory, I haven't overdone it that much, have I?* "What makes you think you look like a hooker?"

"Because I'm wearing a lot of makeup."

"Do you know what a hooker is?"

"Mommy says hookers are women who wear too much perfume and makeup."

"Well, not exactly. There are a lot of women who wear too much makeup, but they aren't hookers."

"Like old ladies that we see in department stores."

"Well that's one kind that aren't hookers."

"So what are hookers?"

Sidney grabbed a brush and began combing Megan's hair. "How about we braid it? You always look so cute when it's braided."

Megan said, "Sure. So, what's a hooker?"

"Well," said Sid as she braided Megan's soft and silky dirty-blond hair, "Hookers are women who sleep with men for money."

The little girl's jaw dropped, and her eyes filled with excitement. "Really? People will pay you to sleep with them? That sounds like a pretty easy way to make money. Sleeping's easy, but sleeping with boys seems kind of gross."

There's a lot of truth to that. "Well, there's a lot more to it than just sleeping with them."

"Like what?"

Be straight. "Kissing."

"Like sex kissing?"

Sidney eyed her reflection in the mirror. "Uh, something like that."

"Like I see on TV. I see lots of kissing on TV. Are all of those women hookers?"

"Only if they're paid for it." *Oh geez.* She stopped braiding. "What kind of shows do you watch?"

"Just what Mommy watches. I have a TV in my room, but the screen's all fuzzy. Mommy says she'll get me a new one now that she has a job."

"Okay, listen to your Aunt Sid, and I'll explain to you a little bit about hookers." *I shouldn't be having this conversation.* "Hookers sleep with men for money, but it's against the law. They can be arrested for it. So, talking about hookers, also known as prostitutes or call girls, is a bit of a no-no."

"Oh, I see." Megan smiled. "Thanks, Auntie Sid. That clears that up."

"Good." Sid resumed braiding the girl's hair.

"Aunt Sidney."

"Yes?"

"What happens if people sleep with each other for free? Is that illegal?"

Morning Glory!

CHAPTER 9

A FTER A RESTLESS NIGHT OF sleep, Sidney rolled out of her sister's bed and rubbed her eyes. It was daybreak, and a soft light illuminated the edges of the bent mauve-colored window blinds. Megan slept at her side, curled up in a ball. A gentle rise and fall was in the little girl's chest and her face, despite some smeared makeup, was at peace.

Sidney kissed her forehead and brushed her cheek with her thumb. *Such a sweet thing.* She picked her way through Allison's bedroom. Drawers were half open, stuffed with clothes spilling out. Her closet was cramped with shoeboxes and fancy dresses. Sid rubbed the satin on a pearl-colored evening dress.

This would cost me a paycheck. How does she get these things? The conversation she'd had with Megan about hookers came to mind. Sid's neck tightened. *No. She wouldn't. Would she?* It would explain plenty of things. The clothes, the shoes… she opened a white jewelry box that sat on the dresser and gaped.

Look at this stuff!

She held up a tennis bracelet loaded in bright diamonds and shook her head. *And she can't buy any damn groceries!* There was more. More precious stones and fine metals of all sorts. A small hoard. Sidney slipped a ruby band flecked with diamonds over her finger. *Hmmm, I might keep this for myself.* A gold-leaf brooch studded with rubies caught her eye. She snatched it up. *That's Mom's!* She clutched it in her hand. *Is she stealing this stuff, or was it given to her?* She plucked another item out of the box. A pair of silver and onyx cufflinks she had seen their father wear. *Sonuva—?*

A rustle in the living room caught her ear. She scooted over to the bed and grabbed her Glock from under the pillow. On cat's feet, she crept down the short hallway. The back of a man's head could be seen sitting on the couch. He was leaning over the coffee table. She charged the slide of her weapon, readying a round in the chamber. "Get those hands up where I can see them."

Slowly, the man's big hands rose toward the ceiling.

"Clasp your fingers behind your head," she ordered, making her way to the kitchen.

The man let out a grunt but complied. He turned his face toward hers.

"Smoke?"

The man looked amazing even in blue jeans, work boots, and a nondescript brown jacket. He swallowed. "Yeah. It's me."

She kept her gun on him. "What in the hell do you think you're doing?"

He grimaced. "Just keeping an eye on things, I guess." He eyed the barrel of her gun. "Do you mind?"

"Oh, I don't mind putting a bullet in your head. No, not at all."

"Maybe you should call the police." He started rubbing his neck.

Now that she looked closer, she noticed that his arm was skinned up. And the thigh of his jeans was torn, revealing a bloody gash.

He said, "You wouldn't happen to have a Band-Aid, would you?"

"No," she said, lowering her weapon. "But there's a hospital a few blocks up the road. Did you miss it on your way over here?"

"Guess so," he said, leaning his big frame over the coffee table. He clutched his side and eyed the Black Slate file that was opened on the table. "Interesting."

"There's nothing in here for you to see," she said. She stuffed everything into the file and tossed it onto the kitchen bar.

"I disagree," he said, running his eyes up her legs.

She was wearing only a long black shirt and panties and made no effort to hide it. Instead, she took a seat on the barstool and rested her gun hand on the bar. "Out with it. Why are you here—and why do you look beat all to hell?"

"Traffic problems."

"You didn't escape, did you?"

"Who, me? Nah, nothing like that. Just a simple misunderstanding on the way over, is all." He rubbed a lump on his head. "Got any ice?"

"No." She fidgeted on her stool, foot kicking. She was still mad at him for the cold shoulder in the detention center. She wanted an explanation for it. At the same time, Smoke was hurt. Bad enough to get stitches, maybe worse. *What is he up to?*

Smoke sat quietly eyeing the décor and pressing his jacket against the cut in his leg. "Look, I'm sorry for the brush-off, okay?"

"What are you talking about?"

"You know, back in the detention center. But I was in a hurry. You came at a bad time."

"Oh, were you missing out on some Bingo?"

"Something like that." He eased himself up off of the sofa and stretched his broad shoulders back. There was some popping of tendons and sinew. He lumbered toward the front door. "I guess I better get going." He glanced at the file. "I got all I need for now."

What is he up to? There was a strange thing about the file: no letter from the bureau and no mention of Smoke, either. *Is he still on my side?* "See you around, Mr. Smoke."

He stopped turning the doorknob. "You're one stiff lady."

"What did you expect, a welcome wagon?" She put the gun down and balled up her fists by her sides. "What kind of friend sneaks in while you're sleeping? It's creepy."

Smoke's face darkened a little. "I wouldn't do anything without good reason. Did you ever stop to think that maybe I was here protecting you and the kid?" He approached her, stretched his arm across the kitchen counter, and grabbed some paper towels off the roll. "We've been through enough together. You should trust me by now."

"That's not how it works."

"Guess not," he said, pressing the paper towels against a notch on his head and opening the door. "Later, Agent Shaw." Stooped over, he exited and closed the door behind him.

Sidney started out of her seat, then stopped. Something thumped into the door.

Wump.

She hopped out of her chair and opened the door. Smoke lay stone cold in the stairwell.

CHAPTER 10

S MOKE'S PULSE WAS STRONG BUT slow. Careful not to get any blood on the concrete stairs, Sidney dragged the man inside. "Geez, you're heavy." Closing the door, she left him on the floor, rushed into the bathroom, and grabbed alcohol and washcloths. In the kitchen she found a pair of scissors and cut the jeans off his leg. The sticky, matted blood was worse than it looked, and it had a rough stitch job on it. More blood still oozed out of the wound. "You need a hospital."

She grabbed her phone and had started to call 9-1-1 when a text popped up from an unknown caller.

Don't call the hospital. He'll be fine.

"What?"

The text continued.

I think.

She scanned the apartment, checked outside through the blinds, and checked the front door's spy hole. She had started to text back when another message popped up.

It's Mal Carlson.

"I'm getting a little sick of Mal Carlson." She kneeled alongside Smoke and applied pressure to the wound on his leg. His clammy face soured. "What kind of scrap did you get into this time?"

It wasn't the first time he'd shown up battered. It had happened when they were dealing with Night Bird. He had been slightly hobbled then, but this was worse. *What on earth was he doing?* She got up, fixed a damp washcloth, and put some ice in it. A knock sounded at the door.

Picking up her gun, she then checked the spyhole. Phat Sam and Guppy stood outside. She opened up. Guppy bustled through first and opened up a kit of some kind.

"Care to fill me in?" Sidney said to him.

Sam eased her way inside and said, "We have this covered. Just give him a moment." The gorgeous woman's tone was somber, and her forehead was creased with concern. "It's been a long night."

Sidney opened her mouth to speak but opted to close the door. "Fine."

Guppy pushed up his sleeves, revealing his thick and hairy forearms. He plucked a syringe from his kit and filled it with a clear liquid from a vaccine bottle. He injected it into Smoke's wounded leg.

"Care to tell me what that's for?"

"Smoke has a thing," Sam said, moving over to the sofa. She eyed it and sat down on the coffee table. "I think you're going to need a new blanket, but that leather upholstery should be good to go."

"Again, what is the shot for?" Sidney demanded. "And what kind of thing are you talking about? You make it sound like he's a diabetic."

Guppy tucked a penlight in his mouth and peeled Smoke's eyelids open with his thumbs. "He's gonna be out for a while. Better put him in the bedroom." In a slow but fluid move, he hefted Smoke up into a fireman's carry on his shoulder and headed down the hallway.

"Hold on a second," Sidney said, cutting into his path. "My niece is sleeping back there."

"She's not sleeping in both bedrooms, is she?"

"No."

"Then," Guppy said, "I'll use the one she's not using." He smiled. "And which one might that be?"

Sidney opened the door to Megan's bedroom and stepped aside. "Don't make a mess."

"Hmmm," he said, stepping inside. "Lots of pink and purple. I like it. It's not manly, but it's soothing. Good colors for healing."

Sidney shut him in and took a peek inside the master bedroom. Megan slept easy. Sid closed the door and headed back down the hall. Fat Sam had her nose buried in the Black Slate file.

"Do you mind?" Sidney said.

Sam waved her off. "Oh, we're all part of the same team. Get over it." Wearing only a dark-green hoodie and blue jeans, Sam was still an impressive sight. Her words somehow carried authority.

Sidney glared at her.

"All right," Sam said, closing the folder. "I guess we can sit here and stare at each other."

"Or you can fill me in on what happened to Smoke."

"Do you have any coffee in this rat hole?" Sam said toward the kitchen. "It goes great with conversation."

"No."

"Donuts?"

Sidney shook her head. "You don't look like someone who eats donuts."

"I have amazing genes."

"Yes," Sid said, taking a seat beside Sam, "you appear to have a lot of amazing qualities, but not pissing me off isn't one of them. Out with it, Sam."

Sam smiled. "Huh, I like that. A compliment with a dash of insult. Well done, Agent Shaw."

Sidney raised her brows at Sam.

"All right," the woman said, "Smoke got in a fight last night, but we've been keeping track of him and ended up here."

"With the help of Mal Carlson?"

"Yes."

"So you've met him?"

"Yes," Sam responded.

Sidney's tone tightened. "In person?"

Sam started to nod her head and then shook it. "No. But he sends us stuff."

The muscles knotted between Sidney's shoulders. Again, everyone seemed to know what was going on but her. "What kind of stuff?"

"Oh, a few software programs and some other gadgets, like that kit Guppy has." Sam checked her black-coated nails and mumbled. "A few weapons and articles of clothing." She huffed on her nails and rubbed them on her hoodie. "Hasn't he been sending you stuff too?"

"Not lately. Does the FBI know you're in on this?"

"Oh no. No no no no. Honestly, my skin crawls a little, hanging out with you, but it's fine since you're a shadow agent." She eyed Sid. "You *are* still a shadow agent?"

"Oh, I'm a shadow all right." Sid glanced down the hall. Inside, her feelings stirred. "He *is* going to be okay, right?"

"Sure. Believe it or not, he's even tougher than he looks." She nudged Sid. "And he has us looking after him."

"So, are you going to tell me what he got in a fight with and why he got in a fight with it? And how exactly did he get out of prison? I need some answers."

"Well, I don't know how he got out of prison. I was only notified after he got out, but I do know what he got in a fight with." She peered down the hall, and her beautiful face filled with excitement. She looked into Sid's eyes and squeezed her forearm. "It was a gargoyle."

CHAPTER 11

"A GARGOYLE, HUH?" SIDNEY SAID, STARING at Sam's fingernails digging into her arm. "And you saw it?"

"Well, no." Sam let go. "But I'm pretty sure that's what it was."

Sid recollected the gargoyle theory from back when they were in the cemetery during the last investigation. Smoke had claimed that was what he'd seen. "And where did this happen?"

"Smoke sent us word that he was investigating something at some old cemetery. And he told me what he saw that last time. He said it was a gargoyle." She pulled her chin up. "And I believe him. And," she poked Sid in the shoulder. "I believe in the werewolf and the harpy and I'm not alone."

You're a kook. Sidney squeezed her eyes shut and shook her head a little. *And I'm a hypocrite. I've seen these things—but I still don't believe anyone else sees them.* "I'll make some coffee." She headed into the kitchen and spied an espresso machine on the counter. "It's going to be pretty stiff."

"That's how I like it."

"Who are you?" said a little girl's voice with avid curiosity. Megan had made her way out of the bedroom and waltzed into the living room. She yawned and squeezed her teddy bear. "And why is my bedroom door locked?"

"Uh, hi," Sam said. "I'm Sam, and it's nice to meet you. You must be Megan." She looked at the bear and stretched out her hands. "And who do we have here?"

"This is Agent Fluff, and he doesn't like strangers." Megan sat down on the sofa, still staring at Sam. "But you're kinda pretty, so I guess it's all right." She handed over the bear.

"Nice to meet you, Agent Fluff," Sam said, shaking his paw.

"Aunt Sidney, I'm hungry."

"Okay," Sid said. She checked inside the fridge. No eggs. No milk. She closed the door and opened up one of her bags of groceries. "You still like cinnamon Pop-Tarts?"

"Yep!"

"Maybe the three of us should go out," Sam suggested. "I know a great place nearby that makes awesome pancakes."

"What? No." Sid rejected.

"Yeah! Let's go, Aunt Sidney. Pleeease!" Megan pleaded.

"What is *with* you people and pancakes?" Sidney said.

"Come on," Sam said. "I think it would be best." She eyed the hallway again. "If you know what I mean."

Sid shut off the coffeemaker and agreed, "Okay."

They spent the next couple of hours eating at the International House of Pancakes. Megan had a hundred questions for Sam. Sam had a thousand answers. All went well until they returned to the apartment and found out Smoke and Guppy were gone. Otherwise, everything was just as they left it, and even Megan's bedroom was cleaned up and organized.

"I guess that's my cue," Sam said, making a break for the door.

Sidney blocked it. "You aren't going anywhere until you tell me what's going on."

Megan took a seat on the couch and turned on the television. "Do you two mind taking it somewhere else? My show is coming on. Got to get me some Halley and Baby."

Sidney pointed down the hall and said to Sam, "March." Inside the master bedroom, they both took a seat on the bed. "So tell me something. Why did Smoke come here?"

Sam shrugged.

"All right then." Sid rubbed her hands on her thighs. "Since we're a team, and I'm pretty sure you pride yourself on being an honest woman, I'll rephrase the question. Why do you think Smoke came here?"

Sam's eyes brightened. She crossed her legs and said, "I think he was protecting you."

"All right, and what do you think he was protecting me from?"

"Gargoyles?" Sam lifted her shoulders a little. "Maybe that Mason Crow fella." She made a bitter face. "That's a scary-looking guy. And then, of course, as usual, you have the Drake to contend with, which I think we know is behind all this."

Sidney shrank back on the bed. Things began to click. "It's the file. They want the file!"

"You think?"

Sidney retrieved the file from the kitchen counter. She had taken it with her on the trip to eat but had left it in the car. From now on she'd be more careful. Back inside the bedroom, she dropped it on the comforter and opened it up.

"What are you doing?" Sam asked.

"Someone made sure the last file got burned up in a car accident. We still recovered pieces of it, and that was enough last time, but..." She studied the faces in the pics, looking for marks, tattoos, or distinct features. There were several notes and records too. "Everything is a clue, a puzzle piece, and each file ties them all together to complete the picture."

"In theory." Sam picked one of the pictures up. "Or Smoke missed you."

"Now that's a theory." Sid plucked a shipping manifest out of the file and noted a tiny logo on it. It matched some markings on people's arms, and one of the soldiers with Mason Crow had the image sewn on his camouflage shirt. "I think this is probably a good place to start."

"Assuming you survive until Monday. You and your niece both."

"We'll be fine." Wheels turning inside her mind, Sidney wanted to get out on the hunt, but that wasn't going to happen with Megan. She had been right about not looking at the file, but now that she had, she was hungry. Starving with curiosity.

"I can see this is eating at you. Tell you what," Sam suggested, reaching for the file. "How about I take the file, and you can pick it up on Monday, or Sunday night if you like. Out of sight, out of mind. Have some piece of mind with your little sunshine."

"I don't know about that." Sid stared at the file. She knew she couldn't control everything all the time. "You know, it wouldn't kill us to make a copy."

"Wouldn't that be breaking the rules?"

"I suppose, but I don't think you're going to tell," Sid said. "Come on. I know a place we can go."

Sam took her by the wrist with a firm grip. "Let go, Sid. Just let go of it."

Sidney started to pull away, but then she sighed. "All right. Let's do this. Take some pics with your phone."

"No, too many Cloud issues," Sam said. "Just let it go for a while, will you? Besides, I know you remember most of what you saw."

True. Sidney's sharp memory retained plenty, but she had only glanced through what she'd seen. She ground her teeth, eyed Sam, and released the file. "I want it back Sunday night."

Sam got up with a smile. "Oh, don't you worry. You'll have it back."

Sidney followed her to the front door and let her out. "I better."

Sam's shoes echoed off the concrete steps, and out of sight she went.

Sidney closed the door and rested her shoulder on it. Her hands clutched at her aching head. *Am I crazy?*

"Aunt Sidney," Megan said, popping up over the back of the couch. "Can I still have a Pop-Tart?"

"Sure, sweetie." Sid headed into the kitchen. Outside in the parking lot, a woman's voice cried out for help, and a blood-curdling screamed followed.

"AAAAIIIIEEEE!"

CHAPTER 12

"**S**TAY PUT," SIDNEY SAID, SNATCHING up her pistol, "and lock the door behind me. I'll be right back." Rushing outside and into the parking lot, she found Sam sitting on the blacktop clutching her leg. "What happened?"

"They got it! They got the file!" Sam pointed toward the parking lot exit. A dark blue sedan without any plates swerved and clipped the back end of a car that was backing out. Without slowing, it sped away and out of sight onto the highway. "I'm sorry, Sidney. I'm sorry."

Sid kneeled alongside Sam. The woman had a nasty gash through her jeans on the side of her thigh. "Are you okay?"

Grimacing, Sam nodded. Tears streaked down the corners of her eyes. "That's going to leave a scar, isn't it?"

"That's what you're worried about?"

"Well, that and the file," Sam said, stretching out her hand. "Help me up. I need to get out of here."

"Let's get you inside so I can take a look at that."

"No." Sam pointed at the car whose bumper had been clipped. A man with fuzzy hair was pointing and screaming. Sam started limping toward an all-white mustang convertible. "Cops will be coming. You'll have to cover for me."

"I need my file back!"

Sam closed herself in the car, fired up the engine, and drove away. Seconds later, Sidney closed her jaw, headed back for the apartment, and knocked on the door. "It's Aunt Sid, Megan. You can let me in now."

The door cracked open, and Megan peeked out. The chain held the door from completely opening. "Is everything okay?"

"It is now," Sid said, squatting down. "Are you okay?"

Megan nodded and closed the door.

Sid heard the chain come off, and then the door opened again. She eased her way inside and locked the door behind her. "You did good, Megan. You did just like I said. I think I'll let you eat the entire box of Pop-Tarts for that."

"Yippee!"

It took less than an hour to sort everything out when the police arrived. Sidney told the officers most of what she saw, but she didn't claim to know anything about who Sam was. Instead, she opted to not be forthcoming with all that she knew. It left her steaming inside. She wasn't big on half-truths and lies. Especially ones told to her. Telling them herself left her feeling dirty.

Somebody really needs to explain all this.

She was sitting on the sofa hiding her glum face with a smile when Megan asked, "Aunt Sid, can we watch a movie?"

"Sure, whatever you want. You pick."

For the latter half of the day, she played with Megan, feeling guilty because her heart wasn't in it. Her thoughts raced through every detail of her visit from Smoke, Sam, and Guppy. Perhaps the entire thing had been staged to get that file. A ruse. A deception. Was someone playing a game with her?

"Can we order pizza?" Megan asked at dinnertime.

"Sure. Whatever you want." Sidney scratched some images on a note pad. It was a picture of Mason Crow. His broad face and features gave him an inhuman quality. On a separate pad she made a list of people, places, and things she'd seen in the file. A tiny finger tapped her on the shoulder. "Huh?"

Megan looked up at her. "You need to call it in."

"Oh, I'm sorry." She set down her pad. "Where's the phone?"

Megan cocked her head. "You have it. In your pocket."

"I thought there was a phone in the apartment."

"There was, but it was discontexted."

Sidney laughed. "You mean disconnected."

"Yeah, that's what I said, discontexted." The little girl yawned. Her light eyes were weak and tired. "I like Hawaiian Style, with thin crust and extra ham."

Sidney readied her phone. "Your mommy likes that?"

"No. That's Grandpa's recipe."

"So it is." She knew that. They had practically grown up on it as kids. "And you want it from Husson's Pizza, I take it?"

"Either there or Grazianno's." Sidney curled up on the couch, sniffled, and closed her eyes. "Wake me up when it gets here. I think I need a little nap time."

The next twenty-four hours were more restless ones. On the outside, Sidney tried to entertain Megan the best she could, but the Black Slate was eating her alive on the inside. There was no word either. Not from Smoke, Mal, or anyone. She stewed over whether or not to report that the file had been lost, but it could wait until Monday. *Maybe later.*

Megan lay on the sofa napping again. Sid covered her with a blanket. The little girl's energy ran high in spurts before turning low. *She needs to see a doctor.*

Sid watched television on and off, but nothing eased her restless mind. It was 3:16 Sunday afternoon, and Allison wasn't expected back for hours. *I'm not going to make it.* She rubbed Megan's leg. *She must think I'm a horrible aunt.*

A jingle of keys sounded outside the door, and the knob rattled. Sidney unholstered her gun and slipped over to the door and peered through the spyhole. *Allison?* She removed the chain just before the door swung open.

Allison shuffled inside with her head down and tossed her luggage on the floor.

"You're home early," Sidney said, "Is everything all right?"

"I'm fine. Thanks." She made her way over to Megan and huddled at her side. She kissed her daughter's cheek. "I missed you."

"Are you all right?"

"I said I'm fine," Allison said again, not making eye contact. "And I appreciate it. I really do. But if you don't mind, I could use some time alone with my daughter."

"Well, if you don't mind, I'd like you to tell me that face to face."

Allison stood up with a sigh and faced Sid. She had a split lip, and her chin was bruised. "I partied too much and fell. And I don't need a lecture. I've embarrassed myself enough already."

Sidney reached for Allison's sleeve. "Let me see your arms."

"What? No!" Allison backed away. "I'm not using."

"I didn't think you were, but I can see a bruise on your wrist that wasn't there when you left. How'd that get there?" She reached out again. "And what's that on your neck?"

Allison smacked her hand away. "Get out of here!"

CHAPTER 13

THERE WAS NO ARGUMENT. SIDNEY gathered her things, kissed Megan on the forehead, and left. She'd been driving around in the Hellcat ever since. Three hours of lonely road. She drove around Interstate 495 at least four times before pulling into a gas station.

The chill nipped at her ears as she pumped high-octane fuel into her car. Finished, she headed inside the store, fixed a large coffee, paid with a card, and hit the road. Inside her, a conflict stirred. Allison infuriated her. Whoever had hurt her sister made it worse. And the last thing Sid wanted was for Megan to have to see such things. It pained her heart. She said the serenity prayer.

"O God, give me the serenity to accept the things I cannot change,

The courage to change the things that I can,

And the wisdom to know the difference."

She took a swig of coffee and thundered down the road. *I can't do it all. At least not on my own.*

Cruising through the biting wind of the late-winter day, she headed toward Smoke's apartment. She wanted answers to her questions. *And somebody better be there to answer.* Off the interstate she went, onto the highway until she hit the back road that rolled right up to the remodeled service station that was now Smoke's home. The brakes squeaked as she came to a stop. No lights shone from within, and no cars were parked outside.

I thought Sam would be here.

She shut off the engine, made her way to the front door, and turned the knob. It was unlocked. She swung the door open and was greeted by a burst of warm air. Inside, the light was dim, but the gas furnace rattled above. She closed the door behind her. "Smoke?"

"You're early." Smoke sat in a chair that seemed too small for his frame, hunched over his computer desk, studying something.

"Am I? I didn't realize I was on your schedule. As a matter of fact, I'm not aware of any schedule."

He kept his back to her, igniting her blood.

She marched over and spun him around. "Tell me what in the hell is going on!"

Smoke tilted is head back and gazed up into her eyes. His color had returned, and his strong, handsome features were more pronounced in the dusky light. He offered a smile and shrugged his brawny shoulders. "I'd be happy to fill you in, Agent Shaw." He reached behind him and grabbed a sealed manila file and handed it over to her. "You might want to start here."

The file had some heft to it. She wanted to hit him with it. She ripped the top off and removed the black file that was inside. The tab on it read, Mason Crow. "What is this?"

"You might want to sit down."

"I'm fine where I'm standing."

"Suit yourself then, Agent Shaw." He got up and took a seat on the old black leather couch and sunk in. "It was all a setup. Sorry."

She opened the file. Most of the pages and pictures were identical, but there was more information. A notable amount. There was a smaller envelope inside with bureau letterhead in it. "What do you mean by 'setup?'"

Smoke rubbed his neck. "The other file was a ploy to draw the enemy out."

She stiffened. "And I wasn't consulted on this!"

"No. *They* agreed that it might interfere. That it was too risky. Keeping you in the dark was better. At least that's the version I got." He looked her in the eye. "I didn't agree. Things got dicey on Friday, and that's why I showed up."

She walked over, leaned down in front of him, and hit his knee with the folder. "Who are *they?*"

"Good question. I don't have the answer."

She let out a disturbing chuckle and flopped down on the sofa. "Am I even on the FBI's payroll anymore?"

"As long as the checks keep clearing, I'd say so. Besides, there are plenty of folks on the payroll that people never see or hear about."

"Yes, I know." From the file, she took out the letter and opened it up. "Everything's a conspiracy."

"And you still doubt that after everything you've seen?"

"No, I believe what I see, and I believe in things I don't see. I just don't share your disconcerted views."

He sat up. "Disconcerted?"

She read the letter to herself.

Agent Shaw,

Due to the unorthodox arrangement of this assignment, you will need to keep the following items under consideration.

John Smoke is a convicted criminal with special skills. Don't underestimate him. He's dangerous. Unpredictable. Possible escape risk.

You have eyes on him, and we have eyes on him. Allow him free range. We'll let you know if he needs reeling in.

If any alien objects or circumstances or individuals encountered, notify your superiors immediately.

Seek Mal Carlson for assistance when needed.

Shadow cover authorized on this Deep Black assignment.

Trust your instincts and good hunting,

The Bureau

"Care to share?" Smoke asked.

"You mean to tell me you don't know? Huh?" She handed him the letter. "Go ahead. Read. Have yourself a chuckle. After all, this is becoming a joke."

"It's anything but that," he said, staring at the letter and then chuckling. He did his Batman voice again. "*He's dangerous.* Hah. I just love that part. *Unpredictable.* I guess that's 'cause I'm Batman.*"

Sidney held her lips tight to keep from laughing and stuck her nose in the folder. There were a few more photos, and one of a woman stood out in particular. There was something about her, standing alongside Mason Crow with an M-16 assault rifle resting over her shoulder. A deep intensity shone in the tall and lanky woman's eyes. *She seems familiar.*

Absorbed in the photo, she hadn't even noticed that Smoke had gotten up until she heard a rustle behind her. "What are you doing?"

Smoke stood by the kitchen wearing only a pair of boxer-briefs. His long frame was layered in corded muscles. With a panther's ease, he slid the sweet heart suit up over his powerful legs. His arms were scarred and knotty. His smooth, strapping chest revealed something primal and powerful about him. A giant cat of a man ready to spring. "Getting ready," he said.

Sidney swallowed and caught her breath. Something stirred inside her. She ingested him with her eyes. It was just her. Just him. And nobody else for miles. He slid the rest of the suit over his brawny shoulders. "Where'd you get that suit?"

"Mal sent me a new one."

"Mal? Oh, your buddy Mal." Her urgings cooled. Her temper flared. "You sound like old buddies."

"I said he *sent* it to me." He put on his jeans and a burgundy hoodie that was similar to Sam's. "Do you happen to have yours?"

"Yes, why?"

"Because those people who stole the false file, well…" he strapped two guns to his hips, "I know exactly where they are."

CHAPTER 14

"Y OU KNOW EXACTLY WHERE THEY are, huh?" Sidney said. They stood outside her car in the rain twenty miles south of DC, looking at an open field. "Lead the way then."

Smoke stared at an app on his phone. According to him, *they* had planted a tracking device in the dummy file. That explained how Smoke had known Sidney was staying at Allison's apartment. He tapped the side of his phone with his palm.

"Really?" Sid said. "Is it named Ziggy, too?"

"Huh, good one." He stuffed his phone into his pocket and sauntered out into the field. "Something's here. I can feel it."

Huffing through the drizzling rain, Sidney followed his lead. On the ride over, she and Smoke had made amends and discussed the file—and a few other things. His apologetic words had given her some comfort, but there was still plenty of tension between her shoulders, even with the sweet heart suit on. Smoke had given her a hoodie too, like the ones he and Sam had, saying it was another of Mal Carlson's devices. Hers was dark blue.

"I see something," he said, pointing ahead.

Squinting her eyes, she made out a very high chain-link fence.

Smoke marched straight for it, stopped, and gawked at the crooked sign. "No trespassing."

"No surprise." She made her way a little farther down along the fence. "It says here, 'Property of Drake Real Estate.'" She cocked her head and stretched out her hands. "I wonder if it's electrified." She grasped it and started shaking uncontrollably. "Aaaaaiiiiiieeeeee!"

Smoke shook his head at her. "Really?"

She stopped shaking and let go. "You know, you're the first person that hasn't worked on."

"And you've done that how many times?"

Once. "I can't remember." *I'm really losing my humorous touch.* "It seems odd that the people who took the file would come this way. There isn't a road or anything."

"I'm not right on their trail. I'm staying a quarter mile off." He reached up, grabbed the lip of the fence, and pulled himself up and over. He eyed her through the fence. "I don't want them to see me. Are you coming?"

"I kind of like the view from right here," she said through the fence. "And I assume you're accustomed to it."

"You're cold."

She felt a little bad, but made no apologies. "Sam mentioned that you fought a gargoyle. Is there any truth to that?"

"Yep. Now are you coming over, or are you keeping the car warm for my return?"

"Just hold on a second. I think we need a little more planning before we do anything."

He put his hands on his hips. "Fine, let's hear it."

"First, the objective. Mason Crow. They want him alive."

"Yes, same as always." He shrugged and came closer, almost pressing his face to the fence. "Nothing new. Listen, I can go this alone. Retrieve. Report. Then we'll take step two. You can count on me."

They both clutched the fence, and her fingers touched his. She climbed over and hopped down. "We'll see."

Night had fallen. The pair cut through the darkness of the meadow. The rain slid right off their hoodies, and the second skin she wore left her feeling energized.

"I've got the signal back," Smoke said, staring at his phone. "Maybe a couple hundred meters that way." He pointed.

Wading through the tall grasses, she caught a whiff of manure. The landscape flattened and large bales of hay were scattered throughout the area. Peeking out of the night against the trees were a handful of silos. When they made a bead for the structures, several storehouses appeared.

Smoke stayed her with his hand and hunkered down. He produced a small pair of binoculars and put them to his eyes. He handed them to her.

Gazing through them, she got a better look at the ranch. A huge log cabin sat in the middle, with smoke billowing out of the chimney stack. The windows showed a warm glow within. The binoculars detected something else as well: heat signatures of men standing or strolling on the porch. With assault rifles in their arms. She surveyed more of the area. Guards were posted all around the complex. They stood among the silos, storehouses, and barns. There were vehicles too. Humvees. Vans. Farm trucks. Beyond the buildings was something else. A helicopter. *Morning Glory.*

"I counted fifteen, what about you?"

She handed him the binoculars. "Twenty."

"Hah," he said, pulling out his pistol. "I was testing you. Good eye. Besides, I like these odds better." He clicked out the magazine and slapped a different one in. "The more bad guys, the merrier." He tossed her a magazine. "Blue tips. Have fun."

"More presents from Mal?"

"Yep." Smoke stood up in the grass and grinned. "I don't know about you, but I'm ready to put some holes in things." He glanced at her. "So what's the plan?"

She switched magazines. "Tell me yours. If I don't like it, I'll tell you mine."

"Plan A, we disable the chopper first and recon. Plan B, we secure the chopper, find Crow, unleash a distraction, take him down, and whisk him away in the chopper."

"Are you flying the chopper? Just because I was in the Air Force doesn't mean I'm a pilot." Her fingertips tingled. "I'm a cop, remember?"

"I've got it covered."

Sidney didn't remember reading anything about him being a pilot. "Let's just find out if he's in there first. And stick together."

Staying low, the two of them circled around the ranch toward the chopper. Her nerves were on fire, and butterflies fluttered in her stomach. A step ahead of her, Smoke prowled with the finesse of a jungle cat. It eased her doubts. She split off to Smoke's right, stumbled over something, and pitched forward. *Crap.* She gathered her feet under her.

Smoke stopped and turned back.

"I'm fine."

He turned his back and marched forward again.

Sidney took her next step. Something seized her legs and jerked her down to the ground. A rock-hard fist clocked her in the side of the head, drawing bright spots. Cold and clammy hands clutched at her throat. Uncanny strength pinned her down. Dead yellow eyes found hers. It was a deader, stuffing her face down in the earth's soft grime. *Help!*

CHAPTER 15

FIGHTING AGAINST HER AGGRESSOR AS quietly as she could, she released her gun and fumbled for her knife. Her hand found the hilt and jerked it out. She stabbed wildly over her shoulder. The blade bit deep into flesh but the strong arms held her fast. Thrashing, she twisted onto her back and stabbed at its chest. The blade sunk into its belly.

Its expressionless leer didn't change. Its fists flailed at her head.

She covered up.

Wop! Wop! Wop! Urk!

The beating stopped. Her eyes snapped open. The deader that straddled her swayed with a knife tip sticking out of its chest. It teetered over into the grass.

Smoke stood there offering his hand. "How are you?"

Heart thundering inside her ears, she got back on her feet. "Fine." She kicked the monster. "Damn dirty deaders."

The monster still twitched.

Smoke kneeled down and wrenched his blade like a key, making a sickening crunch.

The deader's body went limp.

A beam of light shone from the compound.

She huddled down, hissing, "Great."

Smoke whispered back, "You didn't fire your weapon. I'm impressed." He offered over to her the gun she'd lost in the struggle. "Don't worry. I won't tell Cyrus you lost it."

She snatched it out of his hand, whispering harshly, "I didn't lose it."

As the light passed over their hiding spot, she took a glance. Three men were spread out and coming their way with assault rifles ready. Assuming these men knew what they were doing, it would be her last gunfight if they saw her first. A few quick blasts into her spot and it would be over. *This is bad. Really bad.*

Smoke crawled over to her side and whispered, "We could surrender."

"Are you nuts?"

He shrugged.

The light swept over their heads again, and she took another glance. The men were twenty yards away and closing in. *Do I shoot or not? Do I shoot or not?*

Smoke wiggled her knife in front of her eyes. "I'll handle this."

Suddenly, a buck rushed through the grasses and bounded over them. A cry of alarm went up. Shots were fired.

Blat-at-at! Blat-at-at!

"Stop shooting, you idiot!" said one of the guards. "It's a fricking deer!"

Still huddled beside Smoke, Sidney watched one guard in a pea coat march toward the one she thought had fired. He snatched the man's weapon away.

"Give me that!" He cocked the weapon back and stuffed it into the man's belly.

"Oof!" the man gasped, collapsing to the ground.

"Now I have to explain this mishap to the boss." The lead guard lowered the muzzle on the fallen one. "I should probably shoot you myself. It'd be better than seeing you turned into one of those deaders." He tossed the rifle at the man. "Let's get this over with. Better hope they're feeling merciful."

The guard pushed himself up with his weapon and trudged behind the other two. Near the log cabin, a small force had gathered. The lead guard held his arm up and waved. Before long there were some angry mutterings cutting through the steady rain.

Smoke nudged her. "We need to move while they're distracted. Come on."

Heart racing and keeping low, she pushed through the tall grasses with her gun barrel lowered. The thought of deaders prowling the grounds kept the alarm sounding in the back of her mind.

Smoke led her behind a barn that stood adjacent to the back porch of the cabin. The smell of hay and manure tickled her nose. She sneezed into her sleeve.

"This isn't the time for that," Smoke hissed.

"Then maybe we should vacate."

"Are you allergic?"

"No." She pressed her ear against the barn. Soft rustlings came from inside. She crept along the way, running her hands along the boards. Her fingers found an open knothole about knee high. She crouched down and peeked through. She stiffened. Children aged eight to twelve were busy packing, taping, and stacking boxes. A fire erupted inside her. *Not again!*

"What is it?" Smoke said, bending down.

She scooted away.

Smoke took a look through the hole, grunted, and eased back. "They'll have to wait."

"I'm sure they've waited long enough." She took out her phone and started to dial.

Smoke pushed her hand down. "One thing at a time. This is Drake space. Your comrades at the FBI aren't going to drop in without more evidence."

He was right. She didn't want to admit it, but he was. All she could think about was Megan. What if her niece were in that situation? The horror of it all. She took another look. There were five kids, wearing khaki jumpers. They all seemed so familiar. Their movements were purposed, fluid, and eerie.

"Hey," Smoke whispered. "I think I have an idea." He twisted a silencer onto the muzzle of his gun. "See that propane tank? How about I put a hole in it?"

"I think we need a more subtle course of action."

Smoke offered a smile. "I don't." He took aim and fired.

Ptew!

There was a metal *ting* sound, but no explosion.

"Idiot!" she whispered through her teeth. "Good thing it was empty."

He took aim again. "I see another one."

"No, it's too loud." She pushed his gun barrel down. "We just got here. Just wait a minute."

"Don't worry about it. We'll draw them out and then scatter. Easy peasy, Agent Shaw."

"Easy peasy?"

"You didn't have to come. And frankly, you're slowing me down."

"You arrogant sonuva—"

Smoke clamped his hand over her mouth.

The door on the back porch of the cabin opened. A towering man stepped out of the inner light and into the porch roof's shadows. His head was partly hidden by the rafters. Two guards sidled up to him, and he waved them away. There was a flicker of light, and a cigar was lit. Its fiery ashes burned bright and dulled again.

"That's him," Smoke whispered in her ear.

She peeled his hand away and said, "I know, you sonuvabitch. And you better not do that again."

The giant man took the wide-plank steps off the porch and into the rain. It was Mason Crow. Tall. Dark. Black bearded. Much bigger in life than in the pictures.

One of the men in pea coats came down the steps and said a few words to him.

Crow was every bit of seven feet tall. Maybe four hundred pounds, all muscle. He bent his ear toward the man and nodded.

Sidney whispered, "You really think you can carry him out of here?"

"Yeah, but I'm not sure the chopper can lift him." Smoke let out a strange chuckle. "I've never seen such big shoulders."

"Excuse me, but what are you doing?" A little girl in a khaki jumpsuit appeared beside Sidney, half-stopping her heart.

"Where did you come from?" Sid said, clutching her chest.

The little girl stood in the barn's shadows with them. She was a straight-haired towhead, pale-eyed, with a maturity about her. "Where did you come from?"

"We need to go," Smoke said with a sense of urgency.

"Can you tell me what your name is?" Sidney asked the girl.

"We need to go now," Smoke said

"Sure," the little girl said, "My name is—" Suddenly, she let out an ear-splitting scream.

CHAPTER 16

S IDNEY CLAMPED HER HAND OVER the little girl's mouth. "Sssssh!"

It was too late. The alarm sounded. Forces scrambled. Mason Crow, their target from the Black Slate file, ducked back inside the cabin.

"Way to go, Princess," Smoke said. He laid down a round of cover fire. Men screamed and fell. "Get inside!"

Gunshots rang out all over.

Budda-budda-budda… Budda-budda-budda…

Sidney lifted the girl onto her shoulder and scrambled for the barn entrance. The barn door opened, and a man in a pea coat stepped outside. Sidney cracked off a shot into his leg.

"Aargh!" he cried out, falling to the ground.

She leapt over him and dashed inside the barn. Children, four that she could see, stood inside handling the boxes the same as they'd been doing before, packing them into a black van's cargo doors. "Get in the van!" she said.

They all gave her a mute look.

She popped off a few rounds into the ceiling and yelled. "Now!"

The frightened children scrambled into the side door of the van. She jumped in the back with them and slammed the door shut behind her.

Smoke sat in the driver's seat and said, "Hang on!" The van lurched forward and powered through the barn wall and barreled through the ranch. Gunfire erupted all around. Bullets tore into the metal.

"Get down," Sidney said, covering the children as best as she could. "Stay down!" The van bounced up off of its wheels and landed hard. "What was that?"

"A person." Smoke cut the wheel hard and surged through the ranch. Bullets blasted the windshield. Smoke hunkered behind the wheel and stomped on the gas. "Here we go!"

The van's tires dug in, and the vehicle roared ahead, bouncing over the rough road. Sidney climbed into the front seat. The van was speeding down the driveway. Checking the side mirror, she saw other vehicles were in pursuit and closing in.

"Are you happy?" Smoke said.

"Happy?"

"Sure. Looks like this turned into a rescue after all." He flashed his teeth. "Happy?"

"Just drive."

The van now barreled down a country road toward where they had parked the Hellcat, slinging from side to side.

"You're going to crash!"

"No, I'm not," he said, slamming on the brakes and accelerating up a hairpin turn. "See? Besides, they can't get around us. The road's too narrow. Once we get around this crooked neck, it's practically a straight stretch to the city." He glanced at her. "What are you doing?"

"Calling backup."

"We don't need backup."

"Yes, we do—unless you plan on adopting these kids."

Smoke checked the rearview mirror. "Oh, them." He smiled. "Hi, guys." There was no response. "Pretty shy, I guess." He slung the wheel back and forth more times until they found themselves on a straight stretch of gravel.

Sidney could make out a faint line of cars traveling down the highway in the distance. Her breathing eased. "Everything's going to be fine," she said to the kids. "Just stay down."

"Yeah," Smoke said, looking up and out of the front window. "Everything should be just fine, assuming we can get past that."

A helicopter buzzed overhead, rattling the van. It landed on the road a half mile ahead.

"That's a problem." Smoke said.

"Go around it," Sidney said.

He shook his head. The straightaway had a steep valley on either side. "The only thing we can do is pull off and run for it. Maybe we can get to your car from here, but not with these kids—unless they're really, really fast kids."

One of the children popped his head up and said, "I'm fast."

"Yeah, me too," said one right after the other.

Ahead, the helicopter lifted off the road.

"Whoa!" Sidney said, squinting. A lone man stood in the middle of the road. His arms were spread wide, shaking toward the sky. Lightning flashed. Thunder boomed. "Is that Mason Crow?"

"It's something," Smoke said. He pressed on the gas. "And it's about to get rolled over!" The closer they got, the bigger the man became, filling the road. "Sweet mother of Pearl!" Smoke slammed on the brakes. "That's not a man…"

From less than fifty yards away, Sidney got a closer look. It was at least eight feet tall and padded in brawny muscle and coarse hair all over, and it had the head of a bull and the body of a man. It shook the horns on its head and let out a strange roar. Its hooved foot scraped over the ground, and it charged. *It can't be! It can't be!* She finished Smoke's sentence, "It's a minotaur."

Horns lowered, the man-bull made a bead straight for them.

Smoke put the van in gear and sped straight for it.

Frozen in her seat, Sidney said, "Why do I not like our chances?"

"Because this defies reasonable explanation." Smoke's knuckles were white on the wheel. "But can it defy the laws of momentum?"

Speeding toward each other, the van and the minotaur crashed. Twisted metal and shattered glass erupted from the impact. The van's wheels dug into the gravel road. The minotaur's horns pierced the hood. Its monstrous face growled and began shoving the van backward.

Sidney took out her pistol and started shooting. *Blam! Blam!*

The minotaur twisted its mighty neck and flipped the van over. The machine rolled over the hillside and slammed into the trees. Flames and smoke spilled out from underneath the hood. Smoke lay slumped on the wheel with his head bleeding. She shook him.

He groaned.

Dazed, Sidney clawed her way into the back that now lay sideways. The children were disheveled. Some had been knocked out. She found the latch to the cargo doors, twisted it, and shoved them open.

Wham!

The roof of the van buckled. Children screamed.

Wham!

Something had jumped on top of the van and started pounding on the roof. A horn ripped through the metal. A huge hand peeled it away. The minotaur leered inside, snorting.

Sidney went for her other gun and started shooting it in the face. *Blam! Blam! Blam!*

The minotaur let out a booming laugh, reached inside, and pulled her out of the van by the arm. It shook her like a doll and hopped down off the van. Her struggles were child-like against its raw power. Its animal eyes stared her down with hunger in them. Slinging her over its enormous shoulders, it said in a cavernous voice, "NICE. YOU'RE GONNA DO JUST FINE."

CHAPTER 17

T HE MINOTAUR HAD STARTED INTO a jog, jostling her entire body. It stopped at the sound of Smoke's voice. "Put her down."

"Move aside, mortal," said Mason Crow the minotaur, "your weapon is useless against me." He stomped his hooved foot. "Or watch as I run rough-shod over you. Oh, how I like the sound of splintering bones and cracking skulls."

Sidney twisted enough to get a look at Smoke. He stood tall, pointing the gun at the monster's skull. "Just shoot it!"

Crow jostled her. "Be silent, woman." He leered back at Smoke. "Go ahead. Let's see what your bullets can do. Be careful though. I don't want this woman damaged. That might make me angry. Crow likes his pretty playthings."

Ka-blam!

Crow let out an awful howl. "Mah-Rooooo!" He whipped Sidney around the front of his body. "Where did you get those bullets?"

"Where did you get those horns?" Smoke took aim. "Put her down."

The minotaur eyed the upper road. The forces from the ranch had gathered. He crushed Sidney against his powerful chest. "You have nowhere to go. And your bullets only sting. They cannot kill the likes of me."

"Is that why you're bleeding?" Smoke said, maintaining his aim. "Or is that blood a figment of my imagination?"

"It's only blood. I have plenty of it." Crow started to squeeze Sidney harder. "Let's see how much she has."

Sidney's eyes bulged. Her body felt like it had been stuffed inside a trash compactor. She let out a painful gasp.

Ka-Blam! Ka-Blam! Ka-Blam!

Crow dropped her in front of his hooved feet, lowered his horns, and charged.

Smoke skipped away and kept shooting.

The minotaur kept running up the hill, crashing over small trees, and bellowing, "Kill them! Kill them!"

The throng of men above opened fire. Smoke caught Sidney up in his arms and dashed behind the van. Bullets riddled the vehicle by the dozens. Smoke returned fire.

Sidney shook her numb arms and searched for a gun, finding nothing. *I'm useless.* She spied another gun tucked in the back of Smoke's pants and took it. It was an old single-action army, cowboy style. *Are you kidding me?* She pulled back the hammer and cracked a shot off up the hill. A man tumbled into the tall grasses. *Pretty accurate, but I've got a whole five shots left against their hundreds.*

"How do you like it?" Smoke said to her, talking about his gun.

"This iron would make a great paperweight." She took another shot. "But I bet it was quite the conversation piece a hundred years ago." She squeezed off another, and one more goon rolled down the hill. "Eh, it's a good shooter. But 'game over' once we're out of bullets."

"Never imagined it would end like this," he said, blasting away until he emptied his magazine. "A bad ending to a bad western. Nice knowing you, Agent Shaw." He snapped in another magazine. "I'll stay with the children, you run. Your car's just over that ridge."

"No."

"Yes!" he said. "Just go! Get help!"

"I'm not leaving you, and I'm not leaving these kids." She patted down his pockets. "Got any more bullets?"

"No."

She cracked off her last shots. "Then maybe we need to give ourselves up. Keep our lives a little longer."

He eased back behind the van and hunkered down beside her. He looked her in the eye and said, "If that's what you want to do, then so be it."

She grabbed his face and kissed him hard. Finishing, she said, "It's sexy when a man listens to me." She tossed her gun away and Smoke tossed his. They raised their hands up over their heads and waved them high. She said, "We give up."

The gunfire stopped.

She took a breath and eased away from the van. *This sucks!*

Wumpa! Wumpa! Wumpa! Wumpa!

A chopper soared overhead with searchlights burning bright. A voice came over its loudspeaker. "FBI! Drop your weapons!"

The mercenaries on the road tucked away their weapons and turned tail.

"FBI! Halt!"

Engines started up and headed back down the country road, disappearing into the night. A small convoy of cars with sirens gave chase, and the chopper landed.

Sidney let out a ragged sigh. "And you didn't want me to call them."

"I just said that because I knew you wouldn't listen to me." He touched the lips she had just kissed and added, "It was all worth it."

"I don't know about that." Stiff legged, she opened up the doors to the back of the van. Her jaw dropped. All of the children were gone. "That's impossible."

CHAPTER 18

"**W**E SURVIVED," SMOKE SAID, STARING out of Sidney's car window. "I think that's a good thing. Soon enough we'll get another shot at that monster."

"Huh?" Sidney replied. She had barely heard what he said. Instead, she was in deep thought about those kids. What happened to them? They couldn't have snuck off so fast. "Oh, I suppose."

They spent less than an hour at the scene before the FBI let them go. Four men who had been wounded in the battle were taken into custody. Two more died from their wounds. Sidney and Smoke were lucky. The entire battle took place just outside of private property. Cyrus Tweel, her current supervisor, was there. The conversation was unpleasant. She wanted to go back into the compound and get the children. His response was a flat-out no.

"Are you going to take Smoke now?" she said to Cyrus.

His brow crinkled. "No, not this time. You don't have the mark yet. But it would be for the better. This is a mess." And with that, Cyrus departed.

"I wouldn't worry about them," Smoke said.

"About who?"

"Those kids. There's something strange about them."

"They're kids."

"Very odd ones." He shifted in the car seat. "You know what I'm talking about."

She did. The children's faces were almost identical to the ones they'd rescued months ago at Ray Cline's place. Their complexions and hair color were different. Otherwise, they were the same. "I know."

Cruising down the highway, she continued to gather her thoughts about all of the detail7s. Mason Crow was a minotaur. None of it seemed real. Not to mention the fact that there were dozens of men and women who had seen him. They had lives, family and friends, and they knew about this. *How can this madness be hidden?*

"Makes you think, doesn't it?" Smoke said.

She downshifted and let off the gas pedal, then accelerated into the turn. "About what?"

"About how these monsters are hiding in plain sight." He drummed his hands on the dash. "With all of the security videos and social media, you would think the entire world would know about it. Certainly someone has posted something, somewhere, and lived to tell about it."

Russ Davenport, the reporter for *Nightfall DC*, came to mind. She needed to check and see if he had survived or not. He was just the kind of person Smoke was talking about. "I guess the powers that be pick the stories that matter." She rubbed a knot on her head from the van's rollover. "Sometimes I feel like I'm in an episode of *The X-Files*."

"Yeah, where are the Lone Gunmen when you need them? So, where to now?

She hadn't given her next move much thought. "I guess I'll drop you off at your place."

"Well, the cupboards are kinda bare. I wouldn't mind a round of pancakes. Fighting a minotaur can really work up your appetite."

Her tummy rumbled. "Fine. And I imagine you have a place in mind."

"Take the next exit and hang a left."

Her phone buzzed. There was a message on it. It read:

Time to meet. Carlson.

She showed it to Smoke.

His brows lifted. "Huh. An address and everything. But I'm getting my pancakes first."

Mal Carlson's home was a round structure full of glass windows, sitting on a massive stone, partially hidden in the trees that overlooked a place called Henson Creek. The unique circular architecture was odd to say the least, but beautiful the same. Sidney knocked on the red door. Smoke stood on the broad granite steps behind her, cleaning his teeth with a toothpick. She glared at him.

"What?" he said.

She plucked the piece of wood from his mouth and flicked it away. The door opened, and a pretty, oriental woman in an ivory silk gown bowed and said, "Please, come in."

They eased their way into the home. The woman led them down the landing into a room that appeared to be a combination of a living room, a bedroom and a kitchen. Like a massive studio apartment, it was wide open and decorated in tasteful décor from various cultures all over the world. There was only one little closed-off area, which Sid assumed was the privacy of a bathroom. The furniture was anything from colonial American to Italian Renaissance. There were small busts and statues on pedestals of figures she did not recognize. Nothing striking, but odd. She stared at one marble statue that had a bald head, an eye patch, and the grisly look of a pirate.

"That's Carl the Reaver," said an unfamiliar voice that spoke with what sounded like an early American accent, "eighteenth century hero, that is."

Sidney turned. Alongside the oriental woman, who stood just outside of the kitchen, was an elegant man with olive skin, in a simple white cotton outfit. His eyes were ancient and inquisitive, his demeanor purpose-filled, more charming than handsome.

"Finally, Agent Shaw, you can put a face to all of those troublesome texts." He walked over and offered his hand. "I'm Mal Carlson, and this is my wife, Asia. Welcome to our home. Ah, and this must be Mr. John Smoke." He looked up into Smoke's eyes. "I think you and Carl would have gotten along quite well. He was a Navy man."

"Who lived in the eighteenth century," Smoke said. "How would you know what he liked?"

"I'm a bit of a historian and very knowledgeable about peculiar things." He moved toward a dining room table that offered a wonderful view of the outdoors. "Come and sit. We have much to talk about. Asia is preparing some food for us. Something to drink first? Coffee, water, whiskey, wine—or Mountain Dew perhaps?"

"This is it?" Smoke said, taking a seat. "I was expecting something a little different."

"Like the Bat Cave?" Mal said, chuckling. "Be patient. This is only the first floor. I have a basement. So, drinks or no drinks?"

"Water's fine," Sid said, taking a closer look at Mal. He had strong features in his slender face, and high cheekbones. His nearly black hair covered his ears and rested on his neck. There was some gray in it.

"Asia!" he blurted out. "Bring out some water!" He leaned across the table. "Don't be alarmed. She's a little hard of hearing. Asia!"

"I'm coming!" She hurried into the room and rolled three bottled waters down the table. "There!" She smiled. "Anything else?"

"I'm sure our guests are hungry. A prepared meal would be nice."

Asia narrowed her eyes on her husband. "You did not tell me guests were coming. How about I order pizza?"

"I was thinking you could make one of your home dishes?" Mal said, pleading and whining a little.

"A Philly cheesesteak?"

"No! That thing with the rice."

"Rice-a-roni?"

"No!"

"Jambalaya?"

"Never mind," Mal said, shaking his head. "What do you two like on your pizza?"

"I'm not hungry," Sid said.

"I love everything on mine," added Smoke.

"Asia, one order of supreme will do," he said in a rich voice.

Asia slid a phone across the table. "You order. My show's coming on." She smiled at Sid and Smoke. "Nice meeting you." Then she planted herself on the sofa, turned on the television, and started laughing.

A little embarrassed, Mal said, "I didn't marry her because she could cook. I just married her because I love her." He picked up the phone and called in a pizza.

CHAPTER 19

A POLISHED METAL STAIRCASE SPIRALED BENEATH Mal's home. A security door waited at the bottom with a red light glowing on the pad. When he pressed his thumb to the scanner, the light turned green, and the door popped open. Inside was a large computer lab. A wall of oversized monitors was the first thing Sidney saw. The rest was cosmetic by comparison.

"Fifty screens and over a thousand camera feeds from all over DC," Mal said in admiration. "I know it's overkill, but it's quite effective."

There were plenty of places she recognized. Hotel lobbies. Monument buildings. High-rise apartments. Traffic lights. Bank buildings. *How does he have access to all of this?* "You're an employee of the government, Mr. Carlson?"

"No. I like to think of myself as a freelancer. 'Contractor' is such a rigid word, although I am under contract, so to speak." Mal glanced at Smoke. "Somewhat similar to your arrangement."

"I didn't sign any paperwork." Smoke took a seat in an ultra-modern scoop chair beside a long oval table. "I'm done signing my life away. This way, I can cash out whenever I want to." He rubbed the table's polished surface. "Is this pewter?"

"A hybrid metal." Mal motioned for Sidney to sit. "Please. I'm sure you have many questions about what exactly is going on."

She took a chair alongside Smoke and crossed one leg over the other. "So can you tell us why there's a minotaur on the loose in DC?"

Mal's jaw dropped as he gasped at the same time. He plopped in the seat beside Sidney with an excited look in his eye. "Mason Crow is the ancient beast?"

"Pretty sure," she said.

"Horns and everything," Smoke added, making little horns with his fingers.

Mal covered his mouth, uncovered it, and said, "I can't believe it. But I shouldn't be surprised. That's even worse than I suspected."

"You said ancient. What do you mean by that?" she asked.

"Of course." He made his way over to an alabaster bookshelf that was filled with many heavily bound tomes. He pulled a couple of books free, brought them over, and dropped them on the table. One was the Bible, and the other was a book filled with pages of Egyptian hieroglyphics. "Do you know the story in the Bible where Aaron confronts Pharaoh with his staff?"

"Exodus seven," Smoke said. "Aaron casts down the staff. It turns into a snake. Pharaoh's sorcerers cast down their staffs. They also turn into snakes, but the snake from the staff of Aaron devours them."

Mal pointed at him and said, "Right. That's the kind of evil powers we're dealing with. In theory anyway." He opened the Egyptian book of hieroglyphics and pointed at various pictures.

Sidney leaned forward. He pointed at people with bird heads and dog heads, the Sphinx, and more. A funny feeling overcame her.

"Seem familiar?" Mal said.

She made a reluctant nod. "I thought these were pagan images of gods?"

"Well, in most circles of history and archeology, they'd have you believe that. The truth of the matter doesn't fit the agenda of the powers that be." He flipped through the pages. "What they can't bury, they destroy. That's how *they*," he made air quotes, "control the information. It's the same today as it was thousands of years ago. *They* do their work in the dark. Behind the scenes. Pulling unseen strings."

"Who are *they*?" Sidney asked. *And do I work for a good* they *or a bad* they?

"That's much easier to ask than to answer. Even I don't know for sure, but I'll share my theories. Fallen angels, demons, evil spirits, nephilim, annunaki—those are a few of the more common names. They carry the supernatural seed that spoils humanity." He moved over to the computer and pulled up ancient images of Greek, Roman, Hindi, and other gods. "I believe these beings really did exist. Men and women of great renown and stature. Some records report them as being over twelve feet tall. The legends of Medusa, Prometheus, mermaids, sirens, unicorns—I think they are all various accounts of the truth."

Sidney started to say something.

Mal held up his hand to indicate he wasn't finished. "Over the centuries, or even the millennia, good men and women have been fighting these dark forces that continually try to take the world of men over. Empires rise and fall. Great cities are built up and buried. The truth gets distorted into lies or fables. The both of you have seen it for yourselves, and you've lived to tell about it. It's impressive."

Sidney's throat became dry. She glanced at Smoke. His eyes were fixed on Mal Carlson. A single thought ran laps through her mind. *This is crazy.* "Shouldn't there be a bigger team fighting against all this? A team of priests or archeologists, maybe?"

"There have been. There have even been knights and many kinds of crusaders," Mal said. "Not to mention our pirate friend you noted above, Carl the Reaver. They say his sabre dripped wet with giant men's blood."

Smoke let out a short gusty laugh. "I like this."

"So you wish to continue?"

"Without a doubt."

"And what about you, Agent Shaw?" Mal said, eyeing her with intent. "Are you still comfortable with your assignment?"

"I'm not sure what my assignment is anymore." *Or why they picked me.*

"Try not to overthink it. The mission is the same. You're going after what is believed to be a band of supernatural criminals that are listed on the Black Slate." He popped up a couple of pictures on the screen. It was Adam Vaughn the werewolf and Angi Harlow the harpy. "Ho ho. When you brought these two in, you opened some eyes. You certified this effort, and they had to acknowledge that sorcery was afoot. Still, they want discretion. And what you two are doing is working. Cutting out these two threw a big wrench into Drake's network."

"So Drake is *them*?" she said.

"So to speak. Yes. They are the ones behind this. AV and Night Bird were a pair of their top commanders. You sent ripples through that network when you took them down. Their cult-like henchmen scattered, and that made them angry. So now, the pressure is on in Washington."

"What do you mean?" she asked.

"They'll start digging around. Trying to figure out who's behind these efforts. Bribe and bully the congressmen and senators they have in their pockets."

On the monitors, pictures of Congressman Wilhelm and several others popped up.

Daggers of ice shot through Sidney's veins.

"They have their people in there," Mal said, "but don't fret. We have ours. So far as I know, the details of your missions are under wraps. There's still plenty of good people in the bureau protecting you both."

"But Wilhelm's already made us, and they've tried to kill us more than once. Not to mention they know we're in possession of the files. So whoever is protecting us is doing a lousy job."

"Well, I didn't say they were good at it." He tapped some more keys, and dozens of pictures of kids popped up. "If these faces seem familiar, it's because they are. We call them the Forever Children."

CHAPTER 20

S IDNEY GOT UP FROM HER seat for a closer look. Young boys and girls with different-colored hair and complexions were scattered all over the screens. The faces of all the girls and boys were almost identical. Some had freckles. Others red hair. Black. White. Asian. Many different styles of hair. "Who are they?"

Mal put on a pair of glasses and studied one of the faces on the screen. "Simply put, they're clones."

"That doesn't sound very supernatural."

Mal rubbed his chin. "Well, there is a supernatural element to it. That's what makes them breathe anyway. Genetic manipulation. Experimental. Combined with other things that defy scientific explanation." He pulled up another picture. A burly man with clammy skin was strapped to a table. "This is a deader we found wandering around the woods at AV's hospital site. Remember that. Blood runs through him like a reanimated corpse. It's fascinating. As long as his heart pumps, he won't die, at least not until the spell wears off. It happens sometimes."

Sidney took a closer look at the children on the screens.

"Why children?"

"Don't let these little minions fool you, Agent Shaw. They are faithful to their hive. Soulless slaves." He cleared his throat. "No one has any fear of a child. They throw your instincts off. They're the perfect workers. Remember the ones you found. Have no doubt they are back on the job again."

Sidney's stomach turned. Clones or not, they were children, just as real as any. Using adults was one thing, but using children was sickening. "It's not right."

"None of it is. Mother Nature is being turned inside out. Perverted. Most of these monsters volunteer for it. They want money. Power. The promise of immortality. They become roaring lions that prey on the weak humans who stand too close to the darkness." Mal faced her. "There are only good and evil. There is no in-between. Few know the difference, such as you and Mr. Smoke over there."

"What do you mean?"

"When it comes to battling these shape shifters, one has to come from a very solid foundation or else be lured in. That's one of the reasons why the pair of you were picked." He pecked on the keyboard and the screens went black. "You'd be surprised at the number of good people who have fallen victim to their temptations."

Sidney swallowed, remembering how AV had ignited a passionate fire inside her that she'd never felt before. Dark, lurid, and sensual. Her eyes drifted to Smoke. He sat back, reading the Bible in one hand and switching the pictures with the remote in the other. *Pancakes and Butterflies.* If Smoke hadn't been with her, where would she be today? Was she that close to becoming one of them? An evil minion of Drake?

"Any thoughts, Agent Shaw? Doubts? Concerns?" Mal resumed his seat at the table. "After all, these are some extraordinary items that you've been presented with."

"It's an awfully big undertaking for a single agent and a bounty hunter."

"And me, naturally," Mal responded. "That's why I'm careful how we pick our battles. Much thought and consideration goes into it. The Black Slate is a unique list of people, or shifters. And I am convinced that one of those names is in charge of it all. Who knows, we might be lucky and capture the top dog by accident. Maybe Mason Crow is the one."

Sidney sat back down beside Smoke. His face was a mask of concentration. She could almost see the wheels turning inside his head. *What is he thinking?*

As for herself, after taking in all that Mal had shared, something began to stir. Her inner fire was stoked. An awakening charged in her blood. She had seen the face of pure evil. Her civilly tempered senses had denied it until now. She took out the postcard that Deanne Drukker had mailed years ago and set it on the table. It read, "Ted, monsters are real. Avoid the Slate."

Mal leaned over and read it. His eyes widened a little.

"You recognize it, don't you?"

"Yes," Mal said.

Smoke closed his books and picked up the postcard and studied it. "An interesting item."

"An even more interesting warning about the Black Slate," Sidney said.

"You aren't going to let a little postcard scare you off, are you?" Mal said. "Not after you've come this far. At least now you know what to expect."

"I'm more concerned about the message, not the monsters. The fact that it is seven words caught my attention, along with the sketch of the black sun. I think there's a greater message behind the warning.

"No doubt seven is special," Mal said. "There are seven days of the week, seven seas, seven continents, not to mention the seven deadly sins. I could go on for a long time. Some say seven is the number of completion and perfection."

She got the feeling there was something Mal wasn't telling her. "Maybe that's how many villains are on the Black Slate?"

"Er, no, not that few," he said, rubbing his finger under his lip. "That might just be a mystery between her and Chief Howard. Don't overthink it, hmm? We need to move on."

"Are we in a hurry?"

"Well, Mr. Smoke's free time is limited, and our objective, Mason Crow, is now on full alert to our presence, so we need a plan to take him." He made his way over to the desk and began typing away on the computer. The monitors came back to life with a myriad of city scenes. "Seems he's still holed up at his ranch, which is a good thing. Perhaps we should brew some coffee." He pulled up an image of his living room. His wife Asia lay on the couch snoring. He spoke into a microphone by the computer. "Asia." She didn't stir. "Asia," he said again. She shifted a little. "Asia!"

She jerked up into a sitting position, looking around in many directions and holding her head. "I hate it when you do that."

"Would you be a dear and bring us some coffee down?" Mal said in a charming voice.

Asia stood up, yawned, and rubbed her eyes. "Okay."

"Thank you, dear," he said, switching the screen to something else. "She actually loves to make coffee. Has a little thing that she does. Wait until you try it."

Sidney eased back into her chair and let Mal talk. He was doing his best to keep things simple. According to his own archives, the shifters had risen from the shadows over and over, aided by the forces of darkness. Good men and women would beat them back only to see them surface somewhere else and rise again. That somewhere was now DC, the most powerful city in the world. And the shifters could be anybody. She rubbed her temples with her index fingers. *I hope one is not the president.*

CHAPTER 21

"WAKE UP," SID SAID, WAKING from her sleep. She was resting on Smoke's shoulder. She pushed off of him and gave him a nudge.

The ranging man slumbered over the table with drool dripping from his mouth.

Sidney made a face and shoved him again. Mal had gone off on a tirade that had taken until early in the morning. She felt like she'd been trapped in a dream, drifting between bizarre comic stories, movies, and reality. She stretched out her stiff limbs and groaned. She wasn't sure if all of this information was helpful to her cause or not. *Avoid the Black Slate.* Why would anyone want a part of this? But she did.

Smoke, who had been silent the entire time, helped himself out of his chair. He lumbered over toward a fresh pot of coffee that Sidney hadn't seen Asia bring in. "Want another cup?" he said, filling a mug. "It's good Joe. Nice kick to it."

"Sure." Looking for but not seeing Mal anywhere, she got up and cruised around the room. "Seems our host is gone." She rubbed her head. "I didn't think he was going to ever stop talking. Did you catch all of that?"

"I did, well, at least until I started sleeping. But I'm firm on the gist of it. These shifters are murderers, and murderers have to die." He rolled back his brawny shoulders and sent a heated glance her way. "Huh?"

"Huh, what?"

"You just have that morning air about you," he said, coming closer. "A swelteriness."

"I don't think that's a word. And it's creepy." She remained standing where she was and took the coffee that he offered. It was warm in her cupped hands, and for a moment she wondered if that was what she would feel like in his arms. "Care to try again?"

"Enticing."

"Really?"

"Enchanting."

She pushed her hair away from her face. "You're a strange man."

He made his way up to her, coming almost toe-to-toe. "I know, but you're all right with that, aren't you?"

His commanding presence drew her inches toward him. She could feel the warmth from his body. In the morning her juices started flowing. Apparently so did his. She set the coffee mug down on the metal table, bit down on her lip, and gazed up into his eyes. "What are you thinking?"

He gently rested his hands on her shoulders. "I'm thinking I don't want to go out of this world without kissing you again."

His hand glided down her back, sending shivers down her spine. Her heart raced. She eased her body into his. He leaned down and brought his lips to hers, delivering a soft kiss. It wasn't anything like the ones she'd give him. It was deep. Passionate. Real. Her fingernails dug into his lower back, and she returned his efforts in kind.

"Good morning, all!" Mal interrupted in a chipper voice.

Sidney broke off the kiss, gasping for breath a little. There was a thin stream of saliva still connecting them. She brushed it away and backed up with wide eyes. Smoke stood still with his eyes closed and lips still parted.

"Is he all right?" Mal said, sauntering over. He had a covered silver platter that he set down. "What's he doing?"

Sidney backhanded Smoke in the thigh. "Meditating, I think."

"Never seen that technique before." Mal took the lid off the platter. It was filled with steaming eggs, bacon, and pancakes. "I figured we could eat down here so I could continue."

Smoke plopped down into a seat and eyed Sidney. She lifted her brows. He said, "I think the food is the only course left that is needed. What do you think, Sid?"

"I agree."

"But there's so much to go over."

"We get it," Smoke said, grabbing a handful of bacon. "Just give us what we need to hunt the bad guys. I know you're dying to reveal something."

Mal's face lit up. "I'll be right back."

After Mal left the room, Smoke started to nuzzle back up to Sidney. She stopped him with her hand, only to find her palm pressed against his rock hard abs. *Morning Glory.* "Just what do you think you're doing?"

"I thought we'd—"

She cut him off. "Keep your thoughts to yourself. And to be clear, you took advantage of a moment of weakness, so get ahold of yourself."

He stepped back. "What do you mean by that exactly?"

"Funny," she said with a smirk. "Now just back away."

"But—"

"I'm not talking about this right now," she said, drinking her coffee. "And maybe never again, for that matter." She couldn't look him in the eye. "It happened. It's over. Move on."

"Okay," he said with a nonchalant shrug. "But just so you know, I thought that was a great kiss, and I think you thought so too." He walked out of sight.

He's right about that. She stared into the chocolate-colored coffee. *What is he thinking? What am I thinking?* She liked Smoke. What woman wouldn't? He had rugged good looks and a boyish charm about him, but he was odd too. Something about him unsettled her, leaving her uncertain whether or not she was truly attracted to him. *Probably just lust on both sides of the fence. But Lord can he kiss.* A fantasy of her and him started to unfold in her thoughts.

"Agent Shaw?" a voice said. "Agent Shaw?"

"Huh?" she said, twisting around and spilling her coffee.

"Oh, don't worry, I'll have Asia get that," Mal said, walking over and taking her by the arm. "It's time for the next stop." He eased her up out of her chair. "Come on now."

"Where's Smoke?" she said. The man was nowhere to be seen.

"He's a step ahead."

Sidney noticed one of the shelves in the back of the room was swung open. "A secret passage? Really?"

"Just a room actually," Mal said, leading the way inside. "Filled with many dangers."

CHAPTER 22

T HE ROOM WAS HALF AS big as the one they'd been in and laid out like a weapons locker. Pistols and machine guns hung on black racks. Another wall displayed a host of archaic weapons guarded by two burnished statues of full plate armor. Smoke stood at a table, wearing only his second skin. He was trying on a pair of western gun belts. He had a grin on his face.

Sidney didn't hesitate to share her thoughts. "That looks really stupid. Take it off."

Smoke handled the chrome-plated, ivory-handled Colt .45 pistols with ease. They blinked in and out of the holsters and spun on his fingers before he shoved them back inside the black leather. To that effect, he added a mild, "Yeehaw!"

Sidney turned her back. *At least he didn't say Hi Ho Silver.* She ran her fingers over several objects on the table. Bullets, magazines, hand grenades, and a silvery pair of flex cuffs. *Hmmm.*

"I thought you might like those," Mal said from the other side of the table. "Unlike your unfortunate experience with AV, those will hold just about anything."

"Even a minotaur?" she said.

"In theory."

"Are these stun grenades?" Smoke said, picking up a pair of flat black metal disks.

Mal walked over, plucked them out of his hand, and set them back down on the table. "Yes. They're on timers, and they can be activated by a radio signal or app—which reminds me." He opened up a heavy-duty plastic toolbox and withdrew a pair of boxes and tossed them over.

Inside, Sidney found a black watch with a flexible wristband. "No, thanks," she said, setting it down on the table. "Not my style."

"But it's sophisticated technology. Very helpful."

Smoke tossed his box to Mal. "No thanks for me either. These guns and bullets will do." He eyed the wall filled with swords, axes, spears, and other ancient weapons. "Some of those blades will, too."

"Those are antiques from my personal collection. Leave them alone."

Smoke's hand stopped short of a double-bladed battle-axe with a spike on it. "Are you sure? I really would like to have this battle-axe. It'd fit perfectly between that minotaur's horns." He plucked it off the wall and swished it through the air.

Slice! Slice!

"Stop drooling over it, and put it away," Mal pleaded. "It's a priceless piece in my collection."

Smoke twirled it in the air one last time and then placed it back on the rack with a clank. "So be it." He started stuffing weapons and ammo into a duffel bag. Looking at Sid, he said, "I'm ready to go. Are you?"

She found an empty case on the floor and dropped guns, bullets, grenades, and a few other things inside it. She found a dark pair of sunglasses and slipped them on. They enhanced her sight. "Yeah, I'm ready."

Mal pushed his hair back. "You aren't taking all that."

"Why not?" Sidney said. "Who else is going to use it?"

"That's not the point."

"Come on, Smoke," she said. "You only have one more week, and we've got monsters to kill."

Mal cut off their path at the doorway. "A reminder. Bring Mason Crow in alive. And it's best to find him in the daytime. Most shifters prefer to change at night. That's when their power is at full zenith, especially when the moon is full." He poked Smoke in the chest. "And don't lose that *Zweite Haut* suit again. If you only knew what I had to go through to recover it."

Sidney landed some heavy slaps on Mal's shoulder. "Don't worry. I'll see to it that he wears it the whole time." She started to push by.

"No wait," Mal said, "Just hold on one more second." He rushed over to one of the walls that had a drawer in it, pulled it out, and produced a pill bottle. "Look. They're ready for you this time, and I'm not going to lie. You two are on your own. The truth is, no one thought you'd get this far on this project."

"You mean they thought we'd die," she said.

"Well, you in particular, yes, Agent Shaw, but you've proven to be a formidable survivor." His eyes brightened. "They're impressed."

"Well, they can kiss my ass," she said, "And I'm not taking any drugs." She squinted at the pill case.

"It's my own brand of sorcery," Mal said, dumping two bright-emerald pills into his hand.

"I thought magic was bad," Smoke said, leering down on him.

"No, it's not that kind. Sorcery comes from the Greek word *pharmakia*, hence it means drugs or pharmacy. Just a concoction of my own making." He tried to hand the bottle to Sidney.

"No, thanks. You know the FBI does random drug testing."

"You're going up against great evil. It might take more than bullets or brawn to stop them. These little pills," said Mal, shaking them in the bottle, "will certainly help level things out."

"How, by turning us into one of them?" Sidney said.

"No," Mal replied, "by enhancing your senses. Really. No side effects, but temporary. You'll thank me later."

"No," she said, pushing by him. "I'll put my faith in my wits and the guns on my hips." She'd heard enough. Seen enough. And now she was ready to get away from this place. Breathe some fresh air and find some normality. Without looking back, she made her way upstairs and passed by Asia, who was once again napping on the couch. Shaking her head, Sid exited the round glass mansion and walked to her waiting car. Shoulders slumped, she set the heavy case of munitions down. She rubbed her neck. *Damn, this is going to be a weird commute with Smoke.*

CHAPTER 23

REST. SLEEP. THAT'S WHAT SIDNEY needed. At 5:03 in the morning she sat up bleary eyed in her bed, contemplating her situation. She'd departed with Smoke the night before last, after leaving Mal's home. Little had been said about what was going on between them. Instead, they had talked about how they were going to find Mason Crow the minotaur. It was a little disturbing that conversations like this were beginning to seem normal. She flopped back onto the bed.

This is crazy.

She stuffed her face in her pillow and let out a scream. She followed it with an odd laugh she'd never let out before. The FBI had given her this nutsy assignment. It was loose. Dangerous. Mysterious. She had been a rigid by-the-book soldier, but now she was beginning to like the freedom of being a shadow agent. She could tell Smoke was into it too. A fire lit behind his dark eyes when he talked about it.

I wonder what he's doing now. She put her bare feet on the cool hardwood floor and shuffled into the kitchen. *Probably feeding hay to the minotaur by now.* She put on a pot of coffee, leaned on the granite kitchen counter, yawned, and rehashed their plans.

She and Smoke had decided to separate for the next few days. Supposedly, Mal was keeping tabs on any activity from the ranch and would let them know if anyone left. She didn't buy it. The ranch was pretty far out of sight and mind, and there had to be more than one exit. There was the helicopter too. There weren't video feeds in air space. Hm, but there was satellite tracking.

I hate counting on others.

She took a seat on the sofa, grabbed the remote, and turned on the twenty-four-hour local news. A reporter was on site at a fire scene. Fire trucks and flames were the landscape of the background. She turned up the volume and took her first drink of coffee and listened to what the reporter said.

"There are no confirmations of any casualties, but firemen are still clearing the building," he reported. "I can feel the intensity of the flames from where I'm standing, a good fifty feet away. Again, no casualties reported so far, and they are a long way off from clearing the building."

"Probably some bloody arsonist. What's wrong with the world?" She started to change the channel, but for some reason the reporter kept her attention. She leaned forward, hanging on the concerned tone in his voice.

The man on TV with a Geraldo mustache cleared his throat and continued with a worried look on his face. "I talked to one resident earlier, and she said it all happened so fast. Another witness said flames erupted in one lone apartment and then spread like wildfire." He glanced back at the burning building and shielded his face from the flames and added, "But it looks like DC's finest have the fire under control here at Rochester Apartments."

Sidney almost spit out her coffee. "*What?*" Her hand trembled. *That's Allison and Megan's place!* She rushed into the bedroom and snatched up her phone. She didn't have any texts. She punched one in to Allison. *Come on. Come on.* No response.

She practically jumped into her clothes, grabbed everything she typically needed, and in less than a minute she peeled out of the parking lot in her car. "Oh God, let them be all right. Please!" She dialed her contacts at the local police and fire department, but she couldn't get through. "Damn." She voice-texted Allison again. "Are you okay? Please answer!"

The Dodge thundered down the streets, but it was fifteen minutes later when she got there. The blaze was out, but half of the apartment complex lay in a smoky ruin against the day's first light.

Sidney parked and rushed to the scene, hollering out, "Megan! Allison!"

Two firemen approached and one female police officer. "Miss," the woman said, "can we help you? Do you live here?"

"Uh, my sister and niece do," Sidney said. Her heart was pounding. Her thoughts racing. "Did you get them out? Did you get them out?"

"Ma'am, it'll be fine."

"Is that where the fire started?" Sidney said, pointing. "Oh my, oh my!" Allison and Megan's second-floor apartment was nothing but charred remains. "Did it start there? Did it start there?" She rushed toward the remains.

The two firemen grabbed her and pulled her back. "Ma'am!" said the female officer. "You can't rush in there. Our people are on the scene. Let us handle this."

"Let me go! I'm FBI!"

"Then you understand standard protocols." The woman made sympathetic gestures. "Just trust us, and I'm sure everything will be okay."

Sidney's body slackened, and she eased out of the grip of the men. "Okay." It was torment. She couldn't stop visualizing her family being burned to death. In her gut, she knew something was wrong. She could feel it. *This can't be happening. Please don't be happening because of me.*

"Come on," said the female officer. She was a veteran lady with silver-black hair showing underneath her blue ball cap. "Guys, get her a blanket. She's shivering."

Sidney didn't even realize she was trembling. The firemen put a blanket over her shoulders, and she sat back on the hood of a black and white squad car. A stiff breeze kicked up, blowing the smoke into her face and stinging her eyes.

"Phew," the policewoman said, covering her nose. "I can't stand the smell of melted plastic." She squeezed Sidney's shoulder. "It's gonna be all right, uh—"

"Sidney."

"I'm Kate McFadden," the woman said, offering her hand. "I'll stick around, if you don't mind. Besides, I could use the overtime. When things like this happen, they need a little crowd control anyway." Her head swiveled around, and her eyes locked on a pair of reporters sliding through the police barrier. "Oh, no they don't. Excuse me." She darted away. "Hey! Hey! You two better get back behind that barrier. I'm not warning you again."

Sidney checked her messages again. Nothing from Allison. She sent another text out anyway and remained seated. She couldn't fight the fear swelling up inside of her. At this time of day she couldn't imagine Allison and Megan being anywhere else. All she could do was hope that maybe they escaped the fire, and Allison lost her phone in the process. Of course it wouldn't be beyond Allison to ignore her calls, especially after the fight they'd had earlier.

She said a prayer and started walking around the lot, searching the faces. Families and children were scattered all about. Tears streaked down a lot of faces. One woman was wailing. A man was arguing with the firemen and police officers. If Sidney had to guess, the apartment complex housed about fifty people, and judging by the looks of things, everything was gone. Her little thread of hope turned to despair as another section of the building collapsed in a whoosh of smoke. People started screaming.

A voice of authority caught her ear, and a handful of firemen gathered on a section of steps that hadn't burned in the fire. They vanished into the building with a pair of hand-carried gurneys. Teeth clenched and nails digging into her palms, Sid watched for them to emerge again. The female officer, Kate, stood by her side, humming. Sidney eyed her.

Kate stopped humming and said with a sympathetic look, "Sorry, but I get nervous sometimes."

"It's all right."

The second-floor fire exit door opened, and a group of firemen carrying two loaded gurneys made their way down the stairwell. Sidney started forward, but the officer grabbed her arm.

"Sidney, stay put, and let me take a look. It could be anybody." The woman ducked under the barrier tape and headed straight for the firemen.

Sidney felt her heart pounding inside her chest. *Please don't be them. Please don't be them.* Her keen hearing caught the brunt of the firemen's conversation. One said, "Pretty sure it's a woman and a little girl." Sidney leapt the barrier and charged over. Kate cut into her path, but Sidney slipped away. She jerked the blankets off the gurneys and choked out a sob at the sight of the lifeless charred remains.

CHAPTER 24

S IDNEY SWAYED OVER HER BUCKLING knees.

Kate caught her beneath the arms and steadied her. "Come on now. Come on. You don't know that's them for sure." The policewoman turned Sidney away as the firemen covered up the bodies again. "Just walk away. Walk away."

Sid shuffled through the parking lot and swallowed back the bile building in her throat. The strong stench of burning flesh hit her nose, and she began to gag. She covered her mouth with her clammy hand. *Get a grip, Sid. Get a grip.*

"You're in shock, honey. You're in shock," Kate said again, hugging her around the waist. "Just keep walking. Keep walking."

On spaghetti legs, Sidney managed to make her way back to the squad car. People were commenting and murmuring. Her rattled mind didn't comprehend anything they said. She squatted down and leaned on one of the hubcaps, huddled up with her head down. Tears streamed down her cheeks, and she shook uncontrollably. "Oh Lord. Oh Lord. Why?"

"It's probably a tragic accident," Kate said in a comforting tone. "But maybe it wasn't them. You never know. Hang in there."

No. Sidney had known something was wrong from the moment she saw the flames on TV. Her instincts had warned her of the danger. Emptiness filled her stomach. "Oh, Megan. Oh, Allison." She pounded the pavement with her fist. "No. No. No!"

"Easy now," Kate said, kneeling down beside her and trying to put a blanket over her shoulders. "You're gonna hurt yourself."

Sidney pushed the blanket aside and rose back to her feet. She wiped the tears from her eyes. "I need to walk."

"Sure. I'm right here if you need anything."

Hands on her hips, Sid took a shuddering breath and made her way through the crowd into the parking lot. *What do I tell Mom and Dad?* She could hear their hearts breaking. *What if this is all my fault?* The last thing she'd ever do was put her family in danger. A memory flashed in her mind. The text that had come with a picture of Allison and Megan and the message that read,

Watch your step.

Her blood turned to ice. *Wilhelm!*

Had Allison seen something? Maybe the congressman was covering up his tracks. Perhaps something worse had happened over the weekend while Allison was gone. *What kind of people play these games?* She found herself standing on the sidewalk across from the building. A flood of feelings rushed through her. Anger. Sadness. Despair. *Maybe the cop is right. Maybe it isn't them at all but someone else.* She closed her eyes and gathered her thoughts.

Be patient.

She'd find the cause in the fire marshal's report. An autopsy would have to be done on the bodies. There wasn't any sense in getting anyone upset until everything was confirmed. She checked her phone again. "Come on, Allison. Please. Be alive somewhere else," she muttered to herself.

"Excuse me," said a man who was passing by. He was much older, wearing a fedora hat and a brown trench coat. "Did you say something to me?"

"No, sorry," she said.

"Quite all right," he said, tipping his hat. "My hearing isn't what it once was. He gazed at the apartment's ruins and twisted the end of his grey moustache. "It's almost a tragedy to see such bad things happen."

"Almost?" she said.

"Oh, why yes," he said, without looking at her. His voice took on a sinister tone. "You know, Agent Shaw, bad things happen to those who dicker with the Black Slate."

Sidney slugged him in the jaw, knocking his hat from his head. He tumbled hard to the ground and lay out, on his back. She pinned him down with her knee and stuck the muzzle of her gun in his face. "Who did this? Who did this?"

The eerie man with a bleeding lip laughed and spat blood. "I don't know for certain. I'm just the messenger. Hahahaha."

She punched him in the face again. *Whack!* And again. *Whack!*

He continued to laugh. His watch started beeping. "Oh. It seems my time is up, Agent Shaw, but I'll give you a hint. The Drake send their condolences."

"You sonuva—"

The man convulsed and shuddered, and then his eyes froze upward to the sky. A foamy spittle oozed from the corner of his mouth.

She checked his pulse. He was dead. She checked his coat and grabbed his hat. They had a very musty smell, and the style looked to be at least seventy-five years old. She found a wallet and a paper driver's license belonging to Dwight Guilden. It had expired over sixty years ago.

"What's going on over here?" said Officer McFadden. She had a gun on Sid, and she wasn't alone either. "What did you do to that man?"

Another cop checked the pulse and said, "He's dead."

"Agent Shaw," Officer McFadden said, "put your hands down where I can see them."

"Why?" she said, holstering her weapon.

"Because you're going downtown until we get this all sorted out. Bart, cuff her."

"*What?* For what?"

"Assault and suspicion of murder."

"I'm a federal agent! I didn't kill this man."

"Then why's his face bleeding?" Kate took out her taser. "Now, Agent Shaw, don't make me use this."

"Have you gone mad? My family just got burned alive in there." Seething, Sidney took a pleading step forward.

Kate pulled the trigger on the stun gun.

Zzzzzzap!

Sid's body twitched, her teeth chattered, and she collapsed hard on the ground. She couldn't move her shocked and numbing limbs, but she could still see and hear.

Kate pulled out a card and read the Miranda rights to Sid. "You have the right to remain silent…"

CHAPTER 25

S IDNEY NIBBLED ON HER NAILS. For the past eight hours she'd been in the local PD's lockup while the FBI got everything sorted out. Cyrus Tweel had picked her up, and it had been a long trip back to headquarters.

"You can't cut loose like that, Sid," Cyrus said, pushing his spectacles up onto his nose. "It's bad for the agency, and you know we hate attention in the papers."

She sneered at him. One thing the weasel of a man lacked was compassion. He was all image. All agency from day one. If they made you walk around with your hat on fire, Cyrus would do it. "I don't need an academy lecture," she said, facing the passenger window. "And you don't know what the hell is going on either, so don't act like you do."

"Why don't you explain it to me then, *shadow agent?*"

She didn't miss the venom in his voice when he said it. "Ah, that's it, isn't it? You're jealous, aren't you Cyrus? They picked me over you, and it's just bugging the crap out of you."

"I could not care less about the Black Slate and your little ghost chases. Doesn't mean a thing to me at all. But as for you? Well, you're an excellent agent, but this assignment is a joke. Everyone thinks so."

"Everyone who, and how do they know about it?"

"Your special little assignment isn't a secret. Do you really think a bunch of special agents don't notice when someone like you," he glanced at her legs, "goes missing from time to time? The Slate is nothing but snickers at the water cooler."

"Oh, I see, so I'm making you look bad, huh Cyrus? I'm sorry." She reached over and patted his leg. "I really am sorry, little Cyrus."

"Geez, cut it out. Even you are above such mockery."

She dug her nails into his thigh. "Do you even give a shit about Allison and Megan? How can you sit here and act like you don't even know them?" She jerked her hand away. "That's your problem, Cyrus. If it doesn't help you and your career, it doesn't matter. You don't care if your fellow agent's family just perished in a fire. Jerk."

"You know I'm not like that, Sid. Look, I'm sorry." He steered the car to the exit ramp. "An autopsy revealed that those bodies were not your niece and sister."

She straightened up in her seat. "*What?* And you're just now telling me this?" She wanted to pound his face in. Instead, she punched him in the arm.

"Ow!"

"You're a rat, Cyrus. Just a little rodent who gets off toying with other people's feelings."

"No, I don't. I just have my orders. Chief Howard was going to brief you at his office." He rubbed his shoulder. "Geez, you hit like a dude."

She snorted. "You know Cyrus, this was one of the reasons why our relationship couldn't go any further."

"I beg your pardon."

"I never could put my finger on it. I mean, you do and say all the right stuff. But between us, I always knew the agency would come first." She sighed. "You would choose them over me. I could just feel it. And I think the agency, and the authority that comes with it, is how you get away with some bad things you like to do."

"Like what?"

"Like shooting people. Keeping secrets. Manipulating a situation. You thrive on it. I see that spark behind those icy eyes of yours. You delight in it. It disturbs me."

Cyrus turned on his blinker and turned into the headquarters garage. His face was stone cold. The brakes squeaked as he brought the SUV to a stop. He turned and looked at her. "I'll keep that perspective in mind."

"Sid," Ted Howard said, sitting behind his desk, "we're trying to help. Honestly, you know that." He took a swig of bottled water. "It hasn't even been a day yet. You know how these things go."

She sat back in one of the chairs, arms folded, legs crossed, and foot kicking. "It's a little different when your own family is missing."

"It hasn't even been twenty-four hours yet," Cyrus added. He was sitting in the seat beside hers, facing Section Chief Howard. "Give our people, your people, a little more time. They'll turn up."

"Yes, they'll turn up dead if I don't get moving." She started up out of her seat.

"Sit!" Ted said, rising up from his chair. He lowered his voice again. "Please, Sid. Let's work on this together."

Reluctantly, she took a seat. "I know you don't have anyone on this. You don't have time for it. I'm only here because I got carried away and busted that freak Dwight Guilden in the face. What about his autopsy? Certainly you checked on him."

Ted and Cyrus looked at each other. Cyrus shrugged.

"You two are dropping the ball," she said. "How did you do an autopsy on the burn victims but not follow up on the man who got me arrested for attempted murder? Huh?"

"The man, Dwight you say," Ted said, checking out some papers. "He's at the county morgue. The burn victims went to the state where we have better connections. Look, I'm sorry. I'll get a man down to county as soon as I can find one."

"No hurry, Ted. He's dead, so I don't think he's going anywhere. At least not until the Drake make him disappear, just like they did with my niece and my sister!"

"Keep your voice down, Sid. Please. You aren't being yourself," Ted said. "It worries me."

No, she wasn't, and she knew it. Instead, she was coming unglued. It wasn't like her. But this was different. Her family had been taken. And by the sound of things, the two men she knew best in the agency didn't believe her.

"Look Sid," the chief said, "run this by me again. This Guilden fella. What exactly did he say?"

Cyrus took out his notepad and added, "Yes, walk us through it one more time. Word by word."

She got up again. "I've got a couple of words for the both of you." She pointed at each one. "Screw you, and screw you."

"You better button it up, Sid!" Ted said.

"I'm a shadow agent. I don't have to be here." She headed for the door. "You have no idea what I'm up against, because if you did, you'd be in the thick of this with me." She swung the door open and marched straight out.

Sitting behind her desk, Jane gave her a disapproving glance and opened her mouth to speak.

Sid cut her off and shot her a hard look. "Not a word if you know what's good for you." She made a bead for the elevator and noted the group of male agents mumbling and watching her go. "Worry about your own sorry cases, you bunch of jackasses." She punched the elevator button, tapped her foot on the tiles, shook her head, and blasted through the door to the stairs.

I'm beginning to hate this building.

She jogged down four flights, crossed through the lobby, and pushed her way outside through the main entrance doors. Taking the steps two at a time down onto the street, she realized something. *I don't have my car!*

CHAPTER 26

S IDNEY STUFFED HER HANDS INTO her jacket pockets and meandered down the sidewalk. *They're idiots. Then again, maybe I'm the idiot.* Throughout all of her career, everyone had preached teamwork—until the Black Slate. Now, it seemed no one wanted anything to do with her—or it. She felt like an outsider looking in. It hurt. It made her angry.

She took a breath and tried to flag down a taxi. It was getting dark now, and the busy streets had begun to thin. She didn't see a taxi anywhere and cursed. *Get ahold of yourself. What would you do if you were in their shoes?* She had never bent the rules before, but now things were different. Everything she knew about life was turned upside down.

"Hey! Hey! Taxi!" She dashed into the street as one went by. The driver waved. She smacked the back of his trunk with her hand. "Thanks for nothing!"

She headed back onto the sidewalk. A woman and her son were staring at her with widened eyes. *What are you gawking at?* She didn't say it. Instead, she tucked her chin down, picked up the pace, and marched down the street. She took out her phone. *I suppose I could call a cab.* She pressed the info button.

"How can I help you?" said a male computerized voice.

"I need a—"

A nearby car let out an awesome exhaust note.

Vrrrrooom! Vrrrrooom! Vrrrrooomm!

Sidney turned around. Her phantom-black Dodge Hellcat with orange highlights awaited in the street.

Smoke was in the driver's seat. He rolled down the window. "Need a lift?"

She walked over to his side, bent over to eye level, and said, "I'm driving."

He got out, walked in front of the hood, and entered the passenger side door.

Sidney took her place in the driver's seat. She adjusted her mirrors and seat. Cars honked as they passed by. She popped the sunglasses holder. The glasses from Mal's house fell into her hand. She slipped them on. The dark streets became brighter, distant images crystal clear. She squeezed the wheel. "Do you know what's going on?"

"Yeah," Smoke said, eyes forward, switching the magazine on his gun.

"You might want to get out. I'm going to see Mason Crow. Don't try to talk me out of it."

"I didn't swing by to give you a shoulder to cry on." He slapped the magazine into the gun.

"Good." She slapped the gear shifter into drive and punched the accelerator. The front end lifted off the ground and the rear tires dug in. "Now let's go get those bastards."

You can count on me. Smoke's words echoed in her mind. It was clear now. He meant what he said. It strengthened her. There weren't too many people she trusted in this world. Whenever she had trusted someone, they'd let her down. *Maybe my expectations are too high for most people. Not everyone can be a 'do the right thing or die' kind of person.*

The car engine purred as they traveled down the road back toward Mason Crow's estate. Or the Drake estate. It didn't matter to her whose it was.

"So, you plan on driving straight up to the front porch?" Smoke inspected the keen edge of the knife he had in his hand.

"I've got a feeling they're expecting me."

"You have a good sense of things. Guts too. I like it," he said. "Let's just hope they stay in you."

"I've got my sweet heart suit on. I figure my guts will be just fine. Getting my hair messed up is what worries me." She eyed his shaved head. "At least you don't have that problem."

He let out a low chuckle.

"You need to let that hair grow back out if we make it out. Just saying."

"All right, Delilah. If we live, I'll never cut it again."

"No, don't go all hippie on me, either." Her phone buzzed. She turned on the car's Bluetooth. "Hello, Mal."

"Good guess, Agent Shaw. Is Smoke with you?"

"Yes," she said.

"And I see that you're headed back. You need to turn around." Mal's voice was urgent. "Now."

"Can't do that," she said.

"It's a death wish. Turn around."

"It was nice meeting you, Mal. But we have to go now. If you recover our bodies, make sure it's a nice funeral."

"And if I'm gored to death," Smoke added, "be sure to hide the hole if it's in my head."

"Have you two gone mad? You're on a suicide mission. You need a plan."

"We have one," she said. "And it involves using all of your ammo."

"At least take the pills," Mal said. "Please, take the pills. Take them now. They're time release."

"I don't have any pills."

"I do," Smoke said, holding up two liquid green pills. "Sorry, but I couldn't resist. Reminded me of *The Matrix*."

"Well, you can take one for you and one for me then."

"Agent Shaw, listen to me. Your lives depend on it. So do your niece and your sister. Turn around."

"Good-bye, Mal." She disconnected the phone and powered it down. "I don't like being talked out of things."

"I know," Smoke said, "but if you don't care, stop for just a few seconds."

"Why?"

"Because I'd stop for you if you were asking."

She slowed the car down and put it into park.

Smoke shifted around in his seat and faced her. He held up the two green pills. "Who knows what sort of real monsters we'll find in there. I think we'll need an edge this time. These super vitamins might help."

"It doesn't seem like you," she said, eyeing the pills.

He shrugged his shoulders. "I won't take it if you won't."

Now the pressure was on her. She rubbed her palms on her jeans. "Don't you put this on me. If you want to take it, then take it. Don't blame me for dying if you don't."

His dark eyes bore into her. "If you won't do it for yourself, then do it for Allison. Do it for Megan."

"Fine." She snatched the pill from his hand and swallowed it down.

Smoke did the same. "See, that wasn't so bad."

She put the car into drive and hit the gas, pinning them both to their seats. "We'll see about that."

After they rounded the last bend, about a quarter mile in front of the ranch was a gate under heavy guard. Suddenly, a spotlight beamed on her car.

Sidney stopped the car about an eighth of a mile away. "Huh. I get the feeling they're expecting us." She squeezed the grip on her pistol.

Smoke held a gun in each hand. "They haven't started firing yet."

The sounds of small engines roared to life. Four ATVs zoomed in from the tall grasses, surrounding her car. A dozen gun barrels were lowered on them.

"Get those hands where we can see them!" yelled one of the men.

"Yep, they were expecting us." Smoke eased his hands up.

One of the men hopped out of an ATV, holding his fist up. He pecked on Sidney's window with the butt of his weapon. She rolled it down.

"Are you Agent Shaw?" he said.

"No, I'm the tooth fairy."

The man lifted his bushy brows. "Nice car, tooth fairy. Now take a nice easy drive up the road, and come to a stop at the log cabin. Someone will meet you there." He spit tobacco juice on the ground. "I hope you're up for a long night. It's gonna be hell. It's gonna be death."

CHAPTER 27

INSIDE THE OVERSIZED LOG HOME, a fire burned beneath a great hearth of cut stone that rose up through the ceiling. Sidney's face dripped sweat from the heat of the blaze. Her hands were bound behind her back, and she was on her knees. Smoke was in the same position beside her, with sweat dripping off his chin.

"Hot, yes?" said a man with a booming voice. It was Mason Crow, sitting in a grand chair carved from wood and animal bone. He was larger than life. Dark skin with large eyes underneath a head of shaggy brown hair. His shoulders were inhumanly brawny. A large machete rested on his lap. "Enjoy it. It's much warmer than the grave."

Sidney shifted against the bonds biting into her wrists and gave him a defiant look. "Where's my sister? Where's my niece?"

A tall well-built woman wearing a dark purple and gray suit with short salt and pepper colored hair strolled over and drove her booted foot into Sid's gut.

"Ooof!" Sid teetered over onto the floor, coughing and spitting.

"I doubt you are in a position to ask any questions," Mason said, rolling up his white cotton sleeves. "If I want you to speak, I'll ask."

Sid fought her way back onto her aching knees. She didn't care what he wanted. She hadn't come here to play games. She just wanted to know if Allison was alive or dead. "Just answer me, you fricking animal."

The woman launched a punch into her jaw. *Whap!*

Sid swayed, kept her balance, and leered up at the woman. "You hit like a girl."

Whap! "You bleed like one." The woman drew her fist back again. *Whap!*

Sidney's stinging eye began to swell. Her split lip tasted like blood. *I hate these people.* Like a fool, she had rushed into the lion's den, and now she would have to face the consequences.

"She is a spirited one, isn't she?" Mason said, cocking his head and giving her a study. Nostrils flaring, he took a deep draw through his nose. "I don't smell fear in her. Nor in him, for that matter. Much unlike her family."

Sid's head snapped up, and she stared him down.

"Yes, Agent Sidney Shaw," Mason said. "I have seen them, and you'll be glad to know that they live... for now."

"Show me!" she fired back.

The woman cocked her fist back to strike.

"Hold!" Mason said. "Let her save her energy, Double Dee. She'll need it. Humph." He picked up his machete, stood up, and made his way toward them. He brought the blade up under Smoke's chin. "You are the one who shot me. Humph. It takes a special bullet to penetrate my skin. My attendants marveled when they plucked it out of my hide. A breakthrough in ammunition. It will take more than that to kill me, but it's more than enough to kill mortals like you. I'm all about heavy blades and horns." He hefted the machete high over his head and brought it down hard with a tremendous yell. "Haaaaaaaaaaaaaaaaaaaaa!"

"Smoke!" Sidney yelled.

The blade quavered less than an inch from Smoke's skull. The man remained still as a stone.

Sidney gasped. "You're sick! What's wrong with you people! Are you nothing but bloodthirsty vampires?"

Mason withdrew the blade and stuck it into the hardwood floor. "Please, no need to insult us. We are nothing like those blood-sucking leeches. Leave those vermin to the European world." He backed up and resumed his chair. "Humph. Survivors. I like that. It's been quite some time since the attendants of the Drake have been tested. You took down the wolf man and the bird lady. Quite a feat." He stroked the coarse black hairs on his chin. "I'd say they underestimated you."

"That's an excuse," Sid fired back. "Your friend Night Bird didn't like lab rats who fought back. Well, we do fight back, and given the chance, we'll kick your hairy ass too."

Mason's chest heaved with great laughter. Some of the other guards in the room chuckled. The woman called Double Dee smirked. "Said like a true warrior. It's no surprise that *they* chose you, bold woman. You have guts." He stomped his foot, shaking the room. "And I aim to see them splattered underneath my hooves."

"Doesn't make for a very nice memory of the petting zoo," Smoke said. "Say, do any of you fiends turn into llamas? You know, half man, half llama. Now that would be formidable."

Sidney laughed.

"Fools," Mason said, "but cocky fools. Humph. That makes for great entertainment, but unlike the battles you had with my lesser colleagues, this one will be quite different." He snapped his fingers. "Let me see their weapons."

One of the soldiers carried Smoke's duffel bag over, bowed, and set it down at Mason's feet. Slowly he stepped off to the side.

Mason reached down and pulled the duffel bag up and into his lap. *Clank.* "Let's see what our dear enemies have in store for us." He fished his hand into the bag and withdrew one of the daggers Mal had given them. He thumbed the edge. "Interesting." He ran the blade along his arm. A hairy clump of arm hair drifted toward the floor. "Now that's a sharp knife. I like it." He eyed the point, stuck it deep into his forearm, and sliced back until he drew blood.

Sidney grimaced. Blood dripped down Mason's arm and splashed onto the floor.

"'If it bleeds, then it can die,' the mortals like to say, eh, heroes?" Mason held his forearm out. The nasty gash closed itself together, and the shaved hairs grew back. "And that's true in most cases."

Sidney glanced at Smoke.

His eyes were on hers, and he said, "I've always wanted to be a matador."

"Yeah, me too," she added. "Do we get to wear those funny hats?"

"No," Mason said, "but you will be seeing a lot of red." In a lightning-swift move, he jammed the blade to the hilt into the soldier's chest. *Chuk!*

"Urk!" The man in the pea coat sagged to the floor, eyes wide and gasping for breath.

"Take this mess out of here," said Double Dee.

Two men rushed over, hooked the dying man under the arms, and bore him out of the room.

Sidney's nerves were on fire. She shifted on her knees. Eyed the exits of the room. *Maybe coming here wasn't such a good idea after all.*

CHAPTER 28

"T HIS IS INTERESTING." MASON HAD fished a gun magazine out of the duffel bag and was eyeing it. He plucked a bullet with a red tip out and cocked his head. "Humph. Looks to be a little more than a tracer. What does it do?"

Sidney pulled her tongue off of the roof of her mouth and tried to speak. She was on a roller coaster of mixed emotions, fear and anger intermingled. Sweat dripped into her eyes. She wiped it with her shoulder. *Be brave. Be bold. Do it for your family.* "It kills people. And animals."

"Oh, I see." He slapped the magazine into the gun and handed it over to Double Dee. "Show me."

Double Dee charged the weapon's slide and took aim at Smoke. "It's gonna leave a mess," she said.

"Good, I like messes."

"Double Dee?" Sidney interrupted with a sneer, "What kind of stupid name is that?" She glanced at the woman's chest. She couldn't stop the words from coming. "Did you have a reduction and forget to change your stripper name?"

"You've got a pretty big mouth for a woman whose boyfriend is about to get shot in the head." Double Dee recharged the weapon's slide. "Anything else, *Agent Shaw*?"

"Nope."

"I'd like to state, for the record, that I'm not her boyfriend," Smoke said. "And I'd like lilies sent to my funeral. If I get one."

The woman huffed a laugh and said back to Mason, "Can you believe these two?"

"They'd make excellent jesters, Dee. Humph. I like it." He pointed at the guards posted at the windows. "Shoot one of those. Or both."

One man stiffened, and the other man moved.

Ka-Blam! Ka-Blam!

Sidney squeezed her eyes shut and hunkered down. Two explosions rocked the floor. *Boom! Boom!* Glass shattered.

"Holy shit!" Dee said.

Sidney opened her eyes. There was blood and guts splattered on Dee's face.

Dee wiped it off, held up the gun, and said to Mason, "Can I keep this?"

He nodded.

Sidney glanced over her shoulder. The pair of men lay dead, each with a massive cavity in his chest. Her tummy soured, and she turned away. "I told you they killed people. Pretty sure they'll work on livestock too."

Mason wiped the bits of scattered flesh from his arms and removed another item from the bag. It was the special flex cuffs that Mal said would hold anything. "They can have these. Humph. " He tossed the bag onto the floor. "The rest is now acquired by our arsenal."

Dee cozied up to Smoke and tugged at the sweet heart suit hidden underneath his collar. "What about this? I think this suit's made of fibro-gynnsynn."

"Leave it. It might save their skin, but it won't stop their bones from breaking or their innards from being crushed. If anything, it will only prolong their suffering." He cracked his knuckles. They each made a loud pop. "I love the sound of bone and sinew breaking."

"What about my family?" Sidney said. "I don't care what you have in store for me, but just let them go."

"Oh, but I'm going to leave their fate in your hands, Agent Shaw. Yes. All you have to do is find them. If you can find them, then you can save them. How does that sound?"

"It sounds like another one of your twisted games."

Mason shrugged. "When you've been around as long as I have, you find creative ways to entertain yourself. I'm so glad you volunteered your services." He stood up to his towering full height. "Dee, have them prepped and sent to the catacombs." He stood over Sidney. "I hope to see you both at the end." He turned his back and exited the room with loud and heavy footsteps.

"What does he mean by prepping us?" Sidney asked Dee. The woman had a vague familiarity about her.

Dee waved a few guards over, but she addressed her comments to Sidney. "It means search them again and take off their shoes. No one wears shoes down there. It's a thing. Now sit down on your ass."

Knees aching, Sidney was almost happy to comply. "How can you do this, Dee?"

"Please don't start trying to pick at my conscience. I don't have one." Dee started untying Sidney's boots. "Besides, you've only seen a glimpse of the power they have. Let me give you some advice. Let the devils in those holes take you quickly. They'll have more mercy than Mason will." She jerked Sid's boots off one at a time. "You'll understand once you get down there."

"I saw what you were thinking," Sidney said to Dee. "You have that gun, that power. You were tempted to shoot him, weren't you?"

"You're mistaken."

"No, I'm not. Women of your disposition often want to kill their lovers."

"Ha, well, I don't think you were paying attention." Dee tossed the boots aside. "He can't be killed."

"That's what AV and Night Bird thought. You know, Mason reminds me of my boss, Ted Howard."

Dee froze for a moment and then said, "Good for you."

"Huh, so the legendary Special Agent Deanne Drukker lives."

"I don't think so."

"What's the Double for then, Dee?"

"Just a stupid pet name for me," Dee said, looking Sid in the eye. "You should be able to figure it out, Special Agent." She then spoke with a hushed breath. "I warned Ted. Now you've come to die."

Something clicked deep inside Sid's thoughts. *Extraordinary Caution. Did Ted put me on this assignment hoping that I would find Deanne? Damn him!* "He misses you."

"He always was soft."

"Probably started after his mentor left."

"Uh-huh."

"Dee," Sidney said, pleading a little. "I don't care what happens to me. I just want to save my sister and niece. Free them."

"How noble." The rangy woman stood up. "But that's entirely up to you and him." She shook her head. "I really hate to see good troops go, but I'm excited to see how this ends." She pulled out her pistol and raised it behind the back of Sid's head. "Have a good death, Agent Shaw."

The gun came down. The butt of the weapon struck her skull. Sid's head filled with painful bright spots, stars, and then blackness.

CHAPTER 29

S IDNEY AWOKE WITH A SHIVER. Rubbing her bleary eyes and aching head, she managed to make it to her feet. *Where am I?*

She was in a round room about twenty feet across, with walls that were made of cut rock on a framework of iron beams. It was illuminated by dim yellow lights. The ceiling was maybe ten feet high, and a heavy metal door, no window, was closed behind her. *This must be where they dropped me off.*

She ran her fingers along the door's edge. There were no handles or latches, and the door was sealed up tight. "Great. Welcome to the catacombs, Sid."

The room she stood in was cold and lonely. She already missed Smoke, and despite the warmness her suit provided, a chill went through her. *Not a fan of caves. Or the dirt that's in them.* She'd gone spelunking once in her teens and sworn she'd never do it again. Getting trapped a few hundred feet underground had unnerved her then. It was worse now. She had a feeling she was so deep that no one would ever hear her scream.

"Well, Sid, let's go find your sister."

She shuffled forward. Something sharp bit into her foot. "Ow." She braced herself against the damp wall and hoisted her foot up. A sliver of something was stuck inside her foot and she plucked it out. *Is that bone?* She flicked it away. Something else caught her eye on the grimy floor. It was a few pairs of flex cuffs. "My, won't these come in handy." She looped them into her belt and shuffled—foot bleeding—down the corridor.

The walls and floor were slick and damp in some places but not all. Her feet found some cleared-off tiles cut from marble. Her nose found something else. She sniffed. Something somewhere was rotting. She balled up her fists and carried on, eyeing the ceiling from time to time. Every twenty steps or so she'd notice a small device mounted on the beams. *Are those cameras? What a bunch of sick people.*

The corridor winded left and right, making right angles and sharp bends and sometimes crossing over. Its grade went up and down, giving her the feeling she was inside some sort of military bunker. She'd been in them before, great man-made caverns and tunnels beneath the ground or built into the mountains. They were stockpiled with weapons and all kinds of other devices. She walked for minutes, twisting and turning, losing all sense of direction. *Morning Glory. I really am a lab rat.*

Her stomach groaned. A strong hunger gripped her. *Crap, how long was I out?* It could have been hours, and the suit tended to make her more hungry than normal. It gave her energy, but it made her want to eat more too. *Forget about it, and keep going.*

As her feet slapped over the wet floor, the foul odor became stronger. She covered her nose and forged ahead into an open room. A lone metal desk sat in the middle of the room with a body, seated in a chair, slumped over it. It was a man in uniform. The back of his blue shirt was stained in blood and showed a gaping wound. His flesh was rotting from his skin and it looked like rats, really big ones, had nibbled on it. He wasn't wearing any shoes.

Geez. Poor guy.

She gave his body a shove, and it collapsed onto the floor. She held back her shriek. The man's face was chewed up. His eyes were missing, and his mouth hung open in a silent terrified yell. There was a name badge on his shirt. She ripped it off. John Carter, DCPD. She remembered reading about how he'd gone missing. She glared up at the cameras.

"I guess I'm not alone fighting you minions! Screw you!"

She tucked the nameplate away in her back pocket. She ground her teeth thinking about his family and all they had been through since he went missing. It charged her blood. She patted down his body, searching for a weapon of any kind. Finding nothing, she searched the room. There were some empty shelves, boxes, and crates. A bunch of crap long abandoned. *Oh well.*

There was another corridor across, identical to the one that she came from. She started toward it and stopped. She heard footsteps coming her way. Steady. Purposed. She hid on the other side of the desk and waited. On her hands and knees, she peeked from underneath the desk. A pair of bare feet emerged from the corridor and slowly began to circle the room.

"Muh… muh," muttered an inhuman voice as something sniffed the room.

Sidney shifted her way around the desk, staying out of its line of sight. Her skin crawled at the sound of its voice.

"Muh… muh," it said, feet shuffling over the floor. Its movements stopped. Its voice fell silent. Only the hum of the yellow lights and the sound of dripping water remained—along with the foulness of the air.

Sidney swallowed and took a peek over the desk. Her eyes locked on a burly man with stringy hair and hollow eyes. A huge bloodstained club was in his hand. *A deader!*

Its eyes locked on hers. "Muh!" The weapon came down with all of its might, pounding at the desk. *Whack! Whack! Whack!*

Sidney sprang to her feet and backed away. A second deader emerged—bald and bearded— from the other corridor, dragging another crude club behind it. It raised the weapon up and came right at her, swinging left and right. The pair flanked her behind the desk, leaving only a straight path down the corridor where she had not been. *There might be another deader back there!*

The clubs came up and slammed down. Sid dashed between the pair of deaders and circled around the room. Their moves were mechanical but quick as a man of the same size and with unrelenting purpose. The clubs clanked off the walls, toppled the shelves, and ricocheted off the floor.

Chest heaving, Sidney ducked, twisted away, and spun through the pair of them. A bludgeoning blow ripped through the air, missing her and cracking the skull of the other deader. It teetered over and fell. Its club clattered to the ground. Sidney went for the weapon.

The shaggier one with the club charged. *Whack! Whack!*

It missed her curled-up legs. Her fingers stretched out, grabbing the club by the bottom and catching it up in time to block the next thunderous blows that rained down on her.

Clack! Clack! Clack!

The thunderous blows jarred her arms. She drew back her leg and kicked out its knee.

"Muh!" It said, teetering over and spilling to the ground.

Sid scrambled to her feet. A powerful hand snatched her leg and jerked her down. The first deader had her in its fierce grip. It balled up its fist and punched her hard in the thigh.

"Aargh!" Sidney yelled. "No more of that!" She hit it in the head with the club. *Whack! Whack!* "Die, monster, die!" *Whack! Whack! Whack!*

Its grip loosened.

She tore away, scrambling to her feet. Her lungs were burning, and her face was dripping with sweat. Sidney stumbled back against the wall. Two more deaders emerged from the corridors with clubs bigger than the last. "I hate you things."

CHAPTER 30

"Muh! Muh! Muh! Muh!"

"Oh, shut up!" Sidney swung with all of her force into the nearest one, dismantling its chin. *Clak!*

It fell backward, jostling the others.

Sid made her move. Fueled by another burst of adrenaline, she sprinted by the other deaders and darted into the corridor. *Catch me if you can!* She ran, leaving the distant 'muh muh' echoes of the deaders behind her. She slowed to a stop, legs cramping, and gasped for air. Her heartbeat was pounding inside her temples. The wound in her foot burned, but she ignored it.

Think of something, Sid. Think!

Feet splattering over the wet stone floor, she headed toward the sound of rushing water. Perhaps there was a drainage tunnel leading out. She picked up the pace, following the lights around a series of sharp bends in the tunnel. The path split off from time to time, but she followed the sound. It grew louder and louder. She turned down a narrow corridor until the sound of crashing water roared in her ears. The ceiling lowered and she stooped down, traveling toward the sound until the tunnel came to a stop.

No!

A wall of metal bars blocked the exit. Beyond them a series of tunnels roared with water rushing through them. She hit the bars with the club. The grid of iron rang out. She hit it again and again. *Clang! Clang! Clang!* She turned and slumped back against the bars. Took some deep draws through her nose and clutched the stitch in her side. It had been awhile since she'd run so hard.

"Muh…"

Her head snapped up. A deader bore down on her on stiff, fast-moving legs. Closing in, it swung its club. She sidestepped and walloped it in the side of the head. The creature's head tilted and snapped back. It swung again. She parried. She blocked. *Clack! Clack!* The unrelenting creature of the dead laid into her with heavy blow after heavy blow.

"Muh!"

"Muh you!" she yelled back. She clobbered it in the face, busting its nose. She was skilled. Quicker. She blasted it in the teeth. In the knee. The back of the head. She beat it down. Blasted it full in the neck. It lumbered aimlessly then cut loose a wild swing.

Crack!

"Aaaah!" Sidney cried out. It had busted her in the hand. The club slipped from her fingers. Tucking the wounded hand beneath her arm, she backed away. "Where's a flamethrower when you need one?" She shuffled back and ran into another deader. "Ugh!"

It locked its arms around her waist and held her fast. The other came at her and unleashed a furious swing.

She ducked her head. The club skimmed over her face and cracked the head of the deader holding her. It let out a ghastly groan, stumbled back, and slammed her hard on the tunnel floor. She grabbed its hands and tried to break free of its grip. She kicked, elbowed, and flailed. The other deader with the club attacked again. *Whap! Whap! Whap!*

It missed her and hit the other one. Sidney twisted in its loosened grip, pulled her feet under her, and shoved her way free. It fell back into the other, creating a pile of undead flesh. Gasping for breath, she found herself pinned between the deaders and the barred gate. *Morning Glory! How can I stop these things? I need my weapon!*

The deaders gathered themselves, blocking the path of any escape out of the tunnel, and closed in once more.

Sid's frantic hands found the handle on the club she'd lost. She got up on her feet. "Fine! Come and get me!"

"Muh!" one said with a dangling jaw.

"Muh!" said the other with a crushed eye socket.

She charged with her club high and brought it down with all of her might on the nearest one. The club clocked off of its skull and the handle busted. *No!* She tossed the broken weapon aside and launched a kick into one deader's gut, doubling it over. She locked her hands around the swinging club of the other and hung on for dear life.

Whop!

Something hard crashed into the side of her face.

She kicked back and kept kicking. Something hit back and kept hitting. She fought with everything she had, but she got tired. They didn't. She lost her grip on the club and sagged onto the tunnel floor. She looked up at her undead aggressor, spat out the words, "I can't go down like this," and launched a futile punch into its groin. "Not to some undead bastard."

CHAPTER 31

THE DEADER'S CLUB STARTED TO descend.

Glitch!

A blade erupted from the front of the deader's chest and ripped back out of it. The deader collapsed on top of Sidney. She shoved it off. *What just happened?*

The remaining deader whirled away from Sid and faced the new attacker. It was Smoke, standing tall with a gory spear in his hands. The deader charged. Smoke rammed the spear into its heart and clean through the back.

The deader let out its last cry. "Muh!" Its body slumped to the floor.

Smoke braced his boot on the deader's chest and pulled the spear out. He offered Sidney his hand.

She took it. "Where did you find a spear?"

Blood was dripping down from a gash in his forehead. He wiped it away. "Another deader. Come on. These tunnels are full of them."

"Hold on." She took the spear away from him, glared at one of the deaders, and stabbed it again. "Okay, now we can go."

Nodding, Smoke reached down for one of the clubs. "This all right with you?"

She shrugged. He led. Still catching her breath, she followed. Smoke moved with ease through the network, not moving too fast or too slow. They tread on bare cat's feet, stopping and listening. Deaders roamed. She could hear their heavy steps slapping the wet stones, but it was hard to tell where they were coming from.

Smoke stopped and held up his hand. Something was coming on heavy feet, but she couldn't see around the bend. "Go back," he said.

Turning, she crept back down the tunnel toward the last intersection that they passed. Just as she was pressing her back against the way, two more deaders, one very big, lumbered by carrying machetes. *Cripes!*

Smoke's hand gave her shoulder a gentle squeeze. His breath was on her ear. A tingling sensation raced through her.

Now's not the time for these kinds of feelings. Something crawled over her feet. A rat the size of a cat was sitting on her bare toes. "Eek!" She kicked it off of her.

The two deaders turned around and ran right for her. Charged with adrenaline, Sidney lowered the spear and ran the first one through. *Glitch!* She ripped it out, looking for the rat. "Where are you, little vermin?" She jabbed at a rat scurrying over the floor. "Not sure which I hate worse. Rats or deaders."

"Sid!" Smoke yelled. "Sid!"

She spun around.

Smoke—swinging two handed—was clubbing away for his life against a deader that towered over him swinging a machete like a butter knife.

She jammed the spear into its back. She missed the heart.

It twisted, breaking the spear shaft off in her hands and backhanding her in the face.

She landed hard on her ass. "Ooph!"

Smoke renewed his assault, hammering it in the face. "Can't hit what you can't see!" Whack! Whack! Whack!"

With a spear poking out of its chest, the deader chopped back. The blade slit Smoke's abdomen, doubling him over. The machete went up. Smoke's decapitation was soon to follow.

"No!" Sidney screamed. Her long legs churned. She slammed into the back of the deader's legs and knocked it from its feet. *Wump!* It tried to split her in half. She rolled away.

Smoke sprang like a panther and locked up its arms and neck. "Kill it!"

"With what?"

"The spear," he said. The veins in his neck bulged like purple roots. "Hurry. I can't hold it much longer!"

She crawled over, grabbed the gory spear in her hands, jerked it from the deader's chest, flipped it around, and plunged it into its heart.

Its long legs shivered and went still.

"That was gross," Sid said.

Smoke shoved the deader aside and said nothing, wincing and clutching his belly.

"Are you all right?" she said.

He fingered the clean slice in his clothes, revealing the black second skin underneath. "I can't believe my guts are still in me."

"Me either," she said, scooting closer. "You almost lost your head too, you know." She winced and glanced at her throbbing hand. Her pinky finger was out of joint. Her stomach turned sick.

"That looks nasty," Smoke said. "Let me take a look."

"No."

He made his way toward her and said it again. "Let me take a look."

Reluctantly, she showed her hand.

"Ever dislocated it before?" he said.

"No."

He rubbed his chin. "Hmm. I think you better let me fix it, Sid."

She shook her head.

"Come on. You can count on me. Just let me do it. You can't let yourself be distracted by that aching pain." He nudged her shoulder. "Come on. Time's pressing."

She stretched her hand toward him, looked him right in the eye and said, "Do it."

Smoke took her hand gently in his palm, looked right back at her and said, "Easy peasy."

Pop.

Pain lanced through her hand, back, legs, and shoulders. She winced and sucked through her teeth. Eyes watering, she said, "Thanks."

He stretched out his hand and took her other one in it. They pulled each other up together.

He looked deep into her eyes and said, "I'm glad I didn't lose my head."

"Oh," she replied.

"But it wouldn't be so bad if you were the last thing I ever saw."

"I can't believe you just fed me a line."

"I can't believe you're scared of rats."

She rose on her tiptoes, eyed the floor, and said, "If I see any more, you might have to carry me through here."

"It would be my pleasure."

CHAPTER 32

THEY WANDERED: LONG TEDIOUS MINUTES avoiding the unnatural sounds that roamed the corridor.

"This looks different," Smoke said, scratching the dirt wall with his fingers. He eyed the ceiling. The beams were wooden instead of steel and iron, but the lights were still there.

"Do you think they used to mine something down here?" she said, bending over and picking up a small chunk of coal. "Or is it just another hideout?"

"It's a catacomb. Not sure what else you'd call it. The pattern's purpose is to confuse." He led her up a gentle slope that opened up into an oversized alcove. There were tables and chairs, and the shelves were stocked with dry rotten rations of some sort. Decayed corpses and piles of bones lay dormant in the corner.

Sidney ran her fingers over the table. Checked the grooves and markings. She had a knack for such things. Her parents had been avid antiquers. "This is early American," she said, looking at an emblazoned rising sun carved in the backs of the chairs. "Probably worth a small fortune."

"Maybe we can get Mark Wahlberg and *The Antiques Roadshow* down here," Smoke said, taking a knee alongside one of the corpses. "They might take a keen interest in these uniforms too. These are redcoats."

"You're kidding."

Smoke picked up the tattered uniform and what was left of the bones in it. He played with the skeleton's jaw and made funny talk with it. "The British are coming. The British are coming. Wait. I *am* the British. Say, how'd my legs get so bony?" The jaw broke off in his hand. "Whoops. The roadshow's not going to like that."

"I think we need to get moving, Smoke Revere."

Smoke picked up a redcoat hat and dusted it off.

"Don't put that on," Sidney said, easing her way around the alcove. It felt like she'd stepped back in time more than two hundred years. "You look silly enough already. Let's go."

"After you." Smoke gestured and shrugged. "I think we've survived the first wave of danger. They want us to be here. I can feel it in my bones."

Sidney resumed her trek, opting to take the tunnel on the right, rather than the option on the left or going back. For some reason the tension between her shoulders eased. Perhaps Smoke was right. It seemed that their pursuers had been called off. Trudging over the sloppy floors, she came to a stop at the top of a stone-cut staircase. Torches lit the stairway that spiraled downward. A lump formed in her throat. "Uh, Smoke?"

Like a big hawk, he leaned down over her shoulder. "Looks like a gateway to Hell, doesn't it?"

"I really wish you hadn't said that."

"Sorry," he said, brushing by. "I'll go first."

Heart racing, Sidney followed the stairs deeper into the bowels of the earth. *Allison and Megan better be down here.* One thing she remembered from spelunking was that you never could tell how deep you were on your own. It practically terrified her. When she was a girl, she'd found the Loraine Caverns fascinating. Now, she'd avoid those historic caves altogether.

This shadow agent stuff really should come with a hefty boost in hazard pay.

The tunnel got cooler and even damper. Her thoughts were on the rushing waters she'd seen earlier. Those had to be above her now.

Do heavy rains fill these tunnels? This is crazy.

Smoke stopped. "I think we finally hit bottom."

"I can't imagine being any lower." She stepped from behind his broad shoulders and gazed ahead. Her mouth formed a small 'O'. A monstrous black chasm loomed. The glimmer of two torches looked to be a hundred yards in the distance. A low howl of wind caught her ears, nipped at her toes, and finally chilled her straight to the marrow. "There has to be another way."

Smoke moved forward, fixing his hands on the wood beams that supported a rope bridge that looked to be in poor condition. It was the only thing between them and the other side. He looked back at her. "Can you do it?"

Her fingers twitched at her sides. "Uh…"

"I can piggyback you."

I would like that… Damn my pride. If he's not scared, I'm not either. She stepped onto the bridge, glanced back at Smoke, and said, "Don't get any crazy ideas, Dr. Jones."

"Huh, good one."

Squeezing the ropes with white knuckles, she ventured forward. The bridge swayed. She clutched the ropes with her arms.

"Just stay in the middle, Sid," Smoke said in a reassuring voice. "It'll be fine."

She sucked it up and moved on, one short step at a time. The wind licked at her toes and howled in her ears. *Where is that wind coming from?* There was nothing but darkness as black as pitch above her, below her, all around her. The void was the most terrifying thing she had ever seen.

"You're doing good, Sid. Keep going."

"Oh, shut up."

She lengthened her stride. The boards beneath her feet began to creak. *Morning Glory.* She took another step. *Morning Glory.* And another. *Morning Glory.* She thought of her mother's mother. 'Morning Glory' was the harshest thing Nanna Nancy ever said. Even though she'd been widowed at a young age, she had great patience with everything she did. *Her heart probably wouldn't skip a beat if she were on this bridge.* Sidney turned on her tiny engine and continued forward. *Morning Glory. Morning Glory. Morning Glory.*

Squawk!

Sid froze. "What in the hell was that?"

"A Night Bird," Smoke said.

She peered around. "That's not funny."

"Just keep going."

She did, but with ears honing in on the strange rustling that came from all around and on the scattered flaps of tiny wings. She summoned her inner strength. She'd closed at least half the distance to the other side, where an archway awaited, lit by torches. *Screw it.* She picked up the pace. The rope bridge jostled and twisted.

"Slow down," Smoke warned. "It's sensitive to our movements. Cat's feet, just like before."

Sidney felt exactly what he was talking about. The ripple effect moved up and came back stronger, pitching the bridge from side to side. Anything too rushed would twist the ropes right over. "Okay," she said in a hushed voice. "Okay. But we better find a shovel, 'cause I'm digging my ass back out of here."

She made it five more steps. Ten. Twenty.

Squawk!

The black sea surrounding them came to life.

Squawk! Squawk! Squawk!

Sid envisioned ancient winged predators darting down, plucking her off the bridge, and dropping her into the hungry black gorge, where gnashing teeth waited. *Keep going. Keep going!*

"Ignore it, Sid. Just go." Smoke said.

Something zipped overhead, clipping her skull. On instinct, she swung. The bridge buckled hard to the left. She lost her footing and started to fall. *Nooooo!*

CHAPTER 33

DANGLING OVER THE BRIDGE WITH just fingers locked on the ropes, she hung on for her life. *This is bad. Really bad. Squawk! Squawk!*

Barely able to make out what she was holding onto, she climbed back on the swinging bridge and lay belly down. Huffing for breath, she said, "Smoke? Are you back there?"

No answer.

Oh no! Oh no!

"I'm here. Just be still, will you?" he said in a strained voice.

Slowly, she managed to look back over her shoulder. *Oh no!* Smoke held onto the lower rope of the bridge with one hand. "Hang on, Smoke. I'm coming."

"The thought had occurred to me," he said, "but don't you move. Stay flat and wide. It keeps the bridge stabilized."

"Okay."

Smoke began a gentle swing, swaying the entire bridge, and with a heave he latched his other hand onto the ropes. He pulled himself back up onto the bridge and said, "Let's get moving again."

"What about those bats?"

"Those aren't bats. Bats don't squawk."

"What are they?"

"Just go," he urged.

"Fine, but I'm crawling," she said.

"Suit yourself."

"Did you just drop a line on me from Moonraker?"

"Huh," he said, "I suppose I did. But really, you should get going."

Another stony screech erupted, followed by a burst of flapping wings.

Squawk!

She crawled onward and said, "You know what those things are, don't you."

Silence.

"Don't you."

"Yes."

"And?" she said, digging her hands between the planks.

"You don't need to worry unless you see the yellow glow in their eyes."

"Yellow glow?"

"Yes."

Something landed on the bridge, jostling the entire thing.

"Sid," Smoke said.

"What?"

"Run."

"I thought you said to go slow," she said, checking behind her. Smoke had his back to her. He was eyeing something else on the bridge. It was a small figure, little more than two feet tall, with burning yellow eyes, claws, and black wings. Her neck hairs stood on end. "Never mind."

"Run!" Smoke said again.

Up on her feet, Sid stretched her long legs out in full stride and raced to the other side. The bridge bounced, buckled, and swayed. She surged on, pulling at the ropes, closing on the glimmering torches. Something zipped overhead. Claws scraped over her ducking skull. She cried out. "Ow!"

"Go!" Smoke said. "Go!"

Almost there! Almost there! She wanted to get off the bridge more than anything. Her hands raced along the rope railing, steadying her balance.

Squawk!

A little gargoyle-like creature landed on the end of the bridge, barring her path. Another one landed on its shoulders. They grabbed the bridge ropes and started shaking them.

Sidney didn't know which was a worse fate: facing the grey-skinned fiends with burning-yellow eyes or being pitched into everlasting darkness. *Screw you, little monsters!* She lowered her shoulder that last ten steps, let out a cry, and charged. "Eee-Yaaaaaaaah!"

She plowed into the gargoyles, toppled them over, and spilled off the bridge onto the landing. She rose to her feet, shaking her head, and raised her fists up to fight. "Come on, whatever the hell you are!"

Smoke emerged off the bridge fighting two creatures that were latched onto his legs and arms. He ripped one off and stomped on its chest. He squeezed another by the neck and held it at arm's length. Its taloned fingers tore at his arms in an angry frenzy. He punched it in the face. "Ow!" He flicked his hand and flung it off him.

Sid searched for a weapon. They had left theirs on the other side to cross the bridge.

Squawk!

A creature landed on her back and dug its fingers into her neck. She grabbed its arm and slammed it hard into the rocky ground. She kicked it in the face, skipping it across the ground. "What are these things?"

"Gargoyles," Smoke said, ripping another monster from his leg. "Can't you tell?" He hurled it into the abyss, only to see it fly back and attack him again. "Argh!"

"How do you kill them?" she said, peeling another fiend from her waist. The gargoyles were strong for their size. Strong like animals and hard like stone.

"With a hammer. Preferably a big one."

"I don't have a hammer!" she said. She kicked and swatted at the two gargoyles that squawked and hissed at her. "Got any other ideas?"

Smoke held a gargoyle by the feet and started smashing it into the cave floor. The little monster started to chip and bust. *Wham! Wham! Wham!* It crumbled to dust.

"Good one," Sid said. She launched a kick at one, missing it. Another gargoyle latched onto her arm. She tried to shake it off. Punched it in the face. "Ow!" She shook her stinging hand. The other monster locked onto her free hand and let out a screech to the other. Their wings fluttered with new life and Sidney felt herself being lifted into the air. *Oh snap!* The gargoyles flew straight for the abyss. "Smoke!"

CHAPTER 34

F EET KICKING, SHE CRIED OUT again. "Smoke!"

The ranging man's head snapped up. He took two tremendous strides, jumped up, and locked his fingers on her ankles. The gargoyles shrieked. Their wings beat with fury, pulling them both toward the abyss.

Sidney's arms and legs groaned under the strain. Muscle and sinew popped. "You're ripping me apart!"

Smoke's toes dragged across the ground. He bunched up and heaved. The gargoyles faltered. Their efforts sagged. They let go.

Smoke landed on his feet and caught Sidney in his arms. "Are you all—"

She slipped out of his arms, let out a growl, and plucked the nearest gargoyle out of the air. She slammed it face-first into the ground and stomped her bloody foot on its back. Pinning it to the ground, she reached down, grabbed its wings, and tore them off its back.

It let out an ear-splitting shriek.

She tossed the wings aside and stuffed its face in the ground. "Shut up!" She grabbed it by the legs and slung it far into the abyss, listening to its fading horrified cry.

"Eeeeeeeeeeeeeeeeeeeee!"

"Almost makes you think they have feelings," Smoke said. He pinned another gargoyle to the ground. "I like the way you think." He tore its wings off. *Riiiip!* Casually, he flung it away. "I think that's the last of them."

"For now," Sidney said, peering into the black chasm. She wiped away the blood that dripped into her eye. Ran her fingers over the gash in her head. *That feels nasty.*

"Let me take a look," Smoke said, easing up to her. He had deep scratches all over his hands and face. He examined it. "It'll clot."

"Gee, thanks."

"Did you want me to kiss it for you?"

She leered at him. *Yes.* "Shut up." She moved by him and stared at the door between the burning torches. It was a solid-steel door, modern by the looks of it, sitting just behind an archway cut from large stones. "That's a big door."

Smoke knocked on it with his knuckles. It made a hollow sound. *Bong. Bong. Bong.* "Makes you wonder if it's supposed to keep things in or out. Open sesame."

"Please don't." She placed her hands on her knees and caught her breath. Her lungs burned, and her body ached. She licked her dry lips. She'd worked out hard, but nothing had ever pushed her like this. "Are you sure this isn't Hell?"

"Hell isn't this much fun." Smoke rapped on the door again. "I want a peanut butter sandwich." He knocked again. "Kazam. Shazam." He spread his arms wide. "I am Batman!"

Sidney still struggled for her breath.

Smoke tilted his ear toward her. "Are you wheezing?"

"No," she wheezed. "Okay, yes?"

"You have asthma?"

"Yes, but I haven't-*wheeze*-had an attack in years." She practiced some deep breathing she'd been taught long ago. "I'll be all right, just give me a minute." *Damn. Not now of all times.* It had been so long, she'd almost forgotten the mild suffocation she suffered. It was demoralizing.

"Might be these moldy caves," he said.

"Or all of the life-threatening excitement." She gulped down some air and exhaled through her nose. Sometimes the attack would last for minutes, other times days, even weeks. *Well, at least we're not going anywhere.*

In an instant, the steel door slid upward.

Ssshluuuk!

"You ready, or do you want to wait?" he said.

Sid righted herself and headed for the door. In stride, the pair crossed the threshold at the same time.

Ssshluuuk!

"I guess we're staying," Smoke said.

The stone and mud-walled tunnels were gone, replaced by something far more modern. The dry floor had black-and-white checkered tiles. The walls were painted a medium gray, and fluorescent lighting dangled ten feet overhead. Sid ran her fingers over the wall and pecked her knuckle on it. It was limestone block. She wanted to hug it. "Not nearly as bad as I expected."

"Nope," Smoke said, moving forward. "Gray's still a depressing color though."

"I find its neutral base very soothing." Her breathing came a little easier.

"Well, spend a few weeks in prison, and then tell me what you think."

The corridor burrowed another hundred feet and came to a stop at a pair of double doors. They were yellow heavy safety doors, similar to the ones at her high school. She grabbed the handle and depressed the thumb lever. She eyed Smoke, he nodded, and she shoved it in.

"Welcome," boomed a voice within. "Please, come in."

Inside was an oval room with exits and doors similar to the one she'd just come through. The first thing Sid noticed was the floor. It was an archaic network of multicolor tiles with bloodstains splattered all over them. The musty smell of death lingered, and more corpses, some in dark aged armor, huddled dead along the walls.

There were large windows too. All the walls were cinderblock, and up above glowed gas lights in glass bulbs. There was a terrace, high above them, forming a platform around the room. Mason stood with his great hands on the rail in full minotaur form.

He snorted and shook his horns. "I am surprised you made it, humph!" It was strange how the words came from his bestial lips. "But I'm glad as well. Please, go ahead, take a look around."

"Where's Allison and Megan?" Sid demanded.

"As I said, take a look around."

In the center was a stone staircase that led up to a dais. An automatic pistol sat on the pedestal in the middle, locked in a case of glass. *That's my gun.*

Mason snorted above and paced over the catwalks. He was a monstrous figure, thick in muscles and hide hair. AV and Night Bird were rodents by comparison. His hooved feet made clopping sounds that echoed in the chamber. He held a great machete in his powerful paw.

Sid's breathing started to thin again. *Calm down, girl.*

"Sid," Smoke said, nodding her over. He was peering through one of the glass windows she'd noticed earlier.

"What is it?" she said, walking over. Smoke stepped aside. She gazed through the glass. "Megan!"

CHAPTER 35

S IDNEY POUNDED ON THE GLASS, but it made no sound. The sheet felt thicker than metal. Megan was inside, in a daycare-like facility decorated in fun colors and with tables, TVs, and shelves loaded with toys. She was playing with other children her age. Laughing and smiling along in a pair of pajamas adorned in pink and purple colors.

"Megan!" Sid hit the glass again. "Megan!"

"She can't hear or see you, Agent Shaw. It's a one-way mirror, similar to your interrogation rooms but made with impervious glass," Mason said from somewhere above. "But you can see that she is well cared for."

Sidney stormed to the nearest door. It was sealed tighter than a drum. She kicked it and moved on to the next one. It was the same result. She backed into the middle of the room and found Mason's bison-like eyes. "Where's your trough?" she said.

He cocked his horned head. "Pardon?"

"Your trough! I need to know so I can take a dump in it, you cud-chewing bastard!" She marched toward one of the fallen warriors and picked up a spear. She hurled it straight at Mason.

The minotaur plucked it out of the air and huffed a laugh. "I like your spirit, woman." He snapped the spear in half and tossed it aside. "But you'll need something far more deadly than that."

Smoke slid alongside her with a concerned look in his eyes. She was still wheezing. "Save your breath," he whispered in her ear.

"Please," Mason said, extending his hand. "Continue looking around. Make the most of it. After all, you'll need all the advantages you can get."

Sidney sauntered over to the next glass window. A group of men in a mishmash of uniforms lumbered aimlessly around an empty room. *Deaders!* Each had a bludgeoning weapon in its hand. Some carried two at a time. Bloody feet sticking to the tiles, she shuffled over to the next window. It was a supply room with an assortment of things: fire extinguishers, backpacks, rations, microscopes, other scientific equipment, and five-gallon jugs of water. "See anything useful?" she said to Smoke.

"No."

Her jaw dropped as she peered through the last window. Allison lay back in a salon-type room with cucumbers on her eyes. Two Forever Children in light-colored robes were in the room. One, a girl with frosty blonde hair, was giving Allison a manicure while the other one, a straw-headed boy, massaged her feet. Allison's creaseless expression was pure bliss. *She would be comfortable in this devil's pit.*

"These people really have a screwed-up way of doing things," Smoke said.

"Who are you calling people?" Sid marched out into the room, looked up at Mason, and said, "So, what's your game?"

"You kill me," Mason said, drumming his fingers on the rail, "or beat me into submission, humph, and you can all go free. Pretty simple."

She stepped onto the dais and eyed the gun encased in glass. There was a heavy padlock on it. "And this is the only thing we can kill you with?"

Mason lifted his monstrous shoulders up and down and said, "In theory." He stroked the coarse fibers of animal hair under his chin. "The key is in one of those rooms that you've seen. All you have to do is get the key and the gun before I get you. But be careful. In my labyrinth, not all is as it appears to be." He shifted over toward a great lever that jutted out from the wall behind him and laid his hand on it. "Ready?"

Smoke hustled over to the vanquished bodies lying along the walls. He plucked out a sabre and a bayonet. "Gear up," he said, tossing her the bayonet.

The bull-faced man brought the lever down a notch. There were sounds of metal moving against metal. *Clunk! Clunk! Clunk!* The chamber Sid stood in started to spin. She backed toward Smoke. "How come you gave me this and not that?" she said, eyeing Smoke's sword.

"Ever use a sword before?"

"No."

"A bayonet's much easier to learn."

Above, Mason ran his fingertips along his rack of black horns. "I'm going to enjoy this." He reached for the lever again and pulled it down. "Go."

All of the doors slid open, but because the room was spinning, all of them were blocked.

Mason laughed, "Humph! Humph! Humph!" In a single bound, he leapt over the rail and landed down inside the chamber, making a thunderous sound. Towering at eight feet tall, he spread out his muscular arms that were as thick as tree trunks. "If you only understood how much I enjoy this." He scraped his hooved foot over the tiles and lowered his head. "Goodbye now!" He charged.

Smoke took Sid by the arm and jerked her into one of the portals just as it opened. Eyes fixed on the minotaur, she watched it slide to a halt and rear up just as the portal closed. It was laughing. "Humph—Humph—Humph—Humph—" The sound was cut off.

"Are you finished standing around?" Smoke said, tugging her deeper into the limestone-block tunnel. It was wide and tall, an ideal fit for something as big as a minotaur. "Come on."

Sid hurried along on legs of jelly. The raw power of Mason rattled her. Suspended her thoughts and action in time. She shook her head. "I'm fine now, sorry."

They crisscrossed. Zigzagged. Doubled back. The minotaur man hadn't lied. It indeed was a labyrinth. A maddening one. As they ran along a curved wall, a door appeared on their right. Sid could only assume it was one of the rooms they'd already seen, but she was too disoriented to know which one.

Smoke pressed his ear to the door. "I can't hear a thing." He grabbed the door handle. "Are you ready?"

Brandishing her bayonet and wheezing, she said, "Yes."

He shoved the door inward. It was the colorful daycare room, but it was completely empty. A dark feeling sunk into Sid. *Lies! Nothing but lies!*

"Let's go," Smoke said.

Clop! Clop! Clop!

"I can smell you," Mason's grizzly voice said. "That means I can find you as easily as my fingers in front of my face. Humph."

"I've got a finger for you!" she yelled back.

Mason stepped into full view only twenty feet away from where they stood. "Do you now?" He lowered his horns and charged.

Sid was fast. Smoke was fast too, but the minotaur was faster. Sprinting, it closed the gap with great, powerful strides. They ducked into the next turn and weaved through the labyrinth. Mason thundered behind them. Sid's lungs burned. Her energy was fading. Smoke was pulling her along. She'd run marathons. Won ribbons in track. But all of her accolades and efforts were negated. "Go," she wheezed. She tried to peel Smoke's hand away. "Just go."

He came to a stop and said, "I don't think either one of us is going anywhere." He stared at the wall that closed off the corridor in front of them. "Dead end."

Clop! Clop! Clop! Clop! Clop!

CHAPTER 36

"I LIKE TO CALL IT 'DEAD MAN'S END,'" Mason said, blocking their only avenue of escape. He took a great snort. "I can still smell the blood. Can you see it?"

Crushed bones and tattered clothes were on the floor. Bloodstains graced the walls.

Slowly, the minotaur closed in, toying with the tips of his horns. "When I stick it to the good guys, I stick it to them good."

Smoke rushed in with his sabre high in the air and delivered a devastating chop.

Mason caught the blade in his hand and ripped it free from Smoke's grip. The monster clobbered Smoke in the chest with his fist, sending him staggering backward into the wall. Mason took the sword, bent its blade, and tossed it aside with a rattle of steel. "So young. So futile. So stupid." He cracked his knuckles and scraped his hoof over the floor.

Sid sagged, fighting for breath.

Slumped over, Smoke clutched at his chest.

She'd never seen the big man down like that before. Mason's punch was like a sledgehammer. She reached over and grabbed the cuff of Smoke's pants then glared up at Mason the Minotaur. "Do your worst," she said, shielding herself and Smoke with the bayonet.

"Humph. I plan to." He came forward, hooves thumping on the ground. A smirk formed on his bestial face. "Goodbye, Agent Shaw." He raised his hoof.

A spark ignited inside Sid's belly and spread. Her breathing eased. Time seemed to stop. Everything moved in slow motion. *What is happening?* A spring of limitless energy coursed through her body. Aches and pains disappeared. She felt like lightning in a bottle. And it was time to come out. She sprang like a gazelle. Jammed the bayonet in the monster's eye.

"Aaaaargh!" he said, clutching his face. He unleashed a wild swing.

Sid ducked under it. Smoke rushed into the minotaur, toppling it over and bounding along his side. Eyes as big as moons and smiling just as wide, Smoke said, "I feel awesome."

"The key!" Sid said. She sprinted off, feeling like the fleetest of deer. Her memory was crystal clear. Her focus razor sharp. She knew every twist and every turn of the labyrinth. Old memories and overlooked evidence from long-forgotten cases popped up inside her thoughts. *Oh my. I think I missed something back when. Poor bastard.* She weaved through the maze until she found another door. Breathing just fine, she said to Smoke, "Ready?"

"Oh, yeah!"

She swung the door open. It was the supply room. The pair of them rushed inside and rummaged through the goods. They opened boxes and crates. Tore through the shelves. Scoured through tables with beakers, microscopes, boxes of slides, and tuning forks. It looked more like a classroom than anything else. "Find anything?"

"No."

"Mah-rooooo!" The sound echoed down the halls.

Sidney stopped. "Sounds like beastie boy is angry."

"Yep, I don't think he liked the contact you gave him."

She laughed. She felt fearless. Invincible. *Whatever this is, I love it!* "Nothing in here. We need to move on."

"I think you're right." Smoke snapped his fingers. "I know where it is."

"You do?"

Smoke's lips curled as he said it. "The deader room."

A memory flashed inside Sid's mind. One of the deaders had on a necklace with a key on it. "Clever. Oh well, let's do it."

Clop! Clop! Clop!

Smoke slammed the door shut.

"What are you doing?"

"I have an idea." He gathered himself in front of the mirrored window.

Taking her place beside him, she said, "I think I know what you're thinking."

Horns first, Mason crashed in the door with one hand holding his eye. "See what you did? See what you did?"

"I thought you said it would heal," Sid said.

Smoke held his gut, pointed, and laughed like Bugs Bunny. "What a maroon!"

Mason perked up. "What!" He removed his hand. His eye was fine. "It did heal, you fools!" He charged, plowing straight through the tables.

At the last possible moment, Sid jumped left, and Smoke jumped right.

Mason's rack of horns shattered the thick glass into hundreds of crystals. His huge body became wedged between the walls and the spinning room.

Smoke huffed a laugh. "I can't believe that worked."

Mason's feet stomped at the floor. He roared on the other side.

Sidney and Smoke were on the move again. She followed the maze through the last paths she'd not yet taken. It took five minutes, and they were at their destination. The deader room.

"Do you think this is it?" Smoke said, taking the door handle in his hand. "Or somewhere else."

"Hey, it can't be any worse than that minotaur." She bounced on her toes. "Let's go for it."

"All right then, ladies first?"

"Said like a true gentleman."

Smoke shoved the door in. The dry stench of rotting flesh slapped them in the face. Sidney darted into the fray of decaying men. She ducked, dived, and disarmed. Every move the deaders made was in slow motion. She was on high speed. She stole a sword from one and impaled another. "And you thought I couldn't use a sword."

Smoke waded through the throng, letting loose skull-crushing blows with his club. "That one," he said. *Whack! Whop! Whack!*

Sid spied the one that he talked about, ducked under a chop, and skewered it through the chest. She jumped over the swinging blow of another and landed in front of the one with the key on its neck. With a lightning-quick swing, she severed its head. She grabbed the key from the body as the head tumbled to the floor, telling it, "Thank you." Back at Smoke, she yelled, "Let's go!"

Smoke pummeled through the broken bones and flesh for them, clearing a path to the door. Seven minutes and sixteen seconds later, they were standing back just outside the main chamber. The portal was only a quarter open. She and Smoke had to squeeze through.

Clap! Clap! Clap!

Still wedged inside the room and chamber, Mason continued to bring his oversized paws together. He stopped and said, "I have to admit. This has been one of the more entertaining challenges in my lifetime."

Sid ran up to the dais where the gun was displayed and took hold of the lock. She tried to jam the key in it, but it didn't fit. "Damn!" All of her strength and energy fled as quickly as it had come, and down on the floor she went.

Mason laughed. "Humph—Humph—Humph. Such a priceless expression. I wish I had my camera." Using his powerful back and hands, he pushed the entire chamber, freeing up his body, and stepped into the room. "Humph! Now it's time for you to play dead, forever."

CHAPTER 37

SIDNEY HUDDLED UNDERNEATH THE GUN pedestal. With all of the strength that she had left, she shoved the glass case off the stand. It bounced off the stone and landed at her feet, intact.

"It seems you found the wrong key," Mason said, marching straight for her.

Smoke climbed onto his back.

The minotaur slung him off like a ragdoll. "Too bad for you. But I am curious what got into the both of you. I think a dissection will be in order. Maybe you'll be alive, just paralyzed while it's happening. Humph."

The super vitamin had worn off, leaving her completely exhausted, but Sid's spirits didn't dim. "I'll be just fine, but you'll always be an evil bastard."

He glowered at her. "Humph."

"Hey, pack mule," Smoke said, chiming in. He held a silver object up in his hand. A tuning fork. "Maybe this is the key you were talking about." He tossed the fork to Sid.

Mason's eyes became bigger than moons watching the object tumble through the air.

Sid snatched it and rapped it on the stone. The tuning fork wavered with life. She touched it to the glass case. It shattered.

"No!" Mason said, rearing up on his haunches.

In one fluid motion, Sid scooped up the gun, charged the slide, and took aim. "Yes."

Blam! Blam! Blam! Blam! Blam! Blam! Blam! Clik!

Mason stood tall as a statue with a grim smile on his face. He dusted the lead from his chest and watched it clatter to the floor. "Nice shooting."

"You cheated. Those weren't red-tipped bullets."

"And you believed me? Humph. Don't you know evil always lies?"

In a sudden move, Mason snatched Smoke up in his arms and bear hugged him. His mighty arms knotted up and Smoke's face turned purple. He started to gag. "Now listen, woman. Listen to the sound that makes your friend's spine snap."

"You mean you aren't going to gore him?" she said in a listless tone, trying to buy time.

"No, I'm going to gore you."

"I thought you were going to dissect me."

"Fool of a woman," Mason snorted. "You'll both be dead soon enough."

"Sid." Smoke somehow managed to croak out the word. "Catch!" He spat something from his mouth.

It was a bullet with a red tip on it. She snagged it from the air and loaded it into the weapon.

Mason cocked his horned head. "Eh, what trickery is this?"

Sid rose up and took aim between Mason's eyes. "Bye bye, Big Horns." *Blam!*

The minotaur's arms flung wide, dropping a gasping Smoke to the floor.

"Impossible!" Mason roared.

Boom!

Shards of bone, horn, and bull brain showered the room. There was nothing left of Mason above the shoulders.

Sid wiped the muck off her face and took a seat. Smoke crawled up alongside her. "Bye bye, Big Horns?"

She leaned against his shoulder. "What would you have said?"

"Actually, I think that's pretty good. Now we just have to figure out how to get our bounty out of here."

"Did you regurgitate a bullet?"

He showed a faint smile. "Sometimes I do strange things."

"Sometimes?"

The sound of metal grinding on metal brought the spinning room to a halt. Dee was standing by the lever, and another dozen men in pea coats had weapons pointed at them.

"For the first time in my life, I'm speechless." Her eyes locked on Sid's. "You're one helluva troop. The both of you."

"And now?" Sid fired back.

"And now, to my dismay, I'm going to let you go."

Leaning against the elevator wall, Sid allowed herself to breathe. She had never been fond of elevators, but this was the best ride she'd ever taken. It came to a stop, the doors split open, and prompted by Dee, who had a gun on her, Sid walked outside into a barn-like structure. She inhaled the air and rubbed her nose.

"Let's move along," Dee said. She poked the gun into Sid's back. "Quickly, before I change my mind."

"What about the body?" Smoke said to Dee. "There's a bounty I want to collect."

"If someone wants the body, they're more than welcome to come here and get it."

"Why, is the Drake going to blow another place up?" Smoke added.

"Well, maybe they'll just blow you up," Dee fired back. "I suggest you quit while you're ahead."

They made it outside of the barn and found the log cabin waiting under the moonlight. Allison and Megan were on the porch. Allison was kneeling down in front of her daughter, who was shaking her head and crying.

"What's going on?" Sid said, taking a step forward. A wall of guards shoved her back.

"Give it a moment, Sid," Dee said in her ear. "Not everyone wants to leave the Drake."

Allison hugged her daughter, took a quick glance Sidney's way, and hustled back inside the cabin.

"No! Allison!" Sid started to run for the porch.

Dee punched her in the ribs. "I said behave. Your little niece needs you now. Alive. Not dead. Stay away from the Black Slate, kid. Stay away for both your sakes."

EPILOGUE

TWO DAYS LATER, BACK AT FBI headquarters, Chief Howard's office.

"Sid." Ted stood up behind his desk and waved her over. "Please come in. Sit."

Cyrus remained seated in his chair and gave her a nod. "Uh, fascinating report." Sweat glistened on his balding head and upper lip. "Can I get you a drink? Some water perhaps?"

"No."

"Will you have a seat then?"

Eyes forward, she remained standing with her hands behind her back. "Where's Smoke?"

"Given the circumstances and in concern for his own safety, he's been relocated to an undisclosed location."

Her nails dug into her palms. The FBI had whisked him away within an hour after Sid contacted them.

"What's the matter?" Cyrus said, toying with his tie. "Didn't get a good-bye kiss?"

Ted stretched out his hand. "Cyrus, that's enough. She's your responsibility, you know."

The frosty man shrugged.

"Ted," she said, "when did you become such a putz?"

"Now, let's not get all insubordinate. I've warned you before. This time I'll write you up." He loosened his tie. "Will you sit down?" He eyed her. "Fine. Sid, the Black Slate, well, *they* want to move on. And they want me to talk to you about your next assignment. Given your situation with your niece, I think you'll like it. A forty-hour week supervising the range and armories and assisting the ballistics teams." He smacked the top of his desk. "It'll get your life back to normal."

She looked up, shook her head, and said, "You're such a putz."

Ted's cheeks reddened.

Cyrus jumped up from his chair. "That's it. I'm writing you up."

She glared into Cyrus's eyes and backed him down into his chair. "Go ahead." She tossed her badge and gun onto Ted's desk. "I resign."

CRAIG HALLORAN

THE SUPERNATURAL
BOUNTY HUNTER
FILES

SMOKE ON THE WATER
BOOK 4

CHAPTER 1

PPROACHING HER STAND AT A public outdoor firing range, Sidney donned her headset. There were signs everywhere: "Hearing Protection Required Beyond This Point." There were rules. She knew them all by heart. She took a deep breath through her nose. The smell of black powder and roasted brass awakened old military memories.

It was morning, warm and hazy. She wore sporty gym wear, black mixed with neon green. She set a soft leather duffle bag on her stand and unloaded her gear. Ten boxes of 40-caliber ammo, each box fifty rounds. *This will be fun.*

She pulled out her Glock 22. It wasn't the one the FBI had issued her. It was her own, a backup. She swung another bag up onto the table, beige and marked with a red Ruger stamp. From inside, she pulled out a small, short-barreled assault rifle with bipod legs built in. It was called a Charger. It had a built-in laser sight and a grey, camo-wood finish. She pulled out a box full of 22-caliber ammunition, a thousand bullets in all. *And this will be even more fun.*

Four magazines for the Glock 22 were already loaded. A typical Glock 22 held fifteen rounds. She had two that held thirty. The Ruger Charger held thirty as well. She slapped the magazine in and checked the sights. Down range, at forty yards, were barrels loaded with sand. At close range, fifteen yards, were metal silhouettes mounted in the ground.

"That's some fine weaponry you have there, young lady."

Sidney glanced back over her shoulder. It was an older man, big boned with a frosty mustache. He wore an NRA ball cap and a pair of six-shooters on his hips, nickel plated with pearl handles. Bowlegged in his jeans and wearing a Cabela's sweatshirt, he spoke louder than he needed to.

"Mind if I use this stand?"

Sidney glanced around. The range had more than fifty stands, and fewer than ten people were out there shooting. She shrugged. "Sure."

"I won't be crowding you, will I?" the older man said, lifting a brow. His voice was warm and friendly. "I'm just partial to this area on this side of the range. Eh, my name's Jake. They call me Big Jake."

"Hi, Big Jake," she said, extending her hand and shaking his. His calloused hand had an iron grip. "I'm Sidney."

"A pleasure, Sidney." He smiled, revealing a gold tooth toward the back. His bottom lip stuck out, and his breath had a minty scent of tobacco. "My, we sure don't see many gals out here. And you're a mite prettier than the last one I saw. She was coyote ugly and couldn't hit a barrel if she stood inside it. Woo! But, judging by her girth, she was a heckuva good cook. Wouldn't be surprised if she didn't have a stick of butter named after her."

He kept going.

Sidney kept laughing. Before she knew it, half an hour had passed, and she knew everything there was to know about who came and went at the range. For some odd reason, she enjoyed every bit of it. The last three months had been rough. Taking care of Megan was a delight, but still a chore. She needed some time to be around adults. Finally, she'd left Megan with her parents for a long weekend. Sally and Keith were about to leave on vacation, and it would do them all good to spend some time together first. It was the first time she'd been separated from her niece since they'd left Allison at the ranch.

"Sorry for talking your ear off, Sid," Jake said, plucking his six-shooter out of his holster. He opened up the cylinder and loaded in the bullets super quick and slapped the cylinder shut. "I don't get to talk to the ladies much since my wife died."

"Aw, I'm sure you get plenty of talking done when the opportunity presents itself."

He let out a Santa-like chuckle. "I sure hope you come around here more often." He loaded up his other pistol, holstered it, and squared up on his target. He turned his ball cap around and checked his earplugs. "Sid, this is where I like to show off a little. Watch this."

"Oh, you've got my attention." She leaned back against her stand and checked her headset. "Go for it."

Standing like a big ape, stooped over with his thick wrists hanging to his knees, Jake twitched his fingers and narrowed his eyes. His target was twenty yards away. It was a row of six small metal bull's eyes the size of fists. With uncanny speed, Jake eased one of his six-shot revolvers out of the holster. Two handed, he blasted away.

Blam! Blam! Blam! Blam! Blam! Blam!

Lead smacked into metal, making sharp plinking sounds. The bull's eyes spun around and around and steadied again.

"Woo hoo!" Jake twirled the gun on his finger before stuffing it into the holster. "Didn't miss a one!"

Smiling, Sidney clapped her hands. "That was awesome, Jake."

He pulled out the other loaded revolver and held it toward her butt first. "Care to give it a try?"

"Sure," she said with a shrug, "why not?" She took it from his grasp.

"It's heavy compared to that polymer thing you carry, so keep a firm grip on it. That forty-five will kick." He pressed his hands into her back and lined her up in front of the targets. A father helping a daughter. "Now listen. It's got a hair trigger. Put that in myself. It'll get away on you if you ain't careful." He gave her a little pat on the hip and eased away. "Show me what you got, girl."

Sidney pointed the heavy weapon toward the ground, closed her eyes, eased her breathing, and visualized herself shooting the targets. She loved the range. The smell. The muffled sounds of shots being fired. The wispy scent of gun barrel smoke. *Show this old fart what you got.*

Simultaneously, she opened her eyes, raised the gun, took aim, and squeezed the trigger.

Blam! Blam! Blam! Blam! Blam! Blam!

There was no triumphant sound of lead hitting metal, only six fresh holes in the dirt.

"Morning glory," she said, lowering the weapon with a frown.

Jake chuckled. "I told you. A big gun like that takes some getting used to." He took the gun. "Next time, take your time between your shots. You would have hit the other five if you'd taken enough time to think about it."

Shame on me!

CHAPTER 2

SIDNEY SPENT THE REST OF the day sharpening her aim. Hot and sweaty, she'd stripped down to a grey cotton T-shirt with a dragon logo on it. Taking command of the Ruger Charger, she emptied another magazine on the metal diadem 100 yards down the range.

"That's better," she muttered under her breath. Mopping the sweat from her brow, she reached over and upturned the box of .22 long rifle rounds. It was empty. She checked her duffle bag, fishing around inside. No ammo was left. With a sigh, she got out her cleaning kit and started breaking down her weapons. *At least I got my shot back. I hope.*

She ran a cleaning square into the barrel. Feeling disgraced by the lack of control she'd had with Big Jake's weapon, she hadn't stopped shooting until she'd gotten her edge back. It had taken a few magazines with her own weapon before she was back on the mark again. It ate her up. She'd been a crack shot since the first time she fired a weapon. She'd never before lost her touch once. She'd only lain off a few months, and she shouldn't have been off that much.

"Wrapping it up, I see," Big Jake said as he walked by. He'd been working the range all day, speaking with plenty of older hands. He seemed to make a point of knowing everyone. "I'm guessing you have things under control again?"

"I'm pretty sure." She ran the cleaning rod out of the barrel and checked the grimy square. "Thanks for the advice."

Drumming his fingers on the pommels of his guns he said, "Care to try it again?"

"No, I'm good, Jake. Certain of it."

"I know you are," he said. "Say, where'd you learn to shoot like that, anyway?"

"My father. The military. The fact that I love it."

Jake sauntered over and took a seat by her stand. He took his hat off and ran the back of his arm over his bushy brows. "Always feels hotter on the range than it is." He looked her dead in the eye. "You've seen some real shit, haven't you."

"What do you mean?" she said, wiping down the small rifle.

"I can see it in your eyes, Sid. They're pretty, but hard as iron." He huffed a little laugh. "When you missed those targets with my pistol, I thought your head was going to explode. That look. It was dismay. And then suddenly, a light went on behind those pretty eyes, bright as a furnace. You set that little jaw and started getting it on."

"These bullets don't shoot themselves."

"Heh!" He slapped his knee. "I suppose not!" His face reddened, and he started coughing. He tapped his chest with his fist. "Pardon me. Felt like I swallowed a butterfly. Anyway, what is it you do, if you don't mind me asking?"

"I used to be a cop."

"And what are you now?"

"Just between jobs."

Big Jake narrowed one of his eyes on her. "You aren't one of those mercenaries, are you?"

"What? No, why?"

"Eh, well—"

A very loud gunshot rang out. *Pow!*

Sid's head jerked up. "Geez! Was that a fifty cal?"

"Yep," Jake said, turning his head over his shoulder.

Two men on the far left end of the range were hunkered down over their .50 caliber rifles. They wore black ball caps and black T-shirts stretched over their muscles.

Pow! Two hundred yards down range, a canister of yellow paint exploded.

"Those two punks have been coming down here for weeks, blowing the crap out of everything. They're weird. Almost spooky." Jake spit juice on the ground. "They rub everyone the wrong way. Pushy types. You know. They talk, but it's like they see right through you."

Sid squinted her eyes. The pair of dusky-skinned men with slicked-back hair reloaded the monster bullets into their guns, speaking little. They were big men, like professional wrestlers. The one who wore mirrored sunglasses that looked small on his head glanced her way. He rolled a toothpick from one side of his mouth to the other and smiled. They had tattoos and triangle-shaped earrings in their ears. The other twisted his long neck around, revealing his cold, dead eyes. He sneered and turned away.

"Weird and ugly, ain't they," Jake said.

"Nothing surprises me these days," she said, wiping down her weapon and placing it in her satchel. She kept her eyes fixed on the men. They were different. The way they moved. Sat. Stretched. Talked. It raised the hair on her arms. "I think I might go say hello."

"What? Why?"

Sidney didn't say. She wanted a closer look. She needed to look for the mark. A black sun rising. The sign of the Drake. It ate at her. Every time she went out, she'd notice a little something she hadn't before the Black Slate. She had a new awareness. The way people spoke and dressed made all the difference. The weird signs on doors and even the slogans she read. Somehow, some way, there seemed to be subliminal messages that were tied to the Drake, or maybe to an even darker evil. "I'll be right back."

"Hold on now, Sidney. Uh," Jake looked over his shoulder. "I'm about as tough as they come, but those guys make even me a bit nervous. I did two tours in Vietnam, you know. Got a Purple Heart to show for it."

"I'll be fine." She glanced at the guns on his hips and gave him a wink. "Just keep those peacemakers ready in case things get a little hairy."

"Fine, just stay out of my line of sight."

Sid slung her jacket over her shoulder and headed down the range. Both men caught her coming their way. Both of them twisted around in their seats and faced her.

The one with the mirrored glasses spoke up. He had a heavy inner-city accent. "Something we can do for you, Miss?"

"I just wanted to get a closer look at those big cannons."

The stockier, bald one crossed his meaty arms over his chest. "Is that so? I think you need to move along, lady."

The other sniffed the air. "I smell cop. You a cop?"

"No," Sidney said. "Just a gun enthusiast." She eyed the weapons.

The first man, in the glasses, stood up, blocking her view. He was tall and rangy like Smoke.

"Awfully big for this range. You guys military?" she said, looking at the triangle earring in his ear.

"We're rabbit hunters," said the one sitting down. He slipped a buck knife out of the sheath on his waist and shaved a few hairs off his forearm. "I like to skin them. Cook them. Eat them."

"I don't imagine there's anything left once you shoot them with that," she said.

"Oh, I don't shoot them. I sneak up on them." He showed his calloused hands grasping in the air. "Catch 'em and squeeze them until they snap." He made a breaking motion. "I've killed lots of them like that."

Sidney's stomach soured. The man wasn't talking about rabbits. He was a killer. Both of them were. Hard-eyed, compassionless men. She ran her eyes up and down their arms and over their necks, feigning fear and fascination. No black suns. Mostly snakes, skulls, sharp blades, and guns. She started to back away.

"Where you going, little lady?" the first one said, tilting his head to the side and coming closer. "Don't you want to hear more about our rabbit hunts?"

The second man slid in behind her. "Yeah, why don't you come with?" he bumped up against her.

"Watch it!" she said. She tried to move around them, but the pair of them hemmed her in. Her cheeks flushed. "Move it."

"Or what, sweetie?" said the one with the long neck. He cornered her against the stand. His eyes were like a hungry predator's. Hypnotic like a snake's. Paralyzing her limbs.

Her knees weakened. "Go, go away," she said, trying to tear her eyes away from the long-necked man.

"You're coming with us, honey," he said.

Her shoulders sagged and her mouth dropped open. Heart pounding, she said, "Okay."

CHAPTER 3

"**B**OY!" JAKE SAID, STICKING HIS gun barrel against the long-necked man's ear. "You might want to step back, unless you want a ravine in your head."

The man who had cornered Sid froze and slowly lifted his arms. "That would be foolish, old man. And I'm unarmed."

"Don't give a damn." Jake pulled the gun's hammer back. "Get the hell away from the lady."

The man slipped to the side of the one in mirrored glasses and lowered his arms. "Just having a little fun with your daughter. She shouldn't be so nosey." He flicked his nose with his thumb and narrowed his eyes. "And you, foolish old one, shouldn't be so, heh, bold. You don't know who you're dealing with."

"I know your kind. Seen my share of men with venom in their eyes." He glared at them both. "My gut's telling me I outta shoot you both down where you stand." He stuffed his pistol back inside his holster. "Damn me for letting you live. Come on, Sid."

On instinct, she took his hand. Her eyes widened. She took a deep breath and followed him back down the range without looking back. Behind her, she heard the two huge men laughing. She swallowed. She'd lost herself to them somehow. Their hypnotic stares had sapped her will. Much like it had been with the wolf man, Adam Vaughan. "Thanks."

"You all right?" Jake said, helping her to a seat. "I hate to say this, but I saw your lights go out. You don't have a medical condition, do you?"

She rubbed her temples. "No, no." She couldn't shrug off the horrible feeling she had inside. She started stuffing her guns into her duffle bag. "Thanks, Jake, but I've got to go."

"Let me get you a beer. Settle your nerves." He looked beyond her shoulder. "Besides, those grease balls are moving out. Probably drug dealers." He hitched his thumbs in his belt. "I'm gonna have a few words with the owner about guys like that. Their kind seem to be coming around more often."

She slung her bag over her shoulder. "I'm fine. Don't do anything on my account. I'm a big girl. Nice meeting you, Jake."

Back inside the Dodge Hellcat and roaring down the road, her nerves began to settle. She wanted distance between her and the men at the range. The abnormal men. Long-faced and fluid. Smooth. Crass. Seductive. *This is exactly what Allison fell for.*

When it came to men with power, her sister was a moth to a flame. The Drake probably didn't have to promise her too much to get her to stay. A nice place to live and a line of credit. Allison would be all over it. Those were Sidney's first thoughts about her sister. She hated herself for it. *Shame on me.*

Allison wasn't without a heart. Not entirely. She loved her daughter, but she was weak. Still, Sid held out some hope that maybe, just maybe, Allison had done what she did to save her and Megan. Any loving mother would do that for her child. And a loving sister would do that for her sibling, too. It was that part that Sid struggled with. After all the years of bailing Allison out, had Allison made a sacrifice that bailed Sid out?

"Crap!" She banged on the steering wheel. "I don't know."

For the last three months, she'd put all her energy into Megan. She put the FBI behind her, even though they still called. She blew off Sam and Guppy whenever they reached out. Mal Gunderson had sent her a box, wanting his gear back. She'd been happy to oblige. And Smoke … she did her best to forget about the man. His handsome façade and odd musings. It angered her that he'd come into her life only to be gone again.

She eased off the highway and pulled into the first gas station. She exited the vehicle and scanned her card. Pumping the gas, she leaned against her car and sighed. She noticed a couple police officers coming out of the convenience store. They were loaded up with sodas and hotdogs. They were smiling and laughing, too. She grimaced.

I miss Sadie.

She'd been blowing off her best friend. Her excuse was that Ted and Cyrus wouldn't want them communicating. The truth was, Sadie had called and texted numerous times. She'd even gotten pretty ugly about it when Sid fired back a bunch of canned excuses. Sid thumbed through her phone and read the last text Sadie had sent.

It read, "You see! This is why you're going to die single!"

Laughing, Sid took the nozzle out of her gas tank and placed it on the rack. Seconds later, she was driving down the road again, trying to sort everything out inside her head. Keeping Megan around kept her distracted from other things. The news. The job. The lies. With the girl gone to her grandparents' house, Sid's thoughts raced through everything that had gone on. It was driving her crazy. She didn't like not being able to carry a gun like she used to. She felt naked without it. Her concealed carry permit still hadn't been approved. *I should move to Texas.*

Her phone rang. Her mother's picture popped up.

"Hey, Mom. How are things going?"

"Hey Aunt Sidney," Megan said.

"Oh, hey, Megan. How are *you* doing?"

"Well, Grandma and Grandpa keep taking me to places that smell really old." Megan sighed. "And I'm getting tired of biscuits and gravy every morning. And smelling like bacon. They always eat bacon." She kept rambling on another ten minutes. Finally, she said, "When are you picking me up? I miss you."

The words crushed Sid's heart. It had only been a couple days, but Sid felt guilty. *How do parents do this?* She had decided to sacrifice everything for Megan, but not having a steady paycheck was starting to take its toll. At some point, she needed to find a job somewhere doing something. But she wasn't going to just take anything. "Can you hang in there until tomorrow?"

"Morning?"

"Come on, Grandma and Grandpa aren't that bad."

"They're boring. Nice, but you know, boring. And my bedtime is way too early."

"All right, no promises, but I'll try to be there by morning. Okay?"

"Okay. Bye."

The line went dead.

Sidney shook her head. *How long can I keep this up?*

CHAPTER 4

THE FOLLOWING MONDAY MORNING, SALLY and Keith had left on their vacation and Sidney was back inside her apartment getting Megan ready for school. The little girl sat at the kitchen table, eating cereal. She had a yellow bow in her hair and wore a khaki skirt and a white Oxford dress shirt. "I like cereal, so long as it doesn't taste like bacon," Megan said.

"You need to finish up and get the rest of your lunch packed," Sid said. She signed off on Megan's homework and stuffed the notebook in the girl's backpack. That was the thing she liked about the private school she'd enrolled Megan in: They ran a tight ship. And the school uniform made her life a lot easier than picking out different clothes. She could relate to the uniform. "And don't forget your milk."

"I won't," Megan said. She loaded a milk box, a juice box, chips, and a cheese sandwich into her lunchbox. "Can I take a chewy granola bar? I get hungry."

"Sure." Sid slung Megan's little backpack over her shoulder. "Let's go."

The drive to school took about ten minutes. There were two teachers, a man and a woman, standing outside at the student drop-off.

Sid waved at them.

They waved back.

"Aunt Sid," Megan said, "are you going to look for a job today?"

"Uh, I don't know, why?"

"Well, you need something to do. You can't just wait around on me all the time."

Sidney caressed Megan's face, looked her in the eye, and said, "I like doing this."

"I like it too, but…" Megan's voice trailed off.

"But what?"

"But you've got to be you." Megan popped the door open and hopped out. "See you later." She slammed the door shut and ran into the school.

After Megan made her way inside, Sidney pulled away. *What did she mean by that?*

Sid jogged around the Lincoln Memorial Reflecting Pool. It was one of her routines while Megan was in school. Jog. Work out. She was as fit as she'd ever been. And the time between that and when Megan got out of school was torture. She'd read the paper. Skim the news. She'd picked up reading books again. Fiction. Biographies. Maybe go home and watch some old shows on Netflix. She tried to avoid anything that made her think of the Drake or the Black Slate. Huffing for breath, clothes clinging to her body in sweat, she kneeled down and tightened her shoelaces. She walked over to a bench and sat down.

The DC campus was beautiful, but there was darkness hiding in the shadows of the magnificent architecture.

Washington, DC. Home of the greatest truths and the greatest lies.

That's what Smoke said. It had all been so very true. Sidney had learned the hard way that nothing in the world was as it seemed. More than she ever imagined was saturated with evil. Good men and women died for no reason because of it. People were careless in how they lived their lives. She couldn't be that way. She wanted to keep herself and Megan away from those shadows. They had taken her sister. They could take anything.

Never underestimate evil.

She rubbed out the tightness in her calf muscles, watching other joggers and walkers make their way around the great pool. It was midmorning, and the sun warmed her face. People loaded down with strollers and fanny packs took pictures. Some moved at a brisk pace, others with more leisure, noses stuck in their smartphones. Every one of them seemed lost to her.

Just a bunch of people wandering around waiting for someone to tell them what to do.

She got up, ran in place a bit, and took off around the reflecting pool. She picked up the pace, made one more lap, and then fast walked back to her car. There was a small newspaper pinned under her wiper blade. She didn't see any on the other cars parked nearby. She removed it. It was the size of a tabloid, only a few pages, similar to a college newspaper. She unfolded it, exposing the front. It was a copy of *Nightfall DC.* Her fingertips tingled as she scanned the area.

Grumbling, she spread the paper out on the hood of her car and started to read. There weren't any pictures, just bolded headlines.

Missing Girl. Strange Lights in the Park. Senator Howser, Man or Alien? Muggers in Fur Coats. Loch Ness Monster in Mallows Bay. Man Shot Ten Times and Walks Away.

She skimmed through them. The stories were bizarre. Odd. And clearly designed for the gullible. Her eyes froze on the next headline that she read.

Vietnam Vet Murdered. *"Jake Miller, known to his neighbors as Big Jake, was found dead inside his apartment, having been shot with his own revolver."*

She gasped.

CHAPTER 5

Russ Davenport's home was on wheels, with no engine. The old trailer was long and weather beaten, with a railed ramp leading up to the front door.

Sid shut off her engine, checked the surroundings at the trailer park ten miles west of DC, and exited the car. With that edition of *Nightfall DC* crushed in her hand, she stormed up the ramp and pounded on the door.

"Geez!" a rugged voice said inside. A glass bottle fell and rattled on the floor. "Aw, great!"

Sid pounded on the door again.

"Who is it?" said the man on the other side.

"It's Sidney Shaw."

Things got quiet for a moment. Then the familiar voice of Russ spoke up. "What do you want?"

"Answers."

"Ever hear of a game called Jeopardy? Give that a try," he said.

"Russ, are you going to open the door or not?"

"Eh." The door handle started to turn and the door swung open. Russ sat in a wheelchair on the other side of the threshold. He wore a Washington Senators jersey. A sawed-off shotgun rested back against his shoulder. "I don't like visitors."

Sid stepped inside and tossed the copy of *Nightfall DC* into his lap. "This isn't a social call."

Russ wiped a little bit of drool from his mouth and rubbed his eyes. The husky man backed his wheelchair toward a small table and picked up some glasses. He put them on, studied the paper, and grunted. "So, what do you want? It's my rag. So what?"

"Why'd you stick it on my car?" she said, noting all the newspaper clippings hanging on all his walls. The wood-paneled place was musty but organized. A computer was hooked up to three monitors, and a flat-screen television was on in the tiny living room. The trailer was plenty big for a single person. "Or did you have one of your reporters do it?"

"It's nice to see you too, Agent Shaw," he said. "You could at least ask how I'm doing, seeing how I'm back from the brink of death."

"Looks like you're doing fine. You even have new wheels. Good for you."

"You're cold."

She stepped closer and glared down at him. "I'm angry."

"I didn't put this on your car. And even if I did, why are you so bent out of shape about it? It's got nothing to do with you. Just more of my imaginary rubbish." He folded the paper up and set it aside. "What happened? One of the articles cut too close to some FBI informants?"

She eased back, shuffled some papers over on his couch, and sat down. "What happened?" she said more softly.

"With what?"

"The wheelchair. Why are you on wheels?"

"Oh, *now* you ask." He rolled his eyes. "Well, ever since I got shot, I have moments. I lose feeling in my extremities from time to time. It's scary. Sometimes it lasts a few hours. Other times, for days. Doctors can't figure it out." His eyes became sad. "I woke up this morning and couldn't move them at all. It's like I'm cursed or something."

"Sorry to hear that, but at least you're alive."

"Yeah, well, it's not much for living. If it keeps up, I'm going to have to give up on *Nightfall DC*." He wheeled toward the refrigerator. "Want a drink? I have cold beer and Gatorade."

She made a stop gesture and shook her head no.

"Suit yourself." He found a bottled beer and twisted the cap off. He flicked it with his thumb across the room into the trashcan. "I never miss." He grabbed a prescription bottle, took out a large white pill, flicked it into his mouth, and washed it down with beer.

"I didn't think you were supposed to take medicine with alcohol," she said. She'd noted the label already. It was a narcotic for pain. "And I thought you didn't feel anything."

"Sure, from the waist down. But this wound in my chest still hurts like hell." He took another drink. "You've seen action. You telling me you don't have aches and pains? Surely you've got monster scratches on you."

She did. Her scars and bruised bones would ache in the cold. Her knees would ache if she sat too long. Sometimes tiny, painful needles raced up and down her neck and arms. "So you still believe in monsters?"

"I know you've seen them. That's good enough for me. There've been others, too. That look in their eye when I asked them questions and heard their stories. I know the truth when I hear it." He wheeled closer and eyed her. "What brings you to me?"

"The Big Jake Miller story," she said.

"Oh." Russ nodded his round, scruffy face. "You knew him?"

"I met him, and I think I know who killed him."

Russ's eyes shone like moons. "You don't think I did it, do you? Are you investigating me?"

"No."

"Is this one of your cases?"

"No," she said. "I don't work for the FBI anymore."

He cocked his head. "You're serious."

"I resigned."

Russ smiled.

"What?" she said.

"I know you did. I just wanted to see if you'd admit it to me."

"I'm not very fond of games, Russ."

"Me neither. Since you're being up front with me, now I'm going to be up front with you." He reached back and found the local newspaper. "Your friend Big Jake. Huh. He wasn't the only one dead. The truth is, I was too scared to report all that I found, and anyway, the cops did a pretty good job covering up the rest."

"What do you mean?"

"Big Jake was shot with his own gun." He winced. "Poor guy was in the middle of a *Matlock* marathon, too. And that ain't all." He opened the paper up to the crime section and jabbed at it with his meaty finger. "In that same area, a woman was killed with a knife and another man was run clean over. Dead. Those were witnesses." He eyed her. "How come you think you know who did it?"

She told him the story about the two goons at the range.

Russ's face turned pale.

"What is it?" she said to him.

"I've heard about those guys before. They call them the Buffalo Brothers Assassins, and they say they can't be killed."

CHAPTER 6

"**W**HERE DO YOU COME UP with this stuff?" Sid said. "I've never come across any files dealing with any Buffalo Brothers. And why would they take out Jake?" She hit the arm of the plaid sofa. "Damn!"

"He probably shouldn't have stuck a gun in their face. Guys like that, they don't take threats lightly." He wheeled his chair back and eased his way in front of his computer. He started typing. "Sounds like they were making a point."

"If they can't be killed, why worry?" Her nostrils flared. Her face got flushed. Were the Buffalo Brothers the ones that had put the paper on her window? "Sickos!"

"My guess is they wanted you to know about it. Look, Agent, er, well, Sidney—that all right?"

"Yes."

"Seems to me they wanted you to know about it. Or somebody did for some reason." He eyed his screens. "Huh, this is interesting. Seems Big Jake had quite a unique history."

"What do you mean?"

"He was an ex-cop that worked a lot of strange cases. Looks like they made him retire early." He clicked through some more articles. "Yup. The top brass didn't like him. Hmmm, now that I think about it, his name's pretty familiar. When I started my rag ten years ago, he was one of the few that would talk. Not much, but better than nothing." He pulled up a picture of Jake, younger. Clean shaven and in uniform. "That's him. Now I remember what he said. I quoted it in one of my papers. He said, 'Monsters pull the strings, not men.' Huh." He rubbed his lip. "I burned my lip with my coffee when he said that one."

"That was the last time you saw him?"

"Yep. Of course, I was pretty self-absorbed back then. I moved on. He retired. He had an edge about him, though. I wouldn't be surprised if ol' Jake knew something. Or made some enemies. They decided to take him out."

"When you say *they*, who does that mean, to you?" Sid asked.

"Oh, well, you have the Black Slate. The Drake. The Hierarchy Enslaving You. Probably several more they go by." He plunked away on the keyboard. "Who do you think *they* are?"

"The same, I guess." Sid's fingers drummed on the sofa arm. Were the Buffalo Brothers coming for her, or were they satisfied having gotten Jake? Who had put the paper on her car? It all seemed so convenient. It didn't help that she felt like someone was watching her all the time, either. The people she passed. The cameras in the streets and stores. They controlled all of them. "How do you know about the Buffalo Brothers?"

"Huh. It's another one of those dirty little DC secrets. That pair's been killing people around here for years. They're assassins. Hit men. It was the weird earrings, sunglasses, and the one's long neck that gave it away. When they show up, death follows." He guzzled down some of his beer. "Yep, real spooky. And they take out criminals mostly. Rats. People no one even cares about. The faces that don't make the papers. I think they're part of the Drake's cleanup crew, to be frank. Those monsters that leave tracks in the blood they spilled. They need looking after, too." He shook his head. "I sure hate to see someone go like that. Seems Big Jake was one of us."

"Us?"

"Yeah, us. People who aren't scared to shine the light on evil."

Sid nodded. "Tell me more."

"There was this one fella, worked the door in town at one of the strip clubs. Well, he said there was a scuffle in the alley. Said he saw a guy in sunglasses take a few gunshots at point-blank range and walk away." Russ finished off his beer. "The guy doing the shooting survived because the guy he shot vanished just as police arrived. The bouncer said it was lucky, because he saw murder in that assassin's eyes. The bouncer said that look scared the piss out of him. And he was a big dude."

"Maybe he wore a vest," Sid suggested.

"Well, that's one account. There was another club, the Night Ranger, where I met a pair of gals who'd stumbled on a murder victim. A guy was stabbed to death. No one saw anything." Russ turned toward Sid and leaned forward. "After the detectives left, I asked if they noticed anyone standing out in the crowd. They mentioned those guys. The weird earrings and glasses. Their eyes haunting them. One gal said she blacked out just from looking at him. 'Hypnotic,' she said. 'Evil.'"

Sid's throat tightened. *Those sound like the guys.* "Why do they call them the Buffalo Brothers?"

"Good question. Simply put, they started this stuff in Buffalo, New York. Oh man, I haven't talked about them in a long time. Uh, could you reach behind you? See those ratty books on the shelf?" He pointed. "Grab that one in the top right corner, third book over."

She turned, got up on her knees, reached over, and grabbed the book. "This it?"

"That's the one."

It was a small hardback book with a brown cloth cover. The title read *The Buffalo Murders*, by Jim Johann. She scanned the title page. "This was published in 1955."

Russ tossed his beer bottle in the trash can. "Yep."

Sid leafed through the pages. In the middle were some black-and-white photos of murder scenes. At the end of those pictures were mug shots. Her blood curdled. It was the faces of the two men from the range. "Impossible."

"You don't really believe anything is impossible, do you?" Russ said.

She'd already encountered more than a few corpses that came back to life. It was unsettling. "Says their names are Warren and Oliver Ratson. They were convicted. Went to prison for life and disappeared."

"There's a lot of people that have gone to prison and disappeared. You'd be surprised. Especially back in those days." He rubbed his thighs. "Legs're starting to tingle. That's a good sign. Anyway, the Buffalo Brothers are ghosts. Living and breathing ghosts. But you've seen them for yourself. Now what do you do?"

She thought about Jake Miller. He had been a good man. You took him seriously, but he was warm and friendly. He was the kind of fella that would help you move furniture on a rainy day. "So no one investigates these guys."

"Seems so. Not unless they trifle with someone that really matters."

Sidney got up, still holding the book. "Can I take this?"

"Sure. So what are you thinking about doing?"

"I'm thinking I'm going to find these bastards and take them down."

CHAPTER 7

D RIVING DOWN THE ROAD, SIDNEY thought to herself, *Who am I kidding?* She had to take care of Megan. That didn't leave her any time to launch her own investigation. But what had happened to Big Jake ate at her. She had to do something. Protecting people. Serving people. It drove her. *Damn my pride!*

She missed being an agent, and it was beginning to catch up with her. She'd had access. Authority. The badge had given her an air of invincibility, and now that was gone. She'd given it up because she'd gotten mad. Because she felt guilty. She'd convinced herself that she couldn't trust her fellow agents anymore. Cruising down the highway, she pulled over into a Wendy's parking lot. She put the car in park, took out her phone, and sent a text.

The text read, "Looking for the Buffalo Brothers."

Her thumb hung over the phone. She was about to dig into something that she might not be able to finish. But those men! The arrogant sneers on their faces riled her. They had a dangerous air about them. Same as all the other monsters she'd encountered.

Morning glory, think about what you're doing, Sid.

Somewhere in her heart, she knew that she and Megan were safe so long as she didn't go nosing around. That was the deal she suspected Allison had made with the Drake. It was a cop-out, too, but a sacrifice nonetheless. But if Sid moved out of that lane, trouble might quickly find them. She held her breath.

I have to do the right thing. I have to be me.

She pressed send. The text went out to Phat Sam and Guppy. Sid let out her breath. She figured they'd probably changed their numbers anyway. She gave it a few moments. Nothing happened. Probably for the better. She put the car in drive, eased on the gas. The engine rumbled, and the muscle machine surged ahead to the thrill of a few gawkers that showed a thumbs up as she passed by. She smiled.

Maybe I should come here more often.

While she was merging onto the highway, her phone buzzed. There was an emoticon with an excited mouth wide open. The message read. "Never heard of them. Doing research. Very interesting. We're in. Meet at Smoke's. Tonight."

At the stoplight she texted back. "No, tomorrow."

"No," Sam's text read. "Tonight. Bring Megan. We have plenty of ice cream."

Morning glory! I was afraid of that.

"Where are we going, Aunt Sid?" Megan asked.

They were heading down the highway after finishing up homework and dinner at Sid's apartment. She'd chewed one of her nails off contemplating what to do. She needed to get back in the action. But it killed her to think she might be putting Megan in danger.

"We're going to go see Sam and Guppy. Remember them?"

"Oh, that really pretty lady. Yay, I like her. She's funny." Megan checked her nails. "Do you think she'll give me another manicure?"

"I'm sure she'd love to."

"Good," Megan said. Her face had brightened. "I love getting my nails done. BTW, it looks like you need yours done, too." The little girl, now eleven years old, always carried some sadness within her.

Sid felt guilty. She couldn't keep Megan isolated all the time. They needed to get out. Be around people. It was finding people you could trust that was hard. Sam and Guppy could be trusted.

"I know."

"So, are you going to be doing cop stuff again? I hope so." Megan straightened the bow on a purple stuffed bear with burnt-orange plastic eyes. "I know you miss it. You can't just sit around on your butt and babysit me all the time."

"Megan!"

"Well, it's true. Listen, Aunt Sid, I know I'm only in the fifth grade, but I'm reading at a twelfth-grade level. And I've always been able to take care of myself. Not that I don't need you. I do. But you can't stop living your life because of me."

Sid's mouth dropped open. Recovering, she said, "You're starting to sound like your grandmother Sally."

Megan slapped her head.

Sidney laughed. Megan was a little adult. She had been since she was five. A lot of that came from taking care of her mother. Sid reached over and brushed her hand over Megan's soft hair. "You're something else."

"I know."

"Look, Megan. What I did before was dangerous, and I don't want to dive back into that. If something happens to me, who's going to look after you? It's not worth it."

"Nothing's going to happen to you, Aunt Sid. Besides, at some point you're going to have to go get my mother. That's what heroes do, right?"

Sidney sank behind the steering wheel. Her eyes started to water. Of course Megan would expect her to go get her mother. Why shouldn't Megan expect her to save her own sister?

"Besides," Megan said, "most of the time, Mom doesn't know what's best for her."

"Well," said Sid, swallowing the lump in her throat. "I wish it could be easy."

"Haven't you been looking for her this whole time? Like when I'm in school?"

Lord, I'm a fool! How do I explain this? Megan was staring at her with her round pretty eyes. The young girl deserved an honest answer. "Megan, the people your mother is with are very dangerous. If I go after her and get too close, they'll come after us. I can't risk losing you again. Do you understand that?"

Sadly, Megan nodded her little chin and curled up into her seat. She hugged her bear tight to her chest.

"Megan, do you trust me?"

"Yes," the girl said, still looking away.

Sid took a deep breath. "Then I promise I'll find your mom, my sister. But you have to be patient."

Megan's face brightened. "Okay. Thanks, Aunt Sid."

It's going to be hard to find someone that doesn't want to be found. And they'll be waiting for it. "You're welcome."

CHAPTER 8

S MOKE'S GAS-STATION APARTMENT HADN'T CHANGED a bit since the last time she had been in there. The room was warm, and there was a lingering sent of oil in the air. Even after only being there a few times, Sid felt at home there.

"This place is cool," Megan said, gazing up at an old *King Kong* movie poster on the wall.

Sam shook Sid's hand. The gorgeous older woman was casually dressed in Buckle jeans and a snug designer T-shirt with a sequined design. She gave Megan a hug. "How about some ice cream while we get those nails of yours done?"

Megan clapped her hands and bounced up and down like the kid she was supposed to be. "Yay!"

It made Sid smile before she looked expectantly at Sam.

Sam winked. "Good to see you. Once we finish with this little angel, we're doing you next." She took Megan by the hand. "Come on."

Eyeing the studio apartment, Sid's eyes landed on Guppy. The short, burly man stood up from behind the computers as she approached. He gave her a warm embrace, locking his powerful forearms around her waist. "I was starting to think you weren't going to come around."

"It's not easy staying away. I'll admit that."

"It's in your blood," Guppy said. "It's who you are. It's probably who you've always been."

Nodding her agreement, Sid sat down in the chair beside Guppy. "So, what have the two of you been up to?" She eyed him. "Have you still been bounty hunting?"

"You know we keep our jobs confidential," he said, smoothing his hand over his bald head. "But we've been paying the bills, if that's what you're concerned about."

She wasn't. She wanted to know if they'd seen Smoke, but she wasn't going to ask. She set Russ Davenport's book, *The Buffalo Murders*, on the desk. "Have you dug up anything yet?"

"Maybe. Are you hiring us for a job?"

She leaned back. Her chest tightened. "Well, no. I just thought—"

"I'm teasing you, Sid. You're family to us. You know that. Any friend of Smoke's is a friend of ours." His chestnut eyes locked on hers. He patted her knee. "Till the end."

Relieved, she said, "I don't want to be any trouble. I just … you know … this guy, Jake Miller. He's dead. I feel like I'm a part of it somehow. She clenched her fists. "Oh, I don't need to drag you guys into this." She went for the book.

Guppy covered the book with his rugged hand. "Take it easy, Sid. Look, I'm not going to lie to you. We have things going on. That doesn't mean we can't squeeze you in."

Oh man, they're going to blow me off. "Are you shelving me?"

"No, no," he said, picking up the book. "Now you should know better than that. We trust each other, right?"

"A lot can change in a matter of months. For all I know, you have a really cushy gig." She tipped her head toward the window. "I noticed that Porsche Cayenne outside. That looks pretty new. Nice cream color." She started to get up.

"Sid, please sit down and let me finish my thoughts. Geez. I guess I do talk too slow. Either that or all women are impatient. At least to me. Sam really wears me out telling me to spit it out all the time."

"You're rambling now."

He sighed. "Okay, let me spit it out, then. Me and Sam have been talking. We want you in."

"In? What do you mean, in?"

"Become a bounty hunter. Like us. It's got great hours, and you'd be good at it."

Something ignited behind her chest. A spark. A flurry. She liked the idea. "I'm at a loss for words. Uh, how's your dental plan?"

Guppy rumbled a laugh. "And you'd fit right in."

"How do you do what you do and fly under the radar?"

"We have a legit operation that's our cover, and then we do other things as well." He shrugged his heavy shoulders. "We manage."

"I just thought that Smoke—"

"Did all the field work? No, no." He rolled up the sleeve of his plaid shirt. "Dog bite." He exposed his neck and ran his finger down a white scar. "Knife wound. I have many more, but I'm a gentleman. And nothing against Smoke, but he hasn't been around. We don't close shop without him. If I gotta bust heads to get my dough, so be it. "

"I didn't realize you did that. And so does Samantha?"

"Oh yeah. She's the hook and I'm the hammer. Her face works like a stun gun. Men are putty in her hands." Using his hands, Guppy made goggle eyes. "Thugs get that deer-in-the-headlights look." He glanced at Sam, smiling. "Never seen a mortal man that can resist her wiles."

Sid laughed. "You make her sound like one of Charlie's Angels."

"Lord, don't tell her that. The last person that said that to her got punched in the throat." He made a bitter face. "She just hates that show for some reason."

"Okay, I'll think about it. In the meantime, what have you dug up on the Buffalo Brothers?"

Guppy leafed through the pages of the book. He stopped on the mug shots. "Them's some ugly boys. Faces like that shouldn't be too hard to recall." He snapped a picture with his phone and uploaded it to the computer. He pulled the picture up on the monitor and cropped each face out. "I'm going to load this into the facial recognition database. See if we get any bites."

"What facial recognition database?" she asked.

"The taxpayer-funded one," he said, giving her a shifty glance, "that the FBI uses."

"You've hacked into the FBI?"

"Not exactly," he said. "Let's just say we have people on the inside. You know, like you used to be."

Sid's hands turned clammy. "They pick up on everything in there."

"No they don't. Trust me. I've been doing this awhile." He glanced at her. "Should I not have told you that?"

"Hey, Guppy!" Sam shouted across the room. "Stop incriminating yourself!" She started laughing and resumed painting Megan's nails. The little girl had headphones on, and her smile was as wide as the room.

"We'll be fine. He eased back in his chair and rested his hands on his stomach. Now tell me everything about these Buffalo Brothers."

Sid recounted the entire story all the way through her visit with Russ Davenport. "Say," she said, "you guys didn't put a copy of *Nightfall DC* on my windshield did you?"

"No," Guppy said.

"Not me," Sam said from across the room.

She believed them. "All right. So there you have it. Look, these men or whatever they are, they're bad. I want them."

"And if you find them," Guppy said, "what are you going to do with them? So you think they killed your friend, Jake Miller. You need evidence to convict them."

She got up and started to walk the room. "They'll have kept his gun, the one they shot him with. We find them, we find it. I'm sure of it."

"It's pretty thin," Guppy said. "Even if you root them out, you still have the powers that be to deal with. They might not even arrest them."

Sid made her way toward the door that opened into the garage. She put her hand on the knob.

"Sid, come back here. Let's sort through this conversation."

She pushed open the door. Her heart skipped inside her chest. The garage was empty. "Guppy, where's Smoke's Camaro?"

CHAPTER 9

"**H**OPEFULLY IN THE JUNKYARD," SAM said, averting her eyes.

"Guppy?" Sid said to him. "Any insights?"

The stout man's brow furrowed as he twiddled his thumbs. "We just got here ourselves. We don't know all about the comings and goings of Smoke."

"What do you mean, comings and goings?"

"He's got other people aside from us, you know. Perhaps one of them borrowed it."

Sid crossed her arms over her chest. "One of whom?"

"Uh, them?"

Agitated, Sidney brushed her hair out of her eyes. "Is he out?"

"Can't say if he is or isn't," Guppy replied. He turned back to the computer monitors. "All I can say is I haven't seen him."

Sidney didn't know whether to be mad or happy. She didn't like the thought of Smoke being in prison, but if he was out, he could have contacted her. *Why would he contact me? He doesn't owe me anything.* She sat down on the couch and eyed Guppy. He was hunched over the desk with his back to her. A quick glance over her shoulder, and she saw Sam had her back turned as well. *They know something.*

"He's out and working on the Black Slate, isn't he." She got up and poked Guppy in the meat between his shoulder blades. "Isn't he?"

"I can't say."

"Damn! He is out!" She squeezed Guppy's shoulders. "What's he working on? Tell me."

"I can't say. Look, Sid, we have to keep our mouths zipped. You know that."

"Then why did you bring me here?" she said.

"Well, er, that's more of a coincidence," he said, pulling out of her grip. He looked up at her. "And, well, it wouldn't be our fault if you happened to run into him. Seeing how you are a client and potential team member and all."

"All in favor of making Sidney Shaw a team member, say 'Aye'!" Sam blurted out. She raised an arm.

Guppy raised his hand. "See, you have two out of three. Of course, it has to be unanimous."

"Oh, stop it," Sid said. "I'm not in the mood for games." She huffed. "And I don't guess it's any of my business anyway."

"Yeah, but you miss him," Sam said. "Or else you wouldn't have come here. We miss him, too, you know. But we haven't seen him. That's word." She squeezed Megan's cheek. "So cute."

"Look," Guppy said. "He hits us up. We feed him. You know the routine. It's all pretty down-low unless he calls us." He cleared his throat. "He could be in prison somewhere for all I know. The truth is, we get odd requests from him all the time."

"What was his last request?"

"I can't tell you that," Guppy said. "Not unless you're a team member."

"Quit being silly; there is no team." She rubbed her forehead. She wanted to leave, but Megan was having such a good time. She looked happier than Sid had seen her in weeks. And there was always a lingering warmth about Smoke's place. It was like a cozy cabin in the woods. "There's just you two, covering for Smoke."

"Somebody's getting awfully frosty over there," Sam said. "I better put a sweater on if this keeps up."

"Oh, be quiet," Sid said. "Geez, can I make some coffee or something?"

"Oh, let me," Guppy said, jumping out of his chair. "I'll love making fresh brew."

Sam resumed her seat on the couch and sank in. Before long, the strong aroma of coffee drifted into her nostrils. Sam was quiet, but Guppy rumbled an old hymn of some sort under his breath. Considering her options, Sid decided to hang out for a while. She hadn't had much adult company in weeks. *Why not?*

"Here you go," Guppy said, handing her a ceramic mug with a handle on it. "You take it black, right?"

"The blacker the better." She took a sip. "Good. Very good."

Guppy eased in behind her. "This is one of the best parts of being a bounty hunter, enjoying some joe until all the action starts. The truth is, we've been pretty bored. I mean, we've been working the routine stuff with bail bondsmen, but not the, you know, supernatural stuff."

They all spent the next hour talking about black suns, the Drake, and the Black Slate. Even though Sidney wasn't really supposed to talk about the confidential information, she didn't care. She wasn't an agent anymore. She filled them in on what she and Smoke had seen. The Minotaur and the gargoyles. Sam especially hung on every word while Megan watched a kids' movie on the television with the headphones on.

"You really saw a minotaur?" Sam said, filing Sid's nails. "I mean, bull's head and everything?"

"Horns too," Sid smiled. All this talk got her juices flowing. That was one thing about Smoke. They had that bond. All the things they'd seen together. She loved talking about it with him. And for some strange reason, she enjoyed watching him eat, too. "But those gargoyles were some weird little things."

Sam grabbed her by the shoulder of her shirt and said, "I want to see those gargoyles! Man, Smoke didn't tell us anything!"

"Didn't tell you anything when?"

"Well, you know, whenever." Sam started filing Sid's nails really fast. "Don't be so paranoid. Smoke never tells us as much as he should. He's tight lipped about a lot of things."

"So are you," Sid said. "The both of you." She pulled her hand away. "Look, this is a bad idea."

"Ooh, you are testy," Sam said. She snatched Sid's hand back. "Now let me finish this."

"No. Megan!" Sid yelled. "Come on, let's go."

Megan took off her headphones. "What?"

"I said it's time to go."

"Aw, but I want to stay. Just a little longer," the girl pleaded. "Please?"

"Yeah, Please?" Sam said. "We haven't even had ice cream yet."

"No, we're going." Sid finished off her coffee, got up, and took the Buffalo book off the table. "Thanks for the coffee, Gilmore. And thanks for doing Megan's nails, Samantha."

"But," Samantha started to speak.

But Guppy held her off with his hand. The roughhewn man stood up. "We're here if you ever need us, Sid."

"Hey, what's that mean?" Megan said, pointing at one of the computer screens.

It was flashing red.

Guppy rushed over and squinted his eyes, then said, "I'll be. We got a hit on the Buffalo Brothers already."

CHAPTER 10

S IDNEY CRUISED DOWN THE ROAD. Guppy was buckled into the passenger, seat eyeing the dashboard of her Hellcat.

"You picked a fine machine," he said. "What's the fastest you've taken her up to?"

"One-fortyish," she said, cracking a smile. She felt good, being on the road, tracking some thugs down. It felt so good that she felt a little guilty leaving Megan behind with Sam. But the girl and woman hit if off great. She didn't want to ruin Megan's evening. Her niece deserved a little pampering and ice cream once in a while. Sid put her foot down on the gas. It pinned her and Guppy to their seats. They blasted by a pair of tractor trailers.

"Like that?"

"Love it," he said, eyeing the speedometer. "Man, one-twenty in a flash. I like it." He unzipped a leather pistol case on his lap. Inside was a pair of .45 caliber semiautomatic pistols. They were stainless steel 1911's. He charged the slides on both of them. "The boys haven't been out to play in a while."

"Interesting hardware," she said. "Are those Detonics Combat Masters?"

"Boy, you sure know your guns, girl."

"Yes, well, uh, those are pretty old school."

"Well, I'm pretty old. But I hated school." He laughed. "So, hotshot, what's your plan if we find these guys? You gonna take them down and haul them in to the judge? Or maybe we just gun them down, like Matt Dillon."

"I'd like that, but I'm not sure. I'll think of something when I get there."

He leaned back in his seat. "Really? I took you for a planner."

"We'll see what happens when we get there."

"Works for me."

They cruised back toward DC, got off the highway a couple miles outside the heart, and parked the Hellcat at a small shopping plaza. The mall's best days had been over decades ago, and the blacktop had cracks sprouting grass. Most of the yellow markers for parking spaces had faded away.

"Huh," Guppy said. "I haven't been down here since I was a teenager. Boy, half the places look closed."

"Well, it *is* after hours," she said, tucking her key inside the pocket of her jeans and opening the door. "But I smell danger."

"Huh-huh," Guppy said, closing his door. "I hate to say it, but I hope you're right."

There were cars spread out all over the parking lot. Small crowds gathered here and there in little tailgate parties. Many of the cars were souped up. Men and women sat in their cars' seats, doors open and engines revving. There was loud music pumping and beer bottles being sucked on, and the smell of weed was in the air.

A young woman approached. She had a dark complexion, ratty black hair, and smoky olive eyes. Her lip was pinned with rings. She smelled like she had just rinsed off in bong water. "Nice wheels, lady friend. Nice wheels. Hellcat. Woo. You got to enter. Got to enter." She held out her hand. "Take a look around. I'll keep an eye on it for you." She winked. "A real close eye."

"Sure," Sid said. "I'll set you up when I get back."

"No, I need something now."

Sid stepped on the girl's toe and got right in her face. "You be here when I come back later, and I'll take you for a spin, understand?"

The girl grimaced. "All right. All right. Tough lady friend. I like."

Sid eased off her foot. "See you soon." She and Guppy walked off.

"You sure have a way with people." He chuckled.

"Funny." Sid looked at all the loiterers. "Makes me wonder if any cops ever come around." She started to stroll through the parking lot with Guppy at her side. No one paid them any mind. It gave her a feeling that she was in a bad postapocalyptic movie. A scene from *Escape from New York*, perhaps. She glanced at the lampposts above. Most were out, and the lights flickered on some of them. Looking up at the cameras mounted on the posts, Sid said to Guppy, "Is that where you think you got your hit?"

"I'd say so," Guppy said, rubbing his short beard. "Eh, let's take a look around. All this funny smoke is making me feel a little lightheaded."

"You're worried about that? I didn't realize your bounty hunter department did drug testing. I might not be eligible."

"You! Really?"

"I'm not an agent anymore, you know."

Guppy stopped and looked at her. "Pah, you're just kidding. Right?"

"Come on." They walked the sidewalk, passing several stores. Most were still in business. Others had realtor signs in them. Sid stopped in front of a pair of glass doors with a realtor sign hung inside. "Drake Real Estate. No wonder this place stinks."

"You can say that again." Guppy scratched his back. "Just looking at those people makes me feel like something's crawling all over me."

"Let's keep walking," she said, rubbing her arms. As she walked, her keen eyes sorted through the crowd. If this was Drake property, then there was no telling what sort of fiends were running loose out there. The sound of revving engines caught her ears. Really loud exhaust notes were blasting across the lot. The people started heading toward the sound. "I guess it's time to see what this racing is all about."

Easing in with the throng of hoodlums, they made their way to the main strip of road that circled the mall. Sid checked her phone. It was ten past eleven, and she didn't have any messages. She didn't see any signs of the Buffalo Brothers, either. The closer they got to the action, the louder the exhaust notes became. She fought the urge to cover her ears. Beside her, Guppy said something that the engines cut off. "What?"

"I said, let's get a closer look!" He took the lead and pushed his stocky frame through the crowd until they made it onto the curb running along the main street. "This outta do."

Flames burst from the tailpipe of a lightning-black truck. It had four doors and giant off-road wheels and was lifted an extra foot off the ground. The plate said, "So Long."

"Ford F250," she and Guppy said at the same time. "Wish I could see who was driving," she said. She grabbed a frail young man in a dark-grey sweatshirt. "Give me the story here."

"One lap around the mall. The straight stretch here gets nasty. Those dudes in that black hulk got lots of nitrous. They usually win. But maybe not tonight."

The crowd started to cheer as another car with dim lights pulled alongside the black truck and revved up the engine. It was a primer-grey Camaro. Smoke's car.

CHAPTER 11

A JOLT OF ELECTRICITY WENT THROUGH Sid. "It can't be."

"It is. It is," the dude said. "That's Grey Racer. People been talking about this race all week long. No one's beat the Black Hulk, and no one's beat Grey Racer. They've never faced off before." He pulled out a wad of cash and squeezed it between his dirty fingernails. "Wanna make a bet? If not, I got to hustle."

Sid turned her back on the frail little creep. "Come on," she said to Guppy.

"Where?"

"To get a closer look." Keeping herself out of sight, she marched up through the crowd to the two revving vehicles just as the Black Hulk smoked all four tires. She covered her nose. Through the stinky mist, she noticed the passenger hanging his arm out the window. He stuck his head out and started screaming and waving his arm up and down. The crowd squalled with glee. "Idiots."

Suddenly, the hood of the Camaro floated up. The back wheels spun. The engine roared.

Sid coughed. *That's enough of this.*

The truck revved up again.

Sid turned and found herself looking at the man in the truck's cabin.

A pretty girl in high heels and little else was standing next to the truck, talking to him through the window.

Sid grabbed Guppy by the sleeve. "It's them."

"I'll be," he said, fanning the smoke from his eyes. "I don't suppose this is a coincidence."

It was them, the Buffalo Brothers. Both men had an air of superiority about them. They yucked it up with the girls that scurried around their windows. Now standing on Smoke's passenger side, Sid noted many other women fawning all over his car and blowing him kisses. His windows were closed, and the glass was tinted. She couldn't tell if it was him in there or not. "I'll be back."

"No, Sid!" Guppy yelled out after her.

She slipped away from his reaching hand and snuck up to the Camaro's side. Two girls blocked the passenger-side door. "Move."

"Yeah, right," one said, chewing a mouthful of gum. The other had her nose down inside her phone.

Sid shoved them both out of the way and popped the door open. Leaning inside, her eyes widened at the sight of the passenger. It was the little blonde, Agent Rebecca Lang, in a burgundy miniskirt. That rookie data analyst Cyrus Tweel had been dating. "What are you doing in here?"

"Me?!" the younger woman said. "I'm on a case. Now *you* need to go before you blow my cover!"

Crammed in the driver's seat and strapped in was a man wearing a navy-blue driver's suit. A gunmetal-grey helmet covered his head. He flipped up the mirrored visor. "Hey, Sid. How've you been?"

Blood charging, Sidney roared, "Get out, Rebecca!"

"I'm not getting out. Hey! Get off my seatbelt!"

Sid fumbled with the clasps on the harness that was like what you saw in racing cars. "Get out!"

"You are assaulting a federal officer, you retiree!" Rebecca squealed, swatting at Sid's hands. "Go away, or I'll press charges!"

"Sid," Smoke said. "Go. I'm on a gig." He motioned to the front.

A woman with a long white scarf and even longer white hair stepped out between the cars and raised her arms.

Smoke revved the engine. "It's racing time."

Sid glared deep into his dark eyes. "We're going to talk when this is over."

"No," Rebecca said defiantly, "you won't."

"We'll see, you little ferret." Sid backed out.

Rebecca slammed the door shut.

The crowd erupted in cheers just as the woman with the scarf dropped her arms. Powerful engines unleashed throaty roars. Wheels spun. Rubber burned. Everyone was left standing in the smoke as the two cars sped away.

Shoulders sagging and chest heaving, Sid watched the cars disappear around the first bend. *What is she doing here?!* Scanning the crowd, which was now on the move, she saw no sign of Guppy. Instead, her eyes met up with a pair of frosty eyes.

Her ex-fiancé was storming her way. "What in the hell are you doing here?" he asked her, his jowls jiggling and his glasses fogging up.

She looked him up and down. He wore some torn-up jeans over sandals, a dingy grey sweatshirt, a camo ball cap, and glasses that had clearly been designed for birth control. "I love racing. You know that."

"Get your ass out of here, Sid!" He was gritting his teeth and obviously fighting the urge to yell, knowing that a scene would blow his pathetic attempt at being under cover.

"Are you and Rebecca working the Black Slate?" Sid asked, sweetly feigning friendliness.

"You need to shut your hole," he said, glancing around. "That's an order."

"I don't work for you anymore, Cyrus. I'm free to be anywhere I want."

"Look, I don't know how you wound up here, but you are interfering with a federal investigation." Looking around, he was fighting even harder to keep his voice down. His arm shook when he pointed back toward the highway. "You need to get the hell out of here. Now!"

"I don't have to do anything." She tilted her head and smiled her sweetest smile. She would have batted her eyelashes if she thought he would have noticed.

"You are endangering us. Not to mention yourself." When Cyrus saw that line of reasoning wasn't getting him anywhere, he adjusted his ball cap and tried another tactic. "Of course, I'm not surprised that you and Mr. Smoke managed to hook up again. You know, he was under strict orders not to work with anyone on the outside. Especially you. And now you show up? Heh, he's not going to get out again anytime soon. He blew it."

"Wait a minute," she argued. "I didn't have any idea he was here, and I haven't seen or heard from him since before I left."

"Sure, Sid. Sure. I should have known he was sneaking in a little something on the side." He started away. "Look at you, giving booty calls to criminals."

She balled up her fist.

"Oh, seems I hit a little close to home," Cyrus said. He looked so sure of himself now that he could see he was getting to her. It made her even madder. "Go ahead," he said, "Take a shot if it makes you feel better. That way, I can take both of you out with one stone." He shook his head. "Man, Sid, you're such a disappointment."

"Are you friggin' kidding me? This is how you act?" She poked him in the chest. "I'm not a liar, and you know that. I'm here because those goons in that truck killed my friend."

Cyrus eyed her. "What friend?"

"Jake Miller."

Cyrus's brows lifted. Rubbing his chest, he said, "Huh, even Smoke didn't know about that. Look, I'll give you a pass, but you need to stay away from this case. Far away. I mean it, Sid."

"Well, I can't."

"Why?"

"Because I've been hired to bring those murderers in."

"Oh really, you're a bounty hunter now?" He laughed. "Who hired you?"

"Me."

A clamor rose up from the crowd. The grey Camaro screeched around the corner. The black truck was on its tail. One man was hanging outside the truck's window, aiming a gun. The sharp pop of gunfire rang out above the roaring engines.

"They're shooting!" Sid said, going for her gun.

A man running by said, "Anything goes! Anything goes! It's only lap one of the Death Race."

CHAPTER 12

W EAVING IN AND OUT OF the onlookers, Sid sprinted for her car. Clearing the massive gathering of crazed people clamoring to get closer to the gunshots, she made a bead for the Hellcat.

The young woman from earlier was standing on Sid's hood, whooping it up with her arm. She wasn't alone, either. A small horde of miscreants surrounded the car. They saw Sid coming and showed some tough looks on their faces.

"Get away from my car!" Sid yelled.

The woman on the hood waggled her finger. "You got to take us for a ride first. You promised. But we'll make it easy on you. Just give us the keys, and we'll do it for you." She opened up her palm. "Hand them over, and we won't hurt—"

Sid whipped out her Glock, took aim, and fired. *Pop!*

"Eek!" The woman screamed, clutching her ear. "I felt that. Shit! I felt that."

The horde scattered. The woman jumped off the hood, started to run, stumbled, and fell. She looked up at Sid. "You're crazy, lady thing. Crazy." Still clutching her ear, she scrambled up and fled.

Sid got inside her car and fired up the engine.

Cyrus hopped in the passenger side and shut himself inside with Sid. His chest was heaving.

"What are you doing?" Sid said, putting the car into gear. "The FBI doesn't have jurisdiction over my car."

Panting, he pulled out his badge and said, "I'm commandeering your car." *Puff-puff.* "Geez, I forgot how fast you were." He fanned his hand forward. "Go. Just go!" Cyrus mopped his forehead with a grimy and stained white handkerchief.

She stomped on the gas. The Hellcat surged forward, scattering miscreants like a flock of seagulls. She hit the main road, the pseudo-racetrack, and drove the opposite direction of where Smoke was headed. Between her teeth, Sid seethed at Cyrus, "Did you know this was a death race?"

Cyrus shook his head. "No." He buckled up and pulled out his phone. "I'm calling in backup."

"So you're going after the Buffalo Assassins? Why? Are they on the list?"

"You know I'm not saying." He checked his key pad and started dialing.

She smacked his phone out of his hand. "Don't call it in. You'll blow your own cover."

"Like you haven't? You're chasing them."

"I am," she said. "But not you. Just let me handle this." Doing eighty, the tires screeched around on the blacktop.

Ahead, Smoke the Grey Racer was side by side with the Black Hulk.

Sid saw a series of bright muzzle blasts. She locked up the brakes and formed a roadblock on the main drag. "Roll down your window!"

Cyrus was searching for his phone. "What? Why?" He glanced out the window. "Shit, you're going to get us pulverized, Sid! Move! Move!"

"They won't hit us." *I hope.* She pulled out her pistol. "Just shoot at the truck!"

She and Cyrus both started blasting away. The Camaro juked around the front end of the Hellcat. The truck swerved around behind her trunk.

"See?" Sid said, punching the gas and speeding after them.

Cyrus was on his phone again. "The steer is out of the stable! The steer is out of the stable!"

"Really?" she said, letting out a hearty laugh.

He sounded embarrassed when he said, "I didn't make it up."

Ahead, the F250 and the Camaro raced. Suddenly, the truck veered left and plowed over a handful of onlookers who were standing too close to the makeshift racetrack.

"No!" Cyrus cried. "Geez! That was intentional!"

Sid's heart sank. A pit in her stomach formed. "That's what monsters do. Haven't you met any before?"

"Damn, Sid. No. Not like these two freaks." He got back on his phone. "We have casualties. Send an ambulance." He glanced at the carnage and shock-filled wailing as they zoomed by. "Make it two."

The black truck veered off the track, off the road, bouncing over the berms toward the main highway.

"I think they're on to you," Sid said to Cyrus.

"Onto *me*? You're the one chasing them."

"You commandeered my car. Do you want me to stop and let you out?"

"No," he said. "Go. Just go!" He shook in his seat as if he could make the Hellcat speed up from there.

Sid followed the two racers to the highway, laughing the whole time and not being at all careful to avoid the bumps.

She just about lost it when she heard Cyrus gulp down some barf.

Smoke the Grey Racer's Camaro sped along, weaving through the traffic signs and lights after the Black Hulk, which picked up speed now that it was on the highway.

Sid swung her car left and right, fishtailing, spinning her tires before they bit into the road. Up the entrance ramp she went, right after Smoke.

"Rebecca," Cyrus said into his phone. "Are you okay?" There was a pause. "Good, good. Tell Smoke to follow. Don't engage. Let's just see where these bastards go. Be careful." He disconnected.

Sid eyed him. "'Be careful'?"

"What? It's a dangerous situation."

"I think being careful is implied in the FBI academy," she said. They were doing about ninety, weaving in and out of traffic and passing one car after the other. "So, she's my replacement on the Black Slate?"

"I can't answer that," he said, texting.

"I can only imagine you had a hand in picking her. Isn't she a little green? What kind of field experience does a data analyst have, anyway?"

He ran his forearm over his brow. "She's a good actress. Discreet and deceptive."

"Oh, a cute young female version of you. That's nice."

"Smoke seems to like her," he said. "They've gotten a lot done in the past six weeks."

She squeezed the wheel. *He better not have been out for six weeks.* "Well, I'm sure she finds him better company than you."

"Funny, I could say the same about you." He tipped his head up. "What did he say to me? She gives him a much longer leash. Something like that."

Sid ground her teeth. *It doesn't bother me. What do I care if he spends time with another woman? Dammit! It bothers me! Six weeks with Prissy Pants! Cyrus better be lying! Change the subject.* "So tell me. What do you want with the Buffalo Brothers?"

"No. Not going to say. But I'd be curious to know what you know about them."

Fine. I'll play.

"They're the Drake's cleanup crew. And the rumor around town is that they can't be killed."

"Interesting," Cyrus said. "I bet a pair of men like that have a lot of good stories to tell."

"Huh." *I'll be. They want to capture these guys. Interrogate them. Why am I surprised?* She glanced in the rearview mirror. Cop cars with flashing lights had filed in behind them. "We have company already."

"Yep," Cyrus said, sounding sure of himself and no longer about to puke. "And just a few miles up the road, a blockade will be set up. We have these jokers on manslaughter now." She could hear him smiling, imagine him showing his tiny little teeth. "Busted."

Cruising at high speed, Sid saw flashing cop lights up ahead.

The black truck screeched to a halt. In seconds, it was hemmed in by a fleet of cop cars, and so was Smoke and Rebecca's ride. The trapped truck did a circle of donuts, smoking up the area.

"What are those freaks doing?" Cyrus said, getting out of the car.

Eyeing the scene, Sid waved the drifting smoke from her face. The black truck's windows were rolled up. She couldn't make out the men inside. She tilted her head. Above and flying toward them was a black helicopter.

Whuppa! Whuppa! Whuppa! Whuppa! Whuppa!

A police officer was shouting through a bullhorn. He could barely be heard over the chopper that now hovered over the truck. Someone dropped a ladder out of the chopper. Suddenly the doors to the truck burst open. The big men hopped into the bed of the black truck and grabbed onto the ladder.

"No!" Cyrus screamed. "Halt! Halt!"

The helicopter soared away. The Buffalo Brothers gave them all a middle-finger salute and vanished into the night.

Pounding his fists against his thighs and stomping his foot, Cyrus screamed, "Dammit!"

An FBI cruiser pulled up. A small team emerged and approached Cyrus.

"I want a forensics team all over that truck. Now!"

A second later the truck exploded.

Boom!

CHAPTER 13

W ATCHING THE FLAMING TRUCK BURN to the ground, Sid heard Cyrus say to her, "This is your fault!"

"My fault?" she argued. "You're the one watching a pair of mass murderers run around on the loose. I bet you could have apprehended them weeks ago, but you wanted to follow some ridiculous protocol."

"You know what, Sid?"

"What?"

"You're a joke. You can't even see your error in all this." He lifted up his phone like he was going to smash it into the ground. He held back. "Damn. Everything was fine until you showed up."

Two more people approached. Smoke was still in his racing suit. Beside him, Rebecca Lang lumbered along, holding her shoulder. Her face was wrought with pain.

Cyrus rushed over to her. "Are you all right? What happened?"

"I got shot," she said, sucking her teeth. "Sort of."

Cyrus rolled up her sleeve. She was wearing a dark mesh shirt Sid recognized. "Is that a Sweet Heart suit?"

"Part of one," Smoke said, taking off his helmet. His dark, wavy hair hung below his ears. His chiseled face was shaven, giving him a touch of a boyish look. "She wouldn't wear the whole thing. She said she wanted to sell it."

"I sold it, all right," Rebecca said, glancing at Sidney. "And I could have gotten more money if you hadn't ruined it. Ow!"

"Sorry," Cyrus said, inspecting her shoulder. "That's going to leave a beauty mark, but you aren't bleeding. Still, you better get that x-rayed. There might be a hairline fracture in there. Come on." He turned toward Smoke. "Don't either of you go anywhere. As a matter of fact…" His head swiveled around. "Lee! Lee! Keep an eye on these two."

A slender-faced man, tall and broad shouldered, sauntered over. He wore a dark navy suit, tinted glasses, and an earpiece. He clasped his hands in front of him and said, "Will do, sir."

Sid didn't know the man. She turned her back and faced Smoke. He had a funny look on his face. "What?" she said.

"I was wondering if you wanted to hug me."

Yes. "Not going to happen." Looking into his dark eyes, she found something she hadn't admitted to herself she'd been looking for. "Where have you been staying?"

"Can't say." He set the helmet down and started to unzip his racing suit. "Man, this thing's hot. It's nothing like the Sweet Heart suit."

"You don't have one, and she does?"

"Your ex-fiancé took it," he said.

"You didn't need to say that," she said, "but at least I know that still bothers you."

"That makes you happy?"

Yes! "Maybe."

"Huh. Well, it's good to see you, too. So, how did you stumble upon this?"

"Aw, crap. Guppy." She pulled out her phone and noticed a text.

It read, "Don't worry about me. On my way back. G."

"So," Smoke said, leaning back against her car, "I guess you've figured out I've been out of prison six weeks. And maybe you're mad that you haven't heard from me?"

Furious. "You could have let me know." Taking a place near him against her car, she shrugged. "Besides, Megan's asked about you."

"How is she?"

"Fine."

"You have to understand, Sid. I'm keeping things pretty close to the vest. If things go well, I can get out. Early." He glanced around. "Not that I trust them, but that's what they offered. And don't be bent at me because I haven't checked in. You're the one who left the Agency. Why'd you do that? I thought we had a good thing going."

She stiffened. There was a deeper meaning in his tone. He sounded hurt. "I had to. For Megan."

"When they came for me, it was like the first time we met. Remember? Except it was Rebecca, not you." His eyes found the little blonde, who was sitting in the back of a nearby ambulance. "She's a clever little bird. She asked an awful lot of questions about you in my interview. That said, for the record, I was disappointed."

"In what?"

"That it was her and not you. I knew something was wrong. I didn't want to take the job, but the offer, time plus money… I had to."

Sid leaned toward him. "You almost make it sound like they forced your hand. I don't take you for the kind of man who does things he doesn't want to do."

"She made it clear that if I didn't do what they wanted, things would get a little tougher on me. Besides, I thought I'd take the risk and hopefully bump into you. And here we are. Quite the coincidence, isn't it?" He eyed the star-filled sky. "Such a pretty nightfall."

She backhanded him in the shoulder. "You did that, didn't you."

Smoke feigned a look of surprise. "Did what?"

"You put that paper on my car, didn't you!"

"What sort of paper are you talking about? Notebook? Typing? News?"

"*Nightfall DC!*" She pushed him sideways along her car.

Chuckling a little, he let her. "Oh, never heard of it." Giving her an all-too-knowing smile, he said, "You look like you want to hug me now."

Heart pounding, she reached over and squeezed his hand tight.

His warmth raced through her.

Throat tightening, she quickly released his hand and his warmth. "No."

Cyrus approached with a handful of men. "I hope you two enjoyed your little reunion, but now it's over. I've got orders. Mr. Smoke, you're going back. This investigation's over." Several of the armed men closed in. "Don't try anything."

Smoke raised his arms over his head. "No problem, Cyrus."

"It's Agent Tweel to you."

"Cyrus, what is your problem?" Sid said, watching the men cuff Smoke's hands behind his back. "He's put his neck out for you, and you treat him this way?"

"You should have minded your own business, Sid." Cyrus had a familiar mean look in his eyes that scared Sid a tiny bit.

"What?" she cried. Numb from head to toe, she watched everything move in slow motion.

Smoke was led away in cuffs. His eyes caught hers one last time before he was shoved into a black SUV.

Cyrus got in Sid's face, pointing at her with anger. "And you interfered with an FBI investigation and have at least a dozen other charges, too. And I'm not even sorry to do this. Agent Lee, cuff her."

CHAPTER 14

SIDNEY SAT ON A COLD grey metal chair bolted to the wall of a small solitary holding cell. The walls were stark white. The fluorescent lights overhead flickered. The room was stuffy and warm. She stared at the heavy metal door. There was a square portal at the top. The last time a head had gone by had to have been an hour ago. Maybe longer. Using her T-shirt sleeve, she wiped the sweat from her lip.

Morning glory! What have I done?

Elbows on her knees, she sank her face into the palms of her hands. It was real. She was arrested. Spread out and searched and thrown into the slammer. Her nails dug deep into her hair. Her arms flexed. She had to have been in there a long time. Three hours, she guessed. She was good with time. But inside this little room, things had gotten weird. The isolation threw her off. Worry beset her. She stomped her foot.

"How stupid of me!"

Megan. That was her concern. Her niece should be safe with Sam and Guppy, but no doubt the little woman-to-be would worry. Sid's heart ached. She felt trapped. Helpless. More than a little scared now. She shifted in her chair. Got up and stretched her legs. Rose up on her tiptoes and peered through the portal. There was only the opposing wall of the corridor. She couldn't see much at all from left to right. She hit the door with her fist. The blow made almost no sound at all.

Keep it together. Don't act like a criminal.

Cyrus was right. She had interfered. If she'd kept her head down and lived the normal life, she'd be back home right now. Not waiting.

She sighed. The processing of paperwork took hours.

It might even run until tomorrow.

She'd been on the other side of that heavy metal door many times before. Taking her time. Getting the paperwork ready. Not giving the person in the cell a single thought. Guilty or not, no one ever rushed for them. No one heard their pleas. Their screams. No one asked about their responsibilities, their families. They just left them. Let them rot until the system sorted it out.

She sat back down on the bare-bones cot, pulled her legs up to her chest, and leaned back against the wall. All she heard was her own breathing. Her heart pumping in her chest. She swore her brain spun around in her head, running through every scenario and detail.

I'm a fool.

She had jumped into the action feet first, feeling justified. She had wanted to find Jake Miller's killers. She had opened up a can of worms. It had gotten her cop juices flowing. She had abandoned her responsibilities because of it. All because she wanted to go out and play.

Now Megan would pay for it.

What if they stick it to me? What if they don't want me out?

What if the Drake was calling the shots all along and this was what they wanted? What if they stuck her in an orange jumper, released her into the general prison population, and let a bunch of burly cons with shivs come to kill her?

Don't think like that, Sid.

Her stomach groaned. Above, the vent rattled as the air conditioner came on. It was icy cold. Chill bumps rose on her arms. Although she felt refreshed for a moment, it wasn't long before her sweat-slicked body chilled. She started to shiver. She rubbed her crossed arms up and down. She moved away from the vent, but it didn't do her any good. She couldn't go far.

Man, that's cold.

The temperature in the room must have dropped from ninety degrees to sixty in a minute. She stood up on the cot and stretched her fingers toward the ceiling vent, wanting to close it. She was at least a foot short.

"Come on," she said, teeth chattering. "This can't last forever." She rubbed her arms. Paced back and forth. She fought the urge to curl up under the cot like an animal.

Come on, Sid. You're tougher than them. Get mad. Don't give in. Fight them.

She'd trained in severe situations. Been through survival camps. Combat camps. Interrogation camps.

This should be a cakewalk.

Picking up her knees, she ran in place for fifteen minutes until the air shut off.

Yes.

Taking a seat and gathering her thoughts, she thought about Smoke. It stuck in her craw that he might not be getting out sooner because of her. Now he was gone again. Just when she had started to feel close to him.

Why do I hate to admit that I miss him?

The cold air kicked on again.

"Damn!" She stood up. "Fine. I can take anything you can dish out."

The cold air went on again, off again, minute after minute, hour after hour.

Finally exhausted, Sid let out a tormented scream.

CHAPTER 15

E XHAUSTED, COLD, AND HUNGRY, SID huddled in the corner of her cell. A sound caught her ear. The cell door's lock tumbled over, and the door swung open. Muscles stiff as boards, she pushed up into a standing position.

A guard stepped into full view, an average guy in plain clothes, wearing an FBI jacket and ball cap. "Come with me," he said, stepping back out of view.

Sid headed out of the cell. The air in the hall was like a warm blanket. She followed the man down the hall and to the left, cutting across an office filled with a handful of empty cubicles. He cut into another hall, took a right, and opened a door. "Go on in. Have a seat," he said, running his eyes over her disheveled body. He gave her a funny look. "Someone will be with you in a minute."

"That's what they said last time."

"Sorry, I just came in. I've barely been briefed on it." He smiled. "I'll see if I can get you some coffee, but don't count on it."

"Oh, I won't." She entered the room. It was a typical interrogation room. A hard table and chairs. A big mirror and a camera in the corner. She turned as the door closed behind her and the lock was turned into place. "Great."

Rubbing her hands up and down over her cold bare arms, she yawned and sat down, glancing up at the camera in the corner. The little red light wasn't on, but that didn't mean anything. Often, they'd watch without recording.

Who's watching me now?

"Do you think I can get something to eat?" she said to the mirror. "Any chance I can make that phone call? I seem to have misplaced my phone."

Silence was the answer. She got out of the chair and walked around the table. At least the interrogation room was warm. That was intentional. The hotter the better. They liked to make the guilty sweat. She'd conducted plenty of interviews in places like this. The FBI had little offices all over. She didn't recognize this one, and she'd been inside many.

How many things does the FBI do that I don't have a clue about? Man, and they're only one agency.

The door popped open, and Cyrus Tweel entered. He was in a suit and looked refreshed.

Right on his heels came Agent Lang. The petite woman in a snug pantsuit wore a sling on her arm and a frown on her face.

"Sit down," Cyrus said to Sid.

"Good morning to you too, Cyrus," she said, resuming her seat.

He pulled out a chair for Rebecca then seated himself. "I'm sure you had a long night, but you know how paperwork goes."

"I know exactly how it goes! You can't hold me like this. You threw me in a cage like a hardened criminal. Like an animal!"

Cyrus held up his hand. "Don't raise your voice. You're in enough trouble already. Just so you know, I don't have to be here. Consider it a courtesy."

"I'm sorry," Sid scoffed. "Did I interrupt your morning? What's the matter, no time for you and your little bird to snuggle?"

"Sid, there's no need—"

Rebecca cut Cyrus off by whispering something in his ear.

He cleared his throat. "Tell us everything you know about the Buffalo Brothers." He pushed over a pad and pen. "Write it down."

She shook her head no. "Why?"

"Because I said so." He pushed his thick glasses up on the bridge of his nose. "You really need to do yourself a favor here, Sid. Things aren't looking good for you at all. Do you know how hard it is to get a job with felonies on your record? And what about your niece, Megan? Do you want her going into a foster home?"

"She has grandparents."

"That's for the state to decide. Everything doesn't always go your way, you know." He tapped the table with his fingers. "The charmed life you led is finally over."

In disgust, she said, "What are you talking about?"

His frosty eyes locked on hers. "Just start writing."

She slid the paper over and started to draw, humming as she did it. She lifted the top edge of the paper so that they couldn't see it. "No peeking." Like a schoolgirl, she bit on her tongue as she drew an obscene gesture on the paper.

Cyrus and Rebecca glared at her.

Finished, Sid tore the paper off the pad, folded it in half, and slid it over.

"A little quick," he said. He unfolded the paper in front of him and Rebecca and huffed. "Cute, Sid. Real cute."

"That's for the both of your eyes only," Sid said. "I'm sorry. You and your little bird look upset. Am I going to be additionally charged with insulting a federal officer now?" She leaned back in her chair. "I wonder if you can make that stick."

Cyrus wadded up the paper and tossed it aside.

Rebecca whispered something else in his ear.

He nodded. Rising from his seat, he said, "I gave you a chance. You blew it."

"What, you're leaving me?" Sid said, rolling her eyes. "How disappointing."

The door opened and the agent from earlier came in with a cup of coffee in his hand. Rebecca slid into his path, plucked the coffee cup from his hand, and said with a smile at Sid, "Why, thank you."

Cyrus followed her out, saying, "Have fun in the hole. I hear it can be rather chilly at times."

CHAPTER 16

S ITTING IN THE CELL WITH her knees bouncing up and down, Sid pondered her situation. Cyrus was using coercion. Trying to pick her brain for some reason. She didn't really have anything, but she wasn't going to let him know that. She leaned her head back against the wall.

"Shoot."

She'd broken at least five laws in the last twenty-four hours. Sure, it was minor. Scuffing up against Rebecca while she sat in Smoke's car didn't seem like much, but it could be a problem. She'd seen things like this happen all the time. Agents getting out of control with their authority. It wasn't a problem agent on agent. But civilian on agent? Especially with an agent who had a grudge against you? That was different.

What cards do you have, Sid? Let them think you know something? Get them to drop the charges then exchange nothing? Maybe my unlawful imprisonment is a good example. No food. No visits to the bathroom. No calls. She slapped her head. *Megan. I need to be taking Megan to school right now!*

She hit the wall, winced, and shook her hand. The air conditioning fan kicked on. She balled up. Her eyes started to swell and her chest tightened.

I'm such a fool. Such a fool I am. Get it together, Sid. Don't let Cyrus and that little twit win.

She shuddered a breath and then recited the Serenity Prayer. "God, grant me the serenity to accept the things I cannot change, the courage to change the things I can, and the wisdom to know the difference." Her head sank between her knees. "Amen."

A moment later, the A/C fan kicked off. The cell door opened.

She lifted her head and saw Section Chief Ted Howard standing there.

"Sid," he said, stepping inside and clasping her hands. "I'm sorry about this. I just got word and made it over here as fast as I could. Come on. Let's get you sorted out and back on your feet."

She studied his face. Ted was a hard man at times. Tough. Old school. The hard lines on his face were softened by the sad look in his eyes. She took his hand. "No games, Ted."

"No, friend."

Sid was inside a small office furnished only with a desk and half a dozen chairs. There weren't any decorations or evidence of personal effects. It was a typical satellite office, a place agents used when they went undercover. A place to meet. To plan. Off the radar from the main office. For the most part, the building was run by a skeleton crew that might consist of one field agent acting as a supervisor or guard.

Ted sat behind the metal desk in an old wooden swivel chair. His navy-blue suit jacket hung on an old coat rack in the corner. He rolled up his sleeves, exposing his husky forearms, and loosened his tie. He helped himself to something from a box of donuts and shoved them over.

Sid sipped coffee from a Styrofoam cup that read Donut Connection. Ted had given her some time to get cleaned up and make a call. Megan was fine, thanks to Sam, and had made it to school. Starving, she eyed the donuts, reached in, and plucked out an apple cinnamon. "So, did you pick these up as you rushed to come and see me?"

Taken aback, Ted said, "Well, I figured you'd be hungry. And it was on the way."

"Isn't there always one on the way?" She bit into the donut and chewed. *This is the best donut I've ever had in my life.* Washing it down with coffee, she grabbed another. "Bavarian. Interesting variety, Ted. Looks like it might have taken some time to pick out."

"Oh, don't start, Sid. I didn't have to bring anything at all, you know."

"You've known I was in there since last night, haven't you."

He looked her dead in the eye and said, "No."

She believed him.

"Okay. So what's happening now? Am I under arrest or not?"

"Yes and no."

"Yes and no? What does that mean, 'yes and no'?"

"I've gotten word that *they*," he said, making air quotes, "want you back on the Black Slate."

"Aren't Cyrus and *Agent Lang* handling that now?" she said, easing back into her chair. She made a face and tilted her head sideways when she said *Agent Lang*.

"Your sudden departure had consequences, Sid. Cyrus hounded me. Hell, he hounded everyone he could, trying to get into the Black Slate." Ted shook his head. "He'd kill to be a shadow agent. I really think he would. Well, somebody above gave him the pass. They even let him pick his team. He picked Rebecca."

Sid hitched her brow. "His girlfriend?"

"Actually, I think she has some connections that even I don't know about. I've never seen an agent so young promoted so fast. Anyway, as I understand it, the powers that be gave Cyrus what he wanted. Part of the reason was his familiarity with John Smoke and you. They even apprehended somebody on the Slate already."

Sid sat up and scooted her chair closer. "What? Really? Who?"

"I can't say."

Suddenly, the office door was flung open. Cyrus and Rebecca stormed in.

Cyrus slapped a document onto Ted's desk. "This is not happening!"

Rebecca, blue eyes smoldering like fires and arms crossed over her chest, huddled up to Cyrus's side and added, "You better not do this, Ted. You need to butt out!"

CHAPTER 17

"Excuse me," Sid said. "What is going on here?"

"You shut up!" Rebecca shot back at Sid. "You washed-up has-been!"

Sid sprang out of her seat, pinned Rebecca down on the desk, and growled in the petite woman's ear, "Don't ever tell me to shut up."

"Get off her!" Cyrus said, taking Sid by the arm.

Sid twisted away and released Rebecca.

"I'm pressing charges! I'm pressing charges!" Rebecca cried out. Adjusting her glasses, the mousy little woman practically screamed, "Arrest her, Cyrus!"

Ted stood up with his fists on his desk and shouted over everyone in a thunderous voice. "No one is arresting anybody! Now sit down!"

Scowling, Rebecca pulled a chair over to the left of Cyrus, who took a seat to the left of Sid.

"I expect better from my agents," Ted said, slowly sitting back down.

Kicking her crossed leg, Rebecca said, "She's not an agent."

"Agent Lang," Ted said.

"What?"

He glared at her. "Call me Sir or Section Chief. Got it?"

Rebecca stuck her chest out and saluted. "Yes, Sir."

Ted took a breath and picked up the document Cyrus had slapped onto the desk. Examining it, he said to Cyrus, "I have no problem with this. You shouldn't either."

"Sir, I'm already working with one ex-con. Now I'm supposed to work with another? This is ridiculous."

"Sid's no convict," Ted replied. "You know better than that, Cyrus."

"What are we talking about?" Sid inquired.

"As I was about to say before I was interrupted, we, or rather the Agency, want to acquire your services, Sid."

"What do you mean?"

"We want to add you on as a consultant for the Black Slate," he said.

"We as in you, Ted?"

"We as in the same Agency folks who lined you up before. *They* want you on the Slate, Sid."

Beside her, Cyrus clenched his jaw.

Beside him, Rebecca lifted her chin and turned her head away while she sat there with her arms crossed tight over her chest, still kicking her leg.

"Tell me more," Sid said, sounding very interested. She swore she could hear both Cyrus's and Rachel's butts pucker. *Make 'em suffer.*

"The paperwork's ready. You'll be given consultant ID, and your former security clearances will be restored." He rubbed his chin. "Sorry, I'm making it sound simpler than it probably is. Anyway, you and Agents Tweel and Lang will work as a team on this."

"Just us?" she said.

"Mr. Smoke will be coming along, but he's not in a position of authority, hence not a team member, so to speak."

She heard Rachel shift in her seat. *Squirm, girl, squirm.* "What's the objective?"

Ted reached into the desk drawer, withdrew a black file, and slapped it down on the desk. He kept his hand over it and said, "Are you in or are you out?"

Eyes fixed on the file, Sid sorted through her thoughts. There was Megan to consider. Other than that, there was nothing else—aside from the satisfaction of pissing Cyrus and Rachel off. "I'm in."

"What!" Rebecca blurted out. "You have a nanny job to attend to. You don't have time for this! Sir, we don't need her. She'll just slow us down."

"Says the woman she just pinned to my desk," Ted said. "And you're borderline insubordinate. I'm getting tired of it. Don't make me warn you again."

"Or what?" Rachel said, getting out of her chair. "I'll have your job before you know what hit you, you frickin' dinosaur." Shooting Sid a look, she left the room.

Ted's face darkened. Normally, the veteran leader and agent would have taken immediate action. But something held him back. Sid wondered what that was.

"You need to get a better handle on that," Ted warned Cyrus. "That better never happen again."

Unfazed, Cyrus said, "I'll do what I can."

"I'm sure you will," Ted said, shoving the file toward Sid. "That's your copy. Now, we want to get the Buffalo Brothers, Warren and Oliver Ratson."

"We had them until she showed up," Cyrus said.

Ted clasped his fingers and rested them on the desk, staring at Cyrus until the flabby man backed down into his seat. "Continuing. We don't know much. They work for the Drake. And whenever they show up, someone important gets killed."

Thumbing through the file, Sid came across some familiar names and faces. Politicians and other high-ranking DC officials. Names that often made the papers. Important men and women. They were all dead. The papers reported natural causes. Maybe suicide. The photos showed something else. Grizzly photos. Blood and mutilation. Torment. "How is this possible? How is this covered up?"

"That's not the issue," Cyrus said.

"He's right," Ted said, giving Cyrus a warning glare, "not that it doesn't matter. The point is, these guys need to be brought down. Because they're here, we know someone's hired them to kill someone else. Mr. Jake Miller tipped us off to that."

"How's that?" she asked.

"The Buffalo Brothers have a calling card." He produced a transparent evidence bag and slid it over. "Those were in Jake's eyes."

Studying the contents, Sid observed two buffalo nickels. Her heart sank a little thinking about Big Jake. Like Ted, he was an old soul from a different era. "I imagine there is one for each of them."

"Of course, Jake's death didn't fit the profile. It looked more like vengeance. Sick thing is that they left fingerprints. And in the system, they are both registered to dead men. Got graves but no bodies."

Sid swallowed. If she'd stayed away from those men at the range, perhaps none of this ever would have happened. Jake's death was on her conscience. She gathered herself. "But Cyrus says he and Rebecca have been tracking these brothers for weeks. What tipped you off?"

"Check the dates in the files and you'll see where City Councilman Jeffery Ryson died in an automobile accident. Well, that's not what happened. As you can see."

She found a picture of a man pinned between a brick wall and his car. *I wonder what he knew. I wonder what he saw.* "They all have ties to the Drake, don't they."

Ted shrugged his husky shoulders.

Sid went on and told them about her encounter with the Buffalo Brothers at the gun range.

"Not good," Ted said, rolling his eyes. "It's bad enough what they're doing, but now they're using a sniper's weapon? Whoever they're after must be really high up. Damn. It could be anybody."

CHAPTER 18

"**L**ET HIM OUT," TED SAID into the intercom. "And bring him in."

Sid's heart raced.

A minute later, Smoke entered the room. His towering frame was back in his racing suit. He walked up to the desk, picked up the box of donuts, and sat in the vacant chair to Sid's right. He stuffed an entire donut in his mouth. Chewed. Swallowed. Stuffed in another. Repeated. And another, until the box was empty. He held it up and shook every last crumb into his mouth. And then he set the box back down on Ted's desk and dusted off his hands. "What's the plan?"

"Uh," Ted started, lifting his jaw up off the desk. "Well, Mr. Smoke, you've already been briefed. You might need to fill in Agent Shaw, excuse me, Liaison Shaw, on what you know. We have killers out there. An unknown target. We need to track them down before someone else dies." He rubbed the back of his head. "Cyrus, you're the lead, but the four of you have to work as a team on this. I mean it."

"You know I can't be accountable for these two," Cyrus said with a sneer. "They're reckless."

"They're proven. And if you want to continue to work on the Black Slate, you'll need to deal with it. That's the impression I get, anyway." Ted got up out of his chair and stared down at the empty donut box. "Looks like I'll have to make another stop on the way back to my office. Cyrus, report to me in the morning. You all can see yourselves out." He grabbed his jacket. "I'm out of here."

The room was very still and quiet after Ted left. Sid broke the silence. "So," she said to Cyrus, "what's the plan?"

Cyrus walked over to the window and pulled back the blinds.

Sid heard the sound of a car driving away.

Cyrus turned to her and said thoughtfully, "You two find something to do. I'll call you this afternoon." He took his phone from his pocket. "Sid, what's your new number?"

She gave it to him. "So that's it. Just wait."

"I have to wrap things up, seeing how you trashed the last assignment. We had them, Sid. We almost had them." He stuck his phone back inside his jacket pocket. "And you messed things up. Now we have to start all over again. Unless of course you have something to add?"

"Nope."

"See you around. Enjoy your conjugal." He walked out.

Smoke started to speak.

She held her hand up to his mouth. "Don't you dare say anything about me being engaged to him."

"I was just going to ask you if you wanted to get something to eat." Smoke smiled.

"You just ate half a box ... Oh never mind. Let's go."

They were back in one of the diners they'd been to before. An old rail car with blue booths miles from the heart of DC. Smoke had a stack of pancakes almost up to his chin and a Coke big enough to drown in.

"Aren't you eating?" he said, stabbing with his fork a pile of buttermilk pancakes slathered in syrup.

"Watching you eat fills me up somehow." She drank her coffee. "Just take your time. Sometimes you eat like an animal."

"Sorry." He wiped his mouth with a napkin. "Folks aren't really big on etiquette in prison. So, how have you been?"

She didn't want to get into it. For the moment, she was just happy to be with him. "Fine."

"You don't look fine," he said, adding a little grin.

"I'm sure I don't. But you've seen better days yourself. It's good to see your hair back, though. Even with the helmet hair."

He choked on his food and started laughing. "Helmet hair. If I'd shaven it, I wouldn't have that problem, now would I?"

"Don't shave it."

He made and air circle with his spoon. "Oh-kay."

"Let me ask you a question. Ted said that you and Cyrus brought in someone else from the Black Slate already. Who was that?"

"Maddy Ryan. A hunchback." He swallowed his food. "He wasn't anything like the ones me and you brought in. I mean, tougher than he looked, but not a big threat."

"So he was just a hunchback? Did he shift into anything?"

"No. He was just strong as a bull and exceptionally cruel." He stopped the waitress walking by. "Miss, could I get some whipped cream?"

"Sure, hun." The waitress in powder blue and white squeezed his cheek. "Anything for you." She looked at Sid. "He's a keeper. I think it's sexy when a man eats like that. And stays so fit. He's a keeper."

"Yeah, thanks," Sid said, watching the woman walk away. She eyed Smoke, who'd resumed his eating. "You were saying."

"Oh yeah. Uh, Maddy could hop like a rabbit. It was really weird. Scaled walls and ropes like a monkey."

"Was he wearing a Notre Dame jersey?"

"No, why?"

"Are you making this up?"

"Nope," he said.

"So, what was he doing?"

He pointed his fork at her. "Funny thing. I think he was running a day care. It was full of all those weird little kids. The Forever Children Mal told us about."

Sid felt a chill go up her spine. Something about those children disturbed her. She had no idea what to make of them. Were they dangerous, or were they in need of help? "What happened to them?"

"I don't know."

Of course not. "What about Maddy Ryan? What happened to him? Is he dead or alive?"

"Well, he should be dead. I beat the tar out of him." He huffed. "I'd knock him down, and he'd bounce right back up. I swear, that hump in his back, it's got a battery in it or something."

"Did Cyrus and Rebecca help?"

"Sure, they were a big help."

"Really?"

Smoke shook his head. "No. Not really. They're pretty useless without their guns, which of course Maddy deprived them of. It's a long story."

She leaned forward and rested her chin on her fist. "I'm not going anywhere, unless you are." Her phone buzzed on the table. She answered. "Hello?"

"It's Cyrus," he said in his snide voice. "Need you and Smoke to stake out 8505 Rummel Avenue. Be there now." *Click.*

CHAPTER 19

8505 RUMMEL DRIVE WAS A business park off Interstate 395 in Falls Church. Sidney parked her car in front of a UPS distribution warehouse. Drumming her fingers on the steering wheel, she glanced over at Smoke, who was looking out his window. His strong chin and muscular arms were appealing. Very appealing. She rolled down her window and fanned herself.

"So," he said without looking at her. "Do you think he'll be long?"

"I doubt it. He's pretty anal."

"Yep. But his little counterpart likes to play games. I bet they don't show for at least an hour. Maybe two." He rolled down his window. "At least it's a nice day."

"What do you mean about his counterpart?"

"Oh, Rebecca. Yeah, she's trouble. You better watch out for her. She'll get you killed."

"Get me killed?"

"Yeah, like she almost got me killed trying to take down Maddy. Music?" He reached for the radio.

She slapped his hand away.

"Uh, news?" he said, taken aback.

"How about you fill me in on this killing thing?"

"Either it was intentional or it was incompetent, but she had a clean shot on Maddy the Hunch and didn't take it. I took a beating because of it. Part of me thinks she let that happen. Plus, other things that don't add up."

"Like what?"

"Like the whisper thing. And she's always sneaking off. I don't think she's done anything helpful. All she's been is there." Looking out the window, he popped open the door and picked something up. He showed a copper coin to her. "Like a bad penny, she always turns up."

Sid flipped on the radio. Something cheesy from the eighties about balloons was playing. Smoke started to sing along, which was very awkward for a big guy, but he could carry a tune. Preoccupied, she remembered her early encounters with Rebecca. The younger woman had seemed fine. Just eager. She'd fooled Sidney entirely. It angered her.

"Well surprise, surprise, surprise," Smoke said, "look who's already showed up.

A black Cadillac Escalade pulled along their side. Cyrus got out of the passenger seat and walked over to Sidney's window. He had on dark sunglasses and gave her a file. "Sherman Investments. There's a man, Winslow Swift. Handles Drake Properties. Big community guy and donor. Well connected." He pointed to another building in the distance, a five-story building, all glass, with a big sign in front of it. "That's Law Park Offices. He'll be coming in and out of there. Keep an eye on him."

"I will until I have to get my niece," Sid said.

"Make arrangements," he said, glancing over at his SUV. "If you can't handle it, then you need to step away."

Sid stooped her head down and looked under Cyrus's arm at the black SUV he'd parked next to her.

Rachel, who was watching and listening intently, sneered at Sid from the passenger seat.

She's like a little blonde life-sucking rodent. Sid looked back up at Cyrus. "Sure thing."

Cyrus leaned down in her window. "Screw this up and you're gone, Sid."

"Got it." She fired up the engine and revved up while Cyrus was still speaking. *Vroom! Vroom!* "Sorry, what was that?"

Cyrus backed away and yelled something.

She pulled the car out and sped away, leaving Cyrus and Rachel out of sight but not out of mind. She tossed the file over to Smoke.

Without opening it, he said, "You know this is a decoy."

"Why do you say that?" She pulled the car into the parking lot of the Law Park Offices building and took a parking spot with a good view of the front entrance. A security guard at the desk could be seen inside the lobby. "Let me see that file."

Winslow Swift was a short, heavy man, very well dressed, dark headed, and with a devilish smile. "He looks like a Drake guy. A real shyster."

"That's right. Why would the Buffalo Brothers want to kill that guy?"

"Maybe he'll lead us to them," she said.

"But Cyrus says he's a potential target. No, this is a decoy. Keeping us on ice while they conduct their own investigation." He opened up the glove box. "What, no gun?"

"Sorry. I'm traveling a little light lately. Don't you have anything in your car?"

"No, little miss prissy picked me clean during our operation. Need to get back to home base to get them." He eyed the back seat. "Do you really not have anything else?"

"Why? It's just a stakeout. We aren't in any immediate danger, I don't think. Besides," she patted his leg. "You know I'll protect you."

He eased his seat back and closed his eyes. "Okay then. Wake me up if he shows."

Good idea. She yawned. Gazing at his body, she found herself thinking about taking him back to her place and curling up with him to … sleep. *Bad idea. Get it together.* She poked his shoulder. "Did I really blow up your situation with the Buffalo Brothers last night?"

"No. You've seen those guys, right? We weren't going to catch them. There's something seriously different about them. Did you read the file?"

"No," she said, a little irritated. She reached into the back seat to grab it and accidentally braced her hand against Smoke's rock-hard belly. *Oh my.* "But what the heck. Why not take a look now."

"They're like deaders on steroids," he said. "At least that's what Mal said."

"And how's he doing?" she said.

"He's not happy," Smoke said. "He got ahold of me, briefly. Said his funding was cut off and they took all his stuff."

"So, no Sweet Heart suits? Blue-tipped bullets? Super vitamins?"

"Nada. He sounded pretty pissed off. Said to call if I needed help but that he couldn't offer much."

"Have you called him again?"

"I did, but he hasn't called back."

"Great." For all Sid knew, Cyrus and Rebecca might have a little bit of everything Mal had to offer. *Wouldn't that be something.*

Things fell quiet. The pair of them sat, listening to the local news radio. The minutes turned to an hour and cruised well past lunchtime.

Sid broke the silence. "I'm going to get Megan. Screw this stakeout." She drummed her fingers on the wheel, eyeing the Law Park building. "You can stay if you want."

"I don't want to stay. I want to go after the Buffalo Brothers. Besides, I already know where they stay."

"What?!"

CHAPTER 20

"Excuse me?" Sid said. "You're joking, right? How can that be?"

"No joke. It just is."

Sidney pulled out of the parking lot and headed for the highway. "And how long have you known where they were?"

"A few days. Well, more like eight days. Six hours and eight days."

"And you haven't shared this with anyone?"

"No."

"Why? If you brought them in, you could go ahead and get your time reduced."

"So they say, but that isn't always true. Besides, I'll need some help on this." He glanced at her. "And there aren't many people I trust to work with."

"Are you telling me you strung this hunt out so you could bring me in?"

He reached up and grabbed the handle over the car door. "Sort of."

Sid grinned. She'd been thinking about him every day, and now she knew that he'd been thinking about her.

"That makes you happy, doesn't it."

She clammed up. "No."

"Then why were you smiling?" he said, gazing at her.

"Because you screwed Cyrus."

"Huh, good answer. But I don't think that's really why."

Well it isn't, but there's still truth in it. "So where are they?"

"I don't know where they are right now. But I know where they hide out," he said.

"And how did you come across this information?"

He glanced at her. "You know me. Cyrus and Rebecca are pretty caught up with each other. That gave me a good bit of leash. I followed the brothers one night. They're cautious, but I pinned them down at Mallows Bay."

"The ship graveyard."

"None other." He pushed his hair out of his eyes. "Gave me the willies, too."

"What do you mean, the willies?"

"I watched them drive over the water and disappear," he said, shaking his head.

"They drove on the water?"

"Like a bad episode of *Knight Rider*. Pretty bizarre, huh?"

Mallows Bay rested on the Potomac River south of DC. It was filled with old steam ships and the ruins of other vessels that had been sunk in the 1920s. It had been a historic park up until recently. Now it was privately owned. Sid stared at the No Trespassing sign mounted on the chain-link fence. Beside it was another sign, a new one that read Drake Properties. She wanted to spit. "Boy, they own a little bit of everything, don't they."

"I'd say so." Smoke stepped over the metal gate that consisted of two steel bars crisscrossed over the road. "Ready to get a closer look?"

She grabbed a small gear bag, and then she and Smoke walked up the road. Before long, they found themselves in a parking lot that led to the boat ramp. The skies had darkened with grey clouds, and the wind was picking up.

They followed Wilson Landing Road to the edge of the dock. From there, Sid could see the ruins of ships scattered all over the bay. With the silt buildup caused by the tides, most of them had been clumped together into a small island, forming their own shoreline. A few of the boats still stood against time in the middle of the bay, fading ever so slowly into the murky waters.

"They drove over the water?" she said to Smoke. "From right here?"

"Yep." He took off his shirt, shoes, and pants.

"What are you doing?" she said, glancing at his legs.

Smoke handed her his pants. "Hold these." He waded into the water. It was murky.

Sid couldn't see his ankle-deep feet from where she stood.

Wearing only his boxer briefs, Smoke ventured out farther and farther, up to his knees but not sinking.

"Get back here!" Sid yelled, looking around. There weren't any people for miles, but she didn't like this place. It was too quiet. Odd. The water smelled a little rank. She rested her hand on her gun. "Smoke! Come back!"

"The water's a little chilly," he said, sloshing around from side to side. "But, yeah, there is definitely a road here." He resumed his walk farther out into the bay.

He must have been forty yards out before he came to a stop. He turned and waved. His lips were moving, but the wind ripping over the water drowned his voice out.

"What?" she yelled.

He waved at her. Then, suddenly, as he ventured farther out toward an old abandoned tanker-type ship, he disappeared.

"Smoke!" she cried. "Smoke!"

CHAPTER 21

ARMS CROSSED OVER HER CHEST, Sid paced back and forth over the boat ramp, holding Smoke's pants and seething. "I'm not going after him. I'm not going after him."

For all intents and purposes, Smoke had been missing for more than thirty minutes. The clouds had darkened in that span of time, and now rain began to sting Sid in the wind. Calm so short a time ago, the bay's waters now crashed against the shore.

She stowed Smoke's clothes in her gear bag and procured a pair of binoculars. Putting them to her eyes, she scanned the waters. The place Smoke had vanished had a shadowy look to it. She stepped out on an old floating dock that shifted beneath her feet and then spied the huge metal craft in the distance, maybe a hundred yards away. Sea birds rested on its edges. Nests jutted out from the anchor portals. Birds on the boat erupted in flight.

He's on there! I know it.

She noticed a figure drifting along topside on the boat. It looked like a man in an old trench coat. His shoulders were slumped, and he moved really slowly. She adjusted the focus on her binoculars. She watched the back of the man's head. He had a captain's hat on and was moving away. Slowly he turned. Sid's heart skipped a beat. The man's skin was taut and leathery, his chin whiskers grey and ragged. His spacy, dark eyes were sunken into the sockets.

A deader. Dammit!

The head of the man disappeared. Sid scoured the edges of the bay with the binoculars. It was just woodland beyond the bay that contained one sunken ship after the other. The rain began to come down a little harder.

I'm going to be soaked. I'm going to kill Smoke. I should just leave him.

She backed off the dock and onto the hard top. She found her gear bag and stuffed the binoculars back inside it. Grabbing her phone, she checked the time. Megan would be out of school in an hour. She started to text Sam. *Crap!* Sam wouldn't be able to pick Megan up. She didn't have permission and probably wouldn't ever be able to get it.

"I'm a horrible aunt."

Frustrated, she kicked off her shoes, rolled up her pants legs, and waded into the water. The icy river sent tingles up her legs and through her neck. She felt a hard surface like a road under her feet. She slipped on the grime, bashing her knees and soaking her pants.

"Morning glory!"

She pushed herself up, teeth chattering, soaking most of her arms and shirt.

Lightning flashed in the distance. Thunder rolled across the river.

"Screw this." She turned around and stomped back toward the dock.

A deader popped up in front of her. It seized her leg in an iron grip and jerked her down into the cold water.

In an instant, Sid was fighting for her life. Water filled her mouth, and she was choking. Squirming against the force, she braced her legs against the wall of the underwater bridge and shoved upward. Head clearing the water, she gasped for breath, only to be submerged again.

Fighting for her life, she kicked at the undead person. She jammed her thumb in its eye. Bit its finger.

Mindless, the deader held her down in the water, trying to wrap its paws around her neck.

Somehow, Sid got her head up, took a breath, went under, and drove her feet into its chest, pushing free of its grip.

Gasp!

She swam for the boat launch and made her way to where she could walk up its slope. When she was shoulder deep in the bay, the deader pounced on her again.

It tore at her, relentless. Fearless of a death that had already come for it. Now it wanted hers.

Sid fought. Kicked. Screamed. Her water-soaked clothes felt like lead blankets. Her chest heaved. She punched its face. Broke free of its grip and staggered up the ramp.

God help me!

Arms heavy as anvils, chest heaving, she found her gun and pulled it out of the holster. She turned. The deader crashed into her. Sid squeezed the trigger. *Blam! Blam! Blam! Blam! Blam!*

Chest full of lead, the deader slumped. Waters washed over its decaying body.

Sidney half crawled up the ramp, soaking wet. Making it out of the bay, she coughed and heaved. Blood dribbled onto the pavement. She raised her hand to her head and felt a gash. A little woozy, she got up and stumbled to the dock and held onto the post. The rain kept pouring.

I hate deaders.

More movement on the water caught her eye. Someone approached, walking on the water. They were moving fast. She aimed her gun. Her wrist was shaking. She started to squeeze the trigger.

"Don't shoot!" said a strong, reassuring voice. Smoke emerged in the rain, wearing nothing but muscle and shorts. He caught up to her and took her by the wrist. "Run!"

There was the whine of a motorboat engine. A fast craft appeared from around the other side of the tanker. Gun flashes sparked in the air. Bullets whizzed overhead and skipped off the ground. Smoke snatched up her gear bag and ran straight through the parking lot and into the woods.

Lungs burning, Sid fought to keep up. Her soaked clothes weighed a ton. Fighting for her life had taken a toll on her. She needed time to recover, bullets blasting away at them or not. She collapsed.

Smoke scooped her up in his arms. "I'm sorry. I've got you now, Sid."

She managed to drape her elbows over his neck. She was aware of Smoke laying her on the reclined passenger seat in her car. The roar of the engine. The screech of tires. Barreling through the rain, she took a long draw through her nose, put the seat back up, buckled herself in, and slapped Smoke in the arm. "As soon as I catch my breath, I'm going to kill you."

"You'll have to get in line," he said, checking the rearview mirror.

Sid looked back behind her. A car was giving chase. A Mustang, judging by the looks of it. Black as coal.

"I guess you found something," she said. Her eyes widened. A man hung out of the passenger side window with a large rifle in his hands. Even in the rain, she could make out the weapon. It was a sniper rifle. Its bullets were as big as her hand. "Those are the Buffalo Brothers!"

Smoke swerved the car just as the man fired.

The bullet rocketed into a passing semi-truck's cargo trailer. The entire back end exploded.

"That was nasty," Smoke said.

Chest pounding, Sid watched their pursuers take another shot. It hit some power lines ahead. They fell and barricaded the road.

Smoke slammed on the brakes, coming to a stop inches from the live power lines.

"Get out," Smoke said. He shoved her at the door. "Get out!"

CHAPTER 22

S ID JUMPED OUT OF THE car and scrambled onto the berm. The Buffalo Brothers' tires screeched as their car came to a sudden stop. The brother hanging outside the car window with the rifle took aim on her car. The Hellcat. She heard him speak before he fired. "Nice car. Too bad." He squeezed the trigger.

The Hellcat exploded, shaking the ground. *Boom!*

Face first on the ground, Sid rolled onto her back. One of her car's wheels was falling out of the sky. She rolled out of the way. The tire bounced off the berm and disappeared somewhere in the nearby pines. Gaping, she stared at what was left of her car. It was nothing but flames and black smoke. She clutched her head. "No. No!"

Nearby, the Buffalo Brothers were laughing. The one with the mirrored glasses lit up a cigarette. The shorter one, still tall and oddly long necked, held the rifle out so he could spit on the ground. He hefted the rifle back onto his shoulder and eyed her through the smoke. "Ah, there's the little bird." He started Sid's way.

She pulled out her gun and pointed at his chest. "You're going to pay for that."

He stopped in his tracks. "What do you mean, pay for that? Is that a revenge thing? Or do you mean I'm going to buy you a new car? That's so cliché."

She fired a round into his leg.

"Ow! You stupid bitch. You shouldn't have done that!" He started to lower the barrel of his gun.

Sid unloaded her magazine into his chest.

He staggered backward with his face aghast and toppled to the ground.

The other brother rushed over. "No! No!" he said, kneeling at his brother's side. "You killed him! You killed my brother."

Loading in another full magazine of ammo, Sid made her way over to the men. The one lay on his back, booted toes up, twitching. The other put his hands over his head. "I surrender. I surrender," he said, pleading. "Don't shoot. Don't shoot. I don't want to die like him."

Sid removed a pair of flex cuffs. She eyed her surroundings, looking for Smoke. He lay face down on the ground, not moving, several yards from the burning car. She approached the first man on his knees. "You're Warren, right?"

"I am he," he said. "Look, lady, I'm really sorry about your car. Really. But your friend, well, he shouldn't be snooping where he doesn't belong."

She had started to cuff Warren when the brother on the ground, Oliver, caught her eye. He wasn't bleeding. Suddenly, he sat upright with a big smile on his face.

The closer brother, Warren, backhanded her in the face.

Sid staggered backward from the powerful blow and dropped down to one knee. Raising the barrel of her gun, she squeezed off a shot, but all it hit was the ground.

Warren clamped his hand over her wrist and wrenched the weapon free. "None of that now," he said. "It can't kill us, but it stings." He tugged her off the ground, twisted her arm behind her back, and held her fast.

"Uh!" she said, grimacing. The man who held her was strong, his grip a vise. She couldn't move.

Oliver chuckled a deep rumble. He inspected the bullet holes in his shirt. He dug in, squeezed a bullet out from under his skin, and flicked it away.

Sid's skin crawled.

He continued, saying, "I love it when they fall for the possum act. So stupid." He pinched Sid's cheek. "Huh, you're that gal from the shooting range. The nosey one. You know you got your friend killed, don't you?"

Sid kicked at him.

"Oh, ho, ho," Oliver said. "Now, now. You don't want to do that … Sid, isn't it?"

Her eyes widened.

"Of course we know who you are, Agent—well, former Agent Shaw. We do our homework." He cocked his head and eyed her. "I thought you'd be a lot more tomboy, though. So, this is probably going to hurt worse than I first figured it would."

"What do you mean?" she asked.

He slugged her in the belly.

"Oof!" Sid sagged down to her knees.

"Quit playing around, Oliver," Warren said. "Just take care of the other one. We'll deal with her later."

Oliver shrugged. "Sure. Sure. I was just softening her up a bit. Besides, AV and Night Bird were my friends." He walked over and picked up the sniper rifle. He charged the chamber and stepped into the firing line of Smoke.

The rangy man was gone.

Oliver grunted.

"Well, go and get him," Warren said. "I can smell his scent. Get on it!"

"I am on it." Oliver marched forward.

Smoke stepped out from behind the front side of the burning car. His head was bleeding and he held his side. "Let her go," he said.

"Oh, he likes you," Warren said in her ear. "He wants to play hero. Dead men can't be heroes." He yelled over at Smoke, "I don't think you're in any position to negotiate, Mr. Smoke. You should have stayed in prison."

Smoke shuffled forward. "You don't want us. You have bigger things to deal with. Let her go. She's harmless."

"You're both harmless," Warren said. "At least that's what the others thought. No, I think it's time to finish you off, Mr. Smoke, but I think they have other plans for her."

"What do you mean," Sid said, "for me?"

"You'll find out soon enough. Oliver, just kill him."

The assassin slicked back his jet-black hair under his palm, hefted the weapon up to his shoulder, and aimed. "Bye-bye." He squeezed.

CHAPTER 23

S MOKE DOVE RIGHT.

The bullet exploded somewhere in the forest.

"How'd he do that?" Oliver said. "It's impossible."

Smoke charged through the pouring rain and slammed into Oliver. The two big men went down. Smoke clocked Oliver in the jaw. In the ribs. Oliver Ratson roared and countered with a flurry of his own. Then the two men were locked up. Warriors with fire-lit eyes slugging it out with everything they had.

"Oh, this will be fun. For a moment," Warren said in her ear. "Your friend will put up a good fight. Then, his lungs will burn like fire. Feel like they burst inside his chest. He'll be unable to move his limbs at some point, and then my brother will grind him into the dust. He should have just let Oliver shoot him."

"Don't be so sure about that," Sid said. "He's killed your ilk before. I'm sure he'll kill them again."

"You had help before. You don't have it now, foolish girl."

A glint of sharp metal appeared in Smoke's hand. He jabbed it into the back of Oliver's knee.

Oliver howled and staggered backward. He had a limp now. A bad one. If Sid were to guess, Smoke had torn out a tendon. "Looks like that hurt," Sid said. "Do you want to put a wager on it?"

Warren applied more pressure on her neck with his forearm. "Don't aggravate me, mortal."

Wary eyed, Oliver circled Smoke. "I'm gonna take that knife and gut you with it."

"Please," Smoke said, "by all means, try."

With a roar, Oliver charged. He sprang the last few feet like a wild beast pouncing on its prey.

Smoke leap-frogged the man, landed on his feet, turned, and pounced on Oliver's back. He drove the blade deep into Oliver's long neck. The huge man's muscular body went limp.

"No!" Warren yelled. He shoved Sid hard to the ground and glared at Smoke. "You will pay!"

"What's the matter?" Smoke said, rising back up to his feet. "Can't your brother handle a severed spinal cord?" Smoke waggled the knife. "You see, I'm quite the surgeon. Now, why don't you come over here and try to take the knife from me?"

Warren edged closer. "All you've had is a stroke of luck, but your luck has just run out." Warren coiled back like a predator ready to spring.

A helicopter buzzed overhead. *Wuppa-wuppa-wuppa-wuppa …*

A voice came over the loudspeaker. "This is the FBI."

Warren looked up and sighed. "Yadda, yadda, yadda."

The chopper landed between the black Mustang and the road leading to the dock. FBI agents with assault rifles poured out of the chopper. A swarm of FBI vehicles blockaded the other side of the road. In seconds, Sid, Smoke, the burning Hellcat, and the Buffalo Brothers were surrounded.

Warren raised his arms over his head. "You got me, little G-men." He looked at his brother. "Get up, Oliver."

With a grunt, Oliver pushed himself up off the pavement. He cracked his neck from side to side and glared at Smoke. "That hurt," he said, spinning in a circle without a limp. "Next time—and there will be a next time—leave the knife in."

The Buffalo Brothers dropped to their knees and locked their fingers behind their heads. Warren glanced at Sid as they cuffed him. "See you around, girl."

She watched the agents bind up their hands and legs. They even put muzzles over their mouths and covered their faces. *That's really odd.* She breathed a little easier, but she wondered how many agents understood what they were dealing with. *Where are they taking them?*

Cyrus and Rachel appeared. He held an umbrella over her head. "You two are finished!"

Sid rolled her eyes.

Cyrus stared at her car and continued. "You're both too smart for your own good. I put a trace on your car when I gave you the assignment on Winslow Swift." He glared at Smoke. "I figured you knew more than you were telling. And as I suspected, you led us right to the Buffalo Brothers." He pointed at Smoke. "You're done, mister."

"It sounds to me like you got just what you wanted," Sid interjected. "So what's the problem?"

"The problem, Sid, is that he, like you, hindered our investigation and apprehension of two known murderers!"

"It's all a coincidence," Smoke said, putting away his knife. He rubbed the bruise on his jaw. "Dumb luck. We just came down here to go fishing."

"Have fun fishing another five years out of your prison toilet bowl, jerk!" Rachel's face went oddly calm then, and she turned and whispered something into Cyrus's ear.

He motioned a couple agents over. He pointed at Smoke. "Cuff him." He pointed at Sid. "Cuff her. Throw them in the van and get them the hell out of my sight."

"Will you get off it, Cyrus!" Sid said. "We still have to report everything that went down. You need to know the details. You can't just fill in the blanks yourself."

"You can do it later!"

"Boy, when did you become such a yeller?" she said, getting cuffed.

"Since I had to start putting up with you!" he pointed at her, "and you!" he pointed at Smoke. He rubbed his temple. "Just go. Get them out of my sight."

"Hey, I have to get my niece," Sid yelled, fighting against the agents. "Cyrus. You've got to get off this. Please."

Rachel whispered in his ear again.

Cyrus said, "Don't worry, I'll let Child Protective Services handle it."

CHAPTER 24

SITTING IN THE BACK OF the FBI van, Smoke said to Sidney, "Sorry."

She was turned away facing the window, which was being splattered by pouring rain. She didn't want to talk. She was mad. He'd pulled one of his stunts, and it had failed. Now she had no way of getting ahold of Megan—or anyone, for that matter. Her hands were literally tied. Not to mention, her car was gone.

I hate him.

"I know you hate me," he continued. "I figured we would nip this in the bud. Of course, when I went down into that tube, well, it was just kind of awesome. You see, it worked like a drainpipe, or one of those pools with an infinity edge. The water just gushed right over it, and into a tunnel I went. It reminded me of the Bat Cave."

"Just shut up," she said to Smoke, shivering. "Hey!" she said to the front seat. "Do you think you could turn the air conditioning down? I'm freezing."

The agents didn't respond. Their eyes were frozen on the road ahead.

"You have insurance, don't you?" Smoke said, trying to sound positive.

"Sure, I'll just tell them I lost my car to an exploding bullet."

"Well, it should qualify as a catastrophic accident." He cleared his throat. "You can use my Camaro while I'm back in prison. No problem. But I only have liability on it, so be careful."

She turned and gave him a deadly look. "Be careful? You turned my life upside down by being stupid. I don't know what I was thinking."

"At least the assassins are off the street, and we unveiled another one of their secret lairs." He pushed his hair back. "I think those ships are loaded with smuggled goods. It's going to cause them a problem with distribution."

"It's under water. Don't you think they'll just flood it?"

Smoke shrugged. "I guess that's what I would do."

"Hey, I need you guys to make a phone call for me. Just one," she said to the agents driving the van. "I'm begging you. Please."

"You need to keep silent," said the agent in the passenger side, a woman. She flashed a Taser that zapped with blue light. "I'm dying to use this."

Sid's chin dipped. She couldn't let Megan wind up with Child Protective Services. It would take weeks, maybe months to get her back. Megan would be distraught. Hands cuffed in front of her, Sid balled up her fists and started hitting Smoke. "You idiot! You idiot! You idiot!"

"Hey, I told you to shut it!" said the female agent. She came back at Sid, Taser ready.

Smoke grabbed the Taser and zapped the woman. Smooth as a cat, he slid into the passenger seat and slugged the driver, knocking him out cold, unbuckling him, and flinging him back at Sid. He took command of the van. "Unlock yourself and let's roll."

Sid found the keys and uncuffed herself. She checked the agents. Both were breathing easy. "Have you gone mad?"

"You know this doesn't feel right," he said, looking at her in the rearview mirror. "Right?"

She couldn't ignore the pit in her gut. Cyrus, stiff necked as he could be, wasn't himself. "Wrong!" She jumped into the passenger seat. "Stop breaking the law!"

"Sure. Look, let's go get Megan, all right? It will be a great field trip."

"I'm sure the FBI will be expecting us, once these two fail to check in," she said.

"We'll find a way." He ran the van up the highway entrance ramp.

Sid settled back in her seat, picking at her lip. All her plans had turned to disaster. She was a better planner than this. *Who cares about the Buffalo Brothers? Who cares about any of this?* "So, you know what school Megan's in?"

"Uh, yep. Unless it's changed recently."

"Fine."

Flying down the road, it took twenty agonizing minutes to make it to the school. Sid, still wet from head to toe, rushed inside. Megan was waiting in the gym. Ignoring all the strange looks, she signed Megan out, saying to the lady, "I left my umbrella at home."

Outside in the parking lot, Smoke pulled up in the FBI van.

"Where's the Hellcat?" Megan asked.

"Somebody killed it," Sid said. Looking the confused little girl in the eyes, she added, "Megan, you trust me, right?"

"Of course."

"Well, get inside and don't ask any questions." She opened up the passenger door and pushed Megan inside. Smoke pulled out of the parking lot and shot out onto the main road.

"Hey, Smoke!" Megan said.

"Hey, Megan."

"So, what's up with the van?" the girl said, looking everywhere. And then she saw the bodies in the back and screamed.

CHAPTER 25

T HEY DITCHED THE FBI VAN in a hotel parking lot and caught a ride on a city bus. Sidney had done her best to explain to Megan everything that was going on. The little girl, somewhat distraught, quietly nodded. It had taken some convincing to show her that the FBI agents in the back were alive and just knocked out.

"I'm hungry," Megan said. She sat with her backpack clutched on her lap. Sid sat beside her, and Smoke sat across from them, staring out the windows. "Can we eat soon?"

"Sure. Just a little longer," Sid said. *I'm a horrible aunt. Horrible.* She didn't have any of her gear. No gun. No phone. No connections. Nothing. She felt powerless. Across from her, Smoke looked at ease. He caught her staring at him. "The bus was a good idea," she said.

"Thanks. And don't worry about money. I borrowed from those agents." He looked at Megan. "So we'll get you whatever you want to eat."

Even Sid was relieved. And hungry. She put her arm over Megan's little shoulders and kissed her head. Taking the bus was a good idea. It took them off the grid. Away from the cameras and other prying eyes. It also gave them something they needed: time. She scanned the bus again. There were only a handful of other people on it. A young woman with two toddlers and a sack full of groceries. An older black fellow who mumbled a lot. A pair of old women wearing scarves on their heads and speaking Italian.

It didn't make for bad company. But the bus driver, a heavy fella with nervous eyes, stared back at them in his mirror from time to time. She and Smoke certainly weren't his typical fares. Soaked, cut, bruised, and swollen, they looked far from their best. She'd be suspicious, too.

"What are you thinking, Sid?" Smoke said.

"I think I should call Ted."

"It's your play. If I were in your shoes, I'd do the same, but …"

His conditional word jolted her. She knew what was coming.

"… they'll probably expect that."

"They're going to find us. I need some kind of dialogue with somebody, and it has to be Ted. He's the only one I can trust. I think."

"You can trust me," Megan said, looking up into her eyes.

"I know I can." She stroked the little girl's hair. "I know I can."

They remained on the bus until the first wave of passengers got off and another one got on. That's when the bus driver said to them, "This isn't a tour. Are you going somewhere or not?"

"Are we committing a crime?" Smoke said to him.

"No," the driver answered.

"Then shut up and drive."

The bus driver stiffened in his seat.

"Aunt Sid, I'm really hungry. Really bad."

"Okay, Honey. Here's fine!" she said to the bus driver.

They all exited the bus into the rain and dashed up the sidewalk and into a café. It was humid inside, and plenty of people were in there avoiding the rain. The three of them crammed into a small booth made for two people. A waitress came by and said, "I'll be with you soon. Sorry, I'm the last one on duty."

"So, did you borrow any change?" Sid asked Smoke.

He slid some coins over.

"Get her something to eat." Sid got up and made her way toward the back, down the corridor to the bathrooms. A pay phone hung on the wall in between them. She dropped the coins in and dialed.

A young woman with pretty nails walked by and gave Sid an odd look.

She probably doesn't know what this thing does.

The phone rang. "Uh, hello?" said a woman on the other end of the line.

"Sadie, it's Sid."

The woman's voice was very excited. "What are you doing? I was wondering if you were ever going to call me. So, let me guess, no let me hope, you found a man and you want me to be the maid of honor in your wedding."

"No."

"Oh, well then I have to go."

"Wait, Sadie, this is important."

"It is? So you're calling to apologize, then?"

"Apologize," Sid said, "for what?"

"That's what I thought. Click."

"Did you just fake hang up on me?" Sid asked.

"Yes."

"Okay, I'm sorry. I should have called. Stopped by. Please forgive me."

"Hmmm, well, that's better. So, what do you want?"

"You don't know I'm back in the thick of this stuff?"

"What stuff?"

"My old stuff. I'm an FBI liaison now. Supposedly, but things are a bit upside down."

"Go on."

"Listen carefully. Being discreet, I need you to get a message to Ted. Avoid Jane, his secretary—and avoid Cyrus and Rachel if they happen to come in."

"Oh, that won't be a problem," Sadie said. "I'll tell you what, ever since you left, that Rachel acts like she's running the place. She has most of these three-legged hounds wrapped around her finger." She huffed. "They act like a bunch of horny puppy dogs."

"Sadie!"

"It's true. Now, I'll get the message to Ted. What is it?"

CHAPTER 26

TWO HOURS HAD PASSED SINCE Sidney had gotten off the phone with Sadie. Three empty plates sat on the café table flanked by four empty milkshake glasses. Sid picked at her lip. Megan was asleep against her side.

"I don't like this," Smoke said. His eyes were narrow and wary. "He should have been here by now."

"I'm sure he's being cautious," Sid said.

The waitress walked up to the table and refilled her coffee. "Aw, how sweet," the woman said, glancing at Megan. "Can I get you anything else?"

"No, we're fine," Smoke said. After the waitress left, he added, "I don't suppose we can consider this a date."

"After you destroyed my car? No, I don't think so."

"I didn't destroy it."

"Let's not get into it." She locked her eyes on his. "I need you to tell me something. The truth."

He leaned forward. "Okay. What?"

"How did you dodge that bullet?"

"Oh." He leaned back. "Well, that's just really good anticipation. I have a knack for it. And it wasn't point blank. I was fifteen yards away, at least."

His answer didn't satisfy her. She grabbed his forearm and squeezed. "Look, John. I don't have a lot of faith in people. Not lately, anyways. I need you to be straight with me. Are you like them?"

"Like who?"

"You know who. People with powers. Extra senses. I've seen you do some things that seem superhuman."

He made a smile. "I am pretty impressive, aren't I?"

"I'm not toying around with you, John."

"I'm not toying around with you, either. Sid, you can count on me. I swear I'm not one of those freaks." He sucked some residual milkshake out of a straw. "Sure, I'm gifted. I've always been. And sometimes I get carried away and venture a little too close to danger, but I can handle it. At least I think I can. And I'm sorry that I put you and Megan in danger. But I'm not one of those people. Let God strike me down if I am."

Her breathing eased. If anything, she felt a little sorry for Smoke. He was odd. Not one to fit in easily, even though he had his charms. He probably saw right through people. He probably knew exactly what they were before they even opened their mouths. Staring into his dark eyes, a thought occurred to her. *I feel like he knows what I'm thinking.* She let go of his arm.

He caught her hand in his. It was warm. Strong. Just what she needed. "Sid, I've come to a conclusion about something."

She tried to gently pull away, but he held her fast. His handsome eyes were caught up in hers. "About what?"

"Us. The truth is, every day I think about you. And when I saw you again yesterday, I realized that I didn't want to go another day without seeing your face."

She swallowed before she found something to say. "Now's not a good time for us. I mean, this. Don't do this to me,

John." Her heart tapped like a hammer inside her chest. She wanted him, and he'd just confessed he wanted her. "We have to get out of this mess first."

"Life will always be a mess. And without this mess, I never would have met you."

She squeezed his hand. Her body became hot, her breath bated. "Not now. The timing's bad. And you'll be going back to prison. I'll probably be going to prison. Please, Smoke, don't make my life harder than it already is."

"You can count on me. Let me help make it better."

She wanted to curl up in his muscular arms and bury her face in his. Her body was a flame. It was clear now, in her heart, in her mind, that she wanted him as much as he wanted her. "I-I need time to think."

"Go with your heart."

"I—"

Smoke released her hand. The connection was broken. He leaned back in his seat and eyed the entrance to the café.

She turned.

Section Chief Ted Howard was coming. There were deep creases in his forehead, and he was sweating. He pulled a chair up to their table. "I don't know what in the hell is going on. I swear it." He touched Sid's shoulder. "Are you all right?"

She filled Ted in on everything, from the time he'd left that satellite office up to now. Glancing at Smoke from time to time, she noticed a lonely expression on the hardened soldier's face. He seemed lost. Almost alone.

"Sid, I'm going to make some calls and get this cleared up. In the meantime, go rest. Go home. Take care of the little one." He eyed Smoke. "As for you, well, I don't know. The Buffalo Brothers are in custody. I can only imagine interrogations will begin soon. At least they're secured, but we need their target. There's a lot of people still nervous about it. Rumor is the Buffalo Brothers might have been a decoy."

"What does that have to do with me?" Smoke asked.

"You'll probably be going back in the hole. Sorry for the expression."

"My time better be shortened."

"I'll find out. I'll find out." Ted took out a handkerchief and mopped the sweat off his head. "I swear, I'm having the worst time figuring out where the orders are coming from. I'm told to do one thing and Cyrus and that little witch do another."

"Get rid of her, Ted," Sid insisted. "You know what effect people like that have on the team. She's a cancer. It might be hard, but you have to get rid of her."

"I know. I know." He shook his head. His hands clutched in and out.

The waitress walked up and asked if he wanted something.

He said, "No thank you." He gazed at Sid. "I don't think there is anything I can do to her, Sid. I don't even know how she got hired. Her personnel file's nonexistent, but she's on the payroll somehow."

The little bell on the café door rang.

Smoke rose to his feet.

Sid looked around the booth.

A tall blonde woman in leather pants and a black jacket stood with her back to them. She locked the door and turned the Open sign around. Then she started closing the blinds. That's when Sid realized they were the only ones left inside the café except for the waitress and the man behind the grill.

"Hey," the waitress said to the woman. "What are you doing?"

The woman turned around and stuck a gun barrel in the woman's face. "I'm here for a reunion."

CHAPTER 27

"**D**EANNE!" TED SAID IN ASTONISHMENT.

Deanne Drukker. The imposing blonde was striking, her voice full of authority. "Have a seat, princess," she said to the waitress. The woman scurried into a booth, hands up. Deanne said to the man behind the kitchen counter, "Don't make me say it, dough boy."

The man scurried into the booth alongside the waitress. "The money's in the regist—"

Deanne stuck the gun barrel on his nose. "I'm not here to rob you, stupid. Didn't you hear? It's a reunion. And listen, boy, don't think I haven't killed people for being stupid." She kept the gun on him and turned her attention to Ted and Smoke. "And the rest of you sit tight. I talk. You listen."

"It's good to see you, Deanne," Ted said, gathering his composure. "What's on your mind?"

"You look older, Ted. Older and fatter. What did I tell you about all the snacks?"

"You said 'They'll make you old and fat.'"

"And I was right," she said. She rapped the butt of her gun on the table. "Wasn't I?"

"Yes! Yes!" said the waitress and grill cook, nodding their heads feverishly.

"Boy, it sure is a nasty day out there. I hate coming out on nasty days. Now I'm all wet and sticky." She took off her jacket, revealing nothing but a tank top. She was built, with well-defined muscles. "It pisses me off. I don't like coming out into the city. Especially to do shit like this."

"Maybe you should have brought an umbrella," Smoke said.

"Shut up, John. Pain in my ass number one. Well, actually, in today's case, it's number two." Deanne looked at Sidney. "You know, you had a good thing going, girl, but you had to stick your big nose back in it. You even got your sister's little girl all involved. Stupid. Plain old stupid. And I was beginning to think you were smarter than that." She waved the gun around. "But I have to hand it to Allison. She was right. You had a way out, and you jumped right back in it."

"So my sister's doing well?" Sid said.

"She's doing great." Deanne moved through the room and lined up on a view of Megan. The little girl was fast asleep. "She's longing for her baby, though. It's tough."

"You aren't taking her, Deanne."

"Oh, if I want to, I will, but be at ease. That's not why I'm here." She moved over to the counter and hopped up onto it. "You see, our boys, Warren and Oliver. Well, they won't talk. In less than twenty-four hours, they'll be out. And soon after that, someone is going to die. And you all need to let them do their job or else there will be more casualties. Take those two nitwits that work here."

The waitress let out a sob.

"Oh, don't cry. You aren't worth the bullet," Deanne said.

"What happened to you, Deanne?" Ted said. "You were one of us. One of the good guys. Now you're a megalomaniac."

"I enjoy megalomania. Living life without a conscience is so…" She cast her eyes up for a moment. "…liberating."

"So you're liberated," Ted said, "because you help people die."

"Oh, Ted, you wouldn't understand." She walked over and squeezed his shoulders. "Your heart's too big. Just too big. Like your belly."

Sid held Megan a little tighter. Deanne had an air about her. Like the Buffalo Brothers. Fierce. Fearless. She noticed a bead of sweat running down from Ted's hairline. *There's something else going on between them. He's scared.*

"So here's what's going to happen, boys and girls," Deanne continued. "Because I'm not a complete devil, I'm going to make you an offer. Forget about the Black Slate. Move on. Do something else and live. Keep at it and die."

"I didn't ask for the assignment," Ted said, pushing her hands away. "I don't think any of us did. And you know how it works. *They* choose you. And you don't have much of a choice in the matter."

"*They* are a problem, but I don't have any sympathy for your dilemma. Just think about it. Your family. Your friends. Their lives are on the line." Deanne shrugged. "Look, I'm here as a courtesy. You'd be wise to consider it a favor."

"I'd say you're here because we're getting too close to something," Smoke said. He pulled his shoulders back. "You're cocky. Why don't you just come out and tell us what that is?"

"Well, that's super-top-secret information, John." She gave him a little smile. "If you really want me to share it, I'll play your game, but I'll have to clear the room."

"Fine by me," Smoke said.

Sid's nerves fired. Deanne turned her gun on the waitress and fry cook. Sid tensed to spring. Ted plowed into Deanne and tackled her to the floor. The waitress and fry cook rushed for the door. Gunshots rang out. Bullets burst through glass.

"Get off me, Ted. I'm warning you," Deanne growled, fighting against the big man who had her pinned to the floor.

"Those are innocent people," he said, half spitting. "Are you mad?"

"Yeah," Deanne sneered, "I'm mad!" *Blam! Blam! Blam!*

Ted's large form sagged. His blood leaked onto the floor.

Megan screamed.

CHAPTER 28

DEANNE SPRANG BACK TO HER feet. Smoke crashed into her. He wrenched the gun from Deanne's hand and locked her up in an arm bar.

Lip bleeding, she started a nasty laugh. "You better save your friend Ted. Poor old guy. I used to like him."

Sid was on her knees. She rolled Ted over. His hands were clamped over his bleeding gut. Blood seeped through his fingers. His face was in torment. "Are they safe?" he said, spitting blood.

The waitress and fry cook were gone.

"Yes," Sid said, half choking.

Ted's eyes were glassing over.

"Hang on Ted, please, hang on."

"Fight the good fight, Sid," Ted said, spitting more blood. "Don't let those devils win."

Sid squeezed his hand.

"Such a sad thing to see. A decent man dying over a couple of nobodies," Deanne said. "Never understood it much myself. It's time you released me, Johnny Boy, if you know what's good for you."

"You aren't going anywhere," Smoke growled. "You're a murderer."

"Attempted murder on those sock puppets maybe. But I think in this case, it was self-defense. Oh well." She spoke something that sounded like German. The metal bands on her wrists lit up. A spark came out of her body.

Smoke jerked and spasmed. His grip on Deanne loosened.

The formidable woman slipped free of his grasp and drove the heel of her boot into his calf several times.

Smoke lay on the floor twitching.

As Sidney applied pressure to Ted's belly, Deanne retrieved her gun.

Walking casually over to Sidney, Deanne held the barrel on her head. "You need to let it soak in, what happened here this evening. Next time it could be you, your family, your friends." She cast a glance down at Ted's dying face. A glimmer of sadness was in Deanne's eyes. "I always liked him, but he was always kinda stupid."

"You're sick," Sid said. Her eyes swelled with water. "There's a special place for people like you."

"I know," Deanne said, backing away. "It's called the top." Police sirens squalled from outside in the streets. "Time to go. Sorry it ended this way, but maybe this was the plan all along." She backed toward the rear door of the building.

Sid felt Ted's hand find hers. Somehow, he stuffed his gun into her hand. His voice was barely a whisper. "Take her down. That's an order."

"Good-bye, Sid," Deanne said, still pointing her gun at Sid's chest. "Remember, stay away from this." Deanne turned and started to vanish into the back corridor.

Sid ripped out Ted's gun and unloaded several shots. *Blam! Blam! Blam! Blam!* She sprang to her feet and gave chase: down the hall, through the back door, and into the alley. Deanne was gone. Disappeared. Looking down, she noticed blood in the alley. *Damn! I shouldn't have missed. I shouldn't have missed.*

"You're lucky, Sid! Lucky!" Cyrus said, tapping his finger on the table. "But thanks to you, Ted is gone. How do you feel about that?"

Sitting inside an interrogation room painted with army-green walls, Sidney finished writing down the details of the incident at the café. She wiped a tear off the form and rubbed her eyes. She was hollow inside. Ted C. Howard, FBI section chief, friend, and mentor was gone. Another FBI agent was down, and to another ghost no less.

Cyrus had his sleeves rolled up over his flabby arms. He took his Coke-bottle glasses off his face. He continued his ranting. "Two witnesses saved your bacon. If it weren't for the both of them, I'd have you in jail again. You just can't play by the rules, Sid, can you? You're selfish. Dangerous."

"Shut up, Cyrus," she said in a stone-cold tone. "Everyone is hurting from all of this aside from you, it seems. I just lost one of the few men I trusted. It hurts. Hurts bad. And now you want to rub it in?" She shoved the paper across the desk and glowered at him. "I thought you'd be happy. You'll probably get a promotion."

"Huh," Cyrus said, picking up her statement. "You need to initial here." He set it back down. "Look, I'm mad that Ted is gone." He pulled out a chair and sat down. "I'm mad that you refuse to work with me on the Slate. I'm mad. I'm mad. I'm mad." He took out a handkerchief and cleaned his glasses. "We're supposed to be on the same side, you know? Deanna Drukker. Boy, a psychotic rogue agent." He leaned forward. "You see, Sid? That's what bothers me. What happened to her could happen to you. I'm looking out for you. You need to trust me."

She wanted to believe him. He was an agent, and she wanted to trust agents more than anything. But there were too many unanswered questions, and there was way too much weirdness with Rebecca's ear-whispering. *Let's wait and see how all of this is reported. What the papers say.* Deanne Drukker burned in Sid's mind. The older woman had half enjoyed Ted's death. *Why?* "Cyrus, I know you've always meant well." She paused. "So now what?"

"Well, we have two agents that were assaulted during your little incursion. Again, lucky for you, Mr. Smoke is going to take the fall for all of that. I'd say it's going to add a few more years to his sentence. But you are free to go. And so is Megan."

Her heart stung inside her chest. *This is my fault. All my fault.* She wanted to help. Be involved in the fight. But now Big Jake was dead. Ted was dead. Smoke was gone again. "So I'm not a liaison anymore?"

"It's early, Sid. Nothing is official yet. And you know there will be a ton of paperwork to follow." He leaned back. "I'd assume it's done, though."

"What about the Buffalo Brothers?" she said. "Deanne said they'd be out in a day. That they'd get their target one way or the other."

"Don't you worry about that."

"But I'm still official, aren't I?"

Cyrus's eyes narrowed on her. "You need to take Megan and back away from this thing."

"And if I don't?"

"Then I can have Child Protective Services over here right away."

CHAPTER 29

FBI AGENT SLAIN IN ATTEMPTED **Robbery**. That's what was all over the news the day after the incident. The story was nice and neat. It made Ted Howard out to be a hero. There were crystal-clear statements from the waitress and fry cook. It all added up. No one would suspect a thing.

Sidney set the remote down on the coffee table. It was about 6:30 a.m. Megan was still asleep in her bed. The little girl had cried until she soaked her pillow. Sidney had finally gotten her to sleep just before midnight by gently caressing her hair. Sid had been up ever since.

Why me?

All night long, she had rehashed everything. Doubted everything she'd done since high school. She was smart. She could have been anything. Why a cop? It was hard on families. Death and danger lurked at every traffic stop, routine building check, and simple apprehension. People were desperate. It made them deadly. Sidney was drawn to it.

I'm a foolish little girl.

She got up and poured another cup of coffee. She couldn't help but think of Ted's wife. His children. The funeral would be miserable. The tears would flow in streams. Her throat tightened. Her eyes swelled. She couldn't bear it. She made her way into the second bedroom. Megan lay on her back with her teddy bear tucked under her arm. Her chest gently rose and fell.

We should move south. To the beaches.

Back inside her living room, Sid turned on the television again. It was all bad news. Muggings. Murder. Scandal.

Mayhem. "Fight the good fight." Those were some of Ted's last words. There had been power in them. An intense look in his fatherly eyes. He believed in what they did. What she did. She felt that in her gut. Ted used to say, "You know you're doing something right when you start pissing rotten people off."

But I don't want all this blood on my hands.

While she stared at the television, a familiar face came up. Her stomach soured. It was Congressman Wilhelm. Finely dressed and well manicured, he was a little pudgier than the last time she had seen him. His eyes had dark circles under them, and he sweated under the camera's light. He was accompanied by his son and two Secret Service agents.

"Agent Ted C. Howard," Wilhelm said, "was a dear friend of mine. A banner of law enforcement. Everything right with fine government agencies like the FBI. Let's pray that his colleagues and their associates bring the fugitive murderer to justice. My thoughts and prayers are with his family." He straightened his jacket. "Now, if you'll excuse me, I need to get to session. We've got an important bill to push through." He gave a thumbs up and walked away with his entourage in tow.

Snake.

Her sister Allison had come home battered from her last job with Congressmen Wilhelm. Defiant. Angry. It was people like Wilhelm that put people like her sister in bad places. They made promises to them then preyed on them. It was disgusting.

Now, for some odd reason, Sidney took comfort from knowing that her sister was safe with the Drake. Or perhaps it was more accurate to say Allison was just where she wanted to be: among the powerful. Standing alongside the ones calling the shots. Maybe they gave her the protection she needed. The attention that Allison always craved.

No. That's not what is best. But it's her choice. I have to help make a better life for Megan. Somehow.

She curled up on her couch and started to reassess things.

Put it together, Sid. You have to make sense of this. Did everyone die because of me? If I'm the problem, then why don't they just take me out? I'm just one person.

There was something Cyrus always said that irked her. Well, just about everything he said irked her, but there was one thing in particular. He said she led a charmed life. That she was lucky.

She never felt any more special than anyone else. Sure, she moved ahead of some people and excelled at many things, but she never thought of herself as special. It wasn't as if she used her looks to get away with things like Allison, although Sid knew being pretty did help her from time to time.

But when Cyrus said "charmed," it always felt like he meant Sid had an advantage that went beyond just being pretty.

Megan entered the room. She wore pink pajamas with cartoon characters on them. She yawned and stretched out her arms. "What's for breakfast?"

"Whatever you want."

"Pancakes and chocolate milk," Megan said. She shuffled over and snuggled up to Sidney on the couch. "I had a lot of bad dreams last night."

Sidney pulled her little niece closer. "I'm sorry. Is it anything you want to tell me?"

"Not until after I eat." Megan looked up into Sid's eyes. "I'm sorry your friend died."

"Me too." Sid kissed Megan's head. "Me too. I'm sorry you had to see that. Do you feel like going to school today?"

"You mean I have an option?"

"Of course. After all, yesterday was a bad day, and you probably didn't sleep well."

Megan yawned again. "No. School's fine. I have a math test, and there's a mobile petting zoo coming in for a visit. I want to see the llama. They make the funniest faces."

"Like this?" Sid contorted her lips and made a funny face.

Megan burst out in giggles.

Sid tickled the little girl and kept making the face.

"Stop it! Stop it, Aunt Sid!" Megan cried, laughing.

"All right," Sid said. She pulled Megan out of the couch pillows and dragged her to her feet. She gave her a big hug. "Now get ready. We'll swing by the Country Kitchen and eat there."

Megan's eyes widened. "Before school?"

"Yep."

"Yay!" Megan vanished into the bedroom.

Taking a breath, Sid turned off the television and drank down more coffee. *Now that's a much better way to start your day.*

Heading for the kitchen with her empty mug, she heard a knock at her door. Slowly, she turned. On cat's feet, she made her way to the door and put her eye to the spy hole. Sadie stood on the other side. Sid opened the door.

Sadie burst in with tears in her eyes. She sounded a little hysterical. "What happened? You need to tell me what happened!"

CHAPTER 30

S ADIE WAS DRESSED IN A tunic dress that hung just above the knees. She was an older black woman, always well dressed, and her decorated nails rivaled Sam's finest work. Right now Sadie's eyes were all puffy. She sat down on the sofa and blew her nose.

"Why, Sid? Why did you call me? I sent Ted to his death." Sadie sobbed. "I can't get over it. I read the paper and, and …" She blew her nose. "I knew it was my fault."

"Sadie, he was just in the wrong place at the wrong time."

The woman stiffened. Her eyes fastened on Sidney. "Don't you lie to me, Sid. Don't you dare lie to me. I'm not stupid."

"I know. But the news …"

"Don't you think I can put two and two together?" Sadie grabbed Sid by the arm. "You call. He dies. And with everything going on since you left, it makes perfect sense." Her eyes started to water again. "And now I'm part of this mess. I have to live with it." She fell forward into Sidney's arms and started sobbing. "I can't do this. I can't do this. They're going to come after me. I only have ten months, and I can retire."

Sidney felt like her chest was going to collapse. She'd gotten another friend into the crosshairs. "I don't think they're going to ask you anything."

"Why do you say that?"

"They'll move on," Sid said.

"How do you know?" Sadie leaned back and straightened up her dress. Using the tissue, she wiped her eyes. "I couldn't even get my makeup on. Now, out with it."

"Don't get mad at me for saying this—"

"Oh, I'm already mad."

"The less you know, the better."

"Huh, I figured." Sadie studied Sid's face. "You know who killed him, don't you. You were there, I bet. This whole thing is all a charade, isn't it?"

Sidney's eyes drifted away.

"Look at me," Sadie ordered.

"Not just this. A lot of things."

The room fell silent. Finally, Sadie said, "I knew it was all a bunch of horseshit. Heck, I've always known. I could feel it in my bones." She cupped Sid's cheek. "Aw, I'm sorry, Sid. I know you'll miss Ted. I'll miss him, too. He always brought me flowers on Secretaries' Day." She shuddered a sigh. "I think he knew too much. He was acting kinda nervous the last few weeks. Almost jittery. Man, I just wish it was Cyrus or that little vixen of his, Rebecca. There ain't nothing good in that one. It took me some time to figure that out, though. She's crafty like a bad Beastie Boys song."

Sid cracked a smile. "You know, I don't think Ted would want us to be whining around. Why don't you come with me and Megan to get something to eat?"

"Well, I'm not really hungry."

"Could you at least give us a lift? It's either that or a cab."

"What happened to your car?"

Sid headed for her bedroom. "I'll tell you on the way over."

Days later, Sid was lying in her bed staring at the ceiling. She wondered if she had told Sadie too much. She had held back as much as she could, but Sadie was pushy. Smart. She'd put it all together before she backed off. *I hope she's okay.*

Megan was in school. Sid had rented a car for the weekend and used it to go to Ted Howard's funeral. That had been a long, hot, miserable, rainy day. It had made her think of Jack Dydeck, her old supervisor who'd had his head ripped off by AV the wolf man. Jack's wife had been at the funeral alongside Ted's, with their kids in tow. Some young. Some old. All of their faces long, with not a single dry eye.

I live. They die. Charmed life.

She rolled onto her side and checked the clock. It was 9:40 a.m. She had no place to be. No word from Cyrus. There was just silence. A dead quiet that made her question whether she was even alive at the moment. She lay back down and rubbed her temples.

Maybe I should go for a run? Maybe I should go drink?

She ran through a mental checklist. Smoke was gone. The Hellcat was gone. Ted's murderer, Deanne Drukker, was gone. Someone needed to find that woman. Make her pay. Deanne had been so cold and calm after what she'd done. Soulless. *Is that what's in store for Allison? Can she be saved?*

"You can't save someone who doesn't want to be saved." Sid's dad, Keith, had told her that when she was a girl. He'd arrested so many people and had tried to help countless faces. He wanted to help get their lives back on track. But almost all of them didn't want to dig themselves out of the hole. No amount of convincing could change that. Her sister was like that. It was scary. Not even the love Allison must feel for Megan was enough to pull her out of the abyss. So it seemed. Perhaps Deanne Drukker was the same way.

Maybe I should move on.

A battle stirred inside Sid. One side wanted to quit. The other wanted to fight. Deanne needed to be brought to justice. Murderers and other monsters were running free. Someone had to stop them. She eyed her guns hanging inside the door of her closet.

Bounty hunter by day, babysitter by night?

Quickly she got up off the bed and made her way to the closet door. She checked her wallet. It still had her FBI liaison card. She had some access left. Some authority. Maybe Cyrus was wrong or lying. He just wanted her away from the case, but if anyone had answers, it would be him. *Him and that little snake, Rebecca.*

She strapped on her shoulder holster and gun. "That's better." She got a little bit of a charge from it. A feeling of wholeness. She picked up her phone from the nightstand and sent out a text to Sam:

"We need eyes and ears on Cyrus and Rebecca," Sid wrote.

A text came back. "We're on it like flies on stink. Glad you're back in the game."

CHAPTER 31

O VER THE NEXT TWO DAYS, Sidney lay low. She kept things routine. She took Megan to school in the silver Dodge Charger she'd rented. She texted with Sam a couple times a day. She paid close attention to the local news, both on TV and on the Internet. She even logged into *Nightfall DC*, but there weren't any new stories. Things were quiet. Oddly so, leaving her too much time to think. She couldn't help but think that the Buffalo Brothers were going to strike.

She pulled the car into the parking lot near the Washington Memorial. Wearing her bright-green-and-black jogging clothes, she donned her headphones and took off at a trot, thinking a few miles would do her some good. She made her way toward the Reflecting Pool and had finished two laps when the phone buzzed. She checked her screen.

The text from Sam read, "Cyrus is headed to Law Park Offices. Murder scene. Bad."

"Morning glory."

On long legs, Sid sprinted back to her car. The Law Park Offices were where Winslow Swift worked. She and Smoke had been assigned to stake it out that day, to keep an eye out for Winslow Swift. She'd pretty much forgotten about him. Now it seemed another mistake had come back to haunt her.

Back at the rental car, she hopped inside and fired up the engine. She noticed a case in the passenger seat. "You've got to be kidding me." The silvery metal case was just like the one she'd gotten before—from Mal Carlson. Glancing around the area, she shook her head and popped open the case.

There was a typewritten note on a small piece of white parchment paper. It said, "You'll probably need this. MC."

A Sweet Heart suit was inside. Special bullets in clips that fit her Glock. A matching pair of razor-sharp knives that would fit her hands. There was even a small bottle with a cork in it. She rattled around the glimmering emerald pill that was inside. It was a little different than the super vitamin she'd taken the last time.

"I'll be damned. Everyone knows what I'm doing but me." She got out her pistol and slapped the clip of green-tipped bullets into it and charged the handle. Looking around, she ducked down in the front seat and started to slip out of her clothes to put on the Sweet Heart suit, saying with a smile, "Why not fight the good fight."

The parking lot at the Law Park Offices was almost empty. People in business attire were filing out of the building. It was more like a fire drill. No one hustled. There wasn't any panic in their voices. Calmly, they chatted among themselves, loaded into their cars, and headed home.

Sid got out of her car and approached a middle-aged woman in a dark-grey business suit. "What happened?"

"The power went out," the lady said, lighting up a cigarette. "They told us all to go home. Heh. I've been here twenty-three years, and I've never had a break like this. Hell, I never even get Christmas Eve off. I'm taking it." She looked Sid up and down. "Uh, you got business?"

"Yep."

"Well, you better reschedule." The woman blew smoke into the air and stared at the misty clouds. A power truck pulled up to the building's curb, and two men in white jumpsuits hopped out and rushed into the building with metal boxes. "I'd hate to be those guys. My bosses are a bunch of real a-holes, if you know what I mean. This'll cost somebody a buttload of money. It's always money." She sucked the cigarette down to the last ash and dropped it. She crushed it with her shoe. "Money, money, money, money. See you around."

Sid made a quick scan of the parking lot. There were only a couple unmarked FBI cars. She was pretty sure the black Navigator near the front was assigned to Cyrus. Some other men and women agents, in plain clothes, had positioned themselves at the corners of the building. The best that she could tell, no one coming out had any idea that somebody had been killed.

Feeling spry in the Sweet Heart suit, she navigated through the people and slipped unnoticed into the building. All of the lights were out, but the daylight illuminated most of the lobby with dim light. She found the directory near the elevators. Sherman Investments was on the top floor. Finding the emergency stairwell, she swung open the door. The emergency lights were on. She jogged up three flights of steps and peeked through the stairwell portal.

The office was dark but not without window light. The secretary's desk was abandoned. A flashlight beam flashed over cubicles deeper in the room.

Sid pushed through the door and quietly closed it behind her. The Sherman Investments lobby was top flight. Leather chairs and sofas. Chocolate marble walls. A waterfall dripped into the pond full of large goldfish. She passed the break room. There was an industrial-sized cappuccino machine. The scent of rich coffee grounds lingered in the air. On cat's feet, she pressed deeper into the facility. There were low voices and rustlings coming from a conference room that was enclosed in glass. Sid's heart skipped. There was blood splattered all over it. A flashlight glared in her eyes.

"Freeze!"

CHAPTER 32

IN A LIGHTNING-QUICK SWIPE, SID knocked the flashlight out of the man's hand. She wrenched his hand behind his back and drove him into the wall. Two more men burst out of the conference room with their guns lowered on her chest. One of them was Cyrus.

"Dammit, Sid!" he said. "What are you doing here?"

"Serving as a liaison," she said.

"I oughta shoot you." He shook his head and holstered his weapon. The other man did the same. "Since you're here, well," he stepped aside, out of the doorway, "be my guest."

She tilted her head to the side. "Really?"

"I don't think it's going to make a difference. Your life is finished anyway."

She walked into the conference room and surveyed the grisly scene. Five bodies sat around in office chairs with buffalo nickels inside their eyes. Four men. One woman. They'd been cut to ribbons. A knife still protruded from one man's chest. Another's neck was shoved backward. The woman had darkening bruises around her neck.

"I don't see Winslow Swift," she said. "So, where's your partner?"

Cyrus was texting someone when he looked up. "Huh? Oh, don't you worry about her. So what do you make of this?"

"Do we have anything other than the bodies? Any video?"

"Power's out."

"The power is out thanks to you."

"Heh. Look, you've seen. Now you can go."

"Just like that?"

"You stuck your nose into it, Sid. Get a sniff, offer some advice, and move on. I don't know what else to tell you."

She noticed a folded letter in the crook of his arm. She snatched it and opened it up to read it out loud. "This is what happens to thieves." There was a Drake stamp on it. "Interesting." She laughed. "He robbed the Drake, and we're worried about it? Excuse me, you're worried about it? So how much did this swindler steal?"

"Uh, Zed," he said to the other agent in the room, "give us a moment." Cyrus watched the man leave and then continued in a low voice, "Over a billion."

"Oh, now that must have hurt. So now the FBI is helping the Drake find their money?"

"No, we are following the money," he said. "And Winslow Swift has it. This is a message. A nasty one."

Her eyes searched the dead bodies. There were signs of torture on all of them. Broken fingers and missing ones as well. Sadistic carnage. "So the Buffalo Brothers came to deliver a message?"

"Er, and to find Winslow," he said with a twitch in his eye. "Naturally."

She knew he was holding back. The FBI, or someone over the FBI, was protecting Winslow for some reason. There was something bigger. Something deeper going on. Watching Cyrus text, she said, "You have Winslow, don't you."

Cyrus kept texting.

She stepped closer and covered his phone with her hand. "Look at me, Cyrus."

He glanced up. His eyes were all jittery. His forehead beaded in sweat. His Adam's apple rolled inside his neck. "I-I don't know what you're talking about."

Sid had never seen Cyrus nervous before. If anything, he had ice in his veins. Perhaps Ted's violent death *had* gotten to him. Perhaps he knew he could be in the crosshairs next. Something was on the man's conscience. Something bad. She decided to play nice. She put a little honey in her voice. "Come on, Cyrus. You've always known that I was trustworthy. And I've never lied to you. It's not like we haven't shared secrets before. Let's be a team again."

He stepped over to the door and closed it, leaving them in a stuffy room filled with the dead. "We have Winslow. We're using him as bait to capture the Buffalo Brothers. *They* want those guys off the Slate. They want them bad." He blotted the sweat from his brow with a handkerchief. He started shaking his head. "I shouldn't have agreed to this. I never should have let her do it." He kicked the chair. "How stupid of me!"

"Let who do what?" Sid said.

"Rebecca was guarding Winslow. Back in the same place we held you." His face filled with strain. His voice cracked. "They took her. They took Winslow." He handed her a cell phone. "Look."

There was a picture on it. Rebecca was bound up in a chair. Her face was bruised and swollen, her blonde hair matted. Two men with knives were in the picture as well, but their heads weren't showing. She moved to the other picture. Winslow was stripped down to his undershirt and lying on the floor. His nose was busted open.

There was a text message: "Return the money or they die."

CHAPTER 33

E VERY MAN HAD A WEAKNESS. Cyrus's was women. He fell too hard for them. He'd fallen hard for Sidney and overdone it. Now that same thing was happening with Rebecca. Sid could see it in his face. He was all torn up inside over it. The same tormented look was on his face like the day she had walked away from him. It tugged at her own heart a little. "We'll get her back," Sid said to Cyrus. "I swear it."

Over the next few hours, they worked with a tactical team. During that time, Cyrus came clean with a few more things.

"Winslow embezzled one billion from the Drake," Cyrus explained. "Sort of. You see, according to Winslow, the money was supposed to be spread out among several political fund-raising organizations. As it turns out, that money never showed up. Instead, it wound up in the Cayman Islands and Switzerland. Maybe some of it's buried in Swaziland, for all I know. Well, May is coming up. Election time, and a whole bunch of incumbents are about to get burned." Standing outside the Law Park Offices, he strapped on his body armor and checked his gun. "So that's why we're involved. I hate to say it, but some congressmen and senators are all up in this, and they aren't happy at all. It's just a damned dirty business. Not what I signed up for." He holstered his gun. "I just want to get Rebecca out of this jam. But Winslow, he's screwed. He has names. They want to either control him or shut him up. I don't know. I just want to get Rebecca out."

The information was a lot for Sid to swallow, but she felt a chuckle inside. The Drake was out a billion in resources. It would cost them power and influence. The dirty politicians were screwed because many of them would be out of jobs. And it was all on account of one greedy little SOB.

The snakes devour each other. How poetic.

Sidney eyed the little case Cyrus had in his hand. Another agent had delivered it an hour earlier. It had a coded chip in it, and on that chip was an account for one billion in bitcoins. "So, if the money's hidden, how'd they scrape up a billion?"

"Huh. I don't even want to know, but clearly Winslow had insurance," Cyrus said. "He had names. I'm pretty sure if anything happens to him, then all of that dirt under the rug is going to be exposed. You'd think they'd kill Winslow, but it's like *Catch 22*. He's their lawyer. If he dies, then I think all their hard work is set back a decade." He almost laughed. "One way or the other, a lot of heads are going to roll because of this." He glanced at Sid. "So, are you sure you want to do this?"

A light rain began to speckle her rental car. The balmy day was unusually cool for this time of year. "I guess this is what liaisons do. Let's deliver the mail. My car or yours?"

The plan was simple. Per the request of the Drake, they were to deliver the chip to Mallows Bay. If everything was in order, Rebecca and Winslow would be released, and everyone could walk away. Sid pulled into the Mallows Bay parking lot. She was surprised Cyrus had let her drive, but he was preoccupied with his phone. He talked. He texted. She wasn't entirely sure who with. It seemed he had access to whoever was calling the shots, but the odd thing was—why was she included? Again, someone knew what she was doing before she did. It ate at her.

The brakes squeaked as she brought the vehicle to a halt at the edge of the Mallows Bay boat ramp. "Are you ready?" she asked Cyrus.

Cyrus rubbed his hands on this thighs. "Why do you think I let you bring your vehicle and not mine?" He coughed out an uncomfortable laugh. "I hope you got the damage waiver on this rental."

Sid studied the choppy waters of the bay full of sunken ships. Now that she knew what she was looking for, her keen eyes could make out the faint outline of a road underneath the water. She peered at the edges of it, envisioning the deaders crawling up onto them. *Come on out so I can run you over.* "All right, let's go."

The car eased into the water, tires almost a foot deep, following a straight line toward the half-sunken tanker. A dozen yards out they were surrounded by the murky waters on all sides. Sid sat up straight in her seat, peering over the edge of the car's hood. The hairs on her arms tingled. A gaping hole appeared in the middle of the bay. A rush of water poured around the tunnel's mouth, spilling into a great vat surrounding the submerged road. It was a marvel. A feat of engineering or something else. Something unnatural. The road moved deeper into the waters.

Cyrus looked at her and said, "I think I'm going to vomit."

"You can swim, right?" Sid asked.

"Yeah. Now why did you have to ask that?"

She made a little smirk and eased on the gas. The car's hood dipped down, and in seconds, they were below the waters and driving through a tunnel of glass or plastic. It was something similar to what Sid had seen at the massive National Aquarium in DC before it closed. There weren't any colorful fish, however, just glimpses of sunken ships in the muddied waters.

After they had driven along at five miles per hour for what seemed a long time, the great tanker's hull appeared. The tunnel led right into its belly. She kept driving, headlights on, into the darkness until some lights appeared ahead. After another thirty yards, they were inside the sunken ship's belly.

Cyrus's mouth dropped open. "You have got to be kidding me."

The inner hull of the ship gleamed with new metal. There were catwalks. Rows of metal shelving. A forklift. A Bobcat bulldozer. Several cars. Sid brought the car to a stop and turned the engine off. She and Cyrus got out. Behind them, a white cargo van with the Drake markings blocked their exit.

"Looks like we're staying for dinner," Sid said. Her thoughts drifted to Megan. *I'm a lousy aunt.*

The van groaned as the big man stepped out the door. It was Warren Ratson, mirrored glasses and all. Coming from the other side was his brother, Oliver. His chin jutted out from his long, crane-like neck. A nasty smirk was on his face. The two imposing men flanked them.

"Time for a patdown," Oliver said, closing in on Sid. "Don't get all excited, pretty girl. My sap doesn't rise like it did in the good ol' days among the living."

She turned her head. His breath was like the rot of the dead. He ran his hands down her shoulders and over her chest and stopped. He took her gun and tossed it aside. "Wouldn't do you any good against us anyway, but there's still a few other warm bodies around." His gruff hands rested on her hips. He swayed a little. "You know, I used to like to dance back in the day. I liked that Chuck Berry's Twist. Ew, what do we have here?" He slipped out the knives she'd pulled out of Mal Carlson's case. He thumbed their edges. "Very nice. I bet I could skin your eyeball with this."

"Or you could cut your tongue out with it," she said.

"Heh-heh," Oliver said. "You've got spirit." He ran the tip of the blade down her cheek, making a paper-thin cut. "It's going to be fun watching you bleed."

CHAPTER 34

SID BALLED UP HER FIST.

Oliver glanced down at her side and said, "Don't get wise, little lady. You'll only bust a nail, and I'll bust you." He slapped her hard on the ass, half lifting her out of her shoes. "You liked that, didn't you."

Sidney lashed out. Turning into a back spin, she drove her elbow into his face. It crushed the cartilage that formed the bridge of his nose.

Oliver staggered back. "What the—"

Sid drove her booted foot into his gut, doubling him over. In a cat-quick move, she leg-swept his feet, knocking him flat onto his back. She heard laughing. Warren Ratson held Cyrus by the neck. His fingers were crushing his throat.

"I could snap it like a chicken's," Warren said. He shook Cyrus. "What a fleck of a man."

Sidney's ears caught a rustle on the metal deck. She turned.

Striking with speed that defied his size, Oliver pounced on top of her. He pinned her down, clamped his hand over her throat, and pulled his fist back to strike.

"That's enough!" A strong feminine voice echoed in the hollow metal chamber. "This is a business transaction. Not a bar fight."

Deanne Drukker stood on one of the catwalks overlooking the main floor. She was dressed in black cargo pants and a sleeveless camo shirt. Her hips sported a pair of Luger-like guns.

Oliver released Sid's throat and leaned back. He pushed his nose back into place with a sickening crunch. He took a big snort of air. He pointed his sausage-sized finger into Sid's face. "I'll get you." He stood up and moved away.

Sid gathered her feet beneath her and rose back up.

Warren Ratson dropped Cyrus to the new-metal floor.

The flabby man fell to his knees and started coughing.

Sid helped him back to his feet and said up to Deanne, "I was hoping I'd see you at Ted's funeral."

"I bet you were," Deanne replied. "Sorry I couldn't be there, but hey, I just didn't care." She put her fingers to her lips and made a sharp whistle. "Let's get this over with. I've got things to do."

A pair of upright gurneys with two bodies strapped to them were being pushed her way. On them were Rachel and Winslow. Both of them had bizarre masks over their faces, something similar to what Sid had seen in *The Silence of the Lambs*.

"Looks like you forgot the straitjackets," Sid said with disdain. "Is that really necessary?"

"The Ratson brothers have a twisted sense of humor," Deanne said from above. "Which is odd for deaders."

"We're not entirely dead," Oliver said with a grunt. "Just mostly dead." He rolled the sleeves up on his meaty arms. They were coated in mesmerizing tattoos filled with what seemed to be living arcane symbols. "Bet you ain't ever seen anything like that before, have you, Sweetheart?" He gave Sid a wink.

"They say anything you see on TV can become reality," Sid said, "so it doesn't surprise me. Who knows, if you survive long enough, maybe you'll get your own reality TV show."

"She's a funny one," Oliver said up toward Deanne. "I can see why you like her."

"Charming, aren't they?" Deanne said. She walked over the planks of the catwalk and made her way down a set of spiraling stairs. Upon hitting the main floor, she approached, stopping in between the undead Ratson brothers. "They are quite the marvel. Bloodless but still alive, thanks to the supernatural and some arcane medical advances. How can you kill something that cannot bleed?"

"Are you a deader too?" Sidney said to Deanne.

The woman stiffened at the remark. Regaining her composure, she said, "No. I can still bleed. For the time being," she said with a wink. "Now, I believe you have something for me. If all goes well, then we can part ways in peace. And Sid, you really need to get away from all this."

"I won't stop until I've taken you down. You can count on that."

Deanne huffed. "We'll see. You never know. You might just change your mind about that. I thought like you once." She laid her eyes on Cyrus. "All right, Specs. Get the payment." She patted the gun on her side. "And don't try to be clever."

Cyrus slid over to the car and retrieved the little silver case with the bitcoin codes in it. He tried to hand it to Deanne. She sneered at him. "Open it."

Cyrus complied. The inside of the case revealed a small chip tethered to a smartphone cable. He plucked it up and dangled it in front of her face. "I don't think it's dangerous."

Deanne received it and plugged the device into her phone. "Bitcoin. Pretty hard to trace the source. What will the world of greedy men—and women—think of next? And the funny thing is, bitcoin is pretty volatile right now. But a few well-placed articles posted in the *Wall Street Journal*, and boom, one billion becomes ten. I just love how those one-percenters think."

"Of course you would," Sidney said. She was making a little small talk while scanning the insides of the ship. Her stomach filled with butterflies. Her hands turned clammy. Other than Deanne, the Ratson brothers, and the two deaders, there wasn't anyone else in there. It seemed odd. There had to be more. There was merchandise everywhere. "I hope you enjoy your cut," she added.

"It's uploading to our account," Deanne said, staring at her phone's screen. Keeping her eyes fixed on that, she said, "Oh, I don't do it for the money. I do it for the power. I do it for the thrill of it. It's so exhilarating." Her mouth fell open, and her brows buckled. "What's this?" She stormed over to Cyrus and stuck the phone in his face. "What's this?"

"Uh," Cyrus said, blanching, "it looks like only a hundred million dollars. Look, I didn't have anything to do with that. I'm just here to pick up and—"

Deanne punched him in the face. *Whack!* She smashed her phone on the floor. "Kill them! Kill them all!"

Quick as a snake, Oliver Ratson caught Sid up in his arms and picked her up off her feet.

Deanne then pulled out her guns and pointed one down at Cyrus and the other at Sid. "Aw, hell, I'll do it myself."

CHAPTER 35

C YRUS BALLED UP INTO THE fetal position and peed his pants.

Sydney could feel Deanne begin to squeeze the trigger. "No, wait!" she said.

"You had your chance," Deanne said.

Out of nowhere, the unexpected happened. The trunk of Sid's rental car, the silver Dodge Charger, popped open.

Deanne pulled her gun barrel up and cocked her head. "Check it out," she said to Warren Ratson, who stood to her right.

"Okay, Boss." The muscle-packed deader started toward the rear of the car. Just as he started to pass the hood, the car bounced a little. A tall, rangy man stepped into view.

Sid's heart leapt.

Smoke stood tall. Dressed in black attire from neck to toe, he seemed to leer down at all of them. In his large hands, he held a monster of a machine gun like a toy. It was an M-60, just like the one Rambo used in the movies. Smoke had two bandoliers of ammo crisscrossed over his shoulders. He lowered the barrel at Warren. "Don't move, dead man."

Warren froze but managed to cluck a chuckle. "You can't kill me. Go ahead. Take your best shot."

Smoke pulled the weapon tight to his chest and took aim. He squeezed the trigger.

Buppa-Buppa-Buppa!

Buppa-Buppa-Buppa! Buppa-Buppa-Buppa!

The first burst of ammo bored a hole through Warren's head so big that you could see clean through. The second burst tore out his heart. The third left the undead man disemboweled. Warren Ratson staggered around on clay feet before collapsing with a heavy *thunk* onto the ship's hull.

"Any more volunteers?" Smoke said. He pointed the smoking barrel at Deanne. "We're going to be leaving, and you'll be coming with."

"You! You! You killed my brother!" Oliver Ratson screamed.

He was still bear hugging Sid. His powerful arms were squeezing her ribs.

She winced.

All puffed up and chest heaving, he rambled on. "You'll pay! You'll pay!"

"He might not be dead. He's still twitching," Smoke said. "Now, make yourself useful and get down on your hands and knees. Both of you."

"I don't think so, Mr. Smoke," Deanne said. She had both guns out, one pointed at Sid and the other at Cyrus. The woman was filled with eerie confidence. "You see, this ship, it's filled with deaders. And the only live person walking away from here will be me." She tipped her head toward Winslow. The man was wide eyed on the gurney. "And probably him. I guess we'll just have to skim our money off him. And of course, I'll have to put a nice hole in your girlfriend."

"She not my girlfriend," Smoke said. His eyes found Sid's. "Are you?"

Hands half up, she said, "No."

"You don't sound very certain," Smoke said. "Are you sure about that?"

No. "Yes." Sid glared at him. "This isn't the time for that."

"Oh, I think it is. I love to hear the famous last words of people who are half in the grave," Deanne said. "Believe me, I've heard the worst of them. So cliché almost every time. They tell me, 'You'll burn in hell' for this or that. Or, 'I'll see you in hell.' I'd be curious to hear what the both of you have to say. It's always so much more delicious watching people who care about each other go down."

"We aren't going down," Sid said. "You are."

"No, I don't think so." Deanne took a full step closer and pointed her Luger at Sid's nose. "Mr. Smoke. Set your weapon down or watch your, well, wannabe girlfriend die. I'll do it, you know."

"You're a murderer," Smoke said with a dark threat in his voice. "And murderers have to die."

"Oh, you won't kill me," Deanne said. "That's why they picked you out over many others. Sure, you'll kill the monsters, but you always spare the men—and women. It's such a weakness for those who hold onto such lofty standards. That's what separates the haves from the have-nots, you know. Conscience. People like me prey on fools like you. Now, set down the weapon, Smoke, and slide it over here."

"You're a murderer, and murderers have to die," Smoke said again.

"Stop saying that!" Deanne said. She jerked her head. "I'm only going to say this one more time. Give up your weapon."

Smoke set the machine gun down and slid it far away. He held his hands up. "You're a murderer, and murderers have to die."

"Ugh," Deanne sneered. "You really shouldn't have said that again." She took aim at Smoke with her left hand and fired. *Blam!*

CHAPTER 36

S ID'S LIMBS FROZE.

The shot rang out, echoing loudly inside the metal hull of the ship.

Smoke spun around and fell to the deck.

Sid fought against her captor, Oliver, but he held her fast. Finally, she pulled her tongue off the roof of her mouth and said, "You're evil!"

"And a good shot. Don't forget that," Deanne said.

"Not that good," the voice of Smoke said. He stood on his feet again. His countenance was fierce. Stark. "You missed."

Face contorted in rage, Deanne started to blast away with both barrels. *Blam! Blam! Blam! Blam!* The loud shots echoed all around. Bullet holes peppered Sid's rental car. Smoke, like a panther, slipped into cover and vanished.

From somewhere behind the car, Smoke said it again. "You're a murderer. Murderers have to die."

"Deaders," Deanne said to the two goons behind the gurneys. She motioned to Sid. "Seize her."

Just as Oliver released her, the two deaders latched onto her arms.

"Oliver, kill Smoke!" Deanne ordered. She started to circle the vehicle, firing shot after shot until her magazines emptied. "Dammit!" She bounced the guns off the floor. "Dammit!"

Sidney noticed Cyrus was still huddled on the new-metal hull with his eyes squeezed shut. He hadn't even cracked them open to see what was going on. Deanne walked over and kicked him hard in the back several times. Cyrus groaned. Deanne kicked him again.

Now, in front of a captive audience, Smoke and Oliver circled Sid's rented Dodge Charger.

"I'm going to tear you in half for what you did to my brother," Oliver said. He drove his fist into the car and put a dent into it. He crossed over the front of the car, shifting back and forth, trying to figure out which way Smoke would go. "What's the matter? You chicken?"

"No," Smoke said, mostly hidden by the popped-open trunk. "I'm just reloading." He slammed the trunk shut and stood with a synthetic shotgun in his hands. "Come and get some."

"Huh. Those little bits of grain won't stop me!" Like a great ape, Oliver leapt onto the hood of the car and scrambled over the roof.

Smoke opened fire. *Ka-blam! Ka-blam! Ka-blam!*

Chunks of flesh were ripped from Oliver's body, but he churned on and pounced on top of Smoke. The two vast men thrashed back and forth. They punched. Kneed. Kicked. A heavyweight bout of two relentless champions.

"This is good," Sid heard Deanne say. "Real good."

Smoke broke free and backpedaled away. His face was bleeding, and his shoulder dangled. Oliver circled him with hands clutching open and closed. Half of his face was shot off, revealing lots of teeth. A chunk of shoulder and another of leg were gone as well. "I'm going to make you feel every bit of what you did to my brother."

Sid recoiled in her captors' arms. Her heart sank. It was clear that Smoke's shoulder was dislocated. Oliver, with his supernaturally charged hulking frame, would make good on his words. He'd tear him apart. *I hope he has on his Sweet Heart suit.*

"I don't guess you'll be getting an engagement ring anytime soon," Deanne said to her. She put her fists on her hips. "This will be good. Just wish I had some popcorn."

Oliver charged.

There was a flash of silver like a strike of lightning. Oliver stopped in his tracks and glanced down. A blade was sunk hilt deep into his chest. "Aw, shit." He dropped onto his knees and toppled over on his side.

Smoke limped over to the car and leaned against it, panting. Bracing himself against the car, he shoved his shoulder back into place and yelled. He sagged to the hull floor, beaded in blood and sweat.

"Bravo," Deanne said, plucking up one of Sidney's knives. "And after all that, I'm still going to kill you all." She came at Sid. "You first."

CHAPTER 37

HELD FAST BY THE DEADERS, Sidney used their strength as an anchor. She leapt upward, launching a kick, disarming Deanne, and flipping over. Using her leverage, she pulled the deaders' heads together, loosening their grip. She twisted free.

"Seize her," Deanne ordered again. "Seize her!"

The deaders clutched after Sid.

Gunshots rang out. *Blam! Blam!*

The deaders recoiled. Each had a hole in the head. Adjacent to them, Cyrus had his Glock on them. The deaders resumed their attack on Sid. "Why aren't they falling?" he said with wide eyes.

"They aren't zombies," Sid cried out, trying to free herself from their clutches.

In a burst of movement, Deanne dashed away and wrenched the Glock from Cyrus's hands. She then said, "You have to shoot the heart." *Blam! Blam!*

The deaders fell flat.

Deanne cracked Cyrus between the eyes with the butt of the weapon and sent him bleeding to the shiny metal floor. She then turned the gun on Sid. "It's still over."

"Over?" Sid said, cracking her neck from side to side. She shifted into a fighting stance. "If you're such a badass, why don't you show me what you got?"

"Oh ho, I see the golden princess has some vengeance in her eyes." Deanne smiled. "I trained Ted. Ted trained you. This will be interesting. I tell you what. You win, I'm your prisoner. You lose? Well, you all die. And just to make sure that my efforts are secured," she put her fingers to her lips and let out a sharp whistle, "I'm bringing in some special referees."

The interior of the sweltering ship started to rattle. From the dark exterior of the ship's hull came a shuffling of feet. Deaders were coming. They moved slowly but determined. A mix of men and women, half-animated with blank faces. They held heavy working tools like clubs. On their heads were metal bands with faint blinking lights. They wore dark-navy pea coats with beige jumpsuits underneath. Twenty or so encircled all of them.

Sidney took a deep draw through her nose. She thought about Ted. His family. His friends. She set her jaw. "Let's do this."

"Let's do," Deanne said. "Ding. Ding." She came in high, feinted down, and executed a perfect leg sweep.

Sid landed flat on her back. "*Oof!*" On instinct, she pushed herself back to her feet. *That was fast. Really fast.* Sid had fought plenty of people in her days. Men. Women. She had a case filled with trophies from tournaments, but none of that compared to what it was like when your life was on the line.

"If you want, you can just give up, and I'll make it easy," Deanne said.

"No thanks."

"Suit yourself." Deanne lunged in. She kicked high. Punched low. Landed shot after shot after shot. *Wap! Wap! Wap!*

Sid counterpunched. Counterkicked.

Deanne slipped away, drove in again, and lit up her ribs. "Stings, doesn't it, little Sidney?" Deanne backed off and circled. "Yeah, those Sweet Heart suits are really good against puncture wounds, but that won't stop me from jangling up your innards." She mopped the sweat from her eyes. "This is where I'd normally say you'll be sore tomorrow, but you'll be long dead before sunrise."

"We'll see about that," Sid said. Nostrils flaring, she rushed in and unleashed her rage. Locking her hands over Deanne's head, she started driving her knee into the woman's ribs. She locked her fingers in the woman's hair, jerked her head back, and punched her in the jaw. Deanne's head rocked backward, and her knees buckled. Sid hit her again. And again. Bone smacked into bone. *Wap! Wap! Wap! Wap!*

Nose bleeding, Deanne spit out a mouthful of blood. In one swift move, she executed a judo throw and toppled Sidney over. She shoved her forearm into Sidney's throat and put her full weight on it. "You're tough. I'll have them put that on your tombstone."

Face reddening, Sidney pushed back against the woman's power. Deanne was strong. Solid. She had the leverage and the glazed look of a killer in her eye. Sidney drew her fist back and launched it hard into the woman's ear.

Deanne's teeth clacked together. Her taut body went limber.

Sid slugged her again, smiting her in the jaw.

Deanne's eyes flashed with anger. She still had Sidney pinned down, legs clamped over her waist. "I've had enough of this." She unleashed a flurry of hard punches.

Sid blocked some. She caught the full force of the others. Fighting against the unrelenting surge, her arms began to get heavy. Her arms juddered against every blow. *She's a maniac. She's a machine.* Fighting for her life, her limbs failed just as Deanne's fingers locked around her throat.

"Time to die," Deanne said, ramping up the pressure.

Sid took a halfhearted swing. The blow scraped off Deanne's brow, cutting a little slit above her eye. Blood dripped from the wound and onto Sid's face.

I can't die like this. I can't die.

CHAPTER 38

MEGAN'S FACE FLASHED IN SID'S mind. Who would take care of her? New strength surged through her veins. She dug her fingers into one of Deanne's hands. *I won't die like this!* She locked onto Deanne's thumb and wrenched it backward.

Deanne let out a pained yelp. "Ouch!" The woman jumped up and away.

Sid held onto Deanne's arm and slung the rogue agent back down. Jaws clenched, she wrestled the older woman onto her stomach and rammed her elbow into her kidneys.

Deanne let out another yelp.

Sid shoved her onto her back and pinned her down the same way Deanne had her before. Like an MMA fighter, she started punching, one blow after the other. "You're going to pay for what you did to Ted!" *Whap!* A glint of steel caught her eye. It was one of her knives. Sid plucked it up off the metal floor and raised it over her head. You're going to pay!"

Deanne's body was limp. Her eyes were wide open, and she was panting. "Go ahead if you have the guts. Go ahead."

"Rrrrah!" Sid cried, bringing the knife down with all her might.

Deanne lurched. Eyes blinking, she stared at the blade stuck in the ship's hull by her side. She let out a ragged sigh.

On her knees, Sid rolled Deanne over.

Cyrus tossed her some flex cuffs, and with a knife, he cut loose Rebecca and Winslow.

Still, they were surrounded by deaders. The strange half-dead people clutched oversized wrenches, pry bars, and chains in their hands.

"Call them off," Sid said to Deanne. "Call them off."

"No. I can't do that. It would be disloyal." Deanne took in a sharp breath and started to whistle.

Buppa-Buppa-Buppa!

Buppa-Buppa-Buppa! Buppa-Buppa-Buppa!

Sid, Cyrus, Rebecca, and Winslow hit the deck.

Smoke stood like a giant unloading one blast of rounds after another into the deaders with the M-60 machine gun.

Bullets tore through their flesh. Heads were chopped up and severed. Body parts became tiny bits and pieces. It was carnage. Raw. Overwhelming. Smoke cut one deader clean in half. Its torso fell from its pelvis. One after another they fell under the heavy barrage of bullets. The gunfire stopped.

"Hold on," Smoke said, eyeing the heap of twitching bodies. He loaded up another belt of a hundred rounds of ammo. "Resume fire."

Buppa-Buppa-Buppa!

Buppa-Buppa-Buppa! Buppa-Buppa-Buppa!

Seconds later, all the deaders were nothing but a pile of rotten cat food. Smoke unslung the M-60 from his shoulder and tossed it back into the trunk. "Let's roll."

Everyone regained their feet. Cyrus's eyes were fixed on the leaf pile of exterminated bodies. He turned toward Smoke. "I'm not sure if that's sick or not." Taking out a handkerchief, he blotted the bloody spot on his forehead. "Ow."

"I'm glad I don't have to do all those reports like I used to," Sid said to Cyrus. "This case is all yours."

"Oh, you're still going to have to make a statement." Cyrus faced Deanne. "And you are going away for a very long time."

Deanne stood hunched over, listless eyes on the floor. Her spark was gone. It was as if a shroud of death had fallen over her.

"I bet she's chock full of useful information about the Black Slate," Sid said, still trying to catch a full breath. "Just don't let her get a reduced sentence."

"I won't."

An engine started up. Smoke was backing up the Drake van that was blocking the exit. "Hey, I've got shotgun!" he yelled out the window.

"Okay, let's load up, everyone," Cyrus said. He shoved Winslow into the back seat of the car. "Rebecca," he said, looking around. "Rebecca?"

Blam!

Sidney spun around. Rebecca had a gun pointed at Deanne. She intently watched the woman's figure collapse on the floor. Deanne had a bullet in the back of her head. Her eyes were glassy. She was dead.

"Rebecca!" Cyrus said, rushing over but showing some hesitation. "What have you done?"

Sidney found the woman's next statement eerie. With a bit of a deranged look in her eye, Rebecca said, "She's a murderer. All murderers must die."

CHAPTER 39

Back inside FBI headquarters, Sidney sat in the lobby just outside Ted Howard's old office. Smoke sat on the opposite end of the contemporary orange sofa, leaning back with one leg crossed over the other, reading a law enforcement magazine. Across from him was Ted's secretary, Jane, pecking away at the keyboard. She looked stunning as usual, but her posture was stooped a little. Sid noticed a box of tissues on her desk where there had never been one before. Not ever.

I miss Ted.

Inside Ted's office, an occasional outburst caught Sid's ear. The offices were well insulated, but nothing did well to muffle raised voices. Sid had already been sitting there for more than thirty minutes, and Smoke had already been there when she came. He wore work boots, jeans, and a black T-shirt with a white dragon logo on it. All they did was say hi. She hadn't seen him since they left Mallows Bay, and that had been two days ago. She glanced at the nameplate on the office door for the twentieth time. She rubbed her swollen hands.

Cyrus Tweel. Interim Section Chief.

It gnawed at her gut. She could have been a section chief one day. She'd often thought about it. It was just part of the natural progression of the career path. But she wouldn't have wanted it under these circumstances. Still, that was how things happened sometimes. Usually people moved on. Sometimes they just died. In the case of Ted, he'd been murdered. She couldn't help but think there was a greater design to it. Deanne had made a strong hint about it. Now Cyrus was in place. Her eyes glided over to Smoke.

How can he always be so relaxed? He's going back to prison.

He looked over, and his face lit up in a pleasant expression. He turned back to his magazine. He'd made a confession to her. A deep one. She'd rejected it without any kind of good reason. "Love isn't a convenience. It's a commitment." That's what her mother Sally always said. Sid wanted Smoke, though. At least she thought she did, but she resisted. Every time he went back into the system, it tore her up a little more. She wasn't being selfish. She just couldn't commit to that. She scooted over toward him.

"Hi," she said.

He put the magazine down. "Hey, Sid, what's up?"

"Something's been eating at me."

His handsome, dark eyes widened a little.

She continued. "How'd you wind up in the trunk?"

His brightness dimmed. "I'm a hero. I had to be where I had to be."

"Huh," she said. "So, you're a hero. Sure, I guess I should have known that. Makes perfect sense. We're all about to die and you pop up out of the trunk like a jack-in-the-box."

"More like a Smoke-in-the-box," he corrected.

"Maybe more like a jack-ass-in-the-box."

Jane stopped typing.

Smoke bobbed his chin. "If you say so."

"Look, I'm sorry, that wasn't right. I just—"

Ted's office door popped open. Rebecca, dressed in a skinny business suit and high heels, exited. Her cheeks were flushed red. She glared at Smoke and Sid as she stormed by.

I hope that psycho got what she deserved. The electric chair, perhaps. Bzzt!

Cyrus stuck his head out. His entire forehead had a white bandage taped over it. "Come on in, you two."

Inside they went, and Cyrus closed the door behind them. "Have a seat."

One of the three chairs in front of the desk was already filled. A man sat in the chair on the right. He was older, wrinkle faced, with soft brown hair and wearing a light-grey suit. His eyes were saggy but with a deep intelligence behind them. He held out a pack of Big Red gum. "Help yourself," he said in an old, Southern voice.

"No thanks," Sid said, holding up her hand. She took the middle chair.

"Sure," Smoke said, taking a stick.

"I'm Leroy Sullivan. One of the *them* in *they*." He unwrapped a piece of gum and stuck it in his mouth. He placed the pack in his jacket pocket, revealing an early model 1911 pistol. An old Army issue. "We are impressed. With both of you."

He didn't say anything after that. He just stared at them, back and forth, with soft blue eyes.

Sidney felt like a schoolgirl on pins and needles. She rubbed her hands on her thighs. She jutted her chin out and said, "Thank you?"

"Heh," Leroy said. "Well, keep up the good work. I'll be in touch." He pushed himself out of his chair and extended his hand to Sid.

She shook it. His grip was gentle but with iron behind it.

Leroy shook Smoke's hand after hers, gave Cyrus a nod, and departed the room.

Sidney stiffened at Cyrus. "What was that?"

"One of the most powerful people in Washington, DC," Cyrus said. He gave a little shrug. "I think. Anyway," he pulled out a black file thicker than a Bible and dropped it on the desk, "he's one of the men behind the Black Slate." He nodded his chin. "Seems like there's an awful lot of people on the Black Slate."

"So ..." she said.

"They still want you on as a liaison." His eyes drifted up at Smoke. He rubbed his chin. "And you, too."

There was an awkward pause after that. Then Cyrus produced another document and slid it over the desk to Smoke. "And you can't be both a liaison and a prisoner."

Smoke picked up the paper and started to read. Sid leaned over to see it, but Smoke turned away. "I'm pardoned." He glanced up at Cyrus. "A free man?"

Cyrus nodded. "Just don't go on any big vacations. Either of you. We'll be in touch."

"But I haven't agreed to anything," Sidney said. She was still thinking about Megan.

"You'll agree. Now get out of here. We'll sort out all the details later. I've got another meeting at three." He glared at them. "Adios."

Smoke and Sid made it all the way out into the parking lot without saying a word. She swore there was a little bounce in his step. Maybe there was in hers, too, and her heart was racing. Smoke was free.

Inside the parking garage, they both stopped behind her rental car.

"I guess I'll see you around," Smoke said. He fingered one of the bullet holes in the quarter panel. "I hope you got the damage waiver."

Sid draped her long arms over his neck and said, "Shut up and kiss me."

He took her by the waist and pulled her lips up to his, and they both settled in for a long, passionate kiss.

EPILOGUE

I**T WAS DINNERTIME A DAY** later. Sid, Smoke, and Megan were at another one of Smoke's chosen diners. Megan was all smiles from ear to ear. The entire table was filled with food. Greasy hamburgers that half soaked the bun. Chocolate milkshakes in tall glasses with whipped cream and a cherry on top. Megan had whipped cream on her nose, and Sid was laughing. Smoke stuck his nose in his. Megan cracked up.

"You two need to stop it," Sid said, wiping off Megan's nose. "You're supposed to eat it, not wear it."

Megan giggled. Sidney's heart swelled. She hadn't had a moment like this for as long as she could remember. Still, she was a little stressed about how things with the Black Slate would work out. She thought of an older classic rock song she had heard earlier in the day. "Love Will Find a Way." She gave Megan a hug. She felt like she had everything she needed.

And then the tiny bell over the door to the restaurant rang.

A moment later, the conversation inside the diner fell silent.

Sid lifted her head.

Smoke turned and looked over his shoulder.

A woman stood in the aisle. She was stunning from head to toe. Her blonde hair was shoulder length and exquisite. A tight celery-green dress accentuated every curve. Jewels adorned her neck and fingers. Bright and tasteful. With a smoldering look, the confident woman approached, dropping every man's jaw.

Megan stood up on her seat and said, "Mommy! Mommy!" She jumped over Sid's lap and rushed into the woman's arms.

Sidney's heart dropped. She whispered in astonishment, "Allison?"

Allison hugged her daughter tight and kissed the little girl on the cheek. "Oh, I missed you, baby. I'm taking you home."

"Yay! I missed you too, Mommy!"

Sid's throat tightened. This wasn't the same Allison she'd grown up with. No, this woman was different. She had an air. A renewed confidence. A swagger very much like what she'd encountered with everyone from the Drake. Monsters and all.

CRAIG HALLORAN

THE SUPERNATURAL BOUNTY HUNTER FILES

SMOKE & MIRRORS

BOOK 5

CHAPTER 1

S IDNEY COVERED HER NOSE WITH one hand and held her Glock in the other. A small beam of light shot out from a gadget mounted on top of the gun's barrel. Her feet sloshed through the muck inside the dark sewage tunnel. "There's got to be a better way to make a living."

"You wouldn't have it any other way," Smoke said. He walked step-for-step behind her, a shadowy protector with a pump-action shotgun in his hands. "Plus, it's good for the ole ticker. Keeps you from getting fat too."

"What's that supposed to mean?" she said, easing around the next bend in the tunnel.

"Just an expression."

"From where?"

"Somewhere."

Four months had passed since they took down Deanne Drukker at Mallows Bay. Allison and Megan had vanished. Sid hadn't slept well since. Now she was stuck in a sewer pipe hunting down another criminal on the Black Slate. She felt a tug on her arm and turned.

Smoke had a finger to his lips and was pointing at the light on her gun.

She turned the beam off, leaving only the two of them in the blackness. Reaching out her hand, she found his chest. His heart pounded slow and steady under her palm. Smoke was never in a rush. Never panicked. Her breathing eased.

With his soft breath on her ear, he whispered, "Listen."

The past few months with Smoke had been nothing short of odd. All business for the most part. A little pleasure in between. A strange platonic romance that neither one of them seemed to have figured out yet.

Footfalls splashed and echoed through the waters somewhere nearby.

Smoke took her hand and guided her deeper into the network of tunnels.

She followed.

This wasn't their first rodeo. Just in the last few months there had been several others, but not from the Black Slate. Instead, they'd hauled in local criminals. Thugs. Bail jumpers.

Smoke called it 'easy money'.

She'd learned a few more things about Smoke that she'd never had time to notice before. He had instincts. He did things. Extraordinary things that she hadn't figured out yet, but she liked it.

Trying to ignore the stench, she followed along, one grime-soaked step after the other. She slipped and caught herself by grabbing one of Smoke's jean loops.

"This isn't the place for that."

"Hah, hah," she said, still keeping her voice low. "But I'd say our chances here are as likely as anywhere else."

Smoke didn't respond to her quip. Instead, his strong frame came to a stop.

Ahead, something soft scurried in the ankle-deep waters, sending chills down her spine. Swallowing hard, she aimed her gun barrel toward the sound.

"Easy," Smoke whispered.

The new mark on the Black Slate was just as trying as all the others. His name was Swift Venison. It was one of the stupidest names she'd ever heard. The man behind the name, a pale-faced rat of a man, was the definition of sinister. Six FBI agents had died at his hands over a month ago. That didn't count all of the innocents who had perished in his bloody wake, either.

It hadn't taken long for Sid and Smoke to catch up with the man in a frumpy diner. However, he had scurried away like a rat as soon as Smoke put a gun to his head. The man was fast, impossibly quick, and a street race on foot had led them down into these sewers.

Now Sid, twitching her nose, walked through the foul muck below the city. And there was more than stink all over it.

The scufflings ahead got a little louder then came to a sudden stop. The wretched tunnel had been deadly quiet, but now tiny voices made little squeaks. Stomach starting to knot, Sid said in a low voice, "I really need to shed a light on this."

"Go ahead."

She pressed the button on the small laser light mounted on her pistol. The bright beam cut through the darkness, illuminating the tunnel. There, at ground level, her eyes locked on dozens of others. She gasped.

Rats bigger than cats blocked the tunnel. Their eyes were small ruby beads. The sharp teeth in their mouths dripped with hunger.

Tugging on Smoke's pants, she started to back away.

Smoke remained.

"Let's go!" she urged.

"Not yet."

"Let me guess, you speak giant rat?"

"No, but he probably does." Smoke lifted her gun light higher.

A man stood just behind the horde of rats. His eyes were a deep red and his slender face was covered in grey fur. His supine figure bulged inside his clothes, in which several stitches were ripped. He removed the tie that hung from his neck and slung it aside. Showing a mouthful of rat-like teeth, he hissed more than spoke, but what he said was clear. "Eat, brothers and sisters. Feast on their bones!"

CHAPTER 2

S MOKE SAID SOMETHING. THE WORD was barely audible, but the meaning was clear. "Run!"
Sid took off at a full sprint.
Smoke was on her heels, with the sea of rabid rats nipping after him.

To make matters worse, the angry tide of rats squealed so much it hurt her ears. She hated rats. She hadn't even liked to feed squirrels when she was a girl. But rats, why? "Where am I going?" she yelled as she closed in on a junction of tunnels. She turned left and slipped to a complete stop.

More of the monster rats were coming right at her.

She unloaded a round of shots.

Blam! Blam! Blam!

"Ulp!"

Smoke jerked her up to her feet and took her by the hand. "This way." He crossed the junction in the other direction. The way was clear, nothing but smelly sock-soaking waters.

"We need to get aboveground now, John!"

"I'm working on it."

They'd already been inside the tunnels for more than an hour, and Sid didn't have any idea where they were. She wasn't so sure Smoke did either, but they didn't have any other choice but running at the moment. She glanced back. The rats couldn't be seen, but they were heard. A loud, continuous squeal from Hell itself. She cracked off a few more rounds that ricocheted off the walls and ping-ponged down the tunnel.

Blam! Ping! Pong! Pow! Blam! Ping! Pong! Pow!

"Save your ammo," Smoke said.

"I do what I want with my ammo, and you do what you want with yours."

They stopped in the middle of another intersection where the tunnels crisscrossed. The sound of more rats was coming from all directions. The path they were traveling was cut off. The turn to the right was another swell of rats.

"To the left it is," Smoke said, forging ahead.

"Brilliant choice," she said, running after him.

Hoofing it as fast as she could, Sid fought the urge to cover her ears. It sounded like the entire maze of tunnels was stuffed full of rats—hungry flesh-eating vermin.

Don't look back! Don't look back! Don't look back!

She did.

A lone rat—bigger than a cat—had surged ahead of the pack and started to nip at her heels.

She screamed. She fired.

Blam!

The little monster fell over dead and was instantly trampled and devoured by its brethren.

Sid's legs churned faster.

Lord, please don't let me die like this!

She turned and let the light on her gun find Smoke's back.

His broad shoulders blocked the view, leaving her chasing his back. He stopped on a dime.

She slammed right into him.

"What are you—*ack*!"

Smoke slung her around his back and formed a wall between her and the rats.

Ear-shattering shotgun blasts fired from his barrel.

Ka-blam! Ka-blam!

With her back to a sealed-off door and her ears ringing like bells, Sid took aim.

The entire horde of rats had come to a stop. They were all bunched up, one row on top of the other. A knee-deep wall of fur.

A squeaky sharp voice spoke.

The sea of rats parted from side to side.

There stood Swift Venison. Part human. Part rat. Another abomination of nature gone mad. "I see you both have finally found the end of the tunnel. Good. Now I just need to decide if I should let my friends devour you or not."

Sid started to squeeze the trigger.

Swift held up a finger. "I wouldn't do that if I were you. You see, if I die, then there is nothing to keep these rats from devouring you." He looked back behind him. "And notice, they stretch back as far as the eye can see. Besides, why waste a bullet? It can't hurt me." He made a command-like squeal.

The rats pressed closer. They were little more than a foot from Smoke's boots.

"Be wise now and set your weapons down."

Eyeing the rats, Sid set her gun down.

Smoke tossed his on top of the rats, drawing some squeaks.

"Very smart of you." Swift sniffed the air with his tiny nose. "Oh, how I love the smell of fear. It's in your eyes. In your sweat. All the way down to the hair on your toes." He flicked the shotgun up into his hands with his toe. "Now, turn around and open that door."

Sid and Smoke didn't move.

"Aw, I'm not going to shoot you in the back," he said in a calm and trustworthy voice. "It's just not my style. And I could easily tear the both of you to pieces. Oh, but how I hate to get my nails bloody. I just had them manicured."

"Really? Which veterinarian did you use?" Smoke asked. "I've been looking for a good one. You see, I have these little Pomeranians—"

"Shut up!" Swift pushed back the long rat fur on his head and took a breath. "Anyway, typically I let the rats eat you, which I probably still will. But a funny thing happened. I recognized you. John Smoke and Sidney Shaw, bounty hunters." He let out a shrieking laugh. "Heeeeeeee! The funny thing is, our kind has a bounty on your heads! It's the oddest thing. I only recently became aware of the facts. You see, so many of our special kind don't frequent my abode. I can only assume it's my gruesome exterior and preferred décor." He bounced the shotgun on his shoulder. "You took out the wolfman, Night Bird, the Minotaur, and those vile Ratson brothers. It seems you've really gotten the Drake's attention. Now there are bounties on your heads, big ones. More power. More territory, and it has all fallen right into my—eh?"

Sid and Smoke turned their backs to him and put their hands on top of their heads.

"Just shoot us in the back," she said. "Anything is better than letting you bore us to death."

"Wh-What?"

"Come on, just get it over with," Smoke added, shaking his head. "A talking rat. Say, are there any mutant turtles down here?"

Sid burst out in laughter. "Ha ha ha ha ha!"

Swift let out an angry howl. "Grrrrrrrrr! You dare! What are you fools babbling about?"

"Come to think of it, why are you pursuing us?" Sid asked. She wiped the tears from her eyes. "Shouldn't you be pursuing Shredder?"

The next warning from Swift froze the marrow in her bones.

"I'll shred you. I'll shred you both."

Out of the corner of her eye, she saw something come at her with blinding speed.

Smoke's head rocked forward.

A split second later so did hers. Pain filled her eyes, and everything in the world turned black.

CHAPTER 3

WITH PAINFUL EFFORT, SID LIFTED her chin from her chest and blinked her aching eyes. Skull throbbing, she found Smoke's eyes.

He sat adjacent to her with his hands behind his back. He was struggling. "Enjoy your nap?" he asked.

"I've had better." Grimacing, she fought against the bonds that had her arms pinned behind her back as well. She started digging into them with her nails. Her nostrils flared. The cell was a dingy spot with mold, mud, and who knew what else on the floor. Surrounded by concrete block, the only way out was through an iron grate with a solid but haphazard door. "Aw, great."

"Don't worry," Smoke said, "I'm sure the ninja turtles are around here somewhere."

"Ha ha." A desperate nagging started in Sid's stomach. "We really need to get out of here."

"I had a plan," he said, grunting with effort. "But you set ole Fuzzy-face off with that Shredder comment. He must have hated the show. But he was fast. I'm talking AV fast, and—"

"Hold up a second. Are you blaming me for us getting captured?"

"I was merely distracting him. Like I said, I had a plan." He winked at her. "Don't worry, I'll figure something else out."

She stretched out and kicked his boot. "You'll figure something out? How about I figure something out?"

Smoke sat still. "Okay, then you figure something out."

She leaned her head against the wall. "Sometimes I don't know if we make a good team or a bad team."

"Lighten up, Sid. I'm just stoking your fire."

"Why?"

"Because he's coming."

"I don't hear—"

"I hear voices!" It was Swift. The creepy shifter stood in front of the bars, holding a giant rat in the crook of his arm. It had a long tail and pink-painted toenails. "So it seems the little smart-alecky people are awake from a pain-filled and nightmarish slumber. Good." He stroked the rat's fur and added, "My friends are getting hungry, and I won't be keeping them at bay much longer."

"Just out of curiosity," Sid said, "why didn't you just kill us?"

"An excellent question, thought out. Most people just plead for their lives. But I have to say, the two of you are special." Swift stepped back, and another foreboding figure stepped in. It was a deader. An iron-thewed male with a long expressionless face. He wore bellbottom jeans and a black Styx concert T-shirt like a cursed body guard. "This is Jax. He's been with me a long time. You'll have to forgive the smell. I don't think he's had a shower since 1983." Swift rubbed the fiber on Jax's sleeve. "But look at the quality of these clothes. Not a hole in them. Sometimes I wonder if it's the bloodstains that keep them together."

Sid swallowed as Jax opened up the door.

The formidable figure lumbered in, bent over, and picked her up into its arms.

She coughed. "Morning Glory, he's foul! Put me down."

Jax walked out of the cell.

The door slammed shut behind them with a loud clang.

Sid flinched. Her heart raced. She craned her neck around, only to catch a glimpse of Swift blocking the cell door.

"What's the matter, dearie? Didn't I give you time to say a proper goodbye to your boyfriend?" Swift flashed his teeth and chomped them really quickly as he lowered his hand and snapped his fingers. "Oh rats."

The deader hauled Sid into another room, where oversized rats scurried over the floor.

Beady red rat-eyes bore into her.

This is bad. Really bad.

The room was nothing but slime-coated stone with some old tables and chairs. It looked like a guard shack from the fifties. There were chains and shackles hanging from metal loops in the walls. Skeletons hung all over the death chamber.

Gaping, she finally realized Jax had set her down, unbound her hands, and shackled her wrists to the chains.

He strung her up with her arms raised over her head and moved away.

Swift mounted a digital video camera on a tripod and pointed the lens toward her.

"What are you doing with that?" she said.

"Proof of life. Proof of death." Swift clasped his hands together. "My kind just loves this stuff. It's for our own version of YouTube. And just look at how happy my little brothers and sisters are." He waved his hand over the rat-covered floor. "Eating the homeless and those drug addicts isn't quite as filling for them as the likes of you." He squeaked to the rat in his arm, "Reeee!", and it licked him on the nose. He set the rat down on the table behind him, patted its head, and turned to Sid. "Now, try to look pretty as long as you can."

Sid started to tremble.

I can't believe this is happening! No! No! No!

"That's perfect!" Swift said. He stuck his eye to the camera. "Yes, they'll eat that up." He moved toward Sid and faced the camera with flare. "Let loose the rats of chaos and cry havoc! Oh wait, the record light isn't blinking. Damn!" He marched back to the camera and pressed a button until the red light stayed on. "Now let the show begin."

"Wait, wait, wait," Sid pleaded. She stomped her feet. "Wait! Don't I get a last request or something?"

"No. What you are supposed to do is beg and plead for your life. Promise me everything. Tell me you'll do anything." Swift grabbed her by the chin and looked her in the eye. "Anything."

Sid's shoulders drooped. "Okay."

"That's better." He leaned his ear towards her lips. "Tell me. Tell me what you'll do for me."

Her chin dropped. "I'll do anything you want."

CHAPTER 4

SWIFT PETTED HER FACE. "GOOD. Very good."

Sid rammed her knee into his groin.

"Ah!" he cried out, and then he slapped her across the face, drawing blood with his nails. "Fool of a woman. How miserable this is going to be for you! My brethren will eat you alive one chunk at a time."

"I don't think so!"

Swift whirled around. "You!"

Smoke stood beside the camera. He held Swift's pet rat by the neck and had Sid's pistol to its head. "Let her go, or the rat gets it."

Swift threw his arms up and pleaded. "No, no, not my baby!"

Jax the deader closed in on Smoke.

Smoke cocked the hammer back. "Your pet is going to be a pelt if you don't call off your goon."

"Stop, Jax!" Swift ordered. Hands up, palms out, he said to Smoke, "Now, let's be reasonable about this. There is no escape for you. You know that. And if anything happens to me, my rats will swarm you."

"True, but this critter will be dead, and so will you."

Swift the rat shifter eased closer. "Come now, be reasonable. You can't kill me."

Dangling the rat by the neck, Smoke turned the gun on Swift. "I have an exploding bullet in here, and trust me, you won't be doing anything after I blow a hole the size of your head through you."

"Impossible," Swift said with a grin, "we made a thorough check of both of you."

"You didn't check everywhere," Smoke said.

"That's gross." Swift looked back at Sid and added, "Do you date this man?"

"No, he just does strange things."

"And I thought I was weird."

"I regurgitated it," Smoke said, shaking his head.

"Oh, well, that's much more sanitary. I thought you—"

"Smoke, will you get me the hell out of these shackles!" Sid said.

"You heard the lady, Swift. Snap to it."

"Jax, free the woman," Swift said to the deader.

It took some effort, but the lumbering deader finally managed to unshackle Sid.

She rubbed her wrists and backed alongside Smoke. Keeping her eyes glued on Swift, she said, "Can I have my gun back?"

"Sure." Smoke handed it to her and said to Swift, "Get your hands behind your back and call off all your rats. I don't want to see a single one of them, except this one." He shook the pet rat. "Do you understand?"

Swift's eyes narrowed. He started to bend at the knees. His clawed fingers clutched in and out. "You're bluffing. There's no explosive round in there. I don't believe it."

Smoke held a red-tipped bullet in front of the rat man's face. "No, there isn't one. There's an entire clip of them. Now come quietly or come in pieces."

Swift cringed and followed it up with a quick shriek. "Eeeack!"

The rats scurried in all directions, stuffing their bodies into cracks and holes before vanishing, tail last, completely.

Swift put his hands behind his back. "Happy?"

Smoke put the flex cuffs on him and secured them tight. A knife appeared in his hand, and he held it under Swift's eye. "Now this blade, I think you know, will cut through anything. It's a real heart-stopper." He shoved Swift forward. "Take us out of here."

Head down, Swift said, "Jax, lead the way."

The undead man took them back into the next room. It was there that Sid gathered more of their things from a metal table. Everything seemed to be in order, but her heart still raced. She'd been certain she was a goner. How Smoke had appeared was nothing short of amazing. Still, she couldn't shake the dreadful feeling that something was wrong. Very wrong.

And from every crack and crevice, hungry rat eyes were all over her.

"Tell you what," Swift said. "I'll make it worth your while if you leave me be, hm? What do you say to that? I'm certain the FBI doesn't compensate you that well. Whatever it is, I'll double it."

"It's not about the money," Smoke said.

CHAPTER 5

S WIFT CHUCKLED. "OH, IT'S ALWAYS about the money. But I'm curious. If it's not about the money, what are you in this for?"

Smoke replied, "I just hate rats. I tell you what though. Maybe we can make a deal."

The rat man stopped and turned his ear. "A deal. What sort of deal?"

"We want to know who the heart of the Drake is."

Swift started laughing. "Ha ha ha! You'll never know that unless you become one of our kind. Heh-heh. But that can be arranged if you want to know bad enough."

Sidney's thoughts raced to her sister, Allison.

What kind of madness have they done to her? What about Megan?

"Let's get out and get paid, Smoke." She pointed the Glock's barrel at Swift's nose. "I'm running out of patience."

After a long and winding walk, the deader Jax led them through some metal double doors and up a stairwell. Soft light crept through the cracks in the doors above. Jax pushed them open, revealing the ground floor of a warehouse. It was empty, save for long rows of shelves and abandoned multipurpose appliances that were scattered all over.

Sid took a deep breath and dialed up the FBI on her phone. While she waited, she sent a text to Cyrus Tweel. She kept the gun on Swift. "You've been extremely cooperative."

He shrugged. "What can I say? You're a formidable pair that outwitted me. In truth, it's your bravery that I admire most. So many cringe. Cry. Some are so terrified that they have a heart attack and die. But not you two. It's no wonder you are wanted and hated so bad."

"Sounds like we're doing the right thing then," she said, checking her phone. There wasn't a text from Cyrus yet, which seemed odd. "It feels good keeping the vermin off the streets."

"Hah," Swift scoffed. "Who do you think really keeps the vermin off the streets, law enforcement? Hah. You see, that's part of what we do for your kind."

"Pardon me?" said Sidney.

"You know, long before I became what I am, I used to be a priest." Swift's form started to change. His bulging sinews and body hair thinned, leaving only a small man with a rat's head and thinning grey hair. "I took care of many. Drug addicts. The homeless. The wayward and desperate. There was no end to it. Then, a friend of mine introduced me to the Drake and showed me true power that let me embrace my inner nature." His eyes filled with lust. "There's nothing like it in the world."

Smoke tightened the flex cuffs on him. "And your point is?"

"That power can be yours, eh? And you won't have to answer to these fools that run your cities. Most of them work for us anyway. They are the ones who pay us to keep the unwanted off the streets. They become dinner for my rats." Swift glanced at his pet that Smoke still had in his hands. "Could you show some compassion and let my pet go before local law enforcement arrives? I fear they just might shoot her."

"Sure," Smoke said. He slung the rat up high in the air.

Sid took aim and fired.

Blam!

The rat exploded into bits and pieces.

Swift screamed, "Noooooo!"

"She's gone now," Smoke said. "You were saying something about dinner and compassion?"

Trembling with rage, the rat-man said, "You'll pay! You will pay!"

Sid caught a glimpse through one of the upper warehouse windows of a helicopter coming in for a landing. She kept the gun pointed at Swift's nose. "Looks like your ride is here, Mister Venison. Gee, I wonder who is going to feed all your rats when you're gone? Maybe DC's finest pest control will have to euthanize them."

"Don't you dare!" Swift said, puffing himself up.

Two squads of men stormed into the warehouse carrying automatic machine guns, dressed from head to toe in helmets and Kevlar body armor. One of them flashed an FBI badge.

Sid recognized him.

It was Agent Jonnie Wok, a stocky but short Asian with a Southern accent.

"We'll take it from here," said Agent Wok.

"I'm not releasing anyone until I hear from Cyrus Tweel." She checked her phone. There still wasn't any text from Cyrus.

The agents had them hemmed in, gun barrels on everyone's chests.

"Miss Shaw, we can't stand here and dilly dally," said Agent Wok. "I've got a job to do, and yours is finished. Now, step away and let us handle this."

Sid looked down at Agent Wok. "I need to hear from Cyrus."

Agent Wok stepped closer. "Well, maybe he's on vacation. Or maybe he's taking a sick day. Or maybe he's in the shitter?

I don't have time to wait for him, and I don't have to either." He looked hard at her face. "Say, that's a pretty nasty scratch. You might want to get that looked at."

"Don't try to butter me up now, Wok." She texted Cyrus again, saying, "Wok here. Need your clearance." She hit 'send'.

"Agent Shaw—I mean Bounty Hunter Shaw or whatever the hell you call yourself—we need to move." He glanced over at Jax the deader. "Shit! Someone cuff that thing!" He focused on Swift Venison. "What's he do?"

"He's the Pied Piper," Smoke said.

"The what?"

Sid's phone buzzed. There was a text from Cyrus. It read, "On my way. Stay put."

Agent Wok took out his phone, checked the text, and rolled his eyes. "Aw, great. Looks like we're all staying. Damn, I was hoping to avoid Cyrus. Just seeing him gives me a brain freeze." He stuffed his phone inside his pocket. "Didn't you use to date that guy?"

"Yes."

"Man, what were you thinking?" Agent Wok twirled his finger beside his head. "Let's get these prisoners secured. Head to toe. We can't have these freaks getting loose. "

The agents put Swift and Jax into security straitjackets and muzzled their mouths. Their feet were shackled with short chains. After that, they sat them both down on the floor.

Agent Wok took off his cap and wiped the sweat from his brow. "Say, how much are you getting paid for this gig anyway?"

"More than you make in a year," Sid said, stuffing her weapon into her holster. "Why, you looking for a new job?"

"No." Wok fanned his face. "I'd rather not smell like a sewer. Besides, this gig pays well enough. I like it."

"Prisoner transport? Hah!"

"There's more to it than that," Agent Wok said. "I meet a lot of interesting people."

"Tell me more."

Smiling, Agent Wok said, "Maybe we should have dinner sometime and I'll tell you all you want to know."

Sid's eyes glided over to Smoke. He stood with his back to her, facing the prisoners.

She leaned in toward Agent Wok and asked, "Just tell me. Where do you take them?"

"Sorry, can't tell you that, even though I feel compelled to." He glanced over his shoulder and then said to her, "But I might give in over dinner and breakfast."

"Keep dreaming."

He shrugged, nodded, and stroked his chin. "I always have, and I probably always will."

Sid slipped away and found herself at Smoke's side.

He was staring at the prisoners.

Their hands and feet were covered in mitten-like gloves and booties. Their ears were covered with hearing protection, and blindfolds were on them. Both of the freaks seemed calm and at ease.

"What's on your mind?" Sid leaned close to Smoke.

"Maybe you should have dinner with him."

"What?" She leaned away again. "No! Why?"

"Well, the truth is, I want to know where they take them."

"So you want me to sleep with him?"

"Well no. Just get him drunk and make him think you'll sleep with him. He'll fall for it."

Sid's neck muscles tightened. "You'd better not be serious."

Stone-faced, Smoke turned and looked her in the eye. "No. I don't think I'd like that."

"Well, now that I think about it, maybe it's not such a bad idea. After all, Jonnie is pretty funny, and he loves to party."

Smoke's stone-faced expression turned dark.

Good. "So do you have any more stupid ideas?"

"No, but I do want to know where they take them."

Sid's breathing eased. She brushed her hand against his. "So do I, but why are you so worried about it?"

"Sometimes I have a hard time believing they're actually incarcerating them."

"Me too."

"Look sharp, everyone," Agent Wok said, "Section Chief Tweel just landed."

Here came Cyrus, marching through the warehouse doors wearing a beige trench coat and looking as thin as ever. He wasn't alone either. Rebecca Lang was with him.

"Damn," Sid said, "she's back."

CHAPTER 6

S WIFT VENISON WAS GONE. Jax the deader, gone. Agent Wok the Chinese redneck and company, gone. Only Sid, Smoke, Cyrus, and Rebecca Lang remained. Sidney hadn't seen the mousy blonde since the day she killed Deanne Drukker in cold blood. 'She's a murderer, and murderers must die.' That's what Rebecca had said, and it still gave Sid chills to this day. And now, the woman who should be as far away from law enforcement as possible was back.

How in the hell did this happen?

"My bitcoin account is awfully low," Smoke said, holding up his phone. "About twenty-five grand by my count."

Sid checked her account as well and shook her head. "What's the deal, Cyrus? The bounty was one hundred grand split between me and him. This is only half. Where's the rest?"

Cyrus opened his mouth to speak, but Rebecca—wearing a blouse and a knee-length skirt—cut him off. "I can answer that. We aren't paying you that much. Budget cuts."

"I don't care about your budget cuts. We are going to be paid what we're owed."

Rebecca faced off with Sid, made a sour face, and stepped back. "Ew, what have you been into?"

"It's not what I've been into that should worry you, but what I'm about to get into." Sid balled up her fist. "Now release my money!"

"The way I figure it," Rebecca said, "you stand to make a lot of money if bitcoin soars again. So be patient and make do."

"You aren't my financial advisor, and we didn't just risk our necks for a measly fifty K. We just about died down there!" Sid wanted to knock the woman's head off her shoulders. It wasn't about the money either, even though she could use it—she was way behind on all her bills. No, it was principle. A bargain struck. A deal. But worst of all, she hated Rebecca's involvement. That tramp was an arrogant, prissy, conniving little witch. "I'll just get ahold of Leroy then."

"Leroy's dead," Cyrus said. He was cleaning his glasses with his tie and put them back on. "Heart attack, I believe. Hey, he was old."

"Very old," Rebecca added, "and very dead."

"When did this happen?" Sid asked.

"A couple weeks ago," said Cyrus. There was something different about Section Chief Cyrus. He was more reserved, less arrogant. He rubbed his hands together, caught Sid looking at them, and stopped. "I didn't find out about it until after he was buried."

"And you couldn't have told me this?"

"It wouldn't have made any difference," Rebecca said with a sneer. "It's not like you'd quit. After all, you need the money."

Sid shifted her hips and prepared to let loose a roundhouse kick.

Smoke stepped in her path of attack. "Are you going to pay us the rest or not?" He addressed Cyrus, but Rebecca answered.

"No, I'm not. And seeing how this is all off the record, consider yourselves lucky you got what you got."

Towering over Rebecca, powerful arms crossed over his chest, Smoke looked down at her. "Do you want to know what happened to the last person who didn't pay me what they owed me?"

Rebecca swallowed. "I could not care less." She spun around on her heel. "Let's go, Cyrus."

"Hold on!" Sid said. "What about the Black Slate?"

Rebecca kept walking.

Cyrus turned to look at Sid as he walked backward. "We'll let you know."

A week later, Sidney lay in bed inside her apartment. It was early morning after what had been another long and restless night. She rubbed her temples. A nagging headache hadn't left since she'd seen Rebecca and Cyrus.

I can't stand that woman.

Sid had blown Smoke off too. She needed time to think. Sort things out. She was supposed to be getting some steady pay as a liaison for the FBI, but the deposits weren't coming through. Now, Rebecca had stiffed them on their last bounty. Even worse, Bitcoin had taken a twenty-five percent hit the day after that last deposit. She tugged at her hair.

Am I an idiot?

Then there was the other odd thing. Leroy Sullivan. He was a big shot with the FBI who was supposed to be overseeing her dealings with the Black Slate. Now he'd died. Supposedly. Allegedly. Had he really? Sid had exhausted herself searching the obituaries and found nothing. It was more than odd. More than strange. The ice-blue-eyed old man had vanished.

Her financial stability had vanished with him.

What am I going to do?

She picked up her phone and pulled up the photo album. She found some pictures of Megan in there. She stopped on one of her favorite pics. Megan was on a swing with her teddy bear, looking as happy as she could be. Sid's eyes started to water. Working on the Black Slate gave her hope of finding Megan and saving her sister. If she could find that monster at the top of the Drake, then she could put an end to it. But now, she wasn't any closer than she'd ever been. She wiped her eyes and sniffed.

"I'm so sorry, Megan."

She swung her legs off the bed, got up, and shuffled into the bathroom. Looking in the mirror, she said to herself, "Good Lord, I'm a mess." She ran her fingers over the gash that Swift Venison had given her. She huffed a laugh.

What a stupid name, even for a rat.

The claw marks were still red and itchy. From the vanity drawer she pulled out a tube of Neosporin. She squeezed some on her finger and rubbed it in. "At least I don't have anywhere to go."

In the kitchen she scraped out just enough coffee grounds to make a cup of coffee. Her machine was out of coffee pods. It was one of the first expenses she'd shaved, by whittling down her coffee budget to a plastic can of Folgers. As she took a seat at the kitchen bar, the smell of fresh brew got her going a little bit again.

Routine. That was what she needed to get out of this funk she was in. She closed her eyes and made a mental list.

Coffee.

News.

Stretching.

A long run.

Workout.

Hit the heavy bag.

Kick the heavy bag.

Smoke popped into her mind.

Sex.

She squeezed her eyes tight.

No. No sex. No Smoke. Morning Glory, Sid. The man eats bullets!

Oh, but those eyes.

CHAPTER 7

SID COMPLETED THE GAUNTLET OF activity she'd planned for herself and returned to the apartment. Sweat soaked, she removed her neon-blue-and-jet-black jogging suit and tossed it onto the overstuffed hamper.

Oh boy, I can sit at home and do laundry today. Whoopee!

She took a hot shower, dried off, and slipped into the only clean clothes she could find: the gunmetal-gray Darkslayer T-shirt Guppy had given her and a pair of khaki shorts. She threw in the first load of laundry, headed into her small living room, and sat down. She turned the TV on to the local news.

A hard rain started outside.

Glad I got my run in.

The outside weathercaster was getting drenched. The sewer drain behind him was overflowing.

Sid thought of the massive rats inside those tunnels and cringed. She'd almost died … again. Devoured by rats like in an Indiana Jones movie. Her father, Keith, loved those movies. It got her thinking again about Swift Venison. The things he'd said about power. Money. The temptation.

He said he'd been a priest. He made it clear that the Drake worked for or with the politicians. They cleaned up the streets in grisly ways. And he'd said there was a bounty on her head. On Smoke's head. But she didn't feel any less safe than she had before. And Swift Venison hadn't seemed that worried when they took him in. He'd almost seemed relieved.

It had all been too easy.

"Something stinks." She rubbed her cheek. "Stinks bad."

Knock! Knock! Knock!

The sound jostled Sid from head to toe. Images of fiendish bounty hunters ran through her head. She found her Glock and took a quick peek through the blinds. Her breathing eased, and she opened the door.

"Hi," Smoke said with a sparkle in his dark eyes. He was clean shaven, and his lustrous hair was combed back in waves. He wore a burgundy polo shirt in a nice cotton blend and dark-blue jeans that stopped at the toes of his leather boots. "Nice shirt."

"You should call first," Sid said, stepping aside and closing the door behind him.

"But that would ruin the surprise," he said, taking a seat on the couch.

She crossed her arms over her chest. "Well, I'd rather you ruin a surprise than ruin my day."

"That's kinda harsh." He patted the sofa cushion beside him. "Why don't you just sit down?"

"Look, I'm sorry, John. I really am. But that's not a good idea." *He smells good. Really good. And the semi-preppy thing really works for him.* "And what's with the clothes? Did you swing by the mall on your way over here or something?"

"I thought we could go and have lunch? Somewhere nice."

"Like a waffle house?"

"Maybe a little nicer than that. I know a great 24-hour breakfast buffet at Truck Stop Ninety-nine."

"Shut up," she said, letting loose a little smile.

There was something innocent and boyish in Smoke's expression. He seemed a little nervous, maybe.

"So, is this visit business or pleasure?"

Smoke's eyes brightened. "Pleasure?"

"Just an expression. Bad choice of words. I should have said, 'social.'"

"But you said 'pleasure'. You've been thinking about me, haven't you."

She cozied a little closer to him, just a hair out of his reach. "You're all my dreams and nightmares wrapped up in one."

"You just can't give in to the plus side of me, can you."

"I guess that's just the woman in me."

"Well, I like the woman in you." He reached out and tried to grab her hand.

Sid drifted back. "So, I take it this is a social visit? Or is it business? Do we have a case where you get to go undercover as a mall dad?"

Smoke started laughing. "You really are cold, aren't you. Come here."

"No. I'm not in the mood. I've got a lot on my mind."

Striking fast, Smoke seized her wrists and eased her onto his lap. "Now this isn't so bad, is it?"

"Yes." *No.*

He coiled his arm around her waist and squeezed her thigh with his hand. He leaned in and kissed her.

Lips to lips, heart to heart, she gave in. It wasn't the first time either. She and Smoke had moments here and there, but nothing serious. She was holding back because there was something mysterious about Smoke that she didn't understand.

Something also seemed to hold Smoke back, an innocence or lack of experience.

She was drawn to it. She tangled her fingers into his thick locks, straddled him, and kissed him harder.

He returned in kind.

It went on for minutes until she broke it off, gasping for breath.

"Is something wrong?" he said.

"No. Do you think something's wrong?"

Smoke shook his head no.

Sid could see something was still on his mind, eating at him. Panting, she swiped her hair back over her shoulders.

Here we go again.

"Okay, do it."

"Do what?"

"*You* know what. Do what you always do that screws the moment up so that we can get on with it." She grabbed him by the collar of his shirt and kissed his handsome face, broke it off and then said, "Make it fast."

Smoke rubbed her thighs with his big hands. "Let's just keep doing what we're doing?"

"What, keep making out like we're in an episode of Happy Days? I'm a woman, Smoke. I want you, you want me. Take me!"

Smoke's face paled. His expression grew uncertain, almost embarrassed. This was the man who faced down death with nothing short of ice-water in his veins. Nothing rattled him. Now, he seemed confused.

Sid's engine cooled. She pushed herself up off his lap.

Smoke reached for her.

But she glided away. "Do you want me or not, John?"

"Of course I do. It's not you though, it's me."

"'It's not you, it's me'? What the hell is this, a bad Matthew McConaughey movie?" She drew back her fist and kicked him in the knee instead.

"Ow!" he said. "And who's Matthew McConaughey?"

"Ow!" She hopped over to the kitchen counter, shaking her hand and wincing. "Just get out of here!"

"Sid, it's not that. It's not that at all. I just want to do things right."

Without looking at him, she said, "Are you sure? Because you really seem to enjoy doing things wrong."

"Look, I'm good at a lot of things. Shooting people. Beating up people. Killing people. And eating pancakes. But relationships? Well, they aren't my strong suit. Of course, you seem to have figured that out on your own."

She could see him fidgeting with something, but she kept her gaze fixed on the kitchen.

"That's the reason," Smoke continued in his strong but gentle voice, "why I don't want to mess this up."

The stiffness in her back started to melt a little. She almost turned her head.

"Sid, look at me."

She turned on her stool and lost her breath.

Smoke was on one knee holding a diamond engagement ring in his hand. "Will you marry me?"

CHAPTER 8

S ID'S EYES FASTENED ON THE jaw-dropping diamond ring.

The cut, clarity, and color were astounding. And it was big. It winked at her from the gold ring in which it rested. It spoke to her, saying, 'Take me.'

She glanced at Smoke then back at the ring. She leaned closer. Her keen eye didn't pick up a single inclusion. She found Smoke's eyes again. Sweet and innocent. "What did you just say?"

"Will you marry me?"

She couldn't feel her fingers or toes. She held her head as the room began to spin a little.

"Sid, are you all right?"

"I–I … did you just ask me to marry you?"

"That's what the ring is for ... a wedding." Smoke rubbed his sweaty palms on his jeans. "Like I said, I want to do things right."

In a hushed breath, she replied, "You're crazy." She shook her head a little and felt her senses start to return. She checked out the diamond again. Her heart was pounding. "That really is beautiful, John, but this ... this is crazy. Uh, I'm sorry to ask this, but why?"

Smoke rose up, looked deep into her eyes, and touched her chin. "Because I love you."

"Me?"

"Yes, you."

It wasn't sinking in.

"John, you can't just walk in here and ask me to marry you." She moved away and curled up in the chair. "It's crazy. What are you trying to do to me anyway?"

"I'm trying to marry you. Take care of you. Be your husband if you'll have me." He sounded nice about it, but there was a hint of irritation in his voice.

"You couldn't have possibly believed that you could come in here and ask me to marry you and that I'd just say yes."

"I wanted to do it over lunch."

She made a frustrated growling sound. "Most people talk about these things. They don't just do them." She stuck her face in her hands. "Nobody does that."

"Well, don't get mad at me. I didn't realize there was a rulebook."

"Well, there is!"

Smoke took a seat on the couch, set the ring box down, and didn't say a word.

The silence was uncomfortable.

Sid's thoughts were a tangled mess. She wasn't much different than most women. She too dreamed of a diamond engagement and a nice wedding. She and her mom and Allison had even talked about those things from time to time. Of course, Allison had done most of the talking. She'd always had big plans, and Sid knew that her sister would be full of envy if she saw a ring like this. "It's beautiful," she whispered.

Smoke eased forward. "Would you like to try it on?"

Yes! "No. I can't."

"Why not?"

It was a fair question. Smoke deserved a fair answer. She gave him the best one she had. "I don't know why." She qualified it. "Yet."

Smoke rubbed his clean-shaven chin. "Look, I realize this might not have been in your plans, but you really shouldn't have expected anything different from me. It's supposed to be a happy moment, you know."

She let out a little laugh. "Heh! No, you're right. But I honestly think I would have been less surprised if you'd asked me in the sewers. But like this? Something's not right."

"Maybe you don't feel the same way about me that I do about you. I can live with that. Well, maybe I can't. But since the first moment I saw you, I knew I wanted to marry you." He closed the case on the diamond. "I don't know how long 'yet' takes, but I can wait."

His closing of the box felt like her own coffin being sealed as she watched Smoke get up to leave. Her wide eyes were on his back as he started walking for the door. His long, dark hair. His powerful, rangy frame.

Tall, dark, and handsome—and I'm going to let him get away. He's saved my life and almost died for me. Am I crazy, or is it all him?

Smoke put his hand on the doorknob and started to turn it. "Just call me."

Sid's heart started to break.

What do I do?

But then it was too late. Her heart had broken the moment the door closed behind him.

Clutching her chest, she took a seat on the couch.

What just happened?

She reached over, picked up the ring box, and popped it open.

The ring was as bright as a shining star.

Morning Glory!

She hopped out of her seat, ran to the front door, and opened it up.

Smoke was gone. There was only the rumble of his primer-gray Camaro pulling out of her parking lot and vanishing into the traffic on the streets.

"Dammit."

She closed the door and sagged down with her back against it, holding her head. With the ring box still in her hand, she started laughing—a bit derangedly—as the torrent of mixed emotions toyed with her brain. Smoke loved her! He had said so. She knew she loved him too, but marriage? Was it really that kind of love? Deep. Long lasting. Meaningful?

As she ran her finger over the diamond's edges, a smile crossed her lips. "I guess I could be a big girl and talk to him like a woman about this. Boy, I sure didn't handle that very well." On her hands and knees, she crawled over to the couch to lie down on it. She tucked the ring box under her arm.

I need to call him. What do I say? Yes? No? Maybe? Not now? Good Lord, why did that man have to propose to me?

She yawned, and her chest shuddered. She reached over to the coffee table, grabbed her phone, and pulled up Smoke's number.

Should I text, or should I call him?

The phone buzzed in her hand.

"Eek!" Expecting Smoke, she got another surprise, a text from Cyrus Tweel. It read, "Turn on the local news and don't go anywhere! On my way over."

"What in the world is going on now?" She found the remote and turned on the television to the local news.

Ambulances, police cars, and fire truck lights were flashing like the Fourth of July fireworks. Behind them was the site of a new construction project, a new mega-shelter for the homeless that Congressman Wilhelm and some other prominent business leaders had been working on. If Sid's memory served her well, today was the grand opening. She turned up the volume.

A black female reporter stood just inside the building's overhang, out of the pouring rain. She was soaked, but unaffected. "This is Angie Gentry, TV1Y News, and we have confirmation from local law enforcement officials that Congressman Augustus Wilhelm has been shot and presumably killed. The congressman has been rushed to Mercy Angels hospital." She read more details from a rain-soaked piece of paper. "Witnesses at the ceremony reported that a tall white male in a ball cap and raincoat stepped out of the crowd and opened fire. Security has already released this video footage." She held up the paper, revealing a crystal-clear picture of John Smoke.

Sidney dropped the ring box and gasped.

CHAPTER 9

S ID'S UPSIDE-DOWN WORLD HAD JUST been turned inside out. Two FBI agents were posted outside her front door. Inside with her were Cyrus Tweel and Rebecca Lang. Neither were happy. Both showed frowns as long as football fields. "I could have come down to the station," Sid said as soon as they arrived. It was all business though. Pressure. A congressman had been shot. DC's entire world was rocked. And her want-to-be-fiancé was the prime suspect. "This isn't an ideal place for an interrogation."

"Do you have any idea where he is?" Cyrus said, staring at her with his hard, beady eyes. "And don't play any games, Sid. We're not in the mood for them."

"We're?" Sid replied, looking at Rebecca.

The petite agent was every bit as frosty as she'd ever been. Her eyes gave Sid's apartment the once-over more than once.

"What did I say about the games?" Cyrus said.

"I'm not playing games, and no, I don't know where Smoke is. He just left twenty minutes before you got here. Cyrus, there is no way he did this. He was here, not there."

Rebecca stepped over. "The shooting was an hour and a half ago. That's plenty of time to come over here and have a booty call before he goes back to prison."

Sid's eyes flashed. She was up on her feet, shoving Rebecca into the bar stool.

"You bitch!" Rebecca hauled back, ready to unload a punch.

Cyrus caught her arm.

"You dare!" Rebecca said to him. She smacked him hard in the face.

Cyrus's eyes filled with astonishment. A blue vein popped out on his forehead. "This is no way for agents or former agents to act. Rebecca, Sid, sit down!"

"Don't you dare tell me what to do!" Rebecca straightened her business coat and sat back down on the stool. "I'll legally castrate you."

"Sid, I know you like this guy, but we warned you, me and Ted. He's a loose cannon. A bit of a nut job." He rubbed the back of his head and sighed. "And I also know about your history with Congressman Wilhelm. You and him, his son, and your sister, well, let's just say you have a colorful history."

"Wait a second. You think I said something that triggered this?"

Cyrus and Rebecca glanced at each other, then Cyrus said, "So you think he did it?"

"No. Absolutely not. He'd never do such a thing. John might be a lot of things, but he's not a murderer."

"He's psychotic," Rebecca said in a cold voice.

"You're the one who's psychotic."

"I spent some time with him too, if you remember," Rebecca said. "He's crazy. Certainly capable of doing a lot more harm than good."

"I think you have him mixed up with yourself. You're the only one I ever saw gun anyone down in cold blood. Yet here you are!"

The door popped open. A black agent filled the doorway. His head was shaved clean, and he had a dangerous look about him. "Everything okay?"

Cyrus gave him a nod. "We're fine, Calhoun."

The man closed the door behind him, but not without giving Sid the eyeball first.

Her skin prickled. "Calhoun? I thought he was fired. I thought he was in prison!"

"That's not your concern, Agent—I mean Sid." Cyrus took out his iPad and pulled something up on the screen. He set it down in front of Sid. "Now, I need you to watch this closely."

She did.

It was video surveillance footage from the new homeless center. It started out on the open streets where a man in a raincoat, on foot, weaved through the traffic in the pouring rain. He made his way up the steps and tilted his chin up just high enough for the camera to get a perfect shot of his face.

It was Smoke. No question about it. Even the height and build were right.

Heart empty, Sid glanced up at Cyrus.

"Keep watching if you're not convinced," he said.

New footage continued inside the shelter. Dripping-wet people from all walks of life were standing inside the lobby. Smoke stood among them, half a head taller than all the rest at least, wearing a Washington Redskins ball cap.

In front of the crowd was a podium where Congressman Wilhelm was making a speech. There wasn't any audio, though. Just a camera shot right over Wilhelm's shoulder and into the crowd.

Not too far into the speech, Smoke pushed his way through the throng, aimed his semi-automatic pistol, and cracked off several shots.

Wilhelm fell.

Everyone scattered, and Smoke disappeared with the masses.

Sid's stomach seeped down into her toes. "It can't be him."

Cyrus put the iPad in his coat pocket. "Sorry, Sid, but it's him. And you need to do whatever you can to help us bring him to justice. Anything you can think of that will make this easier will make a difference."

Sid's throat was dry and she didn't have any words to say. She'd seen him on the video. But it wasn't him. It couldn't be. There was no reason for him to do something like that. Not unless there was something else. Something bigger that no one else knew about. Maybe the Drake had blackmailed him. Feebly, she managed to say, "I assume you checked his place?"

"It's clear. No sign of him anywhere. We're keeping an eye on it though." Cyrus took a seat on the barstool and sat with his hands clasped together. "Have you and him talked about your relationship with Wilhelm?"

"He knows enough. I don't like Wilhelm. Neither of them. And they don't like me."

"Be careful what you say, Sid."

"Well shit, Cyrus. You make it sound like I pulled the trigger. I didn't!" She caught Rebecca rummaging through one of her end-table drawers. "Excuse me, do you have a warrant?"

"This is interesting." Rebecca held the ring box in her hand, opened it up. "Wow. That's one fine rock. Where did you get this?"

"Let me see," Cyrus said.

Rebecca tossed it over.

He snatched it from the air. "Whoa. That is impressive. An engagement ring, Sid?" His expression was twisted. "Who gave this to you?"

"That's none of your business." She averted her eyes for some reason. "Long story, just hand it over."

"No," Cyrus said, "I think I'd like to hear that story. Hmmm." He tapped the ring box on his chin. "There's only one man in your life that I know of. Is this ring from John Smoke?"

"I don't want to talk about it." She held out her hand. "Hand it over, please."

Cyrus removed his spectacles and huffed on the lenses. He cleaned them with his tie and placed them back on his head. He brought the ring in for a closer look. "My, I can't see a single inclusion, and it's so … white. Mister Smoke gave you this, didn't he?"

Sid didn't reply.

"Well, it's certainly a superior product compared to the one I presented you with. It kinda makes me feel like a turd."

"Excuse me?" Rebecca said, tapping her foot on the floor.

"Nothing, dear," he said, still gazing at the stone. "So when did he give this to you?"

Sid didn't want to say it, but she did anyway. "Today."

"Hmmm, interesting timing. You know, until today, we were working on another case. A jewel heist of sorts. I hate to break it to you, Sid, but I believe this ring was stolen."

CHAPTER 10

S ID SAT WITH HER FACE in her hands.

It can't be true. It just can't be true.

Her heart told her one thing, the presented evidence said another. The pragmatic side clashed with the gut. Doubt swelled inside her. If there was one thing she was sure of, Smoke was a good man. But he might just be crazy.

"We could take you in for possession of stolen goods," Rebecca said. She'd found one of Sid's emery boards and started to file her nails. "Not to mention the fact that you might be an accomplice to murder. Aiding and abetting a known fugitive. Tsk tsk. Looks like the deck is quickly stacking against you."

"You're really starting to get on my nerves," Sid said to Rebecca. She faced Cyrus. "You know I don't have anything do to with this, right?"

"That's not for me to decide, Sid. Love can do funny things to a person. For all I know, you and Smoke might be today's Bonnie and Clyde. And you know how the FBI is. They don't like to take any chances." He picked up a picture frame that stood on the end table. It was an image of Megan. "And people not only do unordinary things, but sometimes extraordinary things for family." He glanced at Rebecca.

She gave him a little shrug.

He got up and straightened his tie. "Sid, if you know or find out anything, I'd better know first. Don't leave town."

Really? Wow.

She found Rebecca's face.

The mousy woman seemed satisfied.

"I won't."

Cyrus closed the ring box and stuffed it in his pocket. "I need to check this out. I'll let you know."

As soon as Cyrus and Rebecca departed, Sid took a long, shuddering breath. Her head pounded. Life was upside down again.

Smoke, what have you done to me!

She took a peek through the blinds.

The parking lot was in full view. A little farther down the lot was a black Chevy SUV. She wasn't certain, but it looked like Agent Calhoun was in the driver's seat.

Great!

She wanted to go see Sam and Guppy, but that would be a bad move. That left her with nobody to talk to. The only other ally she thought she had was Smoke, and maybe Mal Gunderson, but she hadn't heard from Mal in what seemed to be forever. Wringing her hands, she sat down and watched the TV again.

It was all over the news. Every major network. It seemed like every channel.

It isn't every day that a high-ranking Washington official is shot. Even though Augustus Wilhelm is a good start.

She squeezed her temples.

Don't even think it, Sid. Geez!

Her phone buzzed. An image of her friend Sadie from the FBI office popped up.

"Hey," Sid said.

"Hey, are you all right?" Sadie said. She sounded really worried.

Pacing throughout the apartment, Sid said, "You have no idea. Cyrus and Rebecca just left. Look, Sadie, don't get involved in this—"

Her phone vibrated. Her mother Sally was calling.

"Crap. My mom's on the other line. Look, I'll check back in with you. I'm fine."

"Just let me know if you need anything, Sid," Sadie said. "You know you can count on me."

"I will." Sid switched lines. "Hi, Mom."

Her mother was all over the place. The woman couldn't even get a complete sentence out.

"Mom, slow down. I'm all right. ... No, I don't think it's him, it just looks like him. ... Yes, I know he seemed like a nice guy. ... No, I'm not in any danger. ... I don't need money. ... No, don't come down here."

Sally rambled on and on.

Sid paced. She found a notebook of paper and slapped it on the table. She put the phone on speaker, set it on the counter, and began scribbling down notes, half listening to her mother as she wrote. "Uh-huh. Uh-huh. Uh-huh."

Watching the television, she jotted down the dates and times the reporters gave. She noted the hospital. Paid attention to the details on the police cars, ambulances, and fire trucks. She watched the replays of the brutal shooting, looking for things that she should and shouldn't see. She wrote down the times that Smoke, Cyrus, and Rebecca had come and gone. She included the things they'd said and not said, too.

"Sidney, are you there? Are you listening to me?" Sally asked on the other line. "And you know your father can't handle all this excitement. He doesn't know that I'm calling. Don't you dare call him."

"I won't, Mom. Look, I need to run some errands while all of this mess gets sorted out. My love to you and Dad. Got to go."

"But—"

Sid disconnected and sagged onto the counter. "Morning Glory, who's going to call next?"

In case her line was being tapped, it was good that she'd maintained a normal conversation. That was real. Genuine. It would be odd if no one called at all. That would have aroused more suspicion.

All of a sudden, Sid sat up straight.

Damn, they probably planted a bug.

Gently she inspected every place Cyrus and Rebecca had been. Thankfully, they'd been confined to the kitchen/living room the entire time. Sid ran her fingers under the counters and tables, and then she rummaged through her two plants and vases.

Nothing, but it doesn't feel like nothing.

Eyeing the room and spinning around slowly, she saw one place she'd almost overlooked: the picture of her and Megan. Without touching the frame, she bent over and took a look behind it. There was a tiny black chip mounted on the velvet back of the frame.

Ah-hah.

Her phone buzzed again. She walked over and picked it up. The screen was blank. It buzzed again, but not in her hand. It came from somewhere else.

Buzz. Buzz. Buzz.

Standing inside her kitchen, Sid slowly spun around.

There.

The sound came from inside a set of jars for baking ingredients. They'd been a house-warming gift from her mother, and not a single grain of salt, flour, or sugar had ever been placed in any of them.

Sid took the lid off of the one in the middle and found a burner phone.

Oh my. It's got to be Smoke.

She answered and put the phone to her ear.

"Ah, Sid. Don't say a word. We need to meet. The Reflecting Pool. Forty minutes. I'll find you." The line went dead. It had not been Smoke.

CHAPTER 11

S IDNEY THREW ON A HALF-DRY pair of blue jeans, gathered some gear into a backpack, and headed out the door. The hard rains had subsided, and she made her way across the water puddles and opened the door of her car. The automobile, a dark-blue 1995 mustang GT, wasn't the Hellcat, but it was cheap. Lousy on fuel but good on speed. The door groaned as she closed it and fired the engine up. Three seconds later she was on the wet main roadway. At the first stoplight she checked the rearview mirror.

"Ah, there you are."

Agent Calhoun was four cars behind her. She could see him hunched over the steering wheel. There was a story about him. Several that she recalled. He abused power. Abused criminals. He'd even abused his supervisor. A couple of witnesses had died in his protection. Fleeing criminals had been blown away—and one of his partners, an agent named Muriel Davis, had vanished without a trace. There were question marks all over the man. He was supposed to be gone. He was a troublemaker, but he was back—and with eyes on Sid.

"So, how do I lose him?" She tapped her fingernails on the steering wheel. The light turned green. She didn't move. It couldn't have been a split second later when the honking started. Horns blared. Car windows filled with angry faces. Sid got out of her car and threw her arms up. "Sorry."

That was when the obscenities started. Everything foul from A to Z with many F's in between. Not one person offered to help.

So much for chivalry.

Sid popped the hood and checked the engine.

I can't believe I'm doing this.

Out of the corner of her eye, she watched the other lanes of traffic blast by until the light turned yellow. She slammed the hood shut and jumped back into her car. She stomped the gas as the light turned red and cruised through the intersection unmolested. Agent Calhoun sat stuck in his lane. His hands slapped the steering wheel.

Sid smiled. "Thanks, Dad. If you hadn't made me watch 'Beverly Hills Cop' with you twenty times, I might never have thought of that." She chuckled. "Every cloud really does have a silver lining."

It didn't take long for her to get to the Reflecting Pool. She even parked in her usual spot. After getting out of the car, she slung the backpack over her shoulder and headed for the pool.

There weren't many people out. The rain was between a mist and drizzle. The Reflecting Pool was usually a pretty popular place during lunchtime. Plenty of joggers, walkers, and tourists. But not today. It was quiet.

Sid tied her hair back and started walking.

Great.

As she headed toward the Lincoln Memorial, a flash of light caught her eye. She figured someone was taking a picture with a huge flash until the light hit her in the face again. Picking up the pace, she marched up the stairs and inside the monument where Abe Lincoln sat. He wasn't alone.

A wrinkle-faced man with soft blue eyes and brown hair wore a black trench coat and was chewing gum. It was Leroy Sullivan.

"I thought you were dead," Sid said, walking up to him.

"Oh, you should know better by now. You can't believe everything you hear." Leroy stuck out his hand. "Gum?"

"No thanks."

"It's everlasting cinnamon."

"Don't you know by now that nothing lasts forever?" she said.

Leroy half cackled and half laughed. "Shit, that was kinda funny. Good for you, Sid." He tucked the gum away. "So, my little buddies Cyrus and Rebecca paid you a visit. Told you I was dead. Boy, they're something, aren't they?"

"So they know you're alive?"

"Oh yeah. They're just trying to cut me out of the Black Slate. You see, they want control of it, and they don't have that. Some people just can't stand to not have control of everything. That's the problem with this country. Well, the world for that matter. Anyway." He came closer and put his arm over her shoulders. "We got a helluva problem. The manhunt for John Smoke has begun."

"So you don't think he did it?"

"If he did it, he wasn't in his right mind when he did. There's always things, dangerous things, lingering out there. Mind control. Hypnosis. It would be mighty hard to get him to go against his nature, but they want him off the streets. You two are causing problems. They don't like it."

"How can we clear him? I mean, there's video. Eyewitnesses."

"Yes," he said with some admiration. "Clever, aren't they. The only thing I can tell you is that you need to find out who really did it. But Sid, it could be him. And if Congressman Wilhelm doesn't survive, then this will never be over with. Even if he does survive, I'm not sure Smoke won't be buried out of sight for a long, long time."

"How am I supposed to do anything with the FBI all over my ass?"

"I'll take care of that." He squeezed her shoulder. "It's time to suit up, soldier."

"So I'm supposed to trust you now?"

"You don't really have anyone else." He handed her a set of keys and pointed back to the parking lot with his other thumb. "Everything you need is in the car."

"What about my Mustang?"

He offered his palm. "I'll see that it's properly retired. Goodbye, Sid. And happy hunting."

CHAPTER 12

Hands stuffed in her pockets, Sid made the long walk back to the parking lot. She hadn't even looked at the keys Leroy had given her. Instead, she squeezed them tight.

Where am I even supposed to start?

Deep in thought, she kept walking, eyes forward, not really paying attention to what was ahead of her until she stood in the space where her car should have been.

Where's my car?

She spun around. The old Mustang was gone without a trace. She checked the keys in her hand. Dodge. With a curious look on her face, she pressed the auto-start button. A throaty engine note followed.

Vrrrooooom!

About ten car spaces away and partially concealed by a silver Volvo crossover rumbled a Dodge Challenger. Sid closed the gap between her and it and came face to face with a new phantom-black Hellcat. Her fingers tingled. "I'll be."

She ran her fingers over the triple coat of black on the hood. Traced the edges of the orange racing stripes. It was just like the one she had lost, but better. She opened the door and sat inside. The leather welcomed her like an old friend. She checked the console and glove box. All of her belongings were there. The registration and insurance were even in her name. She revved it up. "Purr, Hellcat, purr."

Vrrrooooom! Vrrrooooom! Vrrrooooom!

A charge went through her. New life. Exhilaration. She rubbed the dash, leaned back, and with one leg still hanging out the door she took in a deep breath and closed her eyes. "Man, I love fast cars."

Ring! Ring! Ring!

It sounded like the ringer from the old Adam West Batmobile. Sitting up, she fidgeted with the dash and answered the console.

The small digital screen in the middle came to life.

Mal Gunderson's face was on it. "Hi, Sid, how have you been?"

"It hasn't been the best day, but it's getting better."

"Do you like the car?" he said, smiling. The older, olive-skinned man looked as refined and studious as ever.

"Love it."

"Good."

Someone shoved into him, and another face crammed into the screen. It was Sam, stunning and happy. "Hey, Sid. Check out the trunk."

Guppy pressed his face into the picture. "Hey, Sid, did you check out the trunk yet? Check out the trunk!"

"Why, is Smoke in it?"

Sam and Guppy froze, and a frowning Sam said, "That's not funny."

"Oh, sorry."

Sam's face brightened. "Just kidding. No, he's not in it. Only God knows where he is. Now check out the trunk."

"Will you two get back!" Mal said to the both of them. Regaining his composure, he politely said, "Sid, go ahead and check out the trunk."

"All right." She headed outside, checked over her shoulder, and popped the trunk open. "Oh my."

Guns. Big and small. Ammo. Loads of it. A pair of L.A.W. rockets.

Is that a flamethrower?

There were two small metal cases too, like the ones Mal had equipped her and Smoke with before. She unfastened one and opened it up. A sweetheart suit. A vial full of pills. A Glock 22 with a pair of 30-round clips of ammunition. There were bullets too: red, blue, and green tipped. She picked her way through some other supplies. More knives. An ammo belt. A lighter. Watch. Glasses. "Are you trying to turn me into Jane Bond or something?"

Chuckling erupted inside the car.

She closed the trunk, got back in the car, and closed the door. All three faces were crammed onto the screen. "Am I being deployed? That arsenal was full of everything but a parachute."

"Oh, there's one in there," Guppy said with a wink.

"You know, all of that extra weight is going to infringe on my quarter mile time," she said.

"I think you'll be fine," Mal said. "Now Sid, do you think you're ready?"

"Ready for what?"

Sam said, "To kick some bad-guy ass."

"I think you all know I was born ready." Sid adjusted her seat and locked in her radio channels. "What's the plan?"

"We need you to come in," Mal said.

"To the Bat Cave?"

"No."

"The Hall of Justice?"

"No."

"The Avengers—"

"We are staying at the Hyatt Regency Downtown, suite 1111," Mal said, shaking his head. "See you soon."

Just before the image faded, Mal's Asian wife, Asia, popped her head in the screen. "Pick up some good food. Hotel food is shi—"

Sid cut her off, dropped the car into drive, and laid her foot down on the gas. Shoulders pinned to the seat and smiling from ear to ear, she made it to their hotel in no time flat.

CHAPTER 13

ROOM 1111. A BUSINESS SUITE. Suitable for all occasions.

"What do you mean Cyrus took the ring?" Sam said. Her face was red, and her perfect brows were creased. "It wasn't stolen. I'm the one who picked it out. Geez!"

As soon as Sid entered the room, a new interrogation had begun. Half embarrassed, Sid had told them everything, and Smoke's proposal was the worst part of all. "You knew about it?"

"Of course we did," Sam said, shaking her head yes.

"All of you knew?"

"It was a pretty ring." Asia was lying on one of the beds in a hotel robe, watching a soap opera on TV. "I prefer princess cut."

Sid grabbed a pillow and screamed into it. "Eeeeaaaaahhhh!"

Why does everyone but me always know what's going on!

Red-faced, she said, "So did everyone go out shopping for my ring? Guppy, were you there too?"

"There was a lot of shopping going on. Somebody had to hold the bags."

"If it's any consolation," Mal said, "I was the last one to know. Well, obviously you were the last one, but I certainly would have picked a better day to pop the question."

"You can say that again," Asia said. "Fool of a man proposed to me behind a liquor store. Can you believe that?"

"It was a nice view of the river. The liquor store just happened to be there," Mal said. "And I was, well, nervous. It's not like I'd ever asked anyone to marry me before."

"Aw, it's all right, honey," the little woman said. "I've forgiven you, but I'm still waiting on that second honeymoon to Vegas."

Sid sat down on the edge of the bed, exhausted and embarrassed. Smoke sure had awfully weird ways of doing things. She recalled the first time she'd read his profile. No hint of a schoolboy romantic anywhere in there. If anything, it had said he was a dangerous, lawless terror.

How can I marry an enigma?

Sam threw her arms up. "We can't have a wedding without a groom, so I suppose it's time we got to work."

"Indeed." Sitting behind his laptop, Mal pecked at some keys.

Guppy fed some paper into a portable printer. "And pardon everyone, Sid. This certainly is serious business, having to clear Smoke."

"Clear the Smoke. Funny," Asia said.

"You'll have to pardon my wife, Sid. She suffers from a mild but still annoying form of Tourette's."

"What is Tourette's?" Asia asked.

"Continuing," Mal said, "I don't think anyone here believes Smoke did what we think we saw him do. We're going to have to find out who did do what we saw." He turned on a projector, and his computer's image appeared on the wall. "Lights."

Guppy lumbered over to the door and turned off the lights.

The projector's light kept the room lit up.

Mal ran the video that the television stations had played during the assassination attempt. "We should be able to find some clues right here. Let me know if any of you sees anything out of the ordinary."

Sid had a very strong memory, borderline photographic. Several things jumped out at her. When the video stopped, she spoke first. "The shooter wore gloves. I don't recall seeing Smoke in a ball cap before, either. Back up to when Wilhelm is behind the podium."

The video image cruised backward.

"Stop it there. See this," she said, pointing with her finger. "This is a full view of the entire stage. One of the first things I said to myself was, 'Where's the Secret Service?' Wilhelm always has two of them nearby. There weren't any today."

"Very good," Mal said.

"Also," Sid continued, "Smoke doesn't move like that. This guy's stiff. Smoke is graceful. And look at Wilhelm. His eyes land on the audience and freeze on Smoke. If he felt he was in danger, then he would have moved out of harm's way, but he doesn't. He keeps talking." She put her finger on Wilhelm's image. "Run it right up to the point when the gun is fired."

Mal did, and then he froze the camera angle on Wilhelm's face.

"Look," said Sid. "He's tightening up. You can almost see that paunchy face of his pucker up, and the shot doesn't come until a couple of seconds later. If I were to guess, I'd say he was expecting it."

"Pretty good, Sid," Mal said with admiration. "I didn't even pick up on all that. Of course, it's not my forte."

"Good work, Sid," Guppy said while he rolled up the sleeves of his flannel shirt. He dabbed his sweaty forehead with a handkerchief. "I'd be lying if I said I wasn't worried. Still, how are we going to prove that it wasn't him? We weren't there, and whoever did that looks just like him—and he has disappeared."

Sid sat down at the table.

Sam and Guppy joined her.

Every eye was fixed on her, looking for leadership. Looking for answers.

She took out the notepad where she'd jotted her notes in her apartment. "Let's start with what we do know. Time. Place. Hmmm. Witnesses. Did anyone see any interviews with the witnesses?"

"A couple," Guppy mumbled.

Sam was checking her nails until she found Sid's eyes on her. "Uh, nope."

"Tell you what, Sam. Maybe you and Guppy can contact Russ Davenport. If anyone else is on this who we can trust, it's him."

"Listen, Sid," Mal said, "all of this that you are suggesting is fine and well, but I don't see how any of it will help Smoke. We need a body and a gun. We aren't a bunch of attorneys who can clear his name. No, this is deep, and it's got the Drake's stink all over it. And as we all know, they have deeper pockets than we do."

"Aw, quit being such a sissy," Asia said.

"Will you shut up?" Mal fired back. "Now, I do think you should follow your instincts. That's fine. But I need to dig into some deeper things." He pecked at the computer and pulled up a new screen. "Look at this."

Images of faces from the Black Slate showed up. AV, Nightbird, Mason Crow, the Ratson Brothers, the forever children, the hunchback, Swift the rat-wolf, gargoyles and a handful of deaders.

"Creepy," Sam said with awe, "but kinda cool."

"What are you getting at, Mal?" Sid asked.

He gazed at all of them. "These are shifters. Men and women that change forms. What if there's one out there who has shifted to look just like John Smoke?"

CHAPTER 14

SID RUBBED THE CHILL BUMPS racing up her neck and shoulders. "Are you telling me that might not have even been him in my apartment at all?"

"No, that's not what I'm saying," Mal said. "Did you get a creepy feeling? Was there something odd about him?"

"Yeah, was he creepy?" Sam said.

"No, not exactly. Just the fact that he proposed to me."

"Aw, did he get down on one knee?" Sam said. "I love it when they do that."

"I take it you've been proposed to before," said Sid.

"Oh yeah, lots of times." Sam studied her nails. "But I only said yes once." She winked at Guppy.

"Let's not get ahead of ourselves," Mal said, closing the laptop.

Guppy powered down the projector. "It's only a theory."

Sam and Guppy got up and headed toward the door.

"Where are you two going?" asked Sid.

"After Russ Davenport, like you said." Sam was giving her a look.

"Forget it, I'll go."

"What? Wait a minute, why?" Sam said. "I think we can handle it."

"It's not that," Sid said, "it's just that I don't know where to start, so it might as well be there."

"I don't see any reason why we can't come with," Guppy said.

"Because three's a crowd." She felt someone tapping her on the shoulder.

It was Asia. The little woman said, "And four's even worse. No, let's go get something to eat. I'm tired of sitting in this stuffy room. Feels like a hospital." She made a sour face. "Uck!"

Asia sat in the front seat of the Hellcat, staring straight ahead and stuffing her face with French fries. Sam and Guppy were in the back, and neither one of them stayed quiet longer than one second at a time.

"You know, this car's fairly roomy back here. Needs more leg room, but heck, it's a sports car," Sam said. She had a copy of Nightfall DC folded in front of her. "Hey, it says here there are giant rats living in the sewers." She shoved Sid's shoulder. "Duh."

"Why don't you lay into this thing, Sid? I want to feel that power. Say, I know a great track that we can take it for a spin on," Guppy said. He pushed himself up toward the dash. "Maybe time the quarter mile. See? You have a timer in your console here, and you can figure out your G-forces as well. Look, see the race light?" He poked it with his pudgy finger. "Sweet, huh."

Sid smacked his hand. "Do you mind?"

"Can't say that I do."

Sam shoved him back in his seat. "Behave yourself."

Asia stuck her hand in Sid's face. "French fry?"

"No thanks," Sid said.

Geez, what is wrong with these people?

That was one of the things that bothered Sid about these people most. They didn't seem to worry. It was both weird and refreshing. Since she graduated high school and went into the service, most of the training had been intense. The job was serious. She pushed herself to the highest levels and gave herself the biggest challenges. Heck, there were plenty of days when she probably didn't crack a smile. And come to think of it, the FBI was notorious for its frowns.

Sheesh.

But this crew, they seemed to delight in danger.

"How much farther, Sid?" Guppy asked.

"A few more miles of highway and a few miles of old roadway after that," she said. "Why?"

"Oh, I think I'm starting to get a little carsick is all."

"Oh honey," Sam said, petting his head, "do you want us to pick you up some Dramamine?"

Sid tuned them out. Or at least tried to until they got to the camp where Russ Davenport kept his trailer. She shut off the engine and popped open her door. "We're here."

Guppy hustled out, a little green. "I call shotgun on the ride back."

"Tell you what," Sam said, stretching her long frame out of the car and putting on her sunglasses, "this is pretty much how I imagined it."

Russ's two trailers stuck together looked just as shabby as they had before. The wooden deck needed paint, and the wood was aged grey. Rust was apparent on the corner edges of the trailers, and the screen door banged a little in the wind.

"Why didn't you just call?" Asia said, crinkling her nose. "This place is shitty."

"He doesn't like phones," Sid said.

The steps creaked beneath her feet on her way up to the front door. She pounded on the frame. "Russ! It's Sid. Sidney Shaw."

No answer. She scanned the camp area. A white convertible Chrysler LeBaron was parked nearby. Its best days had been at least two decades ago.

Guppy walked over to it, put his hand on the hood, and showed Sid a shrug.

She banged on the trailer again. "Russ!" She opened the screen door. The main door was cracked open behind it. She looked back over her shoulder and pulled out her gun.

Asia's eyes popped open.

Sid went inside.

Russ's trailer was a mess. The books were all over the floor. Computer equipment was busted. Anything that opened had been pulled out or torn off. Glass crunched under her feet. "Russ?"

Thump. Thump. Thump.

Swallowing hard, Sid ventured deeper into the trailer toward the bedroom. There was nothing but ruffled sheets, torn up pillows, and loose papers. "Russ?"

Thump. Thump. Thump.

She whirled and faced the tiny door that led to the bathroom. Gun ready, she grabbed the handle and jerked the door open. Russ's heavy frame rolled out. His mouth, hands, and legs were bound. He was barely breathing—and bleeding from the head.

CHAPTER 15

"**A**W MAN," RUSS SAID, HOLDING a wet towel to his head. He was propped up on his sofa, surrounded by Sid and everyone else. "I gotta tell you, I'm sure glad you guys stopped by. I thought I was a goner."

"What happened?" Sid asked.

"I'm sitting at my computer, you know, doing my thing and working on my paper." He sucked his teeth and winced. "When I hear a sound. I turn, and *pop*, I get hammered right between the eyes. The next thing I know I'm bound up and lying on the floor. Some dude's tearing up all my stuff, and I yell at him. He turns, and then things get spooky. His eyes are pitch black, and his face is weird and pasty. His hands are huge. He snatches me up off the floor with one hand and tosses me back onto the bed. Man, I thought I was dead."

"Did he say anything?" she asked.

"He—or it—asked me where Smoke was. I said, 'I don't know, ask the fuzz.'" Russ's breath shuddered. "That's when everything went black. Well, after his fist exploded into my head." His eyes found Sam's face and brightened. "But it looks like my day is getting better."

"Looks like you're going to make it," Sid said. "You might want to check and see if he—or it—took anything."

Russ leaned forward with a groan and let Sid help him to his feet. Scanning everything, he shuffled into the other trailer. It was a little more suitable for company and had a bigger desk with more intact computer screens. He took a seat behind the desk. "Well, doesn't look like anything is broken in here. So, uh, can one of you grab me a beer out of the fridge? It'll do me better than this rag."

Asia—petite, expressionless, and pretty—brought over two bottles and set them on his desk. She twisted the caps off both of them. "The only thing decent in here is your beer. Everything else sucks." She gulped some down, took a seat, and turned on Russ's TV.

"Uh," Russ said, grabbing his beer, "so what brought you guys over here?"

"You know about the Wilhelm shooting?" Sid said.

"Of course. That's what I was working on when that goon showed up."

"What were you working on?" Sid asked.

"Ah, well, like everything else I write about in the city, I was working on the conspiracy." Russ took a long sip of beer. "And that shooting is another doozy."

Arms crossed over her chest, Sid said, "What do you mean?"

"You know, one thing that I do all the time is interview. I've done hundreds of them, heck, maybe thousands, I don't know, but I'll tell you this. I know when someone's not being honest. And, I'm pretty good with faces." He turned his screen around so that everyone nearby could see. He typed on the keys, and a pair of images showed up. "For instance, this guy who I like to call jackass number one."

Sid, Sam, and Guppy leaned closer. The man on the screen had kinky hair and was going bald. His cheeks were saggy, and so was his jaw. Russ played the eyewitness interview, and the man sounded like a real know-it-all. He recalled a lot of interesting details: how many shots were fired and what the shooter was wearing.

"Okay, where are you going with this?" Sid asked.

"Well, watch this other interview. Same guy, right, but different shooting. This was from a taping just outside of Atlanta. Remember that shooting at the university? Guess who was there." He played the video.

"Hah!" Sam said. "That SOB recited the same MO. I'll be damned. You know I read an article that said the Atlanta shooting never happened."

"That was my article," Russ said, giving her a smile.

"Well, it was a good one. But reading that, and seeing this all for myself, now that is something." Sam walked away. "I need a beer."

"I'll take one," Guppy added.

"Sure, help yourselves," Russ said. "And I can only assume you guys are going to stick around long enough to help me clean up this mess."

"*Phllyyt!*" Asia said. "This place is hopeless."

"It ain't that bad." He shook his head. "Tough crowd. Anyway, I've got this guy on two other videos and two more separate incidents. And he's not the only one. There are others too. He's just the one I hate the most."

"Why do you hate him? Have you met him?" Sam said, coming back with two beers.

"The man's a liar. I just can't stand liars."

"Maybe you should consider moving out of this city," Sam said, taking a seat on the edge of his desk. "Ever consider that?"

"Nope." Russ guzzled down the rest of his beer and tossed the bottle into a little trash can that toppled over. "Because that's just what they want."

"So you think Congressman Wilhelm wasn't even shot?" Sid said.

"Have you seen his body, dead or alive? Has anyone? No, this stinks, and it's got the Drake written all over it. Crap. Uh, can someone beer me?"

Asia got up and returned with a beer. She tossed it to him. "Hope you can take the cap off by yourself, sloppy man." She returned to her seat.

Looking around his screen at Asia, Russ said, "I can't tell if I like her or not. Pretty and mean. Huh. What's her story?"

"Mean," Guppy said.

"Russ, what's your theory then? Why the setup?" Sid asked.

He twisted the cap off his bottle and replied, "It's pretty clear to me. They have a DC-wide manhunt going on because they want your pal John Smoke dead."

CHAPTER 16

S MOKE DEAD. SIDNEY FELT HOLLOW inside on the drive back to the hotel. It didn't help that everyone else was a little quiet as well.

"Oh, he'll be alright," Sam said, reaching up and rubbing Sid's shoulder. "He hasn't been caught."

"It hasn't even been a day," Sid said, cruising the streets of DC. A tingle went up and down her spine as she passed by a police car with flashing lights on. A man was handcuffed and being stuffed into the back of the patrol car. Everyone in Sid's car was looking. "Has anyone heard anything at all from him?"

"No," Guppy said. "And I don't suppose we will either, too risky. You know what I mean."

"Your weird boyfriend likes to hide," Asia said. She was checking her makeup in the visor mirror. "He be fine. Say, how about we stop and get something to eat before we go back to the hotel? I'm in the mood for some Indian cuisine, eh? Spicy food makes your worries go away."

"I'm not hungry," Sid said, irritated, "but I'd love to drop you off so you can gorge your little self."

"Don't be so frosty," Asia said.

Sam chuckled. "Forgive her, Sid. It's taken us some time to get used to her too."

Sid had gotten used to Sam and Guppy over the last few months, since they'd all been working together as bounty hunters. The pair had been nothing short of reliable, sharp witted, and effective. They would make great FBI agents, but they were pretty heavy on the big government conspiracy side. On the one hand, they seemed pretty kooky with their theories, but on the other hand, there was the Black Slate. It made it kind of hard to rule out anything they said. "I think we need to see if we can figure out where Congressman Wilhelm is. If this was staged, he's probably alive somewhere."

"He's at Angels of Mercy Hospital, right?" Sam said. "Me and Guppy can handle it. I'm a pretty persuasive woman when I put my mind to it."

"You're always persuasive," Guppy said.

"Aw!" Sam kissed Guppy on the forehead. "You're so sweet, honey."

"Honey?" Sid and Asia both said together. Sid continued. "Are you two dating or something?"

"Dating?" Sam took out a compact mirror and started putting some lipstick on. "Certainly not dating."

Guppy chuckled. "We're married."

"What?" Sid and Asia both said with alarm. "You're serious?"

"Of course. Geez, didn't you know that?" Sam said. She held her hand out and flashed the many rings on it. "See that rock. Or those rocks?"

Sid had noticed Sam's bejeweled fingers before. The woman had plenty of rings, and she changed them out all the time too. Sid had never paid any mind to the small engagement ring that was always there. "Interesting. So where's your ring, Guppy?" she said into the rearview mirror. "I don't see any rings on your fingers."

Guppy pulled out a heavy chain around his neck. There was a gold band attached to it along with a pair of dog tags. "I've gotten a little heftier since we got married, so it don't fit no more."

"Then go on diet," Asia said, "chubby dwarf."

"Great," Sid said. She took pride in figuring things out for herself, but she'd totally missed on Sam and Guppy. The pair worked so well together, and neither ever fawned or argued. Of course, she wasn't with them most of the time, but still …

How did I miss that?

She'd even done background checks on them and didn't recollect anything about them being married.

Guppy, sitting in the back, eased up between the front seats. "I know what you're thinking, Sid. How'd you miss that? You see, not everything's on public record. That's just what they want, and they can use it against you. But don't worry." He pointed up and gave her a wink. "He saw the entire ceremony."

Sid showed a little smile. "So, are there any other secrets I need to know about that my thorough research missed?"

Sam and Guppy sank back into their seats.

Asia started humming.

Sid smacked the wheel with her hands. "Seriously? There's a bigger secret than you two being married?"

"No one said it was a secret," Sam said, tucking her lipstick away. "You just missed it."

"What else did I miss, then?"

"Uh, well, there's only one other oversight I can think of," Sam said. "I'm Smoke's sister."

Sid pulled the car over into a grocery parking lot, slammed it into park, and turned her shoulder toward Sam. "What?"

"Well, half-sister, sort of."

"Which is it?"

"It's complicated?"

"Do you have the same father or the same mother?"

"More complicated than that," Sam said. "Look, I don't really want to discuss it. But at least now you know." She flipped her hands up. "There. No more secrets."

"You can't just leave me hanging," Sid said, taking a demanding tone.

"You know enough. That's it." Sam made the zipped-lips motion and looked out the window.

"She won't talk now," Guppy said. "Trust me."

"True, but I'm sure you know as much as she does," Sid said.

"That is true, Sid, but I know better than to open my mouth and tick off my wife. You'll have to get it from her someday. Or him."

"Yeah, right." Sid put the car in gear and headed toward Angel of Mercy Hospital. A long twelve minutes later, she dropped off Sam and Guppy at the hospital's ER entrance. Getting out and letting Sam out of her side, she took the woman by the arm, a little torn between mad and happy when she said, "The more I know, the more likely I am to say yes. I don't like secrets."

Sam gave her a tough little nod. "I'll be in touch."

Sid sat back down in the car and looked at Asia. "Do you have any secrets that you want to share?"

Asia patted her belly. "No secrets here. Hungry."

Sid started pulling out of the emergency room entrance.

A man walked right in front of her car toward the hospital.

She hit the brake and laid on the horn. "Idiot."

The man kept moving. Head down and clutching his side, he vanished through the sliding glass doors.

"I can't stand hospitals," Sid grumbled.

"Me either," Asia agreed.

While she was driving down the parking lot, a crash of glass exploded from somewhere outside. A man toppled out of a third-floor window. The bushes broke his fall. Another man sailed out of the window and hit the pavement hard.

"Holy crap!" Asia said. "Men don't fly so well."

Standing inside the third-floor window was a tall and ranging man with his back to them. He moved fast, fading in and out of sight. He wore green scrubs and had a surgeon's cap and mask on his head. The sharp pop of gunfire sounded from somewhere inside the building. The man dressed as a doctor jumped out of the window and landed in the bushes.

"Looks like another person going to need emergency room," Asia commented.

The man sprang up out of the bushes and took off at a full sprint.

Men in dark suits and glasses hung out of the window and started firing.

"What kind of hospital is this?" Asia said, folding her arms over her chest. "They shooting at the doctors!"

"Asia, that's not a doctor," Sid said, "that's Smoke."

CHAPTER 17

"**R**EALLY?" ASIA SAID. "HE'S A doctor and a bounty hunter? Looks like he's probably a better bounty hunter."

"Shut up, Asia." Sid stomped on the gas, peeling rubber.

Smoke's head popped up between the cars in the parking lot briefly, and then she lost sight of him. "Damn!" She cruised up the parking lot, looking left and right. "Where did he go?"

"I think we better get out of here," Asia said, peeking in the side-view mirror. "Angry patients everywhere."

Men in suits poured out of the emergency room exits and spread out all over the parking lot.

Sid counted eight of them with guns ready.

What have you done now, John?

"Look, Sid, you need to get us out of here." Asia tapped on her shoulder. "Look!"

Police cars with flashing lights were coming. In seconds the entire parking lot would be sealed off.

Sid couldn't get pulled over and have the trunk searched either. She eased on the gas and squeezed off the lot and onto the main road just as two cop cars blew by. She pulled off on the berm and looked back for Smoke. "Whew!" she said, heart racing and looking forward.

The whine of a motorcycle engine caught her ear.

She looked back.

Smoke was on a street bike, hemmed in by Secret Service and cops. The only way off the lot was through the police barricade. Officers from all over were swarming in from all directions now. Smoke revved up the bike and took off straight toward the shooters.

"No!"

Like a bullet, the bike screamed down the parking lot straight into the path of the shooters. Smoke and the ultra-fast bike covered the distance to the barricade in two seconds.

The shooters jumped aside just as Smoke squeezed between the bumpers of two cars and jettisoned out onto the main road. A hail of gunfire and screams of shock and alarm followed.

The wide-eyed Asia turned to Sid. "If you marry him, you better get a lot of life insurance."

"I will," Sid said, gunning the engine, "if I don't kill him first."

The Hellcat's engine revved. Rubber burned.

Pinned to their seats, Sid and Asia chased after the diminishing speck of John Smoke.

"Slow down, slow down!" Asia screamed.

Sid did no such thing. She blew by three cars merging onto the highway and was up to a hundred miles per hour before Asia screamed again.

"Aiyeee!"

The Hellcat closed in on Smoke.

With Smoke's hair flying in the wind behind it, the big green ghost had slowed, but it still weaved in and out of the cars on the highway.

"Where are you going, John?" Sidney checked her rearview mirror.

Police lights sparkled, but they were still far behind. It wouldn't be long before every police car in town packed the interstate. She pressed on the gas. A hundred and twenty. A hundred and thirty.

"You're crazy!" Asia yelled.

It was crazy. Illegal. Dangerous. Stupid even, but she had to catch up to Smoke. Ahead, she saw the helmetless man glance over his shoulder. "But he's crazier than me. He doesn't even have a seatbelt."

Asia balled up in the seat, clutching the seatbelt with her eyes squeezed shut, chanting, "Please don't wreck. Please don't wreck. Please don't wreck. I don't want to die yet!"

Smoke's motorcycle slowed and moved over to the right lane. Sid caught up and pulled alongside him. They both backed off to about seventy miles per hour. She rolled down her window.

"Hi, Sid!" Smoke yelled.

"Don't you 'Hi' me, you idiot. What do you think you're doing?"

"Evading law enforcement." His eyes scanned the Hellcat. "Nice ride. Where'd you get it?"

"Never mind that, John! What's going on? What's your plan?" she asked.

"I need to clear my name and probably blow up a few things. Look, Sid, stay away from this. I can handle it." Still cruising down the highway at seventy miles per hour, he put his hand on the car door and peeked in. "Hey, Asia."

"Shut up, crazy man!" said the little woman.

"John, you can't do this alone. It's too big." She could hear the sirens now. "They're going to kill you."

"Aw, Sid, don't worry. You can count on me." He glanced back. "Tell you what, follow me off the next exit ramp. I've got a plan." He sped the bike up, but then he slowed down and approached her window again. "Oh, wait. Do you happen to have an extra gun in there?"

Asia popped open the glove box and tossed over a 1911 semi-auto with an extra-long clip.

Sid handed it to him.

Smoke stuffed it down the front of his pants. "Thanks. Now follow me." He led them off the next exit ramp, where traffic was bumper-to-bumper at the red light.

"Morning Glory. What is he doing? Is he stupid?"

Smoke turned around and saluted. Revving up the bike, he squirted through the traffic, raced through the intersection, popped a wheelie, and roared back up the other side of the entrance ramp.

"No you didn't!" Sid screamed, banging her hands on the wheel.

"Yes he did," Asia said, dabbing the sweat off her brow. "And I'm happy for it. He's crazy, but in a sexy way."

Sid ground her teeth.

I can't believe he did that.

Police sirens roared by on the interstate over their heads. Looking up through the window, Sid saw two choppers zoom overhead. Men were manning the machine guns on both of them. Helpless and gaping, Sid felt doom creep between her shoulder blades.

CHAPTER 18

"THE MANHUNT IS STILL ON for this suspect the authorities have not identified," said the female reporter on the television screen. She was standing outside the Angels of Mercy hospital. A picture of John Smoke, a little blurry, appeared in the right-hand corner. "Authorities say this man is armed and dangerous. If you see him, do not approach him, but send any information you have to the contacts listed on your screen."

Sid turned the television off and lay back on her couch, rubbing her temples. "What are you doing to me, John Smoke?"

"Did you say something?" Sam said, popping her head out of the kitchen. She wore an apron, and her hair was up in a bun. "Say, why don't we make some cookies? It will make you feel better." She rummaged through the cupboards, opening and closing the doors. "Or maybe not. You don't cook very much, do you."

"I don't eat a lot."

"That's a good thing. Too much gluten in everything."

Sid leaned over on her side, facing Sam. "And you're wanting to make cookies?"

"I didn't say we had to eat them. I usually just give them to Guppy. Maybe that little Chinese lady. She eats like she has a tapeworm or something."

Sid put her feet on the floor and rubbed her eyes. It had been two days since Smoke lost her on the highway, and she'd barely slept a wink because of it. And things had been quiet. Too quiet. It didn't seem possible that Smoke could have escaped just about every law enforcement official in DC. And those helicopters really put the fright in Sid. What if Smoke was already dead?

"Don't do that," Sam said.

"Do what?"

"You're biting your nails."

"Oh. Thanks."

"Why don't we go out and get some fresh air?" Sam suggested. She took off her apron. She was wearing a sequined shirt with a dragon on it, jeans, and high heels. "Maybe some good news will find its way to us."

Sid headed for the bedroom. "I need to change."

"Why don't you put that sweetheart suit on? It'll make you feel better. Besides, you never know when we might run into danger."

"Then why don't you wear one too?" Sid said. She took off her shirt and opened the case to the sweetheart suit.

"Not my thing," Sam replied. "But if I were you, I'd be wearing it. Especially after what you told me about those rats. Ew!"

Sidney removed her jeans, took up the suit, and started slipping it on. It was snug but energizing, a warm second skin that made her body feel alive.

Her stomach groaned.

Sam stuck her head into the bedroom. "Was that you?"

"The suit does that."

Sam eyed her up and down. "It does look good on you. Hmmm ... Maybe I *will* try one of those things."

Moving to her closet, Sid slipped on some new jeans and a shirt over the suit. She grabbed her boots—light but durable hiking ones—and laced them up. After she cracked her neck from side to side, she strapped on a pair of shoulder holsters and adjusted them in front of the mirror.

"Not bad," Sam said. "You look like the Punisher."

"Ha ha." Sid gathered her gear, and out the door they both went.

Agent Calhoun was leaning on the trunk of the Hellcat. He was a little bigger and thicker than Smoke, heavy shouldered with a dangerous and lazy look in his eyes. His hair was really short, bald in places, and his voice was a warning thunder when he spoke. "I see you upgraded to a better set of wheels. Nice."

"What do you want, Calhoun?"

"Oh, just the same thing every officer of the law in DC does: John Smoke." He pushed off the car and rose to his full height. Looking down on Sidney like a drill sergeant, he added, "Dead or alive."

Leroy Sullivan had told Sid that the FBI dogs wouldn't be a problem. Yet, here Calhoun was. It put a crimp on things. "I don't like your chances," Sid said. "You can't even keep up with me. What makes you think you can keep up with him?"

"A quarter of a million dollars," he said. "That's the bounty on his head."

"You can't collect that. You're an agent."

"Was. You see, I'm on an extended leave of absence." He flashed a broad smile. "Family problems." He opened up his long coat, revealing a pair of guns and a long knife hitched in his belt. He took out a handkerchief and mopped the sweat from his brow. "It's gonna be a hot few days, Sid." His eyes gave her and Sam the once-over as he walked away. "Real hot."

"That's one shady bastard, isn't it," Sam said, getting into the Dodge.

"To put it mildly." She pulled the car out and stopped in front of Calhoun. He was hunched over the wheel inside his black Suburban. She loaded some blue-tipped bullets into her Glock's clip, charged the weapon, took aim on Calhoun's engine block, and squeezed off a few rounds.

Blam! Blam! Blam!

The armor-piercing bullets ripped through the SUV's metal, and the engine started to smoke. Agent Calhoun's face darkened, and his eyes narrowed on Sid.

"Let's go eat," Sid said as she drove away with Sam's laughter filling her ears.

The long lunch that went into evening was good. The return back to Sid's apartment was bad. The front door was busted open, and two police officers were inside. Her entire apartment had been ransacked.

CHAPTER 19

"**I**S THIS YOUR PLACE?" THE one officer said. He wasn't very tall and had a friendless demeanor. A real sourpuss. The other cop, much younger and taller, had a cocky smile.

"It's mine," Sid said, forcing her way inside. The cabinets were empty. Glass was broken. Her bed was overturned, along with many other things. The padding on the sofa and chairs was cut open and the stuffing pulled out. "What happened?"

"Anything missing?" the older cop said, writing on a small notepad.

She held up a picture of Megan that sat on the end table. The glass and frame were broken. Sighing, she said, "Let me look around and see."

"Do you have a boyfriend or husband, miss? Maybe a fallout?" asked the younger cop.

"No."

"Er, what's your name, Miss?" asked the older cop.

"Who called this in?" Sidney fired back.

"Beg your pardon?"

"Who called this in?"

"Er, it was a 911, I guess. Look, I'm asking the questions here. Name?"

She pulled out her badge and held it in his face. "Sidney Shaw."

He leaned in and tilted the cap back on his head. "FBI Liaison. What's that mean? You some kind of consultant or something?"

"Maybe you should call them and find out," she said.

"Hey, we're just doing our jobs," the older cop said. "You just need to cooperate, Miss FBI Liaison. I can still haul you in for obstruction, you know."

There were plenty of obstinate cops she'd crossed before, but there was something different about this one. His uniform was a bad fit. The buttons were tight, the cuffs on his pants too low. The other cop's pants were too high, and the grin on his face was a bit abnormal. He leered at both Sid and Sam with a hungry look in his eyes. "What is your badge number?" Sid asked.

"My what?" the older cop asked.

Sid enunciated. "Badge number."

"It's, uh—" He looked down at the badge on his chest. "Five. Four. One. Two."

Sid eased away and took Sam by the wrist and led her toward the front door. "You know, I didn't notice a police car outside. Did you two walk over from the station?"

Both officers' nostrils flared. Their eyes narrowed and dimmed. Hands clutching in and out, the taller one said in a throaty voice, "Where's Smoke, woman!"

Sid went for her guns.

They were halfway out when the old officer collided into her. He clamped his hands over her wrists and wrenched the guns out.

"Run, Sam! Run!"

The gorgeous woman made it down two steps. The tall cop snatched her by the hair and yanked her back. "Hey!" She started to scream, only to have the man's hand clamped over her mouth.

He dragged her inside and slammed the door shut.

Sid launched a kick into the cop that had her.

He laughed it off.

She twisted away, only to have him pounce on her back.

He pinned her down with inhuman strength.

"Damn. You're a deader, aren't you."

"In the undead flesh," he said. "It's the price we pay for being superhuman."

She drove her head into his chin.

His grip loosened, but he held firm. "Aw, you're only going to hurt yourself more fooling around like that. Now tell me, where's Smoke?"

"That seems to be the question everyone is asking, but I don't know."

The deader cop forced her onto her back and slapped her in the face. "I don't like your tone."

Grimacing, Sid managed to snake a knife out of the back of her pants. She sliced his throat. "I don't like yours either."

The man staggered back, holding his throat but not bleeding.

Sid scrambled for her gun and got the drop on the first deader cop. "One hole through the chest will end you!"

The first cop froze. The second cop had his arm wrapped around Sam's throat. "Yeah, but one hard squeeze and her trachea will cave in. Who's going to save her then? Now tell us where Smoke is!"

Blam!

A bullet ripped through the tall deader's forehead. He staggered back with a face full of alarm.

Blam!

Sid's second shot tore clear through the dead man's heart. He dropped to the floor.

The other deader cop rushed out the door.

Sid couldn't get a clean shot at him.

"That was crazy!" Sam said, catching her breath and rubbing her neck. She kicked the deader cop lying on the floor. "He's not even bleeding, but he was so real." She glanced up at Sid. "I thought deaders were slow and stupid."

Tucking her weapons back inside her holsters, Sid said, "They were, but they're getting better. More real." She kneeled down by the dead man on the floor and pulled down his collar. There was a Drake tattoo of a black rising sun on his neck.

"Spooky, huh," Sam said, trembling.

"You okay?"

"I'm just getting the chills." Sam pulled out her phone and started texting. "Let me get the word out to Guppy. He gets worried if I don't check in."

"Tell him we need some cleanup. Cops, real ones, will be all over this place. Not sure we have a good explanation for this man down here." She gave her apartment a long, sad look. "I think I'm going to need a new place to live."

Looking at her phone, Sam said, "We need to get out of here. Guppy and Mal will handle the cleanup."

Sidney got a sinking feeling she might not ever see her apartment again. All she had left that hadn't been destroyed fit in her two suitcases. And then she picked up the picture frame, removed Megan's picture, and tucked it inside her shirt. Taking one more quick glance around, she said, "Let's go."

Driving her new car, she made her way out of the apartment complex. It being midday, there weren't too many people standing around. A couple of old ladies stood on the sidewalk, wearing colorful robes. A maintenance crew in a golf cart passed them by.

Eyes forward, she pulled out onto the main highway and let out a breath. "You know, I don't really understand why they want John so bad. Why him and not me?" she said to Sam.

"You're easier to control, I guess."

"What's that supposed to mean?"

"Think about it. You have more family than he does. Or at least you don't think yours are expendable."

"Does he really think that way?" Sid asked. "That you're expendable?"

Checking her makeup in the vanity mirror, Sam replied, "Eh, we're covered. Besides, Smoke's a 'kill them all, let God sort them out' kinda guy."

"I think he's more compassionate than that."

Sam shifted toward Sid. "Let me tell you something, sister. Where we come from, we don't compromise with evil."

CHAPTER 20

S ID LAY LOW THE NEXT couple of days. She slept at Sam and Guppy's place, a tiny apartment on the other side of town, much like the one Sid had to abandon. It was morning, and coffee was brewing. Sam had some eggs and bacon on a griddle. Sitting on the sofa with the television on, Sid rubbed her bleary eyes.

Every day, on every channel, they talked about the manhunt. They never mentioned John's name or anything about his past. They just called him the unknown man and showed a slightly blurred picture. The experts were popping up on every outlet too. They had all kinds of theories about who Smoke was. Prior military. An ex-con. A deranged madman. A jilted employee.

Sid smiled.

They don't know how close they are.

Sam set a steaming mug of coffee on the table.

"Thanks," Sid said. The hot brew stung her lip. "Say, Sam, you didn't see Wilhelm in the hospital, did you?"

"No, everything was chaos when we went in there. I only got a glimpse into the room, but it was cleared out."

"Nothing odd?"

"No, nothing's come to mind since the last time you asked. Or the time before that." Sam fixed up a couple of plates of food and sat down beside Sid. "You aren't doing all right, are you."

Sid nibbled on her bacon and shook her head. "I am. I just have a feeling someone got to him before we did."

"It's not hard to hide in a city like this. It's pretty big, and Smoke knows it pretty well. I'm sure he's blending in with a stack of hot cakes somewhere right now." Sam stabbed the scrambled eggs with her fork and ate. Swallowing it down with some coffee, she said, "Don't worry, something will surface."

Digging into her meal, Sid fished through the news channels. She needed to find something, anything that would be a good starting point. Everything had happened so fast two days ago that she was just now getting a chance to sort things out. She flipped from channel to channel, and then there it was. An eyewitness. And not just any eyewitness, but the same slob that Russ Davenport from Nightfall DC had pointed out. Elbows on her knees, Sid leaned forward.

"What is it?" Sam said, squinting her eyes at the screen.

Sid paused the TV. "If this guy is indeed an actor like Russ says, then maybe he can provide a few answers."

"Yeah," Sam agreed, "he really has been making his rounds, hasn't he? I'll get right on it."

Sid finished up her breakfast, slipped some clothes on over the sweetheart suit, and loaded up her gear.

"Where are you going?" Sam asked.

"Out to catch the bad guys."

"What? I thought we were gonna hang out and watch the Bewitched marathon." Sam leaned over the back of the sofa. "Say, which Darren did you like better?"

"Dick York, of course." Sid slung her pack over her shoulder and nodded at the TV. "Let me know what you find out about that witness, I mean that camera-hogging bearded tub of lard. I'm on my way."

"I'm on it like Larry Tate on ad money."

Sid departed with a chuckle. The Hellcat's engine roared, and before long she was cruising down the highway. With the radio off, she had some time to think, but she liked Sam's company.

Sometimes you need time to yourself.

Thirty minutes into the drive, she got her first text from Sam. It was the location of a small television station just outside the northwest rim of DC.

Man, she's good.

She pulled into the parking lot of the station ten minutes later. She backed the car in with a good view of the front door. It was a one-story white building made from long channels of concrete. The groundskeeping had seen better days. Two people were smoking inside a nearby gazebo. There was one parked news van. Everything was quiet.

She texted Sam. "Are you certain he's here?"

"He wouldn't miss it for the world. Dude has a Twitter account. Blowing up all of his appearances. Loser."

"Gotcha. Tks."

Social media might be one of the greatest windfalls to law enforcement of all time. People just can't keep quiet about their business.

The phone buzzed. A picture of the man she was looking for popped up. Bald and bearded, the heavyset man's name was Clarence Williams.

Tap. Tap. Tap.

Sid's heart jumped. A man was standing by her window.

She trained her gun on him.

"Whoa," the man said with his fingers spread wide. "Don't shoot."

It was Russ Davenport. She lowered her window but kept the gun aimed on his chest. "What are you doing here?"

"Same as you," he said, scratching his nose, "just following the clues. Heh, I'm impressed. Widened my eyes when I saw you pull up in this big black machine." He eyed her gun. "Do you mind? I've been shot before, if you don't remember."

She put the pistol away. "So you're after Clarence too?"

"Yep." He rubbed the back of his neck. "I've been here since he went in. He ought to be out any minute. Say, you think I could have a seat? Kinda hot today."

"Why don't you take that jacket off?"

He peeled back his coat, revealing an old wheel gun. A stainless steel 357 Magnum by the look of it. "I'm a lot more cautious these days."

"You know that's illegal."

"Every Constitutional right seems illegal in DC these days. I say screw 'em."

Sid nodded. "Get in."

"Thanks." Inside the car, Russ adjusted the seat back and dabbed the sweat off his face with a handkerchief.

"So, do you have anything else?" Sid asked.

"Like what?"

"Anything on Smoke or anyone else?"

"Nah, it's been quiet. No one's talking. And it's a pretty big city. Lots of ground to cover—and lousy parking."

Sid shook her head. It didn't help that Russ smelled like sweat and a submarine sandwich. She sat there for quite a while, hands on the wheel and eyes on the television station door.

A pair of people came out.

"That's him," Russ said with a scowl. "Man, I can't stand the look of that guy. He reminds me of a walking gourd or one of those killer space clowns."

"What? Never mind." Sid noticed the other person with Clarence. She was a bulldog of a woman. Black jeans and a grey T-shirt, short dark hair and husky arms. "Who's that?"

"I'll be damned," Russ said in awe from the edge of his seat. "It's Jean."

CHAPTER 21

WHO'S JEAN?' WAS THE OBVIOUS question, but Sid didn't have to ask. Russ became a burbling fountain of excitement. Sid put the car in gear and followed Clarence and Jean, who pulled out of the parking lot in a beat-up white painter's van and then drove through town, light to light, street to street.

"Man, I can't believe it. I can't believe it," Clarence said, sweating again.

"Believe what exactly?"

Russ caught his breath. "That's Jean Moffat, a legend."

"What do you mean by a *legend*?"

He took out an asthma inhaler and took a puff.

Sid cocked a brow. "Asthmatic, huh?"

"Only when I get really excited." He gasped for breath. "I just didn't expect this."

She could relate to the asthma, but not the excitement. "Settle down and spit it out."

"Well, me and a bunch of my cronies, well, not a bunch really—most of them are dead—but anyway"—he sucked in some more breath—"we studied a bunch of old films. I mean archived stuff from any old tragedies that we could find. The stuff's not sealed up or anything, but still hard to come by. Finally, on YouTube, a bunch of good stuff showed up." He wheezed and pounded his chest. "Oh man, this attack's bad. So as I was saying, like our boy Clarence, who shows up at all of these disaster interviews, so comes out Jean Moffat." He went into a fit of coughing.

Sid leaned over, still eyeing the road and the van, and thumped his back.

"I'll be fine. Thanks." He tucked the inhaler away in his pocket. "Remember the Hindenburg?"

"Of course."

"Well, she was there, being interviewed. I swear it's her. And the Kennedy assassination, Dealy Plaza, the Grassy Knoll. She was an eyewitness. Same woman, same pug face, and same mole on her chin. You would really think she'd get that thing removed."

"Maybe she has family, a daughter."

"I can't imagine anyone procreating with that. Not because she's ugly, but flat out mean looking. I'm talking scary." He wheezed in another breath. "I'm telling you, that face has been at all kinds of disasters. Some of the guys say they saw pics of her at the Holocaust."

A chill raced up and down Sid's spine. Goosebumps rose on her arms.

"See?" Russ said, looking at her arms. "You know it's true. Put your friends on it."

The van pulled off to the side of the road in front of an old apartment building. It was small—just five stories—and crammed between two business-office juggernauts. Clarence and Jean got out and headed up the steps of a red brick building and vanished.

Sid parked half a block away. "Wait here."

Russ grabbed her arm. "No wait, are you nuts? Be patient. Wait."

She bent his thumb backward.

"Ow! Cripes, lady!"

"Don't do that again," Sid said. She hopped out, closed the door, and took some strides up the sidewalk.

The streets weren't too busy in this part of town. Some folks hung out on the staircases she passed. One of them asked her for money.

She moved on. She spied the building from the bottom of the front steps. It was old, maybe a hundred years or more, a testament to a time long forgotten. She took the steps one by one to the top. The entrance door was painted with decades of chipping black enamel. The door groaned open at the hinges as she pulled and slipped inside. A narrow stairwell going up. The hanging lights were dim, and there was a heavy musty smell.

Smells even older than it looks.

Up she went, steps creaking beneath her shoes. She pulled her gun and crept up to the first landing. Two apartment doors were at the top, and everything was quiet. She made her way up the next flight of steps, unable to shake the feeling she might be the only person in the building. Up on the second floor landing, she listened at the doors. Stark silence. It fed her, pumped more adrenaline that mixed with the sweetheart suit and charged her blood. She peered around the corner on the next level of steps. Her nostrils flared.

Tobacco?

She hadn't noticed either Clarence or Jean smoking. It was probably a tenant passing through with the smell lingering. Up she went to the next level. Two more doors. No more sounds. No scuffles. No breathing came from the other side. There was only her heart pounding inside her ears. Up she went toward the next floor.

Halfway up, the stair underneath her foot made a mechanical sound. *Click.*

Sid froze. Her instincts fired.

Morning Glory! It's a trap!

Above, the stairs groaned under heavy footsteps.

Clarence appeared on the landing with a shotgun in his hand and a cigar in his mouth. "Looks like we caught ourselves a little squirrel. Heh." He came down a couple of steps, his big body filling the stairway. An over/under shotgun was pointed at Sid's head. "I'd toss that piece you got if I were you."

She kept the gun barrel pointed at his head. "You're the one who needs to disarm, not me."

"Is that so?" He shrugged his shoulders. "Well, I'm not the one standing on a mine now, am I? I suggest you give yourself up unless you want your legs blown to pieces."

Maybe's he's bluffing, and I have the suit on.

Sid fixed her eyes on his.

Clarence's expression was stone cold. His eyes said, "I dare you."

Sid hunkered down and set the Glock down behind her. "Now what?"

Clarence let out a short whistle. The doors on the landing behind her opened up, and two well-knit men emerged in black T-shirts. One had a black sun rising on his neck. They seized her arms and bound them up behind her. Clarence popped open a concealed panel on the wall and pressed something downward.

Click.

The pressure plate beneath Sid's feet seemed to deactivate.

"Smart girl," Clarence said, hefting the shotgun over his shoulder. "Bring her up. Jean would like a word with her. But not now. Later. Time to take a nap, Miss Shaw."

Sid lunged forward. She twisted and kicked, but the men held her fast.

One covered her mouth with a rag.

Chloroform!

Life turned blurry and black.

CHAPTER 22

SID LIFTED HER CHIN AND opened her heavy eyes. She was tied to a chair. Ropes dug into her wrists. Her struggles were in vain. Sitting still, she scanned her surroundings. It was an old apartment room, sparsely furnished, with paint peeling from the walls and ceiling. The glass on the window was painted over. It smelled of smoke and grime.

"Ugh," a voice said. Russ Davenport was bound to a chair on her left. His face was swollen. Lip bleeding. "Did you get the name of that anvil that hit me?"

"Keep it down," she said.

A television set was on somewhere. Footsteps approached. A man came in the room and eyed them both. It was the goon in the black shirt who had clocked her in the head. He had an assault rifle strapped over his chest and a hunting knife tucked in his belt. "Say, Clarence, they're up."

The floorboards creaked, and Clarence stepped into the room with a smirk on his face. The man seemed even bigger than the last time. He had an unnatural swagger about him. He bent down and held Sidney's head up by the chin. "We've caught quite a fish in you, it seems. Heh. Sidney Shaw. Fallen FBI agent and now a bona fide bounty hunter." His dark eyes gleamed. He toyed with her hair. "I can see why the Drake wants you, but I'm not so sure about him."

Sid recoiled. Clarence's breath was worse than stagnant pond water. She launched a kick into his groin.

He didn't flinch. His expression darkened. "None of that now!" He backhanded her across the cheek.

Sid teetered onto the floor.

"Clarence," a female voice squalled. Jean stormed into the room. She looked about half as tall as Clarence, but far meaner. "We'll have none of that. If you want to slap somebody, slap him. I don't like the looks of him."

Clarence backhanded Russ so hard he toppled the heavyset man to the floor.

"Feel better?" Jean said.

Clarence shrugged.

"Well, pick him up!"

Clarence rolled his eyes and pointed to the goon. "Do it." He walked over to Sid, scooped her up, and set all four legs of the chair back down. "Keep your feet to yourself this time."

Fast as a cobra, Jean drilled Clarence in the groin with her fist.

The man doubled over. "Oof!"

"That's for swatting my prize, Clarence—you oversized idiot."

"I told you he was an idiot," Russ said. "Anyone that looks like that has to be an idiot."

"Quiet, reporter man," Jean said. She rolled up her sleeves, revealing a hard pack of muscle. "Don't make me sock you too. Now—" She reached over and grabbed a chair, dragged it to her, and sat down. "Let's have a little discussion, shall we? Tell me, pretty face, why are you following us?"

"As if you don't know," Sid said.

"Oh, good answer. Of course I know. You want to know who is behind this assassination attempt on Wilhelm. Sticking up for your friend, aren't you." The brute of a woman took a can of Copenhagen from her back jean pocket and put a rub in. "Want some?"

Sid gave her head a gentle shake no.

"It'll give you the giggles. Hah. I'm a country girl. Old, old country. Picked up the habit from my grandma. Grew our own tobacco back then. Makes you tough." She flexed her arm. A rising sun was branded on it. "Real tough."

"You gotta be tough to be as old as you," Russ said. "You're at least a hundred and twenty by my account. Maybe a hundred and fifty."

Jean turned toward the reporter and showed a creepy smile. "Good for you, Nightfall DC. Ha. I read your little pissant paper. Too bad only a handful of weirdos have enough good sense to believe you." She turned back, pinched Sid's face in her hands, and eyed her with cold, dead eyes. "Yes, I've seen lots of things. Things that'll make your worst nightmares seem like an amusement park."

Sid swallowed.

"And if you don't cooperate," Jean said, whisking out a knife hanging from her jeans, "I'll see to it you experience it all for yourself." She pressed the blade against Sid's throat. "Now, tell me, what do you want?"

Not averting her eyes, Sid said, "I want to clear John Smoke."

"He's a murderer." Jean laughed. "Killed a congressman."

"Allegedly," Sid said.

"Ha! The entire country saw it with their own eyes. The only freedom for him is death, and that's coming soon enough, thanks to you."

"What do you mean?"

"Aw, come on, Sidney. As soon as I made some calls and found out who you were, I got a plan. You see, there is a bounty on your head, but there's a bigger one on Smoke's. They want him really bad. A rare breed, that one is. A real hawker."

"Why?"

"I'm not going to tell you that, but I'll tell you this. You're the bait that's going to bring him in."

Sid clenched her teeth. Not so long ago, she'd thought she was getting a handle on things, but now she was in over her head. She wriggled at her bonds.

Jean just laughed.

Just play along, Sid. Play along.

"Of course, it might take a few days to flush your friend out. He'll be careful, but I'm sure he'll make it here to try and save you. They say he has a real shine for you." Jean spat on the floor and got up. "I love that kind of leverage. It lets me twist those tender hearts in circles."

"Where are you going?"

Jean looked over her shoulder. "Aw, miss my company already, do you? No surprise. I do have a special charm. But I'll be back. In a day or so. Just hope you and big boy don't starve to death."

CHAPTER 23

"**W**AIT!" SID SAID.

Jean stopped.

"Look," Sid continued. "Let's quit beating around the bush and playing these games. Just tell me, who's behind all this?"

"Oh, I see. You want to take the boss down," Jean said. She kneaded her dimpled chin. "Well, we don't talk about the boss. Heck fire, not many even know who he is, but I do."

At least I know he's a he now.

"Seeing how the odds are stacked against me," Sid said, showing a struggle in her bonds, "what does it hurt to tell me? Think of it as a last request."

"Giving up so soon, are you?" Jean cackled. "Oh, I doubt that. Look, little miss. You don't meet the boss unless the boss wants to meet you. Hmmm." She rubbed the back of her neck. "Seeing how it's going to be a long wait, maybe we should play a little game."

"What kind of game?"

"I'll give you a clue if you earn it," Jean said.

She'll probably lie about that, but at least it will give me some time.

"What game did you have in mind?"

Jean walked up to Sid and slipped her hunting knife out. It was bloodstained and old crafted. She waggled it in front of Sid's eyes. "This blade was a gift. A gift from an Indian warrior I killed. Heh heh. A handsome savage too. He wanted to make me his little squaw. I told him he'd have to fight me for it. He laughed. We fought. He died."

Sid's fingertips tingled. "That's a very touching story," Sid said with a smirk. "Do you share that at Tupperware parties?"

"You've got a smart mouth." Jean toyed with Sid's hair. "And such a pretty brunette. I'd hate to shave off all that lovely hair." She leaned in close and whispered in Sid's ear, "But I have, and I will."

Damn, she means it.

"You said something about earning a clue?"

"Yes, I did," Jean said, thumbing the knife's edge. She eyed Clarence, who was leaning against the wall, biting his nails and spitting them out. "Think you can take him down? If you can, I'll give you a name. But if you lose, you get shaved."

Clarence pushed himself off the wall and crossed his hairy forearms over his chest. He was at least six foot six and three hundred pounds.

"Kind of a sadistic game, isn't it?"

"Pfft! This is nothing. Boy, you have a lot to learn, and besides, you're the one that wanted a clue. But I'm fair. You don't have to play if you don't want to."

Sid weighed her options. Even if she won, she wasn't going anywhere. Jean would have guns on her and Russ. She could jeopardize his life. And getting her head shaved by that … woman?

That would be grisly.

"Why don't you let her shave him if she wins?" Russ said, glaring at Clarence. "Of course, there ain't much to shave."

"Heh. So what's it going to be?" Jean said. "You want to take a shot at some answers or not?"

"Sure, why not?"

Jean's brows lifted. "I like it." With the knife, she started severing Sid's cords. "Don't try anything stupid. I've been around a long time. Know most every trick in the book."

Sid nodded. Her wrists were free. She rubbed the blood into them. With the sweetheart suit on, she felt like she could do anything. In a few seconds the numbness in her wrists was gone. She faced Clarence.

He had a look on his face that was easy to hate. Arrogant. Crass.

"Kick his ass, Sid," Russ said.

Cackling, Jean slid her knife back into her sheath and backed away. "Go for it, girlie."

Leering down at her, Clarence spread his arms wide. "Come on. Give me a kiss."

Like a cat, Sid sprang. She drove her boot heel into Clarence's heavy gut.

Unmoved, he laughed. He pounded on his belly. "Go ahead, try that again."

Sid went in, kicked hard, pulled it back, jumped up high, and socked him right between the eyes.

"Ow!" Clarence said, staggering back into the wall. "That hurt!"

Wincing, Sid shook her hand. Clarence was solid.

"All right," he said, beckoning with his long arms. "You want to fight, let's fight then."

Rushing in, Sid unloaded some punching and kicking combos.

Clarence's beefy forearms countered with a grace that belied his girth.

Morning Glory, he can fight!

She pressed the attack, jabbing and kicking at his ribs. Her hard blows were muted. His body was like a heavy bag of sand.

What's this guy made of?

Clarence, no longer playing around, starting throwing heavy punches.

Pinned back in the corner, Sid ducked a thunderous punch that went clean through the wall. Skipping away, Clarence tripped her with his long leg, sending her sprawling to the hardwood floor. His fingers seized her by the ankle. "I gotcha now!"

Sid kicked at him.

He kicked back.

"Oof!" The foot to her gut left Sid breathless.

Jean's cackling and Clarence's laughter followed.

"I can't wait to shave that pretty hair!" Jean taunted.

Sid was jarred from the impact and half stunned.

Clarence dragged her limp frame into the center of the floor.

Her nails dug into the hard wood.

"Get up, Sid! Fight!" Russ yelled.

I'm trying. Damn, I can't feel anything.

The big man grabbed her in a vice-like grip and kept her pinned to the floor on her stomach. "Too easy," he said. "How about that kiss now?"

Sid flung an elbow back into his side.

Clarence chuckled. "She's still got plenty of fight in her. This ought to take care of that." He shoved her head into the hardwood planks over and over.

Stars exploded in her eyes. Warm blood dripped down her face. Her body went limp.

"First I kiss her, then you shave her," Clarence said. "I'm not smooching no bald-headed chick."

CHAPTER 24

ARMS DANGLING BY HER SIDES, Sid felt herself being lifted up off the floor. Clarence's iron grip squeezed her neck as he brought her face to face with him. Her nostrils flared.

The stench of his breath was putrid. He squeezed her neck harder. "Now, how about that kiss, baby, though I do prefer a little more fight in them." He leaned in.

"Aw no, Sid," Russ said, head down, "aw no."

Using one free hand, Sid clutched him by the beard. "Kiss this." With her other free hand, she drove her knuckles into his temple with all of her force.

Clarence's eyes popped wide, fluttered and closed. His body flopped over onto the floor and lay still.

"Dammit, Clarence!" Jean squalled.

"That was badass," Russ said, head up and smiling. "Badass."

Gasping for breath, Sid wiped the blood from her eyes and rose to her feet. "You have a clue for me?"

"Boys!" Jean declared. "Tie her up." She eyed Sid. "Sure, I'll tell you. I'm a woman of my word. The man you want is called Kane. But I'm not going to tell you one bit more."

"Fair enough," Sid said, taking a seat in her chair just as the first guard approached. One stood in the front, and the other entered the room from the hall. He had a piece of rope. "You think maybe you can stop this blood from running into my eye?" she said about the oozing gash in her forehead.

Jean walked over and eyed the wound. "Gonna need a couple of stitches. Too bad for you my needle-and-thread days are long behind me. Looks like a duct-tape bandage will have to do. Heh. Tie her up good. I'll be back."

The first guard, in front of her, watched Jean go.

The second, behind her back, started to bind up her hands.

"Not so tight, please," she said, sounding nice.

"Huh, you're the one that's looking tight," the second guard said. "Sad to see a fine woman like you go to waste."

Flirting, Sid said, "Let me go and I'll make it worth your while. Both of you."

The man behind her paused, and the breathing of the leering one in front of her became heavy. Behind her, the man tightened up one wrist. "No chance. Jean would eat us alive. Literally."

"That's too bad," Sid said. She winked at the one in front of her and rapped the side of her boot heel on the floor. A toe blade licked out. *Flick!* Exploding into action, she kicked the thug in front of her just behind the knee with the toe blade.

He went down with a howl. "Yeow!"

Sid drove her head backward into the chin of the man behind her. She sprang on the man in front and ripped the assault rifle free. She kicked him in the chin with her heel, knocking him out cold.

The last guard whirled his gun around toward her.

Sid shot two quick rounds into his legs.

Blat! Blat!

The man howled and fell to the ground.

"Throw the gun away!" Sid ordered.

The man did.

"What the hell is going on in there?" Jean yelled.

Sid was on the move. She took out one of the guards' knives and cut Russ free.

"Thanks," he said, rubbing his wrists. He lumbered over to a nearby table and picked up his wheel gun.

Jean walked in. She had duct tape in one hand and her knife in the other. "Stupid, stupid, stupid men!" She tipped her head toward the chair. "Sit down."

"Excuse me, but I think you're the one who needs to sit down," Sid said, keeping the barrel pointed at Jean. "We're getting out of here."

"Honey, you aren't going anywhere. There's more of us in here than you think. They'll be waiting."

"I'll take my chances."

"You'll die," Jean warned.

"Just drop the knife and toss over the tape."

"No. What are you going to do, shoot me?"

Sid pointed the gun at Jean's head. "You're armed with a deadly weapon. It would be self-defense."

Jean's face darkened. Her throat growled. Her eyes turned pitch black.

"Oh man," Russ said, backing toward the window.

"Screw this!" Sid unloaded a hail of gunfire. Bullets ripped into the changing woman.

Jean slammed into Sid and drove her hard into the wall.

Sid dropped the rifle and fought for her life.

Jean whaled on her. Her face was more hog than woman. Tusks popped up from her lower jaw. Her arms were coarse, powerful, and hairy. Taking Sid by the collar, Jean beat her into the floor. "Foolish woman! You're no match for a shifter!" She champed her teeth. "Dead or alive, they want you! That means I can eat part of you. Now stop squirming before I do."

Blam! Blam! Blam!

Jean recoiled and glared at Russ.

The man's smoking gun barrel shook in his hands.

The pig-faced Jean kicked Sid in the gut and marched toward Russ.

He fired again.

Blam! Blam!

Swat!

Jean hit Russ so hard he spun around like a top and collapsed on the floor. She picked Russ up over her head and hurled him out the window.

Eyes wide, Sid darted for the next room.

"Get back here!" Jean yelled with a snort.

Sid caught a glimpse of her Glock on the kitchen counter and went for it. Snatching it up, she wheeled around.

Jean rammed her head into Sidney's chest and kept charging. Wrapping Sid up in her arms, the boar-faced woman drove her clear through the wall.

Plaster dust exploded everywhere.

Sid found herself on her back and pinned down at the top of the staircase.

Jean wrenched the Glock from Sid's hand.

"Ah!" Sid cried out.

"Shut up!" Jean grabbed Sid's hair and slammed her head on the planks. "See what a mess you made." The woman snorted. Still holding Sid in a grip of iron, she said, "You're too much trouble. I'm gonna have to cripple you." She grabbed Sid's arm and yanked.

Sid's shoulder popped out of the socket. "Aaaaaggghhhhhhhhh!"

CHAPTER 25

THE PAIN WAS BLINDING. SID could barely comprehend the words coming from Jean's sweaty lips.

"Do you still want to play games with me, woman?" Jean said, holding Sid down by the chest.

Gasping, Sid sputtered out the word "No." Tears filled her eyes. Blood still ran in her face. She went limp. "No."

"That's a good girl." Jean eased up. "The better you cooperate, the sooner we get this over with."

"I couldn't agree more," Sid said. "The sooner the better." In an instant, she pulled her knees up into her chest, drove them into Jean's gut, and launched the swine-faced woman down the steps.

Jean bounced down the steps to the bottom and scrambled back to her feet. Pointing, Jean said, "You die for that." She started up the steps.

Sid's eyes searched for her gun and found nothing.

Where are you?

She turned back.

Jean's face was a mask of rage, the self-control gone. She stomped up the steps with murder in her eyes.

A faint familiar sound caught Sid's ear.

Click.

Jean took another step.

Sid turned away and flattened herself on the landing.

Boom!

The stairwell burst into splinters. The hall filled with plaster dust.

Sid started coughing and fanning at the smoky mist. Feeling around the floor with her hand, her fingers found her

Glock. The pistol was an old friend in hand. She pointed it down the stairwell. Heart racing and arm dangling, she forced herself up to her feet.

I have to get out of here. But Russ!

She lumbered back into the living room, cozied up to the broken window, and peeked out.

A hand seized her wrist.

She jerked away and stuck her gun in a man's disheveled face. "Russ!"

"Oh man," he said, rubbing his head. "I thought I was a goner. That freak picked me up and tossed me like a hay bale! I'm a two-hundred-and-seventy-five-pound man." He sniffed the air. "Do I smell bacon?"

Sid glanced down.

Russ was on the emergency fire escape.

"Let's get out of here." She climbed out the window. Both of them raced down the stairs and dropped into the alley.

"Ow!" Russ said. He was sitting down and holding his ankle. "Feels like I broke it."

Shoulder dipped, Sid said, "I can't carry you." She pulled him up to his feet with her good hand.

Heads emerged from high above, and gunfire erupted.

"Hop to it, Russ!"

They took cover behind a dumpster. Sid returned fire.

Bullets skipped and ricocheted everywhere.

"We're toast!" Russ said.

A roar sounded from behind them. A black car thundered down the alley and screeched to a halt. It was the Hellcat.

Smoke popped out of the driver's window with a LAW rocket hefted on his shoulder. He pointed it upward at the apartment Sid and Russ had escaped from.

The gunfire stopped, and the guards vanished.

Still aiming at the apartment, Smoke barked an order. "Get in!"

Sid got in the front seat, and Russ stuffed himself in the back. "Get us out of here, man!"

Smoke got back in the car, slammed it in reverse, and stomped on the gas. The car screamed back out of the alley and skidded into the street. He put it into drive, gunned the gas, and zoomed into the nearest highway tunnel.

Groaning a little, Sid said, "How have you been?"

Eyes forward, Smoke said, "I've had better days."

The car emerged from the tunnel and flowed into the traffic.

Grimacing, Sid shifted in her seat. "Thanks for picking us up."

Smoke nodded.

Odd.

"So, where are you taking us, to the bat cave?"

"No," he said. "Parking garage. We'll lie low there until things cool off." He glanced at her body, but not her eyes. "Shoulder dislocated?"

"Very astute of you," she said. "Thanks for noticing."

"So, what happened up there?" Smoke said, eyeing the road.

Russ jumped in. "I'll tell you what happened. This city is full of crazies! I'm moving to Arizona."

"Well, fill me in," Smoke said, eyeing Russ through the rearview mirror.

Russ offered up the entire ordeal.

Sid filled in some other details.

Smoke seemed unaffected.

"John," she said, "we were trying to find out who framed you. We didn't have much luck with that though. All I got was the name Kane."

Smoke nodded.

Geez, he won't even look at me. He must be having a really bad day. I hope this isn't over the engagement thing. And I'm not going to bring up the ring being stolen.

"You know," Russ said, "that name Kane rings a bell."

"I'd hope. It's Cain from the Bible," Sid said.

"No, not like that. One with a 'K'. K-A-N-E. Like the wrestler."

"Why's that matter?" Sid asked. She was grimacing, her shoulder throbbing.

"I did a story a long time ago—geez, at least two decades, maybe longer—about the Lancasters."

"The crime family?"

"Yep. They really hated the cops. Back in the seventies they blamed the cops for the death of their son Kane. Things got brutal for about ten years but quieted after that. The Lancasters kind of faded away in the nineties, but there's been some murmurings of late. A Lancaster here, a Lancaster there. Arrests. Mugshots. Kinda weird."

Sid had read some of those files on the Lancasters. They'd taken two FBI agents down in the late seventies. It was an extremely rare thing back then. But it was one of those things that Ted Howard, her now-deceased boss, had told her about. Fallen agents. The FBI was family, disjointed sometimes, but still family. They took things like that personally, but more so then than now. Things had changed. Ofttimes now, the agency seemed divided.

Smoke took the next exit in south DC. It was a rougher neighborhood than downtown. More poverty. More homeless. He cruised the car into a parking garage that drove down underneath an old office building. The tires squealed on the hairpin turns. The motor sounded like thunder down below. There weren't many cars parked either. The ones that were pulled in looked abandoned and dusty, a graveyard of bad car models from the eighties and nineties.

"Hey look, a K-Car. I used to have one of those," Russ said. "Love that Cream-of-Wheat yellow."

Smoke backed the car into a slot near the elevators, shut down the engine, and got out.

Struggling with the door, Sid finally got it open.

Russ squeezed out.

"So, what's the plan?" Sid asked Smoke. "I could use a sling, you know."

Smoke sat back on the hood and crossed his arms. "We're waiting on somebody."

Aggravated, she asked, "Care to fill me in?"

Smoke turned toward her. His dark eyes fastened on hers and started to change.

The blood drained from Sid's face.

Smoke's eyes turned black as eight balls, and then he scowled. "No."

CHAPTER 26

S ID PUT A GUN ON Smoke.

He showed a wicked sneer.

"Who are you?"

"Oh, put that away," said the man who looked just like Smoke. "You don't want to get hurt."

"Me hurt?" said Sid, trying not to wince. "You're the one looking down the barrel."

"True," said the black-eyed man, calmly, "but you can't know for sure. After all, maybe I really am John Smoke and you've been fooled all along."

"I say shoot him," Russ suggested. "We'll figure out the truth later."

"Oh, I doubt that," the man said. He reached into his jeans and pulled out a soft pack of cigarettes. A black Zippo lighter appeared in his other hand. He flicked the Zippo open, started the flame, and lit his cigarette. He snapped the top shut and tucked it all away. It was just him, smoking, with a smile on his face. "I've probably smoked more of these things than anybody, and it never gets old. Always wondered why."

"Nicotine, dumbass," Russ said.

"No, not with my chemistry," the man said. "I can't be harmed by the usual mortal means."

"I doubt that," Sid said, easing herself into a better position. She pointed the gun toward his back. "You're the one who shot Wilhelm, aren't you."

The man shrugged. "It doesn't take a genius to figure that out at this point. Of course, I've shot a lot of people. You know," he chuckled a low laugh, "I've been around since Lincoln. Makes you think, doesn't it."

"You're coming with me," Sid said.

The man turned. His eyes were dark blue like Smoke's. Every detail was just right on the outside. Only the voice was off a little. "Oh, I'm not going anywhere, and neither are you, Miss Shaw. You see, we're all trapped. Well, not me so much, but you certainly don't have a way out."

A dreadful feeling dropped into her stomach like a cup of castor oil. She summoned her courage. "I'll make a way out. Now get back in the vehicle."

The man held his hands up. "Shoot me, Sid. Shoot me, the man you love." He winked. "I'm a murderer, so shoot me. It will do me some good. But shoot me, and you'll never see me again."

"Screw this." She squeezed the trigger. *Click!*

The man chuckled. "Such a fool. You know, Sid, we switched your bullets out. Yes, those fancy ones with the blue tips. Very nice. Very gone. You're lucky Jean didn't kill you back in the apartment building. But it seemed your resourcefulness prevailed. We anticipated it."

"What are you talking about?" she said.

"Why, your audition. You know, the Drake could use someone like you: a loner, but loyal. We can make all those bills go away. Reunite you with your sister and niece. You'd never have to worry about your parents, their safety."

"I don't want any part of what you're offering. I just want to take you in."

"Really? Which one of me to you want to take in?" The man changed. He had Cyrus's face. "This me?" He turned again. Rebecca Lang appeared. "Or this one? Hah. No one has ever captured me. No one ever will. I'm the greatest shifter of them all. Why, I could even be the President if I wanted. Maybe I have been before. So many strange goings-on these days." He changed back to Smoke. "So do you still want to kill me—or kiss me?"

"Kill you. Definitely kill you."

"You know, I was like you once."

She rolled her eyes. "Oh please, I don't want to hear it. I've heard it twice now: once from Double Dee and a second time from the rat guy."

"Miss Shaw, take it from me, there is no better life than what we have. Power. Money. You, like your sister, should consider it." He blew a smoke ring. "It would be best for you and your family."

"They can take care of themselves just fine."

"Don't be so sure of that." Rubber tires rubbing on cement echoed above. An old black Cadillac limousine with a very high roof pulled up in front of them. "Well, if I can't convince you, perhaps they can."

A deader in a limousine driver's cap lumbered out of the car and opened the back doors.

Someone swung a leg out. The foot attached to it was impossibly big. The limo groaned as the most towering figure she'd ever seen stepped out. A huge man, eight feet of solid muscle packed into a grey gym suit. His head almost touched the ceiling.

Sid tilted her neck just to look at him.

The towering figure would make Shaq look like a child. His face was fierce and hard. Dark wild hair hung over his eyes.

"Holy shit," Russ muttered. "That just ain't possible."

The deader limo driver walked over to the other side of the limo and opened the doors. Sid expected some man or woman, maybe her sister Allison, to step out. The limo groaned and bounced again. Another giant stepped out, bigger and taller than the first.

The man posing as Smoke let out a sinister chuckle. "Let there be giants."

CHAPTER 27

SID FELT ALL OF HER blood seep down into her toes. AV the minotaur hadn't been as big as these men.

She heard the door of the Hellcat shut. The door locks popped closed. Russ tapped the window, said to her softly, "I'm not here. I'm not here," and crawled into the back seat.

The monstrous men stood still. Shaggy. Hairy. Beastly. They each must have been six hundred pounds easily.

That's really not normal! I need to get out of here.

"Big fellas, aren't they?" The man who looked like Smoke puffed on his cigarette. "You can't find them that big at the carnivals. Well, that was a long time ago, anyway. Care for a cigarette? It'll settle your nerves."

Sid gently shook her head no, still gaping at the giant-sized men. They made NBA players look like dwarves.

Just when I thought I'd seen everything.

"Do you have a name?"

"Me?" said Smoke's double. "I've had many. My given name is Reginald, but you can call me Reggie. No need to be formal."

"Are there any more like you?"

"Ah, now that's a good question. Well, the truth is, so far as I'm concerned, I'm the only one that matters. The doppelganger. One of a kind. That's all you need to know." He fixed his eyes on the limousine. Another person was getting out. "And now it's time to meet our next guest."

Sid's jaw dropped.

Older, heavy and swarthy, a slick politician eased his way between the giants and buttoned his dress coat. It was Congressman Augustus Wilhelm. "Hello, Sidney," he said with brightened eyes, "surprised to see me?"

"More like disappointed."

"Hah. Well, you're not the only person to say that. Oh, and by the way, before I forget, Allison and Megan send their regards. Megan, so sweet and growing up so fast. She's going to be such a pretty thing."

Sid stormed forward.

The giant men blocked her path to the congressman. One of their hands could fully engulf her head.

She could hear Wilhelm laughing behind them.

"Oh Sidney, you're such an overprotective hothead. I can't stand people like you. You get in the way of progress." He stepped out from behind the giants and faced her. His face was smug. "Lay a finger on me, and these two will rip you apart. And you wouldn't want them to do anything to your precious little Megan, now would you?"

Casting a glance up at the giants then back to him, her chin dipped and she said, "No."

"Good girl." He lightly smacked her cheek. "It's good to see that as you grow older, you can grow wiser as well."

"What's this all about, Wilhelm?" she asked. "Why the big show?"

"It's all about me, of course. You see, I live." He spread his arms wide. "Miraculously! Now, my path to the Senate will be far easier than it was. In case you haven't noticed, I'm not exactly the most likeable guy with the people, so I made a deal and got a little boost. Oh, won't it be wonderful to come out of that coma a changed man."

"That's it?" she said. "All this, just to remain in the Senate?"

"Oh, well, I'm being modest. It's certainly not my ambitions alone. The Drake supporters have their interests—and they pay well."

"Of course. Just what we need. Another leader who cares nothing for the people but is all in for himself."

"At least you realize I'm not the first," he said.

"Why Smoke?" she asked, turning as Wilhelm paced around her.

"He wasn't my choice, but your friend, well, he gets under their skin. After all, since he came on the scene, you've rounded up several members of the Black Slate. They're a rare and useful breed, so that's a problem." He stopped pacing and faced her. "Now, I know what you're thinking. You helped too. And to your credit, I'm shocked that you live. But your friend Smoke, he's unique." His eyes scanned her from head to toe. "But you're quite impressive yourself. Some might say, special." He glanced over at Reggie. "Did you mention the offer?"

"I did. She wasn't interested."

"Your sister is thriving in the Drake's organization," Wilhelm said to her. "Really rising up the ranks. You know, you and her are more alike than you think. When she wants something, she'll do whatever it takes to get it. And, Sid, with Deanne Drukker gone, there's an opening for a gal with your talents."

"No thanks."

"Double Dee said no the first few times too, but everyone has their price."

"So what tipped her over, blackmail or murder?"

Wilhelm checked his nails and dusted them on his tie. "She lost someone significant, so I'd say it was a little bit of both."

"You know," Sid said, tilting up her chin, "all of you bastards really need to die."

"Good luck with that," Wilhelm said. He clapped his hands together. "Now, back to business. The offer still stands for you to join the Drake. But just so you're clear, John Smoke will die. Either right in front of our eyes or in some prison, but he will die. But, if you want him cleared, and we can clear just about anything, you can just join us. Maybe he'll join as well."

"I'm not buying it."

Wilhelm's prideful grimace soured. "You're a fool!"

The Hellcat's engine roared to life. Russ Davenport was behind the wheel. The car squirted out of its spot toward the doppelganger. Reginald dove out of the way. Window rolled down, Russ yelled at Sid, "Get in!"

She made a mad dash for the passenger door and dove through the open window.

The car surged forward.

One of the giant men caught the front end of the car with his chest. Car fenders clutched in his humongous hands, the massive man heaved and brought the car to a standstill.

"Holy Schnikies!" Russ said. He laid on the gas.

The 707 horsepower throttled with hungry life. Still on the pavement, the back tires spun. The rubber smoked in great white rolling plumes.

The giant's feet slid over the garage floor.

"Come on baby! Come on!"

The giant's eyes were wide, its face straining against the car's force. It was losing.

The car was winning.

"You've got this, Russ!"

Suddenly, the rear tires lost their grip.

Sid looked behind them.

The other giant had grabbed the car by the back bumper and lifted it up ever so slightly. The engine screamed for traction, but caught only air.

"Oh man!" Russ banged his hands on the steering wheel. "Blasted rear-wheel drive."

With a snarl and a groan, the giant in front lifted the front wheels off the pavement as well.

"Oh, this is bad," Sid said, reaching into the back seat and trying to find anything she could.

"Oh no! Oh no!" Russ said.

"What?"

With a heave, the giant men flipped the car over.

It landed on its hood.

Crash!

Sid hit her head hard. The impact had flopped Russ on top of her. Gathering her senses, she shook her head.

But the car started to spin. Gusty laughter like that of a coming storm could be heard. The giants, like children, were spinning the car round and round, faster and faster like a giant top.

CHAPTER 28

T HAT SID WAS QUEASY WAS an understatement. As soon as the car stopped spinning, one giant reached in and pulled her out by the hair. All she did was hold her stomach.

Please stop spinning. Please stop spinning.

"Mrah mrah mrah mrah!" the huge man laughed. He set her down on her feet.

She staggered around and fell down again.

Nearby, someone was retching.

Forcing herself up to her hands and knees, she caught a glimpse of Russ doubled over.

The second giant put his big paws on Russ's shoulders and lifted him up to his feet.

Russ fell back down.

"Mrah mrah mrah mrah!"

"We don't need that one," Wilhelm said of Russ. "Feel free to tear him apart if you want. No one will miss him."

The giant grabbed Russ by the arms. The second one grabbed him by the legs and picked him up off the ground.

"Hey! What are you doing?"

They started to pull him apart.

"Ah! No! No! Ah! Stop it!"

Wilhelm chuckled. "This would make such a great story for Nightfall DC. Too bad you can't write it, Russ. Or your own obituary."

Sid rose to her feet, holding her shoulder, and managed to mutter, "Stop this. Stop it."

A shadow crept up behind Wilhelm and stuck a gun in his ear. "Yes," the man said, "stop it. Now!"

Something in Russ's body cracked. He let out a horrifying scream. "Eiyaah!"

"Now!" said the man holding Wilhelm hostage. It was the big black man, Agent Calhoun.

"Don't be foolish," Wilhelm said. Sweat beaded on his forehead. "There's been too much of that going around."

"Call off those big shaggy hounds," Calhoun said, cocking back the hammer on his gun. "Or whatever they are."

"Rexor! Thorgrim! Release him!"

Russ hit the ground with a thud.

"Are you happy?" Wilhelm said, trying to turn his head.

"Don't know about that," Calhoun said. "I'll just wait for my colleagues to arrive, and we'll let them sort this freak show out." He eyed Reggie. "That ain't normal." He turned back and surveyed the whole scene. "None of this is. Here I have the congressman that was supposedly shot and killed. I had a lot of money coming for that. Not so sure how I'm going to collect it now, seeing how none of what I've seen's been real."

"Oh ho," Wilhelm puffed. "Is money all that you want? There's plenty of that to go around. How much? A hundred grand?"

"Two-fifty buys my silence."

"A negotiator, how quaint," Wilhelm replied. "Two hundred?"

Calhoun's stature eased. "I don't think you have that kind of cash on you."

With a finger, Wilhelm eased the gun barrel from his neck. "Just stay silent. I'll take care of all your needs and more."

"Boss," Reggie said, cocking his head. "I hear sirens."

"Thorgrim! Rexor! Get in the limo! You too, Reginald!" Wilhelm turned and looked up at Calhoun. "I'll be in touch, eh …"

"Calhoun. Cort Calhoun. You better not stiff me, Congressman."

"You have my word, Cort. Play along, and you'll have even more than that."

Thorgrim and Rexor stuffed themselves into the limo.

With a wink at Sidney, Reggie followed suit.

Wilhelm was the last one in and said to Sid, "You can't say no forever." The door closed, and the limo screeched away.

"Fine job," Sid said to Calhoun. Arm hanging, she made her way over to Russ. His right leg was at an unnatural angle. "Oh Lord!"

Russ was sitting upright, eyes like moons, hands shaking over his contorted legs, repeating, "I'm okay. I'm okay. I'm okay."

Calhoun stepped over both of them, shaking his head. "No, you ain't okay. None of this is."

CHAPTER 29

"Y OU TELLING ME WILHELM'S ALIVE and well?" Cyrus Tweel talked as he typed at his desk at FBI headquarters. "Living and breathing. Made alive again?"

"It's in the report. Didn't you read it?" said Sidney. Her dislocated shoulder had been reset, but she still wore it in a sling. She was sitting in a chair in front of his desk.

Rebecca Lang sat to Sid's left, reading a copy of the report she'd prepared. Rebecca had the same condescending look on her face that she always did.

Sid tried another tack. "What don't you understand about this? You've seen some of these monsters for yourself."

Cyrus huffed and pushed his glasses up on his nose.

Sidney had spent the entire night writing up the incident—in a tiny guest room at FBI headquarters, since they knew her apartment was in shambles and she didn't want to drag Sam into all this. The hollow feeling in her stomach seemed to tell her the FBI wanted the entire incident to go away.

"Eight and nine feet tall?" Cyrus laughed, finally reading her report. "If that were the case, those guys would be playing in the NBA. What a laugh. Huh." He peered at Rebecca. "What do you think?"

"I'm like you, Cyrus. Seeing is believing." Rebecca glanced once more at her copy of the report and then tossed it on his desk. "And I haven't seen anything that I believe." She turned to Sid. "In case you didn't know, we have agents on site at Mercy of Angels hospital right now. Wilhelm is comatose. What do you think about that, Miss Shaw?"

"Seeing is believing." Sid glared at Rebecca. "What about your boy Calhoun, you know, the one you stuck on me? What did his report have to say?"

"I don't have his report yet," Cyrus said. He seemed a little withdrawn.

"He's gone, isn't he," Sid said. "You lost him."

"He's a liaison like you, and if I were to guess, I'd say he was still trying to find your boyfriend Smoke, whom you are clearly trying to protect."

Sid jumped up out of her seat. "Are you serious? Who do you think flipped my car over on the hood? Giants, that's who!"

"Keep your voice down and stay seated!" Cyrus ordered, getting up. "I know what I've seen, and I don't need you to tell me."

Sid stood there and crossed her arms in a way that said, "I don't have to obey orders anymore, remember?"

Rebecca whispered something in Cyrus's ear.

He sighed and sat down.

Frustrated, Sid slapped both of her hands on Cyrus's desk.

He jumped. Just a little, but it gave her a thrill.

"What about Russ Davenport?" she said. "Who do you think bent his leg back over his head, huh? No normal man or woman could do that!"

Rebecca put her hand on Cyrus's back and started to say something.

That woman has to go!

Sid balled up her fist and looked at Rebecca. She had no doubt that everything Leroy had told her about Rebecca and Cyrus was true. They were hiding everything. Keeping it all to themselves. It was infuriating. One day they were helping Sid, and the next they were against her. "I ought to slap that smug look off your face."

"It wouldn't do you or your murdering boyfriend any good."

"It's not Smoke! Geez! Talk to Davenport."

"He's not credible, Sid. Just another kook. You know, your kinda people. Now listen, Sid. I think you saw your boyfriend. Actually, according to Calhoun, he was there. He saw him. And you need to quit covering for the guy."

"Covering for what, an assassination that didn't happen? Look, you two idiots! Wilhelm is alive and well! Before long he's going to rise from the dead and talk about his run for Senate."

Cyrus and Rebecca burst out into mocking laughter.

Cyrus said, "Nobody even knew he was a Congressman until he got shot. Boy, why didn't you put that in your report?"

Shaking her head, Rebecca said, "I can't believe even you are that stupid. I think it's time we had you reevaluated." She whispered some more to Cyrus.

Sid's jaws clenched.

Please really be shifters so that I can kill you both. Maybe someone will turn you into deaders. Oh, that would be nice. I can't believe you! Either you are complete idiots, or else you are paid extremely well. Morning Glory, I don't understand it.

"Are we finished?" was all Sidney said.

"Sid, I have to tell you, the entire Reginald-the-doppelganger theory almost had me. After all, that would explain this entire mess. It's believable. Actually, it's so believable I think they made a movie about it." Cyrus pecked on his keyboard and turned his screen around. "Yes, they did make a movie about it. It's called *Doppelganger*, and it starred Drew Barrymore. See, there she is."

Rebecca slapped her knee, held her gut and laughed.

Sid struck. She grabbed Cyrus's hand that held the mouse and twisted his thumb back. "I'm not in the mood for this. You know these things exist. We all do. Now quit treating me like some kind of fool!"

Rebecca hopped out of her chair and closed in on Sid.

A quick kick to Rebecca's gut sent the mousy woman toppling over her chair. Still holding Cyrus by the thumb, Sid said, "I'm going to clear Smoke. You"—she cranked the pressure up on his thumb—"better stay the hell out of my way." She released him.

Cyrus gasped. His face was a mask of pain. He started rubbing his hand.

Looking at Sid full in the face with hatred, Rebecca started to rise.

On her way to the door, Sid stopped and said to her, "Get up and I'm going to Ronda Rousey you."

Rebecca stayed down.

Sid opened the door and found herself face to face with Ted's old secretary, Jane. "Step aside."

Without a word, Jane shirked away.

Sid headed for the stairwell and flung open the door. On her way down she got a text from Sam. It read, "Meet at the Hyatt."

"Great." Sidney didn't even have a car. The FBI had impounded it, or so she'd been told. She was low on money, too, and the Hyatt was a long walk. Not that she minded long walks, but storm clouds loomed above. She'd made it one block and was crossing a four-way intersection to another when a hard rain started coming down. Her shout startled other passersby. "Great!"

Seething, she stepped out onto the curb to hail a cab.

A dull-orange minivan pulled alongside the curb.

Sid flung open the door, hopped in, and slammed it closed.

The cab driver locked the doors, pulled out into the street and barreled down the road.

"Hey, I didn't even tell you where I was going."

"I already know where you're going," the driver said, eyeing his rearview mirror.

"Smoke!" she exclaimed. She eased forward and then eased right back, withdrew her gun, and pointed it at his head. "Or is it Reggie?"

CHAPTER 30

T HE MAN DRIVING THE CAB, the one she hoped was Smoke, wore an Irish tweed cap and glasses. The usually clean-shaven hair on his face was overgrown. He didn't turn or stop driving. Instead, he kept his eyes between the road and Sidney's.

"You got a text from Sam, right?" the man said. "Meet at the hotel?"

"Maybe the text wasn't from her," said Sid, still holding the gun on him. "After all, you can't believe everything you read. Now pull over."

"Aw, you won't shoot me, Sid. Look, I'm not the doppelganger. You know that. Besides, I saw him. His eyes aren't as dazzling as mine."

She warmed up inside a little. "So maybe you aren't the doppelganger. That still doesn't mean I won't shoot you."

"Why would you shoot me?"

"Because you're you."

"Or I'm Reggie? Or," he posed, "I'm—"

"Don't say it."

"Batman!"

She lowered the Glock. "Only an idiot would say that, so it must be you."

"That's my girl. I knew you'd come around. So, how have you been?"

"How have I been?" She couldn't believe how calm he was about everything. There was only an enormous manhunt out for him. She sank back into her seat. "You're nuts."

"I thought you'd be happy to see me."

I am. "Well, I'm not. I mean, what have you been doing the past few days, playing cab driver?"

"Actually"—his voice brightened—"yeah, I have been. I've met some of the most interesting people. There sure is a lot of foreign interest in DC. But the most interesting fare I had was this family from West Virginia. Super nice bunch. Good tippers. I got a big kick out of them because they were here for, get this, a Supernatural convention. They said I looked like one of the dudes that stars on the show."

"Never heard of it."

"Oh, it's about these brothers—"

"Will you shut up!"

"Sorry," he said. "Did you have something you wanted to share?"

Stress. It didn't exist to Smoke. It infuriated her.

"So," he continued, "have you given any more thought to my question?"

"You aren't serious?"

"No, I'm Smoke."

Sid leaned forward and knocked the cap off him. It revealed a nasty wound stitched in a bare spot on the back of his head.

Oh my!

"Hey, that's my disguise." He put the cap back on.

"What happened to your head?"

"I got cornered by some deaders. Those things seem to be getting a lot deadlier."

"You can say that again. There were a couple of cops I had to deal with that I think were deaders. They were looking for you." She eased closer. Something about his presence, aggravating though it might be, drew her to him. "Look, John, we have to get you cleared. I don't know how to do that yet, but this isn't going to stop until we clear you. We need to think. We need to plan. You might need to leave the country."

Smoke pulled the taxi over, and the brakes squeaked as it came to a halt.

They were parked in front of an old church. It was quaint and laid out with heavy stones. He turned and faced her. "Seriously, have you given my question any more thought?"

"About marriage?" *Yes.* "No. John, now's not the time to talk about weddings."

"I didn't say wedding," he said, smiling. "I was only talking about the engagement." He bobbed his chin. "So you have been thinking about it. You know, you're going to have to be more honest with me if we're going to pursue a long-term relationship."

"People are trying to kill you, and some of them are trying to kill me, and you're worried about our courtship?"

"A good man has to have his priorities straight. And I like the sound of that."

"The sound of what?"

"Courtship."

She sank back into her seat, hand over her head. "Morning Glory."

"You know I'm not getting any younger, and you aren't either." Smoke was staring at the church as he spoke. Rain splattered on the window. "And we might not have that much time left on this earth, you know. I mean, seeing how a bunch of people want us dead and all. At least me. I just never thought I'd die single."

"Really? With all of the stupid risks you take, it never occurred to you that you might die single? That's the dumbest thing I ever heard." A sliver of uncertainty slipped through her.

Geez, maybe he thinks he won't survive this.

"Smoke, are you okay?"

"Of course. But I have pissed off a lot of people." He caught her eyes. "Bad people."

"I can't even begin to imagine what you do when I'm not around. Aside from eating pancakes and taxiing people around. And being annoying."

And charming.

She fixed her eyes on the church doors. She eyed him. "You don't have anything set up in there, do you?"

"Only one way to find out."

"I'm not going in there."

"If you knew this was your last day, what would you do?"

Sid's heart beat a little faster.

I suppose I'd marry you. But I'd prefer more sun, rice, and some church bells. Huh, Sidney Smoke. Not too bad of a ring to it.

"I'd take down the Drake."

"I see," he said, a little dejected. "Oh, and by the way… Sam, Guppy, and Mal are in there."

"I thought they said meet them at the hotel."

"No. I found some eyes there." He got out of the cab, fished an umbrella out of the back, and slid Sidney's door open. He stood like a gentleman, holding the umbrella for her. "Coming?"

"Fine, but this better not be a surprise wedding."

Without a word, Smoke led her up the steps under the alcove and put the umbrella aside. He opened the door, saying, "After you."

CHAPTER 31

A SIDE FROM THE WOODEN PEWS and stained glass, the church was empty. Sid's heart sank a little.

Smoke's soft-strong voice echoed when he spoke. "You look disappointed."

I guess.

Just above a whisper, Sid replied, "I thought you said we were meeting Sam and Guppy here?"

Smoke took her hand. "Come on." Down the aisle they went together.

She glanced up at the marble arches in the ceiling. The angels carved from the stone. The podium and flowers that waited ahead. Her throat tightened.

What is he doing?

A door squealed somewhere in the church. A tall figure emerged from behind the choir chairs on the stage.

"Hey, Sid!" It was Sam, and she was waving. Her loud voice echoed everywhere. "Come on down. We've been waiting for you." Her eyes widened. "Aw look, they're holding hands. How sweet." She stepped out of sight.

Taking the steps up onto the altar, Smoke brought her to a stop. He took both of her hands in his and faced her. It was just them and rows of empty pews. He looked deep into her eyes. "You know, we might not make it until tomorrow."

She swallowed the lump in her throat. "Well, then if you want to marry me, we better."

With the side of his mouth turned up in a smile, he bent down and kissed her.

She felt her body melt in his strong arms. It was a great kiss. Soft. Sweet. Everlasting. One to live for. One worth dying for.

"Ahem," a voice interrupted.

They broke it off. It was Sam. "Sorry, but they're pretty eager downstairs."

Gathering her breath, Sid rubbed the palms of her hands on her jeans, glanced at Smoke, then to Sam. "Okay."

Behind the curtains they went, and down an old set of well-built stairs crafted from a fine dark oak. The area beneath the church was a lot of stone archways and alcoves, a little damp and musty.

Sam ducked into one of them, and they followed.

Inside was a large chamber filled with wine racks and whiskey barrels—hiding a modern lab that had been set up inside. Large computer monitors, a network server, conference table, and chairs. A coffee pot was brewing.

"Hey, Sid," Guppy said. He sat reading a magazine at the conference table, which was piled with papers. "Nice place, huh?"

Mal Carlson was behind the monitors, pecking away. "Actually, it used to be an old speakeasy. Can you believe that? Right below a church, of all things. But it's been a safe house for well over a century. Almost two."

"And it stinks," Asia said. She was propped up on an old loveseat that looked like it came out of a fraternity house. She faced a television and held a steaming mug of joe in her lap. "TV reception is crap."

"So what's the hurry?" Sidney said, making her way to the table and pulling up a chair behind Mal. A familiar scene was on the screens. It was live images of the battle with the giants in the garage. "Hey, how did you get that?"

"I've got cameras in the Hellcat," Mal said, taking a sip of coffee. "Among other things."

"So when I was down there fighting for my life, you sat watching?" she asked.

"We were close," he said. His eyes drifted to Smoke. "At least he was. You're all right, aren't you?"

She moved her sling and elbow. She'd dislocated it before, but it still felt like hell to move. "My wing's busted, but I can still shoot if I have to."

"Asia!" Mal called out.

"What!" the Chinese woman yelled, still glued to her TV.

"Fix up Sid's shoulder, will you?"

The little woman huffed, got up, and shuffled over. She eased around the table. "Which shoulder?"

"Uh, the one with the sling on it."

Asia yanked it off.

"Ow!"

"Shut up and be still. Take your shirt off."

"What? No!"

"Don't be so modest. You have nice body. You can leave your brassiere on."

Sam and Guppy started chuckling.

"Look, I think I'll be fine."

A pair of scissors appeared in Asia's hands and she began cutting Sid's top off.

"Hey!"

Asia tossed the shirt aside. No one was looking at Sid except Sam, who walked over and handed Asia a tube filled with long needles. "You'll love this, Sid." She cleared the papers off the table and rolled out a sleeping bag on it. "Here, lie down and just relax. But don't look. That makes it kinda weird." She produced a small dowel rod. "Oh, and bite down on this. You might not need it, but every little bit helps."

Sidney lay down on the sleeping bag. The smell of something calming filled her nostrils.

Asia's warm hands began massaging her shoulders.

She's got strong hands for such a little woman.

"Relax," Asia said, but her voice was far from soothing. "You are too tight. Stiff like old woman." She continued to rub. Her fingers dug deep into Sidney's skin and bore into the muscle.

Sid's forehead burst out in sweat. Something in her shoulder popped and cracked. She bit into the dowel rod hard. "Ugh!"

"Be still," Asia ordered.

Sid saw a long sliver of silver from the corner of her eye. Something sharp pinched her skin. It pierced deeper and deeper. It burned like fire.

"This is the cool part," Sam said, "but maybe you should close your eyes."

"Why?" Sid mumbled with the dowel in her mouth.

Sam's eyes were glued to Sidney's bad shoulder.

Sid glanced at it. The skin began to poke out. Her head broke out in a cold sweat just as the long needle poked clean through the skin. Sid's first instinct was to jump away. Her courage held. It was rewarded. The throbbing pain in her shoulder was replaced with pure euphoria. The dowel rod dropped from her mouth. "Morning Glory! How did you do that?"

"Ancient Chinese secret," Asia said. "Just stay still. I'm not finished yet." She poked more needles into Sid's back.

Sid didn't feel a one of them. She said, "Again, what's the rush?"

"Well," Mal stated, "We've come to a conclusion about this fine mess we're in."

"And that is?"

Mal rubbed his temples, shook his head. "We need to close in on them before they close in on us. If we don't pull this off now, Sid, I'm afraid it's all over."

CHAPTER 32

"**O**VER?" SID GLANCED AT SMOKE, whose dark eyes were fixed on Mal. "I don't follow."

"We've got a pretty big mess on our hands. They want Smoke gone. They want the Black Slate team defunded, and they're getting pretty close to pulling it off. The main concern is Smoke's safety, and they've gone to an awful lot of trouble to get him out of the picture." Mal sighed. "An awful lot."

"What did you do to piss them off so bad?" Sid said to Smoke.

Smoke shrugged.

"It's not what he did; it's what he didn't do," Mal said. "Well, that's not entirely true. Smoke's been throwing wrenches into their missions right and left. It really gets them bent out of shape. Of course you know that. But in this case, they made him an offer and he refused. Actually, they've made him several offers."

"Like they did me?" Sid said. She turned to face Smoke. "And why are they so interested in you anyway? You aren't a shifter, are you?"

Taken aback, Smoke said, "Me? No."

Sid's eyes narrowed on him. There were plenty of things Smoke did that were hard to understand. Being a shifter would explain a lot of them.

"You say they made you an offer?" Mal asked Sid.

"Wilhelm did. He said they needed a replacement for Deanne Drukker." She squirmed a little. Asia was still over her, doing some insane method of acupuncture. There was a little biting here and there, but the sensation still felt good. "Basically he says they'll keep asking until I say yes."

Mal pulled more video up on the screen. It wasn't the best picture, and the angle was bad. "I can't read lips as well as I used to, but it seems what you said was truth. I need to get that microphone on the Hellcat fixed. It should have been working. Then we would have had Wilhelm talking."

It was a little bit surreal watching herself having a conversation with Wilhelm and Reggie. She was transfixed. She felt violated. "Wait? Microphone? You can record me inside the car?"

Sam leaned over Sidney's shoulder and said into her ear, "Just because we can doesn't mean we are."

"I only activate the surveillance systems when needed," Mal said, "so you have your privacy most of the time."

"Where is the Hellcat?" she asked.

"We got it back," Guppy said. "It was a heck of a thing getting it flipped back over."

"Yeah, play that giant thing again," Sam said, twirling her finger, "the part when they flip Sid over and spin her around like a carnival top."

Mal pulled it up. The two giants' strength was freakish. Everything about them was. The one that Sid could see didn't even strain when he helped flip the car over.

Hanging by Sid's shoulder, Sam said, "Those guys are awesome. And really gruesome."

Sid eyed her.

"But evil, of course."

"I'm sure an exploding bullet will take care of them," Sid replied.

"Maybe. Maybe not," Mal said. He zoomed the screen in on another image of the giants. "Based off our analysis, the bigger these shifters are, the tougher their bones and skin. It might take more than an exploding bullet to upend them. But those giants aren't the mission; Reggie the Doppelganger is. We need him to turn himself in, for Smoke's benefit." He removed a jump drive. "So the goal is to blackmail them. After all, we have Wilhelm on video, alive and well. With giants. It might be enough to call this manhunt off Smoke. Call it an ace in the hole."

"And if we deliver it to them and they don't bite?"

"Then you and Smoke will have to bring Reggie in yourselves." He handed Smoke the jump drive. "Like I said, the walls are closing in. This needs to be done, now."

Sidney winced. Asia was taking the needles out of her shoulder one by one. "So, who are we supposed to take this to?"

"We were able to track that limousine. There's an estate several miles out of town. It parked there. It's all loaded in the Hellcat's GPS now." Mal turned and faced her. "Since they're recruiting you, I think you should deliver the package. We'll stay close by in case things get too scary."

"Can't we just call them out and meet them on neutral ground?" Smoke said.

"I don't think they'll hurt Sid." Mal looked up at her. "Do you?"

"No, I don't guess."

"Look, we can't talk all day. At first I wanted to hit them hard and heavy. Rattle things. But I think this tactic is better. It will at least get them off our backs for a while. Give us some time to figure out who Kane Lancaster is."

"Don't they have a bounty on me and Smoke?" Sid said. "Do you think this is enough to settle them down?"

"I think you can convince them of that," Mal said, "but just in case there's going to be a fight on your hands, you might want to take a super vitamin and suit up before you go." He handed them each a sweetheart suit.

Sid made her way into the next alcove and put hers on.

"Shoulder feel better now?" Asia asked her, suddenly right there.

Sid rolled her shoulder. "I can't remember the last time it felt this good."

"Good, then don't screw it up again."

Sam was there too, holding out a long-sleeved T-shirt.

Sid put it on and smiled gratefully at Sam.

"Um, you guys?" Guppy interjected. "You might want to take a look at the breaking news on the television channels."

"What? Why?" Sam said, making her way to Guppy's side. "Oh crap. It's a conference at the hospital. It's Wilhelm."

Sid ran over to the television.

Guppy turned up the volume.

Wilhelm was speaking to a host of reporters from a hospital bed. "I pulled through. Thank the Almighty, I pulled through." He shifted in his bed and grimaced. "But I think it was the good news that woke me up. A little bird whispered in my ear telling me that they caught my so-called assassin. Well, looks like I fooled him, didn't I?"

The captivated reporters chuckled.

Wilhelm started coughing. "Anyway, I want to thank the fine men and women of so many law enforcement agencies that came together to bring this man to justice, though I am sad that he won't see a day in court. Death seems like an easy way out to a menace like him."

Sid stood staring at the screen with her mouth half open. She wasn't the only one either. "They're covering the entire hoax up. I can't believe it."

CHAPTER 33

WILHELM DROPPED A NAME: REGINALD Baker. There were pictures too. A dead man on the streets who looked a little like Smoke, but his face was bloated.

"I don't suppose that video is going to do us a lot of good now," Sid said to Mal, "but does this mean Smoke's off the hook?"

Mal rubbed his chin. "I've still got a bad feeling that the walls are closing in." He started pulling up images from the cameras on the streets around the church they were in. It was pouring rain so hard you couldn't make out anything. "You know, it wasn't supposed to rain today."

Sid hadn't been paying attention, but of course strange weather patterns often happened when you lived near the coast. She pointed at one of the smaller camera views on the screen. A tight knot of men were rushing up the church steps through the pouring rain.

"We've been breached." Mal pecked away on the keyboard. "We need to get out of here."

"Too late," Smoke said. He started loading clips of ammo into guns. "Did you say you had some more of those vitamins?"

"Yeah, why?" Mal said.

Smoke pointed at the screen. Two monstrous men strode up the outside stairs, great arms swinging five steps at a time. "That's why."

Mal took an Rx bottle out of his pocket, filled with bright green pills. "Take these. There's still some issues with the time release." He tossed one to Sid. "Better something than nothing."

Heart racing, she said, "Bottoms up," and swallowed down the pill.

Mal, Sam, Guppy, and Asia scurried to gather whatever equipment they could get their hands on.

"We'll hold them off," Smoke said, slapping a clip into his gun. "You guys just get out and get out now."

The four of them fled out of the alcove and down the corridor. Smoke and Sid faced the opposite way out to the upstairs. "Maybe this church is sacred ground to them. You know, like in Highlander." He eased forward. "What do you think?"

"I don't think anything is sacred to them," she replied. She loaded a clip of blue-tipped armor-piercing bullets. "I just want to shoot them."

Things were quiet, dead quiet, for just a few seconds. And then a rush of fleet feet clamored down the steps. Half a dozen men, maybe deaders, appeared—decked out from head to toe in tactical gear.

Sid and Smoke fired.

One of the deaders tossed a grenade. It seemed to float in the air.

Sid heard Smoke yell, "Stun grenade!" He shoved her into the alcove. The grenade hit the floor.

Boooomph!

Sid's entire body shook with ram-like force. The tight confines of the basement made the stun grenade's impact ten times worse. She saw bright spots. Felt the floor moving. Every nerve in her body was a jangled mess. As she fought her way to her knees, the floor spun. She started to puke.

Smoke was on his feet. He staggered between Sid and the oncoming deaders, holding only a knife in his hand.

That's when it happened.

A deader emerged from the shadows behind Smoke, slack-jawed and ugly. It swung a crude piece of steel like a club and landed a blow in the meat of Smoke's shoulder.

The knife fell from Smoke's fingers.

The deader cocked back to swing again.

No!

Sid lifted her hand and squeezed the trigger.

The gun didn't fire. The Glock wasn't there.

She spread her fingers wide and stretched them out for the gun that lay inches from her grasp. It might as well have been ten yards. She couldn't get it in time.

There was a heavy thud as Smoke got whacked again.

Another deader emerged in full tactical gear. Wielding its club like a cleaver, it closed in on Sid and chopped at her.

Summoning all she had, Sid rolled. Her fingers wrapped around her gun and she opened fire.

Blam! Blam!

The bullets ripped through the deader's face. Its club still came down on her hip.

Whack!

Shrugging off the blow, Sid kicked out its leg, climbed on top of it, and blasted into its chest with a scream.

"Aaaaeeeeeeh!"

Blam!

The deader died.

Game over.

"Smoke," she said, looking around. "Smoke?"

The rangy man was gone. Only a trail of blood remained that disappeared around the bend of the alcove. Forcing herself to her feet, Sid stumbled headlong into the corridor. It was packed with deaders.

They swarmed her.

She unloaded her clip.

Blam! Blam! Blam!

Some stumbled, others fell. The rest covered her like bears on honey.

She fought and kicked with all her might.

But they dragged her battered body across the floor like a soaked mop, bouncing her head off the tiles.

She couldn't see anything. All she could do was smell the wretched stench of the decaying bodies.

They propped her up against a wall and backed away.

Smoke was there, holding his head. Blood seeped through his fingers. He said something to her about a helmet, or forgetting it.

She still could barely hear. The sweetheart suit had absorbed a good bit of the stun grenade's impact, but she thought it might be a long time before her senses returned to normal. Panting, she surveyed her surroundings.

"Oh no."

Mal, Sam, Asia, and Guppy were bound up and held at gunpoint.

There were at least twenty deaders in the basement room. It was some old auditorium of some sort, maybe a municipal room. The deaders weren't the only ones in there either. There was a man, the mirror image of Smoke. And behind him, heads just inches below some colorful banners, were the giants, Thorgrim and Rexor. One held a huge hammer, the other an axe with four blades.

Reginald the doppelganger applauded. "The bounty on your heads is still good. I think it's time I cashed in on it. Oh, and I don't need the money. I just like drama."

CHAPTER 34

EVERYONE HAD A GUN ON them. Sid. Smoke. Their friends' hands were bound up behind their backs. Their mouths were gagged. Sam's eyes were wide with fear. Mal's face was a mask of concentration. Guppy's eyes were hard and cold. Asia looked agitated. But the group's intent was clear. They wanted Smoke and Sid to get them out of there.

"So are you taking us dead or alive?" asked Sidney, eyeing the barrel of an assault rifle.

It was a man holding it. She could see the whites of his eyes. He wore dark-gray tactical gear and had a black rising-sun tattoo on the back of his hand.

"Oh, well, the price is the same," Reggie said. "But the Drake like to keep things entertaining." He scanned the large room they were in. High ceilings. Old stone architecture blended with new painted drywall. The tiled floor was marked off for volleyball and basketball. A rim stood at either end. "This place should make for an interesting arena."

"Beg pardon?" Sid replied. Her voice echoed a little.

More men funneled in, some of them holding video cameras. The deaders huddled up in tight formation in front of the only exits. There must have been twenty of them. Two other men rolled out some bleachers. The odd auditorium had enough room for a few hundred people. Extra incandescent lighting hung from the ceiling.

Arms folded over his chest, Reggie's form started to change. The visage of Smoke was gone and replaced by a face far more vicious and sinister. With high cheekbones, a hawkish nose, and shoulder-length white hair, what Sid assumed was the real Reginald stood in front of them. He slipped a cigarette pack from his jacket and popped open the lid to a black-logoed Zippo. With a flick, he charged the lighter.

"There's no smoking in here," Smoke said to Reggie.

"Funny," the doppelganger replied. Some of his men-at-arms took to the top of the bleachers and aimed their cameras down on the center court.

Sid felt the hollow feeling expand on her stomach. A memory flash occurred. She remembered what the rat-shifter, Swift Venison, had been going to do to her. The Drake wanted her death recorded. They wanted to see the whole thing. It was their sick brand of entertainment.

"For the record," Smoke said, folding his feet under him and sitting cross-legged, "any unauthorized use of my image will be subject to the full prosecution of the law."

Reggie laughed.

So did Sid.

"I'm sure you both have excellent lawyers," said the doppelganger.

"He's a fine notary too," Smoke said, laughing.

"Oh, that's good," Reggie said, blowing out a puff. "The audience loves a sense of humor. You know, we have our own dark network at the Drake and lots of video of both of you in the most unlikely places. We call it Deathflix. As a matter of fact, part of your bounty is based on the viewers wanting to see the two of you in action. Some of it is just for study. That whole thing with the minotaur, Mason Crow, do you know we have most of that on film?"

"Film?" Sid laughed. "You didn't use digital media? Doesn't sound very efficient."

Narrowing his eyes, Reginald glided over to the bleachers and climbed halfway up. He placed a hearing device in his ear and spoke into a device on his wrist. "How's the view?" He nodded. "Excellent. I'll send in the deaders first. Let the wagers begin."

"So people are out there betting on us?" Sid said, shaking her head. "You're a sick bunch."

"No, not at all. We just like to have fun, at your expense. And it's not just us, but your own representatives as well. You know, those helpful elitists who give gobs of money to charity." Reggie rubbed his hands together. "They love a bloody fight as much as anybody." He held his finger to his earpiece and spoke into his wrist. "Roger that." He gave a quick nod to the men holding guns on Smoke and Sid.

The henchmen backed away.

Glancing over at Sid, Smoke said, "Time for round one, I guess. You ready?"

"No," she said, putting her fist on the ground. "I'm angry."

"Just so you don't try anything too clever," Reggie piped in, "remember we have guns on your friends over here. However, I feel generous. If even one of you survives this, I'll let them all go. But if you don't … well, what difference does it make anyway?"

"Why don't *you* fight us?" Sid said. "After all, you were boasting about how you were the greatest shifter."

"Oh, I'll be hanging around, don't you worry. But you'll have to at least beat Rexor and Thorgrim before you ever get a crack at me." He checked his wrist. "And right now, those odds are about one thousand to one."

"I like those odds," Smoke said. He shrugged at Sid. "It's much better than flying through an asteroid field."

"The audience is getting antsy," Reggie said. He pointed to a row of undead men sitting on the first row of bleachers. "Deaders! Kill!"

CHAPTER 35

S LACK JAWED, SLOW AND STEADY they came, one heavy metal pipe in each deader's hands.

Sid and Smoke rose to meet the deaders head on.

She swayed a little.

Smoke stepped between her and the threat. The back of his head was still caked with wet blood. "I'll handle this."

Moving at a stiff fast walk, the first deader came in hard and fast. It brought the long rod of steel down with a fierce two-handed chop.

Smoke sidestepped the blow and kicked the deader hard in its side, knocking it off its feet. Still moving, Smoke closed in on the second deader and in one smooth move, he twisted the pipe free from its swinging arms. A split second later, the pipe Smoke had stolen collided with hard bone, making a sickening smack.

The deader teetered over, holding a hand on its temple.

Smoke didn't slow.

The first deader started to rise from the marked-up tile floor.

Smoke busted its knee. *Whack!* Its chin. *Whack!* He hit it in the head so hard its skull cracked. *Whack!*

The pipe fell from its fingers when the final blow collided with its temple. *Whack!*

Both of the deaders lay on the floor, not dead but twitching oddly. They fought to get up, only to fall back down.

Smoke hit the second one, which had almost managed to make it to its feet, in the temple again.

It flopped to the floor.

He tossed the pipe he had to Sidney. "Aim for the temple. It won't kill them, but it screws them up really good." He picked up the other pipe. "Got it?"

Sid clutched the cold steel in a tight grip. "I've got it alright."

"Well, the odds were only two to one, in your favor," Reginald said. He sucked on his cigarette. "The next round is three-to-one odds. Against you." He turned and spoke to his men. "Send in four deaders. The fast ones. Edged weapons."

Four more men in tactical gear popped up. Their faces were taut, eyes dark. They reminded Sid of the cops who'd invaded her apartment. Two of them had axes like firemen carry, and the other pair wielded big machetes. The tallest was bigger than Smoke, and the smallest was shorter than her. They all had stringy, dry hair, sneers, and crooked smiles. A flash of evil marked all of them.

"It's a good thing you have those German-engineered suits on," Reginald said. "They'll slow down the process of them carving you to pieces."

Sid swallowed. Wary eyed, she watched the deaders close in.

Their blades whisked from side to side, cutting the tension in the air.

Aim for the temple. Aim for the temple.

The smallest deader waggled his machete, eyeing her with fierce intent. He flicked his tongue in and out as he said, "I'm going to cut that hair. I'm gonna cut that pretty, pretty hair." The little man snaked in.

Smoke busted that deader's teeth out.

That was the last thing Sid caught out of the corner of her eye. Right in front of her, she saw a hefty man with a deadly axe swinging her way. She ducked beneath the blow and cracked him in the knee.

He rumbled with slobbering laughter and brought the axe down with a hard chop.

Sid skipped away.

The axe chipped the tiles on the floor.

She had a clean shot on his temple and put all of her weight behind the swing. The steel pipe hit hard.

The deader dropped even harder.

Instincts on fire, Sid whirled around.

Smoke delivered a lethal blow to another deader's head.

Two others were already on the floor. All four were down now.

Chest heaving, Sidney gasped for her breath. "You could have saved at least one more for me."

Smoke gave her a funny look and said under his breath, "You're wheezing."

"I ain't got time to wheeze."

"Two. Four. Hmmm." Reginald lit up another cigarette. "I guess eight will be next. Oh, and now, the odds are heavy against you. But one man from China is still betting on you. Odds of your survival are twenty to one."

"That's better than I thought," Smoke said. He picked up the axes. "Come on," he said to Sid.

They backed toward one of the corners of the room, on the opposite side from the giants. The huge men stood quietly with their arms folded over their weapons. A dangerous look was glimmering in their eyes.

"Send in the next eight!"

Smoke lifted two axes high over his head. "Eight would be great! Why not ten!"

"Are you crazy?" Sid said, wheezing. There was a wild look in Smoke's eyes. A savage fury that had come to the surface. It stirred her blood.

The deaders came at them in a dangerous and shambling mob. Crossing the small expanse, they hemmed Smoke and Sid in without hesitation and attacked.

Smoke's axes sang a riddle of hard steel.

Two deaders' faces collapsed under their unrelenting weight.

Sid went for the temple on the nearest. Her steel club glanced off the fiendish man's arm and skipped off its head.

Something sliced into her arm.

"Ugh!" She held onto her pipe, unleashed a hard swing, and connected with bone. She swung again.

The enemy cut and stabbed.

So far, the sweetheart suit had kept her from being cut to pieces, but the blows of the deaders were heavy—not accurate, but heavy. Her lungs burned. Blood dripped into her eyes from a small cut on her forehead. She kept swinging and swinging and swinging until she felt she couldn't swing anymore. "Smoke," she wheezed.

Deaders were piled up at his feet. His axe strokes were like lightning from the sky.

One deader somehow still fought him without a head.

And then Sid heard Reginald scream, "Send in the rest!"

There were more deaders and men than she could count, and she didn't have anything left.

Smoke dropped to a knee. Covered in gore and sweat, he said to her, "Got any plans for Saturday?"

CHAPTER 36

IT WAS A SEA OF monsters. A rising tide.

Sid stumbled to Smoke's side, fighting for her breath, and they faced the oncoming horde together. She lifted the rod in her hands and shifted her feet. "We gonna make it?" she said.

"Not sure," Smoke replied. "We just have to keep hitting and hope the bodies keep falling. Stay close." He stepped over and drove the axe's back spike into the nearest monster's head.

Sid summoned all of her reserves.

Ignore it. They're just lungs. Who needs them?

The deaders didn't. They were tireless automatons. Dangerous. Unrelenting.

Sid caught a devastating chop with her pole. It jarred her arm. Clacked her teeth. It ignited the survival instinct in her. She felt no pain. Avoided some stinging blows, fought through the others. She was a little faster than her assailants. Smarter. She unleashed wild and clumsy blows. Some connected. Others did little to slow the deaders.

"Just keep swinging," Smoke roared.

She couldn't see him. She could feel him. Her shadow. Protector. It inspired her.

Clack!

Something hard glanced off the back of her head. She fell into a pile of bodies.

Hands from disabled deaders clutched at her wrists and hair, pinning her down, where more deaders closed in for the kill.

Chest burning, barely breathing, she glared at them. "Screw you dirty deaders!"

One with a busted eye socket let out an ugly laugh. It raised the axe over its head with two hands. "Good-bye."

Sid's heart quickened. Her eyes popped wide. Her lungs filled with air. Lightning raced through her veins.

Yes!

Mal's super vitamin had finally kicked in.

She sat up. "Hell yes!"

The deader's axe came down.

Swish!

Sid laughed. Popping up right in front of it, she smashed in the temple of its head.

Now I'm cookin'.

She unleashed all of her outrage. Her hatred. She waded into the deaders. Piece by piece, skull by skull, she felled one right after the other. She was Neo. She was Electra. She was worse. She was a pissed-off Sidney Shaw.

Crack! Crack! Pop! Pop! Whack! Bang! Smack! Smack! Smack!

Limbs were broken. Skulls were smashed. The floor was slick with greasy blood.

Sid danced to her own deadly song. She weaved between attacks. Executed flawless counters. It was fun. Exhilarating.

"Feeling better, I see," Smoke said, sliding alongside her.

She dropped another deader. "Yep. And how about you?"

"Never deader. Er, I mean better."

Only four deaders remained. Standing firm, they crowded in.

Sid and Smoke turned them into dog food and strode out in the center of the room. Not even winded, she looked over at Reginald.

His ageless face was creased.

She yelled over to him, "What are the odds now, jackass?"

Reginald opened up his clenched jaws. "Rexor. Thorgrim. Kill them both!"

Something about the way the giants moved tempered Sid's electrified nerves. They were fluid. Carnal. Savage. Primordial. It was all bundled up in their soft brown jumpsuits ready to be unleashed.

Smoke cracked his neck from side to side. "Which one of you wants to die first?"

Sid looked over at him. "Did you just quote a line from Conan the Barbarian?"

"It seemed fitting." Chin up, Smoke took center stage.

Rexor stepped forward with his oversized four-bladed axe. The massive man, standing over eight feet tall, was built like a train station. With his oversized paw of a hand, he beckoned for both Smoke and Sid. "Come," he said in a cavernous voice, "taste the steel in my hands."

Smoke and Sid charged.

The giant's devastating axe was swift, but not swift enough. It cut over their ducking heads.

Smoke chopped the axe into its thigh.

Sid cracked it in the nose with her pipe.

"Fleas!" the giant said. "You cannot hurt me." Rexor pressed the attack. His axe blades fell with speed and precision.

Morning Glory, he's fast!

She busted him behind the knee. Cracked a kneecap. Smacked his jaw.

Smoke attacked him like a lumberjack hewing down a tree, heavy chop after heavy chop.

Rexor swatted. Jabbed. Chopped. His strikes were getting closer and closer. "See, you cannot hurt me. My bones are iron. My skin is steel. Haaruagh!" With a flick of his wrist, he made an incredible back swing.

The flat of the blade smacked hard into Sid and sent her flying from her feet. Bones aching, she struggled to rise.

"Sid, watch out!" Smoke yelled.

She glanced over her shoulder.

The other giant, Thorgrim, brought his hammer down.

She sprang back like a cat.

The great hammer busted up the tiles between her legs.

"How are we supposed to kill these things?"

"Try kindness," said Smoke.

"What!"

Thorgrim's hammer came down again and again.

She ducked and dived. Evading his blows wasn't the problem, not being able to hurt him was. And the clock was ticking inside her brain. The super vitamin wouldn't last forever.

"Aaargh!" the giant man Rexor bellowed. He staggered back, covering his eye.

"Aim for the softest spot you can find," Smoke said, pressing his attack.

Sid drifted back toward the heap of fallen deaders. She needed a better weapon. She needed an edge.

Thorgrim, hammer high over his head, closed in on her.

She slung her pipe at his face.

He deflected it with his elbow and laughed.

Sid snatched a machete off the floor. She was fast, but the giant's strength and size negated some of that. It didn't help her much if she couldn't hurt him.

Got to find a weakness. Everything has a weakness.

She leaped away from a powerful downward attack.

Thorgrim's hammer made a sickening smack into a deader. Bone crunched. Guts squished out.

That was nasty!

As the giant brought the hammer back up, Sid poked the machete at the giant's eye, clipping the skin just below it.

Thorgrim jerked back and kicked her feet from beneath her.

She flipped head over heels and cracked her head hard on the tiles, pulling up onto her elbows just in time to see the massive hammer closing in on her eyes.

CHAPTER 37

SID SQUIRTED AWAY. THE HAMMER fell again and again. Closer and closer. She rolled away.

Crap! Is he getting faster, or am I getting slower?

In a sudden move, she leapt down between Thorgrim's legs and slid through. Using both hands, she swung the axe into the back of the giant's heel with all her might.

"Rargh!" Thorgrim hopped up on one foot, spun around in a half circle, and took an off-balance swing.

Sid jumped back up to her feet and skipped away.

The giant hunkered down, hammer ready, eyes wary. Blood seeped from his ankle.

Yes! I found his weakness!

"Smoke! Go for the Achilles."

Smoke fought Rexor with the grace and power of a striking panther. He chopped into the monster man with precise blows.

Rexor's chops were devastating and angry. The massive four-headed blade was an arc of death, striking just an inch from the evading Smoke.

The elusive man hammered away on Rexor's blind side. He started cutting at the enormous man's ankles.

Rexor parried with his arms, his axe. "Fat chance, little man! You may have clipped my brother, but you'll not clip me! Rargh!"

The axe came down hard and fast. The blow would have split a horse in half.

Smoke slipped away and unleashed a fierce backswing into Rexor's good eye.

The giant lost his grip on the axe and teetered back, holding his eye. "Aargh!"

Thorgrim averted his attention from Sid.

She charged in and cut out his other Achilles tendon.

Flailing and roaring, he tumbled hard onto the tiles with visible blood oozing from his wounds. "You still can't kill me."

Rexor dashed the blood from his ruined eyes and said to Smoke, "I can't see you, but I can smell you."

Smoke picked up the humongous battle axe that was almost as tall as him. He hefted it over his shoulder and faced off with the giant. "Smell this!" He rushed in hard and fast, swinging. He sank the blade right between the giant's eyes. *Split!*

On his hands and knees, Thorgrim abandoned his hammer and began crawling toward his brother. He bellowed. "No, Rexor! No!"

Sid tossed away the machete and grabbed Thorgrim's hammer. She teetered off balance.

Holy bat crap, this thing is heavy!

She hefted it up on her shoulder and marched right up behind Thorgrim.

The giant man clutched his brother's arms with tears in his eyes.

"Put him down, Sid!" urged Smoke. He was covered in sweat and down on one knee. "Hurry."

She raised the great hammer and dropped it down hard on the back of Thorgrim's shaggy skull. *Crack!*

The giant went limp.

Her legs turned to noodles. She fell, almost face-planting on the floor. The super vitamin was done for. Her stomach started to growl.

"How are you feeling?" Smoke said, resting his hands on his knees.

"I need a plateful of pancakes."

Holding his stomach, he huffed, "Make that two plates." Smoke's head twisted around.

Reginald was coming down the bleacher steps. He was softly clapping his hands, but there was a look of disappointment in his eyes.

Smoke said to him, "So what were the odds on that one?"

"Fifteen hundred to one." Reginald removed his jacket and flicked his cigarette away. He started rolling up the sleeves of his dress shirt. "Needless to say, some heavy hitters lost a lot of coleslaw. Heh. Even though I expected better, I should have known. After all, giants are stupid. That said, I'm still not so sure how you pulled off what you just did. That … adrenaline surge was quite unique." He glanced backward at Sid's friends. "I suppose one of them will supply the answer to that."

Can't let that happen.

Sid groaned on her way up to her feet. Even with the suit on, her arms felt like lead.

Smoke rose up on two legs and swayed in place a little.

She'd only taken the super vitamin once before, and she'd forgotten the tremendous toll it took, not to mention what the sweetheart suit demanded of her.

At least I'm not wheezing anymore. I'm just so hungry I could eat a goat.

Reginald checked his watch. "Looks like the bets are in." He turned and said to his men, "Keep the cameras rolling, boys."

Even though all of the deaders were down, more men with assault rifles still remained. Half of them were operating the cameras. Two others had guns on Mal and company, and the remaining men's eyes were locked on Sid and Smoke with barrels pointed right at them.

She wiped the blood from her mouth. "So now what? We fight you and it's over? You let us go?" Sid asked. She nodded at Smoke. "What are the odds on that one? Two to one in favor of us?"

"Oh, no no no. Let me assure you, it's more like five thousand to one. In my favor."

"Why's that?" Smoke said, lifting a brow. "Are you going to turn into a snake or something?"

"Funny, but no. It's simply because I'm awesome. But I could turn into a snake if I wanted." His muscular arms were covered in tattoos that seemed to slither like snakes. "Oh, and pick up a weapon of your choosing." He picked up one of the metal pipes that the deaders had used and bent it end to end. "Make it two of them if you like. I'm ready when you are."

CHAPTER 38

"**I** THINK HE'S A TERMINATOR," SMOKE said, and he followed up with, "I'll be back." He stepped around the giants and picked up a pole and axe, shook his head, and tossed them away. "I think I'll try something different this time."

Sid balled up her fist and closed in on Reginald.

The doppelganger was a statue. Not the slightest hint of worry in his eye.

She lunged in and threw a roundhouse kick.

He ducked away from it and hid his arms behind his back.

She kicked.

He evaded. His head bobbed and weaved.

She let loose a side kick.

Reginald countered this time, unleashing one quicker and more powerful of his own.

She left her feet and landed hard on her back. "Oof!"

"Wah-tah!" Reginald unleashed a roundhouse kick on Smoke. The doppelganger had changed into some weird combination of Bruce Lee and Chuck Norris. "Wah-tah!"

Wap! Wap! Wap!

Smoke countered with a flurry of his own. Hard, heavy punches landed all over Reginald's body.

The doppelganger shrugged them off and hit back even harder. A nasty front kick sent Smoke sprawling all over the floor. "Wah-tah!"

Sid regained her feet and renewed her attack.

Reginald had changed again. He was a woman now. Not any woman either. He—or it—was Samantha.

Sid cast a quick glance over to the prisoners. Sam was bound up. One of her eyebrows was perched. "Screw it!" Sid unloaded a combination of kicks and elbows.

Sam the doppelganger swatted them aside and danced away laughing.

"Come now, Sidney. Don't hold back." Reginald started to shift again. He turned into Rebecca Lang. "I know you hate me."

A new fire burned in Sid's belly. She attacked.

The doppelganger squared up and took punch after punch after punch.

Sid hit and kicked until she couldn't anymore.

Rebecca's Lang's body didn't have a scratch on it.

Hands on her knees and gasping for breath, Sid said, "I hate you."

"Me, or Rebecca?" said Reginald's Rebecca-like voice.

Sid unloaded a kicked in its gut. "Both!"

The doppelganger shoved her down. "Be wise and stay down."

Sid wasn't sure she could get up again. She felt her face swelling. She was wheezing again.

I hate shifters!

Smoke crept up on the doppelganger with another axe in his hand and turned loose a decapitating blow.

Elation raced through Sid. *Yes!*

Reginald ducked with a split second to spare. The axe swished over his head.

"No!" Sid cried out.

Smoke had missed. Still chopping away, the rangy ex-SEAL fought to connect on a new mark.

Reginald skipped away. Baiting. Laughing. He shifted again. Into Sid. "I hate that thing."

Smoke backed off. He labored for breath, and his brawny shoulders sagged. Sid could see in his eyes that he didn't have much left.

"As I said," Reginald added in Sid's own voice, "I'm the greatest shifter in all the world. There's a reason for that. I don't have a weakness."

Smoke spat on his hands, rubbed them together, and lifted the axe up by the handle. "Everything has a weakness."

"Well, certainly, at least in your cases. You're both human." He blew Smoke a kiss with Sid's lips. "I'm your weakness." He pointed at Sid. "Or at least she is, and you're hers. You'll see soon enough what I mean." He strolled over the gore-slickened floor and picked up an axe like Smoke's. He flipped it around a few times and transformed into Smoke. Glancing at Sid, he said, "See if you can keep track of who's who." And then, axe high, he charged.

Axe heads collided together. The brawling men were identical, but their clothes were different. Sid wanted to help, but she barely had the strength to move.

Find a weakness, Sid. Find a weakness!

She made a pleading glance at her friends. They weren't going anywhere. All eyes were fixed on the battle.

"Oh please, this is too easy," Reginald said. He blocked or dodged everything Smoke threw at him. "Really, I don't know what kind of speed you were on earlier, that was thrilling, but this will be a disaster."

The pair of men locked axe heads.

Reginald ripped Smoke's free from his hands, sending it skipping away.

Shoulder dipping, Smoke limped forward.

Reginald brought down a brain-splitting swing.

"Nooooooooo!" Sid wheezed.

Smoke's hands locked on Reginald's wrist, and the pair of formidable men stood eye to eye. "Drop it," Smoke said in his face.

"Done."

The axe clattered to the floor.

Both versions of Smoke circled one another.

Reginald removed his shirt and tossed it aside. He had a black sleeveless T-shirt underneath it. He lifted up his fists and transformed into a hulking black boxer. "It's time for a knockout."

Smoke rushed in with a flurry of punches. Hard and fast, he pounded on Reginald's face with swift, hard smacks.

The doppelganger's bullish neck didn't yield. His big meaty hands unloaded a pair of heavy uppercuts into Smoke's gut and ribs. "Oh! That's got to hurt!" Reginald said. He tore into Smoke with a rapid fighter's frenzy.

The punches were so hard Sid swore she felt them.

Smoke was down, and the punches were still coming. Hard and fast. *Wap! Wap! Wap! Wap! Wap!* Smoke's legs twitched.

Reginald reared up and shifted again, this time back into Sid. "You're killing him, Sid," Reginald said. *Wap! Wap! Wap!* "You're killing him, Sid!" *Wap!* "You're killing him!" *Wap! Wap! Wap!*

Sid's heart exploded inside her chest, and she screamed, "Stop! Please! Stop!"

Reginald held back his punch. Blood dripped from his knuckles. "You have something to say?"

"Spare him. Spare them," she said, wheezing. "I'll come to the Drake. That's what you wanted all along anyway, right?"

Reginald flung the blood from his fingers. "Well, not me. And I do like punching him. He's tough. But I think he's dead." He rubbed his knuckles. "It's been a few weeks since I beat my last man to death."

CHAPTER 39

S ID CRAWLED OVER TO SMOKE and huddled over him. His face was a battered and bloody mess. Eyes swollen. Nose broken. Lips split. She almost didn't recognize him. "John," she said, pushing his matted hair from his eyes. She held his head in her lap. "John?"

Smoke's eye popped open. He rolled over on one elbow and spat blood, saying, "I didn't find a weakness." He coughed. "I will next time." He eyed Reginald, who had shifted back into his normal self. Smoke leaned back onto Sid's lap. "Don't deal with them, Sid. It's not worth it."

"I already gave him my word." She held his face in her hands. "I couldn't let any of you die. Not on account of me."

Grimacing in pain, Smoke forced himself to a knee and gasped. He held his ribs. His face was wracked with pain. "Don't go."

"She has given her word, Mister Smoke. You know how that goes. Reneging would result in the painful deaths of every last one of you." Reginald put his jacket back on, found a pack of cigarettes, and lit one with his black Zippo lighter. He eyed Sid. "Are you having second thoughts, Miss Shaw?"

She glanced at her friends—Sam, Guppy, Mal, and Asia. All eyes were glued to her.

Smoke rubbed a knot on his head. "Don't give them what they want."

"I can't watch all of you die," she said, still wheezing. "I can't. What else am I supposed to do?"

Gritting his teeth, Smoke rose to his feet. "I know I'd rather die first."

"Don't worry, Mister Smoke. I'm sure that can still be arranged." Reginald beckoned to Sid. "We need to leave now. As in right now. Precious seconds could wipe this deal away. And remember, I still have men with two barrels on each and every one of you."

Empty hearted, Sid got up and draped her arms over Smoke's shoulders. There was tension in his iron limbs, like a great cat ready to spring. She expected a surprise. A last-ditch effort. A miraculous rescue. His iron jaw gave a gentle shake. His eyes said there was nothing left. He'd lost this fight. They both had. "You look like you could use some pancakes."

"Don't say that. I'm one of those stress eaters. They used to call me big boy when I was a kid."

She choked out a sob.

"Oh please, don't be so tiresome," Reginald said. He puffed out some smoke rings. "Give him one final kiss, and let's be gone. The things I do for humanity. Death is such a greater mercy than this sickening forlorn suffering. Rexor! Thorgrim! Get up, you two lazy bastards!"

What? Really?

Smoke's best eye popped wide.

Sid looked over Smoke's shoulder at the giants.

Thorgrim sat up and started rubbing the back of his head. He eyeballed Sid and grabbed his hammer.

Rexor's great arms came to life, and with the help of Thorgrim, he wrenched the four-bladed axe from his face. The mutilated giant gave Smoke a nasty leer. Rising up to his towering height, he pointed at Smoke and then turned and walked away with his brother.

"Stupid and lazy. It's their biggest flaw. They aren't used to fighting so long, so they took a little nap. Pathetic," Reginald said. "Guards, take Miss Shaw into custody and see that she's well secured. I don't want to come looking for her or her friends again. Not for a while anyway."

"I guess this is goodbye," Smoke said with a bit too much finality.

She searched his pummeled face for a place to kiss and ended up kissing his chin.

"That was awkward," he said.

The guards started pulling her away. "Well, you shouldn't have gotten your face all messed up."

"If you think my face looks bad, you should see my heart."

Sid's own heart dropped into her stomach. Being hauled away, she yelled toward Smoke with tears running down her cheeks. "Smoke ..."

"Don't say it," he said back. "I already know you love me."

EPILOGUE

D AYS LATER, SID WAS BROUGHT into a magnificent dining room, the largest she'd ever been in. Aged wood was everywhere. Exquisite china like one might see in the Smithsonian Museum. All around was nothing short of old family wealth. It was the kind of stuff you'd see in the Biltmore or the Vanderbilt. There was a grand fireplace, but no flame, no warmth. The room was cold.

Rubbing her elbows, Sid ventured in. She'd been cleaned up and adorned in the finest evening gown and jewels her eyes had ever beheld. She'd been treated like nothing short of a queen the last few days. She tried not to gape at the sparkling crystals on the mammoth chandeliers.

"Enjoying your stay?"

The strong and rich voice startled her. A man appeared in the room. He was refined, powerfully built, and wearing a dark suit. His salt-and-pepper hair was slicked back. His skin was dark, and his moustache was waxed.

Sid kept her silence.

"Please, Sidney, sit down." He beckoned toward her seat. "And allow me to introduce myself. My name is Kane, Kane Lancaster, and we have much to talk about."

ANGI THE HARPY

CRAIG HALLORAN

THE SUPERNATURAL BOUNTY HUNTER FILES

UP IN SMOKE

BOOK 6

CHAPTER 1

S ID WAS GONE. IT HAD been weeks. Smoke still hadn't fully recovered from the worst ass-kicking he'd ever had. His cracked and bruised ribs still ached, but he'd recover. It was his heart that hurt. Bad. He missed her. He sucked on a straw that was stuck inside a chocolate shake.

I'm going to kill that bastard.

"Honey?" said a sweet voice with a little spunk in it. It was a waitress, a nice-looking gal with a twinkle in her eye. "We're about to close. Are you finished?"

Smoke eyed the empty malt glasses on the table. There was half a stack of pancakes he hadn't finished. He shrugged. "I guess so."

She smoothed her hands over the snug uniform that accentuated her nice figure and started picking up the plates. "You look like you could use some company. A good-looking guy like you shouldn't be alone on a night like this."

Looking into her pretty eyes, he said, "And a good-looking woman like you shouldn't be alone, either."

She smiled. "Is that a yes?"

"My body says yes, but my heart says no," he said to her politely. "Sorry, Kim."

She tugged his chin. "I'd be hurt by that if you weren't so darn cute, Smoke. As for your lady friend, she'd be a fool not to come back around. Now get out of here before I lock you in and do something stupid."

He put his money on the table. "All right. See you tomorrow then?"

"No, I'm off," she said, walking away. "So yes, tomorrow the coast is clear." Kim laughed at him good naturedly. "And you might want to cut back a milkshake or two. Your cheeks are getting a little chubby."

He rubbed his scruffy jaw. "Really?"

Laughing some more, she said, "Goodbye, Smoke."

A little bell rang as he exited into the dark, drilling rain. It was closing in on eleven p.m., and the parking lot was empty aside from his car and a group of young people hanging out between the diner and a convenience store with a gas station.

Traffic from the highway whizzed by, mostly eighteen wheelers. A rush of wind hit Smoke every time one went past. As he approached his old Camaro and briefly admired its new coat of cosmic white paint, a new figure stepped into view.

It was a girl, maybe twenty. Her hair was black with pink streaks, and all of her clothes were black and grey. She leaned up against the driver's door of his car.

"Got a smoke?"

He chuckled. "Get your butt off my car, little lady."

She sneered at him. "Little lady? What's that supposed to mean? What are you, like forty? Give me a cigarette."

"I don't smoke."

"I don't care," she said, giving him more attitude. "There's a store over there. Go get me some."

Four young guys came into view. They weren't a bunch of slouches, either. They were fit, and dressed with Daddy's dollars. Their eyes were busy, fiendish, and rebellious. Two of them were as big as Smoke. Heavy hitters at the gym. Cocky.

"Jenna, is this guy bothering you?" said a good-looking fellow with too much gel in his brown hair. There was nothing but attitude all over him, and he sniffed a lot. Eyeballing Smoke, he tossed an empty beer can on the ground. "You, guy, you bothering my woman?"

"No," Smoke said, "she's bothering me, and now you are too."

The young man huffed and thumbed his nose. "I tell you what. Give me the keys to your car and I'll forget you said that."

Smoke felt his nostrils flare, taking in the fumes from all of them. Cigarettes, pot, alcohol, and other toxins seeped from their skin. The young men were tense. Charged up.

One big one smacked his fist into his hand.

But Smoke's instincts told him that was just a show. His attention was drawn to the leader, whose eyes were glued on Smoke's shirt for a second before he pointed at it and started to snicker.

"Get this, guys. This big doofuss's shirt says, 'Always be yourself, unless you can be a unicorn, then always be a unicorn.'"

Two of them started laughing. One of the gang said, "What a wuss."

"You read pretty well for a slimy little turd." Smoke glanced at the others. "You girls don't have anything against unicorns, do you?"

They all stiffened up.

"Let's roll him, Jimmy." One of the bigger goons stepped forward. He was built like a lineman for a college football team. There were old bloodstains on his T-shirt. "I want to drive his car when we're done with him."

"And I want my cigarettes." Jenna poked Smoke in the chest. "And an apology."

The small group of spoiled young punks hemmed Smoke in by the side of his car.

He only looked at the one in front of him. "You might want to reconsider, Jimmy. I'm not the typical person you usually trifle with."

Jimmy's laugh was part wheeze. "Oh, I know that. There aren't too many big pussies running around in unicorn shirts these days. Haha. Look, hand over the keys, give us your money, and the four of us—"

"Five," Jenna corrected.

"Yeah, the five of us won't beat the hell out of you." Jimmy sucked his teeth and licked his lips. "Now, hand over the keys."

"Let's just whip his ass and take them," said one of the young men to Smoke's left.

Smoke had long ago noticed the car the street punks clung to. It was a black-out BMW X5 SUV. New. There weren't very many things that made him angry, but spoiled and entitled young people like this really irked him. It was hard to reason with people whose parents never told them no. When they were supercharged with drugs and felt invincible like this, it was nigh on impossible. But he considered himself a good guy, so he tried.

"You know Jimmy, I don't usually give second chances, but because all of you are so young, I'm going to." Smoke glowered down at Jimmy. "Back off."

Jimmy snaked a knife out of the back of his pants. "I don't think so. Take him!"

CHAPTER 2

THUGS COULD BE FAST. THUGS could be slow. These were fast. From all sides they came, high and low.

Smoke back-kicked the one straight behind him, driving his boot heel into the abdomen muscle.

The man collapsed like a tent with a groan.

Meanwhile, Smoke evaded the first swipe of Jimmy's blade. The young man had overextended his arm. Using the punk's momentum, Smoke locked his hand on Jimmy's wrist and slung him into another thug.

Three down, for the moment.

That left the two big ones. They had moved with the explosiveness of football players and were now on him.

From behind, the one that spoke the most caught Smoke in a bear hug and lifted him off the ground. "Nail him! Nail him!"

Pain exploded into Smoke's brain from his ribs. They were still tender from fighting with the doppelganger, Reginald.

The second big punk had slipped some brass knuckles over his fingers and was coming straight at him.

Smoke caught him in the face with his boot and crunched his nose.

"Aagh!" the thug moaned, holding his nose. He pulled his hand away and gaped at the blood. His eyes became flame. "Hold him! Hold the bastard!"

From the vice-like grip of a goon hopped up on cocaine and built up with an extra muscle layer from steroids, Smoke kicked again at his bloody-faced assailant. His boot hit the nose again, dead center.

The man screamed and backed away in shock, trying to push his nose back into place.

"That looks pretty bad," Smoke said. "You'll probably need to use your momma's plastic surgeon, assuming you haven't already." He launched his head back into his captor's chin, bringing spots to his eyes.

Roaring, the bigger man's knees buckled, but like a bear he held on.

Toes touching the ground, Smoke executed a Judo move, flipping the big man over his front and landing on top of him.

His assailant now lay flat-backed on the pavement. A whoosh of air escaped from the man's lungs, and his mighty grip loosened.

Quick as a mongoose, Smoke slipped free, stood, turned, and drove a boot into the man's ribs. Blood flowed like a river through his veins, and his milkshake-dulled battle instincts ignited.

Behind him, Jimmy had bounded to his feet and now came right for Smoke, knife flashing under the parking lot lights.

Smoke caught Jimmy's wrist and wrenched the weapon free. "You like knives, Jimmy?" Without looking, he stuck it in the leg of another punk who was coming for him.

The young man let out a scream and hobbled away, clutching his wounded leg.

Smoke raised his right hand up. "I like fists, Jimmy. Especially this one." He punched Jimmy in the chest so hard that all the air came out of him. His next uppercut lifted Jimmy off the ground. He didn't let up.

Every one of the men who moved toward Smoke was hit until he moved no more. Two of them hobbled away. Jimmy stared blinking at the sky, holding his busted jaw.

Chest heaving and lathered in sweat, Smoke cocked his head toward a distant noise until he could make it out. Sirens were blaring in the distance and getting closer by the second. The young people wouldn't be able to hear them yet.

Good. Let them explain what happened here and why they're out after curfew.

Smoke dusted off his hands, got in his car, and rolled down the window. "And that, kids, is why you shouldn't do drugs—or make fun of people who like unicorns." Back wheels smoking, he peeled out of the parking lot and onto the highway just as the punks showed signs of hearing the sirens.

Adrenaline pumping like gas in a top fueled engine, Smoke roared down the road. He stuffed some classic rock into the 1986 Camaro's cassette player and turned the tunes up. The fight had his juices flowing again. His hands drummed on the wheel. He'd stayed calm since Sid departed under uncertain circumstances, but now he was peeved.

He downshifted and stomped on the gas to roar up the interstate. A question he didn't have an answer to plagued his mind.

Where is she?

Since she departed with Reginald, there hadn't been any trace of her at all. There weren't any signs of her sister Allison or her niece Megan either. As for The Drake and all of their foul alliances, they'd gone quiet. No one from the FBI had approached Smoke, either. Things were odd. Aggravating. It wasn't like him to be aggravated about anything, but he was now.

Sid was gone, and it seemed a part of him was gone with her.

He sang along to the cassette he played. It was a mix, and it wasn't his mix, either. It had come with the car when he bought it, and he liked it. Classic rock before his time. Styx. Def Leppard. Van Halen. Dio. AC/DC. Foreigner. Rush. Devo. He'd gotten quite fond of it. He dropped his shades out of the visor and put them on. The darkness went with his mood.

Sid being missing wasn't the only thing aggravating him. There was also Reginald the doppelganger. The shifting fiend had beaten him like a drum, and he didn't like getting beaten. It left a foul taste in his mouth. Sure, everyone else could be beaten, but not him. Not Smoke. He was special for a mortal. He'd always known so.

Miles down the road south of DC, he geared down on the next exit to enter the stretch of road that led to his service-garage apartment. The tall pines he passed were stark on either side of him. They always had been, but it was even more ominous when the full moon glowed over the horizon.

Shifters.

On nights like this, Mal Carlson said, the shifters were at full power. On a night like this, they would be causing trouble. Killing. Tormenting. Humiliating.

Evil does what it does.

He turned the car off the main road down the long stretch that led to his driveway. Rounding the bend, he found himself face to face with a black helicopter that had landed between his car and his apartment.

He slammed the Camaro into reverse.

Two Humvees burst out of the woods behind him, blocking him in.

He shoved the Camaro into park.

You've got to be kidding me.

CHAPTER 3

Hands glued to the steering wheel, Smoke remained inside his car. In truth, there wasn't any reason to run. No one had exited the Humvees. Nobody was pointing a muzzle at him. It was just the Camaro, the Humvees, and the helicopter that sat like a bird of prey, no movement at all.

And that full moon.

Smoke's eyes scanned the details of the chopper. It was shiny black without any distinct markings on it. There weren't any logos from The Drake. No deaders. No shifting monsters or men bigger than two NBA players. Things were just cold and black. Odd. Mysterious.

I guess they want me to come to them.

He popped the door open and got out. There was a pistol in the back of his pants and a knife inside each pant leg. After casually closing the door, he approached the helicopter the same way. It was sealed up. No one sat in the cockpit. He peered around the tail of the chopper and spied the front door of his apartment. It was cracked open.

Breaking and entering. Illegal. I might have to blow someone away for trespassing.

He pulled out his gun and approached cautiously, peering into the front room from a distance. Chimney smoke was rolling out of the black pipe of a wood-burning stove he'd put in years ago. The summer evening was too warm to warrant burning anything for warmth.

Jaw clenched, he was headed for his front door when a figure shuffled out through it. Ranging and a little stooped in the shoulder, its slack jaw marked it for a deader. It wore a pea coat and slacks. Had that dead look in its sunken eyes.

Smoke dotted its chest with his laser sight.

"Easy now," said a familiar voice. A man, well dressed and slender in build, came outside and stepped right into the laser. It was the doppelganger, Reginald. "We have business, Mister Smoke. Please, come inside."

"You're inviting me into my own home. That's funny." Smoke stuffed his pistol into the back of his pants. "Real funny. I never took you for a comedian, Reggie."

Reggie was a fit man, good-looking, cool and calculating in demeanor. He wore an expensive golf shirt and slacks with a little room to grow in. "Actually, I did do a shtick in Vaudeville back in the day. You look to be doing well for a man I thought I'd beaten to death. How are the ribs?"

Smoke headed inside his own place, feeling like a guest and hoping the ever slightest that Sid would be in there. She wasn't, but a dazzling pair of legs did catch his eye.

It was Sid's sister, Allison. Full-bodied and gorgeous as ever, she sat on his sofa wearing a short skintight black dress with tiny sequins woven into it. Diamond and ruby-laden earrings hung from her lobes, their radiance oozing with the fortune of kings. A playful smile started on her full lips when she saw him.

Getting up, she said, "Hi, John." She pressed her body into his and gave him a firm hug, her soft warm lips landing on his neck. "You look well. Very well."

He started to speak.

But she put her finger to his lips. "My sister is fine. That's why I'm here, to give you assurance about that. But let's not spoil the moment with thoughts of her. I want all your attention."

"Please, Mister Smoke," said Reggie, "sit down. Have a glass of wine. It's from our cellar, French, 1763."

"You know, your treating me like a guest in my own home is starting to get under my skin." Smoke picked up a bottle with an old weathered label and chucked it out the front door. "Now, Reggie, can I offer you a cup of nothing?"

Allison's beautiful face darkened. "I was drinking that. It was a ten-thousand-dollar bottle."

"It's nothing." Reggie snapped his fingers. "Harvey!"

The deader stepped inside the door frame.

"Another bottle of wine from the chopper. And make it quick, you stupid dead thing."

"I wouldn't bother," Smoke said, not hiding his irritation. "You won't be staying long. Whatever you showed up for, make it quick. And remember, you're in my castle."

"Castle?" Looking around, Reginald huffed a laugh, sat down on one of the chairs, and crossed his legs. "It's far from even a quaint establishment. Smells like an old grease pit. I never monkeyed around with cars and things."

"I find it sexy." Allison leaned forward in her seat, smiling at Smoke.

The deader stepped into the doorframe with a bottle of wine hanging in its grip.

Smoke pulled out his gun and fired.

Bang!

The bottle burst into a thousand pieces.

Reginald didn't flinch.

Allison cursed, "Stop doing that, dammit!"

"My castle, my rules. No booze."

"You're absolutely no fun at all. It's no surprise my sister's so fond of you."

Smoke ignored her and addressed Reginald. "Does your dirty deader know how to shovel glass into a dust pan?" He walked over to his kitchenette and fetched a broom and dust pan from the tall cupboard. He took them to the deader. "Well?"

"Clean it up, Harvey," Reginald said. "Mister Smoke, you and I have business to discuss."

Smoke crossed his arms over his chest. "Such as?"

"Well, you're a bounty hunter, and we'd like you to track someone down for us. Actually, not just one someone, but a small group of thugs we want eliminated." Reginald pulled out a cigarette case, opened it, and put one in his mouth. "Care for one?"

"You might want to refrain from lighting up."

Reginald flipped open the top of a black Zippo and flicked the primer that produced a flame. "Why? This clearly isn't a *Smoke Free* zone."

Allison laughed. "You're such a clever man, Reginald."

"True." The doppelganger lit his cigarette, took a puff, and blew fumes into the air. "I think the fragrance enhances your abode's stale character." He put the lighter away. "Now where were we?"

"You were about to put out your cigarette." Smoke still had his pistol in hand.

Allison leaned forward again. "Ooh, I like the tension."

Matter-of-factly, Reginald said, "You can't kill me, Smoke. A million of these cigarettes can't kill me. Trust me, I know. Now put that toy away, have a seat by the pretty lady, and let's talk about things."

Smoke stowed his gun, walked over to Reginald, and plucked the cigarette from his mouth, then made his way to the buck stove and tossed it inside. He walked back over to the couch and sat down.

"Now we can talk."

Allison scooted close beside him.

"You're a brave man, John Smoke," said Reginald. "Perhaps a little too brave for your own good. I thought you'd have learned not to trifle with me by now."

"In my house, I don't compromise for anybody."

"You really will have to learn to compromise at some point. Unlike me, John, you're mortal. You need to realize your limitations." Reginald cleared his throat. "My, I sure could have used some wine, but let's get back to business. Mister Smoke, we want you to hunt some people down for us." Reginald tossed a black file on the coffee table. "Track them down and kill them."

CHAPTER 4

S MOKE LAID HIS EYES ON the file. It was interesting in how it resembled the files from the Black Slate. He wondered if this was The Drake's own version of what the FBI had. Perhaps it was all the same. He picked it up and looked inside. There was a picture, a black-and-white 8 x 10 photo of several men with haunting looks. He squinted his eyes. There was something strange about the picture.

"What do you see, John?" Reginald said. He sucked his teeth. "Go on, tell me."

Allison nuzzled her warm body right up against Smoke's some more. She rested her chin on his shoulder. He didn't mind it, not at all. Her perfume coupled with her form was intoxicating. It was like she emanated pheromones that ignited lust.

He scooted away. "I don't see anything special."

"Really? You don't see anything special?" Reginald said. "Why, I'm surprised."

Smoke wasn't being completely honest. Sure, he didn't see anything special to him, but he did see something. There was another man in the group. His body was outlined by the rest of them. It was a picture with one person missing. That person was invisible.

"Surprise can be a good thing." Smoke closed the file and set it on the table. "So go ahead, fill me in on all the details."

"I want you to kill those men."

"I'm not an assassin."

"Oh, you won't be *killing them*, killing them. They're already technically dead."

Allison put her hand on Smoke's thigh.

Doing his best to ignore her, he said to Reginald, "You have plenty of resources. Why me?"

"At Drake, we like to make use of different resources so we can keep our hands clean. I decided to use you because you want to see Sidney. If you take care of this problem, then the two of you can be reunited once more. Doesn't that sound swell, Mister Smoke? You get to be the hero. A knight in shining armor."

"I'm already that." Smoke took Allison's hand off his thigh and stood up. "And if you think I'm going to do this hunt over a woman, you have me all wrong. I want money. I don't do anything for free."

"Ooh, a mercenary in tainted armor," Reginald said, "I like that. A nice twist. What kind of finances are we talking about, John?" He glanced around. "Judging by your environment, I think twenty thousand is more than reasonable. It will keep these florescent lights on. And maybe you can buy some more unicorn shirts."

"Two hundred thousand. Half up front."

"Surely you jest." Reginald stood up from his seat. "That's a bit steep."

"This, coming from a man who drinks ten-thousand-dollar bottles of wine? I don't think so. The offer is on the table. I suggest you take it before it goes up to a million."

"I think you're a decent bluffer, Mister Smoke," Reginald said. "I know you're dying to see Miss Shaw."

"If it's meant to be, it's meant to be."

"Allison, go and get him the money, if you please." After she left, Reginald stood in front of Smoke, looking up into his eyes. "You want another crack at me pretty bad, don't you."

"I just want you to get out of here."

"I see. Well, keep practicing. I could always use a sparring partner. Not that I need to stay sharp, but just because I enjoy beating the hell out of people." He removed a business card from his front shirt pocket and held it in front of Smoke's eyes. "It's a lead."

Smoke took it. "Sounds like you already know where your enemies are."

"I always know everything I need to know." Reginald patted Smoke on the chest. "See you soon, Mister Smoke, and be careful. This brood you're going to cross, there a little different." He glared at Harvey the deader, who was still sweeping up the broken glass. "Put that down, you dead-headed buffoon."

From inside, Smoke watched Harvey and Reginald board the chopper.

Allison emerged a few seconds later with a satchel and came back. She closed the door behind her and said with a playful smile, "Alone at last."

Smoke's throat tightened. He wasn't one to charm easily, but Allison's Venus-like figure could melt a typical man's limbs. With a dry tongue, he said, "Just leave the money and go. I have work to do."

Approaching with want in her eyes, she said, "All work and no play? Please, just give me a little something. After all, you owe me for destroying my wine." She locked her arms around his waist and pulled him tight. "Kiss me. You want to, I can see it in your eyes."

That's an understatement. A huge one.

His longing for Sid seemed to amplify with Allison's presence. Something about her made his knees a little weak. Searching for a way out, he said, "Tell me how Sid's doing."

Running her hands down his back, she kissed his neck. "Oh, don't spoil the moment. Just take me, John."

He got ahold of her wrists and gently pushed her away. "Not without Sid's permission."

"Will you quit saying her name? I don't want to hear it."

He searched Allison's eyes. "She is okay, isn't she?"

"Well that's the whole point of this mission, isn't it? Do what Reginald says and you'll get to see her." She rolled her eyes. "But don't expect a rosy welcome. Sid's changed, you know. She's tasted the Wine of the Kings now. She's changed."

The chopper's engines whirred with life.

"Looks like your ride is leaving." Smoke walked over to the door and opened it up. "I don't think you want to miss it."

Chin up, Allison stormed out. "Your faithfulness is your folly."

"No, it's my strength."

He closed the door and watched through the window as the chopper took off and the Humvees departed. At long last, his Camaro was the only thing left outside. The chopper became a speck in the dark sky and vanished. He wished he'd shot it down. If Allison hadn't been aboard, he would have done just that. Killed them all and found Sid later.

He got a Coke from the fridge, cracked it open, and sat down on the sofa. He stared at the file, but a vision of Allison was burned in his head. Her scent lingered. He took a swallow of Coke and cleared his dry throat.

Crom, what a woman.

CHAPTER 5

"IT'S A GAME, JOHN, JUST another game," said Samantha, also known as Phat Sam. She was sitting at Smoke's computer desk, typing away. Her husband Guppy, built like a tree stump, stood right behind her, nodding. She finished by saying, "It's just one thing after another with these twisted people. Don't worry. We'll find her."

Smoke prided himself on being able to find anyone, but Sid's departure had been troublesome. He didn't have any idea where she was, and he'd been looking, too. He just found himself at one dead end after the other. Things were quiet. Too quiet. He flipped over the business card that Reginald had given him. Perhaps the people in the black file had something to do with that.

"Did you find The Guillotine?" he said as he laced up his boots.

"Oh yeah, no problem there," Sam said. "It's one of those dungeon bars. Real creepy place near the Potomac. We'll need to get a little gothic if we're going in there. I hate gothic. I look good in gothic, but I hate it."

"You look good in everything," Guppy said, rubbing her shoulders, "and I wouldn't mind seeing the gothic thing. It's been awhile."

"Yeah, I think you had hair last time I dressed that way," she said, patting his hand. Her bracelets rattled on her wrists. "But I like that shiny head better. It's like a beacon of love. I'm drawn to it."

Guppy stopped massaging her shoulders and picked up the picture of the men from the black file. "So John, are you really going to kill these guys?" Looking at the pic, he tilted his head to the side. "They have strange markings on them."

"I noticed that." Smoke finished lacing up his boots and started loading one of the automatic pistols on the table. There was a sniper rifle too, and the stack of Reginald's money. "I'll figure out what they are first, and if I have to waste them, I'll waste them. Besides, The Guillotine is only a clue. Or a set-up. I'll play it through."

"We're all going," Sam said. "I'm curious."

Smoke wasn't going to argue with her. Once his half-sister made her mind up, there was no changing it. He just hoped this wild goose chase wouldn't be too dangerous. He didn't have much doubt that Reginald was screwing with him. At least he'd gotten a hundred thousand dollars out of him. He opened up the black file and flipped over the photo. There was some information on it. Names. Places. Contact numbers for Reginald and other high-ranking people at The Drake. Vague stuff.

The beginnings of a new game.

"Hey, John?" Sam spun around in her chair and faced him. "You might want to come see this. I have something on that picture you sent. Pretty weird."

He got up and made his way over.

The picture was on the biggest monitor, the one where the creepy goons surrounded an invisible figure. Sam had filled it in with an eerie green that revealed the large man in the center. Some of the details were still filling in.

Leaning forward, Guppy said, "Is he wearing an invisibility suit or something?"

"Mal says they have the technology." Sam leaned toward the screen. "But look, his hair is showing. At least, I think that's hair, the way it's flowing. How can you make your hair invisible?"

Guppy huffed a laugh. "You just have to be special."

Smoke studied the image on the screen. "Those marks on their arms are interesting. Are they brands?"

Sam zoomed in on one man's forearm. "Either that, or some 3D tattoo art. Ew, it looks like a nest of eggs or a bunch of different eyes. Creepy. It's got tentacles. Without a closer view, I'd have thought it was just a mole."

There was something odd and unnatural about all the men in the picture. Their features were sharp, but their skin was pasty. Some of them had long black fingernails. They were an odd bunch.

"Look at that one over there, on this guy." Smoke pointed at the screen. "It says *Guermo*. What does that mean?"

Typing in a new command, Sam did a search but apparently didn't find anything meaningful. "I'll send Russ a note. Maybe he'll know." She launched a text.

Smoke and his crew had kept in touch with Russ Davenport. He'd been a solid resource, but he found the recent quiet odd. He'd made that clear. "When things are quiet like this, it means something big is happening," he'd said.

Smoke was inclined to agree. Something wasn't right. He could feel it everywhere he went in DC. He refocused on the group picture. The image in the center. "Can you tell if this photo was digitally doctored?"

"No, it wasn't. At least I'm pretty confident it wasn't. The thing is, the background behind our invisible man is blurred. It's a storage room, and you can see the shelves and boxes behind him, but they're blurred just a bit. Computers can fill that in, but the contrast is too smooth. I'm convinced we're looking right through him. He's invisible."

"Or a vampire," Guppy said. "You can't take pictures of vampires, can you?"

"You watch too many movies." Sam's pretty face frowned. She shivered and rubbed her upper arms. "That thought just gave me the willies. Tell me, Smoke. Tell me there aren't any vampires in DC."

"I thought you liked these supernatural creatures."

"I do, but I don't know, that sent a chill through me. Look, I've got goosebumps up to my armpits."

Smoke tried to recall something that Adam Vaughn the Wolfman had said to him. He'd talked of vampires and called them *Euro trash*. There had been another incident too. At the mausoleum amid the gargoyles, an eerie man called Boss had mentioned vampires to Sid.

Phat Sam's phone buzzed. She eyed the text. "It's from Russ. He says germo or guermo is old Spanish for *The Many*." She stuck her tongue out. "Uck, that explains those eyeball tattoos. Man, I'm thinking you should kill those dudes if we cross them at The Guillotine. None of that sounds right at all."

Her phone buzzed again.

"Russ wants to know what's up. What do I tell him?"

"Nothing. We need to get ready."

Buzzzzzzzzz.

Sam checked her phone screen. "Yuck, it's a pic of that eyeball thing." She showed it to Smoke. "Look."

It was graffiti spray-painted on a wall, a cluster of eyes with wavy tentacles encircling it. Below, it read *Guermo*—in what looked like smeared blood.

CHAPTER 6

"**W**ELL, THIS IS IT**,**" GUPPY said, pulling the SUV into the parking lot of The Guillotine Club. It was late night, and the moon was still full. He shut off the engine of the 1979 blacked-out custom Ford Bronco and peered over the wheel. "I think we have the only American wheels on the lot."

Sitting in the passenger seat and wearing a black dress that would make Elvira proud, Sam added, "You can say that again. Is that a Bugatti?"

Smoke, in dark glasses, sat in the back seat, snacking on some pretzels and finishing off a chocolate shake. Like Guppy, he was in a dark dress shirt and nice dark dress slacks. His cuff links and tie had a little goth look to them. He sucked every last bit of shake out of his straw.

In an agitated voice, Sam said, "Will you stop doing that, Smoke? You aren't five anymore. Oh never mind that. The last time I was at the movies, some thirty-year-old was sucking out every bit of his Slurpee." She shook her head. "People these days."

"Yeah, but I don't think you'll have to worry about that guy ever coming to the movies again," Guppy said with a chuckle. "You scared the Slurpee right out of him."

With smiling eyes, she said to Guppy, "I sure did, didn't I?"

Smoke stuck the cup in a holder. "Sorry Sis, but I've got to have my energy shakes. Let's go."

The Guillotine was in an industrial graveyard along the Potomac River. Dark neon colors glowed in gothic designs on the face of a tall building covered in metal sheeting. The parking lot was full of exotic cars. Most were European, but there were a few classic American muscle machines as well. A few people lingered by their cars—smoking, snorting, and chatting. Their hair, skin, and clothing all had a bizarre dark look to them. Techno, punk, gothic, it was a smattering of darker enriched society.

"Oh man, I hope they don't allow smoking in there," Sam said. "I hate going into places where I come out smelling like a chimney."

Guppy looked at the cigar he'd just taken out of his shirt pocket. "I was counting on it."

"Well maybe you should make some new friends and hang out by the Bronco." She reached for the cigar.

Guppy deftly put it away. "I just want to blend in."

Smoke looked at the entrance. "Let's get inside and see what's happening. If you meet anyone, let me know. If any crap goes down, meet at the car."

There was a line to get in, fronted by a couple of bouncers who looked like they hadn't stopped their cycle of steroids since the turn of the century.

Smoke said to Sam, "This is your arena. Lead the way."

Sam sashayed right up in front of the bouncers behind the velvet robe. "Good evening."

Both bouncers slowly eyed her generous curves.

The biggest one—with a chewed-up ear and a gold rope necklace—removed the velvet rope and stepped aside. "And a very good evening to you."

The bouncers patted the three of them down first, but they were in.

The inside of The Guillotine didn't disappoint: neon lights and a long bar with countless glass shelves of alcohol behind it. The men and women danced wildly and cavorted to techno music that pumped so loud it shook the tiny high glass windows.

Smoke and company squeezed through the hard bodies on the dancefloor and cut toward the tables on the other side. A pair of women showing more skin than clothes rubbed up against Smoke's limbs and urged him to dance. Feeling the beat, he started to shake his head and wiggle his shoulder. The women's decorated eyes lit up with sultry fever.

A hard shove from Sam righted his course when she yelled, "Get moving. You're engaged, remember."

Stuffing his body into the nearest empty seat, Smoke took note of Sam's word, engaged. He had no idea where he stood with Sid. He'd asked her to marry him and then everything had turned to disaster. Engaged or not, he was determined to find her.

"See any big shots?" Smoke said to Guppy.

"Tables up top," Guppy replied. "Those dudes up there are packing some concealed hardware. Want me to check it out?"

Getting up, Sam said to Guppy, "I'll check it out. You stay put."

Smoke got up, and Guppy said, "Where are you going?"

"You stay here. You're the check point."

Guppy got out his cigar. "Fine by me."

Smoke cut through the cigarette vapors and sauntered through the club. He tuned into the voices. There were a lot of Europeans, which wasn't anything uncommon in DC. He just wasn't used to seeing so many clustered together in the same spot. Thick in their accents, their brash talk and laughter caught his ears. He didn't understand most of it, but could pick up bits and pieces. He'd always enjoyed straight-talking people.

They might smoke too much, but they're kind of fun.

Glasses still on, he scanned the many faces and didn't see anything familiar. So far as he could tell, The Guillotine was just another club where the rich and spoiled liked to hang out. In the darkness, hands shuffled small bits of contraband back and forth. Others more brazenly huddled over white lines on the table.

Making his rounds, Smoke was stopped by one of the bouncers, who gave a shove to his shoulder. He wore a T-shirt with The Guillotine's logo on it.

The bouncer spoke with an English accent. "Are you lost?"

"Where's the bathroom?" Smoke replied.

The man eyed him and pointed. "Downstairs. Be careful. All sorts linger in those shadows. They'll probably take to you, though."

"Thanks." Smoke made a beeline for the stairwell, where he now saw neon signs that read Ladies' and Gents'. On his way down, he passed some people wobbling on the steps. One woman in a scanty red sequined dress was gripping the railing saying, "I don't want to ride the roller coaster."

When Smoke pushed his way inside the black door of the men's room, the smells and smoke about knocked him over. It was a big bathroom, along the lines of something in a football stadium, with big metal troughs, industrial steel stalls, and freestanding porcelain sinks from the 1950s. The walls were covered in graffiti, and plenty of men, mostly young, moseyed in and out. He slipped into one of the stalls and closed the door.

This place should be on an episode of Dirty Jobs.

He took a leak, turned to leave, and then saw the image on the inside of the door stall like a slap in the face. *Guermo* was spray-painted over a collage of eyes with tentacles. He headed for the sink. Given the clientele, he'd expected the furnishings to be richer. There wasn't even a washroom attendant. With his hands dripping with water, he discovered the paper towel dispenser was empty. He was headed for the one on the other side of the room when a man with a slender face and broad nose wearing a grey turtleneck shoved in front of him.

"You'll have to wait, heh."

Smoke eyed him.

The man's distinct features popped. It was one of the men from the picture, the one with dark-red hair. He had a Guermo tattoo on his forearm. His skin was more grey than white, almost clammy.

After drying off his hands, the man pulled his sleeves down over his corded forearms. "You're American."

"You sound surprised."

"Nah, not really, we just don't get a lot of Americans around here."

"Is that so? You aren't used to seeing many Americans in Hallorica?"

The man tossed his paper towel in the overfilled waste basket and stuck his hands in his pockets. "Something like that. But don't get all riled up. I know how patriotic you Americans tend to be. I'm just making small talk, as you people say. You look like a veteran? Are you a veteran?"

"I am."

The bathroom was empty aside from them until two men entered and blocked the door. It was a pair of gothic goons. Tattooed faces and several piercings. The sleeves were torn from their tuxedoes.

"Well, that's good to know. I respect America and what it's done, so I promise to see to it that you get a proper funeral." He pulled out a switchblade. "I just hope you have ID on you."

CHAPTER 7

S MOKE LOOKED DOWN AT THE pasty-faced man. "So you're going to try to kill me with a knife?"

"Oh no, I *am* going to kill you, and those two uglies at the door are going to clean the mess up." He shrugged. "Nothing personal, just orders."

"So your boss doesn't like Americans?"

"No, my boss doesn't like spies. Especially spies for The Drake."

Crap! Sam and Guppy are in trouble.

Mind racing, Smoke filed through his options: Keep the man talking. Deny his affiliations. Perhaps they were just testing him. He wanted to say he didn't work for The Drake, but he'd taken their money, so in plain fact he did work for them. He wanted to lie, but he prided himself on being truthful.

Options, options, options.

"You look like the type of man who enjoys a challenge, and I'm unarmed, you know."

"Well, as one of America's favorite cowboys once said, 'You should have armed yourself.'" Quick like a snake, the man lunged at Smoke's throat.

Smoke slid to the side and punched the man square in the jaw. The blow should have dropped the man like a bad sparring partner, but it didn't.

Great Dane.

Staggering back with wide eyes, the man looked at Smoke anew. "Clever, American."

The goons crept closer.

The man said, "Stay back. I can handle this one. It's been some time since I've had a challenge." He withdrew another switchblade and attacked with both hands.

Smoke slapped the strikes away. His arms were long, but the man's blades cut the distance, taking away his advantage. He countered the strikes with punches of his own. He punched the man in the chest and kicked his legs out from under him. Dancing like a boxer, he said, "So, you like American movies? Did you ever see *Rocky*?"

With a scowl on his face, the man rose again. There was fury in his eyes. "A survivor, I see. You won't last, though. No one ever lasts. Now your hope will die just like Apollo Creed's in those boorish *Rocky* films." He pounced.

Smoke saw it coming. He saw everything coming. It was a gift. Seizing the momentum, he rammed the man's head into the wall and bent the man's wrist behind his back, dislocating his shoulder.

The man screamed, "I'll kill you! You can't kill me, but I'll kill you!"

With the man's wrist still locked up, Smoke checked his pulse. There wasn't one.

That's what I thought!

The man was some kind of a deader, but more functional, much like the Ratson brothers.

I wonder how this one dies.

Smoke wrenched the switchblade from the man's dead grip. "You know, you really aren't a very good fighter."

Spitting through his teeth, the man said, "You don't have to be good when you'll live forever!" The man was strong like an animal, but his struggles were in vain.

Smoke had him under control. "No one is going to live on this world forever, especially not you."

The man laughed. "Why, because you think you're Rocky?"

Smoke shoved the deader's head down on the sink and said in a throaty voice, "No, because I'm Batman."

"Will you two fools stop standing there and shoot this man!"

On order, the other deaders took out their pistols and blasted away.

Blam! Blam! Blam! Blam!

Smoke shielded himself behind the one deader, who screamed, "Stop shooting me!"

The firing stopped.

Smoke let the one deader collapse to the floor and seized the pause between the hail of bullets to catch the goons flatfooted. He kicked one in the gut and doubled him over. He punched the other one in the jaw and dropped him. Grabbing a gun and not taking any chances, he clocked the one holding his gut in the back of the head, knocking him out.

"You'll die for this," said a raggedy voice. The red-haired deader on the floor was chewed up with bullet holes. One bullet had clipped his throat, but he didn't bleed. "Vormus will have your guts for dinner."

"Thanks for sharing." With the music still thumping above, Smoke emptied the magazine on him, then tossed the gun away and raced up the steps. At the top, the bouncer who had pointed out the restroom signs to him started to turn. Before he could see that Smoke was still alive and raise an alarm, Smoke punched the deader in the throat and shoved him down the steps.

He needed to get Sam and Guppy to safety. He couldn't have been happier when he saw both of them sitting together at the table. Sam was pale faced. Gesturing for them to follow, Smoke headed into the kitchen behind one of the bars.

"We need to go."

There was an exit in the back, and he led them to it. He pushed his way out and found himself standing on the backside of the building. There was a handful of people that didn't even glance at him. He motioned for Sam and Guppy to come out, and then they casually made their way around the building, through the parking lot, and into the Bronco.

Guppy fired the engine up.

"Thank God," Sam said, holding her head.

"Are you okay?" Guppy said.

"Yes, just go, go, go!"

"Yeah, you really need to get rolling, Guppy. I left some new friends in bad shape back there."

The Bronco's engine rumbled, the back tire grinded on loose stones, and then straight out of the parking lot they went.

Sam was buckled in her seat, her face ashen. Her fingers were locked on the seatbelt.

Smoke spoke to her gently. "What happened, Sam? What did you see?"

"She saw him," Guppy said. Sweat beaded on his head. He wiped it off with his sleeve. "Never seen her like this."

"Saw who?" Smoke fought the urge to look back at the club.

Sam rolled down her window all the way and leaned out. "I need some air."

"She thinks she saw the man who wasn't in the picture," Guppy added. "It made the hair stand up on my arms when she told me. She said his white eyes were like hypnotic moons, or something like that."

Sam was sitting normally in her seat now, but her chest was heaving. "Smoke, I went up there, and the minute I did, I felt cold. Something drew me in deeper, and the next thing I knew, I was eye to eye with that man who was invisible. He was surrounded by people, just like in that picture. At ease. Relaxed. Perfectly in place, like a puzzle piece. Somehow, I tore my eyes away and left. They were laughing. I wanted to get out of there so bad." She reached back and grabbed his hand. "Thank God you came."

Smoke's neck hairs stood on end. A shadow fell over the car.

Out of nowhere, a man landed on the hood, standing. His eyes were bright as moons. His fangs were sharp slivers of white silver.

Sam screamed.

CHAPTER 8

"**H**OW ARE HIS FEET STICKING to the car?" Guppy yelled.

A man with long snow-white hair stood on the hood of the Bronco. His eyes were white hypnotic fires. Rippled by the headwind, his silky clothes tore at his lean body. He stepped forward, and his long fingers clamped into the steel on the car's roof.

"Get him off!" Sam yelled.

Guppy swerved left and right, screeching the tires.

The man clung to the vehicle like a leech, with an evil look in his eye.

Sam balled up in her seat.

Smoke shouted, "Cover your ears!" He started shooting.

Blam! Blam! Blam!

The man on the hood disappeared.

"Stop shooting, Smoke! You're killing my ears! And you just blasted out my window!" Guppy craned his neck around. "Where'd that fiend go?"

There was no sign of the man. The sound of the wind whistling through the windshield was their only company.

"Maybe you got him." Sam was rubbing her temples. "Oh man, I hope you got him. Those eyes."

"Just keep driving." Smoke's skin was still crawling. "And no matter what happens, you and Sam get to safety."

Visibly bewildered, Sam said, "What are you talking about? You aren't leaving."

Like a pair of can openers, two hands burst through and started peeling the steel roof back, leaving a gaping hole over their heads.

Smoke fired upward.

Blam!

A hand burst through the driver-side window and seized his arm. With inhuman strength, it ripped the gun free of his grip and threw it off to the side of the road.

"Get out of here!" Smoke grabbed the hand that had grabbed his and tried to reel the man in. He braced his boots against the car's body and tugged with all his might.

The hand jerked itself free.

Smoke searched for a gun.

Guppy handed him one, saying, "Don't miss."

"Just get Sam to safety," Smoke said. "I'll handle this." He popped up out of the gap in the roof and found himself face to face with the eerie vampire. He unloaded every bullet the gun had into its chest.

The vampire shrugged it off. "Say farewell to your friends."

Smoke propelled himself into the man, knocking them both off the roof of the car and landing hard on the ground.

"Turn around, Guppy! I said, turn around!"

"No can do, honey."

Sam grabbed at the wheel. "You have to go back!"

"You heard what he said. Get you to safety. Nine times out of ten, I do what you say, but not this time, baby. Losing him is one thing, but losing you is another. Sorry Sam, but I can't let anything happen to you. Smoke would agree."

Gawking back through the back window, Sam said, "You'd better hope we see him again, or I'm going to kill you."

Smoke hit the ground so hard it knocked the wind out of him. Every bone in his body was jarred. He felt like someone had just skipped him across a cement pond. Lucky for him, the body of the vampire had absorbed some of the impact, but now it was gone. Forcing himself to his hands and knees, Smoke started to stand.

"You might as well stay down," said a voice with cold and confident smoothness. "You'll be six feet under soon enough."

Clutching his bruised ribs, Smoke rose up and faced the man in dark silks and slacks. There was something powerful in the man's eyes that enhanced his sharp features. Built like a long and rangy fencer, he moved like a serpent, ready to strike at any moment. He approached Smoke and said, "I really hope you aren't going to try and fight me. That would be stupid."

"You must be Vormus."

The man's narrow brows lifted. "Ah, so you have heard of me."

"A little crap bird told me you would have my guts for dinner."

"Is that so? Well, I actually appreciate finer cuisine." He locked his eyes on Smoke's. "Would you like to join me for dinner?"

Smoke's knees locked up. His lips wanted to speak with a life of their own and say yes. His mind and instincts resisted.

Something dark and mysterious insisted on sucking him in, tempted and toyed with his inner weaknesses. Unable to unglue his eyes from the man's, he felt a darkness envelop him and squeeze him like a constrictor snake.

Vormus came closer. Standing face to face, he tilted his head. "Come on, join me, and we both shall have a fine dinner. We can even invite your friends if you like."

A fire ignited inside Smoke. A knife appeared in his hand and buried itself deep in the man's chest.

"Fool!" Vormus roared. He hit Smoke hard in the face, knocking him into the street.

Cars rolled up on him, and headlights blinded his eyes for a moment. Smoke tried to shake away the dizziness as men popped their car doors open and people surrounded him.

Vormus pulled the blade from his chest. "I want him alive. I want him tormented."

CHAPTER 9

I T HAD BEEN A ROUGH ride back to The Guillotine. Taking the back entrance, Vormus's thugs dragged Smoke downstairs into an office and walloped him good. A hard hit on the back of his head with a pistol knocked him out.

When Smoke woke up, the music was no longer pumping through the walls, but his head was pounding like a set of drums. He sat in an office chair with his arms bound behind his back.

"I told you that you couldn't kill me," said a rough voice. It was the red-headed deader that Smoke had filled with lead in the bathroom earlier. He'd changed his clothes and had a scarf wrapped around his neck. Murder was in his eyes. "Having a good time?"

"Not really," Smoke said. "This club sucks. Maybe you should switch to a classic country theme."

The red-haired European slugged him in the gut.

A rush of air whooshed from his lips. The stinging pain watered his eyes. "You're awfully temperamental for someone who thinks he'll live forever. Have you ever considered taking anti-depressants? You seem so bitter."

The man drew back again.

"That's enough, Carl. There will be plenty of time to play with him later." It was Vormus who spoke. He sat behind a nice desk, modern, with lots of metal and glass. The entire office was very contemporary in construction. Soft neon lit the wet bars, shelves, and cabinets. There were more men in the office, too, all the ones from the picture. Five in all. Slick, pasty, and shady. The stench of death was on them. "I still have some questions to ask this man."

Smoke rolled his head back. "I hope it's trivia. I love trivia. What are the categories?"

Carl backhanded him across the face. "Shut up."

Vormus held four fingers up. "Carl, please, be patient. I'm finding some pleasure in this fellow's musings. I like him, such a change from the usual ones who beg for their lives."

Poking his fingers into Smoke's temple, Carl said, "You might not be begging now, but you will be."

Smoke clammed up and looked away.

"That's what I thought." Carl backed away and took a seat on one of the leather chairs. "Punk."

Smoke made a quick scan with his eyes. There were five men plus Vormus. His hands were bound with rope that bit into his wrists when he moved. His fingers were almost numb.

Got to give them credit, they weren't stupid enough to use duct tape.

"So," said the vampire, "we noticed you didn't have any identification on you, but Carl says you are a veteran. Why don't you fill us in on some details?"

Smoke continued to size these super-deaders up. None of them were armed. All of them were cocky and pale skinned, with an air of invincibility. Just like Carl. Smoke was used to blasting away bits and pieces of normal deaders, but these … they were different.

But everything has a weakness.

"Well," Smoke said, "my father was a crop duster back in Iowa, and when I grew up, I decided I didn't like the smell of pesticide, so I came to the big city. And boy, imagine my surprise when I got here only to find that it's full of pests. Isn't that sad?"

A couple of the goons chuckled. Carl started to stand. A scowl from Vormus sat him down again.

"I'm sorry," Smoke said to Vormus, "was that too much detail?"

"It was something," Vormus said. He checked his long nails. "It seems our scuffle chipped one. You know, it won't take much time for my crew to track down your allies and kill them. I suggest you become more forthcoming."

"I don't think you want my name. I think you just want someone to pick on." Smoke eyed Carl. "Red over there picked the wrong fight with the wrong someone and lost. He's just trying to save face, and here you are bailing him out. All because he screwed up."

"Your argument does have some merit, but though Carl might be one to start a fight, I don't think his intentions were wrong." Vormus stood up, walked around the desk, leaned toward Smoke, and sniffed the air. "I can smell the good in you." He leaned back on the desk. "It's quite detestable. In a place like this, you couldn't be less noticeable to us wearing a skunk on you."

"Really? You can smell me?"

"Like bad fish at dinner."

"You mean like good fish at dinner," Smoke said, "because you say you can smell the good in me. So I'm like a well-seasoned Boston cod with a nice squeeze of lemon."

Carl jumped up with balled fists. "Let me shred this disrespectful scum, Vormus! I can't take any more!" His voice was hoarse, probably because of all the new holes in his neck.

Smoke gave the deader a sympathetic smile. "I can recommend some good cough syrup to clear up that itchy sound in your voice. It's a family——"

Vormus clamped his hand over Smoke's mouth and squeezed. The vampire's slender hand had the power of a vice.

Smoke found himself staring into Vormus's bright white eyes, unable to tear his gaze away.

In a strong voice that could enchant a statue, Vormus said, "Who are you?"

"John Smoke."

"Who sent you, John Smoke?"

"Reginald."

"And who does Reginald work for?"

"The Drake."

Vormus nodded. "I see. And why would a good man like you be in the service of an establishment as foul as The Drake?"

"For money."

Staring deeper into Smoke's eyes, Vormus said to him, "No, it's not money. Be truthful now."

Squirming in his chair, Smoke said, "They have my friend."

"Ah, extortion. Such a classic motivational vehicle." Vormus backed away. "Now it all makes sense. And why were you sent? As a spy?"

"No," Smoke said. His stomach was churning. "I was sent to kill you all."

Vormus threw his head back and laughed.

The others joined in.

Finally, Vormus said, "I can't believe they'd send a mortal to take us. Oh, how desperate The Drake has become since our arrival. Well brethren, let's send The Drake a message from us. Have your fun, Carl. Torture this man, whatever you want. Whatever remains, we'll send to The Drake in pieces." He patted Smoke on the head and finished by saying, "Thanks for the best laugh I've had in decades."

CHAPTER 10

AS SOON AS VORMUS DEPARTED, Carl was the first of The Many to rise. Two of the others joined him. Their jaws stretched open wide. Fangs grew inside their mouths. Saliva dripped from their razor-sharp teeth.

Smoke watched a new horror come to life, standing right in front of him. "Looks like you fellas missed your rabies shots. I know a really good veterinarian."

Carl smote him in the jaw.

One of the men cackled like a hyena.

Behind his back, Smoke's fingernails sawed at the cords that bound him. The diamond dust that coated his nails was always a good trick, but could he break free in time?

Keep 'em talking.

"I don't suppose I get any final requests before my execution?"

One of the men slipped in behind him and clamped down on his shoulders. The long nails dug deep into his flesh. It was the one that cackled like a rotten teenager acting out some kind of cheap thrill. "You'll be screaming out plenty of requests between the moments of torture."

Carl snapped his fingers and eyed one of the men sitting on the couch. "The case, please?"

The man reached over the sofa arm and lifted up a burgundy leather case, one of the thick boxy ones that businessmen and accountants carry several files in. He tossed it to Carl, who snatched it out of the air and set it down. He popped open the latches on the top, and the case collapsed into a flat surface loaded with sharp, shiny metal.

Smoke's throat tightened.

Lifting up a medical saw, Carl held it in front of Smoke. "I'm reneging on my promise to give you a proper veteran's burial. You've pissed me off too much." He reached behind him and pulled out a set of steel needles bound in black velvet cloth. "And I intend to make you apologize for every bit of it."

"Seems odd to me that a mortal like me would be able to get under your clammy skin. Perhaps you're full of regret."

"Hah, hardly." Carl lowered the needle and poked it into Smoke's shoulder.

Smoke clenched his jaws. Sweat burst on his forehead. His nostrils flared, and his chest labored for breath. "I love acupuncture."

With one brow hitched up, Carl drew forth another needle. "My, you really can't help that big mouth, can you. But I'll tell you what; this is going to be fun. That was only the first of many needles."

"You mean you aren't going to bite me, suck my blood?"

"We have all the blood we need." Carl shoved another needle into the same shoulder, through one side and out the other.

Pain shot through every nerve in Smoke's body. Black spots burst in his eyes. He didn't scream. He practically spat when he said, "You're not very good at this."

"Why do you say that?"

"It doesn't hurt enough."

"That's because I'm only toying with you. See, I'm slowing your blood flow so you don't squirt everywhere."

One of the other members fetched a roll of plastic and started spreading it out on the floor. Two others picked Smoke up in his chair and set him down in the middle of the plastic.

Carl picked up the bone saw. "It works pretty good most of the time, but it's been a while."

The smaller, younger-looking one let out another shrill cackle.

Smoke eyed him and then said to Carl, "And you think *I'm* annoying."

"I adore Julius's enthusiasm. So should you. Okay gentleman, hold him still. I don't want him kicking when I saw his leg off."

"I thought you were sawing my arm off?"

"Oh, I just said that. You're going to bleed everywhere when we—huh?"

Smoke's fingernails had cut through the last of the woven cord. Summoning his strength and fighting against the inferno inside his shoulder, he tore from his bonds and burst into action, rushing out of the chair, twisting from Julius's grip, and charging Carl. He shattered Vampire Junior's knee with a well-placed kick.

With a wail, Carl crumpled to the floor.

Smoke jumped over the steel and glass desk. Hiding under it, he stuck his fingers into his jeans pocket and fetched out a bright-green pill, popped it in his mouth, and clamped down.

The Many slung the desk off him, shattering the glass.

Smoke leg-swept one of them, only to see him bounce up again instantly. He ripped the needles free of his shoulder just as Julius attacked.

Fast and strong, the younger fiend plowed into Smoke and pinned him against the wall, cackling like a wild hyena. "You just went from worse to worser!"

Smoke rammed the needles through Julius's throat. "How's that for *worser*, idiot?"

These junior monsters might have been hard to kill, but they were only average fighters. Bloody shoulder dripping, Smoke fought them off with anything he could get a hold of. He'd held up for a few seconds when they cornered him and got the drop on him and hammered away with their fists.

Overwhelmed by their power, busted up and bloody, Smoke sagged to the floor.

"Get up, you!" A bit bigger than the rest, this one picked Smoke up like a child and shoved him into the wall.

Smoke hit the wall and bounced back through the cocktail bar.

Carl braced himself against the wall. "You're making a mess, everyone! Vormus won't like it. Let's finish him off without trashing this office. Have some fun, but be done with it."

With his energy drained, Smoke let the men shove him around like a rag doll. One would push and another one would hit him in a brutal game of tag. He addressed himself to Julius, who still had the needles sticking out of his throat. "What's the matter, not speaking to me?"

Julius punched him hard in the ribs and gave him a hard shove into the main office door. The deadbolt on it wasn't locked.

Carl was sitting on the tumbled desk. "Go ahead, Mister Smoke. Run. We're having fun. We can allow you a few precious moments. Please, go ahead."

"You could hear a pin drop when Johnny stopped and locked the door," Smoke replied. He shoved the deadbolt into place, sealing them all inside.

"Johnny? Who the hell's Johnny?" Carl asked.

All of Smoke's attackers glanced at each other. Some of them shrugged.

Smoke staggered along the glass wall, where a fireman's axe hung inside a glass case. He busted it out and took it by the haft. "It's a song."

"About a fireman?" said one of The Many.

"No," said another, "I think it's a scene from The Shining. You know, 'Here's Johnny.'"

Nodding his head, the first member said, "I like that movie."

Smoke cracked his neck from side to side, his blood now racing through his veins. His pain was gone. Every limb ignited with fire. "It's from The Gambler, you idiots, a made-for-TV cowboy movie starring Kenny—"

"I thought the Indians carried the axes in those movies," said the biggest one.

Smoke attacked through the glass wall, chopping the big one down first. The axe bit hard into its knee and brought it down like a falling tree.

One down, four to go.

The fireman's axe had a nasty pick on the back end, made to tear through walls. He tore a hole out of another member's head. Fast as a wild tiger Smoke attacked, hacking down one member after another.

Julius went for the bone saw on the floor.

Smoke raised the axe high and chopped the little vampire's hand off. His next strike cracked the monster's cranium.

Carl hopped toward the door.

"Where are you going, Carl? I thought you said I couldn't kill you?"

Back against the door with fear in his eyes, Carl said, "That might have been a slight exaggeration."

Smoke split his face. "Shut up."

He pushed Carl out of the way and opened up the door. Down the corridor, Vormus was coming straight for him.

CHAPTER 11

"**M**Y, AREN'T YOU THE FORMIDABLE one?" Vormus said, walking toward Smoke with an easy gait. He stopped several feet short and eyed the gory axe. "You might have mutilated my expendable men, but you won't succeed with me. Of course, you're welcome to try if you like."

"Just get out of my way."

"Oh, I can't do that. You're not dead yet. And I have to wrap you up into a present."

Smoke lunged. It was a clumsy telegraphed blow.

Vormus swatted his efforts away. The snake-quick man was a match for everything Smoke threw at him. "This is childish. Put your rattle down and just submit. It's been a long night, and you need your beauty sleep."

Like a burly lumberjack, Smoke kept at it.

Vormus shifted from side to side. "Honestly, I can't fathom how you beat my men."

Smoke puffed for breath. "Well, now I *am* tired."

With his hand, Vormus tossed back his long white hair. "Given your valiant efforts, I think I'm just going to crack your neck and kindly put you in a coffin."

Smoke sucked in a raspy breath in the steel office door frame. "Good, I could use the rest."

Vormus's white eyes bore into his with hypnotic power. "Just rest," he suggested. "Rest."

"I would, but I've got places to go and people to see." Smoke cracked the haft of the axe on the metal door frame. It turned the handle into a sharp stick. Propelled by his vitamin-enhanced legs, he drove the sharp end of the handle into Vormus's heart like a stake.

The vampire let out a loud gasp. The glimmer in his eye went out. He sagged to his knees. "How, how did you do that?"

Still filled with energy, Smoke replied, "It's called possum Stateside, moron."

Vormus fell over with his jaw hanging open and no longer moved.

Smoke strode back into the office, found some car keys, and made his way outside through the kitchen. He punched the button on the keyless remote, and the lights on one of the sports cars lit up—a red Jaguar coupe. He hopped in, fired up the engine, found a classic country station on the radio, cranked it up, and peeled out. He was singing along to some solid country gold with The Guillotine miles behind him when the super vitamin wore off. He could barely lift his head up when he pulled into the parking lot of a convenience store and passed out.

Smoke's head snapped up against the driver's seat headrest. He wiped the drool from his mouth onto his shirt. His head was filled with tiny pounding hammers. Rubbing his temple, he popped open the door and spat blood. The sunrise glared in his eyes.

Blocking the light with his hand, he noticed an older woman with honey-blond hair getting into her car and staring at him. She was in a business suit and held in her hand a white Styrofoam cup with a seven on it.

Squinting, he started to turn away.

"Sir, are you okay?" she said, approaching with caution. Her free hand was inside her purse. "Have you been in an accident?"

"Not exactly," he said with a grimace. "But I'm okay. I appreciate the concern."

"Are you sure you're okay? Because you don't look okay." She eyed his shoulder. His shirt was caked in blood. "It looks like you were in an accident."

"Look, you seem like a decent lady—"

"And you look like a decent man." There was a spark in her brown eyes. "Real decent. Are you sure there's nothing I can do for you?"

"I could use some change?"

"You make an awfully handsome panhandler. Bloody, but clean. I like it."

"I'm guessing you're a morning person."

With an enticing smile, she said, "I did Pilates at six this morning. Never miss a day."

Smoke nodded. "I appreciate the concern, but I really have to get going. Places to go and people to see."

She pulled a business card out of her purse and handed it to him. "I'm Sherry. Call me. I'd like to have lunch or dinner with you sometime. Anytime would be great, actually. I'm very flexible, and so is my schedule."

"You seem like someone who has it all together." Smiling at her, he glanced at the card. It read Cheryl Case, Attorney at Law. It had numbers, a business address, and a tag line: "Let Case Take Your Case." He stuffed it in his pocket. "Nice meeting you, Cheri."

"Nice meeting you too." Searching inside her purse, she said, "Oh, didn't you need some change?"

Walking away and not turning to look back, he waved her off. "No. I got it."

Weary limbed, he made his way over to a pay phone in front of the convenience store. People were bustling in and out, but no one aside from Cheryl paid him any mind. He picked up the receiver and pressed a combination of numbers that instructions on the phone said would make a collect call.

The operator spoke with an Indian accent. "What number would you like to place a collect call to?"

Smoke recited the number.

"And who is calling?"

"Smoke."

The digital tones followed, and after two rings someone picked up on the other side. It was a man.

"Hello?"

"Sir, I have a collect call from Mister Smoke. Do you accept the charges?"

There was a pause and a slight gasp of surprise on the other side of the line.

"Sir, do you accept the charges?"

"Sure."

Before he hung up, the operator replied, "Thank you for using C&P-Verizon-Frontier-Bell Atlantic."

"Enjoying your breakfast, Reggie?" Smoke said.

"Why John, what an early surprise it is to hear from you."

With a growl in his voice, Smoke said, "I survived that death trap you sent me into, toadstool. I bet you weren't expecting that."

Reginald spoke after another brief pause. "As a matter of fact, I wasn't. Kudos to you. Can I assume that you completed my mission?"

"Find out for yourself. I want my money. I want my visit with Sid. Get it together."

"I'm a man of my word," Reginald said.

"You're not a man. You're a gutless turd. Why don't you go down to The Guillotine and get reacquainted with filth like yourself?"

"I may do just that. Mister Smoke, do you think you can fill me in on some of the details so I might know what to expect?"

"I met your rival Vormus and staked a claim."

"You're telling me he's dead? Actually dead?"

"He wasn't moving when I left. The others are probably still twitching. You might want to go and see what's left of them, unless the sun turned them to ashes."

Reginald chuckled. "I'll be in touch."

Click.

CHAPTER 12

S MOKE CLIMBED OUT OF THE hyperbaric tube feeling like he could run a hundred miles. It had given him only a fraction of the energy the super vitamin did, but it was still good. Wearing only a pair of dark-blue boxer shorts and patched and stitched all over, he took a seat on a nearby padded stool.

"How are you feeling, big man?" asked Asia, Mal Gunderson's wife. She wore a unique terrycloth lab coat that could pass for a bathrobe. "You look a few shades better. Acupuncture now?"

He held up his hand. "I'll pass. I've had enough needles stuck in me lately."

He was inside a new estate Mal Gunderson had set up, a colonial in a gated suburban neighborhood on the waterfront. It was two stories high with vaulted ceilings and a full unfinished basement. Down there along with the hyperbaric tube were some bookshelves, a huge computer desk, and several monitors. The cooling fans of a server big enough to run a state department whirred nearby.

Sam came down the steps wearing jeans and a hot-pink tank top with some glitter patterns on it. She had a tray full of sandwiches and two big shakes in tall glasses. She set it all down on the bar where Smoke sat. "I imagine you're hungry."

Smoke grabbed a Dagwood sandwich and bit into it. "I am. Mmm, I like that mustard. You remembered."

She rubbed his head, which was the only unscathed part of him. "I'm just glad you're still around for me to make it for you, stupid."

Two days had passed since Smoke got off the phone with Reginald. Samantha had finally quit grilling him for the details of his fight with the vampires. Since he arrived at Mal's place, he'd spent a lot of time resting and taking moments in the hyperbaric tube while everyone else was doing research on Guermo and all the goons he'd fought.

Asia reached for the other sandwich, and Samantha slapped her hand.

"Hey!" Asia said. "I thought one was for me, you amazon."

"Make your own, Asia."

Asia glided in front of Smoke and batted her eyelashes. "Smoke, will you share your sandwiches with me?" She rubbed her belly. "So hungry."

With a mouthful of food and sucking on the milkshake straw, he said, "No."

"Why do you always tell me no? I take good care of you."

"If you want Sam to make you a sandwich, why don't you just ask her?"

Turning around to face the much taller Sam, Asia looked up. "Will you make me a sandwich?"

"I thought you said my sandwiches were—as you so often put things—shitty."

"They are shitty. I just like watching big white woman make it for me."

Drawing back her fist, Sam said with a snarl, "I'm going to crush you like a fortune cookie."

Asia trotted away laughing. She headed up the steps, stopped and turned, and said, "Here is a fortune, Amazon. The giraffes miss you riding them. Go back to the circus." She vanished upstairs.

"I hate her," Sam said.

"No you don't. You love her like a twisted sister, and you know it."

She shoved Smoke in the head. "Shut up."

He plucked the straw out and started gulping the strawberry shake down, then wiped off his mouth. "Good stuff, Sam. Thanks. Have you dug anything else up on Guermo?"

"Mal's coming. He's going to brief you."

Smoke cocked an eyebrow. "Really? So you've heard something? Fill me in."

"No. He started hollering that he found something about ten minutes after you went in the tube, but then rushed upstairs, saying he'd be back after you got out." She made her way over to an end table, picked up a paper, and handed it to Smoke. It was an issue of Nightfall DC. "Check it out."

The headline read, *Club Guillotine Decapitates Self.*

There was a picture of the warehouse waterfront facility on the front page. The parking lot was filled with Federal law enforcement officials. Smoke opened up the paper and read the article written by Russ Davenport. It mentioned that several dead were found inside and how none of this story was in the local news. He quoted an FBI Agent named Cyrus Tweel, who had said to Russ, "Get the hell out of here or get arrested." It said Russ had overheard another agent, later identified as Rebecca Lang, who was inspecting the body bags say, "They have teeth like vampires." It said she had threatened to shoot Russ Davenport, and that he'd been roughly escorted from the premises.

"Hmmm," Smoke said, "seems those FBI guys are staying up on things. I can't help but think Reginald must have tipped them off. It only figures The Drake has people inside the FBI who are checking my story out. Don't you agree?"

"I'm all about conspiracies. You know that."

Smoke was too, and the more he learned, the deeper it seemed they ran. And he was still bothered by a few other things. The Drake had been quiet. The freak shifter sightings weren't even showing up in Russ Davenport's paper. It bothered him. They had tried to take him out again. Perhaps something was coming after all, and they needed him out of the picture. He tossed the paper aside. "No word from Reginald, I take it."

"No."

Mal came down the steps. The scholarly olive-skinned man wore a dark-green dress shirt and brown slacks. His sleeves were rolled up, but he was tidy. "Well, look who's out of the tube. Feeling even better, I take it."

"I'm ready to go, but I wouldn't mind some more of those vitamins."

"Please, you need to be more self-reliant. Besides, I'm all out."

"Sure you are," Smoke said.

"No, really. You need to remember I'm no longer funded by those deep-pocketed Federal officials. Nope, cut off like a spoiled child from his trust fund, so you'd better be more careful."

"I'm always careful."

Sam handed Smoke a pair of jeans and a shirt that were folded up in nice pressed squares. "Asia. She's good for some things."

Smoke started slipping on his clothes and said to Mal, who had sat down in front of the computer monitors, "So, you have some news on Guermo?"

Tapping away at the keyboard, Mal said, "I do. I contacted a friend in Denmark. I'd almost forgotten about her because it had been so long and she put a curse on me when I broke up with her in favor of her sister who subsequently left me for a higher-ranking government official of the Monte Carlo regime, who coincidentally disappeared on their wedding night, which she was framed for, exonerated, and ended up marrying his brother. They're doing quite well and have three children with alarming similarities to her sister's husband that my friend from Denmark divorced. She says she's doing quite well now." He spun around in his chair and faced Smoke and Sam. "What was the question?"

CHAPTER 13

"T HE MANY. GUERMO. WHO AND what *are* they?" Smoke said.

"Yes, sorry." Mal spun back around in his seat. "I just started reminiscing about my time spent with those twins. You know, one of them had a sixth finger on each hand. Incredible typist." He brought some images up on the screens. A castle in deep green hills appeared on one, the pictures of the members of Guermo on another. The many eyes and tentacles symbol was on another. "Turns out they're a rival force of The Drake. As a matter of fact, according to Darlene from Denmark, The Drake split off from The Many, centuries ago. It was believed they'd been vanquished."

"So are they vampires, or what?" Smoke asked.

"As I was told, they are shifters that reinvented themselves as vampires about a century ago. They aren't the typical blood suckers you see in the movies. More or less a hack job of them. Well, sort of. They have supernatural powers akin to what they want to be like, just like all of the other shifters. Werewolves. Harpies. Minotaurs. Vampire's the form they chose."

Sam shivered. "That Vormus sure seemed like a vampire to me."

"Based off what?" Mal said. "Have you ever really met a vampire?"

Mal's point made Smoke's skin crawl. Perhaps Smoke's stake to the heart hadn't killed Vormus after all. He recalled the giants, Thorgrim and Rexor. He'd thought he'd wiped them out too, yet both had gotten up and walked away.

"He landed on the car, Mal. Dropped right from the sky and stuck to the hood." Sam shoved the scientist in the shoulder. "That's a vampire, and he had hypnotic eyes, too. Not to mention his image didn't show up in the picture. How do you explain that? Huh? Huh? He was a vampire!"

Mal flipped his hands out. "Fine, he's a vampire. It doesn't really make any difference. The powerful shifters can be whatever they want to be. So if Vormus wants to be a vampire, then he is. And if you want him to be a vampire, Sam, then I guess he is too. Does that make you feel better?"

"No." She shifted toward Smoke. "You're sure you killed him, right?"

"I thought so. When I noticed there wasn't a stitch of wood in that building, I started putting things together. I thought the axe handle was an oversight on their part." He drank some more of the strawberry shake. "Figuring Vormus was a vampire, I took a stab at it. No pun intended."

"Did he dissolve?" Sam asked.

"He was intact when I left."

Mal cut in. "Again, these aren't movie monsters. The legends aren't scientific fact. They are what they are: shifters, and with that come certain weaknesses. Perhaps wood does kill them. Otherwise, why wouldn't they have it? That said, it seems that Smoke may have crushed their nest. There aren't any other signs of The Many that I could find. In my opinion, The Drake should be happy."

Smoke didn't hide his frown. If his mission wasn't completed, then he might not see Sid. Also, it wouldn't surprise him one bit if Reginald was jerking him around. He needed to see Sid, though. He was worried. The longer they had her, the more likely things could change. She was strong, but how strong could she be surrounded by such evil beings?

She'd die before she gave in, wouldn't she.

He didn't want her to die though. He couldn't bear the thought. He slipped a black shirt over his shoulders that read, "Fight or Die."

"Maybe you should call Reginald again," Sam said. "I wouldn't wait around on that guy. Just bug him."

Smoke squeezed her shoulder. "I'm heading home. If you hear anything, let me know."

"Stay here, John. With us. Relax," she said.

"Just give me a couple days. I'll be back." Still filled with energy, he jogged in place. "I'm still pumped with energy from the tube. I need to do something."

Without getting out of his seat or looking Smoke's way, Mal said, "Up in the coat closet is a case. Take it with you. Don't go on any more adventures without the sweetheart suit."

"There's a new one? I thought your organization was destitute?"

"You'd be amazed what these crowdfunding campaigns can do. Stay in touch." Mal flicked a pill bottle over his head. "And don't forget to take your vitamins."

Smoke drove his Camaro to the Reflecting Pool, parked, changed clothes, and went for a long run. The hyperbaric tube had given him a ton of energy, but after an hour dripping in sweat, he decided to call it a day. He sat down on one of the benches in the shade and watched the people walk by. Families. Couples. Friends. Children. They all seemed to move in unison. Herds of people all going in the same direction. Making the same circles. The runners were few and far between. He was hoping one of them would be Sid.

A warm breeze ripped over the waters of the Reflecting Pool. Sitting in the warm summer air, it wasn't long before Smoke was dried off. He yawned. It wasn't something he often did. It was practically foreign to him. He never felt tired. He was always filled with the restless energy of a hyper ten-year-old.

Blasted vitamins. I love them. I hate them.

He hated to admit he needed anything to aid him in fighting any man or beast. He prided himself on his own unique abilities. The super vitamin had saved him—and Sid—more than a time or two. It was an equalizer. It gave him an unexpected edge against people with supernatural powers. But it came with a price, drained him for what felt like days.

Take your vitamins and live. Don't follow your pride and die.

He got up, cut underneath the tall green trees, and made his way to the parking lot. His Camaro had company. Cyrus Tweel, dressed in a dark-grey suit, was leaning against the driver's door. Rebecca Lang, tiny with a blond ponytail, was similarly dressed and sitting on the car hood.

Not breaking his stride, Smoke said, "Get off my car."

CHAPTER 14

R EBECCA SLID OFF THE HOOD. "You call this a car? My Jetta's faster than this thing."

Cyrus chuckled.

"What do you two space wasters want?" Smoke eyed Rebecca. "And what are you doing out of your bird cage, Tweety? I thought you had bigger responsibilities."

"Oh, I'm a senior agent, which means I can pretty much do as I please. So, any news from Sidney?"

Both FBI agents knew Sid was missing. They'd contacted Smoke looking for her, during the investigation. He hadn't let it slip, but another one of his gang had told them Sid was last seen leaving with The Drake.

"No, why?" Smoke said.

Cyrus and Rebecca looked at each other then back at him. Cyrus spoke next. "Were you at The Guillotine two nights ago?"

"Why are you asking? What happened?"

With his hands on his hips, the slender man said, "Don't be a punk, Smoke. Were you there or not?"

"Do you have any proof I was there?"

"Suppose we do," Cyrus said.

"Then you don't need me to answer your question, because you already know."

"Okay, let's cut the bullshit," Rebecca said as she got closer to Smoke. "We have you on video from their security. You were there and so were your friends, a Mr. Guppy and a Miss Samantha. We have bodies. No witnesses. Don't jerk us around, Smoke. Just tell us what happened. This is off the record. That's why I'm here."

"I noticed this wasn't reported in the local news."

"The filthy rich know how to cover their tracks." Cyrus took his wire-rimmed glasses off and cleaned them on his tie. "You know that. What happened in there? Why were you there?"

"I like to dance. It looked like a place to unwind and have a good time." Smoke pushed by Cyrus and opened his car door. "Now, if you don't mind, I've got places to go."

"We could always take you in for questioning, Smoke. Lots of questioning," Rebecca said.

"Hours of questioning," Cyrus added.

Smoke didn't care for either one of them. For all he knew, they were vetting him on behalf of The Drake. Especially Rebecca. There was something really strange about her. No one climbed the ladder that fast, at least not without some very deep connections. He decided to play their games a little longer.

"How many bodies did you find?"

Cyrus looked at Rebecca, she gave him a nod, and he said, "Five."

Crap!

It sounded like Vormus was still alive, and if that was the case, Smoke wasn't going to hear from Sid. Expressionless, he asked, "Could you identify them?"

"They aren't on the Black Slate, if that's what you mean. And no, there aren't any records. Smoke, what were you doing there? It's not a coincidence that you were there and they are dead. And we can't charge you for killing men that were already dead. The coroner estimates the time of their deaths to be more than a hundred years ago." Cyrus chuckled. "It's a mess. What happened?"

Judging by the looks on their faces, Rebecca and Cyrus were confused and frustrated. They'd still been struggling to come to terms with the Black Slate. Now, a new element of the supernatural was right in their faces.

"So you're privy to the Black Slate now, are you?"

Cyrus put on his glasses. "Funny you should ask, but yes we are."

Smoke closed the car door. "Oh, I see. They've turned it over to you two nitwits. That's why you haven't contacted me about any jobs. You think you can handle it yourselves."

"We *can* handle it," Rebecca said. "We are handling it."

"That's why you're reaching out to me then?"

"No, you were there. It's an investigation, and you need to be more forthcoming, Smoke. We can and will take you in if need be, and you don't want that." Cyrus sighed. "Look, we don't like or trust each other, fine. But my eyes are open a little wider now that I've seen the Slate. And we can use your services again, if you cooperate."

Smoke sensed the ring of truth in Cyrus's voice. A Black Slate opportunity offered some other options too. Hunting down those convicts might lead him to Sid, and he needed every scrap of information he could get. "Tell you what. Give me a case. Keep it simple, maybe just surveillance."

Rebecca glanced at Cyrus. "Get the file."

Cyrus glared at her. "*You* get it."

"Excuse me?" Rebecca's cheeks turned red. "Do I need to remind you I'm the senior field agent—"

"Senior field agent my ass. You've only been with the Bureau two years."

Rebecca rolled her eyes. "Oh, not this again. Just get the damn file!"

"How about *I* get it?" Smoke suggested. "I'll let you two nitwits talk this out."

"Screw it, I'll get it!" Cyrus stormed off toward a black SUV.

Stiff chinned, Rebecca stood there tapping her foot.

"What's the matter," Smoke said, "still waiting for a ring on your finger?"

"We aren't dating anymore. It's just professional."

"Well, I can't blame him for breaking up with you."

"It's the other way around, you convict!" She stared up in his face. "What happened to Sidney? Seems she isn't missing you. Weren't you engaged? Man, that must be hard. She ditched you for The Drake."

"You're a bitter little woman, aren't you."

"No, I'm just motivated."

"Ambitious is a better word."

"That suits me fine."

Cyrus approached with a black file and handed it to Smoke while glowering at Rebecca. "Here."

The file looked legit. Pictures. Notes. Places. Details. Much like the other files Smoke had seen. "Heh, heh, heh."

"What's so funny?" Rebecca asked.

"I just can't believe they're letting the two of you in on this," Smoke replied.

"Why's that?" she said.

"Because you're so stupid."

Rebecca snatched after the file.

Smoke held it out of reach.

"Just let it be," Cyrus said.

"Shut up!" she replied.

Ignoring Rebecca, Cyrus continued, "You've got the file, Smoke. It's legit. We shared. Now you share. Let's get on with this."

It wasn't going to kill Smoke to give them some information they probably already had. He opened his car door, tossed the file inside, and said, "Have you heard of Guermo?"

CHAPTER 15

REBECCA AND CYRUS'S JAWS HAD hung open while Smoke explained to them a little bit of what he knew. He told them about the vampires and that he thought there were hundreds of them out there, maybe thousands of the European fiends that had infiltrated America. He also told how their organization, Guermo, rivaled The Drake, and how a feud had started between them.

When they asked about his interest, that had been the tricky part. All he told them was he got a tip about The Drake that led him to The Guillotine. He didn't dare admit The Drake had hired him, nor confirm Sid was with them. And yeah, he told them that on the side, he was still trying to track down Sid.

Rebecca had snickered anyway.

As for explaining the attack at The Guillotine, Smoke had just left it as self-defense and left them hanging.

Now, he was back at his service-garage apartment, eating a hot ham and cheese sandwich and drinking a sixty-four ounce Coke he'd picked up on the way home. Seated on his sofa, he grabbed a remote and pressed a button.

Beethoven's 9th Symphony filled the room.

He started into the file. It was two women, a mother and daughter named Willa and Whitney Kerrington. They ran a chain of pawn shops in DC, but they weren't seen very often. Supposedly, they worked for The Drake. It made sense. Pawn shops were great forums for a lot of seedy activities.

He studied images of the women more closely. They looked alike, surly gals with long chestnut hair down to their waists. Willa, the mother, had some grey in hers. They were both fit and casually dressed. One picture showed them in commando gear holding machine guns, but it looked like they were modeling. In another photo, Whitney, the daughter, was in an MMA fight. Another woman lay on the mat with a bloody nose, out cold.

Women these days.

He thought about Sid. He missed doing this with her. He'd done it for years, but it didn't feel right without her. She'd left. Her decision. He couldn't blame her. He'd been about to die, and not just him, either. Sam and Guppy, too. He could only imagine the scenarios Sid must be facing now. The lies. The deceit. He had to have faith that she'd hold up to it.

I need to find her.

It was evening. Smoke sat parked in the Camaro at one of the pawnshops run by the Kerringtons. Cleverly enough, the joint was named W&W Pawn and Jewelry. The store was located off a stretch of highway in east DC, crowded together with a bunch of other places in a strip mall. Traffic was pretty steady. Shady men and women slid in and out carrying everything from video game consoles to TVs. Even though it was quite warm and humid, many of the customers left the store with their hands stuffed deep in their pockets.

Smoke opened up a bag of jerky and started eating. He couldn't see much inside the store without going in. The windows were barred and filled with displays. Cars came and went. No one in particular stood out, but it was still early. He could try some of the other shops or at least put some eyes on them, but he didn't feel like fooling with Sam and Guppy. He didn't want to tell them what he was doing. Right now, he just wanted to be left alone and renew his focus. Sometimes, others got in the way of seeing things.

Lone Eagle.

Music on, jerky gone, moon rising high in the sky, Smoke finally decided it was time to venture inside. He'd popped his door open and gotten a foot out the door when a maroon Corvette ZR-1 pulled in front of the pawn store into a handicapped spot. Two women got out, busy and fast-talking to one another. It was Whitney and Willa. They scurried inside.

Smoke gave it a few moments, locked up the car, and headed in. The store was fairly big. The first thing he saw was a motley assortment of shelves loaded with electronics with white tags hanging from them. There was a power tool section and thousands of DVDs and video game cartridges. It all had a musty smell to it.

A young man in glasses with tattoos covering his forearms sat like a toad, working on a slice of pizza and gazing at a fight on one of the TVs.

Smoke made his way over to the jewelry section, staring down into the glass cases. A decent girl sat on a stool behind the counter staring at her phone. He turned his back to the jewelry and made a quick scan of the place. Half a dozen customers were milling about. There were stacks of army and navy gear: canteens, packs, water jugs. Glass cases of guns and knives. Rifle racks behind them. There was more stolen merchandise here than there were shoes in a shoe store.

What a great American way to make a living.

"Can I help you?" said a female voice with a Southern accent.

Smoke turned and faced the daughter, Whitney.

She was leaning on the jewelry counter, a little buck in the teeth, wearing a tight V-neck top that showed off her cosmetically enhanced chest. Her eyes were all smiles and giving him the once and twice over.

"Uh, I was looking for an engagement ring."

CHAPTER 16

"**G**ONNA GET ENGAGED? I'M A little sorry to hear that," she said, holding out her hand. "I'm Whitney. And your name is?"

Taking her hand, he said, "They call me Smoke."

"Your hands are warm, Smoke. You seem like a man with a lot of fire in you. Are you sure about getting engaged? You look too young to settle into marriage."

"I'm sure." He tapped on the top of the glass counter. "How about that one?"

"A princess cut. Nice choice. You know, we've got great deals on gold chains. I know they would look good around that strong neck of yours. Let me show you some."

"Sure."

She led him to another counter and took out some gold chains from underneath. "This one's twenty-four carat. A real nice rope. Step over here and let me put it on you."

He stepped between two counters and bent his knees a bit so she could reach his neck.

She locked on the chain, letting her fingers caress his neck and stop on his chest. "It looks great on you. Very sexy." She licked the lipstick off her teeth. "You've got one hard body. I bet you've seen some action, haven't you."

Checking himself out in one of the mirrors, he said, "It depends on the kind of action you're talking about."

She pressed up against him and stuck her hand in his back pocket. "We have a better selection in the back."

Smoke swallowed. He hadn't planned on getting this close, this soon, to anybody. His little investigation was traveling down an unexpected path of temptation.

It can't hurt to get a closer look at things, can it?

"Sure."

She took the chain off his neck, tossed it in the case, then took him by the hand. "I think you're going to like the selection I have, Smoke." She was leading him to a door in the back when the mother stepped out.

"Whitney, what are you doing?" The mother, Willa, glanced at Smoke. "Never mind, I know what you're doing." She gave Smoke the once-over. "Can't say I blame you, but we have business. And you aren't supposed to be fooling around until your next fight is over."

"They're always late," Whitney said.

An electric door alarm sounded, and three men entered the front of the building.

"Not today they aren't." Willa's face drew tight. "Get it together."

Whitney squeezed Smoke's hand. "Don't go anywhere."

He shrugged.

That was close.

The first was a bear of a man. Chains hung from his thick neck like a beard of gold.

Willa scurried over to greet him.

Whitney gave Smoke a little shove in the back and patted his butt. "Scoot away, just not too far away."

Making his way away from the crowd, Smoke kept his eyes on the men by glancing at the mirrors in the store. Two men behind the biggest guy held empty duffle bags. Smoke noted the same tattoo on the backs of all their necks: a black sun rising, the sign of The Drake. Not meeting eyes with any of them, Smoke slipped outside as soon as Willa and Whitney had stepped into the back with the men.

A midnight-blue Cadillac Escalade was parked in the slot in front of the building, with its engine running. The Drake goon in the driver's seat was smoking.

Smoke reached into his pocket and removed a transparent sticker a quarter the size of a business card. It was like an inspection sticker.

The heavy eyes of the man in the driver's seat found his. Smoke nodded, took the aisle between Willa's Corvette and the Escalade, and faded behind the back of the SUV. He'd just slapped the sticker on the metal plate over the registration tab when he heard the car door open and close and heavy feet coming right for him.

The Drake goon peeped around the tail of the car and pointed a pistol at Smoke.

Down on a knee, Smoke pretended to tie his shoe. Showing surprise, he looked up at the man. "Sorry, mate. Didn't want to trip."

The man eyed the back of the SUV, gave it a long look. Still pointing the gun at Smoke, he said, "Get the hell out of here."

Smoke hopped up with hands raised. "Sorry. No trouble. Sorry." He skipped through a pair of slow-moving cars and made his way into the parking lot and stayed out of sight until he heard the SUV's door close, then made his way back to his Camaro. He still had a good view of the pawnshop's storefront and the Escalade.

Waiting, he rolled down his windows, took out his smart phone, and pulled up an app that he, Sam, and Guppy had created. It was for the sticker he had placed on the SUV's license plate, inspired by Spiderman's spider tracers. A series of fine wires created a microchip signal that was hard to detect but that he could trace. They'd used it on several cases before, and it worked about half the time. A red beacon on the phone glowed on a digital map.

"Whoop, there it is," Smoke said with a smile.

He pushed the cassette tape back in the player and thumped to the Beastie Boys. The tape had run halfway through the song "Brass Monkey" when The Drake personnel exited the shop. Both of the duffle bags were loaded so full it looked like the seams would burst, and when they were tossed in, the big Escalade sagged on its suspension. The men got into the vehicle, and in seconds the car backed out and was gone.

"There we go," Smoke said.

Checking that the signal on his phone was good, he waited about five minutes before he pulled out. There wasn't any reason to rush with a good signal, but he didn't want to get too far away in case the tracker faded out. Cruising through the parking lot, he was wheeling down the aisle when a woman jumped in front of his car. He slammed on the brakes.

It was Whitney.

CHAPTER 17

"WHERE DO YOU THINK *YOU'RE* going, Smokie?" Not being shy about it, she stuck half of her body inside the driver's side window. "We have unfinished business. You need to come back inside or park this thing a little more private. Or not. Doesn't matter to me."

"Sorry, Whitney, but I'm a pretty faithful guy."

"I've heard that before. Just give me a few minutes and I'll change your mind." She clasped one hand behind his neck and pulled him in for a hard kiss.

He broke it off. "Not now, Whitney."

"I'm not letting you get away. I never lose a man."

"Look, I have to go."

"Aw Smokie, don't be so bashful. It'll be fine. I won't tell anybody."

Judging by the hungry look in her eyes, he could tell she wasn't one to take no for an answer. He had learned over the years that some women you just couldn't let down easy, no matter how hard you tried. "Didn't I hear something about a fight you've been training for? Aren't you supposed to abstain?"

"I never abstain. Ever. I just tell that to my mother. She's my manager." Whitney tried to kiss him again.

Smoke managed to fight her off. "You know, I really like those fights. When's your next one? I'd like to see it."

A new spark lit in her eyes. "Really?"

"Really. Just tell me the time and the place, and I'll be there."

She reared back a little. "You're just saying that. I know how men like you like to lie."

"No, I'm not a liar. I'll be there. You'd better win, though. I don't like losers."

"That's all the motivation I need. Got a pen?"

Following after the SUV from The Drake, Smoke looked at the message on his arm. Whitney had practically carved the time and place of her fight into his forearm with an ink pen. She wasn't too pretty, or too smart, but she did have some cunning and a great body, and he kinda liked her assertiveness.

Smoke dabbed the sweat from his forehead.

That was too close.

With the tracker still working, he managed to get within a few car lengths of the SUV. They maintained a steady speed on the highway before they took a sudden exit and headed south onto another stretch of road. Several miles later, they turned off the main road and vanished down a long stretch that disappeared into the trees. He pulled over and watched the beacon on his phone until it came to a complete stop and didn't move for several minutes.

"Bingo."

According to the map, the goons had pulled into an old industrial complex that had been converted into a salvage yard called Red Mark Materials. It was one of those bits of information he might have had Sam and Guppy look into, but he didn't want to fool with them. As for notifying Cyrus and Rebecca, he'd rather investigate on his own first, just in case he found Sid.

Can't trust them anyway.

He drove another mile up the road and ditched his car in the parking lot of some business offices. He geared up. He had the sweetheart suit on under his clothes, filling him with new energy. It made him ravenously hungry if he wasn't careful, though, so he gobbled down two MREs from his bag. Then he clasped on some holsters that held two automatic weapons and slid in two of those nasty sharp blades that Mal Gunderson made. He put on a pair of sunglasses—also courtesy of Mal—that sharpened his vision at night with a unique type of lens.

"Bat utility belt, check. Heh!"

Blood charging, he dashed into the woods. It made for a decent jog, and Smoke's adrenaline was pumping when he stopped at the tall barrier fence. This salvage yard wasn't some mom-and-pop shop from Sanford & Son. It was a full-blown complex encircled by a mile of security fencing or more. Looking through the chain-link, he could see lamp posts all over. Most of them were out. There were pallets of materials. Old cars. Boats. Campers. Row upon row of pipe, wiring, and similar building materials.

Smoke checked his phone.

There wasn't a signal, so the beacon on the app had gone dead.

Looks like a great place to do bad business.

He glanced up at the top of the fence. There were three strands of barbed security wire, and the fence had a hum to it. Cutting through it was out. Going over it was better, assuming he didn't get the piss shocked out of him.

Great Dane.

He followed along the fence until he found the gate that the goons must have taken. At the other end of the high gate stood a brick security shack, and a guard stood smoking outside under the glow of a lamppost. An AR-15 machine gun hung from a strap on his shoulder.

Smoke crept around through the woods to the other side of the small building and concealed himself in its shadow. He could hear a radio or television. A chair scraped over the floor.

Super. There's two of them.

With only one way in and out, Smoke mulled over his options. He could try to subvert the fence's electricity system to cut through it, but he figured that would trigger an alarm. He could climb over the fence and pray that his second skin saved him from the electricity, not to mention getting cut to pieces. Third, he could distract the guards and hope they were stupid enough to fall for it. Or, he could wait for someone to leave and sneak in while the gate was open.

It's going to be a long night.

Smoke hunkered in the shadows for hours. The guards had little of interest to say to each other. They just smoked and talked about one's wife and the other's girlfriend. It was clear they were outsiders. Contractors. Not privy to what The Drake really had going on.

Hour after hour, Smoke rehearsed a plan of action. He envisioned what to expect inside the salvage yard. It wouldn't surprise him one bit if there were deaders wandering around. Guard dogs. Armed men. Then again, he might get lucky. The Drake's supernatural creatures were often cocky. There wasn't much for them to fear when they controlled men and women that were undead. The way he saw it, all of the real people, like the gate guards, were just well-played pawns.

Souls bought with money.

He watched the bats attack the moths fluttering under the lamppost's light. It reminded him of his military days, standing guard hour after hour, his only company the croaking frogs and biting mosquitos.

Sid had shared a similar story with him before, from back in her Air Force days overseas, guarding a wall and hiding in a washout. He and she had some differences, but they had some things in common as well. He missed her voice. Their conversations. The way she looked at everything.

Where are you, Sid?

It ate him up inside. Sid could be anywhere. Florida. California. Japan. But his gut told him she was still in DC, close to her parents. If Allison was near, then so was Sid. Having seen Allison gave him hope. The game Reginald had played did too. Smoke was patient, but he was losing it a little. He needed to hear Sid's voice. See her face.

Lord, I need a break.

From the inside of the salvage yard, a car approached. The tall wire gate started to rattle open.

Smoke stood up and crept behind the guard shack toward the opening.

Showtime.

It was the black Cadillac Escalade that he had tracked here. The nose of the car eased to a stop just past the gate line.

Both of the guards headed over to the driver's side and started making conversation. The big fella with more gold chains than hair on his head sat in the passenger seat eyeing the road ahead. He was like a statue. Eyes forward, beady.

Come on, fat neck. Say something to somebody.

CHAPTER 18

THE CONVERSATION BETWEEN THE MEN wound down. The SUV eased forward, and the gate guards nodded and offered little waves.

Great Dane. Four hours down the drain.

Smoke started to ease back into the shadows. Before long, dawn would come. His mission would be impossible in daylight. He'd have to go home and sleep and then start over again come evening.

Another day down the tubes.

The SUV was halfway through the gate when it came to a sudden stop. About twenty yards ahead of the front bumper, a family of deer had started crossing the road. They froze and stared at the headlights. One of the men in the car snickered. The grizzly of a man in the passenger side swung his arm out of the window and pointed a Desert Eagle hand cannon at the deer. He shut one eye and studied his aim.

Smoke could feel him squeeze the trigger.

But just before he did, the deer jumped away.

The gun fired.

Ka-BLAMmmmmm! Ka-BLAMmmmmm!

The family of deer vanished into the other side of the woods.

Quickly, Smoke crept into the salvage yard between the gate and the car and buried himself in the shadows behind some racks of wire. From this spot, he watched the black SUV finally roll on and the gate close. Judging by the body language of the guards, no one suspected a thing.

I guess deer are good for more than venison.

Red Mark Materials was a massive complex. The flat blacktop would cover five football fields. There was heavy equipment: cranes, dump trucks, old cars. Huge metal bins full of parts. He climbed on top of a broken-down semi truck's cargo box, lay flat on his belly, and waited.

About seventy-five yards away near the middle of the salvage yard was a factory-like building three stories high, full of glass windows. It had a smokestack coughing out black vapors. Inside the upstairs windows were some bright, eerie, unnatural glows.

A scuffle caught his ear. A pair of figures lumbered between the rows of cars. They wore greasy mechanic's jumpers, and each carried a machete. They teetered a little left and right as they walked.

Deaders.

Smoke's skin crawled. Even as stupid as they were, the faint glow behind their sunken eyes creeped him out. Dead men weren't supposed to be walking. It was unnatural. An abomination.

Dirty dumb deaders.

One of the deaders sniffed really loud, a deep, bone-chilling snort. The second deader did the same. They walked right up to the truck and started climbing up.

You've got to be kidding me. They can smell me?

Smoke's hands fell on his knives. Killing them was best. Put the automatons to permanent rest. Killing them without a commotion was the challenge.

Options. Options. Options.

The truck wobbled. The deaders clamored up the face of the vehicle. Just as they crested the top, Smoke hopped off and jogged away. He cut through the salvage yard, row by row, turned into a deep pocket of stacked-up scrap metal, and came to a stop. He was reminded of the movie *Cool Hand Luke*, of the pepper scene when Luke throws the bloodhounds off. He wondered what it would take to throw the deaders off his scent.

Screw it. I'll just kill them. Some Drake flunky can clean them up in the morning.

About thirty yards from the main building now, he decided the best place to hide would be inside. He just needed to find a way in.

Behind him, a hub cap rolled off the pile and clattered on the ground. Smoke snatched it up. The pile before him shifted like a grinding of metal flesh. A large figure in a suit of welded metal scraps lunged at Smoke.

He dived, rolled, and bounced up again. A deader lurking within the suit of scrap metal armor attacked with a crowbar. Smoke sidestepped and snaked out his fighting blades. The flesh and metal automaton's chest was covered in metal plates. Every time it moved, it sounded like a jungle gym collapsing.

Great security system. An undead iron man. I hate these guys.

Smoke ran. Thoughts racing, he tried to think of a back-up plan. Deaders were stupid. They didn't talk well. Who would believe what they saw? He found another hiding spot and listened. More commotion. Men charging their weapons. Boots pounding the ground.

Ninety-nine out of a hundred men would have abandoned the mission. Not Smoke.

I love a challenge. Let's have some fun.

On fleet feet, he scurried back through the salvage yard until he located the armored deader. It and the others were together now, sniffing him out.

He appeared behind them and whispered, "Hey, jungle gym!"

The deaders rushed after him.

Smoke stopped at a stack of ten-inch iron pipes, cut the ropes, and buried the deaders in an avalanche of metal. The troops merged on his spot, but he was gone. Slunk back into the darkness.

He waited to strike. He heard a leader taking charge and telling men to fan out. Ten minutes into the search, a guard crossed through Smoke's line of sight. Like a lurking panther, he struck. Seizing the man by the neck, he put the man in a sleeper hold and choked him out.

Good night.

He donned the man's pea coat and Kevlar helmet, then dragged him to a port-a-john and stuffed him inside. Taking up the man's assault rifle, he journeyed through the salvage yard pretending to be one of them, using nods and hand signals when he crossed them. He played along for thirty minutes. Finally, he slung the weapon over his shoulder and headed toward the back of the main building, found a door, and slipped inside.

It was an old factory filled with heavy machinery. A strange light lit up the upstairs offices that overlooked the main floor, but other than that, the place was lit only by occasional dim bulbs that hung on long lines from above. On cat's feet, he navigated through the complex. There were voices talking. He eased closer. There were several men inside: more guards in pea coats, other men in fine clothing. All around them were racks of weapons, cases of ammo, and stacks of drugs. Pills. Powder. Fine leaves.

Dirty, dirty, dirty. Let's find out what snake is running this operation.

He headed toward the back of the building and took an iron grill staircase up to the supervising level. From the shadows more than thirty feet high, he could survey everything below. Catwalks crisscrossed from one side to the other, and chains and pulleys hung from the center ceiling, dangling over the floor below. The office complex with that strange glow coming from within was backed up against the exterior wall up here. Staying low, he peeked through a window into the glow. A handful of people robed from head to toe were talking around a table where the strange glow came from. They were several doors down from where he was positioned.

Time for a closer look.

He crept toward the first door he came to and started to twist the knob. Ahead, two more doors down, a robed figure emerged from within the offices. Smoke froze. The person put their hands on the rails and looked down at the activity below. Smoke shoved the door inward. The hinges creaked. The person on the balcony turned his way. Their eyes locked right on him.

CHAPTER 19

THINK FAST.

Smoke started unlacing his boots.

"What are you doing up here?" said the person in the robes. They came closer.

In the eerie dim light from the office window, Smoke got a better look at the figure. Average build. Wearing a set of heavy dark maroon robes. Face concealed in the shadows of the draping hood.

"I have a message," Smoke said, standing up. "I was told to update you that everything is under control outside."

The person's hands appeared from behind the cuff of the robes. They were oversized, and each one had a Drake tattoo on the back. The man pulled his hood down. He was ugly, with a haunting look in his eyes. Older. Rugged. Creepy. He cocked his head to one side as he approached. "I don't recognize you."

Smoke stood at attention. "Sorry, sir. They call me new guy." He added a stammer for effect. "T-They said for me to tell you, or s-someone up here that it was just a varmit raccoon stirring the deaders up."

The man leaned his head to the other side and studied Smoke's face. "My, what a strong chin you have. And your size. Formidable. I'm certain I would have remembered you." He reached over and touched Smoke's chest. "What is your name, new guy?"

"Conan."

"Conan? Like the movie?"

"Yes, the first one," Smoke said.

The man perched a brow. "What do you mean, the first one?"

Smoke walloped the man in the gut, caught him when he fell forward, and dragged him around the side of the offices. His second punch knocked the man out. Removing the man's robes and donning himself with them, he said, "You'd know what I meant if you'd seen it, Child of Set."

In his new disguise, Smoke slipped inside the door he'd tried to enter moments earlier and closed himself inside. The room was hot, almost sweltering. The dim supernatural glow within was the only source of light. He meandered behind the figures that hovered around the table. They were talking in low voices. One of them glanced Smoke's way for a moment then returned his attention back to the metal table. A man was strapped down on it. Naked from the waist up, the man lay spread eagle with a cauldron of green fire bubbling between his ankles. There was no life in his limbs. Cold, dead, clammy hands. From the cauldron, tubes fed into his body. A small motor was pumping the fluorescent green liquid into him.

Smoke's palms started to sweat. The hairs on his neck rose.

Not what I expected.

He'd figured there would be men in here governing the ranks and operations. Instead, he'd found a bunch of acolytes performing some bizarre ritual. Unnatural. Evil. Disturbing. Part of the man inside him wanted to run. The other part wanted to destroy. He edged closer.

The naked corpse on the table had a black sun tattooed on his chest. The others around him were chanting words Smoke did not understand. His skin crawled. The words thundered in his ears. He backed away. The man on the table sat up. His eyes were green fires that turned pitch black.

The robed men stopped chanting. They'd given life to a deader. The robed men raised their arms and gave praise. "Let the dead rise and serve. Let the dead rise and serve. Let the dead rise and—"

Ka-Blam!

Smoke blasted a hole clear through the deader's chest. It flopped over off the table and onto the floor.

Instead of fighting him, the robed men let out alarming shrieks and bolted for the doors.

Let them run.

He'd seen enough. Smoke pushed the cauldron over, spilling its contents all over the floor. Whatever was going on disgusted him, turned his guts inside out, and he wouldn't have it anymore. He scanned the offices for anything useful. Files. Books. Plans. Any clues to where The Drake might be operating. Where Sid might be. On impulse, he'd blown this job wide open.

He found a small leather booklet lying just inside one of the exits. He snatched it up and went out onto the iron balcony. A hail of gunfire erupted from the ground level. Bullets ricocheted everywhere. He found the assault rifle he'd left in the shadows and returned fire. Recon was over. War was on.

He pumped short bursts of bullets down into the tables laden with drugs.

That changed their game plan.

One of the men on the ground level shouted out new commands.

"Protect the merchandise! Protect the merchandise!" the leader said.

The soldiers scrambled, hopped in trucks and vans, and barricaded the goods as best they could.

Smoke ran down one of the metal catwalks. Blasts of gunfire cut off his path. He ran back up toward the offices. He recalled something he'd missed in the moment and went back inside the upstairs office complex. There was a phone hanging on the wall, a landline. He picked up the receiver. There was a tone.

Nothing like a plain old telephone.

He dialed Cyrus's number and got voice mail. "This is the voice mailbox of Agent Cyrus Tweel, please leave a message. If it's an emergency, call the FBI hotline at—"

"Figures."

Smoke left the receiver off the hook and headed toward the back of the room. A huge metal door hung on the wall. The lever for the junction box was there as well. He grabbed the lever and pulled it down. All of the power in the entire facility went out. "Lights out, ladies."

He took off the robe and slipped back out onto the balcony. Quiet as a mouse, he journeyed down the steps through the pitch black. On the next landing he approached, someone was making their way up the stairs toward him. Smoke punched the man in the jaw and caught him before he fell. Keen-eyed with the help of the glasses, he made his way down to the main floor.

Orders were still being barked out.

"Get some flashlights!"

Seconds later, light beams were shining up into the catwalks, pinpointing their locations.

Morons.

Car engines fired up and pulled out of the building. He assumed it was those strange clerics making haste. He probably should have killed those sickos, but that wasn't his way. He'd only kill live people when he had to, but the shifters were a different thing. The deaders too. What bothered him now was who was in charge of this operation. That person could provide answers. Certainly, someone knew something about Reginald. He seemed to be top brass.

I've got to get something out of this mission.

Boot steps shuffled over the ground floor and started coming up the steps again.

Smoke made his way behind the men guarding the trucks. He found a piece of scrap metal and chucked it up toward the offices. Metal banged on metal.

Gunfire shattered glass and tore out the windows.

"Hold your fire! Hold your fire!" commanded another voice, a woman's.

Smoke stiffened. His heart beat faster. Toward the middle, a woman moved among the troops with familiar ease. His heart stopped when she spoke again.

"Close all the doors and block all the exits. Whoever the hell is in here isn't getting out alive."

Smoke's throat tightened as he went in for a closer look. Judging by the height and build on the feminine figure, only one person could fit that bill. In the beam of a passing flashlight, he got a quick look at her face. No doubt about it, that was the face of Sidney Shaw.

CHAPTER 20

IT CAN'T BE.

Smoke wanted answers. He wanted answers now. He shouted out, "I see him," and began firing into the rafters.

Budda-Budda-Budda-Budda

The troops scrambled and started to fire.

Smoke snaked through the confusion, crept up on Sid, clamped his hand over her mouth, lifted her off her feet, and dragged her kicking into the deep shadows of the building. He pinned her up against the wall. "What are you doing?"

"Get your hands off me, fool!"

He covered her mouth again. "Keep it down, Sid. What's going on?"

She struggled with the fierce strength of a wild animal. There was no recognition of him in her eyes at all. She drove a knee into his side, winded back her arm, and clobbered him in the jaw.

He staggered back, holding his chin. It felt like a mule had kicked him. He wiped the blood from the corner of his mouth. "You need to come with me, Sid."

She gave him a funny look, whipped out a gun, and aimed at his chest. "No, *you* need to come with *me*. Hands up!"

Smoke took a step forward.

She shot him in the chest.

Blam!

He dropped to a knee. Fought for his breath. All the air had been knocked out of him. Black spots blinded his eyes. If it hadn't been for the second skin he was wearing, he would've had a hole clean through him. He grit his teeth and started to stand. "Are you nuts? What are you doing?"

"You aren't dead?" she replied. "Guards! Guards!"

The troops closed in.

Smoke was surrounded by gun muzzles.

"Cuff him," Sid said.

Smoke studied her eyes as he finished standing. A sharp blow caught him in the back of the head. Stars exploded behind his eyes.

Aside from the headache, busted ribs, and the continuous feeling of throbbing pain, Smoke was fine. Eyes shut and body limp, he felt the goons carry him back up the steps and into the offices. Inside, they dropped him on the floor. As best he could tell, there were three people in the room, milling about. Somebody shoved the power lever back on.

Sid spoke first. "Get this corpse out of here before it starts to stink. Looks like we have a replacement for it."

The men left the room, and the doors closed behind them.

A busy signal could still be heard on the phone Smoke had used earlier. Footsteps walked over to the sound, and the phone was hung up. Silence followed. The quiet. The unknown. The woman who might be Sid was still in the room. He could hear her soft breathing.

Smoke envisioned the scene from earlier. Sid was strong now, much stronger than she'd been before. In the darkness, he couldn't get a good look into her eyes. There were no answers there. It was her, but it wasn't. A carbon copy. A shifter? Her shooting him could not have been a bluff. Whoever this was couldn't be Sid. But she sounded and moved just like her.

Footsteps approached him where he lay on the floor. Fabric stretched from the woman squatting down. Her hands ran over Smoke's body. She slipped out his knives. Unholstered his guns. She tossed the weapons away with a clatter. Her scent was sweet. Faint, but expensive. It wasn't a scent of Sid.

"You're a big one," the woman said under her breath. She clasped his head in her hands. "Handsome too. What brings you here? Why aren't you dead? My bullet should have killed you."

"You should have aimed for the head."

"What?" she said, rising up to her feet.

Smoke swept her legs out from under her.

She hit the floor hard.

Hands still cuffed in the front, he got her into a choke hold. With his legs wrapped around her, he pinned her in his grip.

She struggled and fought. Her strength matched his, but he had her. Or it. Or whatever.

"Who are you? Where is Sid?"

Choking, she couldn't answer.

Smoke eased off.

"You'll die!" She sucked in her breath to scream.

With a squeeze, he choked off her efforts. Lips to her ear, he growled, "Play nice or you die, shifter."

"I'm Samone. Not a shifter. Wait, you're John Smoke, aren't you. My lover. I can see your face in my thoughts now. My memories. Release me, John."

"Be quiet."

She struggled. The tone of her voice changed to something sinister. "I'm a clone, Smoke. A clone of your precious Sid. You won't hurt me, will you, John Smoke?"

"Tell me where Sid is."

"I don't know and I don't care. I have my own operation to run. Her body is weak anyway." She pushed back into him with seductive effort, her voice a playful purr. "Mine is everlasting. Why don't you play with me and forget all about your little Sidney? I can make you really, really happy. I never sleep."

"That probably means you never shut up. Just tell me where she is."

"Don't be silly. I don't have to tell you anything. The guards will be back here any moment now, and I'm just going to tell them to open up."

"Even you can't handle a bullet in the head."

"And you can? Hah." She balled up in a knot of muscle and started to grunt and strain against his strength.

Smoke squeezed harder. His busted ribs burned like fire. His locked fingers started to lose their grip. Samone was growing. Muscles bulged in her renewed limbs. He lost his leverage. Up on her feet, she backed him hard into the wall, jarring him loose of her, and slung him down onto the floor on his shoulders. She stomped at his neck.

He scrambled away, jumped to his feet, and faced off with her.

Samone had become a full six-and-a-half feet of Sid gone ugly. One eye was higher than the other. Her face was a twisted snarl. She was the Hyde to Sid's Jekyll.

Still cuffed, Smoke said, "So you *are* a shifter."

"And a liar." She looked at Smoke like he was a greasy pork chop. She blew him a kiss. "But best of all, I'm a killer."

CHAPTER 21

WITH A PICK SMOKE HAD concealed in his clothes, he took off his cuffs and tossed them on the floor.

Samone's bulging eyes widened. "You *are* a clever man."

"That's sort of the equivalent of calling you an ugly woman." He backed toward one of the exits. A hand-to-hand battle with the monster woman wasn't the best idea right now. Not after being so busted up and all. "Why don't you just make this easy on yourself and tell me where Sid is?"

"It doesn't really matter. You'll be dead soon enough anyway. But you are a great candidate for becoming a deader. Or you could just be smart and become one of us." She stroked her hair and tossed it over her shoulder. "Beautiful, powerful creatures. We can do whatever we want."

"I'll pass." He took a peek out the door. Guards were coming from both directions.

"What's the matter, Smoke? Nowhere to run?" She winked at him. "Guards! Stay outside! If he comes out, shoot him!"

Smoke had faced enough shifters to know there wasn't much he could do to hurt the more powerful ones, not without some of the bullets Mal Gunderson made. Like the ones in the weapons Samone had slung clear across the room. His blades were gone too. He jammed his fingers in his pockets, searching for one of the pills.

Samone held her hand out. "Looking for these?" Two pills were in her hand, glimmering with a life of their own. "What's the matter, Smoke? Did you forget to take your vitamins?" She popped them both in her mouth and swallowed. "Tasty."

"They're actually time release capsules and great for acne, which you could certainly benefit from." He balled up his fists and approached. "Let's get this over with."

She beckoned him over with her chin stuck out.

Smoke slugged her in the jaw.

Samone started laughing. "You're in for a long day, Smoke. Real long." She slashed at his throat with her long fingernails.

Smoke skipped away, dove back in, and countered. He kicked at her knees and punched into her ribs.

"Now *that's* my kind of foreplay," she said.

Smoke delivered blow after blow that would have punished an NFL lineman. Samone rolled with the punches. She slapped and kicked back. Snarled and clutched. He peppered her, time and time again. A stinging bee. Catching her off balance, he punched her hard in the neck and dropped her to the floor.

Everything has a weakness.

Samone was stunned.

Smoke jumped over her and darted for his guns. When he was inches from snatching one up, a hand with a grip of iron seized his ankle and pulled him down. His fingers stretched for the pistol. Samone's raw power dragged him backward and yanked him into her arms.

She smooched at him. "How about a kiss? Quit squirming. You're helpless as a child against me."

Smoke got ahold of her wrist, twisted it behind her back, and stuffed her face into the floor.

"How did you do that?" she yelled.

"It's called aikido. Join a dojo and learn it."

Pinning a wild boar would have been easier than holding Samone down. "You need to be still."

Samone continued to fight against him. "Or what?"

Still maintaining his leverage, he said, "Be still."

"No!"

Smoke dislocated her shoulder.

Samone howled.

Not wasting any time, Smoke abandoned the stunned shifter on the floor and fetched his guns and knives.

Samone was on her feet again, facing him.

He lowered one gun barrel on her. "I'd keep still if I were you."

Shoulder sagging, she transformed back into the form of Sid and said with an enticing smile, "You won't hurt me, will you John?"

"Take one more step and you're going to find out."

Her pretty eyes narrowed. She came one step forward.

Ka-Blam!

The bullet tore clear through her shoulder and spun her around. Eyes filled with terror, she screamed as she dashed out onto the balcony. "Guards! Guards! Kill him!"

Feeling the walls close in, Smoke picked his special sunglasses up off the floor and grabbed the handle on the power box. "Here we go again." He yanked it down. Everything went black.

Armed like an assassin, quiet as a panther, and deadly as a ninja, he tore through the oncoming ranks in the blackness. A good throat punch disrupted anyone. A sock in the temple. A gunshot in the leg. A jab in the ribs. On a mission, he left the guards in disarray. He hit the ground level and used an assault rifle to break all the lights so they couldn't come back on.

Chaos erupted in all directions.

Perfect.

Using all the explosive elements to his advantage, Smoke found his way to a weapons cache and loaded up with a couple of light anti-tank weapons.

I love these things.

He scurried back up onto the metal staircase, opened up one tube, and got a good view in the dark through the special sunglasses of the weapons and drugs that hadn't been loaded yet. He lowered the weapon on his shoulder, took aim, and fired. The rocket soared. Millions of dollars and months of planning exploded. Smoke pitched the empty rocket tube away and readied the other. He turned around and launched the rocket into the offices above. The entire facility shook.

Ka-Boom!

On the move again, he grabbed a Kevlar helmet and pea coat, blended in, and headed outside. Guards were going in all directions, but there weren't as many as there had been. Smoke knifed through the night and loaded himself into a humongous yellow dump truck, an earth mover with wheels ten feet tall. He turned over the key, put it in gear, and stomped on the gas.

"It's Tonka time."

CHAPTER 22

ALL SMILES, SMOKE PLOWED THROUGH the building. The massive truck crushed everything in its path. Cars. Drugs. Weapons. Vans. He ran it all over. Men tried to climb up in the truck, only to fall off with a hole in them. Smoke was in a zone. A zone of destruction. And he'd had enough of The Drake and all of their foul games. Sid or no Sid, it was time to send them a message. He was coming.

He plowed through the walls, leaving dust and debris in his path. Running over the last pile of drugs and ammo, he smashed through another wall and headed outside. The sun was rising. If there were any Drake soldiers left, they had fled. M-16 ready, he got out of the cab and headed down the giant truck's front stairs.

Here they came, the deaders that hounded the salvage yard, the one covered in scrap metal armor and the others in grease monkey suits.

Smoke filled their chests full of lead.

Budda-Budda-Budda-Budda

They collapsed on the ground, twitched a few times, and moved no more.

"Woohoo!" said a voice from above.

Smoke spun around.

Samone was on top of the dump trunk and restored to her monstrous form. She jumped.

He went for his gun.

She landed right on top of him and plowed him into the ground.

He fished the gun out of its holster.

She wrenched it free and tossed it away. "No more of those bullets, sweetie." She punched him in the face. *Whack!* She yanked him up by his shirt and got in his face. "Some good news, though. Those time release pills you gave me? They've kicked in. I feel great!"

Smoke punched and kicked with instinct and precision. It didn't help.

Samone—quicker, faster, and stronger than ever—pounded and bludgeoned him with fist after fist after fist.

Ka-Blam!

Samone fell over.

Bloodied but breathing, Smoke got up on his feet.

Rebecca Lang was holding his gun in her tiny hands. Cyrus Tweel was right beside her.

Wiping the blood out of his eyes, Smoke said, "Thanks."

Fists on his hips, Cyrus said, "What the hell happened here, Smoke?"

A tremendous groan of metal on metal came from the building and stopped.

"Did you bring your brooms?" Smoke said.

"No, why?" Cyrus replied.

"Because it's a mess."

Suddenly, the entire building collapsed. The sunrise crept through the dust.

Smoke smiled through his busted lips and patted the dump truck's tire. "Ah! I love the smell of destruction in the morning."

Back at FBI headquarters, Cyrus fumed in his office. "You were just supposed to look and then notify me as soon as you found anything!"

Smoke sat in a chair across Cyrus's desk. It was Section Chief Howard's old office. Rebecca was in the chair beside him—legs crossed, foot kicking, eyes intent on him. He held a cold compress on his jaw. "I did."

"You did after the fact."

"I didn't have a signal. I did call as soon as I was able. You didn't pick up."

Cyrus leaned forward on his elbows. "That's beside the point. You shouldn't have gone in there without first making contact."

Smoke had already spent two hours writing everything down. Now, along with the rest of his body, his hand was sore. "You should be glad. I took down a big operation."

"No, you wiped out some expensive assets of a rather big company." Cyrus jammed his finger onto his desktop. "Lawsuit, lawsuit, lawsuit!"

"Is that all anyone cares about anymore, whether they'll be sued or not? What about doing the right thing?"

Rebecca chimed in. "That's too expensive."

"Yeah," Smoke added, "these days, it seems doing the wrong thing pays better." He switched the cold compress from one side of his face to the other. "Can I go now?"

"No." Cyrus was reading Smoke's report. "A shifter who looks like Sid, really? I think you're longing too much."

"You saw her. Little Miss Prissy over here shot her. Or it." He eyed Rebecca. "For which I am grateful."

Rebecca showed the faintest smile.

"Look, Smoke." Cyrus gave him a grim smile and shook his head. "You aren't my kind of guy. To me, you're nothing but trouble. I have to admit, though, what you pulled off today, well, they don't do it that good in the movies. I'm starting to get a better idea what we're up against. It's sinister. Disturbing. I can't deny it any longer."

"What did you think it was, a bunch of clishmaclaver?"

"What?" Cyrus bunched up his eyebrows. "Never mind. I want to help. Let's keep working together." He reached inside his desk drawer and pulled out a ring box. He tossed it to Smoke. "I believe that belongs to you."

It was Sid's engagement ring. Smoke didn't ask any questions, just got up and left.

CHAPTER 23

S MOKE WAS HOME LYING IN bed, staring up at the ceiling. He still wore the sweetheart suit, as it had some moderate healing effects. He felt like it was the only thing holding him together. He'd been on the wrong side of too many beatings. He'd survived, but for some reason it felt like he had lost. He didn't like it. Not one bit. He drifted off to sleep again.

When he woke the next time, he crawled out of bed, groaning and stretching. Barefoot on the wooden floor, he took a seat at his computer. There was a leather notebook on the desk, the one he'd taken from The Drake. One of those strange clerics had dropped it in the scuffle. Smoke hadn't told Cyrus and Rebecca about it.

Maybe I'll let them know later.

Slowly, he leafed through the pages. There were some places and dates. Phone numbers and names. There were chemical formulas. Strange languages. Hieroglyphics and arcane signs. He searched some of the addresses, then leaned back in his chair.

"Huh."

The addresses were people's workplaces and homes. He wasn't sure, but it was possible these were names of Drake members. There were a lot of them.

This is the kind of lead I like.

A phone rang. It was his own house phone that hung on the wall. Only Sam and Guppy ever called that number. He pushed himself over the concrete floor into the kitchenette and picked up the receiver. "Smoke."

"Hi John. It's Sid."

It was her. The very fiber of his being told him so. Her voice was strong with some softness behind it. Unlike with Samone, where something had been a little off from the start, his instincts told him this was genuinely her.

"How are you?" he said.

"You don't need to worry about me, John, but I'm worried about you. We need to talk."

"We are talking."

"In person. Let's meet," she said.

As much as he wanted to see her, a little stubbornness surfaced. Leaning against the kitchen counter, he said, "You know where I am."

"I have another place in mind. Midnight. Federal Express Stadium."

"I'll have to check my schedule."

There was a pause on Sid's end of the line. After a brief delay, she said, "This is serious, John. Midnight."

Nighttime. Whoever was pulling Sid's strings at The Drake probably didn't care for the light. That was how the shifters were. They preferred darkness over daylight. Not that light stopped them most of the time. Still, it did seem to Smoke nighttime was when they were at their best.

"How about noon tomorrow?"

"John, if you want to see me, then don't screw around. You've screwed enough up already. I hope to see you at midnight. And John, be sure you come alone."

Click.

The line went dead.

Fighting the urge to hit *69 and call her back, he hung up the receiver and focused on her words.

You've screwed enough up already.

There was a message in there. A compliment. A praise. He had to believe Sid was still Sid, but he wouldn't know until he saw her for himself. He stripped off the sweetheart suit and headed for the shower. Afterward, he stood facing the mirror, combing his fingers through his hair. "I think it's time for a haircut."

CHAPTER 24

AT 11 P.M., SMOKE CRUISED into the Federal Express Stadium parking lot. Engine still running, he made himself comfortable and rifled through his cassette tape collection. It had come in an old vinyl case with twenty slots in it. A nice mix for only five dollars. He ejected one cassette and put in another. It was a band called Slade. "Run Runaway" played. He cranked it up, closed his eyes, and eased the seat back.

Smoke was the only one who knew about this meeting. He hadn't even told Sam or Guppy. The more Cyrus and Rebecca were in the dark, the better. No, it was just him and the unknown. Was he going to be reunited with Sid once and for all? It didn't sound like it. Something was up, but at least he'd get to see her again. He hoped.

When he tilted the seat back a little farther, his breathing eased and he closed his eyes. All the throbbing in his bones and muscles dulled. He fell asleep.

Peck. Peck. Peck.

Smoke opened his eyes. Someone was standing outside his car, knocking steadily on his window. It was Reginald. Smoke leaned up in his seat and popped the door open. There was a black limousine parked nearby. Two men in pea coats stood outside it.

Reginald stepped aside. "You must be awfully tired, Mister Smoke."

"I've been busy."

"Death will give you plenty of rest." Reginald was nicely dressed in a grey oxford shirt, brown woolen slacks, and no tie.

"It will do the same for you." Eyeing his surroundings, he said, "Where's Sid?"

"Close enough. I need to pat you down. Up against the car, if you will?"

Smoke turned and put his hands on the roof. "I didn't think you guys had anything to fear from the likes of a mortal like me."

Patting Smoke down, Reginald said, "We survive because we are cautious, and I must admit you've proven yourself a very formidable person. You put a real whooping on Guermo. As I understand it, Vormus departed with his tail between his legs. Of course, that brood is quite a bunch of cowards." He huffed and finished patting Smoke down. "Vampires. How juvenile. But thanks to your encounter, you will get the meeting you were promised."

Turning to face Reginald, Smoke said, "I'm sure that isn't it. I'm thinking last night's excursion had more to do with it."

"Yes, that didn't go over very well at all. If it weren't for your lady friend, you'd be dead. If it happens again, well, just imagine the worst repercussions ever. Then multiply them." Reginald walked over to the limo and placed his hand on the door handle. "And don't get all excited. This isn't a conjugal visit."

"We aren't married yet."

"It's not a prom date, either." Reginald opened the door, saying under his breath, "Mind that tongue of yours."

Smoke ducked inside the limo, and the door closed behind him. Adjacent to him sat Sid, looking more beautiful than ever. She wore a long dark-purple dress and was laden with bright jewels like a priestess. Beside her sat a deeply tanned and strongly built man in a tuxedo. His dark hair was slicked back. His big fingers were half decorated in Superbowl-like rings. His voice was a rumbling thunder.

"I'm Kane. Kane Lancaster."

Smoke's gaze didn't leave Sidney's expressionless face. "Hi, Sid."

She nodded.

"Mister Smoke," Kane said, twisting a ring on his finger, "before we begin our discussion, I need to make you aware of a few things. First, you are here and alive because I allow you to be. I can say the same about anybody. That's the kind of power I have. Second, you do not speak unless I speak to you first or give you permission to speak. Understand?"

"I don't need an interpreter."

"Good. It seems that you and Sid are a bit unique. You have a talent for surviving. I like mortals with your kind of, oh, how did that one Texan put it? Eh, grit. So much so, that it got my attention. Even Reginald, one of my finest soldiers, was impressed. That is not easily done. In The Drake family, we want the best. It's useful to us, and a veteran of your skills and aptitude could be rewarded quite well. No more fighting for your life or getting beat up tussle after tussle. Just cruise along and enjoy life. Basically you can have anything you want. What do you think about that?"

Smoke's eyes slid over to Sid. She sat quiet as a church mouse. He looked Kane back in the eye. "I'm not interested."

Kane placed his hand on Sid's thigh. "Then we have a problem, Mister Smoke. You see, your little jaunt last night cost The Drake millions of dollars. You need to pay that back. Every penny. My accountants are rounding up the damage totals as we speak. How do you propose to pay me back?"

"I'm not."

Rubbing Sid's thigh, Kane said, "Oh, that's where you are sadly mistaken. You are in debt for dollars. Real dollars. My dollars. And your wretched little life is not enough to pay your debt. No, you need to consider everyone you know as collateral. Your friends Samantha and Guppy. This precious gem of a woman, Sid. Her sister and niece. Her parents, Sally and Keith. Charming people. They all have skin in the game, but much more skin is needed after you destroyed all that merchandise last night. Are you sure you don't want to reconsider?"

"Yes, I'm sure."

Sid blurted out, "John—"

Whap!

Kane back-handed her hard across the face. "Do not speak."

"Don't you ever touch her again!" Smoke jumped him.

Faster than Smoke could see, Kane had him pinned back against the seat with fingers around his throat. Smoke started to choke in the man's unbreakable grip.

"Listen to me, you worm. I'm granting you an opportunity. It's mercy. But even with my long life, my patience can wear thin." Kane's black eyes were smoldering cauldrons of evil. "I can have everyone you care about killed before you fire up that heap you call a car. Do we understand each other?"

Kane's freakish power was too much for Smoke. Face turning purple, he managed to nod.

Kane released him. "You are way out of your depth and treading deadly waters. You need to back off." He turned his attention to Sid. With a handkerchief from his pocket, he tenderly wiped the blood from the corner of her mouth. "Be more careful when you speak, my dear. You know how precious you are to me."

Smoke started coughing.

Kane gave him a fatherly pat on the back. "You're going to be fine. Tell you what, I'm willing to make you another deal. Let's call a truce, because I'm curious to see whether or not you can handle your own temptations. You back off. Stay out of The Drake's affairs. No Black Slate. No curiosity. No investigations. Cold turkey. So long as you can manage that, I'll let bygones be bygones."

Smoke sat up in his seat, rubbing his throat and coughing. "Only if Sid comes with me."

"Oh ho, no. I'm doing this as a favor to Sid. She's the only reason you're even breathing right now. Don't you get it? Now, I'm sure you love her, and I can't fault you for that, but now you see, she favors another. You need to move on, my good man."

Smoke's eyes searched for Sid's.

Sid's eyes searched for Kane's.

Kane gave her a nod. "I'll give you two a few minutes."

Her eyes widened.

"Go on. Leave," Kane said.

CHAPTER 25

SID KNOCKED ON HER WINDOW, and the limousine door opened. One of Kane's guards on the outside looked to Kane, who nodded. The guard stepped back. She got out and started walking. Smoke followed after her. She kept going until she was out of earshot of the limousine, even to Smoke. The guards and Reginald were far enough away to give them some privacy.

A brisk wind blew her hair in her eyes, and Smoke reached to move it away.

"No," she said, moving it herself.

"You look beautiful."

"Thanks."

"Sid, you can't give in to the likes of them." Unable to fight the urge to crush her in his arms, he eased forward.

She looked over to where Kane could still see them and backed away. "John, no. Listen, you have to move on. It's too dangerous, and you're really pissing them off."

"Heh-heh."

"It's no laughing matter, John. The Lancasters might be different, but they love money as much as anyone else. Money and power. It's an obsession. You need to back off. Move on. I'm sorry, John, but that's just the way it has to be." She closed her hands over his. "Think of my family, John. Your friends. They'll all get killed unless you move on."

Her warm hands stirred his heart. "You're killing me, Sid."

"You're killing yourself. I don't want anything to happen to you or anyone else. Move on to something else. There's still plenty of good people out there for you to rescue."

"Can't you see what they're doing, Sid? Fear. Threats. That's how they control people and make them prisoners. You can't let them do that to you."

She squeezed his hands harder. "I have no choice."

"You're being forced to do this. That's not living. That's imprisonment." He touched her cheek. "Are they hurting you?"

"No. John, you have to let me go. It's too dangerous for everybody. I just can't live with that."

"You can't save everybody, Sid. Sometimes, only people can save themselves. Have faith in them. Make that choice."

"I almost watched you die once, John. I don't want to ever see that happen."

"It's because you love me, isn't it?"

She looked up and nodded. Tears swelled in her eyes.

"Then fight to be with me, Sid. We can get through this. Together, we can get through anything."

The limo pulled up near them, and the window rolled down. Kane said in a firm voice, "Sid, come. Mister Smoke, do you have an answer for me?"

"John, take the truce with him. Please."

He looked down into her pleading eyes and nodded. "Fine."

"What's that?" said Kane.

Clenching his jaw, Smoke glared at him. "I said fine."

"Well done. Now Sid, don't make me ask you again. Come."

Sid kissed Smoke on the cheek and slipped away, saying, "I'm sorry, John. Take care of yourself."

The limo door opened, and she vanished inside.

Reginald waved at Smoke. "Goodbye, asshole."

Moments later, the black machine sped away.

Smoke stood alone in the parking lot accompanied only by the whistling wind and the engagement ring in his pocket. Numb from his toes to his sagging shoulders, he headed toward his Camaro. All of its tires were flat.

CHAPTER 26

A DAY PASSED. THEN A WEEK. A month. Smoke hadn't left his place. Always stocked up, he wouldn't need to leave for another six months, unless he got a hankering for fresh food. He didn't answer his phone either. Or texts. Or turn the TV on. He sat on his sofa chewing on beef jerky and drinking a Coke. There was an assortment of books stacked up on the coffee table, everything from *The Darkslayer* to *The Bible*. Copies of Nightfall DC. A few biographies. Some old history books Mal Gunderson had lent him. Aside from reading all the time and eating very little, he cleaned. Tinkered with his car. Replaced the slashed tires.

Early in the evening, he stretched out his arms and yawned. Rubbed his eyes. Considered crawling into bed. Sleep was hard to come by. He normally rested easy, like a baby. Now, something was chewing him up inside. Tired of the silence, he picked up the remote and turned on his stereo. Mozart played. He grabbed another piece of jerky and started chewing.

On the corner of the table sat the ring box. He thought of Sid, the danger she was in. The company she chose to keep. She had given up her life for his. For the lives of many others. But it was supposed to be the other way around. He was supposed to save her. It gnawed at him. She was suffering for his sake. Wasn't she?

Maybe she's okay with it. Maybe she's gone already.

He didn't want to believe it, but he knew that most people, no matter how good, how strong, they had their limit, their price. He had to have faith that Sid was who he thought she was. Have faith she wouldn't get more than she could handle. His skin shifted when he thought about The Drake and what they could do to people. They had power. An ancient evil that turned men and women into beasts. Was that in store for Sid? Would she become an abomination like her clone Samone or Angi Harlow the harpy? In order for that to happen, Sid would have to embrace the power and want it for herself. That was the deal as he understood it.

No, she'd never do it. She'd die first.

And Smoke would never see her again.

Tires crunched over the pavement. Brakes squealed to a halt. Car doors popped open and closed. He made his way over to the front door and let Sam and Guppy in.

"Are you finished sulking yet?" Sam said, pinching his face. "My, your cheeks are getting a little thin. What are you doing, starving yourself?" She eyed the trash can in the kitchenette. It was filled with beef jerky wrappers. "Yep. You're making a go at it, alright."

"Hey, Smoke," Guppy said with a nod as he shuffled inside. He turned on the TV and sat down at the computer.

Sam sat on the sofa and picked up a copy of Nightfall DC. "It's time to get back to work, Smoke."

"I told you, I'm done." He had told them what happened when he called them to pick him up at Federal Express Stadium. He'd told them to leave him alone.

Sam laughed. "Yeah, and I'm going to quit wearing makeup. Look John, I realize you're broken-hearted and haven't ever been through that before—"

"And you have?"

"Well, no, of course not. Not so long as I have the Gupster."

"Aye," Guppy said.

"The point is, you need to do what you do and let things fall back into place. They will. With or without Sid, it's going to work out."

He took a seat beside her. "She's the one."

She took his hand. "Bless your heart. I know she is, but she's going to have to want to save herself, unless you decide to save her."

"It's too dangerous. You know that. You and Guppy. Her family. The Drake will kill all of you."

Sam's jaw dropped.

Guppy's chair creaked as he turned and faced Smoke.

"What?" Smoke said.

Visibly agitated, Sam said, "Are you kidding me? After all your lectures about not caving in to evil?" She flipped her fingers. "After all your little anecdotes about how we are soldiers and when we sign up to fight, whether it's on the front lines or behind them, it's possible we might die? The old, uh, what was it?"

"'We can't save them all, but we try,'" Guppy said. "Not to mention the classic you so often quote, 'In order for Evil to win, the good need only do nothing.'"

Sam picked up the Darkslayer book and whacked him in the head with it. "And what about the 'Fight or Die' thing!"

Shrugging, Smoke said, "Well, that's just fantasy."

"My ass! You love this stuff! Gobbled it up in the Navy and in prison." She snatched up the ring and chucked it at him. "Now, if you want Sid, go and get her. Be a hero. Save the princess."

Suddenly, another voice cut into the conversation. "And suckle the tit of death while you're at it."

Sam gasped.

Smoke jumped to his feet.

Guppy scrambled out of his chair.

Vormus had come out of nowhere.

CHAPTER 27

S TANDING JUST INSIDE THE DOOR, Vormus said, "Oh great, the gang's all here." He wore jeans and a blue polo shirt with a logo that matched his white eyes. Lean and formidable, he slid aside to let Mal and Asia enter.

Hands up and palms out, Mal, dressed in sensible khaki trousers and a shirt that was too big, said, "I can explain."

Smoke had already removed a pistol from under the sofa cushion. "No you can't."

Remaining steady, Mal continued. "Just let me explain. I know what you think this is, and it sort of is, but it isn't."

"You're out of your mind," said Sam.

"No, no, I assure you, I have all my faculties." Mal looked back at Vormus. "Please, just don't move. I told you I needed to introduce you."

Aristocratic chin held high, Vormus replied, "I always make an entrance."

Asia sauntered inside, walked between Smoke and Sam, sat down and picked up a magazine, and started flipping through it. "Sheesh. He's fine. Don't worry about vampire guy. Creepy, but kinda nice."

Looking at Mal, Smoke said, "Talk."

"Uh, well, believe it or not, Vormus is here to help. He has a bit of a vendetta against The Drake, and we've been talking."

"Talking? How long have you been talking?" Smoke said.

"About a week or so." Mal waved him off. "It's not important."

"It *is* important, Mal!" said Sam.

"Well, no, actually it's been quite educational." Mal's tone picked up with excitement. "He has delivered some incredible insight about his kind, or rather, the shifters. Really, really fascinating stuff that goes back to, as I knew, the pyramids. You see—"

Vormus interrupted Mal. "Oh, you Americans like to ramble so much. Let's get to the point, shall we?"

"We already did that once," Smoke said.

"Ha ha. Yes, Mister Smoke, you almost had me. Quite clever." Vormus's eyes searched the apartment. "However, I was fortunate enough to live through it. The stake you ran through my heart, well, it might have worked if some good Samaritan hadn't come along and pulled it out. I think I might have only had a few minutes left. Close, close call. I commend you."

"I'm sure you didn't come by to give me a trophy."

"Well, no, but I do have something else. Information. I know all about your woman Sidney Shaw and the company she keeps with Kane Lancaster. I know plenty about him and The Drake."

"Of course you do. You're competitors," Smoke said.

"And brothers." Vormus sauntered a little deeper into the silent room. "You see, Mister Smoke, you were indeed sent to kill me, just like I assume that rat Reginald told you. But it was a win-win for them. They figured one of us would not survive. In this case, both of us did, and they aren't very happy about that. However, I've gone to great lengths to convince them I've left the country. What I'm really doing is plotting my revenge."

Keeping the barrel pointed at Vormus's forehead, Smoke kicked on the laser sight. "That's *your* problem, not mine. You can do your own dirty business."

"Not without help. I don't have any reliable people left. You killed them. At least, The Drake did when they found what you left of them at The Guillotine. I can't do it alone. You can't do it alone either."

"I'd just as soon stay out of it. I agreed to a truce."

"Pfft! Do you honestly think Kane is going to keep his word to you, your friends, anybody? It's only a matter of time before he has to scratch that itch from leaving you alive and has all of you slaughtered in the dark of the night." Vormus frowned. "He gave me his word too, you know, and look how that turned out. Think about it, eh? Me teaming up with the likes of you and you teaming up with the likes of me—he won't see that coming."

"Maybe not, but I don't work for people like you."

"You already have. You took the job to kill me, didn't you? Whether you like it or not, they still control you." Vormus sighed. "I don't have a bone to pick with you, Mister Smoke. When you came, I was only protecting myself."

"I was leaving."

"You were sent to kill me, were you not?"

Vormus had made his point, and even though he might be a liar, a shifter, a... whatever he might be, he wasn't so much different than everyone else. The world was run by liars and thieves. Smoke had to put up with them wherever he went. Vormus was just another one of them—just one who had already made his deal with the devil.

I should kill him.

"Mister Smoke, I sense your hesitation, and I don't blame you one bit, but there is more that you need to consider."

"What's that?"

"Kane is my older brother. I loved and trusted him. He dallied in dark mysticism first." Sadness grew in Vormus's voice. "He promised to protect me and our parents, everything I cared about and loved. I was convinced I would never be part of any of it. After all, he was my brother, and we were close. But as time went on, he wore me down. Tricks. Temptations. Threats. Over the years, he convinced me there was only one way to protect those I cared about: to become like him." He gazed into Smoke's eyes. There was a deep dark truth in them. "Time is running out. He's doing the same to Sid. Believe me, no one can withstand his pressure forever. I live with much to regret. She soon will, too."

"Boo hoo," said Sam. "Blast him, Smoke!"

"So what do you have to offer?" Smoke said.

"Like I said, I have information. I know everything you need to know about what they do and their locations. But Kane is mine."

Smoke put away his gun. "We'll see."

CHAPTER 28

S MOKE STOOD ON THE SANDY bank of the Potomac River. His friends were by his side. Vormus was there too, oddly basking in the glow of the moon. The shifter stood in stark contrast to the natural surroundings, a pylon of evil. Smoke's fingertips tingled. He'd gotten accustomed to the shifters, to their vibe. Every single one of them set alarms off inside him. They all reeked of death.

Vormus extended his arm over the river and pointed his slender finger. "There it is."

On the other side of the river, tucked deep behind the trees, a massive estate stood like a castle.

"I never imagined there was such a place this close to DC." Guppy put a pair of night vision binoculars to his eyes. "There's a dock, and a little movement in there. I see bodies. Assault rifles. We might need to find another way in."

"You can only get there by air or by water," Vormus said.

"How do you know that?" Smoke said.

"Oh, I've been there before. My one and only visit. It ended up in an argument." Vormus rubbed is jaw. "A rather nasty one."

Taking the binoculars from Guppy, Sam said, "Do you think you could fill us in a little more?"

"I came for a visit. Told my brother I wanted a piece of this sweet American Pie. He told me no. Go back to Scandinavia, he said. Get the hell out of my country. I really have taken a liking to this country."

"I thought the Lancasters were from this country," Mal said.

"No, pilgrims is more like it. My brother came over on some of those later ships. Decades later. He had a spat with our leadership at Guermo. Said he wanted to go somewhere else and do his own thing. My, I must admit, I never saw it coming, all of what America became. Yet, here it is. Red, white, and bluetiful."

Asia looked up at him. "Bluetiful? That not a word. Even I know that, stupid."

Mal gently pulled her back. "It makes sense. The Lancaster crime family has been around longer than any of the others I've learned about, but they have been by far the most discreet. I don't think any of us would have figured out a thing without the Black Slate."

"Well, they are growing in power now. Just like The Many did in Europe. We have feasts when nations lose their faith."

Smoke didn't vocalize his agreement, but he did agree. Now, he had to put some trust in this man. Or did he?

"How are we supposed to know when they are in there?" Smoke asked.

"That can be tricky. Oft times they either take the chopper or that small yacht at the docks. The Drake has plenty of locations that they just drop in on. Industrial yards and such. It makes it hard to tell when they come and go. It's complicated, but for the most part he conducts his business affairs from this home and doesn't go to any of his many offices. He doesn't have to. He has plenty of minions running his operations for him."

"What makes you so certain Sid is in there?" Smoke said.

"My brother keeps his pets close."

"She's no one's pet."

"If you say so."

Coming alongside Smoke, Guppy said, "What's the plan?"

"Extraction," Smoke said. "Vormus, what should we expect in there?"

"Plenty of pea coats and deaders. Some other things that creep and crawl. Some shifters are always part of the backup guard. But you can take some comfort in knowing that if it doesn't have a body, it isn't security." Vormus eyed Smoke. "My brother is old school. He doesn't believe there is anything his fiends can't handle. Besides, no one has ever stormed his castle."

"It's time someone did." Smoke weighed his options. He'd been on plenty of missions with the SEALS, had brought plenty of people to safety. He and his friends were well equipped. They'd recon their targets and make their move. Getting himself over there wouldn't be a problem. Getting Sid out would be. They'd need a quick way to escape. Either the chopper or the boat. Maybe. One or the other would have to do. "Let's do it."

"Wait, what? Now?" Sam was aghast. "You don't even have a plan."

"Yes I do."

"And what are we supposed to do?" Sam said.

"Find a fast boat and have it ready. Mal, I need everything you have. Guppy, get your sniper rifle ready. I'll be bringing Sid back this way, unless I can take off in the chopper. That's plan 1. Plan 2 is a boat."

"And plan three?" Sam asked.

"We walk on water." Smoke followed Mal off the bank and they headed back to the SUV that they all, including Vormus, had ridden there in. "Is the sweetheart suit waterproof?"

"You know it is." Mal popped open the lift gate to the big car. There were steel cases inside. "You know, I'm still a little low on supplies, even with the crowdfunding. Just make sure you get her back. Use every bit of it, even though it's all I have left."

Smoke stuffed green-tipped, blue-tipped, and red-tipped bullets into magazines then loaded them into waterproof bags. "You have any new toys I can use?"

Mal strapped a plastic band over Smoke's wrist. "It's a step and calorie counter. Like those Fitbits, but watertight."

"Gee, thanks."

"Here, take these." Mal handed him a pair of big black plastic capsules.

"What's this?"

"Super vitamins in a waterproof, flame-resistant shell. You have to crack them open. And don't abuse them. I mean, you'll probably need them, but they are in short supply."

Vormus approached. "Are we ready yet?" He showed his sharp teeth. "I'm feeling very eager, almost alive again, knowing vengeance is at hand."

Smoke stuffed the pills in the pack with the rest of his stuff, slung it over his shoulder, and headed for the shore. "Once day breaks, you guys get out of here if I'm not back. Run. Hide. I'm sure they'll be coming after you. Don't be a hero on my account. This is it."

Sam hugged him. "Be careful."

"I will." Smoke waded into the water and looked at Vormus. "You swimming, or can you fly?"

Vormus floated up over the water and started to drift across, smirking. "I'll see you on the other side."

CHAPTER 29

S MOKE DIDN'T HEAD STRAIGHT FOR the estate on the other side of the river. Instead, he swam downriver about a quarter mile, far off from the eyes of any sentries. Wearing only the sweetheart suit, he trudged out of the water. Dripping wet, he unzipped the waterproof pack, dressed, and geared up. He clamped on two shoulder holsters. Belted his knives on his waist and ankles. He added the special sunglasses for a final touch.

Facing him, the moonlit-eyed Vormus said, "It's so sad you have to rely on those trivial little tools. I don't have any issues like that at all."

Moving forward, Smoke said, "They're just back-up. My brain does most of the work."

Pushing through the greenery, Vormus said, "This is really beneath me. I never imagined I'd ever associate with the likes of you."

"What do you think this is, a Spiderman and Morbius team-up?"

"Who are they?"

Smoke kept going, weaving through the trees and brush until a twelve-foot-high stone wall was in sight. "I assume we can expect company from the courtyard within."

"It's just overkill for varmint control. Kane really hates it when the deer eat up his plants." Standing along the wall, he floated up in the air until he stood on top. Looking over the other side, he shrugged, turned, looked down at Smoke, and said, "Need a hand?"

Smoke leapt six feet up, caught the wall's lip with his strong fingers, and hauled himself up. He hopped down on the other side and made a soft landing. The Lancasters had acres of courtyard, exquisite gardens, and greenery. The estate was more castle than house, built with heavy cut stone. Its ominous presence was old and eerie. Vines crept up some of the walls. There were towers with spires at the top. Unlike most homes of the modern day, there wasn't any artificial lighting other than what looked to be gas-fed lanterns and lampposts in the gardens and on the exterior walls. It was a mix of old America and the flair of Europe.

Talking low, Smoke said, "No technology, huh?"

"I'm certain of it. My brother is a firm believer in the theory that life is just as fine with technology or without it. It really doesn't make a difference either way for our kind. The mortal kind, however, depends too much on it."

"True enough." Staying low, Smoke was slinking toward the house when Vormus's voice brought him to a stop.

"There could be traps, you know."

"If you find one, let me know." On light feet, Smoke went to the tall hedge and made his way along it, peeking through the leaves.

Vormus stayed on his heels. He came to a stop.

Somewhere on the grounds, a soft rustle disturbed the plants. Someone was coming. A pair of men. The breeze from the river revealed the smell of cigarettes on their clothes.

Smoke glanced back at Vormus and held up two fingers.

The white-haired shifter nodded.

Around the edge of the bushes the guards came. Assault rifles were shouldered over their pea coats. As soon as the men crossed their path, Smoke and Vormus attacked from the shadows. Smoke locked up one man by the neck and choked him until he passed out.

Vormus broke the neck of the other.

Snap.

Dragging the unconscious body into the bushes, Smoke said to Vormus, "You're going to kill them all, aren't you."

"Why not? They're just people." Vormus tossed the dead body over the wall.

Smoke shook his head. Killing monsters was one thing. Killing men was another. Plenty of the guards were mercenaries, men with wives and children. A lot of times, men made bad decisions and put themselves on the road to Hell with good intentions. He'd had plenty of friends like that. Any of these men could have been one of them. Of course, chances were they were rotten to the core anyway, but he wouldn't do what he had to do until that time came.

"Try not to overdo it."

Vormus shrugged.

Smoke ventured deeper toward the house. The closer he got, the better vantage point he had of everything else. In the moonlight, he could see the boat dock through the trees, along with a helicopter pad in the next courtyard, with a black chopper sitting on it. He could see the glow of a cigarette coming from one man standing guard. There was a silhouette of another one inside there too.

Facing Vormus a scant thirty feet from the house, he said, "What do you think is going on inside?"

"At this hour? Oh, you probably don't want me to answer that."

"Humor me."

Lifting his brows, Vormus said, "Oh, after another dreary night by the warm fire and plenty of exquisite centuries-old wine, I'd say they are sleeping. One on top of the other. Snuggled up like, as you Americans say, swine in a blanket."

Smoke didn't want to think about it. It had been a while, and time could change people. He just had to hope Sid was still the strong woman he had known. He had to believe that. He couldn't let Vormus's musings distract him. "Any idea where that bedroom might be?"

"Top level, just below that tower under the moon. I can take a peek if you like." Vormus's smile showed a shine in his fangs. "That way you won't have to be exposed to anything unpleasantly raunchy. Shifters' erotic appetites are quite … ravishing."

"Just get on with it."

Eyeing the room above, Vormus said, "Eh …"

"What?" Smoke said.

Shaking his head, Vormus said, "Nothing. I'll take care of this. You, I suggest, should stay put. I won't be but a moment." He sprung straight up into the air and floated through the night sky right toward the third-story window and made a soft landing on the balcony.

I don't like this.

Smoke could observe Vormus's progress. The vampiric shifter was hopping from one balcony to another, inspecting the inside of the house through window after window. He made his way onto the largest balcony that faced the river. A pair of double doors led onto it. Vormus opened one of the doors up and vanished into the darkness inside.

Figures.

Everything around Smoke seemed to stop except his heart pounding in his ears. He didn't trust Vormus. On the one hand, the shifter might be taking this opportunity to exact vengeance. On the other, he might be setting Smoke up. He had to assume the latter, and he wasn't going to sit around waiting for things to happen. If he had to go inside on his own, guns blazing, he would.

He'd give Vormus five minutes. Then it would be time to launch.

Three minutes into his wait, he rested his hand on his gun. Vormus still hadn't appeared. So far as Smoke could tell, nothing in the house was moving. It was like he was staring at a haunted mansion, the way the breeze whistled through the gutters.

A chill went down his spine. Something flapped above him in the sky.

Smoke glanced up.

A gargoyle dropped out of the sky and clamped its claws around his throat.

CHAPTER 30

FIGHTING FOR HIS LIFE, SMOKE grabbed the stony horned devil by its wing, trying to rip it off. One hundred pounds of stone dug in. With all of his strength, Smoke wrenched its wing off. He slammed it into the ground, busting its small hulk of a body into the stones. He grabbed hold of one of its taloned hands and bent it back until it cracked off. He dashed its face into the cobblestones again and again until it had all turned to dust.

Gasping, Smoke wiped the blood from his neck. He popped up from behind the hedge and checked the balcony again. Vormus was back outside. He was waving Smoke up. Scanning the area and seeing the coast was clear, Smoke dashed toward the house. His fingers dug into the rough stones and his feet pushed off the window sills. With the ease of an ape, he climbed his way to the top and pulled up onto one of the smaller balconies. With the stealth of a cat, he hopped from one balcony to the other, finishing up alongside Vormus.

Keeping his voice low, Vormus said, "Today might be your lucky day. No one is inside any of these windows."

"Then where are they?"

"It's a big mansion. I figure we should start at the top."

Below them at ground level, the main door opened and closed. Smoke hunkered down. Vormus pressed back into the shadows along the wall. Three men walked out. One of them was huge, over eight feet tall and built like a lumberjack. Smoke didn't know the other two, but each was exquisitely dressed. They were heading toward the chopper.

"I'll be. My dear brother is departing. Fortune favors you this night, Mister Smoke." Vormus squatted alongside him. "The man on the left, in the tuxedo, with that purposed and arrogant gait, that's Kane."

Smoke nodded. The man had a powerful build and formidable looks. He moved with the strange ease of a jungle cat. All three men entered the chopper. The engines whined. The propellers spun, and up it went into the night sky.

"I suggest we get right to the task of rescuing your lady, though this wasn't what I wanted." Vormus started toward the balcony doors with a vengeance in his eyes. "I want him dead. But I suppose I can help you find your friend. That will hurt him too, whether my efforts fail or not."

The first bedroom was lavish. A huge carriage bed big enough for a horse was the centerpiece. Two lit candles stood on the nightstands. The mansion had an old smell about it. Otherwise, the early American furnishings were in fine shape and worth nothing less than a fortune. There weren't any signs of technology. Not even a phone.

Smoke put his ear to the bedroom door. He pushed the brass handle down, pulled the door open, and stuck his head out. A long hallway went both ways. Fine trim and crown molding the caliber of craft one didn't see anymore. Wainscoting on the bottom, wallpaper on the top that ran from door to door. Handwoven rugs covered most of the hardwood hallway.

As the two of them stepped out into the hall, the floor creaked. Vormus pushed in behind him. The door right across the hall creaked, stopped, and was flung open.

"Vormus!" said a woman. She was old, skin withered and spotted, wearing an old nightgown down to her ankles, and had a shaggy head of white hair. "What are you doing here?"

"Please keep your voice down, Mums. And you should be sleeping." He gently stroked her cheek with his hand. "Go back inside and rest."

"Are you two related?" Smoke said.

"Mums is one of Vormus's most trusted housekeepers. Doesn't she do well keeping up this place?"

Smoke nodded, gave a little smile, and said, "That's an understatement."

She eyed Smoke. "Who are you? I haven't seen you here before. A new guard?"

"Of course he is." Vormus started pushing her back into her bedroom. "Why don't you go rest, Mums. Are you hungry? Maybe something from the kitchen. Milk? I know sometimes your ulcers flare up. After all, you are human."

She gazed up at Vormus. "I thought Kane was mad at you. Does he know you're here?"

"Of course he does," Vormus said with a smile. "We are working out our relationship. You know it's complicated."

"But he left," she said, scratching her head. "He told me so. I heard the whirly-bird." She shook her finger at Vormus. "You aren't supposed to be here. You're a liar!" She took in a lungful of air and prepared to scream.

Vormus clamped his hand over her mouth and twisted her neck. *Snap!* He dragged her into her room, closed the door, and looked at Smoke. "I had to. She might be old, but she screams like a banshee."

"She could have told us where Sid was!"

"Could have. Should have. Sorry, that's not part of her capabilities anymore. Oh, but my brother is going to hate to see her dead. He really adored her. Our real mother perished long, long ago."

"I don't care." Smoke sauntered up to the next nearest door, tested the handle, and pushed it open. That room was empty. Vormus did the same.

Room by room, they cleared the top level and didn't find a sign of anyone. The mansion was a cold dead place. Lifeless. Without energy. Yet every room was lit with candles and free of dust or cobwebs, and every bed was freshly made with the finest linens.

At the last door before the stairs went down, Smoke heard footsteps coming up. He ducked into one room and Vormus another. Smoke kept his door cracked open.

Two guards in pea coats came up the steps carrying assault rifles. Chatting among themselves, they started to pass.

"Hold on a sec," one said to the other. He stepped backward in front of Smoke's door. Stared at the crack. Started to push it open.

Smoke crouched in the dim light beside a wardrobe.

The guard stepped within and peered around. His squinting gaze found Smoke, who hit the guard hard in the chin and knocked him to the floor.

The second guard rushed inside.

Vormus jumped on the man's back and lowered his mouth toward the man's throat.

"No!" Smoke said.

It didn't matter. The man was dead.

Not at all mussed, Vormus took a knee by the body. "Did you say something?"

"Quit killing them. We could get some information out of them."

"I'm not holding back." Vormus looked at the man Smoke had knocked out. "What are you going to do when he wakes up? He'll be nothing but trouble, a loose end. Take one of those shiny knives and kill him. I know you have it in you."

"I'll take my chances." Smoke gestured out the door. "After you."

CHAPTER 31

VORMUS DROPPED A MAN'S CORPSE to the floor and flung the blood off his fingers onto the wall. He'd killed four more people on the second story and ripped the last man's throat out. "Sorry, sometimes my anger gets the better of me."

Smoke had a sentry in a choke hold and said in his ear, "Where's the woman named Sidney?"

The guard was a mule of a man, strong and stubborn. He shook his head.

Vormus squatted down and poked the man in the face with his bloody finger. "Tell the man what he wants to know. Your fate is in far better shape with him than it would be with me."

The man spat on Vormus.

Vormus grabbed the man's arm and bit down.

"Quit it, you devil!" Smoke said. "You act like a dog."

Vormus released the man, stood up, and wiped the spittle from his face. "The mortal will not live to see the day. My patience thins with you, Smoke. Sneaking around. It is not my way. I will have my vengeance!"

Smoke put the man to sleep. They weren't getting anywhere, and so far, Sid was nowhere to be found. His gut said Kane Lancaster would be back soon. Darkness wouldn't last a whole lot longer, and Vormus was getting really agitating. Smoke took out both of his semi-automatic pistols. "Let's get on with it."

They took the grand staircase down into a huge foyer. Gas lanterns glowed, giving off a yellowish illumination. There were murals on the walls. Vases and busts on pedestals. It seemed more like a museum than a home. Smoke led the way from room to room. Dining rooms, living rooms, all with stone cold fireplaces. The kitchen was huge but lifeless, except where a double-doored modern refrigerator hummed in the corner. Smoke pulled open one of the doors. There wasn't much to eat. The pantries had little, either.

Peeking from behind Smoke's shoulder, Vormus said, "He doesn't eat that much. Mums usually prepared the food, but her food wasn't the best. Bland."

Smoke could understand Kane not eating, but what about Sid? There wasn't any reason to believe she was here. If she wasn't here, where *was* she?

"I have to admit, I'm just as surprised as you are." Vormus opened and closed some cabinet doors. "It doesn't make much sense that she isn't residing in one of the bedrooms. It's disappointing actually. As I understand it, she is with him wherever he goes."

"Who told you that?"

"I've been privy to his musings for quite some time." Vormus turned on the kitchen faucet and ran some water over his hands, then dried them off on his clothes. "I hate him so."

"Maybe she's on the yacht."

Vormus shrugged. "Hmmm … possible. Of course, there is another place, though I find it unlikely."

"What place?"

"The dungeon."

"You're holding out on me." Smoke pointed the pistol at Vormus's head. "These bullets aren't made of lead. One shot will turn your chest into a sink hole."

Hands up, Vormus said, "Only the worst of the worst get put down there. It's unlikely she's in there at all. I don't have any objection to checking it out."

"Lead the way."

Smoke followed Vormus into the foyer. Under the grand staircase was a heavy oak door with an arch in the top. The vampire-shifter grabbed the iron handle and pulled it open. A stale breeze of cool musty air wafted out. "After you," Smoke said.

A stone spiral staircase led them down into an area that for all intents and purposes looked like a dungeon. Small gas lanterns lit the grey slab walls. There were open alcoves with wine racks and whiskey barrels in them.

Vormus plucked out a wine bottle and inspected the label. "Shifters drink a lot."

Smoke wandered through the dungeon corridor. There were heavy iron doors, some open, some closed. Alcoves protected by steel bars. Straw beds covered in filth. There were bodies too. Decayed and crumbled. Some shackled. Others mangled. Staring at one of the bodies, Smoke's nose started to run. He sniffed.

"Disappointing." Vormus kicked at a pile of bones. "Usually there are a few folks down here pleading for mercy. More often than not, this is where my brother keeps those who disappoint him. It seems his troops are keeping good order these days. Come on, there is more to this place."

Smoke counted more than a dozen cells and alcoves. Just as many bodies. He followed Vormus even deeper into the den, stopping inside a chamber filled with archaic torture devices. Blood stained the floors, tables, and walls. Covering his nose, Smoke said, "Looks like Uncle Fester's basement."

"You have an uncle with a basement like this?" Vormus asked with surprise.

"No."

"Then who is—"

Smoke moved on, taking the lead this time. He wasn't sure if Vormus was trying to rattle him or not, but he didn't have all day to try and track down Sid. He needed a sliver of her whereabouts now, because soon they would have to leave. He could feel it in his bones. He came across a corridor that he hadn't seen yet. It led straight back to another door, and it didn't have any cell doors or windows on either side. Taking it slow, he approached and came to a stop ten feet away. A stone gargoyle four feet tall squatted on either side of the door. The eyes of the statues were closed. Smoke pointed a gun at each one's head and said to Vormus, "What's in there?"

"I can't say, but I do know this. No one gets in there without Kane." Vormus came alongside him and spoke in his ear. "Certainly there is something important in there. I don't think there is anything more important to him than your sweetheart right now. Come to think of it, maybe that is what he does. Locks her up in here while he's gone. The gargoyles would… secure her."

Smoke considered Vormus's thoughts. The vampire's words were powerfully suggestive. What he said made perfect sense. Kane would stop at nothing to prevent Sid from escaping. Smoke had come this far. He couldn't just leave now, not knowing. It would eat him alive. He might not get a better chance than this. Whether or not Sid was on the other side of that door, he had to find out. He eased forward.

"I wouldn't go any farther if I were you," Vormus said. "I can't help you from this point on."

"You haven't been helping me anyway." Smoke went forward.

"Those gargoyles will shred you—and even me—to pieces."

"We'll see." Smoke kept going.

The gargoyles' eyes snapped open.

CHAPTER 32

SMOKE SQUEEZED OFF TWO SHOTS.

Blam! Blam!

The blue-tipped bullets ripped right through the gargoyles' chests. The demon-faced winged monsters kept coming.

"I don't think those bullets are going to work," Vormus said.

"Criminy!" Smoke aimed at their skulls.

Blam! Blam!

The blue-tipped bullets punched clear clean holes through the advancing gargoyles' skulls.

"They don't have brains," Vormus said.

Smoke's instincts told him to run, but he wasn't going anywhere. He had to know if Sid was behind that door. He kept shooting.

"You fool! You'll get yourself killed!"

The bullets blasted through bits and pieces of the gargoyles. Stone flesh plastered the walls with dusty gargoyle guts. These weren't like the smaller one he'd fought before that had turned into powder with one shot. These were vibrant and living. Powerful and quick.

Like apes, they overpowered Smoke in a violent attack. One gargoyle caught him in a bear hug from behind and squeezed him like a huge stone vice, trying to make Smoke drop his pistols. In front of him, the second gargoyle's clawed hands tried to rip out his throat.

Smoke pulled his knees up and launched a kick into the attacking gargoyle's chest, slamming it back into the wall. It came at him again, a stone cold automaton with death in its black eyes. Smoke managed to squeeze off two shots and blow one of its hands into pieces, but the relentless gargoyle's other hand clamped around his neck and started to crush his windpipe.

He jammed his pistol in the gargoyle's ribs and kept firing off shot after shot. Bullets tore through the monster and into the ceiling. Smoke kept squeezing the trigger.

Blue-tip. Blue-tip. Blue-tip. Blue-tip. Blue-tip. Blue-tip. Blue-tip. Brace yourself, Smoke.

He fired again.

Red-tip!

The bullet entered the stone gargoyle. Smoke squeezed his eyes shut and hit the floor.

Boom!

The entire tunnel shook. The gargoyle turned to chunks of debris and dust. Smoke was lying on the floor with his head pounding and ears ringing. The last gargoyle still had him locked up. Smoke couldn't get a good angle to get a shot off. He climbed up on his knees, got his feet under him, and thrust himself backward into the wall, ramming the gargoyle into the wall again and again as hard as he could.

Its grip didn't loosen. It tightened.

Smoke's lungs burned like fire. His busted ribs that had healed up were sore again. Feeling himself start to black out, he summoned his reserves. With a growling scream, he rushed toward the wall, lowering his head at the last moment, and sandwiching the gargoyle between him and the wall at full force, with jarring impact.

The gargoyle's grip loosened.

Smoke scurried away.

The gargoyle lashed out, grabbed Smoke by the ankle, and pulled him in. The monster opened up its mouth and chomped its fangs.

Smoke stuffed the gun's barrel down its throat. "Enjoy your meal." He squeezed the trigger.

Boom!

Covered in dust and concrete gargoyle guts, Smoke swayed up to his feet. Wiping the dust from his eyes, he surveyed his surroundings. Vormus was nowhere to be seen. Smoke turned and faced the door. A huge deadbolt sealed it shut.

If anything moves on the other side that isn't Sid, I'm killing it.

Pistol ready in one hand and holstering the other, he pulled the heavy deadbolt back with a grunt. The door shoved inward. Sid sat on the bed of a finely decorated and well-lit room with stony walls. Her dark eyes were expressionless. Her athletic form had thinned. Her chin hung a little. "Smoke?"

"Who else would make a midnight house call in a place like this?"

"I-I thought it was you, but I just can't believe it." She pushed off the bed, staring into his face. "You shouldn't have done this. You didn't have to."

"Yes I did." He holstered his other pistol. Deep in Sid's eyes something wasn't right. He could sense her worry, fear, and anxiety. She'd been held captive for a long time. Given everything she wanted, but threatened constantly at the same time. Smoke loved her. He'd do anything for her.

But he wasn't a fool. He sensed Stockholm Syndrome in her, and he knew that snapping her out of it wouldn't be easy. He extended his hand. "You can be free of here, Sid. Once and for all. I need you."

Her gaze drifted away. "I don't know. It's dangerous. The others..." She found his eyes with hers. "I need to get dressed."

She was wearing a long maroon nightgown and looking as radiant as ever. She made her way over to a chest of drawers and pulled it open. She slid a pair of jeans on, grabbed a knit shirt, and with her back to him, dropped the gown and slipped the shirt on. But then she slowly slouched, turned her head, and looked back at him. "I can't go."

Throat tightening, he said, "Why?"

"I don't have any shoes."

"I see some under the bed."

"Oh." Listlessly, she sat on the bed, picked the shoes up one by one, and put them on. And then she sat there, staring at him with a blank expression on her face.

Smoke noticed a bottle of wine on the nightstand and an empty glass that she had been drinking from.

She might be drugged.

"We've got to go, Sid."

"Okay."

Smoke approached, reached out, and touched her hand. He rubbed her palm with his thumb.

Her head snapped up, and she looked right in his eyes. "John, John." Tears flowed down her cheeks. She wrapped her arms around him and squeezed him tight. Her body shuddered with heavy sobs. "John, John."

He held her fast. The warmth of her body sent fire through his veins. "I'm here, Sid. I'm always here."

She beat him on his back. "I can't believe it's you. I thought I'd never see you again. I really did. I knew Kane wouldn't allow it. Ever. He's a monster, John. He wants to turn me into one of them. I've been down here since I told him no."

"They didn't break you, Sid. You held on." He caressed her face in his palms. "That's all that matters. I'm here now."

"I'm starving," she said.

"What are you hungry for?"

A spark showed in her eyes. "At least a hundred pancakes."

"I know a great place."

Strength returned to her voice. "Then what are we waiting for." She pulled the gun from his holster and fired.

Smoke turned around just as a deader collapsed on the floor. Nodding his head, he said, "That's my girl."

Looking at the gun, she said, "That felt good, and who are you calling 'girl'?"

The tunnel was crammed full of three wandering deaders armed with hatchets and knives.

Smoke eased in front of Sid. "Stay behind me."

"I can handle myself. Believe me, I've got a lot to let out."

"I know," he said, putting himself between her and the oncoming deaders, "but I don't want to see a scratch on that great body of yours."

She fired again, dropping another deader. "Don't you think action's sexy?"

"True, just don't lose any limbs. You're going to need them all."

"For what?"

"Our wedding night."

CHAPTER 33

K NIVES IN HAND, SMOKE SURGED forward. "You only have a few blue-tips left in that clip. The last three are explosive. I'm down to one last shot." He waded into the throng of deaders, dodging lazy chops and running his blades into their hearts.

A deader dove on his legs and drove him into a wall. Another one plowed into his body. The third brought a hatchet down at his head.

Blam!

Sid's bullet ripped through the attacker's side, dropping it truly dead on the floor.

Smoke punched knife holes in the other two, sending them to more permanent deaths. Racing forward, they were back in the dungeon. Three skeletons from the nearest cell were reanimated. Two lunged for Smoke, and the other was swinging chains at them. Smoke slipped between the bony fingers stretching for his neck and drove a knife into one skeleton's chest. Its jaw clattered like strange laughter, but it kept on fighting.

"Great."

Sid opened fire on the chain-swinging skeleton, which wore rotting buckskin for clothes. Just when the chains looked like they might reach the two of them and do some heavy damage, the skeleton blew apart into shards of bone and the chains dropped harmlessly to the cold stone floor.

"Guess that's it for the blue-tips."

Frustrated, Smoke put away his knives, grabbed the skeleton that was trying to claw him to death, wrenched the arm free, and busted the skeleton in the head with it.

Whack! Whack! Whack!

He got ahold of both remaining skeletons and rammed them into the wall. Their bodies shattered and collapsed on the floor. One's jaw was still moving. Smoke kicked it down the hall. "Shut up."

Another knot of deaders and skeletons came right at them. Sid unloaded two well-placed shots in the bodies of the deaders.

Smoke covered his ears.

Boom! Boom!

The deaders exploded. The concussive force blew the skeletons too.

"I think that's all of them," he said.

A little dazed, she shook her head. "Too bad. That was feeling good. I just wish Kane was in the sights of my pistol."

"We'll get him. Come on." Smoke pushed through the dust and debris and headed up the twisting stairs.

Exiting the door under the stairs into the foyer, they were both greeted with an echoing round of applause. Kane and Vormus were standing in the foyer doing all the clapping. Smoke and Sid froze in their tracks.

"My, look what we have here, a brave and noble rescue attempt." Kane eyed Smoke. "We had an agreement, Mister Smoke. Did we not?"

"Screw your agreement!" Sid fired her pistol at Kane.

Click! Click! Click!

"What's the matter, no more bullets, my little muse?" Kane said.

Smoke drew his gun on Kane. "I still have some."

Kane stepped forward. "By all means, Mister Smoke, shoot me."

Ka-Blam!

The bullet whizzed straight through Kane and blew up the main doors behind him. Kane was fine. The red-tip had passed through him like he was a ghost.

"My, you are an expensive enemy, Mister Smoke. Those doors cost me a fortune to have manufactured." He sighed. "Well, I'm sure it's just another tax deduction, kind of like the loss I incurred at the Red Mark Materials salvage yard. I'm rethinking taking your skin for that."

Smoke took out a knife and tossed it across the floor. "Come and get it."

Vormus and Kane laughed. They were joined by some men in pea coats and the giant of a man who wasn't one of the two Smoke had seen last time. There were some deaders too, but they weren't laughing. They stood stiff and silent, eyes gleaming with the will to strike.

"So it was all just a game, huh?" Smoke said.

"The classic double-cross," Vormus replied. "And you fell for it."

"I had my suspicions, but it was a convincing act, seeing how you killed so many of his people."

"Well, as I said, they are just people. More than seven billion to choose from. So easily bought, and it's so wonderful to stage these things." Vormus held his finger up. "But it wasn't entirely meant to be so. At first, I did have vengeance against my brother in mind. We talked. He convinced me otherwise, but I did owe him, so I agreed to set up this little game. It's been delightful. Search them."

Two pea coats patted them over and stripped Smoke and Sid of all their weapons, leaving them both destitute of an assault opportunity.

"Oh, the games we play with these mortals. Isn't it delightful?" Kane said to Vormus.

"I'd almost forgotten how much fun it was."

"It was a shame you had to kill Mums, though."

"Eh," Vormus said with a shrug, "she was quite old and a bit senile. I'd be happy to gift you another whimsical old person if you like. There are plenty of willing subjects in those nursing homes."

"Oh, no need. Perhaps Sidney can be that whimsical old dame a few generations from now. Of course, I think she'll turn before then. After all, the last hope she had on this earth is about to die before her eyes." Kane turned to the giant of a man wearing a heavy-duty grey jumpsuit. "Fetch the swords."

Through gritted teeth, Sid said, "I'll die first."

"Oh no, you won't," Kane said. "I won't let you. You see John, it is true that you have been duped. I had my brother come and rattle your cage, but probably not for the reasons you suspect. No, I think Sid's faith in you is what is holding her back from turning over to me."

"No, it's not that," Smoke said.

"Oh, he's humble. Humble and rugged. How charming." Kane slapped his brother on the shoulder. "Why can't we be more like that?"

"It's hard to be humble when you rule everything."

"True enough. True enough." Kane stroked his moustache. "Though—and you might find this hard to believe—I was humble once. Back when I was a child, I begged for food. I told people everything they wanted to hear. 'You are pretty. Handsome.' I shined shoes. Threw out the bath water. I did every imaginable menial chore. And what did it earn me? Coppers and whippings. Coppers and whippings." He snorted the air. "Hah! What a grand character builder! It made me who I am today."

"It's a shame," Sid said.

"What's a shame," Kane replied, "that they didn't love me? Care for me better?"

"No, it sounds like they didn't beat you hard enough, you evil bastard."

Kane huffed.

The giant of a man returned, carrying a large wooden case in his arms. He held it in front of Kane.

The leader of the shifters unlatched the case and produced two magnificent swords. He held them up on display. "Mister Smoke, I challenge you to a duel."

CHAPTER 34

"**I** ACCEPT," SMOKE SAID, EYEING THE swords. They weren't the typical fare one would expect for a duel. These weren't lightweight fencing foils, but rather heavy Arabian scimitars—wicked curved blades. Black handled and steel trimmed, the heavy blades could easily cut off a man's head. "On one condition."

"And what condition would *that* be?" Kane said.

"Even if I lose, you let Sid go free."

"Oh sure, why not. You'll be dead anyway."

Sid squeezed Smoke's arm. "John, no. You can't do this. You saw what he did."

"I know." Smoke didn't understand if Kane was a ghost or what, but he'd seen a bullet pass right through him. It seemed the most powerful shifters had an assortment of special powers. Vormus could fly, hypnotize, and maybe even turn invisible. It made Smoke leery of what else Kane could do. He leaned in toward Sid for a kiss. "This might be farewell."

"Now?" She glanced at all the staring people. "You're kissing me *now*?"

"Oh, go ahead and kiss him," Vormus said with delight. "You Americans are so over the top about things. You act like everything you do will be in a movie. Yes, kiss her, and then tell her, 'Frankly my dear, I don't give a damn!'"

Everyone that could laugh did laugh. Even Sid and Smoke.

In a low voice, Smoke said, "Just kiss me."

"I'd rather not."

He pleaded, "Please."

She moved in closer to him. "Okay."

He put his arm around her waist, brought her in close, and barely whispered in her ear, "They work quick. You'll have to chew it."

"What?"

He kissed her. It was a deep kiss. A probing kiss. An—

"Awkward," Vormus said. "My, it looks like he's tickling her tonsils. Grotesque."

Laughter started again.

Smoke broke off the kiss.

Panting for breath, Sid made a sour face and whispered beneath the clamor of the crowd, "You just regurgitated a super vitamin into my mouth, didn't you."

"Yup."

"You're so gross."

"I know."

"If both of you have finished turning everyone's stomachs," Kane said, banging the swords together, "I'd like to get the slaughter started. Vormus, do you have the film rolling?"

"It's not film." Vormus pointed at the man on the balcony, who held a camcorder to his eye. "It's digital technology. Honestly, people really need to stop saying the word 'film.' There's no film anymore."

"Film or digital, it doesn't make a difference to me. I just want to give our allies a show." Kane tossed a sword over to Smoke, who snatched it out of the air. "I'm even going to let you keep your little scuba suit on. It will not increase your chances of survival, but you might last seconds longer. Vormus, secure Sidney. And Sidney, try to keep down to a minimum decibel level any screaming that might be brought forth. We get a horrible echo in here that makes things so awfully loud. I don't want to mess up the sound quality of the picture."

Vormus secured Sid in his arms and showed Smoke a teasing look with his fangs.

Smoke tested the heft of his sword and thumbed its edge. The blade was razor-sharp, but it would tire his arm quickly. It was made for a far bigger man than him, and he could get both hands on the handle. He glanced up at the man with the camera for a moment. He'd almost forgotten that the shifters had a zeal for recording their atrocities. Swift Venison the Were-Rat had been caught doing it. Smoke assumed the films went to other shifters, straight to the top, to someone like Kane.

Perhaps he's not at the top of the food chain after all. Great Dane, then who is?

Kane snapped his fingers. "Before we get started, I need to test my steel, so as to make sure it is in good order." He pointed at one of the pea coat guards. "You, front and center. Take off your coat and turn your back to me."

The man did as he was commanded. Sweat erupted on his brow. A pleading look came to life in his eyes.

Behind the guard, Kane said, "Hold your arms up over your head. Ah, that's good. Steady. Steady now." He gripped the sword with two hands, cocked back, and swung.

Slice!

Sid gasped.

Kane had cut the man clean in half. Blood spurted all over the floor.

"Now that's sharp. Very sharp. Oh, what a mess you people make when you die. Perhaps I should have chosen a deader. Try not to slip, John Smoke. Now, everybody back up. Give us some room—and move this corpse aside."

Smoke's eyes met Sid's. He could see the concern in hers. Kane was a killer who wanted to break Sid's spirit. Humiliating Smoke by slaughtering him in battle just might do it. He gave Sid a reassuring nod.

Shifting his shoulders, Kane said, "Let's get ready to rumble, eh?"

Two-handed, Smoke brought his sword to his chest. He made a couple of hard chops in the air, flipped it around, and finished off by spinning it back behind his waist and returning it to his front. A score from *Basil Ponderous* played in his mind.

"My, how fancy." Kane raised his sword over his head and pointed the blade at Smoke. "On with it, then." He charged.

Smoke rushed forward.

Steel clashed against steel.

Kane's powerful blow ripped Smoke's sword out of his grip. It clattered across the bloodstained floor. Kane laughed.

CHAPTER 35

"**M**ISTER SMOKE, YOU SEEM TO have dropped your sword. Now that's going to make for some lousy entertainment," Kane said. "We can't have a sword fight without at least two swords."

Smoke lunged at Kane and passed right through him. He spun back around and caught Kane's foot in his ribs. He locked up the shifter's leg in his hands and tried to tug him down, only to lose his grip as the man turned back into an apparition and backed away.

"Come now, if I wanted to wrestle you I would. But I want to sword fight, so pick up your sword and fight." Kane nodded to the sword. "Come on now. Let's get on with it."

Keeping his eyes on Kane, Smoke walked over and picked up the sword. "Alright. Let's get on with it then."

Kane attacked.

Smoke parried.

Clang!

The shifter was fast. He sliced, jabbed, stabbed, and cut.

Smoke parried, parried, parried. The sound of finely hewn steel echoed throughout the chamber. On the defensive, Smoke fought for his life. Kane was an imposing man—about his size but enhanced with supernatural powers. Smoke couldn't even get an attack in. He had to do something. Knocking Kane's blade aside, he counter-attacked.

Slice!

Kane's counter to his counter was quicker. The shifter's blade cut right through the sweetheart suit and drew blood from Smoke's thigh. Kane danced backward on his toes. "Oh, look at that. It seems I damaged your little suit. As they say, 'A sharp enough blade can cut through anything,' especially when a mighty hand wields it. You're going to need an excellent seamstress for that. I know a few. I know some fine morticians, too. They can sew up what remains of you."

The cut in Smoke's leg was bleeding bad. There wouldn't be any stopping the blood either. He needed to find Kane's weakness. Kane had to have one. Smoke had to fight on. He charged.

Kane stood there with his arms wide.

Smoke ran right through him.

Slice!

Kane's sword grazed Smoke's back.

Smoke spun around and let loose a furious assault.

Kane backpedaled. Parried. He caught every lightning-quick attack. A cunning fighter, he kept his eyes on Smoke's the whole time.

Every second felt like a minute. Smoke's lungs started to burn. His arms felt like lead.

Effortlessly, Kane banged his sword away.

Laboring with breath and soaked in sweat, Smoke backed away. He'd given Kane everything he had.

In a mocking manner, Kane spun his sword in front of him in a tight little circle. "Now that was exciting, wasn't it? Whoop! Whoop! Whoop! You are a marvelous fighter, but don't think you fool me. My brother tells me you like to play possum."

Smoke saw Vormus shrug at him. Sid was still tight in the vampire-shifter's grip. Time was running out. Smoke was losing blood. His strength was fading. "I'm not playing possum." Smoke's teeth clamped down on the super vitamin he'd been holding in his jaw, and he swallowed. "I'm going Gotham."

"Gotham?" Kane asked.

As soon as the vitamin went to Smoke's stomach, a charge went through him. New life coursed through his veins. A wildfire of energy filled his body. "As Buckshot Roberts likes to say, 'Let's dance.'"

"Who's Buckshot Roberts?"

As if on the wings of an eagle, Smoke glided in for an attack. The Arabian blade became a whirlwind of razor-sharp fury. Steel smote steel.

Aghast, Kane fought with desperation, parrying stroke after stroke but losing ground. "You *were* playing possum."

"No I wasn't." Smoke hammered Kane's sword down, only to see it pop up again to parry his next blow. "Well, yes I was."

Outraged, Kane countered and fought back. His supernatural strength matched Smoke's strike for strike. Rage filled his dark eyes, and he screamed, "I will have your head!"

A furious battle ensued. Back and forth they went, dueling it out with heavy swings. Smoke matched Kane's every move, further infuriating the monster on purpose, looking for the right time to make his move.

That time came. Kane's eyes lost their focus, the monster was so beside himself with rage.

Smoke sidestepped to counter a lunge Kane had tried before, and then smooth as silk, he pivoted on his foot, spun, and sliced right through Kane's shoulder.

"Arrgh!" the shifter yelled. He sprang back, eyes once again wary.

Smoke raised his chin. "So, you can't attack and be a ghost at the same time, can you."

"Touché, but it will make no difference. I can still wear you down. However, I tire of this game." Holding his bloodied shoulder, Kane tossed his sword to the floor and barked a command. "Kill him!"

Sid hip-tossed Vormus to the floor and kicked him in the head. Swift as a panther, she disarmed the nearest man of his assault rifle and started firing into the guards and deaders. Every shot hit its mark, dropping man after man and deader after deader like bowling pins.

She looked at Smoke. "What are you waiting for? Don't you want to live forever?"

Sword arcing high, Smoke flung himself into the surge of bodies. The Arabian sword bit flesh and bone. But that wasn't what he wanted. He wanted Kane. Vormus. Both had evacuated the scene. He punched a hole through a deader's chest, chopped into another's leg at the knee, filled his hands with his own assault rifle, and started firing off short bursts. Caught up in the heat of battle, he almost forgot the purpose of his mission.

This is an extraction, not an incursion.

"Sid! We need to make a break for it!"

She filled a deader's chest full of lead and then looked over Smoke's shoulder toward the gaping doorway. "Tell *him* that!"

Smoke glanced behind him.

Towering at eight feet tall and built like a mighty oak, a giant barred their path. He had a long chin, nose, and ears, and his eyes were black as coal. In his hands was an assault rifle. He snapped it in half and said in a cavernous voice, "Come. Come get some."

CHAPTER 36

G RABBING ANOTHER DEAD PEA COAT'S rifle, Sid said, "Did he really just say that?"

"That's what I heard," Smoke said.

"Thought so." She squeezed the trigger and unloaded into the giant's chest.

Budda-budda-budda-budda!

It started laughing. "Huh-huh-huh, pretty woman come. Come and die." Fast for a huge man, it lunged at Sid.

Smoke shot a short burst of rounds into its temple.

Not slowing one bit, it grabbed Sid around her waist and picked her up like a doll. "Come-come. Kiss-Kiss."

Abandoning his rifle, Smoke took up the Arabian sword and hacked into the monster man's elbow. The blade bit down to the bone.

The giant dropped Sid and howled. "Eeooowwww!"

Smoke chopped it in the knee.

"No no no!" the giant bellowed like a child. It swatted Smoke back against the wall. Its fingers stretched for Smoke's throat.

Sid came out of nowhere, sword in hand. She cut the giant's hand off at the wrist.

The giant looked at his severed hand with astonished wide eyes. "Come-come—"

Smoke made a hard swipe at the back of the giant's legs.

Hack!

Down the giant went.

Smoke remembered the giants from before in the city, Rexor and Thorgrim. He'd thought he had killed them before, but he'd seen later that they hadn't died. This one probably wouldn't either. "We need to go," Smoke said to Sid.

Staring at the giant with a wild look in her eyes, she said, "Maybe we need to cut his head off, like David did to Goliath."

"Come-Come. No-No!"

"Let's go," said Smoke. "The vitamins are fading, Sid."

She took his hand, and they raced out the front doors with their scimitars. "Where are we headed?"

"Dock." He'd felt the energy start to leave him, and that was bad. He was bleeding already from two nasty cuts, and there wouldn't be any time to patch them up. They needed to go, and go now, in case more reinforcements arrived. The chopper caught his ear. The engines whirred with life, and the blades had started spinning. "Looks like Kane's leaving your farewell party early. We can't let that happen now, can we?"

"Let him go, Smoke. Come on, let's go."

The chopper took off.

"He's already gotten away."

"No he hasn't." Smoke started regurgitating. He spat a red-tipped bullet out into his hand, loaded it into a clip, shoved it in the gun, and took aim. He paused, looked at Sid, and tossed her the gun. "Let 'em have it, baby!"

Sid took aim and squeezed the trigger.

The entire chopper exploded. Chunks of metal and propeller blades whizzed overhead. The chopper bounced off the ground. Metal grinded on stone, made a twisted groaning sound, and went still. Only a huge ball of flame remained.

"Nice shot," Smoke said, "but I'm not calling the fire department. Let's go."

He took a few steps forward. His knees buckled, and he dropped his scimitar.

Sid swept under his arm and gave him support. "I've got you, John."

Exhausted and bleeding, the pair stumbled toward the dock, where the river wind cooled Smoke's aching limbs.

"It's been one heckuva night, hasn't it?"

"You've never failed to show me a good time, John. Why would tonight be any different?"

"Never a dull moment, huh?"

"Not so far." She smiled, and they kissed again, more briefly this time.

They were on the lawn close to the dock where the yacht was moored. There weren't any signs of Sam or Guppy, just the yacht. Stark and sleek in the night, it promised all the frivolities of the uber rich.

"You ever been on a cruise?"

"No. Why, you going to take me on one?"

"Yeah. That one."

"It's a pretty big boat. Can you drive it?"

Feeling woozy and sick to his stomach, he replied, "I can drive anything."

He heard something behind them and wheeled him and Sid around.

With a machine gun in hand, Kane was marching straight for them through the trees. "Don't even think about it, you fools!"

Both of them were supporting each other now. Sid sagged at his side. He did his best to hold her up, but he was losing the battle.

"Sid, you're out of juice too, aren't you."

"Yes."

"What's the matter, you two?" Kane said with a sneer. His clothes were scorched and in tatters. Most of his shirt was gone. He was all flaring nostrils and heaving chest muscles. "Is there no more juice in your caboose?"

Sid rolled her eyes.

Smoke squeezed her close.

Kane spat. "I have to admit, I underestimated both of you. It turns out you would rather suffer than just die. Well, I'm not toying around anymore. Using this technological tool is beneath me, but screw it." He cocked the assault rifle. "I want you assholes dead!"

Caught flat-footed in the wide open, Smoke pushed Sid behind him, saying to her softly, "I've still got my suit. Stay behind me."

"That won't help, fool! I'll be aiming for your head, so unless your skull is made of metal, you'll be oozing brains all over your woman in a moment."

Kane took aim.

Sid squeezed Smoke's waist.

The shifter pulled the trigger.

Click!

"Damn them all to hell! I hate these modern things!" Kane charged the handle again and resumed his aim. "I hope you enjoyed that moment."

A figure dropped out of the sky and landed right on top of Kane's back, knocking the weapon to the ground. It was Vormus.

"What are you doing, fool for a brother?" Kane spat.

"I'm uncrossing my double cross," Vormus said, squeezing Kane's throat. "Or maybe it's called a triple cross. I don't know, but my vengeance is at hand." His eyes were white fire, his fangs pure silver. He looked at Sid and Smoke. "Make haste, you fools. If I don't win, he'll tear us all apart."

With a new surge of strength, Smoke and Sid were off and running. Their feet hit the dock at full speed. Ahead and previously obscured by the yacht, Smoke saw a pair of arms waving. It was Sam, yelling from a speedboat that looked small in front of the yacht. "Over here! Over here!"

Two guards in pea coats popped up on the yacht and started firing. One aimed for Sam, the other Sid and Smoke. Sam went down.

CHAPTER 37

"N oooo!" Smoke jumped forward. A bullet caught him in the shoulder, knocking him flat on his back. He could still see the deaders with machine guns, blasting away. Bullets were zipping by all over when suddenly it stopped. The gunmen teetered on the railing. One dropped on the dock. The other into the river.

Guppy.

"Come on." Sid helped him to his feet.

The two labored forward to the boat Sam was in.

"Sam! Sam!" Smoke pleaded, grimacing. It hurt to speak. The sweetheart suit had blocked most of the damage, but taking a powerful round still felt like getting hit by a speeding train. He climbed down into the boat. "Sam!"

"I'm hit," Sam moaned. Her voice was coming from the cuddy cabin. "I'm hit."

Smoke handed Sid into the boat and then climbed into the cabin. "Where?"

"Oh, my arm, my arm," Sam groaned.

He checked her out. A bullet had torn a sliver of skin from her forearm. He sat her up. "You're going to be okay."

Looking at her arm then back at him, his sister made a face. "Are you kidding me? That's going to leave a scar. I'm going to have to wear long sleeves from now on."

Smoke popped his head out of the cabin and said to Sid, who was now speeding the boat across the river, "She's going to be fine."

"Good," Sid replied with an exhausted and weary smile. "Good."

"Take it straight across," he said.

They beached the boat. Guppy jumped in the water and carried Sam out onto the shore.

"Why'd you let them shoot me for?" she said to him.

"Sorry, dear, it won't happen again."

"Well I hope not."

Smoke and Sid helped each other out of the stern. Both of them were skinned up and bloody, and they enjoyed the cool river water for a minute before they high-stepped their way up the sandy beach. He found a large log and sat down.

Sid did the same and leaned against him and sighed.

"Ditto," he said.

She placed her hand on his. "Smoke, thanks for coming. I don't think I ever would have made it out of there without you. My mind, it was just, just gone. I'm sorry."

"You don't need to apologize."

"Yes, yes I do." Her head sagged into her hands. "Thank God for that super vitamin. It got me out of that funk I was in. Kane, that Kane. He's such a—"

"Monster?"

"Bastard monster." She huffed a chuckle.

Asia appeared. "Aw look, love birds back together. Look like dirty farm boy and farm girl." She sprayed something on Sid's wounds.

"Ow!" Sid replied. "What *is* that?"

"Antiseptic spray. It will stop the bleeding. Clean the wound. Has a nice minty scent. Cover the stink on a pig." She patted her stomach. "I'm getting hungry. Mal! Mal! I need to eat." She started spraying Smoke's gashes. "Aw, these are really bad. I'm going to need my sewing kit. Mal! Mal! Jungle boy here tore your suit. Very bad. Very, very bad. I can't stitch this." She walked away as she spoke.

"She's awfully fussy," Sid said.

"Cause she's always hungry."

"Morning glory, maybe she has a tapeworm."

Smoke chuckled.

Sid joined in. As their laughter subsided, she said, "I'm worried about Megan."

"Do you know where she is?"

"I think. Maybe Kane won't hurt her, though. She's Allison's, and Allison's in league with them now."

"So you've given up on your sister?"

"Only Allison can save Allison. We'll see." Still snuggled next to him, she turned her head toward his. "Do you think Vormus killed Kane?"

Staring at the estate on the other side, he shrugged. It was pitch black over there, aside from the burning helicopter.

I should have planted some C4 over there and blown the whole place up.

"I doubt it."

"I hope he did. I hope they killed each other. I really hate those guys."

"I could go back over and finish the job."

Sid locked her fingers with his. "No, we'll just have to see what happens. It can wait. Besides, if he survives we'll know about it soon enough."

"How's that?"

"I was around Kane long enough to know he'll eliminate anything that threatens him. So if he lives, you can bet your boots we'll be public enemy number one."

"Sounds like a good time. I like being a wanted man."

"You're wanted, alright."

Mal sauntered over and kneeled down in front of them. "What on earth did they cut my suit with?"

"A sword," Smoke replied.

"What sword?"

"There's one in the boat."

Mal fetched it. "This is fascinating." He swung it around a few times in an awkward motion and dropped it.

"Stop playing with that," Asia said. "You'll cut yourself. Enough wounds to patch up already. Now hurry up. It's time to eat some food before my stomach eats itself."

Staring out over the rippling black waters of the river, Smoke said to Sid, "Are you ready to go back to the real world?"

"I've never been more ready." She pushed herself up to her feet and reached down to help Smoke up. "Let's go. I feel like I need a month of sleep."

Despite her tired appearance, Sid looked beautiful in the moonlight. Strength and confidence had returned to her dark eyes. Something about her demeanor stirred Smoke's blood. It always had. He knew it always would. He grabbed her hand, fished something out of his second skin, and took a knee.

"What are you doing?" Sid asked with a look of surprise on her face.

"Yes, what you doing, raggedy man?" Asia said. "Let's get going."

Sam and Guppy approached, and with the others it almost completed a circle.

Smoke looked up into Sid's eyes and showed her the engagement ring in his hand. "With God and our friends as witnesses, I ask you, Sid, will you take this ring and be my wife?"

CRAIG HALLORAN

THE SUPERNATURAL BOUNTY HUNTER FILES

SMOKE SIGNALS

BOOK 7

CHAPTER 1

S MOKE STILL HAD ONE KNEE planted in the soft dirt of the river shore. In one hand he held the engagement ring and in the other hand was Sid's palm. They were surrounded by Sam, Guppy, Mal, Asia, the breeze of the river, and the moon shining down in his eyes.

Sid's brows were creased. Her eyes watered. She pulled a strand of long black hair from her mouth.

He said it again. "Will you marry me, Sid?"

"I—I," she said, swallowing.

"Tsk, tsk," Asia said. She sprayed more antiseptic on Smoke's wounds. "What horrible timing to ask such an important question. Not very romantic. Just answer the man's question, Sidney. Yes or no. I want to go. I'm hungry."

Soft eyed and scholarly, Mal Gunderson got ahold of Asia's arm and said, "Perhaps we should leave them alone for a moment."

"Pfft!" Asia said. "She's going to say no. I already can tell. She's a difficult woman." She patted Smoke on the shoulder. "You'll find another, not so stubborn."

Fists drawn up at her sides, Sam blurted out, "Will you shut up, Asia?" She glanced at Smoke, shrugged, and took hold of Guppy's arm. The pair of them walked away.

Sid took a deep breath and let it out slowly.

"It's just the two of us now, Sid," he said. "What are you thinking?"

"I'm thinking I'm tired and thankful. Also, Asia is right. Your timing is horrible." She sniffed and wiped her face. Her eyes drifted over the river to the bank on the other side. "But I wouldn't expect anything else from you."

He could see the distant flames from the chopper in her eyes. She wasn't there with him at the moment. She was back over on the other side at Kane Lancaster's mansion. There was no telling what all Sid had been through. How much she'd been subjected to. How much suffering? Was there pain? Did she have a case of Stockholm syndrome coursing through her veins? He started to pull the ring back, saying, "I know my timing isn't the best, but nothing in my life has felt right without you in it. You're the one for me and I'm the one for you. Search your heart, look me in the eye, and tell me you don't feel that way too."

A tear ran down her cheek, but she didn't look him in the eye. Without looking at him, she said, "What kind of life will we have together? This world is sick and full of monsters." Her hand squeezed his. "They'll come after us and destroy everything we have. Kane is vengeful. If he lives, we'll be dead."

Smoke tugged on her hand. "Get down here and look at me."

Slowly, she sank to her knees. Her watery eyes were downcast.

Smoke tipped her chin up with his fingers until her eyes met his, and he said, "You aren't the kind of woman who lets someone else dictate life to you. You're strong. You do what you want. And you're allowed to have what you want—unless you're going to let those monsters stop you. But they aren't going to stop me from having what I want. I want you. I need you. I love you."

Her breath shuddered. She sobbed. "I'm a mess."

"We both are."

Trembling, she threw her arms around his neck and squeezed him tight. Her warm tears dropped down his neck. She said, "I love you, John. You know I love you."

His heart pounded. Sid was the one he'd give anything for. He wanted her more now than ever, and he was sincere about it. He'd go to hell and back for her no matter how many times it took. But doubt crept into his thoughts as soon as she parted her lips to speak again. *Don't say "but." Don't say "but."*

"But," she said.

Smoke felt the fires racing through his body start to cool. *Oh no. Of course, "but" is a conditional word. It could be a good thing.*

"I need some time." Cheek grazing his cheek, she slid her face across his, locked her fingers around his neck, and kissed him with grateful passion. She finished off with a gentle bite on his lip and added, "And I need some sleep too. I have to be clearheaded when I decide. You understand, don't you?"

"I'm not pushy, Sid. But I don't want to be alone forever." He brushed her hair out of her eyes. "I'm tired of drinking milkshakes by myself."

"Okay, stop before you get me all choked up again." She eyed the ring, blinked, and said, "It's gorgeous." She closed his hand over it, forming a fist. "Just hold onto it for a little time." She stood up and walked away to the car, opened the door, and disappeared inside.

As Smoke rose, his heart sank.

Asia walked over to him, batted her eyes at him, and said, "If it makes any difference, I would have said yes, bandage man."

"He didn't ask you though, did he?" Mal nudged Asia toward the car. "Let's get you something to eat before you say something even more insensitive than that."

"How is me saying I'd say yes being insensitive?" Asia asked Mal.

"Because you said yes to me, and I know how that turned out." He and Asia got in the car with Sid.

Smoke was left with Sam and Guppy. Sam's face was a mix of pity and anger. "Are you okay?"

"I'm sore, exhausted, and rejected, but I'm alive. What more could I ask for?"

"You deserve an answer." Sam gave Smoke a hug. "But the truth is, your timing did suck."

"Sam," Guppy retorted, "go easy on the guy. He just had his heart broken, and after all that fighting."

"She didn't say no," Smoke replied.

"No, you listen to me," Sam said, wincing and holding her arm that had been grazed by a bullet earlier. "Geez, that stings. But as I was saying. What kind of knucklehead proposes like that? Her hair's a mess, her clothes are in tatters, and she just escaped from God knows what. And you asked her to marry you." She poked her finger at the ground. "Right here? Right now? It's sad and stupid. I'm not sure which is more."

Mal, Asia, and Sidney pulled away. Smoke watched until the red taillights were out of view. He looked at the ring. The round cut sparkled with the moon's enchanting light. He took a quick glance at the moon. *I could have sworn the time was right.* He stuck it back inside his sweetheart suit and said, "Let's go home."

CHAPTER 2

D AYS WENT BY WITHOUT SMOKE talking to anyone. He was back at his place, the old full-service gas station that had been modified into an apartment, working in the garage on his Camaro. The garage door was open and the sun was shining. The radio was playing country gold in the background. With his back to the sun, he leaned inside the open hood of the car. He cranked the ratchet, pulled it away, and twisted out one of the spark plugs. It read NGK Platinum.

"It looks like your days are over," he said to it, then tossed it into a metal trashcan with a black liner in it. He reached over to his roll cart of tools and opened up another NGK Platinum sparkplug box. He stuck the new plug in the engine, twisted away, and tightened it up with the ratchet.

"One down, seven to go. And how about another oil change?"

He liked working on cars, especially the older ones that he could still work on. He'd never been a restless man, but that kind of work gave him satisfaction. It gave him peace. Cars were beautiful things to him. And women like Sid who shared his affection for cars were all the more beautiful to him for it.

Singing along to some Hank Williams Jr., he switched out three more spark plugs and took a swig of whatever from his Tervis tumbler. The throaty roar of a car engine caught his ear. He turned and looked down his driveway. A phantom-black

Dodge Hellcat was coming up the drive. The engine drowned out the sound of the radio. A woman was behind the wheel. It was Sid.

Leaning against the hood of his car, he took a red rag and wiped the grease off his hands. He dabbed the sweat from his brow and checked his shirt. It was a night-grey tank top with a battle axe logo on it. It was soaked with sweat. He gave himself a little shrug.

Oh well.

The rumbling Hellcat engine was cut off. The driver's door popped open and Sidney got out. Her long black hair was pulled back in a ponytail. Her pretty eyes had the fire back in them. She wore a black spandex shirt that enhanced her athletic figure and matching pants with some neon pink patterns woven in.

Smoke's throat tightened and his mouth started to water. He wanted to take her up in his arms and feel her body against his all day and all night. He dropped the rag on the engine and started to speak but held back as soon as her lips parted.

"Hi," she said. She tilted her head a little to the side, staring at him, and added, "Are you okay? You look like I have a deader standing right behind me."

"No, I'm good. I just wasn't certain how you were feeling." He rubbed the back of his neck. Her eyes glided over his arms as he did so. "I just didn't expect to see you so soon. Not that I'm bothered by that. I'm glad you're here. I just thought you would need more time than this."

Crossing her arms under her breasts, she came closer. There was a playful look in her eyes. She said, "I needed time to rest. I slept almost an entire day. I've never slept more than eight hours before in my life." She got closer. She chewed on her lip. "But there's a first time for everything."

"We've spent a lot of first times together," Smoke said. He had to fight to keep his hands by his sides. "Werewolves. Deaders. Rat men."

"True." She started stroking her ponytail. "While I slept and when I awoke, all I've been able to think about is you. I wondered what that next first thing could be. Would we have another great moment like that together?"

"Meaning?"

Standing toe to toe with him, she took his hands in hers and placed them on her waist. Her gorgeous eyes met his. "Yes."

"Yes, you'll marry me?"

Sid nodded with a girlish smile over her chin.

"Uh, great!" He started to pat himself down. He reached into his pants pocket and pulled out the ring. "Here."

"You still have the ring on you? Didn't you have any doubts?"

"Yes, but I like to be prepared—oh," he said, taking a knee and grabbing her hand.

She spread her fingers out. "At least you didn't regurgitate it."

"Well, not this time." He smiled quickly at her and slipped the ring on. They looked into each other's loving eyes for a long moment. Sid came to her knees and embraced him. Her body set his on fire, and before he knew what hit him, he was flat on his back and they were kissing.

Breaking it off and panting with passion, Sidney said, "Do you want a long engagement to think about it?"

"No."

She started kissing him again and broke it off. "I want a church wedding where I grew up."

"I wouldn't have it any other way." He kissed her hands and stroked her face. "Can I ask what gave you such certainty?"

"Life's too short, and I want to spend as much of it as I can with you. Whether we fight together or die together, it doesn't matter as long as I'm with you." She started taking off his clothes.

"Hey now, not until after the wedding."

"Geez! You've got to be kidding me." She flashed him the ring. "We're engaged now. It's okay."

He felt like his body was about to burst at the seams, he wanted her so bad. Leaning back on his elbows, he managed a shrug. "Hey, I'm a traditional guy. It's going to wait until our wedding night."

She kissed him several more times then stood up with the back of her hand to her forehead and said, "You big crazy virgin!" She headed back to her car.

"Where are you going?"

"I'm leaving."

"Now? Why?" he asked.

She opened up the Hellcat door and said with a huge grin, "Because I've got a wedding to plan!"

CHAPTER 3

A**FTER MAKING QUICK WORK OF** the Camaro's tune-up, Smoke showered, slipped into some clean clothes, got in the car, and headed down the road. His hands were tapping on the steering wheel and he was singing along to some Twisted Sister on the radio. He felt good. Better than good. He felt great, but he had to do one more thing. He had to stop by and see Sid's parents.

I hope they're okay with this.

Smoke had a shady past. It wasn't because of any wrongdoing, but it still bothered him. Keith Shaw was a lawman, and Smoke was certain he wanted only the best for his daughter. And aside from what he could give of himself, he didn't have that much to offer.

Great Dane. I live in a garage. I wonder what they'd think if they saw my place.

He squirmed in the Camaro's seat. His fingers tingled. He'd always been even keeled, but now he felt a bit giddy. With butterflies in his stomach. Not much of anything had affected him this much before. The monsters, conspiracies, and flying bullets didn't faze him one bit. But this was marriage. The commitment of a lifetime. Could he live up to those high standards? Would being married take away his edge or make it sharper?

The unknown. How exciting.

He pulled behind an old red Ford truck in the Shaw driveway and put the Camaro in park. As soon as his foot hit the pavement, Sid's mother Sally came running out the front door. She had an apron on and looked as happy as she was pretty. Tears were in her eyes. "John! John! I'm so excited for you and Sidney!" She hugged him.

"You already know?"

Still hugging him, she said, "Of course I know. The mother is always the first to know." She pushed herself back from him. "Why are you so surprised?"

"Oh, well, I was hoping to run it by you and Keith first. It was spur of the moment."

Sally's eyes started to flow with tears again. Sid had Sally's eyes, but Sally was a shorter, home-cooked version of Allison. She dabbed her eyes with her apron and said, "You want to ask for me and Keith's approval? That's so sweet."

"Yes, I do. So, how's he taking the news?"

"Oh, you know Keith. He never gets too excited about anything, but I'm sure he'll be glad to see you. Come on. He's out back." She took his hand and led him through the open garage and into the back yard. She was rubbing his hand the whole time. "You'll be even more handsome in a tuxedo. I can't wait."

The backyard was over an acre of greenery at the bottom of a tree-filled hillside. It was a beautiful spot with a children's playset and stone benches set beneath the shade of the trees. There were birdhouses on poles, several gardens, a fish pond, a big red storage barn, and stacks of wood beneath a metal shed roof with no walls.

Keith was on a John Deere riding mower. He wore a white T-shirt, work gloves, and sunglasses.

"Keith!" Sally yelled as she waved her arms. "Keith! We have company!"

The older man started riding the mower right for them.

"Here he comes," Sally said. She rubbed Smoke's back. "I'll get you both something to drink while you two talk."

"That would be great, thanks," Smoke said.

Sally cut through the grass, up onto the wooden deck, and through the sliding glass door into the kitchen.

Keith stopped a few feet from Smoke and turned the mower off. He got up, took off his gloves and glasses, and set them in the seat. "How are you doing, John?" he said, extending his hand.

"I'm doing great," Smoke said, shaking Keith's hand. The older man had an iron grip for a man in his fifties. His features were rugged, handsome and stern. You could see the decades of a seasoned law man in his eyes.

"Not to beat around the bush, but I came to ask for your daughter's hand in marriage."

"It's a little late for that, isn't it?"

"I suppose, but it was a moment, and I wanted to do this in person. You two snowbirds were in Florida."

Keith picked up his cup of iced tea from the mower holder and said, "She already said yes, and she certainly doesn't need any approval from me, not that she'd ask for it. As for you, John, I like you, and there isn't very much reason for me to vet you at this point. You're adults with your own lives, and I know little about what you do with your free time, but I know Sid, and she wouldn't be with you if you weren't one of the good guys. She has high standards."

"I appreciate that," Smoke replied.

Keith finished off his iced tea and set the glass in the holder. "If it makes you feel any better, I can still ask you some questions. After all, you did come all the way out here. Let's go over there under the trees and have a seat while Sally brews up some more tea." He walked toward the benches that sat beneath a pair of pine trees. "You ever had her tea?"

"No."

"It's great." Keith sat down, and Smoke joined him on a separate stone bench. Eyeing Smoke, he said, "So, she wants to get married in our church. Are you okay with that?"

"Absolutely."

"Are you saved?" Keith asked.

"I am," Smoke replied.

Keith nodded. "That's a good thing for many reasons, and it will help me sleep better, considering the kind of work you two are in. I'd like to see the both of you out of it. She's too much like me and wants to fight that good fight, and I can sense that about you, too." His hand trembled. "I miss the fight, but it takes a toll on you."

Smoke rubbed the stitched-up scar on his arm and said, "I know. It can be a real pain."

"Wait until you're my age. Everything is stiff and moves a lot slower." Keith laughed. "So, what about your family, John? You seem like a loner. Will they be at the wedding?"

"I have family. They're just hard to get ahold of. I promise to have some representation though. Samantha is my half sister, and I'm pretty sure she'll be helping Sid and Sally make all the arrangements. I guess we'll just have to wait and see who shows up at the rehearsal dinner. They love caviar."

Keith's eyes widened. "Caviar! I can't afford caviar. Not on my retirement."

Laughing, Smoke said, "I'll let Samantha know, but there aren't any guarantees."

"You're a real funny guy, John. I'll be right back."

"Where are you going?"

"To get my shotgun." He went into the garage and came back with a newspaper in his hand. He dropped it in Smoke's lap.

"A little odd for a shotgun. Is there a sale on them or something?" Smoke unfolded the paper. It was a copy of *Nightfall DC*.

CHAPTER 4

S MOKE OPENED UP THE PAPER and leafed through the pages. "That's some pretty interesting reading. Do you have a subscription to this?"

"It's no surprise you're making light of it, but yes, I do, and I have a collection. There's been some pretty interesting stories over the past year." Head up and elbows on his knees, Keith leaned toward Smoke. "I've had run-ins with this stuff, and it scared the hell out of me."

Eyeing the pages, Smoke scanned the headline of one of the articles. "You mean you saw a rat man in the sewers, like the Ninja Turtles?"

Keith's voice lowered to a rumble. "Twenty years ago, I saw a man the size of three standing on the highway. It was raining, and he was turning some fella into hamburger meat with his fists. I shot him with my forty-five. Six times. He ripped off a car door and slung it at me like a Frisbee." Keith pushed his hair up at the scalp line, revealing a nasty scar. "I woke up with this, happy to be alive, but almost got laughed out of the station. Hell, no one would believe me, so I blamed it on a concussion. Not long after that, I was at a law enforcement convention in DC when I came across that paper. It opened my eyes."

Smoke could see Sally through the kitchen window. "Does she know about your incident?"

"She's my wife," Keith said. "I tell her just about everything, even that. She looked really worried when I told her, so I kinda backed off of it. Sally's sweet and tough, but certain things she can't handle. The supernatural creeps her out, and I have to hide these magazines from her. I have a boy in town that fetches them for me. I hide them in the garage among my tools." The rugged lawman's forehead crinkled. There was a lost look in his light eyes.

Smoke could feel the man's concern and worry. At the same time, he knew there wasn't much point in trying to fool his father-in-law-to-be. Sure, the less they knew the better, but they might as well be prepared for the unexpected. "Keith, I've seen giants. And rat men that live in the sewers. A bunch of other rotten filth too. So has Sid. Do you want to hear more?"

"I just need to know enough so that I can protect my family. Of course, last time, the bullets didn't do much good." He cocked his head at Smoke. "Can you kill them?"

Smoke smiled. "You can kill anything with the right weapon."

Sally brought a pitcher of iced tea out on a tray and set it down on the bench. "How are you men doing? You look so serious. You should be happy." She handed Smoke a glass. "This will make you happy."

He took a sip. "That's delicious. I'm happier already."

Keith took off his Docksiders and rubbed his feet in the grass. "Ah, that feels good."

Sally handed her husband a fresh glass of tea. "For your feet maybe, but not for the grass." She fanned her face. "Shew! For John's sake I hope a breeze starts up. That's awful."

The phone rang inside the kitchen.

Sally perked up some more. "Oh, I bet that's Sid. We're going shopping for wedding dresses!" She scuttled toward the house.

Keith stretched out his glass of iced tea for a toast. "To exciting times and my future son-in-law." He clinked his glass into Smoke's, took a long drink, and then looked over sideways to where Sally had just closed the slider. "Now tell me everything I can stand to hear."

Over the next three hours, Smoke filled Keith's ears with plenty of what had happened. He told him about the Black Slate and what he and Sid had been hired for. He talked about Adam Vaughn the werewolf, the deaders, the shifters, and Mason Crow the minotaur.

Keith's mouth dropped open until his jaw almost hit the ground more than a few times. A breeze came, but the older man started to sweat a lot. He had the expression of a man who had seen a ghost.

Finally, Keith waved his hands and said, "That's enough. I've heard plenty." He slumped back in his chair and let out a long sigh. "I don't want to believe it, but I do believe it. And my daughter is out in the thick of it. My little baby."

Smoke nodded. He'd left out some items. He hadn't told about Sid being abducted by Kane Lancaster, and he hadn't mentioned Allison or Megan. "I'll always protect her," he said.

"I know you will. Damn. I want to join the fight with you."

"You're better off in Florida."

"Hah, there are deaders there, too." He slapped his knee. "They just call them senior citizens. You ought to see them down there. I'm talking about my father and mother of course. They still get around pretty good. It's a nice community, but dead quiet after seven p.m." He rubbed his knee. "Oh, getting old sucks. So, tell me more about the weapons you use. We aren't going anywhere until you two are settled, and who knows, we might need some protection. I still get the willies thinking about that man that was here from the Drake months ago. He was dead, wasn't he?"

"Edwin Lee," Smoke said softly. "Yeah, I saw his tombstone. There's no telling how many of those kinds of people are out there running around." He felt at little flutter in his stomach. "There are children too, Keith."

"Children? You mean like Megan, but they're dead?"

"Clones is more like it. Honestly, I can't tell if they're real or not. Maybe they're something else entirely." Smoke's broad shoulders sagged. "It isn't easy."

The older man fanned himself and refilled his tea and offered some. "More?"

Smoke held out his glass and said, "Sure."

"You know, it really breaks my heart that we haven't seen or heard from Allison or Megan for quite some time. Sally grieves about it every day. I catch her looking at photo albums and crying sometimes. I can't help but wonder where we went wrong with Allison." Keith pinched his tear ducts. "It hurts, and even worse, my gut tells me they're in the thick of all this. Aren't they, John."

Smoke had hoped the topic wouldn't come up, but there wasn't any point in trying to hide anything from Keith now. One never knew how hard life would hit you. One day you were here and the next day you were gone. Keith needed to know everything he could about his daughter and have some peace with it. "Senator Wilhelm was in league with the Drake, and Allison—as you know—was in league with him. She's still with them. It's the choice she made, Keith, but you can't blame yourself." He looked around at the wonderful ranch home and all of its pleasant surroundings. "I don't have any children, but I've known plenty of prodigal sons. Some were in the military and others were in prison. It leaves you shaking your head. Most times it reminds me of Cain and Abel. One just had faith and the other didn't. It's hard to understand why."

"Yeah, I've thought along those lines before. It offers little comfort and it hurts like hell. I just hope for Sally's sake that Allison will come around before it's too late. I think Sally's getting her hopes up that this wedding will bring us all together, but I fear she'll be disappointed."

"It's going to be a great day for all of us," Smoke said. He gulped down his drink and rattled the ice in the glass. "With tea like this, how can it not be?" He tapped the back of his hand on Keith's knee. "Come over to my car and we'll talk more about those weapons you're so interested in."

With a groan, Keith got up. "Good. I hope I can get a few shots in on those bastards that have screwed with my daughters."

CHAPTER 5

S MOKE SPENT THE REST OF the day with Keith and Sally. They all spent a lot of time in the living room after they finished a wonderful home-cooked dinner. Sally showed him volumes of family photos while Keith watched *Gunsmoke* on TV. It was one of the better days Smoke had had in a long time, being around real people that lived a simple life and cared about one another so much. He'd had days like that when he was young, and the familiarity of the family atmosphere left him nostalgic more than a few times.

He left them with smiles on their faces. Keith thanked him for the blue-tipped bullets that he'd left and one of his pistols to shoot them with. Sally was all tears. The sweet woman gave him a big hug and pecked his face with a kiss. Smoke found a tissue in the Camaro, checked the red smudge in the rearview mirror, and wiped it off. He turned up the radio and tapped on the wheel. "Never enough good days like today."

The Camaro rolled down two miles of gravel road that led away from the Shaw house before hitting the T-intersection of a one-lane highway. Happy to get off the long drive that was better suited for trucks than low-riding sports machines, Smoke laid into the gas and zoomed down the blacktop. He was feeling giddy. Even though his discussions with Keith had been on the darker side, it felt right. A perfect day.

Perhaps it won't be long before Sid and I settle down and start our own family.

Family. That was a sore issue for him. He'd had one when he was growing up, but not with his real parents. He'd been adopted as a baby, and he didn't have any idea who his parents were. There were days, not many, but enough, when he'd wonder who his parents really were. But he had Samantha, his half sister, and her parents—his adopted parents—were just as much his parents as hers. They'd been nothing short of good to him. His life had been normal, but unlike the other kids where he grew up, he was different. Special. In his gut, he felt that everything going on right now might have something bigger to do with him. It bothered him.

I wonder how Sid's doing.

He picked up the phone lying on the passenger seat and didn't see any messages on it. It had been a full day without a word from his bride-to-be. It was as if he expected to be chatting with her all the time like two teenage kids on a sitcom, but he did like the excited purr in her voice. At the same time, there was a nagging in the back of his head that something might be wrong. The Drake was out to get them. Possibly she could've been abducted again. If he had it his way, he'd be with her most of every day.

Maybe I should check in with Sam. She'll know something. Ah, Guppy. He'll know what's going on. Sam tells him everything.

Eyes on and off the road, he started thumbing a quick text to Guppy. The radio station fizzled out and squeaked and became static. He pushed the button for another station. It was static as well. Through the windshield, he looked up at the full bright moon hanging in the sky. He passed by a white big rig that was pulled over on the side of the road. He hadn't seen a car pass by in the last few miles. It was just him and a vacant road. The lights on his dashboard blinked. A chill went up his spine. He gripped the wheel.

Feels like an X-Files moment.

He drove another mile with nothing but static in the speakers. He turned the volume down. The lights on the dashboard flickered from time to time. The engine's throttle skipped more than once. Smoke was taking the same route back to DC as the way he'd come. The vehicle had been freshly in tune then, but now it seemed off. He passed another big rig pulled over to the side. Its lights turned on just after he passed, and smoke rolled up and out of its stacks as it pulled onto the road.

Something's going on.

Smoke wasn't one to be paranoid. If anything, he expected things to suddenly happen. That's what he was trained for. He always had a plan of action. An escape plan. He reached into the backseat and grabbed a semi-automatic pistol. The safety was off and it was ready to fire. He laid it in his lap.

He caught his first glimpse of another vehicle coming his way. Its high beams were bright, almost blinding. He glanced to the right side of the road until the whoosh of the other car that was over the centerline whizzed by his. A huge man with stone-cut features was crammed behind the wheel, looking right at him.

This is getting weird.

Pressing on the accelerator, he sped the Camaro up to eighty miles per hour. Ahead, a big rig started to switch lanes in an attempt to pass another one. Smoke let off the gas. Both lanes were blocked. He checked the rearview mirror. The big rig that had pulled out onto the road behind him was coming, and it wasn't alone. Another filled the oncoming traffic lane.

I'm blocked in like it's a smash-up derby. I get the feeling the Malachy Crunch is coming on.

The trucks in front of him slowed, taking their speed down to about sixty. Between the trucks, Smoke had both lanes to himself. He guided the wheel over to the right and accelerated up the berm. The truck swerved to the right, blocking his passage and kicking up road debris. He pumped the gas and swerved back behind the trucks.

"So are you trying to stop me or to kill me?"

The trucks behind him accelerated toward his back bumper. The space between the four trucks was closing fast.

He patted his dash. "It's moments like this I wish you were a Volvo or that you had about twenty air bags."

Behind him, the big rigs' diesel motors roared with new life and closed in. There was only a car length between his car and the trucks. The doors in the back of the trailers rose. Inside, men wearing goggles were pointing machine guns right at him.

Great Dane. Those goggles look ridiculous. And I'm all out of L.A.W. rockets.

They charged their weapons and opened fire.

CHAPTER 6

SMOKE CUT THE WHEEL HARD to the left. The eighteen-wheeler behind him clipped his rear bumper and spun him off the road into the berm. He stomped on the gas and shot down the berm the opposite way. The huge truck swerved at him, but the speed of the Camaro rocketed Smoke to safety. It was just him and the open road in front of him.

"What was that all about?"

His thoughts went immediately to Sid and her parents. He checked his phone, but there still wasn't any signal. Whatever was going on stank. The men with the guns didn't have any peacoats on, and he hadn't noticed any Drake symbols or black suns on them. His mind was racing through the details. White freight trucks with no markings. Men with goggles and machine guns. They were trying to kill him or stop him from getting back to DC, which meant that somewhere, something was going on.

"Heh, they can't catch me now."

The red taillights of the trucks flared in his rearview mirror. Their tires skipped and skidded on the road.

Smoke brought the Camaro to a stop. The trucks were now at a stop half a mile away. Their cargo doors rolled open, and automatic ramps were let out over the road. Men burst out two by two. On motorcycles.

"Now this is getting silly," Smoke said, tapping on the steering wheel. His car was fast, but the speed bikes were faster. There wasn't much point in a race, and two more sets of headlights filled the roadway in the distance. More big trucks were coming. He dropped the car into reverse, stomped the gas, and said, "Screw it!"

The tires smoked, and he made a beeline straight for the racing bikes. The bikers veered out of the way.

Smoke whipped the wheel around, screeching the tires into a one-eighty turn. He was facing the back end of the trucks again. Laying into the gas, he zoomed over the right side of the berm and sped right by the trucks that were stopped dead on the road.

He left all four eighteen wheelers in his rearview mirror, but the motorcycles were coming. The pursuers closed fast, goggled men with Uzis in their hands.

Smoke rolled down his windows, held the wheel steady, and reached under his seat. He had two small boxes that filled his hand.

With the wind beating into his face, he said, "I never thought I'd see the day when I got to use this. It looks like today's the day."

Checking his rear and side mirrors, he watched the cycles close in. As soon as they got within a car length, he dropped one box out of each window. Two loud pops followed. Hundreds of tiny caltrops covered the road and dug into the motorcycle tires. Both riders went down in a speeding skid of flesh and metal.

Smoke pumped his fist. "Woooooohooooooo!"

He didn't know what was going on, but it was getting interesting. Getting fun. Behind him, the danger began to fade. He turned up the radio, but the static was still there. He hit the play button on the cassette player, saying, "You can't stop rock and roll." He turned up the volume. Electric guitars were playing. "No matter how hard the bad guys try, I can still rock in America!"

Smoke contemplated his next step. Whoever was after him had gone to an awful lot of trouble to get him. They must know where he lived, so going home was out. In the meantime he'd need to check on Sid, Sam, and Guppy. His phone still didn't have a signal. He'd have to go into hiding until he could figure something out. That wouldn't be hard to do once he got back into the city. He'd vanish.

He cruised down the road two more miles at about ninety. A speck of light hung in the sky and was closing in on him. He tilted his rearview mirror and squinted.

Tell me that isn't a chopper coming for me.

He made an air guitar. "All day! All night!"

In seconds the chopper hovered right over him, hung with him like a black bird of prey.

Smoke stuck his head out the window and looked up. A huge metal disk was coming down right on top of the roof of his car. "No! No! No!" He jammed on the brakes.

Clank!

His move was too late. The massive magnet fastened onto his roof and lifted the Camaro cleanly and quickly off the highway with a jerk that slammed him back into his seat. By the time he could move again, he was two hundred feet off the ground and flying.

Hands on his head, he said, "This sucks." Watching the ground beneath him, he said, "But the Adventures of the Flying Camaro would make a great movie, I bet." He grabbed his guns and harnesses. Found knives and strapped them on. Wherever they were taking him, he wouldn't go down easy. The chopper rose another five hundred feet off the ground. A bad feeling sank his stomach down into his toes.

What if they drop me? I'll be the cream filling in a metal pancake.

CHAPTER 7

SOARING THROUGH THE AIR AND veering away from the bright lights of DC, Smoke's palms started to sweat. He was too high up to jump, even into one of the many bodies of water. It would crush him to death. He didn't think any super vitamins would help him out. Besides, he didn't have any.

He leaned back in his seat and took a deep breath. The car had the weightlessness of an amusement park ride.

His phone rang. The screen read Unknown Caller.

He answered, "Smoke Airways."

"Hello, John, how are you?" the person on the phone said with a tone of familiarity. His voice was formal and polite.

"Never better. How can I help you?"

"Well, if you'll just sit still for a change, I'll be helping you out." The man cleared his throat. "So, what's it like inside a flying car?"

"There's nothing quite like a *Man with a Golden Gun* moment. Why don't you come down and join me? I've got an extra window seat." Smoke stretched out into the back seat and pulled the backrest of it down, exposing his trunk. The Camaro hatch was crammed full of weapons, ammo cases, and a variety of emergency kits. He fished through the packages.

Just keep the man talking.

"You sound familiar. I'm assuming we've met before."

"We have, but it's been a very very long time." The man coughed. "So, I understand that you have a big wedding day coming up. That Sidney Shaw is a real catch. I'm certain the two of you would make quite the happy couple..."

Smoke jerked out a puffy army-green pack that looked part life preserver, part backpack. "But," he said.

"But, I can't allow that marriage to happen. You see, the two of you have caused enough trouble already. It's time to put an end to it."

"So put an end to it, already." Smoke slid the pack over his shoulder.

"You seem awfully eager to die."

"I'd rather die than listen to your small talk." Smoke clicked the pack's straps together over his chest. "But since your plan is to kill me, you might as well tell me who you are."

"I'm not trying to kill you, John. I'm just getting your attention, but you make it very difficult, which is something that I anticipated." The man on the phone cleared his throat. "Excuse me. I've been under the weather of late. The plan was to shut down your car on the highway and have a roadside chat."

"Or abduction." Smoke smiled and patted the dash of his car. "But you couldn't stop the old Camaro. It runs without the electrical systems you tried to block out. Heh heh, I was ready for magnetic pulses but not a magnetic chopper."

"You've proven to be every bit as clever as I thought you'd be, John, but you don't have anywhere to go now. Now, you're coming to see me."

"No. No, I'm not."

"Don't do anything foolish, John. You can't survive a fall like this if you jump."

Smoke slipped some gloves onto his hands. "Are you going to tell me who you are or not? Because time is running out for you to tell me your dastardly plan."

"Dastardly? John, what are you doing?"

Holding the phone to his lips, Smoke said, "I'll give you five more seconds to say something reasonable. Five...four..."

"Don't be stupid, John."

"Three...two..."

"John," the man said with irritation, "stay put, will you!"

"One. Time's up. Oh, and you better make sure nothing bad happens to my car. Goodbye, unknown caller." Smoke chucked the phone out the window, then hung his face out there and said, "Now it's just me, the wind, and the madness."

Sitting on the frame of the door, he stuck his body outside, stretched out his long arms, and grabbed ahold of the giant magnet's cable.

"Here we go."

He pulled himself outside and started to climb hand over hand up the rope of steel. The one-hundred-and-fifty-mile-an-hour winds were ripping at his clothes and face. Up he went, shimmying up the thirty feet of cord between him and the chopper.

A couple of heads peeked out of the chopper's cargo bay, gaped at him, and looked at one another. One of the men started laughing and shaking his head. The man waved another man into view, who peered over. He was burly and bearded and wearing green goggles. He gave Smoke the finger and vanished back inside.

Over a thousand feet up in the air, the chopper started to descend toward the ground.

Aw, crap. They're going to land early.

Halfway up the cord of steel, Smoke weighed his options. If he were to guess, he'd say they were more than ready to capture him with numbers and plenty of weapons. They'd probably land somewhere with reinforcements. Whoever they were, they weren't stupid. They had a backup plan. At least he was safely out of his car for now. But at best, that only bought him time. He looked up at the goggled goons.

They had smirks on their faces.

Smoke shimmied back down to the roof of the Camaro, offered them a salute, and jumped into the air.

CHAPTER 8

P LUMMETING INTO THE DARK OF the night, Smoke fumbled for the ripcord of his parachute. He'd almost forgotten he had one stowed away in the back of the Camaro. He'd put it there years ago when he and some other guys used to skydive from time to time. This parachute wasn't your standard fare. It had a smaller rectangular canopy designed for making patterns in the air. His fingers locked around the rip cord handle, and he yanked it.

The chute popped open instantly, slowing his descent. He'd hit the ground or something any second. He aimed the chute as best he could for a stretch of road on the other side of a long row of trees. "Not going to make it."

He crashed into the upper limbs and tumbled through the branches before the parachute cords jerked him to a stop.

"Oof!"

Smoke dangled about twenty feet off the ground. He found a knife and started cutting away his cords. The first slice sent him swinging into a tree trunk. Hanging on to a branch with one hand, he cut the rest of the parachute pack free and climbed down to the ground. He spat pine needles from his mouth and dusted off the small, tacky branches from his clothes. He had a few nasty scrapes on his arms and elbows.

A small sliver of wood had lanced his thigh.

Smoke plucked it out, saying, "Barely a flesh wound."

The chopper's propellers beat the air, but they weren't close to Smoke. The darkness had become his ally, and it would take some time before they'd pinpoint his location. The black chute canopy would make spotting him even harder. He'd turned the tables on them. Cheated whoever it was out of whatever they wanted.

And Smoke liked that.

Never in his life was he ever going to be someone's prisoner if he could help it. He weaved into the forest and made his way toward the road he'd seen before he crashed.

If you want to capture me, you're going to have to earn it.

Staying within the tree line, he walked parallel to the edge of the two-lane stretch of road, miles outside of DC. Traffic was coming and going. The chopper's searchlight cast down, and it made its rounds like a bat in the air. Smoke could still see his car drifting underneath and behind the chopper like a small metal banner. It would disappear into the tops of the trees only to reappear again seconds later.

He heard a click, and the car went into a silent free fall that stopped Smoke's heart for a moment.

No!

A crash in the distant woodland followed.

Great Dane! I just painted that and tuned it up!

Fists balled up, he resumed his trek along the edge of the forest. Kidnapping him was one strike, but totaling his cherished car was two. He watched the chopper hovering above the site where they'd dropped the Camaro for about five minutes before it took off again.

He wanted to go back to the car and see what he could salvage. But someone would be coming. Or waiting. He wasn't about to risk it.

Keep moving. Put as much distance between them and you as you can.

He'd made it about another half a mile up the road when he looked back and a white SUV pulled off on the side opposite from him. Toward the Camaro. Three men got out and vanished into the woods.

Man, they're quick.

He stood back under the trees, watching the vehicle. Part of him wanted to go in for a closer look. Take the fight to them. Beat the information out of one of the goons who worked for the man coming for him.

He gave it a few minutes. The driver of the white SUV was still behind the wheel. He had his arm hanging out the window with a cigarette burning between his fingers.

I've got an idea. And it's a bad one.

Smoke reached into his jeans pocket and slid out a thin slip of paper that looked like a Band-Aid. It was one of the tracking devices that he and Guppy had been working on. A flexible, transparent wireless network of circuits that could be tracked with a radio signal. Sometimes they worked and sometimes they didn't.

We really should be making a fortune off these. I think parents would like them. We just need a good name for it.

He backtracked, crossed the road about a quarter mile behind the SUV, and snaked his way into the forest. Following the edge on cat's feet, he lined himself up to the rear of the SUV. Closing his eyes, he tilted his head. He didn't hear any men moving in the forest. The Camaro had been dropped about half a mile into the woods from where they stood, if he had to guess.

Sounds all clear.

He opened his eyes and fixed them on the vehicle's passenger side-view mirror. Through the tinted windows he could still make out the man in the driver's seat. So long as he couldn't see the driver in the side-view mirror, he should be good. He waited until oncoming traffic started to pass. As soon as the next car zoomed by the vehicle, Smoke scampered right behind the back of the car and hunkered down. Quickly, he peeled the Band-Aid tracker from its seal and stuck it onto the license plate. He memorized the plate number, too.

"Hey Jim!" called a voice out of the woods. A man was approaching. "We made contact. Now what?"

Smoke crawled under the vehicle.

"I'll text. Hold on," said the driver, Jim. There was about thirty seconds before he spoke again. "We're going to stay on it all night, just in case that stuntman comes back."

Stuntman? Me? I like it.

"All night? Hell, it's early. Say, if we're gonna be squatting on that heap all night, we're going to need some eats." The guy sounded a little stupid. And annoying. "Some burgers will do."

"Burgers," the driver said with the rugged voice of a truck driver. "I'm not going to buy you any damn burgers. Now get back out in those woods and stop clowning around."

Smoke's fingers were just inches from the man's toes. The laces were long and dragging the ground.

Sloppy troop.

"Look, Jim. Just go get us some hamdamburgers. That stuntman ain't gonna come within a mile of this place. That piece of junk he drove ain't worth anything. The ammo in it was worth more than the car … and there was some nice guns too. What is this guy anyway, some super trooper?"

"I don't know and I don't care. Just get your ass back out there," the driver said.

"Go get some burgers!"

The engine started up. Smoke's eyes widened.

"Fine," the driver said. "I'm going. Just get back out there until I call you when I'm back. Oh, and by the way, you're a real pain in the ass, Harvey."

"Yeah, I know. My wife tells me every day, but at least my girlfriend likes me just the way I am."

Smoke exhaled and flattened down on the ground.

The vehicle revved up and started to pull away. Harvey yelled after it, "Oh, and hold the pickles! I hate pickles!"

The SUV pulled out, leaving Smoke flat on his back and completely exposed.

CHAPTER 9

L OOKING UP AT HARVEY, SMOKE said, "What's up with the goggles?"

Harvey's eyes filled the goggles that he wore. Jaw dropping, he went for his gun.

Smoke kicked Harvey's legs out from under him and pinned him on the ground.

The pair wrestled for a moment, and a gunshot went off.

Pop!

Smoke wrenched the gun free and slung it into the grass. He slugged Harvey in the jaw twice, knocking the man out cold. "You just had to shoot your gun off, didn't you."

A car slowed to a stop beside Smoke. It was a minivan, and the woman rolled the window down and said, "Is he okay? Are you all right?"

Gunfire erupted from the woods.

Blat! Blat! Blat!

Men in tactical vests were coming right for Smoke.

The red-haired woman in the minivan hit the gas, screeched the tires, and sped away.

Smoke returned fire, dashed across the road, and ran into the woods. The manhunt was on again. He could already hear the chopper closing in.

Man, these goggled freaks have it together. I guess that's the price I pay for being greedy.

He heard the footsteps of two men giving chase. One of them was on a radio. "We've got eyes on him. He ran into the woods near our location."

Smoke took cover in bushes behind the trees and waited. The pursuers navigated the woods with tactical flashlights on the ends of their assault rifles, making it easy to see exactly where they were.

Smoke thanked his lucky stars he hadn't been hit when they had the drop on him. Even well-trained men would miss when they were excited. Eyes closed, he became one with nature and listened to the soft footsteps that were quickly coming his way.

Two men, spread about ten feet apart. Both breathing heavy. See them before they see you.

The goon nearest him was almost right on top of him. Booted feet crept over the soft ground and wandered by. Smoke opened his eyes. The man's back was to him. He rose like a ghost from the grave and cracked the man in the temple with the butt of his pistol. He caught the man before he fell and laid him softly on the ground. He turned off the flashlight on the man's weapon, shut off the man's radio, and searched him until he found his phone. He'd lost sight of the other mercenary. The other light was gone.

Not every thug is stupid. He's buried himself somewhere. Time to play hide and seek.

A breeze rustled the branches in the trees. The chopper whizzed overhead and shined its spotlight through the branches. It was the perfect time to move quickly through all of the noise. He darted behind another tree and peered around it.

A goggled man was face to face with him. A knife slashed at Smoke's throat.

He jerked his head back but still caught a slice across his chin. "So you want to do it the old-fashioned way," Smoke said.

"Why not?" The man stepped out of the shadows into full view. He was long limbed like a distance runner, with a twinkling long blade in his hand. "This is the most fun I've had in a long time. Now put your pretty little gun away and we'll go toe to toe like real men."

Smoke stuffed his gun into his holster. "Believe it or not, that's actually comforting." He held up his hands and wiggled his fingers. "This is probably a better option for you, seeing how bad you guys are at shooting. Maybe it's the goggles."

The man shrugged his narrow shoulders and tapped his goggles with the back side of his knife. "Perhaps, but I'm still not going to show any mercy on you."

"It's your beat down," Smoke said, drawing up his fists. "Let's dance."

Slick as a snake, the man used his long reach and stabbed straight for Smoke's chest.

Slapping the weapon aside, Smoke leaned in and gave the attacker a bellyful of fist.

Air exploded from the man's mouth, and he sagged over like a wilting plant.

"Say, that's a nice chin you have there."

Groaning, the man looked up at Smoke with agony in his eyes just as Smoke laid him out cold.

Smoke took off the man's goggles and pulled them down around his own neck.

I need to see what these things are all about, but it will have to wait till later.

Waltzing through the woods with the chopper hovering somewhere overhead, he dialed Sid's number on the first goon's phone.

"Hello?" she said.

"Hiya, Sid."

"John? What's going on? Is that a helicopter I hear, or are you cruising down the highway with the windows rolled down?"

"Are you okay?" he asked with his eyes following the chopper skimming the trees above.

"I'm fine. What's going on, John?"

Speaking above the whipping winds from the chopper, he said, "Well, someone's after me, and I don't know who."

"Is it the Drake?"

"No, I don't think so. Someone else. Look Sid, go to our safe place, okay? I'll meet you there in twelve hours."

"John! John! Smoke, don't you dare hang up that phone," she said.

"See you soon," he replied. He hung up and threw the phone over his left shoulder.

I just have to get away from these goggled fools.

Smoke glanced into the sky and laid eyes on the chopper. Men were rappelling from the chopper down onto the road.

I don't know who these clowns are, but I'm not sticking around to find out. I've got a date in twelve hours.

He took off running.

CHAPTER 10

S PRINTING THROUGH THE WOODS WITH branches stinging his face, Smoke pushed for distance from his pursuers. The path he took paralleled the highway, and he could see through the foliage the white big rigs that had pursued him before. They pulled onto the road and came to a stop. Men were shouting back and forth at each other, and assault rifles were being charged up to fire.

All this over me? Why?

That was the odd part of it. The stink of the Drake wasn't on these men. Nor did they smell of the European sect called Guermo. This was some private army. Mercenaries. Veteran soldiers, and they didn't seem to want him dead. So what did they want? Was it just him, or was Sidney a part of this too?

She sounded fine when I called. No edge to her voice or anything. I can only hope she's okay.

Moving as fast as he could, there wasn't much Smoke could do to hide his tracks. The men coming after him would have to go slower to find his trail, but it wouldn't be hard for a seasoned tracker to find. On a whim, he grabbed the goggles bouncing up and down on his throat and slipped them over his eyes.

The landscape brightened. The goggles worked much like the sunglasses Mal had given him to help see in the dark.

Hmmm.

He scuttled through the brush and came to a stop at the creek that gently cut through the terrain. By jumping to the other side, he left a deep impression in the mud, then took off a dozen yards into the woods, climbed up a fallen tree that ended on the other side of the creek, and lowered himself into the ankle-deep waters and headed upstream.

That ought to buy me a little extra time.

He skimmed over the water on the rocks jutting up above the brook as best he could, like a frog hopping from lily pad to lily pad. A hundred feet into the laborious trek, he heard the voices of pursuit drifting up the waterway and looked back. Men with tactical lights were in pursuit. Three beams of light in all. They paused for several seconds before they ventured across into the woods.

That should give me a few extra minutes, maybe longer if I'm lucky.

But the bright beam of the chopper's spotlight started up the creek and was coming right for him.

That's what I get for relying on luck.

Smoke found a cove in the creek bank and pushed himself up underneath the long overhanging grass until the spotlight passed. Coated in a new layer of fresh mud and soaked to his knees, he resumed his venture. He followed a straight line until the creek bent back toward the highway.

By land or by sea?

Absent the sound of his pursuers, he opted to stay in the water. About fifteen minutes later he was facing the highway, where a small water tunnel burrowed beneath the road. From the cover of the tall grass, he peeked up at the highway. As far as he could tell, he was close to a mile away from the trucks. The chopper was still making its rounds overhead, with the spotlight glaring into the trees.

Follow the water to freedom.

He slipped back down into the creek, got down on his hands and knees, and crawled through the pitch-black tunnel. About a minute later, he came to the tunnel's end and waited. A moment later, the helicopter's spotlight crossed over the creek again. It hovered in the same spot, crossing over the stretch of highway at the points where the creek tunnel entered and exited.

Come on, black bird, nothing to see here. Keep moving.

The chopper drifted away.

Finally.

Without wasting any time, Smoke darted down the creek for another half mile before cutting into the woodland again. The area around DC wasn't anything complicated so far as knowing where he was. He wasn't close to the major interstate but instead the older, less traveled highways. If he had to hoof it into DC and meet Sid, that would be just fine. He could do it in a few hours. He just wondered if anyone else would be looking for him. The police or perhaps the FBI.

I hate to do it, but I might have to borrow someone's wheels to blend in and go. Man, I can't believe my Camaro is totaled. I hope comprehensive insurance will cover it.

He kept at it one foot after the other until the sound of the chopper faded. Skinned up and wet from water and sweat, he wandered into the edge of a suburban neighborhood. The houses were contemporary and well built. The lights were on in most all of them, with the warm canned lights of television sets that were turned on. It being a warm night, there were people out on back porches grilling food. He could see one woman walking her little dogs on the blacktop roads. It looked like the kind of place where everyone knew everybody. It would be tough to steal a car and not be noticed.

Move on or move in.

He eased his way along the backyards until he came to a house where all the lights were out. There was a chain-link fence but no sign of any dogs. He hopped the fence and slunk into the shadows of the backyard shed. He noticed the grass was long beneath his boots.

Maybe this place is on the market.

He made a bead for the back door that led into the garage and gave the handle a jiggle. The security lights flicked on and the house alarm sounded.

Smooth, Smoke, real smooth.

CHAPTER 11

SMOKE LOWERED HIS SHOULDER INTO the back door and busted through. A fishing boat and an old Volvo Crossover sat inside the two-car garage that was mostly empty otherwise. It was pretty clear the house had been cleaned out but not sold, and the owners hadn't moved the bigger items yet.

He went right for the dark-blue Volvo Crossover and took note of the R-Design logo on the back hatch over the bumper. "Cool."

He opened the door and scooted into the old, broken-in leather seats. The key was in the ignition. He turned it over, and the vehicle purred to life. He clicked in his seatbelt, punched the garage door opener attached to the visor, and watched the door open up in front of him. He dropped it into drive and eased the Swedish machine forward.

An old man with a crew cut who was wearing long pajamas blocked the driveway with his shotgun pointed right at Smoke. "Stop right there, thief!"

Great Dane.

Smoke honked the horn.

Pajama Man flinched.

Smoke hit the gas and zoomed straight for him.

Pajama Man dove to the side and a shotgun blast went off, busting out the passenger-side window and sending glass everywhere.

Smoke was skidding out of the driveway, leaving the house way behind and racing through the once-peaceful neighborhood.

Walkers with and without leashes attached to dogs were shaking their fists at him and yelling for him to slow down. They didn't know what was going on, just that there was a maniac running wild through the neighborhood.

He cut down one street and up another.

It's a suburban maze. Crap. One of those unending gated communities.

Eyeing the landscape, he followed the road whenever it led down the slope until he came to a steep, winding road with the backsides of the houses and condos facing it. After following the twists and curves a mile down the hill, he spied the automatic gatehouse ahead. The black iron gates were closed, and the blue and red lights of a police car were flashing through the trees of the exit road.

Law enforcement is here already. They must get a cut from the homeowners' association.

He brought the car up to fifty miles per hour and drove for the gate.

I hope this works like it does in the movies.

He squeezed the steering wheel.

Here we go!

The black gate smashed open and swung over to one side, shattering the gear box to pieces. He bottomed out at the T-intersection and turned right and charged straight for the oncoming police car.

The black and white parked in the middle of the two lanes.

No good.

Smoke cut the wheel hard, doing a one-eighty in the middle of the road and putting the turbo Crossover into reverse. He pushed the accelerator to the floor and rammed through the rear quarter panel of the police car like something out of a *Dukes of Hazard* episode. Metal ground and glass shattered everywhere. The jarring impact snapped his head into the headrest. He kept going backward down the curvy road until he made it to the next intersection. Backing into it, he got the Crossover straightened back out and put it in drive and floored it until he got onto the next stretch of four-lane highway divided by a concave berm.

"Whew!"

He wiped the sweat from his brow. He was out of the woods and onto the road and trying to think his way through to the next plan, but other things than survival were on his mind.

Let's see. Breaking and entering. Grand larceny. Damage to personal property. Reckless driving. Assault on police officers. It's going to be a bad day in court. I hope I can get my old cell back.

He patted the dash of the car. A lifelong reader of *Motor Trend* and *Car and Driver*, he knew plenty about the specs of the Volvo R-Design. It had racing suspension and a suped-up engine with three hundred twenty-five horsepower. That plus its sturdy frame made for an excellent escape vehicle, but now he just had to get far enough away from his pursuers so that he could hide.

A Walmart would be really nice right now. I could park and blend in with all the wal-nut zombies.

He eased off the gas from about a hundred to eighty, hoping to blend in with the steady flow of traffic. He'd passed by a few cars and trucks when the police cars came firing down the oncoming traffic of the four-lane highway. Smoke switched into the slow lane between two other cars and slowed down a little more. The two police cars passed him by and kept on going.

I might make a great escape after all.

He steered back into the fast lane and accelerated up to eighty again, took his turnoff away from the steady flow of cars, and headed back toward DC. He turned on the radio. No music, just a commercial. He poked another preset button. Hip-hop music pumped the bass and shook the windows.

Nice system for a Volvo.

Smoke adjusted his seat.

Wow. They really do make the most comfortable seats.

The radio turned to static.

A spotlight shone down on him in the Volvo like it was an alien abduction. The black chopper was back.

Whuppa…whuppa…whuppa…whuppa…

CHAPTER 12

I'M REALLY STARTING TO HATE *helicopters. They're ruining my radio enjoyment.*

Zipping past car after car, Smoke took the Crossover up to ninety. He was dead meat out in the open. He needed to get into a crowd, blend in, and disappear. Too bad there weren't a lot of crowds on the highway. He was the pitcher on the mound with all eyes on him. Nowhere to escape.

The road chase continued for several miles, taking him closer to DC. He expected traffic, but as late as it was, the flow was easy. He just stayed in the fast lane and went.

Bright headlights lit up his rearview mirror. Two motorcycles were on his tail. Behind them were some other cars.

Looks like the posse has finally caught up with me.

He stayed on the highway until he found himself approaching Silver Spring, a Maryland city north of DC. Now all he had to do was find a crowded spot to get out and hide before they tore up the city chasing after him. The bright lights of traffic had started to thicken. A red light was ahead, and in a moment he'd be in the bumper-to-bumper traffic with his pursuers right on his tail.

Think fast, Smoke. Real fast.

The light turned green and the traffic started to flow again. People on the sidewalks were looking up at the chopper in the sky and pointing. He could see the bikers in goggles talking to each other behind him. If they had guns, they were kept out of sight.

Hmmm, looks like someone wants to keep a low profile.

Now in the thick of town, the traffic started to slow to another stop, waiting for the light to change. Smoke squeezed the Volvo into the left lane, drove onto the sidewalk, and slipped between the foot traffic into an alley. The passage was narrow, with barely enough room to open a door and get out on the other side. The motorcycles and another car were right behind him. He parked the car cockeyed, jumped out of the sunroof, and took off running full speed toward the end of the alley.

Try and catch me now.

As soon as he made his way to the street, Smoke dove into the crowd where the people were thickest. It was a nice night, and many people were out on the town. Staying low and concealing his guns under his shirt as best he could, Smoke slipped into a joint called Pete's New Haven Pizza, where the line was out the door. Ushering himself inside, he brushed through a couple of waitresses into the kitchen and slipped out the door on the back side. After repeating this several times, he started to breathe easy.

I think I gave them the slip.

He hung back under the awning of a storefront, where he could see the chopper overhead. People were still glancing up from time to time. Once the chopper cleared his view, Smoke headed over to a pay phone, got a paperclip out of his jeans pocket, and bent it into a straight line. He stuck the paperclip into a small black hole between the coin release and the amplification button just above the hook mechanism where the receiver hung. Grabbing the handset, he put the other end of the paperclip in the center hole of the microphone. He used the paperclip to toggle the lever inside the hook mechanism, heard it click over, and got a dial tone without paying.

Works every time.

He dialed a number and got an answer after two rings.

"This is Mal."

Huddled over the phone, Smoke said, "It's Smoke. No time to chat, but I'm in Silver Spring and need to get to DC. No rentals, cabs, or buses."

"What am I, a travel agent?" Mal replied without hiding the offense in his voice. "What do you have going on, anyway?"

"Get it done, Mal." Smoke heard Mal screaming through the room. "Asia! Asia! Silver Spring incognito now!"

"After my show," said her voice in the background.

"It's for Smoke. Go!" Mal insisted.

"I'm so glad I can count on the happiest couple that ever lived," Smoke said without hiding his sarcasm. "Listen, you need to make this happen quickly. They've got thugs all over me."

"Who does? The Drake?"

"No," Smoke replied. "I think someone else is crashing our party. I don't know who or why, but I do have a clue. You can take a look at this Maryland plate. 2DH721."

"Okay," Mal replied. "I've got your ride. Fred's Cars and Auto Care. Westwood and Nickers street. Good—"

Smoke hung up the phone. Hands in his pockets, he crossed the street and approached an older couple coming out of McDonald's. "Excuse me, do you know where Fred's Cars and Auto Care is?"

The old man cupped his ear and said, "What?"

The woman smiled at Smoke and said, "He can't hear anything but bells anymore. You're close, honey." She pointed. "Five blocks south to the multiplex and take the left onto Apple Avenue. You'll be close enough to see it from there."

"Thanks."

"Anytime," she replied.

"What did he say?" the old man asked her.

Smoke walked fast, head down and hands in his pockets. Once he made it to Apple Avenue, he spotted the used car place. There were dozens of cars guarding a double-wide office trailer. It was a warm summer night, and they were open. He ventured up the steps and inside the door. A cute young gal sat at a small receptionist desk filing her nails. Her brows lifted when she saw him. She sat up, picked up a set of keys, smiled, and said, "I'm guessing you're the man looking for these?"

Smiling back, he said, "That would be me. Are we good?"

She got up from her chair and walked over to him with a swagger in her hips, handed him the keys, and said, "I think we'd be great together. Come on, sugar. Follow me."

He opened up the door and said, "After you."

With a little giggle, she led him outside onto the parking lot and stopped alongside a white Camry. "She's a ninety-six with over two hundred thousand miles, but probably still the most reliable car on the lot." Chewing her gum, she nuzzled up to him. "So, where are you going in such a hurry?"

"I'm late for a wedding." He stepped around her and opened up the car door. "Thanks, sweetie."

"Next time you're back in Silver Springs, look me up," she said.

He left her in the rearview mirror, hit the main road, and found his way back onto I-495.

The chopper and its penetrating spotlight glided right over him.

You've got to be kidding me.

CHAPTER 13

B IG HANDS LOCKED ON THE steering wheel and eyes on the road, Smoke hunkered down in the seat. It was a pointless exercise, but he did it on instinct, changing his frame and trying to look smaller. The helicopter lowered until it was about thirty feet above the ground as he raced alongside the cars on the highway. The bright beam shone right inside the cars in front of Smoke, suffocating them with brilliant light one by one.

Go ahead and cause an accident, why don't you?

He couldn't help but think they'd figured him out at the used car lot. Perhaps the men showed up and shook her down for a description. Maybe a keyword in his payphone conversation with Mal Gunderson had tipped them off.

They can't be that good.

Moving along with the steady stream of traffic, he switched the Camry over into the slow lane and eased off the gas until he was alongside a big rig that was in the middle lane. The trailer blocked the chopper's spotlight, and the beam kept going backward, one car after another, until its light faded and it soared back into the night toward Silver Spring.

It's about time.

His belly groaned.

I could use a hamburger.

Having finally given his pursuers the slip, Smoke found a drive-through and picked up three burgers and two milkshakes. Sucking down the chocolate shake, he headed to the rendezvous point to meet with Sid.

It was another bizarre set of circumstances.

He could only assume Sid was being followed as well or that she would be in some sort of danger. He just hoped she remembered exactly where the rendezvous was. Well, and that she could manage to get there without being followed.

The last of the chocolate shake came up his straw.

Sluuuuurrrp.

Things weren't getting any easier for anybody these days with all the security cameras that coated the city like white on paper. The stores, sidewalks, roadways, and restaurants had more than the eyes could count. It was a world full of doubt and paranoia. It had gotten so bad that more and more people wouldn't even leave their homes for the sake of privacy. It left a knot in his stomach some nights. All the time, someone somewhere was watching.

He unwrapped a burger and swallowed it down in two bites.

"Mmm, I should have gotten two more of those. Oh, I did."

Wadding up the hamburger paper and tossing it into the backseat and unwrapping another one, he led the car off the interstate until he got onto Chain Bridge Road. From there he drove southwest, drinking the strawberry shake, until he found the entrance to Emmaus United Church of Christ and pulled into the vacant parking lot. He chowed down the last burger and shut off the engine, leaving him alone in the dark and quiet. There weren't any street lamps in the lot. Outside of the car, he shut the door and cut through the trees onto the Westwood Country Club Golf Course.

No cameras out here. Not yet anyway.

Traveling over the fast green and walking around the sand traps, he stopped at what he believed was the tenth hole. Underneath the trees was the backside of an athletic woman.

Easing in behind her, he said, "You made it."

Sid turned. The wrinkles in her forehead were deep, and her eyes showed signs of worry. She gave him a quick hug. "What's going on, John?"

He told her everything that had happened since he left her parents' house then asked, "Have you called to talk with them? I'm worried."

"They're fine." She pushed the hair out of his eyes and traced her finger over a long scratch on his cheek. Her nose crinkled. "Have you been eating hamburgers? I smell pickles on your breath."

"I got hungry on my way over."

Aghast, she said, "So in the middle of being manhunted, you stopped for food? Are you kidding me?"

"Jumping out of helicopters builds up quite the appetite." He tilted his head to one side. "Are you mad?"

"No." She gave him a little shove in the chest. "I was just worried. Damn, John, what do you think is going on?"

He took her by the hand, and they started to walk together through the dark to the sound of the singing crickets. "I don't know who they were, but I do know they don't have the stink of the supernatural on them. They seem to want me alive. If they wanted to kill me, they certainly could have. There's no doubt about that." He slipped the red-tinted goggles over his eyes. "Do you like?"

"Not really," she said, nudging him. "It hides that mystery in your eyes. So these men, they were all wearing those things?"

"Most of them. Well, all that I could see." He rubbed her hand with his thumb. "Are you getting tired of this?"

"I get tired, but so far as all this is concerned, no. If anything, I've gotten numb to it." She squeezed his hand. "That sounds like a cold thing to say. It's hard for me to say it. But after what I went through, I'm numb. That's what they want, John. They want people like me and you, like everyone, to just give up hope. They're trying to break our spirit by putting us through hell so we just give up fighting. When I was at Kane's place, I'd started to feel like I was done for, like I might as well give up. I was this close. But you came. You fought your way into the pit of Hades and dragged me out. My prayers were answered."

"I'd do it again."

She leaned into his shoulder and hugged his arm. "I know you would, just like I would for you. I think the Drake knows that, and it scares them. If *we* can take them on, then so can the rest of the world." She turned to face him and looked up into his eyes. "So without a doubt you want to go through with this wedding?"

"Until death do us part."

"That might come sooner than expected."

"As long as we last for the honeymoon, I'll be happy."

Sid's face lit up. She put her arms around his neck, rose up on her toes, and gave him a long, soft kiss.

He wrapped her up in his arms and kissed her warm lips back with as much passion as she gave him.

They broke it off with her saying, "I love you, John."

The electric hum of a motor caught his ear. Sid cocked an eyebrow, and her hand drew out her gun.

A man hunkered over the wheel of an electric golf cart was approaching. He was alone. Above, the familiar sound of a helicopter straightened the hair in Smoke's ears.

We've got company.

The chopper spotlight illuminated them both.

Bad company.

CHAPTER 14

"**D**ON'T RUN OFF AGAIN, JOHNNY Smoke. Don't you dare run off. I swear, if you do, it'll be to the peril of you both." The man stopped the golf cart about twenty feet from them. Lit up by the spotlight, the man wore an Irish cap and was a little bit heavy in his knit yellow polo shirt and shorts. An oxygen tank was in the passenger seat, and he had a clear mask over his face. He coughed and sucked for air. "So are you going to run or not, Johnny?"

"Do you know him?" Sid asked.

It was the man he'd talked to on the phone earlier. That vaguely familiar voice. It all started to come together. Approaching the man in the cart, Smoke got a glimpse at the man's gemstone-green eyes. "Uncle Earl?"

The man took a deep breath, pulled the mask down, and said, "Yes, it's me, Uncle Earl. How are you, Nephew?"

Sid stepped up alongside Smoke. "The man who's been chasing you is your uncle? That doesn't sound like family to me."

Earl shrugged and produced a cigarette from his pocket, then reached for his lighter while it hung there stuck to his lower lip while he said, "I love these things." He lit the cigarette, took a few puffs, and went into a fit of coughing. He took out his phone and dialed a number. "Turn that damn spotlight off! The fox ain't running."

The light died, and the chopper moved away.

Earl leaned back in the golf cart seat. "Whew, that's so much better." He put his hands on his bare knees. "So, I hear you two are getting married. Congratulations."

Smoke looked at Sid and back at Earl. Uncle Earl was a sturdy, adventurous character that had been a part of Smoke's life on and off. He was in his fifties now, but when he was younger, he was very fit like a burly Army Ranger, and active. But he'd always smoked like a chimney, and it looked like that had finally caught up with him.

Smoke hadn't seen Uncle Earl since his SEAL school, nor heard from him. "Why all of the fanfare to bring me in?"

"I was trying to make it easy by shutting down your car as soon as you left the Shaws, but no, just like you always do, you kept on going." Earl blew out some smoke. "Driving a car that doesn't have an electric system we can take out. Smart move."

"You had my number. You could have just called."

Earl pointed at Smoke while talking to Sid. "I've never seen anyone like him. You can't corner him or trap him. He fights like a hungry badger to get out of it. Always has a backup plan. Even as a kid. And the instincts. Amazing."

"I know that." Sid's tone was angry. "But you almost killed him."

"I didn't almost kill him. He almost killed himself." Earl finished his cigarette and flicked it away. "All he had to do was stand down."

"You didn't want me to stand down. You wanted to test me. To push. You wanted to see what I'd do, like I was auditioning for something. All that time, you were putting me to the test."

"And you passed," Uncle Earl said. "With flying colors. But I swore we had you this time when we picked up your car with the chopper. I still can't believe you jumped!" He went into a fit of coughing and put his mask on, fist tapping his chest until it stopped.

"Wait," Sid said to Smoke, "you jumped out of a helicopter? You didn't tell me you jumped out of a helicopter."

"You should have seen it, Miss Shaw." Earl's eyes gleamed with excitement. "He jumped right off of it like a Captain America comic book or something. I swear I could hear my men crapping in their pants when he did it. 'That's a soldier,' I said, and I meant it!"

Sidney walked over to Earl and pulled his mask back and snapped it into his face. "My soon-to-be husband isn't some rat in a maze. You pull another stunt like that, and I'll shove that oxygen tank so far up your—"

"Sid," Smoke interrupted. "It's fine."

Wide eyed for a moment, Earl whispered to Smoke, "Boy, I really like her." He gave her the once over. She was glaring at him. "She's got a great, uh, personality too."

"I don't care for your uncle," Sid said, making her way back over to Smoke's side. "He's trouble."

"It runs in the family. Heh-heh." Earl locked his penetrating eyes with Smoke's. His raspy tone softened. "Yeah, I'm a bastard. I could have done this the easy way, but I didn't. Smoke is my Rambo. My super soldier. The prodigy. I couldn't resist vetting him some more. Besides, I needed a good field test for my men. They needed to see a true master in action. Someone who'll do anything to win. The hungry will of a lion in action." He dug out another cigarette, lit it, removed his mask, and started smoking. "I'm thrilled and amazed."

"You're sick," Sidney said.

"No, no he's not," Smoke said. He shrugged at her. "I liked it. It was fun. But I still don't feel so good about myself."

"Why's that?" Earl said.

"Because you still caught me."

Earl showed a razor-thin smile. "You did well. It's hard to beat all the technology that's hovering around. There are satellites. Spy planes. Infrared beacons. Radio towers. And many other technologies you don't know about. I've been with you the entire time, ever since you hurled yourself fearlessly into the air." He started tapping on his phone. A black drone with four propellers shaped in a four-feet-wide square dropped out of the sky. It was silent and hovering over the green. "And there is this drone of mine. Pretty snazzy, ain't it?"

Quick as a snake, Sid drew her Glock and shot it.

Ka-Blam!

The drone's body exploded into pieces, and it flopped to a stop on the green.

"Shit!" Earl said. "You didn't have to do that. I'm on your side, you know. Damn, I can't believe you did that. Are you sure you want to marry her, Johnny? She's got a temper."

"I know." Smoke nodded. "I like it."

Sid stuck her gun back into her holster. "So what's all this about, Earl? You came here with your boys to see Smoke. Why?"

"I'm here to recruit him."

"Recruit him for what?"

Earl took another puff of his cigarette and blew it out noisily. "I want him to lead my soldiers in a war against the Drake."

CHAPTER 15

"**W**HAT DO YOU KNOW ABOUT the Drake?" Sid asked.

"Plenty," Earl replied. "You know, there's more than one Black Slate. The two of you are only dealing with the one here in DC. That's the big one, but these shifters, ghouls, nightmares, or whatever you want to call them, they're all over. My task force has been working the west coast. You can tell by my tan." He pulled his collar back, which revealed nothing in the darkness. "Anyway, we got called to DC because somebody—that somebody being you two—has kicked the hornets' nest, and now DC is buzzing."

"What task force are you part of?" Smoke asked. "Who runs it, the FBI? CIA?"

"We're under contract with the division of the federal government that oversees the FBI and CIA. My people are ghosts that don't exist. I don't exist." He hacked really hard and spat on the ground. "I literally won't exist soon, that's for certain. Look, I don't have much time left to live. Look at me. I'm dying. Well, I might make it a year. But I need an heir apparent, and that is you, Johnny Smoke. You are best suited to run the Black List operation."

Smoke shook his head. "No. I'm not answering to anybody. You might as well go."

"Johnny, this is another way to serve your country, and this time you'll have everything you need at your disposal. Armor. Weapons. Cars. We have lots of toys."

"You have lots of red tape that comes with that, too." Smoke made his way into the cart and gave Earl a long, hard look. There wasn't any weakness in his eyes. "You aren't dying."

"Sure I am."

"Not anytime soon. You're too stubborn, Earl."

"Okay, I'm not dying that soon, but I could. Look at me. I'm on oxygen and down to my third unhappy wife. I can't hold up that much longer." He grabbed Smoke's arm. "My job is what you are meant for. I've seen those evil bastards and what they do. They are pollution. Poison. But they're weak right now, and we need to take them before they strengthen."

Smoke pulled away and glanced at Sidney. "I've got different priorities."

"Sure, sure, I know," Earl said. "You want the happy life and happy wife. A family. Kids to bounce on your knee. Well, you're both in the thick of this, and it ain't going away. At least equip yourselves with the best and be ready for the battle ahead."

Smoke got up and walked back to Sid. "I don't even want to think about it until after the honeymoon."

Earl eased the golf cart closer to Smoke. "Listen to me, both of you. They're coming after you."

"Maybe, maybe not," Sid said. "How would *you* know?"

"I'll tell you what I know. I know where Kane Lancaster's mansion is. I know what went down there with you and him. I saw it. That mansion might be archaic, but it's not totally primitive. There are recordings."

Sid's eyes grew wide. "What kind of recordings?"

"Discreet ones."

"How discreet?" she said.

Earl's eyes slid over to Smoke and back on Sid. "I'd rather not say."

Taking Sid by the hand, Smoke said, "It wouldn't make any difference if you did. We're okay." He truly felt that way no matter what Sid had been through. But the pain in her eyes told it all. She was barely able to hide a deep, dark shame. Sometimes Smoke hated being able to read people so well. "Listen, Uncle Earl, it's been good catching up with you, but we'll be on our way. Take care of yourself."

"There is strength in numbers, Johnny," Earl said as Smoke and Sid walked away. "Just come and check out our operation. I swear you'll like it."

Smoke waved goodbye. "You owe me a ton of gear. And a car."

"That wasn't a car. That was something that should have been laid to rest in the eighties." Earl went into another fit of coughing. When he regained his composure, he yelled out, "Enjoy your honeymoon! That's the best part of the marriage. Trust me, I've been through three of them, and everything goes down the crapper after that." There was a raspy sigh. Earl drove the golf cart away and was back on the phone. "Hey, someone get their ass down here and pick up the pieces of my drone."

Hand in hand, Smoke and Sid kept on walking until they were just across the parking lot where Smoke had crossed onto the course. He looked down into Sid's eyes and said, "You all right?"

"Smoke, things happened in that mansion that I still have nightmares about." She swallowed. "I, uh, think you should know more about me and Kane."

"I don't care about that."

"You say that now, but later, that might change, and you need to understand what you're getting into." She hugged herself, shivering. "I don't even know who I was back then. My mind is fuzzy. It's like waking from a horrible dream. Honestly, I don't know how long an effect it will have on me, and I feel like maybe I'm trying to fill the gap selfishly with you by getting married. Marriage isn't going to fix me. I'm broken."

Smoke took her cheek in the palm of his hand, put his forehead to her forehead. "We were born broken and we're going to die broken. It'll never change how I feel about you."

She grasped his wrist. "Those aren't the most comforting words, but I think that's just what I needed to hear. Fine, you still want to get married, then let's quit standing around and get married, but just remember that once I put that ring on your finger, you're mine."

"Till death do us part," he said.

CHAPTER 16

"T his is it," Sidney said to Smoke. It was a sunny morning, and they were standing outside of her church. It was a single-level red-brick building with a high, gabled roof and a white cross on top. On the right side the building extended out into a newer addition that looked to be more classrooms, with a fellowship hall in the back. To the left across the lawn, a little white concrete bridge went across a charming creek to the church's parking lot. "What do you think?"

Nodding, Smoke said, "I like it. It looks humble. Holy. So you grew up here?"

"Every Sunday up until college. You know, there'll be a lot of people here you've never met before. Plenty of single older ladies." She nudged him. "They're going to have their eyes on you. Lots of pinchy fingers and decades-old compliments. Think you can handle it?"

"I like old people. They have the most interesting things to say." He studied her eyes. Sid was in a white cotton summer blouse and a short pair of khaki shorts that really showed off her long legs. The feminine sandals and painted toenails were a nice touch. "You look beautiful."

"Thanks." She blushed. "Geez, you're making me feel like I'm sixteen again. Look, I have goose bumps."

"I have that effect on people." Smoke studied the stained glass windows on the church. It had been a week since his run-in with Uncle Earl. Earl's warnings still weren't sitting well with him. The nagging in his neck told him something was coming. Something bad. It was hard to ignore it, but this was more important. "So, two days."

"Yep, two days and we become a permanent team."

"Like Batman and Batgirl?" he said.

"I don't think they ever got married."

"I know, I was just testing you. Maybe Superman and Lois Lane?"

Sid stroked her silky long hair that hung over the shoulder. "I'm not a very big DC fan."

"Me neither." Smoke switched to his Batman voice. "But I just love saying—"

"I'm Batman!" Sid said in her own imitation.

"That was really horrible." Smoke shook his head. "How about Yellow Jack and Wasp?"

"Too small. Vision and the Scarlet Witch?"

"Nah. Spider-Man and Mary Jane?" he offered.

"No, too nerdy, but I always liked Patsy Walker and Nighthawk. I can't remember if they got married though." She shrugged. "How about Daredevil and Electra?"

"You look too good to be Electra," he said. "And if I were Daredevil, I'd never get to see you. I can't have that." He kissed her briefly. "How about we start our own comic book team?"

"Sure," she agreed. "How about *The Supernatural Adventures of Sid and Smoke*?"

"Let's just call it *Sid and Smoke*. Shorter is cooler."

"If you say so, husband-to-be." She took his hand. "Come on. Pastor Stanley can't wait to meet you."

CHAPTER 17

THE DISCUSSION WITH PASTOR STANLEY lasted about an hour, and then Smoke and Sid were back in her car. She was behind the wheel of the Hellcat with a childish grin on her face. "So, what did you think of Pastor Stanley?" she said. "I like him. He really knows his stuff."

"He should, he's been pastor here since my dad was a kid." Cruising down the highway to the sound of the Hellcat's throaty engine growling under the hood, she reached over and touched his hand. "It means a lot that you're comfortable about all this."

"It's not so different than how I was raised. It makes me think about good times. I like it. Not as much as I like driving, but I like it."

"Are you saying you don't like my driving?" she said.

"No, I'd just like to drive the Hellcat. You know, once we get married, half of this car is mine."

"Oh no, if that's the case, maybe we need to get a prenup."

"Fine by me, but you're more than welcome to half of all that I have. Heck, you can have all of it." His belly rumbled. "Man, all of this wedding business is making me hungry."

"Of course it is. We'll hit a drive-through on the way back to your place. Sound good?"

"Yep."

She gave him a quick glance. "You know I'm only kidding about the car and prenup."

"Of course I do. Don't fret about it."

"I won't. I just don't want you thinking I care about those things. I'm not like my sister. I couldn't care less about money or power." Sid's features tightened. "I just don't know why she's such an idiot."

"I'm worried about Allison and Megan too, Sid. Look, I hope they'll be there. Good or bad, I think you want that too."

Sid drove the car off the exit ramp and merged onto the two-lane highway. "I always thought Megan would be my flower girl and my sister would be my maid of honor. Now, I don't even know where they are. I feel like it's my fault."

"Let's just do what we're doing and see what happens. Who knows, it wouldn't surprise me one bit if they showed up. Doesn't Allison call your mom from time to time?"

"It's been awhile."

They pulled into a drive-through. Smoke ordered a bag full of food and two large shakes. Sid ordered a bottled water.

"You really should eat more," he said, stuffing his face with the first of four hamburgers.

"I have a wedding dress to fit into."

"I can't wait to see you in it." He took the top off the first shake and gulped half of it down. "You're really embracing this wedding. I didn't think you'd be that into it."

"Is that so surprising?" she asked, pulling the Hellcat back onto the highway.

"Sort of. You're gorgeous, but not so girlie. I just never envisioned you planning a wedding."

"I have my softer side. Besides, I have my mom and your sister organizing things. They know what I like. They get the samples and I make the final choices. But there's one choice I need your help with."

"I'm fine with whatever you decide. Just thrilled to be in the ring with such a knockout."

She punched his leg. "No, you need to take this seriously. We haven't talked about the honeymoon. Where would you like it to be?"

"The bedroom."

Sid rolled her eyes. "Yes, but a bedroom where?"

"It can be anywhere that has a bedroom."

She shoved him in the shoulder. "Come on, do you want something remote, tropical, a beach? Niagara Falls? Maybe a European vacation?"

"I'm partial to the continental U.S., if that helps."

"Wow," she said, "you really narrowed it down. Haven't you ever given any thought to where you might want to honeymoon?"

"No."

"Just give me something, a hint. You're a big part of this. I mean, not the most important part, obviously, but a movable part." She rubbed his thigh. "Come on, tell me something."

Smoke swallowed down the last bite of his first burger and said, "I would prefer that the wedding night be somewhere close. Very close. If we have to drive too far before we get there, my head might explode."

With a purr in her voice she said, "We can't have that now, can we?"

"I hope not."

"It's done then. I'll make the arrangements. A honeymoon suite just outside of DC." She gripped his hand. "I can't wait either."

Smoke tugged at his collar. "It might be a good idea to change the subject."

"Why's that?" she said, running her hand farther down his thigh.

"Let's just say I don't want to consummate the marriage prematurely." He pressed his hand down on her hand, stopping it short of its course. "Please, I've been holding off this long. I've got to last two more days."

Sid's cheeks turned rosy. "That's so sweet."

"A honeymoon in Vegas or at a beach is fine by me. I like the sun and the heat."

"I think I'd like to see you at the beach playing in the surf and sunshine. No shirt. Short swim trunks. Rubbing lots of warm suntan oil all over each other."

"You're killing me, Sid." He shifted in his seat and crossed his legs. "Let's go for the sand. Next plan?"

She let out a teasing little laugh. "Fine, I'll be merciful. New subject. You never really told me much about your Uncle Earl. Did you say he was also Sam's uncle? Because he seems like something other than that."

"No, well, yes. He is her uncle, but he was also the one who recruited me to the SEALS." Smoke started in on another burger. "He's something else. A real taskmaster..." Smoke kept on talking about Earl and their long history together. It went on until they arrived back at his place. His white Camaro was sitting in front of the garage. Its frame was crushed, wheels bent into the fenders, and most of the glass was smashed. He tossed his head back and laughed. "A real practical joker, too."

CHAPTER 18

"THIS IS IT, YOU LUCKY dog," Guppy said to Smoke. They were inside the church, in one of the classrooms. The tables were small, and the colorful chairs were designed for little kids. Guppy finished tying up Smoke's bowtie. "Do you feel like vomiting yet?"

"Nope," he said, checking himself out in the mirror. His hands were clammy, and his stomach squirmed a little. The black tuxedo and grey silk cummerbund looked nice. Adjusting his cufflinks, he said, "Bond. James Bond."

Guppy laughed.

"What are you laughing at?" Smoke said.

"You ain't no James Bond, that's for sure. Not handsome enough or scrawny enough, but if I had to pick one, I'd say you were more like Connery. He could have been something if he pumped some iron." He poked Smoke in the belly with his sausage-link finger. "You feel a little soft. Have you quit working out?"

"Says the man who looks like a penguin on steroids."

Pushing in front of the long mirror in his own tuxedo, Guppy thickened his arms and flapped them stiffly at his sides. "I *do* look like a penguin on steroids. I like it."

"You would."

Smoke was putting on his jacket when another man entered the room. It was Sid's older brother Jerry, who he'd just met for the first time last night. Jerry looked very much like his father, Keith, a well-built fella with the look of a frontier lawman. His tuxedo was slung over his shoulder and still covered up in the plastic cover.

Smoke extended his hand. "Hey, Jerry."

"Hey, Smoke." Jerry spoke with a brassy voice. "Sorry I'm running late, but Cecilia kept me up all night, if you know what I mean." He winked at Smoke and started taking his tuxedo out of the cover. The man was about Smoke's age and wore a striped golf shirt and blue jeans. An automatic gun was tucked inside a shoulder holster. "Weddings really get her hot for some reason. That's where I met her, at my partner's wedding."

Smoke had just met Jerry last night at the rehearsal dinner, and he'd concluded two things about him: the man talked too much bull, and he was always late. But otherwise, he wasn't a half-bad fellow. He was a New York City detective who had worked in homicide and narcotics.

"Thanks for being here, Jerry. I know it means a lot to Sid."

Dropping his pants, Jerry revealed some nasty bullet scars on his thighs. He caught Smoke and Guppy looking and said, "That was a harrowing night. Mobsters. They popped me in the legs." He patted his sidearm. "I popped them in the head. I can't talk about it to Cecilia so much. She really hates me being a cop. But man, sometimes you have to vent. So Smoke, you and Sid are bounty hunters now? That's a pretty unique career path. I understand you're a veteran, too. In the navy? I always thought those dungarees looked silly. Do they still wear those?"

"Pretty sure."

In about three minutes, Jerry was dressed and ready to go. He faced Smoke and said, "Look, I don't know you really well, but everyone seems to think you're a pretty good guy. I pride myself as a damn good judge of character." He looked Smoke up and down. "You look like an okay guy, but don't most guys look okay before the wedding?"

There was a brief silence.

Guppy lifted his shoulders.

Jerry continued, "Listen, she's my little sister, and I just want you to know from me that you better not hurt her. She's family. We look out for one another. *Capisce?*"

Cheeks flushed, Guppy stepped into Jerry. "Boy, you don't know what the hell you're talking about. You've never met a better man, aside from your own dad."

Dusting off his sleeves and without looking at Guppy, Jerry said, "Well, I don't know about that. You see to it that you behave yourself, Smoke. I'll be paying attention."

Keith opened the door to the classroom and said, "It's show time, gentlemen."

Jerry followed his dad out.

Guppy sighed. "What was all that clishmaclaver about?"

Smoke shrugged. "I don't know. Maybe it's Biff Tannen complex."

CHAPTER 19

S MOKE STOOD AT THE ALTAR with his hands clasped over his waist. His throat was a little tight. Eyeing the double doors that led into the sanctuary, he felt his fingers tingle. Was this finally going to happen, or was something dark and sinister going to swoop in?

Is this happening? It better be.

There were several small arrangements of flowers on the stage, and Pastor Stanley stood with his Bible in hand. He was a picture of wisdom and peace in his dark-blue suit and burgundy tie. Candelabra held tall candles lit with warm golden flames. The sun shined through the stained glass windows. A young girl in in a honey-colored dress with many curls in her hair played something soothing on the piano. The church pews were overflowing on both sides of the quaint brick-and-mortar building. The faces were warm, wrinkled, tearful, and friendly. The place had a spirit of its own.

The gentle stroke of the piano keys changed its tune and swelled to fill the room. Everyone stood up and turned to face the doors that split open at the opposite end.

Guppy had Samantha on his arm. Sam was tall and gorgeous, with her rich chestnut hair up in a bun. She wore a soft lavender dress that hugged her curves with class and sensuality. The husband and wife split apart and took their places on the dais.

Jerry and Cecilia came next. Cecilia was a vivacious Italian with short black hair and penetrating eyes. Jerry walked with a strut and had a bit of a smirk on his face. They kissed briefly and sauntered into their respective spots.

The wedding march started to play.

Smoke took a glance at Sally. She sat alone in the front pew. Her sweet face was already streaked with tears. On the groom's side were some of Smoke's other brothers and sisters and his adoptive parents, Charlotte and Larry. They were a pair of hardworking and well-dressed people. He gave Charlotte a little wink. Her eyes watered up.

At the top of the aisle, the young boys parted the doors again.

Sid stood arm in arm with her father Keith. The crowd erupted into complimentary murmurs as they walked down the aisle. Smiles were broad on everyone's faces, seeing one of their own little girls all grown up and so beautiful in a marvelous wedding dress with inlaid pearls and a silver lining. The dress touched the floor but stopped there. Sidney's face was covered in a white veil, but the swooping neckline and tight waist enhanced her sumptuous figure.

Smoke's heart pounded in his temples. He couldn't wait to feast his eyes on her. He was a little surprised too, as he hadn't envisioned the veil. He teetered on his feet a little.

That better be her under there.

Keith led her up to the bottom step, whispered a few words in Sid's ear, and took his seat by Sally. Sid slowly made her way up the steps. As she did so, Samantha took the bouquet. Smoke extended his hand to Sid. Her gloved hand touched his.

She really did go all out.

He searched for her eyes through the veil, but he couldn't see them.

The height is right. The build is right.

So were those of Samone, Sid's clone. And those of Allison. He started to wonder if any of these people were real at all. He never got the jitters this bad, not ever, before anything.

Pastor Stanley spoke. "Please sit down, everyone. I wish I could join you. Standing just doesn't come as easily to an old preacher like me these days." There was some laughter. "So, let's get right down to it, shall we?"

Smoke nodded. Beside him, Sid was stiff as stone, her hand firm in his.

"Please face one another," the pastor said. As they turned, he chatted. "So I've done more weddings than I can count, and I know many of you know what I'm about to say, but I'll say it again and I'll try not to be so long, because so many of you look hungry."

Smoke squeezed Sid's hand so as to say, "Is that you?"

She squeezed back once.

But anyone can do that. Sid? Is that you? Please be you.

"Marriage is a mystery. Even in scripture, God does not fully declare its purpose, but He is very clear about the guidelines. You see, in the beginning God created man and saw that he was alone, and He made him a companion. This is the reason why a man leaves his mother and father and is united with his wife, and they become one flesh…"

Pastor Stanley kept on talking, and Smoke soaked the words in while at the same time he was trying to fight off a nagging sensation that seemed to be invading him. Everything had happened so fast that this very moment became surreal.

"And this is an important verse that I cannot implore upon the husband often enough. It will get you through those difficult days if you can abide by this." The pastor's finger scanned down the pages of the worn black leather Bible. "Husbands, love your wives, just as Christ loved the church and gave Himself up for her to make her holy, cleansing her by the washing of water through the word, and to present her to Himself as a radiant church, without stain or wrinkle or any other blemish, but holy and blameless. In this same way, husbands ought to love their wives as they do their own bodies. He who loves his wife loves himself."

Smoke nodded. He was certain that Pastor Stanley was the real deal, but the lingering doubts were coming at him from everywhere else. The whole veil thing was really bothering him.

Get it together, John. That's Sid under there. It couldn't be anyone else. This is happening.

"Now, do we have the rings?" Pastor Stanley said.

Guppy fished them out of his pocket and handed them to the pastor. Pastor Stanley held them up for all to see and said, "Very nice. Endless circles of gold that will last for all eternity."

Sid and Smoke unclasped their hands. She slid her gloves off and handed them to Sam.

Pastor Stanley looked at Smoke and said, "You might want to unveil her for this part."

Gently, Smoke took the veil in his fingertips and lifted it up over her face.

"It's me," Sid said. She was a perfect vision of beauty with a little sparkle to her skin. Her dark eyes were enigmatic and captivating. "You were worried, weren't you."

"A tad."

"I couldn't resist."

Pastor Stanley handed them the rings. "Now the couple will recite their vows. It's always one of the most exciting parts of the ceremony that I so enjoy, particularly because they agreed to the vows that I already have memorized."

Smoke looked deep into Sid's eyes, and she looked back into his.

Smiling, Pastor Stanley added, "But first, for the sake of fun and tradition, I have to ask that if anyone objects to this couple being joined in matrimony, let them speak now or forever hold their peace."

The audience was all smiles, and Sid offered Smoke a childish grin and a little shrug. "Whew," she whispered.

They turned their attention back to Pastor Stanley. Just then, the double doors at the top of the aisle burst open. Allison and Megan appeared, and they weren't alone.

CHAPTER 20

NECKS CRANING AND CLOTHES AWKWARDLY twisting, everyone turned to see who had entered the room. Sid grabbed Smoke's hand and squeezed it. Under her breath she said, "I can't believe it."

Smoke's jaw clenched.

Allison stood tall and proud in a black, knee-length dress. Decorated in jewels, she twinkled with the allure of a movie star. Sid's niece Megan was taller now, her sweet face more slender. She wore a pink dress like a little lady, but her expression was distant. The third person of the trio was Reginald the doppelganger. His suit was a sleek dark grey, and a smirk spread across his face.

Nobody said a word as the three of them strolled down the aisle with the haughty look of royalty and sat right down in the front row beside Sid's parents.

Sally and Keith's expressions were blank.

Smoke felt Sid clenching his hand like she wanted to break something. He ran his thumb over the back of her hand and said under his breath, "Almost there."

Sid faced him again. Her cheeks were a little flushed, but she gave him a quick nod.

"Er, it seems we don't have any objections." Pastor Stanley's eyes slid over to Allison, then he focused again on Smoke and Sid. "So let us continue. Where were we?"

"The rings," Smoke said.

"Yes, the rings. We will start with you. John, repeat after me," Pastor Stanley said.

"It's okay, Pastor. I got it." Smoke slid the wedding band over Sid's finger and said, "With this ring, I thee wed, to have and to hold from this day forward, for better or for worse, in sickness and in health, to love and to cherish, so long as we both shall live. In the eyes of our Lord, I pledge my undying faithfulness."

Sid's eyes watered up.

Sally started to sob and sniffle.

"And now it's your turn to recite your vows, Sidney. Will you be needing my assistance?" Pastor Stanley asked.

She nodded and said, "I think I will." She slipped the gold ring onto Smoke's finger.

Pastor Stanley led her through the recital of the vows. Smoke wiped the tears from her eyes as she did so with his own heart trying to burst from his chest.

"Now, with great pleasure I can say that by the powers invested in me, I now pronounce you man and wife." Pastor Stanley smiled and said, "Now, Mister Smoke, you may kiss the bride."

Smoke hauled Sid into his arms and kissed her soundly.

In a strong voice, Pastor Stanley finished up the ceremony, saying, "Ladies and gentlemen, allow me to introduce to you Mister and Missus John and Sidney Smoke."

A well-decorated but modest reception was held in the church's fellowship hall. Smoke and Sid met with everyone, friends and family, and posed for plenty of pictures. The time quickly came to cut the wedding cake, and both of them did their best to stuff cake into each other's faces. Finally, after about two hours of eating and shaking hands, Sid kissed Smoke on the cheek and said, "I need to spend some time with Megan."

He nodded and said, "Okay, Mrs. Smoke." He tickled her as she walked away and she giggled, and then Smoke reached over and patted Guppy on the shoulder. "I'm going to get some air. Will you cover for me?"

"Sure thing," Guppy said.

On his way out, Smoke spied Sid sitting at Allison's table with Megan on her lap. They both had smiles and tears on their faces.

Good.

After pushing his way out through the fire doors, he followed the sidewalk around to the front of the church. Reginald was stooped over the side of the concrete bridge, smoking. He flicked the butt into the creek and lit another one. A pair of older women who were crossing the bridge frowned at Reginald as they walked by.

"Nice day, isn't it, ladies?" Reginald said, lighting another cigarette.

Smoke stepped up on the bridge. "What are you doing here, Reginald?"

"We just came to see the pair of you off to a good start is all."

"Uh-huh." Smoke moved across from Reginald and leaned back against the rail. "You aren't one to mince words. You're here. What's going on?"

"Allison and Megan begged to be here, and I was charged with being their escort. That is all." He puffed on his cigarette and eyed Smoke up and down. "You clean up pretty good for a country fellow. Not good enough to fit in with the royal types, but you could pass for something a footstool short of noble if you had to."

Crossing his arms over his chest, Smoke asked, "How's your boss Kane doing?"

Studying Smoke's eyes, Reginald tilted his head. "You still think you can take me, do you? I mean, most men don't survive the beatings I give them, but you did. Do you really want another shot at me?"

"If the opportunity ever presents itself, I'll be ready."

Reginald glanced around. "It looks like an opportunity has presented itself."

"Not today, messenger boy. Now tell me about Kane. You say Allison had to beg someone to come, and it must have been him they were begging. I'm guessing Vormus didn't get the best of him?"

"Vormus? Hah! That vomitus pisswaller went back to Europe in pieces." Reginald reached into his coat and revealed a pack of cigarettes and extended his hand. "Take a smoke, Smoke."

"Nah. So what's the end game here? Does Kane want Sid back? Because that isn't going to happen."

"If he wanted her back, he'd have her back and you'd be dead already." Reginald blew smoke out his nose. "This little marriage ceremony, it's just entertainment to us. It humors us that you find something so meaningless to be so meaningful. Your eyes watered, and you're supposed to be a tough guy. I beat the hell out of you and you didn't shed a tear. But now I know where that soft spot is. Your wife Sidney. Your family and friends. It's all such a weakness. No, Kane's got bigger fish to fry, but he's going to make you suffer. You'll come around, or you'll die."

"What do you mean, come around?"

"Just like Allison, one or both of you will become part of the family." He tapped his temple. "And I saw the faces of your own family, too. Mom and Dad. Wouldn't you hate to see their funerals?"

Smoke uncrossed his arms and stood tall. "So your wedding gift is a warning."

Reginald tossed yet another cigarette butt into the creek and watched it float under the bridge. He said to Smoke, "Either you join, or you back way off. Or else things are going to get sticky. Real sticky."

CHAPTER 21

THINGS PERKED UP AT THE reception after Allison, Reginald, and Megan departed. The crowd of friends and family was filled with happy faces and waving hands as Smoke and Sid drove off in the Hellcat to the sound of a roaring engine and the rattle of tin cans. He was driving. Sid picked rice grains out of his hair. "You didn't tell me you had lice," she said with a goofy grin.

"You didn't ask." He smiled.

She started kissing his neck. "Do you think you can last until we reach the hotel? It's a fifteen-minute drive, and I'm not sure I can wait that long. You look so handsome."

Aroused, he replied, "Maybe we should change the subject, briefly. How's your sister and Megan? I didn't get to speak with them."

Sid eased back into her seat. "Weird. I've never seen Megan so distant, and Allison, she's not Allison. She gave me chills. I just feel like she's trying to reel me into some deep and bottomless well. Everything she said was nice, but it all had a veiled warning behind it." Sid put her warm hand on his arm. "But I'm not going to let anything she said ruin my wedding day."

"Me neither." He leaned over and quickly kissed her on the lips, keeping his eyes on the road.

"So you disappeared for a while. What happened to you?"

"I was talking to Reginald."

"And you didn't try to kill each other? Smoke, look, I don't like you around him. I saw what happened the last time you two tangled, and it scared me half to death."

"I was having an off day that day." He turned the air conditioning fan up. "Man, these tuxedos get pretty hot."

"That's because of me." She traced her finger over his ear and down his lobe. "So what else did Reginald say?"

"He gave me the 'join or die' speech. He says Kane's alive and well, too. Are you going to be okay with that?"

"I'm okay if you're okay, John. I say screw 'em. I'm not going to play their little head games."

"They're all talk, aren't they?"

"So far as I'm concerned, yes. The only thing that matters right now is today, and I plan on making it the most memorable day ever."

"More memorable than werewolves, minotaurs, and harpies?"

In a soft, seductive voice, she said, "After tonight, you're not going to remember anything but me."

The hotel suite was much better than nice but far from extravagant, with a distant view of the capital city. The lamp was a small beacon that warmed the dimness. Classic music played on the radio that sat on the nightstand.

Smoke was sitting on the bed wearing only a pair of black boxer briefs. Sid had told him to wait and vanished into the bathroom. She'd been in there for over fifteen minutes, and it felt like an eternity. He rubbed his bare feet on the carpet and smoothed over the sheets with his hands.

Sid came out of the bathroom in a black silk negligée. Long hair cascading over her shoulders, she slunk closer to him with hungry eyes. "Do you like it?"

Her exotic fragrance filled his nostrils, and he said, "You look stunning and smell incredible." His hands reached out for her thighs, and he drew her body into his. With his free arm he pulled the sheets back while he kissed her. Picking her up in his arms and still kissing her with passion, he lowered her seat-first into the bed.

She broke the kiss off, panting, and said, "Take me."

With gentle fingers he lifted her negligee off her wanton body. She peeled his boxers down off his legs and pulled him into the bed. Under the sheet, the tussle of lovemaking began, lasting on and off through the night until the dawn woke them from their slumber.

Snuggled up in his powerful arms, Sid said to him, "That was special."

Propped up on the pillows, Smoke said, "I never thought a word like 'consummate' could be made so erotic." He squeezed her closer to him and kissed her on the forehead. "I love you, Sid."

"I love you too, Smoke."

"Are you hungry?" Smoke asked.

With a brilliant smile, she giggled. "I'm famished."

CHAPTER 22

"IT'S BEEN AN EXTRAORDINARY TWO weeks." Sid was sitting at the patio table of their beachfront hotel suite that had a splendid view of the sun setting over the ocean. The salt air was warm and breezy. She reached over and clasped Smoke's hand in hers. "And I mean that with a big X in extra."

"It was certainly the best honeymoon I ever had," he said.

She leaned back in her chair and said, "Oh really? Are you implying that you've had a honeymoon before or that you anticipate another?"

"Well, given the nature of this one, I thought perhaps a second or third honeymoon would be an excellent plan."

"Good answer. Good, good answer. You really do have a knack for squirming out of dangerous things." She took a sip of coffee. "You know, *husband*, you really did surprise me."

"How so?"

"Well, even with all we've been through, I just didn't anticipate that we'd live every day like it was our last day together. It's been incredible. Joyful." She set the rose Fiestaware cup down. "I just thought we'd keep it simple, but you made it incredible and fun. I mean, most honeymoons are spent in one place, but we've had three or four honeymoons in one." She offered a different giddy smile for each one as she counted them off on her fingers. "Beach bungalow at Paradise Point in California. Vegas, lounging at the Venetian—which was incredible, by the way. Niagara Falls. And now here, snuggled up by the sand at Hilton Head, South Carolina. I just never envisioned it this way, did you?"

"I just wanted it to be special."

"Oh, it was special all right. Especially all of the nocturnal festivities." She pushed her hair back out of her eyes. Still smiling at him, she said, "Thank you, John."

"You're welcome."

"So, you know, we never talked about money, and merging accounts and things like that, but are there any issues paying for all this?"

"Nope."

"I mean, I have … I just…"

"Don't worry about it, Sid. I've had a nest egg for quite some time, set aside for a special occasion like this. It really built up a lot while I was in prison. That's one thing pretty good about prison. You can't spend any money."

"Yeah, well, I guess I've just been having so much fun that I haven't even taken time to think about things. Like, are we moving in together? Do I keep my apartment? Do we live in your garage?"

"I don't know," he said, "but one shared place is fine with me. We can look for another place if you want to."

She sat up in her chair and leaned toward him. "You'd do that for me?"

"You're my wife. I'd do anything for you."

"I know, but you're so damn agreeable."

"I'm just not that attached to places and things. The only thing I want to be attached to is you."

Sidney's body sagged as if her heart had melted from within. She said, "That's so sweet. Too sweet." She took a deep breath and wiped her eyes. "I guess we're going to have to start packing sometime. Man, why can't life be like this all the time?"

"Someday it will be." Smoke stood up and stretched his limbs. He picked up their breakfast plates and napkins and started heading toward the kitchen. "But in the meantime, there's work to be done."

"You're getting restless, aren't you."

From inside the sliding doors, Smoke fired back, "Well, sort of."

Sidney eased her body out of her chair, rushed over to Smoke, and hugged him. She let out a deep sigh and said, "Thank God. I thought it was just me, and I didn't want to be rude."

"You're bored?"

"No, no," she said, "just complacent. I miss my runs and my guns." She pretended to draw her Glocks from her hips and then relaxed her posture and clasped her hands around his bicep. "At least I have these guns to hold me over, but with all of this travel, I've felt a tad vulnerable without them."

"Ditto that. I say we get rolling too." He kissed her forehead. "How about I clean up and you pack?"

"How about I clean up and you pack?" she said.

"Sure, honey."

She gave him a little punch in the arm. "Quit agreeing with me on everything. I don't like that."

"It's just a little thing."

"Yeah, but you pretty much go along with everything I say. That's not you, so stop doing that. I still like the mystery about it and I don't want to lose that."

"I got it. Crystal clear, honey."

"Good. Now that that's settled," she said, walking her fingers up his arm. "Why don't you join me in the bedroom for a final honeymoon farewell?"

"No," he said.

"No? What do you mean, no?'

"I'm just not in the mood."

Dropping her hands to her hips, she said, "Why, do you have a sudden headache or something?"

Chin up and looking away, he said, "Maybe, and looking at this kitchen, I have a lot of work to do."

She started pulling Smoke toward the bedroom. "You're coming with me."

Feebly holding himself back, he said, "But I don't want to."

After pushing him into the bedroom, she shut the door behind her. "Good. That turns me on even more."

CHAPTER 23

WASHINGTON, DC. HOME OF THE greatest truths and the greatest lies. The sparkling city of deceit.

Smoke sat on the sofa in his garage apartment, staring at the television. Senator Wilhelm was on FNN News giving a rousing speech.

Sid sat at the computer desk, shaking her head at the screen. She was back in her normal clothes, blue jeans and a navy-blue shirt but with a shoulder holster on, looking official.

"It's good to be home, isn't it?" he asked her.

Strapping on an ankle holster with a tiny automatic gun, she said, "One thing I certainly didn't miss was the smell of bullshit."

Laughing, Smoke said, "Agreed."

They'd been back for two days, and for the most part they had spent their time back at Smoke's place and seemed to be settling in.

"You kind of like my spot, don't you?"

"You mean our spot?" She tied her hair back in a ponytail. Looking around, she said, "You know, I actually do. I could make this work for a while. I mean, we have space and some land. A nice garage for my car."

"Heh-heh, I see adding a new bay in my future."

"Not as far as I'm concerned."

Picking up the remote, Smoke turned off the television. "So, are you ready to get back at it?"

"Yep."

"And you've called your folks and everyone is a-okay?"

"Mom's begging us to come by for dinner, which is a good sign that things are normal. I promised her we'd be out in the next few days. But I just have to get back into the swing of things." She picked up a sheet of paper on the desk. It was a mug shot of a rough-looking woman with scraggly red hair and prison tats up to her neck. "This is a five-thousand-dollar mark, Annie Wilkins. It's time to hunt her down and scoop her up. The electricity in this place doesn't pay for itself."

Rising from the couch, Smoke said, "It will once I install a windmill."

"Sounds like Senator Wilhelm's got you convinced."

Smoke pulled his boots on and laced them up. "I think a windmill on top of the Washington Monument is a great idea. Doesn't everybody?"

"Shut up." She walked over and kissed him. "That's better."

Smoke patted her on the rear, walked away, and fetched his knives and guns. "Let's catch this cat."

"After you."

Outside, Smoke stood in front of his Camaro, frowning. It had been a good car. Cheap. Easy to fix and modify. Now it was totaled.

Getting into the Hellcat, Sid said, "We'll find you another one. There are junkyards all over this place. You'll have dozens to choose from."

Cheerfully, he said, "I hope so. This would be a great home for all of them."

"No, I don't think so. You're a married man now. You need something a little more respectable." She rubbed the dash of the Dodge. "A nice Dodge, perhaps."

"You mean one like Al Bundy had? I could go for that."

Dropping the car into drive and pulling out, she said, "I was thinking a Dodge Caravan. It's just perfect for a family man."

"Family?"

"Eventually. You'll make a great stay-at-home daddy while I go out and do all the hunting."

"Sounds good to me."

Sid tossed her head back and laughed. "Oh come on, you can't possibly agree with that!"

"Then I disagree vehemently. I hunt. You stay home with the babies. I insist."

"Now I like that." Grinning, she turned up the radio. "That's my kind of sweet talk."

Smoke's phone buzzed in his jeans pocket. He plucked it out just as Sid was picking up hers. At the same time, they both read, "BS. My office. Now. Cyrus."

"I'm guessing that means Black Slate," Sid said.

"Yeah, but it's still BS. Are we going?"

"So far as I know, I'm still a liaison. I'm not aware of any changes in my status since I've been gone."

Smoke glanced at the crinkles on her forehead. "Are you sure you want to dive back into this?"

"Yes. Besides, you know you want to."

He nodded. "Yeah, I do."

"Hi, Jane," Sid said to Ted Howard's old secretary, who now worked for Section Chief Cyrus Tweel. "We're here to see Cyrus."

"Congratulations, Sidney," Jane said, squirming in her seat and giving Sid a little smirk. Eyeing Smoke, she added, "You two make a handsome couple. A very handsome couple. Just have a seat and I'll buzz the chief. He's been wound up pretty tight lately."

Smoke sat beside Sid in the padded office chairs. Just as he sat down, Sid's best friend Sadie appeared from behind the cubicle. Her face lit up like a Christmas tree.

"Well look who's back from the honeymoon!" Sadie grabbed Sid and hugged her. "Oh, you look great, just great! And you looked so beautiful at your wedding, in case I didn't tell you."

"You did, too," Sid said, unlocking from the long embrace.

"And you, mister?" Sadie gave Smoke a big hug and kiss. "You were something else yourself. Damn, look at you two with your tan on. It looks good! Real good! Now listen, me and Alex want you two to come over for dinner." She wagged her finger in Sid's face. "It better happen within thirty days, or you're dead to me. Now, it's been fun catching up, but I gotta go. A bunch of big shots need their TPS reports." She hugged Smoke and Sid again. "Bye, sugars."

"You can go in now," Jane said, pressing something on her desk. The red light on the security door turned to green. "Don't just stand there. Get moving before it turns red again."

"Really?" Sid said. "A mag lock on his office door?"

"You shouldn't be surprised. I'm just glad I'm on the outside. You don't want to get locked inside with him." Jane waved. "Have fun."

The door closed softly behind them and then locked with an ominous *click*. Cyrus was sitting in his chair, white oxford shirtsleeves rolled up and round wire rim glasses down on the bridge of his nose. "Well, if it isn't the newlyweds. Thanks for the wedding invitation, by the way."

"It was spur of the moment, and I didn't think you'd be interested," Sid replied.

"Oh, I wasn't interested, but I at least expected some courtesy. You invited Sadie, and I'm pretty sure if Ted were still here, you would've invited him too." With a long frown that seemed to fill his entire face, he pointed at the chairs. "Have a seat!"

CHAPTER 24

R EMAINING STANDING, SMOKE SAID, "WHAT'S with the attitude?"

"I'm sorry," Cyrus said, "am I being impolite? Let me rephrase it in such a manner that might make you a little more comfortable. Sit your ass down."

Smoke said to Sid, "Let's go."

"Agreed. Have a nice day, Cyrus."

Smoke was the first person to the door. He tugged the handle, but it was locked. He turned toward Cyrus. "You might want to open this. Now."

Hands up in front of his chest, Cyrus said, "Look, Sid and Smoke, you aren't going anywhere. The truth is, you're here because you're needed, and I'm up to my eyeballs in boiling water." He pulled out a file from a desk drawer and tossed it over into one of the guest chairs. "Just take a look. Please."

"Am I still acting under the capacity of a special liaison?" Sid asked.

"You're still getting a check, aren't you?'

"I am."

"Well, you're still on board then." Cyrus flopped into his chair and produced a prescription bottle from the top drawer of his desk. He took out a pill and swallowed it down. "Yeah, never needed any medication before I took this gig. Now my hair's thinning and my skinny ass has lost another 10 pounds. I thought I'd get fatter with a gig like this."

"You should eat more." Smoke picked up the manila envelope and sat down in the chair.

Exasperated, Cyrus said, "Who has time to eat?"

The file was filled with a dozen pictures. Smoke split the stack and handed half of them to Sid. Each picture depicted another part of the same gory scene: a battlefield of dead bodies in a parking lot covered in blood, guts, and gore. Heads were missing from shoulders. Limbs were torn apart. A man appeared to be gored through the neck, and another person looked to be clawed to death.

"Geez," Sidney said with her face drawn up in horror. "Who are these people? When did this happen? What killed them?"

"Oh, I don't know—deaders, shifters, clones? You tell me, Sid." Cyrus's forehead was sweating. "Well, that's not entirely true. We processed and fingerprinted all of them. Do you remember Senator Randolph of Maryland?"

"No," Sid said.

"Oh, oh, of course you don't. You want to know why?" Cyrus rapidly tapped his knuckles on the desk. "I'll tell you why. He's been dead for fifty years. Yeah, fifty years. You know what happened when he showed up as a murder suspect in the system? I'll tell you what. DC went off! Somehow that little tidbit of information slipped through the cracks and found its way into the heart of this country's leadership. And that axe is falling on me. Senator Wilhelm was in here grilling me with questions. Try telling that jerk what he doesn't want to hear."

Still sorting through the pictures, Sid asked, "What are you so mad at us for?"

"Because I've been waiting on you two idiots to come back from your honeymoon, that's what."

"Take a breath, Cyrus," Sid said, mocking a little. "We're here now, so everything's going to be okay."

"Ha-hah, funny."

Cyrus kept talking, and Smoke continued with the study of the pictures, one by one. The men weren't FBI agents or any segment of law enforcement. No, they were something else. Men he'd met before. All of the dead men were wearing goggles. They were Uncle Earl's men, and the picture he was looking at was Uncle Earl's severed head.

"John, are you all right?" Sid said.

He handed her the picture of Uncle Earl.

"Aw, geez, I'm sorry," she said.

"What? What?" Cyrus said.

Sid placed the picture on his desk.

Cyrus picked it up and curled his lips. "Ew, friend of yours?"

"Where's the body?" Smoke asked, ignoring Cyrus's question.

"So far as I know, they've all been processed and identified by family. Look, this was one of those hush-hush deals that didn't make the papers," Cyrus continued. "You know that. It's got the Black Slate all over it. And this operation of these goggled goons? The FBI's never even heard of them. They're some mercenary company from here in the U.S. that has set up shop here." He scratched his head. "It's just been a huge mess."

"You make it sound like all this is our fault," Sid said.

"Is it your fault? No. But despite the leadership's urgings to get to the bottom of this, I'm not being given any more people." Cyrus gulped down some bottled water. "Sure, there's plenty of money for windmills by the sea, but nothing extra to help us prevent massacres and tragedy. Idiots. So that leaves me with you two."

"Both of us?" Sid said, thumbing between her and Smoke. "You don't get two for the price of one."

"Oh, I figure I could," Cyrus replied. "I'm certain your loyal hound of a husband will be wherever you go. But yes, we'll put him on the payroll."

"I don't want to be on your payroll," Smoke commented.

"Oh, is that so? Well I'll just dump the money in my bank account then. How does that sound?" Cyrus said.

"Just give us the paperwork," said Sid. "We'll put it in my account."

Cyrus stood up. "Listen, I need results this week. I have to have them. Today is Monday, and I need something solid before Friday morning." He opened up another drawer and produced a black folder. "Your old pal Leroy Sullivan dropped this off. It's a lead filled with another freak. There are details in this about the other incident that went down. Just find out who's behind it. Maybe it's the Drake, and maybe it isn't, but I have to know before Wilhelm comes back." He rubbed his temples. "Man, what I wouldn't do for some sick leave right now."

"See you, Cyrus." Sidney said, picking up the file. "And try to smile. It does wonders for a headache."

"Friday, Sidney. Friday or else."

CHAPTER 25

S MOKE WAS READING AND SID was driving. Inside the Black Slate file was the dossier of another person of interest. Smoke's eyes drifted over the notes and ledgers. There were pictures of odd places, too. Cemeteries, morgues, funeral homes, and mortuaries. There were strange groups of people congregated in all of those locations too. There was an air about them. A darkness in their eyes. Evil without expression.

"You're being awfully quiet over there." Sid's hands graced the steering wheel like a ballerina's feet graced the floor. The car seemed to move like a panther in the weeds as she maneuvered effortlessly through the traffic. Her fingers glided over the wheel when she turned. "Look, it's okay if you aren't all right about what happened to Uncle Earl. I guess you had some sort of closeness with him."

"I was as close to him as any other man I know. He pushed me. Tested me. But I respected him for it. Even though I was young, I got what he was doing. But he never had to do it. I think it was because he saw something I didn't." Smoke's heart was heavy and aching inside. He felt like what had happened was on account of him. "Perhaps I should have taken him up on his offer. Maybe he'd be alive today."

"You know we can't go down into the valley of blaming ourselves, Smoke."

He nodded. "I've noticed you're calling me Smoke a lot more lately."

"Am I?" She switched lanes and accelerated by a pair of J.B. Hunt rigs. "Huh."

"That's it? Huh?"

"Okay, *John,* I kinda like calling you Smoke, and I figure maybe when we're working, it'll keep things more professional so I don't lose focus. When we're at home, it can be more personal. Does that make sense?"

"It does, and it's just fine by me—not that you were asking my permission." He closed the Black Slate file but left the rap sheet out. "You're a Smoke too now, you know."

With a wide and playful smile on her face, she said, "I *am,* aren't I!"

"Yup."

"So," she said, "what do you have?"

Smoke held the rap sheet up and started to read. "His name is Titus Tolliver. He's a runt of a man that looks as ornery as a hungry hog. Like Guppy, he's built like an elephant's leg. Hangs out with a weird crowd at mausoleums and funeral parlors."

"Creepy."

"Yeah. Well, I suppose that comes with the territory of being a mortician, hm?"

"What?"

"We've got names and several locations. I'm going to have Sam and Guppy take a look and see if they can find some ties to the Drake." He took out his phone. "It's best we exercise some caution." He typed some names into the phone and hit send. "That should do it."

"Don't you think Sam needs to know about Uncle Earl?" she asked.

"Yeah, I'll let her know next time we actually sit down with them. She's not going to take it well. She was pretty big buds with Earl."

"I see. So, are you still dead set on seeing the scene of the crime? I'm certain the FBI's already done a cleanup."

"I want to go. These pictures don't tell the entire story."

About twenty minutes later they arrived at a business park filled with empty parking spots. A small two story white block building with endless windows was surrounded by a yellow construction fence with "Do Not Enter" and "FBI" signs all over it.

Sid pulled alongside the fence and put the car in park. "Let's go."

It was a hot and breezy day. Smoke put on his sunglasses and found a gap in the fence and pushed it open. Seeing Sid through, he said, "I guess they aren't too worried about security."

"You'd think they'd have guards posted out here or something," she said. "I guess they just don't have the manpower for it."

Smoke made his way over to a lamppost mounted on a small cement island that was overgrown with weeds. There was blood smeared on the blacktop and on the yellow paint that trimmed the lamppost island. The lamppost had a huge notch in the metal, like it had been hit with a sword. Smoke fished his hands through the weeds and found an object of interest: green bug-eyed goggles. One lens was cracked and the other one was bloody. There was also a 40-caliber brass casing in the grass.

About twenty yards away, Sid said, "Find anything?"

"Just some sloppy cleanup, but confirmation that something did indeed go down here."

Sid replied, "You mean all the blood stains baked on the blacktop weren't enough?"

"Ha-hah. I suppose I like to be a little more thorough."

"Look at that," Sid said, pointing at another lamppost closer to the building.

The metal post was bent over at the bottom as if a car had rammed into it. Smoke made his way over to the post and eyed it up and down. He ran his hands along the bend in the metal. "It's warped, but it doesn't look like anything hit it."

Sid knelt down and pushed the grasses aside. Giving the base a close inspection, she said, "It's come loose at the base. The metal snapped clean through the bolts in one place, and that's why it's leaning to." Glancing up at Smoke, she said, "Are you thinking what I'm thinking?"

"Giants."

Standing back up, Sid said, "Let's hope just one giant. What do you think was so important in this building? It looks like it's been abandoned for quite some time. I mean, do you think they just met up to do battle? Or were Uncle Earl and the gang launching an assault at whatever was inside?"

"I guess we need to take a look-see." Smoke extended his hand toward the building. "After you."

Sid hadn't taken more than two steps when the high throttle of engines caught Smoke's ears. He turned. Three black pickup trucks were racing into the business park, headed toward the construction fence. In the truck beds were men in black hoods. The trucks blasted through the fence and skidded to a halt. The hooded warriors rambled out. Their eyes had a red glow to them. They moved fast but were stiff.

CHAPTER 26

"**D**AMMIT! DEADERS!" YELLED SID.

Backing quickly toward the building, Smoke said, "How do you know?"

"If you've seen one deader, you've seen them all!" Sid's guns were out, and she started firing shot after shot. The bullets ripped into the deaders, but they kept coming. "Body armor!"

Among the stiff-gaited deaders were a handful of others whose movement was more fluid, and they had shotguns in their hands. They took a knee and started firing from behind the ranks of the deaders.

Ka-Blam! Ka-Blam!

"Let's get inside!" Smoke laid down some cover fire at the shooters. They flattened on the ground.

Standing outside the building's entrance facing the door, Sid fired some shots into the lock. She tugged on the handle, but the door didn't open. "Bad news, Smoke!"

Running straight for Sid, he yelled, "Stand aside!" Hitting the steps to the building at full speed, he charged straight for the door and crashed right through. Covered in debris, he stretched out his hand and said, "Come on."

There wasn't anything extraordinary about the interior of the building. The outer offices had the windows, and it was just cubicles in the center. It was barren, however, stripped down from top to bottom. No phones or computers were on the desks that Smoke and Sid rushed by. Fiber optic and phone cords hung from the drop ceiling. There was some spray-painted graffiti on the walls, and some of the cheap built-in office furniture had been vandalized.

Like a shadow at Smoke's side, Sid said, "What's your plan?"

"Stairwells and up."

"Don't you think we'll get trapped up there?"

Smoke made his way to the back of the building and shoved on the stairwell door handle. It wouldn't open. It was a heavy wooden door, the kind you'd need a truck to run through. "That's a problem."

Sid broke away from him and headed for the elevator. He followed. The doors were split open, but the elevator was suspended above. "And that's another problem," she said, checking her magazines. "I'm down to twenty rounds. I'll make sure they all count."

Smoke cocked his head toward the far corner of the room. "There's another door to try. Let's go."

But before they'd taken three steps, deaders spilled into the room from the other side. Stiff-legged bloodhounds shoved through the cubicles with their pasty hands clutching. A creepy aura of red emanated from their faces.

Smoke tried the door handle again. The locking mechanism gave, but the door wouldn't budge. He noticed the metal around the frame of the door was charred black. "These doors are welded shut. I think we've been set up."

"A trap? You think Cyrus did this?"

"I don't know, but it looks like this is going to be our first 'till death do us part' moment. You keep an eye out for those shotguns. I'll handle the deaders."

With her pistol aimed from the cup-and-saucer position, she said, "I will, but I'm not going to let you have all the fun."

A deader rambled out from behind one of the cubicles.

Sid blew out its knee with a single shot, sending it spiraling to the floor. She laughed a little. "I like shooting deaders."

"Just stick with me." Smoke fired at a pair of deaders that came down the row from the far left side. *Blam! Blam! Blam!* They dropped to their knees but still tried to walk, straining with unnatural effort. "We're going to have to blast a hole through them to get out of here."

A shotgun went off.

Ka-Blam!

A chunk of wall to the right of Sid's head went missing. She returned fire and pumped a single slug into the man's hooded face and watched him drop dead. "A man, not a deader."

The damaged deaders came after them, crawling over the floor on rotting hands and elbows.

Staying beneath the tops of the cubicles, Smoke glided behind Sid toward a hooded man with a shotgun.

Another man peeked out from the far right row of the cubicles, pointing a shotgun at Smoke.

Sid cracked off a shot, dropping her second hooded man dead. She started blasting away at the deaders that had managed to creep right up to her at arms' length. The shots she fired didn't slow them. Hungry fingers locked around her ankles. The bullets she blasted into their heads did no good. "Smoke!"

Smoke filled his hands with the shotgun and pumped the slide. At close range he blew off one deader's entire skull. He pumped the slide again.

Ka-Blam!

And again.

Ka-Blam!

The black hood became a tattered sack of brains and ooze. The deader bodies flailed and flopped like fish out of water.

"We gotta get," Smoke said. He saw something coming at him from the corner of his eye. Three more deaders emerged from the aisle. He shot one right in the face just as the other two collided into him and Sid.

Sidney let out a pain-filled scream.

Smoke looked in horror to see that a deader had clamped its jaws onto her hand.

More were coming.

CHAPTER 27

WITH THE DEADER'S TEETH SUNK into her hand, Sidney unloaded her clip into its head.

Blam! Blam! Blam! Blam! Blam!

Smoke rammed his fist into another deader's jaw. Its fist remained fastened to his clothes. He grabbed its thumb and twisted back until it snapped and then yanked his arm free.

"There they are! Blast them!" said one of the men in hoods who had just emerged out of the aisle.

The man behind him said, "What about the assets?"

"Screw 'em, they're dead already!" The first man pumped his shotgun and took aim.

"Get behind me, Sid!"

Sid dove behind Smoke.

He grabbed the deader by its protective vest and used its writhing body as a shield just as the men started blasting away.

Ka-Blam! Ka-Blam!

Chunks of clothes and deader flesh blasted through the room.

Smoke let out a roar and charged at the men, still holding the deader up in front of him. He slammed into both men, knocking them through the cubicle.

The hooded men fought back, punching, kicking, and screaming.

Smoke throat punched one.

"Gak!" the thug exclaimed.

Smoke forced the deader out of the way with a hard shove to the floor. He caught the second thug by the collar and started to wail on him, one hard punch after the other. Gunshots went off behind him, and he turned. Sid had filled another deader's head with lead.

"I'm empty," she said.

Smoke snatched up one of the hooded men's shotguns and tossed it to her. "Let's get."

Moving faster than the oncoming deaders, they rushed back out the front door.

A lone deader stood in their path and got to kiss Sid's shotgun blast.

Ka-Blam!

In stride, they raced for their car. Sid slid over the hood and jumped into the driver's side.

The surviving deaders were coming back out of the building's doors. A helicopter soared overhead and then hovered near the building.

Smoke couldn't see a soul in the midnight-blue chopper, but it was armed. Rocket missiles fired out of the chopper's guns. White smoke streaked through the sky. The entire building exploded.

"Quit gawking and get in!" Sid yelled.

Eyes on the flames, Smoke did as he was told.

Sid laid into the gas, spinning the wheels, and they raced out of the business park like bats out of hell. Checking her mirrors, she said, "Is the chopper coming after us?"

The helicopter became a speck in the sky going the other way. "No," Smoke said. "How's your hand?"

"It feels like a hungry deader tried to eat it."

Smoke reached for her hand.

Sid jerked away.

"Just let me see it."

"No, I'm fine."

Smoke gave her a disappointed look.

"What?" she said, trying to hide her grimace. "I'm driving."

"Just let me take a peek and make sure nothing's broken. Besides, you don't want to get rabies."

"Rabies? Deaders have rabies?"

"I don't know. Let me take a look at it."

Reluctantly she gave him her hand. "Fine. Smoke, what the hell was that all about? Who were those guys with masks on?"

With the ginger fingers of a surgeon, Smoke lightly explored her hand. "Does that hurt?"

"No."

"Does that?"

"No."

"Does—"

"Ow!" Sid pulled her hand away and gave it a little shake. "Morning glory! Is it broken?"

"Hairline fractured maybe." Showing a look of concern, he added, "It's those bite marks that I'm more worried about. We need to get someone to look at that."

"Why? You don't think I'm going to turn into a deader, do you?"

"I hope not."

CHAPTER 28

"**S**HE'S FINE. NO RABIES," Asia said. The little Asian woman was dressed like a geisha, and her face was painted like a doll's. "Can you move your hand?"

Sid looked at the dark bruise on her swelling hand and said, "Yeah, it's just stiff."

"I'll wrap it up," Asia said, pulling out an Ace bandage from a modern leather medical bag.

"No, don't bother, I'll be fine."

"Suit yourself." Asia neatly tucked her supplies back into her medical case, snapped it up, walked over to the sofa facing the television, and sat down. She picked up the remote, mumbling to herself, "Monsters with rabies. Stupid."

"Are you going to be able to shoot with that hand?" Smoke said to her.

Slowly and forcefully clutching her fingers in and out, she said, "I'll just have to make it work."

Mal Carlson was in the kitchenette of Smoke's garage apartment, fixing coffee. The scholarly olive-skinned man was wearing kimono robes, white and reds and inlaid with dragons. He took a sip of coffee and winced. "Ew, that's hot."

Smoke glanced at Sid and said, "Should I ask, or do you want to?"

"Go ahead," she said to him.

"So Mal, what's going on with your outfit?"

Without taking her eyes away from the television, Asia replied, "The pervert is role playing. He's the shogun and I'm his geisha." She started taking the pins out of her hair and letting it down. "I'm supposed to be part of his harem."

"Now now, that's not the case. This was your idea as much as mine," Mal objected. Showing a little embarrassment, he said to Smoke, "You said to get right over here. I was worried."

"It took you long enough to get here," Sid said. "Did Asia pull you over here on a rickshaw?"

Frowning at Sid, Asia said, "No! Smart-aleck American."

"It's not like you aren't American too, Asia. She was born in Kentucky, you know. Went to public school."

"Not true, not true!"

Mal shrugged and said, "It is. Anyway, danger averted for now, but I'm glad you called. I had a special visitor while you were gone. Asia, will you go to the van and get the silver cases?"

Shaking her head, she answered with a long, "No."

Clanking his coffee mug down on the table, Mal said, "I'll be right back."

Sid took a seat at the computer desk and started tapping on the keys. Images popped up on all six monitors. "So what do you think, Smoke? Were they after us or not? I just don't think the Drake is out to kill us. Maybe it was Guermo. I thought one of those black-hooded thugs had a sliver of accent when he spoke."

"I noticed that too. I guess there must have been something in that building that they didn't want us to find. Or maybe one of them didn't want the other to find it." He walked over to the refrigerator, opened it up, and grabbed a can of Coke. He cracked it open.

Asia's head popped up from in front of the sofa, and she said, "Soda is bad for you. What do you have, a death wish?"

Ignoring Asia, Smoke resumed his place standing behind Sid. "What are your thoughts on Cyrus?"

"I believed him."

Smoke nodded. They had called the section chief on their way back to Smoke's place. Cyrus had been oblivious to the danger they'd just been in, just his usual adamant and nasty self, telling them again, "Get me some answers by Friday!"

"I suppose we're still on the same side with him," Smoke said. "Funny how people can change."

"So do you think the Drake were following us?" Sid said.

"I just assume they always have eyes on us. We're going to have to get better at disappearing. Then again, maybe it was just bad timing. Perhaps they thought we were somebody else. In a way I felt like we were caught in the middle of a turf war."

"Maybe so."

Mal came back in through the front door. He had two briefcases, one in each hand. He walked over to the kitchen island and set them down on it.

Getting up from her chair, Sid said, "Wedding presents for us?"

"I guess you could call it that, but they aren't from me." Mal was smiling. "Go ahead, open them up."

"Are they the same?" Smoke said.

"Uh, no," Mal said, patting the one on his right. "This one is Sid's."

"So who are they from?" Smoke asked.

"Leroy Sullivan."

"You saw him?" Sid replied.

"I got a call. Just open them up."

Smoke popped his case open at the same time as Sid popped hers. Inside was another sweetheart suit, matte black mixed with dark-grey trim. It still had the look of twinkling metal in it. He lifted it up. "Nice. Feels lighter."

"It is," Mal said, "and it's improved since the last one. We noticed that sword from Kane's place could cut them. Well, somebody knew that, so we made some improvements."

"We?" Sid said, eyeballing Mal while at the same time admiring her suit.

"I've still been acting in an advisory capacity."

"To who?" Smoke asked.

"Leroy."

Smoke put the suit aside. It seemed Mal had always known more than he'd let on, but so far he'd been trustworthy. Smoke lifted a flap to reveal the bottom compartment of the case. There were magazine clips loaded with blue-, green-, and red-tipped bullets. Lots of them. There was a clear yellow vial with bright-yellow pills, too. Blue goggles with a thick black strap were staring right back at him.

"You like?" Sid said, staring at Smoke. She had her own set of goggles on.

"Actually, they don't look half bad. Much better than the ones Uncle Earl's men had on. How does everything look?"

"Great. I feel like they're adjusting my sight. Kind of a rush." She took the goggles off. "So what's going on, Mal? All of this stuff. It looks like we're going to war."

Mal nodded and said, "You aren't going to war, you're already in it."

CHAPTER 29

SMOKE HAD HIS ELBOW OUT the window and the wind running through his hair. He and Sid were back on the road. Titus Tolliver was the mark they needed to track down. They had half a dozen locations that they needed to look into. It would take a couple of days at least, but he felt kinda good about being on the hunt again.

"Enjoying the ride?" Sid said.

"Maybe a bit too much. This suit feels great. Now, I always feel great, but this? It's like I'm in a different body, charged with new energy."

"I know how you feel. I'm feeling pretty energetic myself." She glanced him over with her eyes. "In a distracting kind of way."

"You can say *that* again. These close quarters aren't helping things."

Swallowing, Sid replied, "Let's try to change the subject over the next few miles. We've got a war going on between the Drake and maybe Guermo. Doing our job, we're caught in the middle. Maybe we just need to help them take each other out."

"That's what I was thinking. If we can get our mitts on this Tolliver guy, maybe we can get a new perspective." Smoke drew out his semi-automatic pistol and popped out the clip. The bullet tips were blue. He had fifteen rounds loaded up top and two red tips at the bottom. He pulled a green-tipped one out of his pocket. "I forget. What do the green tips do?"

Sid gave a little shrug. "Maybe it's a tracer? Load it in the top and we'll see what happens to the next lucky bastard that crosses us."

"I like the way you think. It's sexy."

"Sexy is as sexy does," she replied.

Wind in his face, Smoke enjoyed the ride, but his thoughts were heavy. There were too many variables now. The Drake and Guermo were competitors. Kane Lancaster was still out poisoning DC, if not the entire country. Uncle Earl was dead, his men slaughtered. There weren't any clear-cut answers. It was chaos and madness. Smoke wanted answers. He wanted revenge. Deep inside, he felt he had let Uncle Earl down, and it was eating at him. Was there some calling inside him that he was ignoring?

Sid put her hand on his thigh. "You okay?"

Shifting in his seat, he said, "Yeah, sure, why?

"You just look a little distant."

"Well, I was thinking about your sister and niece. Ultimately, we have to get them plucked out of that nest," he said, placing his hand on hers.

"I know. I've been thinking the same thing. I don't know if it will change Allison back, but at least we can save Megan. It's a terrible thing to say, but it's true." She shook her head. "Megan looked and sounded okay at the wedding, but I know she's not. I don't want her to turn out like her mother."

"Let's just take it a day at a time. I'm sure they'll approach us soon enough, with all the trouble we cause." He patted her hand. "You know they can't stay away from us."

"True."

Sid took the car off the interstate and down a long stretch of highway, where they came to a smaller suburban area called District Heights. She pulled into Garland Funeral Parlor, an old, big, red-brick house with alabaster columns adorning a huge front porch with green ivy taking over. She pulled around to the back of the building. A pair of black Cadillac hearses was parked underneath the overhang. She parked in the side parking lot and shut down the engine. "Did you see those hearses?"

Popping the door open, Smoke swung his legs out. "Yeah, pretty sweet 1958 Caddies. Just like the one from *Only the Lonely*, starring John Candy. I was thinking something big like that would be a nice replacement for the Camaro."

"I don't think so," she said, shutting her door.

"Of course not. I'll be fixing up the Camaro anyway."

"I'd scrap it."

Smoke headed up the stairs and onto the front porch. The plaster was cracked on the columns, and the hinges squeaked when he opened the front door. A little bit of debris floated onto his hair and into his eyes. Dusting himself off, he said, "I'm not so sure they're staying very busy these days." He pulled the door wide open and stepped aside. "After you."

The décor on the inside matched up well with everything on the outside: old and dated. Smoke sniffed. A staleness lingered in the air. He gave Sid a shrug and started making his rounds. The shag carpet was a seafoam green, wallpaper covered the walls top to bottom, and furniture trimmed in dark wood with soft, colorful velvet cushions flourished in every room they could see. There were three funeral parlors, plenty of bathrooms, and water fountains. A small room with a fireplace had been converted into a breakroom with a coffee station and a nice stainless steel refrigerator.

Smoke moseyed deeper down the hall toward the back. There was an office with a big cherry desk and a green leather office chair behind it. He ventured farther inside and noticed a man peering out the window.

"Excuse me?" Smoke said.

The wide-shouldered man in an old, dark-grey suit turned. The oak floorboards creaked under his shifting weight. The man's dark-brown eyes looked almost as black as coal. It was Titus Tolliver. The thick-necked man in a bowtie looked Smoke up and down and said, "Did you come to bury somebody, or to be buried? I've been expecting you, Smoke."

All around the house, the hallways echoed with doors slamming shut.

Titus added, "I've been expecting both of you."

CHAPTER 30

S MOKE PULLED OUT HIS PISTOL and pointed it at Titus's head. "Expecting us? Care to explain?"

"Certainly." Titus lumbered behind the desk and sat down. His face was cold and expressionless. "We all know about you, John Smoke. Sidney too. Now put the gun down and have a seat so that no one gets hurt."

Smoke backed up with the pistol still aimed at Titus and checked the door that led back outside. It was locked in place. Solid. He approached Titus, leaned over the desk, and pointed the gun in his face. "I disagree. You're going to hurt once I put a bullet in you."

Leaning forward, Titus said, "Try me."

Smoke gave the stone-cold face a hard look. There was something different about Titus. Just like the rest of the shifters, he had an overconfident edge about him. Smoke didn't know what kind of powers Titus had, or if he had any. The unknown was dangerous. He eased back and holstered his weapon. "What about my partner?"

"Partner? How quaint. You mean your wife? I'm certain she's fine." Titus straightened up some of the paperwork on his desk. "For now."

"If you know so much about me, then you know that I don't play games. If you want to talk, then bring Sid in here, then we can all have a nice polite conversation."

Titus cocked a brow and said, "My, you are cocky, aren't you? Well, Mister Smoke, my funeral home, my rules. And please, don't give me the whole 'If anything happens to her' speech. I've heard it a hundred times."

"That's not my style. Besides, she can take care of herself." Smoke gave the office a closer look. The brass floor lamps were antique, early nineteenth century. Behind Titus was a wall-to-wall bookshelf with many black-and-white framed photos layered in. Everything but the 1970s carpet was old, maybe a century or more, but nothing was dusty. It wouldn't surprise him if Titus had been working here for a hundred years. "So are you going to bring her in or not? You might want to do that before she comes knocking."

"She's fine just where she is. Safe too, very safe." Titus slid open a desk drawer and produced a clear jar of about twelve ounces with a pale fluorescent-yellow fluid in it. "Do you know what this is?"

"A urine sample?"

"Hah, good one, but no, not a urine sample. No, this is embalming fluid. You know what embalming fluid is, don't you?"

"Sure, I watch a show about embalming fluid all the time on the undertaker network. Get on with it before I put a hole in your head."

Holding the jar up above his eyes, Titus said, "This embalming fluid is special. You see, this is what we use to make the deaders. In part, that is. It's like blood, new blood, and it doesn't take very much. As a matter of fact, it can redirect the living and reanimate the dead. Well, with a little bit of help from our sorcerous ways." He stared at the jar with admiration. "It's taken me decades, but I finally have it perfected."

Smoke crossed his leg over his knee, pointed at Titus with one finger, and said, "But do you have it patented? Because if you don't have it patented, well, then anyone could go around and start animating the dead." He cleared his throat. "What you need are investors, and I'm listening, but I think we should angle for a spot on *Shark Tank*. Those venture capitalists will eat this up. But let's work on the package and a nice logo first. What do you say?"

Titus looked like he'd swallowed a cat when he said, "What in Hades are you talking about? I'm not pitching you a business deal. I'm threatening you and your wife. I'm going to take this serum and shoot it into her veins, stopping her heart and reanimating her into an abomination. It's going to be painful. Miserable. Insufferable. And you are going to watch it all happen, unless you cooperate."

"Yeah, I'm not feeling it. You're going to have to work on your approach. And smile. Can you smile? You look like you're swallowing sand when you talk. Tell you what—"

Titus smashed his fist on the desk. "Shut up! Shut up, you irritating man. Do you not understand what is about to happen if you don't cooperate? Your wife will die!"

Smoke rubbed his neck. He was getting to Titus just like he wanted, but something was getting to him too. Everywhere they went, they were expected. It was as if the Drake knew their every move, as if he and Sid were mice in some mysterious maze. A twisted form of entertainment and experiments. It was as if the likes of Kane and Reginald were trying to wear him down. But why? Why him? He was getting sick of it. "Titus, if anything happens to my wife, you'll pay for it."

"Oh ho." Titus rolled his eyes. "What are you going to do, kill me? Have you not figured it out yet? You can't kill any of us, you idiot. That's what's so entertaining, watching you fools fight a battle you cannot win."

"We've won plenty of battles, and the Drake's losses are stacking up."

"Pfft. Are you a total fool? Who do you know for sure that you killed? Let me fill you in, Mister Smoke. Adam Vaughn. Alive and well. Angi Harlow. Alive, beautiful, and well. Swift Venison is having some of the best days of his life." Titus tucked the jar of fluid back inside his desk. "You are our entertainment. You are Jason. We are the labyrinth."

Smoke felt tiny spiders crawling up his arms under his skin. Titus's words rang true. Nothing they'd done so far had mattered. They hadn't accomplished anything. He wanted to think it was a bluff, but it didn't feel like one. "You left out Mason Crow, the minotaur. I'm pretty sure he's dead."

"Oh no, he's not dead." Titus smacked his lips. "Just incapacitated." The chair squeaked when he leaned back. "Feeling a little foolish now, are we?"

"No. I'm kinda excited actually. Once I'm done with you, I can go after them."

Holding up one finger, Titus replied, "You might want to hold that thought." There was a black remote controller on his desk that he picked up. He pointed it over his shoulder at the bookshelf behind him. A section of the cabinet split open, revealing a flat-screen monitor.

Smoke's heart skipped a beat when Titus said, "How's your wife doing now, John?"

CHAPTER 31

CHIN UP AND HEAD TILTED, Smoke examined the monitor and said, "Fine, I suppose."

"You can't possibly be so coy," Titus said with a sneer. "This is your wife we are talking about. What kind of husband are you?"

"Did you make Sidney invisible or something? Because I don't see her."

The confidence vanished from Titus's face. He turned in the chair and gazed at the screen. His mouth hung open. "Idiots!"

A ruckus kicked up on the other side of the locked office door. Something big and heavy slammed into it.

"Smoke! You in there?" Sid yelled from the other side.

"Impossible!" Titus exclaimed.

With his gun on Titus, Smoke stood up and said to the shifter, "Don't move. The cavalry's arrived."

There was punching and grunting on the other side of the door. Bodies were being slammed into the walls. The floor shook under the power of heavy footfalls.

Sid was shouting with anger on the other side of the door, "Come and get me, you big ugly—"

The body of something huge slammed into the door again, this time busting it off the hinges and turning the wood into splinters. A giant of a man, big boned with a teased-up head of hair, lay on the floor. He fought his way back to his feet.

Sid stepped into the room. Her face was scuffed up, but her eyes were vibrant and full of energy. Gun in hand, she took aim at the young giant of a man and said, "Stay down, jughead." She eyed Smoke. "How are you doing?"

"Couldn't be better. Glad to see that you're taking care of things, not that I'm surprised. It seems like you turned the tables on these guys," Smoke said, keeping his gun on Titus.

"I took my vitamins," she said.

Titus's eyes started shifting back and forth, and his fingers began to fidget in his lap.

"Don't try anything," Smoke warned. "So who's your new friend, Sid?"

"Some oversized skateboarder who got the jump on me. The damn Lurch of a man was hiding behind the curtains and swallowed me up in them." Her eyes danced with excitement but remained fixed on the giant. The young fella wore jeans and a heavy cotton T-shirt and looked perfectly normal aside from his extraordinary size. "I played possum. He turned his back, and I slipped out of that basement morgue that your buddy has up on the screen. They have a lot of cadavers down there. Lots of doors, too."

"Get over here, Titus," Smoke said, fishing out a pair of specially made flex cuffs. "You're a wanted man, and I'm taking you in."

Titus scoffed. "Are you joking? You can't arrest me."

"It's not an arrest. Think of it more as an apprehension."

"Absurd." Titus swiveled around in his chair, hiding himself from Smoke's view. "Tell you what. I'll play your game, Smoke. Just give me a moment."

The secret panel in the bookshelf closed back up, hiding the monitor.

The young giant chuckled and said, "You guys are really messing up."

"Stick a sock in it, Diesel," Sid said. She moved toward the windows, eyeing the chair.

Smoke felt those spiders crawling up his arms again, under his skin. "Front and center, Titus, or I'm going to put a bunch of holes through you and that chair."

"Have I not told you that you cannot kill the likes of me?"

The stretching sound of the fiber in Titus's suit caught Smoke's ear. The leather in the chair groaned. Smoke's glance slid over to Sid. Her dark eyes widened, and she took aim at the chair.

"I can hear your hearts racing," Titus continued. From the confines of the chair, he stretched out his arms, revealing scaly grey hands with fingernails like claws that could rip through flesh like knives. The chair pushed back into the desk. Titus stood and turned. His face was a grey mask of ruddy skin that had the heavy-laden features of a gargoyle. A long chin and ears. A heavy brow protruding over his glaring yellow eyes. Built like a boulder, Titus shoved the heavy chair into the wall, held out his wrists, and said in his dangerous gravelly voice, "Come on, Smoke, cuff me."

CHAPTER 32

S MOKE TOSSED THE CUSTOM FLEX cuffs at Titus and said, "Cuff yourself."

As the cuffs bounced off of Titus's suit, he said, "That's one of the most ignorant things I have ever heard." He leaned down and shoved the entire desk at Smoke. "Do it yourself, puppet!"

Smoke hopped backward and fired a single shot at Titus. The blue-tipped bullet bounced off the gargoyle's chest.

"Your weapons cannot hurt the gargoyle." Titus's massive hands clutched in and out like a pair of savage can openers. "But most certainly I can hurt you." He grabbed the corner of the heavy desk, lifted it up off of its feet, and flung it aside.

"Smoke, watch out!" Sidney cried.

The young giant swept his leg at Smoke.

Smoke leapt to one side.

Sidney started firing bullets into the giant.

The huge man shielded himself with his arms.

"Back off, big boy!"

The big fella bolted down the hallway toward the front doors.

Sid gave chase.

"Sid, no!" Smoke said. He blasted several rounds at Titus.

The grey-skinned terror came at him with the speed of a charging bull.

Still shooting, Smoke skipped out of his path.

Titus stuck out his arm and swept a leg out from under Smoke, sending him tumbling to the seafoam-green floor.

Hitting the planks hard, Smoke regained his aim on Titus and unloaded the clip.

Blam! Blam! Blam! Blam! Blam! Blam!

Bullets ripped through the fine threads of the gargoyle's suit only to ricochet off his stony skin. Smoke brought his arms up just in time to catch the full force of Titus landing on top of him like a battering ram dropped from the ceiling.

"Oof!"

"Careful, you might break something," Titus said in a voice filled with confidence. "But if you don't, I will!" He held Smoke down by the neck and punched him with the force of a stone hammer.

Smoke groaned. Eyeing the next descending punch, he snapped his arm up and locked his fist around the gargoyle's wrist.

Titus's brute strength was like that of an ape, raw and powerful. The gargoyle swung his arm back and forth, saying, "Delay, delay, you can only delay the inevitable." With his free arm, he grabbed Smoke's wrist and started crushing it.

Smoke groaned. The viselike grip felt like it could snap his wrist. It sent shards of fire into his eyeball.

At almost point-blank range, Sid started firing shot after shot into the temple of Titus's head. His head and burly neck recoiled against the bullets that hit hard and bounced away. His grip slackened.

Drawing his knees into his chest, Smoke planted the soles of his boots into the gargoyle-man's abdomen and launched him back over his head.

Titus crashed into the bookcase, scattering books and papers all over.

Up on one knee, Smoke slapped a new clip into his weapon. "You thinking what I'm thinking?" he said to Sid.

Charging the hammer on her gun, she said with a nod, "I've been wanting to do this all along."

In his bullet-torn suit, Titus rose to his feet, straightened his tie, and said, "You mortals should have run while you had the chance. The both of you should have taken the deal. But now, I'm going to tear you apart."

"Those first shots were just a warning," Smoke said. "You'd best come along quietly. All you're doing is making a mess of your nice office here."

"You cannot stop me. You cannot kill me. Your mortal weapons mean nothing to me."

Smoke aimed for the head.

Sid aimed for the belly. "On three?" she said to Smoke.

With a bitter sneer on his face, Titus advanced.

"Three," Smoke said, and they both fired while diving behind what was left of the cherrywood desk.

Blam-Blam!

Boom-Boom!

The red-tipped explosive rounds shook the entire room. Paper and shards of wood flew everywhere.

Ears ringing, Smoke said to Sid as they got up, "Are you good?"

She plucked a sliver of wood from her face. "Never better. Morning glory, that was nasty." The glass was blown out of all the windows behind her. "You?"

Smoke tilted his chin at the body of Titus lying out cold on the floor. "That's what I call a plan coming together." Holstering his weapon, he rummaged around on the floor until he produced the flex cuffs from the debris. He cuffed Titus's hands behind his back then got out some more cuffs and really secured the shifter. Looking at Sid, he said, "Did we even discuss our payment for this gig?"

"Hm? I don't think we did," Sid replied. "I'm thinking a hundred K should fit the bill."

"At least." Smoke rolled Titus over. The gargoyle was a man again. "What about the teen giant?"

"Another problem for another time, I guess." She helped Smoke get Titus to his feet. "He's not going in the Hellcat."

"Don't worry, I have an idea. Come on."

They half dragged, half walked Titus into one of the parlors. A black coffin was on display and vacant. With a grunt, Smoke heaved the bulky body up and inside, face down in the coffin.

"Heavy?" Sid said.

"Like his limbs were filled with sand." He closed the coffin lid.

Sid helped seal the latches. "I don't suppose he'll suffocate."

"He says they can't be killed, but I bet we can make them uncomfortable." He found one of the decorative coffin gurneys in a nearby hallway and wheeled it in. Together, they shoved the coffin onto the gurney and started to take it outside. Smoke stopped Sid short of the door. "You might want to go out front and do some damage control."

"Suggestions?"

"Gas explosion?"

"I like it." She gave him a quick kiss on the lips. "See you in a bit."

Checking to see that no one was outside, Smoke pushed the coffin out onto the funeral home's parking lot behind one of the Cadillac hearses. He surveyed the area again. There wasn't any sign of anybody yet, not even the giant, but the distant whine of sirens caught his ear.

Make it quick, Sid. We gotta go.

Sliding the gurney to the side, he grabbed the chrome handle to the Cadillac's back door.

I hope it's open. I didn't see the keys. I'm sure I can hotwire it if need be.

He tugged on the back door latch and popped it a hair open. The door slammed right into him, knocking Smoke backward and crashing him into a motorcycle that was parked there.

The giant teenager crawled out of the back of the hearse, smashed his fist into his palm, and said, "You're toast, little dude."

CHAPTER 33

ATHERING HIMSELF, SMOKE WENT FOR his gun. The giant closed the gap in a moment, swinging his long arm like a whip and slapping the gun free of Smoke's hand.

"You're fast for a big fella."

Towering over Smoke with his fists balled up like hammers, the giant said, "No, I'm very fast for a big fella, you little tool. And I can't wait to crush your little head."

Smoke drew his knife and said, "You're welcome to try, but it won't happen. Got a name, boy?"

"Lance."

Shrugging, Smoke said, "Sounds like a little punk skateboarder name. Well, come on then, Lance. Let's dance."

Lance lunged at Smoke.

Striking like a snake, Smoke sliced a deep gash into Lance's forearm.

"Argh!" Lance recoiled. Astonished, he said, "You cut me!"

"Sharp knives will do that to you. They can lance you too, Lance."

They circled. With a tremor in his voice, Lance said, "I can handle everything you got. You can't kill me, mortal."

"I'm getting tired of hearing that. Keep saying it, though, so I can prove you wrong."

Licking his lips, Lance eyed the knife in Smoke's hand. "Look, I don't want to do this. I'm just doing what I'm told." He backed into a pair of trashcans and lifted his hands. "Just take Titus and leave me alone."

Backing off, Smoke said, "If that's the case, why did you attack me?"

"I don't know. I was scared. Hell, I hid inside that hearse. I thought I was safe until you showed up."

Surprised by the confession, Smoke lowered his guard.

In a burst of energy, Lance twisted around, grabbed a metal trashcan, and hurled it at Smoke.

Balling up, Smoke caught the full force of the half-empty can that skipped off his shoulder and clunked on the ground. "Bad move, Lance." Smoke drew from his shoulder and ankle holsters. "I'm going to make you hurt."

Lance snatched up the motorcycle and hoisted it over his head. "I can handle anything you got! Come on, shoot me, little man! Shoot me!"

No longer armed with the red-tipped bullets, Smoke settled for the blue-tipped and regular lead in his guns. He aimed for the gas tank and fired. The cycle turned into a ball of flame. With the second pistol, he shot at Lance's eyes.

The big boy teetered backward into the funeral home wall, screaming with rage.

Smoke shoved the coffin into the hearse and closed the door.

Sidney showed up, gaping at the enraged Lance. He was swinging blindly at everything. "What's the plan?"

"Call Cyrus and tell him to send a cleanup crew and that we'll meet him near here."

"Great," Sid said, watching Lance and grabbing her phone. "So where are we going to meet?"

The sirens were getting louder.

"Somewhere with milkshakes."

CHAPTER 34

Sid and Smoke were standing outside in a truck stop parking lot, hidden from plain view behind the semis. Her phone was on the hood of the hearse and the external speaker was on.

Cyrus's voice was erupting from the phone. "Where are you? I've got people all over a blown-up funeral home and no sign of you guys or the mark!"

"Did you find a giant?" Sid asked. "He should have been easy to find, seeing how he was on fire when we left him."

"Quit screwing around, Sid!" Cyrus replied. "Now where are you?"

Her eyes played with Smoke's and she said, "We never discussed our fee. It's one hundred thousand."

"That's outrageous! And you're on the payroll!"

"No, no, no, we're still in business as bounty hunters. I'm only on payroll as a liaison and special advisor. This is hazard duty you have us on."

There was a pause on the other side of the line, and finally Cyrus said, "You know we're on a tight budget. Purchasing limits me to twenty-five thousand."

"I guess we let Titus Tolliver go then." She looked over at Smoke. "Go ahead and let him out."

"Sure thing," Smoke said, opening up the back door of the hearse. He rolled the coffin out and lowered the bottom end to the ground.

"Listen to me, Sid. I can't just pull that kind of money out of my crack. You know that. If you want those kinds of funds, I'm going to need to see some proof."

She walked over to the coffin, watching Smoke open the latches. He pulled the top half of the coffin's lid open. Titus had woken up and managed to wriggle himself around facing front, but he was tightly secured with ten pairs of flex cuffs. His beady eyes were full of hate.

Sid held up her phone.

Smoke said, "Say cheese, horn head."

"You'll regret this," Titus spat. "The both of you!"

Sid tapped the buttons on her screen and said into the phone, "Coming over, Cyrus. Take a look and give us a call when the money hits our bank account. We'll give you an hour before we set him free."

Cyrus said, "When did you get this greedy streak in you?"

"Bye." She hung up.

"Well played," Smoke said to her. He held his gun on Titus. "Don't even squirm."

Titus scowled at him, but there was a little bit of fear in his eyes. They'd gotten under his stone-hard skin. "I'll double what they aren't even willing to pay you if you let me go," he said.

"It's not about the money. We just like jerking the FBI around. As for you and your ilk, well, you need to go down. You're a cancer on this place."

"People are the cancer, not us. So destitute. So depraved. You can't stop what we're doing. No one ever has, and no one ever will." Titus's eyes glanced back and forth between the two of them and settled on Sid. "You should do like your sister did. Be a part of this. The both of you."

"Why do you want us so bad? You have plenty of willing people who won't hesitate to take you up on your offer." Sid tucked her phone into her pocket. "What is going on with you people?"

"This is just a last-ditch effort to recruit you. Both of you, but you're too stubborn to see the light." Titus craned his neck. "The pair of you are legacies."

Smoke's eyes found Sid's on his. The look in her eyes was more of an affirmation than puzzlement. It left him off guard a little. He was thinking the same thing though. The missing piece inside of him started to be filled by what Titus had just said. "Keep talking, gargoyle."

"Fine then. I'll tell you. I'll tell you both." Titus's heavy stare went back and forth between the two of them as he spoke. "You're offspring."

Smoke bent his ear and said, "I beg your pardon."

"You heard me. Offspring. The both of you." A wily smile formed on his face. "You are very much like me. You know your heart is tainted with black. Really, John Smoke, do you think any mortal man could do what you can do? Your instincts and abilities are far greater than the average man's. You've tried to deny it too long, but now your family has come calling. You're the rebel son."

Sneering, Smoke replied, "I'm not anything like any of you. I die and bleed like any man."

"Have you actually died?"

Smoke had backed up, pondering the thought, when Sid jumped in. "You said both of us."

"Yes, sister—"

"Don't call me that."

"Don't be so touchy, but you are part of a tainted generation. You have your own skills too, though they are more latent. According to the record, the pair of you will produce mighty offspring."

Sid's expression turned clammy, and Smoke said to her, "Don't believe him. They're all liars."

Titus gave a shrug. "True, we all do lie. Quite often. But that's only because it's so effective on people. Stupid people." He chuckled. "Let me take a moment to explain your dilemma, which you should by all means have sense enough to embrace as a blessing. You are the offspring of shifters who mated with humans. Normally—well, quite often—a male shifter impregnates a female mortal, who dies in childbirth. The children rarely survive. They just turn out to be monstrosities.

But in your case, things are a little more special. A female shifter is impregnated by a mortal male. Typically, there is no conception, but rarely, it takes. Bing bang boom, here you are."

Hairs standing up on his neck, Smoke shut the coffin lid and sealed it closed. He shoved the coffin back into the hearse and slammed the door.

"Let's go."

CHAPTER 35

S ID SLIPPED THE HELLCAT IN between a couple of semis and placed the car in park. "That was a pretty short trip," she said. "Care to fill me in?"

Smoke opened up the door and hopped out. The truck stop was a big one, about the size of a football field, and busy. Diesel engines roared with life, and the black exhaust rolled into the hot summer air. Smoke made his way around the front of a bright-red Peterbilt and stood in front of the chrome grille. He had a perfect view of the trucks coming in and out of the stop.

Sid cozied up beside him. "Again, what's going on?"

"I want to see where they take him."

"I know that, but what's bothering you?" She blocked his view. "You don't believe that *offspring* story, do you?"

"I don't know," he replied. He felt like something was eating him up all over. Titus's words were ringing true. They had seeped into his bones, and now they were sapping his strength.

"Come on, you know they're liars," she said, giving him a reassuring smile. "He even suggested that *I* was an offspring. It came off weird and desperate, Smoke. Don't let them get into your head. After all we've been through, you're the man I love, even if you wind up being the son of some demon spawn."

Shaking his head, he said, "Are you serious?"

"No. If you were demon spawn, I'd have to kill you." She grinned. "Sorry."

"I'd do the same for you," he said.

"I appreciate that," she replied.

They stood side by side, faces to the wind, watching the traffic on the incoming and outgoing roads. About ten minutes later, the FBI came in a small fleet of black SUVs. It took them less than a minute to find the hearse, and thirty seconds later, they were departing. Two cars in the front, two in the rear, and someone driving the hearse in the middle.

"Time to go," Smoke said.

"Why don't you drive?" Sid suggested. "I think it will make you a little more comfortable."

The phantom-black Hellcat let out a nasty exhaust note that startled a trucker in a ball cap who was walking by. At first he shouted a curse, but then, seeing the car, he smiled and gave them a thumbs up.

Accelerating out of the truck stop and merging onto the highway, Smoke caught up with the FBI convoy but remained several truck lengths back.

Sid's phone buzzed. Checking the screen, she said, "Well I'll be. It looks like our money has been deposited. Why don't we just take the money and run?"

"Because that's not any fun."

"Agreed." She drummed her hands on the dash. "I kinda hate to admit it, but this is more fun than the honeymoon—but just the parts when we weren't fooling around together."

"I can't disagree with that."

Sid reached over and rubbed his shoulder. "You're all right, John."

"I suppose, but there are too many questions that need answered. The truth is that I don't really know who I am and where I come from. It's always been a mystery. But somebody knows, and that somebody is screwing with me."

"Either that, or they're using that tidbit of information against you," she reminded him. She eased the seat back and closed her eyes. "I need a power nap."

"Knock yourself out."

"Just keep your eyes on the road and don't follow so close," she joked. "Man, that super vitamin really drained me, but it doesn't seem as bad as the last time."

CHAPTER 36

SID SLEPT. SMOKE DROVE. It gave him plenty of time to hash over the things Titus had said. The mere thought that he might have something inside his blood that would cause him to be some sort of abomination made Smoke sick to his stomach. But he *was* different. He knew that. He had always known, but not in any extraordinary way. He couldn't change shape or anything like that, but he could sense things other people couldn't. He could anticipate the moves of his opponents before they happened. He could feel what was going to happen next, like a sixth sense. It gave him an edge. Most of the time.

Maybe I should get some blood work done.

Sid rested in the passenger seat. Her chest rose and fell with the ease of a slumbering baby. He found it hard to believe she had some sort of curse inside her too. She was good, too good. She, like him, would rather die than become evil.

Don't let them get in your head, Smoke.

He squeezed the steering wheel until his knuckles turned white. Nothing rattled him, but today, he felt worn down. Frustration had settled in. Things were getting deeper and more personal. When he was young he had thought he was normal, but at some point he realized he wasn't. There were too many things he could do and see that the other kids couldn't. Without exacerbating it, he'd lain low. As time passed, he'd stopped wondering why he was different and just let himself be. Until today. Now he was wondering again. The long drive wasn't helping. The FBI convoy was heading north toward Baltimore.

Where are they going?

After an hour-and-fifteen-minute drive, Smoke got his answer. The convoy slunk off the Baltimore Beltway on interstate 695 and cruised up to a place called Hawkins Point, right on the bay. With nothing but a dead end ahead, he pulled the Hellcat onto the berm and shut off the engine.

Sidney stirred. Her eyes blinked open, and she wiped her mouth.

"Enjoy your little nap, honey?" Smoke said while he reached into the backseat and snagged their goggles.

"How long have I been out?"

"Over an hour." He put his goggles on and handed hers to her. "An hour and fifteen minutes, to be precise."

She sat up in her seat, yawned, and stretched her arms out from side to side. Putting her goggles on and peering out the front window, she said, "Why are we in Baltimore?"

"Good question." With his eyesight magnified by the goggles, he got a clean look at the FBI crew. There were eight men and women, looking official in their black FBI ball caps and short-sleeved black summer uniforms. Moving with the purpose of black ants, four of them pulled the coffin out of the hearse and carried it over to the concrete dock. A boat was approaching from the Patapsco River. It was a thirty-foot-long pontoon boat with two men on board. They ran the boat alongside the dock, splashing up and down on the edge.

"Someone's picking up our friend." Smoke started the engine and backed the car up off the road into a small grove of trees. Less than a minute later, the four FBI vehicles flew right by them and disappeared up the road and out of sight. He drove the car down to the dock, where he picked up the sight of the pontoon boat again. He pointed. "There."

"I see it," Sid said. "It looks like they're heading to Fort Carroll."

"What a great place to hide…something." Fort Carroll was a hexagon-shaped three-and-a-half-acre artificial island. Even with the goggles, all Smoke could see were three tiers of stone wall, some overgrowth of vegetation, and ugly trees hosting local sea birds. "It was designed by Robert E. Lee and constructed in 1847, designed to protect America's most important ports, back in the day. In 1921, the army pulled out the last of its assets. It's been pretty much abandoned ever since."

"That was a fine history lesson. Maybe we should put you on *Jeopardy*."

With a little shift of his shoulders, he said, "I know things."

The coffin-laden craft disappeared around the island.

"Huh." He put the car in gear and drove away. "Why don't you get Sam and Guppy to see what they can find out about Fort Carrol? Last I heard, they were going to turn it into a casino. That was the rumor when I was a kid. But I'd be curious to hear if it's still privately owned."

"Sure." She started texting. "Anything for my man."

"Anything?" His brow arched. "I like that."

Crossing the Francis Scott Key Bridge, Sid had a bird's-eye view of the island through her window. "I don't see the boat anywhere. It has to be in there. Why would the FBI be taking Titus there?"

"Do you see any other activity?"

"Uh…as a matter of fact, there's a small crane and Bobcat loader. No people though." Her phone buzzed. Checking the screen, she said, "I can't believe it."

"What?" Smoke asked.

Sid let out an angry sigh. "I can't believe this. According to Guppy, Drake Properties owns it." She dug her fingernails into Smoke's thigh. "I'm going to kill Cyrus!"

CHAPTER 37

BACK INSIDE FBI HEADQUARTERS, SMOKE and Sid were in a heated conversation with Cyrus Tweel and Rebecca Lang. They'd been going back and forth for ten minutes when Jane, Cyrus's secretary, popped her head in the door and said, "I can hear you. Loud."

Red cheeked with his sleeves rolled up over his flabby arms, Cyrus said, "Everyone, take a break and take a seat." He sighed through his nose. "Please."

Smoke and Sid took a seat in front of the desk across from Rebecca. The mousy little blonde had shortened her hair, and she'd added a few pounds to her little frame as well. She'd been nothing but nasty since Smoke came through the door. She slumped into her chair, crossed her legs, and kicked her foot like an edgy person. "You two are quite the pair. We pull strings to pay you and now you question our intentions."

"Your intentions?" Sid looked like she was about to come out of her chair and pound the little woman. "You took Titus to a secret facility owned by the Drake! What are we doing any of this for? I want to see what happens to these people after we catch them."

"You don't have the right to see anything!" The tendons in Rebecca's neck were strained. "You were paid to capture the man, and that's what you did. What we do with them is not your business. That's our business!"

Sidney's eyes lit up. With a coy smile on her face, she calmly said to Rebecca, "You said *them*."

Rebecca looked like she had swallowed her foot. Stammering, she said, "I meant him."

No she hadn't. Smoke could tell. Cyrus and Rebecca had been playing dumb all along. They knew a lot more than they were letting on. He caught Cyrus rolling his eyes just as she said it, too.

"At some point," Smoke said to Cyrus, "you're going to have to come clean with us. We do what we do to put these monsters away. We're better off putting them down than turning them in if they're being let go."

"We can get someone else to do what you two do, and for less money." Rebecca crossed her arms over her chest and continued kicking her leg. "Please excuse yourselves."

"You really are one little head case, aren't you," Sid said. "You two really deserve each other. Bonnie and Clyde."

Rebecca fired back. "And who are you two supposed to be, Boris and Natasha?"

Smoke let out a little laugh and started speaking with a Russian accent. "I am invincible! Why does she talk to us like this for? I don't understand, Natasha. Little woman is rude. Nasty like bad vodka."

In a husky woman's voice, Sid replied, "I don't know, Boris. Maybe because she's so short and stupid. Look at her. A puny rabid chipmunk."

Red faced, Rebecca came out of her chair.

"Rebecca, Stop!" Cyrus cried out.

It was too late. Sid had the little woman on the floor with her arm twisted behind her. "Just give me a reason to break it, you mouthy little—"

"Sid, please!" Cyrus pleaded. "She's been out of whack since she found out she's pregnant."

Smoke swiveled around in his chair, looking at Rebecca. "Out of wedlock. Shame, shame. Are you going to be a daddy?"

Stiff necked, Cyrus replied, "I don't know. She won't say."

Sid released her. "Fine, but I've had enough of this. From now on, if we want answers, we'll just get them on our own. Let's go, Smoke."

"Everybody just hold on." Cyrus resumed his seat with a furrowed brow. "Fort Carroll is a prison. Or rather a holding facility. All of these shifters that you catch are taken there for processing. As for what happens after that, I don't know."

"You're an idiot, Cyrus," Rebecca said. She rubbed her wrist and glared at Sid. "They don't have the need to know any of this."

"Maybe not, but they deserve to know. Geez, you really need to work out your issues, Rebecca. I've never seen even a pregnant woman who was so mean before."

Rebecca's eyes watered up, and her face sagged. "I hate you, Cyrus." She rushed out of the room.

Cyrus threw his arms up. "I just keep rolling. Every hour it's a different personality with her, and I can't let that stand in the way of me saying what I need to say. Back to Fort Carroll. Look, I haven't been there. All I know is that's where the Black Slate captives go. And I had to find that out on my own. Actually, agent Johnnie Wok told me. As for the Drake owning it, that's news to me. I've just been following orders."

"Has anyone besides Senator Wilhelm been on your back about all this?" Sid asked.

"No. That's plenty. If another one of those blustering Senate suits comes in here, my head will explode." Cyrus took off his glasses and pinched the bridge of his nose. "Man, I've got a headache."

Smoke asked, "So what's your next step? Who do you call?"

"I've already made the calls. One to the Black Slate handlers and another one to Wilhelm. Lucky for me I haven't heard back from either one of them yet," Cyrus said.

"So what's next?" Sid asked. "Are we supposed to just wait around for another call about the Black Slate?"

"You got paid. Go spend your money." Cyrus put his glasses back on, and his eyes drifted toward the door. The disheartened look on his face couldn't be about anything other than what he was feeling for Rebecca. "I'll be in touch."

CHAPTER 38

Smoke and Sid were back at her apartment at Angel Brook, packing. It was the next morning, and the sun was up and gleaming in her bedroom window. In the background, the television was on and the smell was of fresh coffee brewing. She was in jeans and a black-and-grey Steelers T-shirt, folding up clothes into neat stacks on her bed. She grabbed a suitcase out of the closet, set it on the bed, and unzipped it. Stack by stack, she set her clothes in the suitcase.

Taking more clothes out of her closet, Smoke said, "So, you want to take everything?"

"You're wondering where we're going to put it all, aren't you."

"Ah, no, not at all. We'll make room for it. We can always build an add-on if we have to." He held up a long maroon evening gown. "Wow, this is nice. We definitely have room for this."

"You don't have to worry. Most of the extra stuff I'll take to Mom and Dad's. But we'll certainly take that if you want to." She walked over to Smoke, took the dress, and kissed him. "Have you ever had a roommate before?"

"I've had roommates, but they were always men."

With the playfulness of a vixen in her eyes, she said, "Well isn't that a shame. Wait here. I'll be right back."

Smoke watched her go into the bathroom and emerge moments later with the fine dress slipped over her lovely figure. The maroon and black mixed together enhanced her alluring qualities.

"You know, before we pack everything up, I think we should make a few memories of the old place together." Her eyes slid over his body and onto her bed. "What do you think?"

Smoke shoved everything off the bed, saying, "I've been thinking the same thing all morning." He scooped her up in his arms, and she let out a squeal. He dropped her on the bed and climbed over her. Looking into her eyes, he said, "You're so beautiful."

She ran her fingers through the hair over his ears. "And you're amazing, but don't you ever toss my clothes off the bed again."

"As you wish."

Later that day, they'd finished up most of the packing in Sid's apartment. She walked a box down the steps into the parking lot, where Smoke waited by Guppy's van they'd borrowed. She said to Smoke, "I'm just doing this to keep me busy. Get my mind off things. We haven't talked much about what went down in Cyrus's office, but I'm curious to know where your mind is on that."

Smoke took the box from her and stuck it in the van. "I've kinda enjoyed not talking about that, but you know me pretty well by now. Where do you think my mind is on that?"

"You want to explore Fort Carroll and see what's going on."

He nodded.

"You know, I'm also thinking that Wilhelm is the X factor in all of this. He's the Drake's pawn or something bigger, maybe even a knight. What if that guy becomes president and our entire government is being run by a bunch of clones and shifters?" Sid shivered. "Who's going to be able to control them then?"

"I think you're right about Wilhelm. I'm starting to think maybe Wilhelm really isn't Wilhelm. Maybe he's something else. He could have been a shifter all along. Terrifying, isn't it?"

She picked a box up off the ground. "As if the government weren't terrifying enough already. Can you imagine it being even worse?"

"I can."

"Of course you can. Listen to me, John, I don't want you venturing into Fort Carroll without me. I know you want answers. I want answers too, but I can't get it out of my head that you're going to turn into the ultimate frog man and swim over there as soon as I close my eyes and fall asleep."

Parting his hands in a peaceful gesture, he said, "I'll make it quick."

"So you *were* planning on leaving me."

"No," he said, "but I have been running through a plan of action about fifty times in my mind. Sid, I need to know what's going on. We've taken these monsters down, and I need to make sure they stay down. Too many people suffer because of them."

"Just keep loading boxes, okay?"

Sid's expression was one of concern and worry, and he could empathize with that. Loving another person could be a dangerous thing. Evil would use it against you. Everywhere they went, Smoke was on high alert, watching and listening for the enemies that might try to take Sid away from him again. He had to protect her, but the funny thing was—she was trying to protect him.

"Once we finish up, maybe we should have a sit-down with the gang," he suggested.

"The gang?"

"You know who I mean."

Sid fanned away a bumble bee. "No. Are you talking about the Apple Dumpling Gang?"

"Hah-hah. No, but I like it. Come on, let's finish up and go. We need to get you settled into your new home." He lifted another box into the van. "I will say this. I'm glad you don't have that much to pack. Kinda surprising for such a pretty woman. You have more guns and ammo than anything else. Well, that and a nice selection of feminine underwear."

"You can call them panties. It's okay, we're married now. It would even be okay if we weren't, John Boy."

"I'm old fashioned. I just don't want to say any words that might get me worked up."

"Panties? That word excites you?"

"You saying it does."

"Are you wanting to make my bed again?"

Smoke shrugged.

Taking him by the hand, she started back up the steps to the apartment.

Nearby, a throat cleared. "Such a lovely day, isn't it?"

A tall, slender man with flowing white hair stood on the sidewalk holding a black umbrella against the sun. It was Vormus.

CHAPTER 39

T HE DEEP-PURPLE SUIT VORMUS WORE looked brand new, but the style was at least two centuries old. The top hat he wore was even worse. Smoke said the first thing that came to mind. "Well, it looks like Willie Wonka is back out of the chocolate factory."

"Willie who?" Vormus said.

A woman approached him on the sidewalk at a quick pace as if he would step aside. He didn't. She dropped off the edge of the sidewalk and scuttled along at a quicker pace and started calling a number on her phone.

Vormus raised an eyebrow. "Am I going to have to stand out here all day? It's rather uncomfortable."

"Why would we want you to be comfortable?" Smoke said.

"Pleasant surroundings will make my news more fetching to your ears. After all, you want answers, and I have them."

Smoke and Sid looked at each other, and she said, "We aren't looking for any answers."

"Of course you are. Listen to me," Vormus said. "I know what the Drake has plans for, and you should want to know too, seeing how your family is involved in all of this. Please, just let us speak of this somewhere alone." He stretched his fingers out into the sun. There was a sizzling and cracking of skin. "I'm not at my full strength in the daylight. You clearly hold the advantage."

"Morning glory, come on up then." Sid gave Smoke a shrug.

He jogged down the steps and slipped behind Vormus, who proceeded to follow Sid up the steps and into the apartment. Closing them inside, Smoke pulled his gun on Vormus.

Sid did the same and said, "Talk."

Taking note of his surroundings and closing his black parasol, Vormus said, "This certainly is a modest little place. What will you do with all of this delightful furniture? Will it find a home in that *Goodwill* place?"

"Just sit down," Sid said. "And keep your hands where I can see them."

Edging closer to the sofa, Vormus sneered at it. "I hope you aren't implying that you think I would steal any of your dime-store decorations. That's awfully insulting to me."

"Just talk," Smoke said.

"Oh, I'd be happy to, man of many short words." Vormus sat down like he was about to sit on a pile of manure, then shifted in the seat. "It's not horribly bad. So, where were we?"

Sid stood behind the kitchen counter that overlooked the small living room. "You were about to tell us why you're here."

"Aren't you going to offer me some tea or coffee? Not that pod stuff. A finely percolated French roast will do just fine. Or some Earl Grey tea, but that's not as common among you commoners."

"It's all packed up. Now out with it, Vormus. What the hell do you want?" Sid said.

Vormus's air of superiority started to sag. His slender shoulders slumped, and he said, "I want your help."

Smoke and Sid burst out laughing.

"If there is one thing that I still envy, it is the mortals' way of finding humor in just about everything." Vormus tried to laugh, but only a strange cluck came forth.

"What was that?" Sid said, still laughing. "Are you about to spit up a hairball on my Goodwill sofa?"

"It was a desperate attempt to laugh," Vormus sneered. "The sensation of joy is lost to me." His fingers dug into the cushions, and his voice became serious. His hypnotic eyes sucked their eyes into his. "I want my mortality back, and I want you to help me!"

A brief silence fell over the room before Sid spoke up and said, "That can happen?"

"According to the record," Vormus replied.

"What record?" Smoke wasn't inclined to believe anything Vormus said, but the shifter did have his attention.

Sid had perked up a little too.

"Ancient texts and files the Lancasters have stashed—and it's not all a bunch of mysticism. It's science and chemistry too. To become a shifter, there are injections and rituals, but they can be reversed." He sighed. "My kind doesn't do it because it won't be long before you die if you reverse it, but I'm ready."

"And how are we supposed to help?" Sid said. "Why don't you use your own people, Guermo?"

"I tried that, but all of my loyal minions are dead, and I can't do it alone. Kane is after me. That night we fought was a close one." Vormus took off his top hat, dusted off the top, and set it down beside him. "I wasn't equipped to beat him then. It was a moment of inspiration."

"Inspiration? What kind of inspiration?"

Vormus's jaw shifted back and forth. It was clear that he was uneasy with something. A struggle was within. The cold and compassionless shifters didn't feel anything for anyone. They were arrogant, overconfident, and proud. People were like sheep to them. No, worse. Like insects to be crushed beneath their toes. But something about Vormus was different now. There was doubt. Shame. Finally, he said, "You two."

Sid came out from around the kitchen counter and stood beside Smoke. "Us?"

"I've never seen two more stubborn people in my life. The way you fought for each other. That fire in your eyes. Kane tried to break you, Sidney Smoke, but you didn't break. They wanted John to give up, but he didn't quit. My kind despises that. It reminds us of our past. The life we gave up selfishly that we once had." Vormus gave them both a look of desperation. "I had what you have once and gave it up. Now I'm nothing but a void that cannot be filled."

"Forgive us for not breaking out a violin and playing a song for you," Smoke said, "But you're all a bunch of cold-blooded killers."

Vormus held up his hands. "Guilty as charged. The blood on my hands is thick, and I won't deny it. But I'd be glad to confess and finish out my life on death row just to have my mortality again."

"And what do you have to offer us?" Sid asked.

"I know how to stop the shifters."

CHAPTER 40

S MOKE PUT HIS GUN AWAY and took a seat on one of the barstools. "Go ahead, we're listening."

"I'm not going to spill the beans now, as you like to say," Vormus replied. "I need you to help me first, but I will give you some information that will make it worth your while." He locked eyes with Sid. "Your sister and niece are in certain danger. As a matter of fact, your sister is becoming a shifter now."

The blood ran out of Sidney's face. "Don't lie to me," she said to Vormus.

"I'd like to believe that I was, but I'm not. Allison was drawn to the power the same as anyone else. Immortal beauty. External strength. It's hard for the youth to see that everything they have been presented with is just a charade. An illusion. She'll have regrets soon enough. It may take a few years or decades even, but the regret will be the same. Deep as a bottomless well."

"You said, 'becoming a shifter'? What does that mean?" Smoke asked.

"As I've said, there are rituals and injections that she must agree to. She'll then pick a form that she identifies with. Me, I chose to become a vampire, more or less a charming type of horror. You've encountered the other beasts that the others become. Their powers blossom at night. But not all survive the process. There aren't too many true shifters. But your sister Allison is a prime candidate, just like the both of you are."

Smoke leaned forward. The words of Titus Tolliver filled his mind, about him and Sid being a legacy of the shifters. "Fill us in."

Vormus's long face brightened. "Ah, so you've been told. A good thing. The sooner you both deal with it, the better. As a matter of fact, that is another reason why I am here, to tell you of your value. The shifters are not so many. We don't need many to survive, but the more the merrier. There is strength in numbers, and that is why you are being recruited. Tested. A pair such as you could be an asset, and that is what they want."

"Who is 'they'?" Sid asked. "The Drake?"

"Yes and no," Vormus said. "You see, the Drake thinks they are in charge of shifters, and the shifters think they are in charge of the Drake."

"Aren't they one and the same?' Smoke asked.

"Yes, but the mortals of the Drake are very manipulating, while the shifters are overconfident. It's very difficult to tell who is using who. You see, when you have a short life, you tend to fight very hard for what you want out of it. We have long lives. Hence the fight is not hard, it is entertainment. Do I think the madness will ever end? No. At least not until the end of the age. I don't think any person can withstand the self-devouring circle, but perhaps I can feel what it is like to live again. Even for a day. And your sister Allison? I know you, Sidney. Perhaps you can give her a reason to not give up her life as well. Though it will be hard to change her mind."

Vormus being a fountain of information was odd, and his comments were vague, leading to more questions in Smoke's mind. It wouldn't be easy to accept Vormus as an ally again, but Smoke wanted to know everything he could. Every bit of information he had about the Drake and the shifters would give him an edge, and he needed every bit of it. He was about to speak when Sid spoke up first. It was as if she had read his mind.

"What is the Drake's end game?" she asked.

"The same as it always is. Take over the leadership of all the nations. Use it to destroy any enemies that are a threat to them. If it's not the Drake, then it's always some other organization. A rival government or business. The Drake has its competition too, but it uses people like me to take it out. Nothing new is under the sun, but we are all caught up in the middle of it.

"As for the pair of you, I think you've pissed on Kane and his minions enough. To be truthful, if they can't break you—which I'm pretty sure they have realized they can't—then they will kill you. Because you're always a threat to them. People like you keep coming. I've seen it before in my time. You're bloodhounds. And that little visit from your sister on your wedding day? Well, I think that was a last-ditch effort to turn you to their side. You don't have long. It will be war after that." Vormus snorted something like a laugh. "They can't even blackmail you with your families. Believe me, I was there when they talked about it, but they realized you'd keep coming anyway. They don't understand it and I don't understand it, but I want it. They think you both are crazy."

"As long as people like us stick together, we'll always land on top," Smoke said.

"I know that is a true statement. It wasn't so long ago that there were a lot more of you, but now your packs have thinned. People like us have worn you down." Vormus rose to his feet. "But I've never been surprised at what a couple of people can do. Particularly people such as you. Not to press, but I must ask, are you willing to help me as I am willing to help you?"

"We still have a lot more questions." Sid picked a box up off the floor and handed it to Vormus. "You want to be mortal again, then help us with our moving. It's a real character builder."

"Oh, the laborious tasks of the mortals," he whined. "It's been at least a century since I did anything called work. How exhilarating."

Smoke loaded another box on top of Sid's, which concealed Vormus's face. He stuffed the shifter's top hat on the shifter too and said, "Time to find out how that centuries old back of yours is doing." He hefted another box on to his shoulder and headed toward the door. "Follow me."

After three trips up and down the steps to load the van, Vormus said, "I'm starting to regret my decision entirely." He ran his thumb over his brow and eyed it. "Perspiration. Blecht."

Sid tossed a duffle bag into the van and said, "So where do you start this adventure?"

"All of my sources lead me to Fort Carroll," Vormus said. "We'll get more answers there. We might get all of the answers there."

"What's so special about Fort Carroll?" Smoke asked.

"Remember, I'm an outsider, a part of Guermo. But as I understand it, the minions that fail Kane are taken there for punishment and rehabilitation. We're going to need their help."

Aghast, Sid said, "So you want to rescue them?"

"Just the ones that are helpful."

CRAIG HALLORAN

THE SUPERNATURAL BOUNTY HUNTER FILES

HOLY SMOKE

BOOK 8

CHAPTER 1

F ORT CARROLL SAT IN THE middle of the Patapsco River like a ghost city. Smoke and Sid were at the docks where the FBI had dropped off Titus Tolliver days earlier. Beside the phantom black Dodge Hellcat, Sid squeezed into the sweetheart suit. Her skin tingled. A coppery taste filled her mouth. She fought the urge to spit.

"You okay?" Smoke's sweetheart suit only covered him above the waist. The refined sinew coating his muscular frame rippled with every movement. He blew into a small inflatable raft they were going to stow their weapons and gear in. "You look a little nervous." He gazed at the river. "It's not the easiest swim."

Sid loosened up her arms by doing small windmills. She cracked her neck from side to side. "I was feeling a little tight, but I'm feeling better with the suit on. I bet I can beat you over there."

"Hey, I'm hauling all the gear." Smiling, he shoved a pair of guns into the floating sack. He stood up with a knife and belt in his hand, wrapped it around Sid's waist, and fastened it with a snap. Backing up, he said with an approving nod, "You've got that Bond girl thing going on. I like it."

"Bond girls aren't half the woman I am. They're scrawny."

Smoke put his arms around her waist. "And not half as sexy."

"Why don't I take a picture?" Sam, Smoke's sister, was dressed in black, grey, and white camouflage. Her hair was pulled back in a long ponytail. Guppy stood beside her, dressed the same, with a grin on his face. His black truck was parked behind them. Sam pulled out her phone. "You two look so adorable together. No one would ever suspect you're a couple of lunatics."

"I'd rather you didn't. This isn't the best place for a flash," Sid said.

"OK, fine." Sam put her phone away. Looking around, she said, "So what about this Vormus guy? Isn't he supposed to be here?"

"He said he'd meet us on the island," Smoke said.

"And doesn't that seem a little suspicious, coming from a guy who tried to kill us all?" Sam replied.

Smoke shrugged.

"Are you okay with this, Sid?" Sam asked.

Adjusting her knife belt, she said, "I have to find out where my niece and sister are."

"I don't like it," Sam said, "but if you don't make it back, I promise to take care of the Hellcat. The keys are in it, right?"

Sid laughed. "You're more than welcome, Sis."

"Aw, come here." Sam clomped over on her high heels and gave Sid a firm hug. "You'd better make it back. That place is creepy out there. I can just imagine all those monsters spilling outside."

"And I can't imagine you running from them in those high heels."

"Oh, I won't be running. I'll be driving the Hellcat." Sam made a cat sound.

"Boy, you really do want my car, don't you!" Sid said.

"I'm sorry, I have to say funny things when I'm nervous." Sam shouted at Guppy, "You make sure they've got everything Mal gave you?"

"I did," Guppy replied.

"Well, double check it."

"I did."

"Triple—"

"Done!"

"You're a good friend and sister, Sam. We'll make it back."

Sam swatted at a mosquito buzzing near her face. "I hate mosquitos." Stepping away from Sid, she said, "Guppy, I've got a mosquito."

Sam's burly husband sauntered over with an aerosol can. He sprayed mist around Sam. "Don't get it in my mouth," she said, adding a little cough.

Smoke slung the inflatable pack over his shoulder. "I guess it's time." He and Sid walked toward the boat ramp at Hawkins Point. There wasn't anyone else around. He said to Sam, "We'll be back before dawn."

"You'd better be."

Sid and Smoke waded into the cold waters of the river, sending shivers up from her bare feet.

Smoke handed her a pair of flippers. "These will make the swim a lot easier."

"You know, I didn't even think of that. I guess I should have expected this from a former frogman."

He snapped his green-lensed goggles over his head. "What can I say. I love the water. So are you ready?"

As the waters splashed against the rocks from the wake of a barge passing by, she waded in deeper. With a nod, she eyed Fort Carroll. Her heart pounded. Even though the sweetheart suit sent steady energy into her body, there was quavering inside. It was a long swim. Even longer thinking about the unknown that waited for them on the island. She slipped on her goggles. "See if you can keep up."

"Hah!" Smoke submerged himself to the neck. With the floating sack tethered to his waist, he swam alongside her. His strokes were long and steady. He cut through the water like a great fish.

Sidney pushed off on a rock. The sweetheart suit gave a little extra buoyancy, and the flippers helped a lot. It didn't take long for her freestyle stroke to get into rhythm.

Boy, I wish I could have swum with these on swim team.

Smoke edged out in front, glancing back from time to time. Before long, they were halfway to the fort. With her competitive instinct kicking in, she swam faster. Her long fingers chopped and pushed through the water, but no matter how hard she tried, she couldn't catch Smoke.

Good Lord, he's fast.

A spotlight hit the waters nearby. It came from Fort Carroll.

CHAPTER 2

S MOKE STOPPED. THEY BOTH TREADED water. The spotlight brushed over the waves. Its beam came from just over the fort's fortification wall. The bright lens moved from side to side, just west of them.

"Get behind me," Smoke said. "When I say duck, go under."

"Okay."

The beam cruised right toward them.

"Duck."

After taking a small breath, Sid half swam, half sank into the water. Smoke did the same. The two hovered just below the black water's surface. The light cruised over their location. The illumination wavered above. The light searching for them was the only hopeful sight in the blackness.

The beam moved on.

Smoke took her hand and led them up. Resurfacing, she gasped for air. Smoke's head panned left and right. Her head was on a swivel. The searchlight was gone.

"What do you think?" she whispered.

"I don't see anything." Smoke's stare was fixed on the wall where the light had come from. "Nothing at all. Even with the goggles."

Treading water and taking a breath, she said, "We need to keep moving. This water's choppier than I figured."

Smoke's eyes lit up. "Are you getting tired?"

She nodded.

He pushed the sack over to Sid. "Use this. Besides, we need to take our time if eyes are watching."

"Fair enough." She took a breath. "I didn't think I'd get so winded. At least not with the suit on."

"We're fighting a current. Most of the time, when you fight the water, it wins. Let's go."

They swam at half the speed they had been. Before long, Sid got a second wind. She pushed it again, legs kicking faster just under the water. Ten more minutes' hard swimming and they both hit the stony base of the old fort's rim. She climbed up on the ledge and sat. Chest heaving, she caught her breath.

"It's not the asthma, is it?" Smoke asked.

"Maybe a little." She rolled her shoulder. "Man, that was a swim."

"Going back will be easier." Smoke remained in the water, staring up at the fort's stone walls. The large cut stones, stacked eight high, made a wall much higher than expected. "We'll need to ease around the rim and find a spot to squeeze into."

Sid remembered the long gaps between the stones. She stared at Hawkins Point, where they had started out. It looked far away. She eased back into the water. "After you, John."

Hugging the fort's base, they moved hand over hand, eyeing the top of the wall. Sid read a marker: PRIVATE. KEEP OFF. GUARD DOG.

Eyeing the same thing, Smoke said, "And I thought we only had to worry about shifters."

"You worry about shifters? I don't."

He kept working his way around the wall. "And that's why you wear the pants in this family."

They came to a stop at a lower section of the outer wall, where there was a big break between the stones. Smoke helped Sid up into it. He climbed up after her. With the water splashing against the walls, he looked around. "Creepy."

"Just like the magazine. Sometimes I feel like I'm on the cover." She slipped through the gap, climbing up the broken wall, and made it to ground level. The eerie island was covered in dry trees and brown bushes run amok. None looked like anything she'd seen before. "Strange place for things to grow."

"Life finds a way everywhere." Smoke found a spot where the bushy ground gave way to a clearing on the old pavement. Still huddled behind the brush, he opened the waterproof sack. He and Sid strapped on their guns. They'd loaded the magazines earlier. Red tips at the top. Blue and green tips in the bottom. Smoke was smiling.

"Getting a little excited, are you?"

"Sometimes I feel a little giddy among the uncanny." He holstered both his weapons. From inside the sack, he pulled out a small bottle. He rattled the pills inside.

Sid couldn't hide her surprise. "More supervitamins in stock?"

"I think Mal likes to pretend he's low. He thinks we'll hoard them all."

"Did he say that?"

"No, but I can tell." Something buzzed inside the sack. Smoke produced a phone. "It's for you."

It was a message from Sam: "Status?" followed by several concerned emojis.

Sid texted her back. "Doing great." She tossed the phone in the sack. "Better leave it."

Smoke swallowed a vitamin.

"Isn't this a little premature?"

Rolling his finger in front of his face he said, "It's got a special coating, and I can do my regurgitation thing. I'd love to teach you."

Sid's face crinkled. "I know you're my husband and I need to accept you as you are, but that doesn't mean I have to like everything you do." She opened her hand. "The old-fashioned way will be just fine."

He gave her two pills. "It doesn't bother you too much, does it?"

"I'll say this: better hope nothing I ever feed you comes up again at the dinner table."

"Ha ha. I'm pretty sure that won't happen. You're an excellent cook." He sniffed. "Do I smell lasagna?"

She rolled her eyes. "Let's go."

Even though they were wearing the sweetheart suits and armed to the teeth, her belly had still quavered until a minute ago. Smoke had a way of easing the tension. The rugged man was fearless in the eye of anything he faced. She had no doubt there was something special about him.

They picked their way through the fort, staying hidden in the trees and brush. The center of the compound was cleared off. Someone had used the spotlight, but there weren't any other signs or sounds of people. A chilling thought came to mind. Perhaps there was a shifter on guard, skulking in the brush, waiting to pounce.

And then Sid went to step over a heap on the ground and froze. It was a body. Sid squatted down and gasped. The man's head was twisted past his shoulder, and his dead hands gripped a spotlight.

CHAPTER 3

S ID COULDN'T FIGHT THE SHIVERS that made her hairs stand on end. The man's head brought back thoughts of Adam Vaughn, the wolf man. He'd killed her supervisor, Jack Dydeck, and many other agents in the same horrific fashion. This time, there wasn't all that blood.

She looked back for Smoke. He was gone. She whipped out her weapon. The Glock quelled her earlier fears. Her dark eyes searched the night. A scuffle in the brush caught her ear. She turned and took aim.

Two men approached.

"Don't take another step," she commanded.

"Which is it?" said the man in front with his hands up. "He says march and you say halt." It was Vormus. The vampire shifter's white hair was tied back in a ponytail. He wore large sunglasses and grey slacks, and his lavender sweater stood out against his alabaster skin. "Well?"

Keeping her gun on him, Sid said, "Did you kill this guy?"

"No, one of those raccoons did," Vormus said in his formal and condescending manner.

Smoke shoved his gun into Vormus's back. "Answer the lady."

"Of course I did."

"If you're going to work with us, you need to stop killing people." Sid stood up. "We aren't murderers."

"Pfft. If you're going to take that attitude, then you've lost. These guards, they know what side of the fence they are on. They have it coming as much as anyone else. Nobility." Vormus lifted a brow. "I was raised with nobility. Neither of you have any idea what that is. No one in this heap of a country does. Here, everyone thinks they're so special."

Vormus made a good point. It was something Sid had contemplated more than once. Some of the people they fought were just doing a job. It made it tough when she had to deal with them. Sometimes if you left a man alive, you might lose your own. How do you fight a secret war that is off the books? But they had to know what was going on. They had made a choice.

"Compared to you, most all of us are special." Sid holstered her gun. "How'd you get here?"

"I jumped off the Francis Scott Key Bridge. You should have seen the faces those brats made when I jumped. Oh, how I wish I could still find the joy in that." He dusted off his hands. "So I floated down here. About an hour later I noticed your little party across the way. That dead man had a watchful eye, too, so I ended him."

She tilted her head. "Too? You mean there are more dead?"

Looking at his nails, Vormus said, "Maybe a couple. What? You should be thanking me. It's not on your conscience, it's on mine." He leaned back and said to Smoke, "But we both know I don't have one."

"You have something," Smoke said, "Or you wouldn't be helping us."

Taking a glance at the dead man's body, the shifter replied, "He means as much to me as, what do you special ones call it, ah, as killroad means to you."

"It's roadkill," she said. "Smoke, do you want to scout around before we take this investigation any deeper?"

"I've cleared the area," Vormus said.

"Sit down," Smoke replied.

"Here? On the ground?"

Smoke drove his boot into the back of Vormus's knee.

The shifter collapsed, but he popped right up again. Fangs bared, he got in Smoke's face. "Don't take my cooperation as softness. I might not feel much, but I still have a temper. Take warning, John Smoke. Don't treat me like chattel."

Staring Vormus in the eye, Smoke said, "You're worse than chattel. Don't forget it."

Vormus sneered.

"I've got this, John," Sid said.

Smoke gave a quick nod and moved out of sight.

Facing Sid, Vormus said, "It's only a matter of time before he embraces what he is. The deeper you go down this Lewis Carroll rabbit hole, the more his true nature will reveal itself. It's the same for the both of you."

"It's not something we can avoid?"

"No, you can't. Sidney, I'm grateful you have shown me a degree of trust. After all, we both want the same thing. You need to save your sister. I need to save myself. I'm sincere about that."

"I'll be convinced when my sister and niece are out of harm's way." Keeping her eyes on Vormus, she said, "How do I know she's not a shifter already?"

"I know there is much to discuss on that, and I don't have any intent to be vague, but there is a proving ground. It takes time to show commitment."

"What sort of proving ground?"

"Think of what you know about a gang's initiation. Multiply by ten."

"Are you saying she'll have to kill somebody?"

"I'm saying she will kill somebody, and somebody could be anybody. It could be somebody close to her. It was for me."

"Who did you kill?"

"My parents."

"You don't mean that."

"You have every reason to believe I'm a liar, but I'm not, as I have no reason to lie. But you have to kill someone dear to you. I've known shifters who even took out their own children." His stone-cold stare didn't change. "They didn't shed a tear."

Megan.

Two thoughts coursed through Sid's mind. First, Allison wasn't the best mother to begin with. She was selfish by nature, and she never gave Megan the attention she should. Second, Vormus, if all he said was true, deserved to die. He didn't deserve redemption of any kind. But she needed him. She didn't like it.

Smoke glided back into view. "It's clear. Everything good here?"

"Peachy," she replied. She turned to Vormus. "Where to?"

"You're asking me? This is the first time I've been here too. I'm not much of what you call an investigator. I just know who to fetch when we get in there, wherever there is."

"I've got it," Smoke said. "There's a boat docked on the bridge side. It's got to be close to where they go in. Follow me."

"After you," she said, waving her gun at Vormus.

CHAPTER 4

T HE THREE-AND-A-HALF-ACRE ISLAND FORT DIDN'T prove difficult to navigate. Amid a small crane covered in vines and a Bobcat loader with a busted tread, Smoke found a path beaten down by human traffic. It led down a staircase into a network of tunnels and stone archways. The ground was muddy and wet, filled with silt from the bay. Critters scattered in the darkness.

Sid's goggles enhanced her sight enough to make out the faint outlines of the walls. The forms of Vormus and Smoke were clear. Still, it was a little unsettling moving in the pitch-black without a single source of light.

Smoke engaged the laser sight on his pistol.

Good idea.

Sid did the same.

The red beams cut through the darkness, tracing the walls, giving them the appearance of something real and not some maze hidden in the night.

Smoke moved with his eyes low, burrowing farther into the tunnel. He stepped up on a ledge that led into another alcove. The storage chamber of the old fort was big enough to hold about twenty men. There was nothing inside except the stainless steel frame of an elevator.

"You've got to be kidding me," Sid said, stepping forward and inspecting the frame. "An elevator? Here? Huh, it needs a proxy card."

Smoke dangled a proxy card in front of her eyes. "I patted down one of Vormus's dead guards." He went to scan it. "Going down, I suppose?"

She stopped him. "If this place is so important, shouldn't it be under heavier guard?"

"Again, the shifters are overconfident," Vormus said.

"Huh," said Sid, "and who's to say there isn't some other way out? They probably have a tunnel under here that leads to the Pentagon."

"You mean the Pentagragon," Smoke added.

"Don't start." She brushed a strand of wet hair from her eye. "Of course, at this point, nothing would surprise me." She filled both hands with pistol grips and took a breath.

Smoke scanned the card.

The doors parted. A small halogen bulb inside the elevator was a beacon of bright light. Head turned aside, Sid stepped in. Vormus and Smoke joined her. The new illumination gave her a close look at Vormus's slacks and sweater. "What's with you and lavender?"

"It was a dear aunt's favorite color."

"Did you kill her, too?"

"No, something else did."

"OTIS," Smoke said, eyeing the lettering at the top of the elevator panel. "Wow, they make elevators everywhere. I bet contractors know a lot more than they should." He glanced down. There were two buttons, one over the other. "Going down?" Smoke said with a Steven Tyler chuckle.

"Funny, just don't bust out the air guitar," Sid said. The doors closed. The elevator began to move. Her adrenaline surged.

With a quizzical expression, Vormus asked, "What's an air guitar?"

Sid's fingers rubbed her clammy palms. The elevator ride was either really long or really slow. She looked up but away from the light. She'd toured an elevator shaft when she was a girl. She'd been amazed at how deep it went and how dark it was. Her skin had crawled the entire time. There was only one way out. What if that way failed?

"It's deep," Smoke said. "It has to be deeper than the bay. At least fifty feet."

"How could anyone make such a thing without anyone noticing?" she replied. "This is worse than Mallows Bay."

Vormus snorted. "You haven't seen everything man can do. You only see what is in the world above. They let you see that. Evil lurks in the depths where the light is not wanted. You'd be astonished what is buried in Europe and beneath the great pyramids." He made an effort to chuckle. "And not just mummies."

The elevator stopped with a wobble. Sid lifted both barrels toward the exit. The stainless steel doors parted. Her lips did too. "Morning glory."

CHAPTER 5

I T WAS A CAVERNOUS VIEW. Sid couldn't see from one side to the other. Steel girders held up a dome roof made of yellow concrete block. The cavern floor was solid rock and uneven in many places. The stone was slick with a thin sheen of water. Metal lanterns with glass bulbs and dim yellow gas lights grafted to the walls and hanging above gave off an eerie glow. The air she breathed was damp. It made Sidney think of a subway tunnel but a dozen times bigger.

Smoke stepped out. His broad back blocked her view. She nudged him forward. His head turned in all directions. Under his breath, he said, "It's like the Batcave."

"More like a watery tomb."

Vormus stepped into the cavern. The elevator doors closed. "Interesting, I don't see anyone."

Careful where she stepped, Sid moved forward with Smoke, toward the center of the room. There were desks similar to something one would see in a World War II army base. The rest of the wooden furniture appeared to be two hundred years old. Damp papers lay on the desks and floors. There were old glass-panel cubicles against the walls on the right. She noticed something familiar and gave Smoke a nudge.

The coffin they had put Titus Tolliver in lay on the floor. Smoke kneeled down and picked up a pair of flex cuffs that had been snipped. "At least we know he made it in here."

"True, but where, exactly? It doesn't look like anyone has been in here in days."

The sound of metal being struck echoed in the great chamber. It came again. In the vast open space, the sound's source was hard to make out.

Head tilted and eyes closed, Sid said, "It sounds like someone tossing a rock through a ventilation duct."

"Just bigger," Smoke added.

"Maybe the rats are much bigger down here," Vormus suggested.

"There wouldn't be any rats down here. Well, not unless you've met Swift Venison. Could he be down here?" she asked.

"They might all be," Smoke said.

The tapping became steady.

"That's Morse code," Smoke said. He cupped is ear.

Vormus opened his mouth to speak. Sid shushed him.

"Left," Smoke said, heading that direction with Sid and Vormus in tow. He came to a stop at the edge of a metal trapdoor. It was about four feet by four in size. The hinges were heavy iron. Flush to the floor, the door was a solid plate, aside from a large keyhole.

Sid noted more metal tombs. There were dozens, spaced out evenly and lined up all the way to the yellow block walls. "Geez, I hope these things aren't full of shifters."

"That would be a lot of shifters." Smoke kneeled down and looked in the keyhole. "I think I see an eyeball." He leaned closer. "Yup, it's an eyeball." He rapped his knuckles on the door. The same knock came back.

"Any ideas?" she said to Vormus.

The vampire shifter shrugged. "I suppose you'll just have to open up the box."

"I'll see what I can find." Sid made her way to the desks and sorted through the papers, which were old and damaged. There was Drake letterhead on what appeared to be invoices and shipping manifests. The contents weren't described. It was just a list of packages. She opened desk drawers and rummaged through them. She found several fountain pens. "Huh, I bet these are worth some money."

Vormus puckered a brow. "A pen?"

"An antique pen."

"Yes, but still, just a pen. I can't imagine it would have any notable value."

"Why don't you quit standing around in your Barney sweater and help me look for a key?"

"Who's Barney?"

"Just look."

Vormus began milling about in imitation of what Sid was doing. He didn't seem to have any idea what doing real work was like. She made her way over to the glass-paned cubicles on the right side of the cavern, where she found a clipboard hanging by a nail hammered into the wooden frame of a cubicle. There was a gridded box with names on it. "Oh, snap."

"What?" Vormus said in her ear. He'd crept right up on her heels.

She shoved him back with an elbow. "Don't ever do that again."

He inhaled through his nose. "Your hair smells nice. What kind of shampoo do you use? It has a floral luster to it that I like."

Sid's eyes were fixed on the page. Her lips said the words but not out loud.

Angi Harlow.

Swift Venison.

Adam Vaughn.

There were others. Among them in fresh ink was Titus Tolliver. She headed back toward Smoke and lined up the grid boxes from the clipboard sheet with the ones on the floor. They matched up.

Smoke glanced up at her. "What's up?"

"I think I have a prison manifest."

"Really?" He made his way over and checked it out. "I had a feeling they weren't dead. Well, maybe we can finish them up now."

"I told you shifters weren't easy to kill," Vormus stated. "It's our thing."

"Everything dies eventually." Smoke fingered the manifest. "So who do we have communicating in this box here? Ah, our old buddy Toad Man. Remember him?"

"How could I forget?"

"He's the one pecking inside. Did you find a key?"

"No." Sid paced along the trapdoors. She lingered over the one with Adam Vaughn's name. He'd killed her friends. He should be dead. She pointed her gun down at the keyhole and noticed it was turned to three o'clock. "Smoke."

He slid over and gave a nod. He grabbed the handle on the door. Sid stood on the other side with her gun ready. She gave him a nod. He lifted the trapdoor. Nothing popped out, jumped, or scurried from the hole. The chamber wasn't very deep, but it was empty. Just a metal door over a stone hole.

They checked all the locks in this row. All of them were unlocked except for the one marked "Toad Man Eugene Green."

She tossed Vormus the manifest. "Who was the one you were looking for?"

"Ah, the keeper of secrets, Manson Bay." He pecked his neatly trimmed fingernail on the clipboard. "It says he's here. A good thing." Vormus pointed. "Three over."

She moved. "It's unlocked." The eerie quietness in the room bothered her. They weren't quiet, and their presence had to be easily known. No one else, if they were there, was scratching or pecking.

Smoke came over and took her hand. With a nod from Sid, he opened the small prison.

"Empty," she said.

"That's disappointing," Vormus replied.

One by one, they opened all the doors. Every cell was unlocked and empty aside from the one with Toad Man. The three of them surrounded it.

"I don't know if this is a good thing or bad." She sighed. "If we want answers, we're going to need a key. Let's keep looking."

CHAPTER 6

WHILE SIDNEY AND VORMUS SEARCHED for a key, Smoke sat on the trapdoor, knocking his knuckle on the metal in Morse code. The person inside the tomb pecked back. "So far as I can tell, it's Toad Man. He's angry."

Talking loudly from across the cavern, Sid said, "Why isn't he talking?"

"I think this metal is too thick. Sounds are probably muffled. I don't know. Any luck with a key?"

"No." Sid searched everything there was to search. She looked under desks. Pulled out drawers. Turned over tables. She looked through shelves of rations and supplies. There wasn't a key of any kind. Worry set in. The captured shifters had been here, and now they were gone without a trace. She wondered why they might have been moved. Or were they still inside the cavern, just elsewhere? "Vormus, did you find anything?"

Somewhere inside the underground complex, Vormus said, "As regards a key, no."

Sid stepped outside the wood-and-glass cubicle. She didn't see Vormus. "Where are you?"

"South of you. In the shadows where the walls of block turn to solid stone. There are some smaller offshoot caves down here. Possibly a tunnel, but it looks quite small."

"I got it," Smoke said.

Sid hustled over to him and asked, "You got what?"

Smoke lay flat on his belly. His hands were filled with slender metal tools. He worked the keyhole. Metal scratched on metal. The keyhole clicked. "We're open for business now."

"Toad Man, huh? I wonder if he'll be excited to see us," she said with a smile.

"I have to admit, I'm looking forward to seeing his face." Smoke took the handle.

Sid readied her gun.

Smoke opened the door.

Slowly, Eugene Green, Toad Man, crawled out. All he wore was a pair of jeans, but his skin was brush brown and clumpy. Even in man form, his eyes were extremely large. They widened when Smoke removed the gag from his mouth and he said, "You!"

"How are you doing, Eugene?" Sid said.

Eugene's frog neck turned toward her. "You too?" He gathered himself into a dangerous crouching position. His thick legs coiled to spring. "I can't believe it's you. Of all the despicable people. I swore if I ever saw you again, I'd bury you both."

Smoke lowered his gun to aim between Toad Man's eyes. "That's not a nice thing to say to someone who just let you out of captivity, now is it?"

Blinking, Eugene said, "I don't care. I still hate you both." His long tongue flicked from his mouth. He had a little tic when he talked. Slowly he pointed at the both of them. "I hate you and you. You got me put in this hole. They called me a failure. Took my glory. My money. My everything."

"We don't care," Sid said. "What happened to the others? Why did they leave you here?"

"What do you mean?" Eugene looked around. His jaw dropped. "Oh my. Are all the others gone?" He scanned his surroundings. "Where did everyone go? Did you kill them all?"

Smoke popped the ugly frogman on the top of the head with the butt of his pistol. "Don't play stupid, toad neck."

Wincing, Eugene rubbed his neck with his long toad fingers. "Beat me all you want." His tongue snapped in and out. "I can take it. I'll heal. I'll be damned if I help you with anything."

"Then you're going back in the hole." Smoke gave him a shove.

"No, wait. At least let me breathe the air. Is that lilac I smell?" Eugene's small nostrils sniffed. "Lilac and bay water. It's funny, but women always have a smell." His eyes combed over Sid's body. He batted his lashes. "You're a fetching morsel. I could get over my hate if you were to—"

Smoke cracked him in the head again.

"Just put him in the hole. If he's not talking, we're wasting our time." Sid motioned to Smoke with her gun.

"Perhaps if he will not talk, I should deal with him." Vormus appeared.

Eugene moved away from Vormus. "What are you doing here?"

"That's my business, Toad Man." Vormus loomed over the smaller man. His eyes became hypnotic. "Tell me everything you know. Particularly about Manson Bay."

"Why are you asking me? You're further in than me." Eugene got all fidgety and sweaty. "I'm nothing. You're royalty."

Vormus pressed. "Where did they all go?"

"They locked me up. I don't know. You saw how they left me to rot." Needling his fingers, he shifted his bulging eyes between Smoke and Sid. "I don't play well with the others. They don't care for me. I never cared for their snobbery."

"You're testing my patience, amphibian," Vormus warned.

Toad Man pleaded. "Just take me to the top. To the top. Heh. I'll tell you all you need to know." His tongue licked out over his eye. "Or at least all I know. I swear it."

"Near a large body of water so you can squirt free? I don't think so." Vormus pushed up his sleeves, revealing his wiry forearms. He clamped his fingers around Eugene's neck. His eyes flashed, and he opened his mouth and expanded his jaws, revealing very long, sharp teeth.

Sid's hairs stood on end. Vormus had gone from gentle snob to monster. She pointed the gun at his head, saying, "Vormus, what's going on?"

"I don't know." Vormus's eyes swirled. His features stretched.

The room started to spin. Sid's knees bent to keep her from falling. "Vormus?"

"Okay! Okay!" Eugene cried out. "I'll tell you everything. Just stay out of my mind. I hate that." He panted for breath. His body curled into fetal position. "I'd rather be in the hole than go through mind crap."

Vormus's contorted face resumed its natural state.

Sid swallowed. Her chest pounded. She'd seen Kane do something similar before when she was his captive. The man had an unexplainable power that went well beyond his dominating appearance. Apparently there was also more to Vormus than met the eye.

Smoke took her hand. His eyes were filled with concern.

She squeezed his hand.

"Out with it, Toad Man. Where are the others?" Vormus said.

"They set them free," Eugene said with a sob. "They set them all free but me."

CHAPTER 7

THE WORDS TOAD MAN SPOKE ignited Sid's inner fire. "You mean to tell me they're all out there on the loose again?" The balled-up Toad Man nodded.

"Well, that just pisses me off," Sid said. Her words were venom. "I'm going to kill Cyrus. We've been hauling them in just so they can let them out again? What is this, Guantanamo Bay? I could kill somebody!"

While Sid stormed through the chamber, Vormus asked Eugene, "What about the Keeper of Secrets. He was here, was he not?"

"He was. We all were," Toad Man said weakly. "They'd let us out one by one to feed us. Beat us. Torment us."

"Who did that?" Smoke asked.

Eugene glared at Smoke. "The other shifters. You know," he air quoted his fingers, "'the cherished ones.' Please, please, please, just take me with you out there. I don't want to slowly die down here."

"I didn't think shifters could die so easily."

Eugene scowled at Smoke. "Well, you haven't been living in a hole!" His face softened. "Sorry, you must sympathize with my frustration. I've been stuck in a hole since you hauled me in. I'm bitter. Can you blame me?"

The lights flickered. Everyone froze. Their eyes looked up and down. The flames quavered once more.

Eyes up, Sid said, "I don't like this. We might not get out of here."

"Does this normally happen?" Smoke asked Eugene.

He shrugged. "I don't know. I'm in the hole all the time. Besides, you're deep. The light is not meant for the deep dark belly. Mortals aren't either."

"Toad Man, what is Kane up to?"

"He has plans. Big plans. That's why he let them all out. He needs them. All of them. He wants to restore his disrupted operations. You know, the ones these two ruined." Toad Man had a clear second set of lenses over his eyes when he blinked. "He says with them out of the picture, it will be business as usual."

"Well, we aren't out of the picture," Sid commented. She sat down on one of the old wooden office chairs. The thought of all the shifters they'd captured run amok out there made her sick.

"No, clearly you aren't out of the picture...yet."

"What's that supposed to mean?" she said.

"Just wishful thinking. So are you going to take me out there with you? Please. I'll try to control my tongue." He flicked the long thing in and out of his mouth. "It just isn't easy."

"You haven't told us anything useful," Smoke said. "No names. No locations. No nothing. Just big plans. How gullible do you think we are? You're delaying. I'm just wondering what for."

Touching his chest, Eugene said, "Me? Delay? I'd never trifle with the likes of Vormus."

Something scurried in the blackness on the edges of the enormous cavern.

Sid got up off her chair so quickly she knocked it over. "Vormus, did you see anything over there?"

"A large burrow-like tunnel. I didn't have time to search it due to all the commotion."

Something slunk in the darkness. The lights flickered. The effect was more like a strobe light. Sid pointed her laser at the black spot. The beam died in the dark light.

"They move," Eugene said in a sinister whisper.

Backing toward Smoke, Sid said, "What moves?"

"The guardians. They wake from their slumber. They feast on the sweet marrow of mortals." Eugene hopped into the nearest cell in a single leap and slammed the door shut. "Goodbye, mortals!"

Smoke nudged up alongside Sid. "Stay close."

A centipede-like creature, thicker than a man's leg and longer than two, snaked out from the darkness. The plum-colored monster moved on thousands of silent legs. Its face had huge green eyes filled with many smaller lenses. A sharp horn was on its head. Double sets of black pinchers guarded the monster's mouth.

Smoke and Sid backed up. Sid said, "Vormus, have you seen one of these things before?"

"They call them the vorpeen. Extremely deadly. "

"It looks like a tobacco hornworm," Smoke remarked. "Just ten times uglier."

The vorpeen came right at them.

Smoke and Sid fired. Bullets ripped through the beast's body. It reared up on its thousands of back legs, squealing an ear-splitting shriek. "EeeEEEeeeeeEEeeeee!"

Covering his ears, Vormus yelled, "Don't shoot it! It will only attract more. They aren't easy to kill."

Sid figured that out soon enough. The vorpeen advanced. Sid shot it in the face.

Blam! Blam!

Its bullet wounds oozed. It stopped coming. Its body twisted and writhed.

"I said not to shoot it," Vormus said with disappointment. "They come."

Three more vorpeens appeared from the darkness. The silent things crept right at them with their horns lowered. Their pinchers clacked.

Aiming from one vorpeen to the other, Sid said, "So how are we supposed to kill them?"

"You don't. You run from them. They'll just keep coming unless they're fed."

Sid and Smoke's gunfire echoed in the chamber like the sound of a raging thunderstorm.

The vorpeens wriggled and squirmed. Their guts splashed the cavern floor.

"Looks like they die to me," Smoke said. "And I've got plenty of bullets. How many can there be?"

With anger in his voice, Vormus said, "How many bees are in a hive?"

Three vorpeens became six.

Sid and Smoke looked at one another and said simultaneously, "Elevator!"

Backing away from the monstrous bugs, she took a glance over her shoulder. Eugene the Toad Man stood in the elevator with a broad smile on his face. He smiled and waved. "Goodbye, mortals!" The doors started to close.

"Wait!" Sid screamed.

Smoke turned just as the doors clicked shut. "That sucks."

CHAPTER 8

VORMUS FLOATED UP OFF THE floor.

Still shooting the monsters, Sid said, "You get down here and fight!"

"I didn't start this fight. Besides, I don't want to get my sweater dirty." He picked off a fragment of debris from his shoulder. "I'm rather fond of it."

She pointed the Glock at him. "Get down here and fight, or I'm gonna shoot you!"

A knot of centipedes stormed her feet, at least a hundred pounds of them. It made her skin crawl. She sent two bullets through one's face. The blue-tipped rounds ripped the back of its head out. The second vorpeen devoured the first. The third one kept coming.

"Crap! Smoke, I'm down to the red tip!" She popped out one clip and exchanged it for another. Suddenly, a sea of vorpeens appeared by the dozens, snapping at her legs with pinchers. She blasted off round after round. "I'm going to run out of ammo."

"I knew I should have brought a machine gun." Firing with two hands, Smoke cracked off shot after shot. The bugs piled up in heaps.

It wasn't enough. Within seconds, they were surrounded by the vermin again. Pinchers fastened on Sid's leg and held her tight. She screamed, "Aaaaaaarrgh!" She fired. *Blam!*

The entire chamber became a bug bath. The wriggling masses devoured their own dead, filling their mouths with their brethren's flesh. The insects came *en masse* at Smoke and Sid.

Covered in gore and sweat, she fought the masses. They tangled her ankles and crawled up her spine. She grabbed one by the neck, slung it through the air, and shot it.

Out of nowhere, Smoke appeared. He ripped the bugs away from her ankles, tearing them apart with his hands. "They squish," he said. A bug crawled up his shoulder. He grabbed its pinchers and ripped them apart. "I bet these would make great bait for really big fish."

"Too bad we aren't hunting whale today," she said.

"Maybe tomorrow."

"Ugh!" She kicked another vorpeen free, then stomped its head under her heel. "Can't you regurgitate some bug repellent or something?" She sprinted by the next wave of bugs and jumped up on a desk. "Vormus! Get the elevator back!"

The vorpeens didn't chase after Vormus. He had a clear path to the elevator. He floated over and pushed the button. "You see? I helped, but I don't think anything is coming. You know, it's the blood they so enjoy. If you were immortal like me, it wouldn't be a problem."

"Shut up!" Sid shot another and another.

Fighting at her side, Smoke said, "I have an idea. Vormus, did you say they were coming out of a cave back there?"

"I don't see them coming from anywhere else."

Smoke snatched Sid's clip that held one red bullet. He winked at her. "I'll be back." He ran through the field of centipedes.

Fighting the centipedes, she watched him disappear. Within moments, gunfire cracked off in the blackness, followed by loud booms. The floor shook. A billowing dust cloud spilled out of the darkness.

"Smoke!" she screamed as she fought.

The rangy man emerged from the hazy mist. He killed everything crawly in sight, working his way back to Sid. "I think a cave-in might hold them."

At a furious pace, they fought off every last vorpeen until they were all dead. No more came. Coated in bug splatter, he said to Sid, "Did you use a vitamin?"

"No. You?"

He shook his head. Surveying all the mutilated bugs, he said, "That was awesome."

Sid turned. "Vormus, is the elevator back?"

"No." He applauded them with a gentle clap. "Marvelous work, but I think we have another problem."

"What's that?"

The block walls cracked. Water squirted through. The lights quavered again.

"This place is going to collapse at any moment."

CHAPTER 9

"**T**HEY'VE BEEN IN THERE TOO long," Sam said to Guppy. They stood outside, leaning on Guppy's truck. He held some binoculars to his eyes. A fog had covered Fort Carroll in a hazy mist. The outline of the island could barely be seen. "I knew we should have brought a boat."

"It's barely been an hour," Guppy said. "They're usually gone much longer than that."

Looking down at her husband, the high-heeled woman took away his binoculars. "Excuse me, honey?"

"Er...I can swim over and check on them if you like."

"I might just have you do that." Her long nails dug into her hands. "Aw, I'm sorry, hon. You know I hate waiting. I have a bad feeling, too. Something just doesn't seem right."

"The fog and the moon don't help much either. They bring the stink of the supernatural. They'll be back soon. I'm sure of it."

Sam sent a text to Sid. Her painted eyes were intent on the screen. "They've gone dark, all right."

The ground shook under her feet.

Sam's body straightened. "Did you feel that?"

"I sure did." Guppy glanced at the ground. "That was weird."

"What the hell was it?"

He shrugged his brawny shoulders.

"They don't have earthquakes in DC, do they?" she asked.

"Not that I remember." He scanned the traffic zooming by on the Francis Scott Key Bridge. "I don't see or hear any big trucks that could have moved the ground like that. It felt like the ground farted."

Sam pinched her nose. "Or maybe you did? You didn't, did you?"

"No, no, honey, it wasn't me."

She eyed him.

"I swear."

"At least we're outside." In the corner of her eye, she saw someone moving through the fog. She hit guppy in the arm and pointed.

A man approached, dripping from head to toe. He wore nothing but a pair of jeans. The rest of the stocky figure was difficult to see in the fog and darkness. His attention was elsewhere when he noticed Sid's car. He stopped and looked.

Guppy reached inside his truck and grabbed a shotgun then eased in front of Sam. She drew her nickel-plated 1911 semi-auto from her belt. It had pink pearl grips. Together, they approached. Guppy charged the pump on the shotgun. It caught the man's attention. He stepped full into the light.

Sam made a face like she had swallowed a bug. The squat, dripping-wet guy hunkered down on his thick legs. His skin was toady. His hands and feet were webbed. His huge eyes bulged from the sockets.

"Good evening," he said. His long tongue licked out, snatching a bug. He sucked it back in between his thin lips. "Is this your car? It's a fine machine."

Nerves tingling and skin crawling, Sam said, "Get away from the car, frog lips." She charged the slide on her weapon. Trembling a little, she pointed the weapon at him. "Or I'll blow your warts off."

"Heh." The Toad Man lifted his webbed hands. There were pronounced claws on them. A sliver of a smile crossed his fat face. "I'm not a frog but a toad. Toad Man, they call me. Humph. I suppose you're with those other clowns who sought to detain me. How humorous." His bulging eyes blinked. "They are dead."

"You're lying," Sam said.

"No. They're finished. Soon, you will be too." Toad Man gave Sam a lusty once-over. "I might keep you alive for a bit. You are a feast for the eyes. It's been a long, long time since I've shared company with a woman." He took a step forward.

"That's not going to happen, tadpole," Guppy said. "One more step and I'll scatter your guts all over this place."

"Hah. Your friends' weapons didn't work on me. Your weapons can't harm me either, mortals. What's your name, pretty lady? I'm Eugene 'Toad Man' Green. And you are?"

"Not interested." Sam squeezed the trigger.

Toad Man sprang over both of them.

She turned. Toad Man was gone. "Where'd he go?"

"Not sure," Guppy said.

Hands beat on the hood of Guppy's truck. It was Toad Man. He laughed.

Sam and Guppy took aim.

Toad Man vanished. His laughter carried in the night. From out in the darkness, he said, "I hate mortals. I enjoy killing them one at a time."

"Stay close, Sam," Guppy said.

"I will." Her heart pounded in her chest. She stood back to back with Guppy. Together they turned slowly, searching all around. Something bounded across her path and vanished. "He's so fast."

Toad Man cackled. "You have no idea, dear."

A rock skipped over the pavement. It cracked Sam in the ankle. "Gah!" She fell to the ground, clutching her leg. Tears watered her eyes. "Man, that hurt!"

Shotgun low and eyes wary, Guppy crouched over her. "I'll find him. Hang in there."

Sam didn't see any sign of the man anywhere. She looked in all directions. "I don't see him."

With a wild-eyed look, Toad Man dropped out of the darkness right behind Guppy. His clawed hands locked on Guppy's shoulders. He slung the burly man aside like a small child, smashing Guppy into the truck's quarter panel.

Guppy lay still.

Sam took aim.

Toad Man swatted the gun from her hand with alarming force. He licked his lips. "You're mine now, pretty lady."

CHAPTER 10

WATER POURED THROUGH THE WALL of the cavern like it would through a huge crack in the Hoover Dam. It was up to Sid's knees and rising fast. The vorpeen floated among the inner tide, splashing in the surge. The ones that still lived wrestled with their fate. Sid was glad. It appeared the vorpeen couldn't swim. It was a small victory.

"Smoke, how are we going to get out of here?" she demanded.

The rangy man's hands were digging into the slit between the elevator doors. His face filled with strain. "Man, these doors are stubborn!"

Sid sloshed through the waters. She grabbed hold from the other side. The doors wouldn't move. The lights quavered in and out. The darkness came and went like the door of a coffin opening and closing. She glanced up at Vormus, who floated just beneath the ceiling. "A little help?"

Frowning, he said, "I'm not fond of getting wet."

"You're going to get wet one way or the other. Now get your ass down here!"

Vormus complied, sinking in the air and landing beside Sid. She stepped aside. The shifter sank his nails into the crack between the doors. He eyed Smoke.

"On three," Smoke said. "Three!" Putting all his muscle into it, he grunted. His face filled with strain.

A notable amount of concentration formed on Vormus's pale face.

The elevator doors parted a foot with a groan, revealing emptiness. No elevator.

Sid jumped into action. She wedged her body inside the seam and pushed with her knee. While water spilled into the elevator shaft, she pushed with all her strength. There was a pop. The metal doors gave way. "We need to climb," she said.

Smoke nodded.

Vormus slipped inside the shaft and floated up, saying, "I'd carry you if I could, but my power is limited. Good luck." He vanished up into the pitch-black shaft.

"Over here," Smoke said. The water was up to his chest. His hand locked on an emergency ladder built into the shaft. He grabbed Sid by the hand and pulled her over. "You go first."

Hand over hand, she raced up the ladder. In the black, she could no longer see a thing. It was like climbing inside a tunnel with no end. The water rose under them, trying to swallow them whole. Sid felt like the entire island was sinking.

"Hurry, Sid," Smoke said.

Fueled by adrenaline, she climbed. It seemed to never end. One rung after another, she hoped to see a glimmer of light. She hollered up the shaft, "Vormus?"

There was no reply.

Panic set in. She didn't have any idea how deep the shaft was to begin with. The elevator ride had been so long. Her limbs grew tired. They'd just battled countless vorpeen to the point of exhaustion. Now she was fighting for her life again. And at the top, she knew the elevator would be blocking their way out. Another enemy to fight in the pitch black. "Smoke, how deep are we?"

"I don't know, but the water is almost on my toes. Keep moving!"

She stopped. "I'm not going out like this without a fight." She dug out her supervitamin pill, stuck it in her mouth, bit down, and swallowed. She resumed the climb. The higher she went, the more her shoulders ached. At last, the pill kicked in and the throbbing eased. She climbed faster. "Vormus, where are you?"

The shifter shouted back, "Under this albatross of an elevator."

Sid practically ran up the ladder. Her head smote a metal beam. She shook it off. She could sense Vormus. The vitamin enhanced her sight just enough to make out an outline of the shifter above. "Get out of the way."

Vormus drifted aside.

Holding onto the rung by one hand, she leaned over and punched the bottom of the elevator with the other.

"Heavens, what are you doing?" Vormus asked.

"I'm getting us out of here!" She cocked back and punched again. *Wham!* Hitting the metal over and over, she found a soft spot in the floor. She punched several times. It wouldn't give.

"Sid, the water's rising fast," Smoke said.

"I know that!" She laid into it with everything she had. The water was still flooding the shaft. She took a breath. They were all underwater now. She lost the force she needed to put behind her swing. Her fingers found the edge of the metal panel.

Please, Jesus, don't let us die like this!

She began peeling it back. More strong fingers joined hers. With a wrench and a heave, the panel peeled away. Sid shoved herself up and burst through the elevator's flooring. She grabbed Smoke's arm and pulled him through. Smoke did the same for Vormus. All together, they pulled open the elevator doors. The three of them spilled out into the tunnel under the forest. The water spilled out, too, and vanished through a grate in the floor. Sid coughed and gasped for air. Smoke and Vormus did the same.

Sucking for air, Smoke said, "That was close. Nice job, honey. How's your hand?"

Still filled with energy, she opened and closed her fingers. "Well, there's probably going to be some swelling." She grabbed Smoke's hand with her other one, and the two of them helped each other to their feet. "Come on."

With some feeble coughing, Vormus fell in behind them, and on their way out of the tunnel, he said, "Assuming Toad Man was the rat, I can only imagine that within minutes, Kane will know we're coming after him."

Sid was climbing the steps to the topside. "I'm pretty sure he knew that. Why else would he have moved the prisoners? The entire thing was a trap. They knew we'd go in there."

"And to think they almost got all three of us at once." Vormus toyed with the hem of his sweater. "Oh dear, I have a snag."

"It's possible there is a rat among us," Smoke said. He led the way back to their gear. "Either that, or we missed something."

Sid got her phone and texted Sam. "We're out. All is well. Be alert." She didn't get a reply. Sam always replied within seconds. "Something's wrong."

"Why do you say that?"

Sid lurched up. Her enhanced senses picked up a blood-curdling scream in the air.

CHAPTER 11

"**S**UCH A PRETTY FACE. IT's almost sad to see it go to waste." Toad Man had Sam by the neck. His tongue licked her skin. "Mm, you taste good."

Sam punched him in the groin.

The shifter didn't flinch. "Really? Have you any idea how many times that's happened?"

She drew back and hit him again.

His eyelids flicked up.

"That's two times I know of, tadpole."

A heavy force collided with Toad Man. It tore his grip from Sam.

Guppy had his powerful arms locked around Toad Man's head. He scissor locked Toad Man's legs with his own legs. Face reddening, he held onto Toad Man. The silent ball of muscles did everything in his power to crush the life out of the shifter.

The supernaturally powered shifter shed the burly man. He pummeled Guppy in the face several times.

Guppy staggered back on wobbling legs. His nose was bleeding. He steadied himself and advanced.

"Oh, so pathetic. Brave mortals so eager to test their mortality. It's no wonder the Drake finds them so entertaining." Toad Man set his shoulders. "Come on then. I like the screams that come when I break bones."

"Hey wart-face." Sam stood behind him with the shotgun. "You forgot somebody."

"Oh, how dreary." He spread out his arms. "Fine, shoot me with your little shotgun. I could use the tickle." He scratched his shoulder with his webbed fingers and claws. "As a matter of fact, I have an itch right here."

She squeezed the trigger. With a *pow*, a net made of metal webbing burst from the barrel. Expanding in an instant, the net covered Toad Man from head to toe. The links engulfed his body and wrapped him up from side to side.

Toad Man gaped. "What the hell is this?" He struggled against the bonds. The more he wiggled, the tighter the net became.

"It's called a toad catcher," Guppy said. He marched over and slugged Toad Man in the belly. "That's for touching Sam." He pushed the shifter to the ground and kicked him repeatedly in the ribs. "This is for all those others you killed, murderous fiend!"

A boat skidded up the boat ramp. Sid and Smoke jumped out and rushed over. "Oh my, you got him!" Sid said with a wild look in her eye. "I can't believe it." She hugged Sam. "Thank God you're safe."

"It was nothing," Sam said. "I just hope he doesn't give me warts. If I get a wart, I'll kill him myself."

"We can't be killed, mortal!" Toad Man yelled.

Vormus floated down to the ground. "On the contrary, there are plenty of ways to kill a shifter. Totally destroying the body is one. That's going to happen to you, Eugene." Lording over the man, he added, "I suggest you cooperate."

"Never. You know as I do you can't defeat Kane and his minions."

"His thick skin is thinner when the sun is up. I'm sure he'll be more willing to talk then."

Sirens and lights were racing across the Francis Scott Key Bridge.

"Time to go," Smoke said. "Pop the trunk, Sam."

The back lid of the Hellcat opened.

Smoke picked Eugene up by the net, dropped him inside, and shut the trunk lid. Sam tossed him the keys. He snatched them out of thin air then glanced at Sid. "Care if I drive?"

Her head was swimming. The vitamin had worn off. "Go for it."

CHAPTER 12

S MOKE PARKED THE HELLCAT BEHIND an old strip mall in a bad neighborhood. Graffiti covered the exterior walls. Train tracks ran behind him. He got out of the car. Sid and Vormus joined him. Sam and Guppy hadn't followed. They'd set out on another mission.

Facing a metal door, he pressed the button on the side then glanced up at the camera overhead. Moments later, the door popped open and a little head appeared around the door's edge. It was Asia. "Aw shit, it's you."

"Good to see you too, Asia," Smoke said. "Is Mal in?"

"No. Goodbye." She tried to close the door.

Smoke held the door fast. "After you, Sid."

Sid shoved by Asia.

"Watch where you're going, hippopotamus!" Asia said with her usual disdain, but then she got her first look at Vormus and snarled, "What the hell are you?"

"A vampire."

She fixed her slanted stare on his chest. "Very ugly sweater. And why are you all wet?"

"Hold the door," Smoke said to Vormus. He fetched Eugene out of the trunk and hauled him inside.

"What the hell is that?" Asia fanned her nose. "And why do you all smell like the river? Mal! Mal! Your spooky friends have returned. They smell like bad sushi!" In her bright-orange kimono, she hustled away. "Mal! Take care of your visitors. I'm finishing *The Young and the Restless*."

The strip mall had a sublevel to it. The walls were concrete like an unfinished basement. The lighting was all fluorescent. It was filled with a bunch of secondhand furniture consisting of a king-size bed, sofas, tables, and several desks. Mal sat in front of a wall of monitors with active images on all the screens. The scholarly man wore a rumpled lab coat. His hair was long and frazzled. He looked like he hadn't shaved in days. He clicked on the mouse.

Sid slumped on the couch. Her head was leaned back in the cushions. She could barely keep her eyes open. She'd never felt so exhausted before. It was like she had just swum the English Channel—not once but twice.

Smoke was talking. His voice was low and soothing. He caught Mal up on everything from the time Vormus came up until right now. Eugene Green lay on the floor, huddled up and whining.

It was morning.

Toad Man was all man. The net was off. He was secured by two sets of flex cuffs that bound his wrists and ankles. He had griped when Asia applied the cuffs. She'd smacked him in the back of the head, saying, "Shut up or I'll chicken fry your frog legs, ugly man."

Mal's body language didn't sit well with Sid. He was a little bit out of it. She leaned forward and gave Asia a nod.

Asia shuffled over and leaned down. "What?"

"Is Mal okay?"

"He's never been all right. We used to make love three times a day, and now it's barely three times a month."

"That's not what I meant." Sid pulled at her imaginary beard. "Why's he so shaggy?"

"What do you expect? We're living in a strip mall. There isn't even a shower. I have to go to the YMCA and take a shower after I work out. All the round eyes are always staring at me. Burly men." Her face soured. "I don't like them. I like them scrawny myself. Except Smoke." She eyed the dark and handsome man. "He's a fine specimen. How many times a day do you two—"

"Is Mal sick?"

Asia popped back. "No. Not sick. Just goofy. I have to go." She hustled out the door and upstairs.

Sid found Smoke looking back at her. She could tell he had heard what she said. That was when she heard Mal speak out loud for the first time. "I am sick, Sidney, but it will pass." He turned around in his chair and let out a rough cough. "Asia says I'm not taking enough vitamins and I work too hard. Both are true."

"Me and Vormus know a cure for that," Eugene said. He sat on the floor, straining against his bonds. "Though I don't think they'd take the likes of you, professor."

Vormus swatted Eugene in the back of the head so hard his chin hit his chest. "Be silent, fool. I'm close enough to ripping you apart that one wrong syllable will trigger me."

Eugene clammed up. His eyes attached themselves to the floor.

"We need more information from him," Smoke said to Mal. "He's not talking. You got anything for that?"

Mal lifted a brow. "So, you want to use a truth serum on a shifter? I've never tried before. Humph. I'd be delighted."

"Let's get to it then," Smoke said.

"Eh, the problem is I don't have one. I'm not the CIA, you know."

Smoke pushed the sleeves of the sweetheart suit up to his elbows. The muscles rippled in his forearms. "I guess we'll have to do this the hard way then."

"What hard way?" Sid asked.

"Torture."

"Do you even know how to torture a shifter?" Eugene said, choking out a laugh. "What are you going to do, waterboard me? I'm more amphibian than man. I can take all the pain you can dish out."

Walking over, Smoke stooped above the shifter. "So it won't bother you if I push your eyes back into your head?"

Eugene swallowed. "Er...no?"

"Don't fret, everyone." Mal forced himself out of his chair and sauntered over to a lab table. He opened up an alligator-skin doctor's bag and dug out a metal case. Unclipping the hasp, he opened it up. There was a vial and a syringe inside. "This poison may or may not kill him, but he's going to feel like he's had a heart attack at least a dozen times." He filled the syringe with the clear contents of the vial. "Should I do the honors or should you, Smoke?"

"Vormus, help me hold him." Smoke said, taking Eugene by the arm.

"Disappointing," said the vampire. "I wanted to see you push his bulbous eyes back inside his head. Honestly, I can take care of this dilemma myself."

"You didn't do so well back in the fort."

"His bluff fooled us all." Vormus held the shifter fast. "It happens."

Mal sank the needle into the shifter's neck.

Eugene screamed.

CHAPTER 13

EUGENE'S EYES BECAME FEVERISH. THEY darted from face to face. "What did you do?" he shrieked desperately. "What have you done to me?"

"Does it burn?" Mal said, tapping the syringe. "Hmmm, I accidently took some of his fluids out, which could be helpful for my research."

Smoke took out his knife and held the blade in Eugene's face. "I could take some skin from him. It'll grow back. I think toad DNA heals up. Isn't that what they used in the first Hulk movie?"

"No, that was *Jurassic Park*," Mal corrected.

"Actually, they used frog DNA in both of them," Sid added.

Smoke gave her a nod.

Mal checked his watch. "Eugene Green, is it?"

The shifter licked his lips between shudders and gasps. "Yes, Eugene Green."

"Those severe heart palpitations should start up any moment," said Mal. "Just remember, it will go on for hours. Your chest will feel like it's caving in on itself, like an earthquake inside your frame, but I have an antidote." He fished through the doctor's bag. "At least I use to have one. Oh crap, I'll be right back."

"What?" Eugene lurched up. "Where's he going?"

"Just sit back, Eugene. He'll be back." Smoke talked nice and easy. "Mal's not one to lose things. Besides, you're tough. A few heart attacks will feel like a walk in the park for a tough guy like you. Say, where would a guy like you be from, anyway? I'm guessing Jersey. Are you a Jersey boy, Eugene? Where are you from?"

"I'm from King of Prussia near Philly."

Sid eased over.

Smoke gave Sid an approving glance. He continued. "I've been there before. Nice place. They have a pretty big shopping mall there, don't they?"

"Yes. But that's well after my time." Eugene strained his neck. Peering at the stairs, he said, "Where is he with the antidote? I feel like my heart is pounding out my ears."

"He'll be back. Do you want a drink?" Smoke asked.

"Yes."

"Good. Sid, will you check the fridge over there?"

"Right away."

Eugene shuddered. Wide eyed, he stared at Smoke. "Where is he with the antidote?"

"Hmmm, it looks like the travails are just beginning. That was a pretty bad tremor. Your teeth clacked. Uh," Smoke looked around, "we might want to get him something to bite down on."

Vormus handed Smoke a pencil. "Here."

"I was thinking something more substantial."

Sid returned with a can of Coke. She cracked it open. "Do you like Coke?"

"I once did." He took a sip. "Where's the antidote?" Eugene's eyes were all over the place.

Sid took a seat in front of the computer monitors.

Smoke asked Eugene, "Where can we find Manson Bay?"

"145 Allen Towers."

Sid typed it in. A picture popped up on the screen next to a map, the gate of a condominium duplex community west of DC as one headed toward the West Virginia border.

"Where did Kane take all the shifters?"

"Drake Headquarters." Eugene jerked in his bonds. He slobbered. "Where's the antidote?"

"It's coming." Smoke said. "Where's Drake Headquarters?"

"Near Hillcrest Mausoleum."

"What are Kane's big plans?"

"He wants to replace Washington leadership with clones. He wants to capture you and Sid. He wants domination over the world."

"Does he have Allison and Megan with him?"

"I don't know. But they will change if they haven't already. Where's the antidote?"

Sid typed up everything he mentioned, in a message to Sam and Guppy. They'd start pulling up all the information they could find.

Vormus had a question. "Manson Bay—was he in the prison very long?"

"No, he was never there when I was there."

"Why'd they all leave?"

"They knew you were coming."

"How did they know we were coming?"

"Because someone in your group is a clone."

CHAPTER 14

S ID'S HEART SKIPPED A BEAT. Her fatigue evaporated when Eugene said what he said. It was entirely possible one of them was a traitor. It was the only way.

The next question Smoke asked was the obvious one. "Which one of us is the clone?"

"I don't know. Where's the antidote?"

Mal came down the steps and entered the basement room. "Oh dear me, as it turns out, there isn't an antidote after all."

"What!" Eugene's husky neck bulged. "What do you mean?"

"How did our session go?" Mal asked Smoke.

"I think we have everything we need. He did admit one thing I didn't expect. He says one of us is a clone."

"Really?" Mal adjusted his glasses. "Which one?"

"He doesn't know."

"I don't have much of a lab set up here, but I'm certain we could run a test."

"We don't have time for that now."

"Hold on," Eugene interrupted. "You say there's no antidote?"

"No, you don't need one. I injected you with a truth serum. It will wear off."

"But you said you didn't have the truth serum," Eugene said.

"I know. I lied." Mal took an open chair in front of the monitors. His fingers got busy on the keyboards. "I'll see what I can find. In the meantime, what are we going to do with him? Or it, rather?"

"We can't count on the FBI anymore. It would be another catch and release. We could leave him here," Sid suggested.

"This isn't a prison. We aren't equipped to handle him." Mal shrugged. "I bet your new pal Vormus has an idea."

"It would be best to kill him. Just let me handle it." The vampire shifter pulled Toad Man up by his hair. "I can see to it he never returns again."

"Killing is not an ideal way to restore your humanity," said Sid.

"No, but just think how many lives I will save. But if you insist, I'll let him live. Live in misery."

"Screw it. Just stick him back in the trunk. We'll take him with us." Smoke glanced at Mal. "We're going to need all the supplies you have if we're going to take these shifters out. They've freed all the ones we caught before."

"Give me a few days," Mal replied.

"We'll be in touch," Smoke said. "And see what you can whip up in regards to a DNA test. If one of us is a clone, the sooner we know, the better."

"I'm working on it as we speak. Chow."

They left the building and stuck Eugene in the trunk. Vormus faced both of them. "I'm going after Manson Bay."

"No," Sid objected. "You're staying with us."

"Hardly." Vormus's feet left the ground. Up in the sky he went. "I'll be in touch."

"Do you get the feeling we aren't any closer than we were before?" she asked.

"Uh-huh." Smoke cupped her cheek in his hand. "How are you feeling?"

"I'm not going to lie, I could use some sleep. So, do you really think one of us is a clone? Sam or Guppy? You'd think we could tell."

"True. What did you think about Mal?"

"He's off."

Smoke opened up her door. "I thought so too."

CHAPTER 15

"**W**ELCOME HOME, EUGENE," SMOKE SAID. He opened up a single-car garage in an old neighborhood. The brick garage was at the bottom of an old abandoned colonial house that was deteriorating. Heavy growth covered the front porch. The lawn hadn't been cut in years. The place was spooky.

"You aren't really going to leave me here, are you?" Eugene said.

Smoke pushed the man into the garage. It had one single-pane window, dingy with dirt. Daylight crept in, forming pools of yellow light on the floor. He strapped Eugene to the support beam. He lifted another pair of flex cuffs to Eugene's eyes.

"What are you going to do with those?"

"Seal your mouth shut. Even though we are far from many, I can't afford to have you screaming. Anything else you'd like to tell us before we leave?"

Turning his chin away, Eugene said, "No."

"Good." Smoke secured the shifter's mouth with the flex cuffs. He tested all the bonds to make sure they were secure. Once he finished, he took out his phone and took some pictures of Eugene. "I don't think the Drake is going to be very happy when we let them know you told us everything. You say you can't be killed, but I'm pretty sure shifters know how to kill shifters."

Toad Man slumped to the floor.

Smoke took one last glance around the garage. He stepped outside, where Sidney waited, and closed the door. He locked it shut. "Ready to go?"

Yawning, she said, "Ready as ever."

They got in the car and took off. Smoke drove. Sid leaned her seat back and closed her eyes. They were miles out of DC on some back roads that didn't have much traffic. "So whose property was that?"

"That's one of the hideouts of some marks I tracked down years ago. Last I checked, they were still in prison."

"You keep tabs on them?"

"Yep."

Sid shifted in her seat. "I can't wait to take a shower. This second skin is starting to stink."

"We're going home, but I have to make a stop first."

"Milkshake run?"

Smoke smiled.

"I knew it," she said. With her hand on her stomach, she said, "I think I could use one too. I'm starving." Fighting the sleep that was wanting to take over, she said, "What's the plan?"

"As much as I hate to say it, I think you and I might need to go it alone for a bit. We have the addresses. We just need to do our thing until we figure out who is who."

"So you don't think I'm a clone? I could be Samone."

"No, you aren't her. She wasn't nearly as pretty. Besides, she had a unibrow. I just didn't make the connection until it was too late."

Sid burst out laughing.

"I thought it was a new trend or something. Like the Europeans. She had a moustache coming in too."

Still laughing, she hit him in the arm. "Stop it. I can't take anymore. I'm too tired to laugh."

Smoke grinned. He hit the interstate ramp and gunned the gas, accelerating long enough to merge with the morning traffic. "Great Dane. So, Sid, do you think I'm a clone?"

"No, but the thought of two of you is pretty intriguing."

"How so?"

With a little smile on her lips, she shrugged. "It just is."

"Sounds like somebody needs a cold shower."

"And a hot man. Sorry, I'm so tired I'm feeling giddy."

"That's fine by me. After all, you are my wife."

It took an hour to get to Smoke and Sid's garage apartment. Together, they hit the shower and went to bed.

Sid woke up in the early evening. Her stomach was queasy. She padded over to the bathroom on bare feet and closed the door. She leaned over the sink and stared into the mirror. Her eyes were tired. "I need to get more rest. I feel like I've been up for days." She rinsed off her face with some cold water. Her stomach quavered. She patted her face dry with a towel and sauntered out of the bathroom as quietly as she could.

Smoke was up. He stood in the kitchenette brewing coffee. Eyeing her, he said, "Are you okay?"

Pushing her hair back, she replied, "Don't I look okay?"

"You always look okay, but you're a little peaked." He filled the coffee pot with water, stuck it in the coffee maker, and flipped the switch. He walked up to Sid. Placing the back of his hand on her forehead, he said, "You don't feel hot."

"Gee, thanks, Mom." She brushed his hand aside. "I'll be fine once I get some caffeine back in my system. That vitamin really took it out of me."

"How's your hand?"

She lifted her fist. Her knuckles were swollen and scraped. Clutching her fingers in and out, she said, "Maybe a hairline fracture is causing my queasiness. Lord, I hope not. I need my shooting hand."

With a furrowed brow, Smoke said, "Maybe you need to check in with a doctor. When's the last time you had a physical?"

"Now I'm starting to think you *are* a clone. Are you seriously suggesting I visit some—as you like to put it—overeducated quack?"

"I know a guy."

"Of course you do." She patted his chest and made her way toward the coffee. The rich aroma aroused her senses. "Yesterday was quite a day. Not to mention the extended nocturnal activities. No, I'll be fine."

A glare shined into the kitchen window. Outside, a rubber tire screeched.

Smoke pushed the curtain aside.

An SUV sped toward the building, swerving from side to side.

Smoke snatched a shotgun and rushed out the front door. He took aim at the oncoming car. He fired one shot in the air. The car skidded to a halt. It was a banged-up white SUV. Someone slumped over the wheel. It was Vormus.

CHAPTER 16

S MOKE OPENED THE CAR DOOR. Vormus fell into his arms. The disheveled vampire shifter's clothing was torn to shreds. His face was bruised and swollen. "What happened to you?"

Barely able to stand, Vormus pointed over his shoulder. "Get him out. Get him out."

Gun in hand, Sid flung open the back door.

A little olive-skinned boy was buckled in the back seat. He appeared about ten years old. He wore a blue suit and necktie. His hair was gray and hung over his eyes. His mouth and arms were tied up.

Vormus's exposed skin sizzled in the sun. He staggered under the garage apartment's canopy and inside the building.

"Smoke, he's got a kid in here," she said, unbuckling the boy's belt.

From inside the apartment, Vormus said, "He's not a child. He's much older than I. Bring him inside."

Sid scooped the boy up in her arms. She took him inside and set him on the couch.

Vormus leaned against the kitchen counter. Dabbing his forehead with a silk handkerchief, he said, "I never thought daylight would be my ally."

"What's going on, Vormus?" Sid started tearing the tape away from the boy's mouth. "You're kidnapping children now?"

"I wouldn't do that. Again, he's no child. He is Manson Bay, the keeper of secrets. He's far from harmless."

Smoke entered the room and closed the door behind him. He said to Vormus, "So, who got the best of you?"

"The deaders. Not to mention Titus Tolliver."

"The gargoyle?" Sid said.

"Yes. Kane keeps Manson under a heavy watch. Manson is notorious for giving Kane the slip." Vormus rubbed his jaw. "That's why I thought he'd be in Fort Carroll. The little trickster would be secure there."

Manson's eyes were like black soul-searching pearls. They searched every inch of Sid's face. The boy's body was clearly controlled by an intelligence far beyond his appearance.

"So what do we need him for?" Sid asked. "What kind of secrets does he keep?"

"Manson knows the cures. Not just for me but for your sister."

"You say that as if she's already been changed."

With his eyes glued on Sid, Manson nodded. It sent chills through her.

"I thought you said they were going to change her, not that she'd changed!" She stormed over to Vormus. "How do you know this?"

"Manson told me."

"And how does he know everything?"

"Because he is the one in charge of the process. He converted your sister from a mortal to a shifter."

Sid slapped Vormus across the jaw. "Don't say that! Don't lie!"

Smoke moved between the two. "You said she'd have to kill someone first, right, Vormus? A loved one? Only then would the process be complete."

"Why are you asking him?" Sid moved over to Manson. "Let's just ask this little twerp." She finished ripping the tape from his mouth. "Out with it, Manson!"

"Ow!" Manson cried out. "Geez, woman, go easy on an old man." The child spoke as if he was a venerable eighty. "I'm all wrinkly inside, and I don't feel anything like I look on the outside. Don't let the appearance fool you. Heh."

"You're a shifter. Shifters don't age."

"No, that's where you're wrong, we do age. The process is just slow. Everything on earth deteriorates. It's the second law of thermodynamics. That's what shifters refuse to understand. They think they are immortal, but they are not." He glanced at his surroundings. "You look like a reasonable, very fit, and attractive woman. I need to pee." His brows clenched. "I'm at the point where it's painful."

"Vormus?"

The elegant shifter shrugged. "He's harmless from a physical standpoint."

"Then why did you tie him up?"

"I've kidnapped many. It's always best to tether them with something."

Sid unfastened the tiny man's bonds and led him to the bathroom. Leaving the door open, she said, "Make it quick."

"I certainly don't have any desire for it to take any longer than it has to." He pushed the door shut. "A little privacy, please."

"Vormus?"

"He's harmless."

She moved away from the door. "I don't believe that. He's a shifter, isn't he?"

"Point taken. But he's mild mannered. You'll see."

The commode flushed. The bathroom sink water ran. The door opened, and Manson came out. He wasn't the same olive-skinned boy as before. Now he had a full head of straight blond hair and blue eyes. A quizzical look was on his face. "Ah, now I feel much better." The boyish figure walked like he was in his seventies. He tried to climb on a stool by Vormus. "A little help."

Smoke gave him a boost into the chair.

Manson felt Smoke's bicep. "See, I'll never have those. Sad, isn't it? This body never even hit puberty, but my mind sure did. I've been like this since the eleventh century—you know, when King Arthur and Lancelot were around." He winked at Sid. "I bet you thought that was only a legend, didn't you?"

"Thanks for the info, Benjamin Button, but I never gave it a shred of thought."

He shrugged. "Do you have any tea?"

"In a minute. Tell me about my sister."

"Oh, Allison. Boy, that woman's trouble. She's side by side with Kane day and night. He's not letting her or Megan out of his sight. They're the bait. He's patient. He knows you'll come. That's why he let all the shifters out. He's not taking any chances when you guys come around again. Nope. He's sinister. He always has been, but today, boy, you really screwed up his plans."

"What do you mean?" Sid reached into the cupboard and grabbed a box of tea bags.

"Well, now you have me. I'm his prized possession. You see, now I'm the bait, and he will come after me." He leaned over to Vormus. "Haven't you told them that once the sun drops, he'll be coming?"

"I haven't had the chance."

"Vormus, must you always be so contrary?"

"I like contrary. It suits me. Just like this modest establishment suits them."

"Sounds like it's time to gear up," Smoke said. "How many can we expect?"

Manson's eyes widened. "You're not going to wait for them here, are you? It will be a slaughter."

Smoke opened up an army-green footlocker set beside his computer station. Inside were two L.A.W. rockets. He said to Manson, "I'm counting on it."

"You really are crazy, but your maddened bravery won't defeat them." Manson drummed on the counter. "There aren't enough of you. There are plenty of them. You need to hide, at least until daylight. Best to strike in the daytime."

"You know how to stop them, don't you," Sid said. "Tell us."

"Why? That would be to my peril."

Smoke pointed the light antitank weapon at the man. "Not telling us would be to your peril as well."

"Oh, don't be so dramatic."

Smoke tapped on his computer keyboard. "We're set. Let's go."

"Go where?" Vormus asked.

"You'll know when we get there."

CHAPTER 17

SMOKE WAS IN THE PASSENGER seat. Vormus and Manson rode in the back. Sid drove, but her head was swimming with information. She was having trouble keeping track of everything that was going on. Allison may or may not be a shifter. Megan was in danger. At least one of her friends was a clone. All of the shifters they had captured were out loose, and now that night had fallen, they were hunting them. It came down to her and Smoke against a twisted army of fiends. She couldn't even trust her friends in the FBI. And to top everything else off, perhaps she and Smoke were shifters themselves.

Has life always been this insane and I just didn't see it?

She toggled the car's shifter on the wheel, dropping it down a gear. She pushed on the gas, accelerating into the curve. Vormus squished into Manson.

"Hey, slow it down, will you? I'm not into tasting the G-forces. Get off me, vampire."

"I'll ease off as soon as you start making more sense. I need to know how to stop Kane. It's time to bring the Drake down."

"Again, you're talking about my life, little lady. I'm not so eager to part with the few remaining years I have left."

"No, but the two of you sound like you seek redemption."

"I'd be lying if I didn't say I'd think about it. Personally, I just want to stick it to Kane. He stuck me in a hole for years. I only got plucked out when he needed me." Manson leaned over the headrest. "Sure, redemption would be nice, but I'm more on the side of vengeance. Personally, Kane is the problem. His ambition overwhelms him. He wants it all at once. You need to take him down if you can."

"That's the plan. But that's only one shifter."

"True, but it will disrupt all the others. A power struggle will ensue. It will buy the mortals more time. At the moment, Kane is replacing leadership with clones. It's weakening our country's policies on many things. Law and order will cease to exist. You'll live in a nation of wild things. But there is a caveat. He has some clones out there, but he can't make any more without me."

"How many clones are out there now?" Sid asked, fearing the answer.

"Dozens." Manson leaned back and peeked out the window. "So, where are we headed?"

"Weapons cache," Smoke said. "I sent a message out to Mal. He sent the coordinates to his latest stockpile. Shipyard. We've got a drive ahead of us. Are you sure you don't have anything you want to fess up? Frankly, I tire of not getting answers to our questions. If the pair of you aren't going to help, then we might as well drop you off right here."

Sid buzzed through a green light in the heart of DC and then parked right in front of the FBI building. She put the car in park and turned around in her seat. "I'm certain the FBI will keep you two fugitives safe."

"You might as well turn us over to Kane," Manson sneered. "Heh, we are fugitives, aren't we." He elbowed Vormus. "Fine. I'll give you something to cut your teeth on then. I know how to kill the clones. One power source controls them all. It works like a server. It's a pyramid, ten feet wide and ten feet tall. It glows with a life of its own. Waters run through it. It's mysticism and technology fused together. It's where the clones are harvested."

"Drake Industries?" Sid asked.

"Hillcrest Mausoleum."

"Just like Toad Man said. We just didn't know what we were looking for."

"What's the security like?" Smoke asked.

"The pea coats are thicker than pea soup," Vormus said.

"So you knew about this?" Sid said.

"No, I know nothing about the clones, but I've been inside that place before, long ago. It's an ordinary building with mortal workers by day, but the shifters guard it by night."

Sid put the car in gear and drove away, headed straight for the shipyard. She shut the engine off as soon as she made it through the gate. Everyone got out of the car. It was a cargo shipyard. Massive steel storage containers were stacked as far as the eye could see. Smoke led the way with a long, easy stride, pistols nuzzled in his palms. Both he and she had on the sweetheart suits and their goggles.

Smoke checked his phone. His head tilted.

Talking quietly, Sid asked, "What?"

"We're about thirty meters from the mark. We need to keep an eye out and see if anyone else shows up."

"Shifters?"

He shrugged. "If Mal's a clone, then they'll know we're here. That's why I texted him, to draw them out." He scanned the sky. "Who knows? They could come by land, sky, or sea."

"Why don't you go after the weapons cache? You draw them out and I'll back you up?"

"I was thinking about it the other way around, but I'm game." Smoke gave Vormus and Manson a look. Manson turned into a black kid with curly white hair. "What about these two sandbags?"

"They'll just have to stay out of the way," Sid said to the shifters.

"We can help, you know," Vormus said.

"You need to make sure you don't lose Manson. And stay out of the way." Sid motioned Smoke forward with her gun. "Let's go."

Smoke weaved his way through the graveyard of metal shipping containers. Sid stayed one box length away from Smoke, checking high and low. Nothing but them moved or scurried, aside from the soft breeze that kicked up debris from time to time. Smoke came to a stop in front of a blue container sitting by itself beside metal containers stacked four high. He looked all around. His eyes found Sid's.

Sid held up her palm. He waited. She moved quick, scouting the area high and low. She circled the containers and stood face to face with Smoke. "It's all clear. Not a shifter in sight, aside from the two we brought." She rapped her knuckles on the container. "So, this is the one?"

"Yep."

"Well, let's hope Mal is clone free and he's got some nice toys for us." She worked the container's handles. "Still, I hate to think Sam and Guppy are clones. We'd be able to tell, wouldn't we?"

"You'd think." Smoke grabbed the handles and pulled. The doors groaned. Something smashed through the doors, knocking them backward. A wolf man had Smoke pinned down by the throat.

CHAPTER 18

S ID KNEW THE CREATURE INSTANTLY to be Adam Vaughn. The hairy figure was a knot of muscular limbs and power. He wore only a pair of trousers. His savage fury had Smoke flat on the ground. Saliva dripped from the wolf man's jaws. Dazed from having the door smacked into her head, Sid took aim on the wolf man's broad back.

Smoke twisted away from the wolf man in a wrestling move that reversed their positions. Now he had the wolf man on his back.

But in a burst of primal power, the wolf man swatted Smoke aside with his paws. The blow sent Smoke reeling into the container. The wolf man rose, ready to pounce for the kill. He leered at Sid. "You're next, pretty."

She fired several shots. The bullets tore into the wolf man's body.

A.V. staggered back and laughed. "You mortals and your bullets. How pathetic."

"We'll see how you feel about it once I unload this clip into your skull."

"It will be a lesser effect than when I rip your skulls from your heads." A.V. closed in on Smoke.

Sid continued to fire. Regular bullets, unfortunately. They really needed to get to this cache. As A.V. lunged for Smoke, she drew her knife and lunged for A.V.

A shadow dropped from the sky and plowed into her. The blow knocked the knife from her grip. Her head smacked hard into the ground. Shaking it off, she found that a figure loomed over her. It was Angi Harlow, the Night Bird, head to toe in all her feathered glory. The exotic woman was radiant, her smile beautiful and deadly, her eyes cold and merciless.

"We meet again," Angi said. The talons on her feet opened and closed.

Sid drew her other gun and fired.

In a blur of feathers, Night Bird slipped aside. In a moment, she had Sid's hands locked up by the wrists. She squeezed.

Sid gasped. "Ah!" The shifter's grip was iron. She kicked at the feathered woman.

With taloned feet, Night Bird pinned down Sid's legs and pinched her thighs.

She felt the blood stop flowing through them.

"You cannot hurt me, mortal! And I won't underestimate you this time!" Night Bird's face was a mask of anger. "You embarrassed me in my house. In front of my friends. You will pay!" She punched Sid several times with lightning-quick strikes. And then the harpy's wings flapped.

Sid's eyes rolled up in her head. Her body left the ground. Weightlessness overcame her. With blood dripping from her lips and through her swelling eyes, the world below became smaller.

Smoke lay still.

A.V. moved in.

Using his legs, he tripped the wolf man.

The wolf man stumbled.

Smoke struck. He jammed his knife between the shifter's ribs, burying it hilt deep in his heart.

A.V. let out a howl. His arm cocked back. His fist smashed Smoke in the chest with the force of a kicking ram.

Smoke turned aside just enough to evade the full force of the strike. Reeling from the glancing blow, he locked the wolf man's arm up and yanked it out of the socket.

The savage shifter became unglued. The slavering jaws snapped at Smoke's neck. With one arm, he shoved Smoke away. Kicking his elbow back with a pop, A.V. got his shoulder back into place. The hulking brute pulled the knife from his chest and pointed it at Smoke, panting. "That was close. Mortal blades can cut me, but they can't kill me." He eyed the blade in the moonlight. "Ah, but this is special steel. Maybe my claws can't peel the second skin from your limbs, but this can." He showed a fierce smile. "I can poke a hole clean through you with this."

Smoke spat blood on the ground. "We'll see."

Brandishing the razor-sharp steel, A.V. pounced. He stabbed, jabbed, and cut with raw skill. His savage power and speed more than made up for his lack of refinement.

Smoke blocked and countered with every move he had. He parried the lighting-quick strikes with fists, forearms, and elbows.

A.V. countered his counter.

The knife snaked through Smoke's defenses.

Grinding his teeth, Smoke felt like a ball of fire exploded in his shoulder.

A.V. laughed.

CHAPTER 19

THE HIGHER THEY SOARED, THE more Night Bird laughed. "I should drop you, but that's not the plan. I must say, that would be delightful. But Kane is obsessed with you, like some sort of prize." She sneered at Sid. "I don't see it."

Gathering her senses, Sid stared down at the ground. She felt as helpless as she was weightless. Night Bird's powerful wings beat against the wind, moving them away from the shipyard. "Where are you taking me?"

"You'll know when we get there."

Something flew up from the shipyard. It was Vormus. He wrapped his arms around Sid's body and tried to pull her free of Angi's talons.

"You!" Night Bird screamed. "Vormus, you are ever the pest!" She flapped harder. "Let go!"

"Oh, Angi, you are as lovely as ever, but I fear I cannot let go. This prize is mine."

Sid felt whatever power Vormus commanded pulling against her like a great weight.

Night Bird began to sink in the sky. Enraged, she shrieked, "Release me, Vormus! Don't be a fool! Release me!"

"Release her, Angi, and I'll release you," Vormus said, and then he whispered in Sid's ear, "She's one of the more difficult women I know. We dated a century ago. She was quite entertaining but too needy for my liking in the end."

"Save the story and just get me back on earth," Sid choked out. Angi's talons were squeezing her to death. "Hurry."

The three of them spiraled in a downward pattern like a plane landing with one wing. Fifty feet. Thirty feet. Twenty feet. Night Bird squalled. The three of them hit hard.

Without hesitation, Vormus punched Night Bird in the face. Her grip loosened.

Sid squirmed free.

"Help Smoke," said Vormus. "He needs it. I'll handle her."

Sid took off at a full sprint. Dashing through the containers, she chased the sound of bodies slamming into metal. She darted back to the spot where the battle had started.

A.V. had Smoke hoisted over his head. He hurled Smoke into a wall of steel.

Smoke lay on the ground, unmoving.

Heart racing, Sid took a clip of bullets off her belt and flicked out the regular rounds with her thumb, one by one. *Please be in there!* The last bullet in the clip was green tipped. She didn't even know what it did. She snatched up her gun, dropped out the last magazine, stuffed in the new one, and charged the slide.

A.V. turned. "Huh?"

She squeezed the trigger. The bullet spun out of the chamber at hypersonic speed and smacked into A.V.'s chest.

A.V. the wolf man grunted. His part-wolf, part-man face looked down. The bullet had grafted itself to his skin like a tick. He plucked at it with his fingertips. "It tingles." His eyes slid Sid's way and froze. His jaw hung in an open expression. He looked like a wolf man who had just come from the taxidermist.

Groaning, Smoke knocked on A.V.'s leg. "He's stiff as a board."

Sid fanned her hand in front of A.V.'s eyes.

The eyes didn't move. A rugged sigh came from the shifter's mouth.

"It's probably going to wear off," she said. "We need to secure him."

A.V.'s hardened limbs didn't budge. Smoke put his flex cuffs away. "These are useless, but I have an idea." He picked A.V. up by the waist and walked him inside the shipping container. After unceremoniously dropping the wolf man on the floor, he stepped outside just as Vormus arrived.

The vampire shifter held Night Bird in his arms. She was unconscious. "She tires more easily than the rest." With a heave, he tossed her into the container like a hay bale.

Smoke closed the huge metal container and locked it shut, checking that the locking mechanism was secure. "I think this was meant for us."

"Why's that?" Sid said, holding her ribs. It hurt to breathe.

Smoke lifted his hand and pointed. A painful grimace marked his face. A flatbed truck and loader were nearby.

Sid got it. Her attention zeroed in on Smoke's shoulder. His sweetheart suit was caked in blood. "John, you're hurt."

"Yeah, the werewolf stabbed me. Doesn't make much sense, does it?"

A hollow clapping sound came from nearby. Manson was sitting on a nearby container with his feet dangling over the edge. He was a blond-haired, blue-eyed boy again. "I found this mildly entertaining. You folks really make a great team."

"If you're so old, how'd you manage to climb up there?" Sid asked.

"Well, they have ladders."

"No they don't."

"Oh." Manson hopped off the container. He landed softly on his toes. "So maybe I'm a little spryer than I let on."

"You're a lot spryer than you let on." Sid picked up her guns and holstered them. "How come you didn't run?"

"Well, I never felt like a prisoner. And I could use the protection." He clasped his hands. "It looks like I'm in pretty good hands, even though Mister Smoke is bleeding. I have to say, that wound looks awfully painful. It's going to need more than just stitches. I'd say surgery. Months of recovery. Oh, but you heal faster than most, don't you."

"Nothing extraordinary."

"I know better than that." Manson adjusted his navy-blue tie, then checked his sleeves. "I think this suit is done for. Can we swing by the mall? I need some new duds."

"Quiet." Smoke's eyes narrowed.

Sid caught the scuffle of soft shoes on the pavement. She braced herself against a nearby container, moving Manson back as she did so.

Who on earth do we have to deal with now?

CHAPTER 20

A PERSON PEEKED AROUND THE CORNER. Sid stuck her Glock in the man's temple. It was Mal Carlson.

"Easy now," the scientist said. His hands were up. "I'm here to help."

Sid disagreed. "You set us up."

"No, on the contrary, it wasn't me," said the disheveled man. "I didn't. Why would I set you up and then come here? I drove, for Pete's sake. Have you ever seen me drive before?"

"No, Asia always does."

Mal's shoulders drooped. "Uh-huh."

"Asia's a clone!" Sid said. Her stomach turned queasy. She shoved by Mal and upchucked right behind him. Leaning on the container, she tried to catch her breath. "Sorry about that. I guess all the excitement is getting to me."

Smoke laid his hand on her shoulder.

Sid waved him off. "Just give me some space. I need to breathe." She fanned her flushed face with her hands, taking in as deep a breath as she could. And wincing. It felt like someone had driven a nail into her ribs. "I think I've got a cracked rib. Damn."

"Just take it easy." Smoke took over. He gave Mal a little shove with his fingers. "What's going on?"

"I've been feeling a little worse each day for several weeks now. I wasn't sure what it was, but I never get sick. I dine on my fair share of crap, but I load up on vitamins and apricot seeds. After you left, I did a little more investigating on my own. Thanks to microtechnology, I was able to spy on my sweet Asia. The little witch from the Orient was poisoning me. Still, I lay low. That's when I caught your message. She sent you here, not me."

"Where's Asia now?" he asked.

"I have no idea. I pretended to be so sick I needed rest." He took off his glasses and huffed on them. "I still feel awful, but what she fed me is wearing off." He planted his glasses back on his nose. "I heard her leave not long after I pretended to sleep. If that was a clone, then where is my Asia, Smoke?" Mal sobbed. "Where?"

"We're working on that."

"You don't think she's dead, do you?"

Smoke looked down at Manson. The boy was chewing a piece of gum. He blew a bubble, shook his head. "No. She's probably at the power plant."

"The power plant?"

"Drake's power plant near Hillcrest Mausoleum." Manson popped his bubble. "They keep the cadavers in there."

"Who's this little creep?" Mal asked.

"Manson Bay, the keeper of secrets. He just let another secret out." Smoke grabbed Manson by the tie. "Why didn't you mention that before?"

"Mysteries reveal themselves when the time is right. Now is the right time. Besides, you aren't going to be able to get in there without some sort of arsenal. I had hoped you would find the weapons cache you needed. You're screwed now."

Mal pulled his shoulders back. "The only one screwed is the one who stole my Asia." He looked Smoke in the eye. "I brought the weapons cache with me."

Sid hung back while the men checked out the midnight-blue Chevy Suburban Mal had driven to the shipyard. It was parked beside the Hellcat.

For some reason Manson stayed by Sid's side. He offered her a piece of gum. "You should try it. Bubble Yum watermelon. It's one of the few modern marvels I enjoy. Well, and *Seinfeld*. I think Shakespeare would have liked him."

"I'll pass," she said.

"Your breath is far from fabulous. I'd offer a mint if I had one."

She took the gum. Manson made a nice-looking young boy. He was sharp in his suit. But there were secrets behind his dark-blue eyes, and he carried himself like the ancient adult he was. "Why do you change from face to face?"

"It's just practice, really. I became a shifter when I was young. It was an accident. They hunted me. I learned to survive by changing my face, but I never identified with these monsters or anything. I didn't know what they were back then."

"It sounds like you've had a long and interesting life."

"Right on both counts." Manson cleared his throat. "But it nears its end. I've struggled for centuries knowing I wasn't on the right side of things, but I've been a coward. I let them control me. I created the clones for them. I regret it. They would have never known how to make them if I hadn't done it. I never thought they'd take it to the extreme they did."

Manson seemed innocent enough. She wanted to believe him. But she'd come up with her own rule of thumb. *All shifters are liars.* She played along.

Smoke hollered for her. "Sid, you have to see this."

The back of Mal's SUV was loaded with enough guns and ammo to start a small army. There were boxes of blue-, red-, and green-tipped rounds. Smoke was feeding rounds into an M-16 magazine. "This is going to get nasty."

"You need to take it easy. Your shoulder's still bleeding."

In a rough voice, Smoke replied, "I ain't got time to bleed."

"Well, you're going to make time to get stitched, Blain."

"I feel an action-packed marathon filled with tobacco and graphic violence coming on once this is over."

"Let's hope we can squeeze it in before the aliens, predators, and terminators arrive."

Everyone else had stopped what they were doing and was staring at them. Vormus said, "What's a terminator?"

"Five hundred pounds of steel under a hundred pounds of synthetic skin, steroids, and muscle." Smoke chuckled. "I'll be back."

"We could sure use Asia right now. I can't stitch a shoulder like she can."

"I'll do it," Manson volunteered. "You just have to trust me."

CHAPTER 21

T HE FRONT PASSENGER SEAT WAS leaned all the way back in the Suburban. Smoke lay still in the leather chair. Manson sat in the rear seat overlooking Smoke's wound. He wore Smoke's goggles. The surgical tools in the boyish shifter's fingers moved with the precision and delicacy of a spider's spinnerets.

The large fighter was stripped down to the waist. His jaws clenched. "It feels like you're sticking a piece of rebar in there."

Sid stood just inside the open back door on the passenger side. Smoke's powerful grip held her hand tight. "You know you love the pain."

"Yeah, that burning, throbbing sensation really elates me."

"What," she smiled, "you aren't going to give me the 'Pain don't hurt' line?"

"I guess it slipped my mind."

"I'll be needing one of your little pills, Professor," Manson said to Mal, who was assisting from the driver's seat.

Startled, Mal said, "What do you mean?"

Manson rolled his eyes. "Not that kind. The supervitamins."

"Oh, I knew what you meant. Er, let me see. Uh, Sid, could you reach inside the glove box? There's a vial in there."

She retrieved the bottle of pills and twisted off the lid. "How's this going to help?" She started to put one in Smoke's open mouth.

"No, no, no," Manson said in an elderly voice. "Hand it to me."

She did.

The supervitamin was a large green gel pill with a glow to it. Manson held it between his forefinger and thumb. He eyeballed it, took a scalpel, and sliced it open. He squeezed out the contents into the wound.

"Woo!" Eyes wide, Smoke looked at Sid. "That's much better!"

"These vitamins have a powerful regenerating effect when applied directly to wounds." Manson leaned over the gap he had pulled open in Smoke's shoulder. "Heh, the muscle and tissue mends. You're fortunate the cut was so clean." He finished sewing up the wound. "Don't move it for a few hours. It should be much better by then, but there are no guarantees."

Smoke nodded.

"Now show me your cracked rib, and that hand," Manson said to Sid, reaching for the vial of pills.

"How'd you know the vitamins had that application?" Mal said. "Even I didn't know that."

"Because I created them, that's why."

The cabin quieted while Manson squirted the contents of two pills into a syringe and shot it into her rib and hand. At first it hurt like hell, but then it felt all better.

"Oh, I didn't create them for the likes of you. I created them for when the shifters make the initial transformation. It helps with the cloning process, too." Manson wiped down the tools and placed them back in the medical kit. "They typically have a disastrous effect on humans. I marvel that you can use them, but it must be the shifter blood in you."

Sid got that sinking feeling again. She spoke up. "I've been curious where all this equipment comes from. If the FBI isn't supplying it, then who is?"

Mal held up a finger. "I've been under the impression it was the people who ran the Black Slate. They're the ones who contacted me. It was easy enough to believe it was from a covert military operation."

Manson chuckled like an old man who was the only one with the answer to the puzzle. "I hate to use the word 'gullible,' because it's not entirely true. Yes, a government entity is behind these gifts you receive. But those factions are run by powers and principalities that are difficult to understand. There's good within their ranks, but there's a dark force, too. The Drake runs the evil faction. They use the clones to infiltrate the government ranks. They're trying to out the Church of Nigil."

Sid leaned forward. "The Church of Nigil?"

"The shifters have been around since ancient times. I'm certain you've figured out that much." Manson scooted down his seat and pushed down his armrest. He turned the cabin light off. "They've been a threat on and off throughout all history. In the Dark Ages, the shifters—typically a bunch of crude and savage individuals who worked alone—began working with one another. That's when some of the earliest knights were formed by a warrior named Nigil. He was a devout man, a minister of the faith. He worked quietly and diligently behind the scenes. To this day, there are many unknown followers of the Church of Nigil. They keep the forces of evil at bay. However, with the help of the clones, the Drake, the shifters, and the likes of Kane are having these good members of the old guard eliminated. It's a very quiet but devastating extraction." He hitched his thumb over his shoulder. "They're the ones behind the Black Slate, the Church of Nigil, but now the Drake has them on the run. It's a nasty business."

"I've never heard of this church," Mal said.

"They are careful to wipe out all traces of their existence, but they walk like angels among us—not so much for my benefit but for yours."

"You say they're knights. Do they fight?" Smoke asked.

"They fight with thought, not fists."

Sid soaked in her thoughts. The answer to every mystery was another mystery. She leaned back and gazed at the stars in the sky. *I guess I'll never have the answers to everything. Not in this lifetime I won't. I'll just march forward on faith.*

Smoke took her by the hand and pulled her into the car. "It's time to take out the clones."

CHAPTER 22

"THEY'LL BE EXPECTING A.V. AND Angi back at the Drake compound." Vormus stood beside the containers with a bored look on his face. "I suggest you execute your plan soon."

Sid, Smoke, and Mal were standing around the hood of Mal's SUV, going over the plan with Manson. The boy shifter had drawn them a map, and he said he had told them everything he could think of about the compound.

Drake Headquarters was nestled in the woods. The concrete building was built like a bunker. The windows were small on the three levels of flooring. The security was tight. There was a checkpoint for all traffic going in and coming out. A barbed-wire fence secured at least a mile-wide perimeter.

"You have the pea coats, deaders, and shifters," Manson said, rubbing his nose. "They don't take any chances with the Pyramid. With me gone, they're going to be a little more paranoid from now on."

"What about electronic security? Cameras, pass codes, key fobs, magnetic locks?" Sid asked as she pressed new bullets into her clips.

"Huh, well, needless to say, the Drake uses plenty of technology, but they're pretty old fashioned about this place. They don't want a digital record on their dealings. Needless to say, they don't want any strangers prowling about. If someone strange shows up, they kill them. Or clone them. They don't want to be hacked, either. Sure, they entertain the elites with recordings of their fights and battles, but that doesn't happen at this location. It's top secret."

"But they have to run power to the pyramid server, don't they?" Smoke asked. Automatic pistols hung on his hips. Machine guns were strapped to his back. He taped two weapons' magazines together with duct tape.

"The server does have power. It's enough power to run a small city. It's in the basement, deep, where it's cool. It's in a glass vault. Shatterproof stuff. I'm not even sure if a bomb could take it out." Manson shrugged. "Destroying it won't be easy. Just getting down there will be a feat in itself."

Smoke said to Sid, "Sounds like a job for James Bond."

"James who?" Vormus asked.

"It sure doesn't sound like we can go blasting through there," she said. Based off what Manson had told her, she didn't like the odds. But she felt compelled to do it. She needed to find her sister and niece. She couldn't help but think something bad was about to happen. "How confident are you that Kane now resides at this compound?"

"Oh, he's there. He doesn't have anywhere else to be at the moment."

"How can you be so sure?"

Manson shrugged. "I suppose I could be wrong, but are we going after Kane or the server? We have to take down one thing at a time."

"I concur with Manson," Vormus said. "I believe Kane is there hiding like the rat he is. He knows you have to come after him if he doesn't haul you in there himself. He just wants the advantage. The shifters who serve him want to redeem themselves. Now's the time to take him."

Typing on his laptop, Mal said, "Let's not forget we need to find my Asia. She's in there too, and we don't need any collateral damage. I won't have any part of that. I have an idea though."

"What is it?"

"Servers need to stay cool. If we cut the power to its ventilation systems, won't the server shut down?"

Manson blew a gum bubble until it popped. "Perhaps. It runs hot, but there will be back-up generators. Those will need to go down too. Everything tied to the server will have plenty of security. I didn't have a hand in those systems. I just handle the clone programming. Also, just because the server is shut down doesn't mean the cadavers will waken."

"You speak like they are dead," Mal said, his voice torn with emotion.

"Well, they're in a suspended state. It's more like a coma one never wakes up from. Many die during the process."

"John, can I have a word with you?" Sid asked.

Her husband moved out of everyone else's earshot with her.

"I'm not very comfortable with this, and I don't trust either of them. It sounds like we're about to walk into a bigger net."

"I guess we won't know for sure until we get there, but I'd rather roll in than wait and see. Let me try to steer this thing, and we'll see if they try to dissuade us."

"You just want to play with those weapons."

"I want to waste shifters." He slapped a magazine into his rifle and slung the weapon over his back. "I'm not buying that they can't be killed. Everything can be killed. We just need to find a quicker way to do that. We'll figure it out."

Sid put her hands on his face, went up on tiptoes, and kissed him. "Okay, I'll follow your lead. If I can't trust you, I can't trust anybody. How's the shoulder?"

"Good enough to support my trigger finger." He kissed her back. "How's the rib and hand?"

"Good enough to do this." She kissed him soundly, putting her body into it.

When they'd made their way back to the others, Smoke laid out his plan. "Operation Trojan Horse."

"Sounds original," Vormus said.

Smoke pointed to the truck and the container with the prisoners in it. "They're expecting the truck, so we'll send them the truck. All we have to do is convince Wolf Man and Night Bird to drive."

"That'll never happen," Vormus said. "They won't willingly betray Kane. He has them wrapped around his finger."

"I can help with that." Manson's small body grew. The seams of his suit burst.

Everyone took a step back.

Transforming before their eyes, Manson became the spitting image of A.V. He said, "I'm going to need some bigger clothes."

Smoke slapped him on the shoulder. "And I'm going to need to know exactly where those generators are."

CHAPTER 23

S ID RODE IN THE CAB of the container truck. Manson, now disguised as A.V., drove. He struggled with shifting gears. He worked the long shift with his hairy, clawed fingers like an amateur. He'd stalled at two stoplights already. Sid's nerves were wearing thin.

"Why don't you let me drive?" she said. "You're doing horrible."

"No, I always liked driving. I used to do a lot more of it in the good old days. Those Model Ts were slow but fun. I could get away with it back then when I was a kid. No one cared how old you were. Lots of kids drove back then, those whose parents could afford to let them drive their expensive machines. Now I look too young, and you have to have a license to do just about everything but pee." The light turned green. He popped the clutch and pushed the accelerator, and the big truck rumbled forward. Bouncing in his seat, he said, "See, I'm getting better."

"It looks to me like you can take on whatever form you want. You don't have to stay a kid. So what are you, a doppelganger like Reginald?"

"Eh, sort of. Old Reggie is a clever bird. Very powerful. Almost as powerful as Kane himself. I'm all boy in the day, but I can change form once night falls. But let's keep that between us. The others don't know I can do it. Hee hee! I'm a kid. I'm supposed to be sneaky."

"Why only at night?"

"Evil thrives in the darkness, I suppose. It's a mystic thing. Just imagine where we would be without the light. Did you know more than eighty percent of all crimes are committed at night?"

"Yeah, I read that once."

Manson looked right at her. "Really?"

"No. Stop looking at me. Just keep your eyes on the road."

"You don't like this face, do you."

"I hate that face." Sid pushed back into her seat and set her stare on the road.

"The first experience with a shifter leaves a deep impression. It taints you. No experience with the supernatural is unforgettable. In your case, I'd say temptation overcame you." The truck banged over some potholes. "The seductive nature. The raw power. It sucks you in. There is a promise of great pleasure. Very few can resist it."

Sid's throat tightened. She remembered the encounter with A.V. like it was yesterday. The temptation was etched in her mind forever. A craving had overcome her. She'd wanted to succumb. Embrace it. Smoke's words had brought her to her senses. *Pancakes and butterflies.* She smiled.

"What?" Manson asked.

"Nothing. Question. I shot A.V. with silver bullets. He clearly feared them. How come it didn't kill him?"

"Oh, that's all stuff from your picture shows. Sure, silver is the weakness in his case. Every shifter has one. But once they removed the bullet, he was revived. Heh, we are truly hard to kill."

"So does Vormus have a weakness for wooden stakes and crucifixes?"

Manson lifted his shoulders. "Maybe. It's different for everyone. I don't think they even know their own weakness. That's why they're so cocky. But it trips them up sometimes. One shifter had a severe allergy to pewter. She was killed by a fork and a butter knife. Heh. That was in the eighteenth century. They wore really big hats back then."

"I'm surprised you're willing to ride right into the lion's den, Manson."

"You aren't surprised. You're suspicious, and I don't fault you. Well, I'm taking a new side." His voice became cryptic. "The signs abound. The sky falls. The walls close in. The end is near."

Goose bumps rose on her arms even with the second skin on. She sat in the quiet for the rest of the ride, going through the game plan.

Now's not the time to worry about what he is or isn't going to do. Just focus on what you need to do, Sid.

Manson drove the truck onto a private road that split from the highway. A green sign read Hillcrest Road. Also, a Drake Properties sign was posted at the split, along with several notable "No Trespassing" and "Private Property" signs. The winding road snaked up into the hills for miles. Trees of all sorts lined both sides. Leaves bent on the branches as the truck rolled by. The road flattened out at the top. They passed a mausoleum on the right. The building was surrounded by hundreds of grave markers in an overgrown field. The mausoleum itself looked to be big enough to hold at least a dozen bodies inside the belly of its sandstone framework. A monolith of stone sat facing the moonlight. Two urns sat on the ledges that confined the steps leading up to the iron door of the mausoleum. Four thick stone pillars held up the front of the roof.

At least I don't see any gargoyles.

Ahead were the guard shack and the perimeter fence. The fencing was ten feet high. The top was covered in coils of barbed wire. Behind it was a stone building three stories tall with small windows, just as Manson had described. There were parking places outside, and a ramp led below the building. Dim lights illuminated some of the windows.

Two men in pea coats stepped out of the guard shack and greeted them with M-16s.

Manson brought the truck to a stop. "I'll do the talking."

The guards flanked the passenger and driver's-side doors. A third man stepped out from behind the shack. A giant of a man over eight feet tall. His hair stood up on top of his head in patches. He wore a beige, Carhartt-like work suit.

Lance!

CHAPTER 24

THE HUGE TEENAGER STOOD BETWEEN the truck and the gate. He stooped, staring right at the windshield, small eyes squinting.

Manson rolled down his window.

The guard climbed up on the semi-truck's doorstep. His eyes popped open when he met Manson's in A.V. form.

"Special delivery," Manson said. "And don't ever get in my face again."

The flat-nosed guard held his ground. "Who's the girl? I don't recognize her."

"She's the delivery, fool!" Manson shoved the man off the side of his truck. The guard fell on the ground, popped up, and with a nasty glance over his shoulder at Manson, he headed over to Lance.

Manson said to Sid, "You seem to recognize that big fella. Got a name?"

"Lance. We crossed with him a little ways back at Titus Tolliver's mortuary. I'm a bit surprised he's here. He's a loner."

"A shifter that big has nowhere else to go. Hmm, I wonder if he knows A.V."

Lance approached.

"I guess we're about to find out." Sid put on a long face. Lance's big head almost filled the window. His little eyes got big. "You! Why isn't she secured?"

"She's not going anywhere, Lance. Her loved one is hostage in the back."

"They should both be in there," Lance said. "Kane's not going to like this. Where's the bird lady?"

Manson leaned toward the windshield and glanced up in the sky. "I'm sure she'll be landing any moment now, if she hasn't already. Why, do you still have a thing for her?"

Lance gaped. "What thing?"

"Oh, people talk. They say you give the little lady a lot of leers. I can't blame you. She's a fine wine even to the likes of myself, though a little moody."

"I don't remember you being so talky," Lance said. He stuck his entire head through the window. Sid crammed into the back of her seat. Lance sniffed. "Anyone back in there?"

"The truck cab? Uh, no, you can see for yourself." Manson popped his door open.

"Forget it." Lance looked at Sid. "You burnt my hair."

"I don't care."

"You will." Lance walked away. He snatched a radio from one of the guards. The radio looked like a credit card in his big hand. He said something. A few seconds later, he gave a nod and then dropped the radio on the ground. Using his hand like a grizzly bear's paw, he grabbed the heavy gate by the chain-link fencing and walked it open, waving the truck through.

Manson jammed the truck into gear, hit the gas, and stalled.

"Really?"

He started the engine again. "Sorry, but this clutch is jumpy."

"No, your driving is shitty."

"What do you expect? It's been decades." He hit the gas, the truck jumped forward, and he eased it through the gate. Lance stepped in front of the truck. Arms swinging easily and with giant strides, the colossal teen led them inside the compound. "Looks like things are going to be chippy. I hope things work out. I don't recall seeing this many people about."

Sid counted men in pea coats. They stood inside the windows and were scattered in the parking lot. Each one carried an Uzi. She noted a head and a rifle barrel on top of the building. Men marched along the fence. There were man-like figures, too. Deaders. They wore clothing like men but walked like zombies. Their jaws were slack and eyes sunken as they creeped around the plaza. "And you made those things?"

"I'm not fully responsible for the juices that keep them alive. Much was passed down through the ages. At least you know stopping their hearts stops them."

"Unless they have body armor on. Which, by the looks of them, they do. Morning glory. How did I ever get into this?"

"The same way we all do. Destiny."

"I don't know about that."

A twelve-foot-high garage door rolled open, just like the ones they used in the federal buildings. Lance crossed the barrier and walked down the ramp into a huge garage bay lit up by fluorescent lights. Lance waved them over toward the middle and motioned for them to stop. Aside from the way they had come in, the only other ways out were a stairwell door and an elevator. The roll-up garage door closed behind them, sealing them inside.

"If you haven't prayed yet, now might be the time to do so. I respect that. We'll be having company soon."

Sid mentally said a prayer. She'd done it several times since they left.

Jesus, I know you know what you're doing, but I'm not sure what I'm doing. Give me strength.

The stairwell door burst open. A dozen pea coats came out. Rushing over on booted feet, they surrounded the truck. The elevator doors split open. She expected to see the brawny Kane. She got a bigger surprise. It was her.

Manson leaned forward. "Oh my, that's you. How quaint."

Samone, Sid's shifter clone, was dressed in a sweetheart suit the same as Sid's. She was identical in every aspect—aside from the cruel sneer on her lips. She wasn't alone. Titus Tolliver was in full gargoyle form on one side. Swift Venison, the were-rat in slacks, was on the other. She hoped to see her sister, but there wasn't a sign of Allison anywhere. "Are you sure Kane is here?"

"I'm not entirely positive, but where else would he be? He's cautious. Can you blame him? Why else send in a clone?"

"To rattle me and Smoke."

"That's what I'd do." Manson shut off the engine, opened his door, and made his way out of the cab. Sid did too. "Package delivered," Manson said.

"I can see that," Samone said. Her eyes never left Sid's face. "At least half of it. Am I to assume the other half of this dynamic duo is inside the container?"

"Even Houdini couldn't make it out of this container. Plus, he's bound up. All secure."

Arms crossed over her chest, Samone stood eye to eye with Sid. "We'll see. Rexor! Thorgrim! Come!"

Two huge men stepped out from behind the support columns of the garage and shambled over. They were the same pair of giants that had tangled with Smoke before, bigger and brawnier than Lance. Both wore heavy burnt-orange jumpsuits. Shaggy, long hair hung over their shoulders. Rexor was bearded, Thorgrim clean shaven.

Glancing at the container, Samone said, "Bring it down."

In a feat of awesome power, the giants snapped the chains that held the container secure on the truck bed. Using their fingertips, they picked it up. Together, they walked it off the flatbed, shaking the metal box and laughing. "Heh-heh-heh-heh!"

"It's not a present. Just set it down," Samone said.

Thorgrim dropped his end.

Boom!

"I said set it down, not drop it!"

Rexor eased down his end.

Sid's mind scrambled for another plan. She hadn't expected to see so many powerful enemies in one place. She fully hadn't expected to see the giants. *Screw this, I'm not taking any chances.* She bit open the supervitamin stuck in her cheek and swallowed.

"Go ahead, Thorgrim. Open it up and see what's inside."

The giant handled the metal locking bars with ease. Metal scraped over the mechanism with an annoying squeak that echoed inside the garage. Many hardened faces cringed.

Looking at Samone with big, sad eyes, Thorgrim said in a cavernous voice, "Sorry." He opened the doors, stooped, and peered inside, then hunkered down and crammed inside. "Hello?" His voice echoed in the chamber. He shuffled back out. "It's empty."

Samone locked her fingers on Sid's arm. "Where is he?"

CHAPTER 25

IN THE AIR, VORMUS FOLLOWED the truck from the shipyard to the Drake Compound. He waited just below the tree line when the truck came to a stop at the gate. Once the truck was through and inside the building, he made his move. Floating above the treetops, he rose higher in a huge arc and then hung suspended above the roof. He counted four men roosted on top of the building, leaning over the north, south, east, and west ledges. Each was armed with a machine gun. In the center of the roof was the chiller plant. The fans from the three refrigeration units spun at high speeds, sending gusts of wind into the air.

I can't believe I'm doing this.

He held a pack of C4 plastic explosives in his hand. Staring at it, he shook his head.

So not me.

Vormus's part was to take down the heating and cooling system in hopes of damaging the server. There weren't any guarantees it would work, but it was only part of the plan. This was also a distraction. It was Smoke's plan. Vormus didn't like it, but he complied.

He drifted down like a falling feather onto the roof and nestled himself between the units, where he then stuck three packs of C4 to three different units and filled the malleable plastic with the remote detonator pins.

"Don't move," a guard said. The man had crept up into his blind spot. The barrel of his gun was pointed at Vormus's face.

Slowly, Vormus turned. "That's no way to treat the air conditioner repairman."

"You don't look like a repairman to—"

Vormus ripped the rifle out of the guard's hands. He punched the man in the face, crushing his nose. The powerful blow sent the man backward, where he tripped and skipped on the roof with a loud scuffle.

"Hey, what's going on over there?" another guard cried out.

Back pressed against the chiller, Vormus sensed the men closing in.

So much for discretion.

Vormus burst into action. Toes lifting off the roof, he glided into the blind spot of the first guard he saw. He put the man in a headlock and squeezed. The guard's neck popped. He let the body down and moved on. He found the third guard leaning over the first guard he had punched. He swooped in and punched the man in the temple.

The fourth guard appeared around the corner of the chiller unit. "Move a muscle and I'll send a hundred bullets through you."

Vormus lifted his palms and searched out the man's eyes.

The guard looked right into Vormus's hypnotizing eyes. The man's body locked up.

Holding the man's gaze, the vampire floated over to him and pulled the rifle from his hands. "Normally, I'd twist your head from your shoulders, little man. Fortunately for you, I'm beginning to enjoy this covert thing. It's not as sticky."

The rigid guard stood with a spacy look in his eyes.

Vormus armed a chunk of C4 and stuck it in the man's pea coat pocket. "I really do hate pea coats. If I could destroy them all, I think I would."

"Not everyone shares your sense of style," said a familiar voice.

"Huh?" Vormus turned. He couldn't hide his surprise. "Reginald. And what brings the doppelganger out on this fair night?"

Wearing a suit, the slender salt-and-pepper-haired man looked like he'd just left a business meeting. He sucked on a cigarette. The tobacco burned bright orange. Smoke vapors drifted in the air. A silent drone hovered in the air about twenty feet above their heads. "We've been watching you since the moment you dropped in." He opened up his hand. "Hand over the detonator."

"And fail my task in this secret mission? Oh, I couldn't do that. I'm hoping to get a medal for it."

Reginald slipped off his coat. "I tell you what. Let's make it fun." He blew smoke out of his nostrils and set the cigarette aside with the fire still burning. "Kane and I discussed your betrayal, and he has a deal for you. A simple one. You won't have to make all this racket and create a big mess. Beat me, and you can go in peace." He was rolling up his sleeves. "It's a good deal. Besides, your new little allies, Sid and Smoke, were doomed the moment they entered the building."

CHAPTER 26

THE GRIP OF SAMONE'S HAND had the power of a vise. Sid tried to pull away, but Samone held tight. "Where is he?"

"I don't know," Sid said. "He was in there when we left. Maybe the stupid giant isn't looking hard enough."

"Shut up!"

"He's slipped us," suggested Manson, still posing as A.V.

Samone's brows lifted. "Oh, so you think he *slipped* us? Are you stupid enough to think anything slipped by us?" Samone laughed. "We knew you were coming since the moment you left, Manson."

Manson's eyes enlarged. "I beg your pardon."

Titus Tolliver, the gargoyle, walked up behind Manson and locked his stony fingers around his wrists. "Nice try, fool."

"I beg your pardon, Samone, but you're making a big mistake. I'm A.V."

Samone just rolled her eyes at that. "So where are the real A.V. and Night Bird?"

"I have no idea."

"It doesn't matter. At least half the problem is solved." Samone jerked Sid's arm. "Let's take you to Kane."

"Rough hand me again, clone, and I'll bust you in the face," Sid said.

"Is that so?" Samone tugged again. "I'd like to see you try it, mortal."

"You will soon enough, you soulless bitch."

Samone smacked Sid hard in the face.

With all eyes on the twin women, a new voice interrupted the scene. In an oddly familiar yodel, a man said, "Hellooooooooooo."

Shoulders swiveled. Heads turned. Heels pivoted.

Smoke stood on top of the container, armed to the teeth. Two L.A.W. rockets rested on his broad shoulders.

Samone tossed her head back and laughed. Gloating, she said, "Smoke, surely you don't think you can escape this complex?"

"That depends on how reasonable we're all willing to be. All I want is the girl," Smoke said, aiming the rockets at Samone.

"And if we refuse?"

"Then your fuhrer has no prize."

"What?' Samone said.

Several faces had puzzled looks. Thorgrim and Rexor scratched their heads.

Swift Venison, the rat man, stroked the rat tail that hung over his shoulder and chimed in. "I believe he just quoted from *Raiders of the Lost Ark*. Actually, I believe you both did."

Samone sneered at the rat man.

"Though it was unintentional," the rat man finished. He cackled. "Humorous though. Even I admit to enjoying how this mortal banters in the direst situations."

"Why don't you come down from your perch, Smoke? Just think how much you can enjoy yourself with the both of us, hm, dearie?" She hugged Sid. "Haven't you ever had twins before? Double your pleasure? Double your fun?"

"Double your enjoyment?" the rat man added.

"Will you shut up?" Samone said. "Come on now, Smokie. Let's talk about this."

The giants spread out, flanking Smoke's position.

"Take another step, and you're going to find out what rockets do in a confined space like this," Smoke warned.

Thorgrim and Rexor froze. Their heavy eyes drifted back to Samone.

"What will you do, Smokie, drop the entire building on us? Now that would be foolish. We wouldn't die, but you most certainly would."

"You know, I'm not really buying into this shifter immortality thing. I'm pretty confident you won't survive instant disintegration." He panned the L.A.W. rocket tubes toward the giants. "I'm quite willing to unleash a test fire. Do you behemoths want to volunteer?"

"That mortal is crazy," Samone said to Sid. "He's going to get you killed."

"True. He loves me to death." Sid felt the vitamin start to kick in. *Yes!* "Too bad you'll never know love, Samone. Oh, what a feeling." In a super-fast move, she reversed Samone's arm behind her back. The clone had strength beyond her appearance, but now so did Sid. She cranked up the pressure so hard the woman's shoulder popped out of the socket.

"Argh!" Samone moaned. "Screw the rockets! Take them down! Take them down now!"

The giants moved in.

Smoke depressed the rubber triggers on the rockets.

Sid shoved Samone aside, covered her ears, squeezed her eyes shut, and hunkered down.

CHAPTER 27

"**I**SN'T THIS A BIT OLD fashioned, even for you?" Vormus said to Reginald.

The shifters squared off.

Reginald shrugged. "Even I need a challenge from time to time. It makes me feel alive. Isn't that what you want, Vormus, to feel alive again? Now is your chance. You can be free to pursue your life as you want it."

Vormus held the detonator in his hand. His thumb toyed with the trigger. There was enough C4 to blow the entire roof off the building. It would end him, too.

"Go ahead, Vormus. Squeeze the trigger. You stand about the same chance of surviving as you do in a fight with me."

"If it's such a mismatch, why bother to fight at all?"

"True," Reginald replied. "But who knows, maybe you'll get a lucky punch in."

"Reginald, you aren't half as durable as you think." He set down the trigger. "And I'm twice as strong as you realize."

"We'll see about that." The doppelganger spread his arms wide and wiggled his hands. "Let the games begin." Reginald charged.

Vormus caught the man's bull rush in his chest. He tried to lock up the man's arms.

Reginald's fists smacked hard into Vormus's face with the jarring force of hammers. He overwhelmed Vormus with fists that swarmed him like bees. The superior fighter peppered him with blow after blow.

Vormus's body absorbed punishment that would have broken an ordinary man. He dropped to a knee.

Reginald kicked him in the chest. The blow sent him flying into the chiller.

Vormus shook it off. Something felt funny. He touched his nose, and it was out of place on his face. Shoving his nose back into its original position with a crunch, he said, "You'd think the nose would be tougher." He pushed his way back up to his feet. "You've always been overaggressive. You can pummel me all night, but you still won't break me."

"This is just a warm-up for when the real battle begins. Believe me, it's coming. But you won't be here to see it. Kane wants you dead once and for all." Reginald picked up his cigarette and took a puff. Blowing the smoke through his teeth, he said, "Let's keep dancing." With the cigarette pinched between his fingers, he said, "Oh wait. A moment please." Reginald reached behind the chiller.

What is he up to now?

The doppelganger withdrew a pair of Arabian swords. The majestically crafted steel blades' curved edges caught the bright glow of the moonlight, giving them a lifelike quality of their own. Reginald tossed one of the blades.

Vormus snatched it out of the air.

"As I understand it, you're a much better swordsman than you are a fighter." Reginald cut his blade through the air a few more times. "At least you had better hope so."

Thumbing the keen edge of the Arabian steel, Vormus said, "Your mistake. I'm much better with steel than you are as a fighter. Big mistake, Reginald. An utter catastrophe." The blade took off a sliver of his skin when he tested it. The steel wasn't anything ordinary. No, it was the same metal as the knives Smoke and Sid used. It could cut just about anything, even a shifter's skin.

"They say a shifter is only as formidable as his parts, useless as an infant when those parts are missing." Reginald bent his knees into a stance. "Eventually, one of us is going to lose his head over this."

Vormus approached with confidence. "The headless shifter won't be me." He struck.

The well-honed blades clashed together. Using his size and length, Vormus pushed the smaller shifter backward. Steel battered steel.

Reginald laughed. "You're a horrible swordsman. I can't believe it. I knew you wouldn't be as good as me, but with all your divine skills, I never imagined you'd be this bad." He put Vormus on the defensive with a display of lightning-quick chops and cuts. The Arabian sword slit the side of the vampire's ribs. Reginald jumped back, pumping a fist and screaming, "Score!"

"No need to gloat. The fight isn't over yet," Vormus remarked.

But it was over. Reginald was twice the fighter he was. Vormus had been feasting on the weak for years, but Reginald had been the shifter who hunted down any threats to the Drake, including overzealous heroes like Sid and Smoke.

"I must say I'm disappointed. After all, you did give your brother quite the tussle back at the mansion. You actually shook him up. It makes me wonder."

"Perhaps you should lead the shifters," Vormus suggested.

"No, too much responsibility. I'm perfectly satisfied being the best at one thing."

"It's good to know your limits." Vormus eased forward with his free hand behind his back. "Shall we carry on?"

"Eager for your own funeral, I see. Who knows, you might even wind up in the mausoleum. After all, you are Kane's family."

"Do tell." Vormus snaked in and stabbed at Reginald's chest.

The doppelganger swatted the blade aside. With a twist of his wrist, he disarmed Vormus. He held the steel tip on Vormus's neck.

Vormus felt the edge nicking his skin. "You're quick. Well done."

"I'm the best."

"It's a shame I'll never get to see your trophy room."

"No, but I might just have your head mounted on the wall."

Vormus swallowed. He'd never been so close to death since the days before he became a shifter. Now, at the foothold of death, he realized he'd never see the light again. "I don't suppose you're open for negotiation."

"No, not with so many eyes watching, but I'm sure the elite have enjoyed this. Goodbye, Vormus." Reginald cocked back to deliver the final swing.

But just then, the entire building shook with the sound of a muffled thunderclap from way down below.

The doppelganger teetered.

Vormus shoved the man away. Moving with the speed of a frightened rabbit, he snatched up the detonator that lay nearby and leapt into the air. His body lifted from the rooftop at startling speed.

Reginald looked up at him, gaping, and yelled, "Coward!"

A drone whizzed in front of Vormus's face. He noted the tiny camera lens staring at him like an eye. He held up the detonator. "Enjoy the show, assholes." He squeezed the trigger.

The chillers erupted in a series of blinding explosions. Wrecked steel and hunks of building showered the air. The rooftop became a smoking and burning crater.

Reginald was nowhere to be found.

Vormus snatched up the drone and looked into its lens. "See you soon, dear brother." He ripped off the propellers and dropped the drone into the fire.

CHAPTER 28

GUNFIRE ERUPTED AROUND SMOKE JUST as he squeezed the triggers. The first rocket smote the giant Thorgrim in the chest with a mighty *kaboom*! The second rocket did the same to Rexor. The explosive's sound was deafening, its concussive force bone jarring. His entire body juddered from the impact. His ears rang like bells. Half the lights in the garage were out. The pea coat guards were on hands and knees. Several held their ears. Others were out cold. Smoke waded through the haze toward Sid. He found her balled up on the ground.

Her dark eyes were alert and searching. She found his face. "You're crazy!"

"I thought that was what we planned on."

Fingers tapping her ears, she said, "What?" She started gearing up with whatever Smoke had hanging off him. She snapped a belt of ammo around her waist.

"What?" he said back.

She shook her head and took a strap from his shoulder. "Where's Samone?"

He caught a glimpse of the clone scuttling into the fire exit. She was accompanied by the shifters Venison and Titus. Gunfire cracked off.

Smoke dropped to a knee.

The pea coat forces had gathered. A hail of semi-automatic gunfire spewed out of their muzzles.

"Let's waste them."

Smoke and Sid picked the men off one by one. The blue-tipped bullets ripped through the armor the pea coat guards wore underneath. They went down in cries and groans. Most of them went dead silent.

Squeezing off round after round, Smoke didn't care. It was war.

It's us or them.

Sid marched right into the line of enemy fire like a gallant archangel. Every shot she fired hit the mark.

Lance stepped out from behind one of the circular support columns.

She unloaded a clip in his chest with a rapid *budda-budda-budda* sound.

Lance dusted off his chest. "Your bullets might sting, but they won't kill me. This suit is bulletproof."

Sid popped out the magazine and loaded the second clip taped to the first, quick as she could whistle. Without looking back at him, she said, "Smoke, no more center mass. It's going to have to be head shots from now on. I like head shots."

Lance stepped forward. "Just try me."

Sid took aim. "One more step and I'm going to turn your brains into dog chow." She charged the machinegun handle. "Try me. These rounds are explosive."

Focused on Sid, out of the corner of Smoke's eyes, he saw Rexor and Thorgrim start to rise. "Sid, the tide's rising." He switched to the explosive rounds. "How many bullets is it going to take to put these suckers down?"

With her senses, strength, and agility enhanced, Sid was ready for anything.

Lance stared right at her, wary.

She didn't know whether she could stop the giant or not. She felt the presence of the bigger, more powerful giant fill the room.

Lance bent at the knees. His oversized body leaned forward.

Aw, Screw this!

"Goodbye, Lance." She squeezed the trigger, and a hail of bullets burst into Lance's face like angry hornets. One small explosion after the other rocked the garage.

Lance stumbled backward. His arms slapped at the air. Chunks of his head flew off. He screamed, "Noooooo!" He bounced off the column then fell hard on his back, crushing a crawling deader beneath him. He looked up at Sid with half his face missing. Somehow, he spoke.

"Why?"

Sid emptied the clip on the abomination. "I hope this keeps a bad man down."

"Sid!" Smoke cried out. He was firing round after round at the giants' heads, but they were covering their faces with their forearms. His clip emptied. He started to reload.

The bearded giant snatched up a dead pea coat's body and hurled it at Smoke.

Unable to avoid the colossal missile, he was sent sprawling.

Both giants pounced.

Sid loaded another clip of blue tips and fired them into the giant Thorgrim's ear.

"Eeeyargh!" the giant screamed. He swatted at Sid.

She slipped from his clutches while peppering his face with bullets.

He covered up again.

She fired shot after shot, keeping the giant at bay. "Smoke, we have a big problem. We're going to need bigger bullets to stop these things."

Slipping in and out of the giant's grasp, he said, "Try negotiating."

"I don't think they know what that means."

Every time the giant peeked through its forearms, Sid fired through them at him.

It drew forth grunt after grunt, but the giant lumbered forward until he closed into point-blank range.

Sid fired everything she had, marveling at how the sleeves of the suit the giant wore held up against bullets that ripped through stone and steel. "Damn chemical engineers. They can think up anything."

Thorgrim backed her into the corner and peeked through his forearms. "Boo!"

Sid pulled the special knife from her utility belt. "Boohoo!" She jammed it into the giant's foot. It sank through meat and bone.

Thorgrim chuckled. The monstrous, hairy man's limbs closed around her body.

She dove between his legs.

The giant turned and fell. His foot was pinned to the cement floor by the knife. He ripped it out with a grunt, rose back onto his feet, and chased after Sid, hurdling the dead bodies.

"Any ideas, John?"

Rexor had Smoke in a bear hug. Her husband's face was red as a beet. He kept cracking the giant right between the eyes with the butt of his assault rifle and screaming, "Detonator! Detonator! It's inside the container. Hurry!"

She rushed into the huge steel box. There was a concealed panel compartment at the front where Smoke had hidden while they drove in. It was something they'd set up before they left. Inside was the entire weapons cache. Sid opened up an ammo box filled with C4. The detonation plugs were set. She grabbed the detonator and two blocks of C4 and raced outside.

Smoke was hitting the giant in the face like he was trying to crack open a fortune cookie as he screamed, "What is the riddle steel? What is the riddle steel?"

"Smoke!" Sid yelled.

His head rolled her way. Eyes wide, he dropped the weapon.

Sid tossed him one pack of C4.

Without looking, he snatched it from the air and shoved it in the nine-footer's mouth. He pinched Rexor's nose with one hand and held his lower jaw shut with the other, saying, "Steel isn't strong. Flesh is stronger."

Rexor swallowed. "Gulp!"

Smoke looked at Sid and said in words he could hardly hear, "Detonate this infidel defiler!"

CHAPTER 29

"**A**NYTHING TO GET YOU TO stop quoting lines from *Conan the Barbarian*." Sidney pressed the trigger on the detonator.

The insides of Rexor's body made a *poomf* sound. The giant's belly bulged, expanded within the seams of his jumpsuit, and collapsed.

Smoke slipped free of the monster man's clutches and landed on his knees, huffing for breath.

Rexor's eyes—which seemed to be the size of headlights—glazed over. His head and shoulders sank into his suit. A strange type of blood and guts seeped out of his pant legs.

Sid had a sickening feeling the innards of the tremendous man had been obliterated. She couldn't contain her gawking as the top of Rexor's body collapsed one way and his legs went the other. The huge man groaned. His fingers clutched at the air as he fell and made a gross-sounding *splat*.

Thorgrim rushed over to his brother's side and scooped his mangled body up into his arms. Rexor's eyes were closed. All signs of life were gone. Tears streamed down Thorgrim's face. He let out a blood-curdling moan. "Aaaaauuuuuuuuuuuugghhh!"

Smoke rose to his feet and lumbered over to Sid. "You've really done it now."

"Me?"

The color returned to the rangy bounty hunter's face. "I'll be back. Make sure he doesn't go anywhere." He hustled inside the container.

Eyes fixed on the disturbing scene of one giant moaning over the other, she said, "John, where are you going?"

Smoke emerged from the container with another L.A.W. rocket. He expanded the tube and prepared it to fire.

"How many of those things did you bring?" she said.

"I always carry more than one spare." He rested the launcher on his shoulder. "Take cover."

Sid crouched behind Smoke.

Smoke yelled at the giant, "Hey, Thorgrim! Sorry about your loss. Should we send flowers or make a donation to the local giant-sized urns and crematorium? I hear they're running a two-for-one special."

Thorgrim looked up with eyes full of murder. His hands released Rexor's body.

Smoke fired.

The rocket burst from the barrel in a sizzling stream of smoke and hit dead center in the giant's gaping mouth. *Boom!* Thorgrim's head blew up like a shotgun blast through a pumpkin. Tiny hunks of giant flesh and bone showered the air. The giant headless body fell over.

Smoke discarded the rocket launching-cylinder. "Kinda cool. Kinda gross."

Standing behind him, Sid wrapped her arms around his waist. "I'll take it." Her knees buckled.

Smoke held her steady. "What's going on?"

"I took a vitamin. It's wearing off."

"Well, we aren't going to have time to lie down and take a nap. Can you make it?"

"I don't have a choice. I'm just going to have to summon all the superhero powers I have left."

"Or take another pill."

"We'll see." She surveyed the carnage. The lights were busted and hanging from the ceiling. A filmy layer of smoke rolled through the room. Bodies lay piled up to the knees in carnage. "I don't see Manson anywhere. Do you think they took him hostage?"

"I lost track of him." Smoke vanished into the container and came out with a weapons chest. He also had the Arabian sword sheathed behind his shoulders. "We'll find him or he'll find us. For now, we need to stick with the plan and disable the pyramid server. It sounded like Vormus did his part. Did you hear that explosion earlier?"

Fingering her ears as she rolled her jaw, she said, "I'm pretty sure I heard everything. Man, there's nothing worse than the sound of gunfire blasting away inside a hollow can." She dug into the weapons chest and reloaded her clips. She packed C4 into a rucksack and shouldered it. "We need to get moving."

The parking garage door opened. Men were shouting and barking orders from the other side. Sid and Smoke stepped into full view of the gap that led out into the night.

Stiff-legged deaders rushed down the ramp, followed by pea coat guards armed with guns.

Smoke raised his assault rifle and fired. The bullets tore into the dual motors of the huge garage door. The steel door dropped, crushing a deader and a man beneath it.

From one knee, Sid took aim with her rifle. She squeezed off short burst after short burst. The bullets ripped through the chests of two deaders. They dropped, flopped, and lay still. The next pair of bullets pierced the brains of the last two pea coats. "That's the last of them," she said. The barrel of her gun smoked. The enemy's hands were at the bottom of the garage door, lifting it again. She sent a spray of bullets their way. The door dropped on the bodies. Painful howls came from the other side. "They're going to keep coming. We need to get going. What are you doing?"

Smoke was down on a knee, taping a cluster of stun grenades together. "I'm making a gizmo."

"Like a MacGyver gizmo?"

"Sort of, but mine is just a tad deadlier than the Comet-and-peroxide bombs he mixes." He uncoiled some tripwire, attached it to the pins on the grenades, and wedged the cluster bomb between some bodies. "Come on."

They entered the stairwell just as the garage door opened again. A surge of men and deaders rushed into the room. Smoke and Sid took cover behind the fire exit door. Bullets riddled the metal door. Lead smashed through the door's safety glass. The guards and deaders hustled down the ramp, pointing and firing. They stepped over the cluster bomb.

"Perfect," Smoke said. He yanked the trip wire. Nothing happened. He looked at Sid and said in a Marvin the Martian voice, "Where's the kaboom? There's supposed to be an earth-shattering kaboom."

The enemy charged right at them.

CHAPTER 30

Hunkered down beside Smoke, Sid pulled the pin from a hand grenade. "Here, try this."

A broad smile crossed Smoke's lips. "Aw, how did you know this was exactly what I wanted?" He cracked open the door and yelled, "Did somebody order a pineapple?" He flipped it out and closed the door.

The grenade exploded.

Boom! Kaboom! Kaboom! Kaboom!

"Ah, there's the earth-shattering kaboom." Smoke said. "It just needed a little nudging."

Sid couldn't see anything but smoke through the narrow glass window. "We need to go."

"After you."

There were three options: Upstairs, through a door into the basement, or downstairs into the subbasement. Sid took the steps down. According to Manson, that was where the main server was that needed to be destroyed. They made it down one level. The stairwell ended at another fire door.

Smoke opened the door.

Sid did a head check into the hallway. "Clear."

They slipped into the corridor. Only the emergency and exit lights illuminated the hall, which went straight about fifty feet and then crossed at a four-way intersection. Nothing aside from them stirred.

"It's feeling a little stuffy," Sid said.

Smoke held his hand up to a return air vent. "I believe Vormus actually did his job. How surprising."

"And you said never to trust a shifter."

"I still don't."

On cats' feet, they hustled down the hallway. Halfway down it were two doors, one across from the other. The doors weren't marked, and they required security access. According to Manson, the server should be in the western corner, the farthest from the garage.

Smoke lingered by the first door they came to.

"The server is this way," Sid said.

"We need to go in here."

"Why?"

"Because they'll be expecting us in the server room."

Looking at the door Smoke wanted to enter, she said, "Maybe they're expecting us in this room."

"Humor me." He pointed his weapon at the door.

Sid shoved his gun aside. "We don't have to blow up everything. Geez, I thought you were sneakier than that." She dangled an access card in front of his eyes. "See? Sneaky."

"Where'd you get that?"

"I lifted it from Samone when I dislocated her arm." She scanned the card. The security light went from red to green. "After you."

Inside was a network of huge floor-to-ceiling metal pipes. The pipes were sweaty, and the room was filled with a suffocating humidity.

Smoke snuck through the steam. He grabbed the wheel handle on one of the valves and turned it counterclockwise. He did the same with several others. Coming back to Sid, he said, "It's going to get hot in here. It's going to get hot everywhere."

She wiped the sweat from her brow with her fingertips and opened the door across from the one they had just entered. "Oh my."

Smoke stuck his head in the door. "Ditto."

Rows of living bodies lay sunken in metal carts. The lights were low and throbbing with the rhythm of a heartbeat. The people lay in pools of a transparent golden fluid. Their faces were connected to breathing apparatus. Limbs were hooked up to strange I.V. bags. The macabre lab pulsated with weird glowing tubes, and wires ran in coils that stretched up to the ceiling like snakes.

Smoke and Sid inspected the rows.

There were dozens of bodies ranging from heavyset men to petite women. Eyes closed, their features were unlively. She studied face after face with her stomach in knots. "This is sick, Smoke."

Smoke's hard stare was focused on one of the bodies. "Sicker than you think."

His dark tone brought her toward him. "What's wrong? Is it someone we know?"

"Afraid so."

She glanced down. It was hard to make out the face on account of all the slime, but suddenly it became crystal clear. She let out a sharp gasp.

CHAPTER 31

I T WAS HER OLD FBI director and friend Ted Howard.

Sid's body went numb. "I buried him, Smoke. I mourned with his family." She stuck her hand in the goo. "I can feel his heart beating. Dammit!" Tears streamed down her face. "I can't take much more of this maddening world!"

Smoke took her by the waist and pulled her to him. Holding her tight, he said, "I know what you mean. But Sid, they're alive."

"They're attached to some sick and twisted machine." She forced herself out of Smoke's hands so she could go up and down the rows searching all the faces. She found Asia's face half buried in the goo. "It's Asia."

"Mal will be thrilled."

Gathering herself, Sid said, "I kinda like her quiet like this. She's so peaceful." She made her way down one row after the other, noting a few more faces she knew. One was an FBI agent whose name she forgot. Another was a female news anchor from television. She discovered the face of another man she knew all too well. "It's Senator Wilhelm."

From across the room, Smoke said, "Yeah, and he's not the only senator here."

"Are you serious? No wonder this country's leadership is so screwed up." She glared at Wilhelm. She hated the man and his son on account of all they had done to her sister. But that relationship had been going on for a long time. *How long has this madness been going on?* "We need to find Manson."

"We need to shut down the server," Smoke said. His gaze was fixed on another body. "Oh man."

Stooped over Wilhelm, Sid leaned back. "What?"

With his palms on the table, Smoke said, "It's Rebecca Lang."

"No way." Sid walked over for a look. It was the petite woman, covered from head to toe in the goo. "But last time we saw her, she was pregnant."

"There's no bulge in her belly now," Smoke said. "A pregnant clone. Now that's weird."

"At least now we know why she's always been such a pain in the ass."

Looking at all the odd wiring that covered the room like modern webbing, Sid slung some goo from her hand. "This reminds me of that scene in *The Matrix*. We've got to get them unplugged."

The main lights flickered on.

"That would be to their peril," a voice said.

Sid and Smoke whirled. Titus Tolliver, in full gargoyle form, stood in the doorway adjacent to the one they came in. The husky creature had a triumphant look on his face. "They are in a fragile state. If you do anything to change it, you will kill them."

"Maybe they'd rather be dead," Smoke said. "I figure we'd be doing them a favor."

The gargoyle slunk deeper into the room. He dipped his stony fingers into one of the patients' pools. The demon-faced man glowered at Smoke. "You don't want to play God with their lives, do you, Mister Smoke? I thought you wanted to saves lives, not take them."

"Anything is better than leaving them in your hands," Smoke said. "I'll take my chances with my maker."

Titus shrugged his brawny shoulders. His approach was slow and steady. "You might just be meeting your maker sooner than you think." He kept coming right at them.

Smoke and Sid backed toward the door they came in.

She lowered her weapon. The last thing she wanted to do was hit these people with friendly fire. Judging by the look in Titus's eyes, he was here to kill her and Smoke if he couldn't take them down. Using Smoke as a shield, she turned to back out the door. Taking a peek, she saw that the hallway was empty. Suddenly her arms and legs tired out. She felt like the only thing keeping her together was the sweetheart suit. Shoulders sagging, it was all she could do to take a breath. The supervitamin's effect had completely worn off. The adrenaline that had gotten her this far was gone too. She just wanted to sleep.

"Where are you going?" Titus said. He followed them out into the hallway. "I thought we were having a friendly conversation." He closed the door behind him. Holding his finger to his lips he said, "Ssssh! We don't want to wake them."

"You talk too much for a gargoyle." Smoke put his assault rifle up to his shoulder and took aim. "I put you down last time with these bullets. Take one more step and I'll do the same."

Titus waggled his finger. "You caught me off guard last time. It won't happen again. My skin is impenetrable." He shrugged. "Besides, you should know I cannot die."

"That's what the giants thought. Did you see what's left of them?" Sid said.

"I'm not one to look back. I'm forward thinking." Titus stepped forward.

Smoke squeezed off two single shots in rapid succession. The concussive force of the exploding rounds shook the walls and flickered the lights.

Titus still stood. A grin formed on his big-eared, broad-nosed face. "You see? I was ready. I am ready for anything. Gargoyles, attack!"

A bat-like screech echoed down the hall. Small gargoyles rounded the corner behind them. The two-foot-high monsters raced toward Sid and Smoke on foot and with wings.

"I'll take the big one, you take the small ones!" Smoke said.

Exhausted, Sid wheeled her weapon around and started shooting out a spray of ammo. The bullets ripped through the first wave of gargoyles, blasting through their screaming bodies and blowing them up like pottery. She blasted off their rage-riddled faces. Bullets tore through legs, wings, and bodies.

A gargoyle hopped at her on one good leg.

With her weapon, she turned it to powder.

Still they came. High and low they attacked.

They latched onto her ankles. A small, hard fist smote the back of her head. One of the little monsters rode on her shoulders, pulling her hair. Using the butt of her weapon, she cracked the ones on her legs in the skulls. Noses and ears came off.

How do these things live? It's impossible.

The monsters swarmed her. They attached themselves with clawed fingers and toes, blanketing her like a net. She sagged under the great weight. They bit, struck, and clawed. With a growl, she rammed the ones she could into the wall but went down in a sea of flesh-rending gargoyle grey.

CHAPTER 32

S MOKE UNLOADED THE ENTIRE CLIP of bullets into Titus in a cadence of tiny explosions.

The gargoyle man stumbled backward on his heels and fell to the floor, then rose with a nasty look and dusted off his burly chest. "That made for quite the finale, Mister Smoke. Too bad it did not have the climax you hoped for." He stormed through the white vapors.

Chucking the weapon aside, Smoke drew one of the special knives from its sheath. He'd fought the gargoyle once before and almost died. Now he had to match the juggernaut in even more confined quarters. He needed to find its weakness.

Titus lashed out with his clawed hands.

Smoke ducked. Striking fast, he jabbed the special blade at the gargoyle's ribs. The blade slid in deep, drawing forth a howl.

Titus staggered backward holding his side. "You wounded me! You wounded me! You've found my weakness. It's my ribs! Oh, the pain! The suffering! The anguish!"

Smoke backed off, watching the gargoyle with wary eyes. "You aren't really hurt, are you."

Titus pulled the knife out with a smile, tossed it aside. "Of course not. I'm the total package."

"True, but Arabian steel can cut your skin."

"It can cut, but it can't kill. You see, I don't bleed, Mister Smoke." He punched his fist into his hand. "But you can, and you will. I'm going to turn your body and that suit you treasure into a bag of bloody smashed potatoes. I can't wait to make your bones snap and pop."

Smoke removed the sword strapped to his back. "Don't forget crackle."

Titus's eyes narrowed on the sword. "Where did you get that?"

"It's a little something I picked up at the gargoyle killer thrift shop." He spun the blade in his hands. The balance was perfect, the edge keen. He drew it two-handed to his chest. "And they even gave me the riddle steel for free."

"You're a fool if you think that blade can stop me."

"Not the blade, but the hand that wields it."

"Shut up!" Titus charged.

Smoke went into a zone. Springing forward with the sword, he chopped down hard. The blade removed Titus's right arm at the elbow.

The gargoyle barreled into Smoke like a charging bull, knocking him to the floor. Titus hammered away with his good hand. His heavy punches rocked Smoke's body.

Smoke clocked Titus in the chin with his knee and squirmed free. He popped up on his feet.

Titus rose up in a deadly crouch.

Smoke hacked into him like a berserker. The heavy blade carved into the gargoyle. Hunks of stony flesh flew. Smoke kept swinging.

Titus surged into him like a force of nature.

Both man and monster were in a maddened state of battle.

The Arabian steel sawed through Titus in another arc. A nasty strike split his skull down to the nose. Smoke ripped the steel free.

Punching at Smoke with powerful stabs, Titus said in defiance, "You cannot kill me."

"We'll see!" Smoke tore into the beleaguered gargoyle with a chop that split his knee.

Titus stumbled to the floor. Helpless agony filled his face. "No," he pleaded. He shielded his head with his arms. "Stop!"

Smoke didn't relent. With both hands he brought he sword down hard and quick.

Chop! Chop! Chop!

The gargoyle shifter had nothing left to fight with. He glared at Smoke. "I hate mortals!"

"Then I won't keep your dead brother waiting." Smoke turned the sword loose for a final blow. The blade whistled through the air.

Titus's head rolled from his shoulders. It bounced off the floor and rolled across the room before it lay still.

The smaller gargoyles collapsed all around Sid, and she lay with her face covered by her arms but bleeding. She kicked the inanimate stone monsters away. "Get off me!"

Smoke rushed over, dropped the sword, and took her by the hand. "It's over."

She fought against him.

He held her fast. "Sid, it's me."

Her eyes found his face. "Is he dead?"

"I think we're getting the hang of killing them." He moved aside, revealing Titus's body. The monster had transformed back into a man that didn't bleed so much as ooze. He combed her hair back from her eyes. "Can you move?"

"Barely. Help me up."

Smoke complied. Sid was about as banged up as he'd ever seen her. She had bad scratches all over her face. Her lip was split, and blood dripped from her chin. "Lean on me if you need to."

"No." She checked her weapons, filling her hands with two pistols. She limped down the hall. "Let's find the damn server and blow the hell out of it." She passed through the intersection, made it to the next door, and scanned the card.

Smoke opened the door. It was the electrical room, steel panels locked up with heavy padlocks. "Looks like you found home base for the electric, fire, and security systems."

"Shoot it. Shoot it all." She fired.

Smoke fired.

Bullets tore through steel. Alarms and lights went on and then out.

Smoke eased inside and set a charge of C4 along the largest conduit he could find. He hustled back out and closed the door. "Get down."

They both crouched.

Smoke triggered the detonator, unleashing a tremendous *boom*. All the lights went out.

"I'd love to go to sleep in this dark, hot mess," Sid said. The emergency and exit lights came on. "How cozy."

"They've got a backup generator running somewhere. I can hear the hum, but those emergency lights are on battery power."

Sid crawled over to the next door. The security keypad lights were still on. She scanned the card and went through the door. Icy air greeted her like the coming winter. "Morning glory, feels good." She and Smoke spilled inside. "Man, look at that thing."

Behind a ten-foot-high Plexiglas shield sat a huge computer server shaped like a pyramid. It was at least ten feet square at the base and stood ten feet high at the top. It was black with brilliant illuminating circuitry that coursed through tight veins of pulsating energy. The colors varied and changed, pulsating to a beat like the heart inside a titan's body.

Smoke made his way over to a control center that stood inside the massive room all by itself. The fifty-inch computer screen showed black. He pecked at the keyboard and shuffled the mouse. A moving image popped up on the screen. It was Kane and Allison. The burly blond man with long curls in his stringy hair had a smirk on his face. Allison appeared as voluptuous as ever in her skintight navy bodysuit.

"Hello," Kane said. "I see you made it to the server room. Well done. As you can see, the server room can be very chilly. 'Course, those elements aren't any concern for the likes of us. Hot or cold, it doesn't matter. And as you can see, the server is operating just fine. You blew up the wrong targets."

Smoke heard the door they came in latch shut.

"Oh, and the card you used to get in won't let you back out." Kane chuckled. "It's good to see you again, Sidney, but you're not looking so well. You look like you need to cool off."

An icy mist sprayed out of the sprinkler system that hung above them.

"Enjoy your hibernation, John and Sidney Smoke. Perhaps a few years in suspended animation will be enough time to let you think about things. In the meantime, your clones will be quite useful in the continuance of our operation. Good night." The screen went black.

"Man, I hate that guy," Sid said with a shiver.

Smoke yawned. His eyes became heavy. His vision blurred. He said in forced speech, "All of a sudden I feel like the Cowardly Lion in the field outside the Emerald City."

CHAPTER 33

S ID TOTTERED ON HER FEET and bumped into Smoke.

He steadied her by holding her beneath her armpits. "Do you know how to clear a gas mask?"

"What?" she said with her head drooping over her shoulders. Her eyelids were drooping, too.

In Smoke's long fingers were a pair of black breathing apparatuses, something like what you'd see in an airplane. He stretched the black surgical cords over her head and snapped the cup over her mouth. He stuck another apparatus over his head, covering his mouth and nose, saying, "Breathe out! Breathe out!" He covered the filters on his mask and, blinking really hard, he exhaled.

Sid fell on the floor, staring up at the ceiling.

I don't want to breathe out. I just want to sleep.

A blurry Smoke leaned over her and attached something to her mask.

As she breathed in short gasps, her languid lungs came to life. The image of Smoke's face sharpened as she sucked in more mouthfuls of air.

Smoke took her by the arm and sat her up. He gave her a firm shake. "Sorry, hun, naptime is over. They think we're asleep. Now's the time to move."

The mist stopped spraying out of the sprinklers.

"Just get me up to my feet," she said. With Smoke's assistance, she finally made it back up. Her arms and legs burned with pins and needles. She shook them. "You didn't regurgitate this mask, did you?"

"No comment." He pulled his mask away from his face and sniffed the air.

"What are you doing?" She tried to shove the mask back onto his face.

"It's clear now." He wiped his nose. "It smells a little funny though." Using the mask, he covered the camera mounted on top of the monitor Kane had spoken from earlier and turned his attention to the pyramid server. From his satchel, he took out block after block of C4 and set them on the desk. "We need to plant this stuff before they show up."

Sid hit the Plexiglas wall that protected the server. It didn't even shudder. "Don't you think it's indestructible? It's inches thick."

"These shifters say everything is indestructible," Smoke said, slapping the C4 into the seams where the glass met with the concrete ceiling, "but the only indestructible thing I know of in this world is my love for you."

Sid stopped what she was doing, and with a smile she said, "Aw, how sweet. Moments like this remind me why I so enjoy blowing things up with you."

Smoke chuckled. With a fierce grin, he attached a disk the size of his fist to the glass in the center of the four charges he had set. He depressed a button. A tiny yellow light flared, and the disc let out a charging whine.

"What is that?" Sid said.

"It's a sonic disrupter. It sends high-frequency sound waves into the glass. It works like a tuning fork. It's not powerful enough to shatter the glass on its own, but hopefully it will weaken the structure just enough for the nasty plastique to do the rest."

Nodding, she said, "I like it. You think of everything."

Smoke stuck the detonation caps into the C4. "Yeah, well, they're overconfident. That's their weakness to exploit."

"And what's your weakness?" she said, taking him by the waist and digging her nails into his ribs. Sid didn't know why she did it, but she tried to tickle him. For some reason, Smoke was driving her crazy right now. The ease and purpose with which he moved made her heart flutter. "Am I your weakness?"

"No, you're my strength." He squeezed her hand in his as he stared at his handiwork. "That ought to do it."

The security latches on the doors to the room popped.

"Time to play possum," he said, crouching on the floor.

"You like this game entirely too much," she said, lowering herself. "Why don't we just beat the crap out of the pea coats when they come?"

Smoke shrugged. "The lady makes the call."

Together they hid out of sight behind the computer station and waited. Within a minute the door and the one adjacent to it opened. Sid could see a pair of pea coats armed with machine guns slip into the room, their hard eyes searching the floor. She pointed in the direction of the two she could see.

Smoke nodded.

Weapons ready, they popped up from behind the computer console and fired off two quick shots.

Two guards dropped dead with bullet holes in their heads.

"Status report?" said a voice on the radio gripped in one guard's hand.

Smoke glided over and picked it up. "All secure. We have the persons detained." He smiled at Sid.

She could see playfulness come to life in his eyes. "Don't, Smoke."

"Also," Smoke continued, "One of the prisoners is really hot. Can you check her marital status? I'm not having much luck on my Matchmaker account."

The voice came over the radio. "Who is this?"

Silently, Sid mouthed the words to Smoke, "Don't say it."

In a rugged voice, he replied in the radio, "I'm Batman." He chucked the radio aside and resumed his normal voice. "Let's go."

Live video of Kane and Allison appeared on the monitor again. Their faces were filled with curiosity as their eyes scanned the room.

Smoke removed the gas mask from the camera and waved at them. "Hi!"

Sid popped her head in. "Hey!"

Together they waved.

Smoke turned the computer camera around, facing the server. He backed up and pointed to the C4. "You might want to cover those big ears of yours, Kane, because your server is about to go boom. Bye bye now!"

Kane's eyebrows knitted.

Smoke and Sid left the images of Kane and Allison screaming at the top of their lungs and hustled out of the room. They sprinted down the corridor, made a turn around the intersection, stopped, and turned.

Smoke held up the detonator. "Would you like to have the honor?"

She grabbed his hand in hers. "Let's do it together."

They hit the switch.

Boom!

CHAPTER 34

S ID WALKED OVER THE INTERIOR carnage that lay on the floor. Her boots crunched over stone. The pyramid server room was toast. The walls were bowed out. The drywall was dust. The doors had been blown from their hinges. Every speck of organization had been erased. The charred cement ceiling crumbled. The center computer console had become nothing but scrap and microbits.

The only things standing were the server and the clear wall surrounding it.

The clear finish of the glass was blackened by scorch marks, but it stood. The glass had cracked all over with spidery veins from top to bottom. She could still see the server glowing with life on the other side.

"I can't believe it," she said as she felt her heart deflate.

"Don't believe everything you see." Smoke walked up to the shield glass and poked it with his finger. Fragments of glass fell like frosty snowflakes.

Chin up, Sid moved forward and hit the glass wall with the butt of her handgun. The glass dropped in larger ice-like chunks. "Screw this," she said, checking her weapon's clip. It was filled with blue-tipped bullets. "Back up."

"You're the boss," Smoke said, stepping aside with a grin.

Sid blasted a ring of bullets the size of her head through the glass. With a kick, she knocked the circle of glass out. Looking up at Smoke, she said, "Got any more—"

"Pineapples?" Smoke handed her two grenades. She pulled the pins and tossed them through the hole. She and Smoke took cover behind a long stretch of board that had been part of the computer console. "This better do it."

A muffled *boom* was followed by the tinkling of shattering glass.

Rising from behind their protection, Sid could see the pyramid server burning.

The pulsating lights of its living network went out. The entire building fell silent. It was as if the heartbeat of the building had stopped.

Sid rested her forehead on Smoke's shoulder. "Finally. Whew! I didn't think we would ever kill that thing."

"Huh, I was starting to doubt it too."

"We need to go check on Ted and the others." She ran out of the room, down the hall, and back into the laboratory. Many bodies shuddered inside the bounds. A gaunt figure had his back to Sid.

"Hey!" she said, firing a warning shot. "Hands where I can see them! Get away from there!"

"I'm reaching for the sky," the man said as he slowly turned. It was Vormus. "Is this high enough?"

"Just back away," she said.

Manson appeared from behind Vormus. He was the blond-headed, blue-eyed boy again. With restless energy, he said, "We have to disconnect all of them now! Yank every cord and breathing apparatus you can find. Without the computer giving the orders, their bodies will shut down and die." He yanked the tube out of one man's mouth and plucked the cables connected to the man's head. "Their bodies need to awaken!"

On a motherly instinct more than following orders, Sid did as requested. She went from body to body, yanking out the slimy tubes and macabre wiring. She found Asia and set her free, saying, "Asia, wake up."

All the little woman did was blink.

Smoke entered and did the same. Many of the people coughed and sputtered. Some convulsed. "This one looks like she's having a heart attack." It was Rebecca Lang. "What do I do?"

"Nothing," Manson said with his head down at the task at hand. "There's no guarantee they can adjust to the real world again. Just keep doing what you're doing."

Sid kept at it. She caught Smoke's eye.

His face was stern. He said to her with a quick nod, "Survivors survive."

Finally she was at Ted Howard's cart, and she removed the breathing tube from his mouth. Her quick hands pulled the needles from his head. "Oh, Ted," she said, holding his cheek.

The husky man's body trembled. He shook the cart so hard it scraped over the floor. His chest jumped. He coughed and hacked. His forearms strained against his restraints.

"Manson! Get over here! This is bad! None of the others resisted like this."

Manson hopped clear over a table and landed right beside her. He stuck his hands in the goo and cupped Ted's straining neck. "Oh my, this isn't good. I believe he actually is in cardiac arrest." He shrugged. "Sorry, Sid, it happens."

"Sorry my ass!" Sid shoved Manson to the floor. Immediately she started giving Ted chest compressions. "Come on, Ted, Come on! You can't die on me now!"

Ted's body went still.

"Nooo!" she screamed. She kept pressing on his chest. After all this time, she couldn't believe Ted was still alive.

The one who died must have been a clone!

It had hurt so much when she'd lost him the last time that she couldn't stand to lose him again. "Ted, your family needs you! I need you! Fight, Ted!" Tears streaming down her face, she alternated between chest compressions and mouth-to-mouth breathing.

His body didn't move.

Smoke grabbed her arm and tried to pull her away.

She shrugged him off. "No!"

Putting his strength behind it, Smoke pulled her back. "He's gone, Sid. I'm sorry."

Every last ounce of strength she had fled her. She collapsed into Smoke's chest, crying and sobbing. She pounded on his chest. "Why?"

Smoke didn't have the answer. He held her upright in his strong arms. "Let's help the others."

"I can't bury him again, John. I can't." She stared back at Ted. He lay in the table goo, lifeless as a mannequin. "No person should have to go through this. What am I supposed to say to his family?"

"So far as they know, he died with honor. I'd leave it that way."

"But that's not the truth. He died like this."

"He lived with honor. That's what matters. It's the truth."

"Let's just try one more thing, shall we?" Manson had a huge metal syringe in his hand and held it over Ted's chest. "Normally, I wouldn't do this, but somehow all this sappiness got to me. But no more blubbering if it doesn't work."

"What is that?" Sid said as she turned and wiped the tears from her eyes.

"This isn't the first time these bodies have had spasms. Every once in a while we have to reboot them. This is my version of an intracardiac injection. Lots of adrenaline. But your friend is old and has a bad heart, probably from too much chili fries and beer, so don't go harping on me if it doesn't work. He's better off dead if you ask me. How would you explain his revival?" He poised the needle over Ted's chest. "Well?"

"Do it!"

CHAPTER 35

MANSON PLUNGED THE NEEDLE INTO Ted's chest. His thumb pressed the fluid down, and Ted's body leaped parallel off the table, where it flopped like a fish out of water and steadied. His eyes were wide open. His lips mumbled.

Sid leaned over him. "Ted, it's me, Sid."

Ted spat goo. "What the hell happened? I feel like a car ran over my chest." His soft eyes darted around. "Where the hell am I?"

She said to Manson, "He's awfully alert."

"It's the adrenaline. It'll wear off. He breathes…for now."

"We need to get him out of here. We need to get them all out of here. Ted, what's the last thing you remember?"

Blinking rapidly, he said, "Eating pizza and drinking beer. Why? Did I have a heart attack? That's it, isn't it. I had a heart attack." He found Smoke looking at him. "Oh, it's you. Smoke, right? Everything's hazy." He strained against his bonds. "Why am I tied up? And why am I covered in pea soup? Sid, what's going on?"

"I'll fill you in on the way home," she said. All over the room, the awakened people began to stir. One woman fell off her cart. It was Rebecca Lang. "Manson, can they walk?"

"Not well. They haven't used their limbs in months. Some haven't moved for years. They might be awake, but I'm not certain we can just waltz them out of here. Let's not forget there's a horde of deaders and pea coats out there, wanting to rip us all apart."

"You stay here," Smoke said to Sid. "Vormus and I will check it out. Are you going to be okay?"

She nodded. "I'm not going anywhere without them."

Smoke and Vormus stood inside the garage bay. It was a war zone. Men shot to pieces. Even shifters lay still. Smoke was relieved to see that the giants—Lance, Thorgrim, and Rexor—hadn't moved at all. The only things moving aside from him and Vormus were the deaders. A handful still moved. Their foul bodies lay on the cement floor, struggling to move without the necessary limbs. Smoke finished them off with bullets to the chest.

"You sure made quite a mess," Vormus commented as he stepped over the wreckage.

"You can't clean up evil without getting messy." Before he headed up into the garage, he'd retrieved the Arabian sword and put it back in its sheath. He slid it out again.

Vormus eyed him.

"Just a precaution," Smoke said. He ran up the ramp that led outside into the courtyard of the compound. "Let's go."

The only thing stirring outside was the wind. The guard shack was abandoned, the gate wide open. A fire burned on the rooftop. Smoke did a three-sixty. There had been several cars and trucks in the lot, but now they were gone. Only one single black SUV remained, parked in the front.

"Do you think Kane left?"

Vormus shrugged. "It's hard to say. He's a stubborn man." His eye caught something moving inside the building.

Smoke turned.

A man walked through the glass doors and down the steps. His nice shirt and slacks were torn up. A cigarette burned between his fingers. Half of Reginald's face looked like it had been skinned off. "Pardon the appearance, but explosions tend to do that. An angry Kane does, too." His skin was repairing itself, his svelte look slowly returning. "I've got a message for you. Kane's pissed."

CHAPTER 36

REGINALD CHUCKLED. "MY, I'VE NEVER seen Kane so angry. You know, that's a rare thing when you make a shifter angry. Normally, our polished resolve does not come unfettered, but today, well, things got ugly."

"So, are you here to congratulate us?" Smoke asked. "Is there going to be a trophy ceremony?"

"Such a clever tongue, Smoke." Reginald flicked off the ashes of his cigarette. "It's that stand-up routine I like about you. But no, you won't be getting any kind of trophy for your achievement. But I have to admit, I never thought you would be able to take that server down. Your fortitude is incredible. Kane literally jumped up and down screaming when the pyramid exploded. I found it amusing, myself." Keeping his distance from his adversaries, he walked over to a light pole and leaned against it. He lit another cigarette. "You managed to wreck decades of work—in an extremely bold move, I might add. 'Course, you had some unique help." He eyed Vormus.

"Changing sides gave my hollow life a dash of flavor," Vormus replied.

"Vormus, you can't undo what you've done. You know that. He's just leading you along, Smoke. That leopard won't change his spots. Once his zeal for entertainment is over, he'll come back to the brood. This isn't the first time he's tried something like this, you know. He did the same thing with Guermo."

Smoke gave Vormus a look. He didn't trust the shifter as far as he could throw him, and he always watched his back. He wouldn't be one bit surprised if Vormus turned on him at any moment. He focused back on Reginald. "So what's the end game? If there's no trophy, then why are you here?"

Reginald puffed out a smoke ring. "To kill you. To kill you both."

"You against us?" Smoke said. He tapped the tip of his sword on the pavement. "I like those odds. I've developed a knack for killing shifters."

"Yes, you have conquered many. Kudos to you. But no, I don't plan to battle you in a melee contest. It's your soul I want to slay." Reginald pushed off the lamppost. "You see, you actually have achieved something quite devastating. You wiped out the clones. Oh, I can't imagine the horror that has erupted all over DC. Just think about it. All of the clones that have been so carefully planted out there have lost their connection to the computer."

He removed a phone from his pocket and eyed the screen. "These little things have made our jobs so much easier. Hah! Listen to these headlines." He cleared his throat. "Mayor Roslyn's speech turns into a babbling nightmare. Police Chief Bannon drops dead. Congressman Agnew races naked in the streets. Oh, a streaker. Now that's funny, but hardly anything shocking from the political ilk. But eh. Just you wait and see, all this current news popping up tonight will be wiped clean tomorrow. Don't you understand, mortal? *WE* control everything. The secret wars we fight have been witnessed by countless eyes, yet the truth is still hidden from the public. You might win one battle, but in the end, you're still going to lose the war. The Drake always wins."

Smoke stepped forward. "You didn't win tonight."

"Don't hoist your trophy up over your head so soon, Smoke. Even though you've proven you have a knack for being one step ahead in most things, you'll never be a step ahead in everything. We aren't so overconfident that we lack a contingency plan." He held out his phone. "As you can see, I have a phone, and with this phone I can do many things. I can call Kane. Order pizza. Play a mind-numbing game. Or I can detonate explosives. You're familiar with explosives, aren't you? Why yes you are. You've been blowing up a lot of things." Reginald pecked on the screen. "But we have bombs in place as well. You see, if the operation of the Drake were ever discovered, we would have to destroy all evidence. So it's armed with explosives."

"You're bluffing."

"No, I'm not. If your little helper Manson was as smart as he thought, he would have known this entire facility could be detonated from outside. You didn't have to smash in here like a bunch of angry pirates. You could have used some sophistication." He flicked his cigarette away. "Anyhow, the entire roomful of people you rescued are nothing but hostages now. That goes for your wife and all her precious friends." He shrugged. "Now, there's a remote chance she'll survive the explosion with the suit on, but I don't think she or anyone else will make it out when the building collapses right on top of them. It will be a crushing defeat."

"I will finish you one way or the other."

"You're perfectly fine with all those people dying when you could save them?" Reginald hitched up a brow. "No, you couldn't live with it. Just imagine the thought of never seeing your wife alive again. No more hugs. No kisses. No making love at the beach. The very love of your life buried in one of the heaviest tombs ever. How sad."

Smoke's fingers twitched. His grip on the sword tightened.

Reginald continued as he paced with an easy stride. "And think about your baby. You'll never get to hold your baby."

"What are you talking about now?"

"Oh, what a surprise, the man with an uncanny ability to be a step ahead of everything doesn't know his own wife is pregnant? Perhaps she doesn't want you to know. How interesting. Perhaps because it's not your baby. Perhaps it's Kane's."

Smoke had his suspicions to begin with. Sid had shown signs of morning sickness several times. "If the child is Kane's, I don't think he would want to see the baby in the grave."

"That's where you're wrong. Kane's sired many, and they're all dead. Typically, neither the woman nor the baby survives the birthing process. If they did, shifters would be everywhere. Wouldn't that be glorious?"

"Is this true?" he said to Vormus.

"Neither of us have any children."

According to Manson, Vormus, and Mal, the shifters couldn't breed with each other, but every once in a while a female shifter would be impregnated by a mortal male. In rare cases the baby could survive. That was the theory behind Smoke and Sid, that they were shifter offspring. The thought of his mother or Sid's mother being a shifter made him sick. "What do you want, Reginald? Or rather, what does Kane want?"

"Surrender and come with me, willingly, to meet Kane."

"And if I don't?"

Reginald held up the phone. "Then your family dies."

CHAPTER 37

Surrender. It wasn't ever part of Smoke's modus operandi. He set the sword on the ground. "I agree, but I want to see everyone out safely first."

"But. Such a troublesome word. But—just this once—I'll reward it in good faith." Reginald gave a sharp whistle. Nestled in the hedges that hugged the building was Swift Venison the were-rat. He slipped out of the bushes wearing nothing but a pair of pants. His fuzzy chest and arms rippled with knots of muscle. He slinked beside Reginald, wringing his pinkish, long-nailed hands. "What is your bidding?"

"Make sure he doesn't have a weapon on him. Vormus, step aside."

Vormus complied.

Venison padded over. With eyes like coal orbs, he picked over Smoke's body, removing the gear belt and, before tossing it aside, snapping on a pair of flex cuffs. "I hate these things." He secured Smoke's hands crossed behind his back with the cuffs. He pulled them tight.

Smoke winced.

Venison touched Smoke's cold ear with his nose. "Uncomfortable, isn't it?"

Smoke lifted his shoulders.

The were-rat shoved Smoke's head aside, reached down, and picked up the sword. He brought the edge to Smoke's throat. "If it were up to me, I'd be done with you. One swing and I'd turn your head into a bloody kickball."

"That's enough, Venison," Reginald warned. "Kane doesn't want him harmed. Maybe roughed up a bit."

"Roughed up?" Venison clacked his teeth together really fast. His long whiskers brushed Smoke's cheek. "Thanks to you, I was stuck in the hole!" He cocked back his elbow and punched Smoke in the gut. The blow lifted Smoke up on his toes.

Smoke groaned. "You hit awfully hard for a rat. A girl rat."

Venison's tail coiled around Smoke's neck and squeezed his face red.

"That's enough!" Reginald ordered. "Just pat him down and take him to the car. Buckle him into the front seat and keep a gun on his head." He turned his attention to Vormus. "Go ahead and fetch your friends."

Chin up and eyes down on Reginald, Vormus floated away with a sneer and vanished into the garage.

Smoke took a seat in the car. The leather squeaked under him.

Venison buckled him in. He kept the gun barrel on Smoke's temple. "Just give me a reason. Any reason at all. I'd love to blast a tunnel through your head."

"And I'd still have more between my ears than you do now, rat. Tell me, why'd you choose to be a rat? Was it a natural affection for waste and filth?"

Venison peeked over at Reginald. He was on the phone with his back turned. Venison punched Smoke in the jaw. "Shut up!"

The were-rat walked around the SUV and crawled into the driver's seat, started the engine, dropped the shifter into drive, and pulled up alongside Reginald, hitching his elbow out the window. "We've got them now. Just blow the rest up. Kane won't be mad. If anything, he'll be glad."

"Don't be an imbecile, Venison. Now turn the car around so she can get a good look at him."

As soon as Vormus entered the room, Sid said, "Where's Smoke?"

"He's outside with Reginald."

"Reginald!" She rushed toward the doors.

Vormus blocked her exit.

She stuck a gun in his face. "Get out of my way!"

"At least let me tell you what to expect."

"I'll pass."

"I insist. Apparently, this building is set for detonation. Reginald holds the trigger. In exchange for your safety and everyone else's, Smoke agreed to become Kane's prisoner."

"No! I'm not letting that happen."

"It's too late," Vormus said. "Your husband made his decision. If he's not gone yet, he'll be gone as soon as you get there. I recommend you stay here. Kane won't kill you, but he'll backtrack and kill the rest of them." He eyed the people stirring in their troughs of goo. Many of them were sitting up and talking.

Manson eyed the ceiling. "You don't want all that blood on your hands."

Sid took a quick glance back. She shook her head. "No, I've got to see him."

Vormus stepped aside.

Sid raced away.

He said to Manson as he eyeballed the ceiling, "Do you really think this entire building is wired to explode?"

"That's what I would do."

"Then why aren't you running?"

"I'm staying with them," said the man in the child's body. "There are worse ways to go. But I don't know what you're standing around for. Someone needs to protect her."

Sid's long legs ached with every stride. She'd never felt so tired in her life. She pushed up the incline and passed under the ruined inner garage door, which was propped open with a ladder. The short sprint left her winded as she reached the top of the driveway. Hands on hips and sucking for breath, she saw Reginald standing beside the SUV.

Smoke sat in the passenger seat. He winked at her. "Hi, honey."

She approached.

"I'm going to advise you not to come any closer, Mrs. Smoke," Reginald said.

"What's going on?"

"In exchange for your safety and that of those left in the basement, your dear husband has agreed to come with me. And if he doesn't come peacefully," he held up his phone, "boom."

"You're a bastard, Reginald!"

"Don't be upset with me. It's not my plan, it's Kane's. He's quite the control freak, and I have to tell you, you've made him very, very angry. But in the end, he will have what he wants: Smoke."

"I thought he wanted me," she said, easing forward. "Take me instead of him."

"That was the idea in the beginning, but now Kane feels you are tainted. He has a sure thing with Smoke, but there is little to gain with you, seeing how you might only have a few months left to live."

Sid stiffened. "What are you talking about?"

"Your pregnancy. It is almost certain death for a woman who becomes impregnated by a shifter." He shrugged. "One would have figured Kane would be more careful about that."

Skin crawling beneath her suit, she said with curled lips, "You're lying."

"I have no reason to lie. Besides, it was your foul copulations that got you into this mess. You should have been more careful." He opened the back door. "But enjoy today's small victory while you still live. It was quite a blow."

"Wait!"

Reginald closed the door.

"John, don't believe a word he says!"

The SUV moved forward with Smoke's eyes on hers. The window started to roll up, and Smoke said, "If he's a boy, name him after me."

"John!" She ran after the SUV all the way to the gate. The vehicle's red taillights outdistanced her and disappeared around the first bend in the road. The echo of the engine faded. She held her hand to her abdomen. The moments of her being sick rushed through her head. It all came together, and she knew her instincts were true. She dropped to her knees. "Morning glory, I'm pregnant."

CHAPTER 38

"ARE YOU OKAY?' VORMUS ASKED her.

She glanced up. The shifter with long ghostly white hair floated inches above the ground with a backdrop of black cloudy sky behind him. The wind picked up, blowing his hair. Sid's chest tightened as she soaked everything in.

"How did Reginald know I was pregnant?"

"Shifters have heightened senses. My guess is he sensed the extra heartbeat."

"Did you sense it?"

"Yes."

"And you didn't say anything?"

"I honestly didn't think you wanted to hear the news from me, did you? Wouldn't that have spoiled the moment?"

"Not nearly as bad as what Reginald just did. Bastard." With a grunt, she pushed herself up to her feet. "It can't be Kane's baby, can it? It's been too long since I've been with him."

"Shifters run off a different chemistry. It's hard to say who fertilized the condemned egg."

"Don't say that."

"Fertilized?"

"No, condemned." Her eyes followed the road. A void filled her. Smoke was gone. He had made a sacrifice to save her and everyone else. She had a sinking feeling it would be more than just his life. She could still see the window rolling up over his face. His lips were still moving.

Oh crap, he was saying something!

Stunned, she closed her eyes, envisioning the scene again. Watching his lips move over and over again in her mind, she mumbled.

"What are you doing?"

"Ssssh!"

She got it. "Get them out!"

"Get who out?"

"The people who were cloned. Oh crap, we have to get them out of there!" With a surge of new strength, she ran for the building, down the ramp, down the stairwell, and into the room.

With a bad limp, Manson was already leading the people outside. He said to Sid, "We're about to go boom, aren't we."

"I'm not taking any chances." She threw a man's arm over her shoulder and started leading him up the stairwell, yelling, "Vormus!"

Vormus appeared in the fire exit door. "Yes?"

"Help us get them all clear of the building."

"Saving mortals isn't something I'm accustomed to. Be wise and just leave before it's too late."

Standing in the garage, she said, "Really? That's funny, seeing how you aren't as immortal as you think." She pointed at the fallen giants with her chin and then shoved the man she was helping into Vormus's hands. "Everyone dies if we don't get moving."

Taking the man by the waist, he said, "I see your point, but I hardly feel threatened."

The outer garage door dropped—past the one Sid and Smoke had blasted off the motors—sealing them inside. Yellow emergency lights flashed. An alarm sounded over and over with a loud buzzing sound. A computerized female voiced counted down. "Sixty...fifty-nine...fifty-eight..."

Hand to her forehead, Sid said, "It's like a James Bond nightmare."

"James who?"

Sid spotted the shipyard container. "In there! Take the people in there!"

She got Ted to safety and then rushed up the steps with two people attached to her hips. It was like carrying sandbags. "Come on!" she said to the shifters. "You have to help me."

Vormus carried two over his shoulders.

Manson did as well, with a slightly embarrassed shrug at how weak he had tried to seem.

"...Twenty-seven...twenty six..."

Sid got the pair inside and made another run. She passed Manson on the way down. The young boy carried a girl in his arms. "How many more are there?"

"Three."

She made it into the hallway, where a man and a woman were slumped over. The man was the heavyset Augustus Wilhelm. She took a peek into the lab and didn't see a third person inside the room.

"Dammit!" Sid hustled over to Wilhelm and the much smaller lady.

It was Rebecca Lang. She looked at Sid with lucid eyes.

Sid's jaw hung open. "Rebecca, get on my back! Wilhelm, get your sorry ass up those stairs and into the shipping container, or you're going to die!"

Blinking, he said from a sagging jaw, "Where am I?"

"You're about fifteen seconds from hell, you sonuvabitch!" She grabbed his arm. "Now get your ass up!"

Rebecca's lithe arms latched onto Sid's back. She was saying, "Thank you. Thank you."

Somehow, Sid made it up the stairs with both of them. She staggered to the container and dropped them inside.

"...nine...eight...seven..."

"I didn't see a third person down there," she said to Manson.

"I'll take care of it."

"There's no time!"

From behind, Vormus hauled her inside with a fling that sent her sprawling on top of all the others.

Manson and Vormus closed the container doors together, with Manson saying, "Goodbye, Sid." The doors shut and sealed. Her world became pitch black. Outside was the sound of the world coming to an end with a repeated ear-jolting *BOOM—BOOM—BOOM!*

CHAPTER 39

WITH A GRIN ON HIS face, Reginald set his phone down on the center console. "All in a day's work."

Venison drove, but the were-rat still had a gun in Smoke's face.

Shifting in his seat, Smoke said, "You killed them, didn't you."

"Again, to be clear, I was only following orders."

Jaws clenching, Smoke replied, "We had a deal."

"You had a deal with me, but Kane supersedes that."

"So you're supposed to be the good guy?"

"On the contrary, I'm glad to see them all go. I'm not a people person. The fewer, the better. But I'm sure your cherished bride survived. I did let her out, you know. My, I just had a thought. I hope she didn't go back inside." Reginald leaned forward. He opened the center console and fished out a hard pack of Camel unfiltered cigarettes. He tapped a cig out from the carton and put it between his lips. Reading the pack, he said, "Turkish and domestic blend. I always found that to be a unique selling point. Have you ever been to Turkey, Smoke?"

"I can't say I have."

"Well, who knows what your new future might bring." Reginald offered a cigarette. "Smoke, Smoke? We have a long ride ahead."

"Funny, but I'll pass. Those things will kill you, you know."

"So I've heard." Reginald eased into the backseat. He took a Zippo from his pocket, flicked the top open, and struck up the flame. Lighting his cigarette, he said, "I love tobacco almost as much as I love killing people. It's so… satisfying."

Venison coughed. "I think it's disgusting." He rolled down his window and checked Reginald in the rearview mirror. "A filthy mortal habit. You should be above that."

"It's my way of blending in. Now roll that window back up. It messes up my hair."

"So where are we going?" Smoke said, adding in a cough to cover the sound of his diamond-dust-peppered fingernails sawing at his flex cuffs. "Is it another secret location buried deep in the heart of DC? Personally, I think it would be cool if it was the White House. I've never been."

"You are being taken to a transformation station. Willing or not, you're going to be subjected to the change. Kane's excited to see how the shifter blood in you will respond. You might want to give a little thought to the kind of monster you want to shift into. I'm sure there is some creature out there you identify with." Reginald stuck the cigarette pack in front of Smoke's face. "A camel, perhaps? Now that would be different."

Venison let out a high-pitched chuckle.

Still clawing at his weakening bonds, Smoke said, "How about a doppelganger? Huh? I could be your replacement."

"No one can replace me." Reginald blew a stream of yellow smoke out his nose. "I'm the top of the line."

"There's always someone better and stronger out there. You just haven't met them yet."

"I'm certain whoever it is, it isn't you." Reginald's eyes drifted to the window.

"Certainly not." Venison snickered and coughed. The gun barrel wobbled.

Smoke rolled his wrists, snapping his bonds just as they passed over a pothole. They were about a mile from the main highway. "Bumpy ride," Smoke said to Venison.

"I like the potholes. I pretend they are people." Venison aimed for a bad patch in the road. The vehicle jostled.

Smoke acted. He knocked the gun aside with one hand and jerked the car wheel with the other. The vehicle sped over the embankment, crashing through the trees. It smacked hard on its side and tumbled side over side, finally smashing hard into an oak tree. Smoke wrenched the gun free from Venison's hands, undid his seatbelt, and squeezed out of the busted car window.

As soon as he came to his feet, Venison was there, chest heaving. A nasty scrape crossed the bridge of his nose.

"You idiot! I'll kill you for what you did!"

"Not as long as I have this." Smoke held up his pistol.

Venison's rat eyes widened.

Smoke filled him with blue-tipped lead with two shots to the heart and two to the head.

Venison dropped on the spot.

Reginald appeared from the other side of the vehicle with his cigarette bent in his mouth. He was clapping. "Clever. Very clever. Another shifter bites the dust." He dropped his cigarette on Venison's face. "Eh, he always was a weak one anyway. A shot through the heart and head is rat poison to the likes of him. But now you're going to have to deal with me. That little gun of yours won't work on me."

Smoke tossed the gun aside. "I won't need it to take you down."

Reginald pushed his sleeves up. "Apparently you've forgotten the beating I gave you last time."

"No, I've been thinking about it every day."

CHAPTER 40

"Y OU'RE A FOOL, SMOKE. I've honed my skills over hundreds of years." Reginald stepped over some saplings down to the open ground where the hillside bottomed out and train tracks bent through the woods. "This level ground makes for a more suitable arena. I'd rather not fight among the sticks. I'm quite fond of this shirt." He rubbed the sleeve. "It's from Italy. I like the Italians. They're very passionate people." His face changed into the image of Rocky Balboa. He hunkered down into a boxer's stance with is lazy eyes fixed on Smoke. "Come on, Apollo. Let's go."

Smoke climbed up the gravel and in between the tracks. "You just ruined one of my favorite movies."

Reginald goaded him on with large white fists. "No talk. Just fight."

Smoke stepped in. He raised his fists. "This is weird."

"Did you take your little pills, Smoke? You're going to need them."

"No pills. Just skills."

"Heh, a fatal mistake. You could have increased your chance of survival by one percent." The doppelganger skipped in and unleashed some jabs.

Smoke slid his chin out of the way. He blocked a flurry of punches with his arms. Reginald might've been smaller than he was, but he hit like a heavyweight. Smoke absorbed the blows on his shoulders.

Reginald ducked, jabbed, and punched like Rocky on speed.

Smoke dropped and took Reginald down with a leg sweep.

The doppelganger landed hard on his back but popped right back up with his neck stretched out. "Yo! What's the deal, Smoke? Why are you fighting dirty?"

Smoke rushed in and clobbered him in the jaw. The powerful blow took Reginald off guard. His knees buckled. Smoke put his full weight on the man. He pummeled him down onto the tracks. He hit Reginald so hard his face changed.

Reginald turned from Rocky to Mister T. "Get off me, fool!"

"Shut up!" Smoke punched him in the mouth again and again.

Reginald's arms sprang into action, swatting Smoke's hammering blows aside. With a smile on his face, he said, "Are your arms getting tired yet?"

"No, but my eyes are!" Smoke drove his knuckles through Reginald's chin so hard the doppelganger changed color.

Reginald twisted out of Smoke's grasp. Like a wild hog, he scrambled away and onto his feet. When he turned, his face was back to normal. The cunning look of an English assassin returned. He spat a tooth out. "You've been thinking an awful lot."

"You had impeccable timing the last time we fought. I'd just battled two giants and didn't have much left. Made it easy for you."

"It wouldn't have made any difference one way or the other. You can't hurt me. All you'll do is tire yourself out, and when that inevitably happens, I'll pummel you to death." Somewhere an owl hooted. "There is no sweeter sound than bone busting up bone. I'm personally fond of the sound when the jaw gives. It has such a quieting effect."

"Thanks for the suggestion." Smoke waded in and threw a series of punches and kicks.

Reginald blocked and countered.

With every punch Smoke made, Reginald came back even quicker. Smoke's uncanny knack for avoiding movement before it started saved him from getting knocked senseless. It was that special ability that made him wonder if there truly was shifter blood in him. He had no choice but to embrace it now. It was survival. Instinct.

Reginald popped him in the lips with a backfist. "You're bleeding, Smoke. That fragile shell of yours cracks."

Smoke took a quick breath. His lungs burned. He went at Reginald again, using his longer reach to keep the quicker man at bay. He feinted with a rib jab, pulled it, and countered with a hard southpaw uppercut. His fist connected with jaw.

The blow lifted Reginald up on his toes. His eyes widened.

Smoke locked up the man's head. He drove the punches home. Ribs cracked. He laid into the shifter with everything he had, one nasty Rocky punch after another.

The shifter slipped out of Smoke's grip and stumbled over the track, collapsing on the ground. Reginald was down on his knees, huffing, with a hand stuck down in the gravel. He leered at Smoke. His eyebrows knitted. "I'm tired of toying with you." He transformed. His body filled out his loose-fitting clothes. "Let's see how you do against this."

Staring down at an image of himself, Smoke wiped the blood from his lip. "You've never looked better, Reginald." He gave his other self an approving nod. "I look mighty fine in those Italian duds."

"Oh, shut up." Reginald climbed up the railway track. "Better yet, I'm going to shut you up."

As soon as Reginald stepped over the first track, Smoke launched some furious punches.

Reginald deflected them with big hands and fluid tae kwon do moves.

Smoke changed tactics. He delivered a fierce kick to Reginald's crotch.

The doppelganger moaned.

Smoke winced. "That sort of hurt me to do that."

Reginald caught the next kick. He pulled Smoke to the ground.

They wrestled over the tracks in an angry tangle of muscle. In combinations of well-executed judo moves, the tussle banged heads and limbs off the metal rails. Fists smacked hard into jaws and faces. Elbows jabbed ribs. Chins tasted knuckles.

Smoke fought like a lion against this stronger and quicker version of himself. His sharp mind sensed every move before it happened, but his tiring limbs reacted a hair more slowly every time.

Reginald's energy was boundless. His fists came down in a rain of fury.

Smoke covered his face.

Reginald went for the stomach.

Smoke guarded his belly.

Reginald smote his face.

The tremendous blows rattled Smoke's grey matter. In a break between blows, he said in a gasp, "Wow, I really am a great fighter."

"No, I am," Reginald replied. He had Smoke pinned. His body grew. His visage was Smoke's but more bestial. The seams in the fine clothing burst. Reginald became a Mr. Hyde version of Smoke and said from slavering jaws, "I'm going to break you into pieces, brother!" He started hammering Smoke into submission.

With his strength quickly fading, Smoke blocked with everything he had left.

Brother?

CHAPTER 41

AGONY. PAIN. THE ONLY THING holding Smoke together was the sweetheart suit. He blocked what he could but couldn't attack anymore.

Reginald had him pinned down by the neck. His powerful hands squeezed until Smoke's eyes bulged. "You are a difficult man to control, mortal. And frankly, I'm tired of holding back."

"I can see you're all puffed up about it." Through Reginald's steely vise-like grip, Smoke struggled to say, "It seems to me I got under your skin."

"You know, not so long ago, Kane and I had an interesting discussion. How do you control a mortal who does not fear death?" Reginald's eyes lit up. "You see, it's fear that holds your kind back. Not so long ago, more of you were quite fearless. Then the ones like you show up. Like a briar in the skin between our toes. Every step we take, the nagging is there. It's aggravating. Especially when it's so hard to remove. Like you, brother."

The rail vibrated beneath Smoke's neck.

Reginald turned his head. "I think a train is coming. Isn't that quaint?"

Straining, Smoke tried to speak.

Turning his ear, Reginald leaned down, relaxed his grip. "Go ahead. Say what you have to say, smartass."

Puffing for breath, Smoke said through his busted-up face, "It makes me think of one of my favorite movies." He regurgitated a supervitamin, one of the ones with a special coating Mal had made for him so it wouldn't dissolve. He crunched down on the pill and swallowed it again, saying, "It's called *Dark Territory*."

"Never heard of it, brother."

"Quit calling me that."

"The truth hurts, doesn't it, John." Reginald watched the distant train clatter down the tracks. "Hmmm, that's a slow one. But we might just have to take it."

The supervitamin kicked in. The blood in Smoke's veins caught fire. His heart pumped like a steam engine's wheels turning. Against Reginald's great strength, his neck popped up. He said, "Let me tell you about *Dark Territory* first. It's about this Navy SEAL named Ryback. A SEAL like I used to be." He took Reginald's wrists and shoved them away.

Reginald's lips curled back. Astonished, he said, "How are you doing that?"

In one fluid move, Smoke bent Reginald's wrists backward. It sent the shifter back on his heels. Smoke found himself free of the monstrous man. He sprang to his feet. "You see, Ryback is a master of aikido, a real bone breaker."

"I'm well aware of what aikido is." Reginald sneered. "It won't do you any good against the likes of me."

"Let's find out."

Fluid as water spiraling down, Smoke attacked.

Reginald tore into him. The bigger, stronger version of Smoke let loose with savagery.

Smoke moved with the prowess of a jungle cat. A flurry of punches and slaps peppered Reginald's eyes.

The shifter now seemed determined to tear Smoke apart. He grabbed Smoke and body slammed him on the ground.

But Smoke popped up to his feet, locked up Reginald's arm, and cracked it back. The elbow snapped.

Reginald howled.

Smoke shattered the doppelganger's knee with a stiff, powerful kick.

Reginald dropped.

Smoke put the shifter in a headlock.

Tearing at Smoke's arms, the doppelganger said, "My bones mend quicker than you can breathe. Your little pill will wear off. How long does it last, a minute? Hahaha—*urk*!"

With the muscles in his arms bulging against Reginald's supernatural might, fueled by the vitamin, Smoke cranked back. "You're going to die, Reginald!"

Reginald twisted his hulking frame like a bucking bull.

Smoke held him fast and squeezed with all his vitamin-induced strength.

The layers of packed muscle in Reginald's neck slackened. His fingers clawed. He swam as if he was trying to surface for air.

Pouring it on with everything he had left inside him, Smoke let out a scream, "Yaaaaaargh!"

Reginald's spine gave. *Snap!* The body went slack.

Smoke let go.

Reginald lay on his back, staring up at the sky. His form reverted to that of the man Smoke had learned to hate so long ago.

The train clattered down the tracks, racing at about thirty miles an hour. Its headlamp glowed through the trees. Smoke picked up Reginald's body and approached the tracks. He looked down at Reginald. "So you heal up pretty fast, do you? I can't let that happen. Let me tell you about a new reality show I'm going to pitch." He tilted Reginald up so he could see the train. "It's called *Shifter Versus Train*. And you get to star in it."

Reginald's eyes turned into moons.

One second before the train passed, Smoke heaved Reginald in front of it.

The powerful locomotive splattered the body all over the tracks.

Smoke watched the big coal train chug by until the caboose was long out of sight. There was little to be found of Reginald. Not even his head. Feeling his energy start to drain, Smoke trudged up the hill. The climb became harder with every step. He found the SUV, gave it a look, and kept going. He needed to get back to Sid. It took more mind than muscle to make it up the hill. When he made it to the top, a luxury sedan waited with the engine running. Kane and Allison were leaning against it.

Kane applauded. "I'll be. You really are the one." Dressed in a maroon leisure suit, he walked right toward Smoke, who raised his swollen fists.

"You might want to take a look at the last guy who messed with me."

Kane hit him so hard the black sky turned red.

EPILOGUE

S ID HELD HER POUNDING HEAD. Propped up against the metal wall of the shipping container with people scurrying and moaning in the darkness, she said, "Everyone, be still. We'll be okay." Ears ringing, she pushed herself up. The bombs had rocked the building and knocked her out. She wasn't sure for how long. All she knew was it was hot and stuffy, like the armpit of some hellhole.

I've got to get out of here.

She noted a slim crack of light through a seam in the metal. She stepped on and over some people, saying, "Excuse me."

"Sid?" said a pesky woman's voice.

She knew it immediately. "Asia?"

"Yes. What have you gotten me into now? Why do I feel so sick? Ugh! I feel like I'm surrounded by giant fish."

"You're in a shipping container," Sid said.

"Damn, I knew it. That's how I got over here in the first place." Asia sighed. "What the hell am I doing in a giant sardine can?"

"It's a long story. At least your mouth made a full recovery." Sid found the handle of the container door. She shoved the lever up. It was stuck.

"What are you doing?"

Sid jumped. Asia had crept right up on her heels. "Geez, you're sneaky. I'm trying to open this door."

"Let me help." Asia's hands found Sid's and started toggling the handle. The mechanism gave. They pulled the lever.

Sid put her shoulder into the door. It cracked open a foot. Cool air kissed her sweat-drenched face. The light she'd seen came from a lone skylight that still gleamed among the rubble. Piles of building lurked up all around. Sid squeezed through, with Asia on her tail.

Asia's jaw hung. "Was there an earthquake or something?"

"It's a long story."

"Who are all those slimy people in there?" Asia took note of herself. "Uck, what happened?" She slung her arms. "It looks like Godzilla sneezed on me."

"We need to find a way out." Basing her direction on the doors of the container, Sid scanned the parking garage the way she remembered it. Lucky for them, part of the interior support hadn't completely given way, but she couldn't see any part of the stairwell or elevator. The ramp leading out of the garage had collapsed. Half the first floor lay inside the garage, covering the shipping container. It gave Sid a chill. If not for the container, they'd all have been crushed.

She climbed over the debris. A light flashed in the corner of her eye. She turned. A light beam glowed where the garage doors closed. She waved her arms and yelled, "Hey! Help!"

Asia mimicked her calls.

"Hey! Help!"

Sid made her way over the scrap-heap structure. Debris sprinkled down into the garage where the ramp dropped off from the outside entrance. Someone was on the other side scooting the rubble aside. When the chunk of cement cleared, a man poked his head inside. He shined a light in her face.

"Sid?"

"Cyrus?"

"Holy crap! I should have known I'd find you here. Are there any other survivors?"

"A bunch. Including Ted—and Rebecca."

Cyrus sat beside Rebecca, who was shivering in a blanket. Mal was with Asia, and the pair of them were doing the same. Ted hunched under his blanket next to Sid, not saying much. The FBI had spent hours getting the survivors out of the ruined building. All the walls and windows had been blasted out, but the structure still stood, a skeleton frame of its former self.

Cyrus kissed Rebecca's head. "I'm so glad you're alive. The other you died. I thought you and the baby were gone forever."

With a quizzical look, Rebecca said, "Baby?"

Sid's hand went to her abdomen.

Mal eyed her. "How are you feeling?"

"I'm just worried about Smoke. Can we talk for a moment?"

Mal looked at Asia.

"Go ahead. I'm fine now," the little woman said. "Just hungry. Don't these ambulances have any food? I want some fish sticks. And beer. Hey, big boy, you got any beer? You look like a drinker," she said to an agent.

After moving to a more private area, Sid caught Mal up with everything Reginald had told her about being pregnant. "And the baby? Can we run a test and find out?"

"Of course we can," he said with a reassuring look. "It won't take long to run it through a lab."

Her fingers dug into her palms. Life had been turned inside out again. She was faced with more questions than answers. And Smoke was gone. Her heart ached. "We have to find him."

"He's resourceful. I'm sure we will." He took her by the shoulders and squeezed them. "I can't thank you enough for saving Asia. For saving all of them. It's like a miracle, Sid. A victory. I swear, you can also count on me. With the clones gone, we've mortally wounded them."

"I know, but it feels hollow to me. They took Smoke. Vormus and Manson are gone. I want to know when the bodies are found. And what about A.V., Toad Man, and Night Bird? Do we still have eyes on them?"

"They were all secure last I checked a few hours ago."

"Good. We just need to figure out what to do with them."

An FBI sedan sped through the front gate. The tires ground to a stop on the shattered rubble and glass. The driver, Agent Jonnie Wok, exited with Smoke's rucksack in one hand and the Arabian sword in the other.

Sid rushed him.

Agent Wok made his way over to Cyrus. His eyes widened on Sid.

"Where did you get that?" she said.

"A few miles up the road. An SUV crashed over the hill."

"Did you see any other sign of Smoke?"

"No, but something got splattered all over the tracks. It looked like a man got hit by a train. Agents are still picking up the remains."

Sid's heart sank.

Jonnie Wok held out a sheet of paper folded up like a note. "I found this."

Sid's name was written on the note. She took it and opened it. The note read:

"Dear Sister, we have Smoke. Changes are coming. Once you're gone, he will be mine... Forever. Allison."

CRAIG HALLORAN

THE SUPERNATURAL BOUNTY HUNTER FILES

SMOKE HAPPENS

BOOK 9

CHAPTER 1

S ID WOKE UP GASPING. SHE sat up, peering through the darkness. Tears streaked down her cheeks. Her body trembled. A chill fell over her. She rubbed the goose bumps on her arms and noticed that her fingers were icy cold. She reached for the glass of water on her nightstand. Her fingers wrapped around the smooth glass, she brought it to her lips and gulped the warm water down. She set the glass back on the stand and turned the lamp on.

Smoke's apartment—or rather, their apartment—was fully furnished but seemed empty. The warmth was gone. The sheets were damp and cold, no longer warmed by their bodies lying together. She covered her shoulders with the blanket. Her bare feet hit the cold floor. Picking up her phone, she checked the time. 3:08 a.m.

"Morning glory."

Sleep hadn't come easy the past couple of weeks since she'd last seen Smoke. There hadn't been a word from Kane or Allison, either. Everything had gone silent, but her head was ringing. She shuffled into the bathroom and turned on the light, squinting against its glare. Head down, she turned the sink spigots on and rinsed off her face. Drying her face off, she checked the mirror. There were puffy rings under her eyes. She couldn't remember the last time she'd looked or felt so bad. She placed her hand over her womb.

"I thought I was supposed to get a glow with a bundle in my belly."

Sid turned off the bathroom light, tossed the blanket on the bed, made her way over to the kitchenette, and filled the empty coffee pot with water. She tossed out the old filter full of coffee grounds and filled a new one with freshly roasted ground beans from a bag. Seconds later, the coffee was brewing. She pulled up a barstool and watched the pot begin to fill. The entire time, she was thinking about John. John and the baby. Her heart ached.

She'd spoken with Mal Carlson about her pregnancy a few days after they lost Smoke at the clone factory. She was supposed to get some bloodwork done. Mal seemed confident that he would be able to determine if the baby was Smoke's or not. The test would be easy, the answer simple, but she was avoiding it. In her heart, she felt the baby was hers and Smoke's. The child would be their son or daughter. But what if she was wrong? That was the hard part. According to Kane and the shifters, if she carried Kane's baby, she would die before labor. Her fist clenched in and out. Her teeth started to grind.

Please, God, let this baby be mine and Smoke's.

The coffee pot was full. The fresh aroma filled the room. The smell was strong to her heightened senses. Smells and scents were now almost alarming from time to time. It had taken her weeks to get used to the smell of coffee, and there were some things she couldn't tolerate. Perfumes were a slap in the face. Bacon—which she and Smoke had often lived on—now repulsed her. As for potatoes, in any shape or form, she had a hankering for those most of the time.

She fetched a ceramic mug out of the kitchen sink and filled it to the brim. Taking a sip, she turned her attention to the newspapers lying on the kitchenette island. The *Washington Post* was on top of the pile. The main headline on the front page of section one was "Shake Up under the Dome!" The picture was Senator Augustus Wilhelm being taken into an ambulance in a straightjacket. According to the article, he'd flipped out at a bill-signing session and attacked several of his cohorts. But he had escaped the hospital, and as of now, his whereabouts were unknown.

Sid huffed. The man in the picture wasn't Wilhelm but a shifter. She'd found Wilhelm alive in the clone factory. The Bureau had the real Wilhelm now. At least, she thought so. Staring at the picture of Wilhelm's clone, she thought, *I'm not sure if bringing him back would be a good thing or not.*

Other people were back in the fold. Agent Rebecca Lang had been a clone, and now the real one was back. Sid's old boss Ted Howard was alive and well. Mal's wife, Asia, had also been saved. Sid hadn't stuck around to see how things sorted out. All she wanted to do was find Smoke. And when she did, would she even know it was him?

From underneath the copy of the *Post*, Sid pulled out a copy of *Nightfall D.C.* The monthly newsletter was more of a tabloid than a real news source, but the front-page headline was also catchy. WASHINGTON GOES BATTY! There was a laundry list—with pictures—of dozens of federal, state, and local officials who had suddenly died from "unknown circumstances" or "gone missing." Sid didn't recognize hardly any of the names, but she knew enough of them to know that they were clones. Maybe shifters. How deeply the Drake had penetrated the ranks of leadership left a pit in Sid's stomach.

There were several bizarre stories about what happened to some of the people before they died. Many of them attacked others. A couple streaked naked in the streets. One woman, a county clerk, was found chasing after deer on a golf course. A federal legal attorney had torpedoed his car through a dry cleaners in a strip mall. Not a single one of these stories had been picked up by the local news channels, so anyone would question whether there was any truth to what *Nightfall D.C.* reported at all. Sid knew better. The scary thing was that *Nightfall D.C.* didn't know the half of it.

She'd drunk her coffee about halfway down when she felt a little kick. "Oh my, good morning." Her fingers spread out over her belly. "It's good to know I'm not all alone. Maybe someone is getting hungry. How about some fried potatoes?"

With a smile on her face, Sid lit the gas on the stove and set the pan down.

The glare of headlights illuminated the curtains covering the kitchen sink window. Tire rubber ground over the old blacktop. Brakes creaked to a stop.

Sid grabbed her Glock from the kitchen counter. She didn't hear any car doors open or close. The car's engine kept running.

Her heart jumped at the sound of hard knocking at her door.

CHAPTER 2

S MOKE SAT ON AN OLD metal prison cot that creaked with his every move. The room he was in was a square twenty by twenty with a concrete floor. The only difference between it and a huge jail cell was the way the concrete walls were painted, by a skilled hand. It looked like he was inside his garage apartment. His computer and desk were on one wall, the kitchenette on another. There was the back wall with the French doors leading to the rear, and the front door. The details were spot on, from the hinges on the old cabinets to the music CDs stacked up by the computer to the pillows on his sofa. Aside from the stuffy hot air and the steel bars for a front door, everything was down to the letter.

Scratching the scruff on his swollen jaw, he stood up with a groan. The old springs in the cot groaned along with him. He made military corners on the mattress with the green military blanket. There wasn't much need for a blanket, hot as it was. All it did was catch his sweat. Without having seen the day or night, his best guess was that he'd been imprisoned for ten days. They'd been long ones, but that wasn't the worst of it. He'd been drugged.

He paced the room. His stomach rumbled. They'd given him food, but he wasn't eating. He was only drinking the water, as little as he could. It had a taint to it. Fighting the hunger and the weakening in his limbs, he did a few calisthenics and some push-ups. He finished up in a layer of sweat that coated the drab grey prison jumper he wore. Taking a seat Indian style, he closed his eyes. The distinct click of hard heels on tiled floor caught his ear, reminding him of the day he first met Sid. He turned his head toward the door. Sweet perfume widened his nostrils. On the outside of the cell door, Allison's body filled his eyes.

"Hello, John," Allison said with playful eyes. She was as mouthwatering as a woman could be. Her alluring features were enhanced by a presence that was even more carnal and vibrant. She commanded a power and sexuality he'd never seen before. "You look like you could use some company. And some food."

She stepped back. A peacoat guard unlocked the door with a heavy key. He pushed it open and stepped aside. Allison entered with a metal-covered dish on a tray with a bottled water. She bent over, revealing the plunging neckline of her black blouse, as the guard closed the door behind her. She wore a thigh-high skirt and black designer boots that came up to her knees. The seams in her skirt stretched at the hips when she sat down on the cot.

Smoke's mouth watered. He could smell the hot food beneath the steaming metal. His stomach growled.

"My, you must be very hungry," Allison said, applying a layer of lipstick. "You need to eat, brother."

"I prefer to eat out."

"Oh come now, John, everything you could possibly want right now is here. A delicious meal. A willing woman." She bounced the springs on the bed a little. "Let's make some noise."

"That's not going to happen." He gave her a quick glance before averting his eyes. "Ever."

"Don't be so sure of yourself, Smokey. I've always gotten everything I wanted when I put my mind to it." She patted the cot. "Come. Sit down. I won't bite you, unless, of course, you'd like that."

He turned his back and faced the wall that looked like the bedroom of his apartment. His blood was churning with hunger and desire. *I've got to hand it to her, she knows how to put the hooks in you. Be strong. Think of Sid, and your baby.*

"Smokey, just sit, please. I won't lay a finger on you."

"It's not your fingers I'm worried about."

"Ah, there's that dash of humor that women so admire. I like that." She patted the bed again. "Either you can sit down or I can stand up. There isn't anywhere for you to run, Smokey. I'll catch you, even in these high heels."

Smoke didn't move.

"I tell you what, Smokey." She picked the tray up and set it on her lap. "I'll harness myself with this delightful platter of food so that I cannot make any sudden moves. Besides, you're certainly going to want to hear what I have to say about my dear sister."

"What about her?"

"Sit, sit."

Smoke took a seat at the other end of the cot with his back to her, as far away as he could get. "Out with it then, Allison."

"First things first." She lifted the lid off the plate of food, revealing steaming prime rib and sautéed vegetables. Every item was cooked to perfection. Allison cut through the steak with the side of the fork. The meat was pink and juicy. "I bet you've never seen steak so tender, have you?"

"We cut meat with a saw where I'm from. A steak is not a steak without some chew to it."

"You're a silly man." She held a forkful of meat just under his nose. "Eat. Enjoy while you still have a taste for such things."

Smoke turned his nose. As badly as he needed his strength, he needed his wits about him more. He doubted the food was poisoned, but he wouldn't be surprised one bit if it was drugged. Whatever the Drake planned to do with him hadn't started yet, but he could sense the fight was coming. If it wasn't, they wouldn't have sent Allison in. "I'll pass."

Allison ate the steak. "That's too bad. You're missing out on much-needed protein. I'm trying to help you."

"It looks to me like you're just helping yourself."

"As I've said, whatever I desire, I will have." She leaned over and nudged him shoulder to shoulder. "You'll see."

"Sorry to disappoint you, sister, but you can't always get what you want. That's never going to change in this world, no matter how hard you try."

"It's working out so far." She sawed through some asparagus and ate. "Mmm, so good. You know what would make this meal even better? Wine. I wanted to bring a bottle, but Kane wouldn't allow it. He said you wouldn't accept it, and he didn't want to waste it. As if one bottle of centuries-old vino matters. I have to admit, I find myself surprised by the shifters' attachment to material things. Of course, who am I to talk?" She flaunted the lavish jewelry that decorated her wrists and fingers. "My vices haven't fled me, either."

Smoke faced her.

Her hungry eyes locked on his.

"You haven't changed, have you?"

She leaned toward him. "You can't tell?" Her voice was a purr. "Good, that's how I like it."

Smoke imagined her turning into an exotic cat-lady of sorts, like Tigra from the comic books. Or Batwoman. *Now that would be a show. Shame on me. Sorry, Sid.* "Even if you did make the mistake of going down that road, I won't do it. I'm not going to become an abomination."

"Most of us have been there, Smokey. I know I certainly had my doubts, but when I tasted the power, there weren't any regrets." She cut into her steak and bit into the meat. Red juice dripped down the corner of her mouth. She licked it away.

Smoke's Adam's apple rolled.

"Give in to your hunger, Smokey. Don't deny what you'll need to survive. Sidney didn't."

Smoke eased away.

Allison set the tray of half-eaten food down. In her miniskirt, she flipped her legs over the cot from one side to the other. Sitting side by side with him now, she said, "Kane's told me everything. I have to admit, my sister is a much naughtier girl than I imagined. She didn't deprive herself of the pleasures Kane offered, nor should you deny yourself what I offer. Believe me, Smokey"—she toyed with his ear—"I'll be worth it."

CHAPTER 3

S ID PEEKED THROUGH THE CURTAINS. Outside was a sedan that she didn't recognize. The heavy knocking came again. Not liking the sound of the thumping, she set down her Glock and picked up the shotgun that was propped up beside the front door. She pumped the handle and said, "Hear that? If you whack my door one more time, I'm going to turn that hand of yours into applesauce. Now, who is it?"

On the other side of the door someone said to another, "Will you cut that out? I told you not to spook her. Hey! Hey, Sid! It's me, Russ Davenport. You know, the journalist."

"Hello, Russ. What's going on with this late-night call? It's four a.m."

"I'm an early riser and figured you and Smoke probably were too. Uh, sorry. But seriously, can we talk? You know I wouldn't come here unless I had to."

"I didn't realize you knew where we lived. It strikes me kinda funny, Russ. Care to explain that?"

"Er, Google Earth? Come on, you know we're on the same team. Right?"

With the gun barrel pointed at chest level, she opened the door. A big black man wearing denim practically filled the frame. His head was shaved. He had a mean look and an ugly scar under his chin. His eyes widened as much as his smile when he got a full look at her. He said in a deep voice, "Good morning, ma'am."

"Russ, what are you doing with this guy?"

"He found me, said he had some good information. He does."

"Give me a second." She closed the door. Until that guy's eyes popped, she had forgotten she was in her skimpy summer sleepwear. She found a pair of jeans and slipped them on under one of Smoke's large T-shirts. Putting her hair in a ponytail, she opened the door again. "Come in, but don't make yourself at home." She watched the big man wander inside. His eyes searched all over the room. "Cort Calhoun, I was wondering when you'd show up again."

"I leave that impression on a lot of people. I like it." Finishing his lookover, he said, "Quaint."

Russ poured himself a cup of coffee. The heavyset reporter wore a beige raincoat that enhanced his shabby appearance. He drank and said, "Good coffee."

"What did I say about not getting too comfortable?" She took the coffee away from Russ. Calhoun started to sit down on a barstool, but she pulled it away. "I'm serious. What do you want?"

Cort Calhoun hadn't been around in a while. The fallen FBI agent had been following Smoke and Sid at one time like a bloodhound, but he'd dropped out of sight. His reemergence had an uncanny feel to it. "I don't even know why I let you in here."

"Ladies can't resist my Southern charm. So where's Smoke?"

"He's out, you know, doing his thing?" She poured Russ's coffee into the sink.

"Hey!" Russ said. "Boy, I expected a little more courtesy." He picked up the copy of *Nightfall D.C.* "Being a world-famous journalist and all."

"Get real."

"I was real, back when I started." Russ opened the paper, hiding his face, and gave it a snap. "I had awards, accolades, popularity, women. I was top flight. Then I got a feel for what was really happening and how no one wanted to report—"

Sid snatched the paper away from him. "I don't care. Just tell me what you want."

"We'd like to share it with Smoke too."

Sid's hands got a little clammy. The way both men weren't looking at her wasn't right. She was being vetted. "Listen, boys. Put your cards on the table or get out."

Russ gave Calhoun a nod. "Go ahead."

Calhoun reached inside the pocket of his denim jacket, revealing a large six-shooter strapped to his hip. He pulled out a packet and tossed it on the table.

Eyes on Calhoun, she said, "That's a big piece of hardware you're carrying. Shot any polar bears with it?"

"Ah, you like my Ruger Alaskan, huh? Big man. Big gun. I haven't shot any polar bears, but I've shot worse things, thanks to you and your partner—or husband, rather."

"What's that supposed to mean?"

"I've seen 'em," Calhoun said. "And they've seen me. I about died the last time. Then I came across this clown's paper and everything came together. I started following you and Smoke a little more, but I kept my distance. I watched, waited, and learned." He tipped his chin at the packet on the table. "Look."

Sid picked up the photograph packet. Leaning back against the bar so she could keep an eye on her visitors, she opened it up. Inside were photos of a black SUV. The windows were down on one side. Her fingers tingled when she saw Smoke and her sister, Allison, getting out of the car at an airfield. "When did you take these?"

Calhoun held his fingers up and made rain, saying, "The same night you brought that building down. I tailed you until you hit that road off the main drag, but I stayed on the main drag. I saw that same car go in and come out. On a hunch, I followed. Sure enough, I wind up at a small airfield and out comes that gorgeous lady and Smoke. The creepy fella came out too. Looked like Ric Flair on super steroids." He picked up one of the pictures Sid had set on the table. It was a picture of Kane. "That's one mean, ugly dude."

Furious, Sid said, "Why did you wait so long to tell me this?"

"Because I just figured out where they landed."

"I'm FBI. I could have figured that out days ago."

Calhoun shook his head. "You forget I'm FBI too, and according to my connections—and believe me, I still have plenty—that plane never landed and never took off from where it started. It's a ghost."

Russ butted in. "Transylvania Airlines."

Shaking her head, she said, "Please don't tell me he's in Transylvania."

"No," Calhoun said. His grin broadened. "That's just what we call it. The plane landed in Las Vegas."

"All roads lead to Vegas," Russ said with some shady emphasis.

"That doesn't make any sense." Sid pushed her sleeves up over her elbows. Still studying the pictures, she drummed her fingernails on the counter. "The Drake is based here. This is the power station. Why Vegas?"

"There are plenty of strange stories in Vegas too, you know." Russ sauntered over to her computer desk and moved the mouse until the monitors flickered on. "They just don't get reported on because there are so many other distractions in Vegas. But this eerie stuff is going on there, too."

"I'm not buying it." Sid fished through the pictures. "Do you have any idea where they went after that?"

Calhoun tipped his chin. "I made some calls. You see, there are people whom I would like to believe are on our side of things. Anyway, they track these planes. Thanks to the web, eyes are everywhere these days. I don't care who you are, someone is watching—and they might even be six thousand miles away. It's just like those UFO and storm watchers. Geeks are into these things. So I did my own homework on the dark web and was impressed with what I found."

Taking a drink of coffee, Sid said, "You know, you're smarter than you look."

"This big melon of mine isn't just good looks, it's filled with knowledge."

The office chair in front of the computer desk groaned. Russ was slouched over the keyboard. His heavy fingers pecked at the keys.

"Hey!" Sid marched over. "That's password protected. What do you think you're doing?"

"Was password protected." Russ kept typing. Different images popped up on the computer monitors. "I'm really good at guessing passwords."

She started forward, ready to rip him out of the chair. "Get off of there—" Sid's eyes froze on one of the screens, where a video played. Rough-handed men wearing peacoats were scuttling a rangy man with a powerful build into a black hearse. A range of desert mountains loomed in the stark evening background. The imprisoned man's face was covered in a cloth sack. Sid knew the body as well as her own. It was Smoke's.

CHAPTER 4

ALLISON'S GENTLE FINGERTIP TRACED THE outline of Smoke's face. Even her touch was a seductive fire. She was a powerful force, drawing him in. Purring in his ear with wet red lips, she said, "Let me just give you a taste of something you've never had. Let me waltz you to the threshold of the halls of decadence. You won't regret it. You'll have good sex for a change."

"I wouldn't know the difference between good sex and bad. I've only been with one woman, and I plan on keeping it that way."

With a swipe of her index finger, she wiped off the sweat that dripped down his temple. She tasted it. "So sweet. You are a passionate man, Smokey." She squeezed his thigh. "Unleash that passion. Ravage me the way Kane ravaged Sid."

His back straightened. He eyed her with growing lust.

"Yes, there's no harm in it. Only delight." She pulled her shoulders back and closed her eyes. "Take me."

Smoke swallowed. His fingers clutched in and out. Allison was more than enticing. She was fresh meat to a ravenous wolf, ready to be devoured. With a dry throat, he said, "You witnessed it. I gave Sid my word to be faithful until death do us part. If you want to have sex with me, you're going to have to kill me."

Allison's eyes popped open. A storm brewed in her pupils. "What do you take me for, a necrophiliac?"

Smoke smiled. "You said it, not me."

She slapped him hard. "I ought to rip your tongue out!"

The blow left Smoke a little woozy. He shook his head. "What about Sid? You had something to tell me about her, so out with it."

Red faced, Allison rose. She stormed around the cot and kicked the platter of food across the room. "Sure, Smokey, sure! My dear sister will die in labor having Kane's baby. No doubt the prude will be fool enough to carry it. So yes, Smokey, you'll see sweet Sidney again, when she's dead. Maybe the two of you can share a special moment then."

Without turning to look at her, he said, "You're bluffing, and doing a bad job of it."

"No, Kane assured me. Don't you understand? That's why we left her and chose you. Her days are numbered. Yours are just beginning. You defeated Reginald! A doppelganger. He was Kane's most powerful ally. No mortal could pull off what you did. You are different. Special. Soon, you will see—and like so many others who resisted it before at first, you, my noble little brother, will embrace it." She banged on the door. "You're going to regret not taking me up on my offer or eating that steak. You'll need all of your strength for what's coming. You're family. I was looking out for you. You had your chance, but now it's too late."

Smoke heard the door open and close. Allison's heels echoed in the hall and faded away. His stomach groaned again. He eyed the steak on the floor. *What did Weird Al's song say? Just eat it.*

CHAPTER 5

SID SPENT THE NEXT COUPLE of hours watching Russ surf the dark web. She didn't have much familiarity with it, but Russ seemed to know what he was doing. That didn't mean as much to her as she would have liked it to, so she sent a text to Guppy and another to Mal. In between conversations, she packed a duffle bag.

Lounging on the sofa with his arms stretched out on the back, Calhoun said, "It looks like the little lady of the house is ready to fly." He cracked his scarred knuckles. Calhoun was bigger than Smoke, and with the build of an NFL defensive tackle, he practically filled the couch. "Have you called Shatner and ordered your Priceline tickets?"

"Funny." Standing over the bed, Sid stuffed more clothing into the bag. "I didn't think I needed tickets for Air Transylvania. Just a pint of your thick blood."

"Why's my blood got to be thick?"

"Because your head is."

Calhoun let out booming, out-of-place laughter. When he finished, he said, "If you fly commercial, what are you going to do for weapons when you land?"

"I'm working on it."

"I've got a guy we can hook up with—"

"You aren't coming." Sid zipped up the duffle bag. "You're going."

"What?" Calhoun twisted his head around. "Hey, Princess Bang-Bang, I'm along whether you like it or not."

"Princess Bang-Bang? Where'd you come up with that?"

Calhoun shrugged. "That was the talk about you in the academy. You had all of those marksmanship records, many of which still stand today. That's what they called you. You didn't know that?"

"First I ever heard of it." She walked the duffle bag over to the front door and dropped it down, hiding the pride that she was brimming with. It seemed like such a long time ago that she was the hotshot on the range. *Yeah, I was something then.* She opened the door. "Thanks for the information, fellas. See you around."

Russ spun in the chair. "Hey, we're trying to help you out here. No need to be rude."

Agitated, she said, "I'm not the one who showed up on your doorstep at four in the morning. Besides, you don't have any skin in the game. You don't owe me or Smoke anything. What's in it for you?" She glared at Calhoun. "Either of you?"

Russ and Calhoun locked eyes for a moment before their attention fell back on her. With a shrug, Russ said, "I don't know why you're giving me heat on this, but I've got friends and family too, you know. Sure, they may think I'm a kook, and maybe they've written me off, but I'm still going to do what's best for them. If we don't fight the real nut jobs, who the hell will?"

"Roger that!" Calhoun said.

Rubbing her head, she said, "Look, guys, sorry to be rude, but I'd rather walk this walk alone."

"You're too deep in this to play the lone wolf routine." Calhoun stood up, tall as a giant. "If you want to walk that plank, then go ahead, but if you drown, so does your baby."

Sid's mouth dropped open a little. "You know?"

"Princess Bang-Bang, please, I've got more brothers and sisters than you have fingers. I know a pregnant mommy when I see one. It's all in the walk. Daddy used to put his hands to his mouth like this and announce, 'Build another chair for the table! Incoming!'" With a nod, he waltzed out the door.

Russ sauntered over. "If it's any consolation, I wasn't going to fly to Vegas with you. I hate flying. Besides, I'm a homebody. I can do just as much here as there. You have everything you need. Good luck, Sid."

Feeling a loss, Sid watched the two men speed away in the old sedan. There was sincerity in the both of them. It seemed strange coming from Calhoun. He had a violent reputation, but something about him had changed. She closed the door, headed back to the computer, and took a seat to review everything Russ had pulled up.

Las Vegas was a perfect grid of construction. The casinos were where the attention was focused, but it was the outlying network that made it all happen. The city had expanded fast, but the grid was advanced. Russ and his resources were able to hack into traffic cameras and follow the hearse Smoke had been transported in to where it resided now: at a funeral home, very similar to the one Titus Tolliver the gargoyle operated. The structure was old.

Sid felt a chill trickle down her spine.

It made perfect sense to take Smoke to a place like that to make the transformation. It was there they'd try to turn him into a monster. But she knew Smoke would never willingly do that. He'd die first. That was her fear—that she'd never see him alive again. She shut down the computer, turned off the lights, and grabbed her bag.

She headed to the doorway that led into the garage. Inside, the phantom black Hellcat waited. She fired up the engine, and it rumbled with thirsty life. She punched the accelerator and roared out of the garage.

Road trip.

CHAPTER 6

S MOKE SAT ON THE FLOOR of the muggy cell and stretched. It was one of those things he made himself do in prison. Living in tight quarters made for stiff limbs. When the time came for him to make his move, he needed to be ready to spring. A split second could make all the difference. It was time to make things happen. It was time to reunite with Sid, possibly.

Up on the ceiling, a film of water gathered in the sweltering little room, dripping into a puddle between his legs. It hadn't been this hot earlier. Someone had turned the heat up. He was determined not to let it break him. He'd spent plenty of time in one of Alabama's finest correctional facilities. That was worse than this. In prison, he didn't have any kind of view, but he enjoyed the solitude, sometimes.

Coming to his feet with the ease of a house cat, he walked over to the wall. His fingers traced the outline of his bedroom that was painted in great detail on the wall. He could see himself and Sid lying in the bed, laughing and giggling over something stupid he might have said. His fingers touched the pillows and the sheets. He could almost smell her on them, even though there was nothing but a hard wall behind the paint.

He looked at the bathroom in the background. The door was half open. The vanity lights were on. Smoke snorted. Why in the world would anyone go to the trouble of painting an entire cell to look like his garage apartment? Such a great scene couldn't be painted in a matter of days. This project had taken weeks. Months. How long had they been watching him? Why such an elaborate setup?

He turned. Kane stood on the other side of the cell door in a tuxedo without the jacket, leering. His wavy hair hung over his bullish shoulders. He tilted his head on his thick neck. "You're surprised to see me, Smoke. Heh. You didn't even hear me coming. Perhaps your acute senses have dulled. You aren't used to someone creeping up on you, are you?"

"Did you come to chit-chat, or do you have something important to say?"

"Everything I say is important."

"If you say so." Smoke walked right up to the bars and stared Kane in the eye. "Let's quit playing games. Start speaking like a man."

"Feeling cocky, are you? Good, you'll need it." Kane's penetrating eyes never left Smoke's. "I have to admit, Smoke, you fascinate me. After all, you killed your brother Reginald. That's quite a feat. I admire it."

"He wasn't my brother."

"No? You're wrong, Smoke. We are all brothers and sisters here. We come from the same fabric that was sewn centuries ago. Bastards, each and every one of us." Kane unfastened his bowtie and unbuttoned his collar. He stuffed the tie inside his pocket. He began rolling his sleeves up. "This shirt, this tuxedo, is decades old, maybe a century. My character has never changed from my mortal days, such as you are now. Do you know what I was before I became a shifter?"

"A used-car salesman?" Smoke eyed Kane's head. "A bad hairdresser? Mmm, perhaps the world's ugliest belly dancer?"

Kane's eyes flickered for a moment. He took a deep draw through his nose. "When you go through the change, perhaps you should become a jester. You'd make a great fool with that clever tongue of yours."

Smoke gave his hand a nice nonchalant flip and said, "Hey, then there would be two of us. A funny fool and one who has the personality of a rock."

"I certainly won't miss that clever wit of yours. As I was saying, back when the blood ran warm in my bones, I was a physician. A good one. I saved many lives. I stitched countless men on the battlefield and gave them life again. It was a grand thing. But you see, for all of my good intentions, hard work, and study, I realized I couldn't save them all. I couldn't even save myself. I would die one day."

"And yet you're still here. How disappointing."

Continuing with just as much intensity as before, Kane said, "Yes, I am here. I'm here because I would not let death defeat me. I became obsessed with beating it. I found the Drake—or rather, the Drake found me. That was a very long time ago, and since then, I've become wiser in the ways of this world. More powerful than I ever dreamed of. It happened because it was my destiny. I didn't collide with it so much as it collided with me. That path you are on, Smoke, it's the same one I was on. You are here because it's meant to be. You are one of us, special. You just need to embrace it."

"You really were a used-car salesman in your former life, weren't you? I can tell, because that pitch was horrible." Smoke started laughing. Then he said in Kane's own voice, "You are one of us, special. You need to embrace it."

Kane's expression didn't change. "You know I speak the truth. My words go straight to the heart. No mortal man can do what you can do. You sense things before they happen. I used to have that ability too. I saved many lives because of that." Kane turned his head to the side and gave a quick nod. "But if my words won't convince you, then perhaps the first test will."

A guard stepped partially into view and handed Kane a rubber gas mask. Kane put it on. With a second nod, the guard slipped on his own gas mask and handed Kane a gas grenade. He pulled the pin and tossed it inside the bars. Pink smoke started streaming out of the metal canister.

Kane said, "I can't wait to see your face when you wake up forever changed."

Smoke squeezed his eyes shut. He held his breath as long as he could. Minutes passed before he finally succumbed to the power of the life-draining mist. His world became a flowerbed of pink and purple.

CHAPTER 7

SIDNEY ROLLED INTO LAS VEGAS with the Hellcat smelling like cold coffee and fast food wrappers. She'd made a handful of stops to gas up and eat, but the entire trip—driving day and night—had taken just over thirty hours. She drained the last drop of coffee she had at the first stoplight she hit in Las Vegas. The traffic was heavy, just short of noon.

She rolled down the windows. The hot, dry air was a slap in the face that opened her eyes. She wasn't sure if the sauna-like heat was a good thing or not. She needed rest. Her strength was ebbing. Her eyelids were heavy. She turned down the radio and soaked in the sounds of traffic. Her yawn caught a mouthful of air. It also garnered the attention of the landscaping crew loaded in the back of the pickup truck in the next lane. The grubby little men were all hoots and smiles. One of them gave her a thumbs-up. Another wanted her to rev up the car. When the light turned, she blew right by them.

I should have flown.

But there were too many rules on the airways, and she didn't have any connections in Vegas. She needed her guns and ammo. The sweetheart suit. If she was going after Smoke, she was taking the entire arsenal. The Hellcat had it all. All by Smoke's company.

She cruised through the city stoplight to stoplight, checking the bright billboards and scenery. The towering casinos were landmarks in the skyline that she wanted to visit one day, hopefully with Smoke. She checked the navigation on the screen. She was only a few miles from the funeral home and mortuary she sought. Her phone buzzed in the seat beside her.

Not again.

There was a message from Sam, Smoke's half sister. She'd sent ten messages in the past twenty-four hours. Sid had replied to one, stating that she'd let them know when she was there. Sid texted back, "I'm here. Getting a room. Check later."

She didn't have any intention of getting a room or checking back. The less distraction she had, the better. She needed the element of surprise. The Drake shouldn't even see her coming. A few blocks away from her destination, she pulled into a motel and backed the car in. Donning a ball cap and sunglasses, she locked up the car and headed down the street. The pedestrian lunchtime traffic made it easy to blend in. People were coming in and out of fast food restaurants and small retail shops. Sid jogged by a tattoo parlor called Manny's. Motorcycles half filled the parking lot, and she could see men in barber chairs getting tattoos inside.

Sid took a knee and tied her shoe at the intersection adjacent to the funeral home. The building was dated compared to its surroundings. It was out of place, like many of the old casinos that had fallen by the wayside. It was easy to assume the old establishment had been built far enough away from the strip, only to see the expanding city grow around it like a jungle of concrete ivy.

Chin up, she spied the dated sign in front of the building. Drake Funeral Home. The sign looked like the old signs that led into state parks from the fifties. It was made up of wood and sandstone. The large front porch was empty of life. The windows were grimy. A wrought-iron fence surrounded the building, but the gate to the driveway entrance was open. She searched the edges of the building for security cameras, but she didn't see any.

She finished up retying the lace on her sneaker and aimed herself toward the other side of the street. A man called out to her, "Hey, chica, where are you going? Hold on, I'd like to speak with you."

The man approached. He was a tall Mexican with tattoos covering his bare arms from the wrist to the shoulder. His long jet-black hair covered his ears to the neck. Dressed in biker's garb, he came right at her, but he wasn't alone. Two other men followed in behind him. "I've never seen you on this street before. You lost, chica?"

"Do I look lost?" she said.

"Hard to say, judging by those shades you are wearing." His hard eyes grazed over her body. "I saw you roll in on those hot wheels. Very nice. Maybe you are looking for a custom paint job, eh?"

Keeping her attention on the man, she said, "I'm just passing through. It's been a long drive, and I needed to stretch my legs a little."

Grinning, he said, "Why don't you let me stretch those legs for you?"

Fighting the urge to stuff his nose back into his brain with a blow from her fist, she said, "I can handle it, thanks." She started to walk away. Just as she did, a black hearse, the same as the one Smoke was seen in, pulled out of the driveway and headed down the street in the direction from where she'd come. Her eyes followed it.

"Chica, what are you searching for? I'm sure I have whatever you need."

"I'm not looking for anything." Wanting to follow the hearse, she tried to pass by the men.

All three of them closed around her. They each had a gun on her. The leader said, "You might not be looking for something, but you found something. Come with us now, chica."

CHAPTER 8

THE MEN WALKED SID INTO the tattoo parlor and led her into the back. Her escorts seized her wrists with strong, calloused hands and pushed her into one of the tattoo chairs. They held her fast as the bigger man drew the curtain, closing them inside.

He put his face close to hers. "You aren't a bit frightened, are you?"

Sid didn't reply.

The leader stuffed his semi-automatic into the back of his pants. "I like that. A strong woman. I can see you have some fight in you. Let's take a look at those eyes." He removed her sunglasses. "Nice eyes. I like nice eyes. Nice people have nice eyes."

He tossed the glasses down on a metal toolbox and picked up a tattoo gun. "Do you have any tattoos, chica?"

"What's your game?" Sid strained against her captors a little. The muscles in their jaws flexed. "Only a fool snatches a woman off the streets in broad daylight."

"I did it for your own good. Only a fool snoops on the Drake in broad daylight. Chica, they could see you coming from a mile away."

"So you're their watchdog?"

He held the tattoo gun up to her cheek. "No, I'm the dog watcher." He hung the tattoo gun on the back of the chair. His tone softened. He gave his men a nod, and they let her go. "My name is Mark." He showed her his bicep. Among the many colors and patterns was a picture of a church and steeple. The pillars in the front were swords. "Do you know what that is?"

"I'm tempted to say art, but art is in the eye of the beholder, so I'm just going to call it a tattoo."

"No, that's a church. The Church of Nigil." He watched her, waiting to see if his words sank in.

Sid's sharp mind was as weary as her body, but finally, the Church of Nigil rang a bell. They were the old knights that fought against the shifters. "I know it." She eyed the curtain.

"Don't worry about speaking out loud here, Sidney. That curtain is a sound baffle."

"How'd you know my name?"

"I know all about you and John Smoke. The question is, what in the world are you doing here? You're supposed to be in Delta Charlie."

Sid fought a yawn. Despite the rugged appearance, Mark had a warm glow when he spoke that he hadn't had before. "No offense, Mark, but I don't know you from Adam. I think I'll keep that information to myself."

Mark rubbed his stern jaw. "Don't rush out of here yet. Just give me a minute." He took his phone from his pocket and sent a text. "Well, maybe a little longer. Listen, Sid, if you got something going on in that hive of darkness across the street, you need to tell me."

"And if you've had eyes on it all this time, then you should be able to tell me."

"Good point. The hearses come and go, day and night, but it's always quiet within. Aside from the days they have actual funerals. They do many. It's all a front for the drugs they turn loose on the streets. Dead dealers need burials."

"Drugs? Are you sure that's the extent of their operation? I'm not so certain you know as much as you think about the shifters then."

"I know plenty."

"I don't think you do."

Mark's eyes slid over to his men. "Give us a moment, eh."

The men vanished through the heavy curtain.

Mark's phone buzzed. He checked the message. "Huh? I didn't realize. Smoke isn't with you because you think he's in there, don't you?" He shook his head. "So sorry."

"What? How did you know that? Who are you texting with?" She started to reach for the phone but pulled back. "You didn't know, did you."

"Sorry, I called your bluff, Sid. I texted my wife and told her I wanted Chinese tonight. She responded, 'Then don't forget to pick it up on your way home.' She has a wonderful sense of humor. She needs it. She's a terrible cook but excellent with takeout."

Mad with herself, she said, "Mark, I don't have time for this. I need to go. If Smoke is in there, then I can't afford to waste any time. I have to find him."

"Ah, I see. You think he's targeted for the transformation. That's bad." He started toggling through his phone screen. He fished out a pair of reading glasses from his pocket. "Sometimes the lettering is so tiny."

Sid caught a wisp of gray hair on his jet-black head that she hadn't noticed before. "You know, Mark, you don't look like a knight, at least not how I'd envision a modern-day version of it."

"I know, it's the tattoos. I became a knight after the fact. The knights are mostly watchers now. They seek out men with good hearts who can blend in. The truth is, despite my age, I'm still new to it. This hub is my first assignment."

"So the knights have eyes on the Drake everywhere?"

"Everywhere we can keep up with, I'd say. But when the Drake catches on to our presence…" He slashed his finger across his throat and made a sound. "It's all over."

She watched him intently study his phone. "So, did you find anything? Any funerals in the near future?"

"No, they don't advertise so much on the web. I'm just checking the Chinese menu. I'm hungry, but the wife has me on a diet where I only eat breakfast and dinner." He rubbed his stomach. "I could eat a cow right now."

CHAPTER 9

S MOKE'S EYES OPENED. HE WAS strapped down to a hospital bed with a bright white light shining in his face. The bed he lay on was tilted up almost forty-five degrees, to the point where he could see his toes. The only stitch of clothing he had on was his boxer-briefs. Electrode patches covered his chest and shoulders. An IV was running into his vein. A heart monitor beeped at his side.

Great Dane, what's going on now?

He thrust against the straps. The leather cuffs binding his arms and ankles held him fast. His breathing quickened. The air from unseen ducts was chill and icy. It broke him out in goose bumps. He twisted his head around from side to side. He was in an operating room not much different than any such room he'd ever been in before. This time, however, he was the patient.

He searched the room, eyes sliding from place to place. A round clock reading 12:12 hung crooked on the wall. The red second hand didn't work. There was another bed pushed to the side of the room. The sheets on it had dark patches of blood all over. The smell of formaldehyde hung in the air. There was the stench of something sour, too. Behind his head, he heard drops of water splattering on the floor with a steady *drip-drip-drip*.

Smoke closed his eyes. He breathed in and out, easy. Until now, he had felt in control of things. The tide had turned. The Drake meant business, and the time to put him through the wringer had come. They were going to change him even if it killed him.

The double doors popped open. A meaty woman entered the room, slouched over a hospital cart whose wheels wobbled and squeaked as if it were a bad grocery cart. She brought it to a stop alongside his bed. She didn't look at him, but she made an awful chewing sound with her mouth.

"Excuse me," he said to her, "but could you call my medical insurance carrier? I don't think I have coverage for this operation."

She turned. Her saggy face had milky eyes.

Under his skin, he felt invisible spiders crawling up his bones.

She sucked her gums. "My insurance didn't help me none either, funny one. But your blood makes a fine deposit." The blind woman shuffled away, muttering to herself, "Days like this, I wish I was deaf instead of blind. I hate the sound of a man screaming."

The chill wore off. Smoke's blood started to churn. He studied the shiny medical tools and concoctions. Everything on the table was more than enough to take a man apart and put him back together again.

Maybe bounty hunter wasn't such a good career choice.

Kane kicked open the doors. His hands were up in the air and clean. Allison was with him. They both wore dark-gray hospital scrubs. So did the handful of nurses who came in with them and surrounded the table.

Allison loomed over Smoke's head. Her scrubs were skin tight. "Miss me, Smokey? I look good in everything, don't I?"

"I'll admit, I haven't seen you look bad in anything yet. It's the company you keep that makes you look bad. Well, that and the fact that your heart is three sizes too small."

She stroked his face. "Oh, don't be a grinch, Smokey. We're going to be one happy family once all this is over. You'll see." She looked at Kane. "I can't wait to see what becomes of him."

"Assuming that he survives." One of the nurse assistants covered Kane's mouth with the surgical mask. A second assistant added gloves to his hands. "Ah, Mister Smoke, just so you know, much of what we are about to do is very painful."

"I suppose it's too late to ask for anesthetic."

"No, we wouldn't want to do that. You're being given a great gift, but you'll have to earn it. Just like the rest of us did." He picked up a scalpel. "But you're a tough guy. I'm sure you won't scream out so much as the rest."

"Did you scream when they did this to you?"

Kane's brows lifted. "You know, it's been so long that I can't remember. But I assume it's safe to say I did." He leaned close. The scalpel hovered inches from Smoke's abdomen.

"Hold on. I don't willingly succumb to any of this."

"We know," Kane said. "That's why we're doing it this way." He nodded at Allison.

Allison stuck another needle into Smoke's arm. She hung a new bag filled with green liquid on the IV pole. There was an arcane symbol on the transparent bag.

"If that's antifreeze, it better be Prestone," Smoke remarked.

"How are his vitals?" Kane asked Allison.

"He might as well be sleeping."

"Good, but that will change soon enough. Turn the juice on."

Allison gave Kane a funny look. "This one, or that one?"

"The electrodes. Set them to number three."

"Say, that's my lucky number." Smoke started to sing, "Man and a woman had a little ba-a-by, and there was three-ee-ee-ee in the family." A current of electricity coursed through his body. He lurched on the table.

"I said three! Not six!" Kane said.

"Sorry." Allison turned down the dial. "I just didn't like that song, but I don't want you biting your tongue off. I'm certain it can be useful." She stuffed a mouth guard in his face and secured it with a strap over his head. "There, Smokey."

The electrodes ran tremors through his body, giving him a sensation he didn't care for.

"Now the green juice," Kane said.

Allison thumbed the roller clip.

The tube began to fill and snake toward his body.

The fluid slid into his vein, burning like fire.

Smoke groaned.

"Very good. Just so you know, Smoke, this is a very slow and agonizing process, but you'll thank me for it later. They always do, right, Allison?"

She nodded.

"Now, turn up the juice, one click at a time, until you hit ten. It's the best way to get the blood and elixir mixing. Days like this I feel like Victor Frankenstein."

With his blood on fire and electricity shooting through his body, Smoke wriggled and bucked fiercely as the dial went up, up, up in agonizing minutes that felt like hours.

CHAPTER 10

S ID CHECKED INTO THE MOTEL where she had parked the Hellcat, cleaned up, and took a power nap. Her phone alarm went off an hour later. With her head grafted to the pillow, she forced herself up and climbed out of bed. Wiping her mouth, she headed into the bathroom. She rubbed her face, rinsed it off with water, and dabbed it dry with a stiff motel hand towel.

This isn't the kind of place I had in mind when I dreamed of coming to Vegas.

Yawning, she headed out of the bathroom, opened up her duffle bag, and removed the sweetheart suit. She needed a kick and a clear mind. She didn't want to take any chances. If the Drake ran the funeral home, no doubt there would be some sinister elements within. She put on the suit. A tingling sensation pushed away the dreary feeling from constant driving. A new energy surged from head to toe.

That's more like it. If I was smart, I would have driven in it.

Gearing up with a concealed Glock and ammo magazines as she put on a layer of clothing, she shrugged off her thoughts. The sweetheart suits would dehydrate and drain a person if worn too long. Now was the time, however. The time to strike. She'd need every advantage she could get. She donned her sunglasses and stepped outside into the dry desert air.

Mark was there, leaning against the roof post in the shade of the overhang. His blue denim had turned black. "Ready?"

Locking the door, she said, "How long have you been waiting here?"

"You said four thirty, and I'm always early."

"So the funeral is on, is it?"

"The cars are lined up around the corner. Visitation has begun. Your timing couldn't be better. See?" He tipped his chin at the streets.

Dozens of colorful cars with expensive paint jobs and custom effects rolled down the street. A few new cars had rolled into the motel parking lot where they stood. People walked down the sidewalk, most in black. Sharp but dangerous-looking men, some with glamorous women on their arms. Mark came forward and stuck out his elbow. "We need to blend, chica. Ready?"

Sid took his arm. "Just don't get too friendly." They headed down the street with the sun shining in their faces. "There won't be any issues with complete strangers waltzing in?"

"I'm no stranger, I'm a neighbor. They know me."

"If they know you, then won't it be strange that you are a married man walking in without your wife?"

"Ha. She's never been to the parlor. Besides, this is Vegas. There will be plenty of crooked married men with their girlfriends. I have to blend, remember. Appearances can be the difference between life and death."

"I see." She scanned the road. Mark was right. Many people were being dropped off at the front entrance to the funeral home. They exited exotic cars and heaps of junk. Every last one of them had "Criminal" written all over them, but they acted and spoke with respect. "So, Mark, have you ever encountered a real shifter before? Or a deader, for that matter?"

"Again, I'm the eyes and ears, so I can't speak to any action. But if things get scary, I'll be ready."

"Trust me, you won't be."

He looked down at her and shrugged. "Let's hope it doesn't come to that. I've never froze up before, and I don't plan on freezing up today. Besides, nothing freezes in Vegas."

"Who died, anyway?"

"Reggie Hyatt."

Sid tripped, scuffing her shoe on a break in the sidewalk. "Did you say Reggie?"

"Reginald. Reggie. He was a big deal around here. It's a shock to the community that he died." He bent his head down and looked at Sid. "Are you okay, chica? You look like you're staring into your own open grave."

There was only one Reggie Sidney knew of, even though it was a common name. The one she knew, Reggie the Doppelganger, had died a few days ago. She'd seen his body splattered all over the railroad tracks, or at least what she thought was him. The FBI would have picked up the remains, and she'd never given any consideration to a burial. Perhaps this was it. "Sorry, I had a flashback. I knew a shifter named Reggie. I'd be curious to see if this is an open coffin or not."

"I usually check in. Show respect. People like to see the faces of the dead, especially when it's an enemy or rival. Sometimes the coffin is closed, though, because the body's … well, not a body. Bad things happen to bad people. It can be pretty bad here in Vegas."

"I see."

Sid and Mark made their way up the steps into the funeral home. Mark signed the guest book, and they fell in line for the viewing. The people in the room reeked of criminal behavior and cigarette smoke. Gaudy jewelry covered calloused hands and leathery fingers. Men spoke softly, sometimes in angry murmurs. Others exchanged small packets from hand to hand.

Respect for the dead, my ass.

Sid and Mark crept forward one step at a time. The criminal element gave their condolences to a woman Sid didn't recognize. The woman was in her sixties and pretty, wearing a black dress and holding a handkerchief to her nose. Her voice was soft and polite when she spoke. As she talked to the people in front of Sid, Sid eased up to the polished black coffin with Mark by her side. The coffin was open. The man lying in a bed of ivory satin within gave her the willies. It was Reginald the Doppelganger.

CHAPTER 11

"**D**ID YOU KNOW HIM?" ASKED a soft-spoken woman.

Sid tore her eyes away from Reginald's corpse. She opened her mouth to speak, but Mark beat her to it.

"No, ma'am, I'm afraid. We are neighbors in the community. I like to pay my respects whenever I have the chance. I'm sorry for your loss, Mrs., er, Ms. Hyatt. Sorry."

"No need to be sorry. I've only been a Ms. for a few days, and I'm still getting used to it myself. Please, call me Carly." She extended her hand, shaking both Mark's and Sid's. "And you are?"

"My name is Mark. I own the tattoo parlor across the street. This is my chica, Sarah." He put his arm around Sid's waist and made a weak smile.

"I see," Carly said. "Nice to meet you. And thank you for stopping by." Carly locked eyes with Sid. "Are you okay? You look a little peaked."

"I had a long drive yesterday. I wasn't expecting to swing by a funeral today, either." Sid kept her tone flat. "I'm not very comfortable in places like this. A childhood thing."

Carly placed her warm hand on Sid's shoulder and rubbed it. "I understand, dear thing. There's a bathroom in the rear if you need to refresh yourself. Thank you for coming."

Sid gave Carly a nod, then she and Mark moved on, wading into the crowded parlor and blending in. They sat down on a seafoam sofa trimmed in mahogany.

"She didn't seem too sad."

"Or happy either. A nice lady."

"Yeah, too nice."

A stick of gum in a tinfoil wrapper appeared in Mark's hand. He offered it to Sid. "Big Red, my favorite."

"No thanks." Sid could still see Carly through the crowd, hugging a man with a shaved head. A tall, athletic black woman was behind that man. Carly's eyes searched the room and found Sid's again. Sid put her hand on Mark's knee and looked away. *She's on to me.*

"What is it, Sarah?"

"Huh? Oh, yeah, Sarah. That was a clever one. I'm pretty sure she knew you were lying."

"Nah, not me. You're the one who might have given it away. You knew that man, didn't you?"

"Maybe. You?"

"No. I'll have to do some digging."

"I wouldn't do that if I were you. That man, Reginald. He should be dead, but he shouldn't be in one piece."

Mark scratched his neck. "Why, what happened?"

"Let's just say the train didn't miss him, or so I thought."

"Ew, sounds grisly."

"You don't know the half of it."

Sid noticed that two of the people Carly Hyatt had spoken with were making their way toward her and Mark. They stopped and stood right in front of them. Sid perched a brow. She gave Mark a glance then resumed her attention on the man and woman. A quick once-over revealed a police shield on the professionally dressed man's belt. His black slacks and dress shirt were dry cleaned. He was handsome, his head shaved but not to the skin, and he carried a few more pounds than he needed to.

"Uh, hi?"

The black woman was a stark contrast to the man. Taller than Sid, she had the competitive look of an athlete, with a hard look in her dark eyes. Her straight face suggested that she didn't trust many and wouldn't hesitate to draw the pistol on her hip. Her attire was black on black, even a little FBI-like. She eyeballed Sid but focused her stare on Mark.

Looking up at the woman, Mark said to her, "What's with the heat?"

The man said to the both of them, "I'm Detective Slade. This is my partner, Detective Hawthorne. How are you doing?"

"As well as you could expect one to be at a funeral." Sid cozied up to Mark. She couldn't help but think she recognized the man. "Did you know the victim?"

"Victim. That's an interesting choice of words," Detective Slade said.

"Very interesting," Detective Hawthorne agreed.

Sid widened her eyes in mockery. "I'm an interesting person." She couldn't take her eyes off the man's face. *Who is this guy? I know I know him.* Slade had at least a decade of life over her. He wasn't threatening but relaxed and sharp. His eyes never left hers. "So, is there something that you're interested in?"

Slade hitched his thumb over his shoulder and said, "We're investigating the death of Ms. Hyatt's husband, Reginald. She says you came in from out of town. Whereabouts?"

"First, I didn't say I came in from out of town. Second, it's none of your business, Detective. I'm here with my boyfriend, pretty much against my wishes."

Mark leaned back against the wall. "I'm a businessman, an honest one. If there is some shady business you're checking into, I suggest you look around. There's probably half a dozen murderers in here who should be in prison. Great job, Detective."

Detective Hawthorne got toe to toe with Mark. "Watch it, burrito breath."

"Burrito breath? What is that, racist? You better watch what you say, Amazon. I've got friends in high places in the LVPD."

"Make the call, chuck wagon," Hawthorne said.

Flabbergasted, Mark said, "What was that? I don't even know what that means. Do you know what that means, Sid?"

Morning Glory! Way to go, Mark!

"Sid?" Detective Slade said. "Ms. Hyatt says you introduced yourself as Sarah. How interesting."

Hawthorne agreed. "Very interesting."

CHAPTER 12

S ID DIDN'T HIDE HER AGGRAVATION. "You two dimwits are easily entertained."

Hawthorne slid toward Sid.

Slade gave her an easy smile. "Mrs. Hyatt's a good woman. She knows when something or someone is out of place. I do too. It's my job."

"I'm pretty sure you don't know nearly as much as you think, Detective. But I can assure you, you're barking up the wrong tree." Sid removed her hand from Mark's knee and reached into her pocket. She had one of her business cards in hand. She took her eyes off of Slade for a moment when a memory hit her. She looked right back at him and said, "I'll be. And to think I almost missed it. But it's my job to notice things too. Or at least it used to be, heh. You're Wade Slade."

The detective smiled and nodded. "You got me. I can fool most people, but I can't fool everybody. I assure you, I am a real detective, and I take my job very seriously."

"Huh." Sid straightened her back and said to Hawthorne, "I think I know you too."

The woman's eyes narrowed.

"Yeah, Vanessa Hawthorne, captain of the 2008 USA volleyball team. Now that's interesting. You both thought we were interesting. That's a laugh."

"So you're a fan?" Hawthorne said. "I don't do autographs."

"You know them?" Mark asked. "I don't know them. Who's he?"

"Wade Slade was a child TV star. Huge about two decades ago. He dropped off the face of the earth. Me and my sister used to watch your show a lot. I'll be. It's a shame about the hair."

"I still have it, but in my line of work, it became distracting." Slade smoothed his hand over his head. "I should have worn my glasses. They hardly catch me with my glasses. Anyway. Sid, is it? I have to say, I don't take you for trouble. The problem is, you move like law enforcement. Let me guess, FBI?"

Sid didn't want to reveal that much about herself, but because of what she knew about Slade, she said, "Former."

"I have to ask, what is a former agent doing in a place like this? You haven't taken a dark path, have you?"

"Let's just say I'm looking for someone, but I assure you, it wasn't that guy in the coffin. The person I'm looking for I haven't seen." Everything Sid said was the truth, even though she knew who Reginald was. He was the last person she expected to see. "Look at the element that surrounds us. There's at least a dozen cases in here."

Hawthorne made a little smile. "You can say that again."

Sid swore that Slade was about to ask her if she knew the man in the coffin. The words were right on his lips. He fished his own card out of his pocket and handed it to her. "I don't know what you're into, and I don't want to know. I have plenty going on. I've got a good feeling about you, Sid. I'll trust it."

Hawthorne gave Slade a little punch in the arm. "You're just saying that because she was a fan. I hate it when you do that."

"No, that's not why."

"Is to."

"Okay, Vanessa, then what's your opinion? Should we take them downtown?"

Hawthorne's lips wiggled. "She's okay, but I'm not so sure about Antonio Banderas. Look at those tattoos. He's shady."

"You think everyone with tattoos is shady."

Hawthorne shrugged.

"You'll have to forgive her. She's a tad judgmental." Slade handed Sid his card. "In case you need some assistance." Sid started to hand over her card, but Slade said, "No, keep it. I'll assure Ms. Hyatt that you're not an issue. Nice meeting you. The both of you. Carry on with whatever you're doing." The detectives disappeared into the crowd of mourners.

"That was different," Sid said.

"Yeah, so now what?"

Sid spied the exit out of the main parlor. "I'm going to check the powder room."

Mark nodded. "I'll keep an eye out."

Sid moved out of the parlor. This funeral home wasn't as dated as the one run by Titus Tolliver. The furnishings, carpet, and wallpaper were old but still decades newer than the home near DC. She passed a woman coming out of the bathroom who had mascara smeared under her eyes.

The woman bumped Sid, saying, "Excuse me."

Sid moved on past the bathroom and a kitchen in the back. Not seeing anybody, she opened a wooden door lacquered in dark stain with brass fittings. Through the window in the back of the building, she could see one hearse parked. A man in a shabby suit leaned against the back of it, smoking and talking on his cell phone. At the bottom of the stairwell, a single glowing light bulb hung from the ceiling. She crept down the stairs.

The basement was damp and musty. Sid rubbed her nose. Old checkered tiles had a thin layer of soot over them. Much like the upstairs, there were parlors, but they were now used for storage and filled with old furniture. On cat's feet, she moved deeper into the basement toward a hallway lined with doors on either side. The smell of embalming fluid strengthened the farther she went.

The first door she came to was half open, spilling yellow light out into the hallway. Sid peeked her head inside. It was the embalming lab. A body lay covered on the metal cadaver table. A half-eaten sandwich and cup of soda were on a nearby desk. A roach raced over the floor.

Whoever is on that table is big.

She moved in. Standing by the table, she stretched out her fingers and pinched the sheet between them. She peeled the sheet back from the face. Just as she did, another presence entered the room.

"Can I help you?"

CHAPTER 13

A LONG-FACED MAN WITH SAGGING CHEEKS and hollow eyes had entered the lab. Very tall and big boned, he blocked the exit. Wearing a white shirt with sleeves rolled up to his elbows and black slacks, the gaunt and creepy man looked like a typical mortician, just giant sized.

Sid placed the lab table between her and the man. "I guess you wouldn't believe me if I told you I'm drawn to weird places."

The door clicked shut behind the man. His eyes found Sid's, and his eyebrows lifted. He swept his thinning locks of hair aside and said, "You'd be surprised at the number of people I get down here. You'd think the smell would keep them away, but many are fascinated by the face of death. Pretty things such as yourself showing up here used to surprise me, but not anymore. I'm Frank."

"Sidney."

"As long as you're here, you might as well get a gander at the rotting gem on the table." He moved slowly across the room in three steps. With the steady and strong fingers of a dentist, he peeled back the sheet. "There you go. Have a look. He's finished, mostly."

The tightness in Sid's face eased. The man on the table wasn't Smoke. It was a big-framed man covered in tattoos from head to toe. The mark of a rising black sun like an eye was on him in many places. *Thank the Lord it's not John!*

"Interesting reaction," Frank said. "You were expecting someone else, I see."

"Everyone's a detective these days. But yes, I was thinking it was someone else, and I'm glad it isn't." Her hand dropped toward her waist, and her fingers stretched for her gun. As she went for the weapon, she refrained. Frank was imposing, but he hadn't posed a threat. Instead, he moved about like an old doctor past his prime but filled with wisdom, taking his own time about how he went about things. Sensing an opportunity, she said, "Has anyone ever told you that you look like—"

"Fred Gywnne? Certainly, I'm his brother."

Sid's jaw dropped.

Frank chuckled. "I'm teasing, young lady. I'm of no relation to that lovable and affable Munster. Unlike him, I have a much darker side. Besides, I was more of a Ted Cassidy fan, myself." He ran his fingers over the dead man's face. "It seems I have a little too much embalming buildup there." With his thumbs, he smoothed out a bulge that formed a crease in the man's neck. "That's better. You know, the tattooed ones are some of the best ones to do. The ink gives them the appearance of life. Especially in the face, but not many have their faces inked. Many of the Indians used paints during their burials," he said as if he had been there way back when. "I learned many traits from the Indians."

"Thanks for the history lesson. If you'll excuse me, I think I'll let you get back to work." She made for the door.

In a long side step, Frank cut her off. A sharp scalpel appeared in his hand. Casting a vulture-like glance down on Sid, he said, "Tell me, who are you really looking for? Perhaps I can help."

"It's private." Sid's thoughts ran through a checklist. If the Drake was making plans to transform Smoke, this man would know something about that. *If Frank is a shifter, just remember how cocky they are.* She decided to play her card. "I'm looking for a big guy. He might have come here with Kane and Allison."

"It takes a lot of guts to drop right into a nest of vipers, Sidney. Perhaps I should remove them from you."

Feeling his cold, fetid breath on her face, she replied, "You'd be surprised at the number of vipers I've killed."

"Bravado. I like it."

Sid went for her gun.

Quick as a snake, Frank seized her wrist.

She punched him in the face with a hard fist.

His teeth clattered, but he held her fast.

Sid kneed his groin. The move drew forth a mocking chuckle.

"Little woman, your struggles are in vain." Frank yanked Sid into him. His arms enveloped her body. He lifted her from the ground and squeezed with the strength of a bear.

"Uh!" Sid moaned. Her ribs cracked. Frank's powerful squeeze made her eyes bulge. "Let go of me."

"It's been a long time since I squeezed a person to death. Long ago, the Kanawha Indians called me Eh-hef-haloom. That was their word for bear breaker. I was the only person they ever saw kill a bear with his hands. Not long after that, I killed them. A lost tribe now forgotten, even in the history books, but there's a county named after them."

Fighting for breath, Sid tried to scream. No sound came, only pain that felt like sharp daggers piercing her spine.

Crack!

Sid's thoughts went into overdrive. *Oh no! My back!* The fear of paralysis surged through her. More cracking sounds followed. She could see her vertebrae popping out of place. The worst of the worst was happening.

Suddenly, her captor wobbled.

She slipped from his grasp and fell to the floor, sucking for air.

The room exploded into a battleground of surging bodies. From out of nowhere, Mark plowed into Frank like a charging bull. He drove Frank back into his desk.

Frank jammed the scalpel into Mark's back.

"Gah!"

Detective Hawthorne swung a length of pipe into Frank's big jaw.

The big man's head twisted away then back again with a broad grin. He slung Mark's bleeding body away.

"What are you, some kind of geriatric terminator?" Detective Hawthorne cocked back for another swing. She turned it loose.

Frank caught the pipe. With a jerk of his hand, he tore it from her grip. Catching her gaping, he clubbed her with it. The first hit busted her arm just below the shoulder. The second blow would have crushed her skull.

But Hawthorne snaked her head out of the way. She didn't stand a chance against the third strike that Frank prepared to bring. He was a mauler with intent to kill.

"Cadavers, cadavers, I like fresh cadavers," he said.

Detective Slade appeared in the doorway. "What in the world is going on here?"

Crawling back on her butt, Hawthorne said, "Shoot that spooky bastard!"

Slade jerked his pistol out. He hesitated to fire.

"Now, Slade!" Hawthorne yelled.

Slade cracked off three shots, center mass. *Blam! Blam! Blam!*

Frank kept coming.

CHAPTER 14

S ID CAUGHT HER BREATH. REGAINING her senses, she freed her Glock from the back of her pants. As Frank closed in on Hawthorne and Slade, ready to unload paralyzing swings, she cracked off several shots, hitting Frank square in the knees. The bullets ripped through his slacks into his flesh.

Frank tumbled forward in a lurch. He hit the linoleum face first.

With agony in his eyes but determination and strength in his limbs, Mark jumped on Frank's back. He wrestled the pipe free. With the help of an angry Detective Hawthorne, he wrenched the mortician's arms behind his back.

"Cuff him, Slade! Cuff him!" Hawthorne demanded.

Detective Slade shackled the man. With his key, he double-locked the cuffs. Looking at Frank's wrists, he said, "That was close. For a minute there, I thought I was going to need bigger handcuffs. What's this goon wearing, body armor?"

Frank laughed when they propped him up against the wall.

"That's creepy," Slade said. He found Sid. "Are you okay?"

"I'm still breathing." She sucked in through her teeth, wincing, and forced herself to her feet. "Keep him quiet. I've got to look for somebody."

"Somebody who?" Hawthorne rubbed her busted arm. "Geez, ugly grandpa almost broke me. I've never seen an old dude move like that before." She kicked Frank but spoke to Sid. "If you're looking for somebody, no doubt this Franken Creep knows something. I say we squeeze it out of him."

"Good luck with that, little lady," Frank said.

"He's not going to be forthcoming, trust me," Sid said, grimacing and avoiding Frank's eyes while she dug his keys out of his pocket. "I'll be back." Before she left, she said to Mark, "You gonna make it?"

"This isn't the first time I've been tapped. I'm sure it won't be the last. I'll live. Just go."

Sid slipped out of the room only to find a shadow behind her. It was Slade. The older man had a cool and steely resolve. He was nothing like the young and flashy characters she grew up watching on TV. There was something hard nosed and old school about him.

He holstered his gun.

"I wouldn't do that if you're coming along," she said.

"Duly noted, but just so you know, I'm not the best shot. I'm more of a 'have wits, will travel' kind of guy." He followed after her down the hall. "So who are you looking for?"

"My husband."

"I see. You know, you could have just asked for some assistance from the—"

Sid stopped in her tracks and put a finger to his lips. "Listen, Slade. You need to know there are more people like that man back there. A lot more. This isn't an adventure of just flesh and blood, but rather powers and principalities. I don't think you're ready for it."

Slade's right brow arched. "I'm not going anywhere, sister. This is Vegas. It's been a long time since I was shocked by what I saw. Lead the way."

The basement tunneled into a corridor of doors. It was quiet and stark. Sid flipped a switch. The fluorescent lights in the hall flickered on with a steady hum. Some of the tubes were dead. Others faded in and out, but the light was ample. One door at a time, she entered room after room. The doors were heavy steel bars that locked from the outside. The first room she entered was painted on all four walls, views of an extravagant apartment looking out over Central Park.

Slade whistled when he walked in. "Whoa, now this is weird." He traced his finger over the huge glass pane window that was painted on the wall. He fingered Central Park. "It's been a long time since I've been to the Big Apple. This makes for an interesting trip. Some of this paint is peeling, though." He turned around slowly, taking in the entire room. "That's odd. This layout is from the sixties, like a scene from *Mad Men*. Have you ever watched that show?"

"No." Sid kicked at the only real piece of furniture on the slab floor, a metal spring cot with a withering mattress on it. "Let's see what's behind door number two."

She unlocked one room after the other. All of the walls were painted in grand, realistic detail. There was a view from Paris and of the London Tower. Niagara Falls was one of the rooms. There were houses, mansions, and gardens. There were blood stains on the floor in some. Cots in most but not all. She was almost to the end of the hall when she noticed that one of the doors was open. Light came out the door.

She stepped inside, lost her breath, and dropped her gun.

Slade edged in behind her. He moved to the center of the room and wheeled around on the back of his heel. "This is pretty crappy. What is it?"

Sid didn't want to say, but she did anyway. "It's my home."

CHAPTER 15

S ID SAT ON THE COT in the middle of the room with the willies dancing up her arms. The images on the wall weren't as perfect as a picture, but the clarity was there. It was the interior of her and Smoke's garage apartment, down to the coffee pot in the kitchenette corner.

"You live here, huh?" Slade said, sliding along the edge of the wall. "Well, it's quaint, I'll give you that. Sorry, I didn't see the initial charm in it." He sniffed. "Smell that?"

Sid wiped her nose. A chemical smell lingered. She leaned down and gave the blankets on the cot a whiff. "Some kind of gas was ignited in here. Maybe a sleeping agent of some sort." She felt dead inside. Her heart was sinking. Smoke had been in here. She was certain of it. Now, he was gone.

"You might want to invest in some better security at wherever this place is. Looks like someone got a good look." Slade pointed at the computer and desk painted on the wall. "These monitors have little cameras in them. Hackers can spy from there, good and bad ones. It's hard to buy a computer without one these days. I put a piece of masking tape over my camera." His eye caught something. He walked over and picked up a metal canister. "Well, looky here. You were right. It's a sleeping agent. XSD10. The lab guys down at LVPD might be able to trace it."

"Or not. No, I think Frank might be able to answer some questions if we can get it out of him."

"Let's take him down to the station. You can file a missing persons."

Sid got up on her feet. "Don't take this wrong, but this isn't your typical kidnapping. All of this is off the books. Besides, we don't really have anything."

Slade pointed at the door. "That man back there, Frank, assaulted two police officers. That's more than enough to get the ball rolling."

"I don't need your help. Just let me talk to him, okay?"

"Fine. I'll give you a few minutes to convince me." Slade made his way to the door. "After you."

As soon as they crossed the threshold, they encountered Mark and Hawthorne lumbering down the hall. Their faces were filled with shock and surprise.

"What happened?" Sid yelled.

Catching her breath, Hawthorne said, "Frankenberry got the jump on us. He's gone."

"Jump on you? How?" Slade was incredulous.

Hawthorne tossed Slade his cuffs. "He slipped out of those like Houdini."

"No way, I double-locked them."

Hawthorne shrugged and rubbed a knot on her head. "We tried to stop him, but he overpowered us. It was like wrestling a mule."

"Then he cracked our heads together like a pair of coconuts kissing." Mark was rubbing his head too. "I still have blinding fireworks in my eyes. He said something just before he did that." He shook his head. "Uh, what was it?"

Hawthorne glared at Mark. "He said, 'Tell Sid that she's far too late. The next time she sees Smoke, it will be all over. Tell her she should go home and enjoy her final days.'"

The drive home across the country in the Hellcat was long and miserable. The stretches of barren highway were agonizing. Sid didn't want to talk to anybody. She sulked. Smoke was lost. He was a cloud of dust.

She had managed to stick around a little longer in Vegas, but after a few hours, the truth had sunk in. Kane and Allison were two steps ahead of her. Now, despite the assistance she was offered by Mark, Slade, and Hawthorne, she had to go home. Go home and wait. Wait and pray.

She tried to find that silver lining in the clouds, but it wasn't there. If Kane truly tried to transform Smoke, she knew her husband would die first. She would too, at least that's what she thought. Driving with her taillights to the sun sinking in the west, she felt the baby kick. The child might be all she had left of Smoke. Might be his legacy. Their legacy together.

Her throat tightened with memories. The first time she met Smoke—tall, dark, and mysterious. Trying to trip her up with clever words. She'd liked it. He had reeled her in with quirky mannerisms and vanishing acts that made him hard to hold. Her heart ached. It was the closest she ever felt to being a military wife, someone married to a soldier who gallivanted off to battle and never returned again. Who would deliver the dark message if Smoke never returned? What if she never knew?

No, I'll see Allison again. She can't stay out of my business. She wouldn't pass an opportunity to gloat. And what about Megan? You still have to fight for her, Sid.

She sped through West Virginia and finally hit DC a few hours later. It was late evening, and traffic was light. Finally, she hit the highway and turned down the state road, where the pine trees lined up mile after mile on either side. She turned down the drive, hoping to see a light in the garage apartment, but the lights were dim. She backed into the garage, locked up the Hellcat, and went to the apartment.

It was cold inside the studio. She started to turn the thermostat up. Instead, she trudged over to the bed, covered up in the blankets, and cried.

CHAPTER 16

SMOKE WOKE UP. HE LAY on a cold, hard floor staring upward. No ceiling lingered above, only darkness. A chilly draft caressed the hairs on his body like mistress death. His feet were freezing. He spied the light sources. Small round domes were mounted in the cinderblock walls. The doorway gave off an eerie glow.

He crawled up onto his hands and knees. The burning in his blood had subsided, but there was still pain, inside and out. He pushed up to his feet and discovered he wore only a clean set of trousers. He shuffled to the outer edge of the room, marking off twenty paces between the center and the wall. The room was oblong. The tops of the walls ended in darkness. They must have been twenty feet tall.

Holding his stomach, he walked along the wall and stopped at a metal door. He started pounding on it. "Kane! Let me out! I'm tired of playing your games."

A flicker of electricity caught his ears. High above him, suspended by chains, centuries-old candelabra hung. The newly installed bulbs lit up one at a time.

Smoke scanned more of the room. It was an arena of some sort, musty and unkempt. It was old, but with a few modern repairs. Rows of chairs encircled the main floor, tucked safely atop a thirty-foot riser. He slowly spun around, stopping when he spied Kane and Allison sitting in one of the rows, holding hands.

"It's good to see you awake, Smoke," Kane said, making a smile full of little teeth. "I didn't think you'd sleep too long. They never do. At least, not the ones that live. Good for you. I must say, part of me is disappointed. The other part, not so much."

"So what's the next step, gladiator games?"

"You might say that. We've all been here. We call this place the Proving Grounds." Kane leaned over and let Allison whisper in his ear. He nodded and smiled. "You've survived the transfusion stage. Now, it's time to see if that transfusion had lasting effects. The burning in your arms, well, a little bit of adrenaline will do you a world of good. It's euphoria, you'll see."

"Are you going to come down here yourself and see if it's working?"

"Clever, Smoke. No, I'm going to watch with a bird's-eye view. Believe me, once you get those extremities going, you'll thank me." Kane called out to someone hidden in the stands. His voice echoed. "Release the deaders."

The metal door slid upward. Smoke dashed for it. The door stopped less than a foot off the floor. Smoke couldn't even squeeze through it.

Kane was laughing. "Oh, I knew you would try that. They all do. But let it be known: that isn't an escape route. It's a labyrinth of death. No, no, no, Smoke. Just look behind you."

Trap doors opened up in the floor. Deaders scrambled out. The concealed doors snapped shut again. Three deaders lumbered out. Each of them carried a baseball bat. Dressed in grimy mechanic's overalls, they converged on Smoke.

Smoke backpedaled.

Kane and Allison got up from their seats and leaned over the edge. "They'll kill you, Smoke. Stop running and fight. That's what we paid for."

Not finding any avenue of escape, Smoke danced out of the shambling men's paths. Their stiff limbs moved with purpose. There was intent in their sunken eyes. Deaders weren't hard to beat, but they were hard to kill. As his mind sought a way out, his instincts fired. It was hard for him not to fight when his body went into survival mode. A revival of energy flowed through him.

The closest deader took a lengthy swing. Smoke grabbed the bat. He pulled the deader off balance. The iron grip of the deader didn't loosen on the bat. Smoke shattered the deader's knee with his heel. He spun the bat head over handle until the fiend's grip freed. He brought it up to catch the second deader swinging. The bats collided with a loud *clack*.

Allison clapped with excitement.

Using his speed, Smoke connected the bat to the temples of the deaders. Bone was hard, but Smoke hit harder. He disabled the undead things with blow after blow to the temple. They sprawled on the ground, crawling all over without direction, senseless.

Kane said, "Well, that was mildly entertaining. To be expected. How do you feel, Smoke?"

Great! That was Smoke's first thought. The truth was, he felt more than great. He felt like he could take on the world. A little like if he'd taken a super vitamin. Not as strong, but whatever was going on, he felt like it was lasting. "This is childish, Kane." He tossed the bat aside. "Come on. Let's make it interesting. For all of the marbles. Me versus you."

"No, that's not part of the plan. You see, I make plans and I stick to them. I don't operate on emotions." He gave a nod toward a silhouette way up in the stands.

A trap door opened far away from Smoke. A man hopped out. He was a big, bearded guy with muscles like a professional wrestler's. "Oh yeah!" he said when he eyed Smoke.

Smoke squared up on the guy.

"Do you remember Wild Jack, Smoke? As I was told, it was quite a fight the two of you had in Night Bird's sanctuary. You should have killed him, but you showed compassion. Wild Jack has wanted a rematch ever since. I promised him that if I got the chance, he would have it."

The retired MMA fighter's eyes were as wild as his name. He was juiced. His pupils were tiny dots in his eyes. Big blue veins popped out in his shoulders, neck, and arms. He wore a skintight Guns N' Roses t-shirt over cut-off jean shorts, with a blue bandana on his neck.

"I supposed he's going to try and kill me, same as he did last time."

"This match will be to the death one way or the other, Smoke." Kane made a crooked smile. "You better not hold back on this one. If you do, the enhanced Wild Jack will tear you apart like a Rottweiler chewing a juicy bone."

CHAPTER 17

S MOKE HAD MANAGED TO BEAT every opponent the Drake had thrown at him. He beat some with weapons and others with wit. In all of those battles, he'd never been as confident as he was now. He'd handled Wild Jack before. He'd handle him again. With a flick of his fingers, he said, "Here, boy."

The bullish Wild Jack rushed right at him.

Smoke connected first with a solid fist, smacking right into the man's jaw.

Wild Jack ran right through it. He overpowered Smoke and drove him hard onto his back.

They wrestled like wild cats on the floor, in a knot of muscles that twisted, spat, elbowed, kneed, and punched.

In a surge of uncanny strength, Wild Jack reversed Smoke's arm bar and put him in a two-handed head lock.

Great Dane!

Wild Jack's powerful muscles went to work, constricting Smoke's throat. The wrestler tried to snap his neck.

Smoke stepped behind the fighter's legs just enough so he could get a surge and hip toss the man. He landed on top of Wild Jack, pinning the man between him and the floor.

Wild Jack held him fast, saying, "You'll die, rookie! You'll bleed, you'll cave, you'll die. Oh yeah!"

Smoke drove elbow after elbow into the man's ribs. Nothing shook Wild Jack free. Smoke clawed at the air and saw Kane and Allison looking right at him, their faces intent. Fighting for breath, he pitched over to the side and balled up with Wild Jack on top of him. He tucked his chin down as far as he could, trying to wedge it between the corded meat of Wild Jack's forearm and biceps. It bought him time, but only a little. He was choking. His air was thinning.

Smoke's savvy wouldn't work the wonders it once did. There was no super vitamin pill to take, only the annoying scratching of Wild Jack's rough beard on Smoke's ear—and Wild Jack's insane mumblings. This savage match was not one of wits. It was survival of the fittest. Smoke let go of his inhibitions. He turned loose his rage.

Flexing, shaking, writhing, and slobbering, Smoke turned into a mass of angry energy. He squirmed and fought against Wild Jack's powerful arms and legs. He fought himself free and bounced to his feet. He took in a gust of air and let it out with a howl.

Wild Jack sprang to his feet.

Smoke jumped him. He peppered Wild Jack's face with lightning-fast, hard punches to the face. He crushed Wild Jack's nose. Blood dripped on the floor.

Wild Jack took the punches in stride. He countered with his own. He turned loose uppercuts and haymakers.

Anticipating every strike, Smoke countered. His fists cracked ribs. A hard punch crushed Wild Jack's throat.

The burly man fought on for a second before he started gasping for air.

Smoke didn't let up. He pummeled the man. His fists were wet with blood.

Wild Jack lay on the floor, dying.

Smoke didn't care. He didn't care about anything but blood. He snatched one of the baseball bats from the floor. He brought it over his head and started to bring it down full force.

Wild Jack's eyes showed no plea for mercy, only hatred. He spat blood and barely managed to say, "Finish it, monster."

Monster.

The word struck a chord. It connected with the man whom the beast had buried. Smoke twisted his head around and upward. Kane and Allison were gloating. Their eyes were hungry for the kill. Smoke cocked the bat behind him and slung it at the both of them.

Kane snatched the bat out of the air. His sideways smile turned up in the corner. "It's not a problem, Smoke. You don't need to finish him. Our project is finished already."

Temper cooling, Smoke tried to sort out what Kane meant. Wild Jack lay on the floor wheezing. His face was swollen. Blood had been smeared beneath the both of them. The brute thrashed on the ground. Smoke knew there was nothing he could do to save the man. His wicked days were over. But the blood was on Smoke's trembling fingers. Wild Jack was a man. Smoke had killed him.

A drop of blood fell to the ground. It made a splash with startling clarity. Smoke looked down. His eyes grazed his bloody fists. His skin was discolored and gray. He opened up his fists, revealing extra-long fingers. The knuckles were big. His fingertips were long and sharp like an eagle's talons.

"What has happened to me?"

Together, Kane and Allison laughed out loud. Kane started clapping. "Welcome to the club, Smoke. You're one of us now."

Smoke looked over his arms and legs. There was fine hair, like fur, all over them. "What have you done to me? What am I?"

"You're a shifter the same as the rest of us. With Wild Jack's dying breath, the process will be complete. You killed the man with your bare hands. Wild Jack was an innocent man who had repented. Now, he's dead. The process is complete." Kane stretched out his arms as if he was the emperor of the arena. With his fingers opening and closing into fists, he said, "Embrace your gift, Smoke. Embrace your power. There is nothing in the world like being a shifter. You will see. Your life will be richer and fuller from here on out. You can't escape it."

Smoke searched for a way out, but there wasn't one. His temperature started to rise. He pounced over to one of the trap doors in the floor. He wedged his fingernails into the narrow seams. With a strenuous heave, the trap door buckled under his raw strength. He dropped inside the hole. The last thing he heard was Kane muttering to Allison, "Oh dear, I didn't see that coming. I didn't see that coming at all. Fetch the horde after him."

CHAPTER 18

"HI, TED. IT'S GOOD TO see you!" Sid threw her arms around her old section chief, Ted C. Howard. She hadn't seen him since they recused him from the clone factory. Gruff as an aging linebacker, he accepted her embrace in his strong, bearish arms. "I've missed you. Welcome back from the dead."

He kissed her cheek. "One thing's for sure. I've never felt so alive. You know, I never got a chance to thank you, Sidney." Ted took her by the hand and sat her down on one of the benches overlooking the DC Reflecting Pool. "I have to admit, when I wake up in the morning, sometimes I have to pinch myself because I think I'm dreaming. To be honest, I'm still not completely sure what happened."

"Your old protégé Deanne Drukker shot your clone deader than a doornail. I was mortified. I don't think my heart ever hurt so much as the moment I first thought you were gone."

Ted adjusted the flap of his overcoat he was sitting on. "Yeah, but do you really think she thought it was me? Maybe she knew it was a clone. I've given it a lot of thought since I've been back. Maybe she was double undercover. Perhaps even she was a clone?"

"You're bringing too many dead back to life." She patted his knee. "Let's just stick with you for now. I don't think I can handle any more."

"You got it. So how are you doing?"

"Fine," Sid lied. She was reeling inside. Sleep was hard to come by. There weren't any signs of Smoke or the Drake.

"Aw, come on. I can see you're hurting. Talk to me about it. We have some catching up to do. As I understand it, you and Smoke are married. I'm surprised, and I'm not surprised."

Sid spent the next couple of hours filling Ted in. It came out like some sort of confession. She even spoke to Ted about Kane. Ted would nod and hold her stare with his soft, understanding eyes. He was a man of wisdom. A true confidante. "I'm sorry, Ted. I'm talking your ears off."

"No, you need this. Heck, I need this. Our lives have been turned upside down and inside out, but you know what?"

"What?"

"We're gonna see it through." He squeezed her hand. "You can make it through this. You and your baby. I know you're worried about Smoke, but even if he doesn't make it, you will."

Tears ran down Sid's cheeks. "I don't want to fight this fight without him. It's not the same. I miss him."

"You know you have to keep swimming, Sid. If you don't, you'll drown. That's what the enemy wants. That's what they're counting on. They want the good guys to quit. Just when they think we're down, we have to stick it to them. Hit them right in the gut. Hard."

"Maybe you should start coaching football now that you've officially retired." She sniffed, wiped her nose, and laughed. "You'd make a great coach."

"Well, I might have plagiarized that speech a little. But who's going to know?" He stretched his arm over the backside of the bench behind Sid and stared into the pool. "Life's such a mystery. Heh. You should have seen Mrs. Howard's face when I showed up at home. I'd never seen her make that face before. She was thrilled but torn. It was strange, and I couldn't figure it out until she finally confessed yesterday."

"Confessed what?"

"That she was dating. I have to admit, I was surprised. I wasn't dead that long, and it really threw me. We had a strong relationship. At least I thought we did. Now, she's a different person. I'm not so sure we're going to make it." He sighed. "I'm some sort of dead man walking." Scratching above his ear, he said, "Aw, listen to me, whining like a baby. My problems aren't nearly as bad as yours."

"Hey!"

Ted nudged her. "Aw, just remember what I always say."

"Don't eat too much fast food for breakfast?"

"No, when you're feeling down—"

"Kick ass and smile."

Ted's pep talk lit a fire under Sid. Not a big one, but enough to get her going. Sitting around and sulking wasn't going to do her any good. She needed to find Smoke or at least find out what happened to him. She watched for tidbits on the news, read the papers, and looked for any unusual activity at all over the next few days. Finally, she headed to FBI headquarters, filled with frustration. The elevator rose to the floor of Section Chief Cyrus Tweel's office. The doors split open. Sadie was there. The pretty black woman's smile was as warm as sunshine. She hugged Sid. "Don't you ever stay away from me this long again, you hear me?"

"Sorry, Sadie. It's been rough."

"Tough times are times best spent with tough friends. Like me. I've missed you, Sid, but my heart jumped when I heard you were coming in. To be honest, I didn't know if I was going to hug you or hit you."

"You hit somebody?"

"Hey, this sweet thing has more fight in her than you know. I had to fight. It was the only way to keep them ornery boys out of my skirt." Sadie wrapped her arm around Sid's waist and marched toward Cyrus's office. She spoke to the secretary. "Tell Cyrus that Sidney Smoke is here, Louise."

The young secretary typed a message into her computer.

"They text everything now," Sadie said. "They have to document everything. Ain't that sad."

"What happened to Jane?"

"She dropped dead of a heart attack a few weeks ago. The entire department went nuts. It's a shame, but I told everyone that's what happens when you get a full moon." Sadie looked at Sid and said, "Speaking of moons, your eyes are as big as them. What's wrong?"

Sid swallowed the lump in her throat. *Jane was a clone. I never would have suspected.* Not certain if Sadie was privy to everything going on with the Drake, Sid replied, "I'm just shocked is all."

"Life is chock full of surprises."

"You can go in now, Mrs. Smoke," Louise said.

"Don't leave without saying goodbye, hun." Sadie hugged Sid again.

Sid entered Cyrus's office. Cyrus and Rebecca Lang were waiting.

CHAPTER 19

REBECCA, AN ATTRACTIVE, SCHOLARLY, PETITE woman, threw her arms around Sid. "Sidney! I'm so glad you decided to come by. I've been meaning to thank you."

Sid peeled the wiry woman's arms off her. "You're welcome." Looking serious, Cyrus started in with a courtesy hug, but Sid stopped him. "I've had plenty of hugs today. Save it for some other time."

"Please have a seat then." Cyrus took his spot behind his desk.

Rebecca sat across from Sid. She was glowing. "Can I get you something to drink?"

"No thanks."

Rebecca seemed more like the person Sid originally met. She was eager but not overly enthusiastic. The blonde's behavior was in stark contrast to the monster she'd become shortly after that. Sid had tussled with her several times in Cyrus's office. Without that tension, the atmosphere was downright weird.

"So what's going on with the Black Slate, Cyrus? I haven't heard a peep about any of it. Aren't there any new assignments?"

"The silence is deafening, isn't it?" Cyrus put his glasses on and pecked on his keyboard. "Sorry, I needed to respond to that." He pushed himself away from his desk. "Anyway, since the collapse at the clone factory, the Black Slate list hasn't been mentioned at all. The Drake investigations are suspended. But don't come up out of your seat, Sid. You saw the news. Government agencies have gone nuts. The cleanup and damage control have been a scramble. We just got our feet back under us a few days ago. I have to say, I'm relieved. I"—he looked over at Rebecca—"we could use a break. Honestly, I don't even want to hear the name Black Slate. As far as I'm concerned, you stopped the clones. They're defeated."

"You know this isn't over yet. The clones were only one layer of the Drake's power. The Drake is still out there." Sid's fingers dug into the arms of her chair. "Besides, I didn't come here for a new assignment, I came for help. They have Smoke, Cyrus. I need to find him. I need something to go on."

Cyrus's eyes slid over to Rebecca's and back to Sid's. "Sid, since this last debacle, I've got eyes all over me. As a matter of fact, it wouldn't surprise me one bit if there were bugs in this office."

Sitting on the edge of her chair, Rebecca said, "We've checked, but we've been really discreet about it. What are you supposed to do if you find them? You can't remove them."

Sid picked up a sticky note and pen from Cyrus's desk and started writing while at the same time saying, "So who do you think is keeping tabs on you, the FBI or the NSA?" Sid held the note up for both of them to see. It read, "Write it down, dumbasses!"

"Oh, it could be either one, I suppose," Rebecca said with a nod. "But you must believe us, Sid. We don't have anything new."

"As a matter of fact, Sid, chances are we're going to be given a new assignment. It looks like I'm going to be relocated. This happens, especially after administrative changes or big shakeups. They like to clean house."

"I know how it works."

"I have to be honest with you, Sid, I'm glad to be free of it. Rebecca and I have another chance. A new start." His chair groaned when he leaned forward and back again. He rested his elbows on the desk. "Maybe you should make a break for it too. And don't get me wrong, Smoke earned my respect as much as any man could, but if he's gone, he's gone."

Sid's eyes narrowed. "It's only been a few weeks, Cyrus. I came to ask for help. All you're giving me is a song and dance. I don't appreciate it. Not after all that we've been through."

"Honestly, Sid, whatever is going on with the Drake, well, I just think they'd rather ignore it. They took a stab at it, but it ended up creating a bigger mess than they wanted."

"Or maybe they just didn't think you would have any success to begin with." Rebecca crossed her knees and kicked her leg. "I think it's all a show. We're the stars, and the omnipotent weirdoes out there get off on it."

"Let's not go there again. You know it gives me a headache."

"Well, how do you think I feel? I lost months of my life and woke up on a slab of warm goo. You know I can't let that go."

"We talked about this. We agreed to move on."

Rebecca's eyes flickered over to Sid then back to Cyrus. "You talked. I listened. I sort of agreed." She looked at Sid again. "You know, I'm glad you came by. If I were in your shoes, I'd do the same thing. I'm half tempted to join you."

Cyrus's brows knitted together. "Becky, will you watch what you say? They're giving us enough grief already. Let's talk more about it tonight." He scraped his mouse over the desk. "Sorry to make it short, Sid, but I have to go to another meeting. Listen, you have to believe me, we don't have anything." He stood. "If we did, I'd let you know."

As Cyrus headed to the door, Rebecca scribbled something down on a yellow sticky note. She slipped it into Sid's palm and gave her a hug. "I really am grateful for you and Smoke. Best to you."

Sid shook Cyrus's hand on the way out. "Take care, Cyrus."

"You too."

After Cyrus closed the door, Sid said to Louise, "It was nice meeting you."

Louise smiled. "You too. Have a good day."

"Uh, Louise, where's Sadie's station?"

Louise pointed. "Second row and three cubicles over."

"Thanks."

Sid pretended to head that way but slipped into the break room. She opened up Rebecca's note. It read, "We don't know anything." Sid wadded it up and threw it away. "Damn."

CHAPTER 20

S ID RETURNED HOME THAT EVENING only to discover an old white Ford Bronco pulled underneath the overhead. *Sam and Guppy. Great.* She'd visited with enough people for one day, but she guessed she'd avoided Sam and Guppy long enough. *I might as well get this over with.* She parked her car in the garage and entered through the side door. Sam and Guppy were sitting on the sofa, eyeballing the TV. Sam was stretched out, end to end, and Guppy sat with her legs on his lap. He was rubbing Sam's bare feet.

Sam was eating nuts. Her eyes didn't even meet with Sid's.

"Hello?" Sid said as she closed the door behind her.

Guppy made a weak smile. "Hi, Sid."

"Hey," Sam added. She was barely interested.

Sid rolled her eyes. She'd been around long enough to know when Sam was being pouty. She stepped between the sofa and television. "You're here, so just come out with it."

"Out with what? I'm just chilling." Sam munched on a handful of nuts and washed it down with a diet soda. "Could you get out of the way? It's the fourth quarter, and we're down by a field goal. Stupid Tomlin and those two-point conversions!"

Sid switched the TV off.

Sam sat up with a gasp. "How dare you?"

"It's my home. Besides, that game's not live. It's Wednesday night." Sid took her boots off and left them by the door. "I'm going to make some coffee. Anyone else want any?"

"I'll take a mug," Guppy said.

"You just rub my feet, bald man."

"I am." He turned back to look at Sam. "Rubbing her feet is the only thing keeping Sam out of your face, Sid. If I stop, she's going to run wild on you."

"Oh, I am not, Guppy."

"You're not, huh. Well, let's see what happens if I stop."

Sid put fresh grounds in the coffee maker while eyeing Sam and Guppy at the same time. Sam squirmed for a moment while Guppy lifted up his sausage fingers to see. Sam's expression darkened the room. She jumped up off the couch and stormed Sid. "Okay, I am!"

"Told you so," Guppy remarked.

Pushing up the sleeves of her Steelers hoodie, Sam laid into Sid. The tongue-lashing was an endless stream of absurdities and profanities. Arms gesturing in angry articulation, Sam made her case like a firebrand attorney. "…you're inconsiderate, cold, condescending, stupid, irresponsible, back stabbing, mullet loving, long necked, peacock loving, peccadillo making…"

By the time Sam finished, the coffee was done brewing. Sid poured three steaming-hot mugs. She offered one mug to Sam, whose chest was heaving, and said, "I'm sorry. Will you forgive me? I'm not myself. I miss Smoke. It's hard."

Sam's eyes watered. "Oh, don't you dare turn this around on me. I'm mad. You know I can't stand being ignored." She sniffed. Taking the mug, she said, "Oh, hell, I'm madder at the Steelers than I am at you. It's out now. I understand."

"So tell me you didn't come over here just to yell at me. You must have found something about John, right?"

Sam made a sorrowful shrug.

"Nothing on the dark web?" Sid asked.

"They abandoned that funeral home you were partying in," Guppy said. "At least, it's got a new sign and all. Aw, barnacles! Tomlin just went for two again!"

"Stop reliving it, Guppy! Shut it down. We can't keep torturing ourselves when we know the outcome. Sorry, Sid. Look, I don't know what to say. I'm sick about my brother too. All we can do is keep looking. Did you have any luck at the FBI?"

"Have you been tailing me?"

"Tailing you, no. Tracking you, yes. It's what we do."

"Cyrus had nothing. The entire operation's gone dark. I don't know what to make of any of it. It's like we're chasing ghosts. I figured Allison would have showed up among DC's debaucherous media enclaves, but even that hasn't happened. It's been so bad that I've considered approaching Senator Wilhelm."

"You saved him. I'd say he owes you," Sam said.

"True, but I can't stand that pig of a man."

"No, but maybe the pig of a man you knew was the clone."

"I've considered that. I just find it hard to believe I'm that desperate." Sid sat down on the stool. Sam joined her. "I am that desperate."

"Sorry to change the subject, but what about the baby?"

"You've been talking to Mal, haven't you."

"Asia, mostly. She's one hungry chatterbox." The beautiful woman rubbed Sid's arm. "You really need to make sure everything is all right. If there's something wrong, then there might be something we can do. We don't want to lose you."

"I don't believe them. I'm fine."

"I think you're scared. If you're fine, then know for certain. Mal's got a place set up to see you tomorrow. You need to meet him there. I'll be there with you if you want."

"It doesn't matter what he learns. I'm going to see this through. I have faith that things will be just fine." She took a long draw from her coffee. "Besides, what do you think women did before we had all of this technology?"

"Many died in childbirth, with normal babies."

CHAPTER 21

T HE NEXT EVENING, SID WAS parked outside a closed urgent-care facility. She'd texted Mal and said she'd go through with it. With some prodding from Sam, she had managed to convince herself to make sure that not she but the baby was safe. Her hand rested on her middle, which had started to pop out a little. The baby wriggled inside.

She said a prayer.

The back door popped open, and a little woman poked her head out. It was Asia. She yelled at Sid, "Shut down that rumbling dragon and get your tail inside. It's cold out here!"

Sid shut off the engine, grabbed a bag, and hopped out. She handed Asia the hefty bag of Chinese takeout. "Here."

Asia inspected the bag. "You didn't forget the scallion pancakes, did you?"

"No." Sid slipped inside the building. The lights were partially lit in the halls. The atmosphere was clean but dreary. Asia passed Sid, saying, "Follow me."

Mal stood inside the exam room, wearing a white lab coat over scrubs. His expression was warm. "Hi, Sid. I'm glad you came. Please, make yourself comfortable."

She removed her jacket and set it aside. "How comfortable?"

"Comfortable enough where I can see your entire abdomen."

Sid stripped down to her sports bra and low-rider jeans. She sat down in the chair and reclined, putting her feet up. The vinyl was chilly on her back. Mal pushed the ultrasound machine to her bedside. The monitor was on. Out of the corner of her eye, she caught Asia sucking in a noodle that flicked her nose.

"Do you have to eat while we do this?"

With a moaning sound, Asia set down her oyster pail of food. "Sorry. I'm hungry."

"Maybe you have a tapeworm."

"Maybe you have a demon inside you," Asia fired back.

"Asia, given the circumstances, that's beyond impolite."

"So, I'm cranky when I'm hungry. You both know that."

"Just eat!" Sid said.

"Geez, cranky woman sounds like she's in labor already." Asia retrieved her oyster pail and had at it. "Mmm, still hot. Still good."

Mal lubed up the ultrasound probe with clear gel. "Believe it or not, she's truly thankful for what you did. Just think of her eating as a way of showing it."

Sid nodded. "Let's get this over with."

"Of course. This might feel a little cold at first."

The probe was cool but not icy as Mal slowly moved it over her abdomen. Sid hadn't seen an ultrasound being done since her sister had Megan. She knew the drill. With her head to the side, she studied the screen. After several seconds, an image of a baby formed. "Is that…"

"Yes, that's your baby. A nice steady heartbeat."

Sid listened to the magnified heartbeat that came across the machine. It warmed her soul. "How old?"

"I'd say you're twenty weeks along. Either that, or you have a very large child inside, or you're going to give birth to a banana."

Asia cozied up to the screen. "That looks like a tail. Babies don't have tails."

Sid's eyes got big.

"It's probably the umbilical cord, Sid," Mal assured her. "No worries."

Sid backtracked twenty weeks to where she was and what she was doing. A smile crossed her face. *I was with John. I know it!* "Can you tell me the sex?"

"I think so. Are you sure you want to know?"

"I can answer that," Asia said. "You're having a boy. I can tell by how you walk and your hips are spreading. You're going to be big. Big like a bull. You'll never be skinny again."

Mal scanned Sid's abdomen, froze at a certain point, and said, "She's right. It's a boy."

Sid smiled but contained her excitement. She wanted to share the joy with Smoke. As thrilled as she was, it still hurt that he wasn't here. She wiped her eyes. "So, everything is healthy."

"Well, to be sure, I'd like to take a sample of amniotic fluid. It's the only way to rule everything out."

"How long will it take to get the results back?"

"I have everything I need right here. You don't have an issue with needles, do you?"

"No."

"Let me stick her," Asia said. "I'm great with needles."

"I don't think so," Sid objected.

Mal lifted up a large syringe. "Actually, Asia is more qualified to do this."

"You have to be kidding me."

"Nope." Mal swabbed a patch of Sid's skin with an alcohol pad. "She'll do you right. I met her in med school, you know."

"Asia's a physician? I thought she was a food critic. Either that or a mutated garbage disposal."

Snatching the syringe from Mal's hand, Asia said, "Let's get this over with, wise guy, so I can get back to eating. Now be still."

Sid froze.

Asia stuck the needle into Sid's belly.

Sid watched the screen. The needle's tip was dangerously close to the baby's body. She started to speak, fearing the baby might be harmed, but as she opened up her mouth, Asia pulled the needle free.

The little woman eyed the fluid in the syringe and said, "Bad color. You have a demon baby inside."

Mal eased the syringe out of Asia's hand and said to Sid, "No you don't. The color is normal, so relax. It's going to take a few hours for me to run my panels." He smoothed Sid's hair back. "Just rest if you plan on sticking around."

"Oh, I'm not going anywhere."

"I didn't think so. See you soon."

Mal left. Asia ate. Sid put her shirt back on and said to Asia, "Feel like sharing? We're hungry too."

"Help yourself, but I'm not sharing my chopsticks."

CHAPTER 22

S ID RAN AT FULL SPEED, but she couldn't escape. It was nighttime. The surrounding trees were a web of dreary leaves on one side of her. The Reflecting Pool was a sheet of black ice on the other. Blood-red leaves littered the walk. No matter how fast she ran, she could not get to the other end of the pool. Behind her, a shadow chased.

Panting and straining, she ran harder, stretching her legs to their limits. She couldn't escape what was coming after her like a cold cloud of darkness. The shadow would engulf her whole. It wanted her. It wanted her baby, the bundle clutched tightly to her chest.

Stride after stride, she shot toward the keyhole of light at the end of the Reflecting Pool. The ghostly shadow closed in. Dark tendrils stretched out to snare her. The gangling arms brought a hungry howl with them. A loud moaning. The shadow spoke terror. It awakened new fears.

"No!" Sid yelled. "No!"

She raced for the light. The glimmer grew ever so slowly. The closer she got to it, the farther back her pursuer fell. But panting icy breath, she was quickly growing exhausted. The door of light was there awaiting her at the end of the pool. She looked back. The shadow had vanished. She slowed to a trot then to a walk. Laboring for breath, she approached the warmth of the light.

"Thank you."

A cracking caught her ear. The sheet of black ice that covered the Reflecting Pool had broken. Her limbs froze. A black monster erupted from the bile. Its tremendous arms engulfed her.

"Gah!"

Sid's eyes snapped open. She was still in the hospital reclining chair. Her damp clothes clung to her body.

Asia—huddled in a chair in the corner—stirred. She blinked her sleepy eyes and rubbed them. Yawning, she said, "Bad dream?"

Sid pulled a lock of her hair from her mouth. "Yes."

"Chinese food can do that to you. That and a demon baby."

"Will you stop saying that?"

"What, Chinese food? Why would I stop saying that?"

Sid sat up in the seat and stretched her back. Her hands fell to her belly. She'd always had dreams. Most of them she didn't remember, because none were particularly vivid. But this dream? It felt real. She rubbed the chill bumps on her arms, then fished her phone out of her back pocket and checked the time. It was 6:06 a.m.

"Morning Glory."

"What?" Asia asked while picking through a carton of takeout.

"Are you eating again?"

"Time for breakfast."

Sid sluffed out of the room. The urgent care opened at nine in the morning, but no doubt the staff would arrive between seven and eight. They needed to move on. Better yet, she needed to know the outcome of Mal's tests. Was her son a boy or some kind of demon? *Don't think like that, Sid.*

She called out softly, "Mal."

There weren't any signs of the man anywhere. The muscles between her shoulders clenched. She drew her Glock.

"Mal?"

There was no reply. Something was wrong. She crept through the facility, checking room after room after room. All of them were empty.

"No," she grumbled, moving faster. Panic filled her. "No, no, no!" She raced back into the ultrasound room. "Where's Mal?"

With a mouthful of food, Asia shrugged. "I don't know. I'm not his babysitter. Maybe you overlooked him."

"I wouldn't overlook a grown man."

"You lost your husband, didn't you?"

"I hate you, Asia."

The little woman shrugged. "Hate fits you."

Sid took off to the back of the building. *I'm going to find that bastard.* She flung the back door open. The door hit someone, knocking them over. It was Mal. A cardboard tray of coffee was spilled all over him.

"Hey, what's the hurry? Geez, that's hot!"

"Where have you been?"

"Getting breakfast. The both of you were out like a light, and I figured I'd slip out and grab everyone some breakfast. It's been a long night." He started cleaning himself up. "Why, what did you think happened?"

"The results, Mal. The results!"

"Oh, those." He flicked the coffee from his fingers and began dabbing his clothing with napkins. "Sid, everything is one hundred percent normal. Your son's just fine. Fine as a fiddle. Is that how the expression goes?"

Sid helped him up to his feet. "I think. So you're certain?"

"I have it all packed up in my briefcase. Feel free to scour the results. I went to great length and detail. I'm sorry, Sid. I should have just woken you up. This is awful."

"It's not that bad."

"Yes it is. Asia gets really nasty if she doesn't get her coffee first thing in the morning."

"Just load her up in the car. We'll take her over to Sheetz and fill her up."

Sid shared the news with Sam and Guppy. They were thrilled. She was excited too, and Guppy swore she had a beautiful glow that even he could feel. Still, there was emptiness. Smoke wasn't here to share the moment. Last time she saw him, what had he said with a smile on his face? "Name him after me."

That was the hard thing. As the days passed, she started to wonder if Smoke still lived. It didn't seem possible he could be dead. He was an escape artist. A dodger of death. Now, however, his presence seemed to have drifted away.

Sid pressed on. Perhaps the Drake was out of her life. After all, everything they'd told her was a lie. They'd lied about the baby. They'd lied about her dying. They had lied and lied and lied. Now, there was nothing to go on that would lead her in one direction or another. There was just silence. She missed the lies. She missed Smoke.

Where is he?

CHAPTER 23

"**O**H SID, I'M SO EXCITED. I wish you would let me put something in the paper. At least let me tell the church," Sally said.

"No." Sid avoided her mother's eyes as she packed up her duffle bag in the garage apartment. "Besides, I'm pretty sure you've told somebody."

"No one knows but me and your father," Sally replied.

"And Frenchie," Keith said, sitting on the sofa watching the morning news and glancing at the local paper.

"Frenchie is family. She won't say anything."

"Huh. It never ceases to amaze me how women think telling another woman that something is a secret somehow still keeps it a secret. It's not a secret once you tell somebody else." Keith crushed the can down on the coffee table. "Sid, do you recycle?"

"No."

"Good. Sorting trash is one of the dumbest things man ever created."

Sid's parents went about their business as if nothing was wrong in the world. Keith watched TV. Sally tidied up the kitchen, humming a friendly tune. Having her parents around buffeted the pain she was feeling. She ran her hand over her big baby bump. She was full term. "You know, you could have met me at the hospital. I'll be fine to drive myself."

"Don't be silly. You can't drive yourself to the hospital and drive yourself back with the baby. That's absurd." Sally wrung out a wet dishrag into the sink and started wiping down the kitchenette. "Besides, I'm still kind of mad at you for waiting so long to tell me. You wait until the halfway point to tell me. That's awful, Sid. Allison told me as soon as she knew."

"No, I told you as soon as I knew."

"Oh. Well, that's beside the point. You're the oldest. You should know better. I'm your mother, for heaven's sake."

"She knows that, Sally. You've told her fifty times since we got here."

"You be quiet. What kind of man drinks a beer at six in the morning?"

"It's not beer, it's root beer. Besides, I'm celebrating. Having a boy will carry on my legacy."

Sally rolled her eyes.

Sid zipped up her bag and slung it over her shoulder. "I'm ready."

"Keith, get up. Help your daughter with that bag. Where's a gentleman when you need one?"

"I'm fine, Mother. It's not very heavy."

"Do you have a car seat in that awful car of yours?" Sally asked. "You can always borrow our minivan until you get something more accommodating."

Sid's nostrils flared. "I'm not driving a minivan. Ever. Besides, my boy's probably going to be a rambling man."

"Why would you wish such a thing?"

Sid rubbed her stomach. "I just have a feeling."

Sally dried her hands off and said as she looked around the apartment, "This doesn't look like the best place to raise a baby. No offense, but I don't even see any baby stuff. You needed to have a baby shower, Sid. It was awful that you didn't have one."

"I did have one, here, with Sam and Sadie. A quiet one. We're going to be okay, Mom."

"If you say so." Sally hooked her daughter's arm. "Come on now. Let's load you up into the van."

"I'm not a piece of luggage. Besides, I'm driving and we're taking the Hellcat."

Sally looked mortified.

Keith's grin was as broad as a bridge. "Shotgun."

❋ ❋ ❋

One doctor, one nurse, and a lot of pain. The doctor had induced Sid's labor in the morning, and now the time had come to deliver.

"Push, Mrs. Smoke. Breathe and push!"

Sid strained. "I don't think he wants to come out yet. I told you not to induce me." She huffed, puffed, and pushed. "This is ridiculous."

"It's still going to hurt the same, whether it's now or later." Doctor Endicott spoke in a calm but very stern voice. He was as skilled and professional as they came. "You're full term. It's go time."

"It's go time? What is this, a football game?"

The nurse assistant let out a giggle.

Doctor Endicott cut her short with his eyes. He was an older gentleman with hawking good looks. He went about his business with humility and confidence. "Just keep pushing. The little fella doesn't need to come to a stop in the birth canal."

Sid groaned. "I should have done a C-section. I feel like I'm giving birth to a horse."

"Well, we won't know for certain until you push the baby out. Now push!"

Teeth clenched, she pushed through the blinding pain. She used her anger to give her strength. She was mad. Mad at Smoke. He should be here for this. She'd never imagined him not being by her side when something this important was happening. It left a pit in her. She couldn't do Lamaze class. She didn't have a coach. She didn't have him to share the ultrasound pictures with.

"Push, Sid! The head is crowning."

"I am!"

Even with the baby, she'd never felt so lonely in all her life. She'd been abandoned, but at the same time, she was wracked with guilt. It wasn't Smoke's fault that he wasn't here. It was the Drake's, the likes of Kane and Allison. They had taken Smoke away from her. Busted up her family. If she ever got the opportunity, she would make them pay.

"Keep pushing, Sid! Keep pushing!"

"Gaaaah-ugh!"

The pain shooting through every inch of her body peaked then fell. A draft of cool air washed over her.

"Waaaaaah!"

Catching her breath, she said, "Is that my baby?"

Doctor Endicott held the baby boy in his arms. He stared at the child with silent admiration. He gave a gentle nod, handed the little baby over to the nurse, and said, "He's a gusty little one. A big one too. I'm guessing he's about nine pounds and three ounces. Congratulations, Sidney. Welcome to motherhood."

The nurse assistant cleaned up the baby boy and weighed him. "You're right, Doctor Endicott, nine pounds, three ounces. I don't know how you do it." She swaddled the baby in blankets and brought him over to Sid. "Here you go, Mommy."

Sid cradled the baby in her arms. The little boy had a headful of jet-black hair. She smelled and kissed his head. "Oh, you're so beautiful."

Doctor Endicott took off his mask and gloves. With a caring smile, he said, "You'll be a fine mother. I'll check in with you later." He checked his watch and said to the nurse, "That's five of them today, right, Mona?"

"We've been busy."

"I'm starving. I'm heading down to the commissary, if anyone needs me. I've got a hankering for a hamburger and a milkshake. See you later, Sid." He winked at her. "Enjoy that baby."

Starstruck, Sid didn't even see the doctor leave. She snuggled the tiny boy.

"Do you want me to notify your family? But I can only allow two."

"Uh, yeah, sure. Please go ahead and send my parents in."

CHAPTER 24

BEING A MOTHER WAS MORE hard work than Sid had imagined. The nights were long and sleepless half the time. She catnapped with the baby boy when she could during the day. She called him John, the name Smoke had requested. She gave him her father's name, Keith, as a middle name. John Keith Smoke. She liked it. They all did.

Without having seen any of Smoke's baby pictures, she thought their son looked like his father. Baby John helped fill the gap inside of Sid. Her time was consumed, and she allowed it. Even so, it was hard—and sometimes when she wanted to be alone, her friends and family wouldn't leave her be.

Sam and Guppy would stop by to help. She took long visits to her parents' place. When Sally wasn't showering the baby with love, she was trying to talk Sid into moving down to Florida. Sid considered it but didn't let on. The pattern continued like this for weeks. Weeks that took months. Before she realized it, a year had gone by since she'd last seen Smoke.

She took John out of the backseat of her car—nestled in his baby seat and hidden by the blankets—and made her way into the grocery store. She latched the portable baby seat to the cart and wheeled it inside. Heading down the baby supplies aisle, she heard a familiar voice and found a familiar face.

"Hello, Sid. How are you and the baby doing?" It was Doctor Endicott. He carried a handbasket of groceries that included a carton of eggs, a box of pancake mix, some fruit, a bottle of wine, and a six-pack of sodas. He stood out among the crowd in a very nice gray suit. "Can I take a look?"

"Of course you can. After all, you delivered him." She smiled at him and stepped aside. The cologne he wore stirred her. Doctor Endicott did everything with grace and refinement. His long finger tickled baby John's chin. The infant giggled.

"He seems happy. It looks like the two of you are doing well together."

"Thank you, Doctor Endicott."

"Please, call me Steve." His dark eyes were smiling. "Say, Sidney, I've actually given you some thought, and if you don't mind me asking, has Mister Smoke stepped back into the picture?"

"Uh." She paused and scratched her head. "I, well, no."

"I'm sorry. I didn't mean to make you uncomfortable."

"No, you didn't." She bit her lip. "I mean, you caught me off guard, but it's a fair question."

"Actually, it was probably unfair. I just, well"—he made an uneasy smile—"I was hoping you might consider joining me for dinner sometime. You can even bring John along if you have trouble finding a sitter. I just feel like I would enjoy your company."

Sid's heart started to race. She felt drawn to the man. There had always been something about him that she liked, ever since the first time she met him. Everything he did or had was impeccable, from his hair to his clothing. "I, uh, well, I appreciate the invitation, but I'm just not ready to move on yet."

"I understand. But when the time comes—and I hope it does—you know how to reach me. Take care, Sid." He wiggled his fingers at John. "Goodbye, little fella."

Doctor Endicott disappeared around the end of the aisle. Sid closed her mouth that was hanging open. *I don't know if I should be ashamed or delighted. He's a good-looking man, and I've been without a man too long.* She threw some diapers and wet wipes into the cart. Flushed, she checked out.

John Keith fell asleep on the way home. Sid swam through a current of emotions. It was starting to look like Smoke wasn't going to return at all. She was going to have to move on. Smoke would understand. He'd want that. *Wouldn't he?* It just didn't seem possible that a man so alive could be dead. *Lord help me.*

Back home, she parked the car in the garage. She unloaded the groceries and placed them on the kitchen island. Flipping the light switch, she went back into the garage and took out John Keith. "How's my little JK doing? Are you still sleeping? Good."

She turned the dial up on the heat. Then she set JK, portable baby seat and all, on the bed. JK slept well in the baby seat most of the time. Over at the computer, she logged in. She went to YouTube and played Mozart with a background of rain at 432 megahertz. It was one of her favorite selections. Yawning, she slipped off her tennis shoes and hung up her jacket.

A soft knocking sounded at the front door.

I didn't hear anyone pull up. She drew her Glock. It was late in the day, with the sun falling. She looked outside. A white sedan was parked in the driveway but not up close. It was a Tesla. *No wonder I didn't hear it.* The knocking started again.

"Who is it?" she said, clearly but not loudly.

"It's your sweet sister, Allison. I have a gift for my nephew."

Sid flung open the door and stuck the barrel of the gun in Allison's face. "And I've got a present for you. Goodbye."

"Oh please, pull the trigger and make your son an orphan." Allison rolled her eyes. "Just let me in. I have information you need."

"All you have is a mouthful of lies."

Allison held up a small white gift box with a black ribbon tied around it. "You don't have to accept it, but you might need to sell it for money one day." She pushed up her curly locks of platinum-blond hair. "By the looks of things, you'll need it."

"Are you alone?"

"I am all by myself. You should feel honored. Do you know how long it's been since I've driven?"

"Who cares?" Sid double-checked the outside and closed the door.

Allison made her way over to the bed and sat down.

"Where have you been? It's not like you to stay away so long and be so quiet."

Allison peeked at JK. "That bothers you, doesn't it."

"Where's Smoke, Allison?"

"Ah. Well, I wish I'd come with more than just a gift, but I'm afraid I have some unfortunate news to share. Kane tried to transform your husband. Smoke didn't make it."

CHAPTER 25

"I'LL BELIEVE IT WHEN I see the body," Sid said. A nest of butterflies fluttered in her stomach. "Couldn't you be honest for just one day? You want John alive as much as anybody."

"I had my fun with him. He was blessed with a great deal of prowess. It takes a lot to impress a woman like me." Allison made some baby sounds. "But alas, the good ones always perish."

Sid marched over to the bed and pulled JK away from Allison. "Keep it down. I don't want him waking up and facing a witch."

"You're so clever, sister. I could never keep up with your wit. But for all of your skills, you won't be getting Smokey back. He's gone, and with him gone, I wanted to let you know it's best that you move on. Have you given dating any consideration? I bet you have. You aren't so different than me. You can't go too long without a man."

"Shut up, Allison."

"I would, but you know you were all too eager to hear what I said. Your husband is gone, and truthfully, we are very sorry for that. Even Kane's disappointed. He had such high hopes for Smoke." Allison opened up a small handbag and applied moisturizer to her lips. "I did too, but sometimes these things don't work out and you have to start all over again. The Drake calls it the Quiet Time."

"And here you are yapping away."

"Sister Sidney, get on with your life. Take care of yourself and have more babies. You've been given a free pass. I suggest you stop nosing around and take it."

"So you've been keeping tabs on me?"

"Sid, we know everything. We might have had a setback, but we are a far cry from crippled. The Drake will be back on top once the changes settle." Allison got up, but she left the present on the bed. Showing the coldness in her blue eyes, she said, "He might not have a father, but at least he has his grandfather. That's more than many children can say."

"And what about Megan? Where is she?"

"She's in private school, where she excels, thank you. She's looking forward to meeting her little cousin. I told her we'd arrange it once you were ready."

"I'm ready now. Go get her."

"I think I'll wait until Thanksgiving. Perhaps we can all sit down and have dinner together."

"We as in who? Me, you, Mom, and Dad? Or did you have something else in mind?"

"Shifters don't celebrate the holidays. I'll be in touch. Soon." Allison made her way to the door. "I'm sorry for your loss. I know how hard it is to meet the right guy. Well, actually I'm not that sorry. I just wish he would have made it."

"I don't believe you. You'd have a body."

"I don't need a body when I've brought you ample proof. It's in little John's present. I don't suppose he can open it, but you can do it for him."

Sid scowled. Glaring at her sister, she said, "I can't figure you out. Are you a shifter or not?"

"I am, the same as the others."

"I'm curious what kind of monster you turn into. You're scary enough already."

"Perhaps I don't change. After all, this body and face are already perfection." Allison opened the door. "See you around, Sidney."

Sid sat down on the bed. She picked up the gift box. *I should throw it away. It's just another game.* She palmed the box, lifting it up and down. *It's got some heft to it. Screw it.* She loosened up the ribbon and pulled the lid off. A black satin bag was inside. It clinked with metal as she removed it from the box. She loosened the neck of the bag and poured out the contents. "Whoa!"

Ancient gold doubloons glittered on the bed. She ran her fingers over the cold metal. The way it felt and shined sent a thrill through her fingers. "Well, that should cover college and then some." Her eyes spotted another object that didn't fit in. Her fingers trembled when she picked it up. It was Smoke's wedding band.

CHAPTER 26

Arlington Cemetery. Sidney stood in front of the Tomb of the Unknown Soldier, watching the Marines stand firm in the stiff wind. She was dressed in black and holding hands with Sam, who was dressed the same. Guppy was on the end of them, wearing a suit and tie. With her free arm, Sid held JK.

Sam sniffed and dabbed her eye with a handkerchief. The memorial was lonely and cold. The ground was wet from a recent rain. "I guess my brother would like this, considering that we don't have any remains."

Sid swallowed the lump in her throat. She'd struggled for days with whether or not she should move on. The wedding ring had gotten to her though, like a nail in the coffin. It was time to move on. She had to, for her sanity. She didn't want to make an event out of it though. There wouldn't be a grave nor a marker. She couldn't do that. Not without a body. A ceremony would have to do. Smoke was an unknown soldier. An ex-Navy SEAL. A man who had perished in combat with remains that had not been discovered. Without dishonoring any fellow soldiers, she felt Arlington was the best place to honor Smoke's life. Quietly.

With the wind nipping at her chin, she stood with tears freezing on her face, reflecting on the times they had. Watching the Marines, she gave thanks to all of the brave men and women who had made the ultimate sacrifice. *All gave some. Some gave all.* Smoke had given his life to save hers and their son's. She'd have to learn to accept it. With a quiet nod, she said, "Let's go."

Guppy led the way back to where the car was parked. He opened the back door of a black Cadillac Escalade. Sid loaded JK into his car seat and climbed in the back. Sam and Guppy closed themselves inside the front, and out of the parking lot and down the road they went. The ride was quiet. Rain started to splatter on the windows.

Sam blew her nose. "So, Sid, are we taking you home?"

"I'm not sure."

"Do you want to go somewhere and grab something to eat?"

"Just drive."

"We can watch JK if you need some time alone. It won't be a problem. You know how much we love him."

"I know. We'll see. We've still got a drive ahead of us. Just head back my way." She fished Smoke's ring out of her pocket. The metal was warm. She slipped it over her thumb, but it was way too big.

"Maybe you should wear it around your neck?"

"I've thought about that." Sid gave a little shrug. "I don't know."

"Sid, I'm not going to hold it against you for moving on. Smoke wouldn't either. I know him. He'd understand."

"I know. I keep asking myself if I'd be okay with that if I was in the same situation. What if I were gone? Would he move on?"

Sam shook her head. "The difference is that Smoke was never looking for somebody. He was a loner. Chances are that he'd just do what he normally did. You know, he's quirky but pragmatic."

"So, you don't think he'd date or marry again?"

"I just don't think he'd be looking. I never thought he'd meet anyone, and I was thrilled when he found you."

"Me too," Guppy said.

"And now, Smoke has a legacy, you and his son. But he'd want him to have a father. A good one of course. He was an orphan, you know. Having a dad would have meant a lot to him."

Sid didn't have any idea what the days ahead had in store for her. She was a bounty hunter, but that part of her life seemed to be closed for now. She needed steadier if not safer work now that she had JK to look out for. Something to dig into. With all of the changes going on at the FBI, now might be a good time to go back and start with a clean slate. She looked out the window, noticing one of the diners she and Smoke had frequented. The restaurant was practically empty.

A man sitting in the window slouched over the table caught her eye. She lost sight of him as they passed. "Hey, let's get something to eat."

"Now?" Guppy said, looking at her in the rearview mirror. "Sure thing, then. Where do you want to go?"

"That diner would be nice."

Guppy shrugged, got off at the next exit, and turned the car around. The three of them rushed into the diner as a downpour of rain started. Inside, they eyed one of the many empty booths. The man Sid had seen slouched over the table was gone, but his dishes were still there. Syrup coated the plate, and three tall soda cups were empty.

Sam gave Sid a push. "Let's take a seat at a clean one." She sneered a little. "If we can find one. You know I don't like these places where I can catch those secondhand carbs."

"You'll live." Sid found a booth, still eyeing the other table. She set JK and his car seat in the booth first.

The waitress came by, wearing a peach uniform and apron. The plump woman offered to get them some coffee with a smile.

Sid asked her, "What happened to the man who was sitting over there?"

The waitress looked around. Sticking her pen in her mouth, she said, "I don't know. He was just here a moment ago." She hollered into the kitchen. "Archie, it looks like we got another dine and dasher. Geez, he was a handsome fella too." A door squeaked in the back. A tall man emerged from the bathrooms in the back. "Oh, never mind. There he is."

Sid's eyes met the eyes of Doctor Endicott.

CHAPTER 27

DR. ENDICOTT'S EYES WIDENED WHEN he saw Sid. He followed it up with a friendly smile. His short beard was a few days old. He was very casual, wearing khakis and a sweater, but his clothing was still nice.

He came right to her. "Sidney, what a pleasant surprise. I was starting to think I would never see you again."

She took his hand, and with a tilt of her head, she said, "Hi, Steven. Let me introduce you to my sister-in-law, Sam, and her husband, Guppy."

Steven shook hands with both of them. "Very nice to meet you."

Sam was giving Sid the "go ahead" eyeball.

"You'll have to forgive my appearance. I'm taking some time off. I'm sort of on a bender. Those long days catch up with me. I tend to overdo it."

"Leading a double life will do that to you," Sid said.

"Excuse me?" he asked, looking at her quizzically. "I don't take your meaning. Uh, may I take a peek at the little guy?" He leaned over the table toward JK.

Sid caught his arm and pulled him back. "No. I'm not a big believer in coincidences, Steven." She pointed at his booth with her chin. "Take a seat."

"But I was just—"

"Sit!"

With a polite nod to Sam and Guppy, Steven took a seat in his booth.

Sid sat down across from him. She took a long draw of air through her nose. "Who are you, Steven?"

"I'm your doctor. Or at least I was. There isn't much of a doctor–parent relationship after the delivery, unless of course you have another baby. Or, say, if we were dating?"

"You haven't been following me, have you?"

"Pfft?" His face drew up with perplexity. "I'm flabbergasted. I admit I have an honest flare for you, but I'd never take it to the level of stalking."

The waitress walked up. "Can I get you anything else, honey? Or are you ready for the check?"

"The check will be fine."

The waitress peeled it off her pad.

Sid snagged it.

"Hey!"

"I've got this."

"Fine by me. I'm just glad he didn't dine and dash." The waitress tended to another table.

Sid read over the receipt. "Interesting. One large order of pancakes, two Great American Breakfasts, three Cokes, and a chocolate shake."

"Again, I'm on a bender."

Guppy and Sam sat up in their seats. Their eyes were glued on Sid and Steven.

"Bender, my ass. Who are you, Steven? This is the same wholesome junk-food diet my husband thrived on. A bit ridiculous, I might add. But coincidence? I don't think so. You're screwing with my head." A sick feeling overcame her. The man who had delivered her baby wasn't the man she believed him to be. "You work for the Drake, don't you."

"The who?"

Sid slapped the table. The fork jumped off the plate. "Don't screw with me, Steven—or whoever you are." She pictured Reginald the Doppelganger in her head. She had seen his body in a coffin, but his remains were supposedly splattered everywhere. Her gut told her he wasn't dead. "Give me a straight answer."

"Listen, I don't know what you're talking about. I just want to leave."

"Problem," Guppy said, sitting down beside Dr. Endicott, pinning him in.

"I think we have a shifter in our midst," Sid said.

Remaining calm, Steven said, "The last thing I want to do is draw unwanted attention to myself. I don't think anyone would want that these days. I just want to lie low. I suggest you do the same." He winked at Sid. "All of this tension is giving me butterflies."

Sid caught her breath. She searched the man's eyes. They weren't Doctor Endicott's. They had changed. They were Smoke's. "What in the world is going on?"

"Listen to me," the man said. "There are eyes and ears everywhere. Just pretend this is normal." He glanced out the window.

A black sedan had just pulled into the driveway. The headlights went out, but no one exited the vehicle. It was still pouring rain.

"Mrs. Smoke, I'll explain when the time is right, but you are still drawing too much attention. Meet me at my office. Tomorrow. Come alone. Room 365, across from Endicott's."

"No, you aren't going anywhere. I can't take these games anymore."

"Me either. Just give me one more day. I have to go. Now. Night falls. It's a problem."

Guppy's face was filled with confusion. He watched Sid and said, "What do you want me to do?"

"Play along. He can go."

Guppy got up. He gave Doctor Endicott a firm handshake. "Nice meeting you."

"You too," the doctor said. He winked at Sam. Then he said to Sid, "Are you still going to pay that bill?"

"I think I've paid enough already."

He tossed a fifty on the table. "Bye for now."

Feeling her soul leave her body, she watched the man exit the diner, get into a white Lexus sedan, and drive away. Shortly after that, the people in the black sedan entered: a man, a woman, and three children. Sid climbed from her booth into another.

Sam said, "What just happened? I saw him. I swear I saw him."

"Me too." Sid shook her head. "I have a feeling I'm not going to sleep a wink tonight."

CHAPTER 28

S ID DROVE HERSELF TO THE hospital center. JK was with her, bundled up and quiet. She paid the parking attendant, crossed traffic, and headed up the sidewalk and inside the building. The hospital was a new establishment with a clean grey antislip tile floor. The walls were painted white and decorated with paintings and other artwork. Avoiding the elevators, she took the stairwell up to the second floor. Down the hallway the doctors' offices were in. White oak doors, pale-yellow walls, carpeted floor. The doors had rectangular portals in them. She could see parents and children waiting in the lobby.

She peeked into Doctor Endicott's office. Pregnant women were sitting in chairs, reading notepads. One of them was fanning herself with an old magazine. That was office #370. On the other side was office #365. There wasn't a name plate on the door. It was open. The hallway was empty, and she went inside. The lobby was barren. The door to the secretary's station was open.

Sid called out, "Smoke?" She headed into the hallway that led into the examination rooms. "Doctor Endicott?"

"Back here," said a solemn voice.

She couldn't tell if the voice was Smoke's or Dr. Endicott's, but it came from the exam room in the back end of the hall. She went inside. A tall man was peering out the window with his back to her. He wore a doctor's lab coat. She set JK down on the exam table. Her hand went to her gun, hidden under her jacket. "It's time to see what's behind door number one."

Slowly, the man turned. It was Smoke. Tall, dark, and mysterious, he faced her with his hands up and the sliver of a smile on his face. He appeared exhausted. "Hi, honey."

"It better be you." She pointed her gun at him. "Swear to God that it's you, John."

"I'll swear it, but I won't take the Lord's name in vain. Sid, it's me."

His voice assured her. She rushed into his arms and squeezed him with all her might. Fingernails digging into his back, she said, "You better be real! You better be real!"

His long, sinewy arms reeled her body into his. He stroked her hair. "I'm sorry."

She shuddered in his arms. Her tears soaked his coat. It was him. She could feel it. She looked up into his face and drowned in his eyes. Her breath was taken away.

He bent down.

She pushed up on her toes and gave him a long, passionate kiss. When they broke it off, she said, "Why all of the games, John? Why?"

"I'm me, but I'm not me anymore." There was sadness in his voice. His face was long. "They changed me, but I escaped."

"So, you're a shifter?"

"I'm something, but I didn't go willingly. I've just been hiding."

The baby cooed under his blanket in the car seat.

Smoke said to Sid, "May I?"

"Of course." She tucked her gun away. "You know, I've been pretty upset that you haven't been around for all this."

"I was there." He shook his stethoscope at her. "Who do you think delivered my little man? I did." He picked up the infant and tucked the boy into his chest. He kissed JK's forehead. "There's my boy."

"That was you, for certain?"

"Yup. I tried to drop some hints when you came in for your checkups. I couldn't help myself. "

"You did all of those? I thought Doctor Endicott was too touchy and feely."

"I didn't get the impression that you minded. It makes me wonder what was going on in that head of yours." Smoke tickled the baby's ribs. JK giggled.

"I should have caught on to the milkshake comment."

"You'd just had a baby. It was easy to slip by you. Besides, the real Doctor Endicott is a health jock. He wouldn't have syrup and pancakes if it killed him."

Sid sat down in one of the chairs. "John, you're telling me you can shape-shift, like Reginald?"

"Sort of. I'm not quite so adept at it."

"And how am I to be certain you aren't Reginald?"

"You know I'm not. Besides, I splattered him on the railroad tracks. Well, the train did. You can be certain he isn't coming back. I promise." He lifted JK high in the air. With admiration, he said, "He's one beautiful boy, isn't he?"

"Of course. Mom's crazy about him."

"I bet." Smoke sat down beside Sid, cradling their toddler in his arms. "Look, I'm far from out of the woods yet, and me revealing myself isn't the best decision. I just couldn't go on with you thinking I was dead. I mean, I wanted them to think that you thought I was dead, but I couldn't stand you thinking that I was. It ate me up."

"I knew you weren't dead. I just didn't feel it. I was still empty, though. Then Allison started flapping her lips." She punched Smoke in the arm. "Oh, I hate you." She hit him again. "But I love you so much more."

"Sid, I don't know if I can be what I once was. I'm changed. Watch what I can do. Cursed blood runs through me."

She palmed his face. "No, I don't want to see what you can do. Just be you. I mean, can't you just be you and still have the power?"

With dread, he said, "Not at night."

CHAPTER 29

"Night? What happens at night?" She could see creases building in his face. His jaw muscles were tightening. She gave him a soft punch in the arm. "Do you howl at the moon or something?"

"Not exactly."

She touched his face. "You know I'll love you no matter what, right? What did they do to you? How did this happen?"

"After the fight at the clone plant, Kane caught up with me and took me out. I woke up in a room painted like our apartment."

"I was there."

"You were? When?"

"I think I missed you by a few days. Russ Davenport and Cort Calhoun, do you remember him? Well, they came across your whereabouts on the dark web. I was so close, John, but I was too late. Sorry. Tell me everything."

"While I was captive, your sister offered me the world, as always. I didn't cave, of course, but then Kane came. They knocked me out, and the next thing I know, I'm strapped to a table. IVs are running through me, strange music is playing, and there are electrodes all over my body. What they did hurt so bad that it blinded me. It was a blood transfusion of some sort. Real nasty."

"Was there a man there named Frank, a long-faced, elderly creep?"

"I don't know. So many things were going on, the faces are a blur. People came in and out. There was chanting, bright flickering lights. I felt myself move through time. I saw a hellish portal. I honestly thought I was a goner."

"Then what happened?"

"I woke up with fire running through my veins. I can still feel it. It's a living thing. I have to wrestle with it or embrace it. Anyway, I was in an old arena, very medieval. Kane and Allison and someone else put me up against deaders and that one fella, Wild Jack? Remember him?"

She nodded.

"Well, I beat him, to the point of death. I'm pretty sure that's what they wanted, for me to take a life. Then I transformed and made my escape. I was being chased from all directions in a network of catacombs. I ran. I hid. I fought shifters off. Finally—and I don't know how—I pictured myself as something else. It happened. I ambled out as a deader. Drove off as a guard in a peacoat. The difference was the daylight. I can shift in the day, but at night, I'm just a monster."

"What have you been doing all this time?"

"Hiding. Learning. Spying. They're still looking for me. They know I haven't just vanished. They've been watching you the entire time. I've been watching you most of the time." He smiled down at his son. "Becoming your doctor was a work of genius, you have to admit."

"So you've been seeing patients?"

"It's been tricky, but you know me."

"Yeah, I do. As for me being watched, I haven't picked up on anything. Who's been watching?"

Smoke stood up. Spying through the window at the parking lot across the street, he said, "Take a look. Black sedan, Section D."

Without standing, Sid craned her neck. Two men in peacoats were parked a dozen paces from her car. One was smoking, and the other talked on his phone. "I guess I need a bird's-eye view. They really must be keeping their distance. So now what?"

"What's going on with me isn't good, but it's power. I like it. It's what I need to stop Kane. To finish him off once and for all. I think he's the key."

"How so?"

"I've been coming and going from their lair, the one I escaped from."

"Lair? What lair? Where is it?"

"Here, but I'm not telling you where. The last thing I need is for you to go snooping around. It's bad enough that I am. But I'm convinced that Kane is the key. They worship him like a god. If he goes down, I think they all go down. I believe it's his blood that spreads the curse. Did you ever notice anything like that when you were with him?"

Sid stiffened. Her chest tightened. She didn't want to think about it. "Come to think of it, I did see him draw blood once. I didn't understand why. Are you suggesting he's the main host of all of this?"

"Yeah, and if the host dies…"

"They all die."

"The question is, how do we get close enough to kill him? I'm not sure I can just take his head. There might be more to it than that. And I have a feeling I'll only get one chance. I'm angling for it before it's too late."

"You sound like a man with time running out. I don't like it. You need to let me help."

"Just stay clear for now. I'm still on recon. I have to be truthful, Sid, this power changes you. It's a rush. I can do things that, well, that I never could have imagined. I thought I was fearless before. I feel invincible now."

"That lack of fear is the shifter's weakness."

"Don't think that hasn't crossed my mind."

"So what am I supposed to do, sit around and wait until you contact me again? That will drive me crazy. You need to let me work on this. I can talk to Mal. He might be able to figure something out."

"They're watching everybody. Just go about your business. I know it's tough, but give me a few days and I'll be back in touch. I'll find you. Just don't shelter yourself back at the apartment."

"I'm not making you any promises."

He hugged her and the baby all in one. "I love you, Sid. I won't make any promises I can't keep either. See you soon."

CHAPTER 30

S ID HAD HAD ENOUGH. SHE wasn't going to sit around waiting for Smoke to show up. He was alive. She was going to help keep him alive even if it killed her. Back at the apartment, she sat at the kitchen island, signing cards by hand. She sealed them up in envelopes and added adhesive Charlie Brown Christmas stamps to them.

"Sometimes the old ways are the best ways."

Without getting too carried away, she wrote out some details about what was going on with Smoke. She mailed them to Sam and Guppy, Mal and Asia, and Russ Davenport. Everyone had a post office box. That had been established long ago. Snail mail might not be the fastest way to get the word out, but it was more secure than email or texting. There were too many spies on the web. In addition to mailing out the letters inside Christmas cards, Sid encrypted the notes. It wasn't anything complicated, but only a trained eye would be able to see the message.

Sid tied her hair back in a scrunchie and set the notes aside. Dressed in casual clothing, she and the baby headed out for a routine day. There were groceries to be bought and some shopping at the mall, but the first stop was at the post office. Smoke never had a mailbox, but he had always had a post office box. It was routine for her to check it. She drove the highways a little slower than she normally did. She changed her route from time to time. Through the rearview mirror, she'd keep an eye out for any black sedans.

There you are.

Hanging back over a quarter of a mile behind her, a black sedan was on her tail. There wasn't anything unusual about it. The vehicle stayed on her like a distant magnet. She made the first stop at the post office. It was a small brick-and-mortar building with white tile floors and hundreds of post office boxes. With the child carrier hooked in her arm, she dropped the cards in the bin inside. Taking out her key, she checked her mail, pulled some out, and tucked it under her arm.

Sifting through the mail, she kept a close eye out the window.

A black Buick cruised by and came to a stop at the light that led onto the main stretch of road. The driver, a thick-necked man with a shaved head, pulled off to the side of the road and into the parking lot across the street. He backed the Buick in front of the offices of the small plaza.

There you are. Now that I know, I can see you as plain as day. Smoke was right.

She got back in the Hellcat, locked in the car seat, and said to JK, "Are you ready to have some fun, sweetie?" His toothless smile shined in her eyes. "Yeah, you're just like your father."

Sid backed the Hellcat out. As soon as she did, she saw the black Buick creep out from between two cars. She pulled back into her slot. The Buick pulled back in too. She saw another car and driver honking the horn at the Buick because they wanted the spot. A woman was leaning out of her window, shaking her fist and yelling at the men in the Buick.

Laughing, Sid said to JK, "That language probably isn't appropriate for a little fella like you. Let's go." She hit the road and at first took the way she'd come but then made a few quick turns into a residential area where the houses were laid out in square blocks. She laid on the accelerator from stop sign to stop sign, drawing a nasty look from an old man walking a black poodle. Sid was laughing. "I'm not going that fast. I just sound fast." She peeked at the speedometer. "I suppose I am going a little fast."

She made a few more turns, cutting through the streets that ran parallel to each other. Finally, she came to a stoplight that led into the main intersection. The light turned green. She didn't slow. She spilled over into the residential area on the other side of the highway. There wasn't any sign of the Buick. *I'm pretty sure I lost them.*

Parked alongside the street, she took a peek at JK. He was fast asleep. "I must be boring my little guy." She turned the symphony music up a hair. The baby stirred. "I'd better get moving. I think my little rambler sleeps better when we're rolling."

Figuring that if she had lost her followers, they'd be keeping an eye out for if she went back the way she came and not wanting to risk it, she decided to go the other way and head in a direction she didn't routinely go. There were a few things that bothered her about her pursuers. She wasn't sure where they had picked up on her, since it hadn't been at the apartment. That suggested they might have more eyes than she initially imagined. Any person driving down the road or walking down the street with a phone could be in cahoots with the Drake. And in the Hellcat, she wouldn't be that hard to notice. She drove a few miles and pulled into a Chick-fil-A drive-through. She ordered a chicken-egg-and-cheese bagel with a large coffee. At the pay window, the black Buick rolled by. "I'll be damned."

"Excuse me?" the polite woman working the window said. "Is there something wrong with your order? We'll be really quick to fix it."

"No, the order is fine. Sorry, I just discovered another problem. Thanks."

"You're welcome. Nice car, by the way."

"Later." Sid pulled out of the drive-thru and headed back toward home. On her way home, a helicopter shot through the sky. She'd seen it more than once since she'd been driving. She'd keep an eye on it. Eating her bagel, she realized there wasn't much she could do about it. The Drake was indeed watching. *They could be using satellites for all I know, but at least they aren't getting too close. Advantage, Sid.*

CHAPTER 31

S MOKE DROVE A WHITE DODGE pickup truck south down the George Washington Memorial Parkway. He passed the Ronald Reagan Washington National Airport, the Washington Sailing Marina, went past Daingerfield Island, hooked a left just past Marina Towers, and slipped over toward the Potomac River by an old power plant. The power plant was surrounded by chain-link fence marked with several warning signs. Some of the signs read "Keep out" and others said "No trespassing." There was only one entrance.

Two peacoat guards opened the gate and let him in.

"Good morning, sir." The guard checked the credentials Smoke was holding out the window. A picture ID with the

Drake logo on it. It wasn't his face, though, but someone else's. The hard-faced scowl of an older flat-top veteran with a caterpillar moustache.

"Good for you, Roy. You remembered to check my identification today."

The roughneck smirked. "I learned my lesson, sir."

"That's right," Smoke said in a voice that wasn't his own. "Don't give me any of that personal recognition bullshit again. Spread the word. If it happens again, you peacoats are going to be licking the slime off the bellies of the boats." He blew smoke in the man's face from a cigar he was puffing on. "At ease now. I'll see you after guard mount."

"Yes sir."

"Eh, how is that boy of yours doing. Tommy, wasn't it?"

The guard started to grin. "Growing like a weed, sir."

"Remember that," Smoke said.

The guard's expression soured. "Yes, sir," he said flatly.

Smoke pulled into the parking lot and shut off the engine. He grabbed a metal lunch pail and thermos, smiling to himself. He'd worked hard for months infiltrating the Drake's lair. Drake Energy was the very place he had escaped from, nothing but a hive of evil. The facility wasn't garish and fanciful like so many other Drake office buildings. Instead, it was low key, barely on the radar and not even identified by search engines like Google Earth. Most landmark buildings had a name with them, but this one didn't.

The truck door swung open with a groan. He slammed it shut hard, leaving the keys inside. He'd stolen the identity of Mack Black, a real hard leader charged with the security of the facility. At first, Smoke had shifted into the form of one of the peacoat guards, but just long enough to figure out how the operation inside the energy plant went. That was when he'd gotten acquainted with Mack Black. The man had access to everything inside the facility and was even on good terms with Kane, who was in and out all the time—via boat mostly, but sometimes by chopper.

Thermos tucked under his arm and lunch pail in hand, he angled toward the side entrance of the facility. He spied the men posted on the high points of the building nestled between the ductwork and bricks. The naked eye wouldn't know they were there if you didn't already know they were there. At the steel doors that led inside was a security camera. Digital eyeballs were everywhere. Smoke held his access card up. The door clicked. He went inside and down a long hallway, where the paint was peeling off the cinderblock.

Smoke fought the urge to whistle. Mack Black would never do such a thing. At the same time, Smoke hated having to keep the man imprisoned, but what choice did he have? There was too much on the line. Posing as Mack was easy. The man didn't talk much and took orders well. The guards didn't cross him, and the shifters that came in and out respected him. In just a few weeks, Smoke had learned more than he ever cared to know about the Drake's operations. The drugs, the bribes, the recruiting were all bundled together as they continued to bring more people into the Drake family.

He entered the main operation center. Rich and Sherry were inside, wearing headsets. The room had huge monitors up on the wall and a dozen workstations facing it. It reminded Smoke of the war rooms he'd seen in the movies, where everyone would be standing around watching the defcon countdown or a new space rocket launch. He took a seat at a station and began typing.

"Report?"

Sherry spoke. She was a mousy gal with short cherry-red hair. "The lair is secure. All shifters and deaders accounted for. No distinguished visitors on the premises last night."

"How are our satellite operations? Our marks make any unusual patterns?"

Rich was sitting at the other station, a short man who was a little pudgy. His thick fingers pecked the keys with lightning speed. A new image popped up on the big screen, a view from space that quickly zoomed in on DC. "Mark number three made a move yesterday that was suspicious. She lost her tail. The satellites lost her in the trees. It went on for fifteen minutes. She was cruising the oaks on the back streets. We found her again at a fast food place. Nothing strange since. Should we put more boots on the ground to follow after her?"

"I don't need your suggestions, cupcake. Play the segment where you lost and found mark three."

With a bird's-eye view, the big screen flashed through the entire fifteen minutes in thirty seconds. It was astonishing being able to see everything at once from such an enlightening perspective. It was good. It gave Smoke comfort, watching out for Sid the same way the Drake was looking for him. Now he had the advantage for a change.

"Show me the other marks."

"Yes sir," said Rich and Sherry together.

"Sir." Sherry pulled an image up on the screen. A black boat was sailing down the Potomac River. "Kane is coming."

Great Dane, why so early?

CHAPTER 32

KANE'S ARRIVAL POSED CHALLENGES. UNPLEASANT and demanding, he never seemed pleased with anything. Smoke headed to the back end of the building, exited, and took the stairs down to the dock. A handful of peacoats were there, ready to tether the small cruiser to the landing. Smoke flicked his cigar in the river.

When Kane wasn't around, he had free range of the power plant. Smoke had taken full advantage of this time, going through every room he could find, making routine security checks. He found plenty of interesting places within. The arena was one of the places, buried underneath the plant. That wasn't all. The plant was built on an old fort built to control passage up and down the river. There were dungeons and chains. Deep and dank, the dreary facilities were way below river level. That was where colonial technology met with the modern days. There were also labs where deaders were made.

Men and women were brought in on boats, like slaves on pirate ships. Addicts were hauled in, doped up between life and death. Their failing bodies, broken in spirit and mind, turned themselves over to the Drake. Promised the golden road to El Dorado and fully deceived, their hearts were stopped cold in their chests. In those critical moments, they were taken from the brink of death and brought back as deaders. They lived, but they didn't feel the pain of life any longer.

Smoke spent his time trying to learn whether it was technology or dark mysticism behind it all. Or was it something else that allowed the dead to walk? Kane's bloodstream seemed to be the source of it all. Vials were filled in the chemistry labs and mixed into dangerous concoctions. The weak became deaders. The strong, if they survived, became shifters.

So far as Smoke could tell, Kane used his power to taint DC one day at a time. If he could control the most powerful people in Washington, he could control the world. He wouldn't need shifters or deaders then. He'd just have to influence the wicked imaginations of men and use their own vices to allow them to destroy themselves.

As Mack Black, Smoke had access to almost everything, but some of the places were sacred, and only the known shifters went in. He didn't have his finger on the pulse just yet.

The roughneck peacoats anchored the custom cruiser to the dock. Putting their backs into it, they locked in the gangplank and shuffled out of sight.

Here we go.

Clad in a heavy black turtleneck, Kane appeared. His stringy locks of blond hair stirred in the river winds. Allison appeared wearing a hot-pink ski cap and a long white winter coat. Kane was barking about something. He came down the plank with his arms swinging like an ape's. He tipped his chin at Smoke.

"Good morning, sir," Smoke said.

"Give me a report, Mack. Any news?"

"It's still quiet." Smoke hustled up to the back entrance of the facility, opened the door, and stepped aside. "No sign of Mister Smoke."

"And what about the marks? Not even the slightest aberration in their patterns?"

Allison caught his eye for a moment, then she slipped inside the inner corridor. Smoke caught up with the both of them. He didn't want to report on Sid dropping off the radar for a mere fifteen minutes but decided not to hold back. "We lost her at mark number three for a short spell, but the satellites quickly picked her up again."

Kane stopped in the middle of the hall. "When did this happen?"

"Early yesterday. I'm not concerned. It's not the first time the men in the field lost her for a short spell. Once we call in the satellites, it's little problem to find her again."

"I'm not worried about finding her. I'm wanting to find her husband. Mind yourself, Mack. You're on thin ice already. You let the man slip through your fingers." Kane stormed down the hall and took the steps up to the top floor. He pushed through the door at the top into a very plush and extravagant penthouse. There was an excellent view of the river. He slipped behind the bar made of polished black wood and cracked open a bottle of whiskey. He filled a tumbler to the rim and handed it to Smoke. "Have a snort, Mack."

"Sir, it's a tad early. You know I can't do my job without a clear head. I wouldn't want to fail you again."

"Nonsense, Mack. Appease me as if your life depended on it."

Smoke eyed the whiskey. "Sir, if you aren't pleased with my efforts—"

"Drink it!"

"Not on duty." Smoke set the goblet down. "I'd rather die first."

Kane spoke into his ear. "That can be arranged."

Smoke stood at attention, staring out the window. "If that is your wish, sir."

With a hard slap on Smoke's back, Kane said, "If I only had ten more like you, Mack. Now that would be something." He roared with laughter so loud it startled Allison. "If I only had more men like you running the show in those polished DC offices. They are so fickle once I give them some power. Bootlicking sycophants." He gulped down the whiskey. "But it's easy to manipulate the greedy. That's how we make our living. That's how we rule the world. But men like you, Mack, aren't manipulated. You do what you do out of duty and loyalty. I provide and you are grateful. That's good."

Kane led Smoke closer to the window. There was some activity on the boat. A man was being pushed down the plank. His face was covered in a pillowcase.

"Who's that, another shifter candidate?"

"Perhaps."

CHAPTER 33

S ID'S PLAN BORE FRUIT. SHE sat inside the food court at Union Station in DC, admiring the classical architecture in the archways above her head. The old train station had changed a lot since she took her first train trip from there as a kid. She wore a scarf, lightly tinted glasses, and a fashionable knit cap. Drinking a smoothie, she waited on the others. If the letters she had mailed garnered the efforts she hoped for, she could put her next plan into action. It was lunchtime, and the station was full of people. Holiday shopping had begun, so the lines were long. She spied Sam. Her sister-in-law's arms were loaded up with shopping bags.

Sam caught Sid's eye and sat down. "How's this for incognito?"

"That's not incognito, that's you."

"What do you mean? I'm wearing a ball cap. Why would I ever cover my gorgeous hair, not to mention covering my gorgeous eyes with glasses?"

"Don't worry, you're still getting plenty of lookers."

"Of course. So what's up? I have to admit, I was surprised by the card. At first I thought it was a thank-you note."

Asia showed up with a red plastic tray covered with food from end to end. She set the tray on the table and flopped into her chair. "Damn people. I can hardly move through here, and I'm little. I can't stand all the tourists. Why do they come here anyway? I bet they haven't ever visited the capitol in their own country." She took a big bite of her bacon cheeseburger. Juice dripped down her chin. "Mmm...now I remember why I came. So, why all the sneaking around, Sid? A letter? Who does that?"

"People that are being spied on." She gave Asia a look. Asia wore nothing on her head. "Nice disguise, by the way."

"Don't worry. I took the rental car out of the parking garage just like you said."

Sid's eyes slid over to Sam.

"I did too. Boy, you really went old school. Where'd you come up with this plan, anyway?"

"I made it up." Figuring the satellites were watching as well as the cars that followed her, Sid had rented cars inside parking garages of hotels and had them waiting. If Asia, Mal, or Sam were being watched, it wasn't too closely. They could drive their regular vehicles to the designated hotel and take the rental. All of them came from different locations far from the others. North, south, and east, they converged at Union Station. "I've confirmed that all of us are still being watched."

Asia looked around. "By who?"

"Who do you think? The Drake."

Sam leaned closer and lowered her glasses down the bridge of her nose. "What's going on, Sid?"

"Smoke's alive."

Sam hit the table. "I knew it."

"Big handsome lives." Asia's eyes were as big as her burger. "I like it. Where is he?"

"He's on the run. He's changed." Sid's finger tapped on the side of her cup. "Says he's a doppelganger, like Reginald. He also says he's something else at night, but I haven't seen it. Or him, rather."

"That's a shame. Tough break for him." Asia drained her Coke. "So are we going to kill him?"

"No!" Sid and Sam both said.

"But he's a shifter. You have to kill him."

"This is why Mal should have come and not you. Smoke needs a cure, and he needs our help. The last thing I want is the word to get out that Smoke is among us. Kane and Allison want him bad. I think he poses a threat to them."

"Of course he does. He keeps screwing up their operations." Sam applied some lipstick. "I'm so glad he's alive. Have you seen him?"

"Doctor Endicott."

Sam grabbed Sid's arm. "No kidding. I knew there was something about that guy. So what's the plan?"

"Smoke wants me to wait until he contacts me again, but my gut tells me he's in over his head. He's going to need our help. We need to be ready. For what, I don't know, but he thinks Kane is the only way to stop the shifters." Sid relayed everything Smoke had told her in the doctor's office. "I don't know what all you can do with that information, but I do think we might be able to find the Drake's lair if we work hard enough."

"We'll figure it out, Sis," Sam assured her. "I'm as motivated to find my brother as ever. Anything else?"

"Get ahold of Russ Davenport. He and Cort Calhoun need to know."

"Sounds like a weak link. Are you sure you can trust them?"

"We're going to need all the help we can get," Sid said. "Trust me. Kane's gearing up for something big. The way I figure it, when the time comes, we'll only get one chance to stop him."

"So what's our next move, super spy? Are we supposed to wait for another letter?" Asia finished her sandwich. "Why don't you just text me?"

Sam rolled her eyes. "Because they watch that. Geez, Asia, all those carbs are clogging your brain. Think."

"I am thinking. Thinking makes me hungry."

Sid slid them each another letter in an envelope.

"What's this?" Sam asked.

"Instructions. Plans. Agenda. Code. Just read it, and give a set to Russ. If I do text or call you, that will help you understand what I'm saying."

With her lips curled in a sneer, Asia said, "That's cheesy."

"You like cheese. That's why I did it. Stop eating and let's go."

CHAPTER 34

"**W**E HAVE A SOUND CANDIDATE in that man, I believe. Blackmail does such delightful things for a cause," Kane said. They were still inside the penthouse, enjoying the view. Kane made his way back behind the bar. He inspected the bottles stacked inside a hundred-slot wine rack mounted on the wall. "It's amazing what people are willing to do for precious things. If they only realized it all comes from the same dust and stone... Fools." He picked up a wine bottle and spun it on his finger like a basketball. "I witnessed an entire kingdom fall over a wine collection. Isn't that stupid?"

"I'd say so," Smoke agreed.

Allison took a spot on a burgundy leather sofa. "See, Kane, there's someone here who enjoys your stories. You don't have to bore me with them."

"You're still new to this. Your appreciation will grow with time." Kane pushed the spinning bottle into the air and snatched it by the neck. He put it back in the rack. "So, we're bringing a new recruit in. Actually, there are many candidates, but we're going to move forward with this one first. That John Smoke did real damage. He's taken down the shifters and wiped out my clones. Many of them were powerful. Such a problem. But not for long. I'm going to raise up more shifters than our enemies will ever be able to count. Imagine having the world's most important law enforcement division at your disposal. That was my problem. I was not being bold enough. Damn board of directors. But now it's time to move the end game forward."

There was a knock at the door.

Receiving a nod from Kane, Smoke moved over to the door and opened it up. Two peacoats led the hooded man inside and sat him down in a chair. The guards departed. Something about the man in the chair bothered Smoke. He was familiar. Too familiar. Smoke looked at Kane.

"Go ahead, take it off," Kane said.

Smoke lifted the hood from the man's eyes. It was Cyrus Tweel. *Not at all what I expected.*

"Welcome, Cyrus," Kane said. "Tell me, what is going on back at the Bureau? Is Sidney still making visits?"

"She comes by to visit her friend Sadie. She's even brought the baby. The last time I saw her, she was polite but didn't mention a thing about the Black Slate. It seems to me she's moved on." His brow crinkled. "I don't see any reason to worry on that front, but I don't know. She might be looking to come back to the Bureau."

"And that's why I need you to stay there."

"Yes, you made that pretty clear. And I've been pretty clear. I'll do this so long as I have full protection for the ones I care about."

"So, you're willing to become a full-fledged member of the Drake's secret society of shifters, eh?"

"I am."

Smoke couldn't believe what he was hearing. He'd been certain Cyrus had figured it out and was on their side. *I never should have trusted you, weasel.*

Cyrus continued, "I just want what's coming to me. Power at the Bureau. Real power. Political support."

"Power is such a wonderful treasure to share, isn't it, Mack?"

Smoke cleared his throat. "I agree. Shall I escort Mister Tweel to the preparation station?"

Kane cocked a brow at him. "I beg your pardon, Mack, but that's not protocol."

Smoke had slipped. He'd spent time questioning the real Mack Black about what happened in the facility. He'd used truth serums. But Mack had been hard to break even then, not wanting to betray Kane, his fear was so great. Still, Smoke had plenty of valuable information that had gotten him this far. He didn't know everything, but he'd have to trust his instincts and gamble. "You know I want to see how this process goes. I apologize, but my wants got the best of me. It won't happen again, sir."

Kane put his arm over Smoke's shoulder. "Maybe you've been working too hard, Mack. You seem a tad off your game." He tapped Smoke's chest. "Your heart races a little. That's not like you. Is your stone-cold demeanor shaken?"

"Never, sir. If anything, I'm a tad envious of this man. I feel my opportunities slipping away."

"Don't be silly, Mack. The only reason you're not a shifter is because I haven't found a suitable replacement for you. Trust me, I've had Allison research your position on—what do you call it, Allison?"

"Monster dot com."

"Yes, isn't that delightful? But I tell you what. I'll give you a peek inside."

"You always say that," Smoke replied.

"I know, and then I say maybe next time. No, Mack, I can't let you see all of our little secrets, now can I?"

"No sir, I suppose not. I wouldn't either."

Kane broke off his hug. "Don't fret. This time we're going to do things a little differently. Cyrus, we aren't prepped to do the shifter transfusion today. I'm waiting on another associate, Frank, to arrive. He'll be handling the big operation. No, instead, I want you to prove yourself in a different way. You see, I've given it some thought, and I'm going to do things like we did in ancient times. If you want to become a shifter, then you need to prove your dedication first. After all, it's a great deal of power that I offer."

"I'll do it. You just name it."

"Good, very good. As I recall, you had strong feelings for Sidney once, didn't you?"

"We were engaged, yes." Cyrus shrank in his seat a little.

"Contact her. Tell her you have some information about the Black Slate. Lure her in. And then kill her."

CHAPTER 35

S ITTING, CYRUS PALED. HIS ADAM'S apple rolled.

"Is there a problem, Agent Tweel?" Kane said.

Even Allison's back straightened. She was sitting on the edge of her seat.

"Uh, no, Kane. I'll do it. It's just that she won't be that easy to kill." Cyrus loosened the collar on his shirt. "But I'll do it."

"Of course you will. I don't mean to be coercive. After all, this deal we are making is one that has to come from your free will. That shows loyalty. If you can't help me, then I don't have any use for you, now do I? And I can't just keep you alive."

"No, no, I'll do as I've been asked. I wouldn't be here if I couldn't make the hard decision."

"Good. Mack, escort him back to the ship. Cyrus, keep me apprised of your situation. Oh, and by the way, I want this done today."

Cyrus stood up and gave a quiet nod.

Smoke escorted him out. His muscles knotted in his back. His stomach was churning. Cyrus had gained Sid's trust, and chances were she wouldn't see what was coming. He had to warn her. To make matters worse, he was stuck at the power plant. Any changes or requests would make Kane suspicious, if Kane wasn't on to Smoke already.

He might be toying with me. Trying to draw me out.

Walking Cyrus down the dock, Smoke said to him, "I envy you. Kane doesn't let many into his inner circle."

"Maybe that's because you don't have what it takes."

"I'm not so sure you do either. You seem weak."

"You never know what someone is capable of until their back is to the wall. Besides, I've seen enough to know we are going to lose this battle, so when the fight is over, I'm going to be on the winning side."

Smoke looked down into the man's eyes. "Me too." He covered Cyrus's head up with the hood. He walked him up the plank onto the boat and shoved him down into the cabin. He headed back to the power plant and went upstairs.

Kane and Allison were arguing on the other side of the door.

Smoke knocked on it.

"Yes, come in, Mack," Kane said.

Smoke entered. Kane and Allison's cheeks were flushed, which seemed odd for shifters. "Will you be needing me for anything else today, sir?"

Kane made a quizzical look. "As a matter of fact, Mack, with all of the excitement going on, I think I'm long overdue for a walk-through. I need to refresh my mind on our operations. Give me a run-through."

"Certainly. I'd be glad to." *Crapola. I've got to get word out to Sid. But how will I do that with Kane shadowing me all day?* He watched the small cruiser pull free of the dock. *God, help Sid.*

He spent the next several hours thoroughly walking Kane through everything he did. They walked the halls, checked the doors, tested security systems, and monitored the cameras. They went over a list of so-called agents loyal to the Drake in the field. The list of people on the Drake's payroll was scary. The corruption in Washington ran deep. Hundreds of people in key positions were faithful crooks and thieves. The few dozen shifters Kane controlled were the enforcers. The bosses.

Kane flipped through the manifest of servants. "The list keeps growing. It won't be long before we control everything, clones or not. That was a gamble, and I told them so. But they insisted. Everyone wants bragging rights about something new they did. Well, there is nothing new under the sun. Trust me." He set the clipboard down. "I tell you what, Mack. I'm feeling a little—oh, how should I put it—generous today." He pulled out from under his shirt an ancient key that hung by a chain. "How about I give you a tour of the deep?"

"Sir?" Smoke said. He'd never seen the key before, and he wasn't sure what Kane was talking about.

"You only have access to the sublevels, not the deepest ones. No, let's take you all the way down to the belly of our operation."

Smoke nodded.

Kane led the way to the basement level. The modern facilities gave way to colonial-period items. There was an old steel door at the end of one of the halls that dated back centuries. Without any modern security on it, Smoke had figured if it was ever used, it was used for storage. Looking at Smoke, Kane put the key in the keyhole and turned. The metal locking mechanism clanked over. He pulled the door open. "You first, Mr. Black."

A gust of air stifled Smoke's nose with the scent of death and decay. A wooden stairwell led down into the darkness. He shielded his nose. His senses were stronger than they used to be as a man. Something foul lurked down there. He started to step over the threshold but stopped. "I'd rather not."

"What ever do you mean, Mack? This is a great honor. For you."

"I have a feeling that what's down there is not for mortal eyes to see."

"Oh, don't be such a baby." Kane gave him a hard shove. "Don't disappoint me now. You're the toughest man I know. Go."

Smoke followed the stairs way down into the blackness all the way to the bottom, where gas lanterns flickered and radiated soft light. It was a huge network of underground caverns below the river. People were hunkered on the floor and along the walls. They were deaders. Deaders in deteriorating Revolutionary War–era redcoat uniforms. Dozens of them, and possibly more beyond. A huge man stood among them dressed in an old rebel uniform. He was every bit of ten feet tall. The huge, bearded man's eyes were black as coals. A rebel cap rested on his head.

Kane was sitting on the steps with a smile on his face. His eyes lit up as he said to Smoke, "It makes you wonder, doesn't it? An entire regiment of soldiers, some over two hundred and fifty years old. Isn't that something you never imagined? I like the mix. One giant rebel—I call him Stonewall—and some of Britain's finest, all held over from Revolutionary times. I love history. I especially love making it."

"That's an understatement. What are they here for?"

"They're guarding something, of course."

"I'm curious. What?"

"I'd tell you, but if I did, I'd have to kill you, Smoke."

CHAPTER 36

BACK AT HER PARENTS' HOUSE, Sid was sitting in the living room, rocking the baby in her father's recliner. The lit fireplace brought a soothing warmth to the room. Keith and Sally were sitting on the sofa watching an episode of *Gunsmoke*. JK's eyes were aglow. He sucked on his binky, staring at the light on the ceiling.

"They sure don't make them like James Arness anymore. Look at him. He's as tall as a horse. Did you know that he was six foot seven? He served in World War II and got a Bronze Star and Purple Heart for his service."

"We know, Dad." Sid had heard it time and again since she was a kid.

"And I'm making sure you don't forget it. I miss Matt Dillon and the like." He held up a bottle of beer and drank it down. "Here's to you, James!"

Sally slapped Keith's leg. "Will you quit being so foolish? You're setting a bad example for the baby."

"He'll not be picking up on it anytime soon. But when he does, I'll mind myself. Maybe."

The telephone rang. Sally perked up. She hustled over to the phone.

The loud ringing startled JK. He started to cry.

"Aw, just when I thought he was about to go to sleep." Sid sighed and tried to put the binky back in his mouth. "We never get enough rest, do we?" Visiting her parents had become routine. They'd watch him while she ran her errands. She hadn't told them about Smoke being alive. She contemplated whether she should or not. If she couldn't trust her parents, who could she trust? But she didn't want them put in danger. She put JK over her shoulder and patted his back.

"Sidney," Sally said. She'd stretched the old yellow phone cord from the kitchen into the living room. "It's for you."

"Me?" Sid didn't have her parents' house listed on any of her instructions that she'd given to Sam and Asia. She got her hopes up. *Smoke.* "Who is it?"

Sally's eyes were as big as saucers. Excited, she said, "Its Cyrus."

"Tweel?" Sid got up on her feet. She handed JK over to her mother and took the phone. Slipping into the kitchen, she said, "Hello?"

"Hey, Sid. How are you?"

"Fine."

"How's the baby?"

"He's wondering what the hell you're doing calling me at my parents'." She could hear traffic in the background. "Where are you?"

"I'm still in DC. My transfer isn't official yet. Look, sorry if I startled you, and I hate to call you at your parents', but I wanted to use a secure line. Well, at least something that no one is keeping ears on. I wasn't sure if anyone would pick up, but I'm glad Sally did."

"Out with it, Cyrus. What's going on?"

"Look, I know you've been wanting some insight on the Black Slate. I came across some information that you might be interested in."

"What is it?"

"It's not something I can explain over the phone. It's more or less a 'see it to believe it' kind of thing."

"You need to be more specific than that."

"Look, I have it on a jump drive. I'm not about to send the file over the net. And Rebecca doesn't know about it. If something happens, I don't want to put her in any kind of danger. Just meet me. I'll hand it over and give you a little more insight. Listen, Sid. I'm washing my hands of this. I'm moving on, but maybe you can do something with it."

"Okay, Cyrus. Where do you want to meet?"

"Remember our favorite place to eat dinner?"

"Yeah."

"Meet me there on the back patio, say six thirty. I won't keep you."

He sounded a little nervous. "All right, Cyrus. Six thirty, then." She hung up the phone and said, "Mom, can you keep an eye on JK for a few more hours?"

Bright eyed and sweet voiced, Sally said, "Well of course we can. Do you have a date? I always liked Cyrus, even though he was a bit frosty. I thought he tried really hard to please you. Too hard, perhaps."

She kissed Sally, Keith, and the baby. "See you soon. And Dad, I'm taking your truck."

"What?"

CHAPTER 37

"I SAID, 'SMOKE?'" KANE HAD A pack of cigarettes in his hand. He was tapping one out. "I know. You're a cigar man, right Mack? What's wrong? You look a little queasy."

"This stench isn't doing much for me."

Kane rose. "No, I imagine the colonial guard hasn't bathed in two hundred years. Hah, it wouldn't surprise me one bit if some of them never bathed at all. You have to appreciate the modern times we live in. People don't stink so much."

Smoke breathed a little easier. *If Kane's playing along, you play along. We'll see.*

Kane started passing out cigarettes to the old soldiers turned deader. The listless men lit the cigarettes with the lighter he gave them. Many of them carried old sabres and muskets with bayonets still attached to them. He handed the rest of the pack to the giant. "Stonewall here is one of my favorites. He's an actual giant turned into a deader, not a shifter like the other giants you've seen. I like deaders. They're completely loyal. They don't cause problems like some shifters do. Like my brother Vormus, for example. He's such a traitor."

Smoke stepped aside when Kane came back and headed up the stairs. With a casual glance back at the deaders, he said, "I have to admit, I'm curious about what they guard. Don't you think we should put some eyes down here?"

Heading up the stairs, Kane said, "No. What lies down here is not meant to be seen by the living."

"Is it a demon?"

"It's something." Kane made it to the top. Smoke moved right by him and closed the door. Kane locked the door and tucked the key in his shirt. "I hope you enjoyed that. Now let's finish the inspection of the rest of the facility."

Tormented, Smoke led Kane through the facility step by step. On the inside he was agonizing over Sid. He needed to get word to her. He needed to do it now. Outside, they cruised the parking lot in a golf cart and counted the cameras. *This is asinine.* To make matters worse, the sun was starting to fall. Dusk was coming, and it wouldn't be long before he changed. He was stuck in a wormhole of the unordinary. *What is Kane up to?*

"My, it's getting late, isn't it? Let's swing by operations and drop our checklist off. Tell you what, Mack, why don't you join me and Allison for dinner?"

"Really?"

Kane laughed. "Of course not. Come on though. I'm tired of this. Ride me down to the dock." He took out his phone and dialed. "Allison, meet me at the dock. We're leaving."

Smoke saw them off. As soon as the boat churned into the river and headed upstream, he went straight to operations. He sat down at a station and pulled up Sid's location on his monitor.

"Is there anything we can help you with, sir?" said Sherry.

"Anything happen while I was out giving Kane the grand tour?"

"No," she said.

"Good." Smoke watched a satellite feed of Sid's car parked at her parents'. He saw Keith's truck leave. *That's her. I know it.* He linked up the satellite connection with his phone, which wasn't anything odd. Mack Black had the authority to do things like that. He stuck the phone in his pocket and logged out his recent history from his search. Getting up, he said, "I'll see the both of you in the morning."

"Knocking off early?" the man said.

"Don't ever ask me that again."

The man shrank behind his console.

Smoke headed out, got in his truck, and left the facility. He pulled up the image of Sid driving on the screen. She was headed east. Smoke dialed a number on the phone. He got a signal that the line was dead. *Aw, crap!* He realized he might have been out of the loop too long. Sam and Guppy would be on different exchanges by now. Mal Carlson would be too. That's what happens when you don't want contact. You cut all those ties.

Smoke laid into the accelerator. He weaved through traffic, watching the sun drop from the sky and settle in the west. The streetlights flickered on over the black streets. The rain came. He checked the image on the phone again. Sid parked in an old neighborhood and got out. There was an FBI vehicle sitting in the rear. Smoke was still a mile away. He banged the wheel. His hands became claws. He saw his face in the rearview mirror, savage and ugly. "No!"

CHAPTER 38

S ID DROVE HER FATHER'S TRUCK to the east end of DC. She wasn't certain if the car switch would work or not, but chances were the goons that followed her would be focusing on the Hellcat. She prayed the satellites would be, too.

She pulled the truck into a slot in the street in front of a small brick building. The sign on the building read, "Fazio's House of Spaghetti." It was a quaint restaurant tucked inside one of DC's smaller suburban neighborhoods. It was a good place away from the hustle and bustle of the city. The houses in the neighborhood were old and the area quiet. Rain came down in a cold drizzle as she stepped out of the truck. The warm lights that filled the window of the small eatery were out. Sid stepped on the stoop. A handwritten sign taped on the inside of the glass door behind the bars read, "Closed for Renovation."

Not seeing any sign of an FBI car on the street, Sid headed around the side of the building toward the parking lot in the back. There, a single car was parked in the small blacktop lot. It was a black SUV with a government plate. Sid found it odd that the lighting in the back was out. That was when she saw somebody standing on the patio in a trench coat. It was Cyrus.

"Good evening, Sid. I'm glad you could make it. Come on up." He scanned the area. "I hate cold days like this, but at least no one else is about."

Sid took the steps up to the patio. "What's going on, Cyrus?"

He took off his glasses, which had become misty from the rain. "Does that suit you wear keep you warm?"

"What suit?"

"You know, *the suit*?"

"It does, but not when you don't have it on." Her teeth chattered. She faced him but didn't get too close. There was something off with him. "Which I regret."

"You know I hate the cold. Sorry, it's just a whimsy that came to my mind when I saw you." He put his glasses inside his coat pocket and produced something else. A black jump drive was in his hand. "This is it, Sid. Now, I'm not saying it's going to take you to the heart of the matter, but it's got names and places. Look, I could have just left it somewhere, but I wanted to wish you luck. I'm also sorry for having been difficult." He came closer, widening his arms out for a hug.

She gave him one. "It's okay, Cyrus. I know you risked a lot with your career by coming here. Thanks. I hope you and Rebecca do well. You deserve a new start."

He broke off his embrace. He showed a weak smile. "Thanks, Sid." He handed her the jump drive. Before he fully let it go, he said, "You should think about breaking away too."

"I will." She turned her back and started walking away. She had hit the first step down when the hair rose on the back of her neck.

Behind her, the sound of a pistol clicking out of its polymer holster caught her ear.

She turned, feeling like she was stuck in time. She caught a glimpse of Cyrus.

Fire blasted out of his gun's muzzle.

She fell backward into a sea of blackness. Her head bounced off a step. Through glazed eyes, she watched Cyrus walk away with a silencer in his hand. He opened the car door and didn't look back. He sat down in the seat, slamming the door behind him.

That dirty bastard. She could feel her blood seeping through her clothing. *I knew I never should have dated him.* The fire burning through her wounds turned cold. Her numb fingers found her gun. She pulled it out, but it slipped through her fingers, falling to the pavement.

The car engine started. The lights came on. The SUV lurched forward.

Something black dropped from the sky, landing on the car's hood. It was a man in form. The face was hard to see in the dark. The ears were large, the expression bestial. The clothing it wore was in tatters. With steel cords for muscle, it busted out the windshield.

Cyrus fired a shot at the monster.

Clawed hands reached inside the cabin and jerked Cyrus out like a rag. The man's entire body was slung over the hard pavement, bouncing before skidding to a halt. The agent didn't move.

In a single bound, the creature hopped over to her side. Gently, he picked her up in his arms and said, "Talk to me, Sid."

"Smoke." She reached up and touched his face with bloody fingers. "It is you, isn't it?"

He nodded. "We need to get you help."

"You look like a bat," she managed to say. "A man bat."

"Save your energy."

"I always liked Man-bat." Her eyes were weak. "I'm not going to die, Smoke. I can't. I won't leave my baby. I won't leave you." Her phone buzzed. "Get that."

Smoke fished through her clothing and found the phone. He read the screen.

"What does it say?"

"Take a pill."

Two seconds later, two vehicles screeched into the parking lot. Guppy jumped out of a Bronco with a gun on Smoke. "Get away from her."

The other car was an old sedan. Cort Calhoun emerged with a big Alaskan wheel gun in his hand. "If you don't back off, I'll take your head off! Whew, what in the world are you, anyway? You look like a bat, man."

Asia, Mal, and Sam spilled out of Guppy's vehicle.

Smoke held his hands up. "It's me, Smoke."

Sid croaked out, "It's him. Get Cyrus."

Mal and Asia rushed beside Sid. "Were you shot?"

"Several times."

"Why didn't you wear the suit?" Mal asked.

"I did wear the suit." She had told Cyrus she didn't, or at least led him to believe that. "I'm not sure what the hell he shot me with."

Mal opened up her jacket. Clean bullet holes had torn right through the suit. A burst had gone through her left side, soaking the fabric. "Take this now." He gave her a pill. "Chew it up and swallow. These wounds are through and through. No shrapnel. We need to get the bleeding stopped."

Asia popped over with a first aid kit. "I'm on it." She made a sour face at Smoke. "Handsome man not so handsome now."

Groaning, Sid said, "What's that, your lunch box? I hate to imagine what's in it."

"Watch what you say. I'd hate to accidently use the hot sauce on those wounds." Asia plucked a bottle of Cholula hot sauce out of the box and handed it to Smoke. "Hold this. Got to operate." She grabbed a metal canister and screwed a long straw on the end. "This is great stuff for humans. Hold her still."

Smoke and Mal held Sid fast. Her tongue started to numb. The burning in her side started to fade. "What did you give me, Mal?"

"Part supervitamin, part pain pill. Very potent, and it slows the heart too. Don't let her fall asleep."

Asia injected foam into her wounds while Sid kicked. "Hold her still. She flop like fish."

Smoke's grip tightened around her legs. "Hang in there, Sid, you're going to make it."

"I know," she replied.

Asia filled Sid's wounds with the concoction. "That has to hold her for now, but she needs to get to a hospital. I need to stitch her up, inside and out."

"I thought the vitamin and the foam would do the trick," Mal said.

"Sometimes it does, sometimes it doesn't." Asia shrugged. "Either way, she'll live, but she might have trouble digesting spicy foods."

Sid's innards tingled. "Whoa, something's happening."

"Take it easy," Smoke said.

Calhoun approached. He had Cyrus in a headlock. "What do you want me to do with this ass-bag?"

Sid glared at Cyrus. "Give me a gun. I'm going to shoot him."

CHAPTER 39

CALHOUN HANDED SID HIS GUN. "I'd be happy to let you use mine," he said.

Smoke took the gun out of Sid's hand. "No, we can't kill him. We need him."

"How could we ever need a piece of crap like this? He almost killed me." She glared at Cyrus.

His face was sagging. "I'm sorry, Sid. I didn't have a choice. Kane's too deep on the inside. He was going to kill Rebecca. I couldn't let that happen."

"That's not true," Smoke said. "Kane wouldn't kill anyone. You had to become willing to be his servant to go through with this. What you did came out of your heart. It's dark and broken."

"No, I swear it. I'm sorry, Sid. I didn't know what to do. Aw, what does it matter? Kane will kill me anyway, and just so you know, he'll kill all of you too."

Guppy appeared with Cyrus's gun in hand. "I found this in his car." He popped out the cartridge. "Blue-tip bullets. Explains a lot of things. It doesn't seem like he was taking any chances."

"Where'd you get those bullets?" Smoke said.

"I snaked them away from you guys. Can you blame me? I saw what was going on out there with all of these monsters. I needed my own protection from them. But you're going to lose, trust me. You don't realize it, but it's over. Kane's always a step ahead of you."

"I really don't like this guy." Calhoun gave Cyrus a shake. "Let me take him away and bury him. I know just the place. I've got a cousin who owns a junkyard. We'll put him in a junker in the compactor and squish him. It'll make an FBI Rubik's Cube out of him."

Sam poked Smoke in the shoulder. He looked up at her. "Hi, Sis."

"Man, this is weird. You always did read too many comics as a kid. Can you fix it?"

"I don't know." He looked at Sid and said to the others, "Give us a moment."

Everyone moved away.

"Sid, what needs to be done needs to be done now."

She touched the outlines of his face. His features were strong, between a man and a bat, but she could still make out the man she loved. "Are you blind?"

"No. You're still as radiant as ever. Trust me. I'm not sure how I ended up like this, because I've done everything I can to resist it." He groaned. His face twitched. The muscles in his arms flexed. "This power coursing through my veins is hard to fight. It clouds my mind. Sid, if you lose me, you have to put me down."

"You're not an animal."

"No, not yet, but I don't want to lose my soul over this. There's a war inside me. I'm trying not to embrace what I have. That's why my blood runs so hot."

Sid pulled herself up to her knees. "You're going to beat this. We're going to beat this. Think of all the evil Kane has done. Use your power and turn it against him. If anyone can do it, you can. I know it."

"I should be able to do anything, now that I have wings," he said, flapping a membrane of skin that was attached between his elbow and lower back. "But I can't fly too well. I more or less glide. I guess I'm a werebat. I guess that's what I get for having a powerful imagination."

Clutching the fur on his chest, she said, "You do wonderful things with your imagination. You've certainly never disappointed me, so don't disappoint me now." Wincing, she stood up. "Now let's do what we have to do. Let's find Kane and bury his ass."

"So be it." Smoke walked over to Cyrus and wrapped his long, clawed fingers around his neck. "You tried to kill my wife. You owe me." He squeezed. Cyrus's eyes bulged. "Contact Kane. Tell him the deed's done."

Choking, Cyrus managed to say, "You won't kill me."

With one arm, Smoke lifted Cyrus off the ground with ease. "Don't be so sure."

"Phone. Phone is in my pocket. But he usually calls me. It'll ring between now and morning."

Smoke set Cyrus down. He patted him down until he found the phone. The phone seemed really small in his hand. He tossed it to Guppy. "See what you can do with this."

Rubbing his neck, Cyrus said, "I'm telling you, Smoke, Kane's not going to lose. You can't beat him. He's a thousand years old! Maybe older. They win. They always win. They control everything. You've got to see that."

"Somebody get me some duct tape so I can silence this man," Calhoun said.

Asia pulled a roll of medical tape from her first aid kit. "This will do." She started to unstring the tape.

Cyrus's phone rang.

"Unknown Caller," Guppy said.

"That's him. He's the only caller my phone doesn't ID."

"Don't do anything stupid," Sid said to Cyrus as Guppy handed the agent the phone. "You've done enough stupid today. Put it on speaker."

Crowded by everyone, Cyrus answered the phone. "Hello."

Kane's voice responded. "Is the deed complete, Agent Tweel?"

"Yes. She's dead. I'm working on disposing of the body as we speak."

"Interesting. I'm sure that was very difficult, seeing how she was a former lover of yours," Kane said.

Calhoun's eyes turned big and white. He started to mutter something, but Asia covered his mouth.

"Now that you've finished your task, come down to the plant. There's a full moon tonight. It's the perfect time to run you through the process. As a matter of fact, why don't you bring the body with you?"

"I, uh—"

"Just stuff her in the trunk if you haven't dropped her in a river already. Yes, bring her back here. She'll make a beautiful deader. Besides, I promised Allison some new company."

"Yes, sir. I'm on my way."

CHAPTER 40

MOVING PRESENT COMPANY TO A more discreet location under a bridge, Smoke told everyone what he knew about the Drake Energy power plant. He had a jump drive that he handed over to Guppy, who sat in his truck with a computer on his lap. His sausage fingers were working the keys.

"I don't expect anyone to go in with me, but it's all or nothing." Smoke snapped a gun belt around his waist. Two pistols were holstered on the sides. "We aren't going to get another shot at Kane. He's the main mark. We have to kill him, but it won't be easy. The plant has security everywhere, not to mention deaders and shifters coming in and out. We're going to need all the ammo we can get. Mal, what do we have?"

"I've got a lot of everything: bullets, suits, vitamins. I've been storing up for this special occasion." Mal slid open the door of his minivan. He took out a metal suitcase and set it on the ground. "Who wants one?"

Russ Davenport held his hands up. "As much as I'd like to think I'm brave enough to go in, well, that's not happening. I'm not much of a lover or a fighter, but I'm more than happy to lend my brain."

Asia grabbed a suitcase. Mal's eyes widened when she said, "Let's wipe them out so I can get back to routine dining."

Everyone grabbed a suitcase. Cyrus was laughing. Calhoun socked him in the head.

"So, Smoke…" Guppy was looking at Smoke as he talked but obviously wasn't sure what to make of him. "Are we going in by land or by sea?"

"It'll be too slow to go in on the Potomac. No, I have another idea." Smoke strapped on a smart watch-type device that Mal handed him. He cringed as he stuck in an earpiece. His enlarged ears must have magnified his hearing ten times. "Just don't speak too loud into this. As for entering the plant, I might be going in by air. On my signal, we're going to drive a wedge right in there."

Sid had a suitcase. He opened it up and began gearing up with sharp weapons and guns. He pulled her aside. Her face was pale, and her heart beat fast. Too fast. "Sid, I'm not going to try and stop you, but, well, you know I'd rather go it alone."

Loading special-tipped bullets into her magazine, she said, "Yeah, well, I don't plan on raising our son without his father, either. I've got to pull Allison and Megan's hind ends out of the fire too."

"This is going to be our little Armageddon, isn't it?"

"This is what heroes do."

Smoke leaned in for a kiss and then remembered his hideous form and pulled back.

Sid eased her fingers behind his neck and slowly reeled him in. "You're mine for better or worse," she said just before she kissed him.

He responded in kind. When they broke it off, he said, "You're excellent."

"And I'll never let you forget it."

EPILOGUE

IN THE CONTROL CENTER OF the Drake Energy plant, Kane and Allison stood side by side, staring at the huge monitor in front of them. The only other people there were two analysts, Rich and Sherry. Both of them were slouched over their stations, unmoving and quiet, as if they were frozen. On the giant screen was a satellite image zooming in on the streets of DC. Cars were pulling out of the parking lot behind a building.

"Do you think he really killed her?" Allison asked Kane.

"I don't know. The satellites don't pick up images so well at night. But that's okay. I'm pretty sure they'll be coming here.

On the one hand, Smoke will want to avenge his love. On the other, if she lives, it won't be for long. But he'll be coming. The bat is flying right into my trap. Sherry, bring up the shifter tracking screen."

Sherry typed. A new screen popped up.

"Pan back," Kane said. "My shifters are so stupid. I have all the new ones tagged like cattle." On the screen were tiny blue dots lit up in a variety of places. There were names and locations that tagged the dots.

Allison stepped forward for a closer look. "That one says John Smoke." She pointed at the bridge Smoke and Sid were currently under. "You've been able to track him the entire time and you didn't tell me?"

"As a matter of fact, he's been right under our noses. He was Mack Black. I knew it."

"Why didn't you take him out?" Her eyes flashed with anger. "Why didn't you tell me?"

"You're new to all this. Besides, I like surprises. This is what we do, Allison. For fun. But after tonight, the game is over, and we'll have to find new mice for the mousetrap." He texted a message. "I'm not going to take any chances this time. I'm summoning all the shifters to the lair. When that pathetic band of mortals shows up, we're going to watch them be wiped out one by one."

The door to the operations center opened. Frank from Vegas filled the doorway. He wore a grey suit, a white shirt, and no tie. He stepped under the door frame and said, "Hello, Kane. You summoned me?"

"Yes, Frank. I want you to meet Allison."

"A pleasure, Allison."

Kane moved between Rich and Sherry's workstations. Facing Frank, he pointed at both of them. "This is Rich and Sherry. As of today, their employment is terminated. Escort them out, if you please."

"Certainly." Frank walked up behind the man and woman. Their mouths gaped open. Sherry's chin quivered. Rich's eyes streamed with tears. Frank grabbed them both by the hair and dragged them out of the room, begging for their lives.

Kane shut the door behind them. Leaning against it, he said to Allison, "I have a sinking suspicion your sister lives. Do you think you have it in you to finish her?"

Allison nodded. "It will be done." She held up her hand. Her fingernails grew long and razor sharp. She transformed into a deadly exotic tigress right before his eyes. "I guarantee it."

CRAIG HALLORAN

THE SUPERNATURAL
BOUNTY HUNTER
FILES

SMOKE OUT

BOOK 10

CHAPTER 1

Under the bridge, Cort Calhoun loaded his big Alaskan handgun. He slipped round after round into the Ruger wheel gun. He was a big black man with short hair and scruff on his face. He reminded Sid of the defensive tackle Reggie White.

"Those bullets aren't going to do you any good, Cort." Out of the aluminum case she handed him a semi-automatic pistol. "You're going to need one of these."

Cort squinted an eye. He took the Glock semi-automatic. It looked like a toy in his hand. "I can barely fit my finger inside the trigger guard."

The night brought hard bits of snow from the sky. Traffic rumbled over the bridge overhead. Everyone was still present. Mal Carlson, the one who fit people with their gear, was helping Asia into a sweetheart suit. Smoke stood beside a Ford Bronco, going over plans with Sam and Guppy. Russ Davenport, the reporter for Nightfall DC, sat inside Sid's dad's old truck, holding a gun on Cyrus Tweel.

Cyrus caught her eye and mouthed the words "You're going to die."

"You were engaged to that geek?" Cort popped the cartridge out of the Glock. He thumbed out blue-tipped bullets. "You, to him? That's like a princess actually marrying a frog, with glasses."

Sid showed a part smile and part grimace. "They say love is blind, and I didn't even love him like that. Honestly, I don't know. I don't get it. Just a phase."

"Yeah, a stupid phase. I never understood women and the bad decisions they make. Sometimes, I see these pretty ladies and these ugly guys. The faces ought to match up better."

"It's not all about looks."

"True, but then again that's coming from someone married to that big-eared thing over there."

Smoke, still in his bat-man form, popped his head out of the Bronco's door. "I can hear you, Cort, all too well."

"So? You're still ugly. It's not like I was trying to hide it. Anyway, what do these blue bullets do?"

Sid's smile hurt. "They'll rip through steel and shifters."

"And sweetheart suits too," Cyrus yelled out of the truck. "Just make sure you don't miss the mark, like I did. Aim for the heart. Of course, in Sid's case, it turned out she didn't have one."

Russ jammed his gun into Cyrus's ribs. "Shut up."

Mal made his way over to Sid and produced some bullet clips filled with cartridges. The bookish man said to Cort, "Is that a forty-four magnum you're carrying?"

"Yep."

Mal handed over the cartridges. "These should do." He started to walk away.

"Wait a second." Cort had a bandolier of bullets around his waist. On it, there were two small leather pouches. He pulled out two round cylinders with six bullets in each. They were speed loaders specially designed for his hand gun. He started loading the bullets into the speed loaders, alternating between blue, red, and green tips. "What do the green bullets do?"

"Paralyze," Mal said. Cort opened his mouth. Mal cut him off. "And the red tipped are explosive."

"Why would I want to paralyze them?" Cort said. "When I shoot, I shoot to kill."

"The shifters come in all shapes and sizes, Cort. Some things are more effective on some than others." Sid snapped both of her Glocks with extended clips into her polymer holsters. "Shoot the deaders in the heart. A regular bullet will stop them unless they have armor on. The peacoats are the same, just people, but they probably have Kevlar underneath. As for the shifters, well, I guess you'll know when you see them. Most of them are kinda ugly, like Smoke." She grinned Smoke's way. Face out of sight, he waved his hand. "Mal, do you have a suit that fit him?"

"Yeah, I think he got it stretched over everything. I'm surprised it didn't rip. It was supposed to be Smoke's. He needs his vitamins too."

"Vitamins? Look, I eat all my fruits and vegetables. I don't need any Centrums or One A Days. I'm a healthy eater."

Sid glanced at his belly, which bulged over his belt a fair bit.

"Beer has plenty of good health effects," he said.

"You'll need the vitamin. It'll make you feel like Superman, but it doesn't last long." Mal handed Cort a small cylinder of pills. "Don't take them all at once."

"I don't want to feel like Superman. I want to feel like Luke Cage, Power Man."

"You will, minus the steel-hard skin," Sid said.

"Yeah, you know your Power Man. Girl knows the books. I like that." Cort stepped closer to her. "You know, if your husband doesn't make it, I'll look out for you."

"Not happening. And he'll make it." Sid slid knives into her boot sheaths. "What if you don't make it, Cort?"

He showed an illuminating smile. "Fine by me. I'll be dancing in heaven with the angel ladies then." He started a little waltz. "That day will be here soon enough, one way or the other."

"Mal!" said Asia. "We need to stop at a drive-through on the way over. This suit is making me very hungry." She was pulling the collar on her suit. The suit enhanced her little curves on her tiny little frame. "Don't look at me like that. We have business to do."

Cort took a knee. He laced up his boots, revealing some knives of his own as he did so. "So, who's this man we have to kill?"

"Kane."

"Cain like in the Bible, or the bad Kane guy from Robocop 2? I love Robocop. Or is it the wrestler?"

"He's not as cool as the wrestler. More like Kane from Robocop 2." Sid's stomach turned sideways. She'd been with that monster. It tore at her sleep at night. She'd never rest well again until he was dead. "He's a big blond, well-dressed, kinda like a pro wrestler. "

"Does he turn into some kind of monster too?"

"I don't know." Sid had never really thought of it before. Kane appeared the same all the time, but she couldn't rule it out. "As always, expect the worst. Oh, and one more thing, don't kill my sister. Leave her to me."

"What does she look like?"

Sid pulled up an image on her phone. "This."

Cort leaned over. His jaw hung. "Damn. No offense, Sid, but she makes you look like a dog."

She punched his arm.

"Sorry, I didn't mean it. It was—"

"A quote," Smoke said. He'd snuck in behind Sid. "From Ted Baxter, off of Mary Tyler Moore."

Cort nodded his chin. "The man-bat knows his MTM."

CHAPTER 2

"**S**O WHAT ARE WE GOING to do with this worm?" Russ asked Sid. The heavyset reporter in a brown trench coat was sitting behind the steering wheel. "Nobody's out tonight. I say we drop him in the river using those cinderblocks over there for a flotation device."

Standing beside the passenger-side window, she said, "No, that's too good for him."

With his hand cuffed to the car door, Cyrus said, "Kane's expecting me, Sid. If I don't show, he'll kill me. He'll kill Rebecca." His neck strained. "You know that. She's innocent of all this."

"No one's innocent." Smoke's body brushed against Sid's back. "But we don't have much time to fool with. Kane's very particular about how he controls things. He's going to be expecting Cyrus with your body. How do you want to play it?"

"I thought we were just going to bust in there and hit them with everything we have?" she said.

"We've been talking," said Smoke, standing close to seven feet tall, part man and part bat, nodding Sam and Guppy's way. His nose crinkled when he spoke. "It would be best to assume at this point that Kane knows we're coming."

"Oh, bravo," Cyrus said. "Listen to that. I told you Kane was more than a step ahead of you, and now you listen. It won't matter though. He'll kill the both of you. Unless, of course, you let me take you in. Once again, we can all be on the same team."

"Boy, this guy really is a piece of work." Russ pushed the gun deeper into Cyrus's ribs. "I don't want to get your truck all dirty, but I do want to shoot this guy."

Cyrus pushed back against Russ. "You'll never shoot anybody. You're a tabloid journalist. Huh. Are all of you a bunch of complete idiots? Haven't you figured it out yet? You can't win! The Drake isn't some elite gang of thugs. They've been around for centuries. Longer. They're part of something that mortals can't comprehend. Unless you're one of them, you're better off fleeing. You'll live longer that way."

"Life on the run isn't my style. You know that, Cyrus. I like to face my problems head-on," said Sid.

"This isn't like what you've faced before, Sid. It's an entire conglomerate. I did my homework when I became Section Chief. I got access to more information." Cyrus poked his head halfway out the window. "The Drake has many heads. Many names. Sure, you may have taken down a few of them—and you can beat your chest about that all you want—but you barely made it. Remember: every time, you almost died. The Drake and Kane, do you think they mourn their losses? No. It's all a game to them. I'm telling you, they are worse than Congress. Hell, they are Congress, don't you see?"

Sid pushed back into Smoke. "Let's have a chat."

"Now you're thinking, Sid," Cyrus said.

"Shut up." Russ rolled up Cyrus's window and his. He took a cigar out of his trench coat pocket, popped out the truck cigarette lighter, and began smoking.

"Do you mind? I hate smoke. Both of them," Cyrus said.

"Shut up," Russ replied.

Smoke and Sid walked away together until they stood at the top of the berm of large stones that led down to the river.

"What's on your mind, honey?" Smoke's eyes appeared larger now. His strong features were more pronounced, but in a good way, even with the fur.

"I have to admit," she said, "I'm not too keen on walking into a death trap. I'd feel better if we had an army with us or something. I just want to wipe those bastards off the map."

"Yeah, but we don't have an army. It's just us, Sid." His brows knitted together. He shut his eyes. "There's a beast inside of me that wants to be let out. I'm not going to lie. It's difficult to resist. I've been fighting it off, Sid, every night, but I don't have much time, I'm afraid." He opened his eyes and took a breath. "Listen, whatever happens, just take care of yourself and little John Rich."

"I was really hoping you wouldn't talk like that, but I know I need to hear it. There isn't any guarantee I'll make it out of this either." She wrapped her arms around his waist and leaned on his chest. "We have to win, John. We have to."

"We will." He snared her into his arms. "You feel good. A little too good, considering I'm in full beast mode."

"It's okay. I like it." Her heart pounded. "Boy, do I like it." She took a deep breath, held on a little longer with her eyes closed, then forced herself to break away. "What do we do about Cyrus?"

"His very name is ice water to the veins." With his clawed hands draped on her shoulders, he said, "Well, he can't go back without you. He told Kane you were dead. He doesn't have anywhere to go."

"You aren't suggesting we let him go, are you? He almost killed me."

"I know. And he's going to pay for that. We just need someone we can trust to turn him over to."

"You don't think Russ can handle it?"

Smoke glanced over at the truck. The entire cabin was smoked up. "No. Maybe we just need to take him with us. It wouldn't be so bad if it was daytime. I could change then. But tonight, with this full moon? Whatever happens is going to be ugly. I can feel it."

"Maybe Mal and Russ can keep an eye on him. We have the flex cuffs. He can't get out of those."

"No, but he can be a distraction. He's a weasel. He knows how to get into people's heads."

"And what about Rebecca?" Sid asked. "No doubt she'll be killed, like he said."

Smoke walked back over to the truck and knocked on the door. A plume of smoke rolled out when the window dropped. "Where's Rebecca?" Smoke said to Cyrus.

He shrugged his narrow shoulders. "Home, I'd assume. Why?"

"You need to call her. Confess. It's the only way to save her."

Cyrus swallowed. He nodded. There was a shift in his composure. His body language changed. He cared for Rebecca, sincerely. Sid could see it.

Russ reached Cyrus's phone through the window. Sid took it. "What's the code?"

Cyrus sort of rolled his eyes. "One, two, three, four, five, six."

"Oh geez, you really aren't a mastermind, are you?"

"I haven't lost one yet."

After one ring, Rebecca picked up. "Cyrus, are you on your way home?"

Sid held the phone up in front of Cyrus's mouth. "No, I'm tied up right now. Listen, Rebecca hon, can you come and meet me? We have to talk with some old friends of mine."

CHAPTER 3

R EBECCA'S FACE TURNED ASHEN. SHE sobbed in her hands. Shaking her head, she said, "This can't be true. It can't be true."

Cyrus had confessed everything from the dealings he had with Kane to his attempt to kill Sid. The more he talked, the more he sank inside his seat.

"Just get him out of there," Rebecca said to Sid.

"Why?"

"Because I'm going to kill him." The petite woman's saddened expression turned to fire and brimstone. She reached inside the truck, grabbed Cyrus by the collar, and jerked his head out of the window. "What were you thinking?"

"I did it for us!"

"You idiot! You don't decide what's best for me. I do!"

"Rebecca, you know Kane can't be stopped. They don't stand a chance. This is our big move! Really big."

The little woman hauled back and slugged him in the jaw. "I hate you, Cyrus! You're insane!" She kept hitting.

Sid pulled her away.

Spacey-eyed, Rebecca chewed on her fingernails. She'd checked out.

"Rebecca, you need to get to safety. I just wanted you to hear it from him for yourself. I'm sorry."

"Sorry?" Rebecca's chin lifted. "He tried to kill you. Don't be sorry. You should have killed the bastard."

"I'm not sorry for him, I'm sorry for you. You've been through plenty. I suggest you get somewhere safe."

"Safe? Ha! You heard him. They must have eyes on me. If they have eyes on me, then they have eyes on you." She started freaking out. "They have eyes on all of us!"

"Calm down."

"Calm down, my ass. We're all dead. I'm probably going to die by this crap-smelling river. I hate the water. Did you know that?" Her lips curled. "It smells."

Sid had shown enough compassion for the night. She didn't want anything to happen to Rebecca, even though the woman had been a pain. She couldn't have that on her shoulders. The woman, though a little nutty, deserved a good life. She'd had to bring her face to face with Cyrus to get the truth. Rebecca never would have believed him over the phone. "Rebecca, we need to get you somewhere safe until this is over. How does FBI headquarters sound?"

"Like a trip to the morgue. But that dirtbag in glasses needs to be taken into custody. You need to press charges, Sid."

"No, this is all off the books. Cyrus will get his once this is over."

Cyrus sat in the truck, slumped over. His nose was bleeding. He sobbed. She'd never seen Cyrus cry before. His spirit was broken.

Why do I even feel sorry for him?

"The things you do in the name of love. Stupid things."

It had been well over an hour since Kane checked in with Cyrus. Without a doubt, Kane would be onto them by now.

As a matter of fact, Sid was surprised the phone hadn't rung. It sent a chill through her. Smoke was right, Kane was ready. The final battle was about to begin.

Guppy and Sam popped over from the Bronco. "I've got a handle on our situation, Smoke, but you might want to move out of sight."

Smoke took a spot behind the bridge's support column just as a blue-and-white police car with its lights flashing pulled down into their spot. With the headlights glaring right at the small group, an officer stepped out of the car.

Guppy greeted him with a firm handshake. He walked the officer over to the truck. "This is Clive, an old military buddy."

Clive appeared to be in his early forties. He wasn't much taller than Guppy, but not in the best of shape. His uniform's buttons were stressed. Carrying an air of authority and the swagger of a seasoned vet, he looked in the truck window. "That the guy?"

"Yes. He got a little rough with his fiancé. She called us and we called you," Guppy said.

"I see." Clive looked at Rebecca. "You going to make a statement? We need one if we're going to hold him until you get your affairs in order."

"Uh, yes, I'll press charges," Rebecca said, and her eyes slid between Sid, Guppy, and Clive. She straightened. "Yes, I'll do it."

"Alright. I'll get my pad. Come with me, miss."

Twenty minutes later, Clive handcuffed Cyrus and stuck him in the back of the patrol car while Rebecca sat in the front with her head down. With a wave, Clive drove away.

"He'll take care of them." Guppy puffed on his cigar. "Clive's seen plenty of strange things. He gets the shadows. Macanudo, anyone?" He held up his stogie.

Sam snagged it from Guppy's fingertips and flung the cigar toward the river. "What do you think you're doing?"

"Have a smoke? It's a big night, you know. Perhaps the—"

"Don't say it, Guppy!" Sam rubbed her shoulder. "This entire night is nothing but bad vibes. I just don't like it…at all."

"We're going to make it." Guppy put his thick arm around her waist and held her fast. "That's a promise."

Everyone was geared up from head to toe. Guns were on hips. Knives were strapped to belts and inside boots. They all wore sweetheart suits.

Sid's innards quivered. Somehow, she felt responsible for getting them all into this mess. The thought of her getting them hurt or killed wasn't something she wanted to live with. But all of them had chosen to make their stand. They were brave. No one was going to be talked out of it. She scanned the open area under the bridge. The fine hairs on the back of her neck bristled. "Where's Smoke?"

CHAPTER 4

"**S**MOKE!" SID CALLED OUT. "JOHN, you better get your ass back here!" Everyone looked high and low. Chins tilted. Necks swiveled. "John!"

"You probably don't need to yell," Cort said. "He's got those giant ears, you know."

"I'm fine," Smoke said.

Everyone did a one-eighty. Smoke was behind them.

He shrugged. "What? I had to relieve myself. Even bats have to take a whiz."

"Just answer the first time, will you, hon?" Sid stated.

"Of course, dear. Sorry, I didn't mean to cause a panic." Smoke adjusted the gun belt strapped to his hips. He wore dark fitness pants that were tight at the waist. His muscular thighs bulged at the seams. "I suppose the time has come."

"Not so fast," Guppy said. He hustled over to his Bronco and grabbed his laptop. "I have some good news and some bad."

"There's good news?" Sid said.

"Sure, hear me out. The jump drive that Smoke brought me held a great deal of useful information. So useful, in fact, I was able to find a back door into the Drake's mainframe. I've been able to watch their entire operation. I can view what they view. I haven't done it yet, but I can even access things." He pecked on the keyboard with his sausage-sized fingers. "Right now, I have one of their primary monitors pulled up. See?" He set the laptop up on the hood of his car.

Sid and Smoke leaned over his shoulder. The others gathered around. There was a map on the screen, much like one that could be seen on Google Maps, but not a satellite view. Bright-yellow dots were lit up in several places. Many of them were clustered in one location.

"What are those dots?" Sid asked.

"Those are markers," Smoke said. "That's how they tag their people out in the field. They use satellites to track them." He touched the screen with his pointy fingernail. "Looks like Kane's gathered us a welcoming party."

"Yes, the good news is I can see what they are seeing. The bad news is they can see us." Guppy looked back at Smoke. "Er, you at least."

"Me?" Smoke said.

Using the mouse, Guppy panned the image on the screen back. He shifted over to a spot in DC, hovering the mouse pointer right over their location. He zoomed in closer and switched the view to full satellite. "I'm playing back from a feed they ran earlier."

Sid could see the bridge they were gathered under. "You mean they know we're here?"

"Yes, but even worse, Kane has known where I've been the entire time. He's been playing us. Well, playing me." Smoke's knuckles crackled when he bunched up his fists. "I was there, right under his nose. Face to face. I was Mack Brown, and he knew it was me the entire time. That even gives me chills."

"Seems to be the case. It's like Cyrus said, Kane is always a step ahead. But this time, maybe, just maybe, he slipped up." Guppy started typing again.

"I feel foolish," Smoke said to Sid.

Rubbing his arm, she replied, "Don't. We've all been played since the first day we met. But they weren't counting on one thing."

"What's that?" Smoke asked.

"That we would become one, giving us the one weapon they can't conquer. Love."

Holding her stomach, Asia said, "Either my sugar's getting low, or that comment is making me sick. Where did you come up with that, The Young and the Restless?"

"I liked it." Sam wiped the corner of her eye.

Cort Calhoun peeked up in the sky. "If they know where we are, you'd think they'd just drop a bomb on us."

"That's the whole point. They don't think we're a threat. They're daring us to come in," Smoke said. "They want me to give in. And if I don't, they'll just kill us all. So, Guppy, you say you have an angle?"

"Everything has a weakness. In the cyber world, I pride myself on finding it. In this case, it might be so easy they don't suspect it." He started typing. "Being an old organization, they aren't so fond of technology. They don't trust outsiders either, so much of what they do is off the record. So, I'll freeze some of the surveillance loops they run. Like on most cheesy shows on television, I'll make us appear to be locked in our location. That should give you a few hours to get inside before they realize what happened. All you have to do is say when, because I'm pretty sure they are wondering what in the world we are standing waiting for."

Smoke fingered his earpiece. "You need to get everyone else miked up, Mal. Once we're in, you can be the eyes for us."

"There's a lot of markers in there, John." Sid pointed out some yellow markers on the laptop screen. "Do you think those are other shifters?"

"I don't know. I'd hoped we'd taken most of them out, but apparently not. Whoever or whatever pops up, it's shoot to kill."

"I know you have wings, but I don't want to leave your side."

He covered her hands in his. "I know, but I'll have to go in first. We need to put that place in the dark. Shut down the generators. I know where all of that is. I think I can slip in if I have a distraction."

Guppy cracked his knuckles. "I can toy with their power grid. Maybe get those lights out for a bit."

"Do what you do." Smoke stretched out his hands. "Huddle in, everyone. It's time to pray."

CHAPTER 5

KANE STOOD IN THE UPPER office of the power plant, staring through the wall of glass that overlooked the river. The oversized moon hung in the air with a dazzling hue to it. Wearing his typical black slacks and white dress shirt, he basked in the light. Hands crossed behind his back, he said, "This is what it's all about, Allison. The night. The hunt. The kill. I may have lost many close associates in this game, but I revel in it. This has been the best, as far as I remember. There's been no better rival than your dear sister and Mister Smoke. Are you ready?"

Allison lay in a cozy position on the leather sofa. She held an antique hand mirror, admiring herself. She combed her fingers through the thick waves of her hair. Her feline face was sensual and exotic. She held out her long, sinewy arms in display. They were covered in tiger stripes and fur. A hungry smile crossed her face. "I'm so gorgeous, and far more deadly. I could rip these coming saplings apart with my bare hands. Of course I'm ready."

Kane turned. "So, no qualms about slaying your sister?"

"We'll see what happens. But with all of those shifters out there waiting, do you really think we'll have a confrontation with them?" She set the mirror down. "I thought this was going to be another one of your sadistic reality shows for the Drake?"

"Our sadistic reality show, Allison. We're in this together now." He made his way over to the mahogany bar and filled a tumbler half full of Baker's small batch bourbon. "Don't think for a moment I won't send you out to finish off your sister, Allison. You're still ripe. It's important that the blood in your veins doesn't run warm anymore."

"My blood was cold long before you did this to me. I'll be fine. It's you I'm worried about."

Kane's brows rose toward his hairline. "Me? That's curious. I can't think of anyone who ever worried about me before. Tell me, why worry?"

Allison sat up. "You've underestimated them before. They aren't dead yet. Perhaps there's more to them than what meets the eye. Maybe there are greater powers at hand."

"Pah. Don't be silly, Allison." Kane approached the window, marveling at the moon. "The glow of Khonshu is ever strong tonight. The Egyptian god of the gods is with us. These mortal deaths are sacrifices to him. The full moon shall see red." He spun on his heel and faced her, his face lit up with hunger. He dropped his gaze to her hands and frowned.

Allison's long fingernails had popped holes in the leather sofa. She quickly pulled them out. "Apologies."

"Oh, don't worry. That piece of furniture is a leftover. I've been meaning to replace it for quite some time. It squeaks too much when you move."

"What happens if they don't show up tonight?"

"John Smoke will. He has to. He's only hours away from losing himself forever. Come, let's take a stroll down to the control room." He drained his glass and set it on the bar. "I'm curious to see when we can expect our guests to arrive."

Downstairs at ground level, the panel door slid open to the control room. Allison entered first, followed by Kane.

Frank the mortician stood inside, staring at one of the many oversized monitors on the wall. The older lanky man was nearly seven feet tall, even with his slouch. He wore an old grey suit, a matching collared shirt, and a tie that would have been in style decades ago. He did an about-face. "Kane and Allison, a pleasure. Please, come inside and I'll fill you in." He beckoned them over with a hand that seemed too big for his body. "It's been interesting."

"Really, how so?" Kane stepped down a level.

In the voice of an old, loving grandfather, Frank said, "Rich and Sherry have been a little slow on the uptake, but they are coming around."

Allison moved down the steps in front of the two people who sat behind their computer consoles. They were a young pair with dead black eyes that had once been brighter colors. Their skin was pale and clammy with prominent veins. With steady fingers, they worked the keyboards.

"I see," Kane said with a little smile. "They've never looked deader."

"Chuckles, my liege. Well said. Thanks to the moon, they are shaking off the sluggish effects."

"Excellent. It's so difficult to find mortals we can trust with these things. And the payroll taxes, such a bear. No more of that anymore." Kane slapped the counter. "After tonight it will be full speed ahead for our operation. Shifters and deaders only. So delightful." He faced the screen. "So, where's that battish shifter Mister Smoke now?"

"He's still under the bridge," Frank said. The image zoomed in. Smoke's mark was prominent on the screen. "I think they're over-planning. Wasting time. Perhaps they have doubts."

Kane checked the clock on the wall. "It's been two hours. What about Cyrus?"

"He and Miss Rebecca Lang were tailed to a police station. He resides in custody there."

"I see. We'll deal with them on the morrow." Fingers needling his chin, Kane moved closer to the big screen. "This is odd. And they are how far away?"

"I'd say under an hour. There's no traffic this time of night. Perhaps forty-five minutes."

"Trouble, Kane?" Allison said.

"Perhaps."

"You don't seem fully confident."

"I didn't live this long without being cautious. The secret to my success is staying one step ahead of my foes." The lights and screens in the room flickered the slightest. "That's odd."

"There's been some very minor surges, hardly noticeable," Frank said. "Did you notice any upstairs?"

"No, the office offers the ambience of gas lighting. Far more reliable than all of these demonic electric circuits that this deteriorating world relies on. Ah, it seems the mark is moving, finally." His fingers rubbed inside his palms. "Frank, keep me apprised. The final stage of the game is afoot."

CHAPTER 6

SMOKE WAS ON THE ROOF of a twenty-story-high apartment complex. From the ledge, he looked out over the Drake Energy compound. The spotlights that typically lit up the compound lot like daylight had been dimmed. Whatever roamed inside the fence, Kane didn't want it to be seen. Typically, there were ten peacoats on duty day and night. In all, there were twenty-five of them on rotating shifts.

The stiff wind bit into his furry hide, but he didn't feel it. His body burned. He was on fire inside. The beast inside coiled back, ready to lash out. He moved toward the river side of the building. Tall pines lining the Drake Complex hid the dock from full view, but he made out the yacht. He spoke into a Bluetooth device strapped around his wrist. It linked him up to Guppy.

"The boat's in the water. I don't want anyone from the Drake getting away. I don't want to see a chopper landing either. Keep eyes on the sky."

"Got it, Smoke. The fish are in the water."

"Literally? They shouldn't be."

"Sorry, I couldn't think of a better analogy. It's covered."

"Good. I'm going after the control room."

"No. Wait, Smoke," Guppy said. "I've got eyes and ears inside. Access to everything. Whatever they see, I can see. And I hear what they hear, in some places. We've got audio on Kane. He's not expecting you for forty-five minutes."

"Are you certain?"

"I heard it too," Mal said.

"And me, John," Sidney added. "Maybe we should go back to plan A and bull-rush this thing."

Smoke heard everyone linked to him perfectly. Everyone was connected. "I'm going to do some recon first. Who knows, I might get a nice window."

"I'll give you fifteen minutes, John. Not a second more. We're coming in after that," Sid said.

"Just stay put. I'll be back in touch. Guppy, if you can see those cameras, tell me, what are you looking at? How many men? Deaders? Shifters?"

"You've got four men at the lone entrance. Three more are posted at the dock. Seven are doing a foot patrol. My guess is there are more inside. It's a pretty big complex. Mal's looking for interior feeds."

"There aren't any interior feeds," Smoke said. "They only care about what's on the outside getting in."

"Well, you have three in the control room. Kane's up in his office — with Allison, I suppose." Guppy cleared his throat. "Aside from the peacoats, nothing else is moving."

"What about all of those marks?" Smoke asked. "None of them are moving on the grounds?"

"No. Huh."

"Huh, what?" Smoke asked.

"I'm guessing they're all inside."

"Fine. I have to go silent. Time to get moving." Smoke muted himself on the Bluetooth. It freed him up a little. The communication gadgets were aggravating. It would be a distraction if they didn't maintain radio discipline and everyone spoke at once.

Then he heard Guppy say, "Fifteen minutes, starting now."

With the complex dark, it gave Smoke an edge. He didn't need Guppy to dicker with the lighting. He could glide right in, but flying wasn't something he'd mastered. His gear would weigh him down too. He stood on the building ledge and spread his arms out wide, then leapt high and outward. He flapped his arms, catching the wind drifting under his wings.

This feels good.

He banked toward the river, staying as high as he could. He could make out figures posted along the dock that led up to the yacht. He glided a little closer down. He could make out the men breathing with his enhanced hearing. He listened for anyone moving on the boat. Rubber soles let out quiet squeaks on the polished wooden deck. Something that breathed really heavily resided in the cabin.

More shifters. It's got to be. Deaders don't breathe.

"Fourteen minutes," Guppy said.

Smoke fought off the urge to pluck the earpiece out.

That's annoying.

Circling, he glanced at the landing spot he had in mind, the roof. It was a field covered in a black tar top. Above the view of the cameras were peacoats posted on every corner. One of them worked with a pair of binoculars, scanning the grounds as well as the sky.

Time to see how good you are, Johnnie Boy.

Years ago, when he was in the Navy Seals, Smoke had crept up on plenty of unsuspecting foes and killed them. It was the same thing now, except he was more than twice as dangerous as he'd been before. It should be easy. All of the guards' backs were turned. Not a one of them looked back at the other. He had to be quick and careful. One stray gunshot cracking off would be like thunder in the night. Chaos would erupt.

A dark and stormy night would have been so much better.

Smoke landed on cat feet several paces from the guard holding the binoculars. He locked up the man's head in a sleeper hold. Seconds later, the man sagged. Smoke dashed toward the next soldier and brought each one down, one after the other.

Easy peasy.

"Thirteen minutes."

Smoke unmuted his Bluetooth. "Just hold your horses. I'm on the roof, counting bodies and looking for an entrance. I can tell time. Lay off until the final minute unless I check in first."

"Roger that."

The building had an entrance on the roof. There was a magnetic lock. He tried one of the peacoat guards' keycards, but it didn't work. He linked back up with Guppy. "Can you unlock the rooftop door?"

"I figure so," Guppy replied. "Now."

Sid cut in, "No, John. Don't go in there alone. It's too dangerous. That place will be full of shifters. This is recon. You hear me?"

"I do." A soft scuffle caught his ear. He ducked. A powerful glancing blow clocked the back of his head. Stars streaked in his eyes.

CHAPTER 7

"**W**HAT JUST HAPPENED?" SID SAID, toying with her earpiece. "John? John?"

"His link is off," Guppy said with a shrug. "Probably nothing, you know him. Twelve minutes."

The group sat inside a large passenger van they'd switched to on the way over to the Drake Energy Plant. They were parked alongside the road a few blocks away. Sam, Guppy, Cort Calhoun, Russ, and Mal sat on the bench seats. Asia was elsewhere.

"All of this waiting around is making me edgy," Cort said, scratching the side of his cheek. He sat in the passenger seat. "Makes me sweat. Turn on the air or something."

"It is on," Russ said from the driver's seat. The reporter dabbed his forehead with a blue handkerchief. Eyes up, he craned his neck toward the front window. "Boy, that moon is big. I wrote my articles based off events that occurred on nights like this. You know, it's really true. A full moon really brings out the crazies."

"Man, that's just superstition stuff," Cort said. Everyone in the van stared at him. "What?"

"You haven't picked up anything superstitious since you started hanging with us nuts?" Russ said.

"Well, now that I think about it, I suppose there could be some truth to it. But I'll believe more when I see more."

"I've got a pretty strong feeling that you are going to see something that you'll never forget." Sid leaned closer to Guppy, who held the laptop on his lap. Sam sat on the bench seat on the other side of her. Mal was in the row behind them. "Keep checking those exterior cameras."

Guppy toggled security views one by one. His seventeen-inch laptop screen managed several images at once. The complex was dead still, aside from the peacoats that walked by the view. All of them moved with the purpose of well-trained soldiers. She winced. A sharp stabbing pain throbbed in her side, causing her to suck through her teeth.

"Are you okay?" Sam said.

"Fine. I'm still mending."

Sam nodded. Lips puckered as she took slow breaths, her elegant fingers rubbed the gun in her hand. "I have a feeling I'm going to have to shoot something tonight. I'm not the best at shooting things that move right at me."

"I'll protect you, honey," Guppy said. "Ten minutes."

"Man, this ten minutes is going to take forever." Cort beat his head against the head rest. "So what's the plan again? We're just going to roll through the main gate and start firing?"

Rocking back and forth, Sam said, "That's the plan unless Smoke comes up with a better idea. Oh, I think I'm going to be sick."

"That's not the best tactical plan," Cort said.

"We're trying to get the jump on them. It's the element of surprise," Sid said, pointing at a view of the complex on the computer. "Listen to me, if we don't hear from John, we're going to bust through that gate and pull up to this entrance door. Guppy can let us in. Just don't take your vitamin until you absolutely need it."

"If we drive in there in this old van, they'll shred us," Cort said.

"No, it's bulletproof." Guppy grinned. "I bought it at a government auction. In this sucker, we're going to roll in just like the A-Team. Eight minutes."

Sid's stomach turned upside down. Her palms started to sweat. She wanted to hear from Smoke. *Something's wrong, I can feel it.* There were too many unknown factors with their mission. She didn't know how many of the enemy were out there. It was one thing to face off with Kane and Allison at some point, but who else? Deaders, giant men, harpies. *Lord knows how many shifters are really out there.*

Sitting in the back, staring out the window, Mal quietly said, "Khonshu."

"What's he babbling about?" Cort said. "Sounded like a sneeze or something."

"What are you talking about, Doc?" Russ asked.

Sid heard Mal's fingers getting busy on the keyboard. "Khonshu is the Egyptian god of the moon. I glossed over that as an option for the shifters' powers before. After all, the ancient Egyptians were very advanced in their technologies. What we have been dealing with are supernatural things, but we've also witnessed some modern biochemical effects. I'm starting to wonder if all of this isn't tied back to some ancient technology."

"Or alien technology?" Russ added.

"Please stop talking," Sam said. "I used to love this stuff, but now, it's too close to home. It's really making me sick. Oh man, I need something for my upset stomach. Does Asia have any Pepto in her backpack there?"

"I'll check," Mal said.

"Five minutes."

CHAPTER 8

SMOKE ROLLED. A HARD FOOT caught him in the ribs, sending him scraping over the roof. He rolled with the momentum. He came to a stop just as another blow was about to belt him. He caught the leg of his assailant. It wasn't a leg. It was a talon. The claws would rip steel. A husky figure lorded over him. It was a neckless man with the feathered face and eyeballs of an owl.

"Release me," the owl-like man said. He jerked his leg and swiped at Smoke with sharp talons on the hands at the ends of his wings. His voice was a windy whisper. "Release me and die." The shifter's clawed fingers ripped the meat of Smoke's shoulder.

Smoke hauled the owl shifter up. In a judo move, he drove the man's face into the black-coated roof.

The burly shifter lurched up, wings flapping at his sides.

On instinct, Smoke stuck his fingers in the owl man's mouth, choking out the screeching sound that was about to come. He unsheathed a knife. Striking hard, he rammed the blade into the owl man's spine. The body went still.

The owl man let out a life-draining sigh.

Putting his blade in the sheath that was strapped on his leg, Smoke rolled the shifter over. The owl man's spacy eyes gazed at the stars. He was lifeless as a stuffed owl perched in an old study. He nudged the shifter with his foot. *I suppose he's dead.* He crept over to the edge of the roof. The scuffle he'd been in had been silent. The peacoat guards walked the grounds. Others were still huddled at their stations.

Good. Smoke checked his Bluetooth link, but the unit on his wrist was busted. *Great Dane.* At least he could hear them when they spoke. He considered going back to let them know. He had time. It was a long way off before Kane thought they'd be coming. Besides, it had been a recon mission.

However, the bodies on the roof now made this a different story. Someone on the inside would be checking on them. When that happened, the complex would become a hive of activity.

This entire mission stinks.

He was seconds away from having Guppy let him in. He was going to go it alone. Nip it in the bud. Now, he was hanging out on a rooftop, waiting for the real fire to start. He made a choice. Counting the time, he waited for the last five minutes.

Smoke raced over the rooftop and took to the air. In seconds, he was a hundred feet up. He circled high above the lights in the streets where the bats dined on the fluttering wings of moths.

"One minute," Guppy said.

Smoke heard tension in the man's voice. He then heard Sidney say, "Ready or not, John, here we come." He counted down. Fifty seconds. Forty seconds. Thirty seconds. Twenty…Ten.

Smoke dove through the sky straight at one of the windows of Kane's office.

Kane and Allison faced each other on the other side of the glass, drinking and talking. Smoke zeroed in. Both of their faces turned his direction at the same time. Their wide-eyed stares were priceless. Smoke hit the window like he'd been shot out of a cannon.

Thud!

He bounced off of the unbreakable glass and crashed into the garden below. Body aching, his hypersensitive ears picked up the vibration waves of their raucous laughter. Shaking his head, he climbed back to his feet. A rushing engine revved. Metal collided with metal. Voices hollered and gunfire erupted.

This is a disaster.

CHAPTER 9

"**O**NE MINUTE," GUPPY SAID. EVERYONE patted down their gear. Sam's hands rubbed on her thighs. "No word from Smoke."

Sid nodded. "Drop it into gear, Russ." She charged the slide on her weapon. "It's time to go."

Russ turned on the van lights. He dropped the gearshift into drive. Slowly he pulled into the street. The traffic they passed was light on the two-block trip down to the complex. He turned the van down the dead-end street that led to Drake Energy's main gate.

Sid noted the signs hanging on the chain-link fences. There were coils of barbwire on the top. Tall rows of pine trees covered in frost on the top branches swayed. She took a breath. Sam's hand clutched hers.

"I feel like I'm in a hearse," Sam said. "My hearse."

"You don't have to do this, hon," Guppy remarked.

"No, my brother is in there. I have to help, somehow."

"Final stop coming up," Russ said as his heavy arms turned the wheel to the right. The chain gate that opened up on a base of small metal wheels was closed. There were dark-green slats in the links that barred the view inside. Rolling the window down, he hit the horn a couple of times. "Hey! I've got a delivery." He laid on the horn again.

The gate cracked open the breadth of a man's shoulders. A peacoat deader guard stepped through. He eyed the markings on the outside of the van. Guppy had prepped the van with lettering that read Drake Industries. The guard carried a small Uzi in his hands that was strapped over his shoulder.

"He's got some heat," Cort whispered.

"We aren't expecting any deliveries," the deader said. He searched out their faces. "This is an awfully big delivery crew."

Russ lowered his voice down to a threatening tone. "Yeah, well, Mack Black knows we're coming. And I think you know what this crew is all about. We just happen to be a late arrival. These hard faces got caught up in customs." Russ held up a fake Drake ID badge. "Go ahead. Check it."

The deader's eyes slid over the badge and hung on Cort. "I don't even want to know what you turn into. Give me a sec to sort this out." The guard moved back to the gate and started talking to someone on the other side of the opening. He gave a nod. Holding his hand up in a stop signal, the guard put his shoulder on the gate and walked it open. The chain links rattled.

Six peacoat deader guards were pointing Uzis right at them.

"Morning Glory," Sid whispered.

The peacoat that opened the fence dropped his arm and shouted, "Fire!"

Muzzles flared. Bullets blasted. Sam let out a bloodcurdling scream.

"Run through them, Russ! Stomp the gas! Now!" yelled Sid.

Rolling up the window at the same time, Russ crushed down the gas pedal.

The juggernaut of a van powered forward.

The deaders split like the Red Sea.

"Where the hell am I going?" Russ yelled.

"Just run them over!" Cort rolled down his window and started shooting.

Spray after spray of bullets rattled off the metal on the panel van, making loud popping sounds.

Ears covered, Sam looked squeamishly at Sid. "I really don't like this!"

"We need to get to the building entrance." Sid was leaning forward to squeeze in between the two front seats. Pointing, she said, "There!"

"I'm going. I'm going." Russ spun the wheel in his hand. The tires screeched. A peacoat popped up right in front of him, blasting away. The van plowed the deader over. The van jostled. "Twenty points!"

Sam chortled a strange giggle. A crooked grin appeared on her face. "That was kinda funny."

Russ drove the panel van through wave after wave of dodging and diving deaders. The van made a nasty weapon, but that wasn't the plan. They had brought it to get them to the building quickly, and then later, to speed them off to safety. But Russ was driving all over the place.

Cort was screaming, "Waaaaahoooooo!"

"Russ!" Sid yelled. "Get us to the door! This isn't a video game! Drop us off and get out!"

Bullets peppered the metal machine.

Russ ran another peacoat down. "Okay! He was pretty big. Thirty points for that one!"

Cort was still shooting. "I've taken out four of them! I don't see any more. I think we have this place cleared out."

The van circled through the parking lot. A small group of deaders dashed over the blacktop and hid behind a sizable storage shed.

"There's some!" Russ turned the wheel in the shed's direction. "I say we oust the last of them."

Sid grabbed the man by the ear. "Get us to the entrance, Russ!"

Russ slammed on the brakes. He was twenty feet from the shed. "Okay, okay, I'll back it up. Geez, I'm not a five-year-old. Just having some fun mowing over evil. How often does a guy like me get a chance like that?" He dropped the van into reverse.

Two huge men burst out of the shed. They stood at least ten feet tall.

Sam screamed, "Aaaaaaah!"

"What in the hell are those!" Russ yelled.

"Sweet butter biscuits, those are the biggest dudes I ever saw!" Cort added.

They were Rexor and Thorgrim, the giants Smoke had fought before. One of them had a missing eye and a bald head. The other was just hairy. Muscles bulged beneath their chestnut-colored jumpsuits. The shambling men came at them with wild eyes.

"Back it out of here, Russ!"

The engine revved. They didn't move. "I'm trying! I'm trying!"

"You're in neutral, idiot!" Sid stretched her arm out and yanked the van into reverse. The tires spun. "Go! Go! Go!"

The hairy giant dented the side of the van's passenger-side fender with a swing from a huge mallet-headed hammer. The blow rocked the van to the side.

"Whoa!" Sam leaned away.

The van accelerated from the giants.

Both monstrous men gave chase. Their long legs closed the distance.

Russ cut the wheel. The van did a one-eighty. He dropped it into drive and hit the gas, making a bead line straight for the entrance. "I don't know about this plan, Sid. We need to shake those giant bearded bastards!"

Sid could see the giants running after them through the portal windows in the back. If they stopped, the giants would have them. "You're right. We need to shake them." She climbed into the very back seat and popped one of the rearmost doors open. "Keep driving."

"What are you doing?" Mal said to her.

"Just keep ahold of me!"

With Mal holding her tight by the waist, Sid started firing her Glock. Blue-tipped bullets ripped through Thorgrim, who led the charge.

He didn't slow.

"Crap! Those won't do it!" She popped out her cartridge and fumbled for one with red-tipped bullets.

The van rocked.

The red-tipped magazine slipped from her fingers and out of the van. "Russ!"

"Forty points!" Russ replied.

A body rolled out from under the van.

Thorgrim hopped over it. Rexor crushed it under his feet. The van cut to the right.

"Russ, what are you doing?" Sid yelled.

"Sorry, I was trying to clip a straggler."

The maneuver was costly. The bald giant angled into the direction that Russ cut the wheel. Rexor bull-rushed the driver's side of the van full force, rocking the heavy vehicle up on two side wheels.

The bald giant closed in. His long arms stretched out. His fingers hooked the open door. He dug his heels into the ground, slowing the van's momentum.

Sid slammed her cartridge of blue tips back into the Glock then unloaded the entire clip in the giant's one-eyed face.

The giant roared. His grip slipped.

Sid grabbed the door and slammed it shut. "I need something bigger to stop those things. Send me up some more red tips!"

Guppy passed his gun over his shoulder. "Yer locked and loaded."

The van slowed.

"Russ, what are you doing?" Sid said.

Stomping on the pedal, Russ said, "I don't know. We've lost gas or something. I think the fuel line ruptured."

"That's what we get for you running over all those peacoats like an idiot!" Sid noticed a wet trail behind the van. "Damn!"

That wasn't all. One-eye zeroed in on the front and the hairy giant full of beard on the rear. Together, they grabbed the van by the front and back bumpers. With a heave of their shoulders, they flipped the van over on its side.

CHAPTER 10

FIFTY FEET OFF THE BOW of the yacht docked at the Drake Energy Plant, Asia treaded water. Wearing nothing but a sweetheart suit and a belt of gear, she mumbled, "Mal owes me a five-star dinner for this. This river stinks." She paddled toward the yacht. "Shitty job."

Asia was accustomed to bad jobs. She grew up in poverty in the streets of a small Filipino city called Mabalacat. She did dirty jobs, just about anything, to make ends meet. The hovel of a town resided alongside Clark Air Base in the Philippines. It was on that base that she got a job working at one of the local barracks for the Third Law Enforcement Squadron as a house girl. Young and with a fetching figure, she ended up marrying a G.I. named Logan. When the volcano at Mount Pinatubo erupted, Clark Air Base was closed. She was relocated stateside. Her husband, Logan, a law enforcement officer, taught her how to shoot. She had a knack for it and many other things. Logan died a few years later from sudden cardiac arrest, but having pursued an education during that time, she made a good living as a nurse. That's when she met Mal Gunderson. He mentored her in other arenas—espionage, surgery—and having taught her all that he would, he ended up marrying her. She'd been his woman ever since, but still had a penchant for doing just about anything for good food.

A handful of peacoat deaders were spaced out on the craft. One of them faced her direction. An Uzi hung from his shoulder. Something caught his attention, and he turned away. One of the other guards was shouting for him. The deader hustled away.

Asia made her move. She swam to the ladder on the aft of the boat and climbed into the yacht to the sound of gunfire cracking off in the distance. The peacoats hung over the railing with their backs to her. Moving with the shadows, she took the steps down into the cabin, passing through a small saloon. Footsteps caught her ears. She hunkered underneath a small dining table. A set of guards walked right by her and up the steps. She darted into the hall that led into the engine room.

She withdrew two small bricks of plastic explosives and planted the tacky plastic under the belly of the engine. There were two small electronic detonators with timers. She fed the contacts into the explosives. There were timers on each, set for one minute. She triggered them both.

"Time to go."

The light-footed woman doubled back to spy through the doorway that led into the kitchen. She sniffed. Something smelled very, very good. She peeked inside the doorway. A small buffet of platters was laid out on the kitchen counter. There were rolls, stacks of sliced meat, and cheeses. Spicy-scented vegetables were steaming inside silver serving dishes heated up by Sterno kits. She licked her lips.

I think I'll take some of my pay early.

Asia filled slices of ham, turkey, and roast beef loaded with cheese into two rolls. She stuffed the food into the chest of her suit. Snagging an eggroll, she stuffed it into her mouth and headed back toward the steps that led out of the cabin.

A short stumpy man sat on the stairs with his fingers knitted together. His features were heavy, his ears were long, and there was an unnatural gleam in his yellow eyes. He wore a bow tie.

"Pardon me, but I don't recall you being part of the crew?" the man said in creepy voice. "Perhaps we haven't met. I'm Titus Tolliver, and I'm responsible for this craft."

Asia had heard the stories about every shifter they'd come across and what their powers were. She knew Titus was like a gargoyle with skin harder than stone. She drew her weapon and said with a mouthful of eggroll, "Get the hell out of my way, Titus. You're going to make me late."

Wearing a nice grey suit that shone in the cabin lights, Titus said, "Those little bullets won't do you any good, tiny lady."

"No?" Asia said. "Well, I was taught that the red one work just fine on the likes of you."

Titus's citrine eyes widened. "Eh, I'm certain you didn't take the time to load those. That would be premature."

"True, but I like big, big explosions. They excite me. Now, Titus, it's time for me to light your stony fanny up like the Fourth of July. Goodbye, Titus."

Hands up, Titus said, "Nooo!"

Backpedaling, Asia squeezed the trigger twice.

Boom! Boom!

The concussive force knocked her back into the cabin. The gun fell from her hand. Her face was filled with bright lights. Clawing for anything she could get ahold of, she found a strip of railing. She climbed through a window portal that had blasted open, forced herself over the railing, and splashed into the waters in a clumsy flop. Using her strength, she swam as far and fast as she could on arms that felt like lead.

"There!" a peacoat guard shouted.

A hail of gunfire blasted into the waters all around her.

Still swimming, she counted down in her head, "Three, two, goodbye, Mother—"

KABOOM!

Asia swam to the sandy bank. Huffing for breath, she sat down, pulled her sandwiches from inside her watertight suit, and ate while she watched the burning boat sink.

"Damn, I forgot the mustard."

CHAPTER 11

FTER A POWERFUL LEAP, SMOKE dug his fingernails into brick and mortar. He scuttled up the side of the building like a tree squirrel before flinging himself onto the roof. Without slowing, he ran to the side overlooking the parking lot, grabbing a discarded assault rifle on his way.

Guppy's van sped through the parking lot. Peacoats gave chase. The guards fired automatic shots that blistered the van. Russ ran two of them over. Cort sat in the front, firing out of the window and hitting his marks.

Smoke shouldered his rifle and took aim. The deader guards converged. Smoke picked them off one by one with semiautomatic shots.

All of their well-laid plans had fallen apart. Kane would have the complex on full alert. The element of surprise was gone. The only thing they could do now was barrel inside and shoot everything that moved. So far, the group was doing pretty well on their own. The peacoats were on the run. The last ones dashed behind the storage shed.

Perfect! Head for the door, Sid! I'm right with you!

That was when all hell broke loose.

The giants busted out of the shed and gave chase. Smoke picked off the last three peacoats that charged after the huge men. But with their impossibly long strides, the giants caught up with the van. Before Smoke could say *gesundheit,* the entire van was flipped over like a toy. The giants laid into the van with a huge hammer and triple-bladed axe, the same weapons Thorgrim and Rexor had used before.

This would all make better sense if I lived in the Hyborian Age.

As the giants tore into the van like it was a giant sardine can, Smoke sprang off the wall and took flight.

Thorgrim ripped the passenger door off and yanked Cort out of the vehicle like a doll.

The black man fired bullets into the giant's face.

The giant grinned then opened his jaws wide. He swallowed Cort's arm up to the elbow and bit down.

Wide-eyed, Cort screamed with bellowing terror.

Smoke landed behind the giant. He shot it in the back of the head with a red-tipped bullet. The giant's chin hit his chest.

Cort fell to the ground, clutching his elbow.

Thorgrim wheeled around with axe in hand. He charged Smoke.

Smoke fired one round after the other into the giant. The crescendo of *boom-boom-boom* slowed the tremendous man, but he kept coming.

Sid bumped her head on the roof of the van. Sam landed right on top of her. Including Guppy, they were tangle of limbs. Something hammered at the van from the outside. The metal walls of the van were caving. The sides bulged under the blows. "Is everyone okay?"

The answer came in the sound of metal groaning. Cort's door was ripped from the hinges. Giant fingers grabbed him by the arm, jerking him from the seat. Gunfire, hammering, and screams ruled the moment. The hammering stopped. The van started to spin like a top. It stopped with Rexor taking a knee and peering inside.

Pushing himself into the door and kicking at the giant's grabby fingers, Russ shouted, "Get this thing away from me! I didn't sign up for this! I'm a reporter, not a fighter."

"Well, you should have thought of that before you started running people over like a moron!" Sid blasted several rounds at Rexor.

Sam and Guppy turned loose their own gunfire. Bullets pelted the giant's face. His expression turned to a face of savage anger. He backed off, picked up his hammer, and swung with rage-filled momentum. His first blow knocked the windshield out.

Russ scrambled to the back.

The entire front end of the van was being pulverized. Bits of metal and glass flew everywhere. The giant reached his long arm through the opening.

"I'm not sticking around for this." Sam fought to open the van's back doors.

Sid found Mal sprawled on his side, out cold. The side of his head was bleeding. Lending her help to Sam, together they shoved one of the split doors open. All of them crawled out. Sid and Guppy dragged Mal by the arms. They all scurried away as far from the van as they could.

The giant rose up. Eyeing them, for a moment he continued his assault on what was now a busted-up metal box. The pounding stopped. He pointed the monster hammer at them. "You're going to be dogfood."

Sid stuffed Mal into Russ's trembling arms. "Get him out of here. Hide! You too, Sam!"

"But—" Sam sort of objected.

"Go with her, love," Guppy said, holding a gun in each hand. "It's on us now."

On wobbly legs, Sam and Russ took off, with Sam saying over her shoulder, "Don't get killed. That's an order!"

Sid and Guppy spread apart, circling the giant, who walked right at them. They gave each other a quick look. Sid gave the nod. With guns in both hands, she pulled the triggers. Guppy matched her efforts as they both fired and backpedaled at the same time.

Between the small bangs and large booms, the one-eyed monster kept coming. The explosions slowed him a little, but that was all. He turned right at Guppy and closed in. The hammer went up and came down hard.

Guppy darted out of the way.

The giant gave chase.

"Oh crap," Sid said, loading in another clip of bullets. Rexor bore down on Guppy like a coyote chasing an old cat. A few more steps and it would be over.

CHAPTER 12

"Allison, it seems our guests have arrived early," Kane said after a lengthy outburst of laughter. Kane wasn't one to laugh, but the hilarity of Smoke hitting the window like a bird tickled him to the bone. "I swear, sometimes I miss being human and laughing so hard that your guts hurt. The only problem is that death thing."

"I never laughed that much as a child. I'm not sure why. I was always about more serious things."

"Ah, yes, women can become quite vain at a young age." Licking his teeth, Kane picked up the receiver of an old red telephone that hung on the wall.

Frank's gauley-deep voice responded on the other end. "Yes?"

"Are you keeping track of our little invaders?"

"Certainly. Do you have any particular orders you would like me to execute?"

"I think we are well prepared. Just see to it that Allison and I don't miss anything from our roost. I take it all is in order and our customers on Deathflix are watching?"

"If money mattered, you'd be happy to know you're making a million dollars a second off this fiasco. Quite impressive."

"Oh, I delight. And money always matters. It's how we control the underlings of this wicked world. I'm pulling up my viewer now." Kane hung up the phone and picked up a remote where a huge digital screen popped up out of the floor facing the sofa. He took a seat and beckoned for Allison to join. Her feline body sat beside him. There was a clear image in the middle of the eighty-inch TV showing the battle with the giants attacking the van. Smaller pictures, three in all, were lined up one after the other on the left. A list of strangers' names and dollar amounts was on the right. There were names and odds. Smoke's chance of survival was three to one against. Sid's was ten to one against. The odds for the others were even worse. Many of them fluctuated.

"I bet they love this in Vegas," Allison said with her eyes glued to the screen.

"The entire world loves this. Entertainment feeds the savage minds of the people. At the rate we're going, it wouldn't surprise me one bit if our secret little society was widely accepted. Deathflix will be the number-one station of the depraved."

Allison shifted in her seat. "I suppose you're right. People do feed off these things."

"Mortals thrive in chaos. They can't help themselves, at least most of them. It's the ones that can control themselves who give us trouble."

"Like Smoke and Sid?"

"Underdogs like them bring hope to the weak. Oh, how I delight in seeing the light go out of those wishful eyes. The sweet kiss of death conquers the ambitious."

CHAPTER 13

Thorgrim chopped and jabbed at Smoke with rigorous strikes. Smoke had emptied a clip into the monster with little effect. He loaded another. He needed more firepower to stop the brute. In the meantime, he led the giant away from Cort. Cort dashed into the cover of the van.

"Stop moving, little bat," the giant moaned. "Be still so I can eat you." Another hard swing bit into the ground where Smoke had just been standing.

Smoke skipped to the side, jumped hard, and punched the giant in the eye.

The giant recoiled.

Smoke locked one hand in the giant's thick locks. With the other hand, he cocked back and punched the pistol right into the giant's eyeball. He pushed in knuckle-deep and started firing into the soft flesh behind the skull.

The giant moaned. His arms flailed. A primordial instinct overtook the massive man's body. He snatched Smoke in his hands. Hauling the smaller man in his arms, the giant squeezed. "Hurk!"

Smoke flexed his spring-tight muscles. He could feel veins pop up in his neck. It was like being crushed in a trash compacter. His vision began to black out. Suddenly, the giant fell over on his side. A stabbing sound caught Smoke's ears. The monster man's grip loosened. Smoke squirmed free.

Cort held the Arabian sword in one hand. He stabbed the giant through the back and chest, piercing the heart repeatedly. Distressed, he said, "Is it dead? Is it dead?"

"The only way to be sure is to go Biblical," Smoke said with his hands on his hips, sucking for breath.

"Meaning?"

"Cut off Goliath's head."

"You don't have to tell me twice." Cort brought the glinting, razor-sharp steel up and dropped it down with wroth force. *Chop!* "Man, that sucker doesn't even bleed."

The scuffle of skin and bone clashing together caught Smoke's ear. Sid rushed after the other giant, firing round after round into its back. Guppy was pinned down to the ground, taking a pounding.

"Give me that sword."

With a weary fling, Cort tossed the sword to Smoke.

Smoke took off at a dead sprint. Moving at inhuman speed, he covered the distance in two seconds. Jumping in full stride, he glided through the air, cocked back the sword, and swung the blade in an arc of death.

The bald giant's head slid from his shoulders. The fists pumping into Guppy slowed. The giant died where it stood.

Sid kneeled beside Guppy. The blocky man was bleeding. His face was swelling. "Smoke, he's in bad shape."

"It's worse than it looks. It always is," Guppy said, wincing. "I've known nuns who swatted harder than that. Just help me to my feet."

Sam rushed over to Guppy's side. "Sweetie, are you okay? Your nose is broken."

"I can't have you looking at a man with a busted nose, now can I? It's bad enough as it is." Now sitting up, Guppy shoved his nose back into place, making an ugly crackle.

Flinging her wrists, Sam said, "I hate it when you do that."

At the moment, the parking lot turned battlefield was quiet. Smoke didn't pick up the sound of any enemies. Looking at the stark old building that seemed to beckon him forward, he said, "Everyone pull yourselves together. This field trip has just begun."

CHAPTER 14

S TANDING OUTSIDE OF THE MAIN entrance to the building, Guppy worked the screen on his phone. Smoke pulled the handle. The door wouldn't budge. The entrance was made from heavy industrial steel. His strength wouldn't be enough for it. His heart raced. The battle had gotten his juices flowing. His focus became unclear. The bright moon in the sky seemed to call to him.

"They have it locked down now," Guppy said, fighting for breath. He could barely move. "Sorry, we missed that window."

"What do we do now, Smoke?" Sid said. "We can't end this if we can't get in there."

"No, we're going in. We have a key." Smoke headed back toward the van. The vehicle was lying on its side, all banged up. It looked like a rhino had attacked it. There was a black plastic carrier on the roof of the van with an air-resistant design.

"Everyone do an ammo check. We're going to need everything we have. I hate to think we used most of our bullets on that first encounter, but I did."

Sam crawled into the van. She picked out an ammo box. It banged hollow on the ground. "You can have mine, Sid. No, we're close to out." She handed over two clips.

Smoke unlatched the top of the luggage carrier. He flung the lid, sled-like, aside.

With her hand resting on his shoulder, Sid looked at the unusual cargo. "I should have known."

"Heh, heh," Guppy said as he rubbed the side of his swollen mouth.

Smoke tossed a green tube over to Cort. The man's eyes grew big.

"That'll make a hole," Cort said. He held up his left arm. His hand was turning blue. The giant's bite had crushed his arm. His black skin had paled. Sweat drenched his face. He locked the LAW rocket tube between his knees, and with his hand he jerked the tube open. "I'm ready to knock that door down when you are."

Smoke picked another weapon out of the container. It was an M-60 machine gun. He handed it over to Sid. "Are you ready for this?"

With a little smile, she said, "It's been a long time, too long." She fed a belt of one hundred rounds into the feed. Every sixth 7.62 had a blue tip. "Is that the real thing?"

"I assure you it is." Smoke grabbed up a matching machine gun for himself and loaded it up. "Time's a-wasting. Cort, let's see what's on the other side of that door."

"You got it." Cort hefted the LAW rocket onto his shoulder. He placed his fingers on the trigger and took aim. "Open sesame, evil bastards."

The rocket streamed out of the cylinder in a straight line. It hit the security door square in the middle. There was a loud *pop-boom*! The building shook. A smoking hole remained.

"That's one way to make an entrance," Cort said. "Is it time to storm the castle?"

"No, wait." Sid stepped around to the front of the van.

A man wandered out of the entrance. He was a deader dressed in the deteriorating uniform of a revolutionary general. A man out of time.

Sid's heart hung in her chest. "Is that a redcoat?"

"Oh yeah, I forgot to mention that," Smoke said. The centuries-old soldier ambled forward a few more feet. He raised his arm and dropped it down. "Wait for the whites of their eyes. The British are coming."

Deaders in British uniforms burst out of the entrance in a steady stream. They carried sabers and old rifles with bayonets.

"Say hello to my deader defense system, creeps!" Feet planted on the ground, Sid opened fire. The old general's chest turned into a window. The gun barrel turned hot in an instant. The blue-tipped rounds streaked into the bodies with the laser-like glow of tracer rounds.

Two-hundred-year-old bodies fell. Their shattered limbs twitched on the ground. They climbed over their own dead in an unfettered wave. Bulging through the entrance in a single column, they fanned out.

Sid hit them all with short bursts. "They don't have any armor!"

The ambling men dropped like flies. Sid blasted into one side, Smoke hit the other. The redcoats were massacred.

"The war would have been a lot shorter if we had these back then." Her gun emptied. She took a knee. Cort fed her another belt. "Thanks!"

Two deaders made it within ten feet. The machine gun chewed off the face of the first one. She mowed down the other with a fiery blast. The raging battle ended after a minute. Every redcoat was incapacitated.

Scanning the battlefield, Sid said, "That was easy."

Smoke's barrel was smoking. "Thanks to these equalizers. Problem is, we're out of bullets."

Setting down the machine gun, Sid drew her pistol. "The way is clear. After you."

Guppy fought his way back up onto his feet. He swayed in his spot. "You aren't going in there without me."

"Stay with Sam and the others, brother." Smoke placed the Arabian sword in its sheath and looped it over his back. "Cort?"

"Don't worry about me. It's on like Donkey Kong."

Led by Smoke, they headed into the building.

CHAPTER 15

SID HUNG ONTO SMOKE'S HIP. The halls were wide and industrial. The smell of the rotting deaders and their musty uniforms still lingered in the air. Aside from that, the main building of the power plant was typical for that era. With her instincts on high alert, she matched Smoke step for step. Behind her, Cort breathed heavily. She glanced back. Cort gave her a reassuring nod.

The big fella was none too quick. No doubt the busted bone in his arm hurt. She could see the pain in his face.

The hall had doors on both sides, all of which were closed. There was lettering on the glass panes on the doors with the names of people long gone. They passed a break room and a conference room that were marked. A T-intersection in the hall turned right toward the middle of the building. It was more rows of doors. At the end was a wide set of double doors. There was a humming on the other side, like the *whirr* sound of generators. Aside from that, the building was stone-cold, much like a mausoleum. There weren't any signs of more deaders.

She nudged Smoke's elbow. Her heart raced so much she only just noticed the cameras that hung at the tops of the walls. The lenses' eyes were silent but gave her the feeling of a ghostly stare. Someone was watching them.

"They all know we're here," Smoke quietly said.

"You make that sound like an awful lot of people, Smoke. What people are we talking about?" Cort asked. "I thought we were just after this fella named Kane."

"Long story. I'll share more when it's over."

"This might be my only chance to get a better grasp on why I might die tonight."

"We're the entertainment. Smile, you're on Candid Camera."

"Oh, you mean the Deathflix thing. I never really took that seriously. I guess I should have known better. Huh." Cort smiled big for the nearest camera. Then he gave it the finger. "Bunch of wealthy degenerates."

An illuminated red exit sign hung over a stairwell. There was a security pad. Sid shoved on the handle. "I guess they don't want any visitors upstairs."

"Nope. We could try the elevator, but I've got a feeling it's going to be the same situation. They only want us to go where we can go." Smoke faced the double doors. "Through there."

"What's in there?" Sid asked.

"It's just the smaller generator stations that still run in there. That's what you're hearing, anyway." He shoved the doors open. "Yup, this is where they want us to go. Do you think it's a trap?"

"This entire thing is a death trap," Cort commented.

Everything was pretty much as Smoke described. There were rows of shelves loaded up with office storage boxes. Fluorescent lights gave off a steady glow high above their heads. In the middle were three electric generators. Each was big enough to be its own garage bay. They were out of place in the room, which looked to have at one time been a cafeteria.

"A natural gas line feeds this place. Those generators run off it. They keep the Drake's operations off the local grids. Drake Energy is just another front. The only energy they supply is the drug supply." Smoke pointed.

There were long metal tables stretched out side by side. Boxes filled with clear baggies were on top of them, remnants of the drug trade. Abandoned lab coats and scrubs. Facemasks, surgical head gear, hair nets, and gloves. Sidney had seen all of the same before, along with little cloned children packing up drugs. Her thoughts went to Megan. She hadn't seen her niece in quite some time. "Looks like they cleared out long before we came."

"They've been gone long before I even made it here. Kane's been planning our arrival for a while. This is the perfect theater for their twisted games." Smoke's head tilted. His dark eyes landed on the shelving. Scufflings scratched inside the boxes.

"What the hell is that?" Cort said.

Lids slid off the tops of the boxes. Little winged gargoyle men crawled out. Dozens of them. The small stony creatures with a gleam of life in their eyes took to the air. Little bigger than cats, the gargoyles swarmed them.

"Aagh! Creepy!" Cort started shooting. His bullets blew two gargoyles into dust. A gargoyle landed on the back of his shoulders. Its claws tore at his eyes.

Sid caught a gargoyle by the wing, slung it to the ground, and stomped the stone out of it. Its body cracked under her feet.

Smoke battled the fiends down like flies. Every one he hit cracked under his blows.

Sid emptied another clip. She cursed when she changed it. "At this rate, we aren't going to have anything to fight with when the time comes!"

Smoke pulled a gargoyle off his face. He pulled off its wings and drop-kicked it over the generators. "Two points."

The little gargoyles had emptied the boxes. Many of them ran across the floor. Others flew. They pinned their thick little bodies to whatever body part they could attach themselves to. The pressure of their tiny grips was mighty.

Sid's skin was pinched on the back of her thigh. A stony face with a wicked grimace bit into her knee. She shot it in the eye.

Cort came up behind her and ripped one off the back of her leg and flung it high.

She shot right through it.

Gripped in Smoke's long hands, two gargoyles were smashed together. The broken bits and pieces fell on the floor. "I think that's the last of them."

All of them were banged up in one way or the other. Sid's face bled from deep scratches. Her hair was in tangles.

Cort sucked for breath. "This feels worse than the first day of football practice."

An overhead intercom system came on. A voice spoke over the loudspeakers. "Welcome, dear guests." It was Kane. "I'm so glad for your visit. So far, it's proven to be quite entertaining. The Deathflix ratings are higher than ever. I applaud you." He cleared his throat. "Excuse me. All of the excitement left me a little parched. Now that the pre-game warm-up is over, it's time for the real games to begin. Unless of course you want to surrender."

"Never!" Sid said.

"Ditto," Smoke repeated.

"I thought as much. Let's see it through then. Goodnight." After Kane finished, there was a loud click. The entire room turned black. Kane laughed, and the mic went dead.

CHAPTER 16

"I HATE BLACKOUTS," CORT SAID.

Smoke found Sid's hand. Her grip tightened in his. There was a quiet click of doors west of him being unlocked. Creatures on padded feet moved into the large room and spread out.

"I don't like this," Sid whispered.

The intercom clicked back on. "Spooky, isn't it, brave heroes? But don't be alarmed. After all, our precious viewers can't see anything in the dark, either. Let there be light." The fluorescent lights flickered back on. "And let there be death." The intercom went out.

Squinting, Cort was the first one to speak. "You have to be shitting me."

Three shifters formed a circle around them. Smoke couldn't tell if two of them were men or women, but they were shifters that looked like rabbits, disturbing and creepy. Their legs were bunched up underneath them while they gently bounced up and down. They were covered in brown fur with white on the chests. Their ears were long, eyes the same as the animals', and protruding teeth. Each of them had nunchucks.

Cort looked at Sid with a bizarre look on his face. "Tell me this isn't Wonderland."

"No, it's Peter Cottontail on steroids," she replied. Her eyes narrowed on the third party. "And our old friend Adam Vaughn, who should be dead."

"True, but seeing how you didn't know what you were up against then, you didn't manage to finish the job. Hence"—the wolfman looked at his nails—"I'm back." Much like Smoke, Adam Vaughn, also known as AV, was covered from head to toe in fur—only his was wolf fur. His face was more human, and his black slacks and grey dress shirt rolled up to the elbows dulled down his bestial appearance. His black eyes burned, however, on Smoke. "I see you've made the change, but I owe you one, John. What you did caused me great pain. I'm going to deliver it back to you, times ten."

Smoke faced AV the wolfman. "You're a loser, wolfman, and you know what they say about losers?"

"Indulge me."

"Once a loser, always a loser."

"Schoolyard banter. Pathetic."

"Enough talk!" Sid fired at the rabbit straight across from her. It hopped away just as she squeezed the trigger. "Shoot, that was fast!"

AV came at Smoke before he could draw the sword.

That was the first option he'd considered, but battling AV in a straight fight would give him a better feel for what he was made of. He was a shifter now, maybe not entirely, but enough.

Ten feet from Smoke, AV sprang, but not at Smoke. AV turned his sights on Sid.

Smoke jumped after the wolfman. He was too late.

AV plowed into Sid, crushing her beneath his powerful build.

Her head bounced off the hard floor.

AV drew back his fist. "I'll end you first, pretty."

Smoke caught AV's wrist in both hands and yanked the wolfman from his feet. His fist landed hard in AV's gut. "No surprise that you attack like a coward."

AV blocked the next punch. "It surprised you. Aw, don't be so mad. I only wanted to give her a little kiss. After all, she wanted it until you interrupted the last time." He hip-tossed Smoke over his shoulder.

Smoke landed on his back.

AV jumped him. His fists delivered precision blows, stinging Smoke's ribs. A split second later his fingers were digging into Smoke's throat. "I've been dying to crush your throat in my claws. I won't be denied."

Smoke chopped at the wolfman's arms karate-style. His efforts were futile.

Shaking the stars from her eyes, Sid climbed up to her knees. The crack of a gunshot caught her attention. That's when she noticed her grip was empty. She spied her Glock lying a few feet from her. She lunged for it.

The bunny man kicked it away then lingered over her, spinning its nunchucks.

Looking up at it, she said, "You've got to be kidding me."

The bunny man bounced up and down with large, glassy brown eyes fixed on her. It seemed more animal than man. The nunchucks whistled with blinding speed. One hard wooden end clocked her in the head. Blurry purple spots burst behind her eyes. She drew her knife. "Screw you, Bruce Bunny!" She lunged. The steel she swung swished through the air. The rabbit man hopped over twenty feet in a single leap. It paired up with the other. The smaller rabbit men teamed up on Cort.

Using the nunchucks in unison, the rabbit men attacked Cort with blinding speed. The *whacks, thuks* and *cloks* fell right after the whistling in the air. They smote knees, elbows, and fingers. Cort was screaming obscenities. The vicious tandem beat him down to a pulp.

"Somebody get these things the hell off me!" Cort yelled. A hard shot in his face followed. "Dammit!"

Sid drew her second Glock. Taking aim, she fired at the rabbit man with its back to her.

It hopped away a split second before she blasted off a round. Both of the rabbit men bounced away from Cort. Each hopped all over the room.

Every shot she fired missed.

The rabbit men didn't dodge, they just weren't in the same spot when she fired. In a staggered and unpredictable pattern, the rabbit men came at her.

Come on, Sid, you've got this. Focus!

She took aim on one of the rabbit men as soon as it hit the ground.

Immediately, it pounced away again. Its long legs sent it twenty feet through the air.

She swung her aim at the airborne creature. *Gotcha!* She squeezed. *Blam!*

The rabbit man's body went limp. The bullet had torn through the ribs and heart. It hit the floor mid-hop.

Sid searched for the other rabbit man.

Nunchucks busted her gun hand. A long furry foot knocked her from her feet. The surviving rabbit man pounced high and fell toward Sidney with nunchucks twirling over its head. It landed right on top of her.

Enough of this! Using the knife she still held in her hand, she gored its heart.

The rabbit man's foot thumped the ground several times. Its long ears sagged as it died.

Catching her breath, she said, "Wascally wabbit." She shoved the stiffening thing off her.

Cort was up on one knee rubbing his face. His eyes fell on her. He pointed over her.

She looked around. Smoke was on his back. AV was on top of him, choking the life from his body. "No!"

CHAPTER 17

"**Y**OU'VE GOT A WEAKNESS, MISTER Smoke. You deny what you are. You hold back," AV said. "Unlike me, you haven't embraced your savage nature. It leaves you weak." Saliva dripped down AV's teeth and over his gums. "It strengthens me! It's amplified my hatred without limits!" His biceps bulged. His efforts magnified. "What a waste."

Smoke fought against the stormy sea that raged in his bowels. Self-control was the only way to win. He needed his wits. If he lost them to his inner bestial passions, Kane would win. He locked his fingers on AV's wrists. He strained to pry the iron limbs apart.

The wolfman laughed.

Sid appeared over the back of AV's shoulder. She dug a knife behind his ribs. "Fool!" AV unlocked one hand. He balled it up into a fist and struck. The fierce blow spun Sid in a three-sixty. Her athletic form slumped to the ground. Her eyelids fluttered.

A spark fired inside Smoke the moment she fell. It ignited. The dam that held back the dark waters within crumbled. The gloating stare of AV hung over him like a red bull's-eye. Smoke cranked back a fist and lashed out. The punch rocked AV's chin.

"That's more like it! I felt that! Good, Smoke! Good!" Still straddling Smoke, AV fought to fasten his grip again. "But you are still weak, rodent! I'm a wolf, and you're a bat. Pathetic!"

Smoke kept punching. He alternated fist for fist, pounding AV's jaw from side to side. It was like hitting a block of cement mounted on a neck of iron.

AV absorbed the first several blows. His brows lifted. His iron chin weakened. Fingers once stronger than steel slipped. With rage filling him from head to toe, Smoke did a reversal. He pinned AV underneath him.

AV's eyes changed. The confident look of the predator faded. He'd crossed the line. The beast he had goaded was out of the gate. He fought against the river of regret that was about to drown him whole.

Smoke beat AV's face like a speed bag. Bone loosened in the skull. The boundless strength of the wolfman's extremities turned to noodles. Smoke sank a blade deep into AV's heart and twisted.

AV let out a long, bloody, ragged sigh.

With instincts flaring, Smoke sprang away toward an approaching enemy. Cort stood a few feet away with a gun on him. The eyes in his battered face were narrowed.

"Whose side are you on, Smoke?" Cort said. He increased the distance between them. "You don't look like yourself. You need to show me some control. What's my name, Smoke? What's my name?"

The man was speaking, but the words weren't registering. The language was gibberish. All Smoke saw was a threat. A weapon that could cause pain. The dark blood of AV dripped from his fingers. The splatters on the floor echoed in his ears. The man pointed at something on the floor. There was a woman sprawled out on the floor. The heartbeat was strong and the breathing ragged. A fragment of humanity slowed the currents that fed the beast.

Sid.

As he took a knee, he cradled her up in his arms. He brushed the hair from her face. Slowly, the lids covering her eyes opened.

"Smoke?" she said.

The language was still fuzzy. The tide continued to rise.

The intercom clicked on. "That was entertaining. The viewers are happy," Kane said. "Oh, the savagery! Time is ticking, Mister Smoke. You're only moments away from fully embracing it. As for the rabbit men, well, that was a special request from a deviant old friend from England. A notorious Monty Python fan. So, dear champions, are you out of bullets yet? Those little jump skippers made you drop a lot of pellets."

"We really need to put an end to him," Sid said to Smoke. Her eyes were searching his. "Are you okay? You don't look right. Stay with me, John. For the love of Christ, stay with me."

Smoke set her down. Standing tall, he stared up at the ceiling. His thoughts raced. He caught a branch that swiftly floated through the river of his jangled thoughts. It read, "When the rules aren't working, change the rules."

"John!" Sid said, holding onto his leg. "John, I know that look. Don't!"

Letting out a loud bat-like screech, Smoke jumped to the ceiling. His fists punched holes in it. He ripped the tile and plaster out.

He left Sid and Cort behind, staring up at the gaping hole.

CHAPTER 18

S ID TURNED HER ATTENTION TO Cort. "You're hurt!"

"No, I just feel like I went fifteen rounds with George Foreman. Probably look like it too. Those rabbit punchers beat the snot out of me."

Kane was still on the intercom. "Where did he go?" He spoke as if he wasn't aware that his microphone was still on. "Frank, do you have eyes on him?"

The name rang a bell with Sid. She recalled the gaunt, hollow-eyed giant of a man with whom she'd had a nasty encounter in Las Vegas.

"Who's this Frank guy anyway?" Cort said, rubbing his jaw with his good hand. "Aw man, I bet I'm too ugly for a casket. Close my coffin if you survive and I don't."

"One of the creeps that turns men into shifters, I believe." She made her way around the room, spotting the cameras on the walls. The room was huge, and there were more than she could make a quick count of. For some reason though, she got the feeling they weren't the most entertaining part of the story. Over the intercom, glass smashed into a wall. She could see Kane's enraged face perfectly in her mind.

Over the loudspeaker he said, "Find him, Frank! Find him now!"

There was a click. The cafeteria became oddly silent.

"What just happened?" Cort moved about the room with a limp, his head swiveling on his shoulders. "I feel I just lost my date to the dance and I'll be dancing all alone."

"And you're complaining?" Sid stared up into the hole Smoke had made. It wasn't too high for her to reach if she stood on Cort's shoulders. "Boost me up."

"Excuse me? You're going after him?"

"Yep."

"We need to stick together, Sid. I might be able to get you up, but with my arm"—he lifted his busted arm—"I'm stuck. We'd best go at this together."

"He needs me."

"I understand where your heart is, but I need you too. Besides, I'm not boosting you up. Where you go, I go, and vice versa. It's not my fault your husband abandoned you. What did you expect? He's a wild man."

"Don't talk about him like that, you know better. He needs me. He needs us. Come on." There were other exits out of the cafeteria posted on all four walls. She checked them all one at a time with fierce tugs. The door they came through had now locked as well. She kicked it. "Morning Glory!"

"They've got us where they want us, I suppose." Using one hand, Cort managed to load in a fresh magazine of ammo. "I can't wait to see what comes after us next. What do you think? A unicorn? Giant teddy bears? I wonder if they have any robots. I always wanted to fight a robot."

She pointed her gun up at the hole in the ceiling. "That's the only exit they don't control. Cort, you have to help me. We can't just sit here."

"Okay, okay, I see your point. But before you go up, you have to promise that you'll come back for me."

"I can't unlock those doors from the other side. I can't unlock them at all."

Shaking his head, he replied, "No can do then. Tell you what. You know something is coming. When it comes, we blow it to kingdom come and shoot through the doors."

"They're watching," she said, looking at the cameras. "They come in the direction opposite … oh, never mind!" Sid marched over to one of the storage shelves. She scooted it over with a grinding screech.

Cort covered his ears. "Woman, what are you doing?"

Sid shoved the shelves under the hole. She climbed. Standing on the top shelf, she looked down at Cort. "I'll be back."

"Shut up."

"Sid, Smoke, can you hear me?" Guppy was speaking into Sid's earpiece.

She'd completely forgotten about the device. She saw in Cort's eyes that he heard it too. Her fingers fumbled for the communication link in her wristband. "Guppy! Guppy, I'm here." She lowered her voice. She wasn't sure if the cameras had microphones or not. She made it look like she was having a conversation with Cort. He had a puzzled look at first, but caught on.

"Thank the Lord! I've got eyes inside again. I got the laptop, started configuring, and even though it took some time — you know, those firewalls — I cracked in. It really took some doing though, seeing how they knew I was looking, but I think they lost sight of the fact that we're out here and you're—"

"I don't need the rundown, Guppy. We're locked inside the storage room where the backup generators are located. Can you unlock the doors? We need a route out."

"Give me a second."

"Guppy, if you have access to their screens, look for Smoke. He's gone."

"No sign of him. I'm searching though. It's pretty easy because it looks like they're searching every camera they have in a frantic wave. Heh-heh. Smoke really knows how to give people fits, doesn't he?"

"He's giving me one right now. He's run off again, and Guppy, he's not himself, he's…scary."

"I see. We'll find him, assuming I don't get cut off again." Guppy groaned. "Darn, this is a little harder than it looks."

Cort gave Sid a worried look.

"He'll get it."

A subtle pop caught her ears. A pair of double doors adjacent to the top of the room wobbled a bit. She and Cort had their guns fixed on it. "Or not."

"I got it," Guppy said. "You should be able to head out whatever door you want. There's a lot of square footage, Sid. I've got eyes in the halls, but I can't see them all at once, plus, there's no telling what's in the rooms. Anything could ambush you."

"I know. I just want to find Smoke before Kane gets to him. I've got an awful feeling about this."

"My suggestion is that you go for the main communication room. That's the nerve center. That will be the fastest way to find Smoke, or anyone else."

She climbed off the shelf. "Good idea, where is it?"

"Hold on, I'm looking."

CHAPTER 19

S ID AND CORT EASED THROUGH the double doors. Without a lot of ammo, the two of them crept down the hall, waiting for Guppy to give them a little more guidance. Sid's patience had run out. She was determined to find Smoke, with or without the use of the control room. She just wished she could have left Cort behind. She didn't want to abandon the man, but he was slowing her down, and Smoke's trail was long gone unless the cameras picked him back up.

Cort caught her elbow. He pointed his chin at one of the hallway doors on the right. At the bottom, a shadow moved behind the gap. She responded with a nod of her own. The office had a glass window, but there was a vinyl blind that blocked the view inside. The blind quavered.

On cat's feet, Sid darted by. She hugged the wall on the other side of the door, between it and the next door beside it. She gave Cort a nod. He moved by the door with the finesse of a hunting grizzly bear. She exhaled. She didn't want to draw any attention to them. She didn't want to waste any ammo either. They'd only be able to fight for so long, then it would be over.

"Sid, it's Guppy. Good news. I've found the control room, and it's on the first floor."

"And the bad news is?"

"That corridor is chock-full of deaders. Don't worry about them until you get there. I'm running loops through the security feeds again. Whoever's watching doesn't know where you are, I think."

"That's not very reassuring." Sid bounced the back of her head against the wall. "How many deaders are we talking about?"

"Mmmm, twenty or so, I'd say. Redcoats. What's the deal with the redcoats?"

Sid shook her head. "It makes no difference. Which way do we go? We'll just have to figure out something when we get there."

The sweat from Cort's chin started to make a puddle on the floor. "Man, I'm getting hungry." He wiped his chin on the forearm of his suit. "Starving like a pregnant lady."

"It's the suit. You won't get used to it. Where are we going, Guppy?"

"Stay south toward the river. Pass the elevators. Corridor bends right, then left. The command center is in the southwestern corner of the building. But again, it's packed with deaders, and I'm just talking about the ones I can see."

"Let's go."

Sid led. It didn't take long before she caught the stench of eroding flesh and musty uniforms. She held off from covering her nose. *Not a priority.* She squatted down and peeked around the corner where the T-intersection started. The redcoat deaders were crammed at the end of the hall like sardines. The brass buttons on their uniforms clinked against one another. Old sabers in scabbards rattled on hips. It was an undead army with dark fires burning in their hollow eyes. She pulled back.

Cort took a look. His body stiffened. He turned back to Sid and said, "Damn." He took a deep breath through his flaring nostrils. "I should have known it would come to this. It's got to be done, Cort. Got to do it, Cort. Got to go."

"Who are you talking to, yourself?"

"Listen, pretty lady, you're sweet and all, but if I survive this, you owe me one!" She caught a crazy look in his eye as if someone turned on a switch that lit up a wild light.

"Slow down, Cort. Cort?"

Cort stepped out into the hallway. He walked right toward the shambling soldiers. With his gun pointed straight at the nearest deader, he fired. The bullet punched through the deader's chest and into another. "Listen up, rednecks! Which one of you bony bastards can tell me where the commissary is?"

At the same time, all of the deaders turned toward him. All together, they charged.

Cort let loose a couple more shots, then turned and ran with a speed that belied his size. He ran down the straight line of the corridor.

Sid slid back into one of the offices. It was just her. Through a crack in the door, she watched the deaders rush after Cort in their startling stiff gait. "Guppy, you have to help him."

"I am. You just do what you need to do."

She moved out of the office. The end of the hallway leading into the control room was empty. There was an alcove entrance with a sign that hung above the opening. It read Command Central. Sid snuck up to the opening with her back to the wall. She could make out the edge of some steps that led down. Back sliding against the wall, she peeked around the corner. A strong bony hand locked around her throat. The fingers dug into her flesh and squeezed with unforgiving strength that wasn't human.

Sid gasped then stuck a gun in the bony ribs of a redcoat deader and pumped two rounds into its heart. The grip of the monster loosened. A second deader tucked in the shadows of the alcove rammed a bayonet at her side. "Gah!"

The rusting metal blade poked at her ribs, but the sweetheart suit saved her. The force of the impact knocked her into the wall, though. The deader continued to stab. Sid planted the barrel of her gun in its chest and fired.

The deader collapsed.

"Sid, are you okay?" Guppy said.

Panting for breath, she said, "Yes." She tugged on the handles of the double doors. "I'm going to shoot my way into the command center."

"No, I can open it, hold on."

Sid's breath became raspy. Her lungs started to burn. She wheezed. *Not now. Of all the times, not now.* Wiping her hair from her eyes, she turned to take a peek down the corridor.

Click.

Before she could turn, something grabbed her by the hair and jerked her clean off her feet and inside.

CHAPTER 20

SMOKE BURROWED HIS WAY BETWEEN the joists in the ceiling and the second-level flooring. Blood rushed through his ears. His savage nature was coming out. He had to run. Hide. Calm himself. Cort had looked like a pork chop to him moments earlier. He'd wanted to kill the man for blinking. He wanted to kill everything that pumped with warm blood.

Fight the hunger.

His fist smashed through the subflooring above his head. He punched until there was a hole big enough to squeeze through. He was inside an office. The bookshelves and desks were metal. An old computer monitor was on the desk. The chair sat on four casters. The place dated back to the late eighties. It was possibly the last time anyone worked there for a living until the Drake took over. Smoke ventured to the door and listened. It was quiet in the hallway.

Get it together, Smoke. You can't give in.

Whatever Kane had done to him was taking a toll. He thirsted for a taste of innocent blood. It wasn't like he was a blood-sucking vampire. But for some reason the urge to kill was inviting. Spilling the blood of the living was a sweet desire to him. He could smell it. Sense it. Something different. It was like seeing life from two different dimensions. In one realm were the living, some good, some not so much, and there was a hue about them. In another realm were the shifters, with an aura as cold as stone. They had no soul. No nothing. Just a living existence full of regret. Smoke clenched his fists.

Just find Kane. Kill him.

Smoke's own regrets began to fill him. When he'd been posing as Mack Brown, he'd had Kane right in the crosshairs. He should have tried to kill the monster then, but hadn't. For some reason, Kane had a hold on him. Perhaps it was the strange injection he was infused with. A mixture of blood perhaps, or strange chemicals. Whatever it was, it was otherworldly, or ancient, from civilizations long forgotten. Smoke's limbs trembled.

You're not a murderer. Kane's a murderer. Murderers must die.

The thought of Smoke becoming something that killed innocent people was appalling. Ever since he was young, he had abhorred those who shed innocent blood. Had felt compelled to fight evil wherever it rose. So often he found himself alone, in a world where people turned their backs to the horrors that devoured the innocent in the night. Now he had become one of those horrors. A man lost at sea only to find himself in the fight of his life against the great white whale. Bringing down Kane would be his death.

So be it.

There was more to fight for now than ever. He had a family. A wife and son. Smoke wasn't about to stand around and let them be the prey of the monsters that tried to besiege mankind. No, he would end the fight here. That was his gift. Fighting. Being a second ahead of where he needed to be. Counterpunching quick and deadly. None of his skills would be effective if he was out of control.

Breathe, Smoke. Breathe.

Kane had been two steps ahead of him the entire time. He'd played right into the shifter's hands. Now, it was time for him to turn those tables. Going through the floor was the first step. It took him off the radar for a bit. Now, he needed to take Kane by surprise. He wasn't sure how closely Kane could track him. There was something in his bloodstream that gave him away.

No, there's only one way to go about this.

Smoke stood up on the desk. It was time to hit the third level. The floor above him groaned. He crouched back. There was a soft click of a gun safety switching off. Smoke dove away. Gunfire erupted in a savage *budha-budha-budha-budha.* The large-caliber bullet holes turned the ceiling into a manhole. The bullet clip emptied.

Smoke sprang into action. He launched himself through the hole and hit the man changing out a clip square in the face. The man was out cold. There was a handheld scanner lying on the floor with a bright-green beacon on it.

Yep, I'm being tracked, alright.

He tossed it aside then turned. Something sliced into the back of his calf. It was the man he'd punched, bright-eyed and bushy-tailed. A shiny knife matched his grin. A familiar sneer formed on the thug's face.

The man propped himself up on his elbows. "Remember me? Perhaps this will jog your memory, hound." He slid on a pair of mirrored sunglasses. It was one of the Ratson brothers.

"I killed you," Smoke said.

"No, I'm Oliver. You killed my brother, Warren. You turned his face into dogfood with that machine gun. But you didn't get me. The blade you used sank, but not deep enough. I played possum after that. Live to fight another day. That's what us Ratsons do." He laughed. "Now look at you, all grown up and hairy. I have to say, I'm glad to take another crack at you."

"Let's crack on then, Oliver." Smoke grabbed the man by the leg and threw him through the wall.

Oliver was back on his feet when Smoke got there. The man turned and loosed a flurry of punches.

Smoke swatted them all away. He twisted the knife free from Oliver's hand then clocked him in the chin.

Oliver's knees wobbled.

"Where's Kane, Oliver?"

Touching the split in his lip, Oliver said, "He's not worried about the likes of you, Smoke. You're practically one of us. Soon enough you'll sign your life over in the office."

Smoke punched Oliver again.

The man dropped to a knee. "I felt that!"

The entire floor trembled. Oliver grabbed Smoke's legs.

A minotaur burst through the door. It rammed Smoke with its massive head of horns.

CHAPTER 21

FRANK TOOK THE GUN AND knife away from Sid like a parent taking toys from a toddler. With a handful of hair, he hauled her into the room. "It seems a little mouse has fallen into my snare. How sad for you, Sidney." He slammed her over one of the desks. The iron strength in his arms nullified Sid's struggles. "You've proven to be quite the difficult catch."

"Save your breath, Frank." She kicked back at his shins. It did little good.

Frank made a hollow chuckle.

Despite being pinned down, she had a fairly clear view of the room. Big monitors were up on the walls. In front of her, a young man and woman with ugly veins in their faces sat behind their desks working at a steady pace. They didn't even turn to look at her. On screen were images of empty hallways and the generator room.

"Looks like a pretty boring Super Bowl party you're hosting."

"I don't party." Frank put more weight on her back.

Sid groaned. Guppy was speaking in her ear, "Hang in there, Sid, we'll get help." She was wheezing, and her bruises burned like fire despite the sweetheart suit.

"My, you are in really bad shape, aren't you? The mortal existence is such a fragile one." Frank stripped the communication link from her wrist. He pulled the plug from her ear and set it aside at a nearby computer station. "All of this wonderful technology that you mortals take such a shine to is your weakness. You rely on it rather than your God-given instincts. It ruins all forms of self-reliance."

"You're the one down here staring at computer screens, not me." *Keep him talking, Sid.* "You track us with satellites, spy on us with cameras. The drug traders you command use countless wireless devices to do business. And you're telling me that somehow you are self-reliant?" She wheezed. "You're delusional."

"There is a cure for asthma, Sidney. Would you like to know what it is?"

She didn't reply. Instead, her eyes searched out the gun and knife Frank had taken.

"Death, Sidney. Death is the answer to all your problems."

"Yours too, Frankenberry."

"I don't follow your jest, but if it makes you feel better, make all the jokes you want. Rich, Sherry, let's give Ms. Shaw a seat."

"It's Mrs. Smoke."

"Yes, if you say so, Mrs. Smoke." He strong-armed her into a desk chair.

Rich and Sherry crept over with their jaws hanging. They bound up Sid's arms at the wrists with duct tape. Frank stood behind, pressing her down by the shoulders. She squirmed, but everything was hard because she couldn't breathe. Her energy was sapped.

"To be clear, Sidney, I find all of these technological wonders to be an abomination. I prefer the simpler times. But, I'm one to follow orders. Plus, I'm loyal. Long ago, I was dying and Kane saved me. So, here I am."

"Who cares?" Sid wheezed.

"Well, you should. After all, once we corral that troublesome husband of yours, I'm going to turn you into something like me. Or, like Rich and Sherry. Aren't they a charming couple? Oh, don't let those varicose veins disturb you. That will fade. You see, the both of them are new to the deader procedure." He massaged her shoulders. "Remember, I'm a mortician, and I want my subjects to be presented at their best. You see, I preserve life. I take pride in it. I promise you, you will be one of my most marvelous works yet."

"You can't win, Frank. The fires of Hell are waiting."

"Now, now, let's not go there. I'm treating you kindly."

Several of the screens flickered. The once-empty hallways now showed new signs of life. A huge minotaur now roamed the halls with other men and deaders.

Sid's heart skipped. Then it started to sink in. Every shifter they had fought was still alive.

"How about that? I can feel your heart in my fingers. You're surprised, aren't you. The shifters keep coming back. Well, most of them." Frank kissed the top of her head. "We are hard to kill, that much is certain. That is why we always win. We are weeds. We spring up in every crack. We crawl out of those dark corners. It's an amazing thing."

The screens flickered. The hallways became void.

An old telephone sitting on the desk rang. "Oh, fudge sticks." Frank stretched out his hand and picked up the receiver. "Yes, Kane?"

Sid could hear Kane screaming. "Get these monitors fixed, Frank! Now! Our customers grow angry!"

"I believe there is a mouse chewing on the lines."

"Then exterminate it!" Kane yelled.

Click.

"It seems that your friends on the outside — Guppy and Sam, is it? Well, they've become more than a nuisance now. Their termination has just been moved up on the schedule." He picked up the phone and dialed. "Mack, we have some pests outside. I need you to exterminate them. I want four dead. Turn them to ash if you wish. It must be done."

"Right away."

"There, Sidney. No more heroes. If they're lucky, there might be something left for a funeral."

CHAPTER 22

"**D**UMBEST IDEA EVER!" CORT WAS running full speed down the hallway with a pack of redcoat deaders hot on his tail. The chase led him back into the generator room. He hadn't done this much running since his days in the FBI academy. Still able to hear Guppy in his earpiece, he clicked on the communication link. "Guppy! Can you hear me?"

"Loud and clear, but I lost Sid. What's going on?"

"I thought you could see what was going on! I've got about twenty deaders on my tail!"

"Hold on. Where are you?"

"The generator room. You know, the one we started in!" The deaders poured into the room. Rickety limbs and equipment made for a macabre vision. Cort's lips curled. He bolted for the next double door entrance and hit the doors at full speed. He bounced right off them. "What the—Guppy, the doors are locked. I'm trapped inside with them!"

"Sorry. I'm battling it out with the other side. Give me a minute."

"I don't have a minute!"

The deaders closed in at a stiff-quick gait.

Seeing no other options, Cort fished the super vitamin out of his pocket, bit into it, and swallowed it down. Energy coursed through his heavy limbs like a bright sunburst in the sky. He grinned from ear to ear. Head bobbing, he said, "This is alright."

Cort's aim was quick. With a squeeze of the trigger, he shot four deaders in the heart. The bullet ripped through the first one, blew up the second, paralyzed the third, and the fourth deader's chest was sheared through front to back. They fell with flailing limbs, except the paralyzed one. Many of their fellow deaders tripped over them. Cort kept shooting. The pop of bullets bursting through the chamber was music to his ears. Two more deaders went down. His wheel gun was emptied. Running away from the surging enemy on legs that made him feel like a running deer, he popped out his speed loader from his pouch and reloaded.

A knot of deaders cut off his path. The first round Cort shot tore through one's skull. Brain matter oozed from the wound. The deader marched onward with a bayonet. Cort pumped it with an explosive round. He knocked aside the deader with a hole in its head like an old grocery cart.

The deaders were slight of build. There wasn't any meat on their limbs. Cort realized with his surging strength he could brush them aside. With dead-accurate shots, he dropped another handful of deaders. Then the trigger clicked behind Cort's finger.

"Empty!" On instinct, Cort holstered the Big Alaskan behind his back and drew his knife. There were about eight deaders left coming at him. He had his suit on. He liked his chances, bad hand and all. "Come on, geriatrics! Come get some!"

The first deader came at him with a rusty saber. It cut down hard.

Cort sidestepped with speed that didn't match up with his bigger size. He plunged his dagger into the deader's chest and gave the blade a twist that made crunching sounds. Still moving like a giant wildcat, Cort attacked the other deaders. Their weapons cut and stabbed. His head slipped aside like a prize fighter's. "You old ladies don't have nothing on me!" With the knife in his hand, he started punching them in the head like he was Apollo Creed.

"I'm the King of Sting! The Master of Disaster!"

The deaders poked and prodded at him. Their clumsy hacks brought pain, but the sweetheart suit held Cort together. He fought on with the eyes of a tiger, putting holes in one beating heart after the other. They kept coming. "What's going on here? What's going on? How much punishment do you devils want to take?" He hit a deader in the face with a few quick jabs that knocked its uniform hat off. A jaw cracked. Rotting teeth rained on the floor.

"I can get used to this!"

Fighting like he was king of the mountain, he jabbed one heart after the other. Right in the thick of it, his strength began to fade. His punches became telegraphed and heavy. He shouted into the comm link. "Guppy, my juice is gone! I need out of here!"

Cort's lungs caught fire. His shoulders sagged. The deaders seemed to pour it on. They locked onto his body and held on with their undead lives. Their sharp fingertips clawed at his face. At first, the deaders hadn't weighed so much. Now they felt like anvil-laden leeches stuck to his limbs. And their strength was unnatural.

"Guppy! Get me a door open now! Now!" Something bit into his face. "Aaaaah!"

Wearing out the keys on his laptop, Guppy said into the comm link, "They're open, Cort! They're open!" The link went dead.

With eyes bigger than saucers, Sam said, "Tell me you didn't lose him."

"I did." Guppy's chin was in his chest. "I've lost them all. Sam, I've got to go in there. They need all the help that they can get." He spat blood out on the blacktop.

"Your ribs are busted. You aren't going anywhere. The best way for you to help is from here. Just hack that system. You can do it."

He let out a painful sigh. "Okay, I'll keep going. Just keep your eyes open."

There was a loud *whoosh* sound. The parking lot lit up from a plume of flame before turning black again.

Sam and Guppy peeked around from behind the cover of a van. There were two men dressed in full suits of body armor. One held a machine gun and a flamethrower, the other an assault rifle. The one with the flamethrower was Mack Black, the man Smoke had disguised himself as. There was no missing the buzz cut and caterpillar moustache. The other had a helmet that looked like a welder's mask. A blast of flame roared out of the thrower, licking the pavement like dragon's breath.

Mack Black called out, "I'm here for a marshmallow roast, but I'm all out of marshmallows. I'll take some volunteers instead."

CHAPTER 23

THE MINOTAUR'S MOMENTUM DIDN'T STOP until Smoke was driven into a concrete wall back-first. "Miss me?" the minotaur said in the voice of the man, Mason Crowe. With burly arms wrapped around Smoke's back, the minotaur power-drove him into the wall again. "I missed you, Smoke!"

Under normal circumstances, Smoke was certain his body wouldn't have held up. His ribs, even if he had a sweetheart suit on, would have been crushed. It was his shifter form that held him together.

"Mason, I'll be honest. I did miss you." He kissed the nose of the bull man's face.

Mason's eyes lit up. His rock-hard body loosened.

Smoke's thumbs jammed into Mason's eyes.

The minotaur dropped Smoke. He let out a bullish bellow. His hooved feet clawed at the floor.

Smoke scrambled away. He made it into the next room only to find himself face to face with Oliver again. A gun barrel was pointed right at Smoke's chest. He sprang to the side, avoiding the spray of bullets, and grabbed a hardback book from the shelf. He flung the book at Oliver's eyes.

The dead man mad at the living didn't flinch. The book bounced harmlessly off his lantern-jawed face, but it gave Smoke enough time to dodge another hail of gunfire and slip out the office door.

"You can run, but you can't hide, Smoke. Our eyes are everywhere." Oliver started whistling. He hustled out into the hall.

Smoke was huddled down at floor level. As soon as Oliver entered the hall, he struck. With a fierce slash, the knife in his hand cut through the man's elbow. The gun he carried fell. Smoke snatched it up.

"Look what you've done. You idiot! You cut off my arm. That will take some doing to repair!" Oliver snaked a bowie knife out of a sheath strapped to his back. "So, you want to fight the old way. Let's do it, Smoke. You like a challenge, don't you?"

"No, I think I'll just shoot you in the face with your own gun. Just like I did your brother."

"You wouldn't do that. You're a brawler, not a co—"

Smoke squeezed the trigger. Bullets ripped through Oliver's face. Brass cartridges fell to the floor. Oliver Raton's body crumbled. "No, I'm not a co-worker."

The minotaur charged out of the room, trampling Oliver with his hooves.

Smoke sprinted down the hallway. He ran as fast as he ever had. Looking over his shoulder, he realized Mason Crowe was gaining. The huge man must have weighed half a ton. He moved like a minivan.

Smoke hooked his fingernails on the corner of another turn in the hallway, pulled himself around, then pressed his back into the wall. He fully expected the minotaur to skid into the turn. Instead, the corner wall that Smoke shielded himself with exploded. Mason Crowe ran right over the top of him.

Mason grabbed Smoke up in his short, stocky arms. He slung him into the walls. "You fool. I've trampled so many, I know every trick in the book. You thought to slip me? An insult!" He flung Smoke into another wall. He lifted one of his hooves over Smoke's head. "I'll crush your head like an egg." Mason stomped.

Flat on his back, Smoke wriggled away.

But Mason's quick hands proved to be formidable. His thick, plucky fingers grabbed Smoke by the feet, and then the minotaur spun around, knocking Smoke's head into the walls.

When Mason let go, Smoke hit the floor and slid. When he stopped, his bell was ringing. He shook his head while fighting to stand.

Smoke had fought about every shifter. None of them was as brawny as Mason Crowe. The minotaur was layers of animal brawn and muscle. The legendary beast would give the giants a fit. Strength for strength, Smoke wasn't a match for the horn-headed man. Yet, his own unique abilities stormed inside him.

"What's the matter, Smoke? Are you getting tired so soon?" Mason clapped his hands. "I'm full of all kinds of energy, brother."

"Don't call me brother."

"Okay, sister then."

Smoke took in a lungful of air and let out an ear-splitting shriek.

Mason covered his big ears. The neckless monster shook his head like bees swarmed his head.

Still letting out the piercing sound, Smoke drew his sword.

Mason started ramming into the walls, yelling, "Stop it! Make it stop! Please!"

Smoke stopped screaming.

Mason froze.

With careful aim, Smoke slid the blade between the brute's vertebrae.

The minotaur fell like a tree, crashing through linoleum tiles to the subflooring.

Smoke sighed. If he had sweat to wipe, he would have brushed it. "Bats don't sweat."

There was a *click* overhead.

"John Smoke, that was delightful. Our viewership on Deathflix is pleased," Kane said. "You have proved to be one of our greatest adversaries yet. But remember, we are still here, and have always been here, so you can't win. The only way to win is to join."

Smoke stared into the camera mounted where the wall met the ceiling. His reflection was in the lenses. His face was that of an animal becoming unhinged. The more he fought, the wilder he became. "Kane, I'm going to kill you today."

"Kill me? Hardly. I've faced foes far more challenging than you. For example, I vanquished Mason the Minotaur with my own bare hands. I didn't need some shiny little sword. Believe me, it took a lot for me to earn his loyalty. So, how do you expect to beat me when you can't even beat him?"

Behind him, Smoke heard Mason rising back to his feet. The bull man said, "Round two."

CHAPTER 24

FRANK WORE A GREY SUIT that loosely fit over his body. Leaning over Rich, he nudged the deader aside, and then his fingers went to work on the keyboard. A small smile creased his face as the images on the screens shifted. He had brought back the live feed. Rich and Sherry began toggling through different images on the screens. The compound was big, but after a few minutes, life resumed in the hallways. In one of them was Cort fighting for his life against a horde of deaders in the generator room.

Sid's eyes scanned the pictures on the screens. She needed a glimpse of Smoke. Instead, another image popped up. There were flames in the parking lot. The van they rolled in on was on fire. She didn't see any signs of Guppy or Sam. She wriggled in her bonds. Groaned behind the tape. It was hard to breathe. It was the worst asthma attack she'd had in a long time.

Frank turned. With a concerned look, he said, "You don't look so well. Perhaps all of this excitement is making your condition worse. Rich, Sherry, take down those images for now."

The screens shifted from the camera views to a satellite view above the facility. Sid could still see the top of the building and the parking lot. The van was burning, but it was too hard to see anything else that was going on.

Frank gave the monitors a quick glance before facing her anew. "Isn't it amazing? On this level, everything is so tangible and immediate. Face to face, the world is in chronic turmoil, but from high above it looks so peaceful. The images are so miniscule. People are ants or something much smaller. They don't seem so important, do they?" He nodded his chin. "No, they aren't important. We are not important, only a speck in the cosmic winds."

"You believe what you believe," she said. "I know what I'm fighting for is important."

"What you are attempting won't change anything if you are successful. It's all in vain." Frank half sat on the edge of a desk. "That's why you should embrace the life we live, Sidney. We enjoy the game of life."

"You pervert it."

"According to who? Who's to say what man is or is not? Who's really in charge?"

"Jesus."

Frank's chin dipped toward the floor, and he sighed. The rhythmic keystrokes of Rich and Sherry typing skipped a beat then resumed. "An awful lot of people in this world disagree with you. I for one."

"That's too bad." *Keep him talking.* "Given the condemning nature of my situation, Frank, why don't you enlighten me as to who is really in charge? I've spent time with Kane. I know he's not the one in charge. He's a big part of the Drake, but he's not the Drake."

"No, Kane is not the head of the organization. The Drake is global and has many facets and forms. What we do is just a portion of the Drake's dealings, though we are the most unique and formidable facet. Most of the Drake, if you dig deep enough, is men and women just like you, content in their mortality. Bankers, brokers, doctors, scientists, lawyers, and so on. We do the dirty work for them. Our mission? Poisoning the leadership of this country from the inside out. We've been quite successful, aside from a few setbacks. Like the clones. I have to admit, that was an impressive act of valor that made Kane's head spin around."

Sid cut in. "There was a computer there. A pyramid. That entire operation was otherworldly."

"Oh yes, but not otherworldly. You see, the Drake are great scholars of antiquities. They employ many archeologists and fund notable museums and preservation societies. So much of the ancient world is buried, a world not so different from the one we live in today. Men in ancient times were not so primitive as the schoolbooks taught people to believe. But many crafts were lost in the sludge of time.

"The Egyptians and Babylonians were highly advanced. Think about it: the pyramids, giant stones cut with laser-guided precision. There are slabs of granite hollowed out in perfected angles that are too big for men to move without great machines. The Drake sought answers to such things, and they found them. The important thing is that they"—Frank made air quotes— "control the information.

"Governments, like this one, are too busy making problems for themselves, rather than trying to solve them. The Drake is a contractor that takes the burden out of government hands. Then, they control these artifacts that common men can't understand. One of them was discovered in a crypt centuries ago. There was a range of large hills, beautiful sights, in Venezuela. Three of them coming together and covered in lush vegetation. Lo and behold, after a thousand years of neglect it was discovered that pyramids were buried underneath. They were lined up exactly as the great ones in Giza. But"—he held up a finger—"smaller. However, they were undisturbed. They hadn't been ransacked by centuries of looters. The Drake was at the right place at the right time on that occasion. Perhaps that's what Khonshu the Moon God awaited. Inside were technologies more advanced than what men could imagine for his time. They brought us to where we are today. It took centuries to decipher it. These computers, smart phones, it all comes from that. Hitler's secret bunker had a trove of this advanced technology too, but the U.S. government, because of the weaponry, secured that."

"So that's how you make deaders and shifters? They're mummies?"

"No, that's all baloney. But, yes, the process of reanimation came from those ancient people. The ability to change into shifters as well. It's a mix of biochemistry, DNA alteration, and powers that we still don't fully grasp yet. We just trust the teachings of Khonshu. Have you ever seen those pictures in history books of Egyptians with heads like dogs and birds?"

"A man's face on the body of a lion, like the sphinx."

"All reality a long time ago." Frank rubbed his saggy cheek. "Think about it, people are living longer as we slowly integrate these ancient teachings into the modern world. But at the same time, we can't let there be too many people. So, we've created war, disease, famine. At some point, the world will be perfect and run by the likes of us. You could still be a part of that."

"Part of a syndicate that decides who lives and who dies?" She wheezed. "I think I'll pass. So, Kane is the most powerful shifter? He has a direct connection with Khonshu?"

"Kane is the father of the shifters. As for Khonshu, no one has seen him since his crypt was opened. I'd say you being with Kane is as close as you'll ever be. Rich, Sherry, go ahead and pull up the screens. Let's see if any of Sid's allies are still breathing."

New images popped up. Sid gasped.

CHAPTER 25

MACK BLACK BLOWTORCHED THE VAN. Sam and Guppy ran for cover. Bullets blasted into the pavement at their feet. Putting their hands in the air, they came to a stop. "Is this it, honey? The end of the road for Guppy and Sam?"

"If it is, it's the best road I've ever ridden on," he said with labored breath. "I love you, Sam."

"I love you too."

Mack Black called out to them. "Turn around. I always enjoy seeing the faces of the people I'm about to put it to." His beady eyes blossomed. "Oh my, I've never roasted such a dish." Eyes on Sam, he sprayed some flames in the air. "And I thought this flamethrower was hot. It's got nothing on you, babe. I'm having second thoughts about this kill. Maybe Kane will let me save you."

"In your dreams, creep," she said.

"Oh, I can certainly promise you that, but there's nothing quite like the real thing."

Guppy took a step forward. Bullets chewed up the ground before his feet. The man in the welder mask said in muffled words, "One more step and you'll die from bleeding feet."

"Get on your knees, the both of you," Mack said. "Hands on your heads."

Sam and Guppy complied.

"My, my, my, I certainly do have a situation here. A tough decision. I hate to go against Kane's orders — or Frank's, for that matter. But I can't make much sense of killing someone so beautiful." He pointed the flaming gun barrel at Guppy. "As for you, anvil-face, killing you isn't much of a problem. I've put down dogs uglier than you before."

The body of the man in the welder mask heaved with chuckles.

"But I can't stand to see such a pretty lady cry. Tell me, gorgeous, you won't cry when I kill him, will you? Even the pretty ones make ugly when they cry."

"I'm not promising anything. After all, he is my husband."

"You and him? You've got to be kidding me. Heh-heh-heh. He must have a big wallet, or something else. That makes little sense to me."

"Hey, I'm not so bad, especially compared to the likes of you."

"Oh, ho-ho, ole brick face is taking it personal. Listen, I'll take good care of your lady." Mack winked. "Real good care of her. But now I have to do what I have to do."

"No, wait," Sam said. "Let me at least say goodbye to my husband."

"Of course, of course, go right ahead. I'm a decent man."

Walking on her knees, Sam butted up against Guppy. She kissed him full on the mouth.

"No! None of that now! I'm okay with words, not lips," Mack said.

The other man cracked off a shot.

Sam broke off the kiss. She said to Guppy, "That really is a nice suit you'll be wearing to your funeral. Make good use of it."

Guppy started to say, "Huh?" but his mouth was full of something Sam had given him with her kiss. He bit down on a super vitamin and swallowed it whole. Not a second passed before he felt like a new man, spry as a stag. He nodded at his wife. "Thanks for everything, baby." He fastened his eyes on Mack. "Listen, mister, at least let me die standing on my feet. It's all I ask. It's a family thing."

Sam started to sob.

"Fine, fine, stand. I just want to roast the dinner so that I can get to dessert."

Guppy took one knee off the ground and planted his foot.

"Slowly now, blockhead."

"My ribs are already busted up, so I'm not one to move very fast. The arthritis doesn't help much either." Guppy groaned, even though there was a spring of new life swelling inside. The stinging pain of his ribs was gone. The spring in his legs was back. "By the way, mister," Guppy said, "that flamethrower you're carrying, I noticed it's got a leak."

"Oh, and I'm supposed to look now?"

"No, I'll check it out for you." Guppy sprang at the man. Flames engulfed his body. He passed right through the scorching heat, colliding with the man's body. He yanked the flamethrower's handle from Mack's strong grip. He pointed it at the other man, squeezed the trigger. Flames spewed out, covering the man in the welder mask in flames.

The man stood in his spot. Burning in his armor, he let out a spray of bullets.

Guppy held the flamethrower hose on the man.

The bullets went astray as the man started screaming.

Mack jumped Guppy. He was strong, but right now, Guppy was far stronger.

Guppy drove his elbow into the man's face. The jawbone gave. "Don't ever talk to my wife like that again." With a few more punches, Mack Black was out cold. He stripped the flamethrower harness from the man's back.

Sam grabbed him and kissed him. "That was awesome! Where are you going?"

"I'm going in. I've got to help Cort."

CHAPTER 26

G UPPY GAVE SAM A QUICK kiss and ran. He noticed Mal and Russ emerging from their hiding place. Everyone was armed. With pure adrenaline racing through his veins, he pushed through the hole in the doorway and barreled down the hall, taking the first right toward the generator room. He slammed his shoulder into the double doors. The heavy metal doors bowed against his strength, but held. He jogged backward, pulled his semiautomatic pistol from the polymer holster, and fired.

The doors exploded inward. Guppy holstered the weapon and made his march inside. It had been a long time since the veteran had seen any action in the field. The smell of gunpowder livened his senses. All of his instincts from multiple tours in Iraq and Afghanistan came back. This was another mission. A rescue mission. He'd done it dozens of times before. But never with a flamethrower.

As soon as he cleared the hazy smoke inside the yawning size of the generator room, deaders rushed him. He pulled the trigger. A stream of flame ignited the deaders' old uniforms like kindling. Skin bubbled and crackled. They marched with their bodies burning and bayonets lowered to impale him. Guppy side-jumped out of their path, watching the old bodies begin to crumble from the corner of his eyes. There were deaders in red coats ambling all over the room. He'd only caught some of their attention. There wasn't any sign of Cort.

Seeing the whites of their eyes, Guppy hosed them all down with flame.

Something jabbed into his back, knocking him to his knees. He caught the flash of a sword bearing down on his skull. His hand shot up, catching the deader by the wrist. He stuck the flamethrower in its gut. "Burn!"

Flames erupted out of the deader's eyes and mouth. It fell over with its head leaving a stream of smoke behind it.

"Guppy!" cried a deep but feeble voice.

Cort was up on top of one of the generators. Deaders scrambled at the base, crawling over one another to the top. The big black man was hitting them in the face with bloody knuckles whenever a deader's face popped up. He was on his belly, with his boots hanging over one end. Deaders had ahold of those boots, fighting against the kicking feet that dangled over the rim.

Guppy turned the deaders on the backside into fire. The entire room smelled like burning flesh and hair. The smoke was so thick Guppy choked. His eyes watered so badly it was hard to see. "Hang on, Cort, I'm coming."

"Hurry up!"

Guppy rushed around to the other side. The flames sputtered from the tip. "Tank's about empty!" He slid the flamethrower tank off of his brawny shoulders and yelled at the redcoat deaders, "Hey!"

The remaining trio of deaders turned on Guppy.

Guppy tossed the flamethrower tank to one in front. It caught it full in the chest. "I don't know what your name is, soldier, but Bonfire has a nice ring to it. Cover up, Cort! The thunder's coming!" With the quick hand of a gunslinger, Guppy drew and fired. The tank exploded. Deader bodies splattered from the floor to the ceiling. A deader head bounced off the floor and rolled. Guppy kicked it away. "Cort?"

There was a pause, followed by, "Please tell me they're all dead."

Guppy scanned the room. "They were all dead before we started, but now they don't move." Guppy's legs turned into noodles. He broke out in a cold sweat and fell on his backside. "Whoa."

Cort's head popped up over the side of the generator. "I know what that means. You're out of gas. Those pills have a nasty side effect, but at least it saved my ass."

"Ditto. Do you need any help off of there?"

"My arm's still broken, but I think I can manage." Cort's face soured. "Whew! The dead stink. If we ever get out of here, the first round is on me."

"I don't drink."

"Then I'll drink for you." Cort managed to slide his body over the edge. He swung his big frame over with one arm. He landed heavily on his feet and fell to the floor. He started laughing. "I feel like I just ran a dozen gassers."

"Me too."

Both men were staring up at the ceiling. Guppy's ribs felt worse than they had before.

"Say," Cort said, tapping Guppy with the back of his hand. "You got any more ammo?"

"Yup." Guppy fished a cartridge out of his belt. "Here."

"Are these forty-four magnums?"

"Nope." Guppy handed over a second gun he had in his belt. "This will have to do you."

Cort took the gun. He popped out the empty cartridge and loaded the new clip. He reached down into one of his belt pouches. He fished out the small vial of pills. "Do you think it's too dangerous to take these too close together without having a meal? I wonder if it's addictive."

"Who knows?" Guppy sat up with a grunt. "I doubt they have FDA approval. I'm sure Mal wouldn't have given us so many if it wasn't safe."

Cort made it up to his elbows. "Man, I just wish they lasted longer. That's quite a rush. Where to now?" He reached out his hand. Together the men helped each other up.

"Sid's in trouble."

"I know where she is."

"Lead the way."

Stiff limbed, the hardened veterans ambled along, completely unaware that someone was watching them.

CHAPTER 27

"**T**HAT WAS A NICE MOVE with the sword," Mason the minotaur said, "but it takes a lot more than that to kill the likes of me."

"Playing possum, huh?" Smoke backed down the hall with the sword still in his hand. It appeared that

Mason wouldn't be a pushover. Smoke had dropped the monster into a deep chasm, yet he had still come back. In the back of his mind he wondered if anyone they killed was ever dead. One and all, it seemed, had come back. "So, if I can't kill you with this sword, perhaps you wouldn't mind letting me take a free shot."

Mason's hooves clawed at the floor. His wide nostrils snorted. The burly beast man with horns as wide as his shoulders said, "Go ahead. I'll give you the first shot."

"With the sword?"

"You can use your sword or your gun." Mason stood straight. His head almost touched the ceiling. "But when I don't die, then I get a free shot at you."

Smoke eyed the bull man up and down. The hairy, husky man appeared as solid as any statue. Smoke knew an explosive bullet wouldn't do it. A blue round would pass through one side and out the other, but if he couldn't stop the beast with a sword, there was little chance that a bullet could. *Why not.* He dug the tip of his Arabian sword into the floor and leaned it against his waist, spat into his hands, and rubbed them together. He took the sword up in both of his hands.

"This is your bet. Stand still."

Mason crossed his arms over his chest. "I will, rodent."

Smoke walked right up to the minotaur and raised the sword over his head.

Mason didn't budge a fraction of an inch.

He brought the sword's razor-sharp blade down with wroth force. The steel split the skull dead center. It cleaved through the thick skull brain-deep before stopping between the eyes. He released the handle and stepped away, fully expecting Mason to drop.

"Boo," the bull man said. Like an anvil on a block, he didn't budge an inch. If a bull could smile, he made one. Mason grabbed the sword by the handle and wriggled it free, making a sickening squishing sound of bone and brain rubbing on metal as he did so. He offered the blade to Smoke. "Now it's my turn."

Smoke took the sword and sheathed it behind his back. He'd just taken the biggest gamble of his life. *I should have chopped off his head. That might have done it. What was I thinking?*

"Don't second-guess yourself, John Smoke. Nothing you tried would have worked. Some of us can't be killed. We'll always come back." Mason's right hoof started to dig. "Now brace yourself — unless you want to chicken out."

Smoke moved back twenty paces. "No, I'm a man of my word. A bet's a bet. I took my shot, now you take yours."

"A shame. You would have made an excellent brother. But now, you have to die."

It was a gamble. Smoke figured if they couldn't die so easily, then neither could he. *If I survive this, I swear, I'll never do it again. Stupid.* Smoke prided himself on being able to escape anything. He could run, but to a point of fault, he kept his word. *I live by my Word, and I'll die by my Word.* "Okay, fatty, give it your best shot."

"With glee." Mason charged. His steps shook the hall.

But when the minotaur was ten steps from Smoke, the flooring gave out.

Mason's momentum shifted. He fought his way at Smoke with a dying head of steam. He plowed his rock-hard forehead into Smoke's chest. The impact sent Smoke sprawling backward into the wall. He left a full-body impression in the drywall. The dark spots in his eyes didn't clear. His chest felt like it had taken a direct shot from a cannonball. Stuffed inside the wall, he nevertheless kept his feet.

"NO!" Mason punched the floor. "I get another run at it!"

But Smoke had a problem. Even though he hadn't gotten Mason's best shot, the jarring impact had still paralyzed his limbs. *I feel like I just got hit by a tank. Ugh!* As Mason climbed to his feet, Smoke began wriggling his fingers. He pulled his shoulder out of the wall.

Mason was on the move again, gaining a full head of steam. Luck wasn't going to stop the juggernaut this time.

At the last possible moment, Smoke broke away from the wall.

Mason dipped his head in an attempt to gore Smoke, but the minotaur's momentum carried him onward. Tripping over Smoke, he busted through the brick wall.

Smoke groaned. A hoof had caught him full in the ribs. He crawled away, got onto his feet, and began running.

Behind him came an angry roar. Hooves stomped the floor. The enraged minotaur gave chase at a fast and steady speed. "I will crush you, Smoke! There's no escape from me!"

I should have cut off one of his legs! That would have done it, John. But no, you had to go for the kill, didn't you?

Holding his side, Smoke ran as fast as he could. Mason continued to gain. There weren't many places to run. The offices ran along the halls, all of which crisscrossed the building. Smoke lowered his shoulder into one of the fire escape doors that led outside. It didn't budge.

Laughing started up over the loudspeaker. "Run, Smoke, run! Watch him go, viewers, as the minotaur closes in. How much more does this cursed do-gooder have left in him?"

Smoke wheeled around into the next hall. A knot of redcoat deaders were crammed in there, four men deep. Mason rounded the corner. There was nowhere to run. *Great Dane.*

"Surprise, John," Kane said. "It looks like your heroics are up in smoke."

CHAPTER 28

ONE SCREEN SHOWED THE GENERATOR room full of burning deader bodies. Another showed that Sam, Russ, and Mal had found safety near a storage shed. The view that had Sid's heart racing was of Smoke. He was in the thick of things, battling the Minotaur.

"Mason Crowe lives," she said, wheezing. Her breathing was a forced effort by design. The constriction in her lungs had begun to ease, but she wasn't letting on. "That's impossible."

"The word 'impossible' is not in our vocabulary, Sidney." Frank laid his hand on her head. He stroked her hair. "Such a sweet child, who only knows what she sees and has been told. That's why the likes of the Drake are so successful. No one wants to tell you what's really happening. You only see what the powers that be want you to see."

"Please stop touching me."

"Oh, get used to it, little pet. Be smart and let your owner care for you. Enjoy the simple life that we are trying to provide for all."

"I had the simple life with Kane. It didn't work on me then, and it certainly won't work on me now." She pulled her head away. "Keep your damn hands off me."

Frank slapped her. It felt like she'd been hit by a sandbag. The heavy-handed strike tipped her and the chair over.

Lording over her, Frank said, "I'm not a violent person, but I don't take kindly to abrasive tones used against me. It shouldn't, but it does, anger me a little. It seems there is still a spark left in this centuries-old frame of mine."

"It's not a spark. It's just evil." Sid lost her view of the screens. "Are you going to just leave me here? Pick me up."

Frank's long neck eased back and forward again. Reaching down, he pulled her up by her head of hair. Fibers of hair ripped out of her skull as he did so. "Behave yourself, or no more television for you."

"So far, all my friends live, Frank. They're beating the odds. I don't think that's an accident." She had a view of Cort and Guppy coming down the hallway that led to her location. "I think visitors are coming. Would you like me to prepare something?"

"No, that won't be necessary. I think I can manage. Sherry, would you please fetch our other guest out of the server room?" The undead woman disappeared through a concealed panel door beside the monitors. Frank picked up the communication link and the earpiece that went with it. He fit it inside Sid's ear. "Tell them you're heading back to the parking lot."

"Why would I do that?"

"Because if you don't, then someone very dear to you is going to die."

"You've played that card plenty of times already. And no one has died so far." Sherry returned, but she wasn't alone. "Megan!"

Held fast in Sherry's grip, the little girl was unresponsive. Her wavy blond locks were in tangles. Her complexion was ashen. The clothing she wore — jeans and a pink unicorn t-shirt —looked like it hadn't been changed in months. Megan held a brown teddy bear in her arms, but her eyes were on the floor.

"Megan, it's me, Aunt Sidney. Come to me, Megan, please."

Megan's head turned slightly, but she didn't look.

"What did you do to her, Frank?" Sid yelled.

"Things have been so hectic of late that she's been given a mild sedative. Besides, she's a prime candidate to become a shifter like her mother."

"What are you talking about?"

"Oh, your most lovely sister Allison has become something quite beautiful. Her daughter will thrive just as well, or, like yourself, die. But as you can see, I don't think the young one has it in her to resist." Frank held the comm link in Sid's face. "Now tell your comrades you are heading back to the parking lot. You'll meet them there."

"Or what?"

"Or Megan will die."

"I thought you said she was a candidate?"

"Yes, and she'll have to die first. Now, Sid, I suggest that you do as I say. I don't bluff." He touched the link to her lips. His voice became gritty. "Tell them."

There was a little crackle in her ear. "Guppy, can you hear me?" She watched Guppy stop in the hallway and grab Cort's arm with his hand. "Guppy?"

"Sid," Guppy replied. "Where are you?"

"I'm out. The control room was a dead end. I'm heading back to the parking lot. We need to regroup."

"What about Smoke?"

"I don't know, Guppy. Let's regroup. We have to gather all the resources we can muster. He's in here somewhere, but I've got to get out. I can barely breathe."

"Yeah, yeah, Sid. The parking lot. Stat."

Sid watched Guppy talking to Cort in the hallway. Cort was pointing down the corridor where Command Central waited. They bickered back and forth a bit, but Guppy appeared to prevail in the argument. They headed back in the direction from where they had come. The monitors tracked their every step.

"Well done, Sidney. Well done." Frank took the Bluetooth plug from her ear and set it aside with the communication link. "Cooperation is an important part of building strong relationships. When the deed is done, perhaps you will become one of my most masterful creations, much like your sister and niece. Along with Smoke, you can be one big happy family."

Sid kept her eyes fastened on Megan. She'd never seen her niece look so pitiful before. She was dark and jaded now. The vibrant marrow of her had been sucked out, leaving her hollow. Panting, she said, "How could you do this? She's just a little girl."

"I consider it mercy. Just think, she won't have to face all those nasty trials and tribulations that plague your corrupt world. She'll be free of that struggle and bondage." Standing behind Sid's chair, Frank rested his spade-sized hands on her shoulders. He started to rub. "Soon, you will be free of it as well. Sherry, kill the girl."

"What!" Sid said. Sherry produced Sid's knife and pressed it against Megan's throat. "No, Frank, no! Stop this! I'll do anything!"

"Sorry, it's too late for that. Sherry, do it."

CHAPTER 29

R EDCOATS. THEY LOOKED LIKE COSTUMED freaks at a bad Halloween party. With bayonets and sabers at the ready, the sunken-eyed men stayed their advance. Sealing Smoke off at the other end was Mason, with murder in his eye.

Smoke's thoughts were clouded. He didn't have a plan other than self-preservation. He was like a cornered animal. Fight or run. But there was nowhere to run. Fight or die, more like.

Don't lose it, Smoke.

"End of the road, jerkoff." Mason pounded his fist into his meaty hand with a loud smack. "I'm going to turn you into a pile of mush. I can't wait."

Smoke fought to find words. He had none. His mind was swirling. Clutching his head, he staggered on wobbling knees.

Focus, Smoke! Focus!

He needed to rip something apart. He ran straight at the deaders. Their bayonets advanced. Smoke leapt high, clearing the jabbing soldiers and gliding over them with his back brushing the ceiling. A strong hand caught him by the ankle. Down he went into a sea of rotting people. His raw savagery was unhinged. Sharp weapons jabbed and poked. His bearish strength broke bones and shattered faces. Joints were pulled from their sockets. Sunken eyeballs were wasted. Smoke hit them with everything he had.

Mason waded into the turmoil. He ripped Smoke out of the deaders that clung to him like flies on tape. Holding Smoke by the nape of the neck, he punched him in the gut. "I will break every bone in you!" The punches kept coming. Mason mashed Smoke's face into the wall. He hoisted him over his head and pounded him into the ceiling like something one would see in a comic book.

When Smoke's body was used up like a sock full of cue balls, Mason started beating the deaders with his frame.

Somehow, Smoke squirmed out of Mason's iron grip. He snaked into the deaders that threw their bodies at him in a wave. Catching them off balance, he pushed them in Mason's path. Surprisingly, Smoke's body held together. His bones seemed malleable in a unique way, something like how rats could squeeze through tiny holes. All he knew was he still lived. A movie quote crossed his mind: *"Bats are excellent survivors."*

"Where are you going, Smoke? Stop running! Start fighting!"

Smoke picked up a deader and flung the man at Mason.

Mason shrugged it off with his horns. He gored another through the head, making for a nasty crunch when he slung it aside.

Before Mason could gather another head of steam, Smoke ducked underneath his crushing arms. Using his own long arms, he scooped up Mason by the legs, lifted the massive shifter up off his feet, and slammed him on the floor. Wild with rage, Smoke attached himself to Mason's body and pummeled him in the face. He jammed his thumbs into the minotaur's eyes. He raked Mason's face with claws. His fists pounded the minotaur's chin.

The flurry of attacks had Mason flailing and kicking. "Get off me, pest!" Mason rolled back on top of Smoke.

Smoke pulled his knees up into his chest and planted his feet in Mason's abdomen. He flung the minotaur over his head, sending him crashing into more deaders. Without looking back, Smoke ran back the way he came.

Come on, Smoke! Think! You have to think!

Shifter or not, there wasn't much more he could take from Mason without his body shutting down. Even worse, he was losing control of himself. His sharp mind had dulled. He clung to his humanity. The inner struggle was worse than the outer one.

Mason's powerful voice echoed down the hard walls of the hall. "You can run, but you can't hide. We own you, rodent." His footsteps were thunder. The pounding thuds grew louder as he picked up speed. "I am strength! I am doom! I am invincible!"

Rounding the next corner, Smoke couldn't make an argument against what Mason stated. The shifter was a juggernaut. Smoke had tried everything, and nothing slowed the monster. He needed a weapon like the one he had used on the giants. He had nothing. In times like this, he usually used strategy, but his mind was so fogged that he couldn't dig anything up. All he wanted to do was fight. Kill.

Keep it simple. What's the mission, Smoke? Keep it simple.

He ran down one straightaway after the other. A single thought kept with him.

Kill Kane. Where is Kane? Kill Kane.

Smoke knew the layout of the entire facility top to bottom. He'd been through every room. He fought to get his bearings. Where was he? Where did he need to be? He was on the third floor. Kane was on the third floor in a concealed location that took extra security to get to. There was only one way in and one way out. No doubt it would be heavily guarded.

"Quit running, Smoke. It's only a matter of time before I catch you!"

As he ran, Smoke caught names on doorways. *God, help me put this together.* Like puzzle pieces, they came together. The layout that was broken mended. A clear blueprint formed in his mind's eye. He knew where he needed to go. Where he had to be. *Kane, I'm coming!*

CHAPTER 30

"**M**EGAN, GET AWAY FROM HER. Get away!" Sid shouted.

Sherry pressed the knife to the young girl's throat.

Sid's stomach knotted. "Noooo!"

"So sorry, Sidney," Frank said with his strong fingers keeping her wriggling form held fast. "One life ends and a new life begins."

The knife slashed a line across Megan's throat. The cute little girl didn't scream or gasp. She didn't even bleed.

With her entire soul haunted, Sid gasped. The horror of what was happening only compounded her confusion. "What, what, what?" she panted. Her heart was racing. New blood rushed behind her temples from a fear-provoked rush of adrenaline. "This is madness. Megan, talk to me, Megan."

Megan's eyes narrowed in mockery. Something devious took over. Devious and familiar. Megan snatched Sherry by the hand. She hip-tossed the undead woman over her shoulder as if she were a man twice her size.

"What's the meaning of this?" Frank said with outrage. "Who are you?"

Megan transformed right before their eyes from a pretty girl to a young, handsome black boy with granite-colored eyes. With a smile crossing his face, the young man said, "You always were such a goon, Frank."

"Manson!" Frank shouted. "Have you gone mad?"

It was Manson Bay. Sid hadn't seen or heard from him since they lost Smoke at the cloning plant. She'd forgotten all about him.

Manson looked down at his pink unicorn shirt. "Certainly my style is questionable, but the bear was a nice touch, wasn't it?"

Frank's fingers dug into Sid's shoulder and neck. The pressure grew. Her breath choked off. "You're supposed to be on our side, Manson. Don't be a fool. You dare sacrifice yourself for one like this? Rich, Sherry, take him."

"Stay put, Rich and Sherry." Manson winked at Frank. "Surprised, big man? I put a little wrinkle in your immortal soup. Now Rich and Sherry respond to me."

Sid continued to choke. Still sitting in her chair, she made the move she'd been waiting for. Securing her wrists with duct tape had been a poor move. Tearing through those bonds was easy. She sawed her elbows back, hitting her bindings just below the knees. The duct tape ripped. She grabbed ahold of Frank's arm and tried to toss him.

"No, you don't." He lifted her clear from her feet. Her head touched the ceiling. "There is no cavalry, Sidney. I'm going to kill you."

A long knife hacked into Frank's arm below the elbow. Manson continued to chop. "What do you mean, there's no cavalry? I'm the cavalry."

Sid slipped out of Frank's grasp.

The large man kicked Manson so hard he landed on another desk.

Choking and coughing, Sid spied her gun on the floor. She staggered over.

Frank tripped her.

She fell on top of the weapon. She shifted over to her back and fired. Bullets ripped through his chest.

Frank staggered away and burst outside of the double doors and ran.

Still coughing, Sid got up and looked at Manson, who was also back on his feet. "Where's he going?"

"Who knows?" Mason shrugged. "Frank's a big coward. He'll run as far as he can go."

"No, he's too dangerous. We have to stop him. He'll just go after more of my friends." Sid grabbed her earpiece and the comm link. "Where's Megan, Manson?"

Manson took a seat behind one of the computer consoles. His fingers were hard at work. "Who?"

"My niece, Megan! The one you were disguised as."

"Oh, don't worry. It's late. I'm sure she's fast asleep at the safe house."

Sid glared at him. She didn't have time for more games. On a good note, she was still alive, and the adrenaline rush had wiped out her asthma. She called out on the comm link, "Guppy! It's Sid! Abort the parking lot. I'm back in the control room. Look out for Frank! He, well, looks like Fred Quinn. Don't let him fool you! Guppy, are you there?"

"Roger that, Sid. Cort and I are on it. Coming back your way," Guppy said. "We got a new weapon out of one of their storage rooms. It should be useful."

"I'm coming," Sid said. "Watch out, Frank is dangerous!" She turned to Manson. "I'll be back. Don't you go anywhere."

Without looking away from his computer screens, he said, "Don't worry, I have plenty to do."

Not taking any chances, Sid shot the magnetic lock that sealed the double doors shut. "See you soon, Manson." She almost thanked him but held back. In all reality, the boy was a shifter. The last thing she was going to do was put her faith in one of them. With her wind coming back, she chased after Frank. She'd caught a glimpse of where he was going on the screen. He was headed right for the exits that led to the parking lot. No doubt he'd prey on the weak. That was the coward's way. He'd hold the likes of Sam or Mal up in some type of twisted ransom.

It wasn't long before she heard his footsteps. He didn't move very fast. She rounded the corner and caught him halfway down the hall. She fired a shot that clipped his shoulder.

Frank didn't slow until Cort and Guppy appeared at the other end of the corridor. He looked back and forth between the two of them. "Shoot all you want. You can't kill me, but you can try. I'd be delighted to see you kill one another in a crossfire."

"We're better shots than that, you idiot." Sid moved flush against the wall. On the other end, Guppy and Cort backed up on the same side. "Aim for the left knee!"

The hallway echoed with the loud sound of bullets bursting out of the barrel. Frank stood his ground for a moment as his knee was shredded. The long appendage fell out of his pants leg and oozed on the floor. Frank stood one legged like a crane. His hollow eyes were filled with amazement. "You still can't kill me."

"We ain't going to kill you." Cort set a chainsaw on the floor and fired it up. The little engine roared with a gas-guzzling and throaty life. "We're just going to turn you into firewood. Time to burn, Franken Face!" He revved up the engine.

Frank's arms waved frantically as he pleaded, "No! No!"

Cort and the chainsaw turned the shifter into kindling. Nothing but oozing body parts and scraps of his suit remained.

"That was gruesome but needed to be done," Sid said to them. She took her eyes off them for a moment and wiped the hair from her eyes. When she looked at them again, someone behind them slammed their heads together. Both men hit the floor out cold.

Sid's tongue clove to the roof of her mouth when Allison said, "Hello, Sis."

CHAPTER 31

S MOKE LED THE CHASE. MASON charged after his heels. Redcoat deaders roamed the halls. If Smoke couldn't dodge, he knocked them aside. Mason ran right over them, but as fast as the minotaur was — with hooves that tore up the old floors — Smoke stayed ahead. The goal was to make it to the southern face of the building. Kane's office was in an overhang that looked out over the river. It was boxed in all by itself, a separate attachment to the building, but solidly built. *Almost there.*

Letting Mason gain a few steps on him, he flung the office door open and ran inside. At a full sprint, he ran through the plaster walls, crossed through another hallway, opened up another door, and ran inside. He leaped a desk and punched through the back wall. Covered in plaster dust, he opened up the adjacent office door. He hit the wall solidly with his shoulder. It didn't give. He clawed the plaster in huge hunks.

Mason came. The minotaur's tremendous frame was running through walls like he was running through sheets of paper.

Smoke's long fingernails tore at the cinder block. *Got to sell it!*

"I have you now, rodent!" Mason roared.

With Mason's footsteps closing in like a crashing tidal wave, Smoke jumped aside at the last possible moment.

At full speed, the bull man's powerful body carried him clear through the cinder block wall and across Kane's office toward the wall of glass.

Smoke caught a glimpse of Mason steamrolling through the room. The minotaur ran roughshod through a television and sofa without slowing. Smoke fully expected Mason to bounce off the glass windows the same as he had. Instead, Mason hit it full speed. The glass gave way, shattering into thousands of pieces that looked like sparkling rain.

"Nooooo!" Mason cried. A notable *thud-glitch* followed.

Smoke slipped into the room.

The refined furniture that hadn't been trampled was still intact. Kane was standing behind his bar, frozen with a drink of whiskey in his hand. His brows were up to his hairline.

Smoke made his way to the window and took a look down. Mason was impaled on some iron fencing that he'd crushed underneath him. He still moved, but like a turtle upside down on his shell.

Kane started pouring another tumbler of whiskey. "My, John, you really are an incredible person. You've made it to the final level. Pat yourself on the back, brother. You passed the test." With the courtesy of a gracious host, Kane approached Smoke and offered him the drink.

Smoke didn't take it.

"Oh, come on. This is the end, one way or the other."

Smoke took the drink, and without looking at it, he flung it outside.

"Oh, come on. That was a two-hundred-dollar shot of whiskey. And you of all people should know that refusal to take what has been offered can lead to unfortunate circumstances."

"I can live with that."

Kane walked closer to the shattered window. "Do you mind?" he said as he leaned over. He shook his head. "I can't believe you duped Mason a second time. You know, it took us weeks to extract him from that cavity you led him into. I almost left him, but he was one of my strongest."

"Let's get this over with, Kane."

"Just give me a moment, dear John." Kane moved over to the sofa and scooted it over the floor with his thigh back into its original spot. Half of the sofa was crushed. He still sat down. "I'd offer you a seat, but... You can pull up a barstool if you like, while we talk."

"We aren't talking, Kane. We're fighting."

Kane's calmness made Smoke uneasy. The shifter gesticulated as if he didn't have a care in the world. If the world was burning down around him, Kane would not sweat. The way he carried himself was like a demigod among mortals. He feared nothing.

"Get up."

"Feel free to pounce on me if you want, but just as a reminder, your friends — what's left of them — are still out there. Your sweet wife, Sid, hangs by a thread. And let's not forget the child. John Keith, is it?" Kane rested his muscular elbows on his knees. "Sleeping in his crib at the in-laws'. They sleep peacefully, but that's only because I let them."

Smoke's foot scraped over the broken glass. The clouds drifted beyond the light of the moon, bathing his backside in white light. His temperature rose. "I know you aren't bluffing. I'm not bluffing either. I'm going to kill you."

"No, like so many others who have come this close before, you're going to serve me." Kane polished off his glass of whisky and set it down on the busted planks of the floor. "Let me just give you a little more history about two of your favorite opponents. Let's start with the bull man, Mason Crowe. He was like you once. A do-gooder, wife and family, who wanted to take out the likes of me." He spread his arms wide like he held a great fish. "He got this close."

"I don't care."

"And then there's Reginald," Kane continued. "I really, really, really didn't think you would whip him, but you did, John. You, a mortal, defeating a shifter. It was uncanny. At that moment, I knew you would be a more than worthy replacement. I just needed to get you to that point. And here we are."

"You're lying, Kane." Smoke's breath became heavy. His fingers clutched in and out. "You're always lying."

"No, there isn't any point in lying at this juncture. Reginald was the best ever, aside from you. I beat him so bad that he finally caved underneath my power. The fight didn't last very long, either. As you Americans like to say, I mopped the floor with him. In regards to me, let me give you a better idea of what you're facing. I'm the best of all of them, but ten times as strong, proportionally speaking. The giants, given their girth, in some cases are an equal match." He removed a dark ring from his finger. "See this? Titanium." Kane pinched the ring flat between his fingers. "Do you still want to fight, or can I accept your surrender?"

CHAPTER 32

"I**T'S BEEN A LONG TIME, Sid**," Allison said with a purr in her voice. She was a gorgeous woman to begin with, but now she'd become an exotic goddess. A flowing mane of hair draped down and over her shoulders. Her cat eyes sparkled green with the fire of a lurking predator. Her full and generous curves were enhanced in the sleeveless, low-cut bodysuit she wore. She was wicked, dangerous. Her pretty mouthful of teeth was chilling. The claws on the tigress were deadly. "What do you think of your new sister?"

"You look like you now have everything you wanted." Sid brandished a knife in one hand and a gun in the other. She kept them down around her knees. "Beauty and power, just at the cost of your humanity. You're a fool, Allison. Why would you do this to yourself?"

"You know me, Sid." Allison stroked the pelt of soft striped fur on her arm. "I've always sought the spotlight. The attention. I hunger for it. I wanted to be the one everyone looks at. Men will swoon, women will be jealous. Yes, I may be vain, but I delight in it. Now, I'll have it all, this voluptuous figure, this gorgeous face, forever."

Sid pointed the gun at Frank's remains. "Did you not just see what happened to him? The same will happen to you, eventually. Fate catches up with you, Allison. This is evil. Evil loses, always."

"It doesn't seem to me that it's losing. Besides, who's to say what is and isn't evil? Look at me, I'm stunning. How can that be bad?"

"You know better."

"No, I knew better, but I know better now." Allison stepped over Frank. She stood inches taller than Sid now. It had always been the other way around. She seemed to gloat over it. "You were always the athlete and the smart one. I don't think that's the case now. Now, you've stuck your nose where it doesn't belong. I'm going to do something I've wanted to do for a long time. I'm going to whip you bloody."

"What have I ever done to you to cause such resentment, Allison?" Sid backed away. She could see Allison's eyes turn into cauldrons of hate. "I've always looked out for you."

"I didn't need your protection. You weren't my mother, though you were Mother's favorite. You constantly made me look like a fool to our parents. Every time I stepped out of line, you tried to correct it." Allison's claws were clutching at her chest. "I hated you for that! I just wanted to have fun, be with boys, experiment. I have a right to make my own mistakes."

"You blame me for interfering with you making one bad decision after another?"

"Yes!"

"That was always your problem, Allison. You never took the blame for anything you did. Your pride wouldn't let you." Sid sneezed. It wasn't a sincere one. Allison's eyes were locked on her, but she needed to fool her. She needed a super vitamin. Things were about to go down. She fished one out of her pouch, and covering her nose, she stuck it in her mouth. "You lied to Mom and Dad constantly. They should have whipped your ass the moment your antics started. Instead, they let you get away with it." She was backing up. "I couldn't stand it! They gave you everything, and you broke their hearts."

"Shut up, liar!" Allison spread out her fingers. The long claws were like sharp files. "I'm going to enjoy killing you."

Sid fired a shot at Allison's leg.

Allison moved a split second before she pulled the trigger, and the bullet missed by a foot.

Damn, she's fast.

Allison bore down on her like a mountain lion stalking a possum.

The full weight of Allison drove Sid to the floor. The pill popped from her mouth.

Straddling Sid, Allison said, "I'm going to enjoy this." She started punching.

Pinned down on her back, Sid blocked the wild punches with her forearms. With grit in her voice, Sid said, "You might have the strength of a wild animal, but you still can't fight worth a—"

Allison snuck in a hard, quick punch that sent Sid's world spinning. "Uh!"

Grabbing Sid by the collar and jerking her upright, Allison said, "You were saying, Sid? No, I can't fight, but I've got more than enough speed to whip you!"

Sid covered up.

Allison slapped at the sides of her head with broad swipes.

The heavy-handed blows knocked Sid's arms aside. Clawed fingertips tore the skin on her face. She tasted her own blood in her mouth. All she could do was cover up and take a beating. Even with the knife and gun still in her grip, she was helpless. One solid punch from Allison would knock her into a sea of blackness. She let the knife and gun slip from her fingers. There was a momentary break in the blows. Sid said, "Do what you will, Allison, but remember, I still love you."

"Oh, shut up." Allison hit her again.

The red spots in Sid's eyes turned black.

CHAPTER 33

K ANE FLICKED THE FLATTENED RING aside, "So, John Smoke, are you still wanting to dance?"

"You bet." Smoke drew his sword. At this point, he couldn't take any chance with Kane. The shifter was too unpredictable and dangerous. He had to go at him with the only weapon he had left. "Get up."

"Really, the sword again? As you can see, I am unarmed. Come now, why don't we duel with our fists, like you did with the others?"

"What's the matter? Does this Arabian steel scare you, Kane?"

"Hardly." Kane stood up. He pointed to the wall behind the bar where several swords hung up on the wall. "Might I?"

Smoke nodded. Kane turned his back. Smoke sprang forward, releasing a decapitating blow at the same time.

Kane ducked clean from the blow. The blade swished through thin air.

Before Smoke could recover, Kane had his arms locked up.

The man with stringy blond hair wrenched the sword out of Smoke's grip. Drove his head into Smoke's chin.

His head felt like it was filled with cement. Smoke backpedaled on weakened knees.

Kane clapped. "Bravo. Bravo! For a moment, I thought you would be foolish enough to actually let me grab some finely crafted tungsten steel, but you went for the kill. Too bad you missed. Oh, and just so you know, John, decapitation won't work on me. This isn't a movie like Highlander. This is reality." He shoved the sofa aside like it was a pillow. "Let the waltz begin."

As soon as Kane stepped into striking distance, Smoke jump-kicked him in the face. The cartilage in the nose crushed at his heel.

Kane faded back and spat. "Nice shot." He straightened his nose. "Let's try it again."

With an attacking style Smoke had never seen before, Kane slipped by Smoke's punches and knuckle-punched his ribs. Bone cracked. Smoke sensed it coming but wasn't quick enough to evade the last counter-shot Kane delivered.

Back and forth they sparred, a pair of dancing cobras fighting to the death.

Smoke didn't expect the burly fighter to fight with the cunning speed of a welterweight or use the deadly strikes of shaolin monk. The only thing saving Smoke at the moment was his lengthy reach. The hard blows of Kane knocked into his arms. Fast feet jabbed at his shins and knees. It was like fighting Reginald all over again. Kane was unpredictable with what he came up with. Smoke landed a jab in the man's face. His fingernails cut the shifter beneath the eyes.

Kane locked up Smoke's arms like a heavyweight and said in Smoke's ear, "You're good, but you're holding back. Don't be such a coward, John. Let go of that famous self-control of yours. It's the only way to survive what I have." He shoved Smoke away. "The only way. I've given you a gift, Smoke. Turn it loose."

There wasn't any walking away. This was what Smoke came for. The only way to win was to destroy Kane. The only weapon at his disposal was his body. His fists.

But Smoke feared losing all control of himself and becoming a savage monster. Once the switch was on, he feared he wouldn't be able to shut it off again.

He locked his mind down on one single objective. He forgot about friends and family. There was only one goal. One mission, God help his soul.

Kill Kane.

With his fists balled up, Smoke threw his elbows and shoulders back. He let out part battle cry and part shriek.

Aghast, Kane covered his ears. "What in Hades are you doing? That's awful! Stop it!"

Smoke let loose his inner furnace of rage. He pounced.

Kane's quick hands stopped striking right at him.

Smoke punched right through him. He peppered Kane's wide-eyed face and iron jaw. His arms pumped like pistons.

Kane ate knuckles. Tasted fist. He covered up his face.

Smoke grabbed Kane by the back of the head and drove his knees into the shifter's ribs. The blows lifted Kane off his toes. Smoke fought like a wildcat.

Kane shoved him away, only to have Smoke pounce on him again.

Smoke ripped Kane's shirt to tatters. Hardened nails clawed at the shifter's eyes. Power coursed through him. Something fed his strength. The limitations were gone.

Kane's awesome strength bailed the shifter out time and again. The titans of battle wrestled back and forth, slamming into walls and rolling on the floor in striking and tangled limbs.

Fighting Kane was like fighting an armadillo that punched back. His rock-hard body didn't give. His determination was eternal.

He talked to Smoke like he would a dog. "That's it, pup! Give it all you got! All of it!"

Smoke found himself flat on his belly, with a knee in his back and his face stuffed in the floor. Kane mashed his face into the wooden planks. Smoke squirmed out of it in a reversal. He had Kane face down in the wood. He locked up one arm and grabbed a handful of hair. He dashed Kane's face into the floor over and over.

Kane was laughing. His body stiffened. The muscles in his arms and back bulged. The seams in his clothing burst. "I haven't had this much fun in decades."

With Kane's body growing beneath him, Smoke shoved the man's head down one more time. The sinewy muscles in Kane's neck seized up.

In a quick burst of motion, Kane shed Smoke aside like a gorilla tossing a monkey. He was up on a knee just as Smoke attacked again. The expression on Kane's face became dark and monstrous. Every feature became more pronounced and ugly.

"It's time to end this game, John. You've ruined enough of my outfit and office for a day. And it's so hard to get contractors that I can trust in places like this." Kane rose to his full height. He appeared to be a full seven feet of stalwart brawn. "I usually turn them to deaders if they ask too many questions."

Like a wild cat defending its den, Smoke attacked.

Kane caught his wrists and body-slammed him. Kicks to the ribs took Smoke's wind. A flurry of colossal punches sapped his remaining strength.

Smoke felt like he was ten heartbeats from being roadkill. Painful needles danced all over his body. Blood from his wounds dripped on the floor. His ragged breathing hurt.

Kane picked Smoke up and slung him over his broad shoulder like a child being taken to bed.

"I won't kill anyone," Smoke said. A broken and bloody tooth fell out of his mouth. His consciousness began to fade. "I won't be your servant."

"Of course you won't. That's what they all say. But, there is a way around everything." Kane kicked aside the broken pieces of the cinderblock wall Mason Crowe had plowed through, then made his way down the hall to the stairwell. He pulled and pushed on the handle. The door was locked. He glanced back at the cameras. "Frank. Get on this!"

Nothing happened. "More repairs, I guess. By the time this is over, I might as well buy a new building. Renovation costs are outrageous these days." He kicked the door off the hinges. Down the stairs he went, with Smoke hanging over his shoulder, barely hanging onto his consciousness. His loose limbs hung over his body. There was almost nothing left in him.

Save your strength.

Kane took him down into the basement, where the entrance to the subterranean level began. "Remember our little visit here, Smokey? You came as Mack Black, and I as myself. I almost took you out then, but letting you go made the game so much more delightful." He walked down the steps, jostling Smoke hard all the way down. "Now you'll get to see firsthand what my operation is all about. Consider this upcoming baptism a blessing, Smoke. A baptism without fire."

CHAPTER 34

ALLISON DRAGGED SID DOWN THE hall by the hair. "I tell you what, Sid, I've often dreamed of the day when your charmed life would come to an end. Everyone always thought you were so brave and so smart. But I didn't. No, you were just lucky. It's going to be really interesting to see how Mom and Dad react when they know I'm the only daughter they have left. Perhaps they'll give me a little more attention then. Maybe then they'll appreciate me and my beauty."

Sid's hands grazed over the flooring.

"Jesus, give me strength."

Her fingers searched for a weapon. She was hiding it, but there was some fight left in her. In her desperation, she found a small object that felt like little more than debris. She dragged her numb arm up to her chest. Her super vitamin was pinched between her fingers.

Yes!

She popped it in her mouth and chewed.

Keep talking, you spoiled little witch!

"Isn't it funny how we are family, but we hate each other? You're jealous of my beauty, and I was always jealous of, well, your homeliness." Allison laughed. "I guess that's a bit unfair. It must have been your ability to hook a worm that Dad so delighted in. It made me sick. And those times when I'd sneak my boyfriend over when Mom and Dad went on vacation, you always tried to ruin my romance."

"It wasn't a boy. It was boys. And they were ten years older than you. You didn't know what you were doing! You don't know what you're doing now!"

Allison tugged on Sid's hair so hard that strands of it ripped. "I liked those boys! They liked me! You ruined it! It embarrassed me!"

"One of them was an assistant coach, Allison. He was married. Why are you so blind? You can never see the wrong you do in anything." Sid's juices started to flow. She played possum a little longer as Allison continued her walking and whining. "No one in our family ever did you wrong, and you know that."

"They did!" Allison screamed.

"Who did? When?"

Allison buttoned up. She always did that when she didn't have anywhere to go.

Sid didn't have any doubt that Allison manipulated the truth. She always suggested that something bad, inappropriate, or twisted might have happened when she was young. There was never any proof of any of it. She just lied to keep true punishment at bay. That was how she became what she was: a spoiled, entitled child who never took responsibility for her actions. Sid had had enough of it.

"You know what your problem is, Allison?"

Allison stopped in her tracks, looked down at Sid, and said, "What?"

"You've never had a real good ass-whooping."

"Excuse me? You mean like the one I just gave you?"

From the floor, Sid gave her sister a steely-eyed look. "No, like the one I'm about to let loose on you."

Allison blanched behind her coat of fur. Her feline brows crinkled. "All you're doing is making what I have to do too easy."

"Easy. That should have been your middle name." With the strength of a python racing through her limbs, Sid snaked her arms around Allison's. Fastening her grip, she jerked Allison down so she bent at the waist. Sid planted her boots into the tigress's stomach and flipped her overhead.

Allison landed flat on her back, screaming, "You dare!" She bounced up to her feet.

They faced off.

At the top of her lungs, Allison yelled, "I'm going to rip your face off!"

"I'd like to see you try…wimp."

Allison's eyes turned to molten lava. "Grrrrrrr!" Claws bared, she launched her body into Sid's.

Sid turned her hips and started to slide back, but she wasn't quick enough.

Allison knocked her to the floor.

Using her sister's momentum, Sid popped back up on top of her. She stung Allison in the nose with a jab.

Claws out, Allison went at Sid like she was a human scratching post. The long nails tore at her face. "I'm going to bore those brown eyes out of your head."

With renewed strength that matched her sister's, Sid started swatting her hands aside.

Allison clawed.

Sid countered with a right cross followed by a left.

Allison's jaw shuddered after the last blow. "What are you doing?" Allison cried out. She swung.

Sid blocked and tagged her face.

"Stop it!"

"You should have watched more boxing with me and Dad when you were a girl." Sid peppered Allison's face with stunning left, right, left jabs. She put her weight behind every punch. Her knuckles cracked and smacked with the stinging blows. "It's called a combination, you idiot."

Blood trickled out of Allison's nose. She blocked with her arms. "Stop it, Sid! Stop hitting me! It hurts, dammit!"

Sid poured it on. She tagged the ribs, belly, and neck. In the back of her mind, she knew the clock was ticking. The vitamin was only good for a minute or so. She punched on. "You're a brat, Allison!" *Whap! Whap! Whap!* "A spoiled rotten little brat. You've had this coming a long time!"

Tears streamed down Allison's face. "Why are you doing this?" she whined. "Why do you hate me?"

"Because you're an idiot who was about to kill me!" She swung her arm back and delivered a haymaker. Allison's tooth shot from her mouth. Sid's strength began to fade. Her shoulders and back burned. She kept punching with a Rocky quote going through her head. "You have to punch and punch until you can't punch no more," she told herself. The last punches didn't have anything in them. Her lungs burned like fire.

Allison balled up on the floor, crying like a little girl.

Sid managed a final stiff kick to the ribs. Sweat dripped off her nose. Someone touched her shoulder. She flinched.

Guppy smiled at her. "You okay?"

"Never better."

The burly man secured Allison's hands behind her back with flex cuffs. He used two pairs and did the same with the tiger woman's ankles.

Cort showed up, rubbing the side of his swollen face. With an approving nod, he said, "Now that's what I call an ass whooping. Your sister's still hotter than you, though. That whole tiger thing is sexy, even with the tears."

Laboring for breath, Sid said, "Don't you have more important things to think about?"

"Nope."

She turned her attention to Guppy, lifting up her hand for help. "Let's find Smoke."

CHAPTER 35

S ID, GUPPY, AND CORT REGROUPED with Manson Bay inside the command center. Manson kept the appearance of a young teenage black boy. His fingers were busy on the keyboard, and his eyes were glued to the large screens.

"Have you found Smoke, Manson?" Sid was leaning over his shoulder, looking down at his monitor.

"Kane's got him." Manson pulled up a digital video feed. Kane had taken on the monstrous form of his own persona. It was a Jekyll-and-Hyde type of thing. Smoke was draped over Kane's shoulders like a pelt. They entered the stairwell and vanished for several seconds before reappearing on the first level. Then the cameras lost track of them in the southwestern quadrant of the building. "They went down into the sub-levels, I think. It's a dark zone. No technology."

"What's down there?"

Manson shrugged. "I don't know. I haven't been down there. I've spent most of my time pretending to be your niece. For the most part I helped out in the labs with the deaders."

Guppy plopped down in a chair next to Rich and Sherry, who sat like mutes in their seats. He pointed at them with his thumb, over his shoulder. "What's their deal? Do we need to shoot them?"

"No, they can be helpful," Manson responded.

With Allison thrown over his shoulder, Cort said, "Can I put Tiger Lady down now? She's crying all over my back."

Sid nodded. "What else is out there, Manson? I need a count of shifters and deaders."

The big screens panned through image after image. Lots of redcoat bodies spasmed on the floors. Several others were moving aimlessly about the complex. Aside from the burning van, the outside parking lot was void of activity. At the dock, the yacht was sinking. "I'm ninety percent certain that you've eliminated all threats." Manson pointed at tiles of betting odds on the screens. Sid, Guppy, and Cort had all beaten the odds stacked against them. "Looks like some rich people lost a ton of money today. I love it when that happens, even though it won't make any difference. Now that Kane's off the grid, they're logging out." His fingers were still very busy. "I'm trying to trace them, but it's not easy."

Sid checked her ammo. She had half a magazine left. "Cort, Guppy, load up everything you have. We're going down."

Guppy could barely make it out of his chair. "Coming."

"I don't know what's down there, but I could use a hand up here," Manson said. "My fingers only work so fast, and I need to find these links before they vanish."

"Guppy, stay," she said.

His brow puckered.

"It'll be fine."

"Here then." He handed over a gun and his cylinder of vitamins. "Come back, Sid. All of you."

"We're going to be pretty short-handed." Cort was eyeing the empty holes in the cylinder of his Big Alaskan wheel gun. "I'm down one arm as it is. And starving."

"Anyway, one of my hands is worth more than ten of yours," said someone standing in the doorway.

"Vormus!" Sid exclaimed.

The long-haired, cotton-headed vampire shifter tipped his chin. He was dressed in a grey tuxedo from the eighteenth century.

"I see you're overdressed for the occasion once again."

"I pride myself in looking my best no matter the circumstances. It's nice to see you, Sid." He twirled a sword in his hand. It was the Arabian blade that Smoke used. "We need to get to your husband before it's too late."

Sid headed for the door. "What's happening?"

"Kane's preparing him for the Kiss of Khonshu. If that happens, it's over for him. Probably us too. Well, you and your friends at least."

"Are we really supposed to believe that an Egyptian god is the one running the show?" she asked Vormus. "Someone or something thousands of years old?"

"I'm seeking out some of those answers for myself. Remember, Sid, I'm with you because I want out. If there's a way for me to become mortal again, then perhaps I can finally find the answers I seek."

The three of them moved swiftly through the halls. Turning a corner, they ran into a pair of redcoat deaders. Without breaking stride, Vormus slipped the sword into their hearts and walked right by their collapsing bodies.

Stepping over the dead bodies, Cort said, "That was quick. I'm going to get me one of those swords."

Sid pressed Vormus. She needed more answers about what was going on. Frank had filled her in, but that was only one layer of many. Even though she was grateful that Manson and Vormus had shown up to help her, the timing was very suspicious.

"Why now, Vormus?" she asked. "You've been gone all this time, and here you are? You could have been helping us all along."

"The truth is I've been on the fence whether or not to help you. Aiding you in the defeat of Kane could result in my own death. Honestly, I didn't think you would make it this far without me. For some reason I can't explain, you inspire me."

"I've heard that before." Sid glanced over to Cort. Behind Vormus's back, she mouthed the words, "Watch him."

Cort gave a stiff nod.

One thought puzzled her. How did Vormus know where they were and what they were doing? It only made sense he'd be working with Kane. Perhaps leading them into another trap. Logically, she knew she couldn't trust him, but his actions showed otherwise.

They came to a stop at a much older door that didn't match up with the rest. The handles were made from solid hammered brass. The keyhole was huge. It was unlocked. "What's down there?"

"Answers." Vormus opened the door. A gust of stagnant air ruffled his hair. "Ladies first."

Sid grabbed him by his fancy collar and shoved Vormus through. She held Cort back for a moment. She took a super vitamin and placed it between her cheek and gum. Cort did the same. The doors led down concrete steps.

"Whew! There's something rotten down here," Cort said, covering his nose.

The stairwell was pitch-black aside from the yellow glow far down below. The steps were many, holding a straight line instead of switching back and forth like most stairwells. Sid's fingers grazed the wall. The surface wasn't smooth, but rough, and slightly damp. Vormus's graceful body blocked the light on and off.

When they got to the bottom, it wasn't at all what Sid expected. There wasn't a basement. Instead, caverns and hollowed-out tunnels ran as far as she could see. Gas lanterns were mounted on the walls with light flames that quavered. It was something like the labyrinth below Mason Crowe's frontier mansion, but not as deep. She was thankful for that.

"What is this, the Bat Cave?" Cort looked at the ground. The floor was wet and grimy. "What's with all these footprints?"

"I think those deaders were stored down here. I don't see any now. Nor do I hear them."

Cort bent down and picked up the butt of a cigarette. "Deaders smoke? There's a bunch of butts down here." Something else caught his eye. "Look at that." He picked up a leather pouch. The tie string broke off when he opened the neck. He poured some old coins into his hand, silver and gold. "Jackpot."

"Come on. We need to find Smoke," Sid said.

The cavern spread out in all directions. There were cave openings and huge stone blocks almost as big as her that might have been from an old fort long ago. In columns and walls, the stones supported the building above. The gas lanterns, to her surprise, were lit up as far as her eyes could see. "Stay together."

Vormus walked ahead as if he'd been there before. There was an air about him.

"I'll lead," Sid said, moving alongside of him. She held her Glock at chin level in a routine tactical position.

Water dripped from the ceiling. The drops echoed when they hit the puddles. Cort's breathing was heavy. Vormus didn't seem to breathe at all. She moved slowly while keeping her head on a swivel. There had to be more deaders or shifters lurking somewhere. "This doesn't feel right. It's too quiet," she said under her breath. "Vormus, do you hear or see anything?"

"Yes." He looked upward.

Sid did the same. The ceiling was over thirty feet high. Heavy beams of wood from the building's foundation linked together with the stone bases. Something crawled along the beams. It was the shape of a man who moved like a beetle. A dark bulk with arms and legs. Sid's bones chilled. There was more than one. She tapped Cort's shoulder.

He looked up.

Something hideous dropped down.

CHAPTER 36

"**W**ELCOME TO THE KHONSHU'S TRIBUTE," Kane said to Smoke.

They were inside a chamber with walls made from big blocks of sandstone. Smoke sat slumped over on the ground, trying to gain his strength. Illuminated by the gas lanterns, Smoke could make out hieroglyphics along the wall. They were lit up and pulsating with their own ambient light that shifted into many colors.

There was a nine-foot-high pyramid made of glass with sparkles that twinkled like stars. A chair was built in, giving it the appearance of a throne. Heavy black cords thicker than the hugest black snakes ran from the pyramid-throne and across the floor. The black cords hooked into a man-shaped sarcophagus that stood up in the floor across from it. The cords rippled and bowed like living things.

"What is this?" Smoke could barely hold his head up. There were other objects in the chamber too. Ancient tables covered in pottery, and small statues of men with animal heads. The moon in its various cycles hung on the walls. Painted figurines faced it in worship. It was all ancient but had the low hum of churning technology. "A museum. How much are you going to charge for admission?"

"That might be your best joke yet. Definitely your last." Kane grabbed Smoke by the arm.

Smoke couldn't break the steely grip. He couldn't do anything. It was hard to even think.

Kill Kane.

Kane shoved him inside the sarcophagus. Living black cords fastened around Smoke's neck, wrists, and ankles. "There won't be any getting out of that until it's all over." Kane retrieved an ornamental pewter helmet made for an Egyptian warrior. He placed it on Smoke's head. Looking Smoke in the eye, he said, "Smile. It's a great honor to receive the Kiss of Khonshu."

Smoke strained against his bonds, trying to head-butt Kane's ugly face. Spitting, he said, "Save your kisses for the grave, Kane."

Kane threw his head back in laughter. "If only you wouldn't lose your sense of humor with this. It would be delightful at my parties. They are often dull. No, John, the kiss is a ceremonial name for it. You see, since you've been so reluctant to receive the gift of shifting that I've given you, I'm going to have to take a greater course of action."

Smoke heard and felt something attach to the helmet that he wore. It hummed. Every hair on his body stood on end. Fire ran down his spine. He choked down a scream as laser-thin needles pierced his skull. Whatever was happening was straight out of a horror movie.

"Don't worry, John, you won't get used to it." Kane moved across from him and sat down on the pyramid seat. He fit it like a king. Chair arms silently slid out of the black pyramid. Kane pressed on the glowing buttons that had tiny images on each. "It's been a long time since I had to do this. It's a sad thing, as the experience is rather delightful. You see, John, I'm not the man the others know to be Kane. I'm actually Khonshu."

Kane pushed the arms back inside the pyramid.

"Well, let me correct that. I'm the essence of Khonshu. You see, centuries ago, the Drake came across the hidden pyramids in Venezuela. I was one of those explorers at the time. Not much of anybody, just a man with a weak frame, strong mind, and fathomless ambition."

The pain coursing through Smoke's body was so great that he could barely hear Kane's words. He focused, searching for a nugget that would aid in his freedom. Part of him was ashamed that he'd come this far, only to be locked up like a child. He'd become helpless.

Don't give in, Smoke. Don't give in.

"Faced with ancient technology that turned our frail minds inside out," Kane continued, "many walked away. Others focused on the treasure within. The pottery, jewelry, precious baubles. Anything that they could get their greedy little hands on. They were all about money, but that was meaningless to me. I wanted power. Outlasting my fellow scholars, I spent time in the ancient tomb, scouring over every crease in the floors and walls. That's when I came across Khonshu's hidden tomb. This pyramid was in there. The sarcophagus too. The odd thing was that it stood empty. No mummy. I'd seen plenty of graves in my day, but never an empty one. It was beyond puzzling.

"This pyramid looked like nothing but a glassy piece of onyx. Smooth as a sheet of ice. It offered no answers, only more mystery. But when I touched it, I knew it lived. Something powerful lurked within. That's when I found myself in a situation very much like the one you are in. Under a strange compulsion, I placed that helmet on my head. Then, when I began inspecting the inside of the sarcophagus, those black tendrils seized me. Those needles you feel, they dug into my head, too. I screamed so loud that it waked the dead. I saw a ghost. The spirit of Khonshu. At first I thought it was a ghost. Turns out that it was a projection. He spoke to me in Egyptian. I understood every word. The pyramid transferred great knowledge into my mind. My body transfigured into something far greater. I was no longer a man, I was a god."

He rubbed his hands together.

"This throne is rife with scientific and worldly knowledge. Like the sun, the moon has power and purpose. It controls the tide, does it not? Its radiant light does more than shine, it reflects a dark energy. Only few can tap it. That's why on a night like tonight, the likes of me, and you, are at full power. With this power, I learned how to reanimate the dead. Clone the living. I learned to change the DNA of men into that of shifters. It presented endless opportunities, but it took much time to master it. It took time, money, and willing participants.

"My colleagues were highly objectionable when I revealed my discovery and my plans. So, I killed them all. That innocent blood sealed my fate. I and the essence of Khonshu have been one ever since."

Smoke's chin was down in his chest. His head felt like it weighed a ton. He was panting. Underneath his fur was sweat. "What are you doing to me?"

"I'm altering your internal programming. Those needles in your head, they know where your memories lie. I'm going to take them away and unleash your more carnal ambitions. When I turn you loose again, you'll shred the first blood-beating heart that comes within a hundred feet of you. Only then will your memories be restored. You'll recognize the shame of what you've done, and you'll be mine forever. John Smoke, prepare to become a permanent member of the Drake."

A clear piece of tubing with a needle on it wormed out of the pyramid. Kane stuck it in his arm. Blood flowed back into the pyramid. That was when Smoke noticed that same clear tubing lying on the floor among the black coils. The dark blood snaked its way into the coffin. Smoke prayed. Smoke screamed.

CHAPTER 37

ORT SHOT THROUGH THE CREATURE that fell from the ceiling. It hit the ground like a rock. It had the tiny face of a man and the body of a black beetle. "Ew! What kind of sick thing is that? It's a ladybug man! I hate ladybugs!" He started shooting at every creature that fell.

The beetle men landed on their oddly shaped hands and legs. With bullets ricocheting off their shells, they scurried right at each of them.

Sid shot one beetle man in the face, stopping it cold.

Cort hollered at Sid, "Get this thing off me!" He pranced like a girl as he flailed wildly with a Rottweiler-sized beetle man latched on his back. With a face full of tiny sharp teeth, it bit into Cort's neck. "Aaaaah! I'm going to turn into a ladybug!"

Using his sword, Vormus flicked it off Cort's back, where it splattered against a wall. "They are virtually harmless unless you're absolutely stupid. Just stab them or shoot them in the head." Vormus stabbed a beetle man that was crawling at his feet. "See? Easy. Besides, I think we've killed all of them. And it seems we have much bigger problems."

Rubbing his bloodied neck, Cort said, "Please tell me it's not some giant beetle thing. If it is, I'm leaving."

"No, just a giant." Vormus pointed his sword toward the deeper bowels of the cave.

Deep in the cavern, a humongous man came their way. He was dressed in a full Civil War army uniform. The rebel giant was full bearded and broad chested, with thick arms and hands bigger than hams. He was the biggest giant Sid had seen. Bigger even than Rexor and Thorgrim. The black-eyed man made the cavern look like a playpen.

"He's not stopping," she said.

"No, I'm fairly certain he's here to kill us. One can only hope this is the final guardian," Vormus said.

"Man, Vormus," Cort said, "he's wearing clothes that are even older than yours." He lifted up his weapon. "I guess it's time to start shooting." The first bullet Cort fired exploded on the giant's chest.

The rebel brute didn't even break his stride. Even his uniform remained intact.

"Dang! I've got to get the name of his tailor!"

Sid fired. The blue tips from Guppy's magazine pierced the giant's uniform, but they had as much of an effect as a bee stinging a bear. As the giant bore down on her, she said, "Aim for the face!"

"I am!"

Bullets explosive and piercing dotted the giant's face.

The huge man didn't even cover up. Like a slow-moving locomotive, he came on.

Within seconds, Sid's gun stopped popping and started clicking. She moved away from the giant. "I'm empty! Cort, toss me some rounds."

"I can't. I'm empty too!"

Sid drew her knife. Cort did the same.

Brandishing the sword, Vormus stepped in front of them. "That's not going to do. Oh, how I hate these menial tasks." He floated upward and glided sword-first toward the giant's chest. He ran the blade straight into its heart. He twisted the steel. "That ought to do it. Oh look, it has a nametag. Stonewall. Goodbye, Stonewall."

Stonewall's knotty arms caught Vormus in a fierce bear hug. His giant fists smashed into Vormus's face over and over again. The giant didn't let up. The sword slipped from Vormus's fingers. His body went limp. Stonewall hoisted Vormus high over his head. He slammed Vormus to the ground. The shifter didn't move. Stonewall's pitch-black eyes locked on Sid.

Looking over at Cort, she bit into her vitamin. "This is it."

Chewing on his vitamin, he rolled his shoulders. "Let's do this."

Flanking the giant at the same time, they converged. Sid worked at one flailing fist, and Cort did the other. Quick as cats, they shredded the giant's tendons at the fingers.

The monster didn't slow. He just kept swinging stiff blows filled with power. A quick counter-backhand aimed at Cort sent him flying from his feet. The giant pounced at the man.

Sid dove on the giant's leg, tripping him up and knocking him to the ground. The vitamin's energy coursing through her veins faded. She got up slowly and backed away, watching the giant rise up and come right toward her. She stared down the giant but said under her breath, "This *is* it."

Once spry as a kitten, Sid found herself barely able to stand. Taking one pill was bad enough, but two within a matter of minutes was too much for the body. She was drained. Somehow, she managed to lift her arms to make her final stand.

"Get down, Sid!" The voice was Sam's.

Sid didn't bother to turn and look, she just flopped on the ground.

Best idea I've heard all day.

The heavy *budda-budda* of a machine gun's roar erupted inside the cavern. Sid got her neck twisted around. Russ carried a belt of ammo. He was feeding it into Sam's M-60 machine gun. The gorgeous woman had turned into a combat soldier. With a tie wrapped around her forehead like a bandana, she opened fire. Bullets tore through the giant's uniform in a tight group, punching in one side and out the other. Explosive rounds popped inside his body. Sam's chest jiggled. Empty cartridges bounced off the floor. The wild-eyed woman let out a crazed battle cry.

Sid low-crawled away.

Stonewall stumbled backward.

Sam marched on. The *budda-budda* kept singing. The bullets ripped and exploded inside Stonewall. She made a straight line right through him. "You need a zipper to go with those clothes, freak!"

Stonewall's upper body started to slide from his low extremities. He looked down just as his legs gave way. His top half landed right by Sid with a *thud*.

Sid logrolled until she couldn't logroll anymore. She stopped against Sam's feet.

Holding the big machine gun in a victory pose, Sam said, "Did you see that? I zippered him. I zippered a giant! Man, I wish Guppy could've seen that." Her eyes became glassy. She wobbled. "Sid, I think I'm going to faint. Catch meh—"

Russ caught her.

Sid fought her way up to her knees. "What happened to her?"

"She took the vitamin. I don't think her body could withstand the withdrawal." Russ's face was dripping with perspiration. "Man, I want to get out of here. I'm not made for this kinda stuff. Say, you don't look so swell either."

"I'll manage." Sid gulped in some air. She grabbed the machine gun and looped a belt of ammo around her arm.

Russ helped her to her feet. "Where are you going?"

"I'm going to get my man back," she said, head hanging and limping away.

"But you're bleeding and can barely walk."

She reached down and picked up the Arabian sword. "If you think this looks bad, wait until you see what I do to Kane."

CHAPTER 38

S ID HAULED HER BODY INTO the cavern's stomach. Without knowing where to start, she trudged on, driven by a yearning to find Smoke that was so strong, she couldn't comprehend it. That desire within burned, gave new life to her body. Passing a variety of cave entrances and alcoves, she finally came across an eroding corridor made from the same stone blocks near the entrance at the stairwell. The gas lanterns—lined up in neat rows—illuminated the long hallway. There were ancient carvings in one row of the blocks. Hieroglyphics somewhat different than the ones she was accustomed to seeing in museums and magazines.

She rolled her shoulders, adjusting the M-60 strap that dangled the big gun at waist level. She brushed the hair from her eyes with the back of her hand. The images on the wall were of people with animal heads worshipping the different phases of the moon. There were images of altars, knives, and sacrifices. That was the portion of what she could make out that made any type of sense to her. The rest of the images were a collage of extraordinary objects and peoples.

King Tut, here I come.

At the end of the corridor was a pair of double doors with their own gas lanterns burning on each side. The doors were cast iron covered in jade-green corrosion. They were split open halfway. The light source was strong within. Sid passed through the doors.

Kane was on a throne built into a black pyramid. He was a bestial man with roots of muscle that ripped out of his shirt. A welcoming smile of oversized teeth crossed his face.

"Sidney, you have such perfect timing." He beckoned her over. "Please, please, come in. We have much catching up to do."

"Where's John?"

"Oh, there isn't a John anymore. Say, what is that you have there? Did you bring me gifts? A machine gun and a sword. Please, lay them down in front of the temple and I'll bless your family and crops when I get around to it."

Sid fired at his feet.

Kane didn't flinch.

"I'm not asking again, Kane. Where's John? I want to see him." She pointed right at him. "Now!"

"Honestly, Sid, you should know by now that putting a gun on me is no bigger threat than taking a swing at me with a flyswatter." He licked his lips. "It is rather sexy though. You know, I really miss our time together. Those long nights and early mornings. Perhaps another go for old time's sake?"

Sid moved closer. The only thing between her and him was a sarcophagus. Black coils that were attached to it moved like slithering snakes. She dreaded taking a peek inside. Crossing over to its back, she stepped over the coils.

The sarcophagus was empty.

Tapping his fingertips together, Kane said, "What's the matter, Sid? You look disappointed. Did you expect to see your mummy? Get it, mummy?"

"Your jokes are as bad as your lovemaking."

Kane blanched in a funny way. "Oh, now that stung a little. Good for you, little woman. I like a mortal who fights to the bitter end. It garners respect. Perhaps I'll let you have a funeral after all."

"Just tell me where John is. Let me see him."

"Oh, you will see, Sidney, but it won't be him that you see." Kane rose from the throne. "He'll be a marvelous creation akin to me. The truth is, you're going to regret that you even asked. You are much better off remembering him as he was — a strange yet extraordinary man who had a curious panache that caused him to do the stupidest things. Honestly, I'm thankful. He's my finest creation yet." Kane looked past her shoulder.

Slowly, she turned.

Smoke stood right behind her, now a more terrifying version of his man-bat form. He'd become a dangerous lurking predator, slavering quietly from his jaws. The soul behind his eyes had been replaced by black pits. His long, ghastly fingers clutched in and out.

Heart racing, Sid unhinged her tongue. "J-John, it's me, Sid." She reached toward his face.

Smoke slapped her to the ground.

Kane burst out in devilish laughter. "I've been wanting to do that forever. But it was so much more fun watching the entire event transpire. Kill her, Smoke. Embrace your destiny and finish this quest. Just do it slowly. I want to enjoy this. I like to hear her scream."

CHAPTER 39

WITH ONE HAND SMOKE PICKED Sid up like a ragdoll. With the other he stripped the sword from her fingers. A swipe of his claws cut through the strap to the machine gun. He lifted her up to her tiptoes. Staring in her face, he let out an angry shriek. Smoke was fully monster. An untamed beast. His clawed bat feet had locked around her throat. His eyes yearned to shred her. Saliva dripped from his mouth to his chest.

"Spill that blood, Smoke, slowly. Let eternity be yours," Kane gloated.

"John, listen to me. You don't have to do this. I love you, John." Sid's voice trembled as she choked out the words. "I'm your wife. We have a son. John Keith."

"Please withhold the soap opera antics, Sidney. He can't hear you. Those fond memories of frolicking with you are gone. I took them away. He is nothing but a blood-hungry beast now, primed to devour you and howl at the moon. Well, screech at it in his case." Kane's towering frame appeared behind Smoke's shoulder. "So long, Sidney. Just know before you go to the grave that this has been the most delicious game I've ever played. But in the end, as in all cases, Kane wins. Now finish her, my faithful servant."

"Smoke, you have to listen to me," she said, searching his eyes. "I know you're still in there. Think of me, us. Butterflies and pancakes, John. Butterflies and pan—*urk*!"

"Butterflies and pancakes? What a strange combination," Kane said as he backed away.

Sid clutched at Smoke's arms. She tore fur from his wrists. Her feet kicked at him as her eyes bulged from her head. Fighting the pain and death pulling her toward the grave, she kept her eyes fastened on Smoke's, thinking, "You can beat this. I believe in you, John. I love you!"

Smoke hungered. The beast that lived within him had emerged. He was free to kill and slaughter. The struggle began on Kane's first order. He didn't want to kill the blood-filled woman slowly. He wanted to kill her fast. Yet, Kane's command was compelling. It tore at him inside and out. Smoke didn't know the woman. She was meat on a rack. Something weak that needed to be killed. Kill her and he'd have complete control of what it was that he lost and was searching for.

Her piercing eyes bored into his brain. The words she sputtered were gibberish, but they echoed inside his brain. Images and memories, good and bad, flashed like lightning in his head. There was a diner. Laughter. The words she said started to make sense. He just couldn't control his compulsion to kill her.

Sid's kicking stopped. Her arms went limp. She held her gaze as long as she could. Tears dripped down the corners of her eyes. For some reason, Smoke's grip softened just enough so that she could share her final words, "Butterflies and pancakes."

Smoke's eyes shifted from coal black to a rusty brown. In a voice that was his own he said, "And milkshakes?"

Sid croaked out a joyful sob when he released her. "All you'll ever want."

"Unbelievable!" Kane yelled. He gnashed his teeth. "I've never seen the likes of it! Oh, I hate love! Love ruins everything evil. Oh well, I guess I'll just have to kill you both myself."

"I promise you, it won't be that easy. After all, it hasn't been so far." Smoke flicked a super vitamin up into the air and opened his mouth to catch it.

Kane snatched it out of midair. Backing away, he said, "Oh ho-ho, if it isn't one of your cherished vitamins. Your little equalizers. How pathetic." He eyed the capsule pinched between his index finger and thumb. "No sense in letting it go to waste. Now it's time to turn the tide and use it against you." He devoured the pill. His expression soured. "Lord almighty! That tastes awful. How do you even stomach these things?"

"We don't," Smoke said, watching Kane start to choke. "That wasn't a super vitamin. That was a heavy dose of cyanide. Your body might be able to handle a lot of things, but it's not worth jack squat if it can't use oxygen to run it. That's science, not mythology."

Kane clutched at his throat. His skin turned pasty white. Blue veins spidered out all over his face. Somehow, he managed to say in a wheeze, "Impossible, nothing can kill me."

"Sure it can. But as a backup we brought this." Smoke picked up the Arabian sword and handed it over to Sid. "He's all yours."

Receiving the sword in two hands, she walked right in front of Kane and said, "Any famous last words?" Kane was down on his knees, doubled over. "I guess not. Goodbye, Kane." She cocked back the sword and swung.

Slice.

Kane's head fell from his shoulders. The pyramid pulsed. The walls shook.

Smoke passed out.

Sid released the sword and dropped down by Smoke, cradling him in her arms. Gently slapping his face, she said, "John, wake up! Wake up!" Tears ran down her cheeks.

In the heat of the moment, she'd forgotten that killing Kane might kill Smoke as well. According to Mal and the musings that Frank gave, Kane was the host with the blood from which all of the shifters and deaders thrived.

She rocked Smoke back and forth. 'I'm sorry, John, I'm sorry."

Smoke's body transformed from that of a man-bat to a man. His skin was cold and clammy.

Clutching his hand and rubbing it against her face, she said, "Please don't die on me, John, not like this."

He squeezed back. "I won't."

"You're alive!"

"And hungry. Did you say something about milkshakes and pancakes?"

Sid gave him a passionate kiss then said, "All you want."

He sat up and leered at the pyramid. "Hold on." He choked and sputtered, regurgitating a sandwich-sized Ziplock bag. "What in the world is that?"

"What else? Plastic explosives." Smoke mounted one bar of the plastic on the pyramid and the other inside the sarcophagus. With a devilish smile, he said, "Let's go. Uh, but we'd better run. I put it on a timer, and there's only twelve seconds."

Hand in hand, they sprinted out of the room and down the corridor past Vormus, who was coming their way.

"Why are you running?" Vormus said.

"Because the power source of Khonshu is about to go boom," Smoke said.

Vormus put his hands on his cheeks. "Noooooo!"

Sid didn't look back, just kept on running, and waited for the *BOOOOOOOM*!

CHAPTER 40
EPILOGUE

EVERYONE MADE IT BACK TO the parking lot. They were all huddled together inside a ring of SUVs. The FBI had arrived. Two choppers had landed on the scene. Ted Howard was there and taking charge. Rebecca Lang was with him. Asia dressed Mal's head wound. "I want a five-star buffet and hotel room. All I can eat, with all the sleep. You got that? I killed a shifter and a boat."

From inside the building, Cort had gathered a large pile of muskets, sabers, and old uniforms. "Man, this is my retirement. This stuff's worth a fortune."

Russ was helping him load it into a van that Ted brought for them to use. "It ain't all yours. I've got dibs on half."

Sam and Guppy sat leaning against the front bumper of one of the cars, wrapped up in blankets. "You should have seen it, Guppy. I turned that giant into applesauce."

"I wish I had," he replied. "Just glad you're alive. That we're all still alive. Tell me it's all over."

"I think so," Sid said, watching FBI agents take Allison away in handcuffs. She was relieved. All the other shifters had died. Their bodies were scattered about in human form, dead. Even Mason Crowe's body was mutilated on the fence. But her sister hadn't shed innocent blood. There was hope for her yet.

Sid sat holding Smoke's hand.

His heavy stare was on Vormus and the kid version of Manson Bay, who were both very much alive.

"Why didn't you die?" she asked them.

"I'm not a child of Kane. Neither is Manson. Our blood is different."

"I thought you were brothers," she said.

"As you would say in your garbage language, brothers from another mother. A long story, but the main thing is Kane is dead. Quite a feat, though I was hoping to find something that might cure me of my own condition. That pyramid held many ancient secrets, but my search will continue."

Sid shoulder-nudged Smoke. "You're awfully quiet."

"All this time, Kane had me convinced I was something else. Yet here I am, normal as ever."

"You mean abnormal as ever," she said. "Maybe your gifts aren't so extraordinary after all."

"No common man could have survived what Kane put you through," Manson Bay said with a bookish look on his young face. "You are a descendant of the Knights of Nigil. The offspring of a vanquished line of royalty." He handed Smoke a black jump drive. "Some fragments of your family tree are in there. To put it bluntly, like Sidney says, you aren't that special, but you are. That sixth sense that you have, well, it runs in your family. It's a warrior's intuition some refer to as tekken. It's passed down your family line, but it skips generations sometimes. It's a physical gift, a great one. You get to enjoy it."

"So I'm not a shifter's kid?"

"As far as I know you're just a plain old mortal who's either going to die from a violent death or tragic old age." Manson offered his hand. "Look, we aren't exactly on the same side of things, but I want you to know: the Drake is still out there. Kane was but a portion of that operation, and just because this burned down, doesn't mean something else won't move in to invade this sullied city."

Sid shook Manson's hand. "May we never meet again."

Vormus nodded. He picked up Manson in his arms and said to Smoke and Sid, "Even though I know you won't, try to enjoy what you have and stay out of trouble. I wish I had." He floated up into the sky right past another helicopter coming in for a landing. The pilot's jaw dropped. Vormus and Manson were gone.

"We probably should have killed those two," Smoke said.

Sid draped her arms over his shoulders and kissed his cheek. "Nah, they're dead already. Now let's get out of here. I'm in the mood for some buttermilk and pancakes."

"Buttermilk?"

"Sorry, I meant butterflies."

"You mean milkshakes and pancakes?" he said as they helped each other stand. "I don't eat butterflies."

"Let's just go before the moth man shows up or something."

Twirling the ring of keys on her finger, Asia said, "I'm driving. Get in."

Miles away, the group filled three blue-and-white checked booths inside a diner. The dishes were piled up to their eyeballs. No one was talking, everyone was eating and drinking. Over the counter, televisions hung on the wall displaying the local news.

A breaking news segment came up. A cute lady reporter bundled up in a wool winter coat and matching ski cap stood just outside the Drake Energy plant.

She reported, "Tonight we are sad to report tragedy on the riverbank. Just minutes ago, a sinkhole swallowed up this old power plant. FBI officials say the hole opened up on the bank, swallowing the facility into the river and leading to a series of fires and explosions. Area residents have been asked to evacuate."

In the background, driving alongside the flashing lights of the emergency vehicles, a semi-truck and trailer pulled into the complex. It had a Drake Transportation logo on it.

"Evil never rests," Sid said.

"No, I guess not." Smoke called out to their waitress, "Hon, could you change the channel?" He held up his Coke glass and shook the ice. "And I could use a refill."

"So John, how did you come up with cyanide to kill Kane?" she asked.

"I don't know. I guess you could call it fighter's intuition. It's something Mal and I talked about a while back."

"You weren't going to use it on yourself, were you?"

With his arms stretched across the table, he rubbed her hands with his strong, warm fingers. "Never, baby."

"It's just a strange plan."

"I'm a strange man."

"I love you, John. I'm glad we're okay."

"I love you too."

She picked up the jump drive that was lying on the table. "So what are you going to do with this?"

He covered her hand, including the jump drive, with his large hands. "I'll let you decide. Right now, I just want to focus on spending the rest of my life with you and JK."

FROM THE AUTHOR

Boy, that was fun, wasn't it? I want to thank you for supporting me during this journey with Sid and Smoke. Wrapping up the ending of a series is never easy, and if you're crying a little because you miss them already, good! I miss them too.

As for future books, I can't say I have any in mind. If you follow my other works, then you know I stay pretty busy. Sid and Smoke need a long time to themselves anyway. With that said, I really had a blast writing this urban fantasy adventure.

Do me a favor and tell your fellow readers about it — and please leave a review. They are a huge help for me!

As always, I love to hear from you, so feel free to email anytime if you have any questions.

craig@thedarkslayer.com

Please leave a review. They are a huge help for me!

*I'd love it if you would subscribe to my mailing list. www.craighalloran.com

*On Facebook you can find me at The Darkslayer Report or Craig Halloran.

*Twitter, twitter, twitter, I am there too. www.twitter.com

*And of course, you can always, anytime, email me at craig@thedarkslayer.com

See my book lists below!

ABOUT THE AUTHOR

Craig Halloran resides with his family outside his hometown of Charleston, West Virginia. When he isn't entertaining mankind, he is seeking adventure, working out, or watching sports. To learn more about him, go to: www.thedarkslayer.com.

CHECK OUT ALL OF MY GREAT STORIES

CLASH OF HEROES: Nath Dragon meets The Darkslayer

THE CHRONICLES OF DRAGON SERIES

The Hero, the Sword and the Dragons (Book 1) Free eBook

Dragon Bones and Tombstones (Book 2)

Terror at the Temple (Book 3)

Clutch of the Cleric (Book 4)

Hunt for the Hero (Book 5)

Siege at the Settlements (Book 6)

Strife in the Sky (Book 7)

Fight and the Fury (Book 8)

War in the Winds (Book 9)

Finale (Book 10)

THE CHRONICLES OF DRAGON: SERIES 2, TAIL OF THE DRAGON

Tail of the Dragon

Claws of the Dragon

Eye of the Dragon

Scales of the Dragon

Trial of the Dragon

Teeth of the Dragon

THE DARKSLAYER SERIES 1

Wrath of the Royals (Book 1) Free eBook

Blades in the Night (Book 2)
Underling Revenge (Book 3)
Danger and the Druid (Book 4)
Outrage in the Outlands (Book 5)
Chaos at the Castle (Book 6)

THE DARKSLAYER: BISH AND BONE, SERIES 2

Bish and Bone (Book 1) Free eBook
Black Blood (Book 2)
Red Death (Book 3)
Lethal Liaisons (Book 4)
Torment and Terror (Book 5)

THE SUPERNATURAL BOUNTY HUNTER FILES

Smoke Rising (2015) Free ebook
I Smell Smoke (2015)
Where There's Smoke (2015)
Smoke on the Water (2015)
Smoke and Mirrors (2015)
Up in Smoke
Smoke Em'
Holy Smoke
Smoke Out

ZOMBIE IMPACT SERIES

Zombie Day Care: Book 1 Free eBook
Zombie Rehab: Book 2
Zombie Warfare: Book 3

You can learn more about the Darkslayer and my other books deals and specials at:

Facebook – The Darkslayer Report by Craig
Twitter – Craig Halloran
www.craighalloran.com